COLLINS
COLLECTOR'S CHOICE

COLLINS COLLECTOR'S CHOICE

Four Novels
SARA DANE
BLAKE'S REACH
FIONA
A FALCON FOR A QUEEN

by

Catherine Gaskin

COLLINS
St James's Place, London
1978

William Collins Sons & Co Ltd
London · Glasgow · Sydney · Auckland
Toronto · Johannesburg

First published 1978
© Catherine Gaskin 1955, 1958
Catherine Gaskin Cornberg 1970, 1972

ISBN 0 00 243130 0

Set in Baskerville
Made and Printed in Great Britain by
William Collins Sons & Co Ltd Glasgow

CONTENTS

FOREWORD

These four novels span a period in my life of seventeen years, years of working at my craft, years of living in different parts of the world, of travelling to others. I often think that for a working novelist there is little rest. While almost nothing is consciously 'marked' for future use, almost anything may come to the surface as one stirs the brew of one's life and experience.

SARA DANE was my first attempt to write an historical novel. I finished it on my twenty-fifth birthday, after two and a half year's hard labour. I do confess to having been rather frightened of the historical form, because I hadn't been trained as a researcher. Having grown up in Australia, though born in Ireland, there seemed to me a great story to be told about Australia's years of birth, and its struggle to gain recognition as something vastly more than a penal colony. For me, there was only one way to tell it – through the eyes of a woman, and one set somewhat in the heroic mould. She would, of course, have to be beautiful, because in those days beauty – and unhappily this still obtains – was so often the attribute that first attracted attention, permitted the first opportunity to rise. But there would have to be more. She would have courage and spirit beyond the ordinary. It was not until long after I had finished SARA DANE that I realized in fact that the real key to the book was that I had written about a land, a place which shaped people, their motives, their attitudes, their total lives. I believed that the girl I had called SARA DANE could not have managed in England what she achieved in Australia. She was no passenger on the ride from obscurity to prominence, from the proverbial rags-to-riches; she rode *with* men, not on their backs. I think that set the theme for many of the books which were to follow.

My marriage took me to live in New York, but the setting which had been the early part of SARA DANE was much on my mind. I had visited the Romney Marsh in the South East corner of England many times, walked its empty roads, traced its dykes, learned the tales of its smuggling past. In an apartment high above the roar of Manhattan traffic I remembered it all, the flowers and the lambs of the spring, the old and often untenanted churches, the wide, wide skies. I particularly remembered a house, set half-way up what would once have been a cliff before the Marsh was drained. In my mind I called it BLAKE'S REACH, and I brought there a girl who was to struggle to hold it, to bring up a young half-brother, to fight against poverty, to try to have what she felt was hers; a girl who grew to love the Marsh. I set it at the time when SARA DANE was making her way forward in Australia, the time of the French Revolution. Only a few miles beyond the edges of the Marsh, across the Channel, the Terror reigned, and my girl was caught up in it. Heroines, it seems, do not emerge in peaceful times, nor peaceful places. They must always act, and react, not be acted upon. Heroines are not peaceful women, although they may indeed be women of peace.

And so, when we lived in the Virgin Islands for a time, quite naturally my mind turned to slavery as the cause of the evil that afflicts us in so many ways to-day. I pictured that lovely Caribbean island at the moment of its highest drama, the moment when the slaves were freed in 1833. My heroine was caught in that drama as inexorably as she was caught in the hurricane which carried away so much. There is little that even the strongest woman can do against the hurricane winds of social change. She must accept and endure, as FIONA did. I began to detect a note of compassion creeping into my women, and they were better for it.

In A FALCON FOR A QUEEN I dared touch on the sort of love that is forbidden, only half-realized by my heroine, Kirsty. Once again, the woman was struggling for a place in a man's world; she fought for her right to inherit and run a small whisky empire in the Scottish Highlands, a woman on the brink of the twentieth century. She both won and lost, which is much the sort of balance life hands to most of us.

With a wry sense of amusement, I look back and realize that for many years I had been writing, in a quiet fashion, about women's struggle to liberate themselves, to use their talents, to be allowed to compete where the terms were equal. I have never written specifically about Women's Liberation. But then, the imagination is always free, isn't it?

Catherine Gaskin

AUTHOR'S NOTE

The story of Mary Reibey has become something of a legend in Australian history – its is the story of a woman, who, sentenced to transportation for what can have been no more than a child's prank, overcame the stigma of her conviction, and rose to a position of wealth and prominence among the citizens of early New South Wales. This novel is *not* her story, but it is based on the assumption that what one woman can do, so may another. The broad outlines of the lives of Mary Reibey and of Sara Dane are similar – the details differ sharply. This book is meant in no way to be a portrait of Mary Reibey, but simply a novel of her times.

In only one instance am I conscious of not having kept to the exact dates of the principal events in the colony. In Part II, Andrew Maclay takes up his grant of land on the Hawkesbury River about a year before the Historical Records show that the first settlers established themselves there.

Lastly, I should like to express my sincere thanks to Dr G. M. Mackaness, of Sydney, for his advice and many suggestions on the early chapters; to Ian Grey; to Katherine MacDougall and George Naish, of Greenwich Maritime Museum; also to my sister, Moira, for whose help with research, and in editing the manuscript, I am deeply grateful.

C. M. G.

SARA DANE

PART ONE

I

'*I am the resurrection and the life, saith the Lord, he that believeth in me, though he were dead . . .*'

There was very little movement among the crowd that packed the *Georgette*'s deck. They listened to the words recited at the burial service, seeming frozen by the unemotional calm of the captain's voice. Only a few of the more curious pressed forward for a better view of the stitched bundle of sailcloth, partly hidden under a Union Jack.

It was noon of a June day in 1792. The *Georgette*, a sixty-four gun, two-decker, of the East India Company, was ten days out of Rio, headed for Cape Town. On leaving the Cape, her orders were to turn south into the Antarctic and then eastwards following a track that only a few ships had ever taken before her. Her destination was the settlement established four years ago on the shores of Port Jackson, in the new colony of New South Wales. It was hardly yet known by its proper name of Sydney – the familiar name, the name that rang through the courtrooms and prisons of England was that of Botany Bay. This was the dreaded settlement raised to house the overflow of the prisons, a prison complete in itself, from which escape was impossible, and the hope of ever returning to England almost futile. The *Georgette* was a convict transport, and the thought of Botany Bay stirred somewhere in the minds of most of those who listened silently to the captain's words.

'*Man that is born of woman hath but a short time to live . . .*'

They made a strange sight herded round the flag-draped sail-cloth. All about, there on the upper-deck, the quarter-deck, and the poop, the crew was arranged in orderly lines, bare-footed and dirty; they stood with faces arranged in careful solemnity; in-different faces, because the identity of that roll of sailcloth meant less than nothing to them. One or two, making a gesture towards the occasion, had braided his greasy hair into a pigtail, much neater than the careless efforts of the rest. They were unwashed; they looked it, and they smelled vilely.

Four officers, the master, his mate, and six midshipmen, stood in a stiff line behind the captain. The ship's surgeon had taken his place at the end of the row – his attitude suggesting that he did not belong to that little hierarchy, because he was not, as they were, wholly a seaman. Each face in the row bore that same frigid look which found its echo in the crew about them; eyes were mostly fixed on the horizon that tilted steadily with the movement of the ship; bodies were drawn up in disciplined rigidity. The words of the service fell on inattentive ears; they had all heard it many times before, and only the midshipmen were young enough and fresh enough to the life of the sea to be greatly impressed. The youngest midshipman, a lad of fourteen, on his first voyage, now and then shot quick, nervous glances towards the sailcloth. But the rest wore an expression of patience, and an acceptance of the monotony, struggle, and death to which their long, slow voyaging had made them accustomed.

A man and a woman, with their two children, stood behind the officers, and a little to the side of them. They were grouped closely together, looking ill at ease, as if they were well aware that their servant, whose body lay under the flag, was no concern of the crew; she had been an ordinary woman, leaving no impression with these men who might have passed her on deck a dozen times in a day. The wind played with the long bright skirts of the woman and her young daughter; it played among the fringes of their shawls. The colour and the movement of the soft materials was a touch of frivolity thrust among those erect lines.

The convicts stood by themselves, farther away from the captain, their armed guards making a sharp division between them and the rest of the crowd on the upper-deck. There were two hundred and seven convicts aboard the *Georgette*, an ill-assorted mass of human cargo, housed down in the darkness between decks, waiting without hope for the arrival in Botany Bay. They were sullenly submissive while the words of the burial service droned over them. But heads kept turning, eyes wandered to the masts and the riggings stretching above, to the endless horizons. They blinked constantly, in the strong light; the distances of sea and sky were painful when they had looked at nothing for weeks but the bulkheads, dark with age and damp. The wind sported pitilessly with the rags they wore. They were a wild-looking lot – men and women; long hair, matted with filth, hung on their frowning brows; their eyes, screwed up against the hard glare, were fierce and unrepentant. There was scarcely an adequate pair of boots or shoes among them, and the flapping of their tattered clothes gave them the appearance of a collection of scarecrows. They shifted gingerly from one foot to another, savouring the relief of stretching their legs and filling their lungs with air.

'We therefore commit her body to the deep, to be turned into corruption . . .'

All heads craned in curiosity as the sailcloth bundle was raised and slid forward through one of the open gun ports. The flag was drawn back, and the body fell with a splash into the sea. The shock of the sound registered briefly on a few faces. There was a strange, choked-back cry from the midst of the convicts, and a child of eleven suddenly bent her face into her grimy hands. No one took any notice, except a woman standing behind who gave her a half-affectionate pat on the shoulder. The child's sobs continued, soft little cries which the captain's voice easily overrode. As though afraid of the noise she made, she ceased weeping abruptly, and raised her head. The tears had made fresh tracks in the dirt on her cheeks.

Finally the captain lifted his eyes from the book he held, reciting the last words of the service from memory.

'Amen.' The crew mumbled the word in a chorus. They waited for the order to dismiss.

Among the convicts there was a sense of tension as they formed up to go below again.

Andrew Maclay, the *Georgette*'s second officer, watched them go below, a tattered, barefoot mob. They were a miserable-looking lot, he thought. There wasn't even a picturesque quality about them – just a collection of thieves and ruffians, some of them lucky to have escaped the gallows. They murmured among themselves as they bunched around the hatchway, waiting to go down. A guard's voice sharply ordered them to silence. Andrew watched only a moment longer, thinking that it would take more than the sort of punishment New South Wales meted out to reform the greater part of this sorry crowd. He turned, starting to make his way to the companion-ladder leading to the cabins. But he was halted suddenly by a woman's voice, rising high and indignantly from the midst of the waiting convicts.

'Here, mind what you're doing! You'll have the child down that ladder on her head!'

'You mind your words, you . . . !' The sentence finished in a stream of oaths.

Andrew wheeled. The group round the hatchway parted at his approach, and stood silently watching to see what would happen. The guard, made aware of an officer's presence by the quietening of the crowd, turned swiftly. He jerked his thumb backwards at the convict-woman who had called out.

'Causing trouble, sir,' he said. 'Holding up the line, she was.'

The woman had her hand on the arm of the child whose sobbing had broken into the burial service. She drew herself up very straight, looking from the marine guard to Andrew, and for a brief moment the filthy remains of the gown she wore seemed to stir and quiver with the force of barely controlled anger.

She burst out: '*You* saw what happened!' The words were fairly flung at Andrew. 'He,' pointing to the guard, 'almost threw her down there!'

'Sir . . . !'

The guard made a savage movement with his musket towards the woman. The circle of convicts closed in, heads craning, tongues loosened with excitement at the prospect of a set-to. In those dulled eyes Andrew saw a flicker of interest build up within a second. This crowd was spoiling for a diversion, eagerly waiting his order for punishment for the woman. He was sickened by the sight of them, the sharp, watching faces, without a trace of pity for one of their own kind, or even for the child.

'Enough! Silence — both of you!'

He addressed the woman then. 'Get below — at once!'

She looked back at him for only a moment longer, and then she urged the child towards the companion ladder. The guard, relieved, began to hustle the convicts forward again. The babel of talk increased.

'Keep them in order, there!' Andrew commanded curtly as he turned away.

'Aye, aye, sir!'

Andrew made his way below, and he found himself thinking of the incident. It was all over in a few seconds — it hadn't even attracted the attention of any other officer. It was no more than the smallest point of discipline, something which happened constantly when the convicts were bunched together in groups on deck. Yet his mind lingered on the scene. The eager, pitiless faces revolted him; he had seen their quick willingness to turn upon one of their own. And the woman herself — there had been a fierce kind of spirit in the way she sprang to the defence of the child. He tried to think what she had looked like; but she was no different from any of the other young women who clutched their indistinguishable rags. All he could clearly recall was the angry flash of an extraordinary pair of eyes when she had first turned to him.

With his hand stretched towards the knob of the wardroom door he halted, remembering, with a sense of shock, that her voice had been that of an educated woman.

2

As readily as any other member of the party, Andrew had accepted Captain Marshall's invitation to eat dinner with him after the burial service. This was a diversion from routine for which they were all thankful; these meals at the captain's table, lengthy and rather boisterous, made up for a whole week of monotony in the wardroom. He settled back in his chair, drowsy, contented, and watched the man opposite, their passenger, James Ryder. Ryder had been a prosperous East Anglian farmer, who now, for some inexplicable reason, was determined to settle and farm in New South Wales. Andrew privately thought this revealed a man of incredible eccentricity, and yet his appearance was perfectly normal. He carried the marks of his class and type — well-cut coat and immaculate linen. Ryder's pretty, frail wife had also been pressed to join them at the table, but the ordeal on deck that morning had tired her, and she had gone directly to her cabin. Also absent was Howlett, the purser, and young Roberts, the fourth lieutenant.

It was mid-afternoon and the meal had not yet finished. They had eaten well; the madeira was good and plentiful. Their spirits were high, though their talk had turned for the second time to the subject of the scene they had witnessed at noon that day.

Brooks, the surgeon, addressed Ryder.

'I'm afraid your wife, sir, will be greatly inconvenienced by the death of her servant. Most unfortunate . . .'

Ryder nodded agreement. 'I'm afraid she will, Mr Brooks.'

Andrew's eyes flicked from one to the other of the company, watching their expressions change as the topic was reintroduced. The men's ages ranged from Lieutenant Wilder's twenty-four years, to the captain's mid-fifties. It was a party of six — the captain, Harding and Wilder, his first and third officers, Brooks, James Ryder, and Maclay himself.

Ryder fingered some breadcrumbs on his plate, then he looked directly towards the captain. He cleared his throat. 'My wife has been wondering, Captain Marshall,' he said, 'if it's possible that you have a woman among the convicts called Sara Dane?'

A silence followed the words. The captain tilted the decanter carefully over his glass. The wine had been brought aboard at Teneriffe by Ryder, and it was uncommonly good. He sipped, raising his eyes to his passenger.

'What name did you say, Mr Ryder?'

'Sara Dane, sir.'

The captain glanced at his first officer. 'Mr Harding, can you recall that name on the list?'

Harding shook his head. 'There are sixty-seven female convicts
on board, sir. I can't, at the moment, remember if this person is
among them.' He turned to Ryder. 'You have some special interest
in this woman, sir?'

Ryder took his time in answering. He was frowning; his leathery
skin was dark and lined, rough against the smooth white of the
linen at his throat. 'My wife, as you know, is a bad sailor. She
is so often confined to her cabin that I honestly don't know what is
to become of the children now Martha Barratt is gone. She was
quite excellent with them, you know.'

Harding nodded, waiting to hear the rest.

But it was Brooks who spoke. His voice was cold and rapid.
'And is that your reason for seeking this woman, sir? Are you
thinking of making her a nurse for Ellen and Charles?'

Andrew saw that Ryder stiffened at the tone.

'Have you any objection to such a scheme, Mr Brooks?'

'Well . . . ' The surgeon hesitated. 'She isn't known to you, is
she?'

'Not personally,' Ryder replied. 'By hearsay.'

They had all become interested by this time. Andrew noticed
that the captain was leaning forward, his elbows on the table, his
glass clasped between both hands.

'Before we embarked at Portsmouth,' Ryder said, 'my wife received a letter from a friend who lives in Rye. The lady writes of
Sara Dane, who was servant to a parson's family there – and sentenced to transportation about twelve months ago. My wife has
hopes that this young woman may be on board. And if so, as she
is domestically trained, she would probably be of great help to her
for the rest of the voyage.'

He went on, 'The doubt is, of course, whether she survived her
imprisonment in England.' Then he lifted his shoulders slightly.
'She may already have reached New South Wales. Or, again, she
might still be awaiting a transport.'

Brooks spoke again. 'Sentenced twelve months ago, you say?
Then I should be surprised if she isn't dead. The gaols are filthy,
and crawling with vermin – and the dogs in the streets wouldn't
eat the food the prisoners are given. When gaol-fever gets going
the poor wretches die off like flies.'

Captain Marshall looked round at his guest. 'I once visited a
gaol, gentlemen – not, of course, of necessity.' Here he waited for

the laughter which dutifully followed. 'The place was in a state of ruin and the gaoler hadn't received any money for repairs. So what do you think the fellow did? He simply chained the prisoners to the good walls, and let the others tumble down about them!'

Andrew listened with interest. He had never seen the inside of the gaols where the gaolers acted as a kind of landlord, and the prisoners were treated according to their means.

'The sight you saw was not an unusual one, sir,' Wilder put in. 'It often happens. After all, what else can these gaolers do? They've got to live on what the prisoners can pay. They can hardly be expected to run their places like inns.'

'Inns!' Brooks laughed. 'There's not much chance of that! Believe me, gentlemen, you've seen nothing until you've been inside a woman's prison. Sometimes they cram thirty or forty women into a ward scarcely big enough to hold ten. I've seen them almost naked, and the few rags they do have are crawling with lice. Most of them haven't even the money to treat the gaoler to a pot of beer, so they're simply left to rot – and they do!' He added quickly, 'If I ever have the bad luck to be sent to prison, I trust it will be after I've stolen a large enough sum of money to let me pay my way out again!'

No one spoke immediately; they seemed content to let Brooks's words sink in. The trouble was, Andrew thought, they were all, excepting James Ryder, half-asleep – the heat, the heavy, drawn-out meal and the plentiful wine were not conducive to a purposeful conversation. But Wilder bestirred himself. Andrew, glancing at him, noted the nonchalantly-raised brows, the slow, studied smile, and wondered if Ryder allowed himself to be irritated by this young man.

'In view of what we've just heard, Mr Ryder, do you really think it's a good idea to have one of these creatures to wait on your wife and children?' Wilder eyed the company with a slight smirk. 'We all know what these women are. It's no secret that they pay their gaol fees by prostitution.'

Ryder was immediately on the defensive. 'I'm quite satisfied that my idea is a sound one, Mr Wilder.'

'Inadvisable, sir, surely,' Wilder murmured. 'These women are felons.'

Andrew looked quickly at Ryder. Here was a man of solid worth, a farmer of considerable wealth and education, and the *Georgette*'s officers still passed time amongst themselves wondering at the nature of his attraction to the struggling colony for which they were bound, why he should choose to drag his wife and children on this in-

terminable voyage to set them down finally among savages and
convicts in a penal colony.

'These felons are what the Governor will assign to me as servants when we reach New South Wales,' Ryder replied, regarding
Wilder coldly. 'I am prepared to take a risk on whatever type
of woman I choose from this ship. My wife must have someone
to take care of the children.' He turned to the captain. 'Captain
Marshall, have I your permission to see if this woman is aboard?'

'Oh, certainly, Mr Ryder! Certainly!' the captain answered,
scarcely taking the glass away from his lips. The top of his head,
bald, and ringed in greying fuzz, was as pink and shiny as his
cheeks.

The old fool, Andrew thought. Captain Marshall was more
than half-drunk, and not at all concerned with the problem Ryder
faced. But, to merit his passenger's generosity – for the madeira
was indeed excellent – he would give all the help he could. The
unwelcome job of routing the woman from the stink-hole between
decks would fall to one of his luckless officers. Andrew felt it likely
that Brooks would be chosen; it was the surgeon's duty to visit the
convicts' quarters each day on a tour of inspection. And then it
suddenly occurred to Andrew that he himself might be the one for
the task. God forbid! He desperately hoped the captain's wandering glance might finally pause on Brooks.

But the captain was leaning towards Ryder again. 'Yes, my dear
sir, I quite agree with you. If you must have one of these women as
a nursemaid, better to put her into service now – get whatever
good you can out of her while you need her most.'

Andrew put in good-humouredly, 'You might not find her so
bad a proposition, Mr Ryder. They're not all desperate criminals,
you know. We have poachers and dissenting preachers down in the
holds. One could hardly call *them* criminals.'

'Then what is one to call them?' Wilder asked.

'Well . . .' Andrew began. 'I wouldn't call a man a criminal
simply because he preaches another way to worship – or because he
steals a chicken or two.'

'Rash words, Mr Maclay!' Harding said with a smile. 'An odd
preacher here and there – what does it matter? But think of hundreds of preachers and thousands of poachers and poultry thieves,
and it becomes a different story altogether. Why, if these people
were left unpunished they'd soon fancy themselves as good as their
masters. It's that same feeling which produced the revolution in
France. From what I can make out, it all started because the King
was weak enough to call these fellows together and give them the

idea that they had something to contribute to the Government. They, of course, seized power the first opportunity they got – and now the Royal family is imprisoned in the Tuileries, and from the temper of these Frenchies it looks as if they might all end up on the guillotine.' He paused, and then said firmly, 'And where did it all begin – with nothing more than letting an odd poacher off punishment, and permitting a few men to roam about the country stirring up trouble!'

Ryder nodded his agreement. '*I* like to see justice done. Sometimes the laws *are* severe on the poor. But rebellion breeds in the masses – and they must be taught that they can't break the law and expect to go unpunished. These agitators are dangerous men. Given half a chance they'll pull down King and Government. That rascal, Tom Paine now . . . His *Rights of Man* is as treasonable a document as ever yet hung a man.'

Brooks, risking a rebuke for Jacobin sentiments, said, 'All Tom Paine wanted was representative government and old-age pensions.'

'Tom Paine wanted to see the monarchy and House of Lords abolished,' Harding said. 'He wanted the poor educated above their stations – and he'd be happy to have us ruled by a gang of labourers, as they are in Paris.'

'Look at the effect Paine's gospel and the French Revolution have had in Ireland,' Ryder said. 'Wolf Tone is a mad hothead! And the Irish have far from finished with rebellion yet, believe me!'

Andrew said thoughtfully, 'I don't think it's altogether fair to blame the French for the agitation in Ireland. In my opinion the Irish simply don't like having their country ruled by English soldiers. And, as for England herself – wouldn't you say, Mr Ryder, that the Enclosures Acts, driving the peasants out of the land into the factories, is the real cause of the trouble? Many of them who were happy and contented before, can't even earn a living wage. So they steal and poach.'

The captain roused himself at that. 'Yes, they steal and poach – and are very rightly sent to Botany Bay for their trouble. Once give them the idea that they can do that sort of thing and get away with it, and it's the end of decency and order.'

'True enough, sir,' Andrew said. 'I don't say they ought not to be punished. But I can't see the decency and order in laws that hang a murderer, or give him life transportation to Botany Bay, and then deal out exactly the same sentence to a man for poaching a rabbit or two. It just doesn't make sense.'

Harding chuckled softly. 'You talk like a Whig Member of Parliament, Maclay! Will you speak for Law reform when you're sent to Westminster?'

There was general laughter among the group. Andrew answered amiably. 'I only become a reformer over a bottle of wine, gentlemen. I'm afraid at other times the state of my fellow-man doesn't worry me much.'

'Well,' Wilder drawled, 'one can't really expect much in the way of politics – or reform – from a Lowland Scots farmer-turned-sailor.'

Andrew, not in the least put out, turned to him. 'Perhaps Scottish farmers don't know much about politics – at least according to Westminster standards. But that doesn't make me altogether wrong in saying that not every man among the convicts is a criminal and not every woman is a slut. I think if Mrs Ryder is prepared to take a chance with one of the women, then it's more than likely she'll find someone to suit her.'

Captain Marshall seemed to think they had spoken long enough on an unpleasant subject. He rose to his feet. The others followed.

'Excellent wine, Mr Ryder,' he murmured, bowing.

Ryder also bowed.

The captain gazed round his assembled officers. He was smiling slightly. The tips of his fingers rested on the table as he leaned forward.

'Well, Mr Maclay, you seem determined to champion the convicts. In which case, I think you'd probably be the best person to find out if this woman, Sara Dane, is on board with us.'

Andrew stiffened, and his face was suddenly hot. 'Yes, sir!'

'And in the event of her not being with us,' the captain went on, 'I'm quite sure we're safe in entrusting the choice of a female to you. Isn't that right, gentlemen?'

Andrew saw the covert grins and heard the chorus of assent.

'Yes, sir,' he said.

The captain bowed again towards Ryder. 'My compliments to your wife, sir. I'm sure Mr Maclay will do everything possible to accommodate her.' He pushed aside his chair and stepped back from the table. 'Good afternoon, gentlemen.'

An hour passed before Andrew sent one of the midshipmen for the list of women convicts aboard. He was in the wardroom, a litter of maps and papers spread on the table before him. He was busy, but the captain's orders couldn't be kept waiting any longer, no matter how he cursed his luck in being the one to receive it. Damn old Marshall!

The door opened and he looked up. The youngest of the mid-shipmen entered, a leather book under his arm.

Andrew reached out for it. 'That's right, Williamson. Thank you.'

'Aye, aye, sir!'

The boy went out again.

The other two occupants of the wardroom, Brooks and Wilder, came over to the table.

Andrew pushed aside the maps and opened the book reluctantly.

'I wish to hell the old man had picked anyone else but me to do this.'

Wilder smiled. 'I'll be interested to see what you produce – to see your idea of a virtuous woman.'

Discipline on board the *Georgette* was strict. Captain Marshall had never turned a blind eye to fraternization between his crew and the convicts. Andrew had little doubt that Wilder would be one of the first to consort with the women if the rule were relaxed. He recalled tales of other transports where the captain was lax, and the crew and convicts mixed riotously, making the voyage one long carousel. Wilder, he felt, was airing his contempt from the safety of his position on the other side of Captain Marshall's fast and set codes of conduct.

Andrew turned the pages distastefully. Feeling ran high among the officers of the East India Company that it was beneath their dignity to accept the contract to transport convicts to Botany Bay. The Company had of late made a number of contracts of this kind, and Andrew, at times, was doubtful that he would ever be transferred to a regular Indiaman run again.

Wilder leaned across his shoulder, looking down the list. He said idly, 'Can't imagine why Ryder should want to go out there. And taking his wife . . . You know, she's a damned pretty woman! And the fool proposes to set her down among a bunch of savages!'

'Ryder will probably make a fortune for her in New South Wales,' Brooks remarked. 'That's good enough reason for any man to want to go there.'

'A fortune, he says!' Wilder nudged Andrew. 'I shouldn't think there was a hope in the world of that! What's to be gained from a penal colony? It hasn't any trading advantages like China and India. It can't export anything and the natives are savages. It wouldn't have been settled at all if the war with America hadn't stopped the Government from sending convicts there. From all accounts Botany Bay is nothing more than a clump of huts – it'll never be other than a dumping-ground for the overflow of the prisons.'

Brooks's brows were lifting slowly while Wilder spoke. He put his hands in his pockets, and threw one leg lazily across the corner of the table.

'Your opinion is interesting, Mr Wilder,' he said. 'But I have a different one.'

From Brooks's expression, Andrew knew that he was about to enjoy turning Wilder's second-hand views inside out. Brooks had sailed as surgeon with the second fleet of convicts to Port Jackson. He was a quiet man, and didn't talk much about any previous voyages he had made. Andrew looked at him inquiringly.

'It's like no other place I've ever seen,' Brooks said, half to himself, not looking at the other two. 'And I've spent quite a few years of my life in ships, and there aren't many ports that I haven't seen. It's a mystery, the whole place – it's desolate, but its fascinating. Captain Cook charted the east coast first about twenty-two years ago. He made only one landing, at Botany Bay. But when the First Fleet went out five years ago, Governor Phillip found Botany Bay impossible to settle. He moved his fleet to Port Jackson, a few miles along the coast. What a harbour that is! He landed and settled at a place called Sydney Cove.'

'And out of all that, where do you get your idea that Ryder has a chance of making a fortune?' Wilder asked.

'Because I agree with Governor Phillip,' Brooks said, studying the amused set of Wilder's well-shaped mouth. 'Phillip has great ideas for his prison-colony. And, by God, I don't care what anyone says, I think he's right!'

'What sort of ideas?' Andrew put in. 'Is the land fertile?'

Brooks hesitated. 'That's a difficult question, Maclay. At the moment they can get almost nothing out of it in the way of crops. They're perpetually on the point of starvation. They depend solely on England for supplies – and you know how precarious that is. The convicts die off in dozens, because if the ships are delayed they just haven't enough rations to keep them alive. But Phillip thinks the place can be made to produce when they learn to manage the soil and the climate. So far there doesn't seem to be a man among them with any real knowledge of farming – and the convicts aren't concerned for the future of the country.' He finished earnestly. 'That's why I think Ryder has a fortune waiting out there. He has the right knowledge, and he has the money to push ahead.'

Wilder's good-looking young face wore an expression of boredom. 'Well, all I say is that it'll be a damned nuisance if Port Jackson becomes a regular call on the way to the East. I, for one, won't have a care if I never see the place after this trip.'

Andrew turned again to the book in front of him. He flicked the pages impatiently. 'Sara Dane . . . Hmm . . .' Suddenly he looked up. 'God, how is one expected to tell these women apart? There aren't even papers sent with them to tell us what crimes they've committed.'

Wilder laughed. 'Perhaps we're consigning the gentle Mrs Ryder into the hands of a murderess!'

'The whole position is absurd,' Andrew said, frowning down at the book. 'The Government has sent these people to the end of the earth without papers of any description. No one has the faintest idea why they were convicted. What's to happen to them when they reach New South Wales? How does Governor Phillip decide when their sentences have expired?'

'That's his affair, my dear fellow,' Wilder said lightly. 'Now, let's get on with the problem in hand. Let's find the fair damsel in the darkness below!'

'I'll warrant she's not on . . .' Andrew broke off, jabbing at a page with his forefinger. 'Here she is . . . Sara Dane! . . . and no punishments marked against her. This is a piece of luck for Ryder!'

'Well, off you go, Maclay!' Wilder said, good-humoured now. 'I wish you joy with your task!' He gave them a half-salute, and adjusting his coat with care, sauntered out of the wardroom. He paused before he pulled the door behind him, looking back over his shoulder. 'A thought has just struck me.'

'Yes?' Andrew said.

'I wouldn't,' Wilder continued, 'for all the wealth in the East, change places with the Governor of New South Wales!'

2

Andrew was never free from his feelings of distaste whenever he was forced to visit the convict quarters. With a curt order he summoned a Sergeant of Marines to accompany him, and went quickly down the companion ladder, trying to stiffen himself for the ordeal facing him. Service with the Navy had hardened him against undue squeamishness, but this was something quite different. This was human cargo carried in worse conditions than the livestock — in fact, the livestock was cared for as something of value, while the death of a convict was of no importance to anyone. As he reached the gun deck, where the prisoners were kept, the confused babel of voices reached him – the women's voices distinct and shrill above the lower tones of the men. He felt the sweat start in a trickle all over his body, and he longed with a kind of desperation to turn again and mount the companion ladder.

He kept his ideas about the convicts to himself – except for the few times, as at dinner today, when he had been rash enough to voice his contempt for the chaos of English law which lumped murderers and petty thieves together in a transport bound for Botany Bay. Men of his class were not expected to feel pity for these prisoners – never once among the officers in the wardroom had he heard a word of sympathy for them. Listening to the way in which they talked of the convicts, he knew that he was quite alone in his feeling for them, a feeling that there was something personal to him in their sufferings, as if, even though he was completely removed from their world, they still had the right to claim his attention and thoughts. Among British ship-owners, and from the men who campaigned against slavery, he had heard descriptions of the slave ships which plied between Africa and the West Indies; it seemed to him that the position of the convicts on the *Georgette* was hardly less terrible.

He hated the crowding, and the struggle for survival which went on among them; he had seen it all before in the crumbling houses in the alleyways of London and Edinburgh. His father had been a Scot with a lucrative practice at the English bar, who had lived only long enough to give his son a distaste for law as a profession, and the kind of reckless purposeless courage which could let him stake his life on the turn of a card, or the throw of a dice. Andrew remembered his gambling father only dimly; he had been brought up by his mother's brother, who owned a small estate near Edinburgh. The only discipline he had known in his life was in the Navy, and after that the milder rule of the East India Company. He grew up with a horror of the crowded swarm of the great cities, and for anything which threatened to put a shackle upon his liberty. A kind of sickness crept over him sometimes at the thought of the packed gloom of the *Georgette*'s prison quarters, of the irons which still remained on some ankles.

Down here the gun ports were closed, and it was dim and airless. In the near-darkness it was always the stench which came first; the overpowering smell of unwashed bodies, the smell of rancid food, and of water, green and half-still with living things. The stench of the prisons had come aboard with the convicts, and Andrew imagined it would be a long time before the ship was rid of it.

The prison quarters had been made by running a bulkhead across the width of the ship, with square openings for the guards' muskets. He made his way reluctantly through the gloom; the guards were both bent with their faces to the holes. When they heard him they came to attention quickly, and one of them produced keys.

Andrew stood before the heavy door; through the grille at the top a confusion of shrill cries and the sounds of scuffling and falling bodies reached him.

He gestured towards it irritably. 'For God's sake hurry yourself, man! What the devil's happening here?'

The guard fumbled with the locks. 'Couldn't say, sir. It's just started – some sort of fight. They're always at it.'

'Well, it's your duty to see that they're not always at it. Why haven't you made some attempt to stop it?'

'Stop it, sir?' The man straightened and threw Andrew an astonished glance. 'Why, it does no good, sir. And besides – I shouldn't like to go in there. They'd tear me to pieces!'

Andrew pushed him aside impatiently, rattling the key in the lock until it yielded. 'I shall take care that the captain hears how you attend to your duties.'

He swung the door open, and stepped inside. With noticeable reluctance the sergeant followed.

Inside, when his eyes became accustomed to the half-light, he could make out the mass of lying, sitting and standing women. The noise was terrible, and in the centre of the space four or five women rolled together in a frenzied struggle. All the others had drawn back from them, watching the contest with vicious interest, lending their own threats and encouragement to the general noise. The combat was desperately unequal; even from the mass of kicking heels and waving arms Andrew was able to tell that one of them, lying so completely beneath the bodies of the others that he could hardly see her, was fighting alone. Judging from the size of the women who opposed her, he imagined that the struggle would have been brief, even if he had not come along.

'Silence!' he roared.

The women in the centre of the floor took not the least bit of notice. Around them, the others became gradually aware of his presence, and their cries faded away. In the growing quiet he could distinctly hear the grunts and sighs of the struggling women.

Suddenly one of them, kneeling on the legs of the woman beneath that incredible pile, was warned by the inexplicable stillness about her, and glanced round. She stared at him for only a second, with a trace of fear on her face; then she tugged at the shoulder of the woman nearest her.

"Ere, Peg! Look!"

The woman she addressed looked up. Her expression altered immediately. She grinned toothlessly at Andrew and made a sort of flourish with her hands. Her harsh Cockney accent rang out over the fading sounds of the others' voices.

"Ere's the 'andsome young officer come to visit us, dearies! Get out the tea-cups!'

Wild shrieks of laughter greeted the remark.

Andrew felt his face grow hot, and he cursed inwardly.

'Silence!' he rapped again. 'What's the meaning of all this?'

The last murmurs died away completely. He knew that no one would answer him. They stared at him solidly, appearing to draw strength from their numbers, while he faced them alone. He watched the stirring of rags as they moved, the cracked, filthy hands plucking at garments which were no more than barely decent. The faces, under their coating of grease and dirt, were indistinguishable. And all the eyes were alike – watchful, shrewd. He looked them over, noting that even the ones who lay ill had raised their heads to see him better. The strongest among them had fought their way to the sides, and had at least the support of the bulkhead, their few possessions were grouped about them like the riches of a kingdom. While he watched them, the three in the centre gradually released their hold on their prisoner. Kneeling where they were, they watched him eagerly, while their victim sat up slowly, holding her head in her hands.

'You all know what the punishment is for fighting!' he said, fixing his gaze on the four culprits. He gestured towards the one he imagined was the ring-leader. 'I seem to remember you've been punished before. Isn't it time you learned to obey orders?'

She answered with another grin. 'Yes, sweetheart, but I'm an old dog to be learning new tricks!'

He flushed, and in the laughter that followed her sally he turned towards the sergeant.

'See that Mr Harding has these women's names.'

'Aye, aye, sir!'

They quietened again at his words. A change at once ran through the crowd. They had been hilarious and cheeky, now they seemed hostile and resentful. There was nothing they could do about it, he thought; they were defenceless against authority. If they once guessed his sympathy for their position they would fasten on it like vultures, and his life on the *Georgette* would be hell. From that minute every appearance he made among them would be the signal for outbursts of wit and insubordination.

He cleared his throat and said firmly, 'Is there a woman here called Sara Dane?'

There was no response.

'Sara Dane,' he repeated. 'Is there anyone here by that name?'

The victim of the three attackers suddenly stirred and lifted her head.

'I'm Sara Dane.'

She struggled to her knees, and then stood up. She began to push her way through the tightly packed bodies towards Andrew. As they moved and shoved to let her through, the suffocating odours reached him more strongly. She reached him at last, stumbling over a prostrate body as she came. This called forth a stream of angry blasphemy such as he had never heard bettered even in the Navy. But the woman moving towards him seemed completely indifferent to the abuse. She was tall; she had to stoop to avoid the low beams of the deckhead.

'Are you Sara Dane?'

'Yes – I am.'

In the dimness he could make nothing of her – what sort of woman she was. But the voice he knew instantly. It was the same one that he had heard raised in protest over the treatment of the child, when the convicts had been sent below after the burial service – the voice which had troubled and puzzled him. He looked at her sharply.

'And what have you got to do with this disturbance? You should be flogged for being disorderly.'

'Disorderly!' She swept the loose hair away from her face to look at him fully. For some reason he felt suddenly intimidated. 'Do you call it disorderly to fight for what belongs to me? Why should I let this scum get their filthy hands on my things?'

'What were they trying to take from you?'

'This!' She raised her hand and swung before his face a dirty handkerchief knotted at the corners and weighted. 'My rations.'

Andrew looked around the sullen faces and fervently wished that he were out of this place. He was faced squarely here with the thought that was for ever at the back of his mind – the hunger of the convicts. They lived mostly on salt pork and weevily ship's biscuits. Brooks, who worked among them daily, had told them that the rations were far less than was needed to keep them in health – there was always the fear of scurvy breaking out. There seemed nothing that he, or the captain, or even the East India Company itself could do about it – they were paid a fixed rate to transport the convicts, and it did not stretch to luxuries. In spite of what Brooks tried to do for them, there were frequent deaths. Andrew had heard tales from other transports of the convicts hiding the

dead for days, in order to draw the extra rations. As always, where
there was hunger, the bullies rose from the mass to take what they
could get by force.

'Is this true?' he asked her.

'Of course it's true!' She gave her head a slight toss – an action
that was oddly youthful, and didn't seem to fit her appearance.
'Why do you think they . . . ?'

He cut her short. 'You've got too much to say! I'll deal with
this.'

He turned to the circle of faces about them. 'One more instance
of this – just one more – and I'll see that you're all punished. All of
you – do you hear?' Then he addressed Sara Dane again. 'And I
don't want to hear any more from you.'

'Well, would you stand by and let them . . . ?'

That will do!

He wheeled, motioning her to follow. 'Come with me!'

As the guard swung the door wide for them to pass, the raucous
Cockney shout rang out again.

'Have a nice time, sweetheart! Be sure and tell the officers there
are plenty more of us where you came from!'

Andrew stopped abruptly and faced them.

'Another word out of you,' he said, 'and you'll be stopped deck
exercise for ten days!'

The guard pulled the door closed with a crash, but the stifled
laughter followed him along the passage to the companion-ladder.
He motioned the woman behind him to hurry.

When he reached the upper deck he turned to watch her as she
emerged into the clear light. She staggered a little, as if the sudden
sweet air and the sunlight were a shock to her senses. He half-
reached out a hand to support her, and then, glancing at the
sergeant, he let it drop lamely again. She regained her balance,
looking about her with an air of ease and composure that mixed
sadly with her rags. His lips parted faintly in a smile of amusement to see there was even a touch of superiority about her. For a
second or two she surveyed the deck with all the manner of a great
lady invited aboard. Then, aware of his eyes upon her, she dropped
her pose, and turned fully towards him.

He discovered that she was much younger than he had supposed. She was slim and straight, and the skin of the throat and
face was unlined. But she carried the dirt of the prison like a
barrier to whatever beauty she might have possessed. Her face
and neck had the greyish tinge of long-embedded dirt; her hair,
fallen from its rough knot, hung lankly upon her shoulders. She

had on a tattered gown many sizes too large; it had been hacked
off at the front of the hem, and at the back it trailed on the deck
behind her. She wore it with an air of impoverished grandeur.

Then she raised her eyes to him. A greenish-blue they were,
almost the colour of the sea, he thought. They had a calculating,
questioning expression.

'It blows fresh up here, Lieutenant,' she said quietly.

He glanced at her quickly, and then, remembering the guard,
looked away. 'That will be all, sergeant.'

'Very good, sir.'

He watched the man across the deck before he turned to her
again. 'Fresh . . . ?'

For all his trying he couldn't keep the curiosity out of his voice,
and was instantly furious with himself for having answered her.
It was a piece of rank impertinence that she had addressed him at
all, and he should have rebuked her immediately. But with those
queer green eyes fixed on him he had, for an instant, lost his
head.

'Perhaps you don't notice it,' she was saying. 'But when one
spends one's time down where I do . . .'

'Haven't I told you to be quiet!' he threw back at her. 'Does
nothing have any effect on you?'

He turned aside, motioning her to follow him to the passenger
accommodation.

She made a little running step to catch up with him, twisting
sideways to peer into his face.

'But why shouldn't I talk to you, Lieutenant? It can't harm
discipline – there isn't anyone to hear us. Besides, it's a long time
since I spoke to anyone like you. Down there' – she pointed to the
deck – 'they don't know the King's English.'

He stopped short and faced her angrily.

'If you're down there with types you don't like – then it's your
own fault! People aren't sent to Botany Bay without good reason!'

'Oh, but . . .'

He jerked his head impatiently. 'Can't you understand? I'm not
on this ship to listen to you talking. Now, for the last time – *be
quiet*!'

'Yes, sir.'

She made a sketchy kind of curtsy towards him, and as she
bowed her head he had an instant suspicion that she smiled. But
she followed meekly enough. He could hear the limp swish of her
skirt as it swept the deck.

2

Sara Dane had been born in London eighteen years ago, in a top room of a lodging-house in Villiers Street, off the Strand. At least that was where her father said she was born; but he had left so many lodging-houses in a hurry, owing money to his landladies, that she often wondered how he could remember which particular one it was.

She had loved her father, Sebastian Dane, passionately and blindly. He was a tall man, shoulders stooped beneath his height, and straight black hair falling over his forehead. She always considered that his thin, dark face, with its fatal lines of dissipation and weakness, was far handsomer than any other she had ever seen. The times when he was sober, or only slightly drunk, he had an infectious gaiety, a good humour that made people love him, and landladies forget that he hadn't paid his rent. There was a strong companionship between them. The only time Sara feared him was during the periods of real drunkenness, when he sat over his rum for days at a stretch, barely able to make the effort of rising from his chair. But this didn't happen often – for the most part he was a merry drunkard. His insidious, habitual drinking gradually drained his strength, and wore the edge of his brilliance.

He was the son of a West Country parson – though his references to the life of the rectory in that pleasantly-wooded Somerset valley meant little to his daughter, for she had never seen it. Sebastian, cynically, did not hesitate in the slightest to make capital from the fact that his father was a baronet's son – although a fourth son. He sometimes found that his name was good enough security for the money he borrowed, knowing, in actual fact, that the name meant literally nothing. There wasn't even a remote hope that either his father or his grandfather might settle any of the debts he incurred. He had seen his father only once since the end of his Oxford days, when he had come down possessed of a brilliant scholastic record, and no money whatever. Since he was obviously not a candidate for Holy Orders, influence was used to find him a position as secretary to a prominent Tory politician. But he was indolent, and already drinking too much, drifting always on the fringe of gamblers and money-lenders. His employer kept him for a year, and then, weighing his touch of brilliance against his multiple failings, finally asked him to leave – not without some regret, Sebastian afterwards told Sara. He then attached himself as secretary to an ageing nobleman, who took him on a leisurely tour of the Continent for three years. The old man was charmed by him, his air of bonhomie and culture, and forgave his frequent lapses from grace. But Sebastian gambled once too often and too heavily with his lordship's money, and one day he found himself travelling back to London with nothing more than a month's wages, and an excellent knowledge of French and Italian.

A few months later he wrote to his father that he had married a woman whom he described as an actress – another proof to his family of the state of utter hopelessness into which he had drifted, for she was a type of woman they believed he would never have become involved with if he had been in his right senses. His father journeyed grimly to London, and found them in their lodgings. His ecclesiastical tongue raked Sebastian over, leaving nothing unsaid which might more minutely describe his horror and dismay over what he called 'this tragic and disastrous step'. The new bride did not escape his scathing comment.

'This is a scandalous affair, Sebastian!' he snapped, enraged at the prospect of having to claim such a daughter-in-law. 'She is sluttish! She is a woman of no refinement!'

The painful interview went on for an hour or more, and at the end of it he offered to take Sebastian back to Somerset – but the bride would have to remain where she was.

Sebastian's reply was prompt. He pointed out that his wife was already pregnant and would soon have to leave the stage. He added that to desert her in such a condition was something not even his father should ask him to do.

'In any case, sir,' he finished mildly, 'I find now that I have little taste for the country air.'

It was the last contact he ever had with his family.

Sara remembered her mother vaguely – a tall, deep-bosomed woman, with a great deal of golden hair, and a bold, undeniable beauty. The image was not clear, and she had never quite believed Sebastian's story that his wife had died of a fever. It seemed much more likely that her mother had gone off with one or other of her acquaintances of the ale-houses or the theatres, whose backstages she frequented, even after her marriage.

During Sara's early childhood, Sebastian passed unsuccessfully from one tutoring job to another, occasionally writing for magazines, until he was shunned completely by editors for trying to publish Parliamentary Reform pamphlets. They lived a hand-to-mouth existence, moving about from one lodging to another; for brief periods they enjoyed modest comfort with outbursts of real extravagance – at other times they hadn't the price of a meal. This state of affairs seemed natural to Sara; she had never known any other. She learned where she could buy food cheapest, and how to haggle over a penny with shopkeepers. She was as adept as Sebastian himself in avoiding the creditors, and when they couldn't be avoided she faced them out boldly. They lived a wandering life, which always had the taste of adventure about it, so long as each experience could be shared by them both. They adored each other, and were only happy when they could be together. Sebastian treated her in every respect as if she were already a woman – she learned to read almost as soon as she could talk, and unconsciously imbibed scraps of learning from him. She and Sebastian were known in every coffee-house and tavern along Fleet Street and the Strand.

When she was eleven she took a position with one of the fashionable dressmaking establishments. Sebastian was helpless to prevent her – by this time he was accustomed to accepting her decisions about everything they did. He talked vaguely of having 'other ideas', about what she should do; she took no notice of his troubled murmurs and flung herself into the business of absorbing this new phase of her experience. One of her duties was to carry messages and packages to the great houses of the city. She found herself more often employed this way because she was quick-witted, and could read and write. Sometimes she was permitted to stand by and watch a fitting, listening eagerly to the gossip which drifted through the scented rooms, the talk of balls, parties and scandals; talk of the dull court of George III. In this way she caught a glimpse of the world beyond her own; her envious fingers touched the velvet hangings and the soft carpets; long mirrors threw back the first full-length reflection of herself she had ever seen. She saw the hustle of preparations for receptions and dinners; occasionally she even waited with the crowd outside to see the guests arrive. She became a general favourite with the ladies who patronized her mistress; she was pretty, and in their presence, made herself docile and amiable. They petted her, and would have spoiled her if she were not too shrewd to be spoiled. Even though she was still a child, they gave her discarded fineries – scarves and scraps of lace. These she either sold or put away, having more sense than to appear to imitate her superiors by wearing them. They encouraged her to chatter to them in her precocious French, which she had learned from Sebastian; altogether she had much more notice taken of her than a dressmaker's apprentice had any right to. She knew her mistress didn't approve the position into which she had manoeuvred herself. But for the moment it happened to be the whim of some of the great ladies to make a fuss over her – and so she was kept on, not without much head-shaking.

It lasted for a year. At the end of that time Sebastian escaped the debtor's prison by taking the first coach he could find out of London with Sara beside him. It happened to take them to Rye. By the time they had found lodgings there, Sara had set the story going that they had made the move in search of better health for her father. He fell into an easier and more comfortable life in Rye; tutoring jobs came readily enough when he gave the names of his grandfather and the Tory politician as recommendation.

The change affected Sara strongly; she settled gratefully to the quieter tempo of life, aware that she was free of the ceaseless bustle of the capital. She became outspoken in her determination that Sebastian should alter his habits, that he should not again uproot them both. Quite suddenly, respectability seemed to her a very desirable state. She made up her mind that Sebastian, from then on, must be respectable.

'So you want me to reform, my love?' he said, playing with her hair, as it lay over her shoulders. 'Well – we'll see! We'll see!'

He made a small effort, and succeeded well enough to give Sara some hope. They gave up the lodgings and took a tiny house; living there alone she managed to keep his drinking hidden. A kind of pact existed between them to excuse his weakness, and when it overcame him, to find a way of covering it up. She invented a story of a rare, recurring fever which periodically incapacitated him. She told her story with great conviction, and it was believed; she had the satisfaction of seeing Sebastian sought after because of his undoubted merits as a tutor.

A year after their arrival in Rye, Sebastian was engaged by the Reverend Thomas Barwell, holder of the living at Bramfield, on Walland Marsh, by Romney. He became tutor to the vicar's two sons, Richard and William; each day he walked the two miles to Bramfield and back again, with Sara by his side. He had accepted the post only on the condition that she was to go with him, and that for half the day she should share the lessons with the boys. The rest of the time she would spend assisting Mrs Barwell in light household duties. It seemed a workable arrangement – the only one whereby Sebastian would have been induced to accept the post, for he would not have left Sara alone through the whole day. Apart from that he wanted her grounded in the classics and mathematics – knowledge, most people told him, quite useless to a woman. But he had his own opinion on the matter, holding to his argument that an education was his only possession to leave with her. Mr Barwell was aware immediately of Sebastian's determination, and he was easily persuaded to give in, anxious, from the first meeting, to have his services for his sons – the West Country scholar had

an excellent reputation in Rye for the job he undertook. Besides, it
was considerably cheaper than having some young man to live
in.

So each day the spidery black figure walked with his daughter
along the dyke roads, twisting and winding by the side of the
water-courses across the flatness of the Marsh. Sara loved the windy
desolation, its greenness dotted by fat Kent sheep. In the winter
the winds tore in from the sea – and when the rain came with it,
Sebastian would put his arm around her, drawing her into the
shelter of his body. Little deserted chapels were sprinkled over the
country in lonely fashion, empty and ruined since the days of the
Canterbury monks. By night the marsh-land was a weird, unwelcoming place, avoided, whenever possible, by those in the villages
and outlying farms. There was no interference, either, with the
smugglers who slipped in from the sea with darkness, their oars
muffled, creeping silently up the dykes. There were inns and farms
spaced about the Three Marshes with unsavoury reputations, where
honest men would whip up their horses sharply until they were far
behind. So Sebastian and Sara left Bramfield with the last light
of the short winter afternoons, hurrying back along the road, thankfully crossing the bridge where the Rother curved under Rye Hill.
It was always with a sense of relief, of a danger passed, that they
climbed the cobbled streets of the town.

Life at Bramfield was pleasant enough. Sara was two years
younger than Richard, and a year older than his brother. Her life
in London had never let her know the meaning of shyness, and
the three worked together peacefully. But outside the schoolroom
the atmosphere was less easy. The vicar's wife was disapproving
of the situation which brought Sara into her household, and she discouraged the girl's contact with her sons. Sara and her father ate
their midday dinner apart from the family, making light of Mrs
Barwell's coldness, and the austerity of the meals she served. They
were excluded also when callers came to the house, and the two
boys were summoned to the drawing-room. Sometimes they witnessed the arrival and departure, in his heavy carriage, of Sir
Geoffrey Watson, who held the presentation to the living at Bramfield. And when he was accompanied by his daughter, Alison, a
dark, sweet-faced child, Sara would gaze at her from the schoolroom window, mildly envious of the richness of her gowns, of the
fur muffs which protected her hands.

Then, sometimes, in the long twilights of the spring and summer, Richard would walk part of the way with them to Rye –
these were hours when they enjoyed an intimacy not possible at

Bramfield. The Marsh was green, the reeds in the dykes bending gracefully before the soft wind. Sebastian taught them the names of the Marsh birds; in spring they sought out the nests together. Sometimes they went as far as the shore itself. The shingle made hard walking, especially if the winds were against them. Pointing out across the Channel, Sebastian filled them with tales of adventure and romance in the coastal towns of Normandy and Brittany. At times like these he seemed no older than Richard himself, his laughter as young and as constant as Richard's own. When a playful mood attacked him, Sebastian would pull at the long braids of Sara's hair, loosening it, to let it fly freely. The wind caught it, whipping it madly across her face, and stinging her eyes. They laughed at this mad confusion of her hair, but there was something secret, something less open in Richard's eyes. She was gloriously happy in the company of the only two creatures she loved. And she sensed, without the need for speech between them, that Richard returned her love.

It was on Sara's sixteenth birthday, an evening of late summer just before the turn of the season, that Sebastian gave Richard his signet ring. They sat together, the three of them, on the shingle, listening to the screaming cries of the gulls wheeling and dipping above them. Sebastian was silent for a time, twisting the ring, a gold one, on his finger. On an impulse he turned to Richard.

'Here, Richard,' he said, 'give me your hand.'

As he spoke he stretched out and took Richard's left hand, placing the ring on the little finger.

'Sir . . .?'

Sebastian waved aside the attempted protest. 'It belongs rightfully, of course, to Sara.' He gave his daughter a faint, rather wistful smile. 'But it's a man's ring, for all that. For her it could only have sentimental value. I've always meant to give it myself – not have it taken from my finger when I'm dead.'

He hunched his shoulders under the sombre black coat, staring out to sea.

'When you leave Bramfield to go into the Army, Richard,' he said, after a few moments, 'things will not be the same. We will still have our friendship, of course – the three of us – but things will not be the same. I want you to keep the ring, to remind you of us three as we are now.'

Sara was thankful that Richard had grace and sense enough to protest no longer against the gift.

He sat gazing at the unfamiliar sight of Sebastian's ring upon his finger. Then he looked up, his eyes moving slowly from Sebastian to Sara. 'As long as I live it will remind me of these evenings – of both of you.' He looked down at the ring again, and then said to Sara:

'Since it should have been yours, may I have your permission to wear it?'

She was aware of a tone he had never before used to her – he spoke to her as if she were a woman, and no longer a classroom companion. Unaccountably, she lowered her eyes rather than look at him. Her father's shrewd gaze upon them both made her uncomfortable.

'I should be glad for you to wear it,' she answered.

Then she sprang quickly to her feet. 'It's getting late,' she said, addressing Sebastian. 'We should go.' She didn't know why she added this – there was no reason to hasten the return.

They were slow, though, in parting – Richard to turn back to Bramfield, Sara and Sebastian to start the walk to Rye. Glancing behind, she had a last sight of Richard as he rapidly paced the winding dyke road.

It may have been some inexplicable premonition which caused Sebastian to present the ring to Richard at that time, for it was the last evening they were to spend together on the shore. Two nights later, when he had managed for once to escape Sara's vigilance, Sebastian was involved – perhaps blamelessly – in a brawl in a tavern frequented by the sailors who made their way in from the coast. They found him next morning lying in a side alley, dying from a terrifying head wound.

He died later in the day, and as the news filtered through the town, the phantasy-world Sara had built up crashed about her in ruins. People came with small bills and debts, tales of Sebastian's petty borrowing and lies. The evidence of his unstable life was revealed, and the stories, drifting from one mouth to another, lost nothing in the telling. From a few of those who knew them both she received pity and condolence, but from the more outraged she received contempt as the daughter of a man little better than a common thief. There was irritation also, among the townspeople, that she herself could not be branded with him.

He was given a pauper's funeral, and Sara had not even the address of the West Country rectory to inform his father of his death. Pride and loyalty to him kept her from making inquiries about the family; she let Rye and the Barwells, and anyone else concerned, keep their belief that the family and background he boasted was simply a further fabrication of lies. She herself denied any knowledge of them.

The day after Sebastian's funeral, she took stock of the situation. There was no money – the proceeds of the few possessions they had owned would have to go to meet the debts. She doubted that she could even keep back for herself enough money to pay the coach fare to London — what then? Back to a dressmaker's workroom, or slaving under a cook in someone's kitchen? She remembered the world she had known before Rye — the grim hopelessness of trying to achieve anything without money, friends or influence.

The memory frightened her enough to send her boldly to the one man she knew who might help her.

She put on her most becoming gown — one that Sebastian had bought her in a moment of extravagance, and probably hadn't paid for — noticing regretfully that her shabby cloak hid most of it. It was a three-mile walk to the gate-house of Sir Geoffrey Watson's estate, and another mile beyond that to the house, but she covered the distance without being aware of it as she rehearsed what she would say to him. On her arrival she was kept waiting for an hour in the hall, and then shown into the room where the business of the estate was carried on.

Although the day was still warm the stout baronet sat before a blazing fire, a litter of papers about him. He stared at her hard for a moment, and then waved her to a low seat facing him.

'Sit down, miss! Sit down!'

She did as he told her, feeling her cheeks already scorched by the fire.

Sir Geoffrey arranged his hands expansively across his stomach. Sara knew from his gesture that he was going to manage the interview although it was she who had sought it. She waited for him to speak.

'They told me at Bramfield about your father,' he said. 'I suppose there's no money for you, is there?'

She shook her head. She needn't bother to deny what the whole of Rye knew. 'My father was often ill, Sir Geoffrey. It was difficult for him to accumulate money.'

The baronet laughed aloud. 'Drinking's the very devil for running away with money!' He thrust out a large, bandaged foot. 'And when the gout gets hold of me I know the other side of it, too!'

Then, seeing her expression, his tone softened. 'You mustn't take it to heart, child!' His head nodded heavily. 'No doubt you were fond of your father — that's just as it should be. Always believe in children minding their parents. Now, my girl, Alison — you've seen her, haven't you? — she minds what I say smartly enough. A good girl, Alison is!'

He stirred in his chair, sending the last of the papers swirling

gently to the floor. 'You have to do something about earning a
living now, miss. Can't live on air, you know.'

She looked at him fully. 'That's what I've come to speak to you
about, sir.'

'Eh? . . . Is it now? And what have you got to say?'

Sara clasped her hands tightly underneath her cloak, and plunged
ahead. 'I've come to ask you a favour, Sir Geoffrey.'

His eyebrows shot up. 'A favour? What is it?'

'I wanted to beg you to recommend me to your sister, Lady
Linton, for employment in her London house when she returns
from India.'

He gasped a little, looking at her more closely.

'How the devil do you know about Lady Linton, and her London house?'

'When I lived in London I was apprenticed to a dressmaker. I
once watched her being fitted for a dress, and then I delivered it
to her house.'

'You did, eh? And now I suppose you think you know all about
her?' When she didn't answer, he went on. 'Well, damn me if I
know what Lady Linton's wishes will be about staff when she returns. Her husband died in India, and she hasn't told me her
plans for the future. The London house wasn't opened all the five
years she's been away.'

Sara pressed her point. 'But surely, Sir Geoffrey, all the vacancies
can't be filled already? Lady Linton has a very large house to run –
her entertainments are famous.' She looked at him appealingly. 'I'd
be very useful. I'm clever with a needle, and I can do household
accounts. And I could write letters for her, and . . .'

He held up his hand. 'A real paragon, aren't you, miss?' Then
he laughed. 'Well . . . I suppose Lady Linton would find some use
for you. I'll ask her to take you on.'

'Oh, thank you, sir!'

'But wait! She isn't expected until after Christmas. What will
you do until then?'

'Anything,' she said eagerly. 'Anything . . . Couldn't I work for
you here at the Hall, Sir Geoffrey?'

He shifted in his chair. 'Well . . . I've never encountered such
a female for knowing what she wants. No doubt you'd like to run
the estate while you're about it . . . eh?' His tone was good-
humoured, but he waved her suggestion aside. 'No, no . . . it
wouldn't do. Too many servants at the Hall already, eating their
heads off in idleness.'

Sara saw she had made a mistake. She remembered that she
was the same age as Alison, and it might have occurred to Sir

Geoffrey that their common friendship with Richard Barwell could prove a link between them. He was not the sort of man to encourage a companionship between his impressionable young daughter and someone of her own dubious standing. Clearly, she was not welcome at the Hall.

'You must go to Bramfield,' Sir Geoffrey suddenly announced.

'Bramfield?' she echoed sharply. 'As a servant?'

'Yes, indeed.' He looked at her with mild astonishment. 'Is there something wrong with Bramfield? I always understood you were employed in domestic duties there.'

'I was *not* a servant!'

'Come, come! This is no time for false pride. You must take what offers.'

She looked at his face, and saw there was no way out. Either she must do what he said, or lose his help. So she managed to smile, while she was raging in her heart against the ill-luck that was sending her back to Bramfield as a servant. But her slanting, greenish eyes were fully upon him as she made a little speech of gratitude. He was charmed, and grew benevolent.

'You'll enjoy being with Lady Linton. She's notoriously indulgent to those who please her – and I don't doubt you'll suit her well.'

He made a gesture of dismissal. 'Be off with you, now, miss. You've had enough favours from me for one day.'

She rose, and made a low curtsy to him.

He stopped her as she was leaving. 'I'm sorry your father's death has left you this way,' he said kindly. 'But you'll get on all right – I can tell. You're not the sort of girl who'll miss her chances.'

Before she left the Hall she was given a meal by Sir Geoffrey's orders, and the groom drove her back to Rye in the chaise. All the way back she hugged to herself the satisfaction of what she had achieved. She remembered Lady Linton's reputation before she had left for India with her husband – an open-handed, generous creature, affectionate and impulsive. In the dress salons they had gossiped of her brilliant receptions, of the extravagance with which she ran her household. Sara knew that in getting a place with Lady Linton she had dropped into what could only be ease and comfort. And much more might be made of it if she used her wits.

She chose to ignore, for the moment, the thought of the months that must yet be lived through at Bramfield. And as yet she could think of no way of seeing Richard Barwell once she left the Marsh. But she would see him again – she was quite determined about that.

Within a week Sebastian's possessions were sold, Sara had packed her few belongings, and was in service at Bramfield. It was now the early days of autumn, and at the same time Richard's commission in the Army came through. Self-conscious in his new uniform he bid her a formal goodbye in the hall of the rectory. Recalling that awkward, uncomfortable parting, she thought miserably that all that seemed to remain of their idyll of a summer evening on the shore was Sebastian's ring on Richard's left hand.

Sir Geoffrey had forced her back upon Bramfield, but the interest he had displayed in her did nothing to improve her status there. She no longer had access to the schoolroom, and the books in the library were forbidden her. The servants themselves made capital of her position in the household, passing on the most menial of tasks, knowing well that she had no possible redress. She slept in an unheated attic with the cook and the one other maid kept at the rectory; she was bitterly resentful of the lack of privacy, hating their rough, country accents, and the coarseness of their conversation. Because they were uncertain what they should make of her sudden relegation from the schoolroom to the kitchen, they became tyrants, taking their cue from Mrs Barwell's own hostility. Sara was unhappy, and bound to Bramfield as securely as if she had been imprisoned there. Only the promise of Richard's return at Christmas made the empty weeks bearable.

But when he did come he was changed. He was stiff with her, and off-handed; she saw early that he did not know how best to face the problem of her altered status – so he avoided it by avoiding her. And, strangely enough, she was able to understand this, and forgive it, too – for she found that she was herself unable to meet the situation. Richard dodged her in the house, and she astonished herself by doing the same thing with him.

She received the greatest blow to her sense of security in his friendship on Christmas Day – a day spent in the quiet and temperate fashion of a clergyman's home, a sober day, making her long for the gaiety of Christmas dinners eaten with Sebastian. In the early evening Nell, the other maid kept by the Barwells, drowsy after the large meal, roused herself reluctantly from her chair before the kitchen fire to answer the ringing of the drawing-room bell. She returned some minutes later, still grumbling and stifling her yawns.

'The parson's mightily in favour when Sir Geoffrey and Miss Alison take to calling on Christmas Day,' she said, shrugging her heavy shoulders. "Tis a time for folk to be staying put at home – unless there be a special reason to take them out.'

The cook stirred herself to poke the fire. 'There'll be a marriage there soon, I'll be bound. Miss Alison has quite a fancy for Master Richard. And vicar'll not stand in the way – not with Sir Geoffrey's money in sight.'

Nell sniffed as she settled back into her chair once more. 'I'm thinking the lass who takes Master Richard will need all the money she can put her hands on – for she'll get nought with him but his handsome face. For all his taking ways and pretty manners, he's not the young man to push ahead for himself.'

Sara leaned far back in her seat, trusting that the dim light of the candles and the fire would not betray the flush on her cheeks. She sat very still, listening to the wind outside, and to the cook's breathing; she repeated to herself over and over again, what had been said about Richard and Alison. Her thoughts were painful to her, like the sudden opening of something secret and hidden.

She needed time and solitude to adjust herself to this new idea that Richard might indeed marry Alison. She could not squarely face it in this atmosphere of servants' gossip, in the unfriendly air of a room in which she was never welcome. Yet even with the desire to be away from them so strong, she schooled herself to sit there quietly, enduring their occasional remarks, waiting until the cook's heavy breathing had become a snore, before she rose silently and went to the door.

Outside in the passage the intense cold struck her, and she heard a querulous voice in the kitchen raised in complaint about the draught. She closed the door, and made her way to the back stairs, mounting to the first floor, and pausing there. Above was the attic where she slept, and where she would be found if either woman in the kitchen came up. But close to this landing was the school-room, forbidden to her, but a secure enough retreat while the family was gathered with Sir Geoffrey and Alison in the drawing-room. Her hesitation was short, because her need for solitude had suddenly become desperate. The door was unlocked when she tried it.

Inside it was dark; the windows were squares of black slightly less dense than the blackness surrounding them. She fumbled and groped, her hands encountering objects long familiar to them, until she found the candle upon the mantelshelf. She lit it, and the single flame thrust its flickering light into the corners revealing the bare, shabby room, no different now from the time when Sebastian had ruled in it. Her eyes rested on the clean-wiped slates, the shelves of tattered books, the huge Latin dictionary upon its stand. The uncurtained windows framed the bleak openness of the marsh, now wrapped in darkness. She moved to the desk that had been

Sebastian's, and sat down, breathing in the remembered smell of ink and chalk. It was very cold. She rubbed her hands together, thinking that there had been little wisdom in her decision to come here at all. There was nothing here but memories of Sebastian, Richard, and William – William, who now, with a new tutor, held sway in this room. Draughts played tricks with the candle, and the shadows jumped in obedience. It was not difficult to fancy that she once more occupied a place on that long bench, and that presently Sebastian, Richard, and William would come to join her. The feeling was so strong that the gossip she had heard in the kitchen faded from reality – it was impossible, sitting there, to believe that Sebastian was dead, that Richard was in the Army, and already there was talk of his marriage.

Carried away by her thoughts, she heard no sound until the door opened. She turned swiftly, guiltily, to encounter Richard himself in the doorway.

'I saw the light,' he said, 'and I wondered . . .'

She half-rose, and then dropped back. The feeling of Sebastian's desk beneath her hand was security. Her spirits lifted a little, remembering her father's refusal to be subservient, and she said, with a touch of defiance, 'I'm not supposed to be here, I know – but I came.'

For answer, Richard stepped farther into the room and closed the door behind him.

'Do you have to talk in that fashion to me, Sara?' he asked quietly. 'Have things altered so much – are we not still friends?'

She thrust her head up. 'More things have altered, Richard, than the new coat you wear.'

He took a few steps towards her, halted, then came the rest of the way, until he stood over her. She waited, watchful. He bent and took her chin between his fingers.

'You've grown up in these months, little Sara. You've altered also.'

The touch of his fingers unnerved her. 'Oh, Richard,' she cried, 'why do things have to change? If only we could be back here . . .' Her gesture indicated the empty desks, the ink-stained floor.

'Are you miserable?' he asked her, gently. 'Are you unhappy?'

She could find no words to reply to him.

'I'm sorry if being at Bramfield has made you unhappy.' His fingers left her chin, and reached up to her hair, stroking it back from her forehead in just the way Sebastian might have done. 'I hate to think of you being unhappy.'

'Does it matter to you, then?' she said, too sharply.

The motion of his hand ceased. 'Of course it matters!'

He straightened, dropping his hand to his side. 'It won't last much longer, Sara. Not more than a few months now. Lady Linton should arrive any time – you'll be in London within three months.'

She didn't look at him. 'I imagine it's possible to be just as lonely in London as here on Romney. Isn't it, Richard?'

'Lonely? Sara!' He gave a rather excited laugh. 'What a silly little fool you are! Lady Linton keeps a fashionable house in London – there'll never be a dull moment! You'll forget what it was like on Romney, never seeing a new face from month's end to month's end.'

His voice was so low now that it was scarcely more than a murmur. 'And, Sara . . . I'll be there too!'

She raised her head, the movement so quick that the candle flame quivered thinly. 'You'll be there? How . . .?'

He smiled. 'Not in London exactly. But near enough to spend some time there.' His smile widened – a sudden return to the spirit of companionship they had known in this room. The smile was accompanied by a twinkle in his eyes, a sense of fun that lurked about the corners of his mouth. She looked at his handsome, smooth face, the thickness of his curling black hair, and the stiff collar holding his head in that position of faint arrogance which somehow seemed natural to him since these first months in the Army. She saw all these things and wondered if this pleasing face and elegant manners didn't bring him all he wanted too easily. He was the son of a country parson, without money or influence, but already he had won a small showing of favour with his commanding officers, and Sir Geoffrey Watson was a powerful ally for any young man to claim. The quick smile and laugh of the favourite came readily to his lips. She guessed that Richard, lacking so many other essentials, would perforce have to climb solely on his good looks and charm.

She moved her arm, as if to stretch it out to him, but then withdrew it. The candle fluttered, casting further shadows across his face. In that brief second she had a vision of him turning into an amiable, smiling lackey of those of wealth or influence.

'Why do you stare at me like that, Sara?' he asked. 'Doesn't it please you to know that I shall see you in London?'

'In London . . .? Oh, yes, Richard!'

'Well, then, why such a long face?' He laughed, returning to his good humour. 'Think of it, Sara! I mean to visit the playhouses. I'll see all the sights I've dreamed about while I've sat

in this room multiplying columns of figures.' He suddenly demanded of her, 'What do you want to do most in London? Tell
me!'

She smiled at his excitement. 'London is not as new to me as
you seem to imagine, Richard. Don't you remember that I was
born there?'

He looked at her, and said more slowly, 'Yes . . . Yes, I do keep
forgetting that.'

He put his hands behind his back, taking a half-step away from
her. 'I keep forgetting,' he said, 'that you have ever had any other
life before you came here. That's selfish, I know – keeping you
locked up here where you haven't always belonged.' He shook his
head then, slightly. 'You're not like me, are you? I was born here,
and I've never been away from it until this year. You've seen a
much bigger world than mine, Sara, yet to me, you belong here and
to nowhere else. Away from here, when I thought about Romney,
I thought about you. When I remembered the way the light was
reflected back off the dykes, I couldn't help thinking of your hair.
It was you all the time. I suppose I was homesick for Romney
. . . I was homesick, and the feeling was all mixed up with you.'

Abruptly his tone changed. 'Do I sound stupid?'

She shook her head.

'I thought a great deal about our evenings on the shore with
your father. You remember them, Sara?' He didn't wait for an
answer. 'Of course, you remember them. Neither of us shall ever
forget. I suppose they're as perfect a thing as we'll ever have to
remember.'

And then he bent down and kissed her softly on the lips. 'That's
for all the beauty you've given me to remember.'

As he started to straighten she caught his hand. 'Are you sure
you want to remember it, Richard?'

'Always,' he murmured, and he kissed her again.

She stood up and gave him her lips fully. It was the first time
she had ever been kissed in this way, and her immediate response
startled her. She could feel his arms around her tightly, and her own
fingers were locked behind his neck. They clung to each other,
bodies pressed together, suddenly firing with passion the memories
of their years of friendship. Sara knew she was casting away her
childhood in that kiss, was altering for ever the relationship between herself and Richard. Yet she went on kissing him, quite
aware now that this was what she had wanted him to do, what
her vague longings for his return had centred upon. Plainly her
reason told her that this wild feeling was her love and desire for
Richard – the emotion to which, until this moment, she had never

given real acknowledgement. Now every particle of her body was deeply satisfied by his kisses.

Their grip on each other slackened at last. Richard drew his lips away from hers to press them against her eyelids, her forehead. Then he put his face in her hair.

'My dear!' he said. 'My sweet Sara!'

She could feel his breath against her face; he was leaning heavily on her, clinging to her. Something in his stance vaguely frightened her. It hardly seemed that he clung to her with love or possessiveness, but as if he sought help and support.

'Sara!' he said again, and now it was like a cry of entreaty.

Hearing it, she suddenly seemed to hear in her ears a rush of wind, a cold wind blowing about her like the whispering of prudence. A touch of reality reached her at last, after the warmth of their passion.

She broke free of him, stepping back and pressing both her hands against her ears to shut out this frightening sound.

'No, Richard!' she said hoarsely. 'You'll leave me and marry Alison!'

His face went white. There was an expression of fear upon it – the expression of a child suddenly insecure.

'Marry Alison!' he repeated. 'Marry *Alison*!' He pushed his hand distractedly through his hair. 'My God, you must be mad, Sara! What makes you think that I could marry Alison?'

'They said . . .' she whispered. 'I thought it was settled.'

He caught her arm sharply. '*Who* said? What are you talking about?'

'Cook said it – and Nell. They said it was almost settled.'

He regarded her sternly. 'How you've altered when you listen now to servants' gossip! And you've accepted this as truth without having asked me about it?'

'What else could I think?' she said miserably. 'How could I ask you? I've never seen you alone until now. You don't make it easy to talk.'

He flushed, turning his eyes away from her. 'I know. And I'm damned sorry about it. But don't think I haven't *wanted* to talk with you.'

Again he drew her to him. It was a gentle, confident movement – and when he began again to stroke her hair, more than ever it felt like Sebastian. The tenderness of his unconscious action caused the tears to prick at the back of her eyes. She wanted to lay her head against his shoulder and to sob out the misery of the last months.

'Dear Sara,' he said, 'I don't think of anyone else but you. How

could I? Forget about Alison! That's all imaginative nonsense –
servants' gossip! I swear to you, that I've made no suggestion of
marriage to her.'

He tilted her face towards him.

'I'll marry no one but you.'

She gasped, stiffening in his arms.

'You can't marry *me* – a servant!'

He answered her with a vigorous shake. 'A servant! You're the
daughter of the man who was my greatest friend. Doesn't that mean
anything to you? Don't you *want* to marry me?'

'Marry you? – of course I do. But *wanting* you and *having*
you are two different things.' Her fingers gripped his uniform
sleeves tightly.

'I mean to have you, Sara. When I get promotion I'll be able
to marry you. If there's war with France I should get it quickly.
Will you promise to wait?'

'Wait . . . ?' Suddenly the knitted points of her eyebrows straightened; she smiled up at him. 'Yes – I'll wait.'

Then she added quickly, 'And we'll manage, Richard, somehow.'

She buried her face in his tunic, and a sense of triumph and joy
swept through her. The future was before both of them, uncertain,
clouded. It was there to make what they could of it – but they
would do it together.

He was stroking her hair again, and murmuring close to her ear.
'*You'll* think of a way, won't you, Sara? You've always been
cleverer at those sort of things than I.'

She listened to him with a sense of shock. His tone seemed to
appeal to her to be strong for both of them, to find a way out. She
knew then that she would have to fight for her possession of Richard,
or he would be taken away from her – not willingly, but inevitably.
He could be taken away because he was too weak to fight the
obstacles facing the marriage. But she accepted this – after all,
she *was* stronger than Richard, tougher than he. In a sense, he was
like Sebastian all over again – needing her love and strength.

'Yes. I'll find a way for both of us, Richard,' she said firmly.
'We'll manage it.'

He bent and kissed her again, his lips seeking hers with a young
eagerness. They were both new to this experience. It was exciting,
like the sour, sharp bite of a green apple. Neither had known
anything like this before. They were flushed and shaken when at
last they drew apart.

Then, for a few moments, they did not meet each other's eyes, feeling some sort of shame that their passion had broken loose, briefly, from the bonds they had learned to impose upon it. Sara, slightly irritated that something so deeply satisfying had of necessity to be regretted, raised her eyes, to find Richard's upon her. There was no apology or repentance in them. Her lips parted, and seeing her begin to smile, he laughed aloud.

Carried on the elation of the moment, he impulsively drew off the ring he wore on his left hand, the one Sebastian had given him at the end of the summer. He caught her hand, pressing the ring into it.

'Keep it, Sara,' he said. 'Keep it until we meet in London – I'll claim it back when we meet again.'

She turned it over on her palm. 'Your ring, Richard . . .'

His gaze upon her was tender and possessive. 'Promise me you'll keep it until I come to claim it?'

She nodded slowly.

He smiled and kissed her, a light kiss that was there and gone before she was fully aware of it. Richard himself was gone almost as swiftly.

The draught of the closing door set the candle fluttering again, and the shadows leaping over the stained floor and the desks. Sara stood still, the ring clasped in one hand, the fingers of the other pressed against her lips where Richard had kissed them. Then she snuffed out the candle; its acrid smell mingled with that of the chalk and the old books. She made her way in the darkness to the door, groping then to the stairs leading to the attic.

She did not talk alone with Richard again before he left Bramfield. They had only momentary encounters upon the stairs and in hallways, and the secret smile that passed between them had to serve as their only communication. There was gossip, too, in the kitchen, about the amount of time he spent away from the rectory. No matter what time he returned, either the cook or Nell seemed to hear the rumble of the wheels of Sir Geoffrey's carriage when it dropped him off at the gates. But in her possession of the ring, hidden carefully in her mattress in the attic, Sara was sure of Richard. His visits to Alison's home hardly troubled her. Aware of the sluggish flow of life about her in the austere rectory, she understood how a nature like his would crave the ease and comfort of the baronet's house on the edge of the Marsh. Day after day, as the curve of the dyke road swallowed up Richard's diminishing figure, she forgave him for the characteristics she loved and feared; she let him carry all his indolence and weakness with him

when he went to visit Sir Geoffrey, and she wondered again and
again if the gentle Alison was completely blinded by his charm.

Spring came at last to Romney – softer winds from the sea, and
a sudden showering of pale, tender greens through the grass, the
reeds and the water-plants; the new colours showed through the
blackthorn hedges and the willows. Sara waited daily for her summons to London, and whenever Sir Geoffrey made a call at the
rectory she hung about the hall until his departure. She began to
fear he would never speak, that the plan would never come to
anything, when he halted her one day as she hurried to open the
front door for him. He strolled in a leisurely way from the drawing-
room with Mr Barwell, where they had been shut up for most of the
afternoon.

'Well, miss!' he said, taking a firm stand upon the elegant silver-
topped cane he carried, 'you'll soon be off to London.'

Her eyes widened eagerly. 'There has been news, Sir Geoffrey?'

'Yes. Lady Linton landed at Portsmouth six days ago. She will
be at her estate in Devon for three weeks, and then she plans
to open the London house. She will send me word when she re-
quires you.'

Sara dropped a curtsy. 'Thank you, Sir Geoffrey.'

He made a move on, then paused, examining her with shrewd,
kindly eyes, almost lost in their thick pouches of flesh. 'You'll be
glad to go to London?'

Sara shot a glance at the ominously still figure of the rector.

'Thank you, Sir Geoffrey . . . but I've not been unhappy here.
The Rector and Mrs Barwell have been most kind.'

'I know. I know,' he answered. 'But you'll have more excitement in Lady Linton's house, I'll be bound.' He chuckled, his
whole body shaking. 'I'm told, Rector, that it's excitement all
young girls look for. Well, there's plenty of it wherever Lady
Linton is!'

He paused, looking hard at Sara. 'Those clothes won't do. Lady
Linton's a great dresser herself – and she likes those around her
to give a mind to their appearance. Here . . .' he searched in his
purse and produced three guinea pieces '. . . take this now and buy
yourself something to wear. Mrs Barwell'll tell you what you'll
need.'

She reddened, and stammered her thanks, which he waved aside.
Mr Barwell's eyes, she knew, were on the money; she knew, too,
that she would have to hand it over to his keeping as soon as Sir
Geoffrey was gone.

'My daughter is looking forward to joining Lady Linton in London shortly,' Sir Geoffrey went on. 'Shopping, y'know. Nothing but the London shops will do that young miss these days. So you'll be seeing something of her.'

Sara replied dutifully. 'It will be a great pleasure, sir, to see a face I know among so many strange ones.'

He chuckled again. 'You'll not lack familiar faces, my girl. I don't doubt young Master Richard will be a frequent guest at Lady Linton's house.'

Sara struggled hopelessly with the colour mounting in her cheeks at the mention of Richard being in London. But it didn't attract attention for the rector had laid a restraining hand upon Sir Geoffrey's arm. The two now faced each other.

'Surely, Sir Geoffrey, this . . . er . . . information is premature? There is nothing settled yet.'

'Nonsense, Rector! Nonsense! It's all as good as settled! – will be anyway, when Richard comes home next time. I'll talk to him myself. There can be no doubt about it. Richard is not unwilling – nor is Alison.'

'That's true, Sir Geoffrey – and nothing could give me more pleasure than a union between Richard and your sweet daughter . . . But, surely . . . Gossip . . .'

Startled, Sara listened to them. The world seemed to wheel about her as she tried to sort out the meaning of their words. This was not what Richard had told her – this was not the truth! And yet the vicar's pale face had never seemed more serious, and Sir Geoffrey was not merely hinting at the matter. Her whole body was taut as she waited for what he would say next.

The baronet faced her again. 'I'll warrant this miss is no gossip. Knows how to hold her tongue, I can tell. In any case, the news will be out soon enough. It is my wish that they should marry in the summer. However, we'll see . . . we'll see.'

Without a further glance at Sara's low curtsy, he turned and went down the steps to where the rector's groom held his horse.

Sara stood and listened to their conversation.

'Looks as if we'll have rain, Rector,' Sir Geoffrey said, 'and I've two calls to make yet. That coachman of mine is a plaguey nuisance – been abed with a fever these last three days, and I'm without anyone to drive me. I'm getting too old now to sit in the saddle for long.'

Then his speech trailed off into a series of harsh grunts while he attempted, with the aid of the rector and the groom, to mount. Sara saw that they were fully occupied, and she sped in the direction of the back stairs and the temporary refuge of the attic.

Once there she flung herself upon the mattress, letting her misery and wretchedness have charge of her body and her thoughts. She shocked herself by the fit of weeping which shook her, taking away all her strength and resistance. She was enraged as well as disappointed.

'Richard!' she whispered. 'Oh, Richard, what have you done?'

She lay there while the spring afternoon faded quickly, and the light fled away down the Marsh. Richard was lost to her, she knew – he was taken beyond her reach for ever, and there was nothing she could do about it. It seemed unlikely that he was fully aware of what was being planned for him, but she felt with certainty that he would not be able to withstand the pressure Sir Geoffrey and his parents would bring on him. They would know how to play upon him, understanding that his was not the sort of strength to hold out against the blandishments of wealth and influence. He was poor and unknown, and he would be offered background and powerful family connections. His nature was not built to refuse such potent attractions. And Alison herself, with her sweet, lovely face and gentle manners, would make a wife any man might well desire. It was inevitable, she told herself. Richard's struggle with his conscience would be true enough, but it would be short. He would remind himself of the long wait, and the battle against family prejudices, before he could marry Sara, and he would say that their love could not last through such a time. He would accept what came easily to hand, not caring to fight for what, in the end, might turn out to be an empty prize. She had recognized these weaknesses in his nature long ago, and excused them. Now she called herself a fool for the excuses she had made. The images twisting and shaping themselves in her mind slowly grew more detached. She saw the future with a sharp clarity, saw Richard's visits to the London house – visits that were to Alison, not to herself. She saw the preparations for the marriage in which she would have a servant's part, the trappings of the fashionable wedding she would be expected to share. Her unhappy mind painted the scenes much too vividly. Fearfully she tried to turn away from them, feeling, even now, the agony of being forced to play her subordinate role.

As she turned restlessly on the mattress, Nell's voice on the stairs roused her.

'Sara? Sara, are you there? The mistress is looking for you this hour past!'

Sara sat up quickly, and called out, 'Coming!'

Nell's rough tones were a sudden spark to her sense of injury. It was Sebastian's unsubdued pride that now flared into resentment against this indignity, and against all the others she would suffer before the summer was out, and Richard and Alison were finally married. And in that instant the thought of flight occurred to her for the first time. It chilled her for a moment; then the simplicity of the plan made her bold. Why not? she asked herself. There could be an escape from her hated position, which was also an escape from watching her lover succumb to Alison, and all the attractions Sir Geoffrey offered. There was no wind of prudence in Sara to cool her impulse, and the idea, once it occurred, was irresistible.

In a fever of indignation and hurt pride she flung herself off the mattress and groped in the stuffing until her fingers encountered Sebastian's ring. She had not held it in her hand since Richard had given it to her on Christmas Day. At the sight of it, her anger rose on a new wave, heating her face, bringing tears to her eyes. Then, with an effort, she put it out of sight, stuffing it in the folds of her handkerchief, along with the gold coins belonging to Sir Geoffrey.

Before she left the attic she changed into her heavy shoes, and threw a cloak about her shoulders. She encountered no one on the stairs; it shocked her sense of importance of the occasion to find how easy it was to leave the rectory unnoticed. She passed the kitchen door like a quick shadow. The heavy smell of cooking food reached her, following her down the passage until the fresh air, at last, gently touched her face. She closed the door behind her, hurrying towards the low wall which separated the rectory garden and churchyard. The daylight had suddenly gone, but scents of the day were still there, drifting, unanchored. Sara was aware of this, and of a fear only half conquered, as she sped past the ghostly tombstones, and the dark, squat church, making for the dyke road, deserted and lonely in the sharp spring evening.

To keep clear of Rye, where she might easily be recognized, was her greatest concern now. She turned in the direction of Appledore. But the thought of reaching Appledore itself brought no heartening feeling of familiarity, for the walks she had taken with Sebastian and Richard had never brought them so far. Behind her, the lights of the rectory cut into the gathering dark, but only faintly. And, having looked at them once, she did not look back again. She felt no regret, her hard bitterness was softening into relief that her flight had not been intercepted, and that by morning she would be far away. She marched grimly onwards, at first unaware of the bite

of the wind, and then feeling it keenly, but never once afraid of
the emptiness about her – not afraid as she had been in the churchyard – the open road seemed to be her own territory, and she had a
sense of rightfully belonging to the Marsh. It was the place she and
Richard and Sebastian had called their own.

She had walked what she judged to be about three miles before
the first rain swept her face. It came on quickly, making her gasp
and twist her head away from it. And with the rain her resolution
palled a little. She became more soberly aware that the lights of
Bramfield lay far behind, and unknown country beyond. At the
same time, the whispered tales of the Marsh stirred in her mind, the
hushed stories of the wool-running to France, the inns and even the
churches which secreted their share of the contraband lace, silk and
brandy. There were rumours of murder committed to safeguard
the fortunes won by smuggling, and the thought struck at her now.
As the rain suddenly worsened, she began to realize her utter de-
fencelessness, and that she faced a night on the Marsh without
shelter. Too late to regret that she had not bided her time at
Bramfield until the morning came – and yet, in the midst of the
fear that had begun to possess her, her heart rebelled at the very
thought of remaining at Bramfield. She began to run, trying to
ignore the continual urge to glance behind; trying to forget the
fact that she had not eaten since the midday meal.

She went on a further two miles. Her steps were slow again
because the rising wind had tired her, and because each step and
each minute brought her closer to the inn, The Angel, which
marked a crossroads about a mile ahead. The reputation of The
Angel, the collection of gossip and rumour which combined to give
it its unsavoury character, brought fear to her heart. She dreaded
the approach of it, yet longed to be past and away. It represented
a goal of distance to her also; once beyond, she would let herself look for some barn or outhouse to shelter until morning.

The wind dropped briefly, and in the lull the sound came to
her of horse's hooves and wheels on the road behind. She stood
still, terrified. They were close, but the wind had prevented her
from hearing them. She had a moment's frightened wonder, thinking that the rector, on finding her gone, had sent one of his nearer
neighbours in search of her. She dismissed the idea as a more terrible one occurred. A horse and cart on the Marsh at night? She
panicked at the thought, for no one cared to question the passage
of a horse and cart abroad on the Marsh once nightfall came, or if
seen, the incident was conveniently forgotten by morning. It was
this thought which started her casting wildly about for cover. The

road was treeless and bare; the night itself, the only shelter. The dyke bounded the road on one side, and it was already too late to attempt to cross to the other. The swinging arc of the cart's lamp came nearer; she turned towards the edge of the dyke, flinging herself full length on the sloping bank. She dug her fingers and nails into the new spring grass, praying that the cold rain might have numbed the unseen driver's watchfulness. With her face pressed close to the earth, she fancied she felt it throb beneath her in response to the steady clopping. There were moments of agonized terror for her while the horse drew level and she sensed her prostrate body was exposed to the wavering light. She waited for a cry from the driver – but it did not come. The cart itself was level now – and then past. And the darkness covered her again. She lay still, relief breaking coldly over her; a sigh of thankfulness escaped her as the distance increased between herself and the cart.

At last she raised her head cautiously to peer at the diminishing light.

As she did, she looked directly into a second lamp, swinging only a few feet away from her eyes. She stared in horror at the hand that held it, and then her eyes lifted to take in the dim figure of a man.

She uttered one strangled sound of astonishment, and shrank back.

He advanced almost gently, then, with a quick gesture, clamped his hand on her arm, pulling her to her knees. The lamp was thrust close to her face.

'Don't touch me! Don't!' she cried, frightened, trying to twist away.

But the man's grip held her tightly.

'Well! What have we here!' he said softly. 'What have we here!'

Suddenly he bellowed over his shoulder. 'Daniel! Wait!'

Sara struggled to find a foothold on the sloping bank, but he jerked her forward beside him on the road. He planted the lamp on the ground, and with one effortless heave, grasped her around the waist and tossed her over his shoulder.

'Put me down! Do you hear – put me down!'

She screamed, but she knew there could be no response along the empty road. She tried pounding her closed fists fiercely into the man's back. If he felt it at all, he took no notice; he picked up the lamp again and started in a half-run to catch up with the cart.

The bouncing gait gave Sara no more breath to cry out; her

terror, in any case, would have prevented it. It was useless to
struggle against the giant arm holding her. The man had enormous strength. She was dizzy and shaken when he put her on her
feet beside the driver of the cart.

'Daniel,' he said, still in that surprisingly soft voice, 'd'y see
what I've found? 'Tis worth-while to tail behind with a lamp.
Never can tell what you'll be lucky enough to pick up!'

Sara gave an indignant gasp as the driver leapt quickly down
from his seat and caught her by the shoulder.

'Don't you touch me!'

She made a swing at his stomach with her fist, but he took a
step out of reach and exploded into a hoarse burst of laughter. He
thrust the lantern he carried level with her face.

'A lass! A right little beauty too! Seems you've picked up a
rare 'un tonight, Harry!' His voice dropped lower. 'But what's t'
do with her now we've found her?'

'I reckon,' the other drawled, 'that folk who hide about the
dykes after dark learn more than's good for them. We'll find out
more about this one later. Better be moving on.'

And, without another word, he swung the petrified Sara, with
the same ease as before, into the back of the waiting cart. She
braced herself for the fall against the bare boards, but it was on
something soft, something rolled into canvas, that she fell.

'Carry on, Daniel!'

As the order was given she sat up, and made a despairing attempt
to scramble over the side of the cart.

'You can't treat me like . . . !'

She received a push that sent her on her back again. This time
she hit her head against the wooden side, and the blow half-stunned
her.

'If you don't be quiet I'll put a sack over your head – understand?'

The young man dropped back into his former place behind
the cart, and Sara, straining her eyes against the dark, could make
out nothing but the swinging light. She lay quietly on the canvas,
exhausted and afraid, with no spirit left to fight. She pulled her
cloak about her, turning her face away from the stinging rain. There
was nothing now but submission to whatever was to follow. Her
own strength was feather-weak compared to this young giant's who
strode along behind. Tears of rage and fear came in a rush to her
eyes; she fought them down, and lay there, cold, but unmoving,
while the cart swung along on its way. At last she felt the wheels
grate on rougher ground, and then they rumbled over cobble-

stones, and were finally still. She sat up and gazed about her.

They had entered a courtyard; stone walls formed three sides of a square which faced out into the blank darkness of the Marsh. Sara could barely discern the outline of some sort of building. The windows were shuttered; there were no lights anywhere. Harry strode past the cart, lantern held high above his head, and hammered upon the door.

'Look lively, there!' he shouted.

After a while the door opened revealing a stout woman who shielded a candle with her hand. Sara's questioning eyes moved from her to an inn sign, swinging dejectedly in the wind. She read the faded lettering before the lantern was lowered – The Angel!

The young man took a step back towards her.

'Here, Mother,' he said, 'I've brought you a parcel of tricks! Come and see what you think of it!'

He swung Sara to the ground, giving her a light push forward. The woman eyed her suspiciously as she stumbled on the doorstep, catching hold of her arm, roughly halting her.

Sara was stung into a fury of irritation by their handling of her. She slapped the woman's hands away wildly.

'Leave me alone – both of you! I'll have the law on you for this.'

The woman took no notice of her whatever.

'What's this, son?' she said. 'What have you brought . . .?' Her voice was as coarse and loud as Nell's, at Bramfield. It contrasted oddly with the voice of the man she called her son.

He laughed now. 'Just what I said – a parcel I picked up along the way. Found it by a dyke.' The idea seemed to appeal to him; he spoke very softly. 'It seemed to me a lass oughtn't to be abroad at this time of night – so I took her along with me.'

The woman stepped back from them, alarm on her fleshy face. 'You brought her here – to The Angel!'

The man's voice now held a hint of impatience. 'And why not? I fancied company for supper.'

'You're mad!' the woman snapped. 'You're drunk!'

He stepped into the inn, squeezing his large bulk past Sara and slamming his lantern down on the table.

Then he turned angrily to the woman.

'You keep your opinions to yourself, until they're asked!' He made a menacing gesture, and she shrank back against the wall, watching him warily as he let forth a stream of curses at her. She ducked before a blow he aimed halfheartedly at her head.

'Now move yourself, you lazy trollop!' he said. 'Bring some
supper – two suppers! Feed up this wench – she looks like a half-
starved kitten.'

As she edged cautiously past, he called to her, 'And remember,
I'm the one who says who shall come to The Angel – and who
stays out!'

She vanished by a door leading into a long passage.

The young man turned to Daniel, standing alongside Sara. His
tones were normal again. 'See to the cart, Daniel. And if you
don't rub down that horse as I showed you, I promise you you'll
not have an inch of flesh on your back in the morning!'

Then he said pleasantly, 'Good night, now. See that you get
your supper when you've finished.'

Daniel went out and closed the door behind him.

Sara had learned by now that it was useless to try to escape,
useless to pour out protests into unhearing ears, so she stood quietly
while Harry attended to the fire in the stone hearth. He threw on
logs from a pile beside it; then he took a candelabrum, lighting its
half-dozen candles from the brightening flames. He lit several
other candles in separate holders, placing them carefully about. She
watched him closely. His movements were light. He was very tall,
with huge shoulders bulging, threatening to burst the weathered coat
he wore; his fair hair, curling above a young face, was glistening
with rain. Now and again he put his hand up and rubbed the
moisture which trickled on to his forehead. She was puzzled by this
giant of a man, who, although so young, appeared to be the master
of The Angel.

He finished his few tasks in a leisurely fashion and kicked at
one of the logs on the fire with his foot. Then he swung round, and
came towards Sara.

'Now we'll see what sort of maid it is who hides by a dyke on a
wild night!'

He caught her, pulled her into the light of the candles and the
fire, and at the same time pushed back the hood that covered her
head. She felt his fingers fumbling with the clasp of her cloak; he
drew it from her shoulders, letting it fall in a heap at her feet. For
a moment he had nothing to say; he gazed at her silently, and she
could read nothing in his face. Then suddenly he caught her shoulders, holding her at arm's length, his eyes raking slowly over her.
She twisted, trying to break away, but he held her as easily as if she
were a child.

Dismayed by the uselessness of her attempt, she looked wretchedly
up at him, and she saw a smile beginning to break on his young-

old face. He started to laugh. Sara wondered how many times she had heard that same laugh since he first pulled her from the dyke bank. The laugh and the smile came too readily after an outburst; they seemed totally unrelated to whatever he might be feeling at the moment. She began to wonder fearfully if he were in possession of all his senses.

He released her after a while, giving her a light push so that she sank down on the settle by the fire. He remained standing, saying nothing, but just gazing at her. Presently the woman he had called his mother appeared again, carrying a tray with dishes and tall jugs. These she set down on a table in front of the fire, arranged two places, and then left the room without saying a word. The man took a seat, motioning Sara to one opposite.

She hesitated, until he shouted, 'Damn you! Do you want to be spoon-fed where you are? Sit down, I say!'

She obeyed him meekly enough now, her eyes fixed upon the food spread on the table. He pushed a steaming plate, bread, and a jug of ale in front of her. She took what he offered, half-afraid that this might be another of his queer ideas of jesting, and that it might be withdrawn. The food was good and there was plenty of it; there was more on her plate than she had eaten in a single meal since Sebastian had died. She ate and drank all she wanted, her thoughts turning now and again to the poor fare served to her in the Bramfield kitchen.

Her companion's appetite was enormous, but, even busying himself eating, he kept his gaze on her.

'Eat up, girl!' he commanded, suddenly pointing the leg of chicken he was eating at her plate.

His expression softened slightly. He went on looking at her, then he said, rather gently, 'You look as if you haven't eaten for days. Finish that up, and if you want more I'll give a shout for it.'

Sara needed no further urging. She went on eating, turning her body sideways to the warmth from the fire. It was almost possible, if she kept her eyes away from her strange host, to forget that she was here, in one of the places most dreaded by the honest farmers of the Marsh; she was here supping royally with the man who was landlord of the establishment. But whenever her glance stole back to him, her fears returned. She recalled the whispered tales of The Angel, and, considering the place called itself an inn, was unhappily aware of the deserted room that should have been full of company, of the windows that showed no friendly light to travellers. She remembered also the careful progress of the cart along the road, and Harry's vigil behind it. Looking at his huge body and unlined face, over which the firelight moved in a kindly fashion, she shuddered to recall the alacrity with which the woman and Daniel had hastened to obey his orders.

He terminated his own meal abruptly by pushing away the dishes.

He leaned back in his chair, apparently fully satisfied; he tilted the chair, lifting the two front legs off the ground, rocking himself while he considered her.

At last he spoke. 'What's your name?'

She raised her brows. 'And what business is it of yours?'

He wasn't at all put out by her tone. 'Oh, come! I must have a name to call you by.'

'It's Mary,' she said slowly.

'Mary? Mary what?'

'Mary . . . Bates.'

'Well, Mary Bates, we'll banter no longer. Why were you hiding by the dyke?'

She flushed at the mockery in his voice. 'I didn't know who might be coming along. The Marsh is not . . . safe . . . at night.'

'Ah, I see you are a prudent maid, Mary Bates! Well, that's a good thing.' He nodded his head in exaggerated gravity. 'But what, might I ask, is a prudent maid doing out on the Marsh after dark? Wise folk are home in their beds.'

She hesitated a moment, then plunged ahead into the ill-prepared story she had devised during the meal.

'I was on my way to Appledore. I have an aunt who is ill there – she sent word for me to come.'

'On your way to Appledore, Mary?' His voice was low, but his eyebrows had lifted noticeably. 'So late in the evening?'

'I've come from Rye – and I took the wrong road. I've never been so far in this direction before.'

'From Rye, eh? And where do you live in Rye?'

'I'm in service to Mrs Linton.'

'Mrs Linton? Mrs Linton? . . . Never heard of her!'

He brought the front legs of the chair down with a crash. He sprang up, hands on the table, leaning towards her.

'It's a pack of lies! And your name is *not* Mary Bates!'

Then, as quickly as his anger had come, it left him. The humourless smile spread slowly across his face.

'But I must have a name for you,' he said, 'until you choose to tell me your real one. I think I'll call you Liza. Yes . . . Liza . . . I like that. Does it please you to have a pretty new name?'

She said carefully, 'My name is Mary.'

With incredible swiftness he edged round the table, catching her arm, and pulling her to her feet.

'Don't lie to me!' he shouted.

He shook her violently, with his great hands spread on her shoulders. She pounded impotently against his chest; it affected him no more than if it were the enraged action of a small child. She was full of terror again, and enraged.

'You beast!' she gasped. 'Leave me alone!' Her teeth clamped together, and she said thinly, 'I hope you hang for this!'

He roared with laughter. She gazed at him in despairing fury, her fingers arched up gradually to claw at his face, and then they halted, frozen by his next action. He bent lower and kissed her fully on the mouth, his hands drawing her closer. His giant's strength engulfed her like a torrent, the shock of his kiss numbing her for a few moments. She felt his searching hands upon her body — but, strangely, they were not rough hands. His lips on hers were determined; although she had never been kissed by any other than Richard, she knew instinctively that this was the determination of a man used to having his own way with a woman. Into the numbness of her tired brain, straining to give even an ineffectual resistance to his demands, a spark of life returned. Abruptly she relaxed her struggle, quite passively allowing her body to be pressed against his. She tilted her head back fully to receive his kiss, and, as he bent yet farther over her, her groping fingers encountered his hair. With a gentle motion, which he might take for a caress, she slipped her fingers beneath the fair tangle of his curls. Then she gripped and pulled, bearing down with all her strength.

There was a second of astonished silence. Then he uttered a sharp exclamation of rage, and thrust her from him. The push he gave her sent her tottering backwards, until she fell against the arm of a fireside settle. She crouched there, shaken, and supporting herself with one hand, while she watched him feeling, with surprised anger, the place where her fingers had torn at his hair.

He took a step towards her. 'My God, I'll teach you . . .'

His clawing hand dragged at the sleeve of her dress as he bent to pull her to her feet. It tore away, leaving her shoulder and arm bare. His nails dug cruelly into her skin. He steadied her on her feet before him, and then deliberately raised his arm. With the back of his hand he dealt her a blow across the face.

She cried out, just once, loudly, with the sudden pain and shock.

He held her quite firmly by the shoulder so that she would not fall, and he raised his arm for a second blow. Sara struggled des-

perately now to break from his grasp. His fingers tightened automatically, and he stepped back from her to have room to swing
his arm. In that instant, while he was unguarded, she blindly
seized his belt with both hands, and, using this to steady herself,
she brought her knee up with a hard jerk to his stomach. He gave
a short gasp, and his fingers loosened and slid from her shoulder.

He staggered back a few paces, clutching his stomach, and bending almost double. Sara's panting breath came painfully; she knew
she had done herself very little good, because her blow had merely
winded him, and it could not be effective for more than a few
seconds. She waited for his next movement.

But he did nothing. His breathing, as he slowly straightened,
was loud in the room. Sara stood there, expecting another swipe
from his huge hand. But, after a minute, she was astonished to see
that the familiar smile was beginning once more to crease his face.
His broad, full laugh rang out.

'My God!' he laughed. 'My God . . . The wench has spirit! And
t'think I've given a wild-cat shelter under my roof!'

Still laughing, he collapsed into a chair behind him, motioning
her to a place on the settle.

'A wild-cat with yellow hair, eh? Well, Liza, I didn't think it of
you. No, by God, I didn't!'

He breathed deeply three or four times again.

'I think I like you, Liza,' he said quietly now. 'Haven't any
use for timid women. Fools, all of them!' He swung his chair forward, leaning closer to her. 'But you're no fool, are you, my pretty?'

Sara didn't answer. She was beginning to feel the reaction from
the desperate effort she had made. She despised herself for letting
him see it; it was impossible now to control the fit of shivering
which seized her. She pressed back farther into the corner of the
settle. Whatever he chose to do, he could do now at will; she had
neither the strength nor the spirit to resist. She looked with hatred
at the blue, pale eyes, with the fair curls above them; she quivered
with pain where he had struck her face, and knew, without even
looking at it, that his nails had drawn blood from her bare shoulder.
She hated him for the pain and the indignity of their raffish brawl,
but all she could do was to stare at the hands that had inflicted
this injury, spread elegantly across the arms of his chair.

'You were on the way to Appledore, Liza? Well . . . I'm going that way myself in a day or two. You'll come with me – I'll
drive you there. And until then, you'll bide your time here at The
Angel.'

She jerked forward in her seat. 'I won't stay here! I won't!

You can't make me!'

'Can't I? Oh,' he went on, grimacing as if her words had wounded him deeply. 'You'll not find me dull company – I can promise you that. After all, Liza, what more could a woman of spirit like yourself want, than a man like me? You'll not be lonely – not with Harry Turner around.'

She listened to him with a cold, fearful heart.

'And,' he added, 'I've some book-learning to suit your educated tastes – in case you fancy a little of that sort of entertainment by way of a change from Harry. Upstairs there are books . . .'

He let out another roar of laughter, reading the expression on her face.

'Are you thinking of *that*?' He jerked his thumb in the direction of the passage leading to the kitchen. 'Yes, she's my mother, all right. But,' and here he winked, 'my father is another story! A gentleman he is, and not too proud, either, to come and visit his son now and then.'

Suddenly his face hardened; his closed fist came crashing down on the table.

'And my God, Liza. I'm more to be proud of than the sons of his lady wife! I've more book-learning, I'll warrant, and a head for business, than those fools'll ever have. Born soft, all three of 'em. They haven't done quarter the things I've done in my time – and I'll be richer yet than the lot put together. You mark my words on that!'

He lapsed into silence, sullenly chewing his lips, staring at the toe of his boot stretched out before him. He slightly raised his leg in its well-fitting, unpolished boot; the sight of it seemed to please him, for after another minute his eyes again sought Sara's, and he no longer frowned.

He said quietly, 'The master of an inn is always concerned for those who pass his door by night – and for those who hide in a ditch beside it.' He tapped the heel of his boot on the floor, still speaking softly. 'You've been lying to me, Liza. Every word you've said is a lie. But I'll have the truth before long. Who are you? Where have you come from?'

She said nothing.

He leaned forward to the edge of his chair; his voice was no longer patient. 'Answer me! Do you hear . . . answer me!'

Sara's back was straight and rigid against the high settle. She knew that her story, slight and clumsily concocted, would not be believed. He would keep questioning her until he got the truth – and the truth would worsen, not better, her situation. He would

then know that he might, without fear, keep her here at the inn
for as long as he chose. Pursuit would not seek her in a place
shunned as The Angel was. This man before her, cleverer than
others of his kind, in an unbalanced crazy fashion, was more than
likely the organizer of the gang of smugglers reputed to use the
place as a store and a rendezvous. In the fanatical brightness of his
eyes she saw no pity – she would be a thing to be used as his mother
was, as Daniel was. Her mind flinched at the thought of what
she faced until the time when she escaped, or he should tire of
her.

'Answer me!' he shouted. He raised his hand impatiently –
his own strength seemed to be a constant temptation to him.

She said slowly, 'I . . .'

Abruptly his attention left her. He looked, with an attitude of
wariness, towards the door. He had caught, above the wind, the
sound of horses' hooves on the cobblestones outside. He sprang
to his feet, and snuffed out all but one of the candles.

Sara watched with awe and a new fear as he stood there, massive,
solidly planted on his outstretched feet, gazing expectantly at the
door.

They heard the thunderous hammering of fists on the panels. A
man's voice cried out, 'Open up, there!'

Harry did nothing. He did not speak, but there was uncertainty in his face. He took a step forward, then hesitated. His mother
came silently from the passage to the kitchen, her candle a second
point of light in the dimness.

The hammering sounded again, authoritative and peremp-
tory. 'Open up, there! My horse is lamed. I need shelter!' The
man outside waited a moment, and then he knocked a third time.
'Open up! Open up!'

Sara looked despairingly from Harry to the door. Whoever
knocked was no associate of the pair here; it was someone who,
innocent of the inn's character, or in desperation, had sought
shelter from the night. Her mind moved quickly. Dare she risk an
appeal to him for help – or at least make him aware of her presence before they hustled her out of sight? From Harry she could
expect no pity, but from the stranger outside there might be a
slight chance of protection. The smarting of her face, and the
memory of the large hands upon her body, told her that she would
fare no worse with this other man, whoever he might be.

She sprang off the settle, avoiding Harry's arm suddenly outstretched to apprehend her, and ran to the door. The latch yielded
easily, and in the cold rush of wind and rain, she stumbled out

against the solid form of a man.

'Good God! What's this?'

The stranger steadied her with his hands upon her shoulders. In the darkness it was impossible to see. He led her back, fumblingly, into the room.

Harry moved forward and slammed the door with a savage kick.

The wildly flickering candle-light steadied, and Sara found herself gazing into the astonished face of Sir Geoffrey Watson.

Sara was charged with stealing Sir Geoffrey's three guineas and a gold ring belonging to Richard Barwell. She was tried at the next Quarter Sessions, convicted, and sentenced to seven years' transportation.

She knew afterwards that meekness and a repentant attitude might have saved her; if she had had the sense to go on her knees to Sir Geoffrey, if she had even told him the true reason why she had run away, he might never have brought the charges against her. But she was unable to bring herself to the point of telling him of her love for Richard, and so she had to listen to him rage on about her base ingratitude, and the notion that he had once trusted her.

During the trial she listened to Harry Turner tell how he had found her, a stranger, attempting to steal food from his kitchen. By repute, Harry was far more guilty than she, but for lack of evidence, he was still entitled to be called an innocent inn-keeper, and qualified to give evidence against her. It mattered nothing to the jury that he denied all other knowledge of her; her very presence at The Angel was enough to convict her. There was no possible appeal against Sir Geoffrey's evidence; he told the court that he had given her money to outfit herself for service with his sister, and that she had run away from Bramfield with the gold and Richard Barwell's ring tied into her handkerchief.

Against one charge Sara had no logical defence; on the other charge she preferred to remain silent. She knew she could not stand before that disapproving, interested court, and tell them that Richard had given her the ring as a pledge – she couldn't bear to hear them murmur and whisper among themselves that she, a servant and the daughter of a man whose name had been dragged through the gutters of Rye, had aspired to marry the parson's son.

Sara's defence – indignant and confused – was useless. The sentence of transportation came promptly.

'*It is the judgment of this court that you shall be transported beyond the seas to such place as His Majesty, with the advice of his Privy Council, shall declare and appoint . . .*'

The people of Rye were loud in their opinion that she was lucky to have escaped hanging.

She had plenty of time, while she waited in the stinking, fever-ridden chaos of a prison for a transport to Botany Bay, to think back to the events of the day when she had run away from the rectory. Sometimes she wondered how she could have been mad enough to have acted on the impulse of wounded pride and disappointment; she cursed her own stupidity in looking upon Sir Geoffrey's three guineas as her own, to do as she pleased with. She rejected the idea of appealing to Richard – he had not been present at the trial and certainly he could do nothing to alter her sentence. In her bewilderment and anger she felt she never wanted to lay eyes on Richard again.

Shortly after she was sentenced, she was moved from the gaol in Rye to Newgate, to wait there until the transport was ready at Woolwich. She learned the lessons of this new world quickly and brutally; weaklings and fools did not survive long, and so she learned to have no concern for any other woman but herself. In order to exist at all she had to be as cruel and feelingless as the rest of them. She meant to survive her term of imprisonment, so she bent her energies towards doing it with the least possible trouble.

When she first went to prison she had only the money from the sale of the few belongings she had been allowed to take from Bramfield. This ran out much too quickly, and soon after she arrived at Newgate she found herself relying upon the indifferent mercy of the gaoler for her food. Her hunger made her savage, but she managed to hold off the one sure way of making money still open to her – prostitution. The gaolers permitted it, and encouraged it because it was their best source of revenue. But Sara watched the women crazy and dying from the results of it, and she decided that she could go hungry a little longer.

After a month in Newgate she managed to attach herself to a woman called Charlotte Barker, a middle-aged forger who had received a sentence of three years' imprisonment. Charlotte lived in great style, paying the gaolers liberally for the food they brought in, and receiving visitors every day. She had brought into prison with her an extensive wardrobe and dishes for her own use. Sara performed little services for her, wrote letters and mended clothes. In return this woman kept Sara in food, and made her presents of odd sums of money. She would never allow any of the fashionably dressed men who often called on her to have anything to do with Sara – and for her part, as long as she had food in her stomach, Sara was glad to be left alone.

Five months after her trial she received Richard's letter. It had been written from his regiment in Hampshire, the day after he received news of her sentence. The letter was months out of date, addressed to the gaol at Rye, and the many greasy fingers which had handled it had almost obliterated her name. She had little idea how it finally reached Newgate, but certainly the sum of money he mentioned enclosing was not with it. That was hardly to be expected after it had been passed round among thieves.

Richard's letter was a cry of distress at the news of her sentence – and he begged her to write and tell him in what way he could help. But his horror wasn't strong enough to cover the doubts he felt – he never mentioned the question of her innocence or guilt. Sara knew instantly that he *believed* she was guilty, and he was struggling with a wavering loyalty to make himself write the letter offering his help. It was a kind and gentle letter, the letter of a friend – but not of a lover.

She folded the greasy paper carefully, and went to Charlotte Barker to beg her to write to Richard in Hampshire telling him that Sara Dane had already left on a transport for Botany Bay.

She felt oddly calm when the letter was written and sent off. After that she tried not to think of Richard again – and she partially succeeded. The business of keeping alive, of surviving from day to day absorbed her, and the world of Richard and Bramfield seemed to fade; she dreamed less and less of the winding dyke roads, of the cries of the gulls on the shore. The crude realities of the prison were themselves effectively shutting off the past; Sara even began to doubt that she had ever known such men as her father and Richard Barwell.

She embarked with the other women in the *Georgette*, off Woolwich in mid-December, and by the time the ship finally took on her full cargo and crew, and slipped down the Thames in early February, Sara's money was exhausted. She spent the months of the voyage cramped in the perpetual dimness of the gun deck, with a daily spell of exercise on the upper deck when the weather was fair. Discipline was strict on board, which meant that the crew were prevented from mixing with the women prisoners, as happened on other transports. The food, although it was inadequate, was fairly distributed; but still the stronger ones always seemed to be in possession of more than their share. The bitter law of the prisoners remained in force here, and the weakest suffered.

3

When Andrew Maclay had appeared in the women's quarters
and called her name, Sara knew at once what was going to happen. After the burial of Mrs Ryder's servant that morning, the gun
deck had buzzed with speculation about who would be selected
to fill her place. They all knew Mrs Ryder by sight, and they
knew from the ship's gossip that she was frequently ill. They had
seen the two lively children, and had the opinion that it would need
more than a sick woman to keep them under control. The chattering prisoners had decided that one of them would be needed, and
they waited hourly for the summons.

It was unfortunate, Sara decided, that the second officer had
chosen just that moment to arrive. She knew she had made a
bad impression on Maclay – she knew just how the scene of struggling, clawing women had appeared to him, and she, with her dirty
bundle of food, must have seemed vulgar and coarse. She glanced
sideways at his face as they walked almost abreast towards the
quarter-deck cabins. He might give a bad report of her to Mrs
Ryder, she thought, but that wasn't the deciding factor. There
was some particular reason why she had been picked from among
the others, and the reason still held good. If she was being given a
chance to act as Mrs Ryder's servant she wasn't going to have it
spoiled by a lack of proper humility and decorum. If Mrs Ryder
expected to see a girl with a meek, pliable manner, she was going
to find her. Sara's hands went to her hair, and she furtively tucked
up some of the straying ends. She looked ruefully at her filthy
gown, in which the rents were almost indecent, and hoped that Mrs
Ryder was prepared to make allowances for her appearance.
Whatever happened she was determined that she was going to
have this chance.

They entered the quarter-deck companion-way, and she clenched
her hands tightly in the first feelings of real emotion she had experienced since the arrival of Richard's letter.

Andrew Maclay paused outside one of the cabins.

'Wait here,' he said, over his shoulder, as he rapped on the
door.

Mrs Ryder's voice called to him to come in. She was lying on
her bunk, and she smiled when she saw Andrew. The cabin was
a little darkened against the direct light from the port-hole and he
could not see her very clearly. She was not much past thirty-five,

still very pretty – a slight woman, dark, and rather ill-looking from the interminable voyage and the sea-sickness which kept her too often in her cabin. She was wrapped in a loose, yellow silk gown. Andrew's eyes lightened at the sight of her; he found Julia Ryder gentle and easy to talk with. She had a sweetness about her which appealed strongly to him.

'Good afternoon, ma'am,' he said, bowing. 'I trust you are feeling better?'

'Indeed, yes, Mr Maclay, thank you.'

She was looking at him questioningly.

'Your husband discussed your need of another servant with the captain at dinner, ma'am,' he said. 'I've brought the convict woman, Sara Dane.'

'Sara Dane!' Mrs Ryder half sat up. 'But this is excellent, Mr Maclay! I hadn't truly hoped for such good news! It seemed barely possible that she would be aboard with us.'

He looked a little confused. 'I trust she will fit your requirements, ma'am. She has, after all, been a prisoner for some considerable time. Perhaps she isn't ... er ... quite suitable.'

She smiled, putting her head on one side. 'Is she as bad as that, Mr Maclay?'

He thought for a moment before he replied. 'She's a convict, ma'am. I know nothing else about her.'

'Ah, yes, but at least she is trained in domestic duties. I might have combed the ship and still not found ...' She didn't finish her sentence; she looked at him directly. 'I know what to expect from Sara Dane. She will be illiterate and coarse, and probably immoral. But I'm desperate for help with Ellen and Charles. I must take this chance when it's offered.'

He wondered if he should try to tell her that Sara Dane did not fit her description very well. But he had no time, because she spoke again, rather quickly.

'Is she waiting? Please show her in, Mr Maclay.'

He opened the door and motioned his charge into the cabin. She stood in front of them, lowering her eyes before their inspection. Andrew was shocked at the contrast between the two women. He saw Mrs Ryder's eyebrows lift, and her face contract in dismay. Her mouth opened slightly, making him immediately aware that this was the first time she had seen one of these creatures at such close quarters.

'Good afternoon,' she said feebly.

The other dropped a curtsy, but did not speak.

Mrs Ryder glanced helplessly at Andrew.

'You are Sara Dane?' she said at last.

'Yes, ma'am.'

'Mrs Templeton, of Rye, wrote me that you might possibly be on board with us. She said you were experienced in domestic duties. Is that so?'

'Yes, ma'am.'

'Have you ever taken care of children?'

'No, ma'am.'

'Mmm . . .' Mrs Ryder looked doubtful. 'Can you sew?'

'Yes, ma'am.'

'I don't suppose you can read?'

'Yes, ma'am.'

'You can?' Mrs Ryder relaxed noticeably. 'Can you write?'

The question seemed to touch Sara Dane's pride. She stiffened her shoulders, and her head was raised until she looked down under her lashes.

'Of course, I can write,' she said shortly.

'Oh, indeed!' Mrs Ryder's gaze was suddenly cold as it rested on the woman before her. Andrew was half-afraid now, realizing that two strong personalities had met and already there were signs of a battle for supremacy. He saw that Sara Dane was no longer demure, her eyes had grown bright and her mouth was set in a determined line.

'You interest me,' the older woman said quietly. 'What other accomplishments have you?'

The other, apparently unafraid, answered, 'I speak and read French and Latin. And Italian, too, a little.' She finished up – defiantly, Andrew thought, 'And I can do mathematics.'

Julia Ryder's expression altered swiftly.

The little baggage! Andrew thought, aware of a growing admiration for her spirit. All Sara Dane's meekness was gone now; she wasn't, obviously, the sort to be content to hide her light under a bushel for long. She was making it evident that the Ryders had found a treasure where they hadn't expected it.

Mrs Ryder spoke again. 'How old are you, Dane?'

'Eighteen, ma'am.'

'Eighteen, only? What crime were you convicted of, pray?'

The ragged figure stirred uneasily, glancing quickly from the woman lying on the bunk to the young officer who stood before her. It was an eloquent gesture, conveying to Andrew a sense of misery and wretchedness. Then she looked away.

'Come, child!' Mrs Ryder urged. 'Tell me what it was.'

Sara Dane's eyes came slowly back to her.

'I was convicted of theft,' she said.

Andrew recalled the conversation at the captain's dinner table — the preachers and the poachers, the petty thieves who filled the courts and prisons. He looked at the girl a trifle sadly, remembering that a short time ago he had loudly defended her and all her kind. He reflected that it was all very well to defend them when they were an anonymous mass, and didn't touch him in any way. But when they emerged sharply as individuals, such as this woman, who had education, some breeding, and still had kept her pride, spirit and touch of humour — then the issue was suddenly confused. It was too close to him; in the space of a few minutes it had become something personal. He was bewildered and a trifle unhappy.

He addressed Mrs Ryder abruptly. 'Ma'am, if,' he gestured towards Sara Dane, 'this woman suits you, Captain Marshall has given instructions that she need not return to the convict quarters. May I report now to the captain?'

'Please do, Mr Maclay. I think Dane will meet my requirements.' She gave him a quiet smile. 'You'll convey my thanks to Captain Marshall?'

He bowed. 'Your servant, ma'am.'

He turned and left the cabin.

3

The two men in the wardroom looked up from their papers when Andrew burst in upon them. Brooks was checking a list of medical supplies in a bored fashion and welcomed the diversion. Harding, flicking over a page of the log, raised mildly astonished eyebrows at the sudden noise of Andrew's entry.

'What is it?' he said.

Andrew had only taken one step into the room. He looked from one to the other.

'Have you seen her?' he said to Brooks.

'Her?'

Andrew was impatient. 'The girl. Sara Dane.'

Brooks smiled slightly. 'I saw her yesterday. Dirty little wretch, but I'd say she had more possibilities than any of the others.'

'Yesterday!' Andrew echoed. 'Then you ought to see her today!'

Harding had taken his cue from Brooks. He began to smile. 'I suppose she's washed away the dirt of the prisons and uncovered a dazzling beauty?'

Andrew slammed the door behind him. 'Well – if I'm any judge of women, she's beautiful enough to set the whole ship talking.'

'The dirt is really gone, then?' Brooks's tone was still bantering.

'Yes, it's gone,' Andrew replied. 'She's washed her hair . . .' He finished lamely, because their faces had too clearly revealed their amusement. 'It's . . . fair – almost white.'

Harding glanced at Brooks. 'There'll be some defiance of Captain Marshall's orders now, with all this beauty let loose among us.'

'Wait till Wilder sees her!' Brooks said. 'She'll give him something to think about. The poor fellow is dying of boredom.'

'If he gets half a chance!' Harding mused.

Andrew turned away from them. He walked to the table, looking down at the papers scattered about. For no particular reason he scowled.

'She's extremely intelligent,' he said quietly. 'Perhaps she's not the sort Wilder likes.'

No one spoke.

He looked up, bursting out, 'God in heaven, what is she doing here on a convict ship?'

After a moment Brooks shook his head, shrugging his shoulders. Harding said nothing.

Andrew left them to their papers. He picked up his own report-book and sat down at a table, resting the point of a quill before jabbing it into the inkpot. He thought unashamedly of the girl he had just seen on deck with the Ryder children, her golden head bare and soft in the sunlight. What a fool he must have seemed – gaping at her. She had worn a blue cotton dress belonging to Martha Barratt, and a bright red shawl about her shoulders. The transformation was unbelievable and, reading his expression, she had looked at him steadily for a second or two, and then smiled. He remembered her eyes, an indefinable colour, more green than blue. He was a trifle shaken by the impression she made on him. It lingered, as the memory of her voice had lingered.

He glanced over at Brooks and Harding, but they were completely absorbed again. Sara Dane was forgotten by then. He dipped the quill in the ink, but his mind was not on the report he wrote. A girl's inquiring eyes came before him. He bent his head, and tried to concentrate.

Sara made her presence felt aboard the *Georgette* in a strange fashion, Andrew thought. Almost from the first day he had seen her in her place by the bulwark with the Ryder children, it seemed as if she had always been there.

The transition from convict to confidential servant might have been an impossible one for almost any other woman. Andrew watched her closely during the long, dull weeks of the voyage to the Cape, and found himself compelled to admire the way she managed it. Her methods were not subtle, but they were clever. She was far too shrewd to make herself a target for disapproval. Day after day, she sat on deck with the children's lesson books open on her lap, her eyes never wandering from them for more than a second. But if one of the officers stopped beside the group to talk to Ellen and Charles, Sara was willing enough to talk also, though she always waited to be addressed first.

The trouble, he thought, was that none of them knew quite how to treat her. They were all conscious that she had been, on her own admission, convicted of theft. On the other hand, she had charm and undeniable beauty and it was too much to expect that men, cut off from the society of women, would not stop to talk with her and the children; too much to expect them to keep their eyes from following her movements. After a while they stopped being self-conscious about speaking to her, they forgot that she had come up from the convict quarters in rags.

She established herself finally in her own niche when the captain paused one morning by the little group to ask how their lessons progressed. Andrew, watching the scene, saw that Sara answered quietly and with no undue meekness. Coquetry or servility would have been out of place, and she did not make the mistake of employing either. Clever minx, he thought. He knew that the captain would soon make it a daily practice to stop to listen to the lessons, commend the children's industry, and watch Sara working neatly and expertly at the needlework Mrs Ryder had given her.

To Andrew, the most astonishing thing about Sara was her gaiety. She made Ellen and Charles laugh continually, and they plainly loved her for it; she was tireless in keeping them interested and occupied during the days that followed each other with dreadful sameness. He admired the spirit which let her throw off the effect of her imprisonment so quickly, and settle to her place naturally in the Ryders' family life. It was quite obvious that she did not expect or want pity from any of them.

He was conscious as he watched her, day after day, of growing approval of the way she set about making the best of her strange situation.

2

The tiny space of the cabin was full of the sounds of rustling
silk, the scents of warm flesh and perfumed clothes, as Sara helped
Julia Ryder prepare for bed. Julia was tired, and had very little to
say; Sara fell in with her mood, folding garments and settling the
cabin to order almost in silence. A gown of pale blue silk, which
Julia had worn that evening at the captain's table, lay across the
cot, and Sara gathered it up in her arms; she smoothed the thin
stuff between her fingers appreciatively, listening to its rustle with
attentive ears. The sound and feel of the material brought back
the London days, when gowns, far more elaborate than this, had
been an everyday sight. With the whisper of silk she could hear
again the light-hearted gossip of the dress-salon; she saw the fashion-
ably-bored faces under feather-trimmed hats, the jewelled hands
slipping into soft gloves. For just a second the crumpled silk in her
arms gave that world back to her.

Then she glanced across at Mrs Ryder, seated before the small,
littered, toilet-table. The other woman's dark hair was loose, and
fell about her shoulders, shining under the swinging lantern. The
picture she made in that gentle light satisfied Sara's sense of beauty;
while Julia Ryder was here, this cramped cabin did not seem
such a far cry from the London salon. She wore now her loose
wrapper of primrose brocade; her nightgown was trimmed with
lace that was hardly whiter than the skin of her shoulders and
breast.

As Sara watched, Julia leaned forward to study her reflection
in the mirror, at the same time picking up a hairbrush from the
table.

'Let me do it, ma'am!' Sara said. She laid aside the gown and
stretched out her hand for the brush.

She took her usual place behind Julia, pulling the brush evenly
through the long hair, watching it tighten, and then slacken and
curl back. She brushed in silence; and Julia's eyelids drooped.
After a few moments Sara's attention wandered to the toilet-table.
The mate of the silver-backed brush she held had been carelessly
thrown down. The mirror, which was always propped against the
bulkhead when they were not in heavy seas, reflected the scene back
in a kindly fashion. The frame of the mirror was a light silver
scrollwork; on a lace mat close to it lay a crystal phial of perfume.
Sara's eyes went slowly from one thing to another while her hands
moved mechanically.

Julia's voice broke in quietly :

'You love pretty things, don't you, Sara?'

Sara lifted her gaze from the table to the mirror; it met Julia's there.

After a pause, Sara said, 'I shouldn't admit how much I like having these things about me.'

'Why not?'

'You know very well, ma'am, that I was transported for theft. If I say I admire them, you may think I want to steal them.'

In the mirror Sara saw Julia frown suddenly, and a look almost of sternness came across her face. Her eyes didn't leave Sara's for a second.

She said sharply, 'Sara, I have only asked you one question about how you came to be on this ship. I don't intend to probe. If you wish to tell me, I'm ready to listen. But I leave the decision to yourself.'

Sara had never felt for any other woman the respect which Julia had won from her. She had worked for her, had tended her when she was ill, and helped her through days when she couldn't stand upright with the rolling of the ship; she believed that in these weeks together she had come to know her completely. She decided now that she must take a risk on her judgement of Julia Ryder.

She didn't attempt to answer the question. Instead she lifted her head and stared into the mirror again.

'Are you satisfied with me, ma'am?'

'Yes, Sara – I'm very satisfied.'

Sara nodded, and said slowly, 'And Mr Ryder – he's satisfied also, isn't he?'

'Yes.'

'And I get on well with the children, ma'am . . .? I mean they're fond of me, in a way?'

'You manage them better than anyone we've ever had. They obviously pay attention to you because they like you.'

Sara's voice went quietly on. 'And the captain, ma'am, *he* doesn't find anything to disapprove of in my behaviour? He doesn't object to the officers talking with me – why, he talks to me himself!'

Julia frowned again, puzzled. 'Yes, Sara. I hear nothing but praise for you from everyone. But why . . .?'

'Why?' Sara repeated. Then she paused to let the other have the full effect of her words. 'Because I *wanted* to hear you admit those things, ma'am! I wanted to hear you say them, so that I'll be certain whenever I admire your possessions, I don't need to wonder if you think I'll steal them.'

At that Julia twisted in her seat, until she was looking directly at Sara.

'I think it's time we stopped this fencing, Sara,' she said. 'Let us be plain with one another.'

Sara's hand, holding the brush, dropped to her side.

'I've watched you very carefully,' Julia said. 'You're ambitious and proud – but you've also got a head full of sound sense. My servant Barratt's death was your good fortune. You seized your opportunity when it came, and I don't imagine you'd be likely to throw it away by doing something foolish.

'We're going to a new country,' she went on. 'The life will be difficult and strange . . . An impossible life, Sara – unless you're prepared to be as fair with me as I'm willing to be with you. I'm not blind. Believe me, I'm as well aware of your good qualities as you are yourself. But I beg you not to forget that in this case we *both* have something to offer. When we reach New South Wales, *you're* going to need my help just as much as I'll need yours.'

She paused, tapping the edge of the table reflectively with her finger-nail. 'As long as you're with us, Sara, I'm willing to forget that you were convicted at all – I'll forget that you have ever occupied any other position but this one. But, if I'm to trust you, then you must stop mistrusting me.'

Sara was disconcerted that the other had read her motives so truly; but swiftly this feeling was replaced by satisfaction because this attitude was exactly what she had sought to bring about in Mrs Ryder. It was the position towards which she had painstakingly worked her way for weeks. This was an assurance of her future.

She dropped her eyes. 'Then I think we understand each other, don't we, ma'am?'

'I think perhaps we do, Sara,' Julia said.

3

In a tiny aft cabin of the *Georgette*, reeking of cooking smells because of its closeness to the galley, Sara struggled with the weight of a studded sea-chest which had belonged to Martha Barratt. Stowed in the small space under the cot, the chest would yield only a few inches at a time to her tugging; she paused frequently to straighten her back and take a deep breath. The cabin had no port-hole; it was airless, and hardly large enough to allow her to move. She had occupied it since the day Andrew Maclay had brought her up from the convicts' quarters. It contained a cot, at the end of which, piled one on top of the other, were three wicker baskets of clothes belonging to Julia Ryder and the children. The only other furniture was a washing-table holding a metal jug and basin and Martha's few toilet articles, which Sara now used. On pegs behind the door hung a cloak and a second striped gown like the one she was wearing.

Her attempts to drag the chest into the space between the cot and the wash-table had brought the first trickle of sweat to her forehead and neck. She passed the back of her hand across her hairline, and stretched out to open the cabin door fully, so that whatever air the passage-way offered might enter the stifling little apartment. Beside the chest was another wicker basket, containing the belongings which Martha had collected during her long service with the Ryders. This basket Sara already had had full access to — the plain, neat clothes excited her very little, apart from the novel experience of having more than rags to wear. But in the chest, ponderously locked, were Martha's few treasures, seldom worn or used, kept more for the joy of possession than any other reason. Mrs Ryder had given Sara the key that morning and told her she might have whatever she found useful. Now, in the hour of the midday meal she had time to herself to haul the chest out and look through its contents.

She dragged steadily at the handle until at last it came clear of the cot. Martha had kept the lock lovingly oiled, and the key turned without protest. Sara gently removed the folded sheets of paper which lay on top, breathing, as she did so, a wordless little apology to the dead woman whose cherished possessions were being touched by strange hands.

She lifted the lid of a white box, and fingered the pieces of neatly rolled ribbon, a few scraps of fancy lace, and lastly a soft pair of embroidered gloves. She laid these aside, turning her attention to a dark blue coat. There was a narrow trimming of fur at the neck which gave a touch of luxury, fabulous in the clothes of a servant; Sara pressed it against her face. Then her gaze fell on a pile of blue muslin; she dropped the cloak and pulled eagerly at the other garment. It was a gown, beribboned and billowing, and neither new nor fashionable. Obviously, she thought, holding it up against herself, this was Martha's best, and only brought out on the grandest occasions. It did not matter to Sara that it was out of fashion — it was still graceful and delicate. She took another look at the soft folds of the skirt and decided to try it on.

But when she tried to close the door before taking her own dress off, she found that the chest was in front of it. Unless she pushed the chest back under the cot again, the door would have to stay as it was. She felt herself flush with annoyance and irritation as she considered what she would do with the unwieldy thing.

It was unlikely at this hour that anyone would pass down the passage-way, the midday meal occupied those on board who might have used it. Sara looked thoughtfully from the dress to the open door, and decided that she might take the risk of leaving it that way. She whipped off the cotton gown, and pulled the blue muslin over her head. Martha had been as tall as she, but of heavier build. The gown was too big; the waist-line fell below her own, and the neck, cut to fit a broader figure, hung open in the front and slipped off her shoulder. She would alter it to fit and some time, she hoped, there might be an occasion to wear it. Certainly, it was rather an elaborate gown for a servant, but if Martha, middle-aged and dignified, thought it suitable, then she, Sara, wasn't going to pass it by.

Searching among the more sober garments for something with which she could adorn the muslin, she came upon a long scarf of the finest black lace. It was probably Chantilly – something she was not unfamiliar with, as smuggled lengths of it were often seen about the shoulders of the richer women of Rye. She examined it critically – it was quite faultless and very beautiful. She draped it over her head, letting it trail across her shoulders. Quickly she turned to the wash-table for the small, handled mirror which lay there.

The only light in the cabin came from the lamp above her head, so that she saw her reflection dimly. She imagined that her mother might have looked a little as she did now. The face she saw pleased her; her pale gold hair and bare shoulders showed through the black lace. She went on gazing, reflecting that it was a comfort sometimes, to be able to take pleasure from one's own face.

She gave a little shrug and adjusted the lace scarf to better effect. Then a sound from the doorway caused her to lower the glass and turn swiftly. She found Wilder watching her.

Their eyes met as they both strove to weigh up the situation. Sara folded her lips, waiting for him to speak. She took in his nonchalant leaning position against the door-frame, and the unpleasant smile that flickered thinly across his good-looking face.

When he spoke it seemed that his drawl was deliberately insulting. He jerked his head on one side, and his eyes moved quite openly over her body.

'Very pretty, my dear !' he said. 'Very pretty !'

She managed to control her anger so that it shouldn't show in her face and give him even that small satisfaction. She kept perfectly still, pressed back against the wash-table.

But his gaze had dropped to the open chest.

'What's this, Sara? Packing? Leaving us? Shame!'

He looked at her inquiringly, and straightening from his leaning position, he stepped into the cabin. There was a touch of petulance in the way in which he banged down the lid of the chest and pushed it back under the cot. He kicked the door closed behind him.

'Mr Wilder,' she said sharply, 'kindly open the door !'

He stared at her, and then laughed.

'Kindly open the door !' he mocked, imitating her tones. 'Mr Wilder has no intention of opening the door !'

Then he stepped towards her, and his hand shot out and gripped her arm. He bent his head close to hers.

'And what can you do about it ?'

She thrust her hand against his chest. He was amused at her efforts to push him away.

'It does no good, Sara. If you make a sound I'll tell whoever comes that I'm here at your invitation. It wouldn't look well, would it, if I were to say that? Not even your frozen air of innocence could stand that !'

'If you . . .' Her voice was weaker and less certain. 'If you don't leave . . .'

He ended her speech abruptly by forcing his lips upon hers, pressing her body against his own until she could no longer even move in protest. Caught tightly against him, she was made strongly aware of the masculine smells he had brought into the tiny cabin, the smell and taste of wine on his lips and tongue, the faint smell of sweat from his armpits, the smell of the dressing he used upon his hair. They clung in her nostrils, and made her afraid. He had a strength and fever of desire to go on demanding with his lips a response she wouldn't give. He released her a little, and she felt him try to push her back on the chest. She closed her eyes and clung grimly to his shoulders, so that her body could be bent back. She had only one thought as she held him – that nothing should make her give in to Wilder, because he would use her without pity or thought. He would use her as long as he wished, and then leave her.

He began to shake her violently to break her grip, but it still held. The smell of the wine seemed overpoweringly strong, and she wondered if she were going to faint. She opened her eyes and saw the beads of sweat on his forehead and upper lip. She realized that it was on her own forehead as well.

Then he slackened his grip, and dropped his arms. She remained clinging to him, staring in a stupid, dazed fashion. It seemed foolish to have fought so grimly to prevent him coming nearer, and now, when he had drawn away, to hold him still. He put his hands up to her wrists, breaking her grip on the shoulders of his tunic with a single jerk.

Still holding her wrists he stepped back, looking her up and down. His gaze moved from her face to the limp muslin dress, hanging awry and falling off her shoulders.

'You didn't count on me coming, did you?' he said. 'You were preparing for someone else . . . for someone else, Sara! You're all dressed up for someone. Who is it?'

He put his face closer to hers. 'If you don't tell me I'll break you! I'll . . .' He gave her a savage shake. 'Is it Roberts? Tell me! Or Maclay? Or is it one of those convict bastards you bed with whenever you get the chance?'

He shook her again, thrusting her with each movement against the hard edge of the chest.

She whispered, her tone thin because of the pain in her wrists, 'If you don't go . . .'

'Go . . .?' He dropped his arms. 'I don't want to go. ' His frenzied rage seemed to have left him.

His expression softened and he put his hand upon her shoulder, one finger moving tenderly upon her flesh, stroking with exquisite gentleness the curve of the bone.

'Why do you fight me, Sara?'

The hand slipped to her throat, the same finger lingering now in the hollow at its base.

'I could make things so easy for you. I'd give you money so that you could buy food when you get to Sydney. I'll get gowns for you at the Cape – and silk . . . Sara, do you hear me? Are you listening?'

His eyes, as they searched her face, were confident, and eager. 'Sara . . .' He spoke gently. 'You like me, don't you?'

In reply she jerked herself free from his lightly caressing hand. Her voice came in a hoarse sort of whisper in the back of her throat.

'If it's a whore you want, Mr Wilder, you'll find plenty of them below! Don't come in here looking for one!'

His hands twitched unsteadily, as if he meant to strike her.

'You blasted little fool!' he snapped. 'You talk as if you were an innocent in arms. Fool . . . Fool! Don't think anyone is deceived by that . . . We all know your kind. But you won't stand out against it long after you land in Port Jackson. You'll see how quickly you change . . . it'll be a choice between your virtue and starvation then.'

His angry voice dropped to a lower level. He breathed deeply, dabbing impatiently with his hand at the sweat on his forehead.

'I'll tell you, Sara, in case you've forgotten, what's going to happen when you arrive in Sydney. You'll be looked over by the military, and, because you've got a beautiful face, and a beautiful body, one of the officers will want to make you his mistress. And you won't refuse. You won't flaunt your virtue, either. You'll be much too afraid of hunger. It's a business, my dear – you'll trade your beauty for bread and salt pork.'

She was looking at him with her eyes half-closed. 'How wrong you are about that, Mr Wilder!' she snapped. 'I'm not up for market. My position in the colony will be as Mrs Ryder's personal maid.'

'Personal maid, eh?' he scoffed. 'And what makes you think that?'

'Because she told me so herself!' she blazed back.

'Did she, indeed? How she trusts you!'

'She hasn't any reason not to trust me – and, what's more, she isn't going to get one.' Her breath was so fast it hurt her to speak. Finally she flung at him, 'Now, get out!'

The thin, unpleasant smile was back on his face.

'Get out? Get out, you say? Why should I?'

And, still smiling, he made a sudden lunge towards her, and caught her to him. To Sara, struggling to avoid them, his lips seemed to be everywhere, pressing into her hair and eyelids and mouth, excitedly seeking a response. Then she felt them against her throat, and on her shoulder where the gown had fallen away. His groping hands were upon her also, and she heard the sharp little sound as the wilted muslin tore. After that her restraint left her. Her anger was a hot darkness before her eyes; it exploded the frightened suggestions of caution; it mattered no longer whether the man who fumbled with such eager hands and lips was the captain or the lowest member of his crew. All she knew was that she must be rid of those hands.

She gave a quick twist, at the same time raising her right hand to his face. She dug her nails into the sweating skin and drew them sharply downwards. For a short space of time they both hesitated. Sara stared in awe at the three long scratches she had made on his cheek. The middle one, deeper than the others, had already begun to bleed.

Slowly his hand went up to touch his cheek. His fingers encountered the wetness there, and he turned them over to examine them. He cursed as he saw the blood smeared across them.

'You strumpet! Where did you learn your tricks – in a whorehouse? I've a mind to break every bone in your body for that!'

He hit her twice. The second blow flung her on to the chest. She struck her head against the bulkhead and slipped down, only half-conscious.

Before her misted eyes Wilder's figure seemed to sway threateningly. He bent over her.

'I'll want nothing more of you – bitch! Stay here! It becomes you well – your chaste little room!'

He swung back on his heel and left her. The door slammed behind him with a thunderous noise which echoed in the narrow passage-way.

4

The dead hours of the middle watch had dulled Andrew with fatigue. He had thankfully handed over to Roberts, and now, shortly after eight bells sounded, he began to make his way below. The night was fine and dark. There was a faint breeze, and the *Georgette* kept steadily on her course in a calm sea. The silence was deep as the ship slept.

The two stern lanterns cast a faint light over the poop deck and touched the helmsmen as they dragged together at the wheel. Looking away from them as he descended the companion-ladder, Andrew saw the glow of a cigar in the darkness, and made out the form of a man leaning against the bulwark. He paused, then went forward.

'Brooks? – Is that you?'

'Yes. Came up to get a breath of fresh air.' Andrew could not see his face, but his tone was weary and grim. 'It's a hell down there,' he said. 'There was a confinement – a convict woman. I've been with her all night.'

'Is she all right?' Andrew asked. He was sympathetically aware of the surgeon's ordeal among the troublesome mob of women.

'The mother is all right – the child is dead. It was born dead.'

Brooks turned back to the bulwark. He puffed at the cigar. 'Just as well it didn't live. These babies born on transports rarely last the voyage. They're sick and starved. This one's mother has no idea who the father is.'

Silence fell between them. Andrew stared out to sea, but was aware of nothing, neither his tiredness nor the blackness of the night. Presently he said, 'The man who was flogged yesterday – how is he?'

'Bad. But he'll get over it, I dare say. He's strong.'

The scene of the previous day's flogging had remained with Andrew. The convicts seemed to possess a fiendish talent for putting themselves in the way of trouble. God in heaven, wasn't their lot bad enough? he wondered. Yesterday's punishment was the result of a brutish attack by a Welshman on an undersized Bristol footpad. The weapon used was a single blade of a rusted pair of scissors. The set-to had been provoked by nothing more than an argument over the number of guns the *Georgette* carried. It didn't take much, he thought, to stir up a spark in the minds of men who had had no occupation for months. The Welshman was flogged before the mast in view of the assembled crew. The cat o' nine tails flew until his back was too bloody a mess to continue; then it fell across the calves of his legs. The little footpad lay below, too weak from loss of blood from the scissor wounds to take his part in the punishment.

'And the other one . . .?' Andrew asked. 'Will he live?'

'Yes, he'll live. He's responding well. In any case, they'll both spend the rest of the voyage in irons.'

Andrew said slowly, frowning, 'I can't get used to seeing them flogged. God knows, there was enough of it in the Navy to harden me. But this is different – and when it's one of the women, it makes me sick. I pity the convicts when they're being punished in a way I'd never pity one of the hands. What else can these miserable wretches do but cause trouble?'

'You've quite a feeling for the convicts these days, Maclay,' Brooks murmured.

Andrew turned to him. 'What do you mean?'

'Perhaps it's not my affair. But I should hate to see you run yourself into trouble.'

Andrew stiffened. 'Yes . . .?'

'The girl, I mean. Sara Dane.' Brooks said this quietly, as if he was feeling his way with care. 'Good God, man, you must know how gossip spreads around on a ship! You spend a great deal of your time with her. You can't blame . . .'

'I love her!' Andrew returned sharply.

'You love her . . .!' Brooks was taken aback. 'You know nothing about her – or almost nothing, how much *do* you know?'

Andrew lifted his shoulders helplessly. 'What do any of us know about her except that she's beautiful and that she has charm and spirit!'

'Beauty, yes,' Brooks replied, considering. 'She has that all right. Oh, and charm and spirit, too! But, God in heaven, Maclay, you don't *love* a convict for having a beautiful face!'

'But that's just it, I *do* love her!' Andrew said quickly. 'She obsesses me, I tell you! I can't get her out of my mind! The thought of her torments me!'

Brooks had turned to Andrew. 'You can't be serious, surely?'

'Damn you, of course I'm serious!'

'Have you told her this?'

For a moment Andrew didn't reply. Then he said, 'That's the curse of it – I haven't.' He went on gloomily. 'You know what she's like – I never get a chance to tell her. She's just the same with all of us – Wilder, Roberts – yourself, Brooks. She's got a smile and a laugh for each of us – and that's as far as it goes.'

'Oh, I'll not deny she knows what she's about. The captain can't have any reason to complain of *her* behaviour! She's a shrewd enough wench, I'll give you that!'

'Yes . . . yes.' Andrew was impatient. 'But what am I to do? I love her!'

'This is a damned awkward business, Maclay,' Brooks said, at the end of a long pause between them. 'I hardly know what to say. The captain won't turn a blind eye to consorting . . .'

'Consorting! I don't want to consort with her! I want to marry her!'

'Don't be such a blasted fool, man! How can you marry her – it's not as simple as that. Have you forgotten you'll be parted when we reach Port Jackson?'

Andrew said calmly, 'I have plans . . .'

'Plans! Damn' good plans you'll need to get you over a situation like this. She's a convict! You know nothing about her – where she comes from, even what crime she was transported for.'

'True,' Andrew said. 'But I'll find out.'

'Then you'll have to ask her herself. None of the convict-papers will tell you.'

The surgeon had finished his cigar by this time. He threw the glowing end down into the water.

'I'm deadly serious about this, Brooks,' Andrew said. 'I mean to ask her about herself. I'll find out as much as there is to know — and you'll see then whether or not I'm in love with her!'

Brooks sighed deeply. 'Well . . . I hope you're not . . . disillusioned. That's about all I can say.'

He added, 'We'd both better get below now. I'm dead for want of sleep.'

Andrew followed the other to the companion-ladder, and as he walked back he glanced at the stern lights standing out against the blackness of the sky. The *Georgette* rode in deep and pervading peace, as if she were an untroubled ship.

Andrew came face to face with Sara the following evening as she descended the companion-ladder from the quarter-deck. He ran up a few steps to halt her progress. She was surprised by his direct approach and gazed down on him inquiringly.

'I want to talk to you,' he said.

She said nothing, but glanced about the deck below her. The passage-way from which Andrew had come led directly to the officers' quarters. Even as they stood facing each other two of the hands passed, and shot quick, curious glances at them.

'Come with me,' Andrew said. He moved past her on the ladder, jerking his head to indicate that she should follow.

Sara faced him squarely when he drew her into the shadow of the lifeboat on the quarter-deck and demanded to know why she was here on the *Georgette*. He asked her outright the reason for her conviction.

She had been expecting this, and shrugged her shoulders, answering with the suggestion of a laugh.

'Oh, I ran away from a rectory — and had the misfortune to forget to return to my employers three guineas, which they claimed did not belong to me.'

He let out an exasperated gasp, took her shoulders and shook her sharply.

'Don't play with me, madam! That's not the whole story!'

'Then you shall have it — the whole of it!' she flung back at him. 'And if you don't like it, remember that I didn't force it on you.'

While his hand still rested upon her shoulders, but more gently now, she told him what he had asked, going back to her life in London, in Rye, and at Bramfield. She left nothing out, not her

mother's doubtful past, or Sebastian's family. He heard about
Sir Geoffrey Watson and Lady Linton. The one thing she could
not tell him, and never meant to tell him, was her love for Richard
Barwell.

'When the time came to go to Lady Linton,' she said, 'I decided
I'd had enough of living with a family in which I'd never be
anything but the daughter of a drunkard and a petty borrower.'
She added a trifle ruefully: 'It was the only mistake I ever made
— to take Sir Geoffrey's money with me. There was no defence
for me after that.'

As she finished he suddenly squeezed both her shoulders tightly
in his hands, and let out a shout of laughter which carried clearly
across the deck.

'You little fool, Sara! Oh, you little fool!' He laughed again.
'To think you let yourself be sent to Botany Bay for the price
of a gown or two! And to think I've wasted sleep over you because you called yourself a thief. A thief — of all things! You're
a borrower, Sara, like your father.'

He had stopped laughing, but he still grinned broadly. 'This is
the best news I've had in my life.'

Without warning he bent and kissed her fully on the lips.

'Remember that until the next time, Sara.'

Then he turned and strode across the deck towards the companion-ladder; she listened to the noisy clatter he made as he
descended it. He whistled softly as he went.

She stayed where she was, within the shadow of the lifeboat.
Below there were many tasks waiting for her attention, but for
once, she told herself, they could wait. She closed her eyes for a
second, and saw again Andrew Maclay's face, gay and yet serious,
as excited as a boy's. But there was bitterness in the knowledge also.
What was the use of Andrew Maclay being in love with her — no
more could come of it than just another offer such as Wilder's.
Though Andrew's would be couched in terms of love and affection,
and the inducement to yield would be all the stronger. Restlessly
she turned her head, looking out towards the dark horizons. Where
could such a relationship end, except in a farewell when they
reached Port Jackson? — and the price she would pay was the loss
of Julia Ryder's confidence. The thought tormented her. Here at
hand was a man who might make her forget Richard Barwell, forget the foolishness two children had committed. Andrew had the
authority about him that could easily command her love, and the
tenderness to win and hold it. Before his reality, the image of
Richard would fade. She acknowledged, despairingly, that it would
be an easy matter now to fall in love.

But inevitably some day the *Georgette* would sail out of Port Jackson, and she would remain behind. Only fools fell in love with a prospect like that.

Four bells sounded – the signal for the end of the last dog watch. Andrew Maclay might carry the air of a man who would carve out an exciting, adventurous life for himself, he might have a swaggering charm and look at her with tenderness in his eyes, but, she decided, he was best put out of her mind before he hurt her as Richard Barwell once had done.

2

Gazing up at the sun, James Ryder breathed deeply, thankful that the seemingly interminable stretch from Rio de Janeiro to the Cape was almost over. More than two hours ago the first excited shout of 'Land ho!' had come from the look-out. The echo of the cry spread abroad the ship, passing like a ripple from mouth to mouth. There was a good wind, and every passing minute brought the African coastline into sharper focus. They had made an almost perfect landfall – a fact that amazed Ryder when he remembered the immense distances of the Atlantic rolling behind them.

He planted his hands firmly on the bulwark, watching the faint shape of the land before him. Julia would be glad of this, he thought. She was weary of the cramped space, the discomforts of the pitching ship, and longing for the entry into Table Bay. Recalling this, and her patience during the long voyage, he was struck afresh by her courage. She was a damned wonderful woman, he thought, journeying half-way round the world with a husband and two children, and very little to compensate at the end of it. After many years of marriage Ryder was still deeply in love with his wife. She was a precious thing who gave him more concern than he cared to admit.

It was now over three years since their sons, twins, had been drowned when a fisherman's boat overturned in the sea off their Essex farmlands. Julia grieved for them mutely and constantly, and the shock of their deaths stayed with her. She became like a ghost, living in a world in which she had no longer any interest. Her husband had seen her apathy, tried desperately, but without success, to rouse her. Finally he begged her sanction to his giving up the farm and taking land in the West Country or the Midlands. But she refused. She would live nowhere in England except with the sound of the North Sea in her ears.

Then at last, in despair, he approached her cautiously with

the suggestion of the colony in New South Wales – and, amazingly, she had welcomed it. The idea was a nebulous thing – so little was known of the settlement, it was a prison-country, its citizens felons. Yet, after their first real discussion about it, she was undaunted by the hardship it offered; its loneliness, its extremity. She was enthusiastic, leaving him no choice but to go ahead with the plan he had as yet only played with. She even insisted upon accompanying him to London for an interview with the Secretary of State, Dundas. From Dundas, they went to Sir Joseph Banks, the botanist who had sailed with Cook and landed at Botany Bay. Here, they imagined, they might expect reliable first-hand information. Banks described the new country as a land of promise, a farmer's land. On the journey back to Essex they were silent, each preoccupied with the story they had heard of the settlement.

They knew that if they settled in New South Wales they would have free land-grants and convict labour; but the drawbacks, too, were great. Reports of flood and famine offered little encouragement to emigrants, so far only a few families had ventured to go there. The sum total of the harrowing tales carried home to England was that they faced a wilderness and starvation. Ryder, contemplating this, might easily have had his enthusiasm dampened. But he was blessed with an imagination and an adventuring spirit which was an easy prey to excitement.

And yet he was not altogether blind to the dangers awaiting the free settlers, and he faced Julia fairly with them, giving her every opportunity to withdraw. But her mind was made up, and she could not be shaken. She left the Essex farm with scarcely a backward glance, meeting the challenge of New South Wales with a formidable determination.

He smiled grimly up at the sky above the billowing spread of canvas. Yes, he thought again, she was a damned wonderful woman!

He began to pace then, up and down the restricted space of the quarter-deck. After about five minutes he halted, his eyes resting reflectively on his two children. They were seated in the shelter of the bulwark, and Sara Dane was beside them. It stirred him to speculate on the possibilities the colony offered his children. If its untapped resources yielded richness, they would be the reapers. They would grow up in loneliness and isolation, estranged from their homeland; but they would grow up with the settlement now in its early infancy, and they would sit astride her promised prosperity.

But what of the ones such as Sara Dane, he wondered, looking long at her – the ones who went out in captivity to populate and work the colony? He shook his head slowly, knowing the uselessness of trying to fathom the thoughts behind those strange eyes. Not Julia – no one, he suspected, except possibly Andrew Maclay – knew why she was here on the *Georgette*. One could only accept the obvious fact that she was not of the type and class usually found in these transports. But, whatever she was, he was profoundly grateful for the qualities she possessed. She was both nurse and tutor to his children, maid and companion to his wife. It was an unexpected combination of abilities. He saw her lift her head then, and laugh at something Charles had said. The sun was fully on her face, and on her skin where her dress was open at the neck. The sight of her young beauty, highly coloured in the sun, held his thoughtful gaze for a long time.

Finally he turned and began to walk again. But he paused almost immediately. Andrew Maclay, relieved of his watch, was descending from the poop.

'Good morning!' he hailed. 'Welcome sight, isn't it?' He indicated the land with a nod of his head.

'It is, indeed, sir,' Andrew replied, grinning and sniffing in the freshness of the fine morning. 'I imagine Mrs Ryder will be glad of a stretch on firm ground. She'll not find it as gay as Rio, but at least she'll have a spell from the ship.'

Ryder smiled. 'I hardly think it's my wife who will miss the gaiety most. I think you younger ones will be the greater sufferers.'

Andrew said nothing, but for a brief moment his eyes turned towards Sara.

Ryder's tone had been bantering, but only to cover the disturbance he suddenly felt. Maclay's attention to Sara was obvious. It was food for ready gossip in a ship which had had little or no diversion since leaving Rio. The attachment was understandable enough, but Ryder puzzled over the fact that each of their meetings took place where a dozen pairs of eyes might witness it. To outward intent they might be conducting a gracious and leisurely courtship, with their whole lives stretching before them. And yet the circumstances mocked this façade. However unlike one she might appear, Sara Dane was a convict, and Maclay an officer in a company whose prestige was second only to the Royal Navy. The whole situation was incongruous. In most other ships he would have been permitted to take her as his mistress, and the affair would end, with Sara considerably richer, when the *Georgette* left Sydney and headed for her regular trading route. Ryder had the feeling that

that was not what Maclay wanted.

The older man studied his companion gravely. In the hard light Maclay's eyes were a deep blue; the skin around them, though young, was lined, toughened and browned by the weather. He had a strong mouth and jaw; his speech, his every action, revealed a typical Scottish determination. The paradox of Maclay's character interested Ryder. He knew that night after night Maclay sat late over cards with whoever he could induce to join him – and he had fantastic luck at them. But Ryder had heard the captain praise his meticulous attention to his duties. He was one of those people who appeared not to need sleep – a seaman with the cool nerves of a gambler.

Andrew, growing restless in the silence that had fallen between them, stirred himself and asked a question.

'Will you be taking on livestock at the Cape, sir?'

Ryder, with effort, brought his thoughts back to the question. 'Yes, I hope to. I'll take on as much livestock as I can get storage for. They tell me it's beyond price in the colony.'

Andrew nodded. 'The plan all round among the officers seems to be to buy livestock at the Cape to sell to the Commissary in Sydney.'

'And will you be joining this trading venture?'

'I expect so, sir. It's reckoned to be a profitable business. And,' Andrew laughed, 'I'm not one to turn down that sort of thing!'

The other nodded. 'I'm told that the man who has livestock does well in the colony. For my part, I don't intend sitting back and waiting on a precarious harvest. I want cows and pigs. And perhaps sheep.'

Andrew considered awhile, then he said, 'I've been meaning to speak to you about the colony, sir.' He hesitated a further moment, beginning again diffidently. 'What is your honest opinion of one's chances of settling there?'

Ryder eyed his companion gravely. 'It'll be no bed of roses. And all who go willingly to New South Wales must go expecting to gamble. Everything seems to be against us – even the floods, and damned hard work on empty bellies.' His voice was rising, his eyes had lightened in excitement. He slapped a closed fist into his other hand. 'But it's a settler's kingdom, Maclay! Why, just think of it, man! It's ground cattle have never trod! It's never had seed sown into it! You cannot tell me that, rightly treated, it will not produce!'

'Yet they still starve.'

'They starve, yes. But only because the colony is in the hands of naval captains and convicts. What does the Navy know about farming? I tell you, Maclay, New South Wales will only be satisfactorily settled by free men – and men who know farming. With each free settler comes that much more hope of prosperity. Put enough good farmers on the land, and then we'll see who'll starve!'

'You seem to have a great deal of faith in this country,' Andrew said.

'Yes, I have faith in it. By God, I have faith in it!' Ryder leaned forward and prodded at Andrew's waistcoat. 'The more settlers the greater the urge for expansion – north and south, they'll go, Maclay, and finally into the hinterland.'

'Expansion behind the settlement? Surely one can't rely on that?'

Ryder sighed. He recalled Brooks's after-dinner tales of the mysteries and dangers of the unexplored continent. They were fetching stories for a man to spin out after a few glasses of wine. With his first-hand knowledge Brooks was able to roll on without fear of contradiction. He was sceptical of the idea of expansion, pointing out that close behind the coastal plains lay a long ridge of smoky-blue, impenetrable hills. Governor Phillip had tried again and again to find a way through them; the expeditions he sent out all turned back, beaten. Brooks believed that they never would be crossed, and that the settlement would stagnate where it was, without ever penetrating farther.

'Ah, you're thinking of the Blue Mountains,' Ryder said patiently. 'They're a barrier, I admit, but they won't stop expansion. Free men will always make room for themselves – as they do in Canada and America. Only if the settlement remains wholly penal will it stagnate.

'Free settlers will be the making of the country.' Ryder's tone dared Andrew's denial. 'In the beginning they'll be so few that they hardly count at all. They'll live in discomfort, Maclay, mind you that. They've got to settle expecting hell. They'll be isolated, and their womenfolk will suffer, too. But my God, man, how they'll be rewarded!' He was smiling, his eyes glinting in the sun. 'When prosperity does finally come, it's the early birds who'll be fat on it.'

Ryder's smile faded slowly and his voice dropped. The conversation was ended. But as Andrew walked away he was turning over his plan – a plan he had already formed, even before he talked with Ryder, which offered a solution for himself and Sara.

3

Even in the strong sunlight Table Mountain seemed to tower
rather sullenly over the neat Dutch settlement and cluster of shipping in the Bay. But Sara and Andrew, standing together by the
bulwark, had no eyes for sights that had become familiar to them
in the three weeks during which the *Georgette* had ridden at anchor
there; there was little interest for them in the prim, yet strangely uncivilized town. Their attention was fixed on the confusion in the
longboat below them, from which a noisy, clumsy cargo of pigs,
cattle and sheep was being transferred to the Indiaman. The warm
air was filled with the protests of the animals, and in an accompanying boat, safely removed from the despairing struggles of the
livestock, the Dutchman who had contracted to supply the *Georgette*
added his shouts and curses to the uproar. The din and the smell
grew; yet the determined activity of the scene held them both
fascinated. Sara's eyes met Andrew's in sudden amusement as a
boatman, grappling unsuccessfully with a young pig, lost his balance
and fell overboard, the pig clutched tightly in his arms. The Dutch
contractor jumped to his feet with a shouted oath. Every eye turned
to watch the incredible turmoil of the water, the mad threshing
that followed the first splash; the contractor, after regarding the
spectacle for a few seconds in fury and contempt, moved into
action. Like a flash he reached the end of the longboat nearest
the struggling pair. In the speed of his movement he showed his
fear of losing valuable property. He leaned down between the two
craft and grasped the pig by its neck. With a mighty swing of his
arms he tossed it into the boat, where it lay coughing up salt water
and squealing in its unexpected misery. Laconically, the contractor
indicated that an oar should be extended to his servant. The
wretched man was eventually hauled into the longboat by two pairs
of hands thrust under his belt.

The work of loading recommenced.

'Will they complete it, do you think,' Sara asked, 'by nightfall?'

'I expect they'll continue by lantern, if necessary,' Andrew said.
'If this wind holds the captain will use it to get under way in the
morning.'

With his words Sara's thoughts were turned to tomorrow's
departure. All day long there had been a sense of unrest aboard
the ship. The officers had made their final buying and trading
expeditions among the shipping in the Bay and the stores in the

town; the final commissions for the captain had been executed. Most of the livestock was, by this time, consigned to the pens prepared, the water casks scoured and filled. The bustle of leave-taking had established itself in the *Georgette*. No one seemed to regret the departure – least of all, she thought, the convicts, strictly guarded during the length of the stay in port, because of the fear of an escape overside.

The ship's officers and company had no great love of the town; it lacked the mystery and heathenish splendour of the trading-posts of the East, nor did the rocky, arid scenery recall memories of the homeland. They met here a sense of isolation which they feared; the grey-green vegetation was unfamiliar, and there persisted a lonely feeling among them that this was the last outpost of the known world. Between the Cape and the South Pole stretched the ocean, and nothing more. Among the sailors there was a superstitious dread of sailing down into those southern seas. The longest stretch of the voyage still faced them, and now, with the hour of quitting the Bay drawing near, there was an atmosphere of urgency to have it over and done with. Thinking about it, she wondered if it could have been this cloud of forlornness and desolation which had swamped one of the hands, Timothy Brown, last night, with a melancholic drunkenness. No one could be certain if his fall overboard was accidental or deliberate. The longboat was launched immediately, but he was already gone. He had slipped down into the dark water of the Bay without a single cry. When the news of his drowning ran through the ship, the women in the holds became unmanageable, shrieking and shouting foul language, believing that Brown had gone overboard rather than face the horror of the voyage ahead. This morning five of the women, the worst offenders, were in irons.

Sara's thoughts were distracted by further shouts from below, and she stood on tiptoe to lean farther over the side. A furious sort of quarrel seemed to be going on between two of the boatmen, but not being able to understand what they were saying, she lost interest.

Suddenly Andrew touched her hand to draw attention; he pointed downwards towards the livestock.

'I've bought my share in that, Sara.'

She answered, 'I expected that you would. You'll sell it for a good profit in Port Jackson.'

He shook his head, although she wasn't looking at him, but still staring down at the loading.

'It's not for sale. I'm keeping it for myself. I'm going to apply for a grant of land in New South Wales, and farm there.'

She dropped back on her heels, turned and looked at him with astonishment. 'Farm . . . You? A sailor!'

'I wasn't a sailor all my life. I was brought up by a Scotsman who was the best farmer in his district – one doesn't forget the sort of things that have been preached at you like the Bible.'

She shook her head. 'But . . . leave the sea and take up farming? Why . . . ?'

'Because,' he said, 'I want to stay in New South Wales and marry you.'

She took a step backward, and her mouth fell open a trifle.

'Andrew,' she said faintly, 'have you gone mad?'

'I expect I have!' he retorted. 'You have driven me crazy – witch! I don't sleep nights thinking about you. And I keep my watches like a drunken fool. I can tell you it's been hell! Sara, will you promise to marry me, and let me have my peace back again?'

'Marry you? Oh, Andrew . . . !'

He brought his hand down with an impatient slap on the bulwark. 'Don't pretend you haven't guessed that I'm in love with you! The whole ship must know it by this time.'

'In love with me . . . perhaps. But have you forgotten that I'm on this ship as a convict?'

'I haven't forgotten that – of course I haven't. But these things can be arranged. If I ask permission to marry you, I don't see any difficulty about Governor Phillip granting you a pardon. He has the power to do it, and, if he doesn't – I'll marry you just the same, and then he'll be forced to assign you to me as a housekeeper until your sentence expires.'

She turned her eyes away from him, looking across the brilliant stretch of water. She said slowly, 'It can't be as simple as you make it sound.'

'It's completely simple! We have to take our chance – we have to do what hasn't been done before. I'm going to marry you, Sara. I'm going to make you free!'

She made no answer.

'Well?' he said, finally.

She shook her head. 'But I don't see how . . .'

'You don't see how!' The words broke from him with an undertone of irritation. 'I've told you how it can be managed. All we have to do is to be firm about it. Everything will fall into place. When we're married we can settle all the difficulties.'

Turning, she answered him heatedly. 'But it's when we're married that the difficulties arise. Don't you see that? Just try to think of the future, Andrew – with an ex-convict wife. And your children . . .' Her voice dropped. 'My dear,' she said patiently, 'see it sensibly. It wouldn't work.'

He took a deep breath. 'But this is a new country we're going to – it's a whole new world! There'll be ways of settling the conventions to suit ourselves. Forget about the rules of society that apply in England. In the colony there are none – or very few. In a new country we make the rules ourselves. It's been like that with America – why not New South Wales?'

He grew excited; his face sharpened with eagerness. 'It's an adventure, Sara! It's something to fix your whole mind and heart to. If I had you with me, there's nothing I couldn't do. Nothing! Are you worried that I'd fail? I have some money invested in the East India Company – I'll withdraw it, and that will be enough to start us. It's not a fortune, certainly – but it's a beginning.

'What do you say, Sara?' he said earnestly. 'Will you chance it with me? There could be wealth at the end of it – perhaps for our children. There's the excitement of a new country, and a new life for both of us.

'You'll share everything I have. It's not a great deal I offer you. I'm a plain man – a sailor, a farmer, and something of a gambler. Is that enough? Will you have me?'

She answered wildly, 'If it were just a question of this year – or next year – I'd say "yes". But marriage is for the rest of our lives. What about the time when that adventuring blood of yours has cooled down, and you've farmed as many acres of this new land as you can count, and you've achieved everything you ever dreamed of achieving? Are you going to look at me then and tell yourself that I'm the one thing in your bright world that doesn't fit? Whatever pardon I might get from Governor Phillip, I'll always be known as an ex-convict. When you make your fortune, can you stomach my past along with it?'

Suddenly he smiled, and an expression of tenderness and joy came into his face. 'My darling Sara, I'll stomach it all! Your past, and your future as well. I'll make you the most envied ex-convict in the world! You'll be so gloriously happy, so much a queen in your own home, that every other woman will wish she were an ex-convict as well!'

A hot flush sprang to her cheeks. 'You're laughing at me, Andrew!'

'Sweet Sara, I'm not laughing! I'm merely telling you how foolish you are. Doesn't it tempt you to consider that I could give you back that empty respectability your heart's yearned after ever since you ran away from your blasted rectory?'

She said in a low voice, 'I'd rather stay a convict than have you look at me ten years from now, and know that you regretted marrying me.'

'Sweetheart!' he said gently. 'Give me the ten years, and let me show you what I'll make of them. Will you?'

'I . . . I don't know.'

He frowned. 'Haven't I a right to something more positive than that?'

'Andrew . . .' she said hesitantly. 'Wait until we reach Botany Bay. You'll have had time to think about it more than once by then. Perhaps you'll find the idea of a convict wife isn't so attractive to you.'

She swung round, making to leave him, but he reached out and caught her hand, bowing over it slightly, and pressing it to his lips.

'It's a very long voyage to Botany Bay,' he murmured. 'Before we're half-way there, I'll have you seeing all this as I do.'

He let her go then, watching her as she made her way, with her erect, even walk, across the deck to the companion-way. His face was taut with excitement and passion. The cries of the animals and the shouts of the men below seemed to swell to an unbearable tumult. He straightened himself, and turned to face the stares of the men who had witnessed the scene.

After leaving Andrew on the deck, Sara went below immediately to the Ryders' cabin. Julia turned expectantly as she entered.

'What is it, Sara?'

For the moment Sara didn't answer. She closed the door behind her, and stood with her back pressed firmly against it. She was breathing quickly and Julia couldn't tell whether it was with excitement or anger.

'Andrew Maclay has asked me to marry him,' she said at last.

Julia drew in a sharp breath. So, she thought, it had finally come, this situation for which she had waited. And not altogether in the way she had expected.

'And what answer did you give him?' she asked quietly.

Sara lifted her chin higher. 'I told him to consider it until we reach Botany Bay. He'll know by then if he still wants a convict as a wife.'

'And if he has changed his mind?' Julia questioned.

Sara shrugged her shoulders slightly. 'In that case, he'll go off to the East when the ship sails again. If he's still of the same opinion, he'll stay where he is and take up farming.'

Julia regarded the other sharply. She didn't like it when Sara assumed an air of unconcern in a matter of such importance to her.

'Sara, you're not fooling me any more than you're fooling yourself!' she cried. 'This is what you wanted. You've worked for this. You've no intention of letting him go – so why, in heaven's name, can't you give him a proper answer?'

Sara took a step forward. She had dropped her defiance, and now looked unsure of herself. Her face was troubled.

'I *will* let Andrew go, if he doesn't want to go through with it. I won't hold him, if I find he's changed his mind.'

'He won't try to back out,' Julia said. 'He's in love with you – everyone knows that. And if he has asked you to marry him, he means to go through with it.'

Sara flared into life again. 'But it's an impossible marriage! I'm a *convict* – and he doesn't seem to realize what that means. He has all sorts of high-blown notions of making his own rules of convention in the colony. He thinks I'll fit in. He thinks he can make me acceptable!' She was passionate in her outburst.

Julia turned away. She sat down at the dressing-table, and let her hands rest idly in her lap. There was enough of an element of trouble in this situation to make a cautious woman draw back – but Julia was beginning to realize, with a mild feeling of astonishment, that, after all these years of placid married life, at heart she had never been a cautious woman. She considered the two young people. Andrew Maclay was nobody's fool, and Sara could match him in spirit and shrewdness, one not out-reaching the other. Supposing she encouraged this marriage? If she were openly to show her trust and respect for Sara, it could be made much easier for Governor Phillip to grant her a pardon. It might be a dangerous thing to do – interfering in the lives of two people who must make their own strange decision. Yet the idea excited her. She saw this marriage as a desperate adventure – it was bold and daring, and it appealed strongly to her. She leaned forward, tilting the mirror so that she might see Sara's reflection. They would be a good pair for a new country, she decided.

She swung around and rose to her feet.

'Sara, I think you must accept Andrew's offer. He doesn't think it's an impossible proposition, and I don't either.'

For a while neither spoke; but Julia, watching Sara's face, saw it soften, and then the excitement came back into her eyes. For the first time, also, she fancied she saw the beginning of tears there.

C.G.O.–C

5

Since rounding the tip of Van Dieman's Land, whose mountains had risen coldly out of the southern ocean, the *Georgette* had followed the eastern edge of the new continent for some six or seven hundred miles. This was the *Terra Australis* of the early navigators' maps – the coast which Cook had charted, the cliffs and inlets that were the fringe of an unknown world. At sunset on the first of October, 1792, the look-out sighted the giant headlands, a mile apart, at the entrance to Port Jackson. The *Georgette* hove to, and waited for the morning light before she attempted the passage through the channel of deep water between them.

All on board, the crew, the convicts, the four passengers, had endured an experience of utter isolation; they had survived, and were now trying to forget it. The weather, almost from the time of leaving the Cape, had been vile. They headed directly south, nearing the Antarctic Circle, then steering a course sharply east to round the promontory of Van Dieman's Land. Few of them escaped sickness; they were all cold, suffering in this last sting of the Southern winter. Supplies of fresh food were consumed too rapidly, and they faced the deadly round of meals of salt pork. The livestock fared badly; some of it died. They had seen whales, and giant albatrosses that circled the ship steadily, dropping below the bulwark and appearing again as the *Georgette* rose and fell in the heavy seas. Their belongings had been soaked by the waves breaking inboard, and with the convicts' quarters awash there was no way of stemming the constant streams of cursing and abuse. There was a good deal of drinking among the officers, and they quarrelled frequently, bickering over petty affairs, gambling listlessly and complaining of each other. The strain grew worse as the journey lengthened, and rations of food and water grew smaller. But somehow, through all this, they managed the unvarying routine of running the ship, keeping her on a course that was always farther south and farther east, plodding on into unknown seas, constantly touched by the knowledge and dread of their isolation. Fear, as tangible and real as the foul weather, hung over them; no one spoke of it – it declared itself in their indulgences in drink, and their stupid, meaningless quarrels.

But there was one incident of the voyage which they would not forget. The *Georgette* was two weeks out of the Bay when the first faint rumour of mutiny among the convicts ran through her, like some soft and eerie piping. An Irishman, Patrick Reilly, transported for life, was the informer; he gave the information to Roberts when he was brought before him, threatened with punishment for insubordination. Reilly's warning was ominous; none knew, nor could guess, what desperate courage and daring the convicts might have gained from their misery and wretchedness. A thorough search for weapons revealed nothing more than a few knives. Yet the unease refused to die. Common sense told the ship's officers that these men, weakened from bad food and confinement, with disease and the threat of scurvy among them, could achieve little in the way of effective mutiny – but the fear persisted. Privately, each wondered if perhaps it might be he who would have the watch when the outbreak occurred, if it might be he who was to feel the sudden stab of the knife, hear the helmsman's warning cry. It was obvious to all that a rebellion on board must necessarily be short-lived, but even that knowledge was of little help. They each felt that he himself would be the one to die as a gesture to mark its beginning.

The sense of crisis oppressed the ship for a week before the climax. It came when the nerves of every man on the *Georgette* were taut with waiting, and even the faintest stir, which might be considered out of the ordinary, was enough to cause a mad and hot-headed panic. It occurred because one of the prisoners, sullenly fighting the pains of dysentery, was gripped in his sleep with hysterical nightmare. He screamed, and continued to scream – the piercing sounds shattered the silence of the watchful darkened ship. The unnerved guards took this as the signal for the mutiny; they fired without aim into the blackness of the convict quarters. There was shouting and confusion and the glaring flash of shot. Four men were cut down before reason told the guards to halt.

Three of these were dead by the morning; the fourth lingered a day longer. They were dropped overside in their canvas swathing without the usual line-up of convicts to witness the ceremony, and if mutiny had ever been planned aboard the *Georgette*, its spirit died with them. The guards were punished as a token of discipline, though the feeling running through the entire company was that these two had been the unfortunate instruments of the wider, deeper fear which possessed the rest.

But other thoughts claimed them when the peaks of the mountains of Van Dieman's Land thrust themselves out of the ocean. The *Georgette* turned north again, and the breezes grew warmer; at times the spring sunshine was hot. They watched the coastline

warily. It revealed nothing beyond long, curving beaches, and vegetation of grey and indefinite greens. Those who had not seen it
before – that was everyone except Brooks – reserved judgement.
The ship's company had hailed the sight with relief, reckoning
among themselves how soon they would be free of their troublesome cargo and sailing again towards more congenial trade with
India and China.

2

In the wardroom Andrew stacked the cards and leaned back in
his chair. His glance flicked briefly over the other three men, Harding, Brooks and Wilder, who sat with him.

'Well, gentlemen, I'm afraid I'll have to withdraw. I'm on watch
in fifteen minutes.'

They said nothing; Wilder shifted in his chair and half-stifled a
yawn; Harding fidgeted with his cigar. Watching them, the ghost
of a smile touched Andrew's lips.

'A lively lot, you are !' he remarked, to no one in particular. 'Are
none of you going to wish me well? This is the last watch I shall
stand at sea in the *Georgette* – it's the end of my commission with
the East India Company.'

Still no one spoke, and the silence grew noticeably heavy. As
Andrew looked at each in turn, their eyes avoided his.

'Well,' he said, 'I see you think it's wiser to say nothing, when
you believe a man is about to ruin his life in one mad act of folly.'
He shrugged. 'Perhaps you're right. A madman never listens to
advice.'

Then he bent over the score. The silence continued while he made
his calculations.

Finally he straightened, passing the slip of paper to Harding.

The first officer noted the total with a resigned air; his lips
moved visibly as he checked Andrew's figures. At last he nodded
slowly, handing on the paper to Brooks, who sat on his left.

'Your run of luck never seems to come to an end, Maclay,' he
said wearily. 'I'm afraid this game leaves me still considerably in
your debt.'

Brooks made no comment; he merely nodded and passed the
paper on to Wilder. The other took it disinterestedly, then frowned
and sat up abruptly as he saw the total.

'I can't owe you as much as this, Maclay !'

'It's not all from tonight's game,' Andrew said. 'You don't forget that you've had steady bad luck since we left the Cape? That's
the total amount you owe me.'

'And you expect me to pay this before we leave Port Jackson?'

'Naturally.' Andrew turned from Wilder to include the other two. 'I've enjoyed your company and your play, gentlemen – but this is undoubtedly the end of it. Within the next few days I'll be leaving the ship, and staying on in New South Wales. You all continue the voyage. None of us can say when, if ever, we'll meet again.'

Wilder said, 'But damn it – you know I can't pay as much as this immediately! I've put all the money I could spare into cargo to sell here and in the East.'

Andrew's expression didn't alter as he listened to Wilder. He flicked the cards between his fingers, appearing not to take any notice of the others. He knew they were each waiting for him to answer, but he was in no hurry to come to terms with Wilder – let him have a few moments longer to consider his position, and to wonder how he was going to find the money. Andrew saw that a frown of impatience was beginning to gather on Harding's forehead. He stopped playing with the cards, and turned to Wilder.

'Part of your cargo is in livestock, isn't it? I seem to remember three cows and eight hogs.'

'Yes,' Wilder said.

'Then,' Andrew said quietly, 'I'll accept the livestock in payment for the debt.'

'Oh, no!' Wilder answered quickly. 'I can't agree to that. I may get a better price from the Commissary than the value of this debt.'

Andrew shrugged. 'That is, of course, your own risk. You may also be offered a lower price for them.'

He drew a fresh sheet of paper towards him, and made some quick calculations on it. When he was finished he pushed it across the table to Wilder.

'The last record we have of prices in the colony is a year out of date. But, reckoning on those prices, the value of your livestock falls short of the debt.'

Wilder sat staring at the figures in silence. Harding was leaning forward in his chair now, watching the faces of both the younger men.

Andrew said, 'As it stands, you're the gainer on the transaction, Wilder. But when we get into Port Jackson tomorrow, you may find the market value of the livestock has gone up – in which case you're the loser.'

Abruptly he banged the table with his closed fist. 'Will you gamble on it? I may as well warn you now that once I leave this

table tonight I'll expect repayment of the debt in full – even if I
have to take part of your cargo for the East as well.'

Wilder flushed angrily. 'You push this settlement as no gentleman would, Maclay.'

'I don't expect to do business in this colony like a gentleman,'
Andrew said sharply. 'Have you ever noticed how very few gentlemen make money?'

He flicked the cards with his thumb again. 'Come, now – take
the offer or leave it – I must go on watch.'

Wilder glanced from Harding to Brooks, but their expressions
gave him no help. He turned to Andrew. 'Very well,' he said
sullenly. 'I accept.'

'Done!' Andrew permitted himself a faint smile, reaching for
more paper. 'Now – perhaps you'll be good enough to sign a bill of
transfer?' He bent over the paper and began to write.

Wilder's lip curved contemptuously. 'I see you don't waste any
time.'

'No,' Andrew answered without looking up. 'I haven't decided
to settle here in order to waste time.'

Wilder didn't reply. The scratch of the quill was the only sound
in the room until Harding, after clearing his throat carefully,
spoke.

'Would you also be willing to settle for livestock for the amount
I owe you, Maclay?'

Andrew raised his head only for a second. 'Certainly, sir.'

Brooks pushed back his chair, and gripping the edge of the
table, swung on the two back legs. It was a rocking motion which
shook the table. 'Well, it seems that I'm the only one with a debt
modest enough to settle out of hand . . . I'll see that you have it
before you leave the ship, Maclay.'

Andrew nodded. 'Thank you, Brooks.'

Brooks got to his feet. 'Only once before,' he said, 'have I ever
known anyone with such devilish luck at cards. *He* won himself
a fortune, and drank himself to death with it.' He leaned over
towards Andrew. 'I sincerely hope you may achieve the first, without the second.'

Andrew stopped writing, and laid down the quill, staring up at
Brooks. Suddenly Brooks thrust out his hand; Andrew took it
readily.

'Good luck to you, Maclay! I'm an older man than you –
and I couldn't do what you intend doing. But I envy you your
courage.'

The bill of transfer was signed, and Andrew went to take his watch. Wilder, Brooks and Harding were left staring at each other; Brooks sat down again, and began to drum with his fingers on the table. Wilder's eyes ran over Andrew's columns of figures for the second time.

'Well,' he said, 'he got a bargain on that deal.'

Harding stirred lazily. 'I don't know that you're right. None of us can tell what price the livestock will fetch in Sydney. It's as much of a gamble for him as for you. Perhaps, after all, he'll be the loser.'

Wilder said, 'I still think it was a shabby thing to do. He pressed an unfair advantage.'

Brooks shrugged. 'It seems to me he's entitled to ask for gambling debts to be settled before he leaves the ship. After all, the livestock's worth more to him in the colony than the money.'

'Oh, you can be calm – you haven't lost much to him.' Suddenly Wilder screwed up the paper petulantly. 'I'll wager she put him up to it.'

'Who?'

'That woman – Sara Dane. I know her sort well – sharper than a monkey, and always with an eye to a bargain.'

Brooks gave a chuckle. 'Then they should be an excellently matched pair. It's the sort of combination which makes wealth quickly.'

'Oh, she'll do that all right,' Wilder said. He straightened out the paper, and was beginning to tear it gloomily into tiny fragments. 'She'll always get whatever she wants – either by sheer greed, or by being suitably demure at the right time. Look how she got hold of Maclay himself! I wonder what story she told him to make him believe she wasn't a thief.'

Harding spoke; his tone was heavy and thick with the amount of madeira he had taken since supper. He gestured vaguely towards the door. 'I'm sorry for Maclay. I think he's ruined himself by this alliance. Supposing the farming fails, as it may very well do? Can he bring an ex-convict back to present to his family at home? And if it succeeds – can he mix with the sort of people he's used to with her in the background?'

Brooks yawned, and stood up for the second time. 'I don't profess to be a prophet – but I've an idea that Maclay and the girl may surprise us all. That is,' he added, 'if we ever hear of them again.'

Wilder said nothing. He swept the pieces of paper to the floor with a single, angry gesture.

3

While Andrew sat in the wardroom bartering livestock for gambling debts, Sara remained still and wakeful upon her cot. A feeling of disquiet possessed her; it seemed to chill even the blood in her veins. The sounds of the ship came to her – the creak and strain of the timbers; wind, like a constant song up in the rigging, the patter of feet on the deck above her head. She listened awhile to the wind, knowing that this, more than anything else, was the reason for her disturbance; tonight it blew off the unknown shore that tomorrow would merge into a land which was to confine her, possibly for the rest of her life.

All she was certain of in the future was her marriage to Andrew. Since the day in Cape Town when he had made his proposal, he had ridden coolly over any doubts she had. He wouldn't even allow her to voice them. Everyone on board knew they were to be married when they reached the colony. Few approved, but no one was wholly disinterested. But there was nothing she could do to alter their opinions; she had to accept the situation as it stood.

Sara had no fears that she and Andrew were not well suited. They had spent many hours discussing the life they planned, the prospects of settling and farming in the great, empty land. She realized that he had no boldness of vision that did not meet an answer in herself; there was nothing he might dare that she was not prepared to dare with him.

She stirred restlessly, suddenly impatient for the coming day. The excitement she had tried to hold down seized her; under the blankets she clenched her hands. She *would* make Andrew a good wife! She'd give him reason to be proud of her. They would have children who would grow up in importance and prestige in the new colony. He had promised her land and her own servants to fill the hungry need in her heart for respect. She knew that one day she would have dignity and graciousness in her life; she would wipe out the memory of years of patronage.

When at last she slept, her sleep was heavy and dream-filled.

PART TWO

I

The following morning the *Georgette* sailed through the heads
guarding the entrance to Port Jackson, and dropped anchor in
Sydney Cove. The sun was bright and hot; points of light glanced
sharply off the waters of the harbour. Those on board rested their
eyes gratefully on the soft colour of the trees that stretched their
grey-green fuzz far into the distance of oddly-shaped inlets and
bays. There was a quiet, aloof beauty about it.

But the settlement itself offered no attraction. The convicts had
built a town of mud and daub huts on the shores of Sydney Cove,
with a crude, whitewashed Government House sitting atop a hill
overlooking it. A few brick houses were dotted among the huts,
but their harsh straight lines heightened the look of dejection about
them. A barracks, a hospital, a public store-house, and a bridge
over the one stream – that was the extent of this newest of His
Majesty's settlements. Here and there garden patches were laid out,
but they were, most of them, no more than hopeful gestures. The
efforts to till and sow the land were half-hearted; the soil was poor.
Drought withered the crop, then the rains washed it away. Food was
the crying need, but the sun-baked earth did not yield quarter
enough. The livestock were lean as they grazed on the sparse,
spikey vegetation.

Andrew Maclay found the Port Jackson settlement a place
of misery. He was taken aback by his first sight of it. It was squalid
in its poverty, and haunted by the now-familiar figures in their
filthy rags. Here the constant threat of the chain-gang and the lash
ruled; there was no law but that of punishment and hunger. Frantic for food, the convicts stole one another's rations, and broke into
the public stores – in the famished colony the theft of food was
punishable by death. They were ill and weak – and they died
easily. Some, in utter despair, broke away into the sly, unfriendly
forest – and perished in the baffling green maze, or staggered back,
exhausted and starved. They muttered among themselves that only
the naked black men, to whom this barren country belonged,
could find a living for himself among those giant gum-trees and
the hard, straggling foliage.

The metallic clank of the chain-gangs greeted Andrew wherever he went. He hated the sight of the women – haggard wretches, with hopeful eyes that followed him about. They prostituted themselves for food, and the dusty tracks between the huts swarmed with their illegitimate children. There was a certain charm about the children, vigorous and healthier, even under the starvation rations, than their counterparts in England – but the thought of settling within sight of their squalid homes disheartened him.

A week after the *Georgette* anchored he took a boat with James Ryder up the river to the colony's second settlement at Parramatta.

He found the beginnings of a planned town there. The land was more fertile than that at Sydney; the country around had a softer, kindlier appearance, laid out rather like English parkland. His spirits rose, and a fever of planning seized him. He listened to Ryder's careful evaluation of the place – it was a ready market-centre for three tiny outlying villages, Toongabbie, Prospect and Ponds, and it was only sixteen easy miles' boat journey from Port Jackson, and the joining road improved with each year of the settlement. Together they watched the market-day barter between officer, soldier, settler and convict of the country's few commodities – fish, grain, livestock and clothing. It was a brisk affair while goods were available; a Government clerk registered all that was brought in for sale or barter, and chits from the Commissary served as currency. This small township had a feeling of permanency about it. Ryder wasted no time in his survey of the district. With an experienced farmer's eye he examined the rich soil of the river banks, and was impatient to return to Sydney to arrange for a grant of land.

But from the officers and settlers – the settlers were mostly emancipated convicts working small farms of their own – with whom he talked, Andrew heard tales of yet another river. This one, far greater than the Parramatta, rose in the mountains in the west, taking a sweep north-east to an outlet in Broken Bay, an anchorage eight miles above Port Jackson. Governor Phillip himself had explored it and named it after Lord Hawkesbury. Here, they said, the soil was richer than anywhere else in the colony, and Phillip had it earmarked for the free settlers he hoped would be sent from England. The vision of the great river burned like a slow fever in Andrew's veins.

He listened with not very great interest to Ryder's planning – the exact position he wanted his grant, how close to the river, how close to the road, which would take his produce either to Parramatta or Sydney. The days passed, and he made no similar plans himself. Ryder sensed that something troubled Andrew, and pressed him to talk. By this time the men had grown closer to each other, bound together by the strangeness and difficulties which surrounded them – Andrew found himself talking wildly of his dream. He wanted to make a journey to the other river, to see for himself the rich, fertile land, the lush river-flats coated with the silt that the floods brought down from the mountains. He wanted, if it were possible, to settle there.

Listening to it all at their camp by the river, Ryder shook his head doubtfully. 'Perhaps you can do it, Andrew – but they say the country is rough going between here and the river. If you settled, you'd have to make some sort of track to bring up supplies.' He gestured to imply all that went with such a venture.

Andrew protested quickly, 'Yes – but if the soil . . .'

Ryder nodded, smiled secretly as he took out his snuff-box. It was always so with young men – the land they couldn't see was always richer, the river broader, the game better. He thought of his own choice, the gentle river, the peaceful acres which wouldn't be difficult to clear, and he was glad that the dream of the Hawkesbury hadn't smitten him also.

Andrew stayed behind at Parramatta when Ryder went back by boat to Sydney. He turned with energy to organizing a party for the journey to the Hawkesbury, and he found himself unexpectedly helped by Subaltern Berry, a young man who confessed that he was dying of boredom, and had an itch for exploration that no one else would gratify. He belonged to the New South Wales Corps, a military force which had been specially raised in England for the new colony – and he had friends among officialdom who listened with sympathy to Andrew's plans, and helped outfit the expedition. They set off with a native as guide – Andrew, Berry, three convicts and provisions for ten days. The country was wild and exotic; the warmth of spring had turned the pointed leaves of the gums red – a fiery tinge that coloured the bush with fantasy. Yellow and white flowers mingled their scents with subtle, elusive smells of the trees, adding to their feeling that they were striking into a mad, new world. They followed the guide along tracks visible only to his own keen eyes. There was no trace of softness in all this beauty, there was no trace of bounty in it for man or plant which was not its native. The tall eucalyptus trees, braks shining white in the sun, were endless and aloof. The going was hard and yet the fascination of the country compelled them to keep on.

They reached Phillip's farthest point of exploration, Richmond Hill, in a thunderstorm of sudden, tropical violence. The naked

black man hunched on the ground, his face, hidden beneath a
mane of matted hair and beard, was pressed into his kness while he
strove to control his panic. A curtain of rain cut off the little group
on the hill; long, brilliant flashes of lightning revealed for a moment the grey-brown waters of the river below. The storm did not
last. It moved on abruptly, leaving them once more in sunshine.
The mountain range, blocking off the west, seemed very close; the
air was as sharp and clear as glass. The valleys were filled with
grey mist and the rising smell of the trees and the rain-splattered
dust. When the hush settled again, the guide rose and beckoned
them to a descent of the hill where they would find level ground
and make camp.

Andrew lingered behind under the dripping trees, his eyes wonderingly on the flat land south and east. This was what he would
describe to Sara, he told himself – this lovely stretch of fertile,
heavily-wooded country with the great river twisting down from
the mountains. There were places here where he could already
see his house built – places on high ground where the floods, if
they came, could not reach. With the land cleared, there was
pasture richer than anything he had yet seen; as he stood there he
slowly raised his clenched hand, opened it, and looked at the soil
that he had scooped up close to the river bank. Soil like this would
give him grain so heavy it bent with its own weight; he raised his
head again and envisaged the fenced fields, with their crops ready
for harvest. It was a silent, uninhabited world he gazed at, full of
mystery, and perhaps unexpected dangers, and yet he knew that
Sara, when he told her of it, would choose this green, unknown
valley, rather than the subdued acres of the Parramatta district.

He arrived back in Sydney exactly three weeks after the date of
landing, and found that the Ryders were on the point of moving
all their belongings by boat to Parramatta; they were going to a
temporary hut on a fine tract of land just outside the township.
Julia, he saw, had got over her first dismay at the sight of the dismal settlement at Sydney Cove. With characteristic quietness and
determination she had set about making the most of what the
country had to offer. She behaved now as if feeding a family on
salt pork had been a lifetime's occupation.

But the greatest change was in Sara. She had gained confidence
in her position as the future wife of a free settler. There was a
vigorous life in her he had never seen before. She was adapting
herself well, and now, for the first time, he witnessed her personality flowering without the restraint placed upon it by the confines
of the *Georgette*. Her smile of welcome caused the hunger for her

to flare in his heart. He kissed her with such longing that the couple of weeks' separation might easily have been years. She responded warmly, and then held him away, demanding news of the trip inland. He told her of the valley he had seen, and the deep, curving river.

She listened without interruption, and at the end she said slowly, 'This is where you want to settle, Andrew?'

He answered her fervently. 'Oh, my darling, yes! Wait till you see it for yourself!' He laughed in his excitement. 'It's rich land there, Sara – rich and green! And it's mine! I can have the pickings before anyone else even sees it!' He demanded of her soberly, 'Could you face it? You'd be there alone.'

But he knew, even as he asked the question, that there was no fear in her eyes – no hint of timidity about the desolation she must know she faced. Her calmness reassured him.

'Perhaps Governor Phillip doesn't want settlers there yet,' she said, a little anxiously. 'Perhaps he won't give you a grant.'

He drew her to him, his lips pressing away the frown on her brow. 'Phillip has a whole continent to give away,' he murmured. 'He won't miss a slice on the Hawkesbury.'

'You'll see him soon?'

'Tomorrow – if he'll see me.' He had taken her in his arms. The warmth of her body excited him. 'I want two things from Phillip – a grant on the Hawkesbury banks, and a pardon for my wife. And then I'll show them what sort of living is to be made in New South Wales!'

He spoke recklessly, his emotions stimulated by the closeness of Sara. For a moment or two his desire for her mounted. He held her to him with his eyes closed. And then, as if she shared his emotion, her arms tightened about him.

'Let it be soon, Andrew,' she whispered. 'If Phillip should refuse . . .'

'He won't.'

Suddenly she looked into his face. The frown had come back to her brow. 'Andrew,' she said urgently, 'promise me you'll marry me as soon as possible. Don't wait for a house. I'll go with you anywhere. I'll . . .'

'Sara, darling!' he said, his lips breaking her words. 'I won't even wait till tomorrow. I'll try to see the Governor this afternoon.'

Andrew faced His Excellency, Governor Phillip, across a table stacked with paper, and gazed with a feeling of faint awe at the man who had pulled the colony through these first five, heart-breaking years. He was an unprepossessing figure, with beaked nose, and only of middle height; his skin had the yellowing tinge of ill-ness. It was now common knowledge in the ragged settlements he ruled that he had been given leave of absence because of ill-health, and would probably sail for England in the *Atlantic*, at present anchored in the harbour.

From the beginning he offered no encouragement to Andrew to choose his site on the Hawkesbury.

'I know it's excellent soil, Mr Maclay, but the help and protec-tion of the Government cannot extend so far. You will be quite alone, without even a road to join you to Parramatta. You're in danger from floods and natives who are possibly hostile – and in the winter you may not be able to get your food and supplies over-land.'

'I've studied all these difficulties, Your Excellency – and I still feel I can overcome them.'

Phillip looked thoughtfully at the map spread before him on the table. 'Believe me, Mr Maclay, I *want* settlers there – it's the finest land in the colony, and we could well do with its produce. But the danger lies in your settling alone . . . if there were others with you . . .'

But he argued half-heartedly, and when Andrew pressed the point, gave in. Once the decision was made, Phillip behaved as if the objection no longer existed – he was now free to encourage the settlement of the land he had first explored and marked down for the free men he wanted to farm the colony. He was generous in his offers of help. The Commissary was short of even the common necessities, but Phillip's order would give Andrew whatever was available. On paper the requisition orders were handsome – a large grant of land, convict labourers, farming implements, seed. But Andrew knew the local conditions well enough to realize that he would be lucky if one-third of the supplies could be filled from the stock of the Commissary. He pocketed the signed order with the same feeling that he would have pocketed a counterfeit coin – won-dering if it had any purchasing power left.

When the maps of the Hawkesbury were pushed aside, the Governor folded his dry, thin hands and looked at Andrew un-blinkingly. He told him in a clipped voice that he had left instruc-tions with his successor that Sara Dane was to receive her pardon on the day she was married.

There was nothing cordial in his tone as he added: 'My com-mission from the King enables me to grant pardons, Mr Maclay. I

allow myself to use this power in view of Mr Ryder's testimonials
of this woman – and the knowledge that she will pass completely
into your care.'

'Thank you, sir.'

Andrew wished his words could have been warmer, but there was
no mistaking the Governor's tone. Clearly, he didn't approve of
the marriage. But his instructions were to encourage settlement,
and in this case the only way it could be done was by permitting
the marriage. He was giving his consent with authority's helpless
shrug of the shoulders.

Andrew brought the interview to an end without waiting for the
Governor to indicate that it was finished. On the veranda of the
whitewashed Government House he paused, wondering if he would
go back and argue Sara's case more forcefully. But his quick judgement of Phillip's character told him that the gesture would be
futile. He slapped his hat on to his head, and stepped out into the
sunshine, hot and resentful.

2

Andrew reached the site allotted him on the Hawkesbury after a
long, tortuous journey. He made an encampment on the river bank
– a small group of tents to house the twenty assigned convicts, two
overseers, and four ex-convicts whose sentences had been remitted,
and who had agreed to come with him for a wage, their food and a
daily ration of rum. From this beginning, he set about to clear the
surrounding forests for the fields where he planned to sow his crops
and the spot he had earmarked for his house. The axes swung and
the trees fell rapidly, but still not quickly enough for him. His impatience was never satisfied.

In Parramatta they had shaken their heads over this impatience;
they advised him to wait until there were other settlers to accompany him to the Hawkesbury. But he took no heed; he went ahead
with his task of collecting the few available supplies, choosing his
overseers and finding extra labourers. He waited to help the Ryders
and Sara with their move up-river from Sydney Cove to the new
land at Parramatta, and he saw his own livestock penned along with
James's, close to the hut where they would live until their house
was ready. Then he made plans for moving his own equipment to
the Hawkesbury. He worked long hours – it was slow, exasperat-
ing work that met with endless frustrations and setbacks. The
colony was short of every single item he needed – shoes and clothing
for the convicts, cooking utensils, carpenter's tools, firearms for

hunting, spades and axes for clearing the land. He endured tedious sessions of bargaining and bartering, fuming over each new delay and hold-up.

Following a hint from his friend, Berry, he sought out an ex-convict settled on a grant of land at Toongabbie, who exchanged him three axes for two gallons of rum, and another at Prospect who let him have two more for only one gallon. He didn't know where the axes came from, and didn't ask.

Berry expended himself in his willingness to help; he produced a carpenter of sorts, a man whose sentence had been remitted, and who was prepared to work on the Hawkesbury property for a guaranteed rum ration. Andrew realized that a carpenter, even a poor one, was a priceless find in this place which seemed to be without trained workmen of any kind. He guarded his prize greedily, already visualizing the house this sullen, toothless man would build for Sara to live in. Fear that someone else might claim first rights on this emancipist galvanized him into action; he swore the man to secrecy and commenced the rum ration immediately.

He found that this high-pressure speed was necessary to get all he wanted. He had to be quick and ruthless. The constant sight of Sara was driving him on, urging him to decisions which, three months ago, would have seemed impossible. It seemed as if, over-night, his gambler's instincts had turned towards trade and barter – he sometimes smiled at the idea of himself so swiftly becoming a man of affairs.

When his provisions and gear were assembled at last, and the nerve-racking weeks of planning and scheming were over, he paid his final visit to the Ryders. He said goodbye to Sara, unwilling to leave her behind, and making no attempt to hide the impatience evident in all his actions these days.

He set out for the Hawkesbury on the first of December.

Through the long, hot days he worked as if he were driven by a demon – he was up at dawn with the convicts, and at night by the fire he was wakeful, planning after the rest of the camp slept. The clearing of the land was slow, yielding to them grudgingly, reluc-tantly giving up each acre that had never known movement other than the soundless tread of its own dark people. Occasionally he shot kangaroo and wild duck to vary the diet of salt pork. He made the most of the game while it was available, knowing that soon – as had already happened at the other settlements – it would retreat from the advance of the white man.

The days of unvarying routine spun out – his dreams were of the grey gums crashing down, and the astonished faces of the natives he sometimes saw standing stock-still and rigid on the edge of the new clearing. They were not hostile, but they never came nearer the camp than the sheltering outskirts of the forest. Neither the white man nor the black interfered with one another – Andrew's orders were that the blacks were never to be unduly noticed, and never molested.

He was not completely alone with his thoughts in his night watches by the fire. He found a companion in one of his overseers, Jeremy Hogan, an Irishman, transported for organizing, with a minimum of discretion, new recruits for Wolf Tone's United Irishmen. He was young, twenty-six, and built like a giant. He had still a touch of laughter about his deep blue eyes that the convict transport had not stamped out. Andrew found it difficult to take Jeremy's politics seriously – he humoured him, delighted by the strange quirk of chance which brought this type of man to share his fire. They talked softly together in the dark, their eyes on the bright, unfamiliar stars of the South. The sound of the River came continuously, like a patter of voices. Of the other's background, Andrew could learn almost nothing; there was, though, the obvious fact of education and breeding. He thanked his good fortune in having been assigned Jeremy Hogan, talking to him easily in the silence of their night camps, telling him without awkwardness of his cherished dreams, for the land over which they both toiled.

Each day a small portion of rum was allotted to the convict labourers. As long as they were assured of this, these men were prepared to work until they dropped; no threat of flogging or any other punishment meant as much to them as a suspension of the rum ration. With reluctant fascination he watched them lining up for the spirit, which was their only hope for forgetfulness. Their eyes and hands were greedy for the sight and feel of it. It was the spirits, he knew, which he had brought off the *Georgette*, that had done far more to bring him to his present position than any of the privileges ordinarily given to settlers. Rum was needed to make his men work; rum would bring the small comforts to make this sort of life possible for Sara. He calculated his store and found that it was dwindling fast. It was obvious that he must find some means to supplement it.

At first he felt his way cautiously, but as soon as the opportunity opened to give him not only rum, but other vital supplies, he took it without hesitation. He risked the money he had invested, the slice of land by the Hawkesbury River, even the hope of soon being able to marry Sara – everything he had he risked on the turn of a card. He played coolly, fully aware of the weight of his gamble. Sometimes he lost, but more often he won.

The officers of the New South Wales Corps were his mark. Since Governor Phillip's departure, the Corps had become supreme. Francis Grose, the Lieutenant-Governor, was steeped in militarism; he was strangely pliable in the hands of his officers, who, each in his turn, was given the position and authority to behave as a small despot. The civil courts had been closed in both Sydney and Parramatta, and a jury of six military officers and a judge-advocate now dispensed rough justice to their own soldiers, the convicts, and the few private citizens. It was a world suddenly ruled by a select military élite, and Andrew found his way into its heart with a pack of cards.

He was accepted in the first place because he had held a commission with the East India Company. Although most of them were contemptuous of his plan to marry an ex-convict, they faced him readily enough over a table set with glasses and cards. He found the little bored groups willing to gamble on anything from five gallons of rum to a chit on the public stores for a frying-pan. As soon as he was quite certain of his place among them, he made frequent trips to Sydney and Parramatta almost with the sole motive of drifting into an evening's play at the barracks.

'He has the devil's luck!' they grumbled, disheartened, but playing on in the hope that his run of luck might turn. Whenever he was beaten he paid up calmly, and came back again the following night.

He played to a purpose which took him some time to achieve. He was impatient, but waited until the debts began to mount up heavily against his partners, and then he suggested that they should be cancelled by concessions for him in the trading-ring they had formed. Their monopoly methods were simple – they had permission from the Lieutenant-Governor to pool their credits in England and to buy the entire cargo of the occasional American ships which were beginning to appear in Port Jackson; they were allowed to charter ships to run to the Cape and the East for the purpose of their own trade. There was no single transaction in the colony from which one or another member of the red-coated ring didn't make his profit. The bartering power of rum was higher than anything else, and it flowed into New South Wales in an increasing stream. Andrew bought his right to share in the rum monopoly with his skill over a card table. He gained more and more ground with his friends in the Corps, until even the arrogant, black-haired John Macarthur, the leader of the trading-ring and the most ambitious, energetic man the colony possessed, no longer questioned his right to share the prized cargoes. Like the rest, Andrew bartered rum for convict labour, rum for food, rum for boots and loads of timber. His supplies were taken inland over the rough track to the Hawkesbury; he went with them light-heartedly, and worked, for a few weeks, as hard as two men on the clearing of his land. And then, when his stocks began to run out, he started back again for the barracks at Sydney and Parramatta.

The walls of his house rose slowly during the months of the autumn and early winter; the forest reluctantly yielded space to sow his crops and run his livestock. The progress was hardly measurable week by week, but at the end of May, Andrew judged that the house would be ready to live in before June was over. It was small – only four rooms, with a lean-to kitchen, whitewashed, half-fur-nished, and uncurtained, patterned exactly on the Ryders' new house. Sara, demanding to hear every detail, begged to be allowed to return with him to Hawkesbury when he made the next trip. Remembering the loneliness and silence awaiting him by the great river, he was seized with impatience. He looked at her eager face, and suddenly knew that he could not wait any longer to have her there with him.

2

The wedding took place in the Ryders' house on a bright, cold morning in June. There had been a frost the previous night, and the sun had scarcely broken it up by the time Sara entered the sitting-room for the ceremony. The sharp smell of the eucalyptus-leaves, which Julia had used for decoration, came instantly to her. James held the door open wide; his gloved hand reached out for hers. She took it, but stood still, aware of the stir her entrance had caused, pleased and reassured by the expressions she saw on the faces of the group waiting for her. She was wearing a gown of white silk brought from China, and paid for in rum; on her feet was a pair of embroidered slippers from Calcutta. She held herself erectly, outwardly calm, yet she sought Andrew's eyes with a sense of relief. Then, after that one brief pause, she went slowly forward to make her curtsy to the Lieutenant-Governor.

Julia was the only other woman present to listen to the words of the marriage service, read in the Reverend Richard Johnston's

prim tones. The New South Wales Corps was well represented
that morning, their red coats brightening the pale sunlight in the
room. The guests, with the exception of the Ryders and Johnston,
were mostly gambling partners of Andrew's. John Berry was there,
and three other officers from the barracks. John Macarthur, whom
Grose had put in charge of all public works in Parramatta, had surprisingly accepted the invitation; Grose himself, up from Sydney on
a visit of inspection, had accompanied him.

But the colony's three women of note were absent. The clergyman's wife and Mrs Macarthur had been invited, but both had declined on the flimsiest excuse. Mrs Patterson, wife of the Corps'
second-in-command, had also declined. Sara had not expected more
or less than this. She had known how she would be regarded by
that narrow clique of female society; she was not abashed by the
snubs, and she carried her head stiffly and proudly among the circle
of red coats.

The ceremony was short. Johnston had no great liking for either
Sara or Andrew, and he wasted no undue sentiment over the duty
he was called to perform. They were married just before noon, and
left – Sara, Andrew, the overseer, Jeremy Hogan, and another convict overseer, Trigg, brought along to help with the baggage on the
return journey to the Hawkesbury – after a gay meal of wild duck
and roasted kangaroo meat. The wine, shipped from the Cape,
was plentiful enough to loosen tongues, and as she changed from
the silk dress into a new riding-habit, Sara could hear bursts of
laughter from the narrow, simply-furnished living-room. She
imagined, with a smile which was half-bitter, half-amused, how
these men would recount the tale of the ceremony they had just
witnessed.

The Lieutenant-Governor led the group which streamed out on
to the veranda to see the party mount, and most of them, in the
heat of wine and good humour, seemed to have forgotten that this
was no ordinary wedding. Sara made her last curtsy to Grose with
a sharp feeling of thankfulness in her heart that, whatever his
reason, he had chosen to come this morning. His presence had given
the marriage the envied seal of official approval. She disliked the
weak, indefinite character of Francis Grose, but for what he had
done for her today, she knew she would never cease being grateful.

Sara had said her private farewell to Julia before they moved
outside, and Julia kissed her softly. 'Do write to me, Sara. I shall
expect a letter each time Andrew comes to Parramatta – now you
will write?'

Sara nodded, and her lips formed words which seemed stuck firmly in her throat. Impossible to thank Julia for the past months together – even for the strenuous efforts which had produced the wedding breakfast. From that first day on the *Georgette* they had grown steadily closer, Sara taking Julia's uncommon good sense to leaven her own impetuous nature, learning from her, copying her in certain ways. Their relationship was complete – still undemonstrative, it had gone deeply into each of them, and there was a comfortable assurance that it would always remain.

Suddenly Sara put her arms about Julia, hugging her fiercely. 'I can't thank you – there isn't any use trying. Nor for all that I've had from you. But I've never loved another woman before – if that counts for anything with you.'

Then she drew back. 'Well . . . that's enough,' she said briskly, dabbing at the faint moisture that had appeared on her lashes. 'I'm not going to make a fool of myself, and a show of you, Julia, for this handful of red-coats.'

Then she stepped lightly out on to the veranda. Julia followed, smiling a little as she thought of Sara's words. Of course she hadn't loved a woman before – and she was nervous and rather reluctant to admit it. Men had been her whole world, and very skilfully she had made use of them. So mature she had appeared as she stood beside Andrew during the service, but she was still like a child in learning some things. Perhaps the last months had taught her more than she knew.

The watching group stayed together on the veranda until the little party disappeared from sight along the Parramatta Road. As she turned to go indoors again, Julia caught the tones of a familiar voice among Andrew's guests.

'. . . I didn't believe he'd have the nerve to marry her in the end. Still, it's done now. An admirable gesture, I'm sure. Let us hope the fellow won't find time to regret it.'

2

When the dusk came they were still seven miles from the Hawkesbury. Andrew ordered the men to make camp beside the rough track which was their only road. He dismounted himself, and turned to lift Sara down. She fell stiffly into his arms; the long hours in the saddle, to which she was still unused, had wearied her almost beyond speech. Jeremy Hogan had spread a blanket for her on the ground; she staggered to it and sat down without a word.

The winter's night dropped down quickly after a short dusk.

In that latitude the light never lingered in the sky. A bitter little wind blew in the tops of the trees, and touched Sara's cheeks sharply. The first stars came out, the big, over-bright stars of the southern hemisphere. She shivered, moving closer to the fire which Jeremy was banking up. She sat still, gazing eagerly into the flames, and listening to the muted sounds of the men's voices.

They ate a meal of cold pork and bread by the firelight. Andrew uncorked the wine which James Ryder had given him. It was a strange wedding feast, the wine slowly warming in their hands, and the cold silence of the bush all around them. The starlight grew stronger, and the tree-barks were white and ghostly. There was a mournful, eerie feeling about the bush at night, aged and remote. By night it had no passion; it was secretive and sly.

Soon after the meal Trigg withdrew to his roll of blankets on the other side of the fire; it was arranged that Jeremy should wake him at two o'clock to take his turn at watching. When the overseer had moved off into the shadows of the spot where he had chosen to sleep, the other three drew into a new intimacy; it was the same sort of intimacy that Andrew and Jeremy had shared by the camp-fire on the Hawkesbury's banks.

Sara's fatigue had lessened. The wine and the cold wind had sharpened her senses, so that when the two men fell into talk, she watched Jeremy closely, seeking in his manner a clue to what her own relationship to him might be in the future. Her mind was already half made up about what she might expect – the smooth-tongued and barely disguised insolence of a gently-born man confronted with his master's wife, who had received her pardon only yesterday. She felt that he had done his own summing-up where she was concerned. He was no fool, and, for the present anyway, seemed prepared to serve her willingly enough. In that first hour, as she sat listening to them talk, Sara sensed that his intelligence and strength had won a kind of ascendency over Andrew; she had a feeling of being shut out of their comradeship. She was hurt and a little piqued, yet she knew already Jeremy's worth to Andrew. She didn't want their intimacy broken; rather she wanted desperately to share it.

She looked at Jeremy, deciding that he must be made to serve her for her own sake – not because it was an order from Andrew.

And then, as if he guessed her thoughts, he raised his eyes and addressed her directly.

'Is it decided yet what you'll call the property, Mrs Maclay?' He seemed amused as he gave her the title.

'My husband,' she said, slyly emphasizing the words, 'wants to call it "Kintyre". It's a Scottish name.'

'Kintyre . . .' He rolled the two syllables softly on his tongue. 'Not so lovely as the name the natives give it. Still . . .' He shrugged and said lightly, 'At least it can be spelled. These picturesque native names are impossible.'

He stared at the fire. 'Well . . . you're the first on the Hawkesbury — but they'll follow you. Within a year . . . a few months even, they'll be settling on your doorstep. A man is never left alone for very long when he farms land like you've got. I doubt, though, if ever any of them will make up the start you've had.'

Suddenly he laughed. 'Thanks to rum you've got it!'

Andrew joined him in the laughter, not in the least embarrassed. 'Thanks to rum, as you say — and the fact that his officers lead Grose around by the nose. Why shouldn't *I* also have what they're all getting? The man who doesn't belong in the circle might as well not be alive as far as advancement in the colony is concerned. As friends their tempers aren't always reliable — but I've no notion to become their enemy.'

Jeremy glanced sideways at him. 'There speaks a canny Scot — you'll prosper in the land, my friend.'

He held up his glass. 'A toast!' he announced. 'A toast to the name of Maclay . . .' Then quickly he added, as if he had just recalled Sara's presence. 'And to the mistress of Kintyre . . .'

They drank it solemnly beneath the full, bright stars.

Sara woke in the half-hour before dawn when the stars were fading. The tent-flap had been flung back, and she could see the sky, now more grey than black. The bush about the camp was very quiet; the wind seemed to have died. She stirred in Andrew's arms. He felt her move, and, without opening his eyes, he turned on his side and drew her closer. They lay under rugs of wallaby skins, the warmth of their bodies and their sense of relaxation defying the cold day breaking outside.

In the dim light she saw that his eyes had opened. His voice was drowsy.

'Too early yet for you to wake.'

She smiled at him. 'But I wanted to wake — do you understand that I just wanted to lie here, and be awake?'

'Little fool!' he murmured. 'You'll learn differently.'

Her head rested on his arm. He felt for her hand and drew it out from under the furs. He kissed each of her finger-tips in turn — and then he began to bite gently at them.

'Oh, woman . . .' he said softly. 'You've tormented me! You've/

driven me mad for a whole year! I don't believe yet that I have you
at last – sharing my *mia-mia*.'

'*Mia-mia*?' The words belonged to the liquid native tongue.
She repeated them again, half-afraid, because Andrew had spoken
them with such spell-binding tenderness. '*Mia-mia*?'

'It's the name the natives have for their bark huts. They spread
the floor of the *mia-mia* with kangaroo skins, and that is their
marriage-bed – no more or less than ours.'

She sought his lips. 'We have the most sumptuous marriage-
bed in all the world, my love. We'll keep it just like this.'

They were quiet for a time, and then he said, 'At the moment I
possess all I ever dreamed of . . . I can see the stars dying, and I
lie here on furs and listen for the wind . . . And in my arms I hold
a woman like you – not submissive, Sara, but acquiescent . . .
sharing my love as if you had always known it would be like
this.'

'I have always known it, Andrew,' she whispered, her mouth close
to his. 'Always.'

For a moment she was silent, then, 'I'll be a trying wife for
you. I'll need so much of your mind and your heart.' Her words
were suddenly fierce. 'I'll make demands on you. You'll have to
be everything to me – husband and lover, brother and father . . .
everything!'

He put his lips close to her ear. 'I'll be everything you want,
Sara – so long as this doesn't alter. I want nothing more of you
than to be able always to lie with you like this – and hold you like
this.'

Then he kissed her, and his tones drifted towards passion.
'Sara . . . Oh, Sara!'

The camp-fire was dead, and the daylight had not properly broken
when Jeremy woke. He opened his eyes and lay quietly beneath
the soft warmth of his kangaroo skins. Sleep still dulled his mind,
and full consciousness came slowly. He remembered where he
was, and the reason – and remembering, he turned to gaze at the
tent where Andrew and his wife lay. He saw the flap open, and
wondered if they were awake, murmuring in the intimacy of lovers
– their words tender, for themselves alone. For the moment he
knew completely the world they held within their arms, and he felt
his flesh creep with longing to have a woman once more beside him,
a woman whose lips would seek his willingly. Desperately he wanted
again to bury his face in a woman's scented hair, and to lie and
listen to her gentle breathing as she slept.

Without attempting to check his thoughts, Jeremy let them wander to scenes of the past . . . Irish skies, and mist, and lakes that spattered the country in silver and shadowed purple . . . Fine horses, beautiful women, and politics had been his playthings. He had used all of them dangerously; often merely for the delight of the danger. To this black-haired man, lying still and wakeful in the early-morning cold, the names of his beloved beauties came flowing back to him. Horses and women mixed in his thoughts like a lovely dream . . . Larry . . . Black Fern . . . Geraldine . . . Rosalie . . . He whispered then, moaning softly in his longing.

Then, with the advance of the daylight, the shrill, maddening laugh of the kookaburra rang out. *Gourgourgahgah*, the natives called it. It perched, its head and beak sharply outlined against the sky, on one of the highest branches of a tree above him. The mockery of its laugh scattered Jeremy's dreams. He was not in Ireland, and he had twelve years of his sentence still to serve. He was an assigned servant, he reminded himself — merely that, to the man who had been given charge over him, body and well-nigh soul. Dreams of beautiful women were not for him — instead he must endure this sense of desolation here in the camp in the bush, with the strong scent of the gum-leaves, and the wood-fire that had burned all through the night. He must lie and endure the knowl-edge of complete intimacy within the tent, and the thought of the golden-haired girl who had yesterday married Andrew Maclay, ly-ing now in his arms, warm under the wallaby skins — the girl who only two days ago had been a convict like himself.

3

The house stood upon a gentle rise facing the river. Sara first saw it at noon, with the winter sun dazzling on its new whitewash, and its uncurtained windows turned blankly towards the mountains. A few trees had been left around it, and on the cleared ground of the slopes was the beginning of an orchard. It was a stark, raw-look-ing building, whose bricks had been carted up from the brick-fields at Sydney. There was no touch of vine or shrub to soften its outlines; its whiteness was harsh against the grey-green of the trees.

The sight touched Sara's heart strangely. She looked at it for a long time without speaking. It was no more or less than Andrew had led her to expect — low, and one storeyed, ugly and crude in its unfinished state, a wide veranda round it, with three or four unornamented steps. But this was the first house that had ever

stood upon the Hawkesbury; only the frail bark of the natives'
mia-mia had stood here before. The simplicity of the house was in
a sense not unworthy of its setting.

She gazed up the slope with a mixed feeling of possession and
pride. The first moment her eyes had fallen on this house, it had become her own – something to be loved and defended with every
ounce of her will and power.

Without saying anything, and still without taking her eyes off
the house, she gestured to Andrew beside her. He interpreted the
vague movement swiftly, motioning to Jeremy behind.

'Go on ahead, Hogan. Tell Annie we've arrived. Mrs Maclay
will want hot water immediately.'

Jeremy nodded and urged his horse into a trot. Trigg followed
closely. The sounds of the horses were sharp in the noon hush of
the bush.

Andrew dismounted and turned to lift Sara down. She stood
stiffly on the uneven ground, letting her gaze move in wonder
across the scene before her. It took in the great sweep of the cleared
land, reaching down to the river; she saw the convicts' huts at the
back of the house, and the railed-in enclosures for the livestock.
The scars upon the virgin woods were raw and fresh, great, jagged
holes torn in the blackman's territory to make way for the usurper's
crops and cattle. She was keenly aware of the intrusion here in
this wilderness; with not even a decent road to link it to the proper
settlement, it was an undeniable fact. But she saw it as Andrew
had seen it – land waiting to be taken, fertile land lying idle, disturbed only by the natives' hunting parties, skilful, hardy young
men, moving soundlessly through the bush in the trail of the kanga-
roos. Every instinct bred in her tough childhood among the London
lodging-houses revolted against the waste of good land. She had
learned something of the thrift and hard-headedness of the Romney
Marsh farmers when it came to assessing the value of land. She
had seen their prosperity based on rich grazing for their sheep, and
supplemented by smuggling. The sight of the broad river, and the
wild acres still waiting beyond the clearings, touched off a fire of
ambition in her. She clenched her hands in excitement, and under
her gloves she could feel a prickle of sweat. The pulse in her throat
leapt with a swift passion. In England, land had meant wealth.
And here in this country land was given for the asking. There was
wealth before her eyes in these miles of winter evergreens stretching
as far as she could see – providing the gods were kind . . . providing
the rain came in the right season, not too little, not too much . . .
providing the river did not rise to sweep the crops away, and the

fires raced through the bush to destroy them.

The gamble for such colossal stakes exalted her. She turned and clutched at Andrew's arm, demanding a reassurance in his eyes.

She found it there, and pride and eagerness as well.

'Don't see it finally as it is now, Sara,' he said tremulously. 'In a few years I'll build you a beautiful house. I've planned it all – it'll be large and white, with a terrace and columns facing the river. I can see it . . .'

She cut him short.

'I don't want a Greek temple in the woods, Andrew. Whatever money there is must go into the land. The house can stay as it is. I'm well content.'

He gave a soft laugh, reaching to her and taking her shoulders between his two hands. His lean, roughened face reflected her own excitement and passion, as if her emotions had spilled over and affected him as strongly. In that moment they both knew that they were one in mind; the union of their marriage was complete. His expression hardened, and his grip tightened.

'You're as greedy as I am – you damned woman!' he said, his lips dry, the skin stretched. 'You ought to have been a man, Sara. It excites you too, doesn't it, all this? You see, as well as I do, what's waiting for a man with the brain and the heart to work?' His hands were feeling their way slowly down her arms. 'But it's just as well you're not a man – you couldn't restrain yourself as I do. You couldn't hold yourself off the rum traffic, could you? Or keep yourself out of every shady transaction this corrupt hole hatches out? You'd be the biggest rum-peddler of them all, my sweet.'

'Probably,' she admitted. 'But I'll find plenty of ways of helping you, all the same, Andrew. As soon as I can mount this wretched horse without fear of falling off, you'll find me as good as three overseers. I'll know every inch of your land – and every ear of corn that grows on it.'

'Be as you are now – I don't ask for any more, Sara,' he said thickly.

Jeremy and Trigg rode into the yard at the back of the house. A mongrel dog, which Andrew had brought home from his last visit to Sydney, started up his barking at the sounds of their approach; he raced round them in a frenzy of welcome. The ceaseless clucking of fowls reached them from the pens in the shade of the big mimosa tree.

As Jeremy dismounted a woman came out of the lean-to kitchen, which was joined to the main building by a short covered passage. She was small and wrinkled, and wearing the graceless garments of a convict. Her face was red from the heat of the kitchen fire.

She approached the two men, wiping her hands in a cloth. This wiping of her hands was a habitual gesture; Jeremy was used to it. She did it now with greater emphasis than usual. As he began to un-strap the saddle-bags, Jeremy glanced back over his shoulder at Annie Stokes's round, bright eyes and button nose, at the low brow furrowed in an expression of acute anxiety.

'They're coming,' he announced briefly. 'Is everything ready?'

The small eyes flashed with a touch of spirit. 'O' course it is. Haven't I slaved myself half to death these past weeks putting things to rights? There's duck for dinner, and if they don't look sharp, it'll be on the table before they're ready!'

Jeremy nodded. 'And see you don't shake the wine more than you can help.'

Annie's thin little frame stiffened. 'Me!' The word was an in-dignant gasp. 'Me, what's served in taverns all me life! What's dished dinners to the gentry! Worked for Lord Delham, I did! 'Tisn't likely I wouldn't know what to do with a bottle of wine!'

Trigg gave a low laugh. 'Y'know what to do with it all right! Dead drunk, I've seen you, Annie – and you praying to the Lord, what you've never prayed to before, to deliver you from this cursed country.'

Annie gave a toss of her head. She took a hesitant step towards Jeremy, beginning to wipe her hands in the cloth.

'What's she like?' she said.

'She?'

'The mistress.'

Jeremy straightened and looked at her. Under his direct stare she wilted, and retreated a little. He snapped a reply. 'You're here to see that Mrs Maclay is served in every way possible – not to ask questions!'

Annie turned on her heel and slipped away towards the kitchen like a scuttling, grey rabbit. Jeremy watched her go, but wasn't in time to check Trigg's coarse shout.

'She's a rare beauty, is the mistress! And looks as if she has a mind of her own! I'll lay she won't stand no nonsense. You'll have to mind yourself now, Annie!'

Trigg's loud, deep laughter boomed across the yard.

Listening to it, Jeremy felt slightly sick. And later, locking the storehouse, where they had laid the provisions brought up from Parramatta, Trigg touched back on the subject of Andrew's wife.

He stood with his hands on his hips, surveying the row of eucalyptus that marked the line of the cleared land.

'She'll have no easy time of it, I'll be bound,' he said in a low voice, half to himself. 'Pardoned or not, I don't envy her trying to show she's any better than the rest of us. Who'll believe it, anyway?'

Jeremy was at a loss to answer him. He knew well enough that Trigg had merely put into words what every convict labourer at Kintyre must be thinking – what was being said in every house and humpy in the colony, and over every barrack-room table. Andrew Maclay was going to suffer for his wife's reputation, he thought. He gestured impatiently to silence Trigg.

'Listen, they're coming! I'll go round to the front and take the horses.'

He hurried round the side of the house and, as he watched the Maclays approach, he saw that Andrew was carrying Sara's hat; he saw the sun on her hair and in that moment he felt that he almost hated her, hated the splendour of the body that the dark habit revealed, hated her faint arrogance and superiority. Even one short day of marriage had seemed to alter her. She was more confident and at ease, sure of Andrew, like a child triumphant over a prize. He looked at the two faces as they came close, seeing in them something which had not been present when he saw them last. They were alive now, he thought, both of them; they were united with a kind of passion that he felt was not wholly the outcome of their physical bond. They had a sort of ruthless eagerness, as if they were both reaching out for something which had just come into sight. Whatever emotion they shared, it was for themselves alone.

He took her horse's head. He had an opportunity then to look at her closely, and he wished that she might have been vulgar and coarse, and then he could have despised her – and ignored her. But he was all too keenly aware that she was not the type of woman to be overlooked. Intelligence and quick-wittedness were there, and she would not allow herself to be ignored. He reflected on Andrew's camp-fire conversations about this unknown girl, and he knew why it was that Andrew loved her. There was intoxication in those greenish eyes if one looked into them long enough, and charm and power in that smile. She appealed strongly to the gambler in Andrew, the part of him that wanted nothing that was tame, or too easily won. He knew from their talks that Sara had not been swiftly wooed, nor would she ever submit meekly to any man's authority. He was angry with her because she had kept

herself aloof, and he was ready to believe that she had schemed
for all she had now, and was triumphant because she had won.

It suddenly occurred to him that he might possibly be jealous
of her.

As he waited for Andrew to dismount and come round to lift
her down, he realized that her eyes were on him.

'Welcome home, ma'am,' he said.

'Thank you,' she replied, meeting his gaze steadily.

He felt himself flushing, realizing that she held a position from
which she might patronize him if she so chose. But her eyes left
his. She turned to smile at Andrew, and Jeremy knew he was forgotten.

3

In the two years following her marriage, Sara watched the Hawkesbury Valleys slowly filling with settlers. Each ship now arriving
in the colony brought its family of free settlers, and the terms of
some of the convicts expired, or were remitted, and they, also,
moved out to take land. By 1795, there were four hundred people
living along the river, and their farms extended for thirty miles
on either bank. A passable road had been made to link the Hawkesbury with Parramatta.

During this time Kintyre had become the most prosperous
farm in the district. This was mainly due to the fact that Andrew
was now firmly established in the trading-ring, enjoying to the
full the privileges of the military – but he had also chosen his land
in the place least likely to be touched by the seasonal floods which
damaged and swept away the crops of those on the low-lying
river-flats. Labour was cheap; many of the ex-convict settlers, having no money and no knowledge of farming, after their first few
months gave up any attempt to cultivate their own land, and
were glad to hire themselves out. As the acres were cleared, there
was more pasture, and Andrew began to make regular trips to
Parramatta for the market-day livestock sales. In a little more than
a year Kintyre's herds and flocks couldn't any longer be reckoned
in a quick glance. The rich river-flats gave a heavy yield of grain –
so long as it could be harvested before the level of the water rose
with the autumn rains. It wasn't much more than a modest kind
of prosperity that the farm enjoyed – the outhouses and stables were
still rough, the fencing incomplete – but, with prices in the colony

always favouring the trading-ring, Andrew's profits mounted steadily. When the first two years were over he had moved beyond the stage where he was haunted by the fear of failure.

To the house itself he added three rooms, setting them at right angles to the main building, so that the whole long veranda faced a complete curve of the river, giving a view in two directions. A dull-green vine climbed the walls, and trailed along the veranda-rails, softening and warming the stark outlines of the house. A small garden was laid out in front, and slender fruit-trees covered the slope at the side – when the trees broke into bloom for a brief time, there was the frail, transient beauty of an English spring to contrast with the evergreens. The house itself was losing its look of impermanence and rawness; its height commanded a fine stretch of the new road, and to those who travelled along it, it proclaimed the Maclays' stature and position in the colony.

Sara felt the great peace of these two years; they were the happiest in her whole life, and it took her some time to accustom herself to her sense of freedom and security, and to the knowledge that there was no longer any need to scheme and contrive for what she wanted. Only gradually could she learn the fact that she was the mistress of a farmhouse, and of Annie Stokes and the two other women who had been assigned to help her; the workers at Kintyre, free and convict, touched their caps to her as they passed, and she had to school herself not to show her satisfaction and delight in that small gesture. Curtains appeared at the windows of the house, and rugs on the floors – there were even a few pieces of indifferent silver exhibited about, which Andrew had bought from a newly arrived settler. Sara was enchanted with them. Each time she passed she gave them a few furtive rubs with the corner of her apron. The plain wood floors gleamed with wax-polish, and the soft light from the lanterns lent some beauty even to the simply-fashioned furniture.

Right from the first month of her arrival at Kintyre, she flung herself into learning the management of the farm. She kept the accounts herself, making them up from the rough notes that Andrew gave her. She learned quickly; after a time she did them with ease and speed, and Andrew, responding to her interest, left more and more of the book-keeping to her. But she was not content to confine her knowledge of the farm to notations on paper. She took to riding every day, accompanying Andrew on his rounds, inspecting the work on the fences, and the deep ditches which the torrential rains made necessary; she began to know something about the condition of the livestock, and the diseases which could attack them –

all matters to which she had paid scant attention when she had
heard them discussed among the farmers of the Romney Marsh. As
time passed the farming on Kintyre's lands became almost as much
her concern as the running of the household, and she listened to
the conversations between Andrew and Jeremy on the subject of
stock and crops. Along the Hawkesbury they began to say that
Andrew Maclay had married a woman as shrewd and businesslike as himself.

The world of the colony beyond the Hawkesbury she knew
only from the gossip Andrew brought back from his trips to Sydney
and Parramatta, and from the frequent letters that passed between herself and Julia Ryder. James was settling well to his
farming, and enjoying it, Julia wrote – her house was gradually
being furnished, and a garden made. In short, James Ryder was
prospering like every other hard-working farmer who had started
either with money of his own, or who had some place in the trading circle. It was a time when money was to be made quickly
from the fantastic privileges which the New South Wales Corps, in
the absence of a Governor to restrain them, granted to themselves. So long as a man was accepted by the officers of the Corps,
nothing could go wrong for him – land was free, rum was cheap,
convicts were assigned without question, and with all this went the
right of buying cargoes offered for sale from every ship entering
Port Jackson.

Sara found little to tempt her to Sydney or Parramatta. There
was hardly more to be seen now than the tired-looking huts and
the few houses that had been there when she first arrived, and
there was no one to visit except Julia Ryder. A few wives of the
Corps' officers had come out from England to join their husbands, but there was no possibility that she would be admitted into
their tight little circle. Over this, she could do nothing but shrug
her shoulders; Kintyre and the work there suited her, and there
wasn't much else she wanted. In the Hawkesbury district itself the
women were mostly the wives of small settlers, many of them ex-
convicts, married to ex-convicts. She knew they envied the prosperity and ease of life at Kintyre, and her appearance on the
Hawkesbury road, mounted on the horse which had been set aside
for her own use, did nothing to endear her to them. Resentful
eyes under faded bonnets peered at her as she went by. There was
no place yet for her in the colony – nothing between these hard-
working women who envied her, and the officers' wives who would
not receive her. She had to content herself with her rather solitary
and aloof place at Kintyre.

So when she knew that she was pregnant, almost her first thoughts were for Julia – whether or not she could be spared from her own farm to make the journey to the Hawkesbury at the time the child was expected. Memories of their former relationship as mistress and servant still remained with her vividly, making her reluctant to write her request to Julia. But before she had finally settled to writing the letter, Andrew carried the news back with him from his next visit to Parramatta that Julia had asked if she might come two weeks before the baby would be born. But when the time came, she was delayed for a week with Charles, who had some sort of slight fever, and when she at last reached Kintyre she was greeted with the news that Sara's son had been born the day before, after only four hours' labour. The surgeon, D'Arcy Wentworth, who had travelled up from Parramatta with Julia, was seriously out of humour over the long journey made to no purpose. He seemed to be of the opinion that no gentlewoman would have produced her first child with so little difficulty.

The baby was christened David. To the scandalized women along the river, the short time which had elapsed between the child's birth and Sara's first appearance on her horse was barely decent. They were not to know what impetus the sight of their first child had given to the ambitions of Andrew and Sara. After David was born they were very close in a way they had never been before; work at Kintyre took on a new aspect seen in the light of a son to inherit it. They had no visitors, and lived with a simplicity which, in Sydney, would have caused slighting comment; but they themselves were satisfied, and each season more ground was broken by the ox-drawn hoe, and better farming equipment arrived out from England. Kintyre took on the trim, whitewashed look of a typical Scottish farm.

It was Jeremy Hogan who caused the only unhappiness Sara knew in those two years. Between them ran an undercurrent of hostility, begun on the day Andrew had brought her to the Hawkesbury as his bride. Plainly, Jeremy considered her not half good enough for Andrew, a common little piece whom, by some misfortune, he had found attractive. They never openly quarrelled, both realizing that Andrew would not have stood for it. But, at best, their politeness to each other was chilly; at worst – when Andrew was not present – they stopped short only of outright rudeness. In every matter their ideas seemed to conflict. Jeremy was an excellent farmer himself; he made no secret of the fact that he, Andrew and Trigg, were capable of running the farm without help from Sara. She said nothing on this score to Andrew, but simply

settled to learning as much as possible from him, without troubling
Jeremy.

She knew well enough why Jeremy took this attitude towards
her. His memories were all of lovely Irish women – gentle, soft-
voiced creatures who bent to their husbands' will, whose minds
never strayed beyond their favourite horse, their children, the style
of their dress, and who would not have admitted to being able to
add a column of figures. This was the sort of woman Jeremy understood – not one who bargained like a gipsy for what she wanted,
who trailed her petticoats in the mud to see the progress of the
work in the fields and garden, and who still called herself mistress
of a farm, and wife to a man whom he respected. She knew there
was no trace of the dependent helplessness in her which Jeremy
wanted to find.

His resentment was never put into words. It remained just below the surface, and the only way he could give vent to it was by
ignoring her when he discussed the farm with Andrew. Clearly,
his object was to show her her place, and make her keep it. She
had no power against him; he was necessary to Kintyre, he worked
on it as if it were his own, and she would have suffered even direct
insults from him in order to keep him there. She often thought
of the wonderful relief if she could have raised her crop and hit
Jeremy just once, as he turned his half-insolent gaze upwards
towards her when she rode to inspect the work he was supervising in the fields.

Sometimes she indulged in a fanciful day-dream of finding
some way of convincing him that a practical, unsentimental woman
was a better wife to Andrew, in his present position, than any of
his own notions of soft-eyed beauties. Then she pulled up short,
and laughed at herself for such indulgence. Jeremy's opinion of her
would have to be worn down by the slow method of proving him
wrong in small ways; but it was a method that was little suited
to her mood.

2

These years, without proper government control, the officers of
the Corps used to form the nucleus of their estates – mostly on the
profits from rum. Sara, watching from Kintyre, could trace the
patterns these men were making – they were uncovering their own
ambitions to establish themselves as the gentry of the new country,
and they were doing it by the classic method of grabbing, in as
short a time as possible, all the land available to them, leaving

the refinements and niceties of their unique position until later. Andrew, except for the fact that he wore no red coat and drew no pay from His Majesty's Government, was hardly different.

The news reached them, almost a year old, of the execution of Louis XVI of France. They also learned that England had joined Prussia, Austria, Spain and Piedmont in declaring war against the French Republic. To the people of New South Wales the events of the world they had left behind were remote and far-off, like a tune heard tinkling faintly in the distance. They were absorbed in their own affairs, and the troubles of Europe hardly touched them.

4

After a week of rain in the early spring of 1795 the Hawkesbury rose suddenly. The lands belonging to several farmers who had settled close to the banks were under water; one man drowned. For three days the swirling brown flood held its place twenty-five feet above the usual level, and then gradually receded. It left behind a generous layer of silt, and scores of dead livestock, bloated, and beginning to smell vilely. The farmers returned to their ruined fields of Indian corn, the mud-caked wrecks of their homes, and they ruefully counted the numbers of cattle either drowned or strayed. They reckoned their losses against the possible return of the floods each spring and autumn. They discussed the prospect among themselves and whatever way they viewed it, it looked gloomy. Some determined to hang on – counting that the yield of one good season here would compensate for two bad ones; others decided to cut their losses and sell.

Kintyre was practically untouched by the disaster that had come to the valley. At the first sign of a rise in the river, Andrew had moved his livestock to higher ground close to the house. When the water went down he had no losses to count, except one field of corn destroyed. He made capital out of the flood. He watched the panic spread among the other settlers, and when the trek began he was able to buy up the small farm adjoining his own, and a further ninety acres a mile or so down-river. More ex-convict labourers were hired, and an overseer found to master them; Jeremy began his task of bringing the productivity of Kintyre's new lands into line with the old.

The spring also brought the *Reliance*, bearing the awaited

Governor, John Hunter, into Sydney Cove. Rumours circulated among the New South Wales Corps that his commission held a paragraph charging him to suppress the rum traffic. On September 11th, the Corps paraded with full military pomp, and with an obvious tongue in the cheek, to hear the commission read, quite fully determined that nothing a King or Parliament on the other side of the world could do was going to stem their profiteering in the rum traffic.

2

'Jeremy, do you think these accounts are . . . ?'

Sara broke off and laid down her pen, as the sounds of a galloping horse broke into the afternoon stillness. Jeremy lifted his eyes from the account-books spread on the table between them. From the bottom of the slope they could hear the heavy beat of a horse being ridden at full speed. For an instant they exchanged a questioning glance. Then Jeremy was on his feet.

'It's news of some sort!' he rapped, flinging open the door of the room Andrew used as an office. 'No one rides like that for the pleasure of it.'

'Wait!' Sara sprang up. 'I'll come with you!'

She swept out, and as she hurried down the passage to the front door, standing open in the spring sunshine, she was possessed of a strange fear. Never before had a horse been ridden to her very veranda steps at such speed – not even when a long-awaited ship arrived, bringing letters from England. Her thoughts flew instantly to Andrew, who had left two days before to attend the reading of the new Governor's commission in Sydney. Her mind envisaged him ill or injured, and the hoofbeats had a desperate, urgent sound. The horseman was almost at the top of the slope now. She gathered up her skirts and ran the last few yards to the doorway.

Here Jeremy sprang past her, racing down the steps to take the bridle of the horse; a scatter of small stones flew up as it was brought too sharply to a halt. Sara recognized it immediately as the dark chestnut which their nearest neighbour, Charles Denver, had brought out with him from England. The man riding it was his overseer, Evans.

At the top of the steps she paused. 'What is it?'

Evans was dishevelled and breathless. He gazed up at Sara for a few seconds while Jeremy tried to quieten the horse. At last he leaned forward and called out hoarsely, unbelief in his voice, 'It's the convicts, Mrs Maclay! They've broken out!'

Sara's own voice was strained, like Evans's. 'What's that? Whose convicts?'

'Ours! They've murdered Mr Denver!'

She clutched the veranda post. She felt an appalling sickness suddenly swamp her, and for a moment she could think of nothing but the closeness of Kintyre to the neighbouring farm. An outbreak! Her hands clenched. This was worse than the flood, worse than the skirmishes with the natives. It was worse than anything the bush could offer in terror and violence. Through her fear she knew her desperate need of Andrew now. Charles Denver had been murdered, and perhaps their own lives were threatened by this outbreak; she and Jeremy faced it alone.

She thought of this a moment longer, and then forced herself to walk calmly down the steps until she was standing beside Jeremy at the horse's head.

'Tell me what happened,' she said.

He breathed deeply, and she could see the sweat matting the lank hair on his forehead. His shirt was soaked, and with a fresh stab of fear she saw bloodstains on his hands. The blood was dry and caked around his nails.

'I was driving six head of cattle back from Sam Murphy's,' he said, panting, and trying to get his breath. 'As soon as I got in sight of the house, I knew something was amiss. Didn't look right, somehow – but I couldn't exactly put my mind to what was wrong. I didn't have time to think much about it because someone started shooting at me from the house. I rode down to the river, out of their range – and that was where I found him.'

'Him?' Jeremy said tersely. 'Mr Denver?'

Evans nodded. 'Aye, Mr Denver. His skull smashed in with a pickaxe – the back of his head.'

'Good God!' Jeremy said.

Sara's eyes moved again to the bloody hands. She stared at them, fascinated and repulsed.

'He was dead, of course?' was all she said.

'Dead, aye! When I left this morning he was supervising the building-up of the bank, in case the river rose again. He must have turned his back on them. There was the other supervisor, O'Brien, with him. God knows what happened to O'Brien. More than likely he's joined the outbreak. They'd loot the house for food and fire-arms, and then, probably, take the boats to cross the river.'

'What about the women on the place?' Jeremy put in quickly.

'There were two convict women,' Evans answered. 'Can't say what became of them. Probably with the men.'

'How many men?' Sara asked.

'Ten, ma'am – and O'Brien, if he's alive.'

She ran her tongue over dry lips. 'How many guns?'

'Mr Denver had four.'

'Four . . .' she repeated. Her eyes searched his tired, taut face. 'You came here immediately?'

'Yes, ma'am. As soon as I found him, I came.'

'Did they see you come this way?'

'Don't see that they could help it, ma'am. And they'd probably guess that I'd make for the camp to get the troops.'

'That's true,' she said. 'Yes, of course they would.'

Jeremy burst out, 'Hell! They've picked their time well for this. I'll swear there's no more than two or three men of the detachment still on the Hawkesbury. They've all been sent to Sydney or Parramatta to make good muster for the Governor's parade.'

The truth of his words struck Sara. She clung to the bridle for a moment in silence, afraid to let go for fear she would stumble and fall. The cunning of Denver's convict labourers enraged her – they had known to wait until the troops stationed in the district to keep down the natives had departed before they rose to their murdering and looting. She looked at Jeremy, knowing well that his face must be a mirror of her own expression, grave and fearful, as they each made a swift reckoning of the extent of the danger. She turned again to Evans. 'You'll ride immediately to Parramatta for help. They can't have sent all the troops on to Sydney. Tell them they'll have to muster horses from somewhere – if they wait to send a detachment on foot, it will take anything up to two days to reach here.'

Evans looked doubtful. 'It's twenty miles, ma'am, and I must stop by each farm on the way to warn them. Unless the moon's clear, I'll not get speed out of this horse. There's no telling what time I'll reach the town.'

Sara said sharply, stamping her foot in impatience, 'Oh, damn you, can't you understand that you must get help here quickly! Whatever time it is they must make up a force and send it immediately. Three soldiers with a musket apiece won't hold down a gang of murderers. Tell them they've got to send all the firearms they can spare. We'll need them.'

She let go of the bridle abruptly.

'Now, go as quickly as you can.'

But Jeremy's hand still held it. 'You'll go as well, Mrs Maclay.'

She regarded him fiercely. 'Go? Why should I go? I'm staying here!'

'You'll go at least as far as the Murphys' house. They'll not reach there too quickly.'

Her voice choked with anger. 'I'm staying here – where I belong! No convicts are going to take *my* house while I run off and leave it to them. I can fire a gun, and I suppose I can shoot a man as well as most if I'm forced to.'

Jeremy's chest heaved. 'The baby?' he said levelly.

'David will stay here,' she replied swiftly. 'At the moment he's as safe here as anywhere on the Hawkesbury. How can we tell which way they'll go? They may pass by Kintyre altogether, to put the troops off their trail. They may cross the river right away, and if they do that, that's the last we'll hear of them. If I take David in the cart, I may meet them on the road. Staying or going – it's a chance.'

Jeremy wouldn't let it go at that. He said loudly, 'But I'm responsible . . .'

'Since when have you been responsible?' Sara demanded hotly. 'In your husband's absence . . .'

'This is one time when I give the orders,' she retorted. 'And that applies to you too, Evans. Now, go – at once!'

With that, she stepped back from the horse. But Jeremy waited a few moments longer, obstinately clinging to the bridle, looking for some sign that she was weakening. She returned his gaze coldly, daring him to make any further show of defiance. Then he glanced up at the grim, white face of the man above him, and with a gesture of hopeless anger, he relaxed his hold. Evans touched the horse with his heels; it wheeled quickly, raising a shower of broken earth, and started down the slope again.

Sara and Jeremy had no time to watch it out of sight; instead they turned to each other immediately. Anger still flared in each face, but it faded in the swift realization they both had of their aloneness in a danger which had come upon them too suddenly. The sounds of the galloping horse were dying fast; with them, it seemed that their link with the world of security and peace was gone. Their eyes met in a moment of full comprehension of their plight. Then Sara jerked her head, motioning him back towards the house.

On the steps she glanced over her shoulder. What she saw made her clutch Jeremy's arm in alarm.

'Look! They've fired Charles Denver's house!'

He swung round. Together they looked in the direction of the neighbouring farm; a faint column of smoke drifted above the trees. It seemed no more than a wisp, but it came from a distance

of almost two miles. On any other day it would have passed for
the burning of timber on a newly-cleared space; it would have gone
unnoticed. But they knew, both of them, that today the smoke
meant that either Charles Denver's house or his stores were burning.

She uttered only a single word.

'Hurry!'

For a second or two Sara stood to see Jeremy stride down the
slope to where the main body of convicts were working under
Trigg. The only hope of stopping the outbreak from spreading
was to lock their own convicts in their huts before they had a
chance to realize what was in the air. The devil of it was, she
thought, that they were never all in the one place at the same
time. Two were working at the moment in the vegetable garden,
one in the orchard, and probably one in the stables. Jeremy was
alone against them, and with the nagging doubt whether or not
Trigg would stick by him if the men broke. She watched him
hurrying purposefully across the field, the gun he had taken from a
locked cupboard in Andrew's office held as inconspicuously as
possible by his side. Her half-closed eyes followed him a moment,
and she prayed desperately that he might be able to fight the odds
against him.

Then she cocked the loaded pistol that he had thrust into her
hand, balancing its weight as evenly as she could before turning
and going back into the house again. She made straight for the
kitchen; the door was ajar and she flung it open, standing squarely
in front of the three women. They all raised their eyes at the
sudden entry. Their expressions altered from inquiry to amazement
and fright as their eyes fell on the pistol.

The youngest uttered a sharp exclamation in a rough Irish
brogue.

'Glory be to God, what's this?'

She dropped the potato she was peeling and jumped to her
feet.

Annie drew her hands slowly out of a basin of dough and wiped
them in her apron.

The third, a heavy creature with the dull eyes of a halfwit, gave
an unintelligent grunt.

Sara stood well back from them, holding the pistol with a steady
hand. She was afraid, but was, more than anything else, terrified
that they would detect her fear.

'Not a word from any of you – do you understand?'

No one spoke or moved. Sara tensed herself, half-expecting that the young Irishwoman might rush forward in a mad attempt to take the pistol. Her only hope of keeping them under control lay in shutting them up before the shock of the situation wore off and gave them time to think or to plan any action.

She waved the pistol slightly towards a small storeroom leading off the kitchen; it was no more than a large cupboard, with a shuttered window high in the wall.

'In there, all of you!' she rapped.

Immediately the gaze of each of them shifted to the storeroom, then back again. No one moved.

Sara looked angrily from one to the other. 'Didn't you hear what I said? In there with you!'

Annie wrung her hands, and set up a faint whining. Sara took not the slightest notice, but she was afraid of the Irishwoman. She watched her anxiously, seeing a brief show of emotion on the thin, white face, the shrewd eyes narrowed down, as if she were rapidly calculating the connection between the horseman's hurried arrival and departure, and now her mistress's unexpected appearance with a pistol in her hand. Sara realized that this woman was intelligent enough to put two and two together and suspect that trouble concerning the convicts was afoot. Again she gestured purposefully with the heavy pistol. But the other woman, defiant, and playing for time, stood her ground.

'Why?' she demanded.

Furious, now, Sara shouted at her. 'Don't ask me questions! Do as I say!'

'But I likes to know . . .'

'Silence! You'll do as I say! Now, hurry on with you!'

The Irishwoman didn't move; she glanced from the cringing Annie to her other companion, standing solidly and open-mouthed. Sara knew beyond doubt that she was reckoning how much support she could count on if she attempted an attack; she knew too that she daren't lose another second considering the chances.

'You wouldn't like a bullet through your leg, would you, Mary?' she said calmly, staring straight into that rebellious face. 'Because that's what you'll certainly get if you don't move before I count three.' She raised the pistol a trifle. 'I haven't learned to handle this for nothing!'

The Irishwoman stirred in an agony of indecision.

'One . . . Two . . .'

Annie let out a despairing wail, and the sound seemed to unnerve the other woman. With a final, defiant shrug she submitted, leading the others into the storeroom.

Sara followed them, the pulse in her throat fluttering with relief, and her wrist suddenly feeling as if its bones had turned to water.

Grimly fingering her bunch of keys, she faced her three captives as they lined against the wall. Her eyes moved from one to the other – Mary's expression of sullen fury, Annie's frightened, cowering stance, the third's look of dumb wonder. She met their stares coolly, knowing well enough how potentially dangerous they were; an unguarded second, or one sign of weakness would bring them down on her like a pack of wolves. Give them only a chance of freedom with survival in the bush, and they would strip the house of food and firearms and be gone within a few minutes.

'Remember this,' she said, sliding a key into the lock, 'if any of you try to escape, I'll see to it myself that the magistrate sentences you to a flogging that won't leave an inch of skin on your back. Remember it well – because I mean it.'

With that she slammed the door and turned the key.

As she picked up her skirts and sped back along the passage to David's nursery, Sara's thoughts were anxiously upon the inadequacy of the storeroom as a prison. Any three women with will and strength could break out of it; she relied, without conviction, on her threats forcing them into docility. It was never safe to rely on the docility of a convict.

David woke up. He made a good-humoured, crowing noise, thumping his fists together energetically. She snatched up a shawl, bundling it around him, fighting down his hands, eager to play with the ends of her hair.

'Be good, David!' she said softly, her mouth close to his ear. 'Be good, now! I'm not leaving you behind to the gang of rogues.'

He gave a crow of excitement, and his hand closed firmly over a lock of her hair. As she hurried from the room with him he began to pull at it; he pulled harder, delighted with this new distraction; tears came to her eyes; David's pulling was painful, and she felt sick with fright and anxiety. But there was no time to stop and quieten his restless hands. Clutching the pistol, and balancing the heavy child against her hip, she ran back through the kitchen. Crossing it, she could hear muffled thuds coming from the storeroom. It was useless, encumbered as she was with David, to investigate. And in any case, she told herself, if she were to catch them trying to escape, she could not stand with a gun levelled at them until Jeremy arrived back to help her. So she hardly

paused on her way through the kitchen; she went out by the back
door, and crossed to the stables.

Once inside them she drew a deeper breath. It was quiet and
dim; the smell of horses and hay came to her strongly, a peaceful,
homey smell on that spring afternoon, a smell that seemed to have
no relation at all to the world so abruptly turned upside down. The
effect was demoralizing; it urged her to rest, to desist from her
fantastic scheme. Above, the hay-loft lured her with its security,
its promise of a hiding place. She shifted David in her arms and
gazed about.

At the same moment Andrew's Arab stallion, Fury, only lately
bought from the owner of a trading vessel, stirred and whinnied
softly, half-turning his head to look at her. The movement broke
Sara's mood of hesitation. The horses were valuable; the three
standing there so quietly, and the one he himself had ridden to
Sydney, represented Andrew's gains of the three years in the colony,
his position among its leaders. Not for lack of effort on her part
was she going to see them ridden away into the bush by a pack of
desperate men, to be most likely killed and eaten when the looted
food ran short. She was filled with a sense of great pride in these
animals and sudden terror in case they should be snatched from her
possession.

'Oh, not you, my beauties!' she murmured to them. 'They'll not
have you if I can help it.'

She turned away quickly, dragging down some hay from a
wall box, and put David lying on top of it. He mistrusted this
strange sensation of being deposited so firmly among the rustling
softness. He gave a cry of protest, and his face began to wrinkle
uncertainly.

Sara looked at him in dismay.

'Don't cry, Davie-boy! Oh, don't cry now!'

She glanced around in desperation, and then, selecting two
long stalks of hay, thrust them into his open hand. For a moment
he regarded them in wonder, tentatively placing one in his mouth.
The taste seemed to please him; he settled contentedly to chewing
on it.

She left him without another word, turning her attention to
fixing bridles on each of the horses. The stallion was always docile
in her hands; he allowed her to handle him without stirring.
The second horse was her own. It hindered her by nuzzling her face
and neck, and thrusting its nose along the folds of her skirt, searching for the carrot she always brought. She talked gently as she
worked, striving to keep her hands calm and patient while her

mind raced ahead to what might be happening about her . . . the possible advance of the convicts from Charles Denver's farm, the women breaking down the door of the storeroom, Jeremy, without help, setting out to round up their own labourers.

Her hands were stiff and clumsy as she fumbled with the straps. The third horse, a young bay gelding, catching her mood of unease, pulled restlessly away from her. It took her a long time to get the bridle secure.

'Well, *you*, my lad,' she said sharply, 'may be more trouble than you're worth!'

She had to decide quickly about David. She took away his shawl, ignoring the cries of protest he let out, finding the hay against his skin no longer soft. Folding it and knotting it at two corners, she hung it over her shoulders like a sling. She picked him up and settled him into it, supporting his weight with her left hand, leaving the right free for the bridles. He didn't like the new arrangement and set up a persistent, lusty howl.

She looked at him grimly. 'There's nothing I can do about it — you'll just have to get used to it.'

His puckered, exasperated face stared back resentfully at her.

Sara frowned down at him. 'I only ask you to lie there, Davie,' she said despairingly. 'If only you'd be quiet!'

His angry cries split the afternoon air, and Sara, with a shrug of her shoulders, decided there was nothing to be done to pacify him.

The stallion and Goldie, her own horse, came forward eagerly as soon as she laid her hand on the bridles. The bay was, by this time, thoroughly unnerved by the child's cries. He stood still and frightened in his box, refusing to come forward. She breathed hard, wondering what to do now. Holding the bridles of the two first horses, and supporting David as she did, she was unable to go into his box and bring him out. Nor could she afford to wait any longer. The only thing was to leave the box door open, and trust that he would follow the other two.

She settled David as securely as possible against her hip, and pulled at the bridles with her tensed, sweating hand. It would take ten minutes, she calculated, to reach the edge of the cleared land. The screen of the surrounding bush was thick and comforting; once they were within the fringe of it, the horses would not be seen by anyone who did not actually stumble on them. Tethered there, they would be safe and unseen. Safe . . . Her mind echoed the word doubtfully. There were still the hours of the night to live through before she could be certain of safety — for her child, the house and stores, and herself. The thin column of smoke above the trees was there to remind her of what she might yet expect.

As she crossed the yard, tugging at the bridles to force the horses to a better pace, she heard a clatter at the stable door. Looking back she saw the bay gelding; he paused a moment, hesitant and nervous. Then, seeing the other two horses, he trotted over to join them, falling in meekly at the rear of the procession.

Sara's mouth relaxed in a faint smile of relief before she turned her face towards the edge of the cleared land.

Sara stood in the kitchen doorway and gazed warily about her. Everything was exactly as she had left it to go for the horses. Annie's cooking-spoon lay on the floor in a pool of congealed fat. The last of the afternoon sunshine threw her shadow before her, long and thin. Her wrist ached with weariness as she raised the pistol level with her waist. Then she stepped inside.

Finding himself once again in the warm familiarity of the house seemed to bring to David a renewed sense of his grievances. He struggled wildly in his improvised sling, setting up a lusty howling that was part hunger and part anger. Sara clamped him firmly to her side with her left hand, and tried to stifle his cries against her breast. The sling, which had taken his full weight during her tramp across the fields with the horses, was cutting into her neck like wire. His waving arms beat at her, and with every fresh attempt he made to escape, the hard knot of the shawl bit deeper into her flesh.

She held back her tears of fatigue and vexation, and paused to listen to the wild hammering on the storeroom door that had greeted David's first cries. The hammering went on, and his screams became piercing. Sara held him tighter, fixing her gaze on the door, pistol held level.

Through the confusion and noise Annie's voice reached her. 'Open up, ma'am! Oh, open up, for God's sake! The others have gone!'

Sara did not reply. Her eyes narrowed in suspicion; she edged closer to the large kitchen table, resting David's weight on it, giving herself better control of the pistol.

'Oh, ma'am . . . ma'am! Let me out, for the love of God!'

The words carried in them a sob of despair and fear; they were cries from a woman, terrified and alone. Two years had taught Sara to know Annie Stokes thoroughly – she was a rogue and an intriguer, but she was no actress. Sara felt that for once she was speaking the truth. She placed the pistol on the table, and fumbled for the key of the storeroom.

She opened the door, and Annie stumbled forward stiffly. 'They've gone!' she gasped, her Cockney's whine rising shrill and unnerving. 'Through the window!' she added unnecessarily.

Without speaking a word, Sara stood looking into the storeroom. The young Irishwoman's shrewd brain had seized upon the situation, and had taken the chance of a breakout. Without being at all sure of what was taking place, she had gambled literally with the skin of her back, on the chance that she might follow the protection of the firearms and food of the men convicts in their escape into the bush. The second woman, slavish in her attitude to Mary, and too stupid to properly grasp what was happening about her, had, as a matter of course, gone also.

Together they had rolled a row of molasses kegs to form a platform beneath the shutter, and then, using their combined strength, they had battered away at the wood with an empty keg. Reflecting on the terrifying power in the arms of that clumsy, slow-witted creature, Sara could well understand that it had taken them only a short time to make their escape.

The wall beneath the shutter was badly scarred, and there were splinters of wood lying thickly on the floor. She turned away dumbly, her shoulders drooping.

Annie had begun wringing her hands. 'I didn't go, ma'am!' she wailed. 'They said I was a fool . . . But I wouldn't go with them, Mrs Maclay, ma'am! I wouldn't leave you . . . now.'

Sara nodded mechanically. 'Yes, Annie. Yes . . . I know.'

Annie had much more to say, a stream of information, comments, and emphatic protestations of loyalty. Sara listened with half her mind, picking out of the flow of words only the bits that were important. Gradually the story was pieced together. Annie gabbled on, telling how they had known of the hasty arrival of Charles Denver's overseer, and had guessed by his agitated manner and the column of smoke above the trees most of what had happened. Being locked in the storeroom at gun-point had confirmed their guesses. Standing on a keg, with her eye pressed to a crack in the shutter, Mary had seen three convicts, whom she did not recognize, armed with a gun, a roughly fashioned pike, and a pickaxe, slip quietly past the house. They had not attempted to enter, but made towards the outhouses. It was then, Annie said, that the Irishwoman had ordered her companion to help her batter down the shutter.

Sara cut her short. 'Three strange convicts, you say? And armed?'

'Yes, ma'am.'

Sara feverishly hoisted the sling around her neck, pulling it over her head.

'Here,' she panted, thrusting the angry, screaming child into Annie's arms, 'take him, and give him something to eat. See if you can make him quiet.'

Cut short in her recital, Annie looked at David with an expression of astonishment, and then gave a gasp as Sara turned and fled from the kitchen.

In Andrew's office Sara unlocked the cupboard again, taking out the second gun of the three he kept there. She loaded it as he had taught her, thankfully remembering the hours of practice he had insisted upon in preparation for just such an hour as the one which faced her now. She loaded and checked the ammunition meticulously, and then turned to go back to the kitchen.

But beside Andrew's desk she hesitated and halted. She thought a moment before sliding open the top drawer. Her hand fumbled among the quills and extra candles, closing over a small, carved dagger, of Italian workmanship, which they sometimes used for cutting paper. It was a delicate, evil-looking thing with a slim blade, and as she picked it up her mind was grimly moving forward to what might happen if the convicts overran Kintyre, recalling too clearly Evans's blood-stained hands and his story of finding Denver's battered body.

As she stood there, she heard the first shots fired – four of them.

She laid the gun down on the desk for just a few seconds she needed to push the dagger into the bodice of her dress, so that the carved handle didn't show. The coldness of the pointed steel between her breasts was a faint comfort to her.

Then she picked up the gun again and started towards the kitchen.

At the sound of the shots Annie had commenced a peculiar, monotonous shriek – something between a howl and a scream. Sara clenched her teeth. She was going to put a stop to that unearthly noise if it was the last thing she did. If she was going to die, it wasn't going to be to the sounds of Annie's shrieking.

As she reached the kitchen she heard the crack of another shot being fired.

The single shot had silenced Annie abruptly. She turned to Sara with a desperate look of appeal.

'It's all up with us now, ma'am! We're finished!' With a halfsob she pointed to the window. 'There's Trigg, now – wounded, by the looks of it. And no sign of Hogan.'

Sara sprang past her to the open shutters, the sickness of fear
deep in her stomach. She was suddenly too much aware of the
dependence of Annie and David upon her, and her own hopeless
inadequacy in defending them if the convicts attacked the house.
It was mainly for reassurance that she raised the gun and steadied
it against the window frame. If the convicts came two guns wouldn't
hold them off for very long. She hoped that Annie wouldn't realize
this too soon.

The principal outhouses were about three hundred yards from
the house itself. They formed a square, facing inwards – two huts
were allotted to the convicts for sleeping quarters, with a smaller
one for Jeremy and Trigg. There were two storehouses for the
convicts' provisions and farm equipment, and the long hut, which
Andrew used to house the extra labourers he hired for seasonal
work – harvesting and sowing, and the quick clearing of new land.
He had built the outhouses at this distance because he had not
wanted the presence of the convicts to weigh too heavily upon
his own life. They were necessary to the workings of Kintyre, but,
beyond that, he baulked at giving them recognition. At this moment, Sara wished that the distance were twice as much.

In the fading light she strained her eyes to see across the kitchen
yard. In the space between the stable and the barn, she recognized
the figure of Trigg. He leant, as if he were breathless and weak,
against the wall of the barn; he was hugging his right arm close,
and his head was thrust back as he sucked in great gulps of air.
He rested for only a few seconds in the shelter of the wall. Then
he lowered his head and ran, with just one backward glance, across
the yard to the kitchen. Sara tensed herself, waiting for some sign
of pursuit, but there was none. Wounded, and unarmed, Trigg was
of no importance to the convicts for the time being.

She lowered the gun, but still kept her place by the window as
Trigg stumbled up the two steps to the kitchen, and stood there,
leaning heavily against the door-frame.

He was very white; his whole right arm, from shoulder to wrist,
was covered in blood. He wore no coat, and the blood was already
running in a thin stream from the tip of one of his fingers. He
tilted his head back, gasping for breath, looking spent and exhausted, as if that last dash from the convicts' huts to the house had
entirely drained his strength.

Annie let out a horrified squawk, and at a nod from Sara,
laid David, quiet now, down on the table, and rushed to help
him.

Sara, unmoving, looked at them both. Annie's loyalty had proved

itself now, but Trigg . . . She was still suspicious of Trigg. His dash
to the house might have been a gallant effort to protect the women
and the baby; it might have been a determination to crawl into
shelter to nurse his wounded arm. She was prepared not to place
overmuch trust in him, but he pushed Annie aside and turned to
her.

'Hogan and me, we had our men rounded up and almost in the
huts when those other devils arrived, ma'am,' he gasped weakly.
'Not a chance they gave us, but came up behind, round by the
stable, and fired. There's about ten of them, ma'am . . . and four
have guns. There was no holding our lot, once they got the gist of
what was happening. I got it in the arm, and then had to run for
it . . . or stay and be murdered.'

His voice had died a little more. He said falteringly, 'Mary and
Bessie have gone with them. I heard them yelling. I knew you
and Annie and Master David were here alone.' He made an
effort to straighten, but it was feeble. 'I'm not much use now. But
I reckon I could still fire a gun.'

Sara nodded, running her tongue across her dry lips. How
wrong she'd been about Trigg; she found it difficult to look at
him without shame.

'And Hogan?' she asked faintly.

'He got it in the back . . . twice. 'Tain't much chance he's alive
now.'

3

There was nothing to do then but wait. During the next hour
Sara did not stir from her post at the window, the gun propped
beside her. In enraged helplessness she watched the plunder of the
storehouses, and then, finally, what she had been dreading – and
waiting for as well. The first pale flame shot above the roofs of
the storehouses. At dusk a stiff breeze had sprung up; it fed the
fire which raced from building to building with a swiftness that
struck terror into her heart. Soon the outhouses were a blazing
fiery square in the early darkness. The wind came in her direction,
and brought the wild voices of the escaped men. The rum they
had plundered from the stores added frenzy to their success. It had
given them a new boldness – a boldness which the certain knowledge that they faced the lonely bush and the river, and the solid,
unknown mountains beyond it, had not yet chilled. They shouted
and yelled to each other in the flush of victory. Sara could see their
figures outlined against the flaming huts; she watched their stagger-

ing progress, their determined shouldering of the bags of food they had looted.

They made no attempt to come near the house. She imagined this was because they had found the empty stable and thought the Maclays had ridden off and left Kintyre to whatever fate threatened it; and because they were already loaded with as much food as they could carry. For a while she waited, terrified that the possibility of firearms and more ammunition might lure them to the house. And then it occurred to her that they wouldn't bother with the house – they were working against time, and once they had their food collected they would be off. If, as Evans had feared, they had seen him ride in the direction of Kintyre, then they wouldn't linger; every minute they expected the arrival of troops. The trek to the river and the two boats moored at the small landing-stage began soon after the outhouses were fairly ablaze.

Sara clenched her hands tightly in an effort to keep her rage in check; she felt sick, and there were tears in her eyes as she watched the roof of the nearest hut cave in with a crash that sent sparks flying in all directions. She knew – none knew better – why they wasted precious minutes firing the outhouses. They were making their only effective protest against their masters and gaolers. Their memories of the holds of the prison ships, the lash, and the chain-gang came to urge them on in their destruction. They called to each other in their drunken courage before setting out to beat the trackless forest, certain that they would find a way across those baffling blue hills, and that somehow they would survive where no white man had lived before. They each of them must have known that the chance of survival was slender; and the knowledge seemed to have made them even more desperate. Sara knew it all, she knew the feeling running strongly among them, one to the other – the anger, the bitter resentment, needing only one spark falling from a hot head to set their fury alight.

When the last of the escaped convicts appeared to have made his way to the boats, and the fires were beginning to die down, Sara roused Trigg and Annie. David was asleep in a basket under the table, so she left him undisturbed. Trigg's arm was bandaged and in a sling made of torn sheeting; he was still in great pain. He followed Sara out of the kitchen and across the silent yard, stumbling several times on the path down to the huts. Sara handed the lamp she carried to Annie, and supported him herself on his uninjured side. In her right hand she carried the gun. The wind blew towards them from the dying fires, bringing a warm breath against their faces, smuts and hot ashes, and the smell of roasting salt meat.

They found Jeremy lying face down in the middle of the square. Annie helped Sara to turn him on his back. He was quite still, making no sound as his body rolled over. There was blood on the shoulder of his coat, and it had clotted in his hair and on the side of his face. Sara wasted no time searching his face, in which there was no sign of life; she tore down his shirt, and bent to listen to his heart.

In a few moments she raised her eyes to the two heads that bent anxiously over her.

'He's alive!' she said.

Then she looked at Trigg. 'Can you manage to carry the lamp and the gun?'

He nodded.

To Annie she tossed a sharp order.

'Give me your apron. We'll have to tie up his head before we try to get him back to the house. Somehow we've got to keep him alive.'

4

Sara gave a final glance at the sleeping figures around her in the sitting-room, before she reached out to take the lantern from the table. She rose with no more noise than the rustle of her skirts.

Annie was sitting on the floor, as far as possible from the window, her back gently sagging against the wall, her mouth hanging open in sleep; every now and then her breath made little hissing noises through the gaps in her teeth. David was beside her, in the basket brought out of the kitchen. Jeremy and Trigg lay against the opposite wall; Trigg in the quiet motionless sleep of weakness and exhaustion; Jeremy was conscious only for brief periods, the rest of the time he twisted and turned in a kind of fever. Throughout the night he had occasionally woken to ask her for water, his eyes flickering over her face in a few moments of clarity before he slipped back into semi-consciousness. Sara paused before him now, holding the lamp directly above his head. He was not as badly hurt as she had first feared – a bullet had grazed his temple, and there was another still lodged in his shoulder. He had lost a good deal of blood.

He turned his head away painfully, and she lowered the lamp. Jeremy wasn't going to die, she told herself firmly – not if a surgeon arrived in time to remove the bullet. Her tongue flicked nervously

over her lips as she calculated the chances of a surgeon being among
the first of the troops to reach the Hawkesbury. It seemed a very
slight chance.

She lifted the latch of the door softly, and moved out into the
passage. This would be her last patrol of the night. In a little
more than an hour the bush would be grey in the first light, and
then she would rouse Annie and Trigg to watch in her place. Her
eyes were blurred with fatigue as she started the rounds of the
window-shutters. First, the dining-room . . . She halted in the doorway, the lamp casting long shadows before her. She had nothing
to do but to try the three windows in a row on one wall, yet it
seemed to require a lot of time and effort to do it. She went to the
kitchen next.

Nothing had disturbed the silence of the house during the long
night. She had sat, the gun across her knees, too frightened to
drop into even a doze while she listened for the sound of anyone trying to break into the house. As the hours dragged quietly out, she
became calmer, and felt safer. But the silence was wearing; sleep
dragged at her body, and yet her nerves, taut as wire, would not let
her relax. It was a relief whenever Jeremy called to her for water,
or when Trigg woke because the dressing had slipped on his arm,
and needed changing.

She walked along the passage to the kitchen, and opened the
door softly. She held the lamp down low, looking towards the
heavily shuttered windows, hoping that the first streak of light might
have appeared against the chinks. It was as black as when she
made her last round, an hour earlier. She stood still, her thoughts
on the escaped convicts on the other side of the river, wondering
what sort of camp they had made to sleep off their drunken stupor.
In the daylight they might raid farms on the opposite bank – or
they might make their way as quickly as possible beyond the range
of the settled areas. She didn't know what their choice would be,
and for the hundredth time that night she pondered the question,
and tried to answer it for herself. She sighed, and rested her tired
body against the door-frame.

'If only it were light . . .' she whispered, her voice coming back
softly to her out of the darkness. 'If only the troops would come . . .'

As she spoke she felt the breeze of the cold spring morning
on her right cheek. It was sharp, coming down off the mountains,
with a hint of frost in it. The thought froze in her mind . . . a sharp
breeze in a room that was shuttered!

She straightened then, leaning forward into the room and trying
to fight off the fatigue that dulled her brain. She raised the lamp,

peering into the gloom towards the storeroom. Its door was open. The shutter that the two women had torn down was letting in the wind in cold gusts.

Her eyes narrowed in fear and bewilderment as she struggled to remember if she herself had opened the door, and left it open. Had she done that in her last round? Her memory fought for recollection. But her mind remained blank – apprehension as well as suspicion crowding into it.

She was certain now that something was wrong, and it seemed to her more dangerous to go back and rouse Trigg than to stand her ground. She put the lamp carefully down on the floor. Then she levelled the gun, and moved towards the storeroom. The weight of the gun made her well aware of how clumsy and cumbersome it felt in her hands; she thought longingly of the pistol, left lying beside her chair in the sitting-room. Fool! she told herself, a little whistling breath of dismay escaping through her teeth.

She couldn't see into the storeroom; the half-open door blocked her view. The boards beneath her feet creaked so loudly that she bit her lips to check the cry that rose in her throat. The lamp threw her shadow in a long line before her, and, seeing it, she stopped still. She stood as if she were frozen, listening. Then, after a few moments of reassuring silence, she took a step nearer.

Before she could move again, a man's figure suddenly thrust itself round the edge of the open door. She raised the gun instantly, and stepped backwards. But he was tall, and moved with the swiftness of a hawk. His hand shot out, knocking the barrel aside before she realized fully what was happening. She fired automatically, but the gun resounded with nothing more than the dull click of a jammed chamber.

The man was huge and bulky, towering over her; he bent to look into her face. She tried to take another backward step, but he gripped her wrist; he twisted it backwards, and she moaned faintly with the pain. One by one her fingers slipped off the trigger. He might have knocked it out of her hand in the first place, but he seemed to prefer to wait until she let it go herself. It fell on the ground between them. She opened her mouth to call Trigg, but his rough hand, smelling of sweat and rum, was clamped over her face. She clawed at it madly, until he reached round her body and, with one arm, pinned both hers to her side.

'Not a sound out of you, or I'll break your neck! Do you hear?' The huge hand slipped down and circled her throat.

Terrified, Sara stared up at him. The hoarse, whispered voice had the tones of a countryman with a London accent overlaid.

He was drunk. The reek of his breath as he leant over her made her stomach heave. His face was shining with sweat, his eyes red-rimmed. He swayed as he held her.

'How many men here?' he said. 'Two?'

She didn't answer.

His hand tightened threateningly on her throat. 'Don't try to trick me – I saw them! Both wounded – dead by now probably.' He touched the gun with his foot. 'The ammunition for this – where is it?'

She made no answer, except to jerk her head backwards in the direction of the door and the passage leading to the rest of the house.

'Any food?'

'Over there.' She nodded towards the shelves lining one side of the kitchen.

He gave a satisfied grunt.

'They left me behind, curse them!' he said. 'I fell and knocked myself out, I did, and the bastards took my gun and left me lying there by the river bank.' He gave a low, expressionless laugh, shaking her a little. 'But I'm not one to be easily beaten – and now I've got more than any of them! I've got a gun and food – and no one to go shares with me. And I have you as well!'

Her eyes widened slowly.

A smile spread itself over his sweating face. 'You don't remember me, do you? You've been playing the fine lady too long now to remember your pals of the *Georgette*.'

She stiffened, and tried to break away.

'Ha! You didn't like that, did you?' He rocked back on his heels. 'Oh, I've watched you – a year it is now since I first came here. I don't forget how it used to be. You, with rags on your back, and not a shoe on your foot. And now you'll turn your nose away from the bad smell of us – from the likes of us who slave on this farm to put silk on your body, and gold in your husband's purse. Well . . . you made the most of it on the *Georgette*, didn't you? You found your way into that fool's bed while the rest of us rotted under the hatches. D'y think I don't remember? I remember every time I clap eyes on you – and I've ached to get my hand round this white neck of yours and choke the life out of it . . . you scheming whore!'

'Who *are* you?' The words were nothing more than a whisper, because of the pressure of his hand on her throat.

'You'd have no cause to remember me, *Mrs* Maclay. Except you might happen to remember that they flogged the skin off my

back twice on that voyage. Johnny's the name. Johnny the Pen-
man, they used to call me in London. A pretty well-known citizen
I was before they hung a sentence of fourteen years round my neck.
Time was when I could have forged the Governor's signature so he
wouldn't know it himself. But not any more. Not since I lost two
fingers cutting wood for your bloody fires! I nearly lost the whole
hand, but did Mrs Maclay know about it, or come to bind it up?
Not a chance! The great lady doesn't put her foot inside a convict's hut!

'But let me tell you,' he said, his face sickeningly close to Sara's,
'you'll never escape it. No matter how long you're in this colony,
or how far behind you leave the *Georgette*, you'll never be allowed
to forget it. Every convict has you marked – and every fresh arrival
hears your story. There'll always be someone to reach up and drag
you down, like I'm doing. Do you understand? You'll never be
allowed to forget it!

'Well . . .' He shook her roughly. 'I won't have to care about
it any more. I'm free, and I don't have to look at you any longer,
or hear you giving orders, or see you lift your skirt out of the way,
in case it might touch one of us. No more of it, d'y hear? I'm
getting away, across the river where they won't find me. And I
don't care if I ever lay eyes on another white woman again. The
native women will do for my purposes.'

Then he spat out of the corner of his mouth.

'The horses,' he muttered, 'where are they?'

'I don't know.'

'Don't lie, you whore! There should be three horses. They
were gone from the stables even before we raided the stores. Where
have you hidden them?'

'I don't know anything about the horses.'

He struck her then across the face. 'Whore! Tell me!'

'I don't know!' she gasped.

He shook her again, his eyes suddenly crazy. 'I'll make you
tell me, gutterbrat!' He struck her a second time in anger. She
reeled back, almost out of his grasp.

Abruptly, his expression altered. His sweating face became alive
with a new emotion, a vicious, drunken lust that hitting her had
awakened. He rode his sensation with deliberate abandon, laughing
wildly. He took one of his hands away from her, and looked down
at it, as if surprised at the power there.

'We'll see now who can touch you, and who can't. You're not
too good for a convict to have, Sara Dane, when he has a mind
to it. Whore . . .' He breathed this softly. 'You were glad to take

what you could get when you were on the *Georgette*. Now I'm not
asking!'

His hand jerked out and ripped open the bodice of her gown
down to the waist. He was half-smiling.

He loosened his grasp a moment to kiss her, and Sara suddenly
tore his hand away, and clutched fumbling at her breast. But she
wasn't quick enough to catch the tiny Italian dagger. It fell to
the floor between them, tinkling, with a sharp little sound against
the gun.

The man looked down, and his slight hesitation gave her time
to stoop quickly and snatch at it before he did. She crouched, with
the dagger in her right hand, facing him. Maddened, he lunged
at her, hitting her again across the face. The blow knocked her to
the ground; she lay there sideways on her elbow. For a few seconds
he stood looking down at her, and then he dropped to one knee,
balancing drunkenly with his hand in the floor. From that position he began inching forward.

She let him come as close as she dared, then, like a flash, she
twisted and rolled on her left side, thrusting the pointed dagger upwards with all her strength. His mouth fell open the instant he
realized what she was doing. He made a clumsy stab to push her
away, but as he bent forward, the blade punctured the skin of his
throat.

A glazed, startled look sprang to his eyes, an expression both of
terror and disbelief. He grasped frantically at his throat, his fingers
encountering the dagger. He dragged at Sara's hand, trying to
loosen her hold, but the movement sent the point further home.
Blood began to gush out. A bubble of blood appeared at the side of
his mouth, and his hand slipped away nervelessly. Slowly he fell
forward, the dagger sinking into his throat up to the hilt.

He fell across her grotesquely, with arms outstretched. He was
already dead when his body struck her, and the blood came in a
bright red stream from his mouth. She pushed at his shoulders until
at last he slid off, rolling to one side. He lay face upwards, his eyes
open, and the dagger slanting downwards at an angle from his
throat. The delicate silver handle gleamed in the faint light.

Sara twisted away from him and began to get stiffly to her knees.
But she paused and shuddered. The man's blood was still warm on
her gown, and on her bare breasts and throat. Her face twitched
with pain from the blows he had given her. She looked down at
her hands, and then over at the dead man. Her stomach heaved;
she wanted to be sick.

And while she knelt there, the sounds of stumbling footsteps reached her from the passage. She lifted her head, too weary to care now who it was. She waited, and at last Jeremy's figure appeared in the shadowy doorway. Her breath came in a little gasp of relief. In the lantern-light she could see the sweat standing out on his forehead and his upper-lip, but his eyes no longer had the mad brightness of fever. He swayed unsteadily, clutching at the doorframe.

'Sara . . . ' he said, using her name for the first time.

'Jeremy!'

She began to crawl towards him.

5

Jeremy watched her closely across the office table. They sat there alone. She poured a second brandy for them both; her hands were unsteady, and some of it slopped over and ran down the edge of the glass. The lamp stood on the floor; it threw the shadow of the table upwards to the ceiling. Sara's features were darkened and distorted by the shadow. Her hair hung down her back in a wild tangle; the blood had dried on her torn bodice, on her breast and hands.

She put the glass to her lips, biting on it to stop their trembling. Then she gripped it with both her hands and set it carefully down.

'There's nothing more to tell you,' she said dully, looking away. 'Now you know the whole of the story that will be ringing through the colony in a few days' time.' She cupped her forehead in her hand. 'I can just hear it . . . "Mrs Maclay, with an ex-convict's special gifts with a knife, kills one of her own labourers." Or what's worse still, "one of her old associates of the *Georgette*." ' Her head sank down farther, and she made a low groan. 'Oh, Jeremy, what meat the gossips will make of it! I have at last fulfilled all their ideas of a tavern-room slut. That's what he called me – a whore!'

'Sara!' Jeremy leaned forward, the movement making his head spin with pain.

She lifted her eyes to his. 'What do you care about that? You've never expected any different from me. If you dared, you'd call me a whore as well.'

He gripped the edge of the table with both hands and made a slow attempt to rise.

'If I were capable of it, Sara,' he said faintly, 'I'd go round and shake you for that.'

She raised her eyebrows. 'Do you deny that you've thought that of me . . . ever since the day of my marriage? Deny that you've thought Andrew no more than a madman to have married me.'

After a long silence, he said slowly, 'I don't deny that I thought it, once. But my views have changed.'

Jeremy focused his eyes on the damp rings the glasses had made on the surface of the table.

'It's not what happened in the last few hours that's changed it,' he said. 'Though, God knows, I owe my life to you – neither of the other two would have gone to bring me in.' He smudged one of the rings with his finger. 'No . . . the change isn't as recent as that. No man in his right senses could have done anything but admire you right along.'

She made a sound that might have meant anything.

He looked at her quickly. 'I was jealous of you, Sara – because Andrew loved you. A man who's cut off from the normal society of women is apt to either hate or love the one woman within his reach – and at the same time out of his reach. I desired you, but wouldn't acknowledge it – even to myself. God knows, that's understandable. You're lovely enough for any man to want to possess.

'Andrew and I were friends before you came. And then you confounded me because you *were* all the things he had boasted you would be . . . efficient, calm, intelligent . . . You've never complained about the sort of life you have here at Kintyre. You never mention the loneliness. I've seen you bear your child away from the company of other women without showing the fear you must have felt. I've watched you grow to meet every fresh demand Andrew made. And I've watched you become more and more vital to his being every month you've been together. He wasn't much more than a small gambler when he came off the *Georgette*. What he is now you've made him.'

She did not move; she watched him closely.

After a pause he said, 'And even in face of all this I was half-disappointed because you hadn't turned out to be the slut I'd hoped. If you want the truth, Sara, I was disappointed that you didn't fall into my open arms.'

He leaned back and took his hands off the table.

'My jealousy was finished when I saw you in there.' He nodded in the direction of the kitchen. 'That made me finally realize that since yesterday afternoon you had done what I didn't believe any woman would do. Whatever you care to do in the future will seem all right with me.'

He lay back in the chair with his eyes closed, his hand gingerly going to the place where the blood had clotted on his shoulder bandage.

'From now on, Sara . . .' He paused and opened his eyes. 'From now on I'll slave for you. You can take that just whatever way you like. But you can take it from me straight what my motives will be. They'll be love and desire – because I doubt if Andrew ever loved or desired you any more than I do now.' His voice had become hard, and his lips too dry. 'I'll have to forget this talk – act as if it had never happened – because you belong to Andrew. You're his . . . but I shall serve you whatever way I can as long as I live.'

She did not reply, merely nodded. Then her head sank down on her arms folded on the table. As Jeremy watched, her shoulders seemed to shake; she might have been weeping, but he wasn't sure. The soft glow of the lamp shone on her skin where the gown had been torn away. The mad disarray of her hair gave her a look of troubled youth. He watched her, and longed to reach across the table and lay his hand reassuringly on her arm. But she gave no sign that she wanted him – or was even conscious of him any more.

They sat in silence for a long time while the daylight grew stronger at the chinks in the shutters. For half an hour Sara did not move; she lay with her head on her arms, like a piece of warm-coloured stone. Finally, the same sound roused them both. Sara stirred and lifted her head to listen. Then she rose and walked with dragging steps to the window.

'The soldiers,' she said. She opened back the shutters and the sounds of the horses came clearly to Jeremy.

'Six of them – and Lieutenant Grey.'

She turned slowly and faced him. Her face was tired and old.

'Do you realize that Andrew will hear this story – everyone else's version of it – long before I have a chance to tell it to him myself?'

She dashed a hand frantically across her eyes.

'And what a story they'll make of it, Jeremy! A dead man lying in the kitchen, and Mrs Maclay hasn't even troubled to wash off his blood!'

Then she laughed; the sound was hysterical and false.

6

Andrew reached Kintyre at dawn the following morning. Sara, lying awake in the shadowed bedroom, heard the hoofbeats distinctly break into the silence. She sat up and listened – she listened also to the footsteps of the soldier who was posted on guard on the veranda.

The horse came up the slope at speed; Andrew's voice impatiently answered the sentry's challenge. His heavy boots clattered over the wooden boards. Sara lit a candle beside the bed, and waited.

He opened the bedroom door, and for a few seconds stood there looking at her. Then he pushed the door closed with his foot. She felt his arms go about her shoulders, and he thrust his face against her breasts.

'Sara! Sara!' His tone was muffled, but she was aware of his relief. His body trembled, and his clothes carried the smell of the horse's sweat.

He raised his face to hers. 'I came as soon as I heard. I've ridden all the way from Sydney without a break. Sara — you're not hurt?'

She shook her head. 'Just tired out — and not able to sleep.'

'The swine!' he said. 'If they've as much as put a finger on you ...'

'They didn't, Andrew. They fired the outhouses — and looted ... That's all.'

'David?'

She gave a little smile. 'David is all right. He slept through most of it.' Then her eyes grew suddenly afraid. 'Andrew, it was terrible. There's so much to tell you. I ...'

His hands moved and gripped her arms. 'Don't try to tell me about it now, Sara. Everyone has the story — in one form or another. I'll hear it from you when you're fit to tell me.'

She closed her eyes, and he gently pressed his lips to them.

'Dearest,' he said, 'when the news first came they said you were hurt — and then that you were dead. I didn't know you were safe until I got to Parramatta.' He thrust his head once more against her breast, gripping her in an agony of possessiveness. 'God in heaven, Sara ... If they had killed you ...'

He looked up at her. 'If you had been dead, I couldn't have lived.'

She lifted her hand and stroked back the matted hair from his forehead. It was stuck with sweat and dirt.

'I'll not let it happen again,' he said. 'By God, I won't! They'll never be trusted again, as I've been fool enough to trust them in the past. It won't worry me if I'm the most hated man in the colony — no convict is going to get the better of me. From now on I'll make every use I can of their bodies for labour, and I'll forget about their souls. If any of them have souls, they're too insignificant to be troubled with.'

He relaxed his grip on her, and she fell back against the pillows.

His lips were thin and determined as he spoke; he had the angry, passionate look of a man thwarted. Sara knew that whatever past leniency he had shown the convicts was finished. Andrew had never been a patient man, and he would not make an effort now to be either patient or forgiving.

At last he straightened and took a backward step away from the bed. He said reluctantly, 'You need rest, my darling. I must leave you . . .'

He hesitated, poised on one foot.

She held out her hand to him. 'But I think there's something else you want to talk about. There's something beside the convicts . . .?'

He shrugged. 'No – nothing. Well . . . it must wait until you've rested.'

She smiled. 'I'm not so tired that my curiosity wouldn't keep me from resting.' She leaned her head a little to one side. 'Andrew, come and tell me.'

He smiled broadly at her; it was a grin that wiped the fatigue from his face. With a single movement he was beside the bed again and had flung himself down full length on it. He lay close to her; he was on his back and he stared up at the ceiling.

'What a girl you are, my Sara! I'd be lost without you!' He reached out and caught her hand. Their fingers laced together, and locked. He closed his eyes.

'I want to start building in Sydney,' he said.

She sat up at that and bent over him, her fingers gripping his tightly.

'Andrew! You mean to give up Kintyre?'

He opened his eyes. 'No, keep Kintyre – and go on expanding, as we've always planned. In spite of what those swine did to the stores, Kintyre will still be the richest farm on the Hawkesbury.'

The grin spread over his face again, and made it, even with its toughened, weathered skin, seem like a boy's face. He drew her down until her lips were almost touching his own.

'Kintyre is only a part of what I want,' he said eagerly. 'Sara, things are stirring in Sydney. The world is beginning to know of its existence – and the possibilities of trade is bringing ships in. More than ever I'm convinced that the colony is going to command great prosperity – and Sydney is the port. As it opens up there'll be need for stores and warehouses and wharves – and I must be there and have land to keep up with the growth. I might even be able to get my hands on some sort of ship, and make voyages to the East for cargoes. It would be a gamble, of course . . . But with you to help me . . .'

She drew a little away from him, and she could see the flame of ambition and a young man's excitement lighting his face. The silence of Kintyre that she loved so much was all about them, and in her mind she saw it replaced by the clatter and confusion of the ugly little town sprawling over Port Jackson's bays. Andrew was asking her to go back to face the world of women and prejudice from which she had broken free. Because of his streak of trader's blood she realized that she was being asked to endure the loneliness of long voyages. Kintyre would become a refuge only to be visited occasionally, a place to be longed for in the midst of Sydney's discouraged-looking dwellings. For a moment her eyes turned to the window. The peace of the Hawkesbury Valley was real and very precious in the early spring dawn. She found it hard to believe that he wanted her to leave it.

But she looked again at Andrew; her fingers moved slowly over his cheek and forehead, and then they curled about the lock of matted hair.

'Dearest,' she said softly, 'tell me what it is you plan to do.'

PART THREE

I

The house that Andrew Maclay finished building for himself at the end of February, 1880, was something as close to a mansion as Sydney was likely to see for some time to come. If it lacked quite the touch of grandeur he would have liked, its proportions were spacious and graceful enough, with wide, cool verandas facing out over the harbour. He built on a site above Woolloomooloo Bay, removed from the noise of the township's dusty streets, from the sounds of horses and oxen teams, and from the stream of raw, undisciplined life that was part of the tiny port.

In the five years since Andrew had made his decision to leave the Hawkesbury, the colony had altered subtly. Twelve years since its foundation, it was acquiring now an air of permanence, although the Colonial Office was tardy about admitting it to the status of something more than a penal settlement. It grew steadily – free settlers dribbled in, and small exploration parties, most of them organized and driven on by the personal need of land, were opening up the hinterland, pushing always farther along the rivers. The mountain barrier still defeated them, but Governor Hunter was encouraging the exploration of the coast. Young Lieutenant Matthew Flinders, with his friend, naval surgeon George Bass, had made a voyage through the strait Bass had discovered earlier, sailed round Van Dieman's Land, proving that it was not connected to the mainland. They were hardly more than boys, both of them, but the southern ocean was giving up its mysteries to their eager adventuring.

But the administrative framework of the colony was very little altered since the hey-day of Lieutenant-Governor Grose. The ruling few of the New South Wales Corps still lined their pockets with the profits from rum and trade, while the rest struggled for their very existence. The military dictatorship had supposedly ended with the arrival of Governor Hunter – its activities had not ended, but were carried on only slightly less blatantly, with a mock deference and a raised eyebrow towards the unhappy, powerless Governor. They retained the monopoly on the sale of the cargoes of ships trading with the port, they distilled and distributed rum illegally – and since very little agriculture was undertaken on the

Government's behalf, the military still demanded and got fantastic
prices for the grain, without which the colony could not survive.
Hunter was hopelessly caught up in the bonds forged during the
three years when there had been no responsible Government. He
had not the cunning to match wits sharpened by greed, nor did he
have control of the troops. The troops obeyed only their officers,
and it was to the advantage of the officers to forestall, frustrate
and even ignore every order the Governor issued. It had never at
any time been an equal match, and Hunter knew that he was fast
reaching a stage where he would be forced to admit his defeat.
Beyond that point there was nothing but his recall to England, and
hope of a pension.

Andrew Maclay had had his generous share in the pickings
of these fruitful years. He had made his profits, with the rest of
the buying-ring. Kintyre's acres had increased and it was still the
most prosperous farm on the Hawkesbury. He had fulfilled his
dream of the store in Sydney; it had not been done easily, but it
stood now, like a banner for his triumph, and a warehouse was
building up beside it. He was the registered owner of a sloop, the
Thistle, which traded regularly in the East. And he was still talked
of as the luckiest man with a pack of cards in his hands that the
colony yet knew of.

But these alone had not built and furnished the house overlooking Woolloomooloo Bay. To do this he had had to go beyond
the colony — to the East, and back to London itself.

The eyes of the colony had fastened with keen, and, for the most
part, rather malicious interest on Andrew when he announced in
1795 that he intended to trade in Sydney. He was given his grant
of land at a noisy, busy intersection of streets close to the public
wharf — hardly the place, the curious whispered, that a gentleman
would want to settle his wife and family. But, after all, when that
wife was a former convict . . . The colony still shrugged its shoulders in amusement and scorn at the very idea of Sara.

After seven months the Maclay store, with living-rooms above it,
was finished, and Sara arrived from Kintyre, household belongings
and bundles piled high in a wagon. The upstairs windows looked
out on to the shipping in the harbour, and to Government House on
the rise above it; close at hand were the uncobbled streets, either
dust-choked or pools of mud, according to the weather, and never
free, day or night, from the clamour of Sydney's rowdy, often
quarrelsome inhabitants. On the day of her arrival, Sara, strained
by the upheaval of the move, gave one backward, regretful thought

to the peace she had left behind at Kintyre, then turned briskly to making a home out of the bare rooms.

Her appearance at the opening of the store was brief, and after that she was seldom seen. Two months later her second son, Duncan, was born. It seemed to the colony that the confinement was barely over when Mrs Maclay gave a sharp impetus to scandalized gossip by leaving David and the new baby in Annie Stokes's hands, and appearing daily in the store to attend to customers. And it was noted, almost immediately, that the store was always crowded with men – many of whom went by the name of gentlemen – at the times when she was known to be there. Seated behind a small desk she took orders, discussed the possibility of securing certain goods in short supply, smiling and talking pleasantly and keeping a wary eye on the young clerks, fresh out from England, who rushed about and perspired freely in their efforts to please her. The women of the colony said that Andrew Maclay must be short of money when he needed to have his wife to attend to the business. The menfolk said nothing, and continued to take their custom to the Maclays' store.

The sloop, the *Thistle*, was Andrew's biggest business venture yet. He bought her after she had limped into the harbour at the end of a nightmare voyage from the Cape, her timbers rotten and taking in water at every seam. Her owner-master was not a coward, but he could not face another voyage in a vessel that was literally going to pieces under his feet. He sold cheaply to Andrew, glad to be rid of his burden. Andrew, trusting to fortune for a good harvest at Kintyre, borrowed money to refit. From amongst the motley host of men that Sydney, as a seaport, was beginning to collect, he found two who claimed once to have been shipwrights. He put them in charge of his hired labourers and the rebuilding of the *Thistle* began. Material was short, labour was short – and Andrew himself spent many days squeezed into the narrow space of the carpenter's walk, working on the hull.

The harvest was a good one; there was more money, and the *Thistle* was ready for sea at last. With a sense of aching relief, Andrew paid back his loan, and got together an oddly-assorted crew from the seamen who had drifted into the port and had been left behind. He engaged a short, wiry Yankee skipper, who was idling about without a ship, to take command. Everything was ready for her to sail for Calcutta, when the first mate fell ill. After an hour's earnest talk with Sara, Andrew took his place. The *Thistle* left with the tide, and Sydney sat back to enjoy the spectacle of watching a woman trying to run both town store and Hawkesbury

farm. It was an engaging item of gossip and speculation, and the
store was always crowded with men anxious to see what she would
make of it.

Sara made a better job of it than even Andrew believed possible.
With Jeremy Hogan beside her, she became a familiar sight on
the road between Sydney and the Hawkesbury. Work went on in
the usual way at Kintyre, as if Andrew himself were there, and
she even took his place in the buying-ring when a ship entered
harbour with a cargo for sale. At first she was an object for
curiosity and slight amusement; later Sydney learned that she had
a business head as hard as her husband's, and that she was never
to be outwitted in striking a bargain.

'No gentlewoman could have done it,' was the general opinion
in the colony.

But Sara appeared to care very little for general opinion. As long
as trade came to her door, as long as the herds of livestock increased each year at Kintyre, and the acres under cultivation grew,
she seemed content to bear her loneliness, and the dust which
drifted into her upstairs rooms during the scorching summer
months.

Both she and Jeremy knew that scandal was waiting to link
their names at the first opportunity. The friendship they shared
since the night of the convict outbreak on the Hawkesbury was
now so strong that they dare not display it. Jeremy never stayed
with her longer than was necessary, and kept rigidly to his rôle
of Andrew Maclay's overseer. He spent all of his time at the farm,
except when he received her request to accompany her to a sale,
or to come to town to bring her back to Kintyre for a brief visit.
The hopes of the gossip-mongers were dampened, but never quite
died.

Winds were favourable, and Andrew was back in the leaking
Thistle months before anyone expected him. He unloaded a cargo
that ranged from frying-pans and silks, to sandalwood and cashmere shawls. His cargo carried the look and feel of the East with it,
and people starved for colour and excitement flocked to inspect –
and those who could afford it, to buy. The store had never been
so crowded before, or the shelves so crammed with goods. Jeremy
rode down from Kintyre to help them, and when he returned,
Andrew, Sara, and the two children were with him.

Andrew basked in the peace of Kintyre for a two weeks' spell,
counted his herds, went through the accounts with Jeremy, and
with thoughtful, careful eyes appraised the startling different quality
of the wool of the tiny flock – three ewes and a ram – of merino

sheep, which Sara had persuaded John Macarthur to sell her. It was well known that Macarthur was experimenting with wool – he was the best farmer in the colony, and he had an unshakable belief in the future of his merinos. Andrew considered him worth following.

The short period of rest at Kintyre seemed to renew Andrew's energies. He had now seen what an entire cargo of his own would realize in clear profit, and he couldn't for long resist the temptation to repeat his venture. As soon as he returned to Sydney he started once more on the job of patching up the *Thistle*. Two months later he sailed in her again, bound for the East. From an upstairs window Sara watched her sails breaking slowly; she watched her out of sight down the harbour.

The colony never learned the full details of Andrew Maclay's second voyage. The captain of an American vessel brought Sara letters from Calcutta. She told no one what news they contained, except that her husband intended going on to London. But the captain himself had a tale to tell, a story he claimed had gone the rounds of Calcutta – a story of the sort of chance of which a man sometimes idly dreams. After a storm off the coast of Bengal, he said, the *Thistle* had come upon a Bristol merchantman, piled with a valuable cargo, and drifting helplessly towards the rocks. It was a feat of splendid seamanship to make contact, and bring the vessel into port, and it was the opinion in Calcutta that Andrew Maclay had truly earned every penny of the salvage money.

That was the story as it was given to the colonists – no one knew if it was the true story. Then, nineteen months after she had sailed from Port Jackson, a sloop bearing the name of *Thistle*, but in no other way resembling her battered predecessor, dropped anchor in Sydney Cove, within sight of Sara's windows. In less than an hour the news had spread through the whole town that Andrew Maclay was back.

Many curious and speculative eyes watched him come ashore, watched him stride along the dusty street towards the store. But there was no one to witness his meeting with Sara, or to hear what they said to each other in the first hour. Not even Annie Stokes, ear against keyhole, heard that.

The result of the trip was a cargo for sale that kept Sydney talking for a month, and buying for much longer; Andrew said he bought the new *Thistle* in London – and no further talk of his voyage would loosen any information about the Bristol merchantman, or of salvage money. But it was noted that he applied immediately for a grant of land, and began building himself a house on Woolloomooloo Bay – a private residence far grander than anything Sydney had yet seen. Within another month the *Thistle* sailed again for the East, still under the command of the Yankee captain; this time Andrew remained behind. Sydney already knew that Sara was expecting her third child.

The child, another son, Sebastian, was born above the store a few weeks before the house was completed. By then, from the evidence of the improvements to the Hawkesbury property, a smaller farm at Toongabbie which Andrew had just bought, and from the furnishings and silk hangings he had brought out from England for the new house, most people were convinced that the story of the salvage deal was true. Andrew Maclay was spending far more money than any small ship-owner and trader could expect to lay his hands on readily. Sara moved her belongings and the three children from the store to the new house – finally given its name of Glenbarr by Andrew – on one of the last summer days of 1800, when the street into which she looked for more than four years was choked with dust. The townspeople watched, smiling broadly at the future prospect of a convict attempting to set up house in the manner of a lady of fashion.

The late summer of 1800 also brought the first ship into the harbour with the news that Napoleon was back in France, having slipped out of Egypt, leaving his army where Nelson's victory at the Nile had bottled it up. He was back in Paris to overthrow the Directorate, and assumed the position of First Consul. Paris welcomed him in a frenzy of joy.

Sydney discussed the news, digesting it warily, remembering that five years earlier they had not even heard Napoleon's name. They could recall too that those five years had also seen the rise of Nelson, and the triumph of the Navy at Cape St Vincent and Camperdown. There had, also with this, been the blow to British security and pride dealt by the naval mutiny at the Nore; and in 1798, Ireland had broken again into open rebellion.

On the colony itself the war in Europe had three direct effects – the Colonial Secretary had neither time nor supplies to meet its growing demands, the backwash of the Irish Rebellion had already hit it in a wave of political prisoners, whose Jacobite views and murderous humour made them singularly unwelcome; and almost the worst effect, from the Governor's point of view, was that, with a war to fight in Europe, there was no chance of fresh Army officers, uncontaminated by rum and power, being attracted by the idea of service with the New South Wales Corps.

The Governor cursed Napoleon for more than the obvious reasons.

2

Jeremy's brows were drawn together thoughtfully. He held his wine-glass loosely as he surveyed the room. After a few days it would take shape as the drawing-room of the Maclays' new house — at the moment it wore the ugliness of bare boards, uncurtained windows, and the litter of half-emptied packing-cases. In the centre, at the table covered with oddments of china, Sara and Andrew stood together, close to the single lamp, concentrating on carving a cold roast duck. There was an eager, restless look about their faces, and neither betrayed fatigue, although the household had been stirring at dawn that morning. The lamplight, seeking out the lines in Andrew's weather-toughened skin, and the warm colour of Sara's hair, also caught the glitter in their eyes, and the swift half-smile which kept appearing on each face. Sara wore a limp cotton gown, faded by the sun of three summers, and Andrew's coat was the one in which he had worked with the carpenters on the old *Thistle*. Their movements were confident, and full of a sense of youth and excitement.

Jeremy listened to their odd snatches of talk.

'. . . and the garden must be laid out properly this time, Sara.'

'Yes — ' Sara paused to lay some of the meat on a plate. 'But not too much. Formal gardens don't suit the landscape here. In any case,' she added, 'it could never be half as lovely as the garden at Kintyre.'

Andrew glanced quickly over his shoulder. 'Do you hear that, Jeremy? I've built my wife the finest house in the colony, and on her first night in it she can think of nothing else but that miserable hut on the Hawkesbury.'

Sara came towards Jeremy with a plate. 'If this house is as happy as Kintyre, then I'll be happy too.'

Jeremy smiled at her. 'A woman's first love is like no other, is it, Sara?'

Her lips pursed a little. 'No, like no other.'

They sat down on packing-cases drawn into a rough circle to eat their food. The lamp stood on the floor between them. One long window looking out on the bay was open to the soft wind of this night at the end of summer. Outside the trees stirred gently; in the house there was no sound to disturb the silence. The working-party had left at dusk, and the three children already slept, with

Annie snoring beside them, in makeshift beds in a room above the wide entrance hall. There was a full orange moon above the harbour, and beyond the rays of the lamp Jeremy could see the pale, white light on the floorboards in front of each of the long windows.

Suddenly raising her head and looking about, Sara caught Jeremy's gaze.

'It's so quiet here,' she said. 'And no lights anywhere. We might almost be back at Kintyre.'

Andrew laid down his knife with a clatter. 'Must you talk of Kintyre that way? One would think it was ours no longer. You know it's waiting there whenever you want it.'

His voice was touched with impatience, but the sharp-edged tone disappeared when Sara turned towards him and smiled. The look that passed between them was meant for themselves alone, and Jeremy cursed silently and wished they would remember that they were *not* alone. They were too prone, he thought, to count him as part of their own happiness, and not to remember that he was a man, someone to be driven half-crazy with an unnamed longing whenever Sara smiled in that fashion. In the years since the convict raid on Kintyre, the relationship between the three of them had deepened into a trust and comradeship that was not definable in words. As far as the rest of the colony was concerned he was merely Andrew Maclay's overseer, and when anyone else was present that was the rôle he assumed; but alone with them he was close-knit in a unity of three people who had worked and struggled for the same end. Nevertheless, it was still torture for him to witness the intimacies of their married life, like the expressions written clearly on their faces now. Looking at them, it would have been easy to forget the years since their marriage, and the three children sleeping in the room above the hall.

Impatiently, he bent and caught up his glass from the floor. He spoke before he could check himself, and the words he uttered were the very last he wished to recall to the Maclays — they betrayed his frustration, and the years of being without women of his own kind.

'Do you remember . . . ?' he burst out. And then he halted.

They turned to look at him inquiringly. He pressed his lips together, and swallowed hard.

'Yes?' Andrew said.

'Do you remember,' Jeremy went on slowly, 'we drank a toast at the camp on your wedding night . . . to the mistress of Kintyre?'

Andrew caught his mood at once. His face warmed with an expression of recollection, of tenderness. Watching him, Jeremy suffered an agony of envy. For a minute they sat there, remembering, all three of them, the cold wind which blew that night, and the stars, too bright and close.

'Do I remember . . .?' Andrew murmured. 'It's almost seven years ago.' He turned to his wife. 'Full years, Sara, for both of us. Who could have known . . .?' Then he shrugged. 'But these seven years are only the beginning. There's still so much yet to do.'

Sara said gently, almost as an aside, 'Will you never be satisfied, Andrew?'

'Satisfied?' He laughed. 'Why should I be? Only fools are satisfied. Why should I sit in a chair and let the world spin about me?'

He stood up. All around his eyes Jeremy could see the lines, too deep, and too many for his years. The eyes themselves were a strained, faded blue, as if the sun of the long voyages had taken the colour out of them.

'I shall be a rich man yet,' Andrew declared. 'But not in the way this narrow corner calls wealth. I want wealth as the rest of the world knows it – wealth that even London would acknowledge!'

Andrew rose and took a couple of paces across the room, hands behind his back. The lamplight revealed the stained coat, the frill of torn linen at the wrist, the unpowdered hair. But how much more impressive now, Jeremy thought, than when he appeared in the magnificence of lace, silver-buckled shoes, and the brocaded coats he had brought back with him from London. He stood with his legs wide apart, as if he were on the deck of a ship.

He turned round and looked down at his wife.

'Some day I'll take you back to London, Sara. You'll have everything you ever wanted then. Some day . . .'

His lips parted in a smile. 'In the meantime, we'll live here – removed from the noise and muck.' He gestured to indicate the township built above the adjoining bay. 'I'll have land – more land and more ships. And I'll make the house here beautiful before I'm finished. Like this . . . I'll show you!'

His enthusiasm flamed suddenly and he stooped to pick up a fisherman's knife they had used to cut the rope around the packing-cases. Then he squatted before the case he had been sitting on, reaching out at the same time to draw the lamp nearer. With unhesitant strokes he began sketching lines in the rough wood with

the point of the knife. The hard surface resisted him, and he
swore softly with annoyance. The other two watched while the
plan of the house, as it now was, became recognizable.

'Now . . .' Andrew said, stabbing with the knife, and turning
towards them.

He broke off, and raised his head. The door-knob rattled softly;
then silence followed. Sara and Jeremy twisted their heads to
look behind. Andrew straightened slowly, the knife still in his hand.
He moved quietly towards the door.

He opened it with a jerk, and stopped. His eldest son stood
there, startled, barefooted, with his nightshirt almost reaching the
floor, and his hand outstretched, as if he were still grasping the
knob.

'Papa . . .'

'David!' Andrew stared at the child. 'Laddie, what is it?'

David took a step into the room. He looked at his mother. 'I
woke up – and I heard you.'

Sara was beside him in an instant, and had swept him up into
her arms. He settled contentedly there, his head against her shoulder, his inquiring eyes roaming round the unfamiliar room. He
glanced from his father to Jeremy, and then gave an excited
wriggle.

'May I stay, Mama?'

Sara smiled over the top of his head at Andrew. 'Let him stay
a little. After a few nights they'll be used to this house – and the
quiet – and then they'll settle down.'

Andrew nodded, reaching out to tousle the boy's flaxen, curling
hair. 'Why not? You've never been up as late as this, have
you, my son?'

He walked back to the packing-case, and Sara sat down again,
with David in her arms. She stretched the nightshirt Annie had
made for him to cover his feet; he promptly thrust one foot from
underneath and wriggled his toes expressively. Sara's left arm was
round him, pressing him close to her. Her free hand rested in his
lap. He clutched it tightly, staring in wonder at the knife his father
held.

Andrew squatted once more before the rough carving. He added
a few lines. 'I want another wing here . . .' The plan cut into
the wood was now L-shaped. 'It will face north-west, to get the
afternoon sun.'

'A new wing?' Sara said. 'What for?'

'That's going to be the new drawing-room – and whatever
other rooms we want above it. And we'll have a conservatory along
this side.'

'A conservatory?' Sara echoed faintly, glancing at Jeremy.

'Yes – why not? The native plants are certainly worth more attention than the people here give them. Think of the orchids we could
grow! We'll have a gardener out from England. And, later on,
we'll terrace the lawns down to the water's edge.'

Sara laid her cheek against David's hair. 'This all sounds very
grand – for a little place like Sydney.'

Andrew winked at her, grinning. 'Sydney won't always be a little
place. When I build my new wing, I'll bring the carpets from
Persia, and the chandeliers from Venice.'

Sara's eyes sparkled suddenly. 'When will this be?'

He shrugged. 'When trade opens up enough to allow me to
carry my plans through – when the population has expanded, and
can support more trade. I will want two ships – even three ships.'

Then he shrugged again. 'All that is for the future – for the
present we'll manage well enough.' His hands opened expressively,
taking in the spacious proportions of the room. He said, 'The new
wing would be merely a showplace – something that represents
land on the Hawkesbury, ships in the harbour, and a store to sell
their cargoes. Give me ten – fifteen – years like the last seven, and
there's nothing I won't be able to do.'

As he spoke he looked directly at his wife and son.

Jeremy sipped his wine thoughtfully. He felt the conviction in
Andrew's words, he felt that these dreams would materialize; he
had now come to believe that, so long as Andrew lived, this fabulous
luck would hold out, and his preposterous fantasy of conservatories
and laid-out gardens in a country still unable to feed itself would,
in time, be realized. He would have his new wing, and the display
of magnificence his heart craved. But he was an adventurer, a
trader, and a gambler; he understood the hard facts of his business
too well to become immersed in the mere trappings of wealth.
It would, as he said, merely represent the solid assets of land, ships,
store, and warehouse. It would be no more than his recreation,
while he gave his life to attending to the things which made it
possible.

Jeremy spoke suddenly, the trace of a smile on his lips.

'Another toast,' he said. 'This time to the house of Maclay!'
He raised his glass to the three of them.

2

Under the low beams of the main room in the Maclay store there was always the mingled odour of sandalwood, spices, new candles, and coffee-beans. Andrew claimed he could supply every need of the settlers; the store's wide rooms, crammed to the ceilings with the cargoes the *Thistle* brought back, almost justified his claim. Ranged about the walls were the deep, fat kegs of molasses, the bins of flour, sugar and rice; huge cheeses stood swathed in white cloth. The shelves were piled high with calico and muslin, and an occasional odd roll of silk; there were carefully stacked boxes for shoes and beaver hats. Beside the door was a long rack holding a selection of walking-canes and riding-crops. At the end of a row of bacon sides hanging from the ceiling, the light from the open door caught the satiny gleam of the wood of a guitar. Sara had secured it to a hook by a bunch of coloured ribbons. It swung there gaily – an incongruous support to Andrew's claim.

On a morning in the middle of April, two months after the family had moved to Glenbarr, Sara sat working over the accounts at the desk in one of the store's curved front windows. The autumn sun fell across her shoulders on to the open books, above her head a green parrot clutched the bars of his cage, and muttered vaguely in French. A year ago he had made his first appearance in the store on the arm of a dark-skinned sailor; David, beside his mother's desk, had seen him at once, and played with him delightedly; Sara gave the sailor an unreasonably large amount of tobacco in exchange for him, and, since that day, he had looked down on the life of the store from his cage, obviously revelling in its atmosphere of orderly bustle. He was given a name at the time, but the children had so persistently called him 'Old Boney' that no one could now remember the original name.

Sara was deaf to his muttering attempts to distract her. She finished re-checking a column of figures, then she looked up, motioning to one of the three young men who ran the store under her supervision.

'Mr Clapmore!'

'Ma'am?'

'If the native, Charlie, comes here this afternoon with fish, send him up to the house with them immediately. And mind you only give him half the tobacco he asks for. He's been getting far too much lately in exchange for his fish.'

'Very well, Mrs Maclay.'

Sara returned to her figures, basking in the gentle warmth of the sun on her back. This was one of the long succession of perfect autumn days which, every year, the country seemed to throw back as a compensation for the fierce heat of the summer. The air had a softness more mellowing than spring; when a wind stirred it brought a smell of the bush and salt water with it. Her lips moved soundlessly as she worked, but her thoughts kept turning to the memory of how Kintyre looked in the autumn – the noon hush of the bush, and the flow of the great river.

The quill halted above the paper, then she sighed, and, with an effort, began the column again. At the moment there was only one customer in the store – she knew by sight this farmer from Castle Hill who was making a careful selection of printed calico for his wife. A midday quiet was beginning to fall in the streets outside. In a far, dark corner a clock ticked loudly; Boney picked at his seed in a bored fashion.

She glanced up as a shadow darkened the doorway. She smiled, rising at once to greet Major Foveaux, of the New South Wales Corps.

'Good morning, Major!'

He bowed. 'Good morning, Mrs Maclay!' He waited until Boney's scream of welcome had died down. 'I hoped I'd find you here as usual at this time . . .'

'Can I be of any help to you, Major?'

'Indeed you can, dear lady. I'm looking for a gift . . .'

He shifted his weight uneasily. 'I thought perhaps a shawl . . . Yes, a shawl would do nicely, I think.'

'Why, certainly.' Sara moved past him, towards the shelves. 'I have one here from China – a lovely thing.' She selected a box, and turned to him again. 'I'm so glad that *you* have asked to see it, Major. I always hoped that someone with taste and discrimination would buy it.'

'Er . . . quite!'

She carried the box back to the desk, opening it and spreading the embroidered silk before him, letting the sun play on it, letting him take his time feeling and examining it. It was like spreading out the East under his hands, and for a time they were both silent.

Then, as Foveaux considered it, Sara said quietly, 'What news of the *Speedy*, Major?'

She spoke of the vessel which had dropped anchor in the har-

bour the previous morning. As always, the interest of the whole
colony had centred upon the ship's arrival – the passengers and
cargo, letters from home, and news of the war. In Sydney, with the
mail and dispatches still on board, twenty-four hours was still not
too short a time to start the ball of gossip rolling.

'The news, Mrs Maclay?' Foveaux turned to her with the
trace of a smile that might well have been malicious. 'There's no
news that we haven't been expecting for some time past. But the
manner of its arrival is – well – abrupt. The *Speedy* brought out,
among her passengers, Philip Gidley King, whom, you probably
remember, was Governor Phillip's lieutenant, and commander at
Norfolk Island. It's now definitely known that the dispatches Mr
King presented at Government House this morning carried the
Duke of Portland's appointment of him as the next Governor!'

Sara's brows lifted, she did not speak.

'Hunter has been ordered to return to England in the first possible
ship,' Foveaux said.

Sara glanced warningly across her shoulder. A small group of
men were sauntering in from the street.

She said, in a low voice, 'Then they're well aware at home of
what has been going on here? The Colonial Secretary knows that
Hunter has failed to carry out his instructions?'

'Obviously.' Foveaux's voice was also low. They were both quite
certain of their own part in the machine that had wrecked Hunter
– they represented the money-making circle he had not been able
to break.

'It's an attempt, then, to tighten control.' This, from Sara, was
a softly emphatic statement.

'It may be – but they'll soon find out that it will take more
than a new Governor to do that. No Governor on earth will stop
us trading as we wish to. After all, it's *we* who bear the risks – we
produce almost all the food of the colony – it's *our* money that
brings in the few commodities to make life supportable. Things
like this . . .' He flicked the shawl, and the silk rose gracefully in
the air. 'What is the price, might I ask, Mrs Maclay?'

Sara told him gently.

His eyebrows shot up. He let the silken fringe slip from his
fingers. 'That's a great deal of money, ma'am.'

She gave him a provoking smile. 'It cost my husband a great
deal also, Major Foveaux. And then, look . . .' She ran the length
of the shawl through her hands. 'There's not a trace of sea-water
on it. So few of these beautiful things arrive here unstained' – she
looked at him fully – 'that the price of those that survive is necessarily high.'

Suddenly, with a flash of exotic colours, she flung it about her shoulders. 'You see, Major, it's quite perfect.'

'I *do* indeed see, ma'am. But the wearer enhances it beyond all that's fair.'

Sara accepted the compliment smilingly, but unmoved. After four years of such compliments, she was able to judge their commercial value to within a hairsbreadth. She reluctantly let the shawl slip from her shoulders.

'In a way, I hate to let it go. Any woman would lose her heart to it.' She gave a faintly audible sigh. 'Shall I have it wrapped for you, Major?'

'Er . . .' He capitulated before her inquiring gaze. 'Er . . . yes, if you please.'

'I'm sure that it will . . .' Sara paused here. Major Foveaux had not mentioned the lady for whom the shawl was intended, and she had long ago learned that, in business, the customer's private affairs were best left to himself. 'I'm sure you won't regret it,' she finished.

'I hope not, Mrs Maclay,' he answered, a little unhappily, watching anxiously as she handed it over to Clapmore for wrapping. It *had* cost a good deal more than he had expected.

She turned to him again. 'Is there anything else I could show you, Major? I have some ribbons . . . And I've quite exquisite lace . . .'

'No,' he replied hastily. 'Nothing more in that line. But I've a list of provisions.' He fumbled in his pocket and drew out a slip of paper. 'My housekeeper tells me that my stocks of provisions are low – which is nonsense. I bought enough of the last cargo to feed an army, but it's quite unaccountably used up. These convict house-women, they have the run of everything – they've stolen my stocks, of course, and probably traded them for rum. But there's little I can do about it. I can't stand to see a woman flogged . . . I suppose I could send them packing and try others – but, then, they'd more than likely be twice as bad.'

While he talked, Sara had taken the list from his hand, noting with surprise the quantities he had marked.

'This is a large order, Major – with tea at six shillings a pound, and sugar at four shillings.'

He frowned. 'As much as that?'

She regarded him calmly. 'Surely you are not unaware of the prices, Major? After all, you buy your own share of the cargoes, and then help to fix the prices at which they will be re-sold. You also know that my husband is not permitted to under-cut.'

'Well . . .' Foveaux shrugged. 'I'm in the unhappy position of being unable to do without these things, whatever the cost. I can't give my guests too bad an impression of the colony in the beginning. They'll know it all soon enough, won't they, Mrs Maclay?' He gave a low, quiet laugh, as if this were a joke only they themselves shared.

She smiled demurely, seating herself at the desk. 'Then you have friends among the new arrivals in the *Speedy*, Major?'

'Hardly friends, yet, dear lady. Captain Barwell and I met only briefly in London some years ago. He wrote that he was coming here – and of course I was delighted to offer him and his wife hospitality until they can make their own arrangements. Barwell was wounded in the fighting in Holland and seems to be unfit for further active service. He exchanged his last commission for one with the Corps.'

Sara sat still, looking up at him. A chilled sense of wonder had fallen on her; the sun still lay across her shoulders, yet she was cold. At the sound of the name on Foveaux's dry lips, a sense of fear, close to panic, possessed her. She put the hand that held the list firmly on the desk to control its trembling.

'Barwell?' she repeated weakly. 'Did you say Barwell?'

'Why, yes – Richard Barwell. Is it possible you know him?'

She groped wildly in her mind for some of the caution the past years had taught her. But it was suddenly gone. In an instant she was like two women – the one rigidly schooled in discipline and discretion, guarding her tongue and her actions from the gossip-hungry colony, keeping the name of Richard Barwell for ever shut away in the secret places of her heart; the other was the girl she once had been, the impetuous girl who ran away from the Bramfield Rectory because of her love for Richard. Now she must sit and listen to herself wrecking the discretion and the long silence, spilling out a claim to having once known Richard. She knew she could not stop herself; it was not possible for her to let Foveaux go without finding out the truth.

'Barwell – from Kent?' she asked.

'Yes. I believe he and his wife are both from Kent. She is the daughter of Sir Geoffrey Watson. Perhaps you know . . . ?'

'I once knew . . . of both families,' was all she would say.

'Oh – I see.'

The Major made no further comment. There was an unwritten law in the colony – gaining strength each year with the increasing number of convicts whose term of sentence had ended, and who were then entitled to call themselves free men – that the past was never to be spoken of, never to be questioned. A man's past might be guessed at, and spoken of behind his back – but never to his face. This rule was applied to Mrs Maclay in a special degree; she was the wife of the most prosperous of the free settlers, and still, as an ex-convict, she was not received by the women of her own standing. It created a delicate problem when her past returned to her in such a tangible fashion. It was implied, in the pause that fell between them, that he was not welcome to inquire into the circumstances in which she had known Richard Barwell and his wife.

Her eyes moved, first to the paper in her hand, then back to Foveaux's face.

'I would be obliged if you would not mention this discussion to Captain Barwell, Major.' She knew she threw this sop of discretion to her own outraged sense of propriety; this was the gesture of the foolish girl to the wiser woman.

'Of course, ma'am – just as you wish.'

Sara acknowledged his half-bow with a slight nod. Until this moment she had always regarded Foveaux as a rather tiresome, amiable fool. Now, as she looked at him, she saw that his eyes were kindly, and that he was perplexed. Perhaps, she thought, he would keep his knowledge of her acquaintance with Richard Barwell to himself. She wished that instead of standing there with his air of helpless wonder, he would go.

'Could you have the provisions sent as soon as possible, Mrs Maclay?' he asked.

'Immediately, Major.'

He saluted her, and left. He walked with the quick, eager step of a man glad to be on his way.

Sara sat there for a long time, the list lying unattended beside her. Her mind did not yet play with the reason for Richard's coming – why he was here, how long he would stay. All that would come to her later, in the hours of wondering and thinking. The only thing that she could clearly grasp was the fact of him coming, unwished and unbidden. He had come back where she did not want him. Sitting so still in the warm sun, with the everyday noises of the store about her, with Boney clawing at the cage practically above her head, she began to question herself about her feelings for Richard since the day she had married Andrew. Her questioning laid open the fact that Richard had been in her thoughts often in the early days of her marriage, and always there with a sense of soreness and grieving; and then he was with her less frequently as Andrew had learned to match all the desires of her heart and body, and as her children had taken her thoughts for themselves. But the picture she had held of Richard was a distinct one, remote from her own life, and therefore never possibly a part of it. He could never seriously interfere with it, dragging the past behind him like a trail of dust. She had loved him once, and she had believed that her love was finished and done with; it destroyed the confidence she had imagined was hers to consider that when he stood before her again she might find her love not so easily put aside a second time. She was shaken and bewildered to realize that, where Richard was concerned, she could not trust herself.

At last her cold fingers took up the list for attention.

'Mr Clapmore!'

He came hurrying forward. 'Yes, ma'am?' Then he paused. 'Why . . . Mrs Maclay, are you ill? You look . . .'

'I'm perfectly well!' she said sharply. 'Please have this order filled out and sent to Major Foveaux immediately.'

He took the list from her hand, and made to turn away.

'And, Mr Clapmore . . .' She spoke more gently, regretting her sharpness.

'Ma'am?'

'Please send for the chaise. I'm . . . going home now.'

2

Bennett placed the decanter beside Andrew's hand, hovered noiselessly for a few minutes, and then withdrew. Charles Bennett was Andrew's latest acquisition – a luxury in which it pleased him to revel to the full. He knew, as the whole of Sydney seemed to know, that Bennett had once been in the service of a duke, and that he was dismissed for insidious tippling. But that could not be counted beside the fact that he waited on table without a clatter which halted all conversation. Andrew guessed that he had probably been nothing more elevated than an under-footman in His Grace's household, but he had learned to preside over a meal with great aplomb; his services had been highly bid for in the colony.

Tonight, however, Andrew hardly noticed the merits of his manservant. As soon as the door closed he rose from his chair, carrying glass and decanter, and moved to where Sara sat at the opposite end of the table. He filled both their glasses, and then he drew a chair up close to hers.

'What is it, my darling?' As he spoke he took her hand in his own, gazing anxiously into her face. 'You've looked whiter than a ghost ever since I came home.'

She smiled at him with her eyes, half-relieved, yet half-fearful of his sure knowledge of her. 'Dear Andrew – you are never deceived, are you? I've been waiting all day to talk to you.'

She sensed him stiffen with apprehension.

'Yes?' he said. 'What about?'

'About . . .' She hesitated, her gaze dropping to the glass. 'Sara . . .?'

She gathered her resolution about her, and looked at him again.

'Andrew . . . Do you remember me telling you about the Barwells – the family my father was tutor to when he died? Do you remember there was a son with whom I used to have lessons – Richard Barwell?'

His hand tightened over hers. 'Of course, I remember. What of him?'

Sara tried to raise her glass to her lips, and was forced to put it down again, because suddenly her fingers had grown stiff and clumsy.

She said slowly, 'I heard today that Richard Barwell has arrived in Sydney with his wife.'

Andrew leaned towards her. 'Good God! He's here . . . Why?'

'I don't know. Oh, Andrew . . .' she said wretchedly. 'I don't know anything except what Major Foveaux told me – that he arrived with the new Governor in the *Speedy*. And that he had exchanged his commission for one in the Corps.'

'And his wife?'

Her mouth hardened. 'It's as I expected. He married Sir Geoffrey Watson's daughter, Alison.'

'Watson? The man who . . .?'

'The man who charged me with stealing his money,' she finished for him. 'The one who found me that night at The Angel, on the Marsh.'

She put her free hand on top of his, conscious immediately of the warmth. 'What shall I do now?' she whispered. 'What shall I do?'

He sat, his unpowdered head bent over her hand; with the tip of his finger he absently traced a vein. She had a moment of dread that he would chide her for being melodramatic over Richard's sudden appearance. How to tell Andrew that she had once been in love with Richard, and that she was afraid of her own emotions when she saw him again? Andrew, she thought, you wouldn't understand. Not even you would have understanding enough for this. This was the hidden Sara Dane who had given her passionate young love to Sebastian and to Richard Barwell, of Romney. In honesty to herself, and in fairness to Andrew, she did not expect his tolerance to extend to the girlish caprices of a Sara he did not know.

He raised his head, and she watched his face closely for his
expression to change; it came slowly, the strange, preoccupied look
that was a habitual when his mind was working too swiftly for
her to follow its processes. He had the wary and suspicious gaze of
a man whose possessions are threatened. It is my happiness he is
concerned about, she thought. He will try to stop Richard spreading any knowledge he has of my past. The look on Andrew's face
chilled her a little, and still comforted her; it meant that Andrew
was not defeated in the way that she was, without a plan of combat, without even a hope of retreat. He had not climbed to his
present position on the backs of other men without having nourished
his own streak of ruthlessness. His eyes grew bright, until they
glittered; the lines about his mouth deepened by the merest frac-
tion, while he continued to stroke her hand with the tip of his
finger.

'Are you afraid, my darling?' he said.

'Yes . . .' Her voice was not more than a whisper. 'Afraid in
a way I've never been before. They can harm me so much. They
can harm you and the children. Everything you have built up here,
they can tear down with a little talk.'

'Then, by God, they *won't* talk!' Andrew snatched his hand
away from hers and smacked it down on the surface of the table.

'*I* have some say in how matters are run in this colony. Mister
Barwell must learn quickly that you are neither a servant at Bramfield Rectory, nor any longer a convict!'

'Andrew . . .' she breathed. 'What will you do?'

'I don't know what I'll do until I can find out more about him
— why he's here to begin with. He must be vulnerable in some
way — and I must find that way.'

She nodded slowly.

'Every man has his vulnerable point,' Andrew said, after a
pause. 'So I imagine the best way of finding Mister Barwell's is to
go straight to the source of the information. Is he staying at Foveaux's house?'

'Yes.'

'Then . . .' He rose, pushing his chair away regardlessly. 'I
think I must concoct some immediate business with Major
Foveaux.'

'Andrew . . .' She stretched out and touched his sleeve. 'I *am*
afraid. The Barwells can tell the whole story if they choose to
— they can give the colony what it's been waiting to hear for
years.'

He bent and kissed her fully on the lips. 'No one will hurt you while I have any power left to fight them. So don't be afraid, my Sara.'

He went then and left her sitting at the table, staring straight ahead, the untouched glass close to her hand. He had taken some of her fear with him; but the real fear, the fear of her old love for Richard, sat like a spectre beside her, a companion for the hours until Andrew returned.

Above the constant patter of rain against the window, Sara heard Andrew's careful footsteps on the stairs. She sat up in bed, and waited for the door to open; the knob turned softly, and he came in. The candle by the bedside fluttered wildly in the sudden draught.

He closed the door, and walked towards her. 'I hoped you'd try to sleep, Sara. You shouldn't have waited . . . It's very late.'

She leaned forward from the pillows to take hold of his hand. 'There was no possibility of sleep,' she said. 'Tell me . . . what is the news?'

He hoisted himself up to sit on the bed beside her. There were drops of moisture on his head, as if he had stood bareheaded in the rain for some time; in the candlelight his face seemed very sun-tanned and weathered in contrast to the immaculate white frills of his shirt.

'More news than I hoped for,' he said. 'I let Foveaux have slightly the better of me in a deal over some cattle. We shared a bottle of madeira, and he grew – talkative. He knows a great deal more about the Barwells than he was prepared to tell you this morning.'

He burrowed his hand down into the quilt, in the hollow between their two bodies. After a few moments he looked at her again, and he said, 'Among the mail that arrived with the *Speedy* was a letter from a friend of Foveaux, who was in Barwell's regiment – the man who had first introduced them to each other. It appears that the Barwells have had money troubles of one kind and another for some time now. They were all right so long as Sir Geoffrey lived, and while he had the money to keep them generously supplied. But it seems that Mister Barwell and his wife have extravagant tastes, and it wasn't easy for them to cut down their scale of living when the old man lost most of his negotiable fortune.'

'Lost it?' Sara said. 'How?'

'He had money in ships. Two were captured by the French in the channel. And another was lost in the Caribbean. The estate, of course, is entailed, and when he died there wasn't much of his money left for Alison.'

'And so . . . ?' Sara urged quickly.

'And so Captain and Mrs Barwell lived merrily on what was left until it ran out.' Andrew was talking slowly, as if he were enjoying the story he told. 'Barwell found that an officer's pay won't keep a lady of fashion for long – nor does it stretch to the sort of tastes he himself had acquired. At the time Foveaux's correspondent wrote, they had been living with Alison's aunt, Lady Linton, for a year. Apparently this good lady was very attached to Barwell – from all accounts she made a pet of him. But being a woman of sound sense, as well as fashion, she soon realized that Barwell would do nothing for himself while he relied on her for support. Foveaux says she's an extremely shrewd business woman. It set her thinking hard when she heard tales of this fabulous New South Wales – how it's possible to receive pay from the army, and still build up quite a sizeable fortune in other ways. It's Foveaux's private opinion that she sent them out to learn the proper uses of money, before she dies and leaves her own fortune to them.'

'Then they'll stay here indefinitely? They'll take up land?'

Andrew nodded. 'It seems so.'

'Are there children?' Sara was quite unable to keep the edge of sharpness out of her voice as she questioned him.

'None – so far. Foveaux says Mrs Barwell is delicate. Perhaps this climate will make an improvement . . .'

'Hothouse plants are likely to shrivel in such heat!' she retorted.

Andrew smiled at her wryly. 'I had the impression from Foveaux that she was a creature of considerable vivacity and spirit – rather the sort who uses up more energy and strength than she can afford.'

'Then she has changed,' Sara replied shortly. 'Or else Richard has changed her. However . . .' She shrugged, and the corners of her mouth drooped. 'We have more information than we hoped for. Now we must wait and see what develops.'

Andrew leaned towards her; his grip on her hand tightened, urgently.

'This is no time for waiting, Sara!' he said. 'I've already taken steps in the matter.'

She caught her breath. 'What do you mean?'

'Quite simple, my dear. I asked Foveaux to present me to Barwell.'

'Andrew!'

His eyes darkened with a touch of sudden anger. 'I've told you before, Sara, that I don't intend to be intimidated by men such as Richard Barwell. Nor have I the time or patience to wait and see which way he will jump. I *had* to know what his attitude towards you would be.'

'Well?' Sara uttered the word through tight lips.

'Foveaux went to bring him from the drawing-room – his wife had already retired. He came – it seemed to me – very readily. We talked of you – he told me he had already asked Foveaux if he knew what had become of you.'

'*What had become of me!*' she repeated. 'He said it just like that?'

Andrew gave her hand an impatient shake. 'How else could he have said it? For all he knew you might have died in Newgate.'

'Exactly! I might have died in Newgate!' She choked angrily. 'But go on . . . I must hear the rest of this.'

'The rest of it is that I've asked him to bring his wife here to dine with us on Wednesday evening. He accepted – gladly, I thought.'

She fell back against the pillows, staring at him unbelievingly. '*You asked them here!* Andrew, you didn't!'

He let go of her hand and caught her firmly by the shoulders. 'And why not? Don't you see how important it is for him to be willing to bring his wife with him here? He means to be friendly – if you will let him.'

'Oh, but Andrew . . .' she protested. 'Richard and Alison here – so soon! I don't think I can face it – not yet.'

'You *must* face it some time,' he answered sharply. 'Far better to do the facing here, in your own house, where you can control the situation. Remember that by now they know the new Governor very well – they travelled out from England with him. They could be powerful friends, Sara.'

'But Alison will soon know – she probably knows already – that none of the officers' wives visit me, or invite me to visit them. She'll come once, and that will be the end.'

'I shouldn't think that our friend, Foveaux, would leave the Barwells long without that bit of news. But, nevertheless, my invitation was still accepted.'

'And what's more, Sara,' he added, 'before long I'll find some way of making certain that the Barwells want to go on claiming our friendship.'

She half-closed her eyes, lying quite still, and thinking over what he had said. His invitation was for Wednesday – and this was

Monday. Two days in which to school herself to the idea of meeting
and talking to Richard, to discipline her emotions so that Andrew's
discerning eyes would not detect it. And there was the dread of
facing Alison, the slight, dark-haired girl whom she had now and
then glimpsed in the hall at Bramfield. Was two days long enough?
– or would she ever be ready to face Richard? In her mind she
sought about wildly for an excuse to delay this meeting – and she
could find none.

She opened her eyes fully, and found that Andrew was looking
at her unblinkingly. She was grateful for the pressure of his hands
on her shoulders.

'I shall send a message to Julia Ryder in the morning,' she
said. 'If she and James could be here on Wednesday evening . . .'
Her words trailed off as she considered the idea.

3

Julia spread herself comfortably in the easy-chair in the main
guest room at Glenbarr, and unfastened her cloak. She looked
about her carefully; her scrutiny was critical, but finally she nodded
in approval.

'It's a fine house, Sara,' she said. 'You have made it very beautiful. And Andrew . . . Well, Andrew is an incredible man. This
place should suit him well. Are you quite settled now? Are you
happy here?'

Sara gestured towards the windows, where the gardens were
already lost in the dusk. She gave a soft laugh, and reached to
take the other's bonnet.

'You've spent too much time with us in our rooms over the
store, Julia, not to know how grateful we are for the space and
quietness here.'

'I shouldn't regret that time spent in the store, if I were you, my
dear,' Julia replied briskly, stretching her feet towards a low stool.
'Young people shouldn't have all the comfort they want immediately – it leaves nothing to work for, and that isn't good. You've
made a handsome profit from the store – and running it has taught
you some valuable lessons.' Suddenly she looked inquiringly at Sara.
'And so far as I can see you've come to no harm by it, have you?'

'Oh, I don't regret it,' Sara said, perching on the edge of the bed.
'But I do find that experiences that are good for one are always
much better when they're over. I still go to the store every morning, and I'm glad to do it. But it is a comfort to have this peaceful, quiet house waiting for me when I return to the midday
meal.'

As she talked she was taking in the changes in Julia's appearance since she had last seen her at Christmas time. At Christmas, Sara and Andrew had taken the three children to the Ryders' at Parramatta for four days. This had been in the nature of a farewell visit to Ellen and Charles, who were both leaving for England in the next ship. Ellen had been enrolled in a young ladies' seminary at Bath, and Charles, showing little of his father's aptitude for farming, but a passionate worship of Admiral Nelson, was to join the Navy. Since Christmas, Sara thought, Julia's face had become worn and thin; it showed the signs of exhaustion and pallor which were the legacy of the long, hot summer. Her movements, too, seemed slower, although the calm tones of her voice were unchanged. There was much grey in her hair now.

Julia broke in on her thoughts.

'Come, now, Sara! You haven't brought me all this way just to be philosophical. What is it? Your note told me nothing of importance. So I packed and came – all on faith!'

Then she gestured impatiently. 'I hope your request that I bring a dinner gown means that you're having some grand entertainment. I'm starving for some diversion.'

'Dear Julia!' Sara said warmly. 'You're always the same. I wonder how many times I've come to you to have my problems sorted out. Do you remember the first time – when we were coming out in the *Georgette*?'

'Yes – and very sound advice I gave you on that occasion, madam.' Julia's brows drew together. 'So it's a problem again, is it? Well?'

Sara took a deep breath. 'This is going to take quite a time, Julia, because I mean to tell you what no one but myself and Richard Barwell knows.'

'Barwell . . . Barwell? Didn't I hear that someone of that name arrived with the new Governor in the *Speedy*? He's married to a baronet's daughter – is that right?'

'How fast news travels!' Sara gave a little laugh. 'Yes, Alison Barwell is a baronet's daughter. Think of it, Julia – a real lady for the colony to fuss over, now. The niece of a countess! What a scramble there'll be to entertain her! Her dress and manners will all be faithfully copied – because, despite all the sudden riches, New South Wales is rather short of genuine ladies, isn't it?'

Julia ignored the tone of the remark. She said with quick annoyance, 'Enough of this, Sara! Come to the point!'

'Well, then . . .'

Sara edged back on the chest and began to talk. The dusk grew deeper in the unlighted room, and a faint swirling sea-mist rolled up from the harbour. She kept her eyes fixed on Julia's face, on which the glow from the fire in the grate played gently. She found it surprisingly easy to speak truthfully to the other woman, older and wiser, and someone to be trusted with the story of her life with drunken Sebastian Dane, in Rye, and at Bramfield Rectory. She told the true reason for her flight across the Marsh on that cold spring night.

'We *did* love each other! I'm sure of that, even though we were hardly more than children. But all the circumstances against us were too much for Richard. I blamed him, and perhaps I shouldn't. After all, *I* had nothing to lose – he might have lost everything.'

'Andrew knows nothing of this?' Julia asked. 'About your feelings for Richard Barwell?'

'He knows that I worked for a time at the Rectory. But I have never told him that I was in love with Richard. Why should I tell him that? When I married Andrew I had no thought of ever seeing Richard again. It was as if he were dead!'

After a moment Julia said drily, 'But now he's here. And Andrew has forced a meeting.'

'Yes,' Sara answered wretchedly. 'You know what Andrew is – he believes in taking the initiative. I knew myself that the meeting must come some time – but this has come too soon. I have only until tomorrow night. Julia . . . I may do anything – disgrace myself, or let Andrew see . . .'

'Nonsense!' Julia retorted. 'You of all people, can't be telling me that you don't know how to take a grip on yourself. You've made it your business, ever since you came to the colony, to see that no one should ever have cause for gossip about you. Surely Richard Barwell can't shake your composure after all this time?'

Sara looked unhappily away. 'How can I tell what he'll do? Once before I made a fool of myself over Richard – who's to say I won't do it again? Even knowing all his faults and weaknesses as well as I did, I still loved him. What if it should be the same way now?'

'Sara! Sara! It won't be the same way – unless you let it.'

'But Richard . . .'

'You must forget that Richard was ever anything but your father's pupil. Stop eating your heart out for something you never could have. And, Sara,' Julia's voice was sharp, 'try to remember that your husband is one whom many women in the colony envy you.'

Sara rose stiffly, and bent close to the fire to light a taper. She put it carefully to the two candles on the mantelshelf, watching them as the wicks sprang into life. Then she blew softly on the burning taper; the smell of the smoke was pungent in her nostrils.

And suddenly, as if she were too weary to do anything else, she rested her forehead against her two hands clamped before her on the shelf.

'If only he hadn't come, Julia!' she whispered, staring down into the fire. 'Oh, why did he have to come?'

4

The crunching of the carriage wheels on the short drive outside brought Andrew to his feet. Sara, glancing at him, also rose, though more slowly. The tension communicated itself to Julia and her husband. James fiddled with his watch, compared it with the little French clock, and shut it again with a click.

They could hear Bennett's hurrying footsteps in the hall, then a low murmur of voices, and again the sound of footsteps approaching the drawing-room. The door was thrown open with a flourish more suited to London than to this raw, colonial town.

'Captain and Mrs Barwell!'

Sara advanced only a step. In spite of having schooled herself, her glance went immediately to Richard. He stood there, in the new uniform of the New South Wales Corps, a smile on his lips, and his eyes wearing a questioning look. The last time she had seen him, he had been standing unhappily in the hall at Bramfield, at the end of his Christmas leave; this evening there was a loose, careless elegance about him that was wholly lacking then.

His face was thinner and more handsome than she remembered it; a white scar, no thicker than a strand of cotton, ran across his forehead, and his hair was streaked with grey where it furrowed into the scalp. She saw at once that he held that indefinable air of confidence and ease of a man who is accustomed to a considerable success with women. She guessed that he had, by this stage in his career, penetrated far into the gay, fashionable world of which he had dreamed naïvely during his dull boyhood on the Romney Marsh. Even with the new coating of veneer, she didn't find it difficult to recognize the Richard Barwell she had once known – he was standing there with a smile for her like a small boy's, his eyes pleading for her forgiveness, and begging to be admitted to her favour again. And at the same time, she felt, he was quite certain that she would not resist him.

She looked then at Alison. Alison was also smiling – a faint, prepared smile. She wore a fabulous gown of kingfisher blue satin, which offset her white skin and dark hair. Beside Richard's height, she seemed incredibly tiny; her small hand rested possessively on his arm. Sara was struck by her appearance – not beautiful, she thought – but Alison had fine eyes, and black eyebrows that were drawn on her forehead like wings. She was slim and erect, and she, like Richard, carried the air of a fashionable world about her.

Sara halted her speculation about these two. She realized now that she had hesitated too long, and she hurried forward with a smile she hoped was welcoming.

'Good evening, Mrs Barwell,' she said, extending her hand.

Alison responded in a calm, level voice. Sara turned to give her hand to Richard.

He took it, bowing over it, and seemed quite unconscious that he held it too tightly.

'My dear Sara – what a pleasure it is to see you again !'

He watched the faint flush mount in her cheeks. He had not intentionally set about to make her angry, but his memory of her told him that in such a situation her pride would be ready to be pricked by almost any remark. He studied her carefully. The years in this southern climate had left their mark; her skin had a darker shade than he remembered, and the sun seemed to have bleached her hair to a colour that was near white in the candlelight. But the promise of great beauty he had seen at Bramfield had been fulfilled beyond his expectations. He had forgotten how tall she was, and the way she had of looking unwaveringly into one's eyes when she spoke. Her gown was the colour of pale jade, and the crusted, gold embroidery on the tight bodice and sleeves told him that it had come from the East. He was anxious to take in every detail of her appearance – to form his own opinion of this woman whose story was now part and parcel of the colony's history. Ready gossip gave her as being ambitious, hard, and grasping; but he had not heard it said that she was anything other than an excellent wife and mother, and that her children openly adored her. He knew, by now, that she had profitably run a farm as well as the store during her husband's absence in the *Thistle*, and he was well familiar with the tale of her having fought off a gang of convicts during an outbreak on the Hawkesbury – of her killing, with a dagger, one of them who had molested her. A smile of admiration spread over his face. He recalled momentarily the young, emotional Sara he had known – and here she was now, the mistress of the best the colony could boast of. All achieved, so gossip said, by a husband even harder and more ambitious than herself. It made curious hearing, this story of the girl who had once joyfully walked and idled away a summer's evening with him along the dykes of the Romney Marsh. She was strange and beautiful. In the years since his marriage, Richard had made his way into many of the great houses of London, and he had found favour in the eyes of many beautiful and distinguished women; yet he was conscious that in all that time no woman had ever looked at him like this, and no other woman had ever managed to disconcert him as Sara did now.

She twisted her hand in his, and broke away from his clasp. 'Indeed, Richard, I'm very glad to see you also.'

Then she turned to present her husband to Alison.

To sit working at the square of tapestry clamped in its frame had always brought Sara calm and relaxation, but now, as she threaded her needle in and out of the canvas, she noticed that her hands still trembled. The interminable meal was finished, and a glance at the French clock told her that Andrew was holding the men an unusually long time over the port. Sitting opposite her, Julia and Alison kept up a conversation – mostly they talked of the items of news that had been fresh when the Barwells left London. Sara was aware that she herself made an occasional contribution, but she gave them little heed. Her mind was back with Richard.

The hour just passed had been dreadful beyond anything for which she had prepared herself. It was a slow nightmare, a struggle to hold herself together in the face of an emotion as strong as any she had ever known before. Throughout the meal Richard had laughed and talked, entertaining and amusing them with his quips and stories, told with a light, skilful touch. And for every minute he had sat there, fingering the excellent wine, drawing the threads of conversation always into his own hands, she felt her resolution ebbing. It was as if he had stretched out his hands and taken her bodily to him. She felt that she might go on endlessly telling herself that Richard was weak, Richard merely played at life while he waited for its best things to fall into his lap, Richard had not one jot of the worth of Andrew – and yet, for all that, he could command her attention as easily now as he had done in the Bramfield days. She was still, she confessed, the girl who had explored the Marsh dykes with him, pale-coloured with the new green of spring; she was the girl who was utterly fascinated by him, obedient to his will, eager to give in to his wishes. An insect drawn by a brilliant light – she knew she was that. Never mind that the light might be transitory and false; it was there, in front of her.

It had been madness to have believed all these years that Richard

could be forgotten at will. Andrew had taken part of her love, and
all of her devotion and loyalty, but the core of her had always been
Richard's. And he had returned now to lay claim to it, just as if
there had been no separation. She was ashamed and fearful, angry
with him that he had revealed her own weakness to her. *He* knew
it, she told herself – under the lightness and the laughter. Richard
knew well that she was again his willing fool, the eager Sara who
had smiled for him when she was bidden, and had been sad when
he was sad.

'Curse you, Richard!' she whispered, under her breath. 'I still
love you.'

She stitched away at the tapestry, half-hearing the conversation.
Thank God for Julia, she thought, feeling truly grateful for the
presence of the elder woman who held the situation as steady as a
rock, covering her own silence, making bearable this awful time
until Andrew should return to support her. Sudden tears pricked
the back of her eyes; she would gladly have cried tears of rage and
dismay at the turn affairs had taken. It sickened her to recall that
four days ago she had imagined Richard Barwell was safely back
in the past.

Even bound up as she was in her own turmoil, she was conscious that Alison had risen and was coming towards her. She
knew the piece of tapestry was going to be inspected, and she
offered it reluctantly.

Alison looked at it, head tilted to the side.

'Oh, but this is quite beautiful, Mrs Maclay!' she said at last.
'And how swiftly you work!'

Sara's temper swelled at the platitude, but she managed a stiff
smile.

'Oh, yes,' she said. 'I've always worked at speed. Perhaps you
don't remember that I was once employed in a London dressmaking establishment?'

Alison turned away, with a sharp swish of her satin, and Sara
imagined she caught a flicker of annoyance cross her face; she
paced the length of the room, pausing before the open keyboard of
the piano. Behind her back, Sara looked over at Julia and deliberately winked. Julia's eyebrows shot up, and then she frowned, shaking her head.

Sara addressed Alison gently. 'Perhaps we can persuade you to
play for us, Mrs Barwell? Have you anything of Beethoven's?
People arriving in the colony speak of him – but it's a matter of
great regret to me that we never hear his work performed.'

'Beethoven is known to be a great admirer of Bonaparte,' Alison returned rigidly. 'I hardly consider it patriotic to encourage the work of such people.'

'Just as you wish, of course,' Sara said, determined to remain unsnubbed.

Alison sat down at the piano. She chose to play Mozart, confidently, and with unmistakable enjoyment. Watching her, Sara wondered what she would do to pass the time in this place, where there were never enough books, and no music at all, where people were mostly too busy making money to have time for the niceties of the cultivated mind. She would want a piano, of course, and Richard would find that shipping a piano from England was an expensive and doubtful business. It would, more than likely, be smashed to splinters during the voyage. But Sara, watch.ng the other's determined little face, felt that before long there would be a piano on the way.

Alison was determined, certainly, Sara decided, watching the slightly swaying figure. She was determined and intelligent – but away from her husband's presence she had changed visibly. During dinner she had been rather gay, amusing at times, and self-possessed, but here she made it plain that she was not at ease in the completely strange company in which she found herself. She was aloof and a little critical; she was more noticeably fragile now – like a painting in her exotic blue gown, a slight child-like figure without physical strength of any kind. Andrew had reported that Alison had suffered terribly from sea-sickness during the voyage, and Sara wondered how this slender, white-skinned woman would live through the long months of the summer.

The music finished, and Alison withdrew her hands from the keyboard.

'Charming!' Sara said. 'Thank you, indeed, Mrs Barwell! Mozart is delightful – though I have always preferred Bach.'

Alison nodded absently, and began to pick out the air-notes of a Bach fugue. The sounds scarcely reached the other end of the room. 'You,' she said, looking up, 'play, of course, Mrs Maclay?'

'Unfortunately, no,' Sara replied lightly, turning the tapestry-frame to examine the back of her work. 'I often think it's just as well my children are all boys – I, alas, have no accomplishments to pass on to a daughter.'

She carefully selected another length of silk from her sewing-basket. 'I understand you and Richard have no children yet, Mrs Barwell?'

Alison's lips tightened as she shook her head. The kingfisher

satin stirred, and seemed to quiver. She rose stiffly from the piano.
But when she began to walk slowly down the length of the room,
she was, in every inch of her small figure, Sir Geoffrey's daughter,
poised, and sure of herself, sure that she was above the vulgar
taunts of a woman who had once been a servant and a convict. She
smiled charmingly at Sara, graciously ignoring the vulgarity, and
seated herself on the sofa beside her. Sara recalled her remark to
Julia that the colony suffered from the lack of real ladies; here,
she thought, was one who would be a match for every situation.

Julia, desperately uncomfortable, was speaking, saying the first
thing that came into her head.

'I'm afraid you'll find it very dull here, after London, Mrs
Barwell. There are so few people . . . and so little to do.'

Alison's eyebrows lifted at that. 'On the contrary, Mrs Ryder.
I don't imagine that I shall find it dull. My husband intends to
farm, and I know I'll be most interested in that.'

Sara paused at her work, laying it aside. She glanced at Alison;
against her will she was moved to a kind of pity over what she had
heard. In all her life, this gentle creature had probably never
done anything more arduous than make herself pretty for a party;
she had come straight from a world of ease and gaiety, and she
was as ignorant as a child of what lay ahead of her. Could she
possibly have any notion, Sara wondered, what sort the country beyond Sydney was, what it was like to handle sullen, reluctant convict women, or see the envy and hatred in a man's eyes, as he
raised them from the garden-patch where he was digging? Did she
know that the natives sometimes murdered and robbed, and the
floods carried away the crops, and fires swept through the dry
bush, which was in itself a sly enemy? She talked of farming as if
this were Kent or Sussex, and that Rye were close by, comforting
and familiar. She faced her new life with the confident, innocent
air of one who had only a four-day knowledge of the colony's
hardships. Her talk had implied that she hoped desperately that
farming would not bore her; clearly, she had never thought of it as
being dangerous.

Sara said tentatively – not to Alison as Richard's wife, but to
a woman who was wholly ignorant of the difficulties she faced, 'I
sincerely hope that when you are ready to begin farming you will
allow me to help you a little. Andrew and I have farmed all the
time since we were married. We were the first settlers in the Hawkesbury – and I think I know as well as most men in this colony what
is likely to be needed.'

Alison's expression changed, hardening a little; she opened her mouth to reply, and then broke off, looking towards the door, which Andrew threw open noisily. She half-rose at the sight of her husband.

Instantly Sara knew that something more than social pleasantries had detained the men over their port. On Andrew's face she recognized an expression he wore whenever something happened to put him in a high good humour. James Ryder was grave and non-committal. As for Richard . . . Sara couldn't read Richard's face at all. He was flushed; his eyes were bright, and moved nervously round the room. He looked like a man who has attempted something of which he is a little afraid.

The little French clock chimed off five quarter-hours, and still the Maclays' guests stayed on. Sara had the impression that Alison would gladly have left, but she waited patiently on her husband's whim. A coldish sea-fog pressed against the windows, but the fire was banked high, and the curtains of gold silk made a false sunshine within the room.

Richard and Alison went to the piano together, and, to her accompaniment, he sang some of the light, sentimental ballads which were going the rounds of the London drawing-rooms. He seemed to have shed his air of disquiet; he was elegant now, and casual. He had a charming, light, baritone, which he had obviously used many times to considerable effect. Watching him, listening to him, Sara could well imagine how he had suited the extravagant, spirited personality which gossip ascribed to Lady Linton. He would have blended with the London of Lady Linton perfectly – Richard, with his jagged scar, worn like a medal for courage; his reputation as an expert with the rapier, and a matchless horseman; his ability to charm a woman – any woman – when it pleased him. This was the kind of man London hostesses always drew about them.

She recovered her sense of humour enough to smile wryly over the picture he made against the gold curtains, and to reflect that gifts of Richard's order would be sadly wasted in such a place as this.

In the last hour since the return of the men to the drawing-room, Sara had calmed herself considerably. She was better able now to sum up the situation, and she was pretty certain, by this time, what sort of relationship existed between Alison and Richard. At her husband's entrance, a mood of gaiety had come upon Alison. She was never still, stirring, twisting, and laughing in an endeavour to hold his attention. She was so easily satisfied – a smile, a nod from Richard was all she required. It angered Sara to see how absently, how nonchalantly he bestowed these light caresses upon his wife, as if she were a child whose desires were never complex or difficult to gratify.

Sara recalled the face of that young girl who had visited Bramfield so eagerly all those years ago – the same pale, determined face now laughingly turned to Richard's, as he came to the end of a rather risqué song. Alison had loved him then with a child's unsubtle passion, and her father had bought him for her, with the lure of a world of which he dreamed. She still clutched her prize as uncertainly as if it had been in her hands no more than an hour.

But when Richard's gaze left his wife, her face dropped back into lines that Sara was beginning to note were habitual. The kingfisher satin became only the bright plumage of a nervous, fluttering bird. Alison is ill, Sara thought – and weary! Her talk of interesting herself in farming was merely to cover her bewilderment over this new life to which Richard had brought her. She didn't dare to stop talking or laughing, in case it gave him a chance to notice that her fine, baby skin was beginning to stretch tightly over her face, and that there were lines about her mouth. Sara was appalled by the thought that suddenly struck her. Alison was afraid! She was afraid that Richard might tire of her!

She watched as Alison ran a finger swiftly along the keyboard, and she said, laughingly, 'Now, Richard – *my* song.'

He glanced at her, an absent, indulgent gaze that did not even see her. 'Certainly, my love.'

He turned and looked directly at Sara as he waited for Alison's introduction.

'*Drink to me only with thine eyes . . .*'

Sara felt herself tense, and then grew cold. Only Richard could do this, she thought, angrily. Only he could sing for another woman a song that belonged to his wife – sing it, and not care what he was doing.

It seemed that every eye in the room must have followed his. Her cheeks burned with shame and rage, and the guilt of her unwilling love.

Sara laid down her hairbrush and listened to the last words between her husband and James Ryder on the landing.

Andrew came noisily into the candle-lit bedroom; his hair was awry, and there hung about him an air of triumph and elation which he so often had at the end of a successful business deal.

He came directly to her, making a place on the littered dressing-table for the candlestick he carried. And then he stooped to kiss her forehead. She sensed the excitement in the roughness of his hands against her shoulders.

He laughed down at her. 'A successful evening, my darling.'

She avoided his eyes. 'A successful evening? I . . . Do you truly believe it *was* successful?'

'Well, they *came*, didn't they? No last-minute, lady-like in-disposition from Alison – which is what I honestly expected. And the dinner was not to be sneered at. They won't get food to better it at any other table in the colony. And the wines . . . Not many people in London itself could offer them wines as good as they drank here tonight.'

He gestured flamboyantly. 'But even had the food been foul, and the wine undrinkable, I think it would hardly have mat-tered.'

Looking up at him, she said slowly, 'Andrew . . . what do you mean?'

He smiled. His smile was too rakish and too mischievous for Sara's peace.

'We've routed them, Sara! Or better, we've captured them! Richard Barwell has committed himself into my hands just about as neatly as he could possibly have done. I'm lending him enough money to buy the Hydes' farm that's up for sale, and to build a house here in Sydney.'

She sprang to her feet.

'You're *what!*'

She waved away his attempt to answer, pacing to the foot of the bed, and back again. For a few seconds the only sound in the room was the swish of her loose robe, and the soft crackle of the fire.

Then she turned to face him. Her voice was low, with the tight control of anger.

'Have you gone suddenly mad, Andrew? *Lend him money!* My God! Why do you think they were forced to come out here? I'll tell you why – *because the pair of them have never been able to save a penny piece in their lives!* Lady Linton is tired of keeping them on velvet cushions. They've been living fabulously. What do you think that gown Alison wore cost? And did Richard look as if he were turned out with an eye to economy?' She flung her hands wide, in a gesture of contempt. 'I tell you lending money to them is simply throwing it away!'

She began to pace again. 'What sort of farmer will Richard

C.G.O.–E

make, do you suppose?' Her back was towards him, and her long
hair hung about her shoulders. 'Hopeless! He may be a pretty
horseman, and a brave soldier, but I'll wager my soul he doesn't
know a hoe from a spade!'

'There'll be an overseer to manage the farm.'

'An overseer!' Sara swung round fiercely. 'Good God! And
will that fashionable pair disport themselves in Sydney on the
money a farm is presumed to bring in? Do they *know* what it's
like to begin farming? Do they know how we started at Kintyre?
Well . . . you may bid goodbye to your money. Once it's in
Richard's free and generous hand, that's the last you'll see of
it!'

There was a silence after her outburst. Then Andrew said, 'Come
here, Sara!'

She was unwilling, but she came because he spoke quietly and
purposefully. He looked down into her flushed and angry face;
he saw the tight arrogance of her mouth, and her heaving breasts
under her nightgown.

'Listen to me, my Sara,' he said.

She raised her eyes, and he thought, for a moment, there was
the trembling brightness of tears in them.

'Have you thought what the money we lend to Richard Barwell
will bring back to us?'

'I know well enough what it will bring,' she retorted. 'When
Richard finally realizes that he can't make a farm pay, you'll discover you've thrown away good money for an unimproved piece
of land. And don't imagine for one second that once the Sydney
house is built you'll ever get them out of it. People of their sort can
sleep happily in their beds with a howling multitude outside their
windows. Shame won't drive them out – and they won't leave until
they have somewhere better to go. *I* know their sort uncommonly
well – do you forget that my father escaped the debtors' prison by
only a few hours?'

'All this is true enough, Sara,' he said patiently. 'But aren't
you calculating only the face value of the money?'

'What other value has it?' she demanded.

He laughed. 'Woman, where is your heart! No wonder they
tell me you managed the business with the coolness of an iceberg
while I was away!'

'Andrew, stop playing with me! Tell me what you've done!'

'I've bought you Alison Barwell's friendship. I've bought you a
past, and a well-born friend.' He was speaking to her as gently as
he would have spoken to one of his children if they needed an

explanation of a difficult situation. 'You see what this means, don't you? It only needs Alison Barwell to call you "Sara" once in public – and you'll have every wretched female in the place fawning over you.'

Her hands dropped down limply by her sides. He saw the flame of colour leave her cheeks, and they became pinched and ashen; he looked at her pale, still lips, and for a moment he was afraid.

'Have I done wrong, my darling? Is it wrong to want to see you in a place you should have had all these years? A woman shouldn't live as you have done – shut off from other women.'

'I haven't *needed* other women!' she declared miserably. 'I don't want them!'

'That may be so. But our children will grow up, and *they'll* feel the absence of the women you ought to have about you, Sara.'

She lowered her head for a few moments, and when at last she raised it, the tears were rolling unchecked down her face.

'But Alison . . .' she whispered. 'She'll never do it. She won't want me . . .'

He brushed her protest aside. 'Alison will do as her husband says – she'll do anything at all for the sake of pleasing him. And they need money – they need it badly if they're ever going to live at anything approaching the style to which they're accustomed. Alison is no different to any other woman in love with a man she's not sure of. She'd rather die than let Richard see her in a gown that didn't dazzle him. When a woman is as much in love as all that – and frightened – there's very little she won't do.'

'You saw that – in Alison?'

'Only a fool could have missed it,' he answered shortly. 'When I recognized it, I knew I had my greatest chance of success. Richard himself would have been easy enough, because for all his airs of worldly knowledge, he's gullible – and greedy. Alison was a different matter. There are some things that just can't be bought, and I feared her co-operation might be one of them. But a woman in love is vulnerable to an extraordinary degree. She's vain. She couldn't bear the thought of living and dressing in any other way than as the soft, precious creature that Richard married. She needs servants around her – and all her accustomed comforts. Do you imagine she'll let the sun touch that lily-white skin? Or will she go outdoors when the hot winds come? Not Alison! Not if she can find a way to avoid it!

'Believe me, Sara,' he said, placing his finger gently under her chin. 'Alison loves her husband desperately. And in face of that, she has no pride, no defence -- nothing. She'll do as Richard says. I'm certain of that.'

He folded his arms about her, rocking her quietly, feeling the sobs shaking her body. With his lips pressed lightly against her forehead, he murmured, 'And I don't give a damn who suffers if in some way you can be made happier, my darling.'

3

The full light of the autumn afternoon was dying on the harbour. The wooded shores of the distant promontories seemed to glide farther back, merging into the darker green of the high ground behind. On the west side of the bay the shadows crept gradually out from the brown rocks, making the water appear thick and oily. Beyond the shelter of the Maclays' own bay, they could see the catspaws of wind darkening the surface. Out there the colour was the particular cold, hard blue of the Pacific in autumn. Sara identified two specks a long way off as native skiffs heading in the direction of the settlement. She watched them for a long time, her fingers tightly hooked in Duncan's belt to prevent him standing up and rocking the boat. Her dreaming gaze saw the two black figures grow larger and more distinct, until an exclamation of triumph from David brought her attention back.

'Mama, look! Another one!'

He held aloft on one end of his line a small fish, and when he was sure his mother had carefully noted and admired it, he pulled out the hook, with a gesture that was meant to appear as nonchalant as those of Ted, the boatman. He tossed it alongside his afternoon's catch, three others, lying in the bottom of the boat.

Sara smiled gaily at him. 'You'll be able to have them for breakfast, darling -- you and Duncan.'

Duncan twisted his face round to look at her. He had impudent blue eyes, bolder even than Andrew's, and young as he was, he had a supreme sureness about life.

'Won't Sebastian have some also, Mama?'

She shook her head. 'Not Sebastian -- he's too little yet.'

Duncan considered that. Then he said, 'How long will it take Sebastian to grow up?'

'Oh . . . I suppose as long as it's taken you,' Sara answered cautiously.

He ran a hand that smelled strongly of fish through his fair hair, and turned away, apparently satisfied.

'Ted!'

The boatman looked over his shoulder at his mistress.

'Ma'am?'

'I think we must put in. It's growing cold. The wind has changed — it's coming off that point now.'

Ted touched the shapeless cap he wore, and quickly drew in his line. He drew in David's also, keeping the child's four fish separate from his own pile, and complimenting him, in his rough, good-natured voice, on his catch. Ted O'Malley had arrived in the colony after the 1798 rebellion in Ireland. He was a Cork fisherman, and a man of such mild serenity that Sara often wondered what attraction rebellion could possibly have had for him. He had once mentioned to her that he had two young sons of his own; sometimes it saddened her to see his gentle devotion to David and Duncan.

With swift strokes he began to pull towards the Maclays' small beach, lying below the sharp drop of the wood. Farther along the bay, through the trees, they could see the roof of Glenbarr. It had a solid comfort about it, that roof; it had a look of permanency which was beginning to appear in Sydney's new buildings. The land on this side of the bay was steep and rocky, useless for farming, and, Sara thought privately, useless for the landscaped terraces Andrew talked of. It was thickly wooded, and the beach itself was merely a narrow shelf of pale sand breaking the irregular line of rocks.

David, from his seat in the stern, suddenly pointed.

'Look, Mama, there's someone on the beach! A gentleman!'

Still holding Duncan, Sara twisted to look towards the little beach. At first she could see nothing — only the whitish trunks of the eucalypts, and the rocks. And then, close to the path leading to the house, she picked him out, a tall, languid figure, sitting, knees drawn up to his chin, on a flat-topped boulder. As she watched, he raised his arm and waved. Slowly she put up her hand in a faint response.

'Who is it, Mama?'

'I think . . . it's Captain Barwell, David.'

David examined the distant figure with interest. 'The one who came to dinner last night? The one who was wounded in the war?'

Sara nodded absently.

'Will he tell us about the fighting, do you think, Mama?'

'I expect so, David . . . some time . . . if you ask him politely.

But not now. He's only been in the colony a few days, and perhaps he's rather tired of people asking him about the fighting.'

'Did he fight against Napoleon, Mama?'

'No – at the time Captain Barwell was wounded Napoleon wasn't in charge of the fighting. Not many people had even heard of him then.'

'Oh . . .' David's interest faded. He looked down at the fish at his feet, and began then to compare the size of his catch to Ted's pile lying beside it. By the time the boat scraped the sand, he had decided that he had done quite a good afternoon's work.

Richard was waiting at the water's edge. He grinned cheerfully at Sara and the boys, as he bent his back to help Ted drag the boat clear of the tide-mark.

'I came for a leisurely afternoon call,' he said, lifting Duncan out of his seat and placing him down on the dry sand. 'They told me you were all out fishing, so I made my way down here. I've been sitting on that rock for the past hour. It reminded me of us two as children to see you in a boat again, Sara.'

'I find myself in a boat frequently these days,' she answered lamely. 'The boys . . .'

He looked at her two sons, smiling, and holding out his hand. 'I'm indeed happy to make your acquaintance, David – and yours, Duncan. I used to know your mama a long time ago, before she came here to New South Wales.'

Over David's head he looked at Sara. 'Yes . . . a long time ago.'

'We have a baby brother,' Duncan announced firmly. 'He sleeps all the time. And he can't talk yet.'

'Sebastian,' Sara murmured, in explanation. 'He is so dark in contrast to these two. My father's kind of darkness. It seemed right, somehow, that I should call him Sebastian.'

'Your father would be very happy about that, Sara. Especially if he grows up as these two have. Do you remember how your father . . .' Richard broke off, shrugging. 'Oh, well, that's all in the past.'

He glanced down at the two children, and then at Sara. 'I expect you'll want to go back to the house now.'

She hesitated. Richard was offering her an escape from him, but she knew he didn't want her to accept it.

She touched David's shoulder. 'Take Duncan, and go with Ted. Ask him to clean the fish for your breakfast. You can stay and watch how he does it.'

David smiled his farewell to her, and less certainly to Richard.

He took his brother by the hand, and they walked to where Ted was waiting, loaded with the sack of fish, his coiled lines, and a tin of bait. He motioned them to precede him; he touched his cap to Sara and Richard, and turned towards the path.

They watched them go, Ted's stocky, bent figure hovering protectively above the children.

'Well now, Master David,' they heard him say, 'the next foine mornin' . . .'

As the three made their way along the winding, sloping path between the trees, the children's clear voices echoed back sharply, Duncan's shrill and dominating his brother's. Ted's deep, soft brogue was lost beneath it.

They vanished from sight among the trees, and finally went beyond earshot. The little bay was abruptly silent; it was a sombre place now that all sound had left it. The sun was almost gone; there were long shadows on the water. The wind that touched Sara's cheek was cool.

Richard turned to her slowly.

'Perhaps I was wrong to come to you like this. But I couldn't stay away any longer.'

She looked, not at him, but across the bay, to the dark colours of the opposite rocky shore. 'You *were* wrong to come. It was . . . unwise.' She faced him reluctantly. 'You have a great deal to learn of our life here. The town is like a village – and gossip is scarce and eagerly sought. Ted will say nothing, because he is devoted to me . . . but the servants in the house . . .'

He checked her with a touch on the arm. 'Can this be Sara I hear talking? How much you've changed! All this caution and prudence! Ah, my dear, the way you used to mock my mother's primness, and shame me into some defiance of it myself! Your father would be astonished to hear you now.'

'Defiance of convention is only for those who can afford it!' she answered shortly. '*I* can't!'

He shrugged. 'That may be – but even gossips can't make anything much of the meeting between two old friends.'

He took her arm, edging her towards the rock where he had been sitting.

'You'll sit awhile, surely? I'll only keep you a few minutes. And then we'll go back to the house – and cheat Sydney gossip of a tit-bit!'

He was smiling slightly as he spoke, and Sara was disarmed. She sat down on the rock beside him, spreading the skirt of the plain, salt-water stained gown which she wore, and patting into some order her wind-tossed hair.

The silence in the bay was so deep that almost unconsciously they had lowered their voices; they were aware of the slap of the small waves against the wet sand, and the occasional rustle of the trees behind them. Yet they were engulfed in a silence of waiting and expectancy.

Quietly, without fuss, Richard placed his hand over hers, lying still on the rock. 'I had to see you, Sara,' he said simply.

When she didn't answer, he went on :

'Last night was unbearable. You were so close, and yet I couldn't talk with you. You wouldn't look at me either. You sat at the head of a table – as beautiful as any woman I've ever seen – but cold.'

His hand tightened on hers. 'And now you look like a girl again – the Sara Dane I remember !' Suddenly his hands were on her shoulders, and he swung her round to face him. 'I nearly went crazy with joy to see you in that boat.' His eyes went to her untidy curls. 'I longed to rush to you and do as Sebastian always did . . . Do you remember how he used to pull your hair free. It blew in the wind, and then you pretended to be angry. *That* was what I wanted to see. I wanted the Sara who was dead to come back to life again.'

He was searching her face in a bewildered way.

'But your children made it all unreal,' he said quietly. 'They spoiled my fantasy – they reminded me too much that you have gone far beyond the girl I remember.'

She twisted her body abruptly, jerking free of his hold, and covered her face with her hands.

'Richard . . . I beg you ! Please don't talk of this any more. You *shouldn't* have come ! And I haven't the strength to send you away.'

'Send me away? Why *should* you send me away? Surely after all these years we have the right to talk with each other – to talk as freely as we please, not as convention dictates.'

She stiffened, and when she spoke there was an edge to her voice. 'Don't talk of "all these years" as if they really meant something to you, Richard. You can't pretend that you've spared me much thought since I left Bramfield.'

'Sara ! I deny that – *completely* ! You couldn't know how much you've been in my thoughts. All these years, believe me, you have meant a very great deal to me.'

There was a silence between them, and then he said, 'You're thinking I didn't care about your conviction. But, damn you, I did! I wrote you immediately I had news of the trial, and months later a letter came back from Newgate, from a woman called Charlotte Barker. She said you had already sailed for Botany Bay. Well . . . what could I do? You were lost to me then. I was young and ignorant, and I married Alison in the firm belief that I would forget you.' His voice changed, hardening. 'But I didn't forget you. You rose like a ghost between me and every single thing in life that could have given me joy and satisfaction. I couldn't cast you off . . . you were a torment to me! If I had been free I would have gone willingly to search for you; but it was too late for that. I went to fight in Holland with the thought that if I were killed I should be gladly released from the torture of self-accusation. I believed that I had no soul above the material things in life that attracted me – but I found that you were in my soul.'

In the fading light he leaned nearer to her, until their faces were close together.

'I wrote you letters that I never sent,' he said. 'I sought news of you wherever I could find it. When ships, returning from New South Wales, berthed in the Thames, I used to hang about the docks, in the hope of picking up scraps of information about you. And finally I had the good fortune to meet Admiral Phillip – he told me that you were to be married to an East India Company officer, and that he himself had given an order for your pardon. After that I insinuated myself with Sir Joseph Banks. I couldn't count the number of Royal Society dinners I sat through so that later I might talk with any of the guests who had recently come back from the colony. It didn't always bring results . . . but gradually I was building up the picture of your life. I knew about your farm on the Hawkesbury, and your two eldest sons. I knew what sort of man your husband was. And then, when he visited London, I almost made myself known to him. He came to a reception in Sir Joseph Banks's house – all the colonists eventually found their way there. Andrew Maclay was pointed out as a man reputed to have made a fortune from salvage, and who was, at the moment, fitting out a new vessel for trading. I was about to ask to be presented . . . I wanted to meet him, and to ask about you. But I couldn't . . . I couldn't make myself go forward. I was jealous, Sara . . . jealous of everything that man possessed. It was a relief when the *Thistle* finally sailed from Greenwich, and took him out of my reach.

'My married life, all this time, was going to pieces. I had begun it in the belief that I would forget you – but I was wrong. I was not happy with Alison – although I knew she loved me and I was fond of her. You, Sara, had spoiled every other woman for

me. But Alison and I had enough distractions to cover whatever dissatisfaction we felt with one another. It changed, though,
when Sir Geoffrey lost his money. He was broken after that —
he didn't live long. The estate was entailed; it went to Alison's
brother. Lady Linton knew the state of our finances — she offered
us a home, and we accepted gladly. She adored Alison, and she
tried to make a son out of me — although she used always to laugh
and say I was not promising material. She spent money lavishly on
us, and we both knew that Alison would inherit her fortune. But,
with all that, she was nobody's fool. No, by God, she wasn't! I
found that she was watching me. She knew every move I made,
and practically every thought in my head. It didn't take her long
to sense that something was wrong — something that drove me to
gamble much more than I could afford, and to ride a horse as if I
cared less than nothing for my own neck. I often stayed out the
whole night — and it wasn't always with women. I would sometimes find myself at dawn, stupid with drink, babbling about
Botany Bay, in some sailor's tavern around the docks.

'All this time my love for you was the fatal malaise that I had
heard others talk of and never believed in myself. You possessed
me — you never left me any rest. Lady Linton suspected something,
though of course she never could reach anything near the truth.
It was I who first suggested New South Wales to her — and I made
her believe it was her own idea. She talked to Alison about this,
and convinced her that I should do well in the colony. I was to
farm — to work out my own salvation. Once the idea was planted,
Lady Linton was adamant. She bought my commission in the
Corps, settled my debts — which were by no means trifling — and
packed us off with barely enough money to cover the expenses of
the voyage. Obviously the cure was to be drastic. "Training for
your inheritance," she called it. Poor soul, she didn't in the least
want us to go.'

Sara shivered, and involuntarily she leaned forward and pressed
her face against his shoulder. 'Oh, Richard, what could you hope
to gain by coming here?'

'The sight of you — that was what I hoped for. I wanted to
live where I could occasionally see you, where your name could
be spoken aloud. Nothing has been right for me since you went,'
he said. 'But I hoped to make something of my life if I could be
where you would see my efforts, Sara. I've taken the offer of
money from your husband because I want the tie with you, and because it gives me the chance to do more than fret my life away
on a captain's pay.'

He put his hand to her hair, smoothed it back from her temple, touching the soft skin of her forehead. 'You have all the witchery of the devil, Sara! I've fought you for ten years, but I won't fight you any longer. I've tried to forget you in other women – I've flirted with many, made love to some, and always with the image of you before me. When I took a mistress, I felt I was unfaithful to you. God, how people would laugh to know of it – that is, if they could believe it!'

Slowly she raised her face to him. 'They won't believe it, Richard, because they'll never hear it. I'm as dead to you, as lost, as ever I was.'

'Not lost, my love,' he murmured. 'I can see you, and talk with you. I'll find peace, perhaps, because I've stopped searching for you.'

'But Andrew . . .' she began.

'Andrew! Do you think I care about Andrew?' he said roughly. 'I can adore the very ground you walk on, and he won't know it. He'll never find out. I promise you that.'

She shook her head wildly. 'But I love Andrew!'

'You loved me once.'

'Once – yes! But I was a child then. Surely even you, Richard, can see what Andrew and I have built up here for one another. We have knitted our lives so closely together that nothing can separate us. We are necessary to each other.'

'Yes,' he said. 'But you love Andrew because he is a copy of yourself. All your ambitions and dreams, are his also. Only a man like Andrew Maclay could match your spirit and energy. Only he could achieve for you what he has.' He leaned towards her again. 'I am not Andrew. I couldn't build a world in the clouds for you. But I am the first man you ever loved. My claim on you is an old one, and it's strong. I need you!'

'No, Richard!' she breathed, afraid and tense. 'You have no claim on me. I owe you nothing. I love Andrew, I tell you! He . . .'

'I need you,' he said again.

'Andrew also needs me.'

'You can love us both, Sara. It's not as a mistress I want you, and there's nothing Andrew has that I could possibly take from him. You can go on being all the things to him that you have been through these years – but for myself, I want what you were at Bramfield. That's the Sara he's never seen or known.'

'I can't let you come here to destroy what I have built up,' she whispered. 'You will destroy my peace of mind – my whole life. I love Andrew – and he won't be fooled.'

He caught her up in his arms, holding her close to him, talking wildly. 'Sara . . . Oh, Sara! Can you deny that you love me also? Say that you do . . . just say it! If I could only be sure of that. I would leave you in peace if I knew.'

Her arms slipped upwards about his neck.

'God forgive me . . .' she whispered. 'I still love you.'

He stood up and pulled her with him, drawing her into his arms, and bending over her upturned face. The last time he had kissed her was in the schoolroom at Bramfield. Now he kissed her in this silent, deserted bay with all the passion and longing of the years in between. Her lips, the warm, sweet lips of a woman, in the place of the child she had been then, moved under his. He was vaguely aware that she was mouthing some protest, and yet giving herself to him at the same time. As he kissed her, the sense of desolation and loneliness seemed to slip from him; the years did not count now, only the mad joy and exhilaration in his heart.

'Sara! Sara! I've found you again!'

2

In an upstairs room of the store – a room once used as a sitting-room when the Maclays had lived there – Sara squatted on her knees before a low shelf packed with rolls of cloth. She murmured to herself as she worked, writing swiftly in a notebook balanced on her knees.

'Calico – dark blue – eight rolls. Calico – flowered – five rolls.' And then she frowned, adding to the last item, ' – slightly water-stained. Broadcloth . . .'

As she wrote, she listened absently to footsteps coming up the stairs, pausing when she realized that they did not belong to any of the light-footed clerks who attended the store. List in hand, she looked expectantly towards the door.

It was Jeremy Hogan who tapped and opened it. He did not smile his usual greeting. He came in, and she saw immediately that he was wet. The shoulders of his greatcoat were sodden; raindrops dripped off the brim of the hat he held in his hand. His boots were splattered with mud.

'Jeremy!'

Sara jumped to her feet, smiling, warmed with the pleasure of this unexpected visit. 'I'm glad to see you, Jeremy! Have you just come from Kintyre? What brings you?'

'I had a note from Andrew,' he explained briefly. 'Stock sales at Parramatta. For some reason or other, he's going to flatter my vanity by referring to my judgement – though in the end he'll buy what he fancies himself, as he always does.'

She put out her hand and touched his shoulder. 'You're wet right through – and hungry, I imagine. Did you call at the house?'

'I did, of course,' he said, shrugging. 'But I was told the master was from home – doubtless drinking the afternoon away and pretending to do business – and the mistress was stocktaking at the store. Annie Stokes's tone rather suggested that it was permissible for you to be here in the mornings, but any *real* lady would be sitting pretty in her own drawing-room at this time of the day.'

Sara laughed. 'I still haven't learned to be the *real* lady that Annie longs to wait upon. Perhaps if I live long enough I'll succeed . . .'

Jeremy cut in, throwing his hat on a packing-case, and turning to look at her with eyes that she suddenly realized were angry.

'You'll live long enough, Sara . . . if gossip doesn't soon have your blood.'

She took a step backwards, frowning. 'Jeremy! What do you mean? What are you talking about?'

He thrust his hands into his pockets, awkwardly. 'I sometimes encourage gossip, Sara. It's a habit of the Irish. Besides, I've been on the Hawkesbury for months now, and news is stale there. So as soon as I got to town . . .'

'Oh, Jeremy, go on!' she snapped.

'I made two calls after leaving Glenbarr. One to leave my horse at Joe Maguire's stable, and then to Costello's for a bite of cheese and some ale. It was the same story at each place.'

'*What story?* For pity's sake, *tell me!*'

He was looking at her fully. 'Oh, it was couched in casual enough terms, but the meaning was unmistakable. Had I heard that great friends of Andrew Maclay's wife had arrived with the new Governor in the *Speedy*? And wasn't it fine now, for Mrs Maclay to be having her friends with her again, especially as they were the quality, no less?' Jeremy's accent was a good imitation of Pat Costello's, as he concentrated on the drawing of a tankard, and the spinning of a story. 'And here, my dear Sara, was a digression while the histories of Sir Geoffrey Watson and his countess sister were related to me. Captain Barwell's history, it seems, is rather more obscure. But the story-tellers returned at last to the original theme. Wasn't it grand, now, they said, that Mrs Maclay had such good friends from the old days to be spending her time with? And wouldn't you all be having fine old yarns about them together? Though, to be sure, *Mrs* Barwell had only once been to dinner at Glenbarr. But the Captain, now . . . Well, *he's* a different matter, entirely. Hasn't he a track worn to the front door, with the number of times he's called? Now, let me see . . . was it four times last week, and twice so far this week? Of course, they quite understand that Mrs Barwell isn't very strong, and couldn't so often make the tiring journey to Glenbarr.'

He broke off, and his voice lost the half-whine of Pat Costello. 'I tell you, Sara, it made me sick in my guts to hear it.'

With huge, angry steps he paced the length of the room, and back again, coming to a halt in front of her.

'And it made me more sick to realize that the tall, handsome officer I passed almost on your doorstep was the same Captain Barwell!'

Sara was deadly white, her eyes like hard green stones, brightened by the rage that suddenly filled her. She was standing close enough to him to raise her hand and strike him fully across the face. He did not move, but stared back at her with a slight look of disbelief. The mark of her hand stood out plainly on his cheek.

'Lies!' she said. 'Gossip! Stable talk that you're not above listening to, Jeremy Hogan!'

'One can hardly help it,' he answered testily. 'All Sydney is listening to it.'

'It isn't true!' she said, backing away from him. 'You know they gossip about me. They'd pin anything they could on me.'

'Yes, I know it – only too well, Sara. And this is the first time you've given them anything real to pin on you.'

'There isn't a word of truth in this!' she said hotly. 'All these gossipers are making a fool out of me!'

His mouth twisted a little. 'No, Sara, not the gossipers. It's Richard Barwell who's making the fool out of you.'

'Jeremy!' She swung away from him, turning her back.

For a long time she didn't speak. He watched her shoulders rise and fall in time to her hard breathing, and then he said, very quietly, 'I'm telling you straight, my dear Mrs Maclay, that I wouldn't have the slightest hesitation in wringing your mercenary little neck if you let this nonsense go on. For it is nonsense, isn't it?' His straight black brows lifted in question. 'It's just gossip? There's no truth at all in it?'

At the soft insinuation in his tone, she turned to him again.

For a few moments she stood looking at him. Finally she said, 'Richard Barwell comes to the house because he wants advice about what he's going to do in the colony.' Her voice rose a little.

'It's advice I have in plenty, Jeremy! There's nothing else to his visits. Nothing, I tell you! If the gossips want to make something else out of them what can I do?'

'*Do!*' he rapped. 'Tell him to go to hell! Or if you won't, I'll do it for you!'

She looked as shocked then as if she had been struck across the face. She ran a hand distractedly over her forehead.

'Am I asking you to do the impossible?' he said.

She shook her head slowly.

'Then what are you waiting for? He's up at the house now.'

She didn't move. Her expression was half-defiant, half-afraid.

'Sara, listen to me.' Jeremy's voice had dropped, and softened, but his eyes, looking into hers, were flinty. They commanded what his words merely suggested. 'Everyone is talking about these visits of Barwell's. Andrew can't remain deaf, or blind, much longer.'

Her lips trembled, and she pressed her hands together to still their agitation.

'Jeremy,' she said, 'will you come back to the house with me? I'll go now and get my cloak.'

'What are you going to do, Sara?'

'Do? Why . . .' she paused, and ran her tongue over her lips. 'If he has waited, then I'll say to him . . . I'll say exactly what you told me to say.'

Sara entered her drawing-room to find Richard standing before the fire, one foot, in elegant riding-boot, resting casually on a low stool. He turned to her, and straightened.

She closed the door, and stood with her back pressed against it. Outside the rain poured down steadily. It made a hollow, drumming sound against the roof of the veranda; the unfinished lawn beyond the windows was a dark sea of mud, with the raindrops cutting the surface. At the end of the planned garden, where it began to slope towards the trees, dozens of little rivulets had forged their own channels. Under the heavy sky the eucalypts had lost their colour, and were a drab, blackish green.

All this Sara saw as she stood with her back to the door, and she realized that in some inexplicable way it all matched the loose, indifferent fashion of Richard's stance, the look of unusual gravity in his face. He came towards her, holding out his hand. She accepted it, and allowed herself to be led forward. With gentle fingers he undid the clasp of her cloak, drawing it from her shoulders, and throwing it across a chair. He was still clasping her fingers loosely, and then he reached for her other hand and held them both pressed between his own.

'You're cold, Sara. And your hair is wet. You look like a young girl. Do you remember how . . . ?'

She shook her head. 'Hush, Richard – no more! This isn't the time for remembering what we used to do, or how we did it.'

Firmly she withdrew her hands from his. 'Or for holding my hands, and dreaming of a time when it was possible to do it. All that is long over.'

'Sara . . .' He frowned uncertainly. 'Just for the little time we're together we could pretend . . .'

'Pretend? What's the good, when we both know the pretending must come to an end?'

'Must it?' he asked quietly.

Without hesitation, she said, 'It *has* come to an end, Richard. Pretence never lasts. I ought to have remembered that – only this time they have taken it away almost before it began.'

'They?'

She nodded. 'The sharp eyes, the busy tongues. I warned you that Sydney was no more than a village. One is watched . . . daily . . . ceaselessly. It's so easy to count the number of times you visit here – and to exaggerate the number. There's gossip about us already. Soon Andrew will hear – and Alison.'

His eyes narrowed suspiciously. 'To whom have you been talking, Sara? Who has put this into your head?'

It was not easy for her to follow Jeremy's advice – to tell Richard he must go, and why. She shrugged her shoulders, as if all this was simple to explain. 'Does it matter? The gossip is something I would have noticed myself, if I had not been blinded temporarily.'

'Sara, tell me!' he said sharply. 'Who was it?'

'It was Jeremy Hogan, if you must know,' she said. 'I have just seen him.'

'Jeremy Hogan? And who is Jeremy Hogan, that he is privileged to say such things about you?'

She raised her hand to caution him. 'Quietly, Richard! You must be quiet! I am not Alison, to be shouted at – or to be affected when you choose to sulk.'

He folded his lips. 'I want to know about this Jeremy Hogan. Who is he?'

'Well,' she said patiently, 'Jeremy Hogan is a political prisoner . . .'

'A *convict*!'

'*You* might call him a convict. To Andrew and myself he is

brother, friend – and our overseer at Kintyre. Before now, I have
trusted him with my life. When he comes to me and says there is
talk about us, Richard, then I trust him in that also.'

He looked at her, scowling like an angry child. 'What fools you
and Andrew are at times. This Hogan is some damned convict
that you both pamper and flatter until he fancies himself a little
god. And it's *his* advice that you listen to, is it? You tell me everything must end between us because an impudent upstart like that
bids you.'

Sara ached to smooth away his scowl then, to kiss him and
tell him that she had not meant a word of what she said. But she
thought of Jeremy, and she knew that she was afraid of the scene
Jeremy might make with Richard if she had to tell him she had
not done as he ordered.

She drew away a little. '*Everything must end between us!*' she
repeated coldly. 'Nothing has happened to make an ending of. I
kissed you once – that was madness, and I freely admit it. And in
the last three weeks you have visited me more times than was
prudent. Nothing exists between us that can't be stopped just like
that!' She snapped her fingers decisively. '*Nothing*, Richard!'

His brows drew together in an expression of disbelief and disappointment. 'Sara, you said you *loved* me! That day on the
beach – you *said* it!'

Her face flamed. 'I said I loved Andrew also.'

'But you loved me first!'

'But I loved Andrew when I was old enough to know what love
meant!'

He said triumphantly, 'But I was first! And you can't deny that
you love me still!'

She gazed long at him, at the handsome dark face enflamed with
self-will and passion. Suddenly she was angry with Richard as she
had never been before. He had changed so little, she thought,
crossly, in all these years – never really learning that there were
some things in life that a display of rage and temperament would
not give him. Alison and Lady Linton had between them ruined
whatever chance he might have had to change this. Together, they
had spoiled and indulged him, and he stood here now, anger
distorting his features because she dared oppose him.

'No, I don't deny it, Richard,' she said steadily. 'It would be
useless. But I want you to understand that what Andrew and I
have made together is going to stand as it is. You aren't going to
be the one to destroy it.' She threw her head back. 'I am telling you
now, and I don't mean it lightly. You must not come here again

unless Alison is with you.'

She held herself rigidly, afraid of softening to him.

'One kiss, Richard,' she said. 'There wasn't anything else – and don't try to make it so.'

He put his hands into his pockets, and looked at her half-sneeringly. 'Is it too much to ask that I should merely come to visit you? I don't expect anything so precious as your kisses, as you're so chary of giving them. Like a well-behaved spaniel, all I ask is permission for a space in your drawing-room. I should also like sometimes to talk with you alone. But no – you prefer to take the word of a low-minded convict that there is gossip about us, and then to turn me out with the high-handedness of a duchess.'

Sara whitened, but she was no longer afraid of softening. She drew herself up fully, her eyes almost level with his, when she spoke.

'I must ask you to remember two things, Richard. Firstly, in my presence, no one may call Jeremy Hogan a low-minded convict. And secondly, that although I am not a duchess, I still am mistress of this house. And now I want you to leave it immediately. And I'll have your promise that you will not come here to see me alone again.'

Richard stiffened, but in his face anger fought with dismay. His eyes held the appeal of a child's.

After staring at her for a few moments, he said quietly, 'I am not Andrew, Sara – and never could be anything like him. I couldn't make a fortune for you, or conquer a world to lay at your feet. But I have need of you – more need, I think, than even he has.' He paused, his voice rising again. 'And what's more, I believe you need me too! However, you've made your very noble choice, my dear. May you be content with it!'

He turned slowly and walked to one of the long windows. He opened it wide, and the damp air stirred in the room. For a few moments he stood staring out into the garden, his hand thrust upwards against a heavy fold of the curtain. The rain came down ceaselessly; it was driven by a light wind across the width of the veranda, and splattered against the windows. The view of the harbour was lost in fine mist. Richard took a step forward, and then stood still, with the slanting rain hitting him. Sara shivered – the misty air, and Richard's unmoving figure seemed almost to cast a spell on the room. It was as if they were locked together in a brief enchantment. He possessed a strange power, just by standing there, to make her feel despair and pain.

'Richard! Richard!' she whispered to herself. No sound came

from her lips, and he did not stir.

The wind rustled in the tops of the trees; the garden was desolate and lonely. At last he turned to her again.

'This isn't the finish, Sara. We will see much more of each other — Andrew has ensured that by his generous offer. And I hope that you will suffer as I have done in the past. I hope that you will know even a small part of my torment.' He gave her a slight bow. 'We have much time before us — you and I.'

Then he strode across the veranda, and vaulted over the rail.

A few minutes later, at the sound of a horse cantering down the drive, Jeremy Hogan rose from his seat in the dining-room, where he was finishing the meal Annie Stokes had brought him. He opened the long windows, and stepped out on to the veranda. As he did so, he caught a glimpse of Sara moving back quickly into the drawing-room.

He leaned over the veranda rail to catch the last sight of the rider, the flash of the bright uniform against the sombre trees. His horse was black, of thoroughbred stock, and shining in the rain.

'Well . . .' Jeremy muttered aloud. 'Well, you might ride as if you and the horse were born together — but I wouldn't weep, Captain Barwell, if I heard you'd fallen and broken your bloody neck!'

3

On an evening three weeks after the Barwells' arrival, Andrew stood by one of the long windows in Major Foveaux's drawing-room, critically surveying the crowd about him.

As yet, only eight or so couples had made their appearance, but outside he could distinctly hear the rumble of carriages, and the bad-tempered tones of their drivers, forced to hold restless horses in line, waiting for their turn to draw up before the open doorway. They would all come, he thought — every one of them; even from as far away as Parramatta they would come, because the pull of curiosity was strong. There was not a woman in the colony who, given the opportunity, would excuse herself from meeting Alison Barwell. And not a few of them knew that King, the Governor-elect, had promised to attend this reception in Foveaux's house.

Across the room Andrew bowed to John Macarthur's wife, standing before the fireplace, but his attention wandered to the group just inside the door. Alison was there, fabulously gowned, and beside her, Richard, a handsome devil, Andrew reflected – a good match for Alison's air of distinction. Foxeaux hovered about them, occasionally signalling to the servants, who moved with their trays among the sprinkling of early guests. On Alison's right hand, just a little behind her, stood Sara. Andrew watched his wife with pride – tall, in her gown of rose silk, and only the heightened colour of her cheeks and the slightly restless movement of the fan in her gloved hand betrayed, even to his familiar eyes, that she was nervous.

There was a buzz of conversation in the hall. Foveaux moved forward to greet his guests. They came, a group of about six people, through the door. Alison was introduced, then Richard. As each guest was about to move away, Alison turned, and with her charming smile, presented Sara.

Earlier, with the first arrivals, Andrew had caught Alison's gentle words.

'Of course, you know my friend, Mrs Maclay . . .'

From some of the women there had been a marked reaction of hostility, a raising of eyebrows, a stiff bow. The more uncertain among them gave shy, rather frightened smiles, and then noticeably drifted off to discuss this unexpected development with friends in far corners of the room. On the faces of the men, almost without exception, Andrew could read admiration, and in some cases, pleasure in the knowledge that at last they were meeting and talking to Sara Maclay elsewhere than across the desk in the store.

James and Julia Ryder came in. The room filled rapidly then and soon it was too crowded for Andrew to see clearly the little ceremony which was being repeated over and over again by the doorway. He moved among the guests, bowing here and there to acquaintances, but not pausing to become involved in conversation, lest he should lose anything of the general trend of talk. The voice of a woman, whose reputation for gossip he knew well, reached him.

'. . . and I'd like to know how that creature, Sara Maclay, happens to be Mrs Barwell's *friend*. It's a perfect scandal that she's invited here to meet decent people . . .'

Then a man's voice, gently, 'But *both* the Barwells say they knew her when they were children.'

With a faint smile, Andrew moved off again.

He stopped to catch the words of a young bride, a recent arrival from England.

'Do you think Mrs Maclay will be *received* after this?' She gave

a slightly nervous laugh. 'I think . . . I should like to know her,
though she rather frightens me. Well, we'll see first how Mr King
receives her . . .'

And a young lieutenant said admiringly to a fellow-officer, 'They
tell me she killed an escaping convict. Jove!'

Andrew made his way towards the group by the door, but he
still did not join them. Alison was a consummate actress, he thought;
or else she had been rigorously schooled by Richard. Every other
minute she turned to consult Sara, tapping her arm lightly with her
fan, laughing, leaning forward to listen to the other's replies. It was
the perfect picture of old friends, familiar and at ease with one another. She kept Sara close, forcing any guest who approached to include her in the conversation. It was all managed with loving
attention to the niceties of social behaviour; never once did
Alison's manner imply her awareness that the women who spoke
now with such tightened lips had never before acknowledged
Andrew Maclay's ex-convict wife. To Andrew, Alison Barwell
made an unforgettable picture that evening – her charming vivacity
never slackened, never faltered. Her poise was equal to every
demand made upon it. He smiled to himself. She was a lady, and
a lady that could be trusted to behave as her breeding dictated
– even if the world turned upside down, as Alison must now
be feeling hers had done.

An abrupt, intuitive hush fell upon the crowd. No one had
announced the arrival of the new Governor and his lady, but
the whisper of it had run through the company like a wave. Heads
turned and craned; any talk that continued was abstracted while
the owner's eyes were fixed on the doorway.

Philip Gidley King and Josepha Ann, his dark-haired wife,
swept in. It was not yet proper to give them the welcome reserved
for the true Governor. Nevertheless, they commanded the attention
of the whole room. Behind them were Captain Abbott, and his
wife, at whose house they were staying.

Andrew watched with keen interest the little ceremony of greetings and curtsies. Alison was known to be a favourite with Josepha
Ann, and King himself smiled upon her warmly. She acknowledged
her introductions to the Abbotts, and then she gracefully stretched
her hand towards Sara.

The silence deepened in the room. One woman among the
crowd, who could not see above the heads of the men, stood on
tiptoe, and almost overbalanced. Her stifled gasp was plainly
audible.

Alison's clear tones reached them all.

'Sir, may I present my dear friend, Mrs Maclay? We have known each other a very long time – almost since we were small children.'

King bowed. 'I am indeed happy to make your acquaintance, madam. Any friend of our charming Mrs Barwell is, of course . . .'

Andrew's eyes were half-closed as he watched the shimmer of Sara's rose silk as she sank in a low curtsy. He knew beyond doubt that King would have been fully informed of Sara's history. The colony was too small to allow a new Governor to live here four full weeks without pressing on him the domestic and financial details of all his prominent citizens. Andrew was aware that King would know, equally well, that this ex-convict's husband was not without power of his own, the power of his reputed wealth, and the weight he carried in the trading-ring. King's main purpose was to smash the monopoly of this ring, either by peaceful persuasion or open warfare. Whichever way events turned, it would do him no harm to win friends among the men he sought to subjugate.

So the Governor-elect of New South Wales smiled upon Andrew Maclay's tall young wife, now being presented to him by a woman of unimpeachable reputation. Always loyal, Josepha Ann hastened to follow his example.

4

For more than two months after the reception at Foveaux's house, Richard did not appear at Glenbarr alone. He came formally with Alison, and sometimes he and Andrew sat late discussing details of the Hyde farm – which by then had passed into Richard's hands. During these visits he was distant to Sara; his detachment lay coldly in his eyes, and she believed that he would never again come alone – until the afternoon Annie came bustling into the nursery to announce that Captain Barwell was waiting in the drawing-room.

Sara went downstairs immediately, to find him leaning nonchalantly against the mantelpiece, his fingers idly toying with the fringe of the bell-cord. He smiled at her, and when his smile met with no response, he frowned and tossed the cord aside.

'It's no use looking like that, Sara,' he said. 'I intend to come whenever I feel like it. No – not whenever I feel like it – whenever I know that I must see you for a few minutes, or do something crazy.'

He tapped the heel of his polished boot against the fender. 'But don't worry, my dear. It won't be often enough to ruin your honour or your reputation.'

She was standing at the back of a big tapestry-covered chair. Her fingers gripped the scroll-work of the frame.

'I could refuse to see you,' she said quietly.

He looked at her, shaking his head. 'No, you won't do that. It would look bad, wouldn't it, if you refused to see me? After all, how could Alison continue to visit here, if her husband is not received? Think of it, Sara.'

She thought of it, and saw what he meant her to see – Andrew's attitude if there was an open break between herself and Richard, Alison's suspicions, and the gossip of the Glenbarr servants sweeping through the town.

Richard, with no small show of triumph, won his point, and throughout the winter appeared in Sara's drawing-room for an afternoon's call, once in every two or three weeks. At first they were uneasy visits – Sara, furious and sullen that he had forced his way in on her, Richard because he knew he was not welcomed. They talked together in clipped, isolated sentences. But familiarity wore down their sense of strain. Sara soon learnt that it was impossible to quarrel politely in a drawn-out fashion. She gave in, and then they ceased throwing words about like a pair of petulant children. Richard relaxed enough to tell her his plans for the Hyde farm – he spent a part of each week there, returning eagerly to report the progress. The house was now in order; he was building hog-pens, and bringing up some oxen from Sydney. Sara shook her head doubtfully over the accounts. Richard was no farmer. He threw himself into the project with the recklessness of inexperience. There was no advice she could give him that he would heed. The farm was his, he pointed out, whenever she tried to dissuade him from some scheme or other – his alone. Andrew might have lent him the money to buy it, but that fact gave no one the right to tell him how to work it. Sara found, when this sort of mood took him, that she kept the peace between them by shrugging her shoulders and having nothing further to say.

During those months there were unmistakable signs that the women of the colony were beginning to take Alison Barwell's lead. They did not immediately call at Glenbarr, but in the streets Sara was greeted with a discreet bow, and in the store their former attitude of ignoring her was abandoned. But as the winter passed, she was more and more certain that Alison had a suspicion of some relationship between her husband and the woman he told her she must call her friend. She came often enough to Glenbarr;

she invited Sara back to the house on the Parramatta road, which
they had bought from an officer returning to England. But she
acted as if she obeyed an order; as if Sara herself mattered less
than nothing in comparison with the fact that Richard must be
pleased. They never advanced towards intimacy – but then, Alison
was the sort to be intimate with no one. Richard was her entire
world, and other people existed only in relation to him. She seemed
to see Sara Maclay's husband as the provider of the luxuries of life
that Richard demanded, the horses, the good wine, the gowns which
were essential if she was still to have him look at her with admiration. Andrew Maclay had also provided the money for the farm,
which, one day, she believed, was going to allow them to live on
luxuries which were not borrowed. She had implicit faith in
Richard's ability to both farm his land, with the help of an overseer,
and carry out his duties at the barracks. New South Wales had
many men now who were doing the same thing – and were succeeding in building up small fortunes. What neither saw was that
Richard was no farmer, and that his chances were slight of ever
catching up with the shrewdness, ruthlessness and frank ambition
of the others. He and his wife lived in a dream of the future, when
the Hyde farm had made them at least moderately prosperous – and
to Alison, prosperity also carried the idea that she would not have
to visit so regularly at Glenbarr, since they would no longer be in
debt to Glenbarr's owners. In the meantime, it was convenient –
more than that, it was a God-send – to draw money as it was needed
from the steady stream that Andrew Maclay showed no signs of
checking. Luxuries were costly, Alison noted with regret, and they
owed a shocking debt already to the Maclays. But, she told herself,
if they were ever to succeed, they must make their start now – and
in the only way open to them.

So, through the winter months, Sara and Alison clung determinedly to their façade of friendship; the wives of the colony's
officials began to bow and nod to Mrs Maclay when their carriages chanced to pass in Sydney's muddy streets. Gradually a
phrase passed among them – 'Of course, Sara Maclay's case is
rather different from that of the other convicts.' One or two of the
husbands suggested that their wives might try inviting Sara Maclay
to their tea-parties. It was well known that she possessed a great
deal of influence over her husband – and there were many people
in the colony who, for one reason or another, wished to retain
Andrew Maclay's goodwill.

And while this went on, while winter gave place to a pale, warm
spring, Richard continued to visit occasionally at Glenbarr, to

tell Sara his plans, to listen to her encouragement, to disregard her
advice. If Andrew were there, he stayed only a short time; if they
were alone, he sat on before the drawing-room fire, talking on and
on, until the intimacy of the walks on the Romney Marsh was once
again established. And always he rode away from Glenbarr at a
mad pace, with a look on his face of a man who has had a great
weight lifted from him. Sometimes he didn't go directly home, or
to the barracks, but turned aside to the road heading to the South
Head.

Once Ted O'Malley, the Maclays' boatman, had reported meeting him on this road, after a visit to Glenbarr. He told Annie –
who promptly repeated it to Sara – that Captain Barwell had
cantered along, singing a soldier's song at the top of his voice, and
with a strange, wild look on his face.

4

Sara gave an audible sigh of relief as the straggling hamlet of
Castle Hill appeared at the end of the stretch of road. There was
not much farther to go now, she consoled herself. Three miles on
the other side of the rough little settlement ahead, a track led off
to the left, curving for a couple of hundred yards to a ragged farm-
building, known locally as Priest's. Joseph Priest had died four
months ago, and for the past six weeks the Maclays had been the
owner of the worked-out, neglected property. Sara reflected happily
enough on the prospect. Within two years, if Andrew was right, this
piece of land would wear the same prosperous, fertile look that
characterized their Toongabbie and Hawkesbury farms. Andrew's
ambition was a restless, growing thing.

He and Jeremy were both together at Priest's, living in the
comfortless, leaking shack, alone except for the one sickly ex-
convict labourer who was the sole remnant of the labour-force of
a dozen men once needed to run the property. The stacks of rum-
kegs piled in the yard at the back were testimony of the reason
why the farm had failed. But the place had promise. After a few
weeks of combined hard work, Jeremy was to stay on, while Andrew
returned to Sydney. It was Jeremy who would guide Priest's
through the difficult years of re-birth, while Andrew's impatient
nature sought a dozen different occupations.

All of this Andrew had written in two hasty letters to Sara.
She pictured the farm as he described it – even its hideous decay

softened and beautified by the burst of spring wild flowers, and
the single, exquisite white gum-tree, bending towards the creek. She
had thrown the second letter aside, and, on an impulse, had packed
a box with a few of her oldest clothes, and ordered the carriage to
be stocked with extra food and cooking utensils. She left the store
in the charge of young Clapmore, Glenbarr to Bennett, and the
children to Annie.

She promised herself in this visit to Priest's a complete return
to the early days on the Hawkesbury. There would be just herself,
Andrew, and Jeremy working and discussing together the problems of over-worked land, diseased, neglected stock, the shortage of
labour. She would cook for them and for two weeks share the unbroken companionship of the two men who had built her world.
She knew she was attempting a flight into the past, and she recognized the possibility that it might be a dismal failure. But, along
with Andrew's letters, she had also experienced that odd restlessness
and dissatisfaction that comes with the spring; this flight was a brief
indulgence of that mood. It was an acknowledgement of her vague
desires for a return to the simplicity of those first years, a simplicity
which, at most times, she was sensible enough to recognize as having gone for ever. The success of this impulse depended upon
Andrew and Jeremy. If they accepted her presence at Priest's as
naturally as she had come, then she would know that the spirit of
adventure and comradeship had survived Andrew's growing wealth
– and she would be satisfied and happy.

At Glenbarr, David and Duncan were still engaged in a struggle,
now a month old, to win supremacy over their new tutor, a huge,
untidy young Irishman of great learning and shy charm, whom
Sara had engaged by letter eighteen months ago; Sebastian, in the
nursery, was beginning to haul himself up to stand totteringly on his
lanky, strong legs. Under Bennett, Glenbarr ran itself, and, short of
the unexpected arrival of a ship with fresh cargo, there was nothing
at the store to need her attention for the next two weeks.

Her carriage suddenly jolted into a rut, and she braced herself
against the back of the seat; the dispirited, whitewashed buildings
came closer. By the side of the nearest house a solitary mimosa
tree had burst into bloom – outrageously yellow against the harsh
blue sky.

Sara shook the dust absently from her skirt, and straightened
her bonnet, acknowledging, in the privacy of her own thoughts,
that she had done perhaps the wisest thing by not remaining too
long in Sydney while Andrew was staying at Priest's. Richard was
due to return after a two-week period of duty at Parramatta, and

she recalled past occasions when Andrew's absence seemed to give him licence, which he didn't hesitate to accept, to visit Glenbarr whenever he chose. Sara sighed, and ran her hand across her eyes. From the doorway of the cottage, in whose withered, brown garden the mimosa flowered, a woman paused to watch the carriage. At her skirts a small child waved shyly. Sara leaned forward, smiling. As she waved back to the little girl, she knew suddenly that she was impatient with the problem of Richard. She wanted to be with Andrew and Jeremy again, in an atmosphere where the greatest problem would be coping with an evil-tempered stove, or deciding how many head of stock the neglected pastures at Priest's would carry in the first year.

They were now among the haphazard buildings which formed the Castle Hill settlement. The heavy spring rains had turned the road between the thatched and whitewashed houses into mud, and the constant passage of horses and carts had cut it into deep ruts. The ruts had dried in the past week of hot sunshine, and there was already a film of dry dust over everything. A flock of geese crossed serenely in front of the carriage, moving on in the direction of the shallow stream at the side of the road. Three men, and two soldiers off-duty, lounged around the door of Nell Finnigan's cottage. Nell was a large, handsome woman, an ex-convict who ran her husband's house as a kind of inn – though it was widely known that she made her obvious profits from the sale of rum. Glancing at the shining neatness of the cottage as she passed, Sara idly wondered which of the gentlemen, living off the fat of the land in Sydney, was responsible for her supply.

The carriage jolted to a halt before the blacksmith's forge. Sara immediately thrust her head out the window, waiting for Edwards, Andrew's ugly, grizzled coachman to climb down.

'Why are we stopping?' she said to him.

He pushed his hat back inelegantly. 'Lor, ma'am! I thought you'd 'a spotted it miles back. Goldie, 'ere, 'as gone lame on me. I reckon the master'll not be too pleased if I take her farther than I have to while she's like this. Carson, the smithy 'ere, can probably let us have another horse, and we could leave Goldie 'ere.'

She nodded. 'Ask him – but be as quick as you can.'

'Yes'm.' He touched his hat, and started, with his bowlegged gait, towards the forge. He vanished into the dark interior, and then reappeared with a small grey-haired man, wearing a leather apron. For a few minutes they talked together; Carson finally called over his shoulder to a young man who came out of the forge and followed him round to the side of it. They headed towards a rough stable at the back.

Edwards approached Sara with a grin lighting up his cracked face. "'Tis all settled, ma'am. Carson has another that'll take Goldie's place. We'll be harnessed up and away in no time.'

He cleared his throat a little, looking at her with concern. She had noticed in the past that whenever he drove her alone he always displayed a solemn interest in her comfort, which he was wont to express with unpolished bluntness. 'Now, ma'am,' he said clearly. 'I was wonderin' if maybe this sun might be too fierce on you – with you just sitting here waiting. Carson sends his respects, and says you're welcome to sit awhile in the forge – if you'll not think it too dirty.'

Sara had already made up her mind not to stay in the stuffy carriage during the change-over. She stepped down on to the road, looking up and down the row of cottages. 'If I go across to Nell Finnigan's, perhaps she'll give me some cold water. I'm thirsty.'

His face wrinkled in dismay. 'Oh, ma'am! Nell Finnigan's . . .' His tone left her no doubt as to what he thought of Mistress Finnigan.

'Go and help Carson,' she said. 'I think I'll hardly come to harm with Mrs Finnigan in the space of ten minutes.'

She heard him muttering doubtfully as she made her way towards the flower-bordered cottage near the end of the row. Outside the soldier's guard-house a dog rose up from his sprawling position close to the steps and came over hopefully to her; a soldier, tacking a notice to the board on the veranda post, eyed her up and down, grinning impudently. The sun seemed to grow hotter as she walked, and the scraggy settlement looked as if not even the spring could shake it from its apathy. When she reached Nell Finnigan's, the small crowd who had stood drinking ale outside her door had drifted, glasses in hand, down the lane running between the cottage and the guard-house. She watched them a moment. They were joined by perhaps a half-dozen others, and on the outskirts of the group three or four children shuffled their bare feet in the dust.

Sara was filled with curiosity. But she had only to take a few steps down the lane before she knew the reason for the crowd. The yard at the back of the guard-house was in full view now, and the people were too sparse to screen what was happening there.

She came upon it suddenly; there were no cries to warn her. The man who hung at the post was unconscious, and the only sound was the whirr of the cat, as it swung backwards and around the hand of the flogger, and then the crack as it hit the naked flesh.

After each stroke a soldier standing near the post recorded it in a sing-song voice.

'Forty-seven . . .'

Another whirr, and the crack.

'Forty-eight . . .'

She had seen it before – too often. It was stamped in her memory from the days of the *Georgette*, and even before that. It was part of the discipline that ruled the colony – as common a thing as, in England, the gibbet, and the swinging corpse at the cross-roads. This was always a public spectacle – as the magistrates wanted it, because its grim warning struck home at even the hardened sensibilities of the ex-convict watchers.

The bright, flowing blood glistened in the sunlight. The ragged trousers hanging on the hips of the man at the post had absorbed all they could hold. It trickled down his calves, and lay in the dust about his feet. The sounds ceased abruptly, and a second man stepped up to the flogger and took the cat from his hand, shaking the knotted thongs, twisting it in his hands to get the proper balance. Then he swung his arm backwards, and then again came the whirr and the sickening crack.

'Fifty-one . . .'

Sara clapped her hands over her ears, turned, and fled back towards Nell Finnigan's door. In the dim, cool passage she saw no one. She leaned against the wall for a moment, pressing her hand against her mouth, and breathing heavily. At last she straightened, groping her way clumsily in the half-dark. She tripped on the hem of her gown, and stumbled up against a door. Her outstretched hand touched the latch, and it opened with her weight. The door swung back with a crash; she clutched wildly at the frame to save herself falling.

She had a confused impression that a man, seated at a bench beside the window, sprang to his feet. Both her arms were gripped steadily, and a pair of dark, shrewd eyes were fixed on her face.

'Are you ill?'

Confused now, Sara shook her head. 'No . . .'

She felt herself being led firmly to the seat the man had just left. It was almost impossible for her to believe, as she looked at the sunlight pouring through Nell Finnigan's curtains, that an unconscious man hung at a flogging-post not more than a few yards away. She rested her elbows on the scrubbed boards of the table in front of her, and put her face into her hands. The sun was fully on her back, but she could not hold back the fit of shivering which gripped her.

Gently the stranger's hand came to her shoulder, giving her a
little shake.

'Drink some of this,' he said. 'It is wine, bad enough to take the
lining off your throat — but it is better than nothing.'

He held a glass close to her lips. She had not yet looked at
him fully — just his eyes, in that first instant, and now, the thin,
brown fingers curling about the glass. She hesitantly stretched out
her own hand to take it, but he wouldn't yield it to her completely.
She was forced to drink with her fingers touching his around the
base of the glass.

The wine was raw and harsh, and made her cough a little. But
the relentless hand held it to her mouth until it was gone. Then a
fine linen handkerchief dabbed at her moistened lips. She crushed
the handkerchief into a ball in her hand, and leaned back against
the window-sill.

'Are you feeling better now?'

For the first time she looked at him fully. He was lean, and very
tall, with unconscious grace in his stance. The shrewd, questioning
eyes fixed on her were almost black; his unpowdered hair was
black also. She wondered if she considered him handsome, and
studied the narrow, well-formed face, dark olive skin stretched
above high cheek-bones. Brows cut thick and savagely across his
forehead. His mouth was too thin, a trifle cruel, she decided — in a
sense, it didn't match his eyes, which regarded her now with
obvious concern.

He repeated his question quietly. 'Are you feeling better?'

She nodded. 'Thank you — much better.' She hesitated. 'I think
perhaps the sun . . .'

'Or the flogging?' he suggested.

'You saw it also?'

'That was hardly to be avoided.' He lifted his shoulders expressively. 'I offer my sympathies, madam. It was not a sight for
a lady.'

As he spoke, Sara's mind was busily storing the details of his
speech and dress, and puzzling over his identity. The colony was
still much too small to allow a stranger, and especially one who
looked as this one did, to arrive without causing a great flutter
of comment and speculation. Her eyes swiftly flicked over him,
taking in the cut of his coat, the fit of his long boot, and the perfection of the emerald he wore on the little finger of his left hand.
His English was perfect, but he spoke it with the slightest of accents.
He was dressed, and he behaved, as any prosperous man in the
colony might, and still in each detail he was somehow a little

more than life-size. He brought a touch of the exotic, a breath of
the civilized and cultivated world into the scrubbed room. Even
the way he spoke of the flogging carried a trace of worldly cynicism
with it. But he was not indifferent to the flogging, she felt – he
merely suggested that such things were painfully necessary and
unpleasant.

Then her mind reached back to some vague, unconnected gossip
she had heard between two clerks at the store the day before.
This was undoubtedly the man of whom they had spoken – a
Frenchman, who arrived in the American sloop which was riding
at anchor in the harbour these past two days. Apparently he had
made the voyage from Ile de France, intending, no one knew
why, to remain for a while in New South Wales. Even the idle
conversation between Clapmore and the junior clerk had managed
to convey the air of mystery which presumably surrounded this
French stranger. Sara realized that he must have been able to
convince the port officials that he was genuinely an émigré, and
entertained no Bonaparte sympathies, otherwise, when the American
sloop prepared to sail again, he would be firmly aboard her. According to Clapmore's gossip, the Frenchman was taking his time
about disembarking – his boxes had not even come ashore yet.
Later in the day she had heard the story over again from two
different customers. And yet, here he was, these many miles beyond Sydney already, and it was hardly past noon. The Frenchman, she thought, obviously moved quickly, once he decided to
move at all.

She saw that his straight, heavy brows were raised in a look
of inquiry, and she realized that she had been staring at him like
any clumsy country girl. It occurred to her that it was possible that
he was bored by the obligation to affect concern over a dull, stupid
woman.

He bowed slightly. 'Madame, might I be permitted to offer you
a little more wine? I grant you that it is abominable – but they do
assure me that it is the best they have.'

Sara flushed, feeling absurdly ill at ease under his steady scrutiny.
Then she straightened, answering him with a trace of hauteur.

'You are very kind, sir. I should be glad of it.'

'It is indeed a great pleasure,' he said quietly. 'I will send for a
bottle.'

He turned to the door, and then stopped and looked back
at her. He came again to the table, facing her across its width.
The concern was gone from his eyes. They held a friendly, faintly
amused air.

'Before we share a glass of wine,' he said, 'perhaps it is better if
I introduce myself.'

He sketched another small, graceful bow.

'Madame – Louis de Bourget.'

He raised his head again, and when his eyes met hers they
were bright and questioning; the corners of his mouth puckered.

'I see by your expression, Madame, that you wish me still to
give an account of myself. Is that not so?' He smiled indulgently.
'Perhaps it will satisfy you if I tell you that I disembarked this
morning from the American ship, the *Jane Henry* – I am now on
my way to Mr William Cooper's house. He and I became acquainted during the few weeks our ships were in port together in
Cape Town. And now I go to avail myself of his offer of hospitality.
I assure you . . .'

Laughingly, Sara waved him to silence.

'Forgive me, Monsieur! I must appear very boorish . . . A
complete stranger is such a rarity to us here! And I must warn
you, you'll have to expect a great deal of curiosity.'

Then she held out her hand.

'You're very welcome to the colony, Monsieur de Bourget! My
name is Sara Maclay.'

A slow, warm smile broke on his face, and it lost its quizzical
look. He took her hand firmly, bowing over it. Then for the first
of many times, he kissed it.

Nell Finnigan had a plump, shapely figure, and, as she stood in the
doorway watching Louis de Bourget, she jerked her sprigged cotton
gown into position in order to define it better. She had just seen
him hand Sara Maclay into her carriage outside the door. Her
curiosity was ablaze about this good-looking stranger – and the
reason why Mrs Maclay had arrived unannounced in the back
parlour. She tossed back her head, letting her black curls swing
coquettishly under the dainty white cap she wore.

She leaned against the door-frame, and addressed de Bourget.

'More wine, sir?' She ignored the fact that the bottle was still
two-thirds full.

He rested back against the sill, as Sara had done earlier, and
looked at Nell carefully. He liked the cleanliness of her, the shining
hair, the soft white skin that this murderous climate appeared not
to have affected. With a touch of amusement, he noted that
deliberately provocative stance she had adopted; she was more than
skilled at displaying her quite considerable attractions. De Bourget
had his own ideas about the type of woman he admired, and this

one was too full-blown, too obvious in type to suit his taste. But
the room was strangely empty now that the golden-haired Mrs
Maclay was gone, and he knew the woman standing before him
would while away the next hour in effortless coquetry. Women who
smiled in just that fashion, who thrust their bodies towards a man,
as this one did, were never hard to entertain.

He gestured towards the bottle. 'As you see, it is hardly opened
yet. Perhaps you'll share it with me, Mistress Finnigan?'

She made no show of reluctance. 'Always glad to share a bottle.'
This was said with a particularly sweet smile.

She seated herself on the opposite side of the table and, without
waiting, poured herself a full glass. She tossed half of it back with
a swiftness that made him wince. Then she seemed to remember
what she had come for in the first place, and turned directly to
her subject.

'Mrs Maclay is probably on her way to join her husband,' she
began.

Louis raised his eyebrows encouragingly. 'So . . .? I'm afraid I
don't know . . .'

'Her husband is Andrew Maclay — he's just bought the old Priest
place three miles farther on,' she volunteered easily. 'Clever as
a monkey with money, he is. He's made himself a rich man in the
eight or so years he's been here — with a bit of gambling on the side,
to help things along. And there was talk of him getting salvage
money — a lot of it — for a ship in India, or China, or one of those
foreign places.' She laughed a little. She was a pretty woman, with
beautiful eyes. 'But there's not so much gambling for Mr Maclay
now, believe me!'

'No?'

'No, he's getting too important these days, too respectable. And
as for that wife of his . . . Well, look at the way she's dressed, for
one thing. You'd never think she'd landed here as a convict, now,
would you?'

He leaned nearer to her. Her wide, bold eyes were fixed on
him unblinkingly. He could smell her faint, clean smell, that
seemed to come from the generous expanse of bosom her gown
revealed.

'So Mrs Maclay was a convict, was she?'

Nell Finnigan shrugged her plump shoulders. 'Oh . . . It's
an old story. Everyone knows it . . . how she had Andrew Maclay
all tied in knots before he ever stepped ashore in this place. It was
this way . . .'

As she talked, Louis refilled her empty glass.

2

Ten years ago, when Joseph Priest first cleared and fenced his
land, he had had dreams of how his property might be in the
future. With reckless disregard of both time and labour, he had
found and transplanted forty young mimosa trees, spacing them
at regular intervals among the eucalypts, twenty each side, along
the avenue leading to the house. He was one of the first who came
to the colony to find beauty in this harsh, austere landscape, and
with the impractical soul of a poet, he had made his gesture to it.
Priest drank heavily. Year by year he and the farm deteriorated
with equal speed; he dismissed more labourers, and the very
promising property gradually slipped into ruin. But every spring
the mimosa trees were a little taller, the avenue turned bright
gold in the midst of the green, and Joseph Priest smiled whenever
he looked at it. He found contentment in the fact that, although
he was counted a failure, he had created here a thing of lasting
beauty — created it out of an untouched wilderness. Crazed with
drink, and overwhelmed by hopeless debt, in the end he could
not wait until the trees bloomed again. He hung himself from the
tallest and strongest of them before winter was over.
    The mimosa were in their golden bloom when Sara drove along
the avenue for the first time. Something of the spirit of Joseph
Priest touched her, she had a sudden understanding of his practical
notion to fashion a thing of ordered loveliness out of the resources
at hand. This was the sort of thing she longed to do for Kintyre —
but at Kintyre, prosperous as it was, and well-run, time and
labour could never be spared, as this madman had spared them.
She breathed a prayer of thankfulness to him for all his wild
folly.
    The house itself was an unpainted ruin. It had a badly thatched
roof, and sagging, rotten verandas around three sides of it. Once
there had been some attempt at a garden, and a straggling orchard
beside it. The garden was choked and overgrown, and Sara's experienced eyes knew that the trees had not borne fruit for some
years, although now they made a show of heartbreaking beauty,
with sparse, frail blossom on every bough.
    She saw Jeremy appearing round the side of the house before
the carriage stopped. Her bonnet, which she had taken off when
they left Castle Hill, lay on the seat beside her. She picked it up
and waved it excitedly. He hesitated, and then came forward at a
half-run. The carriage lurched and halted, and Jeremy flung open
the door.

'Sara! What brings you here? Oh, this is wonderful! Wait until Andrew . . .'

She laughed a little, accepting his hand as she stepped down. 'Am I welcome, do you think, Jeremy? Or is this a time when no woman should intrude?'

For a moment his fingers tightened round her hand. 'What a tease you are, Sara! You know that Andrew will be delighted. We never thought, either of us . . .'

He paused, aware that her smile had grown broader, and that she was looking beyond him. He turned, and saw Andrew come running along the veranda and jump down the three steps. Sara dropped Jeremy's hand as if it had never been there, and he watched her outstretched arms go about her husband's neck. They clung together tightly, quite unmindful of either his own gaze, or Edwards's sardonic grin from the driver's seat.

At last Andrew loosened his grip; his hands slipped forward a little until they rested on Sara's shoulders. He held her back a little, looking at her with a beam of pleasure on his face.

'How good to have you here!' he said.

She laughed delightedly. 'How could I stay away? Your letters made me so envious. Both of you here – and I kept out of all this!'

With a slight gesture she indicated the tumble-down house, the ruin of the orchard and garden.

Andrew patted her shoulder. 'We've needed you here, haven't we, Jeremy? We're killing ourselves with our own cooking!'

Sara's eyebrows shot up. She said, with mock severity, 'If a cook was all you needed, I'm quite sure that there's more than one to be found in Castle Hill.'

Over her head, Andrew winked at Jeremy. 'Oh, of course! And more than one who'd be willing to share the house with a handsome bachelor like Jeremy, I've no doubt.'

They all laughed together, and Andrew began to lead Sara towards the steps, his arm loosely about her shoulders. Jeremy walked on the other side, holding her discarded bonnet, and listening to their talk.

'Come and see the house first,' Andrew said. 'It needs a great deal done to it, of course – but it should be pleasant enough when it's finished. The farm . . .' He shrugged. 'Priest hasn't done a stroke of work, or spent a penny-piece on it for years. But we'll soon have it in shape. I think in a few weeks we can bring the first stock here . . .'

Andrew and Sara went on into the house. Jeremy stayed on the veranda, walking back to the three rickety steps. He could hear

their voices as they planned together. They were excited, he
thought – not bitterly, but a little sadly. He felt the ribbons of
Sara's bonnet between his fingers, pulling them tight, and then
loosening them. He thought of them tied beneath her chin, and
his blood quickened. He wondered when it was that he had first
begun to love her – perhaps the night the convicts broke out at
Kintyre. Perhaps he had always known and loved Sara – might
she not have been the myth of every love-dream he had ever had?
He didn't know.

He leant back against the veranda post, and his eyes were on
the golden bloom of the mimosas.

3

Andrew stood at the foot of Glenbarr's wide staircase, staring
up at the landing above him. He looked at his watch for the
second time in five minutes, brushed unnecessarily at the sleeve
of his coat, listening all the time to the murmur of voices coming
from the main bedroom. Suddenly, madly impatient, he leapt up
three steps. 'Sara!' he called. 'Are you ready?'

The voices ceased. A rustle of stiff brocade answered him, and the
sound of Sara's footsteps. When she reached the head of the stairs,
his quick glance took in the gown of palest blue and silver –
extravagant material he remembered having brought her from
India. She was smoothing her gloves as she came down; a trace
of a smile lingered on her face, as if she had just heard something
that pleased her. Behind her, rigid and thin in a starched apron,
came Annie Stokes. She carried her mistress's wrap on her arm,
and her wrinkled features wore a look of fierce pride and satisfaction.

Bennett opened the door as Sara came forward. She stood
on the doorstep, while Annie adjusted the wrap, sniffing at the
scent of the early dew. The night was dark, though later there
would be a moon. The lanterns of the waiting carriage glowed
warmly; one of the horses pawed gently at the gravel.

Bennett remained by the carriage door until Sara and Andrew
were seated, then he signalled to Edwards perched up on the
box.

Edwards gathered the reins in his hands. Ahead of him was
Sydney's huddle of lighted houses. He squared his shoulders,
and, for the pleasure of hearing it, announced in a loud voice:
'Government House, sir! Right!'

The Maclays' names echoed through the long drawing-room at

Government House, and many heads turned in a puzzled fashion to look at the latest arrivals. They watched Andrew's bow, and Sara's curtsy, noting, with eyes accustomed to discerning the degree of vice-regal favour, that the Governor was affable, and that Mrs King had a welcoming and gracious smile. Eyes turned away rather hastily, in case the inquisitive stares might be discovered, and the buzz of conversation rose louder than before.

The two newcomers advanced farther into the room, to join the Ryders; they were instantly aware that most of the talk was centred on them. Sara's position in Sydney's tiny society was still irregular – although, since Alison Barwell's claims of friendship, she had been more or less accepted and treated in the way that Andrew's position demanded. But society had not let itself go with any noticeable generosity, until the seal of official approval and acknowledgement was offered her. And this evening it was bestowed for the first time in an invitation to Government House.

But the Kings were very new to their position of governing the colony, and more caution had been expected from them at the beginning. A question was asked and repeated among the little groups in the crowded drawing-room. Why was Sara Maclay received, when no other ex-convict had ever been given this privilege? One man in the gathering had the explanation on undeniable authority, and he saw no reason for holding back his knowledge. He leaned forward and whispered in his companion's ear; then, from behind open fans, the tale was spread until no one had cause to wonder any longer.

Mrs King, on acquainting herself with Sydney, had had the idea of starting a girls' orphanage for the illegitimate offspring of hundreds of casual matings – children who roamed the streets, and had already learned how to beg a living, and evade authority. These were to be rounded up and suitably housed; for this purpose Mrs King needed money. The story travelled around the drawing-room that Sara Maclay's invitation to Government House, a graceful gesture on Mrs King's part, had come after she received a donation of a thousand pounds from Andrew, and a firm promise of further help.

Interested eyes turned to look at the man who was a thousand pounds poorer for this evening's entertainment.

Voices grew hard in the effort to be heard above one another; the steady stream of talk continued, almost succeeding in drowning the announcement of each guest's arrival. The soft lap of the water against the rocks below Government House was lost; groups had spilled out through the open french windows on to the veranda,

but, so far, only a few had paused to notice that the rising moon
had cast a brilliant track of light across the harbour. There were
plenty of other nights, Sara thought, for them to watch the moon,
and, sensibly, most of them were concentrating on the business in
hand.

Half a dozen times Andrew was checked by men anxious to have
a word with him, as he made his way, Sara at his side, towards
the corner where they saw that Julia Ryder had found herself a
comfortable sofa. Macarthur stopped them, his dark face bland
and smiling – smiling more broadly, with a bow to Sara, at
Andrew's invitation to call up at Glenbarr the following morning.
Robert Campbell also made a bid for Andrew's attention, desisting
when he saw that the other was not to be side-tracked. Normally
these men were Andrew's business associates, the colony's men of
affairs, the men whose word was power. At any other time he
would have been wrapped in conversation half of the night with
them. But, under the curious stares all around, he seemed bent
on proving that, when his wife was at his side, he had eyes for no
one else.

'My dear Sara – how lovely you look this evening!' In full view
of the room Julia offered her cheek to be kissed.

James Ryder smiled upon her with real pleasure. It touched
his sense of humour to think of the effect on the present gathering if he were to suddenly recall – as he most certainly could –
the picture Sara had made the first time Andrew had brought her
up from the *Georgette*'s filthy hold. She was a beauty, even then,
he reflected – but those rags! He coughed into the crisp ruffles at
his wrist, to hide the chuckle that rose in his throat. Julia twisted
and glanced at him suspiciously. Then her face relaxed, as if she
guessed his thoughts.

'Sara does us great credit, do you not think so, James?'

'Indeed, yes!' he replied, letting his grin out of control, his
eyes on Sara's face. 'There's more satisfaction in watching Sara than
there'll ever be in that prim daughter of ours.' He gave an exaggerated sigh. 'Ellen's a good girl – but a prude. It doesn't seem
possible that any daughter of Julia's brought up in a place like this,
should turn out such a simpering little madam. But Ellen has
somehow managed it.'

'England will change her,' Sara said reassuringly.

'In that select Ladies' Academy in Bath?' James gave a hopeless
shrug. 'She's doomed to prudery, I'm afraid – and my only son
gone off to pin his heart to Lord Nelson's sleeve!'

A shade of fear touched Julia's face, but she spoke quite firmly.

'Charles will be back when he's had enough of the sea. He'll come back because he loves this place more than he cares to admit. As for Ellen . . .'

Sara didn't listen any longer. At the other end of the room she heard Captain and Mrs Barwell announced, and she stepped behind James to get a better view of the doorway. Alison was rising from her curtsy. She wore a white gown that made her look like an exquisitely turned-out doll. In an instant its simplicity caused every other woman in the room to look overdressed, though no feminine eye was deceived about its cost. On Richard's arm she began to move through the crowd. Sara quickly turned her head because Richard was looking about him in a way she had come to recognize. His gaze would find her soon enough, she knew, but she was not anxious to appear conspicuous, and she drew back again behind James.

'Mr William Cooper!'

'Monsieur Louis de Bourget!'

Again Sara's head turned. The volume of talk swelled perceptibly after the announcement of this last name, and there was shifting and craning to get a better view.

'. . . de Bourget . . . de Bourget?'

She could hear the running whisper of it, as he made his bow to the Governor and his wife, and she felt that for the rest of the evening the gathering had found a far more absorbing topic of conversation than herself. She moved her fan gently, watching with narrowed eyes. He and Cooper were detained in talk by King, and she thought that now, with a cluster of English faces about him, his Gallic look was far more pronounced than when Nell Finnigan's parlour had been his background. The magnificence of his dress was yet another feature to distinguish him. The dark red coat and gold-buckled shoes were too grand for this dull little vice-regal entertainment; but Mrs King's face wore a look of pleasure which told Sara that this Frenchman was well enough versed in the art of subtle flattery.

She flicked her fan again, and turned to Andrew.

'This is the man,' she said, 'whom I told you about. He is the Frenchman I talked with at Nell Finnigan's.'

Julia looked at her with raised eyebrows. 'You've actually *met* him? Then that's a great deal more than anyone else besides William Cooper has done.'

Sara shrugged. 'I called in at Finnigan's on my way to Priest's – de Bourget was there, on *his* way to Cooper's house. It seems they became acquainted when their ships were waiting together in Cape Town some time ago.'

James gave another chuckle. 'Then I had no need to waste all
my afternoon gathering information about this fellow. All I need
have done was to ask Sara.'

Sara shut her fan briskly. 'Indeed, I could hardly have helped
you then. We only arrived back from Priest's this morning, and I
know nothing of the man beyond his name. He's a Frenchman, but
as to what he's doing here . . .' She shrugged. 'His nationality seems
to be the only remarkable thing about him.'

Andrew laughed. 'Don't pretend, my dear, that you're the only
woman in the room who doesn't find the cloth of his coat remarkable – and the number of rings he wears! For myself, I'm utterly
fascinated by his look of prosperity. I find this unknown gentleman
extremely attractive.'

James cleared his throat. 'Then do give me the pleasure of relating the gossip I've so carefully patched together from snippets I've
picked up all over the town. No woman could have done it with
greater skill, I assure you. Though, I must warn you, the source is
none too reliable. The tales of this man, de Bourget, were begun by
the captain of the *Jane Henry*, who brought him here from Ile de
France. And *he* claims to have heard the story all over the island.'

His wife reached up and tapped his hand with her fan. 'For pity's
sake, James, *do* tell us! I'm dying with curiosity!'

'Well, in that case . . . The rumour has it that Monsieur de
Bourget is a kinsman of the Marquis de L . . . The name is only
whispered, my dear Julia, in case it should prove to be wrong. De
Bourget was a member of his household – assisted him with some
of his estates, or some such thing. Our young Frenchman has no
money of his own, but he possessed considerable influence with the
Marquis. But he was also, it's said, very well known in other quarters of Paris. In fact, he exercised his full right to mix with people
less well born than his noble cousin. He belonged, in a sense, to
both worlds, as a young gentleman of no fortune is often obliged
to do. He would have been a fool if his influence with the Marquis
hadn't occasionally been sold at a price.'

James was enjoying his audience. He continued, 'The family
tarried too long after the Revolution. The September massacres
came upon them, and the Marquis realized that he would never
escape from Paris. He had often suspected that his penniless cousin
had Jacobin friends, and he begged him to take his only child, a
girl, to London. De Bourget managed to get her away from France
– and with them both went the family jewels.'

Julia caught her breath. 'The child . . . what has become of
her?'

'The child was ill, even before she left Paris. She died in London a year later. Apparently de Bourget had nursed her devotedly.'

'And the jewels . . . ?' Andrew was concerned, and frowning.

James's shoulders lifted a little. 'The jewels? What do you imagine? The whole family was wiped out in the massacres – even the nephews and cousins. The girl was the only survivor – the girl and de Bourget.'

Andrew looked doubtful now. 'And how much of this do you believe?'

The other man spread his hands in a gesture of uncertainty.

'That's the point, exactly,' he said. 'The story has travelled halfway round the world, distorted, no doubt, with each telling. And it's said that de Bourget himself is not to be questioned about it. He neither confirms nor denies it; he expresses neither royalist nor Jacobin sympathies. All that is certain is that he seems to possess a great deal of money, and that he has travelled continuously for the past five years. France was in utter chaos when the Marquis sent his child away. So who can be certain that de Bourget was anything more than a trusted secretary? He might not have been a blood relation at all.'

'Is that possible?' Andrew asked dubiously. 'Surely there were some among the émigrés in London who would have recognized a kinsman of the Marquis? An impostor could hardly expect to live amongst them, and remain unexposed.'

'That, of course, occurred to me,' James acknowledged. 'In the émigré circles in London the story must be well known. Perhaps such a story will only bear repeating on this side of the world, where we're so far removed from the source. Whatever the truth is, the child's death put de Bourget in possession of a fortune, and no one else has come forward to lay claim to it.'

'Has he a wife?' Julia asked.

James nodded. 'That fortune wouldn't escape a woman's hands for very long. He married the daughter of a small Gloucestershire squire. They were together only about a year. She went on a visit to her family, and never returned to de Bourget. There's a child, I believe . . . a daughter.'

'I see you've had a busy afternoon, James,' his wife said mildly. 'The information you've collected in these few hours would do credit to the powers of any six women put together.'

'Oh . . . it wasn't all from the captain of the *Jane Henry*. I fancy William Cooper has been talking also.'

'A fortune in jewels . . . and still his wife can't bear him for longer than a year . . .' Sara pondered the information. 'It makes

very little sense. Perhaps he stays away from England because of
her . . . Or because someone else may come forward to claim a part
of the fortune.'

Andrew touched her arm. 'If you dare to, my dear, you can
question the Frenchman all you please. Macarthur is bringing him
and Cooper directly across to us.'

With burning cheeks, Sara swung round. John Macarthur was
almost beside them now, and de Bourget, with William Cooper, a
pace or so behind.

'Mrs Maclay . . .' Smiling, Macarthur gestured towards the
Frenchman. 'Monsieur de Bourget claims to be already acquainted
with you. Surely he dreams . . . ?'

Sara tossed her head back. 'No, Monsieur de Bourget doesn't
dream.'

Louis de Bourget stepped up beside Macarthur. He took Sara's
hand, and bowed low over it.

'Madame,' he said, 'I am surrounded by strangers. I trust you
and your husband will forgive me for flinging myself upon your
society in this fashion?'

He raised her hand to kiss it, and Sara knew that every eye in the
room was on them in that instant.

5

Some quality in Louis de Bourget answered a need in Andrew,
of which, until that time, he had hardly been aware. At first his
feeling for the Frenchman was scarcely more than curiosity; then
he admitted being amused by the other's cynicism, his air of having weighed up all that life offered a man, his manner of poking
sly fun at the manoeuvrings of the colonials in their race for wealth,
and hiding all of this under his mask of polite concern. Andrew
talked to Louis, and found what he had long lacked – a confidant
who was far removed from the struggle which waged unceasingly
for profits, for concessions, for gain. De Bourget returned to Sydney,
to stay in William Cooper's new house; in the two months following the Government House reception, Andrew began to look forward to sharing a bottle of wine with him, relating the latest
rumours and speculations and then listening to Louis's dry, often
scathing comments on the whole of the colonial scene.

'I despise them all!' Andrew would declare roundly. 'Profiteers!
Land-grabbers!'

'Naturally, you despise them,' Louis answered, with a calculating smile. 'Most of them are not nearly as practised in the art of profiteering as yourself – and I'm beginning to understand that you have very little time for the second-rate.'

Andrew was accustomed to laugh at such a remark. There was about this Gallic temperament a freshness which both fascinated and irritated him.

'Damn me, if I can think why you stay here at all!' Andrew said. 'We appear such bores to you – so bourgeois.'

Louis shrugged. 'The bourgeois are prolific breeders – and their children inherit the earth.' He yawned elaborately, and then finished, 'Though I must confess that the good William Cooper is a rather overpowering example of the species.'

'I can't imagine why anyone suffers your rudeness – unless it's because your politeness is so much worse.' Andrew said this drily, but he was smiling. 'If Cooper wearies you, come with us to Kintyre for a few weeks. We're going to spend Christmas there. We could have some shooting.'

A look of animation crossed the other's face. 'That, my friend, is something I should like very much.'

2

For a time Sara sat quite still, studying Louis carefully. He was perched on the rail of Kintyre's wide veranda; he was booted and spurred, and wore a coat that only a London tailor could have fashioned. Occasionally he swished his riding whip at the midsummer mosquitoes that buzzed about his head. He was turned side-faced to Sara, staring down the reach of the river that Kintyre, from its height on the hill, commanded. He was unusually thoughtful, as if he had forgotten that his role rarely permitted him such moments. There was almost a look of moodiness about him, a brooding air, as he gazed at the twilight stretch of water. Over the bush there was that same withdrawn appearance it had worn for Sara for the first time she had seen it. Clouds were gathering, a dusky purple; off in the mountains she heard thunder, and saw a sudden flash of chain-lightning dancing along a gaunt, mile-long escarpment. A low bar of red above a ridge was all that was left of the day. Down on the river some stray sound disturbed the wild duck. They rose with swift grace, silhouetted, for a moment, against the sky, and then were lost out of sight.

Louis turned his head towards her, and she realized that she could no longer distinguish his features clearly.

'In a week or so, Sara,' he said, 'I intend to go and stay on the Nepean for a while.'

Folding the nightshirt she was making for Sebastian, she answered his remark lightly. 'And who, pray, is next to have the honour of your company?'

He flicked his hand sharply at what might have been a mosquito. 'Sara, you're impossible! You imply that I have not enjoyed my stay at Kintyre. You know, surely . . .'

'I know,' she said soothingly, smiling. 'I *am* impossible. Put it down to feminine pique. I merely wished to know who was to steal you away from us.'

'No one,' he said, shaking his head. 'At least, no one but the river.'

'The river! You can't mean you're going all that way just to look at the river?'

'And why not? I intend to travel along the Nepean as far as settlement has gone.'

'Why?' Sara's tone was no longer light; she leaned forward to try to see his face better.

'I thought that if I liked what I saw, I might apply for a grant of land.'

Sara gave a faint gasp, and leaned back rather limply in her chair.

Louis swished at the mosquitoes as before, and seemed quite unperturbed. He glanced over his shoulder as the thunder in the mountains grew louder.

'I've talked it over with Andrew,' he said. 'It seems there could be no objection to my settling.'

At this, Sara came to life again. She sat up straight. 'No objection, of course – but, Louis, why? What can there be here for you? This is not your country, your background. These are not your people, your customs. Why, hardly anyone even speaks your language.'

He laughed softly. 'You're right – hardly anyone speaks it. *You* do, but you won't give me the pleasure of it, because you say your accent is bad. Sara, shame on you, you're cruel!'

And then, abruptly, the jesting tone left his voice.

'You're right about the other things as well. But they no longer matter to me. I have no care now who my neighbours are, or what they think of me. England, I have never liked – and I am weary of travelling. So why should I not stay here for a while? If I dislike it more than other places, then I shall leave. I have learned enough to know that it makes very little difference to oneself where one lives – or with whom, providing it is not with enemies.'

Sara was frowning. 'But land cannot be taken up for you to play with, Louis,' she said sternly. 'You must be prepared to farm it – and I think I'm right in assuming that you're no farmer.'

He chuckled faintly in the growing darkness. 'No more or no less a farmer than your friend, Richard Barwell. If he can take land, so can I.'

'It's not the same thing!' Sara replied hotly. She knew she betrayed herself in the sharpness of her tongue. She knew also that she was rather afraid of Louis de Bourget, for the depth of his cynicism, for his ability to view a situation, and weigh it up for exactly what it was. She hoped desperately that he would let the subject of Richard alone.

'Sara,' he said, 'you're so feudal in your fashion. Land is your god – you want to see your estates grow, to count your wealth in acres. You would be a small despot if you could.'

Suddenly he flung his arms wide. 'But look at it here – this great, empty land! There are miles – hundreds of miles – untouched. And yet it shocks you that someone like myself might be given a minute piece to play with. If I choose to farm it, or make a garden of it, who is to care? Or who should say that I oughtn't? What if I give myself the pleasure of building a house high above the rivers, as you have done here at Kintyre? A white house, Sara – yes, I should like to build a white house, if only for the joy of seeing it among these dull green trees of yours. And if I tire of my toy when it is completed, why should I not sell it, and be as free to go as I am now? True, the life about me would not be one to which I am accustomed, or one I admire much – but where is one to find the customs of France, except in France?'

'I am told,' Sara said slyly, 'that émigré society has made a miniature Versailles in England. Could you not be happy with them? Or why not in France itself? Many have gone back and accepted the new order of things, or are, perhaps, waiting for a Restoration.'

Louis let out an exclamation of contempt. 'Those who expect the monarchy to return on the old terms are fools. And the émigrés are a stupid lot of fools bleating together, and taking nostalgic trips to Dover. Besides, I don't like England.'

'Then that leaves France,' Sara murmured quietly. 'If you are so contemptuous of the forlorn hope of a Restoration, why do you not return to make your peace with the new order?'

His body was clearly outlined against the reddened sky as she spoke; she watched his head tilt backwards, and heard his slight, mocking laugh.

'Sara, you have been listening to tales.'

'Tales of what?'

'Tales of the dark past of Louis de Bourget.' He waved her to silence as she began a half-hearted attempt to protest. 'Oh, don't bother with denials – I know quite well what they say. It's said that I was once a penniless kinsman of the Marquis de L . . . isn't that so. And it's pointed out that I spend my life travelling, and that I appear not to lack money. All of which is true.'

He went on talking quietly; the distant rumble of thunder was fairly constant now, his voice low against it.

'And don't they also say that I dare not remain in England for fear an heir to the Marquis should suddenly turn up? And that I'm not well received in émigré circles, and so take care to keep out of reach of their power. Isn't that what they say?'

She answered him levelly enough. 'Well, you seem to know it all, Louis.'

'Of course I know it all. Only a fool would not know it. But they who speak without knowledge of Paris in those days are fools. It was a nightmare of chaos and fear. There was no time for second thoughts about anything. Decisions had to be made swiftly, and within the very shadow of death. They were very brave, those people, and rather stupid. Courage was about the only thing their tradition and breeding had given them. It seems to me an incredibly proud and foolish thing to allow oneself to be taken without first dispatching a few Jacobins. But courage was the only virtue of my noble cousin, the Marquis. He had no resources, no imagination. Where better could he turn than to me – who had lived out all my precarious life learning to be indispensable to the rich, and knowing from bitter experience the ways of the poor? Could any one of the Marquis's brothers, or nephews, have got himself out of Paris and to the coast in those September days? There wasn't one among them who knew the value of a sou, and who would not have betrayed himself in travelling the first half-mile. Those who have scattered gold about all their lives cannot assume frugal habits in a single day. No – the Marquis chose rightly when he asked me, the humblest of them all, to take his daughter. I knew the ways of the peasants – I understood their minds, and how they could be expected to act. It took us twelve days to reach the coast – a further two weeks to find a boat to take us across. As soon as I arrived in England, I heard that the Marquis was dead.'

'And the child?' Sara asked quietly.

'Jeanne lived only a year,' he said. 'Three sons and another daughter of my cousin had also died of consumption.'

'And there was no one else?'

'Ah – there!' He shrugged elaborately. 'That is a question which has interested many people. Who can be sure that somewhere in France there doesn't still exist a man with a closer claim than mine? Might there not be a surviving relation who lives in ignorance of the wealth the Marquis placed in my hands? But he also placed a delicate daughter in my hands – and I am owed at least a debt of gratitude. Jeanne died in a soft bed of her own, not at the guillotine. The lawyers may fret over the situation, but I was in possession of the jewels my cousin entrusted to me, alone with Jeanne. His houses were destroyed, his estates parcelled out to a thousand eager hands – but the jewels he gave to me.'

Sara remained silent, thinking back over his words, seeking a flaw in his story, a point on which she might question him further. But there seemed to be none. She thought that perhaps he spoke the truth. It was evident to her that Louis de Bourget was at ease in the ways of fashionable life – she was well competent to judge that quality after her years in London as a dressmaker's apprentice. If he were a low-born impostor, and no kinsman at all of the Marquis, then his manners never betrayed him in the slightest. What man without breeding could dare to be rude and bored, as he often was? Who could wear such clothes as he, and never appear to notice them? His thin, olive-tinted face would have been completely in place among the aristocratic ones that faced the Paris mob from the scaffold.

'And my marriage,' he continued, his voice low, but still distinct, even against the background of thunder. 'That is another subject for idle speculation. I have done no worse in that than many men before me – except that my mistake is more evident. She was so lovely she overrode any feelings of prudence I had that warned me we were not suited. She was so young I believed she would mould herself to my own wishes but I was utterly mistaken. She had the will and the spirit of a woman twice her age. Until she came to London that season she had never known anything but what passed for life in that huge, uncomfortable country house. The only conversation was hunting – in the summer they languished. This was her only world, and I hadn't got the wit or sense to see that she wanted no other. After our daughter was born she went to visit her family. It was then she wrote to tell me that she never meant to return.'

'And you were content to accept that?'

'The truth is, Sara, that I no longer cared enough about her to try to sway that unimaginative soul. Once her lovely face was out of my sight, I found I was not very much affected by her. She was not to be wooed with any gifts but horses, and a woman who cares only for horses can be a tiresome creature to live with. I imagine it's considered an everlasting shame by her family to have had her quarrel with me made so public. But she refused to return to me — not unless I found her a house close by and settled to the hunting routine. The proposition didn't interest me at all. So she lives with her parents still, and we exchange an occasional letter — mostly over money matters.'

'The child — your daughter?' Sara prompted.

'I know almost nothing of her. Her mother has singularly little talent for letter-writing. I imagine, though, that she will learn to ride a horse long before she can spell with any certainty.'

'It's sad,' Sara murmured. 'So wasted . . .'

'Wasted . . . exactly! Both our lives are wasted. She was cold as a splinter of ice. Her greed and selfishness I could have forgiven readily — but not her lack of warmth. I could not live with a woman to whom a husband was something merely to be suffered . . .'

Sudden pity for him touched Sara. She had never imagined that she could pity Louis — the assured and cynical; from that moment her feeling towards him was changed. She could sense the frustration and bitterness where before she had only seen his light, charming manners — his amusing conversation — only those and his bored acceptance of whatever came his way. In a few seconds she knew he would revert to them, but at least he had shown her a glimpse of something else beyond them.

Abruptly she rose and came across to him. A flash of lightning played above the trees on the opposite bank of the river. It lit up Kintyre's well-laid acres, and every detail of Louis's appearance, every feature. He was waiting, a detached smile about his lips, for her to speak.

She held out her hand.

'Thank you for telling me this,' she said. 'My curiosity didn't deserve such rewards.'

He took her hand, not holding it upwards as he had always done previously, but gripping it as if she were a man.

'Reward?' he said. 'Ah, no, Sara! I *cared* what you and Andrew believed of me. The rest . . .' He shrugged. 'Well, let them have their little gossip, if it makes them happy. But if I am to remain in this country, then I must have you both for my friends. You and Andrew — you are the spirit of this place . . .'

He broke off as the thunder crashed about their heads. On a sudden rush of cool wind the rain came down off the mountains. It hit them with a tropical violence and density, slashing against their faces and bodies before they could move back from the rail.

Louis reached quickly to gather up Sara's sewing-bag from the chair, and followed her at a run along the veranda to the door. The noise of the rain was heavy as it hit the sunbaked earth; the lightning lit up the garden brilliantly. They both paused for a few moments to watch it, looking backwards with wonder, as to something they had been lucky to escape. Then Sara turned, trying to smooth down her damp hair with her hand, and stepped into the hall. Louis held the door for her, then followed. As he passed behind her, his eyes held a rare look of softness and pleasure.

3

It had rained all night, the sound drumming and monotonous against Kintyre's roof. But by noon the next day, when Sara took her daily ride along the road in the direction of Parramatta, the rough storm-water ditches by the side of the road were already drying out. The smell of the rain lingered in the scrub, in the eucalypt trees, giving the bush almost the freshness of a spring morning. As she rode along she noticed the curved, prominent heads of a dozen or more kookaburras perched on a high bough of a ragged gum on her left. They remained motionless until she drew level; then their heads went back, beaks opened, and the bush for a mile around was abruptly regaled with their mad, wild laughter. Not in all the years that she had been familiar with the sound had Sara been able to accept it as natural, nor had she schooled herself not to laugh with them. Her mouth curved delightedly; she threw her head back as they did, and laughed inelegantly, and without restraint. The noise they made followed her down the road, infectious, mocking; as strange and different as the country that had bred it.

The next bend would bring her just over two miles from Kintyre. Peering up at the sun, she judged that it was more than time she returned. But at the bend itself she halted, wrinkling her forehead and staring down the road, where the heat conjured up a mirage like water, and the midday haze was thickening. Two horsemen, no more yet than specks, held her attention. She stared at them, shielding her eyes against the glare; then, in a few moments, she raised her crop to wave excitedly.

Both men answered her wave immediately, and urged their horses into a canter. She drew into the shade of a big blue gum to wait for them.

'Richard! Jeremy!' she called, as they came close enough to hear.

And while she sat her horse with an easy smile on her lips, she was pondering the reason for them being on this journey together. There was no feeling of friendship between Richard and Jeremy; their antagonism towards each other was too obvious for them to willingly ride side by side up from Parramatta. As far as she knew, Jeremy had had no intention of leaving Priest's; he was busy there and had even refused Sara's request that he should come to Kintyre for Christmas. The two men must have met on the road, and a desire for company had prompted Richard to stay by Jeremy's side. It would have been more in keeping with Richard's feelings about the Maclay overseer if he had given a brief nod and ridden on.

In the last few yards Richard moved ahead of Jeremy; he was the first to come to her side. His clothes were covered in fine dust, and there were rivulets of sweat on his face.

He smiled his pleasure at seeing her, leaning over in the saddle and taking her outstretched hand.

'Sara! How are you?'

'I'm well, Richard, thank you.' Her answer was smooth, and cool. 'And yourself – and Alison?'

'Well enough,' he said impatiently, staring into her face with a look of disappointment. Then he swung round, only half-stifling an exclamation of annoyance, as Jeremy's horse jostled his own. 'Can't you mind . . .?'

Richard didn't say any more. He sullenly watched Sara's hand go out to grip Jeremy's.

'We'll be glad to see you at Kintyre, Jeremy,' she said. 'But what brings you? Something important, surely – I was beginning to think nothing would ever shift you from Priest's, when you wouldn't even come back at Christmas.'

'In ordinary circumstances nothing would move me from Priest's yet,' Jeremy said. 'But this happens to concern the great John Macarthur.' He tilted his hat back a little, and went on. 'It seems that Andrew did him some service a short while ago – and now he's pleased to inform me that he's changed his mind about selling some of the ewes and a ram from the merino flock. That is, he says, if Mr Maclay still has a mind to have them. I can't help thinking that Macarthur may want yet another favour from Andrew – his merino flock are almost as precious to him as his own children.'

Sara's eyes opened wide. 'The merino flock! Andrew will be delighted! Macarthur's sheep are beginning to produce wool that he believes will better the Spanish merino. We've been hoping to get a few more . . .'

Richard broke in. '*Must* you talk wool and sheep the very moment one sees you, Sara?' His tone was light as he said it; obviously he repented the impatience he had let her see. But his horse moved sideways, and he made little attempt to hold it. The movement, and his words, effectively ended the conversation between the other two, and turned their attention back to him.

Sara laughed, though she could feel a flush of annoyance mounting in her cheeks. 'Why, Richard! I imagined such a farmer as you would be more than interested in the prospects for wool!'

His lips folded slightly, and he shrugged. 'Oh, I leave the experiments in wool to the Macarthurs and Maclays – to the really important people of the colony. Hyde Farm occupies quite enough of my time in its own humble fashion. I'll be content to follow in ten years' time where the pioneers lead today.'

He intercepted the glance that passed between Sara and Jeremy, and it seemed to infuriate him.

'Well, are we going to loiter about here in the sun all afternoon? Let's get on, shall we?'

Without waiting for them, he wheeled his horse, and started at a trot down the road.

They followed, and as he drew level, he addressed Sara again.

'I hear that you have the Frenchman staying at Kintyre?'

'Yes, he spent Christmas with us.'

He nodded vaguely. 'He's trying out the colony, I suppose. What do you think of him?'

'Andrew and I both like him. So will you, I'm sure, when you know him better.' Sara glanced sideways at him. 'He *never* discusses wool and sheep.'

'Obviously not,' Richard said shortly. 'He has enough money to hold himself aloof from matters of mere commerce. But I wonder was he so disinterested in making a little money at any time prior to the Revolution? From what I hear, he suffered an embarrassing lack of the commodity until then.'

'People, no doubt, tell a great many tales of Louis de Bourget,' Sara returned coldly. 'The pity is that they don't tell the full story. What is left out in his history is quite as important as the few facts already brought forward. If one has the inclination to learn – that is, if prejudice hasn't blinded one – there's a great deal more to Louis than the smooth fit of his coat.'

They rounded a bend and were now within sight of the fork leading to Hyde Farm. Looking at Richard, Sara saw his face twist, and then his hands, usually so confident and relaxed on the reins, grow taut. Richard was contemptuous of nervous hands on a horse, but he seemed quite unaware of his own at the moment.

'I don't find this Frenchman's story plausible at all,' he said, looking straight ahead. 'What brings him to a place like this – without introductions, and without any stated purpose? He left a wife and child behind him, too, I believe. It's suspicious – I tell you, no honest man behaves in that way. And if he has all the wealth rumour gives him, why didn't he remain in London where he could enjoy it?'

'It's just possible that he may not regard London as the paradise you found it to be, Richard.' She spoke savagely, and then was furious with herself for letting him see her disturbance.

'I imagine you'll be at Hyde Farm for a few days?' she continued quickly. 'Doubtless you'll come to Kintyre to see Andrew. I advise you to talk to Louis then and judge him for yourself. You'll be in danger of becoming as narrow-minded as the rest of us colonials, Richard, if you continue to place such a trust in gossip.'

He swerved in his saddle so suddenly that Sara's horse halted without warning, nearly unseating her.

'If your husband wishes to see me on business matters,' Richard said, 'I'll be found at Hyde Farm for the next two days. But I'll be damned if I'll come to Kintyre to quarrel with you over that bloody upstart. You and Andrew make me sick with your grovelling to a turncoat Frenchman, who was more than likely a Jacobin before his money forced him to be a royalist. You can find your friends in any doubtful place you choose, Sara – but don't expect them to be my friends as well!'

'You've said enough, Barwell!' Jeremy's voice was thick with anger. He leant across and caught the other man's bridle.

Richard turned on him furiously, unbelievingly.

'What the devil do you mean?'

'I mean that Mrs Maclay expects an apology!'

'Jeremy . . .!' In alarm Sara cried out. 'You . . .'

'An apology is just what Mrs Maclay is not going to get!' Richard snapped. 'I meant every word I said – and, by God, I'll thank you to keep your nose out of my affairs! I'd like to know what right any damned convict has to dictate to me! Take care that I don't have you before a magistrate for this piece of work.'

Jeremy's eyes were glazed with anger. 'Threaten me with what you like, Captain Barwell. But when you insult Mrs Maclay, you insult her husband – and you'll find neither he, nor myself, afraid of you, or a magistrate's court, or anything else you care to threaten.'

'Why you . . .'

With a muffled oath, Richard raised his crop high, and brought it down with his full weight on Jeremy's hand, which still held his bridle. The other winced, and his horse pulled away, almost dragging him from the saddle. But he clung, managing to bring the animal under control again. Richard struck his hand once again, and when the fingers didn't slacken, he swung his crop sideways, slashing it across Jeremy's face. At the same time he dug his heels in hard, and his horse sprang forward. Jeremy was forced to let the bridle go.

Richard galloped away, making for the fork that led to Hyde Farm.

'Curse him!' Jeremy muttered, enraged. 'I'll beat that . . .'

His face was white with fury, and blood was already trickling from the corner of his mouth. His hat had been knocked to the back of his head, giving him a wild, half-crazy appearance that terrified Sara. She saw him dig in his spurs to go after Richard, and at the same moment she hit her own horse smartly. It shot forward in a sudden lurch directly in Jeremy's path. They cannoned together, both almost unseating. Sara managed to pull up before she reached the ditch; Jeremy's horse reared, and he had to fight with it for control. By the time it was quietened, Richard was far down the road.

'For God's sake, Jeremy, don't be such a fool!'

In her anxiety, Sara snapped at him. The fear of the moment had shaken her violently: she was angry now to think of what passion the two men had unleashed in the matter of a few seconds, and over a Frenchman neither of them knew. She was panting, and her fear made her sharp and scathing.

'Don't you know that if you touched him you'd be flogged and sent to a chain-gang? In heaven's name, why do you lose your head like that? You're not a child – and you've had more than enough practice in schooling your temper!'

Jeremy brought his horse beside her. He said tersely, 'There's some things no amount of schooling will rid one of, Sara – and nothing will ever let one forgive. If I were free, I'd call him out and kill him for that.'

'But you're not free!' she reminded him tartly. 'And you're not in a position to make a fool of yourself by challenging him.'

'But all the same . . .'

'A nice figure you'd make, Jeremy Hogan,' she cut in, 'swinging

from the gallows. Now, let's have no more of this mad talk. There's
been enough heroics for one morning to defend the Maclay honour.
We'll get back to Kintyre, and do something to your face before
Andrew sees it.'

Very slowly he ran the reins through his hands. 'You're a woman
without a heart, Sara,' he said. 'I doubt that you've a natural
feeling in your whole body. What a general England has missed
because you're not a man! Rashness would never have outplayed
strategy in your cool head. Even Nelson has his human side in
Emma Hamilton, but there would have been no such indulgence
for you. I wish that you could see yourself just once . . .'

Jeremy's words trailed off; he stopped and looked at her in
amazement.

'Why, Sara . . . You're crying!'

She dashed a hand furiously across her eyes. 'Yes – and I can't
help it! I'm crying because . . .' Her voice rose in an aggrieved
tone. 'Because Richard made such a fool of himself – and because
you frightened me to death by putting yourself in danger over
him. Oh, Jeremy, can't you see – he just isn't worth it! Men are
supposed to be able to keep their wits about them pretty well,
but no sensible woman would dream of behaving as you've just
done!'

She began searching in one of the pockets of her habit for a
handkerchief. Taking it out, she dabbed her eyes, and then said
sharply, 'Well . . . don't just sit there like that! We'd better go
down to the river and do something about washing that cut. It's
bleeding worse now. It would be a nice thing, wouldn't it, if someone rode along and found me snivelling like a five-year-old brat,
and Master Jeremy with the blood running down into his collar! A
pretty pair we make, I've no doubt!'

A ghost of a smile played on his lips, as he followed her off the
road and into the scrub. A Sara who was frightened and shaken
was a rare spectacle; he looked at her gently-heaving shoulders
ahead of him, and was not displeased that he himself was half the
cause of her upset – even if he had to share it with that arrogant
upstart, Barwell. His hot anger against Barwell was fading –
shocked almost out of existence by Sara's tearful reaction to it. He
wished he could again see her face, with the tears sliding down it,
and the look, half of tenderness, half contempt for her own weakness, that it had worn.

She was following a vaguely defined path down to the river, refusing to allow him to go ahead to pick the way through the undergrowth, clinging to the lead, as if she felt the need to assert her own

authority. The sound of the river reached them clearly; the banks here were low, but the trees screened it completely, until almost the very moment when they broke through, and it lay, broad and deep, with the sun on it casting a dazzle that, for a minute, hurt their eyes. On the opposite bank the land had been partly cleared, and a small herd of cattle grazed quietly. Beyond, on a slight rise, was a whitewashed house that Jeremy recognized as belonging to Michael Macarthy, who had come out with Governor Phillip as a marine, and had stayed to take up land. The scene before them was peaceful, and all signs of the rain of the night were gone.

Jeremy dismounted and tethered both horses to the low bush. Then he lifted Sara down.

'Give me your handkerchief,' she said stiffly. 'Mine's useless.'

He offered it and she took it without a word, scrambling down the sandy incline of the river bank with it rolled up in her hand. He watched her bend and wring it out in the water and then come back to him.

'Let me look at that cut.' Her voice was gentler now; it was a little hoarse and rasping in her throat, as if, perhaps, she still held back tears. She dabbed at the congealing blood at the corner of his mouth, making clicking sounds with her tongue, and shaking her head.

'You won't mention this to Andrew, will you, Jeremy?'

She stood on tiptoe as she pressed the handkerchief against his mouth, murmuring absently, as to a child.

He drew back abruptly. 'Mention it to Andrew? You take me for a greater fool than ever! I . . .'

She followed his withdrawal, and began to dab again with the handkerchief. 'Oh, hush, Jeremy!' she said. 'You know I didn't mean that. I was merely trying to reassure myself. Richard behaved like a madman – and the sooner forgotten, the better.'

He caught at her wrist and held it, forcing her to halt her attention to the cut, and look at him directly.

'Richard Barwell *is* mad where you're concerned, Sara. He's mad with love and rage and frustration. He's jealous of Andrew – not only because of Andrew's possession of you, but of his position in the colony, and what he can do. Barwell may have been all that London desired in the way of an amusing drawing-room attraction, a horseman, and a swordsman. But *here*, beside Andrew, he doesn't cut such a fine figure. Envy can drive a man to many things – to drink, for one thing. And to spending far more money than he can afford.'

Suddenly his grip tightened almost brutally on her wrist.

'For how much longer is Andrew going to give this fool money to throw away? Surely, after six months, he can see that Hyde Farm isn't going to pay – at least not while it's run by Richard Barwell.'

She broke her wrist free of his hold. 'Andrew will go on lending Richard money just as long as Richard continues to be useful to him – which, it seems to me, will be as long as he remains in the colony.' She was speaking harshly again, and the bright colour had come into her cheeks. 'Of the two, Andrew is by far the cleverer. He'll profit from Richard and his wife, even if he never gets back a penny piece of the money.'

'Profit? What sort of profit?'

'You're not blind, Jeremy!' she said tartly. 'You can see all of this – you know it, without me telling you. You don't have to ask why Andrew throws his money down a bottomless well. He does it because of *me* – and don't pretend you don't know, because I wouldn't believe you.'

'All right, I won't pretend – I *do* know it. But I didn't think even Andrew would continue . . .'

She cut him short, impatiently. 'Andrew is more ambitious, more tenacious – more ruthless, in a way – than any other man I've ever known. He'll have what he wants, and the cost be damned! In this case, all he asks is Alison Barwell's friendship for me – and he pays for it.'

Her face twitched as she spoke, and then it softened. She looked at him fixedly, and raised her hand to the cut on his mouth. But this time she didn't touch it with the handkerchief. Gently, with the tip of her finger, she traced the thin line running towards his jaw.

'I will never forgive him for this,' she said. 'He is more dangerous than I thought. He loses control of himself, and then he's like a child in a rage – a weak, vicious, brutish child. In these last months he's dangled me on a string – but I swear to you now, Jeremy, that he'll dangle me no longer. For the future, I'll use him as Andrew has done. I'll use him for what he's worth to me, and beyond that I don't care a rap what becomes of him.'

She shrugged her shoulders faintly. 'So don't mock my cold heart again, Jeremy. Be glad of it, because it will need to be wrapped in ice to resist the memory of what Richard once meant to me.'

She turned aside and said no more. She put her foot in the stirrup, and then Jeremy lifted her into the saddle. He held the bridle while she settled herself, and held it long, because some new expression in her eyes seemed to root him there helplessly.

'Come nearer, Jeremy,' she said.

He stepped in closer to the horse, without thinking what she meant to do. Clinging to the pommel, she leaned down suddenly, and kissed him on the cheek.

As if she had struck him, he sprang back.

'Damn you! Don't do that!'

She flushed scarlet at his tone. 'I didn't think you'd object quite so strongly,' she said stiffly.

His eyes were dark and angry, staring up at her. 'You know right well that I don't want kisses like that, not from you, Sara. Don't think you can settle debts by giving me a sisterly peck on the cheek. I'll have from you the sort of kisses I want – or none at all!'

Then he went and untied his horse, mounting without a word.

This time it was Jeremy who led the way back to the road; Sara followed closely behind.

There was silence between them for more than a mile. The heat increased; the road was shadeless, and the sun beat down on their backs. The flies followed them, buzzing about their faces, and settling on their horses' flanks. They met no one; they did not speak to each other, nor did they even turn their heads as they passed the fork leading to Hyde Farm. For all the signs either betrayed, the incident with Richard might never have taken place. The hot, noon hush of the bush was complete.

Then they finally came to the last bend in the road, the spot from which Sara had had her first sight of Kintyre. The same memory returned to them both, like a sudden renewal of that distant day – the day they had discovered their jealousy over Andrew, the day they had found each other's strength, and had been determined to master it. Without a word they checked their horses.

Each could remember, with no trace of sentimental wistfulness, what Kintyre had been then. They remembered the scarred hill, where the trees had been torn out to make way for the house in its crude whiteness, its bare, blank face turned to the river and the mountains. In both their eyes, the vines were, for the moment, stripped from the walls, and the orchard was a few, slender young trees. It was again raw and new, like every other mark the white man had set upon this unused land.

The situation of the house upon the hill was still a challenge, a landmark thrown up boldly to meet the gaze of everyone who

used the road. But both Sara and Jeremy admitted to themselves
that they couldn't for long hold their first vision of it. It was
gently mellowed now, and the years had brought the trees back
on the hill, and soft, English grass grew in the spaces in the orchard.
It was the old Kintyre still, but changed. It no longer represented
Andrew's struggle to hold his own against the bush and the natives,
even against the climate, and the threat of the floods. This was
permanent, secure – the most loved of all his possessions, because it
had been the hardest to win.

Sara took her eyes away from the house and looked at Jeremy.
It did not occur to her to inquire his thoughts. She was certain
that they were on Kintyre, on the part he himself had played in
making it.

'It isn't any use thinking we can quarrel in this way, Jeremy,'
she said at last. 'We all of us – you, Andrew, and myself – need one
another too badly.'

He nodded, accepting her statement as natural – in the same way
he accepted the frustration of having loved both of them through
the years that had gone into the creation of Kintyre, and every
other part of Andrew's scattered possessions.

'Yes,' was all he answered, but his meaning was well enough
understood by them both.

With a slight nudge of his heels he urged his horse forward. He
and Sara started up the hill together.

PART FOUR

I

During the next two years Louis de Bourget startled the colony by doing what he had said he intended to do – he travelled on foot as far as exploration of the Nepean River had gone, selecting his land with more care for the site on which the house would stand than for the quality of the soil, and then announced his decision to settle permanently and farm in New South Wales. Comment, as he had expected, was at first sceptical, then mildly annoyed when it became clear that he would spare no expense to run his farm successfully. Where good livestock was to be bought, he was able to bid a higher price than anyone else; two of the best and most experienced overseers were enticed away from their employers to come to him.

But it was the plans for the house itself that roused most interest. He had travelled in America, and was taken by the mansions the cotton-planters of the Southern states were building for themselves; he decided that his own new house should follow them in pattern. But he had a French love of an ordered garden, and so the gentle slope on which the house stood was to be cut and terraced. There were many raised eyebrows when the news of this went around. So far, no one else in the colony had either labour or money to spare on such a thing. Andrew Maclay had had a like scheme for Glenbarr, but the job was never wholly completed because materials were short and too expensive.

Louis paid little heed to the raised eyebrows; he went on with no more than a shrug to indicate that he had heard what gossips had to say of him. Every ship arriving in Sydney Cove carried goods bought for him by his agent in England – books, marble fireplaces, silk to curtain the long windows, Louis Quinze chairs – the stream of his possessions that travelled the road to the Nepean seemed endless. He tried planting foreign trees, and saw most of them die; he built an aviary and filled it with exotic native birds, and birds from the Indian jungles and the East Indies. He even toyed, for a short time, with the idea of an ornamental lake – but he realized that seasonal drought would defeat him; also his sense of fitness told him that the great river running at his doorstep, and the unsymmetrical blue mountains behind it, were too strong and individual to mate happily with a stretch of smooth water. So he dropped the idea — not without a lingering regret for the future consternation such a plan would have caused among his neighbours.

The house was finished in the spring of 1803. At the time it was completed there were very few people who had yet seen it; the Nepean farms were remote, and the state of the roads didn't invite travel. So the house remained something of a legend while it was being built. By this time, Louis had many friends among the leading families, and each of them knew that, in due course, they would visit at his invitation. But it was Andrew Maclay, with his wife and family, whose carriage was the first to begin the ascent from the road by the river to Louis's front steps.

2

From the bottom of the hill Sara, at the carriage window, had leaned forward to see the house. It stood boldly on the rise, its white walls glistening in the sunlight. The sight of it took her breath for an instant. This was not the cotton-planter's house Louis had talked of; this had the look of what Andrew had once rashly promised to build for her at Kintyre. It was fronted by a portico of ten white columns, severe and unornamented; the building itself was wide and low, and the crest of the hill behind it was visible, crowned with a ridge of eucalypts. At one end of the portico, a short flight of steps led down to the level of the drive. Beyond the drive was the first of three unfinished terraces, cut into the hillside.

Sara was silent, not even listening to Andrew's comments, or to what the children's excited chattering was all about. As the carriage came to a halt, Louis ran down the steps and flung the door open. He welcomed them to his home, and then, smiling, he handed her out. He turned to lift Sebastian, still too young to negotiate the high step.

In the midst of the bustle, with two servants strenuously carrying out Louis's orders about unstrapping the boxes, the high babble of the children, and remarks passing between Andrew and his host, Sara found nothing to say. Taking Sebastian's hand, she mounted the stone steps very slowly. When at last she reached the level of the broad portico, she stood still. The Nepean plains, the river and the mountains, wrapped in their blue haze, were spread before her in one huge sweep. In front of the house, and at its sides, the

SARA DANE253

timber had been cleared, so that the view was uninterrupted. Down
on the fringe of the river, stretching away from the opposite bank,
the gums had turned the reddish tinge of spring, and through the
valley, an occasional wild, flowering tree, scarlet, yellow, white,
thrust itself into prominence. Sara held Sebastian's hand tightly,
feeling that, until this moment, she had not known the true beauty
of this harsh, familiar landscape.

Louis mounted the steps behind her. She did not turn, but
she sensed him standing there behind her, his gaze following hers.
For a few moments longer she looked at the scene, while the boxes
were being carried past her, and Andrew talked quietly with
Edwards, below.

At last she said, in a low voice, 'This is genius, Louis! You
have done what no one else would dare to do.'

He came to her side then. 'Why shouldn't one do what this
place pleads for? Here is sun, and space, and a view! Why build
a house with narrow windows and shut it all out? The skies are
not soft enough, nor the hills gentle enough to allow me to build
something like the sort of house that belongs in an ordered park.
The country here is a challenge – I have done my best to meet
it.'

'You have succeeded – admirably,' she said gently.

As she spoke she was thinking how strange to have to acknowledge that it needed a Frenchman, a stranger among an English
colony, to show them how to blend a house to this uncompromising
background. It lay back against the hill, rested against it almost,
and the ten white columns, of classic simplicity, its only adornment. It faced its outlook superbly, its lines solid and dignified.

'I have called it Banon,' Louis said.

She looked at him. 'Banon?'

He nodded. 'Banon is the name of a town in the south of France.
I went there once on business for the Marquis. I stayed at an inn
outside the town, in the season when the mimosa bloomed. All the
time I have been building this house, I have been able to call it by
no other name.'

Sara smiled, her eyes bright. 'Your house is the loveliest I have
ever seen.'

He bowed slightly. 'If you approve it, then I am more than
rewarded.'

His words were formal enough, and yet she realized his very
deep satisfaction. His thin, sunburnt face was darker now than
ever, but some of the strain was gone from it. He was smiling
a little, his eyes crinkled against the sun. She glanced down swiftly,

and saw that he no longer wore the massive rings, and by the
state of his hands she judged that, perhaps, he himself had taken
a spade when the terraces were being dug away. She was surprised; the suave Frenchman who had arrived in the colony
three years ago could hardly be imagined with a spade in his
hand.

His gaze returned to her, and he said quickly, 'Forgive me, Sara!
I keep you standing here in the sun, when you must be fatigued
from your journey.'

He reached down and took Sebastian's other hand, leading
them both towards the door, where a woman in the plain dress
of a housekeeper stood waiting for them.

3

A cold wind sprang up that evening, blowing towards Banon
from the mountains; but in Louis's white drawing-room they
could only hear its sound in the trees at the top of the ridge. The
leaping flames in the fireplace stained the marble mantel to a pale
rose, and threw irregular lights across the deep red curtains. A single
pair of candles burned on a table at the other end of the room;
they were reflected in a high, silver-framed mirror. Sara, Andrew,
and Louis sat in low chairs, turned towards the fire; their faces,
flushed in its glow, were sometimes bright, then momentarily
darkened by shadow, as the changing light played upon them.
Occasionally Louis stirred to pile on a fresh log, and when the
flames caught it, and burned high, Sara's hair and her silk gown
took on a reddish tinge.

For a time now Sara had ceased to have any part in the conversation. She sat with her hands lying idle in her lap, her eyelids
fluttering as she fought her drowsiness; the wind outside, and the
crackle of the flames, were muted, matching the indefinite under-
tones of Andrew and Louis. She looked towards their host. This
evening he had shed the sober clothes he wore on their arrival; now
he was arrayed as splendidly as ever Sydney had seen him, in stiff
brocade waistcoat, and the finest lace. The rings were back on his
fingers, the jewels winking in the firelight as he twisted the stem of
his madeira glass. He rested in his chair lazily, his feet, in silver-
buckled shoes, were propped on a softly-padded stool. Now and
then, in his talk, he turned with a gesture towards Andrew – but
mostly he gazed thoughtfully into the fire.

It was almost three years, Sara remembered, still looking at
him, since he had perched on the veranda-rail at Kintyre and told

her of what this house should be. That three years had been
favourable to the colony, and kind to Louis. It was still governed
by King, with whom Louis stood in particular regard, though it
was generally felt that King's day would soon be over. A great
deal of the time he was ill with gout, and, while he ruled well
enough, his rule was not enforced severely enough to satisfy the
needs of the Colonial Office. The power of the military was still
unsubdued, and no amount of orders from Government House
could wrest their privileges from them.

But King, even if ill, was not idle. He had a passion to regular-
ize the affairs of the colony – to bring it into line as a typical
English community. The idea of the girls' orphanage had matured,
and the large house now confined its herd of unwilling young
women. The *Sydney Gazette* – the colony's first newspaper – made
its appearance under government sponsorship; exploration, with
King's encouragement, continued steadily. The mountain barrier
had still not been crossed, and the riddle of what lay on the other
side was as yet an open question. But the secrets of the continent
itself had slowly and painfully yielded to young Matthew Flinders's patient seeking. Under orders from the Admiralty, Flinders
had commanded the sloop, *Investigator*, on a voyage to chart the
coasts. He worked his way with infinite care from west to east, then
south to north, from Cape Leeuwin to the Wessel Islands, proving,
beyond doubt, that New Holland and New South Wales were the
one vast island. He had plotted and charted the vague shape which
the old Dutch maps called simply *'Terra Australis'*, and was now
on his way back to England with his beautifully-drawn charts, his
painstaking logs. He went, cherishing the hope that the omnipotent
Admiralty and the Royal Society might adopt his suggestion that
the island, in future, should be known by the name he had always
given it in secret – Australia.

Governor King at last knew the extent of the domain over
which he ruled; but the vastness of the hinterland troubled him
not at all in comparison with the settled areas close at hand. The
farmers were steadily pushing outwards; hemmed in by the mountains, they began moving south – farther, in fact, than King wished.
It would now have needed an army of Government officials to keep
land and farmers continually under inspection – and an army was
precisely what King could not command.

The New South Wales Corps – locally known as the Rum
Corps – was as great and as constant a source of trouble to him
as his own gout. Officers and men, they incessantly harassed, disobeyed, derided and ridiculed him, until he was almost ready to

die from sheer weariness and disappointment. The Colonial Office
was no help – it had little time, and even less money, to spare for his
demands. Macarthur, whom he had sent back to England for
court-martial for his duel with the Lieutenant-Governor, Colonel
Paterson, had somehow managed to win the ear of authority. The
samples of merino wool which he had produced from his own
flocks had forced even the Colonial Office to take notice. Macarthur
had promised that their problem-colony, forever begging money
and supplies, would soon have an export that would fill the looms
of the Yorkshire wool-spinners. His scheme had met with strong support and approval, and he was returning to Sydney, not in disgrace, but triumphant, with a large grant of the most coveted land
in the whole of New South Wales – the Cowpastures district,
where the herds of wild cattle, the property of the Government, ran.
King raged when he heard the news; the troublemaker was returning with power increased tenfold.

The brief Peace of Amiens was over; England was now alone
in facing the genius and organizing might of Napoleon. The
British people were committed to a long struggle, and, on receiving the news, already months old, King acknowledged
sadly that the heads of Government in London would now have
less patience than ever for their remote and unproductive colony.

But there was a threat of violence much nearer to hand than
the future battlefields of Europe. Since Governor Hunter's time
the Irish convicts had made their presence and their grievances felt
in no uncertain way. There were continual rumours of a rising, and
counter-rumours. A year after King's arrival a definite plot had
been discovered; the colony panicked at the news that rough but
effective pikes had been discovered in the hands of rebel convicts.
King sent the ringleaders to Norfolk Island – and he was criticized
for not having hanged them. The passionate outcry of the rebels
died down to a murderous undertone.

Sara felt some pity for the worried, anxious Governor, whom
she had learned to like – to even, in a sense, respect. For herself,
and for Andrew, the years of Philip Gidley King's reign had been
good ones. After she had been received at Government House,
Andrew had, for the sake of the Governor's regard, withdrawn a
good deal from the rum trade. But his prosperity no longer needed
the bolster of the liquor sales, except in a nominal way. He withdrew, also, because his foresightedness saw the end of the trade.
The Colonial Office would some day provide a Governor with the
means to smash it, and all might not go well with the credit of
those who engaged in it right up to the end.

And for Louis, too, Sara thought, the years had been good ones. King was generous in his land-grant; and generous in his friendship. Perhaps it was something of a relief to that harassed man to know that in Louis de Bourget he had found one prosperous farmer, whose money, he knew for certain, did not come from illegal rum sales. Louis had never engaged in trade activity; that fact alone made him something of a rarity in that ring of business men. But, Sara mused, Louis had found the best of two worlds. He enjoyed an immunity from the rivalries of trade, and yet, from it, he made a direct profit. He and Andrew had joined forces to buy two more sloops for trade between the ports of the East. The sloops, *Thrush* and *Hawk*, had appeared only twice in Port Jackson during the two years of their trading, but, in that time, credits were beginning to mount up with Louis's agent in London, and Andrew had every reason to be well satisfied with his side of the deal. Latterly there had been talk of their buying yet another vessel for whaling expeditions to the Antarctic. It was Andrew who controlled these adventures, not by the power of money, but by his own initiative and driving-force. Louis was content to have it so – he rarely withheld his agreement when approached by Andrew in matters of policy; he could mostly be relied upon to shrug and profess no aptitude for business. The arrangement suited Andrew exactly; any partnership in which he played a minor role would have been a brief and uneasy one.

But no such harmony existed in the business relations between Andrew and Richard. Richard had determined, from the very beginning, that he would be absolute master of Hyde Farm, and no suggestions or advice from Andrew, no matter how tactfully given, were received kindly. He was still very much in debt, and, though the farm was beginning to improve and pay its own way, the debt to Andrew increased year by year. The improvement continued, almost in spite of Richard's ignorance of farming – his duties in the Corps kept him in Sydney most of the time, and his overseer had a knack of rectifying his employer's mistakes without seeming to disobey his orders. But the mild prosperity of Hyde Farm only urged Richard and Alison on to fresh extravagances. Their house in Sydney was the hub of whatever gaiety was to be found there. Alison dressed and entertained far beyond her own small income and the salary of an army captain, and when money ran short with them, Richard applied once more to Andrew. But, in spite of the front she showed to the world, each time Sara saw Alison, she fancied that the delicately-shaped face had become a trifle paler, a shade more finely drawn. During the short winters

Alison seemed never to be free from a disturbing cough, and the
fierce heat of the summers sapped still more of her little strength.
However, Sara reflected, for all that, Alison Barwell's vivacious
charm never deserted her. If she were ill, her couch was always the
place to hear the best stories and the tastiest gossip circulating
within the town. Her wit was clever and sharp, and her house was
the gathering-place for the unmarried officers of the Corps.

Of Richard himself, Sara knew very little these days. He attended
to his duties with as much care as any other man of his rank, and
when time allowed, he made the long trip up to his Hawkesbury
farm. But there were tales always circulating of his incessant drinking, and he seemed to lack the will to stand out against Alison's
expenditure. It surprised Sara that he could continue to ask Andrew
for money; and that Andrew had not, long ago, wearied of watching good money go after bad. But it seemed that Andrew's contempt for the Barwells' extravagance was not greater than his
desire to see his wife graciously received in their house. Formal
calls were frequently exchanged between the two women. So long
as Sydney continued to see and note these exchanges, Andrew
turned a blind eye to Richard's growing debt.

It grieved Sara to realize how little knowledge she possessed of
Richard's feelings and thoughts towards herself. Since the day
they had quarrelled on the Hawkesbury Road, she had never
spoken to him alone. When his temper had cooled, he had taken
her invitation, and called at Kintyre; he found her indisposed. At
Glenbarr it was the same; unless Andrew was there when Richard
called, Sara sent Annie to him with her excuses. Finally, he stopped
coming alone; only on business with Andrew, or accompanied
by Alison, did he ever put in an appearance.

Nothing – not loyalty to her husband, nor disgust over Richard's
treatment of Jeremy – had ever quite stifled the feeling of dismay
in her heart over his absence. She was forced to admit to herself
that she missed him acutely, longing to write him the letter that
would bring him back; pride, and a strong sense of prudence, always
restrained her. He was constantly in her thoughts; she worried over
him, wishing that Lady Linton's death might take them both back
to London – and yet, with the arrival of each ship, she dreaded to
hear the news. She had no peace or tranquillity from her decision
not to see him alone again; he could still possess her like a guilty
dream, reproach her with one quick glance in the midst of company, and drive her almost frantic by talking wildly of plans he
had no intention of carrying out, knowing quite well that the tales
would be taken back to her. In such small ways as these, Richard

had his revenge on her.

It seemed that since the days that they had shared the school-room at Bramfield, Richard had possessed an unfair power over her – and he would never let it go. The thought oppressed her, and she turned from it wearily. Outside, the wind had risen, flinging itself against the walls of the house. She listened, and felt that the sound which, until now, had been remote and shut out, was suddenly mournful and close at hand. Despite the heat of the fire, she drew her shoulders together as if she were cold.

Always alert, Louis noticed her movement. He leaned forward in his chair.

'Sara, my dear! I have kept you overlong. It is selfish of me! You would like to go to your room now?'

She smiled faintly, and nodded, rising at the same time. Andrew also rose, and both men came to the door with her.

At a word from Louis to a manservant in the hall, the woman who had waited for them on the portico that morning reappeared, holding a candle to light Sara to her room. She was a French-woman, Madame Balvet, about thirty-five and handsome, in a thin, rather sharp fashion. She had arrived from England three months previously, and acting under Louis's instructions, had come to Banon as a housekeeper. She spoke very good English, and gossip knew no more of her than that she had been in service to a great French family before the Revolution. Sara eyed her with curiosity. Who was this woman whom Louis had brought over from France? Someone trusted? . . . Someone loved? A mistress, perhaps, before his marriage? Sara watched her warily as she strode along the passage; she seemed to have a look of pride and possessiveness in the house, but Sara was prepared to acknowledge that in this she might be mistaken.

The woman opened the door, standing aside silently for Sara to enter. Sara's eyes followed her as she carefully lit several candles in brackets and on tables. In their flare she examined in detail what she had noticed only superficially earlier. The room she was to occupy was furnished with a taste and sensitivity that betrayed – or was meant to reveal – Louis's intimate knowledge of women.

Sara woke when the first streak of light was grey at the window. It was a period of utter stillness – the wind had dropped, and it was too early even for the birds. Within the house there was no sound at all. It would be an hour yet before the dairy-hands stirred – longer before the faint bustle of the kitchen began.

Beside her, Andrew breathed quietly in his sleep. The gentle movement close to her own body was comforting and peaceful. In the darkness her hand went out slowly and touched his arm; she held it there for a few moments, then drew back. The rhythm of his breathing had not altered.

As she lay there in the stillness, she was suddenly reminded of her conversation with Louis on the veranda at Kintyre almost three years ago – the only time he had ever talked to her of his wife. With a feeling of dismay she recalled the words . . . 'She was as cold as a splinter of ice.' The words contained the crux of the reason why his marriage had failed. Probably, in his whole life, Louis had never woken, as she did now, to experience this feeling of tenderness and familiarity, the sense of protectiveness, and of being protected. Louis did not know the security of love in his marriage. The woman who should have lain beside him at this moment slept alone in her father's house, and his own daughter was a stranger to him.

Because of this, Banon must remain without its mistress. It was white and beautiful – and sadly empty. The woman who ruled it was not Louis's wife. With a sense of pity, Sara remembered Madame Balvet's thin, passionate face, her eyes that were not greedy or malicious, but watched over the running of the house with a look of brooding possessiveness.

4

Louis's terraced garden was still unfinished, but a certain order had been brought into it, and even in its rough state it had a free sort of beauty, which Sara hoped it might retain even when smooth, English lawn replaced the tough grass, growing about in spiky clumps. A seat had been placed for her on the highest of the levels, and she took her needlework there on the fifth day after their arrival at Banon. Andrew and the three boys had come out with her, stayed by her some time to talk, and then wandered farther down the slope. Now and again she caught a glimpse of them as they broke from the cover of trees or shrubs, and their voices reached her, the children's high and shrill, Andrew's deeper. She smiled down at them, waiting to see them turn and make for the aviary; so far, they had ended each morning by a visit to the aviary, Andrew no less fascinated than his sons.

But Andrew, she knew, would not remain much longer at Banon. Louis pressed them to stay on – a month, six weeks. But idleness sat uneasily upon Andrew. He enjoyed Banon, he enjoyed Louis's company, and the card games that kept them from their beds until

SARA DANE
261

the small hours of the morning; but Sara observed signs of rest-lessness in him already. Louis's leisured world of elegance and peace was not his; he missed the bustle of the store, the constant journey-ings between Sydney and Parramatta, the bargaining for live-stock and corn, the gossip that was part of every business trans-action. He had been away from it only a few days, and yet at dinner last night he talked rather wistfully of the possibility of mail arriving from his agents in London, and of the fact that there might be a cargo for sale, and he, at Banon, would be out of the bidding. Louis said nothing in reply to this, but he knew as well as Sara that the wilderness of the Nepean would not hold Andrew much longer.

There was a sense of remoteness here that the Hawkesbury, even in the early days, did not possess. Here the soil would grow wheat finer and heavier than anywhere else in the colony, but the land was infinitely difficult to clear. Wherever the settlers had pushed forward to farm their claims by the river-banks, they had done so in loneliness, and with a steadfast will to ignore the silences and the immense tracts of bush about them. Here the natives still roamed in a half-wild state, scarcely touched by the white man's approach; the roads were not more than rough tracks, and civiliza-tion had hardly begun its fight against the bush.

Sara had no pretence of interest in her needlework as she sat with the gentle spring sunshine full on her face. The paradox of Banon fascinated her – the creation of this, the loveliest and most unusual house in the whole colony, merely as a landmark in the wilderness. It faced the unknown, promising mountains like a grand, rather foolhardy gesture to the future of the country. Filled with wonder at the achievement, she turned back to gaze un-believingly at the house; the long windows caught the sun with a dazzle strong enough to hurt her eyes.

It was the sound of a horseman on the drive that attracted her attention. Craning forward, she could see that it was one of Louis's overseers who had been sent to Sydney three days previously with orders for supplies. The sound of the hoofbeats carried to her on the air; but they were not clear, the birds were noisy, and the air was full of the sound of insects. A heat-haze was already rising above the mountains; by noon it would be too hot to sit out any longer. She watched the horseman idly; he took the path that led to the stables, and was lost from sight. Then her gaze returned to the mountains, and the river plains below.

She picked up her needlework again, and worked at it until, about half an hour later, she heard Louis's voice on the portico

above her. He was walking slowly down its length in conversation
with Madame Balvet; their tones were quiet and serious. Sara
imagined, from his gestures, that he was giving his housekeeper
instructions; she nodded several times, and then, with a final nod,
accompanied by a decisive wave of her hand, she turned and went
indoors again. Louis paced the portico a few times, his hands clasped
behind his back. On the last turn he caught sight of Sara. He
waved his arm, and then hurried down the steps and came towards her.

Something was wrong – his expression told her so instantly. At
once her mind went back to the arrival of the overseer, probably
carrying mail from Sydney. Louis's walk was brisk; he brought an
air of excitement and haste that usually was totally lacking in him.
He moved Sara's needlework basket and sat down beside her, beginning to talk without preamble.

'There's news, Sara! Burke has brought mail from Sydney. By
the by, there are several letters for Andrew – I must send someone to find him.'

She shook her head. 'Wait – not yet, Louis! Tell me first what
your own news is.'

'Something I had not expected to hear for many years yet.'
His voice was slower now, its crispness had faded. He was silent
for a few moments, looking past her to the mountains. When his
gaze came back to her, he was frowning a little.

'My wife, Sara, is dead. I have had a letter from my esteemed
father-in-law, telling me in bald sentences that she died from a
chill she caught out hunting.'

Sara grasped at the sense of what he said, but she saw immediately that Louis's expression did not invite sympathy. She felt
it would be hypocritical to offer it; there could be nothing but
relief for him in the news of his wife's death. Relief, certainly –
but, perhaps, also a trace of regret? There were so many things
Louis might regret about this. He may have cherished an un-
expressed hope that she would come, some day, to the colony; he
may often have grieved over the beauty he had loved unwisely.
Surely Banon hadn't been built without the hope of a son to
inherit? But if these were Louis's thoughts, he kept them to himself, and his face told her very little. He had told her his news
within an hour of receiving it, but it was clear that he did not expect her to probe his own feelings on the matter. Whether he was
relieved, indifferent, or sorry, would obviously remain his own
affair. She said nothing, fearful that any words of hers might
intrude clumsily among his thoughts.

263

At last he said to her, 'I'm angry, Sara!'

'Angry?'

'Yes – angry! My wife is dead, but Elizabeth, my daughter, remains very much alive. That blundering fool, her grandfather, thinks he can keep her from me.'

He reached into his coat pocket, and brought out a letter. He unfolded it and laid it across his knees; Sara saw that the handwriting was thick, bold enough, but shaky, as if the writer could no longer control his pen with any certainty.

'Here . . .!' Louis pointed to the lines close to the end of the letter:

> ' "*Your daughter, Elizabeth, now eight years old, will, I presume, remain here with her grandmother and myself. From the reports I have of the colony, I must conclude that it is a wild and savage place, totally unsuitable for such a child as my granddaughter. Moreover, your roving life leads me to believe that you have no permanent home in which she may be properly received and brought up. Nor is there, I imagine, in New South Wales, any woman capable of instructing her in her lessons, needlework, music and painting.*
> ' "*I await, Sir . . ."* '

Louis looked up. 'There it is, Sara! My daughter is the property of her maternal grandfather – too delicate a plant to be entrusted to this harsh manner of living, or to my irresponsible care!'

She had not known Louis as angry as this before. She said, 'And what will you reply to him?'

'Reply!' With great emphasis he thrust the letter back in his pocket. 'I'll reply in person – and I'll show him exactly whose property Elizabeth is.'

Sara put a hand on his arm. 'Louis, what do you mean?'

'I'm taking a passage to England in order to fetch Elizabeth. And then I'll bring her back to the country that in future will be her home.'

'Here . . .! Are you mad?'

'Mad, Sara? If you had a daughter as well as three sons, wouldn't you keep her here with you?'

'That's different. If *I* had a daughter she would have been born here. She would be of the generation that *belongs* here, just as my sons are. She would know nothing of England, or the niceties of manners all little girls imbibe from the time they can walk. And in the end I would have to send her back to England, so that the accepted pattern of gentility could be imposed upon her.'

'Elizabeth shall bring it here with her!' he said emphatically. 'She shall have one of those females who run uncomfortable seminaries for young ladies to accompany her. And nothing – *nothing at all, Sara* – will be neglected in the direction of music, painting and sewing! If she is not precisely her mother's daughter, she will be grateful to me for taking her away from that cold barracks her grandparents inhabit.'

Sara shook her head doubtfully. 'Shouldn't you think again, Louis? You're angry now . . . but later you will see it differently. She is such a child still, yet . . .'

'But she is *my* child!' he burst out. 'She will live in my house, and lead the life *I* have chosen for her!'

Angrily he rose, and stood frowning down at her.

'I am quite determined about this, Sara. The *Dolphin* is in Port Jackson – it was she who brought in the mails. I am going now to write to her captain to hold me a passage for the homeward trip. She goes directly back to the Cape, I believe. With favourable weather, in six months I shall be in England.'

Louis sailed with the *Dolphin* three weeks later. He went, leaving Madame Balvet in charge at Banon, and his business affairs in Andrew's hands, begging Andrew to find time occasionally to ride out to the Nepean, to report progress at the farm.

The harbour was white-capped the day he left, its green shores beautiful and aloof, as they had been the first time he saw them. He kissed Sara's hand, shook Andrew's firmly, and then made his way down the wooden steps of the jetty to the waiting boat. The wind whipped Sara's skirts about her ankles, and fluttered the handkerchief she waved. As he drew into the shadow of the Dolphin, he could distinguish Sara's red gown in the midst of the small crowd on the jetty.

2

On a Sunday evening in March, 1804, Sara stood with Julia and Ellen Ryder on the veranda of their house. She bent and kissed Julia Ryder's cheek warmly in farewell.

'Take care of yourself,' she said, in a low tone. 'Perhaps now that Ellen is back here to take charge, James could spare you to come to Glenbarr for a visit?'

'We'll see . . . we'll see,' Julia answered cautiously. 'I've scarcely had time to get used to the thought of Ellen being back yet, and I very much doubt that the Bath seminary has trained her in the management of a colonial household. But . . . we'll see, my dear. Your Sebastian holds my heart-strings so firmly, I find it difficult to stay away.'

Ellen, beside her, let out a little squeak of protest. 'Oh, Mama, really . . . !'

Andrew, standing on a lower step, turned back towards Julia. 'I wish you could consider quite a long visit to Glenbarr. Sara will need some company while I'm away.'

'Away . . .?' she echoed. She looked questioningly at him. 'I didn't know you planned a trip – is it to the East again?'

'Andrew,' Sara said quietly, 'is thinking about going to England. It isn't definite yet, but perhaps when the *Hawk* comes in again . . .'

James Ryder, who had been waiting with the carriage door open, suddenly spoke. 'What's this about England?' He started to mount the steps again.

Andrew nodded. 'I've had a notion to go for some time. The news about the way Macarthur's wool samples were received has set me thinking. He knows what he's doing, that man. He saw the future of this country was in wool long before any of us.'

Ryder smiled faintly. 'I wouldn't say you'd been precisely slow in following him, Andrew. Your own merino flocks are almost as large as his . . .'

'Ah, yes,' Andrew broke in quickly, 'but look how he's got ahead of me now. He knows the market for wool in England, and has made himself the most talked-of man in the wool trade there at the moment. Why, he got himself out of a court martial almost entirely on the strength of what he could do for the future of the trade in Yorkshire! I've got to get there as well, and convince these men that there are others producing wool, besides Macarthur.'

'Oh, there's more in it than that,' Sara said, laughing a little. 'Andrew has heard the reports that Macarthur wrung a grant of five thousand acres from the Colonial Office for his sheep runs, and Andrew is after the same prize.'

'Well, why not?' he retorted. 'This climate is made to produce wool, and England needs every pound of it she can get. They've got the factories and the workers, they've got the market for their

cloth – the merino wool from Spain comes in at the rate of five
million pounds a year, and still Yorkshire wants more. I tell you
there's a chance to make *real* money here! I have the ships to export the wool, I have the capital – or between Louis de Bourget
and myself we could raise it. What I need is a substantial grant of
land for pasture, and the contact with the leading wool-brokers.
Macarthur believes that the time is coming when our wool will out-
sell the Spanish merino on the London market, and I think he's
right.'

'If he's right . . . ' Ryder began reflectively. 'If he's right you'll
stand to make a tidy pile of money, and money that goes on increasing as fast as your merinos breed.'

'If he's right,' Andrew repeated, with a sideways look at his
wife, 'I'll build that other wing on to Glenbarr, and Sara shall stuff
it full of silk curtains and white marble.'

Sara caught his arm and began to urge him down the steps towards the carriage. 'If that day comes,' she said laughingly, 'I'll
have a design of rams' heads in marble for all the chimney pieces
in the new wing.' Then she tugged more urgently at his arm. 'But
come – we keep Julia and Ellen in the cold.'

She hurried down the steps, James coming to assist her into
the carriage. The two men shook hands, and Andrew climbed in
beside her. James stepped back, giving the signal to Edwards, on
the box above. There were calls of farewell from the two women
on the veranda as the carriage moved forward. Sara waved; the
pace quickened, and soon all she could see was the darker shape of
the house against the night sky, and the lights that streamed from
the hall and the drawing-room windows. Then the drive twisted
sharply, and the trees cut off even the lights.

They were in darkness in the carriage, Andrew's face opposite
her no more than a whitish blur. She felt sleepy and rather disinclined to talk. Two days previously Ellen Ryder had arrived
in Port Jackson, in the *Lady Augusta*, after an absence of four
years. The news had reached Sara and Andrew at Priest's, and they
had driven over to the Ryders' farm that afternoon. Sara had not
cared for the changes she saw in Ellen; the girl was fully a woman
now, with all the self-conscious manners of one lately accustomed
to the fashions of the Bath seminary, and the Twickenham house
of her elegant aunt, Julia's sister. There was worldly knowledge
in the way she greeted Sara, her former nurse, and a one-time convict; if she had dared, she would have snubbed her. But even two
days back in the colony had taught Ellen that Andrew Maclay was
not the man to forgive a snub to his formidable wife. So she dimpled

and smiled, and consented to play the piano accurately and woodenly, to show off the polish of her English education.

The increasing jolting of the carriage told Sara that the drive had now joined the road leading to Castle Hill and Priest's.

'What do you think of Ellen?' she said to Andrew.

He stirred, as though he had been in deep thought, and was reluctant to give any consideration to the girl.

'Ellen . . .? Oh – pert and pretty. I expect she'll improve with marriage and age.'

That was all she could get out of him. She lapsed back into silence, prepared to doze through the journey to Priest's.

She was roused, stiff and a little cold – there was a trace of autumn already in the air – by Edwards's shout from the box. The carriage jerked to a stop, sending her sliding sideways in the seat. It was pitch dark on either side; as far as she could see, they were not near a house of any sort. There was no light anywhere, and, seemingly, no reason for stopping.

Andrew thrust his head out of the window. 'What is it, Edwards? Why are we stopping?'

Edwards's hoarse old voice betrayed unusual animation.

'That light ahead, sir! I've been watching it, I have. That be no ordinary light. That be fire!'

'Fire! Where?'

Andrew was out of the carriage in a second, and had scrambled up beside Edwards to get a better view. Sara, craning out of the window, could hear them clearly.

'We're not more than half a mile or so from Castle Hill, sir. That light be either the village, or the Government Farm, where they keep the convicts.'

'The convicts . . .!' Andrew's voice betrayed his own uncertainty. 'Well . . . it's no more than an ordinary fire. We'd better go and see if there's anything we can do to help.'

But Edwards cautioned him with a weary hand. 'Be easy now, sir! It'll be better to wait a bit and see. There be much talk of trouble among the convicts, and maybe this . . .'

'Nonsense!' Andrew said. 'I'm tired of hearing rumours of rebellion. All the talk never comes to anything. And this is nothing more than a barn that some careless fool has set alight. Come, man, we'll go on.'

'Well, sir . . . just as you say. But I'd be a lot easier if you kept your pistol handy, now.'

Edwards continued grumbling and muttering under his breath,

as Andrew climbed down. In his jumbled stream of words, Sara distinguished 'rebels' and 'mad Irishmen' a number of times. Andrew opened the door to get in beside her again. Worried, she leaned forward and laid a hand on his arm.

'Don't you think we'd be wiser to turn back towards Parramatta, Andrew? If there's trouble . . .'

She was checked by Edwards's shout.

'Hold it, sir! There be someone coming! Someone with a lamp!'

Andrew stepped down on the road again. Leaning far out, Sara could see the wavering yellow light of a lantern far ahead of the carriage. Then someone coming at a half-run and occasionally stumbling. The night was very still and dark – dark, except for the reddish glow of the fire in the distant sky, and the lantern bobbing along close to the road. Andrew turned back quickly and groped in the place under the seat where he always kept his pistol when travelling. He took it out, cocked it, and waited. The three of them hardly seemed to draw a breath as they waited.

It was a woman's voice that reached them out of the darkness.

'For mercy's sake, wait for me!'

She burst into the circle of light cast by the carriage lanterns, breathless, half-sobbing. She wore a white nightgown, with a cloak flung carelessly over it. Her hair was black and long, tumbling in disorder about her shoulders. Her handsome, plump face was flushed from her running.

Sara gave a gasp. 'Nell Finnigan! Andrew – it's Nell Finnigan, from Castle Hill!'

Nell stumbled, and grasped at one of the spokes of the front wheel for support. Andrew took her arm and held it firmly. She leaned against the wheel, her head thrown back as she drew in huge gasping breaths. Andrew bent down, and gently forced the lantern from her clenched fingers. Edwards had scrambled from the box; he stood peering fixedly into her face.

When she had enough breath to speak, it was to Andrew she turned.

'There's a rising!' she cried, clutching him. 'The convicts have broken out of the Government Farm, and burnt it! It's the signal for the rising they've been planning these past months. We must all get to Parramatta as quick as we can. We'll be safe there. They'll . . .'

Andrew shook her a little to halt her panic. 'Tell me quietly, now. Tell me what you know.'

Nell took another great gulp of air, and then restarted her story.

'Well . . . The first I knew of it was the bell ringing up at the farm – the bell they call them in from the fields with. I was getting ready for bed, with my place shut and locked this past hour. Finnigan is in Parramatta, and I can tell you I was scared out of my wits. I looked out of the window and saw the fire – I knew about the talk of rising, so I hoped the bell meant a fire, and not that trouble was starting. Then the boys came pouring into the village, searching every house for food and ammunition. They've scarcely half a dozen muskets between them, though there seemed to be plenty of pikes – you know – the sort they make themselves.²

'Yes . . . yes,' Andrew said impatiently. 'But what happened when they got to Castle Hill?' He gripped her arm too tightly, and she pulled away with a show of indignation.

'Here, mind what you're doing!' She spoke roughly, but then her tone changed in an instant, as she recalled that she was depending on Andrew to get her safely to Parramatta. 'If *you'd* been there at the time, you wouldn't be too clear on it either.'

She made an effort to be calm.

'Well . . . it was like this,' she continued. 'They came from the direction of the Government Farm – at the other end of the village. Most of them made for Carson's, the smithy. They were after the horses, of course. And probably they'd have more chance of a pistol or musket there. They kept away from the guardhouse – though there were only three soldier on duty, and *they* couldn't have done much. I could see plainly enough that they were going into each cottage in the row, so I didn't wait for them to reach *mine*! I took a lantern, and away with me over the wall of my back garden! Some of those boys aren't exactly friends of Finnigan, you understand. I wasn't in much of a mood to see the things in my house pulled about – and I knew if I had anything to say, I'd be done for.'

She was clearly terrified, and Andrew gave a moment's thought to her neat little cottage, well-stocked with rum.

'How long ago did this happen?' he asked.

She shook her head. 'I don't know. I've been shivering in a potato field since I got away – no idea how long. Watching, you know, to try to see how many there were, and if they were using the roads. But it was too dark to see a thing – I could hear them, though. This is the start of the trouble, all right – and, believe me, there were more men in Castle Hill than came out of the Government Farm. They'd collected others. They'll try a march on Parramatta, I'll be bound. I doubt that the road between here and Parramatta is safe. The news will spread like fire, and all the boys who've been sharpening their blasted pikes all these months will have them up from under the floorboards.'

'Has anyone sent word to Parramatta?'

'How should *I* know!' she echoed. 'I tell you, Mr Maclay, you should have *been* there, and you wouldn't be taking it so calmly. Maybe one of the soldiers went to Parramatta – I don't know. But, judging from the numbers of the boys, I don't doubt that Castle Hill has given them all they want for the present. Likely, they'll be spreading out to pick up more men, and whatever arms they have.'

Andrew gave her an absent-minded pat on the shoulder, turning to Edwards.

'We'll have to go back to Parramatta – perhaps the news hasn't reached them there yet. Though, the trouble is, that the sound of the carriage on the road will give the convicts warning before we ever get near there. Yet if we take to the fields, we'll not get to Parramatta before morning, and that'll be no use at all – we daren't delay as long as that. There may be gangs out on the road by now. But that's a risk we'll have to take.'

As he spoke, Andrew was bustling Nell into the carriage beside Sara. She flung herself back on the seat, shivering, her cloak wrapped tightly about her. Andrew held the lantern high, until she settled herself; she seemed subdued, a softer, gentler Nell Finnigan than either had ever seen before. But her black eyes were still bold – her toughened, unsentimental nature faced their danger realistically; she might have fled from it, but she did not wilt at the thought of it.

Andrew drew a rug across her knees, but his last look, as he withdrew to close the door, was for Sara. The lantern light was soft on her face and hair; she gave him a faint smile – a small, private gesture of her confidence and trust. Then he stepped back and closed the door. The two women were in darkness again. They heard him climb up on the box beside Edwards.

The carriage rolled forward slowly – then with increasing speed. Soon Sara and Nell were rocking and swaying to its uneven rhythm. They were shut in the world of darkness, their faces indistinguishable to each other. Sara looked towards her companion, wondering. Was she afraid, when she no longer had the lonely road to watch, and the sounds of the fields to listen for? Sara was well aware that here in the carriage there was no distraction from fear, and no limit to the imagination. Nell Finnigan was brave, she allowed. But could even Nell sit here long, and still not be afraid? Parramatta lay ahead, but on either side were the silent fields, the labourers' cottages, the convicts' huts that might easily have been the scenes of conferences that were carried forward by careful planners. Within a few hours the whole countryside would be aflame with news of the rebellion; muskets, pikes, axes – anything that would serve as a weapon – would be brought out, houses would be plundered, and horses stolen from the stables of employers. The cry of 'Liberty!' would stir up the rebels again, as the night gave way to a revealing morning, when perhaps their hearts had grown faint, and their stomachs empty. There were desperate men, with only the flogging-post and the gallows ahead if they failed. Most of them had brought the spirit of rebellion from Ireland, had fostered it, and nourished its growth among their companions; to-night was the product of their efforts.

Sara grew cold with the thought of how many there might be to join the disaffected. Would the underpaid labourers join the rebels, with land and livestock promised as a reward? The hope of ultimate success was vague – but was it any vaguer when their friends and brothers had stormed Dublin Castle? Military discipline was lax, and all of them knew it. The danger lay in how quickly the word spread, and how many had pledged themselves, during these past months, to take up arms when it came.

The trees lining the road were like a solid menace to their safety. Occasionally they caught the glimpse of a light in a cottage, and wondered at it being there so late. There was no way of telling if the news of the rising was ahead of them on the road, or still behind them. They met no one, heard nothing.

In the darkness Nell stirred, tugging her cloak closer. 'Well . . .' she said, her tone strong and clear. 'I don't know how you feel, Mrs Maclay . . . but, speaking for myself, *I'm* scared!'

With a rush of gratitude, Sara looked at the faint blur of the face opposite. If Nell Finnigan were afraid, then no one else need be ashamed of fear. Impulsively, she leaned forward to take the other's large, roughened hand; she pressed her fingers firmly round it.

'I'm afraid, too,' she said.

Having admitted it, she felt relieved, but there was suddenly nothing more to say; their fear, acknowledged, seemed less terrible.

As they settled themselves back again, the carriage began a rather sharp descent. Sara leaned forward, and peered through the window. She recognized this spot, a place where the road plunged to ford a shallow stream; for the main part of the year it was dry, but now, above the rumble of the wheels, she could just faintly hear a trickle of water against a stony bed. The angle of

the carriage levelled off as they splashed their way through, then
tilted again when they started on the slope of the opposite bank.
A shout rang out as they reached the top.

'Halt! Whoa, there!'

For the next few seconds there was mad confusion, wild cries,
and men shouting, and over it all Sara heard Edwards's curse, and
the cracking of the whip as he urged the horses forward. The
carriage moved with a sudden lurch; Sara was flung back against
the seat, and Nell, unable to save herself, fell on to her knees.
The carriage maintained its progress for no more than half a
minute. Sara knew from the way it was slowing down that their
attackers were hauling at the horses' heads. At last they were
jerked to a stop. Instantly the door was flung open; a man, unshaven, smelling vilely of stale sweat, thrust his head inside. He shone
a lantern on the two women.

'Out!' he snapped, jerking his thumb over his shoulder. 'This is
as far as ye ride, ladies.'

Furiously, without caution, Sara pushed against his shoulder.

'Get out of here! Who are you, anyway?'

For answer, he caught her arm and tugged. He had twice her
weight, and she was dragged forward suddenly, almost falling
from the carriage to the road. Nell received the same treatment; her
curses added to the noise and confusion.

'Take your hands off me, you filthy devils!' She stood with her
feet planted wide, her arms akimbo, scowling defiance. 'A fine
bunch you are, I must say! A couple of pikes and an old musket
between the lot of you. Do you expect to frighten Mr King out of
Government House with that?'

A nudge from one of the despised pikes silenced her.

Andrew and Edwards, down from the box by this time, moved
close to the women. A circle of perhaps a dozen men stood about
them, pressing forward, hemming them in. They were an un-
inspiring lot, standing their ground uneasily, and only the weight
of their numbers appeared to give them any confidence. There
seemed to be some doubt among them still as to which one was the
leader; they looked from one to the other uncertainly. But Sara
could find no reassurance in this. Seen in the light of the lanterns
they carried they might be unprepossessing, but she was not, for a
moment, blind to the fact that they were also desperate. The circle
of dirty, unshaven faces filled her with horror. It was a face such
as one of these that had pressed close to her own the night of the
convict outbreak at Kintyre. So long ago, now, but she recoiled

in terror as she remembered. She looked from each man to the
next; they seemed a little awed by what they had dared, and,
leaderless, they were far more dangerous than a disciplined troop.

One of the gang took the initiative. He moved through the
group and faced Andrew. His only authority seemed to be the
musket he held.

'There'll be no harm done to anyone who behaves peaceful-like.'
He spoke with a soft Irish accent. 'We'll just have yer horses and
yer pistol, now. And then we'll be lettin' ye on yer way. 'Tis a fair
step to Parramatta for the ladies, I'm thinkin'. But like as not ye'll
find some cottage on the way to give ye shelter.'

Andrew, swiftly glancing about him, seemed in an instant to judge
and weigh the temper of the mob facing him. Then he took a
step back, at the same time thrusting his pistol forward menac-
ingly. With the other hand he motioned to Sara.

'Get back in the carriage! Edwards – the box!'

Both Edwards and Nell made a movement to obey, but Sara
stood still.

'Andrew, let them have what they want,' she said, in a low
tone. 'They'll . . .'

'Do as I say!' he said peremptorily.

She drew away from him immediately. At his words, Nell, already
on the carriage step, climbed inside. Edwards began to mount the
box again. Sara hesitated, her mind numbed with apprehension and
terror. Andrew stood quite still, pistol levelled, looking, each in turn,
into the faces about him. She held her breath as she waited for his
next movement; the blood was pounding in her ears, and she felt
herself groping madly at the carriage door for support.

Andrew spoke at last. His voice was as cold as if he were addressing a group of troublesome children.

'You all know that hanging is the penalty for horse-stealing and
armed robbery. You know also that you haven't a chance of succeeding with this rising once the troops are called out.'

Complete silence greeted his words. No one stirred in protest, and
there was no movement among the gang.

'Now . . .!' Andrew continued. 'Stand away from those horses.
I advise you not to add further to the list of your crimes. I promise
you it will go harder for you if you do.'

The self-appointed leader fell back a step, uncertain and irreso-
lute. He looked about him, seeking the opinion of his companions.
There was an uneasy shuffling of feet, a low mutter rose from
someone's throat. Above them a little wind stirred fitfully in the
trees. It was a long minute of agony to Sara – the appraising of

the desperate and yet fearful faces. In the intense quiet, the scraping
of a boot against the ground was like the noise of thunder. The men
wavered openly; their leader's indecision had reached them all.

A few more seconds, Sara thought, and Andrew would win.

Too soon, it seemed to her, he gave the signal.

She climbed into the carriage, craning her head to watch him.
He put his foot on the step of the box.

'Right, Edwards!'

Andrew's sharp voice seemed to break the spell that lay over the
group.

Someone shouted hoarsely from the back.

'Is it a man *ye* call yerself, Matt Donovan? Sure, it's not fit to
lead a donkey, ye are!'

The men parted automatically as the speaker thrust his way
through. He was a huge man; his ugly face was enraged and
brutish. He looked directly at Andrew.

'Stand down, there! B' God, we'll have those horses, whether
y' like it or not!'

There was a general shout of approval from the men. Sara heard
Andrew's voice rise above them.

'Whip them up, Edwards!'

The shot rang out before Edwards could bring down his whip.
Terrified, the horses lunged forward; Andrew crumpled, and toppled
down into the road. Sara heard herself give one piercing scream,
and then she flung the carriage door open. She felt Nell's hands
clutch frantically at her, but she broke free of them. Edwards was
already hauling at the reins, and their speed had slackened. Sara
jumped clear, holding her balance for a few seconds, then falling
on her hands and knees into the ditch. All the breath seemed to
have left her body from the force of the impact, but she scrambled
to her feet again and started to run back to where Andrew lay. By
the time the carriage had finally halted, she was kneeling on the
road beside him.

The circle of convicts stood back from her, watching, muttering
among themselves. They made no attempt to help her, and with
her own hands she turned Andrew over on his back. The bullet
had smashed his temple. He had probably been dead when he hit
the ground.

They took the horses and the pistol, and left quickly – a quiet,
nervous group now. Sara hardly noticed their departure, except
for the sudden silence it left behind. She sat on the side of the road,
holding Andrew's body, aware of nothing but the terrible stillness

of the weight in her arms. Nell and Edwards held a whispered consultation, and then Nell came and crouched down in the dust beside them. Sara didn't feel her presence there until a warm tear splashed on her hand.

She raised her head and looked up incredulously at the other woman.

'You're crying . . . ?'

Nell dashed a hand across her eyes. 'I didn't know him very well. He didn't take much notice of me whenever he passed through Castle Hill – but I liked him.'

Sara bent until her lips brushed his quiet ones.

'I loved him,' she whispered.

They sat there on the road, not talking. Presently, Edwards succeeded in detaching one of the carriage lanterns. With a few words softly spoken in Nell's ear, he set off in the direction of Parramatta.

2

The mainspring of the rebellion did not live out a full day. It died outside Toongabbie the next morning, in an encounter with a detachment of troops under Major Johnston. Cunningham, the leader of the rising at Castle Hill, was killed there, with sixteen other men, twelve were wounded and thirty captured. The remaining two hundred and thirty took to the bush. Pitchforks, pikes, a score or two of muskets, and a desire for liberty, were not enough. Through the week they surrendered in bodies or individually – a ragged rebel army come to heel. When the news swept through the colony, small groups who were waiting to join up with the main movement quietly put away their arms. The rebellion was dead.

On the Thursday and Friday of that same week Sydney, Parramatta and Castle Hill saw the executions of the ringleaders – among them Andrew Maclay's murderer. Some of the rebels went to the flogging-posts and the chain-gangs, others were exiled to Norfolk Island, or sent to that hell-spot on the Coal River. His Excellency publicly commended the courage and actions of Major Johnston and Captain Abbott. Martial law, declared as soon as the Governor had received news of the rising, was revoked. The colony drew a sigh of relief, and prepared to settle back into its old routine. Even from the men in the chain-gangs the spirit of rebellion seemed to have fled.

3

Sara leaned back wearily in her chair, her face turned towards
the small fire that burned in the grate. Glenbarr's long drawing-
room was still and quiet now. Early that afternoon Andrew had
been buried. All day long this room had seen the coming and going
of his friends and neighbours, even the Governor himself had paid
his formal call. David, the eldest, had been there too, stiff and
unnatural in his black suit, his child's face fighting exhaustion and
the strangeness of living through ceremonies which belonged only
to an adult world. Unconsciously, he had seemed to seek his father's
support, and, not finding it, his expression had grown bewildered
and half-lost.

Now they were all gone. The evening meal was over. David
was in his bed this past half-hour, and Glenbarr had returned to
its quiet. Jeremy was the only one who remained. He crouched
on a fender-stool, his back to the fire, watching Sara's face, the
movement of her restless fingers plucking at the rich black silk of
her gown. Her hair was dressed smoothly back off her forehead, and,
above the black gown, its fairness was almost white. He could
trace the ravages of the past week in her face; there was a look of
harsh experience written there, and shadows beneath her eyes that
he had not seen before.

Suddenly she spoke; her voice was tired.

'Your sentence will expire this year – you'll be free, Jeremy. I
have been thinking about you – about the future . . .'

He answered, a questioning note in his voice, 'Yes?'

She looked at him directly then. 'When you're free – when the
time comes – I'm going to ask you to stay. I want you to help run
Kintyre and Priest's and the Toongabbie farm, as you've been
doing.' She stopped him with a wave of her hand, as she saw he
was about to answer. 'Yes, I know what you're going to say. You'll
be free. You'll want to take land and farm for yourself. I'm asking
one – two years from you, Jeremy. No more than that. Stay with
me just that long. I'll pay you . . .'

'We'll not talk of payment just yet, Sara. There are other things.'

Her brows lifted. 'Other things . . . ?'

He gestured meaningly. 'You surely can't have decided to keep
the whole lot on – the three farms, the store, Glenbarr? And what
about the ships?'

'I mean to keep them all,' she replied calmly. 'They belonged
to Andrew, didn't they? Don't they belong to his children?'

'But you're a *woman*, Sara! You can't do what Andrew did! It's beyond your powers – your strength, even.'

Frowning, she folded her lips. 'Do you imagine, Jeremy Hogan, that I've helped Andrew build up his possessions all these years, without the thought of handing them over to our sons? Was there ever a single decision he made that I didn't prompt him? If I should sell the properties now – and the ships, and the store – the money is all that I'd have to give the children. And there is no sense of permanence in money alone. They need to know the feeling of possessing land. They've got to have possessions and roots. They'll forget Andrew – they'll never really know him – if they don't have the things that he built up around them. I want them – David, Duncan and Sebastian – to look at Kintyre, and to know that it took more to build it than luck at a card-table, and a salvaged ship!'

He shook his head very slowly. 'But you're a *woman*, Sara!' he repeated. 'Can you control all of it – the labourers of three farms, the captains of the ships, the store . . . ?'

'Yes, if you'll help me, Jeremy! Give me two years, and then I'll show them that a woman can do it. They'll doubt it at first – and they'll scoff. But I *know* that I can do it!'

'And what if I tell you I believe it can't be done? What if I refuse to help you?'

For a moment she was taken aback. Then she said, levelly, 'If you refuse, then I must try to do it without you.'

He sprang to his feet. 'My God, Sara, you're heartless! You give me no choice!'

He paced the length of the room, paused, then swung round, and returned to face her.

'You've really made up your mind about this?'

She raised her eyes to look at him as he stood over her.

'How can it be otherwise, Jeremy? All these things *are* Andrew. How can I give them up? To lose them would be to lose him again – to lose him a thousand times over.'

Her voice grew choked and stifled; tears were beginning to slide unchecked down her face.

'You, better than anyone else, know what Andrew has done for me. He took me from the hold of a convict ship. Because of me he settled here. Then he grew to love the place, and his heart was here. I'm as sure of that as anything I could be. I *must* hold together everything he's built up – keep it intact for our children. *They* belong to this country, and this is where they will see their father's achievements.'

'And you're prepared to do it alone?' he asked quietly.

She nodded. 'Alone – if necessary.'

Then she bent her head, and he could see her shoulders heaving. She covered her face with her hands. Her next words were blurred and distorted.

'I didn't know it would be like this. I didn't think it was possible to feel so desolate – and lost. Andrew . . .! Andrew . . .!'

Gently Jeremy put out his hand and stroked her bent head. He could remember clearly and painfully the first night he had ever spent under Glenbarr's roof – the night they had dined by candle-light off the packing-cases, and Andrew had strode across the bare boards, his face alight with the vision of the future. Then he had seemed indestructible, nothing was beyond the reach and scope of his energy and genius. Whatever he touched had been golden for him.

But now, four years later, the golden age was finished. And Sara's sobs were a wild protest against its going.

PART FIVE

I

For three weeks after her husband's death, Sydney saw nothing of Sara Maclay. Jeremy Hogan returned to the Hawkesbury without saying anything about her plans for the future; from Glenbarr itself there came no news. All that the servants could report was that their mistress spent her days with the children, walking with them on the South Head road, or down at the little beach; sometimes she took over the lesson hours from their tutor, Michael Sullivan, the young man who came to Glenbarr daily from his lodgings in the town. But Michael Sullivan was not to be probed for information. Richard Barwell appeared to know nothing either. From Annie Stokes came the report that Sara spent her evenings shut up in the room where all Andrew's business had been carried out. She gave orders for a fire there each evening, and Annie, always watchful, knew that it was often the small hours of the morning before her mistress took her candle and mounted the stairs to her bedroom.

For Sara herself they were weeks lived in a kind of daze; it was a period, not of trying to forget Andrew, but of rediscovering his mind, of tracing back the growth of every ambition and plan he had conceived during their marriage. Alone in the small, plain room she took down the heavy books that recorded each business transaction he had completed since the first land grant on the Hawkesbury. The store, the Toongabbie farm, Priest's . . . the first *Thistle*, then the new one bought in London, the purchase of *Hawk* and *Thrush* . . . the accounts of all of them were here, and copies of Andrew's instructions to his London agents. The hours spent here grew to be not only a process of schooling herself, but like a communication with Andrew himself. The records set down badly on paper were the framework of the life they had built up together. '. . . *Store commenced business.*' Back into her mind came the crowded, uncomfortable day, when the store had opened its doors for the first time. '*Purchase of farm at Toongabbie.*' Those words represented Andrew's return from England, with the new *Thistle* – the period when Glenbarr had been building. Each line of his writing could be filled out with a hundred different details; they were bare notations of Andrew's vision and ambition, his belief in the future of the colony. It was like reading the intimate journal of the life she had shared. She gently touched the pages, and seemed to hear again his voice, eagerly explaining the possibilities of some new scheme he had in mind. Andrew had not possessed the soul of a poet, he had left no letters for her to weep over – but the careful entries were a tangible record of his love.

When the last of the account books had been read and studied, she wrote to Louis. It was a long letter, containing the story of the convict rising at Castle Hill, and Andrew's death. In it she outlined her plans for carrying on his affairs, just as he had left them and, there and then, made Louis an offer for the outright ownership of the *Thrush* and *Hawk* – preferring, she wrote, to risk her own money, than to force him into placing their management into a woman's hands. She settled to wait, with what patience she could gather, for his reply. It would take, she imagined, at least a year.

2

It was a morning less than a month after Andrew's death when David came running down the stairs to tell Sara that, from the schoolroom window, they had sighted the *Hawk* coming to anchor in Sydney Cove. Sara heard the news with a sense of misgiving; she felt that she was hardly ready for the problems that were ahead of her over the matter of the *Hawk*'s cargo, but she sat down immediately to write a note to the master, Captain Sam Thorne, bidding him come to Glenbarr.

The next day Captain Thorne waited upon her in the small room he remembered as Andrew Maclay's study. He had already determined what the outcome of this interview would be – not for any money on earth would he remain in the employ of a woman-owner. He, Sam Thorne, was not accustomed to receiving polite notes, telling him the hour at which he might call to discuss the cargo waiting aboard. In his experience, owners had agents, or else they handled the business directly – and, by directly, he meant actually boarding the ship. Transactions with the owner were properly carried out over rum in his cabin – not in a drawing-room, sipping tea!

It was an enlightening two hours that followed. He sensed immediately that the woman who faced him across the table was not completely sure of her ground – but whenever he assumed authority not rightfully his, she had an uncanny knack of stripping it from him. She accepted nothing on faith, examining, one after another, each purchase and bill of sale, in a manner that, had she been a man, he would have considered downright insulting. She was nervous – he knew that very well; and yet she made no mistakes that would give him licence to point out that it was madness to believe she could, from this desk, and from this house, control the fortunes of three ships on the high seas.

The *Hawk* sailed from Port Jackson a month later, bound for London. In that time, Sara and Sam Thorne had reached an understanding. He still didn't approve of women-owners, and he still considered that she didn't know as much about the business as she laid claim to. But, by the same rule, she wasn't as ignorant as might be expected; and, though a haggler down to the last penny, she was strictly fair and just in her dealings. They fought their battle, Sara and Captain Thorne, and the victory did not go completely to either one.

On the afternoon the *Hawk* left the harbour, Captain Thorne called at Glenbarr to take leave of the woman under whose orders he was to sail for perhaps many years.

She walked with him to the veranda steps.

'Well, Captain,' she said, turning to him, 'I hope you have a good voyage. And may God speed your return.'

'Thank you, ma'am, I'm sure. And may you depend that I'll do my best for you. I'll see that those London agents treat you right.'

'Yes, I know you will,' she said quietly. She smiled, then, and extended her hand.

He went down the steps feeling that maybe Andrew had left his business to a head almost as shrewd and hard as his own.

In the town itself there was an outburst of curiosity when it was observed that Sara's first appearance after her husband's death was a visit, accompanied only by Annie Stokes, to the *Hawk*. Then, when it was known that she had made her third visit to the vessel, the idea began to seep through the settlement that she had no intention of instructing the London agents to sell the three ships. People shook their heads, saying to one another what a great pity it was that Sara Maclay didn't realize when she was over-reaching herself.

3

Andrew's death ended the three-year-old quarrel between Richard

and Sara. Although Richard called at Glenbarr several times during
the following few weeks, he had not been admitted; then he came
one day at the time when Captain Thorne was beginning to
spread the news that he could continue to sail under Sara's orders,
and he was not, as before, greeted with the reply that Mrs Maclay
was not receiving visitors, nor was he shown into the drawing-room.
Instead, Bennett led him into the little room where he and Andrew
had so many times talked over business matters. Sara rose from
the desk to take his outstretched hand. He accepted the chair she
indicated, and sat studying her – the set of her head above the
high, black collar, the fine, pale face, and drawn-back hair. It was
three years now since he had been alone with her like this – a long
time in which to regret the words used to herself and Jeremy on
the road to Kintyre, and to reflect on the qualities he had not seen
before or appreciated. He felt an immense, but almost unwilling,
respect for the woman facing him, this person who seemed to bear
little relation to the girl he had known at Bramfield. In the three
years of their separation he had learned her pride and spirit, the
unbending determination he could no longer sway by a mere smile,
or a lightly-expressed wish. He had no longer felt towards her any
of the rash confidence of his first year in the colony. By Andrew's
death, she had reached her full stature; he recognized it immediately, and he approached humbly and cautiously, almost afraid of
her.

He didn't know how to talk of Andrew. He began clumsily,
hesitantly.

'It seems . . . strange to see you here, Sara. Andrew always . . .'

She gestured vaguely – he couldn't tell whether in impatience –
to have him come to the point of what he wanted to say, or whether
it pained her to have Andrew spoken of.

'I know . . .' she said. 'But what else should I do? I was not
made to sit over a piece of needlework all day.' She spread her
hands on the littered papers before her. 'There's enough occupation here for three heads . . . and it keeps me too busy to think.'

But as she spoke, she rustled the papers nervously, and he
did not miss the brightness of tears in her eyes. She spoke with quick,
jerking phrases, and he sensed that, for all her show of calm efficiency, she was afraid of what she had undertaken. He thought of the
ship in the harbour, the captain who was accustomed to taking his
orders from men like himself. Richard owned that, among women,
Sara might be outstanding, almost formidable; but now she was
entering into a world of men where only wits sharper than theirs,
a need more compelling, a sense of opportunity more acute, would

enable her to survive. A petticoat government was a precarious thing; she would need every last ounce of shrewdness and courage that Andrew had taught her to pull off what she was attempting. He looked again at her nervous hands on the papers, and he felt afraid of her.

He faced her directly.

'What I've come here to talk to you about concerns Andrew . . . I've come about the money I owed him.'

She didn't reply, merely raised her eyebrows.

'I've come to assure you that it will be repaid, Sara.'

'Repaid?' she repeated quietly. 'Andrew didn't press for payment. It's not my intention to do so now.'

'You don't see my point at all. There is a vast difference in owing money to Andrew, and . . .' his voice dropped, 'owing it to you.'

Her gaze left his face, and for a moment she stared down at the desk, at the writing materials laid before her. There was a maddening precision in their array, set out by Annie's careful hands.

'How do you mean to raise the money, Richard?' Sara said suddenly, looking up. 'You don't mean to sell Hyde Farm?'

'No – not that. I'll keep Hyde Farm – no matter what happens. Lady Linton would advance the money if I wrote and told her the facts of the case.'

She shook her head violently, holding up her hand to silence him. He thought, for a moment, that her face betrayed anger – a definite irritation at the very mention of Lady Linton's name.

'I don't want you begging money from her. I'm in no hurry . . .'

He cut her short, stung by her choice of words. Her father's arrogance and hauteur were still there, he thought, when she needed them. Since the Bramfield days, she might have learned prudence – but she was never humble. He watched her settling back with a greater show of confidence, into the chair that her husband had always used, watched her spread her hands on the desk and prepare to refuse the money of a woman many thousands of miles away, a woman who had long ago forgotten Sara Dane's very existence.

'I had no thought of applying to Lady Linton,' he said quietly, 'unless you wished to have the money repaid immediately. If you'll give me time, I'll find it myself.'

'How?' she said. Her tone was gentler.

'I'll do what I should have done in the beginning. Expenditure will have to be cut – somehow. There must be ways and means of making Hyde Farm pay more. Alison and I should be able to live on far less than we do. Andrew went on lending us all the money we wanted. It was so easy – too easy – to continue taking it from him – but now we must put an end to that.'

She listened eagerly as he began to talk, outlining plans he had for improving the farm, the ways in which he could cut expenses, of certain business deals which he had, from lack of interest, never entered into before. He was determined he would waste no more opportunities. The flow of his talk ran on, and she didn't check him. She knew perfectly well that he was building up an impossible ideal, he saw himself the man of energy and acumen he never could be. But to hear him talk in this way was to bring back to her the first few weeks after his arrival in the colony, and the months after he had acquired the farm. While she listened, she was able to imagine that their quarrel had never existed; their three years of near-silence was as completely forgotten as if it had not been at all. With brief nods and a question now and then, she encouraged him. If Richard achieved only half of what he planned, he would far outstrip any effort he had yet made in his whole life. She had no particular need of the money he owed, and its repayment was safely insured by Alison's eventual inheritance from Lady Linton, but she would not say a word to halt him. His pride had been touched, and he showed more spirit now than she had ever seen in him before. It wouldn't harm him, she thought, to learn at last how money was made, to watch every penny of expenditure to see if it couldn't be reduced to a half-penny. He would soon get used to wearing last year's coat, and choosing his wines with an eye to the price. For too long Richard had been unhampered by such necessities; he would learn them now quickly, rather painfully, and be far better for having done so.

It was noon before he rose to go. They stood together wordlessly for a few moments, and then he bent and kissed her on the lips.

'Goodbye, Sara. It won't be possible to see you alone like this very often. But it won't be the hell it has been during the last three years – not again.'

She knew quite well what he meant. It seemed that at last Richard had learned the prudence she had tried to impose upon him in the beginning. He knew now the smallness of the society to which they belonged, and the power of rumour and gossip. With a kind of wisdom and gentleness he had not possessed when he had first come to the colony, he was bowing to the inevitable.

She smiled at him. 'We're fools if we haven't learned by this

time that we can never successfully quarrel with one another. You
and I were not made to quarrel.'

Still smiling, she shook her head when he tried to kiss her a
second time. Instead she took his hand and covered it with both
of hers.

4

During the next few months Jeremy watched Sara carefully, concerned that the look she had worn when she arrived in the colony
first, had returned to her face. Her eyes were cold, a little harsh;
when she spoke, her voice was quick and brittle. He thought her
afraid, unhappy, even tormented. She grew thinner, her beauty
sharp and fine – something to touch a man strangely when he looked
at her. And yet she herself seemed to be interested in no man.

Helpless to prevent it, he saw her driving herself to master the
tasks it would normally have taken three people to do. Clapmore
was promoted from his desk at the store to one in the room next to
where Sara herself worked. He took notes at her dictation, toiled
over long columns of figures, prepared letters to the London agents,
and was general liaison between Sara and the people with whom
she did business. The colony was learning the hopelessness of expecting to keep Sara Maclay out of any business transaction which
she made up her mind she wanted to enter. They didn't much like
it, but in time accepted it, and almost learned to regard each communication from her as if it came from Andrew himself. Their
acceptance of her part in the best of their commerce was, after a
while, fairly good-natured – except for the fact that they were,
whether consciously or unconsciously, waiting for the fatal mistakes
to creep in, the false moves that would bring the structure crashing.

When Jeremy's sentence expired, Sara marked the occasion
with a gift of cash and credits with her agents that staggered him.
He returned it promptly, and rather curtly. She took it back, not at
all embarrassed, shrugging her shoulders.

'You're a fool, Jeremy Hogan! You're free now, and you'll need
the money – but, if you choose to be as stiff-necked as a mule, that's
your own affair.'

But he cherished the memory of the dinner she gave him at
Glenbarr to celebrate his day of freedom. David was allowed to
stay up later than usual to eat with them; the dining-room windows
were open to the soft spring air, the wine was chilled and the
candles shed a kindly light on the faces of Sara and the child.

There was laughter between them, and some of the strain that now seemed to be Sara's habitual expression left her.

Suddenly Sara raised her glass, smiling at him down the length of the table. 'To the future, Jeremy!'

He heard her words phrased ambiguously because of David's presence, and caught up his glass eagerly, as anxious as she was to toast his freedom. Fourteen years were gone out of his life, fourteen years since he had seen his home, or the things that made his world – the pretty women, the gentle manners, the beautiful horses to ride to hounds with on sharp winter mornings. It was all gone now, but so were the years of serving other men. He could not return to what he had known, but life here in the colony could be fashioned into something to his liking. He was his own master now . . . Here he checked himself; he was not his own master while Sara chose to have him do her bidding. Telling himself he was a fool, still he drank the wine with her gladly.

The recollection of how Sara behaved to him that evening had to suffice him for the future. He looked vainly for the return to life she had shown then; she was not so much being aloof with him, he thought, as withdrawn and preoccupied. It was almost as if, while she talked with him, her mind was already racing ahead to her next duty. He knew quite well how much she still relied on him, coming to him for advice, and even, occasionally, taking it. But, it seemed to him, he made a useless effort when he tried to come close to her. Andrew was not dead, he thought, again and again – his ships sailed the high seas, his crops grew in rich soil, and Sara lived with his memory and a closed heart.

His freedom had brought little change to Jeremy's life. He divided his time between the Maclays' three farms – up early each morning, remaining in the fields with the labourers while the light held. Often at night, working over the account books in the silence of Kintyre or Priest's, he thought of Sara – probably similarly employed at Glenbarr – and he cursed her for the servitude in which she kept him. Occasionally he rode down to Parramatta or Sydney to find himself a woman, one of the easy ladies who sprinkled the streets after dark, decked in finery probably paid for by one of the soldiers of the Corps, or a farmer in town on a spree from one of the outlying districts.

But there was little satisfaction for him in this, thinking all the time of Sara, who shut herself up at Glenbarr, never admitting him unless Clapmore was there, or Annie paraded the hall. Sometimes he woke in the night, sweating from a dream of her, a dream in which her hair was twined about his throat, strangling him. He fretted

and fumed under her yoke, and yet he could not break free of
it.

As the months passed, her carriage was seen more and more
frequently on the roads between the three farms; in all weathers she
rode, a sober figure in her black, well-cut habit, on horseback
through the fields. She turned constantly to Jeremy at her side,
commenting, sometimes praising – but ever more sparing of her
praise than Andrew would have been. She was afraid to praise, he
told himself – and always afraid that what she had taken on would,
in the end, prove too much for her.

5

To Sara, the only real freedom from the sense of missing Andrew
was complete absorption in her business affairs – absorption to the
point where she was tired enough to sleep at nights, and tired
enough to shut out the growing doubts that, alone, she could carry
out her plans. A faint uneasiness grew in her heart as, each day,
the complication of her work increased. True, the colony was
getting over its surprise at her determination to carry on with
Andrew's affairs, and she was becoming more adept at handling
their diversity. The *Thistle* and *Thrush* had both put into harbour
lately, and their masters had received her instructions willingly
enough; she might well have been pleased with her success, but
she began to sense all about her a growing coolness, a hardening in
the attitude of those people who had cultivated her for Andrew's
sake. In the weeks close to his death, she had shunned callers at
Glenbarr, but, as the months passed without sign of the visitors that
had once come to the house, she began to wonder if they would
ever return. Where, she asked herself, were the women who had
made her acquaintance, those who had followed the fashion set by
Alison Barwell? Were they counting against her the fact that she
was no longer the wife of a prominent free-settler, but merely
a prominent ex-convict? She met them only on Sunday mornings
when she took the children to the service which the Reverend
Samuel Marsden conducted in the temporary church beside the
place where the new stone one was building. Each Sunday when
they had been in Sydney she and Andrew had always attended the
services here, and their walk back to Glenbarr had been slowed by
the number of people who had stopped to speak to them. Now
Sara walked there with David and Duncan beside her, and her
acquaintances, hurrying to be there on time, seemed to go on by
without noticing her. They sat on the hard, wooden benches to

listen to Mr Marsden's haranguing; the convicts dutifully crowding
in at the back; they sang hymns rather tunelessly without the help
of an organ. Afterwards they filed out, spreading about the rough
building as if this were the conventional English churchyard, except that their ears were always listening for the bell that didn't
ring. No one moved away until the Governor and Mrs King had
left; there were bows and curtsies, and often in the past
Andrew and Sara had been among those whom the Governor
had elected to stop and speak to. Now Sara stood with the boys
among the crowd to watch the Governor go – watched also as
Alison Barwell went by with scarcely more than a sketchy bow in her
direction. She noticed that the bows and nods of the other women
were growing more than a trifle perfunctory. They told her plainly
enough what Sydney thought of a woman who didn't spend the
first year of her widowhood sitting quietly in her own drawing-
room.

As the time went on, she knew almost without doubt that whenever she travelled to inspect the farms, or visited the store or the
vessels in the harbour, her movements were marked and criticized.
With a kind of helpless dismay she felt her position slipping back
to what it had been when she had first returned to Sydney from
the Hawkesbury.

The one real satisfaction in that lonely, bewildering year was
the change in Richard. As he and Sara had agreed, they did not
see each other, except for chance encounters in Sydney's streets, or
at the store. But an undeniable intimacy grew up between them,
established on the slender basis of his occasional letters to her, and
the short interview they had when he came each quarter with an
instalment to pay off against the debt he owed.

The card games at the barracks saw Richard hardly at all these
days; as often as he found time, he made the long trip to Hyde
Farm; there were no more tales of his drinking. Alison no longer
gave her evening parties, and, although she was as exquisitely turned
out as ever, she wore last year's gowns – and it was noticeable that
there was no more wistful talk of what Mrs Barwell was expecting
from London with the arrival of the next ship. Richard even made
a hesitant attempt to engage in a little trading on his own account.
He was not very successful – he had no heart and less skill for the
day-to-day struggle for the profits from the rum trade. In Richard,
ambition had been fired too late; energy alone could not compensate for the shrewdness and cunning he had never learned. Sara,
watching him closely, seeing him work as he had never done in his

life before, knew that the rewards of his labour were slight. The sum of money which he paid her each three months represented the ruthless cutting of his personal expenditure rather than his increased profits. But it would have wounded his pride to let him know that she realized this; if his dress these days was more modest, and she heard that he had sold his thoroughbred mare, she had more discretion than to mention it.

She welcomed his rare visits alone to Glenbarr. She settled eagerly to hear of his improvements at Hyde Farm, and encouraged him in the idea of expansion, knowing that she did so as much for the pleasure of listening to him spin his web of dreams, as for the sake of the future prosperity of the farm. It was far too late, she knew, for him to achieve half the things she desired for him; but, in his altered spirit and outlook, she found the slow emergence of a personality less selfish, and less self-centred.

When occasionally he wrote her – in a strange mixture of business and personal matters – she read and folded the letters many times over. And without letting herself consciously acknowledge her reason for doing so, she kept them all locked together in the drawer of the desk where she worked.

The months wore on slowly, filled with a sameness that dismayed her a little when she paused to consider it. In her periods of leisure she found that her own thoughts were dull companions. Jeremy was far away – at Toongabbie, Priest's, or Kintyre. Richard was self-banished. Her children were too young, and Michael Sullivan too shy, to provide the sort of conversation she craved. Not all her multiple affairs gave sufficient outlet to her energies. And the arrival of each mail found her searching eagerly for a letter from Louis.

2

'Will we soon be there, Mama?'

Sara turned to look at Duncan, sitting across from her in the carriage. His mouth had a sticky rim round it from the cake he had just finished eating; he spoke cheerfully enough, but he looked tired, and his clothes were dusty and crumpled. On the seat beside Sara Sebastian was asleep; she supported him with one arm, the other leaned against the ledge of the window, bracing her body against the jolts of the rutted road. Annie, sitting next to Duncan,

was nodding drowsily. Of the five, David seemed the only one with
enough energy to watch the road that wound its way by the
river.

'Yes, darling. It's not far now – not more than a mile.'

David glanced across at her then. 'This is the place we visited
before, isn't it, Mama? Before Papa died?'

His tone suggested that the visit eighteen months ago was already
lost in distant memory. Banon was a place he could only vaguely
recall.

'Yes,' Sara said. 'Don't you remember, David – and you, Duncan
– the white house above the Nepean? And the aviary – you remember the aviary, surely?'

'Yes . . . I remember.' Duncan spoke uncertainly. He did not
much care for moving outside his familiar orbit. 'But when are
we going back to Kintyre, Mama? I like Kintyre best.'

'Perhaps after a week at Banon, we'll go to Kintyre.'

'Why are we going to Banon? Monsieur de Bourget won't be
there – he's still in England.' David swung his foot discontentedly.
Like Duncan, he showed no great enthusiasm for the unfamiliar.
Kintyre was their love, the place that, even more than Glenbarr,
meant home to them. He seemed rather impatient with the thoughts
that Banon was holding them back from the delights of the Hawkesbury farm.

'Well . . .' For a few seconds Sara was at a loss for words. 'Well,
before Papa died, he promised Monsieur de Bourget that he would
ride out to Banon from time to time, to see how it was being kept
while he was away. Papa only managed to go once – and now it's
more than a year since anyone visited the house or farm. As Papa
was Monsieur de Bourget's partner in a number of business matters,
I thought I should go in his place.'

David nodded, and seemed satisfied. He turned his head again to
stare out of the carriage window.

It was a day late in March, 1805 – a year since Andrew's death.
Autumn was creeping gently upon the landscape; Sydney had yet
hardly noticed it, but here in the higher country the nights would
be sharp with frost. There had been no rain for a week, and the
dust rose from under the horses' feet. All around them the afternoon was silent and hushed. Sara was surprised at the change in
the countryside since she had last travelled the road to Banon.
There was now much more evidence of settlement. Rough tracks
led left and right to farmhouses hidden in the trees; whole blocks
of ground were cleared for agriculture, and cattle grazed within
enclosed paddocks. They were close now to the Cowpastures
district – the rich land on the other side of the river, where the

wild Government herds had bred from a few strays since Phillip's
time. No one was allowed to enter the area without official permission, but there was no real order enforced, and settlers who
wanted fresh meat apparently hunted there at will. This was still a
part of the country to which the hand of authority reached only
uncertainly.

To Sara, the remoteness of Banon was, for the time being, a
relief and a blessing. She had looked to it as a refuge, the farthest
part of the settled areas to which she could go. In panic, almost, she
had fled Sydney, bundling children and boxes into the carriage,
clinging desperately to Andrew's promise to Louis as a pretext for
this escape to the quiet of the Nepean. She craved the silence and
the peace, the unfamiliarity of Louis's house. There, alone and undisturbed, she could think around the situation, grown now so
much in magnitude that she could no longer ignore it. It had
reached a new height in Sydney three days before, sending her, with
undignified haste, to seek the solitude of Banon. She knew that,
within the next week or so, she must make some sort of decision
regarding her own future and her children's; she wanted to be
free to make it away from associations with Andrew, away from
any memories of the past which might influence her. The thought
of Banon brought a feeling of great calm.

At the window, David had suddenly stiffened. He craned forward, and then knelt up on the seat to get a better view. Annie put
out a restraining hand, but he shook it off.

'There's the house, Mama! I remember it now! Look, Duncan!'
Sara also leaned forward, glad of the sight of the white columns
and the terraces. She eased Sebastian's weight a little on her arm.
Earlier in the day a messenger had ridden ahead to announce their
coming to Madame Balvet; she had evidently set one of the servants to watch the road, for, as the carriage began climbing the
slope to the house, the housekeeper's black-clad figure appeared on
the portico. With her one free hand, Sara straightened her bonnet
and tried to brush the dust from her gown. As the carriage halted,
Louis's housekeeper came down the steps; despite the servant
standing by in attendance, it was she herself who flung open the
door.

'Welcome to Banon, Madame!'
She spoke warmly, reaching forward to lift the sleeping Sebastian
from Sara's arms.

2

For the next two days Sara worked constantly, leaving the children

to Annie's supervision, and immersing herself in the affairs of
Banon. Her activity gave her no time to think on the problem
which had sent her fleeing from Sydney; she was concentrated
fully upon the business in hand. First, mounted on one of Louis's
horses, she inspected every section of his farm, noting the condition
of the crops, the livestock – and saying little. She listened to the
slightly nervous talk and explanations of the two overseers – she
listened and treated it all with the same degree of reserve that
would have been Andrew's, or Jeremy's. Then she closeted herself
with them for a full day while the account books were gone through.
These had been as honest as might be expected from two men left
to their own devices for over a year. Her experienced eye on the
figures told her that no questionably large sum of money had been
spent on any one item. She knew quite well that the pair had not
run the farm in Louis's absence without a thought for the lining of
their own pockets, but that was to be expected. Louis had known
before he left that he would have to pay in extra, unspecified ways
for the services of men as experienced in farming as these two. Sara
realized that she must accept the accounts without undue investigation. At the end of their long day together the men went off, touching their caps, relief stamped plainly on both their faces.

On the third morning of Sara's stay Madame Balvet came to
her and insisted that she should inspect the house. Rather unwillingly Sara accompanied her; it had never been her intention
to question the Frenchwoman's housekeeping; and she found it
embarrassing to stand silently by while the linen was counted out,
and checked off against a list. The storeroom accounts were in
meticulous order – every pound of flour, every side of bacon recorded and accounted for. Gradually Sara began to see that, far
from being reluctant to display the storeroom, the linen cupboards,
the servants' pantry, Madame Balvet was actually eager to do so.
This was an indirect form of boasting, a desire to show off a perfect
piece of work. The inspection went from drawing-room, with its
delicate china ornaments, and the furniture that had been dust-
sheeted until Sara's arrival, to the bare cleanliness of the scullery-
maid's bedroom – Madame Balvet pausing always to draw aside
curtains, open drawers and point out the fierce polish on the
floors. She turned expectantly to hear Sara's praise. It was given
in a rather astonished fashion, but without stint. The Frenchwoman appeared satisfied; a look of pride and pleasure came to
her face.

When it was over, in a kind of ceremonial fashion, they drank
tea together in the housekeeper's room at the back of the house.
Sara watched the other woman's deft hands at work with the silver

teapot and the spirit-lamp. They performed the ritual with care and ease.

'You don't find it too lonely here, Madame Balvet? The distance from Sydney is so great . . .'

The Frenchwoman shrugged. 'I am busy, you know. There is no time to be lonely. There is always much to be done. Monsieur de Bourget will find I have not been idle during his absence.'

Watching her face as she busied herself with the cups, Sara was startled to see the expression there. It was an unguarded look, telling her how completely, even from the distance that separated them, Louis still dominated this woman.

3

Wearing a loose, silk wrapper, Sara sat before the fire in her bedroom at Banon, holding in her hands a sheet of paper, and reading over the half-dozen lines she had written.

'*Cher Louis* . . .'

She tapped quietly on the edge of the escritoire. She had meant to write him a full account of everything she had seen and heard at Banon in the past three days, while it was still fresh and with her; but even these few lines already had a tired air about them, an air of half-interest. Once more she dropped the quill in the ink, wrote a few more words, and then laid it down again.

It wasn't about Banon she wanted to write.

For the past week a single thought had turned itself over and over in her mind. Thrust into the background while she had worked over the farm accounts, it now reasserted itself and demanded her attention. It had first come into her head at the same time that she had had positive proof of the weakening of her position in the colony since Andrew's death. The leading families had given what sympathy they thought her due, and were now prepared to forget her. And along with her, her children also.

David and Duncan, now eleven and nine years old, could no longer be entirely sheltered from the knowledge of the struggle every ex-convict fought against the stigma of his conviction. Even political prisoners, like Jeremy Hogan, did not escape it. The prominent free settlers, and the officers of the Corps, had banded themselves into a tight little circle which no one who had sailed into Botany Bay for his crimes could hope to break. Through her marriage to Andrew, and her friendship with Alison Barwell, Sara had been accepted there. But with Andrew's death, his power ended, and now she was being pushed surely and quite definitely into the other camp – the emancipists, who stoutly claimed their own place in the colony's society, but who were steadfastly ignored by the ruling clique.

She had had this fact brought home sharply a week ago. Invitations had been issued for a birthday party for the eldest son of Captain Taylor of the Corps. Andrew had done a fair amount of business in London on Captain Taylor's behalf, and David and Duncan had always been prominent guests at young John Taylor's earlier parties. This year no invitation arrived at Glenbarr – and Sara knew none would be forthcoming. David knew it also. He had made only one mention of the fact, briefly, with an elaborate shrug of the shoulders. But before he turned away, Sara glimpsed the bright tears standing out in his eyes, and tears he refused to shed in front of her. Her heart ached for him – so young, and yet already understanding that his mother's past would not be forgiven her, that it would be laid on him and on his brothers.

'It doesn't really matter,' he said. 'In any case, I've always hated John Taylor. And I love you, Mama.'

Duncan would be the next, she thought, as she slipped her arm about her eldest son's shoulders – if indeed he hadn't already realized vaguely that there was something about his mother that was unlike other women. She recalled the day when they had returned together from the township, dirty, with torn jackets, and David trying to wipe away congealing blood from a cut on his forehead. Both had refused to give any explanation of the fight – though Duncan had seemed bewildered, and looked frequently to his brother for guidance. David had hustled him out of the room before he could say very much. Sara had watched them go with disquietening thoughts.

That night she had paced Andrew's study in nervous recollection of the empty, lonely year that was past. Her position in the colony was ambiguous. There had been no invitations to any of the parties or receptions held during that time – and she admitted now that she had gone on desperately believing that this was out of consideration for her mourning. But there was no mention of invitations in the future; nor had one come from Government House for more than twelve months. Another year without social acknowledgement from Mrs King would mean the end of the position Andrew had won for her in the colony.

The realization of this had driven her, early the following morning, to write to Madame Balvet, announcing her intention of bringing the children on a visit to Banon. But the inspection of farm and house was over, and now she must face her problems.

She touched the thick paper before her uncertainly. If she accepted the situation as it stood, she told herself, her sons would

grow up in an unhappy position midway between the emancipists
and the officer-clique. And whom would they marry – the daughters
of ex-convicts? They would, in time, fight Andrew's battles all over
again; however little real thought they gave to it, unconsciously
they would hold her responsible. Sara had no intention of being
pitied by her own sons.

With sudden impatience she ripped the sheet across, screwed
it up tight, and threw it into the fire.

'*Cher Louis . . .*' she wrote for a second time.

If only Louis would return – there was her salvation. Louis
would come back to Banon, wifeless, and with a young daughter
to take care of. No man remained for long in such a position. He
must be made to marry her. If she were the wife of a free settler
again there would be no need for David to pretend that he hated
his friends, in order to spare her feelings – or for him to instruct
Duncan in the things he must not say to her. Louis could do all
this for her – if he would.

She frowned heavily over the words on the paper. This year
of waiting had so far brought no letter from Louis. It was quite
possible that he had married again in England; it was even possible
that he no longer wanted to live here in New South Wales. Many
things were possible, and the power of Madame Balvet must not be
overlooked. The idea had taken only a week to grow in her mind,
but already it possessed her utterly. Louis must return – and somehow be made to marry her.

'Louis! Louis . . .!' she whispered. 'Why do you not come
back?'

She thought with a kind of helpless rage of the distance separating them – the distance and the time. She realized uneasily the
diverse influences which might be at work on him; other women
would find him attractive, either for himself or his fortune; he
might be beguiled by the ease and luxury of life in London; he
might hesitate now to bring a young daughter to the loneliness of
Banon. A dozen different things might combine to keep him away
from her. She looked savagely down at the paper in her hands.
Even this would take six months to reach him – and perhaps by then
he would no longer care for the news of Banon.

The sense of her own inactivity infuriated her. She thrust her
chair back abruptly, and began to pace the room. How did one
influence a man at thirteen thousand miles' distance? How did one,
in the dull, hard-working life of the colony, compete against the
brilliance of London society? Did Louis remember her in fashions
that were outmoded, as the mother of three children who always
seemed to crowd about her? Her conversation lacked the lustre

of the drawing-room – and she did not possess the mysterious
quality of Madame Balvet. She pressed her hands together as she
paced. What could she do? Only write Louis that his farm had
been inspected with the ruthless efficiency Andrew had taught her.
She paused. Perhaps efficiency was not what Louis looked for
in a woman. Would he have preferred a charming bewilderment?

She halted before the fireplace, her hands locked tightly together.

'Andrew would have known what to do,' she said aloud. 'He
would have known how to handle Louis.'

There appeared nothing incongruous to her in the idea that
Andrew would have bent his mind to this problem of Louis. Marriage to the Frenchman, if it could be achieved, would be a business
proposition, a move which Andrew himself would have approved.
It would be a step taken to safeguard the interests of his sons, to
hold together the possessions he had built up, until they were old
enough to take them over from her. Andrew would not easily have
forgotten his own fight against her position as an ex-convict, and
the ways it might affect their children. He would have been prepared to go to even these lengths to protect their interests. She
thought of Louis, his dark, thin face, and his air of worldly wisdom.
Comparing him with Andrew, she wondered if it would ever be
possible to love him deeply, apart from being attracted by him –
and she wondered if he would ever love her. She thought Louis
had the passion of love, but not the tenderness; his knowledge of
women would be wide, but superficial. Probably many had interested him for a time, but she doubted if any one woman had ever
wholly possessed him, absorbed him. Louis would never sit at any
woman's feet to take her orders. He was an individualist, unpredictable; his emotions not to be trusted completely, even in marriage.
He was unbiddable, uncertain – and somehow she must get him
back to New South Wales.

Suddenly she dropped into the low chair before the fire, balancing on the edge, and holding her hands to the blaze. The heat
scorched her face, yet she savoured the warmth, which seemed,
momentarily, to take away her fear and doubts about the future.

Then she cupped her chin in her hands. How would Jeremy
behave if she married Louis? Jeremy loved her; he worked with
the purpose of three men because of that love, and the love he
had had for Andrew. Many times during the past year she had
thought about Jeremy – thought regretfully that his position was no
better than her own. He might love her deeply, but his love would
not benefit her children. Jeremy, who, after Andrew, was of greater

worth than any man she had known, was an ex-convict like herself. Did he ever think of asking her to marry him? That much she never knew. He seemed to understand every thought in her head, the motive for every action; he knew all her harshness and cruelties, as Andrew had never done. It was always Jeremy who had pointed out her failings, forcing her to live up to his idea of what Andrew's wife should be. With no illusions about her, yet he still said he loved her.

Slowly, she shook her head at the thought. There must never be an exchange of love between herself and Jeremy. Emancipist and emancipist . . . If she married again it must be to pull herself upwards, to regain what Andrew had won for her. Marriage to Jeremy would be going over completely to the opposite camp; that was not even to be considered. In ten years from now, her sons should not have to regret the follies their mother had committed.

But she was well aware that Jeremy had the qualities she would never find in Louis. Jeremy was devoted and loyal, with sometimes an unnameable tenderness in his voice when he spoke to her. For her sake he was working himself half to death on three farms that would never belong to him; all these years he had helped build up a fortune in another man's name. She supposed that she had loved Jeremy, in a fashion — not as her love for Andrew, nor for Richard — ever since the night of the convict raid on Kintyre. Perhaps it went back even before that, but her jealousy and suspicion had masked any love she might have felt. If it were possible . . . She shut her thoughts off abruptly. Jeremy was an ex-convict.

She rose and walked back to the escritoire. The blank page with its two written words stared up at her. She felt a sudden weariness and contempt for herself at the realization of what she would do to Jeremy, and what she would do to her own feelings. She must presently sit down and write to Louis, calculatingly telling him how diligent she had been in his interests, convincing him in unwritten words how diligent a guardian she would be to his child. She knew she didn't in the least want to mother this unknown daughter of his, but that was part of the bargain she had made in her own mind.

She sat down again and picked up the quill. The trouble was that the bargain did, so far, exist only in her mind. Louis was thousands of miles away, beyond her reach, beyond her influence. She gave a quick sigh, and then she began to write.

For more than an hour she wrote, and was still writing when she heard the sound of horses and a carriage in the drive beneath her window. She looked up at the clock; it was after ten, and no one travelled so late without good reason on the lonely Nepean road. Puzzled, she went to the window and drew back the curtains. The carriage had halted some distance away; there was a confusion of voices and sounds as servants called to each other and one of them scrambled to the roof to untie the boxes. Suddenly, in the light of the lanterns they had placed about, she recognized the figure of the man who stood talking to Madame Balvet. He turned and leaned into the carriage, and when he faced the light again, he was carrying a child in his arms, well wrapped in rugs against the cold March night.

Louis had come back to Banon!

She waited only long enough to see that no woman alighted with him, and then she let the curtain fall into place.

She hurried across the room, the draught of her passage sending the sheets of her letter swirling. They came to rest on the carpet with a gentle rustle. With her hand on the door-knob, ready to rush out into the hall, she paused, and turned back. Deliberately she walked to the dressing-table, bending close to it, examining her face carefully. Would Louis think she had changed? Had she grown older since he left? To her own eyes she didn't look any different, but how would he see her compared with the cherished pale complexions of London? From a drawer she brought out powder, and flicked it across her face, anxiously peering at the result. Her hair had already been loosened and brushed for the night; it hung over her shoulders, the same bright colour he would remember. She looked at it with satisfaction, and at the slimness of her figure, which the wrapper revealed. Then she went to the cupboard and took down another wrapper. It was sea-green silk, and Andrew had once said it was like her eyes.

Before she left the room she tore the pages of the letter in two; the pieces burned merrily on the fire. She watched them with a flush of excitement on her cheeks. The letter need never have been written. Louis had come back – alone.

The hall candles had all been hastily lit. The front door stood open to allow the manservant in with the boxes. The wind blew down directly off the mountains, and Sara shivered as she paused to take in the scene. Louis and Madame Balvet stood close together, talking excitedly in French; the child had almost disappeared into the depths of a high, winged chair. Her hood had slipped back, revealing black hair, and waxy white skin. Her eyes were closed; she took no notice of the bustle about her. Sara started forward.

Louis turned at the sound of her footsteps. Immediately, he came towards her with both hands outstretched.

'Sara!'

He wasn't changed. His tanned skin was as tightly stretched as ever across the prominent cheek bones; he had the same quick, light walk. He was smiling, and at the same time half-laughing.

'Come, Sara! No word of welcome for me?'

She took his hands tightly in her own. For a moment she found it difficult to speak; she had the sensation of tears pricking at the back of her eyes, and her throat was dry. She was disconcerted; she had not expected his return to affect her in this way. The eighteen months without sight of Louis had made him almost a stranger in her own mind. It was a relief beyond anything she had imagined to find him still familiar, still as he had left the colony. But there was an added familiarity. Crossing the hall, it seemed to her, for perhaps just a second, that she was moving forward to greet her own father. Here was the same thin, dark face, the lean body. Sebastian Dane might also have laughed in just this way.

'Louis!' she cried, in a low voice. 'Of course, I welcome you! No one more than I. But this is so unexpected . . .'

He shrugged. 'Am I to wait about in Sydney until you give me permission to come to my own home? We arrived back two days ago, and they told me at Glenbarr that you had gone to Banon. I told myself, "Louis, there she is – taken possession, as always. She is ruling like a despot at Banon, while you kick your heels here in Sydney. Go and surprise her! Rout her!"'

He bent and kissed her hand. 'And here I am!'

She smiled delightedly. 'Never was defeat more welcome. I shall retreat with all possible speed and grace.'

'Oh, but no, Sara! I shall have to have a few days to get used to seeing you, before I let you go back.'

Her eyebrows shot up. 'A few days . . .! I can't stay so long here alone.'

'Let gossip make what it will of your staying here,' he said shortly. 'Are you not my business partner? And are you not . . . But, enough of this!' Laughingly, he tugged at her hand. 'We chatter too much. Come, I want to present my daughter to you.'

She was led forward to the winged chair. A middle-aged woman who was obviously a nurse stood diffidently waiting orders. Madame Balvet was there before them, touching the child on the shoulder to rouse her. Dark, sleepy eyes opened, and looked up wonderingly at Sara.

'Elizabeth,' Louis said quietly, 'this is Mrs Maclay. You remember I told you about Mrs Maclay's three little boys you should have to play with?'

For a few seconds the child stared uncomprehendingly. Then with an effort she collected her wits, and began to push herself forward in the big chair. She rose on unsteady legs, and started to sink in an uneven curtsy. Sara's hand stopped her.

'I'm glad to meet you, Elizabeth,' she said gently.

The child did not answer, merely turned her eyes down to the floor. Her little white face looked pinched and cold, and she plucked at her cloak in a gesture of shyness.

Sara turned slightly. 'Louis ...?'

He nodded, signalling to his housekeeper. 'She is so tired, ma petite! She has had too much travelling, too much excitement, after all the months of the voyage. In the morning ...'

Madame Balvet stooped and lifted Elizabeth up into her arms. From her new height she regarded them solemnly.

'In the morning,' Sara said, 'you shall meet the three little boys. One of them is just your age.'

For a second it seemed that Elizabeth would smile. But she nodded, with a quick jerk of her head, and then settled down against Madame Balvet's shoulder. Sara and Louis watched her as she was carried away. The nurse trailed behind uncertainly.

'I hardly know what to make of her,' Louis said softly. 'She's still shy with me, even after all the time we've been together. Precocious, I suppose, in ways – and I didn't mend matters there, for I spoiled her shamefully in London. I'm convinced she wasn't happy in that great barracks of a house in Gloucestershire, and yet I can't truly say she seems happy away from it. She might be better here. She rides, of course, as if she had been born on a horse – as she very nearly was. Her mother's nature is in her in parts.'

'Does she look like her mother?'

He smiled. 'That's the one characteristic of her mother's I had hoped for – and Elizabeth has it in abundance. She will be a beauty.'

Then he touched her shoulder affectionately. 'But let us not stand here, Sara! Come with me into the dining-room – Madame Balvet is sending food there.'

Sara sat with him while he ate supper, her fingers curling about the stem of the glass of wine he had poured her. Madame Balvet insisted upon waiting on him herself. She came and went with trays, two spots of unaccustomed colour showing vividly on her cheeks.

Louis talked rapidly as he ate – disjointed scraps of news, and questions thrown at Sara.

'England is at Nelson's feet—but most of them don't care for
Emma . . . Bonaparte has his Grand Army camped on the cliffs of
Boulogne.'

'Invasion?' Sara asked.

He shrugged. 'Nelson is there, anyway.' Then he pointed a
chicken leg at her, laughing. 'But should the good people of England
become too frightened of invasion, there's always the scandals of
the Prince of Wales to divert them. Mon Dieu, how that man
spends money! He lives, in what is presumed to be domestic bliss,
with Fitzherbert—who, happily, has the Pope's brief to tell the
world that she truly married His Royal Highness. Poor Princess
Caroline is always in trouble of one sort or another—but the
people who loathe the Prince rally about her.' He gave an exaggerated shudder. 'What atrocious taste she has! My belief is that
she could have kept him faithful, more or less, if someone had
taken the trouble to show her how to dress. He could hardly be
expected to live with such a guy.'

He finished his wine, and pushed the empty glass towards
Madame Balvet to be refilled.

'I made the acquaintance of the Barwells' Lady Linton,' he said.
'She still entertains the Prince occasionally. She's prodigiously fat.
Always seems to wear purple, though I can't imagine why. Her
complexion is the colour of an orange moon.'

Sara smiled at his expression.

He finished his meal, and turned directly to the house-keeper.

'The box I showed you, Madame—the small one—I should like
it brought here.'

She nodded, and left the room.

Louis turned back to Sara. 'I saw John Macarthur several
times when I was in London. He's pining to be back here. I think
he's expecting to return fairly soon. The court martial, of course,
was all in his favour, and I don't believe our unhappy Governor
has come out of the affair very well. Macarthur has a plausible
tongue, but the samples of merino wool he brought did far more
to win him favour than any other thing. He comes back with a
grant of land in the Cowpastures.'

'Wool . . .' Sara murmured.

'What did you say?'

'I said "wool" . . . Wool will be more important to this country
than anything else. Macarthur has seen that all along. Agriculture
will not expand beyond our own needs, but wool will make our
fortunes abroad.'

'Always the business woman, Sara! You have not altered, my
dear!'

She lifted her head, and her colour heightened a little.

'And why not? What else is there to occupy me here? I haven't
any gossip of the Court, or of Nelson's mistress, to beguile you.
Treat me kindly, Louis!'

'Then give me some of your news – quickly!'

Her eyes darkened a trifle. 'I had been writing you a letter
when you arrived this evening. It was mostly news of Banon . . .
But all that can wait till tomorrow. There is one thing, though,
which I'm sure will interest you. They say the Governor has had
reports of Matthew Flinders. Do you remember him, Louis – the
young lieutenant who sailed in the *Investigator*, to map the continent for the Admiralty?'

He nodded. 'But, of course! What of him?'

'He set out for England in the *Cumberland* – by the route
through Torres, to the Cape. He put into Ile de France for repairs,
and the news is that the Governor there, General Decaen, is holding him as prisoner of war.'

'The man must be mad!' Louis said thickly. 'Flinders was
carrying a passport for a voyage of scientific exploration from the
French Minister of Marine himself. Mon Dieu, what a return for
the hospitality and sanctuary Governor King gave the French expedition, when they came under Baudin! There must be something more to this, Sara.'

'Flinders's charts and maps,' she said, '. . . they're all with him
on Ile de France. You know what that means, Louis. If he is held
there for any length of time, Baudin will publish his own accounts
of the voyage, and the explorations he made for France. And then
Flinders's discoveries may be discredited.'

Louis shook his head slowly. 'So purposeless . . . so stupid! Was
he married?'

'Yes. Three months before he left England, in 1801. Apparently
he was bringing his wife, but at the last moment she wasn't allowed
to sail with him in the *Investigator*. And now she must wait until
Decaen decides to let him go.'

He fingered his glass, moving it round in a circle, and watching
the wine gently tilting. 'These men of science – what sacrifices
they make for their mistresses! Here is young Flinders, with logs
and maps that are exquisite models of skill and patience, cooped
up on Ile de France – and a bride of three months waits for him
in England! Which of them, I wonder, does he love the better?
Which would he sacrifice . . .?' Then he looked up. At a tap on
the door, Madame Balvet entered, followed by a manservant, carrying an iron-bound box on his shoulder.

'Thank you,' Louis said. 'Put it there, by the fire.'

He addressed the housekeeper. 'Elizabeth – is she in bed now?'

The Frenchwoman nodded. 'The nurse has attended to her. I imagine she sleeps already.'

'Excellent! She will be better in the morning. Poor little one – she is so tired.'

Madame Balvet cleared the last dishes from the table. She hesitated before the wine and the two glasses. Louis shook his head. 'No, leave them.'

She made no reply, and did not raise her eyes to either of them while she stacked the tray with dishes. She handed it to the man-servant, lingering for a minute or two longer – purposeless lingering, which Sara quickly noticed. Then she left, closing the door noiselessly behind her.

Louis leaned forward to refill Sara's glass; his action was slow and deliberate.

'Now, Sara . . . we can be peaceful. The voyager has returned to his own fireside, and the clamour of Europe fades! I am glad to be back – far more glad than I would have said was possible five years ago.' He paused there. 'And you, my dear . . .? How has this past year gone with you?'

She hesitated, looking sideways into the fire, twisting her glass nervously. The wine was dark; she moved it to see the play of the firelight through it, struggling to find the words to talk to him. He sat opposite, silent. She would almost have preferred his light-hearted mood of banter. There was no sense of peace here, as he had suggested. Suddenly she thrust back her chair, half-turning to the fire. Her movement shook the table, and a little of the wine spilled.

'This past year, since Andrew died, has been – damnable,' she said. 'Oh, you must be able to imagine how it's been. I'm occupied and busy from the moment I wake in the morning, until I go to bed again – and it all feels as if it's to no purpose. What point is there in the life of a woman who lives as I do now, when I remember what it used to be?' Her voice had dropped, and she kept the side of her face turned to him. 'I'm a successful business woman, I'm the mother of three children, but, with all that, I'm lonely. I go out and inspect the farms, and I'm pleased – but who is there to share my pleasure? I buy a new gown, but it's black, and there's no one to care how I look in it.'

She swung round, looking at him passionately. 'That is not a woman's life, Louis – that is just existence! I grow inhuman and withdrawn. I feel it myself, and yet I can't prevent it.'

Then she sank back in the chair. 'They hung Andrew's murderer as high as the rest of the rebels, but justice gives me so little
comfort. It cannot give me back the reason why I was content –
happy – to work as I did. Now I busy myself in the affairs of my
sons, but I have no heart for it.'

He nodded, his hands resting on the arms of his chair. 'This is
all so true – and I can offer you no comfort. I have thought of you
often, Sara, since I had your letter. Andrew's death brought me
back here sooner than I planned – as soon as I could find a ship to
take me. I suffered for you, but somehow I felt I was merely
hearing news I had known in my heart for a long time. You and
Andrew were too perfectly matched, too lucky. Everything was
yours – and no thought stirred in either that didn't find its counter-
part in the other. Heaven can well be jealous of such happiness.
Mon Dieu, how others must have envied you – as I envied you!'

He lifted his hand expressively. 'Well, it's gone now. Don't
weep for what is gone, Sara. You're a greedy woman if you cannot
be grateful for what you've had.'

She stirred restlessly, frowning. 'That is not enough to make
me stop wishing for that time over again. Have you no heart,
Louis?'

He smiled thinly. 'I have a heart – but it doesn't overflow with
pity for you. You have been lucky, my dear, and luck doesn't
last for ever. I grieved for Andrew, also – I know I shall miss him
in a thousand ways. I cared for him as a friend, more than any
man I have ever known. But he is dead, and, at some time, there
must be an end to one's grief. Be glad for what you have had,
Sara, and forget your self-pity.'

A look, half of surprise, half irritation, crossed her face.

'Self-pity . . . ? No one has ever suggested . . .'

'No. No one has suggested it, because everyone is too afraid of
you. Only I myself am not afraid of you – myself, and possibly your
overseer, Jeremy Hogan. Though even he, I doubt, would dare
suggest such a thing to you. Oh, I knew exactly how you would
pattern yourself to widowhood. I thought about you so often, and
I believed I knew you well enough to see how it would be. And I
fear that I was right.'

Humbly now, she said, 'Tell me!'

He began slowly. 'I knew you would fling yourself into Andrew's
affairs – and work yourself to death in the mistaken notion that you
were assuring the future of your sons. You would shut the world
out of Glenbarr, and at the same time give it a model of how a
widow should behave. You would make-believe that your heart
was buried with Andrew, denying and holding back your own

vigour and spirit – which you'll never succeed in stifling. You could lose the whole world, Sara, and you'd still remain yourself. Tell me, am I right? Isn't this what you've done?'

She answered thoughtfully, without looking at him. 'You could be right. But I haven't learned to look at it in this way.'

'Then it's high time you did. A year has gone since Andrew was killed, and you're not a woman of so little courage that you can't learn to live without him more successfully than you've done in the past. I expected more from you than this – and yet somehow I knew how well you would play the role your notions of respectability set you. Mon Dieu, Sara, you are not like the other gentle, simpering ladies of the colony, who must sit in their drawing-rooms and knit. You arrived here in a convict transport. You have learnt harder lessons than those others will ever know; life can't now give you worse than you've already had. Why pretend that Andrew's death is a blow from which you'll never recover? This is false to yourself – wrong!'

'Enough, Louis!' she burst out. 'You've said quite enough! I won't stand any more of it.'

'Enough, then, it is!' His eyes were crinkled up with teasing laughter. 'You sat there so meekly through it all, that I began to think you had indeed changed since I went away!'

Unwillingly she smiled also, though still annoyed and bewildered by what he had said, and yet unable to resist his mood. She felt his amusement at all her ideas of conventional behaviour, and she resented his parody of her position at Glenbarr. But there was rough justice in his remarks. No one, in recent years, had dared to recall her convict past, or to draw such sharp contrast between herself and the colony's other prominent women. He was right in saying she would never suffer again as she had during her imprisonment and the voyage in the *Georgette* – but only he would have dared to reason in this way, to trace the influence and effects of such experiences through her whole life, and because of them, pronounce judgement on her present behaviour. She thought on and around the subject, and she was forced to admit to herself that he was right in saying that she was false to her true self in this effort to preserve the conventional aspects of widowhood; the young Sara of the *Georgette* would have scorned such practices, would have mocked the older Sara for pretending like this before Louis.

She smiled across at him now, quite broadly, thinking of how, ten years ago, she would have flung herself back into the business of rearranging her life to complete satisfaction after Andrew's death. In particular, she would not have given Louis the picture she had displayed of herself in the last half-hour. Too many years of comfortable, secure existence had dulled her wits, she told herself. Realizing this, she suddenly relaxed completely, laughing, the strain wiped from her face.

He leaned forward again.

'You encourage me now,' he said. 'I thought the time would never come when it would be appropriate to present my gift.'

'Your gift . . .?'

He had begun to search in his pockets, and at last brought out a ring of keys.

'I pictured you languishing in your black gowns, Sara – and in the little time I had to prepare before we sailed, I found something for you which I hoped might bring you to revolt against them.'

With this he rose and put the key he had selected into her hand, motioning towards the small chest

'I should like you to look at it,' he said.

She dropped to her knees before the chest, her fingers trembling slightly with excitement as she fumbled with the lock. It was well-oiled, and it sprang back easily. She was madly impatient.

Behind her, Louis said, 'At great inconvenience, my dear Sara, I've kept it with me in my cabin. I was determined that this was one thing the sea-water would not spoil.'

She was lifting out quantities of soft paper, scattering them on the floor about her; then she came on a loose, calico wrapping, and underneath it, the sheen of satin. She laid reverent hands upon it, bringing it up slowly to catch the light of the candles and the fire. It was a ball-gown of the deepest blue, with clusters of small pearls sewn into its folds – a gown to take the breath away. She sat back on her heels, looking at it.

She was silent for so long that at last Louis spoke.

'I presumed upon our friendship in choosing this for you. A personal gift, you'll think – even an intimate one. Perhaps a set of books for Glenbarr would have been more suitable. But if you'll accept this, you'll show me that you are the woman I believe you to be – that you . . .'

'Wait, Louis!' Her voice was harsh.

Quickly, with nervous fingers, she turned the shining gown around, holding it against her body, fitting it close to her. Its colour swam before her eyes, its richness – and it was like a challenge to her. She recalled the hour she had spent before Louis's arrival, the painfully-written letter, the frustration of believing him beyond her reach. He was so necessary to her plan and her purpose. Should she now try to carry him forward on the mood of their hour here together? Faced with this sort of situation Andrew himself would not have hesitated, nor, ten years ago, would she herself have hung back. She had good reason to curse the caution and prudence she had acquired. Why should she not reach out to what was well within her grasp, to secure it before other influences attempted to take it away? Was he teasing her with the intimacy of his gift? – he was capable of teasing her for many months yet, and Madame Balvet would always be there in the background. If she had the courage, she could end the doubts here – and within a few minutes.

'Louis . . . ?'

'I am listening,' he said quietly.

Still on her knees, she twisted until she was facing him, the gown pressed against her.

'Louis . . .' She repeated his name slowly, conscious of holding back the next words.

Then she looked up at him fully. 'Would you marry me, Louis?'

He dropped to his knees beside her, gently taking the gown from her grasp and flinging it across the chest. He put his hands on her shoulders, looking at her.

'Do you realize what you have said, Sara? Do you know what you have done?'

'I suppose . . .'

'No supposition, this!' he said firmly. 'You *have* asked me to marry you.'

His arms went about her, and he pulled her body in close to his. When he kissed her it was in a calculated fashion, as if he had known how he would do it. And yet she sensed that he found little satisfaction in it. His kiss was not an answer to her question – it might yet be another piece of provocation. She started to draw away from him.

He didn't release her, as she expected. He looked searchingly into her face for more than a minute. There were faint lines puckering his forehead, a look of inquiry. Then it faded, to give place to a gradual smile. The corners of his mouth twitched, and straightened themselves, as if he pulled them back before she should notice. Holding her by his left arm, he reached behind her to take the two cushions from the large chair that faced the fire. They made soft, dull thuds as they dropped to the floor. Carefully he caught her up in his arms, and laid her like a child with her head upon the cushions. She made only a slight motion to rise, and then her lips met his again. This time the kiss was not calculated, nor had she thoughts to analyse it; it gave her an exquisite sense of warmth and life, and the deepening feeling of discontent, which had hung upon her for so long, was stifled. It was deadly quiet in the room, and she heard, with a sharp, gratified pleasure, the sound of their breathing close together. Her hand moved slowly upon the roughness of his face, caressing it, and telling herself that the emptiness which had surrounded and oppressed her through these last months would be there no longer.

At last he drew back from her. She turned her head upon the cushions to watch him. He lay full length on the hearth-rug beside her, leaning on one elbow, his chin resting in his hand.

'I thought,' he said quietly, 'that it would take you many, many months to speak to me like this. In Sydney they told me how it was with you – shut up there at Glenbarr, and never venturing out except for business. I knew I should never ask you to marry me while you persisted with that parody.'

Suddenly he pointed a finger at her. 'I was determined that I would make you want me, Sara. I would make you confess that you were tired to death of living alone – that your own passion would force you to make this demand of me. I swore – yes, I swore I would marry no woman who gave herself to me with a show of reluctance, even if to give herself the desired cloak of respectability. I will not live with this pretence you try to maintain. You will marry me because you *want* to – and not after a decorous interval of courtship, either. It must be quickly, so as to give the gossips nothing to say but that we did it because we wanted each other, and not to suit our mutual conveniences. In a month, perhaps – yes, I will send you away from Banon tomorrow, and in a month we shall be married.'

'A month . . . ?'

'That is not too soon, Sara – because we need each other.'

He leaned over towards her, brushing his lips against her hair, which lay tumbled in a dishevelled mass.

'You are so beautiful with the firelight on you,' he said. 'Your skin is so warm, and I am tired of the marble-white English skins. Your hands are strong and possessive, Sara, and I have imagined their touch on me all these months past. I am filled with a mad longing to kiss your throat, and yet I hold back for the pure pleasure of looking at it. Oh, beauty . . .' His voice was barely a whisper.

He put his head on the cushion beside hers, his lips almost against her cheek. But he was content to rest there only a few moments. He shifted his body closer to hers, and, leaning over her, he gathered her up tightly in his arms.

3

Five days after the notice of Sara's coming marriage to Louis de
Bourget appeared in the *Sydney Gazette*, Jeremy presented himself at Glenbarr. Unannounced, he opened the door of the study
where she was working, filling its frame with his bulk, standing
silently until she turned to see who had entered.

Her startled glance took in his dishevelled clothes, and beyond
him, in the hall, she could glimpse Annie Stokes, wringing her
hands in her habitual, nervous gesture.

Jeremy closed the door with a bang. He took a few steps towards Sara, extending a crumpled copy of the *Gazette*.

'This reached me yesterday,' he said. 'Is it true?'

She looked at him coldly. 'If you refer to the announcement of
my marriage – yes, it is true.'

In sudden fury, he twisted the paper between his hands.

'God in heaven, Sara! Have you gone out of your mind? You
can't be serious about this!'

'I'm perfectly serious. Why should I not be?'

'But you can't marry him! *Not* de Bourget!'

'And what objection have you to him?'

'None – in any position other than that of your husband. There
were never two people less suited to live together. Think of it,
Sara! I beg you to think again before you do this.'

His tone had softened, and she looked at him in a more kindly
fashion. The dust of the roads had gathered thickly on his clothes
and boots; his black hair, hanging on his forehead, was damp
with perspiration. A far cry, this, she thought, from Louis's elegance;
yet it was very familiar, and, after a fashion, beloved to her. She
had never learned to look at Jeremy without recalling the first years
at Kintyre, the happiest time of her whole life.

'Tell me, Jeremy,' she said gently, 'tell me why you think I
should not marry Louis de Bourget?'

The tension left his body somewhat as she spoke; the hand
holding the rolled, crumpled paper dropped to his side. For a moment he seemed bewildered; slowly he walked across to the desk,
bringing his fingers up to rest against the edge, and leaning towards her.

'Does one cage together two animals of a different species, Sara?
Does one try to wed happily two people of utterly dissimilar charac-

ter, purposes, and thought? Louis de Bourget's mind and outlook
is European – more than that – it belongs to France before the
Revolution. To you, this colony is home, and the life, however
crude and rough, is the shape of better things to come. To de
Bourget, the colony is a refuge from all that he finds uncongenial
in his old world. Although he may not consciously see it in this
fashion, to him, the convicts here are like the peasants of France.
There is a great wealth to be won from the soil, and at the expense
of their labour. A new-born France, is how he sees it. It's a country
where the laws of privilege and wealth hold good, where all power
is in the hands of the few, and there exists a level of society even
lower than the French peasant.'

'Careful, Jeremy!' she said. 'These surely are the sentiments
which earned you your passage to Botany Bay in the first place.'

He waved her words angrily aside. 'Never mind the colour of
my political sentiments! Listen to me, Sara! How can you possibly
marry de Bourget, when he doesn't know one particle of what you
have experienced here? How can he ever know the person you
were once – the girl that Andrew brought to Kintyre? And can
you, for the sake of his position, and his ideas of how his wife
should behave, leave behind everything you and Andrew created
together? Will you sell the store, the farms, the ships? Are you
content to sit over your needlework all day? Because, if I am any
judge of Louis de Bourget, that is precisely what he will expect
of you!'

'How blind you are,' she retorted angrily. 'It's to keep the store,
and the farms, and everything else I have, that I am doing this!
Have you thought of that, Jeremy Hogan? Have you remembered that it isn't easy for a woman to carry on these things entirely by herself? Each time I give an order, or handle a transaction it is resented, because it is not backed by the authority of a
husband.'

She drew in a swift, deep breath, feeling the furious colour
spring to her cheeks. Her anger was beginning to match his own.

'And what of my children? What is to become of them? You
know the emancipist problem as well as I do. Since Andrew's
death I have been merely an ex-convict, and nothing more. My
sons have been treated accordingly. Is it fair to bring them up to
face that situation, and the knowledge that they are not accepted
by the people they would wish to know?'

'Your sons are also Andrew's sons,' he said firmly. 'Not one of
the three will be a weakling, unable to fight his own battles. They'll
make their way wherever they choose, and there'll be no barrier

they cannot cross if they so wish. At least, give them the chance to do it themselves – don't impose upon them the worse burden of a stepfather who is at odds with this environment, who will sneer at the commerce and trade which Andrew taught them to look on as their world. Would you give them thoroughbred horses and soft hands – and have them grow up not knowing a spade from a plough?'

'My sons need a father,' she said sullenly. 'And I . . . I need a husband.'

Perspiration was breaking out on his forehead; his hands, pressed against the desk, trembled slightly.

'If it's a husband you want, Sara – then, marry me! Surely I'd fit that role better than Louis de Bourget?'

Her mouth dropped open; the colour mounted again rapidly in her face, until her cheeks were two patches of scarlet.

'You!' She choked over the word.

He looked at her steadily for some moments, his eyes narrowing as they concentrated on her face. The perspiration stood out in beads on his forehead; he put up one hand and wiped it impatiently, his eyes never leaving her face. Then, quite abruptly, he leaned farther forward until his face was within inches of her own.

'No! That wouldn't do for you, would it, Sara? I'm merely another ex-convict. By marrying me you'd be hopelessly ruined, and your children also. But you'll marry this Frenchman without counting whether or not he loves you – or whether you love him. If you searched the whole world you wouldn't find a man less like Andrew in every way – and yet this is the man with whom you choose to spend the rest of your life. Are you going to buy your way into pompous little receptions at Government House with this wedding? Would you rather your sons were bathed in vice-regal smiles – or that they turned out men like Andrew?'

Suddenly he slapped his open hand down on the desk.

'Damn your mercenary little soul, Sara! You're not worth any man's regard!'

He drew back, his expression frowning and dark.

'Well, go ahead, marry your Frenchman – but you've lost your overseer! I'll be damned if I'll slave out my guts to provide more gowns for Madame de Bourget to wear to Government House! Farm your own land in future! Do what you like with it – it's no longer my concern. The day you marry de Bourget, you can stop sending your instructions to me – I won't be at hand to receive them.'

'Jeremy!' she said faintly. 'You wouldn't leave! What would you do . . .? Where would you go . . .?'

'I'll be occupied using my time to my own advantage,' he said shortly. 'You've had enough of my life – from now on it will be my own.'

She jumped up quickly. The papers on the desk fluttered briefly, and subsided.

'Wait!' she said harshly. 'Wait, Jeremy! You can't leave me like this . . .!'

He stepped back from the desk. The crumpled newspaper he had held fell to the floor.

'It's high time that you learned you can no longer say, "Do this," and "Do that," and expect to be obeyed. You seem to forget that I'm free. I do what *I* want now – and that includes telling you that I'm finished with you. I'll bring the farm accounts up to date, and send them here to Glenbarr. There'll be no need for us to meet again.'

He turned and strode to the door; he opened it, and then after a pause, his hand fell away from the knob. He wheeled around, fumbling in his pocket.

'I'd forgotten . . . I called at the Ryder farm on the way down. Mrs Ryder asked me to deliver this note.'

He crossed the room and laid a letter on the desk. He took no further notice of Sara, nor did he bang the door as he left. Outside, she could hear him calling to Annie for his hat. Listening carefully, after a few minutes she heard the smart clop of horse's hooves in the drive.

Only then did she reach for Julia's letter. She tried to control her rage as she broke the seal.

'*My dear Sara,*

'*I trust that in time you will be able to forgive me for writing as I do now. Believe me, I do so only in the hope that you may pause to consider what you are doing in committing yourself to marriage with Louis de Bourget.*

'*My dear, can there be any real happiness in this for either of you? Are you content to give up all you and Andrew have built since the beginning of the colony, to retire to Banon? Or has Louis de Bourget decided to give up Banon to suit your interests? I sincerely hope that you are not attempting to compromise between the two ways of life – for I see the result only as confusion and unhappiness . . .'*

Angrily, Sara read to the end. The whole letter was Jeremy's words over again, though less forcefully expressed. When she reached Julia's signature, she crumpled the paper in her hand, screwing it into a tight ball and letting it fall to the desk. Damn all of them! she thought. They thought they knew what was best for her – they thought they could bid her carry on as she had been doing for the past year, and that she would meekly do as she was told. They strove to see, Julia and Jeremy, a bent in Louis's character that would run contrary to her own, a difference of purpose that would give them no peace together. She clenched her hands in defiance.

There had never been any intention in her mind – and she didn't believe there was in Louis's either – of selling the farms or the store. He knew that they were not hers alone, that they belonged to her sons. When they had discussed them, he had suggested bringing an experienced manager out from England to run the store, and perhaps two farmers, with their families, to help Jeremy. Naturally, after their marriage, Louis would expect more of her time than she was at present able to give – but she felt that he would be patient until her London agents could find such people as she needed.

Suddenly, to her intense annoyance, tears began to slip down her cheeks. She brushed at them with the back of her hand, but could not check them. They were wrong, Julia and Jeremy, and whoever else was disposed to think as they did. She would show them all what Louis was prepared to do for her sake – and what she would do for his. They were not children, either of them, unused to the ways of the world; they had much to give each other, much to contribute to marriage. Louis knew that she meant to hold every part of Andrew's property intact; he had agreed to marry her knowing that. So much for Jeremy's rage and scorn! So much for Julia's cautious warnings!

And still the tears could not be kept back. She was forced to face reality, and the fact that Jeremy was gone. He was gone to the sort of freedom he had not known for fifteen years. She preferred not to recall that he wanted to marry her – the person of Jeremy did not weigh up evenly with the other considerations against him. He was free of her now – free to do exactly as he pleased. But the future without Jeremy was bleak, and somewhat frightening. Very slowly she began to unfold and smooth out Julia's letter again; it was difficult to read, with the blur before her eyes.

2

Until the day she was married, a little more than a month after
Louis's return from England, Sara expected a message, or a visit,
from Richard – but none came. At first she waited eagerly, and then
became resigned to the fact that here was another who anticipated
disaster for her marriage, or who was too jealous even to acknowledge the necessity of this step she was taking. After giving the
situation some thought, she was able to shrug away her dismay; she
should have expected no better from Richard.

She and Louis were married on a morning in April, with no one
but the Ryders, Sara's three sons, and Elizabeth de Bourget to
witness the ceremony. David, Duncan, and Sebastian were quiet,
but, on the whole, Sara judged, they were well content. They remembered Louis, and his constant visits, when Andrew had been
alive, and to them he was a liked and trusted friend. But on Elizabeth constraint and uncertainty were plainly visible. Occasionally
Julia, who had deliberately placed herself near Louis's little
daughter, touched her arm soothingly. The child was obviously
bewildered by the whole situation, and she seemed glad of the
attention Julia gave her.

That night Glenbarr blazed with lights. The rooms were filled
with the scent and colour of flowers; in the dining-room long
tables were loaded with food – Louis's French cook had come
from Banon to prepare the supper, and it was something that would
be talked over for many weeks after. Polished silver gleamed, and
the wine stood waiting. White-gloved servants from Banon glided
through the rooms, lighting the last candles. Bennett stood in the
hall, magnificent in a hunting-green livery of his own design,
directing his helpers. The carriages began to roll up the drive in
their numbers for the first time in over a year.

Sara stood beside Louis to receive their guests. She wore the
blue satin gown he had brought her from London; her hair was
elaborately dressed, her tanned skin lightly powdered. The gown
might have graced a Court function; it was too magnificent for a
place like Sydney, but it gave her satisfaction to wear it and have
Louis look at her as he did. He tapped his foot a little on the floor as
he waited – in his brocade coat and powdered hair he looked more
Gallic than ever in the midst of these English faces. People streamed
in, their glances quizzical, their eyes ready to notice and to criticize.
The Abbotts came, the Macarthurs, the Pipers . . . Smiling, Sara
graciously took the hand of each in turn. The Pattersons, the

Johnstons, the Campbells, the Palmers, all presented themselves. So many of these people were, at one time, Glenbarr's frequent visitors, but had been absent since Andrew's death. She knew that many of them did not approve of her any more now than they had done formerly, but, as the wife of Louis de Bourget, they were obliged to receive her back into their circle. In the midst of all the gaiety her thoughts went to the little bush wedding in the Ryders' house twelve years ago, where the only colour in the scene was not the silks and satins of the women she saw here tonight, but the scarlet tunics of the few officers of the Corps that she and Andrew had been proud to welcome as their guests. She recalled the work and love that had gone into the preparing of the rough, unfinished house on the Hawkesbury, and the happiness she had known there. And then she visioned Banon, white, and elegant, and cool . . . She *would* be happy again, she told herself. They were wrong, the people who believed this marriage would be a disastrous one. She thought of Jeremy, who today would have taken the last of his belongings away from Kintyre. Silently her lips formed his name. The faces passing before her swam in a blur . . . William Cooper's dull, kindly one; Julia's anxious and searching; a young, laughing girl's, whom she did not recognize. She turned from them and her disturbing thoughts, and sank into a deep curtsy as the Governor and Mrs King arrived.

Finally, Captain and Mrs Barwell were announced. They came forward unhurriedly. Alison was exquisitely groomed and gowned in peach-coloured brocade, but, for all her beauty, looking as frail as a piece of glass. Richard, splendid in dress uniform, was sullen and ungracious. He bent over Sara's hand, kissing it, but as he straightened he did not look into her eyes.

And later it was said of Richard Barwell that he disgraced himself that night, and shamed his wife, by being noticeably drunk.

3

Sara and Louis went to Banon immediately after they were married. The countryside was quiet in the dried-out browns of autumn; the house above the river plains looked as settled as if it had been there always. It was no longer a raw, white gash on the landscape, but sank back, and warm against its hill. The days were golden and full of sun; at night they burned wood fires late, and Sara drew from Louis his memories of the months in England. Europe seemed far away, almost a dream; tales of London ballrooms, and the games of faro that lasted through the night, might quicken her imagination, but close at hand her own affairs were absorbing and rich. For almost four weeks she was lazily content.

Madame Balvet was no longer there to disturb the contentment. Her successor was a soft-spoken Irishwoman, who listened with deference to Sara's instructions. Madame Balvet was lodged in Sydney, waiting for the first possible passage back to England. The Frenchwoman's real position at Banon was never explained or discussed; Mrs Fagan slipped into the role of housekeeper as quietly as if there had never been a change at all.

When Sara's idyllic month was almost up, the first disturbing news found its way into the peace of Banon. Clapmore was ill, and the overseer, newly engaged to run the Toongabbie farm, had been killed by a falling tree, as his men worked to clear more land for pasture. Louis tried vainly to soothe her agitation, and, at last, rather unwillingly, agreed to go back to Sydney with her. During the journey she noticed he was often silent.

She found that the month with Louis was to be a pattern of their married life. He made it quite clear that he wanted her at Banon; as often as possible she travelled up from Sydney, diligently organizing the whole retinue of children and servants to come with them. But she always went with a backward glance to all she had left undone in matters concerning the farms and store. Clapmore was well again, and a new overseer had been found for the Toongabbie farm. But, even together, they could not greatly relieve the pressure on Sara herself. Clapmore, though conscientious, had not the authority necessary to deal with the questions that required her attention; the overseer, an emancipist, drank too much, and was too free with the men. At best, they – Clapmore and the three principal overseers – were poor substitutes for Jeremy Hogan.

But she stifled her frustrations and went to Banon whenever she could – and Louis's good humour returned. A week or two they would spend there, while Louis toyed with his farming, smiling indulgently to see Sara immediately assume control of the overseers and labour. He was amused by the children; he seemed to enjoy taking their lesson hours out of Michael Sullivan's hands. Outside the huge, bright room at the end of the portico, that had lately become the schoolroom, Sara often paused to listen to Louis's voice repeating Latin verbs; very soon she noticed that her sons had ceased to pronounce their few words of French with an Irish accent. The happy sound of their laughter, Louis's mingling with it, reached her constantly.

She found that it took time and great patience to adjust herself to marriage with Louis. He was not as easily commanded as

Andrew had been, or as easily pleased. He expected much from a woman; once, he had breathed the heated, over-civilized atmosphere of the Paris salons, and the gaze he now turned on a woman was forever coloured by those years. She strove to please him in a hundred different ways – her costume must be immaculate and appropriate from early morning until they retired late at night; she ordered gowns extravagantly, and they were far too many and too magnificent for the society of the colony. But Louis always dined, even when alone, with great ritual and elegance, and her own toilette must match it. She slipped into the habit of speaking French with him, and in their long talks together she learned that her conversation must never touch more than passingly on the subject of crops or trade. These did not amuse, or even interest him much, and were hardly matters to be introduced over the dinner table, or in the drawing-room. Louis talked as her father, Sebastian, had once done – bringing to the inevitable sameness of the gatherings they attended a whiff of a sophisticated, cultivated world. She was hard put to keep pace with him.

His challenge excited her. Physically and mentally he drained her energy, and still stimulated her – at times to an almost unbearable pitch – able to make love to her, even across a room, by a mere change in his expression, or the tone of his voice. So completely did he absorb and fascinate her, that she began to fear she might lose the struggle to keep her own personality intact. He was capable of great passion and great tenderness; she sometimes wondered uneasily if her preoccupation with him might succeed in ousting her own ambitions for her sons. A battle of wits and strength developed between them; they played at it laughingly in the brittle, clever fashion that was Louis's way, and yet they were deadly in earnest.

The periods they spent together at Banon were always too short. News would reach Sara of trouble at one of the farms, or at the store, and then she would fume impatiently until she could be on her way to attend to it. In swift succession the *Thrush*, *Thistle* and *Hawk* returned to Sydney, and on each occasion there was no possibility of dealing with their cargoes from the remoteness of Banon. The procession of carriages and baggage started back to Glenbarr once again, and Louis's expression was thunderous.

As usual, Captain Thorne came to see her at the house.

'My compliments on your marriage, ma'am,' he murmured, bowing over her hand. 'Doubtless, marriage suits a woman well – but I'm thinking that, if you're to run your ships successfully, you'd best be wedded to your desk.'

His gruff old voice went on.

'Monsieur de Bourget, I recall, was part-owner in your late husband's day. He'll assist you now, surely?'

Louis made no excuses for refusing to have any part in Sara's business dealings.

'I have no intention of turning myself into a slave,' he replied shortly. 'And it will be better for you, Sara, the sooner you realize that that is precisely what you are making of yourself.'

Their disagreements were fairly constant, but not serious, until Louis learned that she was going to have a child. He wanted to take her to Banon, and force her to remain there until the child would be born, the following May. This step she had foreseen, and dreaded; she begged him to remain at Glenbarr. They bitterly fought the question for two weeks, and then Louis finally gave in. She knew quite certainly he believed that, by continuing to refuse his help, she would reach a stage where there was no alternative but to part with some of Andrew's property.

'Sell it, Sara!' he urged. 'Sell it! There's no woman alive who can manage all you attempt, and give proper attention to her children. You'll kill yourself – and break my heart.'

'I can't sell – nothing belongs to me,' was her only reply to this. 'If I leave the farms and the store to look after themselves, they'll go to pieces – the ships' masters will trade just according to their own inclinations. And then what has become of the value of my sons' investments?'

'Oh . . .!' This turn of the conversation always made him furious. 'You talk like a shopkeeper!'

'That's precisely what I am, of course!' she retorted.

In the midst of their quarrelling, her thoughts constantly turned to Jeremy. If only Jeremy were at hand to entrust with all this business – his knowledge of farming was second to none in the colony, his shrewd eye would run over the store accounts in a few hours. But Jeremy was gone completely now; he had bought a farm on the Hawkesbury, and reports came to her that the young, and rather pretty, woman who had been assigned to him as house-keeper was very obviously living quite happily with him as his mistress. As long ago as the days of the first *Thistle*, Andrew had, as a gesture of gratitude to Jeremy, invested a small amount of money for him in the cargo; with every voyage the profit had en-larged, and by the time of Sara's marriage to Louis, he had gained control of enough money to buy the mortgage of Theodore Wood-ward's farm, four miles from Kintyre. He lived there now, with

sixteen labourers, and the young convict woman, whom gossip
reported variously from downright plain, to beautiful. Sara shrugged
her shoulders at the news, and tried to remain unconcerned.

From Richard there was no sign or communication – except
the quarterly instalment paid off against his debt, which he now
always handed over to Clapmore. Occasionally Sara met him
with Alison in various Sydney drawing-rooms, and twice he
attended a reception at Glenbarr. But his face was no more expressive than dull, pleasant William Cooper's might have been, as
he bent over her hand. If he appeared in the store to make a purchase, it was always at a time when it could be safely reckoned
she would not be there. One day, as she set off with David to walk
from the store back to Glenbarr, she saw him directly ahead among
the crowd that thronged the dusty street. It was a terrible moment
when she realized that he had deliberately turned down a side
street to avoid her.

Elizabeth de Bourget could not be counted among the difficulties
that clouded the first year of her marriage to Louis. The three boys
plainly delighted in their little step-sister; she had the makings of
a coquette, capricious, wayward and charming. For the first weeks
she was shy, and rather bewildered by the demands made upon
her by this new country, and by her step-mother and step-brothers,
but her confidence increased as she came to realize the security
of her position, and was petted and fussed over. She rode, as
Louis prophesied, as if she had been born on a horse; she delighted
in showing off, urging her pony to feats which even David did not
attempt. She didn't seem to hold any resentment against Sara;
Louis himself was a person only a little less new in her experience,
and she never appeared to connect either of them with her own
mother. As the months went by she was not more diffident than
her step-brothers in claiming Sara's attention and love. Sara herself
often pondered the situation with vast relief and satisfaction.

At the end of February, 1806, the procession of carriages and
baggages once again set out from Glenbarr. Sara had finally given
in to Louis's demands that she should rest until the birth of her
child, in May. Banon, she had argued, was too far away, and, instead, suggested going to Priest's. Louis countered this by pointing
out that the farmhouse at Priest's was too small to hold themselves,
the four children, the tutor, and the servants; his unspoken objection to the place was that it was too close to the centre of Sara's
activities to give her the complete rest he knew she needed. In the
end they compromised on Kintyre – almost as remote as Banon, but
connected by better roads with Parramatta. Louis listened to her

arguments about getting a doctor and a midwife quicker, if she needed them, and at last agreed.

The final concession she wrung from him as a digression on the journey to visit Priest's, and the Toongabbie farm. Her heart warmed at the sight of the two farms, thriving, prosperous, bearing the marks of Jeremy's care. With a touch of excitement she pointed out to David and Duncan the increase in the merino flocks. At the last counting there were altogether more than twenty thousand sheep in the colony, and the triumph of Macarthur's merino strain was beginning to turn the thoughts of the farmers to overseas markets.

'They need the wool in England, David,' Sara explained, as she stood with him, Duncan and Elizabeth, leaning together on the fencing of the field where the Priest's merinos grazed. 'England can never be quite certain of getting all the merino wool she needs from Spain. And the quality of the wool Spain sends isn't always as good as what we produce here, even now.'

She shielded her eyes from the sun, and gazed across the paddocks, dried and brown by the length of the summer.

'This climate and pasture seems to suit the merino. In a few years we'll be producing a grade of wool that will fetch better prices in London than any of the Spanish stuff.'

Elizabeth hauled herself up on to the first rail of the fence for a better view of these creatures, on whose backs money was literally growing. They seemed unnaturally large by comparison to the sheep she had seen grazing in the quiet pastures of the English shires.

'But if the flocks keep increasing like this, Mama,' David said, putting his hand on Elizabeth's shoulders to hold her more firmly in position, 'where will we put them? I've heard Mr Macarthur say there'll not be enough land.'

Sara gave him a sideways glance – he was twelve years old, and he was beginning to advance beyond a child's acceptance of farming just as it appeared to the casual eye. She had seen him often with books on botany and agriculture; to Louis's amusement he had started to ask him what prices the wheat and wool had brought.

Sara said thoughtfully, 'We need another man with Matthew Flinders's spirit, Davie. We need someone to find a way over the mountains. There's sheep country beyond them – most people are certain of that. When we get over the mountains, there'll be plenty of room.'

4

As the dusk came down on the Hawkesbury, it lent a dark, sinister appearance to the swollen flood-waters, which, since the beginning of March, had swirled and lapped, inch by inch, to forty feet above the normal height of the river. At the dining-room window, Sara paused to look at the desolate waste before her, at the stretch of water where Kintyre's lower fields had been, at the currents and eddies which she judged must roughly mark the submerged trees lining the opposite bank.

The flood was seasonal, but this time it had not come with a spectacular fall of water, sweeping down after heavy rains in the mountains. Its approach had been gradual and relentless. For a whole month the farmers living in the valley had woken to the pounding of rain on the roofs, and day by day the Hawkesbury had crept higher. There had been a brief halt; the level fell a little, and then resumed its advance. Livestock was shifted, and houses abandoned; families moved into the farms of neighbours who inhabited higher ground. The water still rose. In some places the settlers tarried too long, and had to be taken out of their lofts, and off their roofs by boat. The rescue work was confused and uncoordinated; there were reports of drownings. Sara had spoken to soaked, dispirited farmers, whose tales never varied – livestock drowned or strayed, houses under water, haystacks swept away.

From Kintyre's windows they could see, in the centre of the flood-water, a vicious current, which seemed to follow the original course of the river. In the last three days they had watched it tell its own tale of destruction. Sometimes a horse struggled frantically against it, trying to gain the bank; it carried the swollen carcases of cattle and sheep; haystacks rode it merrily, until dragged down into miniature whirlpools; the liberated furnishings of flooded houses sailed past – rocking-chairs, pictures, oak tables. The rain was ceaseless, monotonous – dreary grey skies greeted them each morning, and showed no signs of breaking. An odour of decay hung over the river; there were decomposing bodies of animals caught in the branches of the few trees that remained above water; snakes and enormous, ugly lizards were cast up, and taken on again as the level rose. The air was sour with the smell of mud and rotting crops.

Sara turned wearily from the window and went back to her

task of sorting out the clothes which lay in bundles on the long table. Kintyre had not escaped the reach of the flood, although she knew, almost certainly, that the house itself was safe – Andrew had built it well above the level of the traces left by past floods. But the haystacks were gone and some cattle, not yet counted, were missing. The outhouses down at the bottom of the slope had disappeared five days ago. For consolation, she recalled the sheep, safely penned in tiny, improvised stockades in the muddy fields at the back of the house. It was not pasture land up there, and there was no grazing for them. The sheep, along with the penned-up cattle, had to be hand-fed. They stood desolately in the rain, complaining loudly to the unrelenting sky. The horses in the stables were restless for want of exercise.

She finished roughly sorting the clothes into their appropriate groups. All through the colony there would be an appeal for clothes and blankets for the families forced to abandon their homes to the flood. Kintyre had already taken in its own share of refugees; when the river had risen so sharply three days ago, four farmers, who were settled on low-lying ground bordering the Maclay property, brought their wives and families for shelter. The men themselves went back immediately to continue the work of rounding up cattle, and saving some of their household goods. Two of the wives, waiting only to deposit their children with Sara, and give a garbled account of their losses and the destruction throughout the whole of the valley, left to go back to help their husbands. The two women who remained, Susan Matthews and Emily Bains, occupied the sitting-room exclusively, passing thinly-veiled criticisms of the hospitality Sara gave them. The children of the four families, seven in all, shared the veranda with Elizabeth and the three boys. They had each been forbidden to move beyond it, and they fretted at the restriction placed on their liberty. They played, quarrelled, resorted to blows frequently; their howls and laughter had been part of each daylight hour for the past three days. It could have been much easier, Sara thought resentfully, if either of the women had taken them in hand – but there seemed little hope of that. The six convict servants, which the four families had brought with them, were determined to enjoy their unexpected spell of leisure. Cramped together, they filled a small sitting-room, gossiping ceaselessly, and making no attempt to help Annie Stokes, or Bess and Kate, Sara's other two servants – and no orders to do so were forthcoming from their mistresses. There seemed to be a spirit among the refugees urging them to give as much trouble as possible; Sara guessed that in their years of struggle on the river, they must often

have envied the good fortune of Kintyre's owners, and now when
they found themselves planted here they made their presence felt
in no uncertain fashion. The house was bedlam; it was cold, dis-
arranged, and strewn with rough mattresses. The muddy tracks left
by the children's boots had stained the rugs, their fingermarks were
visible on all the walls. And along with that, the unending sound
of the rain had pitched their nerves near to breaking point.

Sara left the dining-room and made her way down the darkening passage in the direction of the kitchen. Many times in the past
week her thoughts had gone to Jeremy, wondering how he had
fared through this period. He was fortunate that the site of the
farm he had bought was as favourable as Kintyre's own. His predecessor, old Theodore Woodward, had been one of the first
settlers on the Hawkesbury, and, with an eye to Andrew's sound
choice, he had had the pick of the high ground. She supposed that,
like them all, Jeremy's crops had suffered, even if he had managed
to keep his livestock intact. She wished that there might have been
some news of him – that he himself might have come to inquire
how they were at Kintyre. But there was little likelihood of that
– his house would be as crowded with homeless people as her own
was. She was conscious of a stab of annoyance at the thought of
Jeremy's young convict housekeeper playing hostess to a swarm of
refugees.

She entered the kitchen and went to the long trestle table, which
had been set up there for the children's meals, to light the lamps. In
the scullery beyond, Bess and Kate washed dishes and gossiped.
Annie closed the oven door with a blackened cloth, and turned to
speak to her mistress.

'Them, ma'am,' she jerked her head in the direction of the
sitting-room, 'are eating their heads off – and in such comfort, too,
if you please! This is the second baking in three days. If the rain
don't soon end, we'll not be able to feed them.'

Then she laid down the cloth and came closer to Sara. 'Why,
ma'am, you're as pale as a sheet!' Her thin, wrinkled face was
screwed up in consternation. 'Been overdoing it . . . that's what! I
just wish the master was here to see that you rested proper – you
coming near your time, an' all!'

'Yes, Annie,' Sara answered soothingly, bending over the lamps
once more. Hardly an hour of the last three days had gone by that
she had not breathed a sigh of thankfulness that Louis was *not*
at Kintyre. Ten days ago he had left for Sydney, when a message
arrived from Clapmore that the *Hawk* had returned from India.
With a shrug of his shoulders, Louis had prepared to go and meet

Captain Thorne in his wife's place, good-humouredly joking about
the high commission he would demand. Kintyre was lonely without
him. Sara had expected him back within two weeks, but, when the
rains brought the level of the water always higher, and with it,
the crowds of women and children from abandoned homes, she
began to hope that the flood would delay his return indefinitely. It
was impossible to imagine Louis amid this chaos, or to believe that
he would be willing to share communal meals. To see Louis
marooned by floods at Kintyre would be bad enough, but marooned
along with chattering, quarrelling women and eleven children was
unthinkable.

'Perhaps it's just as well he isn't here, Annie,' Sara added. 'With
all this . . .' She didn't finish the sentence, but her gesture indicated the confusion of the house, the noise that never ceased
while the children were awake.

Annie paused a moment, and Sara read in her face a look of
mingled amusement and dismay at the thought of Louis's fastidious
elegance among all this disorder.

'Ah . . . perhaps you're right, ma'am.' Annie threw a shrewd
glance at Sara. 'But don't you fret . . . We'll have them out of
this in no time now, and then you'll be able to rest – as you should
be doing.'

As she spoke, Annie's eyes swept the long table, laid with places
for the children's supper. 'Well, we'd best be calling the young
rogues in now, and have done with this business.' Then, in dismay,
she clapped a hand over her mouth. 'Begging your pardon, ma'am!
I wasn't meaning Miss Elizabeth or your three.'

'That's all right, Annie. It's difficult to distinguish these days.
But, yes – call them in. Perhaps they'll be quieter when they've
had something to eat.'

Annie turned and raised her voice. 'Bess! Go and bring the
children indoors. And see if you can keep them quiet! My ears are
fit t' burst with the noise they're making.'

Bess came to the doorway, wiping her hands in her apron.

'I thought one of them other lazy sluts was supposed to keep
order. Like a circus – that's what this house has been like since
they all came. It's not right . . .' She went off down the passage,
still muttering.

Sara pretended she didn't hear. She couldn't blame Bess, or anyone else, for feeling resentful. These other women had descended
upon them like locusts, taking food and shelter without a word of
thanks, expecting to use Kintyre as if it had been an inn. Sara
flushed with irritation to think of their ingratitude. Moving the

sheep and cattle had meant a great amount of extra work; the
stockades had been hastily improvised, and each man on the place
did the work of three to keep the livestock within bounds. Even
Michael Sullivan had left his pupils, and was working every daylight hour with the convict labourers. But indoors eight women
sat about idly all day, not even making a gesture to help with the
cooking. Sara did not dare to voice a protest; the story would be
wildly distorted, and, years from now, it would be flung up in her
face that she had been chary of hospitality at a time when every
house above water along the river had been regarded as a natural
refuge. She could only hope, along with Annie, that they would
soon be left in peace.

She took a loaf of bread from a side table, and began to cut it.
She glanced across at Annie, briskly dishing out meat and vegetables, and envied the speed and energy in her movements. Her
own body felt heavy and sluggish; she looked down at it with a
frown of distaste, and tried to drape her long shawl more be-
comingly. The seven weeks ahead of her until the child would be
born seemed endless. This pregnancy had been much more irksome than the earlier ones; the time had passed slowly, and yet it
had been crowded with the effort of attending to her business
affairs, and still meeting Louis's demands that she should rest.
Louis waited patiently for the child's birth. He was tender to her,
considerate, and quiet – not talking much about the child, but she
knew that the extra attention he gave to the running of Banon
was given with the thought of a son to inherit it. She glanced
down again at her ungainly body, and prayed, for Louis's sake,
that it would be a son.

The children came crowding in then, pushing a little in the
doorway, and looking expectantly towards the table. Elizabeth
was in the middle of them, a flushed, wild expression on her face,
a frill torn from her hem. Sara couldn't help a smile when she saw
her; Elizabeth's prim manners had slipped noticeably, and now
she claimed her place at the table without any hanging back, her
manner plainly announcing to the others that Kintyre's wide
kitchen belonged to her and her step-brothers. Her gestures were
unmistakably Louis's.

A slight, red-headed son of Sam Murphy's smiled up at Sara as
she placed a plate before him.

'We caught a snake, Madame de Bourget. Killed it, too! It was
this long . . .' His arms stretched to their fullest extent.

Her nose wrinkled in disgust. 'Horrible things! I'm glad you
were quick enough to kill it, anyway. They're . . .' She paused,

her tone growing suddenly serious. 'But where did you find it,
Timmy? It didn't come on the veranda, surely?'

He hung his head, glancing sideways at David, with a look of
appeal.

Sara turned to her eldest son. 'You didn't leave the veranda,
David?'

'Well,' he said contritely, 'the snake was only a *little* way off,
Mama. We thought it might come up later when it was dark, and
get into the house.'

Sara flushed slightly. Her fear made her speak sharply. 'But I've
told you you must never go near a snake. This may have been a
deadly one. And besides, you promised that none of you would
leave the veranda.'

She turned from him, glancing quickly down the table, to where
Annie was seating the last arrival, Tim Murphy's seven-year-old
sister.

'Annie – where's Sebastian?'

The old woman's head flew up. Swiftly her eyes skimmed the
two rows of children, and then came back to Sara's face.

'Well . . .' Annie ran her tongue over her lips. 'He don't seem
to be here . . .'

Sara said to David, 'Was he with you when you killed the
snake?'

He wrinkled his brow in an effort to remember. 'Yes . . . I think
he was.'

'How long ago was this?'

David bit his lower lip. 'I'm not sure, Mama – not long before
Bess came out.'

Annie called to the two convict servants in the little adjoining
room, all her anxiety in her voice.

'Bess! Kate! Have you seen Master Sebastian?'

They came into the kitchen; they shook their heads solemnly.
Sebastian was a favourite with them both, and the concern on their
faces was real and unassumed.

'Lor' ma'am,' Kate began. 'I ain't seen Master Sebastian since
he was in here at midday. One of them others,' she nodded in the
direction of the six women in the sitting-room, 'was supposed to be
keeping an eye on the children.'

Sara looked about wildly. 'But he must be somewhere! Kate
. . . run outside again and call him. Take a lamp with you. Annie,
we'll go through the rooms. He's probably in the sitting-room with
the others. Quickly . . . !'

Ten minutes later they were all back in the kitchen. Susan

Matthews and Emily Bains had now joined them, and the convict women stood together in a nervous group. Sara and Annie had given up their futile search of the rooms; Sebastian was not anywhere in the house. They turned expectantly as Bess and Kate came in, having completed a tour of the outside of the building.

'Well . . . ?' Sara demanded.

Her hands twisted and gripped each other. The children had stopped eating, and they turned to stare at Bess and Kate. In that slight pause, with every sense straining for their answer, Sara noticed absently, as if part of her mind functioned quite separately from her anguish, that a small boy, no older than Sebastian himself, hadn't been given his supper yet. He had no eyes for what was going on, but stared at the plates of the others with an aggrieved air.

Kate spoke. 'It was no good, ma'am. We called and called. He's nowhere around the house.'

Sara let out a sharp breath. 'Oh . . . !'

Annie touched her arm. 'There . . . ! Don't you take on, ma'am! He'll be with the men – yes, that's where he'll be. I'll just take a lantern, and step across to the stables. And Bess and Kate can find their way down to the men's huts. Without doubt he's there – with all he's told not to go near them. The men, ma'am, they encourage him to come. We'll find him yet somewhere down there, hand in hand, with Mister Sullivan. And if he's still not about, Mister Sullivan and Trigg will organize the men with lanterns. You'll see, they'll have him in no time.'

While she was speaking, Annie gathered up her shawl, and took a lantern. Bess and Kate prepared to follow her. By this time the short dusk had deepened into night. With the fading light, except for a few jobs in the stables, the men would be finished their work. The convicts' huts stood behind the house, also on high ground, and well above the water. The emergency stock-pens had been erected in the space between.

Sara went to the doorway with Annie. They could see a dim light in the stables, but the rain curtained out everything else. With a sick terror Sara faced the emptiness of that black space before her. The restless livestock were moving about unseen; she could hear their stamping, and the shifting of their bodies. The light from the stables was friendly, but, down the slope from the house, the water was rising steadily. She could only think of Sebastian's ceaseless curiosity; day after day, he had questioned her about other floods on the Hawkesbury, begging to be allowed to venture out as far as the water had advanced. He was only six years old, and to him the flood was a great adventure – never a danger.

She shivered in apprehension. 'Hurry, Annie! Bess, Kate, hurry . . . !'

When the bobbing lanterns disappeared into the darkness, Sara turned back dispiritedly to the kitchen. She walked to the table and began to attend to the children. A plate was handed to her to be refilled; she poured milk from a jug into two mugs. Surprisingly, Susan Matthews and Emily Bains had fallen to their share of the serving. They both wore frightened expressions, and seemed to walk lightly on their toes, as if any noise on their part was out of place. The twisting, nodding heads of the children were a blur before Sara's eyes; she heard nothing that they said. Sebastian's dark little face, his eager voice, seemed to be all around her. Already the bread was gone from the platter she had filled; she reached for the knife and began cutting again, but her thoughts were with Annie, and Bess, and Kate, as they made their way towards the huts. If they didn't find Sebastian there . . . In her heart she didn't believe they would. When he left the veranda he would have wandered, not towards the back of the house, as they suggested, but down the slope in the direction of the water which had held his fascinated attention for the past week. She thought of him, tall for his six years, but with a slight, wiry body that used its energy in quick bursts. If he should have fallen and hurt himself, out of earshot of the house . . . She flung the knife down with a clatter; she knew she couldn't endure another five minutes of inactivity.

'David, I want you to come with me,' she said. 'I'm going to have just another look around the outside of the house.'

Nodding, David slipped from his chair.

Susan Matthews threw Sara a startled glance. 'Mercy, Madame de Bourget! You're never thinking of going out! Why, the men will be here in a few minutes, and they'll spread around and find him. He can't have got far.'

With steady hands Sara lit another lantern. 'I'll be quite safe, Mrs Matthews. I won't go more than a few yards from the house. When Mr Sullivan gets here, tell him to come out to me.'

'Yes . . . but . . .' Susan Matthews clucked her tongue despairingly. 'I think you shouldn't go. Your husband wouldn't like it – not as you are now . . .'

Sara took no notice. 'Come, David – we'll go out by the front. You can show me where you killed the snake.'

As she made for the door, Duncan stopped her.

'Mama . . .'

'Yes . . . ?'

'Can I come with you? I know where we left the snake.'

She shook her head, giving him a swift smile. 'No, darling. You stay with Elizabeth.'

Then she took David's arm. Together they left the kitchen and walked along the passage to the front door. On the way Sara stopped to collect a coat for David, and to pull a warm cloak about her own shoulders. The sound of the rain greeted them more strongly than ever when they opened the door, the pelting, monotonous sound that had hardly ceased for the past week. In the lamp-light the boy's face was serious. He stared into the darkness ahead, with a bewildered, fearful air.

Suddenly she bent to look at him more closely.

'What is it, my love?'

His lips quivered, and then straightened. 'Sebastian . . . He's the youngest, and you always said that I must look after him. He's only a baby . . . and :f he's lost, it's my fault.'

She put the lantern down on the veranda, and squatted – awkwardly, because of the heaviness of her body – before him. She placed her hands on his shoulders, and looked into his eyes.

'Darling . . . it's no one's fault. One of Mrs Matthews's women was to have stayed with you on the veranda. If she'd done as she was told, this would never have happened. No one expected you to . . . Oh, Davie, don't look like that. We'll find him, pet!'

Then she leaned forward and brushed his cheek with her lips. She rose, taking up the lamp again, and pulling her hood into position. On the top of the steps she paused, reaching to take David's hand in her own.

The ground was churned into soft mud. She carried the lantern low, and placed her feet carefully, feeling them sink with each step. The night was as black as pitch; the rays from the lamp only revealed endless pools of water lying on soil already too saturated to absorb any more. Farther down they could hear the roar of the swollen river.

David tugged at Sara's hand. 'Over here, Mama!'

They found the snake, half-embedded in the mud. For a few moments Sara stared at it, then looked around her helplessly. The lights of the house, dimmed by the curtain of rain, gave her her bearings. From here, the carriageway followed the slope sharply down to join the road that linked Kintyre with the neighbouring farms. She hesitated, remembering how close the water had come to the road when she had last seen it. She drew the cloak closer about her, and took a tighter grip on David's arm.

'We'll just go a little way farther. He may be quite close. He may have fallen and hurt himself.'

Suddenly she swung the lantern high, flashing it over the sodden ground.

'Sebastian! Sebastian!'

Her voice was weak against the noise of the rushing water and the rain. She moved forward as quickly as the soft mud would allow, zig-zagging across the width of the carriageway, swinging the lantern to see as far beyond it as the rays of the lantern penetrated.

'He'll never hear me!' she cried despairingly. 'Call with me, David. Now – together!'

'*Sebastian . . .!*'

No answer came back to them from the rainy distance. They moved on a few yards.

'*Sebastian . . .!*'

Sara could feel a tight dryness in her throat, that made it difficult to produce any kind of sound. Gusts of wind swept the rain into their faces, and the lamp flickered uncertainly. Quite desperate now, she noted the force of the wind. It would increase the strength of the currents; trees that had weathered the other floods would go if it continued; houses would move off their foundations. The thought of that rushing, swirling water, choked with debris, made her frantic. She clutched David's hand for comfort.

'Oh, Davie . . .! We've got to find him!'

They reached the boundary of Kintyre's land, the place where the carriageway joined the road. Sara peered ahead, but could see nothing. Here, the rush of water was unusually loud and close. She hesitated fearfully, and then plunged forward a few steps, holding the lantern high.

Suddenly David stopped. He pulled hard at her hand.

'Mind, Mama! The water . . . It's covered the road!'

Cautiously she took another step, and David advanced to keep pace with her. The swaying light revealed the edge of the water, a black, ominous line, that eddied and lapped almost at their feet – its constant movement hinted at the force of the currents building up behind it. Sara stood dejectedly. On both sides of the point the road dipped lower, one part of it running through a group of boulders, which had been blasted with gunpowder to let the road pass. The land rose again a little farther along, the beginning of the high ground on which Kintyre stood. The road wound about its base, and there, she knew, it would be several feet under water. The realization of this frightened her badly. Never before had the flood waters reached this level; for the first time she began to fear that the house itself might be threatened.

'Just a little farther, David, and then we'll go back. There may be news of him at the house.' She had to shout to be heard above the wind.

They began to trace their way carefully along the edge of the water, their feet finding precious holds on the slope. They continued for about a hundred yards, until they were among the scattering of stones that marked the beginning of the group of boulders. They climbed a little higher, and the noise of the water carving a path through the boulders was much louder. At last she stopped.

'We must turn back,' she said. 'They'll have to know that the water is much higher. We should be ready to leave the house.'

As she swung round, the light fell on a vividly white object, lying against a stone. They both saw it at the same instant, and moved forward with a rush. David bent and picked it up.

'It's Sebastian's wooden horse!' he shouted.

He handed it to his mother. Taking it from him, her feelings were a mixture of fear and relief. It was Sebastian's favourite plaything – a wooden horse, painted white, and splashed with irregular patches of black, carved for him by one of Kintyre's convict labourers. A frayed piece of red cord served for a bridle, giving it the gay, jaunty appearance which had so attracted Sebastian.

Clutching the little horse to her, Sara lifted the lantern again. 'He *must* be somewhere about! We can't leave now . . . If we go back the water may rise further. Sebastian. *Sebastian!*'

David's voice echoed hers. '*Sebastian!*'

He lunged ahead of her. With a furious energy he skirted around the boulders, shaking the tufts of scrub that grew between them. Sara struggled to keep up with him, lest he should disappear beyond the arc of the light she carried. They pushed their way steadily up the rising ground. Sara's breath was soon short with the effort; she drew in great gulps of air, steadying herself with her free hand against the rounded stones.

'*Sebastian . . .!*'

They were beginning the descent of the other side, when she felt the first pain. It went through her body like fire, and then was gone. She took a further few steps before she fully realized what was happening; she shivered with fear at the thought. The pains were starting – a full seven weeks before the time. A choked little cry came from her lips, and she stumbled against a boulder.

'David . . . wait! I can't go any farther,' she panted, as he returned to her side. 'I must go back to the house.'

'But, Sebastian . . . ?'

She shook her head. 'It isn't any use. I can't search any more. The others will have to come back. Let me lean on your shoulder, David.'

A vague comprehension dawned on him. He took the lamp from her hand, and raised it higher, peering into her face.

'Mama, you're ill! Mama . . . ?'

'Yes, darling – but I'll be all right. We must go back now.'

He drew nearer to her, slipping his arm about her waist, and pushing his body close to her side to support her weight.

'Lean harder on me, Mama! You're not leaning on me at all!'

They started down the way they had come, but Sara's steps were less certain now. She was conscious of the desperate need for haste, and yet her body couldn't be urged to the effort she required of it. Determinedly she clung to the wooden horse, pressing it close to her, like a talisman. She stopped abruptly, as yet another spasm of pain gripped her. Longingly she pictured the comfort of Kintyre, and at the same time was worn with anguish at the thought that Sebastian might be somewhere close by, and needing help. But pain and weakness were beginning to blur every other feeling; she forced herself to concentrate on placing one foot carefully before the other. Now her whole body was bathed in sweat, and her wet cloak clung to her icily. She began to lean on David more and more, though aware that his child's strength couldn't support her much longer in this way. Then, at last, her judgement clouded with the effort of resisting the waves of pain, she let her foot slip on a loose stone. David clutched frantically as she was flung forward, but he couldn't hold her; she pitched heavily against a boulder. It broke her fall, and she managed to remain upright; but the breath was knocked out of her body, and her will to fight the increasing pain had evaporated. She clung to the boulder, the side of her head pressing against it, sobbing wildly.

Then David's fingers roused her, plucking gently at her cloak.

'Walk, Mama . . .! I can see a lantern. It'll be Mr Sullivan. Please try to walk, Mama!'

He swung the light he held high above his head to attract attention. A shout reached them thinly through the rain. Sara opened her eyes only long enough to make certain that the flickering lantern ahead was coming towards them, and then she sagged gratefully against the rock.

Again David plucked at her cloak. 'It's all right now, Mama. There's *two* men! It's Mr Sullivan . . .' He tugged violently now. 'Mama, look! It's Mr Hogan!'

Sara turned her head weakly. 'Jeremy? Jeremy, *here* . . .!'

Blackness was crowding in on her as she felt herself lifted into Jeremy's arms.

2

At sunrise Annie came wearily into the kitchen; with Bess and Kate she began to prepare breakfasts for the men who, headed by Jeremy and Michael Sullivan, had spent most of the night searching for Sebastian. There was little conversation between the women as they moved about, handling dishes and pans quietly, so that the sounds did not reach the other parts of the house. A pale sun streamed through the windows, touching kindly Annie's wrinkled, worried old face. Now and again she paused to wipe her eyes on her apron, and to give a loud sniff which could be heard across the room. During the night the flood had reached its greatest height, but before dawn the wind died and the rain stopped. This morning the floor of the convicts' cookhouse was six inches under water; presently the tired, hungry men would come trooping in for their meal. For once Annie had no thoughts of the mud they would track across the kitchen floor.

She paused as a shadow darkened the doorway, and turned to find Trigg and Jackson, the second overseer, there.

'Well?' she demanded eagerly.

But Trigg shook his head. 'The last of the men are back — there's no trace of Master Sebastian. I've had a word with Mr Hogan and Mr Sullivan, and they say we're to have a few hours' rest, and then to start again. The water will be lower by that time . . .' His voice trailed off dismally.

'Mercy on us!' Annie cried, the tears springing to her eyes. 'There's hardly hope now for the poor little lamb . . . and him so bright and full of fun.' Once more she raised the corner of her apron.

Jackson nodded. 'Aye, he was that, all right! A real favourite with the boys, was young Master Sebastian. I've never seen them set to anything with such a will as they did last night. Ah, well . . .'

Then his eyes wandered to the table with its places already set. Annie, interpreting the glance, dropped her apron and moved briskly to the range. 'It'll not be more than a minute now . . .'

Trigg and Jackson took their seats, their heavy movements betraying the fatigue of the long night in the rain.

Suddenly Trigg twisted round to Annie.

'Any news of the mistress yet?'

She looked up. 'Lord, yes! I've been so taken up with Master Sebastian that I didn't think to tell you. Four hours ago – a girl. A little scrap of a thing – but she seems strong enough, and it looks as if she'll live. She has black hair, and she's the living image of her father.'

'The mistress . . .?' Jackson asked.

Annie frowned doubtfully. 'I just couldn't say . . . She had a terrible time, poor soul. Not like the others, this one weren't. She hasn't perked up at all, now that it's over. Not sleeping either – just lying there with her eyes open, and asking all the time about Master Sebastian. Lord, how I wish the master were back! Can't say how long it'll be before he gets through, with the water come as high as it has.'

Then she set their plates before them, and there was silence again in the sunlit kitchen.

'If you could just rouse her in some way, Mr Hogan,' Emily Bains said anxiously. 'She doesn't seem to want to have the baby with her, and she takes no notice of anything I say . . .'

Jeremy nodded, finished the low-voiced conversation that had taken place outside Sara's bedroom. He stepped forward gently, and opened the door.

The large room was flooded with light; the curtains fluttered softly by the open windows. Sara lay in the simple, white-canopied bed, her eyes opened wide, staring up at the cloudless sky. There was a frightening stillness in her body, a sense of waiting. Her face and lips were colourless; her hair, drawn back and thickly braided, lay across the pillow. Low at her throat a ruffle of cream lace showed, and round her shoulders she wore a fluffy blue shawl. The room was immaculate; it gave no sign of the chaos of the night before.

'Sara!' he said softly, closing the door.

She turned her head towards him, half-raised it, and then let it fall back again.

'Jeremy! What news . . .?'

He looked at her steadily. 'None . . . not so far. All the men are back now. They're having a meal and a few hours' rest, before they start again.'

'Oh . . .' The hope that had sprung to her eyes was gone as

quickly as it had come.

He walked to the bed. 'Sara . . . Sara! Don't look like that! There's a chance that we may find him yet. Now that it's daylight . . .'

'Daylight, yes. But you won't find him – not now.' As she spoke she turned again towards the windows. Her face was haggard in the strong light; the look of stillness and brooding had returned to it. He gazed down at her, acutely conscious of his helplessness to rouse or stimulate her. She was as chill and cold as stone lying there. He moved noiselessly and came to stand at the foot of the bed. Now he could see her clearly, and for the first time he noticed that close to her side she clutched the white wooden horse, with its worn bridle of red cord. She gripped it possessively, as if afraid it might be taken from her. In the same way, he remembered, she had clutched it when he had found her last night, refusing to give it up.

'Sara,' he said gently.

Her eyelids fluttered, but she didn't speak.

'Sara, you haven't seen your baby yet – your daughter.'

She twisted her head on the pillow to look at him.

'My daughter? But I have lost Sebastian. He wasn't much more than a baby, either. Look, Jeremy, he took a toy with him when he went – that's how much of a baby he was still.' And with her fingertips she stroked the chipped side of the horse.

Suddenly she put her hand across her eyes. 'Oh, Jeremy!' she cried out. 'Come here . . .! Come here, quickly!'

He went to her side, bending over her. Her fingers sought his hand, and gripped it feverishly.

He dropped to his knees beside her.

'Sara . . .!' he breathed.

'I couldn't believe it when you came,' she said, her voice hardly more than a whisper. 'I remember thinking that I needed you badly, but that you were miles away.'

His lips brushed her fingers clasped round his hand.

'I came when I knew the water was rising,' he murmured. 'I heard Louis was in Sydney – I thought you might need help.'

He laid his cheek against their locked hands, and they were both silent. He could hear her quiet breathing close to his ear. The coldness of her hand terrified him; he drew it closer to his body, and tried to press some warmth into it. Her eyes were closed, and he had a moment of agony wondering whether she might lose consciousness. But then she opened them fully, looking straight up at him.

'I'm so glad you came,' she said faintly. 'I don't believe Sebastian can be alive now. But your being here helps me to bear it. Stay here at Kintyre awhile. I'm so lonely with all those others. You'll stay, won't you, Jeremy?'

He bent over and kissed her quietly on the lips.

'I won't leave you, Sara,' he said.

3

The baby, Henriette, was three days old before Jeremy at last made up his mind that he must leave Kintyre and return to his own farm. He was anxious about his livestock; although penned on high ground, the enclosures he and his men had built were rough and temporary. And the thought that, at the highest of the flood level, his store huts had probably been a couple of inches under water, worried him considerably. As the river went down there would be plenty of work – debris to be cleared, carcases to be burnt, cramped livestock moved and turned out to pasture again. Along the whole of the Hawkesbury Valley a gigantic effort would be made to wipe away the traces of the disaster, and every man was needed on his own property. He felt badly at having to go, leaving Kintyre in the hands of Michael Sullivan. The young schoolteacher from Cork was a good lad, Jeremy thought, but more at home with history books than dealing with the aftermath of a flood. He hoped that Trigg and Jackson might both exert their full energies now, and, not for the first time in the past three days, he wished it was Andrew Maclay's return they awaited – not Louis de Bourget's.

Sebastian had not been found. A disheartened search was still going on up and down the river – but there was no longer any hope held that he might be alive. Sara grieved for her little son, but seemed to have taken comfort from Henriette at last. Perhaps, Annie had suggested to Jeremy, when Sara pressed her face against the tiny head, with its fuzz of black hair, it was Sebastian she was reminded of. She lay in the white-canopied bed, the baby asleep by her side, but she seemed to care nothing for what went on outside her room. She ate little, and said little, except to constantly ask for news of Sebastian.

David and Duncan were saddened and downcast; Elizabeth questioned the men frantically – where was Sebastian? Why didn't they find him? But after three whole days of searching, even Elizabeth grew silent.

By the late afternoon of the third day, the water was down enough to allow Jeremy to make the journey back to his own farm by horse. He was preparing to leave, standing on the front steps giving last instructions to Trigg, when he caught the sound of horsemen on the road below. He watched them as they trotted quickly up the slope – Louis de Bourget, and the surgeon, D'Arcy Wentworth.

Trigg took the bridles of the sweating horses, and Jeremy went forward to greet the two men.

He looked hard at Louis. His shirt was dirty, its ruffles limp; his boots were caked with mud, days old; his coat appeared to have been soaked through several times. Jeremy concluded that he had been caught by the flood at some point along the river, and, like every other available man, had turned out to help move the live-stock to higher ground. He looked tired and worried. By now he would know of his daughter's birth and Sebastian's disappearance – not more than half an hour ago Jackson had set off from Kintyre with one of the farm carts loaded with children and supplies of food and clothing. They were being taken to the Talbot's house – Kintyre's nearest neighbours to have escaped the flood. The offer to take them had come as soon as the news had spread of the state of affairs at Kintyre. If Louis had not known before then, he would certainly have heard from Jackson on the road.

Jeremy had a few moments in which to wonder how he would be received by Louis. He had not spoken to the other – he had done nothing more than glimpse him once in the street, in Sydney, since his return from England. There was no way of telling how Sara had reported their last meeting to her husband, or what her explanation had been for his giving up the management of the three Maclay farms. Louis, gay and charming, but with the temperament and ideas of the French nobility, might regard his presence here, at this time, as damned impertinence. He was capable of walking past without a glance, and going straight into the house.

But Louis approached him, his hand outstretched. He was unshaven, and he had the look of weariness common to them all for this past week.

'I was relieved when Jackson told me you were here, Hogan,' he said. 'You will have been a great comfort to my wife.'

Jeremy gripped the other man's hand warmly. 'I have achieved nothing, so far. Sebastian is still . . .'

Louis cut him short. 'I have news of Sebastian – this morning.'

'What is it?' Jeremy said sharply.

'His body has been found – about six miles down-river. He was caught in a tree on the Sutton farm – they found him when the water went down. They recognized him, of course, and Mark Sutton passed the news to Captain Pierce, who sent a messenger after me. I have told Jackson to go to the Suttons' after he has delivered the children. I told him I would return, as soon as I had seen my wife.'

They looked at each other steadily – Sebastian had stood in almost the same relationship to them both. He was Andrew Maclay's son, and, they both suspected, Sara's most loved child. Because he was the youngest, he had been closer to Louis than his brothers, and Elizabeth had given her heart to him. Jeremy realized that had Sara's child been a son, Sebastian's death would not have affected Louis so greatly. But there was a sense of desolation in his bald words, and Jeremy was conscious, for the first time, of feeling sympathy for Louis.

'Could I not . . .?' He shifted uneasily, wondering how much he dared presume on his past association with the Maclays. He looked carefully into Louis's dark face. 'I should be glad to go immediately to the Suttons' myself, if you would like that.'

A touch of warmth came to Louis's eyes. 'That is kind of you – but you have your own farm, and there must be much work to be done . . .' He finished, lifting his shoulders a little, 'None of us have escaped in this flood.'

Jeremy was momentarily inarticulate. Then he said, 'I have known all the Maclay children since they were born. I would be grateful if you would permit me . . .'

The other nodded. 'Of course. Go now – I will follow as soon as I am able.' He added, so quietly that Jeremy could scarcely hear what he said, 'Sebastian must have his friends to bring him home.'

By this time Wentworth had unstrapped his saddlebags. Trigg still held the horses' heads, and Annie and Bess had come out on the veranda. Both women looked expectantly towards Louis, as if they somehow sensed that news had arrived. He glanced up at them. There were no glad faces to greet his homecoming – this, the first time he would see his daughter.

'And now, Hogan,' he said, 'I must go and tell my wife that they have found Sebastian.'

Slowly his gaze moved along the veranda, until it rested on the windows of Sara's bedroom. He had the look of a man who is afraid. Silently Annie and Bess made way for him as he mounted the steps.

5

On a morning of September, 1806, the de Bourget carriage waited for a long time before the open door of Government House. Edwards sat on the box, blinking in the sunlight, and every now and then raising his head to sniff the fresh, sharp smell of the wild flowers, which for a week had been appearing in a quiet, half-vague fashion to announce the spring. The old man stretched his legs to their fullest extent, grateful for the hot sun which gave him such relief from his rheumatism, but still feeling unaccountably disgruntled at what he saw about him. He sadly missed the English springs, the sudden breaking-out of the young green on tree, hedge and hedgerow, after the long months of nakedness. It was his private opinion that spring in this country of evergreens was no spring at all.

His eyes brightened with the prospect of a gossip as he noticed a man, carrying a pail and a twig-broom, come slowly round the corner of the house. He climbed rather stiffly down off the box, laid a gentle hand on the bridle of the nearest horse, and waited for the man's approach. He and the newcomer, Simon Brand, had shared many a pot of ale in Costello's, while Government House gossip had been bandied about; but he had not seen the other for some time past, and he was eager for news.

'Good mornin' to ye, Simon, lad!'

'Good mornin', Tom! It's a fine sort of day we're havin'.'

'It's that, all right, Simon.'

Brand ran a speculative eye over the carriage, noting the shining paintwork, the rich, fresh upholstery.

'The Frenchman has business with the Governor?' he said casually.

Edwards shook his head. ''Tis the mistress I'm driving.' He winked, laughing a little. 'Nothing but the best for His Excellency – so the master's own carriage was ordered.'

Brand spat reflectively into the neat, clipped shrubs that lined the drive. 'Well . . . let me tell ye, a fine carriage'll not make old "Bounty Bligh" think any better of her. He's not in love with any of the moneyed folk in this colony, because he knows fine well they got it from rum. I tell ye, Tom, that man'll stir up a power of trouble in this place, before he's through. An honest man, Tom, but harsh . . . Let me tell ye . . .'

He came closer, taking out his tobacco pouch and offering it to Edwards, at the same time giving a careful glance in the direction of the windows of the Governor's study. Then, with heads close together, the two men fell into a low-toned conversation.

For the past six weeks the new Governor of New South Wales had been the constant subject on the lips of most of its citizens. On King's request to be relieved of his position, the Colonial Office had appointed yet another seaman, Post-Captain William Bligh, whose name, sixteen years earlier, had swept through naval circles and beyond them, with the story of the mutiny on the *Bounty*. 'Bounty Bligh', they called him now, and his name was a symbol of a feat of courage and navigation unequalled in the annals of sailors. With eighteen of the *Bounty*'s crew he had travelled nearly four thousand miles in an open boat, from Otaheite to Timor; he made this journey in a bare forty-one days, across almost uncharted seas. Bligh was a brave, just and careful captain . . . but made of stern, unimaginative stuff, which invited mutiny from men who had passed six months in a Pacific idyll on Otaheite, and then been forced to give up their native mistresses, and sail with Bligh and his cargo of bread-fruit for the West Indies. But he had piloted his small boat safely to Timor, and now the world knew him as much for his splendid seamanship, as for the mutiny which Fletcher Christian had led.

Later, he had been, unhappily, involved in the mutiny at the Nore, and the tale of his tyranny spread; he had fought magnificently under Duncan at Camperdown, and Nelson at Copenhagen. He proved himself courageous, resourceful, efficient . . . but the legend of the cruel discipline of the *Bounty* died hard. He was a victim of his own passion for perfection; as stern with himself as with other men, he was condemned as humourless and arrogant by those who didn't take into consideration his integrity and his tenderness towards his family. Sixteen years later the world still judged the man on the disastrous voyage of the infamous *Bounty*. It was a ghost that would never be laid. The little colony of New South Wales had awaited his coming with apprehension; unless the temper and disposition of 'Bounty Bligh' had softened considerably, he was not the man to do no more than make feeble protests against those who ignored orders from Government House.

'It's for all the world as if he were back on his own ship, Tom,' Brand said. 'He's up at the crack of dawn every morning, ordering this one and that one about. An' just when you think he's safely at his desk, he's standing right before yer eyes, wanting to know why the path hasn't been swept.' He considered a moment, finishing slowly, 'But I reckon as I like him, for all that . . .'

Then his eyes went back to the carriage. He said reflectively, 'Now, what business do you suppose Madame de Bourget could have with old Bligh? She ain't been abroad much these days . . .'

Edwards looked squarely at his companion. 'I reckon what business the mistress has with the Governor is *her* business, Simon. But yer right about her not being abroad much these days. It's gone six months since the little 'un, Master Sebastian, was drowned in the Hawkesbury flood – but she don't seem able to forget about it for a minute. Poor lady – she were hardly finished wearing black for Mr Maclay, when she puts it on again for the young master. She don't go nowhere, except to attend to business at the store, or one of the farms. I reckon Monsieur de Bourget don't like it much, either. They have words sumtimes, I'm told, about her wearin' herself out. The master – he's not one to take kindly to her givin' half her attention to summat else. But that's summat he ought t' seen before he married her. She's not likely to change for any man, she isn't.'

Simon's expression encouraged him. He took a deep breath, and prepared to launch out on another stream of gossip of the de Bourget household.

In deference to his caller's sex, the Governer had not waved Sara to the usual seat on the opposite side of the desk. Instead, he had indicated the tall winged chair before the fireplace. She settled herself gravely, spread her skirt a little, and gave him plenty of time to take up what must have been a familiar stance, with his back to the grate.

So when she raised her head, she found 'Bounty Blight' looking down at her, his sharp eyes bent upon her with a questioning interest. His black hair was grey-streaked, and he had the thickened figure of middle-age. But he was somehow saved from the pomposity which his commanding attitude might have given him. In the slightly arrogant fold of his lips Sara recognized something of her own characteristics. She reminded herself that this man would have need of authority and arrogance, as well as courage, to bring eighteen men in an open boat across four thousand miles of sea.

Civilities had passed between them when Sara entered the room, and now Bligh shifted his weight slightly from one foot to the other as he waited for her to announce her business. His term of office was only a few weeks old, but the details of Sara de Bourget's history were known to him well enough. He looked at

her carefully, trying to decide if it were the qualities of ruthless
ambition alone which had brought her to her present position
in the colony. But it was said of her that she was an excellent
mother, and Bligh – the father of six daughters – had a strong
respect for any woman who discharged the duties of motherhood
creditably. She puzzled him, for all that – fitting, as she did, into no
definite category within the colony's society. He knew that in the
early days her first husband had been active enough in the rum
trade, but had ended his connection with it about the time of
King's arrival. She herself was an emancipist, and yet had married
a man who was known to have no truck at all with emancipists, a
Frenchman who farmed as a gentlemanly recreation, and who
did not soil his hands with trade. It was an enigma which interested Bligh – the business woman married to the elegant dilletante.

He noted her black gown, and her lack of ornaments, recalling
then what King had told him of the death of one of her children
in the flood six months before his arrival. Apart from the brief
morning call she and her husband had made upon him to pay
their respects, he couldn't remember having seen her at any of the
gatherings he had officially attended. Her hands lay folded in her
lap; instinct told him that, in a woman of the sort who faced him
now, they should have been quiet, still hands. Instead they twisted
nervously.

He spoke at last, feeling that the silence couldn't continue between them any longer.

'Is there some way in which I can be of service to you, Ma'am?
Some matter . . .?' It was a foolish statement, he knew, leaving
him open to a direct request from her. The more money these
people had, the more they seemed to demand privileges from the
Government. He had not come to this country to pamper to such
as Madame de Bourget, but to curb their power.

She answered him firmly, as if she at last knew what she wanted
to say.

'There's nothing I want to ask of you, Your Excellency, except
your discretion.'

'My discretion, Ma'am? I don't see . . .'

He frowned, suspecting her next words. No one came to Government House to ask for nothing – and this woman certainly hadn't
the appearance of a senseless flipperty-jibbet. The histories of
the previous governors of the colony had taught him to be immediately wary of what he did not understand. If the Frenchman
thought he could send his wife, a figure for sympathy in her mourning, to wheedle something from him, then both of them were mis-

taken! He drew himself up to his not-very-commanding height, and waited for his visitor to continue.

'I have come to see you about the grain which I have held at my Toongabbie and Castle Hill farms since the harvest.'

'Yes?'

Bligh's voice had an edge to it which he hoped would be very much apparent. He sensed what she was about, and he believed he had her measure taken. She knew, as did everyone else in the colony, that grain was desperately short as a result of the flood on the Hawkesbury. To try to relieve the situation, Governor King had sent ships to India for provisions, but, as yet, none of them had come back to Port Jackson. In the intervening months the reserves of grain had dwindled alarmingly, and, for the first time in many years, the days of famine and rations returned. As the stores of grain went down, the prices asked by those who still had it to sell, rose. Bligh's mouth twisted as he watched Sara. So this was what she sought from him – she was about to offer the large stock of grain he knew she held, at a price even higher than any farmer had yet got from the Commissary. She had waited until the Hawkesbury settlers were feeling the true pinch of hunger – until no Governor, unless he were completely heartless, could any longer remain oblivious to their distress – before she threw her produce on to the market. On top of that she had the audacity to ask his discretion in the matter! He felt his rage mount at the sheer cold-bloodedness of it. She sat looking at him calmly, this woman who was prepared to bargain for high profits on a flood which had taken her own child's life.

'It was, fortunately for me,' she said, 'an extremely good harvest at both farms.'

His voice broke in coldly. 'Might I remind you, Ma'am, that the Commissary is the proper person to make your offers of grain to. And might I also remind you that he is authorized to offer no prices above these I have already stipulated.'

Sara rose to her feet swiftly, colour staining each cheek.

'You are mistaken, Your Excellency; I came to *give* my grain, not to sell it.'

He stared at her steadily. The quiet ticking of the mantel clock was suddenly loud in the silence which had fallen between them.

'To give it, Ma'am . . . ?' he said slowly.

'To give it, Your Excellency,' she repeated.

The high colour was still in her face, but she spoke evenly. 'I have recently returned from a visit to my Hawkesbury farm . . . and I have seen the distress for myself. Most of the families there cannot possibly afford the price of flour, and their own crops are gone. The children . . .' Here she halted, not trying to fill in the details for him.

He nodded. He locked his hands behind his back, and the gaze he turned upon her was both questioning and reflective.

'There is no need to tell me, Ma'am,' he said quietly. He paced the length of the hearthrug, and then turned back to her, flinging his arms wide in a gesture that conveyed his own distress and anxiety. 'I have not long returned from my own tour of the Hawkesbury, and I have seen the need of the smaller farmer for myself. The plight of the children would touch the hardest heart. But,' he added, 'there are those in this colony who know too well that the possession of a heart does little to further their business interests.'

He shrugged, as if trying to shake away the thought. Then he questioned her directly.

'Madame de Bourget?'

'Your Excellency?'

'Why are you doing this? Why should you *give* your grain, when others every day force the price higher?'

She ran her tongue over her lips. 'I think I've already made that clear, Your Excellency. The distress . . .'

He gave a snort. 'My dear lady, I may only have been in the colony a short time, but already I am well acquainted with the histories of most of the prominent citizens – yours, and your late husband's among them. Do not be offended if I venture to suggest that your past transactions seem hardly compatible with this offer.'

Sara frowned, and seemed to fight for control of her voice. 'Your Excellency – let me remind you also that my past business transactions have very little to do with the fact that my youngest son was drowned in the flood which caused this scarcity. In choosing to make this offer, for once I am not acting as a business woman. I have no desire to have it gossiped about all over the colony – I should infinitely prefer to be known still as a business woman.'

He bowed slightly. 'Certainly, Ma'am. I will give my instructions accordingly . . .'

'Then,' she said, 'I will let you have the details of the grain, and when it can be delivered. Perhaps you would pass them on to the Commissary . . . ?'

Bligh looked at her fully. He was touched and affected by her simplicity and dignity – and more than that, he was impressed by the discipline with which she kept her emotions under control on an occasion when most other women would have been weeping. Even to 'Bounty Bligh' she was formidable as she stood there, and somewhere within him there was not only the warming thought that her grain would be a stop-gap to the famine for at least a short time, but also the surprisingly comforting realization that where he had looked for an enemy he had found a friend. Here was one, he thought, among the circle who controlled trade, whom he could feel was not working directly against him. He knew she could well afford her gift – and yet the fact that she had made it was precious balm to him.

But while he was pondering her action, she had drawn back a few steps from him, and seemed on the point of leaving. He raised his hand in a gesture to detain her.

'Pray be seated again, Ma'am. There are many things I'd dearly like to discuss with you . . .'

But she was already sinking into a curtsy.

'If Your Excellency will permit . . . some other time.'

She rose and turned, walking swiftly to the door. She was gone before he had time to take more than a few paces. It was then he realized that she wasn't any different from other women, after all. As she curtsied, he had seen tears in her eyes.

2

On the afternoon following Sara's visit to Governor Bligh, the spring weather had turned suddenly to rain. In the schoolroom at Glenbarr she stretched her feet comfortably on a footstool before the fire, and turned her tapestry-frame to catch the light from the window. Duncan sat at a small table near her; his tongue hung out slightly as he concentrated on building with elaborate care a house of cards. Occasionally he gave a sigh of exasperation as one card slipped, and the whole structure came down. David sat on the other side of the hearth with a book.

Sara selected a different silk from her workbasket, and glanced at Elizabeth who stood looking over her shoulder. 'It's better to avoid using too much of the one . . .'

Then she paused. The schoolroom door opened, and Louis entered. David glanced up from his book, a smile breaking on his face. Duncan gave a soft groan as his card house collapsed in the sudden draught.

Louis pulled a face of mock tragedy. 'I promise you I'll build it up again, Duncan. They used to say there was no more gentle hand at cards in the whole of France than mine!'

He stooped then to kiss Sara's hand, and bent to receive Elizabeth's kiss on his cheek. He pulled playfully at one of his daughter's black curls.

'I hope you are paying proper attention to all these lessons in needlework,' he said. 'I promised your grandfather you should lack none of the feminine arts.'

Sara nodded in Elizabeth's direction.

'She does very well, Louis,' she remarked drily. 'The other day I heard Annie telling her that she had fingers as quick as a monkey's. No doubt it was meant as a compliment...'

But she broke off and raised her eyebrows questioningly, as he bent over her again to hand her a sealed package, which he had drawn from his coat pocket. She took it, turning it over to read the inscription.

'What is it?' she asked, puzzled.

He shrugged. 'Open it, my love. As I came up, a messenger arrived with it from Government House. Vice-regal letters are never to be ignored, and when they come from such an impatient man as Bligh, then they obviously demand immediate attention.' He drew Elizabeth down on to the footstool beside him, while Sara, with knitted brows, broke the seals and began to read.

Her eyes ran down the bold script.

'. . . I acknowledge receipt of the details of the grain which you purpose . . .'

Then followed more comments about the grain, and Sara's arrangements for its delivery. The business being dealt with swiftly, the tone of the letter changed. She began to read more slowly.

'. . . Those settlers' families who will benefit from your gift, Madame, will never know of your generosity, and can never have the opportunity to thank you. Their present distress touches me sorely and I, of all the colony, am the only person who may make some suitable reply for them. Therefore, I trust that you will accept a grant of land which I have in mind, close to your husband's present property on the Nepean River, and adjoining the Cowpastures District. This land is for you and your children, for however long . . .'

Tears misted before Sara's eyes as she struggled to read on to the end. Bligh wrote that he knew of her interest and success in breeding merino sheep, and he understood the area to be particularly suited for pasture. This was a direct reference to the fact that John Macarthur, to the Governor's extreme annoyance, had chosen his grant of five thousand acres in the Cowpastures itself. Through the concise, rather stiff phrases, there ran a spirit of good-will and humanity. Sara felt herself warm to this irascible, un-imaginative man who was so touched by the plight of the Hawkes-bury settlers – who would, without any public display, seek to reward her with this magnificent gesture, because she had lightened the burden of feeding them, even in a small way. A more subtle man would have found a less obvious way of showing his gratitude – or would have waited some months before making this offer. But Bligh was a sailor, and not one noted for his tact. This was the largest single grant of land, apart from the one which the Colonial Office had given Macarthur, that she could ever recall. The legend that had built 'Bounty Bligh' into a tyrant great enough to provoke mutiny did him a grave injustice – but possibly the small-settlers were the only ones who would never know it.

Sara smoothed the papers, and handed them to Louis.

'Governor Bligh has been more than generous,' he said quietly.

His expression, as he read, grew gentle and reflective. Then he looked across at her, a faint smile on his lips.

'His generosity is not undeserved, my love,' he said, folding the letter and handing it back.

Duncan slid off his chair, coming round the table and stand-ing beside Louis's elbow. 'Will Governor Bligh be coming here, Mama?'

'I don't think so, dear. He's extremely busy.'

Duncan's mouth pouted in disappointment. 'I wish he would. I want to ask him all about the mutiny.'

Sara shook her head. 'I think it would be better not to, Duncan. Perhaps it's something he doesn't care to talk about.'

David put down his book. 'The voyage from Otaheite is the best story. He'd talk about that, wouldn't he, Mama? Lieutenant Flinders said it's the greatest piece of navigation ever known.' As he spoke his blue eyes were full of dreaming; he had the look of a boy in love with the vivid colour that adventure wears. 'Do you know, Mama, that Lieutenant Flinders once sailed as a midship-man with Captain Bligh? That was after the mutiny, of course.'

Sara sighed. 'Poor man . . . The mutiny will never be for-gotten, I'm afraid. How it crops up every time his name is men-tioned!'

Elizabeth turned to her father, and tugged at his coat sleeve. 'Tell me about the mutiny again, Papa! I like the part where . . .'

'No!' Duncan cried. 'Tell us about the boat voyage! I want to hear that again!' He sat down on the footstool beside Elizabeth, wriggling to make room for himself.

Louis laughed at the upturned faces. 'You must, in fairness to the Governor, remember that he did other things besides survive a mutiny and a long voyage in an open boat. He once sailed with Captain Cook, and he was second in line to Nelson at Copenhagen. After the battle, Nelson called him on board the *Elephant* to thank him . . .'

As they talked, Sara, with a nod to Louis, rose and left the room quietly. The even monotone of his voice followed her down the stairs. Bennett, passing through the hall, eyed her as she made her way to the study. Scurries of rain still beat upon the windowpanes; the sky had grown darker with the heavy clouds. Here there was no fire, although one was already laid in the grate. She shivered a little in the chill of the room, and then she lit the candle on the desk.

Spreading out Bligh's letter, Sara read it through again. Here, in this bold script, was the title to land that Andrew had planned to go back to London to obtain. This was what he had dreamed of – pasture in that fertile valley for the flocks of merinos he had envisaged. How the paradox of this gift from Bligh would have astonished him – Bligh, the stern champion of the small farmers, willingly increasing the holdings of one who belonged to the landowning class, because his heart had been touched. She found herself again wondering at the humanity of the man of the *Bounty* legend.

She opened the top drawer of the desk to take out a map of the Nepean and Cowpastures district. But here she paused, her hands wandering down to the bottom drawer. It was locked, and for a few seconds she tugged at it impatiently. Then she searched for the key among the others she carried. She inserted it quickly and turned the lock. The drawer was empty, except for an object wrapped in a dust-sheet of plain, white calico. She drew it out, unfolding it carefully on the desk. Sebastian's painted wooden horse still bore the mud splashes of that night she had found it on the hillside above the road. She set it on its feet, and leaned back in the chair to look at it. The red cord bridle was limp, but the little horse still wore the air of battered jauntiness with which the Kintyre convict had fashioned it.

She touched the frayed cord gently, and then her gaze went to Bligh's open letter. Her stiff lips started to form words soundlessly.

'Sebastian – he never saw you, my darling. But because of you, he's given me what Andrew wanted. No matter what happens, I'll never let this land go . . .'

She reached eagerly for the map, and sought the approximate area that Bligh had indicated. She traced it roughly with her finger, noticing its closeness to Banon, wondering when and how it would be possible to get hold of the land which lay in between. A few small farmers had holdings there, but in time they might be persuaded . . . Her thoughts ran on into the future.

'I'll call it "Dane Farm" – that's for Sebastian and my father.'

6

Bligh's rule in New South Wales came to an abrupt end on a day in January, 1808 – the twentieth anniversary of the foundation of the colony. It was a year and five months since he had taken office.

He had come to the colony determined to carry out his duties as a ruler, but he had been unable to beat the factor that had worn down his predecessors – the army. So long as he could not control the Corps he was virtually powerless; he was thwarted and frustrated at every step by its officers. Without their support, the edicts issued from Government House were just so many scraps of paper. The quarrels between Bligh and the Corps deepened and grew bitter with the months – but it was Macarthur, now a private citizen, who finally brought them to a head. In protest against what they said was a wrongful imprisonment of Macarthur for a slight offence – which Bligh had ordered – the officers then in Sydney, headed by Colonel Johnston, marched to Government House to arrest the Governor. With them went three hundred of the Corps in military formation, and a band playing *British Grenadiers*. Half of Sydney's dusty population trailed behind, like small boys off to a circus.

This was a far cry indeed from the mutiny off Otaheite, but when Bligh, wearing full dress uniform and the Camperdown medal, prepared to meet them, he knew that the mutiny he faced now was no less serious. He was placed under house-arrest, and in Sydney's streets that night many cheered openly for Macarthur and Johnston and others, less openly, pondered the possibility of Bligh's eventual triumph. The 'Rum Corps' had had its hour of

rebellion – and already some of its members were beginning to
fear the day of final reckoning.

2

'This is treason, Sara! The whole regiment is in open rebellion!
They've arrested and humiliated Bligh – the King's representative!
Mon Dieu, how do the fools hope to escape the consequences?'

In the darkness of Glenbarr's veranda, Sara could hardly distinguish Louis's face. The warm summer night was alive with the
song of the cicadas; something about the intimate, throbbing
rhythm of their chorus always excited her, but tonight all her
attention was on Louis. He paced a few yards down the veranda,
his head turned to watch the lights of the township. Then he
came back, standing close to where she leaned against a pillar.

'Bligh will not forgive easily,' he said, his tone reflective now.
'And when the time for the courts-martial comes, no one will be
allowed to forget that it was the King's representative they rebelled
against. Twice in his lifetime it has happened – only his sort of
pig-headedness could invite mutiny twice.'

He looked down towards the township again, where that day
he had been among the crowd that had witnessed Johnston's
march on Government House. He had returned to Glenbarr scoffing
and indignant, contemptuous of the heavy-handed way Macarthur
had chosen to rout his enemy. His French mind deplored the lack
of finesse in the plans, the victory that gave Macarthur nothing
more than a breathing-space in which to prepare a defence of his
act. It was easy, Louis had said, to take a Government by force of
arms – but to take it by arms, as Macarthur had done, and then
try to make it legal, was wholly laughable. Whitehall might be
six months away by sea, but eventually its decisions would be made
known – and Louis felt they would not be in Macarthur's favour.

He put out his hands and touched Sara's shoulder lightly.
'Macarthur will try to justify himself, my dear – he and Johnston
both.'

She stirred, and drew near to him. The white frill of lace at his
throat was sharp in the darkness; always when she could not see
his face, his voice became strangely dominating and she listened
more to the sounds than the words.

'They will start to gather together their friends, Sara. They will
send round documents which we will be expected to sign – documents expressing our heartfelt gratitude that the colony is freed of
a tyrant. We must not be here to sign them! Bligh himself might

be punished, but government still remains – and one does not put
one's signature to treason!'

'Where . . .?' she said slowly. 'Where shall we go?'

'As far beyond Macarthur's reach as we can get. We'll go to
Banon. And we must be diplomatic about this. It will not do to
be unfriendly towards that gentleman either – because until another governor is appointed, it isn't very hard to guess who'll reign
as king here. This is a time when we must both walk a middle-
line, my dear – and it can best be done from the distance of
Banon.'

'For how long?'

He shrugged. 'Who knows . . .? Does it matter . . .?'

He raised his other hand and gripped her shoulders firmly. There
was a faint light from the stars – just enough to let her make out
the smile that had come to his face. Louis, she knew, was well aware
of the power of his smile. The quality of his voice turned a journey
to Banon into an adventure they alone shared; he could suggest
excitement where none existed.

'There's nothing to keep you here, Sara. Now that you have
good overseers for the farms, you don't have to visit them so regularly. Clapmore could run the store blind-folded – besides that, he
wants to get married, and I think it would be a graceful gesture if
you let him have the empty rooms above it. You don't expect any
of the ships back for six – perhaps nine – months yet. Why shouldn't
we have the peace of Banon while we can?'

She moved restlessly. She didn't want to go. The raw, ugly little
town of Sydney had today grown in stature by its act of rebellion;
it had suddenly expanded to a full, vigorous life – if, perhaps, not
the right kind of life, then exciting, just the same. She wanted
desperately to stay and watch its struggles at first hand; but Louis's
shrewd predictions were not to be thrust aside. There would be
more trouble yet, and she would certainly be expected to declare
herself for or against Macarthur – and either decision would be a
dangerous one. Her eyes went to the cluster of lights of the township, and then towards the harbour, where the pale starlight had
given the water a cool, silvered look. The exotic splendour of
Banon did not compare with this world – this place of half-beauty,
half-ugliness. Banon was lovely, remote in its river-valley, but her
heart urged her to stay here among this bustle and intrigue and
worldliness.

'You would be on hand when the first merino flock is brought
up to the new property, Sara. You've always said you'd like to be
there for the first lambing season at Dane Farm . . .'

He broke off as the soft clop of a horse's hooves in the drive reached them. They both peered into the darkness, but could make out nothing but the vague shape of the horseman who had reined to a halt before the front door.

'Hello, there . . . !' Louis called out.

The man turned his head, staring in their direction; then he urged his horse forward at a walk across the lawn, apparently indifferent to the way its hooves would cut up the turf. He halted at the border of the flowerbed beneath the veranda.

'Richard!' Sara breathed.

Her hands gripped the rail nervously. Richard had not come willingly to Glenbarr since her marriage to Louis. At the time of Sebastian's death he had written to her – a letter that was no mere formality, words from his heart, for her eyes alone. Apart from that, the only communication from him was the quarterly instalment paid on his debt. But Richard himself – his thoughts and plans and ideas – had vanished from her life as completely as in those other years following their quarrel over Jeremy. Now, his sudden appearance here, mounted and half-lost in darkness, was like a return from the dead. Her hands against the rail had begun to sweat.

'I must apologize for bursting in upon you like this . . .' Richard said. His voice was like a young boy's – half-eager, half-truculent.

Louis said coolly, 'We are delighted, of course. My only regret is that your horse cannot be accommodated in the drawing-room, otherwise you would be most welcome to come inside.'

'I've just ridden in from Parramatta,' Richard said, ignoring Louis's remark. 'I came as soon as the news of the rebellion reached us there.'

'It is most considerate of you,' Louis replied. 'But we're in no danger, I assure you. Governor Bligh is the only one who might have felt the need of your support today.'

'I haven't time to bandy words with you, de Bourget!' Richard burst out impatiently. 'It was chiefly on Sara's account I came!'

'What is it, Richard?' she said quietly.

He leaned sideways in the saddle, the tone of his voice dropping again, becoming low and earnest. 'I'm on my way to the barracks – I wanted to talk to you before I became involved in this mess. There are some of us in the Corps who think we're well rid of Bligh – and some who don't. But the one thing we are all agreed about is that, although Johnston may have taken over the Government, it's Macarthur who'll give the orders. He'll be in charge until they send someone out from England to arrest him. Perhaps he'll have a year – perhaps longer. But his time is limited – he'll have to make the most of it. And, believe me, he *will* make the most of it!'

Louis spoke, interrupting smoothly. 'But what has this to do with my wife, Barwell?'

'Simply this . . . Macarthur will try to involve as many prominent people in the colony as he can. He'll need support when they call him to give an account of himself. But, for the meantime, those who side with Bligh won't be much in favour with Macarthur and Johnston. It's a tricky business.'

'Well . . .?'

Richard addressed himself directly to Sara. 'It's bad enough for those who have to be involved in this – like myself. But for you, it's unnecessary . . . if you stay out of Sydney. I came hoping to persuade you to stay away for a few months – longer, if you can manage it.'

Sara said gently, 'Thank you, Richard. It was kind of you to think of coming.'

'It's not a matter for thanks!' he returned sharply. 'I came because this business is far more serious than perhaps it looks now. It may affect your future in the colony, Sara – under the next Governor, or Bligh himself, if he is reinstated. Johnston may offer land grants to win supporters like yourself. I hope you won't be tempted . . .'

'I'll remember what you've said, Richard,' she replied. 'I'm very grateful for your warning.'

He nodded. 'Well, then . . . good night to both of you. They're expecting me back at the barracks.'

He saluted stiffly, wheeled his horse, and set it at a canter straight towards the low hedge which bordered the lawn. Clods of earth flew up as the animal jumped. They listened to the sounds of the hoof-beats fading into the distance.

Louis ended the silence between them. 'I expect Barwell is too old to be taught some manners. Or perhaps he likes the dramatic figure he cuts as he ploughs up the lawn.'

'I hardly think he noticed what he was doing,' Sara murmured soothingly. 'He is more upset about today's trouble than I would have expected . . .'

Her voice trailed away wonderingly as Louis turned to her, and suddenly raised his hand to touch her cheek softly. With his forefinger he began to trace the line of her jaw; finally he tilted her chin, so that she was forced to look straight at him.

'He is like an eager boy in his love for you, my Sara. He is either all passion, or all coldness. He leans over backwards to display his indifference to you – but when he thinks he can help you, he is here like a knight to his lady. He is so young and foolish, and always will be.'

Sara jerked her head to break from his grasp.

'You think Richard loves me? How are you so certain?'

'Because, my darling, any fool could have seen it years ago – and I have never been exactly a fool.'

His hands went about her shoulders possessively. He bent until his face was close to hers.

'And now, my love, I hope you are doubly convinced that we must go back to Banon.'

She hesitated a moment, then nodded. His lips found hers in the darkness, and he held her close against him. She closed her eyes, and tried to forget the tumult in her heart at the sound of Richard's voice.

3

The de Bourgets and their family stayed at Banon for almost two years. During that period the rebel administration changed hands several times – from Johnston it was passed on to Lieutenant-Colonel Foveaux, and, on Colonel Patterson's arrival from the settlement of Port Dalrymple, he reluctantly took over what remnants of authority remained. Macarthur and Johnston left for England in March, 1809, to answer the charges against them. In the same month Bligh was released from his imprisonment, and allowed to sail in the *Porpoise*. He had given his promise that he would return immediately to England; but, as he regarded any promise made to a rebel government as no promise at all, he headed for the Derwent River, in Van Dieman's land, and waited there for the help which he expected from the unhurrying Colonial Office.

Each in their turn, the *Hawk*, *Thistle*, and *Thrush*, put into Port Jackson, and for a few days Sara and Louis came to Sydney to see their captains. Whenever they appeared in the town they were almost swamped under the wave of gossip and scandal which greeted them; if the evidence of the Sydney drawing-rooms was to be believed, every member of the rebel administration was engaged in a race to determine who could make himself the richest in the limited space of time in their hands. Seventy-five thousand acres of land had been parcelled out, and the Commissary was wiped clean. But these favours were paid for by a signature on the documents which supported the rebellion. The commerce of the colony had the feel of over-ripe fruit about to fall. It did not need Louis's urging to convince her that she was better away from Sydney while no authorized governor ruled there.

She was anxious over the state of affairs at the store and the farms. Clapmore was doing his best with the harrowing conditions of trade; he managed well enough as long as the de Bourget ships kept him supplied with cargoes. But Sara had given him instructions that on no account was he to buy from anyone within the colony itself, even if it meant that the shelves were to stand empty for months on end.

'Don't give them the prices they're asking,' she said to Clapmore. 'Shut the store, if you have to!'

Clapmore struggled on, facing the hundred-and-one decisions that formerly Sara had made. She was worried about him, but she felt that she dared not remain in Sydney for spells of any length.

On brief visits to Priest's and the Toongabbie farms she saw evidences everywhere that her absences were far too long. At both properties she gave orders for repairs to house and out-buildings, but was never able to wait to see them carried out.

She had no worry over the management of Kintyre. Since the time of the flood disaster, it had been almost completely in Jeremy Hogan's charge. His practice of riding to Kintyre to look over the stock and discuss the crops with Trigg – as they had done together in the old days – had begun during the months following Henriette's birth, when Sara had remained there, still ill and too weak to make the long journey back to Sydney. By now it was an established custom – and Louis had insisted that Jeremy be paid a proper commission as her agent. A letter from Jeremy, giving details of the property, reached her at Banon every few weeks; at times when she was worried about conditions at the other two farms, the letters gave her a picture of Kintyre's acres, as prosperous and as trim as if Andrew himself had been there to attend to them.

But she found that Banon was the refuge from the troubles of the colony that Louis had meant it to be. The valleys and gorges had a haunting, faintly mysterious beauty; it was possible, within a few miles' ride of the house itself, to go well beyond the reach of any settlement; across the river the wild government herds roamed unchecked. Great storms of rain came down from the mountains, but there were long days of sun and perfect stillness, when Sara felt herself becoming part of the silence that surrounded them. She let the peace of those uninterrupted months close over her, like a blanket that smothered all other thoughts.

Louis himself wore an air of contentment. He rode every day
with the children, or with Sara alone, and as time passed she felt
that his attachment to Banon became more and more a decisive
factor in his life. He seemed to desire nothing more than to remain
there undisturbed. Under his hands the gardens were becoming
a place of exquisite and carefully informal beauty; occasionally, with
two or three of the men, he made excursions into the foothills of
the mountains, bringing back young flowering trees to plant among
the eucalypts and Norfolk pine surrounding the house. He added
a library to store the books that arrived for him by every ship.

A governess, Miss Parry, was brought out to take charge of
Elizabeth; she was a prim, softly-spoken young woman, whom Louis
mimicked outrageously. Elizabeth still had lessons from her father
and Michael Sullivan, and went reluctantly into Miss Parry's
charge for music, needlework, and painting. Every morning from
the drawing-room came the airs of Mozart and Handel, executed
efficiently enough, but woodenly. Elizabeth's greatest passion in life
was still her pony, and, latterly, her small half-sister, Henriette,
had begun to interest her. Henriette was very much Louis's child
– with an assured charm which already she had learned would get
her most of the things she wanted. To Sara, it was still something
of a wonder to see the way Louis treated his little daughter – he
adored her, and spoiled her shamefully, delighting in her precocious
baby French. Always remembering the tragedy of Sebastian's death,
Louis engaged a nursemaid solely for the care of Henriette; this
woman had instructions never to let the child out of her sight for
a moment. Sara wished she had the courage to step in and put an
end to the dominance that Henriette exerted over the entire household at Banon, but she was never free of the thought that Henriette had to take the place of the son Louis had hoped for, and he
should be left to spoil and indulge as it pleased him.

With each month that passed, David and Duncan became
more absorbed in the routine of life at Banon. David was growing
into a shy and withdrawn adolescence – much too prone, Sara
noticed, to spending his time ranging through Louis's library, or
riding off alone along the bush tracks. He seemed content to be
led by Duncan – Duncan, who talked enough for them both,
who had Andrew's sense of opportunism, and a boisterous love
of fun. But in their interest and knowledge of farming they were
equal; they knew that Dane Farm, in the coveted Cowpastures
district, was to be theirs some day, and they followed its progress
with interest. Two or three times a week they rode there with Sara

to inspect the clearing and fencing; they knew almost as much about the breeding of the merino as their mother; they were familiar with the prices fetched for sheep and cattle at every stock sale in Sydney and Parramatta. As Sara saw them both, week by week, shed their childhood a little more, she pondered the question of sending them to school in England . . . and, week by week, she put the decision off. Next year they would go, she promised herself . . . next year.

At the end of December, 1809 – almost two years after the rebellion against Bligh – news reached Banon that Lieutenant-Colonel Lachlan Macquarie, the newly-appointed governor of the colony, had reached Port Jackson, in the *Hindostan*. With him in the *Hindostan*, and in the accompanying storeship, the *Dromedary*, were the soldiers of the 73rd Regiment, sent out to replace the rebellious Rum Corps. By placing the Commandant of the regiment in the governorship, the Colonial Office was making it abundantly clear that it would stand for no more of the quarrels that had waged incessantly between Governor and Military since Hunter's time.

With this new governor came the hope of peace within the colony, yet Sara packed for the journey to Sydney with a strange reluctance. These past two years had given to her a life of tranquillity she had never known, and previously hardly looked for. Almost she dreaded the return.

7

A haze of dust rose into the hot air above the Parade Ground, on New Year's Day, 1810. The population of Sydney had put on its best clothes, and in a holiday spirit had turned out to hear the reading of the Governor's commission. Beside the splendid new uniforms of the 73rd, those of the New South Wales Corps were faded and rather sad-looking; but the Corps presented arms as smartly as their fellows. The guns of the Battery on the point roared, the echo sounding back off the hills on the North Shore. A freely-perspiring military band played the National Anthem.

Sara, sitting in the carriage with Elizabeth and Henriette, noted, with a smile she kept carefully hidden, the respectful fashion in which the crowd uncovered its heads as the Great Seal was displayed on the Patent, by the Judge-Advocate. Tall hats and cloth caps were removed with equal alacrity; there was nothing here to indicate that this was the same crowd who had greeted the overthrow of the King's authority so enthusiastically only two years ago.

'*George the Third* : *To our Trusty and Well-Beloved Lachlan Macquarie* . . .'

In the closeness of the carriage, Elizabeth fidgeted with her bonnet, trying, Sara guessed, to keep her face shaded so that the freckles wouldn't appear on her nose. But Henriette, almost four now, was unnaturally still, her eyes fixed in a long stare of concentration. She was fascinated by the spectacle before her. Never, in her short life, had she seen anything to equal the red and gold splendour of the uniforms; to her, the roll of the drums and the royal salute from the Battery were awe-inspiring. She seemed to have forgotten the irksomeness of her many petticoats under the India muslin dress. It amused Sara that Elizabeth, while paying no attention to the ceremony, thoroughly enjoyed looking pretty in a gown that was having only its second wearing.

Louis, standing beside the carriage, wore a slightly bored expression on his face – an expression which, whether intentional or not, plainly said that this little display of vice-regal pomp impressed him not at all. He shifted his hat to the other hand while the Judge-Advocate's voice droned on. The midday heat was intense; the crowd swished irritably at the flies that settled on their faces and arms. Beside Louis, Duncan nudged his brother frequently, and, stretching on tip-toe, made many whispered remarks. Sara managed to lean down quietly and touch his shoulder with her parasol. He turned around, grinning impishly up at her, and then cocking a quizzical eyebrow at Elizabeth's discontented face.

The Governor finished his address, and again the guns roared from the Battery, and from the ships in the harbour. The drums started, and once more the band struck up the National Anthem. The tension in the crowd relaxed.

Louis opened the carriage door with an air of impatience. '*Mon Dieu*, how they love their little ceremonies!'

He didn't make it clear whether he referred to Governor Macquarie's party, or to the eager, gaping population.

As he was about to step into the carriage he halted, his head turned sideways, staring into the crowd which had broken its lines and begun to drift.

'Here's Jeremy Hogan!' he said.

Sara leaned forward. Jeremy came towards them, smiling, his hat still in his hand.

'Jeremy!' she cried, delightedly. 'What brings you here? I thought an occasion like this wouldn't bring you down from the Hawkesbury — not even if the King himself . . .'

Her words were lost in the enthusiastic greeting of the two boys. Even Elizabeth stopped looking bored and smiled charmingly.

'Sometimes an Irish fit of sociability falls on me,' Jeremy said, shaking hands with Louis. 'I suddenly see myself growing dull and rusty in my wilderness, and then I think I must go and drink in some of the cultivated talk and habits of our great metropolis. They tell me there's even to be fireworks tonight — now, fireworks are something I never could resist . . .'

Louis was urging him towards the carriage. 'Then you'll not be able to resist coming back to Glenbarr. Eat dinner with us, and we'll see if we can't persuade you to stay on. This evening we're having a bonfire and fireworks of our own to celebrate the coming of the Lord's anointed.'

Sara saw the broad smile that immediately crossed Duncan's face as he listened. 'You're hardly respectful, Louis . . .'

'Nonsense, my dear!' he laughed. 'I hear the text of the sermon the Reverend Cowper will preach is, "Arise, anoint him; for this is he!" '

As he spoke he climbed into the carriage behind Jeremy, taking no notice of the wail of protest Elizabeth set up when she realized what the extra crowding would do to her muslin frills. Before he closed the door, Louis turned to the two boys.

'David, you'll make your own way back, won't you? There isn't any room in here now.'

David nodded eagerly. 'Yes, of course . . .'

Duncan, as soon as he heard Louis's words, waved his hand gaily, and charged off through the crowds towards the place where the band was still playing. David swung round to follow him.

Louis watched them with a smile. 'That, I imagine, is the last we'll see of them until they're hungry and tired enough to want to come home.'

He sat down and leaned back, and the carriage rolled forward. Its progress was slowed by the line of chaises and carriages ahead. Sara swished her fan to keep off the flies, staring at the throngs of people on foot, listening to them shouting and calling to each other. The soldiers on the Parade ground had been dismissed, and they were now mingling with the crowd, their red uniforms notes of solid colour among the light cottons and muslins of the women. A pretty girl, hanging on the arm of a corporal of the 73rd, stared,

with mildly envious eyes, into the de Bourget's carriage, then her
escort bent and said something in a low voice, and she looked up
at him laughingly, forgetting the silk and the velvet upholstery that
had caused her envy a few seconds ago. It was a Sunday afternoon,
and yet the place had none of the decorum of a Sunday about it.
The dust rose under the feet of the crowd; the heat and the noise
made Sara's head ache, and set her thinking wistfully of the cool
of Glenbarr.

Jeremy was doing a wickedly malicious little paraphrase of the
sermon he imagined the earnest Mr Cowper shortly afterwards
delivering in St Phillip's, greeting the new Governor as the Saviour
of the colony. Louis, shaken out of his boredom, was highly amused,
and lay back chuckling quietly. He had, true to his character, refused to join the small throng of people who had pressed forward
immediately to be presented to Macquarie. He and Sara were
invited to attend a reception at Government House later in the
week, and it did not suit him to be one of the line waiting in the
hot sun to be presented before the eyes of Sydney's interested population.
      As the two men talked together Sara had time to examine
Jeremy carefully, and to note the changes which the last year had
brought to him. He was accustomed to his freedom now; his ease
sat upon him naturally, his speech and humour no longer constrained, as when he had been Andrew Maclay's convict overseer.
His coat was smartly cut, and his linen impeccable; he was stamped
with the prosperity of the Hawkesbury farm. She saw, with some
alarm, the steaks of grey in his black hair, and she realized then
that he was, after all, forty-two, or perhaps forty-three, and his
years in the colony, save the latter ones, had been hard and wearing. His face had a deep tan, and his skin was hardened by the
weather. But he had the assurance of a man who is at peace with
his world; she doubted if he often turned his thoughts backwards
to Ireland. Fourteen years' penal servitude separated him from
the man he had been there – a young man with a taste for women
and good horses. He was confident of his future, and could shrug
his shoulders at the memory of a sentence imposed for sedition.
It had left no mark against his character; here, in the colony, he
was free to rise as high as he wished. While Sara stared at him,
she found herself thinking of the convict woman who was his
mistress, and wondering if he would ever marry her.

That evening the entire de Bourget household, guests, children,

and servants, stood around the huge bonfire that Edwards and
Ted O'Malley were tending. At a smaller fire, Bess and Kate took
turns at slowly turning a pig on a spit. The smell of roasting meat
was heavy on the air.

Elizabeth, standing close to her father, gave a shrill squeak
as a rocket shot into space, exploding in a shower of pink stars.
The whole of the township was dotted over with the lights of the
bonfires that burned to welcome Governor Macquarie. From a
dozen different points that Sara could pick out and name, a series
of fireworks coloured the night sky – from Captain Piper's garden,
from the South Head, from the Parade Ground, from the ships in
the harbour, from Dawes Point. Sydney had never looked so
beautiful – the darkness hiding its ramshackle buildings, and a new
moon over the water. Twenty bonfires glowed in the warm summer
night.

Sara, lost in all the beauty about her, started a little at a light
touch on her arm. Jeremy was beside her. He spoke in a low
voice, which she could scarcely hear above the crackle of the
flames.

'I've been trying to talk with you alone all evening, Sara.'

She smiled, glancing at him. 'Was it important, Jeremy?' Then
her eyes went quickly back to Duncan, who had jumped away
from a cracker which Edwards had let off almost under his feet.

'Important, I think, to you,' Jeremy said quietly.

She turned to him, her smile fading. 'What is it?'

'I wondered if you'd yet heard the news about Richard Barwell?'

'What news?' she said sharply. 'What do you mean?'

'A letter arrived on the *Hindostan*. Lady Linton is dead. She has
left Alison her fortune, of course. I heard this morning that Richard
has been making inquiries about a passage back to England.'

'For them both?' She struggled to keep the note of panic out of
her voice.

'Yes, Sara – both.'

'Well . . . thank you for telling me, Jeremy. I'm glad you were
able to tell me before anyone else did.'

Her lips quivered as she spoke, and the sudden tears blinded her.
The bonfires, and the children's excited cries, belonged to another
world. Sydney's hills, dotted with lights, swam before her gaze.
Touching Jeremy's arm, she stepped back a few paces from the
fire, grateful for the darkness which hid her face.

2

Glenbarr wore a drowsy air as Sara looked at it from across the lawn. It was mid-afternoon, and in most of the rooms the shades had been drawn against the direct sun. A fierce light came off the harbour, and Sara, turning occasionally to glance towards the bay, had to shield her eyes against the glare. Nothing stirred about the house; David, Duncan and Elizabeth were at their lessons with Michael Sullivan; Louis had ridden down to the township to supervise the unloading from a ship of some pictures which had been sent from England for Banon. Beside her Henriette was sitting in the swing, which the nursemaid, Fanny, was pushing in a dreamy fashion. The rhythmic creak of the ropes was a gentle, lazy sound on the warm air. The child's blue dress floated softly as she swung to and fro. From the direction of the stable came the distant sound of buckets clanking together; not even a suggestion of a breeze blew off the water to stir the branches of the group of Norfolk pines under which they sat.

Now and then Henriette spoke, and Sara answered her absently; but the heat made them both lethargic. Sara's sewing lay on the ground beside her in a basket, but she had made no attempt to take it up. It was six days now since the reading of Macquarie's Commission, and, although the settlement was still carrying on its round of celebration, the heat, increasing day by day, was taking the energies and tempers of Sydney's inhabitants. Sara rested her back against the trunk of a tree, listening to the buzz of the insects about her; she stared across the lawn, which was turning brown after weeks without rain, to the drive, and she strained to catch the first sound of the horseman she expected.

But it was Henriette who saw Richard first. For the moment Sara's attention was distracted by the appearance of a fishing boat in the bay below the garden; Henriette's voice recalled her sharply.

'Here's someone coming, Mama!'

Sara turned quickly. She recognized the scarlet uniform of the Corps, but Richard had come on foot. He walked up the drive slowly, and, even at a distance, there was a dejected look about him that touched her strangely. A little nearer he halted, staring across at the group under the dark pines, and raising his hand to shield his eyes from the sun. The quivering heat-haze rose between them like a curtain.

Sara got to her feet.

'May I come too, Mama?'

Sara shook her head. 'No, Henriette. It's time you went upstairs for your rest. Just ten minutes longer, Fanny, and then you can take her in.'

'Very well, ma'am,' Fanny said thankfully.

Sara stepped out from the shade of the trees, and began to walk across the dry lawn towards Richard.

Two days ago Richard had sent a note to Sara, asking if he might come to see her at Glenbarr. The note put an end to her hours of questioning and wondering since Jeremy had told her of Lady Linton's death, and the Barwells' plans to return to England. She had replied, telling him to come at a time when she could be quite certain Louis would be away from the house. And then she had settled to wait, her mind unnaturally clear and calm. She knew what Richard would say to her, almost knew the words he would use. This would be the unsatisfactory ending to the relationship that had existed between them since the day they had talked together on the little beach below the garden. For ten years their lives had run parallel – a time of being very close to one another, of love and tenderness, interspersed with quarrels and estrangements. This was not the feeling they had known for each other in the Bramfield days, when they had thought of love with children's minds; this feeling had brought Richard across the world to be at her side, and had given him ten years of frustration and bitterness.

She knew all this was coming to an end as she walked across the lawn towards him. She came up close to him, and put her hand into his.

'I'm glad you've come, Richard,' she said.

He nodded, but made no reply.

She plucked at the sleeve of his tunic to lead him forward on to the veranda. He followed her up the steps, and along to the french windows opening into the drawing-room. As he passed through into the room beyond, she caught the flutter of Henriette's dress, like a pale blue flower under the lofty pines.

At all but one window the shades and curtains were drawn against the sun, and the room was dim. There was a cool look to the wax polish of the floors between the rugs, and the clean white walls. But flowers that had been put in fresh that morning were already fading in the heat. Many changes had been made in this room since Sara's marriage to Louis, but, in feeling, it was essentially as it was the first evening Richard and Alison had come to dinner. He looked about him carefully as he entered, and Sara guessed that the same thought was running through his head.

He stood by the mantelpiece, one hand resting on it, his gaze fixed on her face as she sat down on the sofa near him. His eyes wore a brooding look as they followed her movements.

'I suppose you've heard my news, Sara?' he said.

She nodded. 'I imagine most people have heard it by this time.'

He spoke hesitantly. 'Then . . . you don't mind me coming here . . . like this? It's five years since I've been here to see you alone . . . five years, Sara!'

Suddenly her composure deserted her. Her mouth worked nervously; she stretched out her hand to him.

'Oh, Richard! Richard! If you hadn't come, I don't know how I could have borne it!'

In an instant he was with her, crouching on a low stool at her feet, both her hands clasped tightly in his own.

'My darling, Sara! I won't let go of you! There isn't any need for us to be apart again. Somehow I'll make Alison stay here . . . She *must* stay, if that's what I want!'

She bent until her face was against his forehead; she moved gently, and her lips brushed his cheek.

'Oh, hush, Richard! Hush! No more of it! This is what we said to each other ten years ago – and it didn't do any good, to either of us.'

He pressed his face to her shoulder.

'God!' he said, in a low voice. 'What a mess I've made of everything! You don't have to tell me that I behave like a child, Sara – I know that I do! And yet I can't help myself. I can no more stop loving you than breathing. But we've been nothing to each other all these years, but a constant torment.'

With gentle hands she stroked his hair. 'Don't blame yourself, my dearest. There's no blame . . .'

Abruptly he flung his head back, so that he was looking at her directly.

'But there *is* blame! Through my stupidity I've ruined Alison's life and my own. She's not happy – she's not been happy since . . .'

'But Alison loves you!' she protested. 'You are her whole world ╷ – she doesn't see beyond you.'

'That's what she would have everyone believe,' he said. 'That's what she made *me* believe. Oh . . . she loves me all right. There's

no doubt about that. She loves me in a way I don't deserve —
there's room in her heart for nothing else. But she also knows and
understands me far better than I thought.'

Sara was frowning. 'What do you mean?'

'I mean that my loving, adoring wife has known what I felt for
you since the first evening she met you.'

'Richard . . . !'

'It's true! When the letter came to tell us that Lady Linton
was dead, I told Alison that I wanted to stay in the colony. I tried
to convince her that, with money in my hands, I could make
much more money — as Andrew did. She told me then.'

'What did she tell you?'

'She said that she wasn't having any more of the colony. She
said she had been bored from the very moment she set foot in
the place — and tired of the dull, stupid receptions, of seeing the
same people every time she went out, of hearing the same talk. It
appears that every year she's stayed here, it's grown worse and
worse. And then . . .'

'Yes . . .?'

He ran his hand distractedly across his face.

'Then she talked about you, Sara. She recalled to me the night
we first came here, and then almost every other meeting we've had
when she has been present. She remembers how we acted, and what
we said. Step by step she built it up, and put it to me. She made
me see what I had done to her life, and yours. I have been useless
to you — *she* pointed that out — it would have been much kinder
and better if I'd left you in peace.'

'And Alison . . .' she said slowly. 'She kept silent all this time
. . . and she still stayed with you, knowing what she did? Why?'

'I've already said that she loves me more than I deserve. I am
not good enough — either for Alison, or for you, Sara. But she still
loves me. It shames me to think of the way I've treated her —
and you.'

She said reflectively, 'A long time ago, when I first heard that
you and Alison had come to Sydney, I remarked to Julia Ryder
that at last the colony would have a real lady to fuss over. At the
time I said it, I didn't mean it generously, because I hated and
feared the very thought of Alison. Now, when I think of her
knowing of our love all these years, and yet being silent, I'm
ashamed also. She is a far greater lady than I believed.'

His grip on her hands tightened. 'It was a strange thing, seeing
the wife I'd always dominated suddenly take control. She didn't
cry, Sara — she didn't cry at all over the love I'd given you use-

lessly, and which she'd wanted for herself. But I hadn't heard the worst of it, even then.'

'The worst of it?' she said, alarmed. 'Richard, what . . .?'

'A few months ago D'Arcy Wentworth told her she hadn't much more than twelve months to live – perhaps more if she took a sea voyage. She hadn't talked of this to me because she knew there was no possibility of leaving the colony until her aunt died. But now she has the money, and she'll go. Her lungs are diseased. You've seen her yourself, Sara – she's like a shadow . . .'

He thrust his head against her shoulder again. 'So . . . whether I want to or not, I can do nothing else but go back with her to England. If I've made her wretched all this time, then at least I owe her the last year.'

Then he let go of her hands, and his arms went around her.

'Oh, Sara! Sara, what can I do? I'm lost without you – and yet I can't stay.'

She cradled his head against her breast, her arms holding him tightly. 'Dearest, go with Alison. You'll find some sort of peace away from me. We're no good to each other – we torture and destroy, both of us. I have Louis and the children, and I will be happy here. And you – in London, when you have money, you will find distractions. That's your world, Richard. That's where you belong.'

'Do I really belong anywhere in the world, without you, Sara? Ever since we were children . . .'

His words were stilled abruptly as she bent over him and kissed him on the lips.

'There is nothing more to say, my dearest. I love you, always. Just kiss me, Richard, and let this be our goodbye.'

Slowly he rose to his feet. He pulled her up to him, and gathered her into his arms.

'Oh, Sara! Sara! What shall I do without you?'

She put her arms about his neck, and as they kissed she could feel the hot tears on her cheeks. Already she had the sense of him having gone beyond her reach.

3

Richard and Alison sailed from Port Jackson, in the *Hindostan*, at the beginning of May, 1810, with the rest of the disbanded New South Wales Corps. To Sara, the period of waiting for their going seemed endless. The *Hindostan* and the *Dromedary* were to travel back to England together, but they had first to be victualled and repaired. The round of farewell parties dragged on, and the months passed slowly.

Bligh, who had returned to Sydney in the leaking old *Porpoise*, too late to be reinstated as Governor, was also to sail in the *Hindostan*. His enforced stay in Port Dalrymple had sharpened his temper, and the delays seemed to give him a perverse delight.

He and Macquarie had hated each other on sight; Bligh's presence in Sydney was a perpetual embarrassment to the new Governor. At the end of April, he gave a ball and a fête in his predecessor's honour, to speed him thankfully on his way.

Sara was nervous and unable to rest while the two ships remained at anchor and she knew that Richard had not yet embarked. She suggested to Louis that they should return to Banon, and he, understanding her unease, made arrangements immediately for their departure to the Nepean.

She was at Banon, in May, when the news reached her that the two ships had at last left the harbour.

The knowledge that Richard was finally gone gave her a peace that helped her feeling of solitude and loneliness. Now there could be no more shared memories of the Romney Marsh – there was no one who might ever mention her father's name. Richard had taken with him the image of the young Sara Dane.

4

Governor Macquarie had small liking for the state of affairs in which he found the colony when he arrived. He knew exactly into what shape he wanted to mould the small world he ruled, and he set about it with determined energy. The dilapidated buildings of Sydney annoyed him – he visioned them replaced by solid, prosperous-looking stone; he wanted better roads, and he got them, paying for them by constructing turn-pikes. A new hospital was started; St Phillip's Church was finished and consecrated. Macquarie's energy touched everything; it reached everywhere.

Offered the example of his own lavish hospitality, the social life of the colony blossomed. It was fashionable to take picnics along the newly-finished South Head Road, and to make an occasion of Sunday morning church-going. There was a regular promenade in the evenings in Hyde Park, to the music of the Regimental Band; private parties and balls – always overcrowded with the officers of the 73rd – punctuated the weeks. A racecourse had been laid out in Hyde Park, and the annual Race Week, in October, became Sydney's greatest social event. On the other side, the fierce, bawdy, often grim life of the town persisted, but in three years Macquarie had pushed it back to its own district – known as the Rocks – and confined it to the convict barracks. He liked and encouraged the veneer of genteel and polite society, and society, such as it was, rewarded him by a determined effort towards elegance.

But there was another quirk to the Governor's character less to the liking of the colony's élite; he had a curious partiality for emancipists. He favoured them whenever possible, and encouraged them to mix in the social junketings. But he was not as strong as the traditions which excluded emancipists. He might bid them to dine at Government House, and appoint them to committees – but he could not force their entry into the drawing-rooms of the officer and merchant class. When His Excellency pointed out the degree of acceptance Sara de Bourget had won, he was gently reminded that all emancipists were not fortunate enough to marry men too powerful, too well-born, and too wealthy to be snubbed.

For Sara the three years following Macquarie's coming were, on the surface, tranquil ones. But she had to learn gradually an acceptance of the fact that Richard was gone; beneath her calmness there was a sense of loss. He had been so small a part of her daily life since her marriage, and yet she had known as much about him as local gossip knew – had seen him quite often at the gatherings they both attended, and had sometimes spoken to him. But with his going even these familiar things were gone. No one spoke of him any more, and there was no excuse for mentioning his name. Hyde Farm had changed owners twice in that short time, so that not even there had he left a permanent mark. Richard had never belonged at the heart of the colony's affairs, and the colony forgot him quickly.

By this time, Louis was reconciled to a life passed half at Banon, half at Glenbarr; Sara no longer went to the store, but merely looked over the accounts when Clapmore brought them to Glenbarr. Nor did she ride so often to Kintyre, Priest's, or Toongabbie; Jeremy Hogan still had the greater part of the control of Kintyre, and the overseers of the other two farms were efficient enough, in their fashion. She had learned by now that she must pay the price of lower profits from both, if she was to have peace with Louis. She was not over-anxious about the fall in the profits from the farms; she looked on this time simply as a period of waiting until David and Duncan were old enough to take charge themselves, and when their own ambition would make it unnecessary for her to exert herself. With each year the acreage of cleared land at Dane Farm was increasing, and the merino flocks spreading wider. The *Hawk*, *Thistle* and *Thrush* carried, on every voyage, a substantial cargo of her wool to the London market. At times Louis still called her a shopkeeper, but she was amused to notice that his former contempt was missing from the title.

It was at the beginning of 1812 that she received her only letter from Richard. He wrote simply and quite briefly, telling her of Alison's death, at Lady Linton's house in Devon. She was saddened by the news. Poor Alison; she thought – she had loved so futilely. Richard was unworthy of such love, and yet Sara knew so well that it was as natural to give it, as it was to breathe. She wondered about his life now, and pictured him, surrounded by the London gaiety he had always leaned towards, left in possession of the fortune Alison had not been able to spend. She tried to make herself believe that Richard would be happy now, in the new wealth and freedom he had found.

8

There were lights and an air of bustle through the whole of Glenbarr as Sara mounted the stairs to her bedroom, on the last night of 1812. Below, she clearly caught the sound of the servants' voices, chattering in the hall, on their way to the kitchen; here, close at hand, she sensed the excitement and the careful dressing that went on behind the closed bedroom doors. Glenbarr was gay; it wore a festive look. She paused at the head of the stairs, and glanced about her. The balustrade was hung with garlands of Elizabeth's fashioning, and bowls of wild flowers, in great masses, stood in every corner. In the dining-room, the supper tables were laid; the drawing-room was prepared for cards, and sofas lined the walls for those who preferred simply to gossip.

Suddenly the excitement communicated itself to Sara herself; she picked up her skirt and half ran along to the window at the end of the landing. The window overlooked the garden at the side of the house, where a marquee had been erected for the dancers. It was brightly lit, two sides open to the warm night, and to the view of the harbour. The sky was clear; later there would be a moon. She stood still and listened, and even above the voices of the men as they put last-minute touches to the decorations, and the scrape of a fiddle from a solitary member of the orchestra, who sat on a wooden box at the entrance to the marquee, playing a tune for the benefit of himself and two gardeners, she could hear the gentle murmur of the water on the rocks below. The tune went on – one of Tommy Moore's lovely, sentimental ballads, which she hummed to herself as she stood there. Then the mood changed – a lively Irish jig this time, with a touch of laughter in it. She could not recognize the man seated there, silhouetted against the light, but she knew she listened to a cry from the heart of an exile. The gardeners moved off, and for a few moments there was nothing but the sound of the water as a faint accompaniment to the tune on the fiddle.

She swung round at a step beside her. David had come out of his bedroom, and was walking towards her with a smile.

'Not dressed yet, Mother?'

She shook her head. 'It doesn't take me as long as Elizabeth. I'm no belle – besides, I've been doing it for many more years than she has!'

'Elizabeth won't outshine you, for all that!' he said, and suddenly leaned forward and kissed her on the cheek. 'You're still the most beautiful woman in the colony – and what's more, you know it!'

Sara laughed, reaching out to take hold of his hair and pull it. Then her hand dropped. 'I can't even do that, can I? You're much too immaculate, David.'

'And that's the way I mean to stay!'

She looked at him with satisfaction. He was nineteen, taller even than Louis, handsome, with his fair hair above the blue coat he wore. He had grown into a thoughtful, quiet young man, but Sara felt that she was very seldom able to reach into his mind and discover what he believed in. She had his love and loyalty, but not his confidences. David was, in a small way, a perfectionist – he attempted nothing that he was not sure could be well and efficiently completed. He had left Michael Sullivan's care now, and was preparing to take over some of the management of Priest's. He seemed happy enough with this, contented – and yet she was afraid that his enthusiasm had no passion in it; he seemed to be doing this because there was nothing else for him. He shot and rode well, he was polite, charming, anxious to please – and yet he constantly wore a slightly aloof air. He shared their family life readily enough, but always seemed relieved when the time came for him to make one of his solitary trips to Priest's, or one of the other properties. She knew quite well that David loved her, but he had never given her his heart completely. She felt a vague disquiet whenever she

looked at him searchingly, especially this evening – handsome, and
suddenly appearing older than his nineteen years; he so completely lacked the passion that had been Andrew's, and which
Duncan possessed in such abundance.

But she shook off the feeling, smiling and tapping him lightly
on the cheek with the palm of her hand. 'Don't you worry, I
won't disarrange you. Although I can imagine the flutter of
feminine hearts . . .'

She broke off as a door was flung open noisily farther along the
passage. Duncan came out of his room, grinning broadly.

'How do I look, Mother? Am I all right?'

'You look splendid, Duncan – magnificent!'

He flushed a little with pleasure, and smoothed an imaginary
crease in his trousers. Looking at him, Sara was touched. His
coat was far too brilliant a red – Louis, she knew, would privately
deplore it – but it was Duncan's own choice, and he was happy in
it. He had a graceless rather untidy charm about him, and a confidence that allowed no difficulties to stand in his way. The whole
household adored and waited upon him; he had a heart for gossip,
and he had friends in every possible level of Sydney's widening
population. He rode his mare and sailed his skiff in the harbour
with a reckless, heartwarming fervour. In Duncan, there was
nothing of his brother's touch of introspection.

Sara reached automatically to smooth the ruffles at his throat.

'Mother, will you be sure to save a dance for me?' he said.
'I've been practising with Elizabeth, but she says on no account am
I to dance with anyone but you and herself – or I'll disgrace us
all.'

'I'll be proud to dance with you, my dear.'

In the hall below, the clock began to chime. Sara looked at her
sons in alarm.

'I must go . . . or I'll never be dressed and ready to dance with
anyone!'

Again she picked up her skirt and hurried along the passage.
David looked after her affectionately; but Duncan was absorbed in
pulling his new coat into a better position.

2

Sara was almost finished dressing when Louis came into the bedroom. He walked slowly across the floor and stood behind her, for
a few moments studying her reflection in the mirror. Then he bent
towards the dressing-table and drew from its case the necklace of

sapphires, which he had given her two years earlier. When he fastened it about her throat, by contrast to her stiff, ivory brocade gown, its colour came to sudden life. He smiled, brushed his lips briefly against her shoulder, and then strolled over to the window.

'The garden looks attractive,' he said.

She nodded, remembering how it had looked when she had stood at the window on the landing outside. Small coloured lanterns had been placed to mark the edges of the lawn and drive; they had been lit now, and glowed softly in the darkness. A sense of expectancy had fallen on the house and garden; they waited for the sound of music and laughter, the voices of couples who would walk arm in arm across the lawn.

'But the mosquitoes will plague to death anyone rash enough to venture out,' Louis added.

Sara glanced over her shoulder at him, but he still stood peering out, his hands clasped behind his back. From the way he spoke she knew that he was merely making conversation, while his mind turned over some other thought. But she waited, knowing that, in his own time, he would tell her what it was. She looked at herself again in the mirror, rearranging the set of a curl in her hair.

'It will be scorching by noon tomorrow,' he said, glancing at the cloudless sky and the moon that was now beginning to appear over the harbour. 'Just the sort of day to put everyone in a thoroughly foul humour for the Races. I have an uncomfortable certainty that I'm not going to beat David for the Magistrates' Purse.'

'That would be a pity,' she said slowly. 'Perhaps it would do David good to be beaten at something. I think he's almost afraid of the race, in case it proves to be an occasion on which he will fail to achieve what he wants. He's a shade too successful at most things. It's not good ...'

'Oh, a race ...' he said, shrugging. 'I think it needs more than a race to shake David.'

A hint of impatience in his tone made Sara turn quickly. Behind his back, Louis's hands clenched and unclenched rhythmically.

'What do you mean, Louis?' she said.

He wheeled round. 'I'm not just talking of David. It's all the children ... Duncan, and Elizabeth, and even Henriette.'

Puzzled, she frowned. 'I'm afraid I don't understand. What's wrong with them?'

He flung his hands in a gesture that indicated his uncertainty.

'I'm not at all sure. But I can't help feeling that it's a great pity there *is* nothing here to shake them occasionally. They've seen nothing . . . This party tonight, for example . . . To their minds, it represents the very peak of elegance and fashion – because they don't know anything better. They live, more or less, at the top of their world – and they're inclined to forget that it's a very small one.'

She turned gravely back to the mirror. 'You're right, of course,' she said, her eyes meeting the reflection of his. 'But what is to be done about it? Whenever I've talked to David about his going to England, he has always said he prefers to stay where he is. It's too late for school, I know, but . . .'

'School! That's not where he'll learn what life in England is like! David is just the right age for London. He is old enough to enjoy it – and young enough to absorb it.'

Sara noticed that her hands were trembling slightly as she reached to pick up her gloves. 'And the others . . .? What of them?'

'They need it, just as he does. Elizabeth is seventeen, Sara. She will fall in love with some young subaltern here from the regiment, without knowing that any other sort of men exist.'

She raised her eyebrows. 'I trust you're not forgetting, Louis, that, in England, marriages for girls are not arranged quite in the same way as they are in France. Elizabeth should be allowed to choose for herself. And if she wants to stay here to marry . . .'

He held up his hands. '*Mon Dieu!* I'm not suggesting an arranged marriage for her! I hope – and I feel quite certain she will – return here to the colony to finally settle. Because this is where she has been happiest. But she should know, while she is still young enough to make a choice, what sort of face the rest of the world wears!'

Sara fumbled clumsily with her bracelet, struggling to fasten it over her glove.

'You suggest the three should go, then?'

'Let all of us go, Sara.'

Startled, her hands flew to her throat.

'All of us! You and I also . . .?'

'A year or two. No longer.'

'But . . . To leave Glenbarr . . . Banon . . . I don't think I want to do that, Louis.'

'But why not? Must you be forever chained here? I'm beginning to think that you need a glimpse of the outside world quite as badly as the children do.'

She made no reply. Her head bent forward, and she began to

pluck at the ospreys in her fan. Louis's fingers on her shoulders tightened a little.

'Sara . . . my darling! What is it?'

Suddenly she flung back her head, and her eyes met his directly in the mirror before her.

'I'm afraid!' she said passionately. 'That's what's wrong with me! I've been in this colony for twenty years, and I'm afraid to move outside of it. Here, they all know my story – and they've stopped whispering over it long ago. I have my own place here – and you ask me to leave it, and go and face the gossip in London? You want me to hear my past raked over and over for all its juiciest pieces? Once, Louis, you reminded me that I arrived in the colony in a convict transport – and you said I'd never again suffer like that. It would be possible to make me suffer in a much worse way. If you . . .'

His thick brows came together. 'Hush, Sara! You let your imagination run away with you! Who is there in London to make you suffer? Truly, my dearest, you're looking at the whole matter in the light in which Sydney would see it. Tell me, who will point to your life and say that you have cause for shame? London has long recognized what Sydney is afraid to acknowledge – that there were many travesties of justice in the sentences of transportation. To those who know your story, you are guilty of nothing more than a childish prank. Have you forgotten the sophistication and cynicism of London? You have position, money – London cares for little else. It would be a happy thing for England if the Prince himself were surrounded by people as guiltless as yourself. Can you not believe that?'

'But that's not all!' she said, shaking her head, as if to thrust aside the reassurances he offered. 'The children themselves . . .! What makes you so certain that they will want to go? Elizabeth, maybe – but will David and Duncan want to go? If David refuses, I can't force him. It would be natural if he wanted to stay here now that he has begun to take over the farming. I can't believe that he will leave it readily.'

'Ah, Sara . . . children are never the creatures we like to believe they are. You and Andrew built your fortune from a rough farmhouse on the Hawkesbury – but you can't expect your children to cherish their possessions as you have done. They haven't had to work for them – and they don't remember much about the time before their father was a man of importance. You'd like to think that it is love of Kintyre that makes their hearts beat – and that they couldn't leave it, or any of the other places, for a year or two.

But you are wrong. To them, the things they own are an established fact – something they've always had, always waiting for their return. When a new side of life is offered them, it's not in their nature to refuse.'

She fingered the sapphires nervously. She said quietly, 'Louis, what makes you so sure of all this? How do you know what they will feel about it?'

He pressed her shoulders back until she leaned against him. She could feel the stiffness of his brocade waistcoat on her bare flesh. He bent over her slightly.

'I know – because I asked them, Sara,' he said.

'You . . . Without asking me first!'

'Don't be angry with me, my love. I knew quite well that you'd be afraid – and I wanted to forestall that fear with every argument against it I could summon. I asked them, because I had to know before I spoke to you about it. Sara, they *need* to get away from this place, so that they can come back to it gladly. How can they appreciate what they've always lived with? How can they be expected to realize the peace you and I have found here, when they've known nothing else? It's for their sakes that I want this trip to England. But they need you with them.'

Miserably she clenched her hands. 'It won't be as easy as you make it sound! Once they get a taste of London life, they'll despise this one. They won't want to come back – and all the work of these years will go for nothing. I've struggled to keep the farms and the store working, so that they should be ready for them to take over. Give them a year of London's gaiety, and they'll want to sell up what they have here. Oh, Louis, don't you see that?'

'Do you have such little faith in their attachment to this place, Sara? My only thought was to convince them that, by comparison, there lives were full and satisfying. You can't possibly believe that they will never want to make the voyage. Let them go now . . .'

He broke off at the sound of running footsteps in the passage outside. There was a knock on the door. He released his grip on Sara's shoulders, and stepped back a little.

'Come in!'

The door burst open immediately, and Elizabeth stood there. She wore a gown of soft, white silk, that seemed almost the colour of her skin. This was her first ball-gown, and her father had decreed that it be completely simple, with none of the elaborate trimmings she had yearned for. Sara looked at her and smiled. Louis's choice was a triumph; Elizabeth was radiant and beautiful in it.

'You look wonderful, Elizabeth!' she said admiringly. 'You're a picture!'

'Yes . . .' Elizabeth gave an excited little laugh. 'David and Duncan have just said the same – though Henriette seemed to think it was too plain, when I went to the nursery to show it to her. She didn't actually say, but I expect she would have preferred something in a bright red. Duncan had paid her a visit before me, and his new coat was much admired by our young despot.'

She stepped into the room, and twirled before them.

'Papa, do you like it?'

'I do indeed, my darling. I'm extremely proud of you.'

Then Elizabeth's gloved hand flew to her mouth in alarm.

'Mercy, I'd forgotten to tell you what I came up especially for! The first of the guests has arrived. It's only old Mr Bridie. He made straight for the supper-room, and didn't seem to notice that you weren't down yet. He *walked* here – that's why you didn't hear the carriage.' Her tone implied complete mystification over people who walked, when they might just as easily have ridden.

She turned to leave them, but paused, looking back slowly.

'Papa . . . have you talked about it yet?' she asked hesitantly. 'I mean . . . you promised to speak to Mama this evening.'

'Yes, Elizabeth – we've discussed it.'

The girl's face lit up. 'Is it settled, then? Are we to go?'

'It's not completely settled,' Louis said. 'Not yet.'

Suddenly Elizabeth ran to Sara's side. 'Please, Mama, say we can go! I'm longing to see what London is like – and to see the country. If I could just *once* hunt with a Midland pack, I'd be happy. Imagine how terrible it would be to grow old and fat without ever having ridden to hounds!' She brushed a fleeting kiss on Sara's cheek. 'Do think about it – and say we may go!'

Then she turned and fled. They could hear her calling to David as she ran down the stairs.

Sara stood up, smoothed her long gloves over each arm, and opened the osprey fan out to its full width.

'It seems,' she said, looking at Louis, 'that my mind is being quite firmly made up for me.'

A slow smile spread across his face. Leaning forward, he kissed her lightly on the temple.

'I've always thought I should enjoy the chance of showing you off to London, my love.'

He offered her his arm, and they left the room together.

3

A sense of bewilderment and disappointment crowded in upon Sara all through the party. The guests arrived, and she greeted them smilingly, but always thankful when each one passed on, and she was spared the effort of making further conversation. The rooms filled with voices and laughter; music floated faintly from the marquee, where, as usual, the men were too numerous, and young subalterns – not so much out of politeness, but simply because they had the urge to dance – danced with grandmothers, three times their own age. The women were surrounded by admiring little groups, and Elizabeth, for whom nothing that evening could possibly go wrong, insisted upon splitting her dances in half, to fit in all her partners. She was the complete coquette, without a trace of shyness, and a flush of excitement on her cheeks. David, when he came to ask her to dance, got a laughing refusal; but when the Governor presented himself, she rose demurely and curtsied. There was no thought in her head of splitting this dance!

At last, when all but the few late-comers had arrived, David came to where Sara stood with Louis in the hall. He smiled, and offered his arm.

'Mother has had enough now, don't you think, sir?' he said, looking at Louis. 'If people arrive as late as this, they don't deserve to be welcomed. I propose to take her to the supper-room for something cool to drink. And then perhaps she'll dance with me.'

Louis nodded, glancing about him. 'And I must go and find Mrs Macquarie . . . David, do you suppose I'll have to join a line of officers waiting for the favour of dancing with the Governor's Lady?'

He wandered off into the drawing-room, straightening his gloves, and searching each sofa and card-table in turn.

In the supper-room, David led Sara to a chair and brought her a glass of champagne. It was chilled, and she sipped it gratefully. He talked lightly to her, criticizing some of the more pompous guests, describing with impudent exaggeration, the florid details of the gown worn by the wife of one of the colony's more prominent citizens.

'. . . purple, Mother – with large yellow bows! Truly, even the natives have more taste!'

Then he hurried away from Sara's side to bring a chair for Julia Ryder, who had just entered on the arm of William Cooper.

He called to Bennett for more champagne, and he went off himself
to attend to the serving of some food.

'David does you great credit, Sara,' Julia remarked, nodding
in his direction.

'Indeed, Madame de Bourget, your son is known throughout
the colony as a young man of the *most* graceful manner!' William
Cooper murmured this with heavy flattery.

Julia interrupted briskly.

'I hope this rumour of your going to England is true. The
children all need it, Sara. They shouldn't grow up in this colony
without a notion of what the rest of the world is like. They'll be better for it – all of them. You yourself have earned a few years of
leisure, and so has Louis. You can't expect a Frenchman not to get
restless sometimes for the sort of life he's known once.'

Sara smiled, making a non-committal reply and thankful when
David returned and insisted upon taking her to the marquee to
dance.

'I think I must have been the very last person to know of this
visit to England,' she said to him as they stepped out on to the
veranda. 'In the minds of everyone here, I'm sure we're already
packed and almost gone. And I hadn't heard a whisper of it until
a few hours ago.'

'Oh, Elizabeth has been talking,' David said. 'She's so excited
about it.'

They walked across the grass in silence. They paused at the
entrance of the marquee, watching the intermingling of the scarlet
uniforms with the more sober coats of the civilians, and the soft
colours of the women's dresses.

'How gay we all are these days!' Sara said. 'Twenty years
ago there wasn't a piece of silk in the whole colony as fine as the
most commonplace gown here tonight.' She spoke absently, as if
the memory was something that did not, even remotely, touch
David. Then she drew closer to him, and her voice changed.

'How badly do you want to go to England, David? Louis says
he has talked to you about it. And I want to be quite sure you are
not agreeing just to please him.'

He turned and looked at her directly. 'I want to go, Mother –
very much. And it isn't to please anyone but myself.'

Then he led her forward to join the dancers.

Sara found the same reaction from Duncan when she opened
the subject of the trip to England. She had a few minutes' conversation with him after they finished their dance together. It had
grown almost breathlessly hot, and they strolled to the edge of the

lawn, where the coloured lanterns marked the flowerbeds.

'There's so much I want to do in London, Mother,' he said eagerly. 'I'd like to take some fencing lessons – and go to one of the riding-schools. And there's the playhouse . . . You know, they say if one rides in Hyde Park in the afternoons, you'll see almost all the swells . . .'

She smiled, and patted his hand. 'I'm sure you do. Do the – swells – mean very much to you, Duncan?'

He frowned. 'Not a great deal. But I'd just like to *see* them.'

The hours were long and tedious to Sara until the last couples reluctantly left the marquee, the card-tables and sofas emptied, and the carriages rolled down the drive. They had toasted the New Year in at midnight, when a piper from the regiment had solemnly strode the lawn, his thin, eerie notes drifting across the garden to the silent guests. Two natives, fishing by the light of the moon in the bay below, heard the piping, and were convinced that it was the wail of an evil spirit. Like shadows, they slipped away in their canoe.

The Governor and his party had left at two o'clock, but it was dawn before the general exodus began. The servants went slowly about extinguishing candles; the coloured lanterns along the lawns flickered feebly in the growing light. The supper-tables were being cleared.

Arm in arm, Elizabeth and David climbed the stairs, laughing together over something Duncan had said. Elizabeth's dark eyes had the fixed look of tiredness about them, but her feet moved as lightly as they had done at the beginning of the evening.

'We're going to England . . .! To England . . .! To England . . .!' she sang, as she mounted the last few steps to the landing. The words, in her sweet, high voice, were a stab at Sara's heart.

4

She laid the sapphires carefully in their case, and sat looking at them, not attempting to begin undressing. She no longer fought her disappointment and fear. They would all go to England – that much was certain now. Since Louis first spoke of it early in the evening, she had been waiting for a denial from the children – at least from David. She was counting on his enthusiasm for the work he was doing at Priest's being great enough to fight the attractions of London. It was difficult, looking at the impeccable David this evening, to remember that he wasn't much more than a boy yet. Louis was right, she thought, wearily. She expected too much from both her sons – she expected them to know, as if they too had been through it, the first years of struggle on the Hawkesbury. In time, she told herself, they would learn their own lessons about the price they must pay as owners of property – but they would not be the same lessons as she and Andrew had learnt. Perhaps, after all, a trip to England was what they needed to teach them the value of their possessions here.

She sighed, closing down the lid on the sapphires. Rightly or wrongly, she was committed to making the voyage now. As she kicked off her slippers, she noticed that at last a faint breeze was stirring. But it would probably be gone when she woke again, and the sun beating harshly against the side of the house. Then she remembered that, in the afternoon, she would have to take her place with the crowds thronging Hyde Park, to watch Louis and David race for the Magistrates' Purse. She slipped off her stockings, wriggling her toes, and relishing the softness of the carpet beneath them. She wished she were at Kintyre, or Banon – anywhere that would excuse her from the dust and heat of the Races in a few hours' time.

She was sitting up in bed, sipping the glass of cold milk that Annie had brought, when Louis opened the door and came in quietly. He wore a long, dark red robe over his nightshirt. He moved rather slowly as he came towards her.

'*Mon Dieu!* How old and feeble I must be growing, when a few hours' dancing fatigues me !' He flung himself full length on the bed, lying on his back, with his hand beneath his head. 'And to think I was fool enough to say I'd ride against men as young as David tomorrow.'

'Today,' she reminded him.

'Today – so it is ! I'll not be fit to climb on a horse by afternoon, much less race.' Suddenly he rolled over, propping himself on his elbow to look at her. 'I have it, Sara ! We must invent a serious malady – a fever that keeps me abed, and you must stay to nurse me. I shall lie in a darkened room all afternoon, away from the heat and the noise of those yelling fools. I . . .'

Then a smile crept across his face.

'What is it ?' she said.

'I was thinking . . . that it would be pleasant if you could lie beside me.'

They laughed together, and she reached out to pull his hair, much in the way she had done with David earlier. He jerked his head away, catching hold of her wrist.

'I shall have to subdue you, Madame! You grow undutiful and insubordinate! In fact, I think an afternoon would be well spent . . .' she put the glass down quickly, and clapped her hand over his mouth. 'Enough! I'll have respect . . .!'

He bit at her fingers until she was forced to withdraw.

'Respect is it? That's the trouble – you've always commanded too much of that. I remember . . .'

'Remember what?'

'I remember the first time I saw you, in the cottage of the amiable Nell Finnigan – who, incidentally, has become monstrously fat of late. Never get fat, Sara – it's so unbecoming!' He pulled himself closer to her. 'When I first saw you, I said to myself, "Ah, here is a woman of great passion!" – and I was driven quite wild by the sight of you. But, *Mon Dieu*, you were so wrapped around in your respectability! When you left I remember lamenting that this was New South Wales and that civilization had not yet touched its shores.'

'What do you mean?'

'It's simple! If this had been Paris, or London, after a little wooing, there would be every chance of you becoming my mistress. But, alas, it was New South Wales – and what could I do but wait until I could marry you!'

Abruptly he reached up and caught her shoulders, pulling her down off the pillows.

'It has been worth even marriage to have you for myself,' he murmured, as he kissed her. 'And once married, I was glad the ways of the civilized world hadn't caught up with the colony. I have the most uncivilized notion of keeping you all to myself.'

5

Sara was standing at the rails with Elizabeth and the usual attendance of young officers, watching the finish of the race for the Magistrates' Purse, and she saw clearly everything that happened. She saw the dog break suddenly from the crowd, and dash madly on to the course as the first horses galloped towards him. Louis was fourth, on the outside, and almost on top of the dog before he saw it. His horse started, swerved violently, and fell; Louis was thrown heavily. Directly behind, the next three riders, unable to pull up, rode straight over the top of them both. Another horse went down in the general tangle, but the rider got to his feet immediately, and began to limp towards Louis.

As soon as all the horses were past, the screaming crowd broke past the barriers and raced forward. Sara closed her eyes tightly, and turned away. She leaned back against the rails for support.

They told her later that Louis had broken his neck in the fall. The surgeon said he had probably been dead even before the first of the other horses had reached him.

9

The storm had broken at about seven o'clock, coming at the end of a day of murderous, stifling heat. For two hours now it had rained without pause – rain that slashed against the houses, and turned the streets into soft mud. In the east the lightning still flickered, followed by cracks of thunder, but the worst violence of the storm was past. Out at sea it raged yet; it had a devilish fury, and the waves pounded the headlands at the entrance to the harbour. The township was deserted; its odd, untidy buildings seemed to huddle together before the onslaught of the rain. One moment they lay in darkness, the next they were suddenly bathed in the eerie blue flash of the lightning. There were pale lamps here and there, and the taverns were crowded out; but the streets were deserted. Sydney had the unreal look of a toy town – the mushroom houses had sprung up wherever they pleased along the crooked, winding streets; the shipping tossed about in the bay like a child's boats – and the sea ran wild at its very doorstep.

In a room above the store that still carried Andrew Maclay's name, Sara watched Clapmore begin to take down some rolls of material. She watched him listlessly, feeling unnaturally weary, as if the long days of heat had drained her energy, and the storm coming at the end of it had no power to stimulate her. She had left Glenbarr as soon as the storm was past its height, and had driven alone to the store. She had come straight to this room upstairs, leaving Edwards huddling into the doorway below, refusing to come inside. A young stable-boy held the horses, shivering, she imagined, half with fear of the lightning, and half from the rain, which, by now, must have soaked him through. The decision to come here at this time of night had been forced upon her by the fact that Louis had been dead only two days, and she had no intention of shocking the town by letting herself be seen driving abroad so soon. In the darkened store Clapmore had cautiously answered Edwards's knocking, holding a lantern high, and then quickly throwing back the bolts as he recognized the carriage and its occupant. His red-headed wife came from the back room to bob a curtsy, murmur her appropriate words of sympathy, and then disappear. Clapmore, as soon as Sara told him her errand, went hurrying before her with a lamp up the stairs to the storeroom above.

'I'd have brought them myself, if I'd only known, ma'am,' he hastened to assure her.

'Of course, Clapmore — I know. But there's been so much to think about all day, that I had no time to send a message. When the storm broke this evening I was too restless to stay in the house. I thought this was a good chance . . .'

He nodded, setting down the lantern, going to the shelves and flinging back the dust-covers. For almost fifteen years now he had worked for Sara, and he would just as soon have questioned the coming and going of the seasons as her movements. If she had cared to visit the store at midnight he would have received her, knowing that she had had good reason for what she did.

He brought the rolls forward, laying them side by side, on the big centre trestle table. The black material glimmered dully in the light of the lantern. Sara fingered it . . . black silk, black satin, black bombazine. All of it black, like the draped windows at Glenbarr, like the gown she wore now, and the bonnet. Clapmore spread out more and more of it, until she began to feel that the whole of Sydney could have taken this wretched stuff and gone into mourning for Louis de Bourget. There were gowns for herself and Elizabeth to be made from it, shawls, cloaks . . . Suddenly she could bear the sight no longer. She turned and moved swiftly away to the window.

Clapmore stared after her. 'Why, ma'am . . . !'

She didn't speak. She gripped the edge of the sill, staring out across the deserted wharf, which the store overlooked. Beyond that, in the darkness, were the tumbled waters of the harbour. With the rain she couldn't even see the navigation lights of the ships. For a few moments she gave herself up completely to her sense of desolation and loss. It didn't matter to her what Clapmore might be thinking. For the two days since Louis's death she had been unable to give way to her feelings; there was always Elizabeth to remember, and Henriette. She had determined that they should not be saddened more than was necessary by the sight of her own grief. But she wasn't disturbed by Clapmore's presence; he was hardly more personal than the furnishings of the store itself. She didn't care that he might see the tears glistening on her cheeks.

He had known her since her first years in the colony, he had known her life both with Andrew and with Louis, and he was not so unperceptive that he couldn't guess at her misery and anguish. Louis's death had left her dazed; she found it almost impossible to believe that he was gone. Louis had possessed her body and soul; he had very nearly succeeded in winning her away from the things she had believed she could never put aside – the farms, the ships, the store. For the last two years she knew that she had been madly impatient for David and Duncan to reach the age when they would take full control of their possessions, and her time would be free to devote to Louis. He had been a demanding, exacting and selfish man, but he was stronger than she; he had bent her will to his own, as no one else had ever done.

She sensed the patient attitude of Clapmore, standing by the table with his sober black rolls. It was a good thing, she thought, that he was not a woman, who might have come forward with mawkish, feminine sympathy; who might put a flabby hand on her shoulder and offer her platitudes Louis himself would have abhorred. Men always understood better about these things. If she wanted to weep alone by the window, that was her own affair, and he had the good sense to know it. She wanted Louis back – and she felt that Clapmore would know that too – she wanted his conversation, his habit of being amused at the things this small world took so seriously, she wanted back the elegance, the charm, and the passion that had been his. He had added to each day a spice of excitement and of pleasure, and she must somehow learn not to expect them any longer.

She hoped desperately that her tears would not turn into the kind of sobbing that had racked her last night, because even Clapmore couldn't be expected to stay where he was and not try to do something to help. She didn't want to be rude to him.

Above the noise of the rain she hadn't heard the voices below the window, where Edwards and the boy waited; the sound of the knocker hammering against the door was shockingly loud and sudden. Clapmore turned in a startled fashion, as if he expected the unknown caller to come straight up the stairs. He seemed to be rooted where he stood.

'Better answer it, I think,' Sara said quietly. 'But there's no need to mention to whoever it is that I'm here.'

'Oh, no, ma'am . . . certainly not.' He took up the second lantern, and ran lightly down the stairs.

Hastily Sara wiped her eyes. She straightened her bonnet, and walked quietly – so that whoever it was below would not hear her footsteps – to the landing. She heard the rasp of the bolts being thrown back. Then a rumble of thunder in the distance blotted out the first words spoken between Clapmore and his visitor. She leaned farther over the banister to listen.

Clapmore's agitated voice reached her. '. . . Madame de Bourget is not here, I tell you! You've made a mistake, Mr Hogan.'

'God damn you, I'm not such a fool as all that! I went to Glenbarr, and her son himself told me she had come here. Now I find her carriage at the door, and Edwards . . .'

'Jeremy!' Sara called. 'Jeremy, I'm here!' She started down the stairs. 'Wait, Clapmore, I'm coming!'

The two men came through the store and stood looking up at her. She was greeted by Jeremy's truculent face, and Clapmore's slightly aggrieved one.

'I was only obeying Madame de Bourget's orders, Mr Hogan. I'm sorry if you . . .'

His voice trailed off. Sara, giving him a quick glance, realized that he probably loathed being in the position of having to offer some sort of apology to Jeremy Hogan, an emancipist, while he, Clapmore, had come to the colony a free man.

'Thank you, Clapmore,' she said, as she reached the bottom of the stairs. 'I'll call you when I'm ready, and you can bring the rolls down here.'

'Very well, ma'am,' he said, withdrawing.

Sara waited until he had closed the door leading into his own quarters before she motioned Jeremy to follow her back into the main room.

Half an hour later they still faced each other across the space of floor where the shadows leapt with each flicker of the single candle. Outside the low growl of the thunder continued, and the lightning flashed occasionally. Sara stood erect, twisting a handkerchief between her hands; Jeremy leaned against the long counter, his arms folded and his sodden greatcoat flung back from his shoulders. The pattern of rain on the windows was like the ceaseless tapping of many fingers; every now and then they heard the stamp of the horse's hooves, and the scrape of Edwards's heavy boots as he took a turn along the length of the sheltered store-front. His shadow, thrown through the big windows by a light in the house diagonally opposite, marched across the floor between them. It fell on the kegs and barrels, the cheeses, the scales; it darkened the rolls of calico and cotton, the sides of bacon, the piles of boxes. It was almost like the swing of a pendulum between one and the other.

'So that's how it is, Sara,' Jeremy said, breaking a long silence.

'Yes,' she said, flushing slightly with annoyance at his tone. 'That's how it is! – as you put it.'

The shadows marked the heavy frown he wore.

'I can't believe it,' he said. 'I can't believe that you'd be so crazy as to throw up all you have here for some mad whim.'

'I've told you till I'm weary of telling you, Jeremy, that this is no mad whim. Louis wanted it – and I fought him over it until he made me see how necessary it was for the children. And as for throwing up what I have here – that's absolute nonsense! A year or two, and then I'll be back. David and Duncan will, I hope, come back with me gladly, because by that time they'll know that their lives here hold something more worthy of love and labour than England can offer them.'

'And you, Sara – what of yourself? What will England have for you?' His voice had a rough edge to it, although he kept it low.

'For me? Very little, I think, Jeremy. I must be with Elizabeth of course, and then . . .'

'Yes?'

'I want to be on hand to prompt the return as soon as David and Duncan begin to think of it. They forget so easily . . . They'll fritter their time away, and the memory of Kintyre and Banon and Dane Farm could grow very faint if I were not there to keep bringing them up.'

Jeremy regarded her in silence again. Then his eyes left her, and watched Edwards's silhouette moving across the two curved windows. Outside, the Maclay name-sign creaked a little in the wind; the candle fluttered wildly as a sudden stronger gust forced a draught under the door.

At last Jeremy spoke, turning to look at her. 'Why don't you tell me the truth?'

She stiffened. 'What do you mean?'

With a loud smacking noise he crashed one fist into the other. 'Oh, damn you! Do you think I'm taken in by your sentimental notions of going to England just to be with the children? You may often have forced me into doing things I didn't want, Sara, but you've never yet succeeded in hoodwinking me!'

Angrily she took a step towards him. 'Tell me exactly what you mean, and stop this quibbling!'

He was breathing heavily. 'You're going to England because of that fool, Richard Barwell. Isn't that it? You've always wanted him, and now he's practically yours.'

She almost recoiled before his words. 'How dare you say that to me! How dare you say it when Louis is only dead two days!'

He tugged at his coat, dragging it back on his shoulders.

'I think I'd say anything to you . . . now that I know what is really in your lying little soul! God, when I think of how long I've tried to believe that you were different! I made excuses for the way you behaved. I told myself that you acted as you did because the hardships of your life had taught you to look after yourself first. When you came to Kintyre, I hoped that Andrew's love for you, the way he worked to give you the things you wanted, might chip away some of that crust of self-love. You assumed a softer façade, but you didn't really change – not ever! For years I've pretended to myself that you've altered – but you haven't. Here you are, now, planning to have yet another prize that you've always hankered after!'

'Don't you preach to me, Jeremy Hogan!' she cried passionately. 'Don't you set yourself up to be *my* conscience! Anyway, what do you know of women like me? Haven't you always told me that you were brought up among women who had soft voices and slept in soft beds? Don't you come here like a twice-a-year parson and tell me what I must do, and mustn't do! You think you know me through and through – you've always thought that – but I'm telling you right now that you couldn't even begin to understand what sort of woman I am. You've only known two kinds – the kind who played the piano in your mother's drawing-room, and the convict strumpet you're living with now! And I'll tell you something else . . . I'm sick to death of having you order me about – I'm sick of your moralizing and your preaching! Ever since I've known you it's always been, "Sara, you must do thus, and thus!" Or, "Sara, Andrew would expect you to do this, and this!" And all the time you've been rotten with jealousy because I didn't fall into your arms when you wanted me. Long ago, at Kintyre, you confessed that to me . . . and I've never forgotten it.'

'Be quiet!' he snapped. 'You're talking like a street-woman!'

'Do you think I care about that? Listen to me, Jeremy. I don't have to ask anyone's permission for what I'll say or do. *Do you understand that?*'

She flung out her hands. 'Oh, I've many reasons to be grateful to you, many reasons – and I'll not forget them, either. But my gratitude doesn't give you the right to tell me how I'll behave. From the day Andrew died, you've tried to tell me how to live my life. Well, I haven't lived it as you wanted – neither has it turned out to be the disaster you predicted. I've had a pretty full life –

but if you had your way I'd still be sitting over my needlework, weeping for Andrew. Louis knew the sort of life I wanted – and *that's* why he married me. Do you understand now?'

He picked up his hat and riding crop.

'Yes. Certainly I understand – very clearly.'

'Well?' she demanded.

He walked up close to her, and stared into her face.

'I understand it all so clearly, that I'm going out of here and I'll marry the first presentable woman I can find. The only thing I'll ask of her is that she has no ambition, and no thoughts beyond her own fireside. I want her to be meek and pliable and biddable. She'll be, in fact, as different from you, Sara, as it's possible for a woman to be. Because, if you're sick to death of me – then I can tell you that I've had my belly and guts full of you, and I hope to God I never lay eyes on your kind again!'

Then he turned and strode across the floor, cramming his hat on his head, and flinging open the door. Edwards, leaning against it, staggered back wildly, clutching at a large keg to keep his balance. The door closed with a mighty crash, setting an assortment of frying-pans, hanging from the ceiling, swaying and tinkling. Edwards stood with his mouth open a little, staring up at them dumbly.

'Mr Hogan has gone, Edwards,' Sara said, unnecessarily. 'You'd better go and tell Clapmore he can come out now.'

PART SIX

I

Sara opened her eyes slowly to the sight of her familiar bedroom in the house in Golden Square, on a morning in June, 1814. Every morning for six months past she had awakened with just the same sense of expectancy, as if this day, above all others, might have something different about it. But within a few moments the feeling of disappointment and indifference had fastened upon her again. The room was dim with the drawn curtains, and she had no idea what the time was, but already the sounds of the London day had begun to penetrate – the street cries, the rumble of heavy carriage wheels, the shrill voices of servants gossiping together as they swept the area steps. These were the sounds with which she had grown familiar but never resigned to – and each morning they struck her ears as if for the first time. She stared up at the silk canopy above the bed, and knew that her resentment was entirely unreasonable; she wasn't any more pleased with herself being forced to admit it. With an almost savage movement she reached out and pulled at the bell-cord.

As she lay waiting for the hurrying footsteps to come in answer to her ring, she thought of the day ahead of her. It wouldn't be much different from most other days – there was correspondence to be attended to, perhaps a visit to her shipping agents, a drive in the Park, and then to end it a party in Lady Fulton's house, in St James's Square. She would hardly be in bed again before dawn. Until a few weeks ago she had been quite willing to accept this routine, hardly questioning it, because it was new to her, and, in its way, exciting. The sharp contrast between the London she now inhabited, and the London of the cheap lodging-houses in and about Fleet Street and the Strand, which she had known with her father, was somewhat of a balm for the boredom and impatience she sometimes felt. To rent one's own London house, to keep a carriage and good horses, to have liveried servants on the box when one drove in the Park – all these things, the marks of belonging in a fashionable world, would have seemed no more than an idle fairy-tale to the young child who had served as a dressmaker's apprentice an almost forgotten number of years ago. She remembered that child vividly, and she remembered how her mind, sharpened by the need to scrape some sort of living from Sebastian's precarious earnings, had seized upon every opportunity towards advancement, and, as quick as a monkey, she had seen her chances and taken them, until the day Sebastian's debts had finally forced them into the coach bound for Rye. Now Sara herself was a respected patron of one of the most fashionable of the dressmakers, but, unlike the other patrons, she had a curiously naïve habit of paying her accounts promptly. She had a strange feeling sometimes, that the young Sara was at her elbow when she attended receptions and parties, giving those same appraising glances to the furnishing of the houses, and the smartness of the carriages in which the guests arrived, and the quality of the clothes they wore.

She turned over in bed and sighed. Once she had taken a chaise – hired, because the servants would have wondered at this mistress's errand if she had ordered the carriage – and driven to Villiers Street, off the Strand. She took it all in carefully – the tall, narrow houses, the street-pedlars, the dirty children, the dogs. This was the street Sebastian had told her she was born in; but it evoked no particular sense of familiarity. She didn't stay long – the young Sara seemed to have deserted her at the crucial moment – and a richly-dressed woman in a waiting chaise excited too much comment in that outspoken neighbourhood. She returned to Golden Square with the feeling that she had lost something definitely precious to her.

A trim, middle-aged maid tapped softly, and opened the bedroom door. She went directly to the windows and drew back the curtains; the clear, bright sun of a summer morning flooded in.

'It's what you might call a fine day, ma'am.'

'Yes, Susan,' Sara returned indifferently. She sat up to take the light shawl the woman had brought for her shoulders, and then the comb, which she ran through her hair.

She took the breakfast tray and rested it across her knees. 'The children . . .?' she asked. 'Are they about – or have they gone out already?'

'Mr David and Miss Elizabeth are still here, ma'am. I believe Mr Duncan has gone, though. And Miss Henriette has just begun her lessons.'

Sara nodded, and waited with an unaccountable impatience for Susan to finish her fussing, and be gone. They exchanged a little more conversation about clothes for the day's programme, and then she was left alone. She sipped her coffee thankfully.

It had been easier than she believed to slip into her present position in London. Louis was more than accurate in his estimation of what London would have to say of her. She could not, of course, escape the tales that were told of her past, but she soon found that there were many people among the smart set who were not anxious to look beyond her obvious wealth, and were then willing to cultivate her society. She knew well enough that most of her new acquaintances – the people whose invitations she received to dinners and receptions – did not belong to the top bracket of the circles in which they moved, but she weeded them out, and accepted the most attractive. To all but the royal circles, elegance and wealth seemed to be the only arbiters of one's acceptability, and in these two factors Sara held her own. Stories of her convict origin, naturally, circulated; but shrewd guesses had been made at the extent of her fortune, the half-forgotten history of Louis de Bourget revived, and the power of money had, in many minds, turned her from a convicted felon into the innocent victim of a judicial blunder. On most occasions she was very well received; she was admired, and made much of. Bligh, now a Vice-Admiral, and living in Lambeth, came to call on her; he seemed delighted to see her again, and, in his embarrassed manner, expressed deep sympathy over Louis's death. He took her to visit his friend and patron, Sir Joseph Banks, who, as president of the Royal Society, wielded an immense influence. To Banks, Sara was something of a colonial oddity, and she appeared to amuse him; but more important, she had brought back with her Louis's meticulous collection of botanical specimens, and, for the sake of possessing them, Banks – the scientist before all else – was prepared to receive her into his house. Those who met her there were soon given the information that she had been pardoned, instead of serving her full sentence. Sara had good reason to remember, in those first months, that she had once done something to earn Bligh's gratitude.

Richard Barwell had played his own part in introducing her to the fashionable world in which he moved. He was now in full possession of Alison's fortune, had taken a town house on the edge of Green Park, and was leading the sort of life to which he had always seemed eminently suited. On his return to England from New South Wales, he had joined Wellington's army in Spain, and he carried the glamour of that successful campaign about with him – added to that, he had a reputation for gallantry, earned by a shoulder wound which would not respond to the treatment of the army surgeons, and was responsible for his being sent back home. He had been one of the great Wellington's soldiers, and he wore the distinction with becoming – but, Sara suspected, not very sincere – modesty.

Richard had greeted her, on her arrival in England last November, with undeniable enthusiasm, coming to Portsmouth to meet

her, and later in London helping in her search for a house. The
Golden Square house had been finally rented through a friend of
his – a Lady Fulton, sister of an earl, and wife of an Irish peer,
who never himself appeared in London, and whose estates were
squeezed dry to meet her expenses. The house belonged to a
cousin of her husband, and Sara shrewdly guessed that Lady
Fulton was herself collecting a commission on the rent. In a practised, skilful fashion she assumed a proprietary air towards Sara,
and more especially towards Elizabeth. With a full knowledge of
what was happening, Sara found herself paying for the parties and
dinners Lady Fulton gave to introduce Elizabeth, David and
Duncan to suitable friends. In a way, this relationship between
herself and Anne Fulton pleased Sara. There was no pretence that,
in other circumstances, they would have been friends; it was simply
that they were useful to each other. Anne Fulton had important
connections, and for the sake of having some of her debts paid
with de Bourget money, she was quite prepared to use them. She
was a friend of that exquisite grandmother, the Marchioness of
Hertford, the *confidante* of the Prince Regent. Sara had once
attended a reception in the house in St James's Square, when the
Marchioness arrived unexpectedly with the Prince. They had
strolled around, played cards, eaten supper, laughed and gossiped
with some of the guests; then, just before they left, the Prince
had indicated to Lady Fulton that he wished Madame de Bourget
to be presented to him. Something of the fabulous story London
society had woven around Sara had been whispered to him, and
his bulging blue eyes were full of amusement as he questioned her
about the colony, which, he said, seemed to be quite beyond the
reaches of the civilized world. He was unpopular, hated by many,
but his taste in the elegant and graceful was unsurpassed in Europe,
and the fact that Sara de Bourget had found favour with him, even
for a brief five minutes, was commented upon and remembered.
With faintly-flushed cheeks she withdrew from his presence reflecting that, in some circles, the cut of one's gown and the arrangement of one's hair seemed to matter more than the sentence of a
judge in a court of law.

The months of winter advanced to spring and summer, bringing the news of Wellington's great victories north of the Pyrenees,
the capture of Paris by the allied armies, Napoleon's abdication,
and his imprisonment on Elba. Europe drew a breath of relief,
and settled down to long-drawn-out quarrels over the spoils of
war. But to London, this June, came the Czar Alexander of Russia,
and the King of Prussia, attended by their victorious generals, on
visits of state. London's welcome to them was wild and exuberant.

The very height of the season's shows were the official entertainments given to them, but in a lesser degree the whole capital celebrated. The Czar was mobbed whenever he appeared; crowds waited all night in the streets to glimpse him. With equal fervour they hissed the Prince Regent's carriage when it passed by.

Sara put aside the tray and lay back on her pillows. It was exciting to even breathe the air of London this summer, but she was appalled to find how weary of it she'd grown – all the endless round of drives and dressmakers, dinners and entertainments. It seemed so purposeless as she faced each new day of it.

Her thoughts were interrupted suddenly by Elizabeth's appearance, after a brief tap at the door. She entered with a rustle of silk, and wearing a new bonnet. She came to Sara's side immediately, and bent to kiss her.

'It's a perfect morning,' she announced. 'Just about as warm as a spring morning at home . . .'

'Home?' Sara said.

'Don't tease,' Elizabeth answered, wrinkling her nose. 'You know what I mean. It's the sort of morning when I long to be riding at Banon.'

Then she stood and surveyed the remains of the breakfast, and began to pile butter on the last piece of toast. 'How is it,' she said, biting into it, 'that you manage to get the only unburnt toast that comes out of the kitchen in the morning?'

'I probably ask nicely for it,' Sara answered casually.

Elizabeth flung herself down in a chair, licking her fingers. 'I don't think I want to go to Lady Fulton's party this evening,' she said.

Sara's eyebrows went up. 'Oh . . .? Lady Fulton says she's particularly asked some young people she thought you'd all enjoy meeting.'

'Oh . . . them!' Elizabeth gave a shrug of exasperation. 'I know their sort. Young men who won't look sideways for fear of spoiling their neckcloths. And besides . . .'

'Besides what . . .?'

'David says he's not coming. I'd counted on him being there. When I run out of talk with these silly creatures I count on him being about to help me.'

'Well . . . you should know David well enough by this time,' Sara said as casually as she could manage.

Elizabeth fingered her dress, straightened the set of her bonnet and looked down at her slippers, carefully avoiding Sara's eye. In the past months Sara had been made aware of her step-daughter's growing attachment for David, and had been equally aware that

David treated her as he had always done, with a mixture of affection and playfulness. She grew afraid as she considered the situation that could develop between them; she knew Elizabeth's nature well enough – she had all of Louis's passion and possessiveness, and a formidable determination to have what she wanted. All through the months here Sara had watched her, and saw her keep her head amidst a surge of flattery and attention that would have made most other young girls breathless. In a few years Elizabeth would inherit the first part of the fortune Louis left to her – a fortune swollen by the careful investments of his London agents. She had a spirited beauty about her that attracted attention wherever she went. Sara knew that Elizabeth was fully aware of all this – and the fact that, if she wished it, she could make a titled marriage here in London. She was aware of it, and at the same time she seemed to understand that it was of very little use to her. For so long as David remained unimpressed she seemed to take little pleasure in her money and her pretty face.

That face now wore a sadly discontented look under the pale yellow bonnet. She twisted on the chair and sighed, looked at the clock, and bent to make certain once more of the smooth fit of her stocking. Sara felt that in some way she was failing Elizabeth. She had spread before her all the things she imagined a young girl delighted in – gave her clothes and an unstinted round of entertainment. But it was obviously not what Elizabeth wanted. Soon after her arrival in England she had gone on a visit to her Gloucestershire relations. Since it was winter, she had bought two magnificent hunters, and had expected to remain until the end of the hunting season. After four weeks she was back in Golden Square, and there had been none of the exhilaration about her Sara had expected. She had little to say about her hunting, and less about the relations. She had come back quietly, flinging herself into an extravagant orgy of clothes-buying which Sara guessed as a futile compensation for whatever had gone wrong. Later David mentioned casually that Elizabeth had written to him from Gloucestershire with an invitation for him to come and hunt also, and he had refused it.

'About this evening . . .' Sara began again. 'Did David say why he wasn't coming?'

'No . . . he merely said he didn't think Lady Fulton would be offended so long as I went. It seems there's something else he prefers to do!' And as she spoke, Elizabeth's hands gripped the edge of the chair tightly, and she scowled.

'Well . . . you don't *have* to come,' Sara answered reluctantly. 'I expect I can make excuses for you both.'

'Good! Well then, that's settled,' Elizabeth said briskly.

Suddenly Sara wanted to smack her – to drum into her a few of the manners that Louis would have expected from her. Louis would never have stood such behaviour in a young girl, and Sara knew she should put a stop to it somehow. But Elizabeth was not her own daughter; she had a mind and temperament which only Louis himself could have dealt with successfully. Then she looked again at the other's miserable face, and repented of her impatience. In the uneasy silence that fell between them, Sara wished she could have gone and put her arms about her – but in her present mood Elizabeth would have resented it furiously.

With relief Sara listened to the footsteps in the passage, and then her feeling faded as David tapped and put his head round the door.

'Good morning, Mother.'

He walked round the side of the bed, seating himself on the end of it and eyeing the tray. 'I see Elizabeth has got here before me and finished the toast.'

'Since you all make such a habit of coming, I can't think why you don't have breakfast here and be done with it. Where's Duncan?' she added, in the same breath.

'Riding in the Park,' David said carelessly. 'I must say he chooses a very unfashionable hour for it.'

'Oh . . . you make me tired!' Elizabeth burst out. 'Duncan is the only one of us who has the sense to go when there's room to ride. There's such a crush in the afternoons – and still everyone continues to go. As stupid as sheep!'

'My dear Elizabeth, if you want to call yourself a sheep you may, but I . . .'

'Oh, hush!' Sara cried. 'Really, I shall have to ask you not to come in here unless you can stay ten minutes without quarrelling. It's too childish . . .'

David leaned over and patted her hand. 'What a nuisance we are to you . . . and yet if you banished me from this room I should feel obliged to do something desperate.'

Sara looked from one to the other with a sick feeling in her heart – from Elizabeth's discontented face to David's bland and non-committal one. She was brought up sharply against the realization that they had both altered alarmingly since their arrival in England, and she felt that long ago she had lost control of the situation. They were growing like everyone else in London – fed on a surfeit of pleasures until they were too tired and bored to care what became of them. Look at them now, she thought angrily – sprawling here, both of them, in her bedroom, at the time in the morning when they should have had other things to occupy them, picking at one another irritably, and yawning as they looked at the clock. At Glenbarr, or Banon, such a thing could never have happened. In the colony David's time had been fully taken up with his own duties, and, in a lesser fashion, so had Elizabeth. She wished desperately, as she looked at them, that they had never left New South Wales. Six months here had very nearly succeeded in ruining both of them – and in a further six months they'd hardly be fit to return to the colony, even if they wanted to. Look at David – the decisions he made these days were over matters no more important than the cloth his coat should be made from, or which of his invitations he would accept, and which decline. Occasionally he went on visits into the country to the homes of acquaintances he made, and when he returned Sara questioned him fearfully, wondering if he was becoming too attracted by the life of the English country gentleman. Was he beginning to think of his life in the colony as too dull and too hard-working by comparison with what he saw here? It was a bitter thing for her to have to question whether any son of Andrew's might be fighting shy of work.

Until this time she had been reluctant to admit what a disappointment David was proving – but this morning, coupling him with Elizabeth in her thoughts, she saw it more clearly than ever before. She wondered if it was her own fancy, or was he beginning to adopt the languid airs and speech fashionable among the young dandies; did he care more now for the fold of his neckcloth than for what was happening to Priest's or Dane Farm? Where was the ambition she had hoped to discover in him? He seemed all too content to accept the world as it was, instead of striving to shape it more to his own liking, as Andrew had set out to do. If this was what money did to one's children, she thought bitterly, then it would have been better if they had never moved beyond the first modest prosperity of Kintyre.

And yet, in his very aloofness there was power. It would only need him to say firmly that he intended to go back to the colony, and Duncan – and probably Elizabeth – would follow him unquestioningly. This was one matter in which Duncan was still too young and unprepared to take the lead. David had the power to change it all – and yet the weeks went by and he said nothing, did nothing.

'Are you driving this afternoon?' Elizabeth asked her idly.

'I thought I might go around to Fitzroy Square to inquire how Captain Flinders is . . .'

David straightened, looking at her directly. 'Flinders . . .? Not Matthew Flinders, Mother?'

'Yes. I've run him to earth finally . . . They've moved so often it's been like a paperchase to follow them.'

'What's the matter with him . . . is he ill?'

'He's dying, David – dying of a disease they call "the gravel". He's in pain the whole time, and only half-conscious these past weeks. And there's very little money . . . He's kept himself alive just to see his book through the press, and I begin to doubt now that he'll live to see a finished copy.'

Elizabeth's face wrinkled with concern. 'Oh . . . how sad! Is he married?'

Suddenly David broke in. 'Yes . . . I remember now. He *is* married. He used to talk about her – Anne, her name was, and he had married her only about three months before he sailed in the *Investigator*. God . . . how many years ago can that be? I was a child then.'

'It must be about thirteen years ago,' Sara said thoughtfully. 'Poor Flinders . . .! As you say, David, he left almost as soon as he married Anne, and he didn't see her again for more than nine years. That was the time he spent charting the coast of New South Wales – and the six and a half years as prisoner of the French, on Ile de France.'

'The book of the voyage . . .?' David said. 'It's completed, you say?'

Sara nodded. 'Two volumes and an atlas. But they've stolen his greatest pleasure, even from that. He called it *A Voyage to Australia*. But they've insisted it should be retitled *A Voyage to Terra Australis*. If ever anyone deserved the honour of naming the continent it's Flinders, but it seems even that is to be taken from him.'

'Australia . . .' Elizabeth murmured. 'How soft it is . . .'

'Whom do you mean by "they"?' David burst out. '*Who's* stopping it?'

Sara shrugged. 'The Admiralty, the Royal Society . . . Sir Joseph Banks is against it, and his word seems to be law where Flinders's book is concerned.'

David frowned heavily. 'So . . . the Great South Land belongs to the Admiralty, does it? And the man who mapped it counts for nothing. He's given his life to putting their blasted continent on paper, but he's not permitted to name it . . .'

He got to his feet, and strode to the window, his hands clasped behind his back rigidly. 'It's the same stupid sense of officialdom

that ruins everything in New South Wales. The Colonial Office is
ten . . . fifteen years behind the most progressive of the settlers,
but still sheafs of restricting orders keep coming from Government
House. Control . . . Control . . . keep everyone bound in tightly.
Look at the question of the sheep. The colony could send England
every pound of merino wool she could use, if only they'd give the
settlers as much pasture as they need.'

'But they're expanding all the time, David,' Sara said.

'Expanding . . .!' he repeated. 'Timidly pushing a few miles to
the north and the south! The Colonial Office won't spend any
money, and so we're all doomed to stagnate on the edge of the
country, until the sheep and cattle eat us out of pasture. I tell you,
it's damnable!'

If Sara had dared she would have smiled for the pure joy of
hearing him talk like this. Not for months had he been roused to
such a degree, and it seemed weeks since he had even mentioned
the colony. She began to wonder if perhaps this very point he
raised was the reason for his disinterest. Had he begun to lose
hope in the future of the colony? He had been given land that was
already cleared and prosperous, and it was not sufficient for him –
the quiet, dull farms needed no gust of energetic planning to help
them. With the exception of Dane Farm, they were well run and
paying good profits while he was still a child. She wondered if he
truly believed the picture he had painted of the future – the population and livestock growing within the limits of their coastal strip,
until there was no room for them all.

'The mountains, David . . . Have you forgotten that a way has
at last been found to cross them?' she said quietly. 'Surely you
can't have forgotten all the letters we had about Blaxland and
Lawson going off with D'Arcy Wentworth's son, and finding a
way through?'

'Of course I haven't forgotten,' he said impatiently. He turned
to face her, and he looked angry. 'And I've been waiting ever since
to hear more of it . . . but there's been nothing. All right . . . I
know Charles Wentworth found a way through the mountains, but
we had that news last January, and there's been not another word
since. It's a nine days' wonder. And what is the Government doing
about it? Precisely nothing. Charlie Wentworth says they saw excellent country from the ridges – But do the Colonial Office direct
that a road be made, so that settlement can begin? – not they!
It would mean that a little section of the community would move
out beyond the control of Government House, and that would
never do. Shall I quote the *Sydney Gazette* to you, Mother, on the

subject of the discoveries of Messrs. Blaxland, Lawson and Went-worth? It called their trek a "trackless journey into the interior", and described the country they saw as one "which time may render of importance and utility". That's the enthusiasm of the Government for you! That's the reason why men like Flinders must break their hearts and their bodies over official stupidity.'

He scowled. 'I tell you it makes me sick to think of it.'

Then he became aware of Sara's startled expression, and his own features relaxed. 'I'm sorry, Mother. I didn't mean to shout.' He gestured expressively with his hands. 'I think I must have a walk and get rid of some of my ill-humour.'

He looked down at Elizabeth. 'Since you've already got your bonnet on, you might as well come with me. It'll do you good. I notice you're not much in favour of walking these days.'

She got to her feet eagerly. 'Yes – of course I'll come!' With misgiving, Sara watched the slow radiance that had begun to shine on her face.

2

Richard Barwell's carriage came to a halt before No. 14 London Street, Fitzroy Square. The sun of the June afternoon was not kind to the mean-looking street, with the rows of shabby brown houses, the paint peeling and chipping from most of them. Farther along a family was moving out; their rolled bundles of mattresses and linen were displayed in their poverty to all the world. The children who made the thoroughfare hideous by day with their increasing noise, had gathered about the removalist's cart, fighting and tumbling over the shabby furniture standing on the pavement. But the arrival of the smart carriage, with the liveried coachman and footman on the box, attracted instant attention, and with whoops they descended upon it to watch for the occupants to alight.

A saucy imp of a girl, about ten years old, wearing a soiled mob cap, came close to the door and peered in.

'Well . . .' she announced to her companions. 'If it isn't the Czar of Russia!'

Shrieks of laughter greeted this remark, but the rest of the children stood shyly back, retreating even farther as the footman climbed down off the box and went to pull at the ancient door bell. After some time a neat, tired-looking woman appeared. Richard opened the door of the carriage and got out. The woman crossed the pavement towards him.

'Good afternoon,' he said. 'I've brought Madame de Bourget

with me – we've come to inquire about Captain Flinders.'

The woman peered uncertainly into the carriage, but as Sara got down, her expression altered. 'Oh, yes . . . I remember,' she said. 'You're the lady who's come before to see the Captain and Mrs Flinders. Well . . . I shouldn't go up now if I were you. Mrs Flinders, poor thing, came down ten minutes ago, and said that he was sleeping at last. She left the little girl with me, and stepped out for some air.'

'How is Captain Flinders?' Sara asked.

The woman shook her head. 'Bad, ma'am – bad! Now that the book's off his hands at last, he's sort of given up. He doesn't seem to know what's happening to him half the time with the pain, and the doctor doesn't do any good. Terrible, isn't it,' she observed, 'what diseases these sailors pick up in foreign parts?'

Sara nodded. 'Well . . . thank you. We'll not disturb Captain Flinders, then. Perhaps you'll tell Mrs Flinders we called?' As she spoke she took the covered basket which the footman had lifted from the carriage, and handed it to the woman. 'Mrs Flinders may find these useful.'

'Oh, yes, ma'am . . . And who shall I tell her came?'

Sara turned back. 'Oh . . . tell her Sara de Bourget and Captain Barwell.'

The woman nodded, repeated the names, stumbling a little over Sara's, and then stood with the basket in her hand to watch the carriage go.

As they turned into Fitzroy Square, Sara touched Richard's arm. 'Would you mind if I didn't come with you to the Park, Richard? It's stupid of me, but I don't think I can face the crowds. If there's the least chance of the Czar driving out, they'll be there in their thousands.'

'Certainly – I'll tell Simmons. Where would you like to go? Shall we drive through Marylebone – or Primrose Hill?'

Sara shook her head. 'I think I'd prefer to go back to Golden Square. Hearing about Flinders has left me in no mood for idling away the afternoon. In a way, Richard, I'm glad we couldn't see his wife. I feel almost as if I'm insulting them by handing over my basket. Flinders deserves so much better treatment from the Admiralty – and yet they're so short of money that they can't refuse even such things as my miserable basket. This morning David . . .'

Richard put his head out of the window and gave the coachman directions to return to Golden Square. He settled himself back against the seat again.

'What was that about David?'

'He was talking about Flinders so wildly this morning. I had never realized before that he felt so strongly about the mismanagement of these affairs. He ranted on about the way the colony was being run – shouted at me. One would have thought he hated it.'

'Perhaps he does – have you ever tried questioning him about it?'

Sara shrugged. 'It's as easy to question David as to question the Sphinx. He's self-sufficient – far too much so. Except when he has one of these outbursts, he's my pleasant-mannered, smiling son, and one can never even guess what's going on in his head. He never speaks of it, and yet I feel his discontent growing with each week we have been here. Elizabeth too – they're so restless, and dissatisfied.'

'Could you be to blame for that, Sara?'

'I? – in what way?'

'Your own discontent, my dear. It's a very catching malady.'

She twisted around to stare at him closely. He sat where the sun came fully on his face, showing the lines that were now deep about his eyes, and the grey in his hair – the streak above the old scar on his forehead was pure white. But he still had the bronze of the long summers in the colony, and his spare-framed body seemed scarcely to have thickened at all since the Romney Marsh days. He was remarkably handsome, and despite the stiff shoulder, which was the legacy of the Spanish campaign, he moved with grace and ease, and still sat a horse superbly. For Richard these days life was a gracious and pleasant affair; his good humour was boundless because there was never anything to disturb it. He had been welcomed back to the drawing-rooms of his old acquaintances with a warmth that might have turned anyone's head; he merely smiled and accepted his popularity with a modesty which he must have known was intensely becoming to him.

Altogether, Sara thought, he was such a man as women fell in love with by the score – the born charmer and favourite. But he was a disappointment to most of them in the fact that he was by temperament too lazy to pursue flirtations once they threatened to become serious. With all this dangled before her eyes, Sara couldn't understand why she didn't marry him. He had wanted that, and kept pressing it, almost since the day she had arrived in England; for one reason or another she had never answered him finally. He had joked good-humouredly about her avoidance of the question. But then, he could afford to be good-humoured and patient; his life spread before him like a golden afternoon, and there seemed little need for hurry when dalliance was so pleasant. No longer full of impulse, he seemed content to wait. She wondered if perhaps it was his contentedness that disturbed her – it was almost as if loving her had become a habit which he couldn't take the trouble to shake off. She knew well enough that if she had not appeared in London as a widow, he would eventually have married someone else. It was not in Richard's nature to live long without the absorbed attention of some woman. But she *had* appeared, and there was enough of the passion of long ago left to them to make him ask her immediately to marry him.

For six months she had hesitated – and each day that passed in which David made no mention of returning to the colony brought her closer to agreement. She knew she was going through the phase in which the unobtainable – suddenly put into her hand – was not, after all, so desirable. All her life she had loved Richard, and she loved him still. But in more than twenty years she had learned to analyse that love, and to know precisely how strong it was. It was not any longer the consuming force it had been for the young Sara, nor could it ever again cause her the anguish she had suffered when he had first come to New South Wales. It could not be weighed against her love for Kintyre, for Banon, and Dane Farm. But her feeling for Richard had its undisputed place in her life, and one that she could never deny.

She held Richard off, and waited for some move from David. If he was going to disappoint her, and treat his inheritance with in-difference, then she would take the consolation which marriage to Richard could give her. She envisaged the life that lay before her – in the small and elegant town house and the Devon estate. In that, and in Richard himself, there would be enough distraction to ease the pain of watching David turn into an absentee landlord.

Yet, she was equally certain that if David had suddenly declared, with any degree of enthusiasm, that he was going back to the colony, she would have gone with him gladly, and Richard would have assumed once more the role in her life that he had always played.

She knew well enough what he meant when he called her dis-contented.

'Discontent? . . .' she repeated the word slowly, not quite know-ing how to meet his charge.

He stirred, and leaned towards her; stretching out and taking possession of her hand quite firmly. 'Sara, you must know what causes your restlessness. You won't settle your future, and you play about with your own emotions and mine like a child with a toy. Why don't you marry me quickly and put an end to this indecision? Once you've made up your mind there won't be any place for restlessness.'

She shook her head. 'Not yet, Richard . . . not yet. I must give David more time – and Duncan and Elizabeth.'

'More time . . . time?' he echoed after her. 'What are you talking about? If you're thinking of settling their futures out of hand before you marry me, you're making a great mistake, Sara. You just can't seem to see that they're no longer children, and they can make their own decisions. Why do you hold on to them like that? Let them go free – they won't thank you to wait your own happiness on their convenience. If you would once settle your own life, you'd find they'd quickly enough settle theirs.

'If David wants to go back to New South Wales – then let him,' he added. 'Duncan also. Elizabeth will, of course, marry here. What is there all the fuss about, Sara?'

'But you don't understand . . .'

'No, I don't,' he agreed. 'I don't pretend to understand your attitude towards them. Whether they stay here or return to the colony, they're well provided for. They cause you no worry – and you're free to marry any time you want. Besides that – I'm growing more than a little impatient.'

'I'm sorry, Richard. I'll try to decide about it soon.'

He smiled as if he were humouring a child's whim. 'Very soon, I hope, Sara. A long and leisurely wooing is pleasant enough, but I must watch that I don't become rather ridiculous by my very faithfulness. After all, we've wooed each other for the greater part of our lives. Isn't it time it came to an end, my dear?'

The carriage turned into Golden Square, and she withdrew her hand from his gently.

'Yes, Richard. Very soon.'

The footman flung open the door with a flourish. Richard got out first and handed her down, waiting with her until her own front door was opened.

She took her leave of him feeling as if she had made an escape.

3

David came to the head of the stairs as Sara entered the hall. Something about the changed expression of his face as she glanced towards him halted her; slowly her hands reached up to the ribbons of her bonnet.

'David . . . what is it?' she said quietly.

'We've been waiting for you, Mother. Could you come into the drawing-room?'

She nodded, and with the ribbons dangling loose, hurried up the stairs towards him. He smiled at her, and she could sense the excitement about him, but his face was serious enough. Inside the drawing-room Duncan got to his feet when she appeared, and Elizabeth, who had been standing by the window, turned and came towards her.

'Mr Macarthur's been here, Mama. He's just left — we thought you'd be back from the Park much later.'

Sara laid aside her bonnet. 'Macarthur? I'm sorry I missed him. What news does he have from the colony?'

Macarthur had become an occasional visitor at Golden Square, though the servants had strict instructions never to admit him if Admiral Bligh happened to be calling at the same time. The court martial which had cashiered Johnston after the rebellion had been unable to try Macarthur. He could only be tried in New South Wales, and he knew that Macquarie had instructions to prosecute him, and that there was no hope that he could escape the verdict of guilty. Therefore he remained eating his heart out in self-imposed exile, and through letters from his wife and colonial contacts in London, vicariously living the life he longed for again. Sara often shook her head over the sight of his energies wasted on such trifles.

'Plenty of news,' Duncan burst out. From a side-table he picked up a letter, and brought it to Sara. 'This is from Mrs Ryder, Mother — it came by the ship that brought Mr Macarthur's mail. He's wildly excited about it — Macarthur is, I mean. He came straight round here directly he'd read his letters.'

Sara began to break the seals. 'But *what* is it?'

David straightened from his leaning position against the mantelpiece. Sara's hands dropped nervously into her lap as she looked at him; never before had David appeared like this — with a light of passion and excitement in his face that might have been Andrew's own. His cheeks had a pinched-in appearance, the corners of his mouth pressed in firmly to a thin line. She drew in a sharp little breath, and half rose from her seat.

'Well ... *what is it?* Tell me!'

'The mountains . . . Macquarie sent Surveyor Evans to follow Lawson's route across them. He went down into the plains on the other side and travelled a hundred miles beyond the point Lawson reached.'

'The land . . . what's it like?'

'As good . . . better than the best on the coastal side of the

mountains. Like laid out park-land – grass three feet high, and none
of the barren patches that occur on the other side. They went
on for as long as their supplies lasted, and they could see no end
to the fertile country. No signs of the desert that people predicted.'

Duncan tapped her shoulder impatiently. 'Read Mrs Ryder's
letter, Mother. She probably talks of it.'

Sara smoothed it out hastily, and the stiff crack of the paper was
the only sound heard in the room. She skimmed the first pages,
which were a collection of small items of news she knew their
impatience would never permit her to read aloud. Finally she came
upon it – Julia's reference to Evans's expedition. With a feeling of wonder she noticed that her hand was shaking as she began
to read.

*'We are in a great state of excitement here over the expedi-
tion which the Governor sent to follow Lawson's route over the
mountains . . . No doubt remains now that they have been
crossed, and that the fine land extends beyond the place Evans
reached . . . The* Gazette *published Evans's report on the journey. I have it by me as I write, and I quote Evans's statements.
". . . this soil is exceedingly rich and produces the finest grass
. . . the hills have the look of a park and grounds laid out; I am
at a loss to describe this country; I never saw anything to equal
it . . ." People say the new country teams with game, and Evans
caught enormous fish in the westward-flowing river which he
followed.*

*'There are authoritative reports that the Governor does not
mean to hesitate over the construction of a road. They say that it
will be no more than a year before the country is opened up
for settlement. This surely is what we have dreamed of all these
years, Sara. James and myself, of course, will not leave Parramatta; we're far too old for such pioneering now. This new
country is for the young ones . . .'*

David broke in suddenly. 'There – that's it! The road! That's
everything. Without the road the land's as useless for settlement
as if it had never been discovered. Think of it – grass three feet
high. What flocks we'll be able to run on that!'

Sara ran her tongue over her dry lips. 'Does that mean . . . you
want to go back, David?'

'Back? Of course I'm going back. I tell you, Mother, that I
mean to have my own land now. Something that no one but myself
had ever worked on – in ten years one could make a fortune from

wool – twenty years one would be a rich man.'

'What . . . what about the other properties?' Sara said weakly. 'Don't they count for something?'

He gestured impatiently. 'They do very well, but with them I should only be following the same old routine that Father worked out years ago. They belong to the old pattern when agriculture was as important as sheep. When I get my own land I don't mean to grow more than I need for myself – over the mountains it's *sheep* country.'

Suddenly Duncan smacked his hand resoundingly against his thigh. 'By God, David, I'll race you for it! Give me that ten years and I'll show you who's the best sheep farmer in the colony. Ships to take the wool to the London market . . . as much land as one wants for the flocks. By God!' he said again, 'this is something worthwhile.'

Sara gave a nervous little laugh. 'To hear you both talk, one would imagine the farms on *my* side of the mountains amounted to nothing more than a few acres for growing vegetables.'

David turned, and answered her quietly. 'It's not that at all, Mother. Everything that you and Father have achieved will give Duncan and myself the money to start in the way we want. But that achievement is still *yours*. If I slaved my guts out for the next forty years I would never believe I had done anything with those farms. They were yours from the beginning, and they always will be. We're not ungrateful – Duncan and I. But there's no crime or ingratitude in wanting something of one's own. I want more satisfaction from life than merely holding together what you've created. Beyond the mountains there's a whole continent – and it will belong to those who go and take it!'

She nodded, and looked down at the letter again. But she wasn't reading it. Back into her mind had come the recollection of that bright morning when the *Georgette* had prepared for departure from Table Bay. Then Andrew had used words almost the same as David's. He had started with a few pounds' worth of credits, and livestock won at gambling. David and Duncan would have far more than that – but what mattered was that they were willing to start before the first rough cart-track over the mountains had become a good road. Like Andrew, they wanted to go and find their lands, to settle for themselves where their flocks should pasture.

Vaguely she heard Elizabeth's voice break in.

'I mean to come back with you – you can't leave me here.' David and Duncan wheeled round at her words. Almost together they answered her.

'Of course you'll come with us!'

Again Sara sought the place in Julia's letter. She felt a choking sensation in her throat as she found the paragraph.

... this soil is exceedingly rich ... I am at a loss to describe this country. I never saw anything to equal it ...

4

'That finishes it, Richard,' Sara said as she laid down her cards. 'I've lost quite enough to you already.'

He smiled broadly. 'I never mind your being in debt to me, my dear. It gives me an incredible feeling of superiority. Besides, after we've had supper I'll give you the opportunity of winning it back.'

She shook her head. 'I said "finish", and "finish" it is! In any case after supper I want to talk to you – seriously.'

A mock expression of concern spread over his face. 'I tremble. When you're serious, you're a very formidable woman.'

He made the remark lightly, and she joined in the laughter that followed, but as they ate supper together, it kept returning to irritate her. Of course, Richard was right. To attempt to be serious over anything but cards in a gathering like this was futile. Lady Fulton's house was thronged with a fashionably dressed crowd, some of the women still displaying the jewels they had worn for the occasion of the Czar's visit with the Regent to the opera in the Haymarket that evening. They had brought with them the fantastic story of Princess Caroline's arrival, a laughable figure in her diamonds and rouge. She had caused acute embarrassment to her husband, the Regent – in which the Czar had seemed to take malicious pleasure – and had been wildly applauded by the audience. It was a story that the whole of London would know by morning, and it made a delicious morsel for supper-time gossip.

But presently Richard caught her hand and led her towards the door of the supper-room. 'I can see plainly enough, Sara, that my efforts to amuse you don't meet with much success. You had better come and tell me what has happened since I left you this afternoon to cause that expression. It isn't becoming to a beauty to keep frowning so.'

He took her along the hall, and opened the door of a small room that Anne Fulton used in the mornings. It was the only room in the house, so far as Sara could judge, that hadn't been decorated to the last inch of space; with its collection of odd

furniture it achieved an air of peace and intimacy completely
lacking elsewhere. Richard indicated a small sofa for her to sit
on, and drew up a fat, padded stool for himself.

'Now . . . this tale that you must tell,' he said. 'What is it?'

She began uncertainly. 'We had a visit from John Macarthur
this afternoon . . . and a letter came from Julia Ryder.'

'Yes . . . ?'

Telling him wasn't easy, but by degrees she built it all up —
her fears over what David would decide about his inheritance,
and his ability to influence Duncan in the same way. She told
him of the months of unease when the conviction grew stronger
that he would never return to the colony, or, at best, return unwillingly . . . her sharp sense of disappointment, the frustration
of searching for a sign of enthusiasm and never finding it. Then
at last the news of the crossing of the mountains, and the change
it had wrought in him.

Richard gave her a hearing in silence, patiently listening while
she groped for words to describe the scene in the drawing-room
in Golden Square that afternoon. He regarded her thoughtfully,
the points of his dark eyebrows almost meeting as he wrinkled his
forehead.

'And what you're going to tell me now is that you're going back
to New South Wales.'

She nodded.

'You're making a mistake, Sara. You can't tie them to you like
that. They'll resent it — and hate you for it. If they want to build
their own new worlds they should be left to do so themselves. Let
them at least make their own mistakes.'

'I've no intention of following them into their bright visions
beyond the mountains.' She shook her head. 'There's quite enough
on the coast side to occupy me — and I think they won't be averse,
now and again, to learning something about farming when they
visit Banon and Kintyre. But my decision doesn't really concern
them, Richard. It belongs to me. I knew quite certainly this afternoon — whether the mountains had been crossed or not — that I
couldn't remain here any longer. There's an itch for power in
me that will never be satisfied by what England can offer. I
grow stifled here and breathless, I'm so cluttered by people and
traditions that I live in mortal dread of tripping myself up.
And none of this I had the courage to admit until this afternoon.'

Richard patted her hand rather absently.

'You'll think me a very faint-hearted suitor, Sara, that I don't go on my knees and beg you to stay. In fact, to be truthful, my dear, I'm not sure that there isn't some relief for me in this. One so often wants what is bad for one – and I think that may be the case with me. You're not my sort of woman, really. But because I've wanted you since I was a boy, it's now become a point of pride not to admit my own mistake. You've still too much energy and spirit for the sort of man I've grown into. I begin to suspect that in old age I'm going to turn into a rather pompous bore and I'll need some cosy, comfortable wife who won't mind in the least. I suppose Alison suited me far better than I knew.'

A smile spread about Sara's lips.

'This is hardly what I expected, Richard – that I should refuse your offer of marriage, and find you no more than mildly disappointed over it.'

He gave a short laugh. 'I'm not going to say I'm sorry – at least we can be honest with each other now. It will do you good to have a little set-back – you've always had men to adore you, and I don't doubt there'll be others in the future. But I can't tell you truthfully that it will break my heart if I don't have you to disturb my comfortable, pleasant life.'

She threw back her head and laughed. Puzzled, he watched her for a few seconds, and then their own ludicrous position struck him. He began to laugh also; he reached forward and took both her hands, and pulled on them, so that they both rocked a little.

'Oh, Sara . . . Sara! *That's* what I shall miss when you're gone. The cosy, comfortable wife of my imagination will never be able to laugh with me like this!'

While she still laughed, he leaned forward and kissed her fully on the lips. Her arms went about him in an embrace, and the laughter was stifled by the kiss.

They were still in each other's arms, when Lady Fulton opened the door. She took in the identity of the occupants in a glance, and stepped back swiftly.

'Do forgive me,' she murmured as she closed the door.

Richard released her slowly. 'How very tiresome! She'll talk about it, of course . . . and when they discover that you're *not* going to marry me, I shall be pitied by the whole of London as the disappointed lover.'

5

The first light of the summer dawn lay on Golden Square when
Sara returned to it that morning. A heavy-eyed manservant admitted her; she paused on the step for a brief moment to salute
Richard, standing still by the carriage. Then the door swung
to with a gentle click, and the hall was dim once more. She took
the lighted candle the manservant held, bade him goodnight, and
started up the stairs.

In her bedroom it was dark; she set the candle down on the
dressing-table and moved to the windows to draw back the curtains. The soft grey light flooded in; she stood looking down into
the square. In a few months this house and this square would be
part of her memories of an interlude – memories edged with gilt
and parcelled together neatly.

'I'm going back . . .' she whispered aloud. 'I'm going back.'

That cruel, austere country had won David, Duncan and
Elizabeth, as surely as it had won her. It demanded a strange
and compelling loyalty, and tolerated no other loves. One loved it,
or hated it . . . but was never indifferent. And once loving it,
one could have little patience for the claims of other places. People
like Richard hated it – and it was harsh with them. From her,
who loved it, it had taken Andrew, Sebastian and finally Louis.
Impartial . . . severe . . . and lovely when one learned where to look
for its beauty.

She sighed, and stretched to relax her taut, excited body. A
faint little wind stirred above the housetops. She stepped back
from the window and turned around.

Across the room she could see her reflection dimly in a tall
pier glass. She tilted her head a little, and stared critically. Then
she began to walk slowly towards it. When she stood before it
she stretched out her arms and gripped the frame. Slowly she
began to examine what she saw – her face with the hair drawn
back and dressed elaborately, her shoulders and neck which the
cut of the high-waisted gown revealed, her slim body behind the
straight, stiff fall of the brocade.

'Sara . . . Sara Dane,' she said quietly to the reflection. 'It's
time you started to remember that you'll soon be old.'

Then the corners of her mouth curved into the beginning of a
smile. 'But you've some time left yet.'

THE END

BLAKE'S
REACH

PART ONE

I

Jane pushed herself forward in the hay, craning to get the last glimpse of the coach before it vanished along the road that led south to London. It was a day of spring unexpectedly dropped into late February; all morning there had been showers, and the air was sharp and clean. From the heights of Hampstead Hill the towers and roofs and steeples of the distant capital were clearly visible – a glittering city, and for Jane, who had never seen it at closer hand, one possessed of a devilish, compelling enchantment, which gave her no peace.

It wasn't that life here at The Feathers was dull, or that they didn't hear enough of London and its doings. A coaching inn on the road to the North from London, placed strategically at the end of the long upward pull to the Heights, would never lack business. They heard the gossip of the capital almost as soon as it reached the coffee-shops in Fleet Street. The excellence of its food and service was well known, and, in its time, The Feathers had served many important political figures, as well as the men and women who made up the world of society and the Court. The Feathers was nothing if not cosmopolitan, carrying out its business as it did, almost on the fringe of the great city. But the fringe, for Jane Howard, was not enough.

Especially now it was not enough. London seemed to be caught in a fever of uncertainty and unrest, and the travellers brought it with them to The Feathers. Now, in the second month of 1792, the fever was mounting. Its centre and starting point was the Revolution in France, carried on in bloody haste and passion in the strange, unfamiliar names of Liberty and Equality. In the minds of most people who stopped at The Feathers to eat and rest – and if the London papers were to be believed, in the minds of most Englishmen – there was no doubt that, sooner or later, they would go to war with France, and in that thought lay their disturbance. War was many things – but most of all, war was change.

The English could think back to their own taste of revolution, when the American Colonies had fought and defeated them; its memory was still bitter. But this business in France was another matter, and uncomfortably close to home. It was difficult – no, impossible – to imagine their own King, 'Farmer George', stubborn and difficult as he was, with increasing and longer periods of madness upon him, being taken prisoner by his own people, and even threatened with death. Such things did not happen in England. But it was a time when strange ideas were drifting about, and it led to restlessness, and questioning. It wasn't only the travellers who stopped at The Feathers who talked of the disturbances and the new ideas. They were on the tongues of the villagers as they sat over their ale. Now it was possible to hear mention of war and revolution mixed with the peaceful talk of crops and weather and the enjoyable scandals of the countryside.

Jane heard the talk as she refilled tankards, or helped Sally Cooper, the innkeeper's wife, serve an elaborate dinner in one of the private rooms. She listened, and thought back on what she heard, and it only served to increase her own personal restlessness. The times were stirring, or was it simply, she wondered, that spring was upon them unseasonably?

She settled back in the hay, and loosened the shawl she had thrown about her shoulders. It was spring, and yet another coach had continued its journey on to London, and, as always, left her behind. She looked at the black oak beams above her head and sighed – a rebellious sigh that only went halfway to expressing what she felt.

The loft was as still as a church mid-week, but Jane guessed that she wouldn't be left long to enjoy its stillness. Sally frequently turned a blind eye to her absences, forgetting to notice that the key to the outside storeroom was gone from its hook in the kitchen. But within the hour a coach was expected from London, bound for the North, and the usual rush to serve the travellers and get them on their way would begin. Jane knew well she couldn't be spared, and so when Sally's deep voice calling her name came floating across the stable yard, she would descend the ladder reluctantly, and exchange the smell of dust and apples and hay for the stronger smells of brandy sauce and pork slowly roasting on the spit before the fire in the kitchen.

Jane didn't dislike The Feathers – but it irked and frustrated her to be continually on hand to serve and help to speed on the travellers, constantly watch their departures to places she had never been, to have to stay while they moved on. The worst times were when coaches from the North started on the last stage of their journey south to London; her heart followed them with a badly-concealed longing and envy, and in the kitchen she would bounce the copper pots on the range, or knead the dough, her arms covered with flour to the elbows, with unnecessary energy. These were the times that Sally's three daughters, Prudence, Charlotte and Mary, had learned that Jane's temper was not to be trusted, and they stayed clear of the sharp side of her tongue.

It wasn't possible to live in a coaching inn, especially one on a road as much travelled as this one, and not share a little in the lives and personalities of the passengers who stumbled wearily from the hard-benched coaches at all hours through the day and the night – the long twilight evenings of the summer or the winter nights when the horses came into the yard caked with mud, and icicles hung inches long from the carriage lanterns. Jane had seen and observed them all . . . the humble ones, the curates in shabby black or the more prosperous parson with tight gaiters, merchants' clerks, governesses – careful of their dignity even when travelling in public coaches – sailors going home on leave. The rich rode in their own carriages, some of them velvet-lined and silk-curtained, the ladies wearing large hats and clutching miniature dogs on their laps, the gentlemen with waistcoats of wonderful colours, and hands that flashed with rings. Jane's eyes were on them ceaselessly as she moved about her tasks, her mind storing up information about worlds she knew only by words dropped carelessly as she poured the wine. Every kind of person came to The Feathers, and The Feathers endeavoured to serve them all to suit their needs and the size of their purse. The demands for food and ale, for fresh bed-linen and warming pans were endless. Jane's body was as strong and supple as a cat's, but by candle-lighting time her legs ached dully, and she understood why middle-aged Sally dropped on the kitchen settle with sighs of exhaustion. If you had to work – and Jane wished she hadn't – The Feathers was a good place to be, with abundant and good food, and brisk gossip to go with it. She always enjoyed the gossip – a whispered piece of scandal about the young baronet who sat over his wine in the front room, tart observances on the manners and airs of the lady whose coach had just rolled away. In a sense gossip was information, and Jane had a great curiosity about things that even remotely touched her life.

But there were times when she had thoughts that weren't to be gossiped about – that couldn't be shared with Pru and Lottie, or even with her favourite, Mary . . . thoughts that disturbed her, and made her restless, thoughts that caused her eyes to follow the coach down the road with greater keenness. There was no way of communicating these things to Mary, though she had the feeling, sometimes, that Sally knew them without being told. On these days

she waited until the quiet of the afternoon, then she crossed the
yard, ignoring the glances of the stable-hands, and climbed the
ladder to the loft, where the loose hay made a couch for her. Here
she felt secure to do as she pleased – free to enjoy the hint of
warmth in the breeze that came through the gap in the wall, to
kick off her heavy shoes and wriggle her toes against her coarse
stockings – free to close her eyes and think aloud the thoughts that
couldn't be spoken elsewhere.

Today her mind followed a track which in the last months had
become routine – though with the remembrances of last night's
angry scene with Sally and Tim Cooper to sharpen it. Yesterday
had been the twenty-sixth of February. Sally was too busy to keep
close track of passing time, but, by her rather loose reckoning of
the year Jane had been brought to The Feathers as an infant,
February twenty-sixth, 1792, was Jane's eighteenth birthday. Her
dark brows knitted sharply over this. At eighteen most other girls
had married and already christened their first squawling infant at
the parish church. Eighteen was almost on the shelf . . . yet here
she was – if not a beauty by the standards of some of the ladies
who called at the inn, then at least more than able to draw and
hold the glances of the men – with no one she considered worth
marrying in sight.

It was over this Tim had quarrelled with her – Sally less violently
taking his part. It was well known in the village that Jane could
marry Harry Black at a day's notice, if she would have him. The
trouble was that she didn't want him – and she didn't know what
she wanted in his place.

The thing that puzzled everyone, Jane included, was that Harry
Black stood for such treatment as she gave him. It wasn't as if he
were of no importance, or had nothing to offer her. Harry was a
giant of a man, famed for his strength through all the neighbouring
villages; he was blond, thick-necked, blue-eyed, with enormous
hands which were slow and heavy in their movements. If Harry
leaned back in a chair it broke beneath his weight; when he wound
a clock it inexplicably came to pieces. He had regular, good-looking
features, he bore himself erectly and was proud of his physical
appearance. He was also boastfully proud of the success he had
with women. Apart from this, Harry was the only son of Thomas
Black – and in the village this meant something. Tom Black owned
the most prosperous farm in the whole district, and had built himself a fine red brick house which was almost as large as the one
belonging to Sir George Osgood; he owned and operated a brewery,
and there was talk that he was doing some trade with merchants
in the City of London. Tom Black was a man of means and

authority, and Harry was his only son.

It followed that Jane was a very foolish girl to ignore Harry as she did. Tim Cooper went beyond that, accusing her of other and less creditable ambitions.

'It's bad blood!' Tim had raged at her last evening. 'You'll turn out like that whore, your mother!'

'Hush! Tim, hush!' Sally said quickly. 'What Anne Howard does is her own concern . . . and Jane's no need to account for it.'

Tim bit at his pipe angrily. 'You've high-blown notions, girl . . . notions that only belong with them as can afford them. Get yourself a dowry before you look beyond Harry Black.' Exasperation seemed to choke him. 'Why . . . why, who are you, when all's said and done? Nothing but a bit of a serving-girl at an inn, and Harry could look much higher if he choose – and find a girl with a penny or two in her pocket, to boot!'

Stung and irritated by pressure which had been building over the last months, Jane became haughty. 'Tom Black started as a common labourer, and I'm more than well enough born for the great Mr Black's son! My mother and father were gentle-folks!'

'Your mother's a whore . . . and your father died in prison! And don't you forget it, miss!'

Jane writhed in the hay at the memory of it. They always spoke of bad blood when her mother's name was mentioned. They used the words with certainty, too, for the whole parish had known Anne's history from the day she had arrived at The Feathers with Jane to leave her in Sally's care. Anne had been twenty then, a vivid young red-head whose clear beauty made strangers gasp. She was the widow of Captain Tom Howard – 'Merry' Tom Howard they called him – who had died four months ago in the Fleet prison, where his creditors had finally put him. Two things were plain – Anne hadn't been bred to work, and she had no money. A young baby was obviously a hindrance in this situation, so Jane was brought to The Feathers. She made no secret of where the money came from for Jane's support : already she clung on the arm of the first of her lovers, and she wore the silks and velvets she loved. There were pearls about her throat.

Anne was as gay and exotic as some brilliantly plumaged foreign bird; she was clever with cards and conversation – good-natured in a careless fashion, and generous in a foolhardy, spendthrift way. No one ever saw her wearied or subdued; late at night when others were heavy with wine and sleep, her wit and spirits were as sharp and pointed as over the noon-day meal. Anne hated to waste time in sleep – she was happiest to see in the dawn with cards and good company.

Over the years she appeared occasionally at The Feathers, and Jane came to look forward to her visits as she did to the coming of spring at the end of a hard winter. She was dazzled by Anne's beauty and vivacity, by the clothes she wore, the sound of her laughter; as she moved and talked she carried with her the breath of a gay, cosmopolitan world. Anne was completely selfish, but that was a failing Jane found easy to forgive. Hopefully each year Jane examined herself in the mirror to try to discover a closer resemblance between them; when she remembered she aped Anne's manners, and the way she spoke. It was safe to imitate her; Anne had been well born, and her air of breeding was unmistakable. What puzzled and frustrated Jane was that Anne would never, even under pressure, speak of her family and background. It was the only aspect in which Anne ever disappointed her daughter.

Sally Cooper was disapproving of Anne's mode of living, and what she called her 'giddyness', and yet she was quite as helpless as Jane under Anne's spell. They both left their tasks unattended to listen to Anne's lively chatter. The talk was of men, always different men. They came and went in Anne's life, rich and powerful men – some that were merely rich, and a few that attracted her for their own sakes, and were no profit to her at all. She could be prodigal of affection, as well as greedy and grasping for material returns. Men there were always about Anne – but none married her.

Sally would shake her head. 'You're no businesswoman.'

'But I'm lucky at cards,' was Anne's reply.

When Anne fell in love finally she blossomed into a new and startling beauty, a mature beauty; even a stranger, watching her speak of John Hindsley, would have known that she was in love. He was a viscount, and reputed to be one of the richest men in England. He paid Anne's debts, and gave her a small, elegant house in Albemarle Street; she wore exquisite jewels. She came, radiant, one day to The Feathers. One look at her face told Sally and Jane her news.

'Johnny and I are going to be married! Lord knows, I don't deserve to have him love me – but this is one time when I'm lucky in love as well as cards!'

The luck ended too soon. They read in a newspaper that Hindsley had been drowned in a river on his estate in Hampshire. There was no word from Anne, and she didn't appear at The Feathers; they felt her anguish in her silence. Then months later came a brief letter. Jane had never forgotten its opening lines.

Two weeks ago I gave birth to Johnny's son. I have called him William. Johnny was drowned two days before the day we had set for our marriage, so William doesn't inherit.'

Sally looked at Jane with stricken eyes. 'Hindsley's bastard – what will she do now, in Heaven's name!'

It was two years before Anne came back to The Feathers. Still beautiful, still with her restless vivacity, but there was a shadow of weariness in her laugh, and her eyes were not so warm. She did not bring William with her, and when Jane asked about him, she replied briefly, 'He's a darling child – and too precious to be jolted about in a carriage just yet.' Jane, diffidently, asked if she might come to London to take care of him. Anne gave a little smile and the warmth returned fleetingly to her face. 'You're too young to take care of William – but soon you shall come to London to pay us both a visit.'

Jane lived through the next years in memory of that promise. She applied herself with greater zest to the lessons that Anne paid for her to have with old Simon Garfield, the retired schoolmaster. Books and learning bored Jane somewhat; she could read and write with fair ease, and add up the accounts at The Feathers. Beyond this she had no accomplishments – but she paid rapt attention to Simon because it had suddenly become vitally necessary that she should be able to speak with the refined accents of the ladies who stopped at the inn. Anne should not have cause to be ashamed of her when the summons came to go to London. Simon, who disliked children, particularly girls, tolerated her, and taught her with a certain efficiency, even trying to give her a smattering of Latin, because he was well paid to do it. The lessons stopped when Jane was fourteen, because by that time Simon was owed so much money he refused to open a book again with Jane until settlement came from her mother. Jane had almost stopped hoping that Anne would send for her.

About the same time one of the real delights of Jane's life vanished also. Years before, generous in a flush of prosperity, Anne had sent a pony, Jasper, to The Feathers. Anne herself was passionately fond of horses, and rode superbly. It was the only accomplishment of her mother's Jane copied with ease. She was without fear of horses, and sometimes in the early morning she rode, in borrowed breeches, astride Jasper on the Heath. When the money from Anne began to dwindle, Tim Cooper good-naturedly paid the feed bills rather than curb Jane's pleasure; Jane attended herself to Jasper's grooming. But in the end even Tim's patience ran out, and Jasper had to be sold. For Jane there was nothing now but the stolen joy of mounting, for only a few minutes, some of the horses stabled for the night at The Feathers.

The money grew less and less, and finally stopped. Anne wrote that she had been ill, and that the doctor's fees were enormous. So as the months went on, Jane fell gradually into the role of a serving-girl at The Feathers. She had learned from Sally how to cook, to sew, how to churn butter; now she learned how to sell and serve a good wine to a discriminating traveller, and to substitute an inferior one when she knew it didn't matter. She already knew how to groom and harness a horse, and from years of listening to it, she also had a fine command of stable language, which she was careful to keep hidden from Sally. She became, in a sense, a fourth daughter to Sally and Tim – sharing the hard-working routine of The Feathers, sharing the bed of the eldest girl, Mary, and sharing, also, the undemonstrative affection they each had for the other.

Anne wrote only rarely, always complaining of lack of money. Vaguely Jane still cherished the notion that some day she would be asked to come to London. Anne still lived in the house Hindsley had given her – there must be some way, Jane reasoned, in which she could be of help to Anne, even if it were to take the place of a servant. She read and reread the few books that were the relics of the days with Simon Garfield; she tried desperately not to let her voice slip into the broad accents of Sally and her daughters. She grew weary of the waiting, conscious of her developing body, conscious of the stares and the talk of the men she served at The Feathers, forever conscious of the time passing. She was always at hand to witness, with longing, the departure of the coaches for London.

The day after her eighteenth birthday she lay in the hay and thought that there must be something more for her than to marry and live and die without stirring outside this one village. There must be something more than Harry Black – but she didn't know what it was to be, or how it would come.

2

Motionless, Harry Black watched the door of the storeroom. His broad, heavy shoulders rested against the stable wall. His attitude suggested that it would have been an effort of will to straighten himself and move, but his mind was busy as it seldom was, flooding with images which brought a flush to his fair skin, and made him swallow jerkily.

He had glimpsed Jane as she entered the storeroom. Without thinking he had started to follow her – and then retreated, cursing his own hesitancy. He wiped his clammy hands against his breeches, and swallowed again. Every instinct urged him to go to her, to take advantage of her being alone to press the claims he had been making for these six months and more; he told himself that if he went now he might be permitted to touch her, hold her body close to him, might kiss her, might even wring from her a promise to marry him. He thought of all this, and still he stood rooted to the spot. He felt himself tremble, and wondered dully what had happened to the strength which made him feared and respected by every man and boy in the village. His determination and his strength both seemed turned to water before this slight girl, whose glance held only contempt for him.

Harry clenched his fists, and his wanting her was a slow pain which burned through him. His mind never encompassed tenderness or love; he knew nothing of his feeling towards Jane except that he wanted to possess her. He had no knowledge of her as a person, for they had never talked together with any intimacy. All he knew was the evidence of his senses. He knew the sensuous, provocative lines of her body, the faint fragrance of her skin; for many hours, as he had sat in the kitchen of The Feathers, his eyes had followed her movements, rested on her shining red hair, her soft young curves.

There were times he hated Jane. She was making a fool of him – he was Harry Black, the only son of a man who could have bought up most of the village; he was strong, and he knew that women called him handsome, and came easily to him. There were plenty of girls in the village who were comely and were willing to walk on the Heath at night with him – he was proud of the fine son he had fathered a year ago by a girl over at Thornton. There were even girls who could have brought him a little money in marriage, and who were fitting matches for Tom Black's son. There were many possibilities open but like a fool he must turn his eyes on a serving-girl who had no possessions, who had not even the dignity of being the innkeeper's daughter. Not a penny to her name, the child of a high-class whore. But her lips were red and sweet, and she walked like a queen. He knew she was conscious of no honour in having his offer of marriage made to her. Her rebuffs filled him with rage, and still she attracted him beyond his power to understand.

Voices in the stable close by reached him, and he jerked his head round. He did not want the two young stable-hands to come out and find him. They would know why he was there; they laughed at him behind their hands for letting a serving-girl play him as if she were a great lady. They knew his long hours of silent waiting in the kitchen – and they knew that Jane didn't walk on the Heath with him. It was almost as bad as the taunts his own father gave him.

He straightened suddenly, and walked to the door of the store-room.

Inside, the afternoon light was soft, and there was no movement to tell him of Jane's presence. He shut the door with what was, for him, unusual gentleness.

'Jane! . . . Jane!' His voice was hoarse as he called.

He hadn't expected an answer from her. His eyes flickered over the accumulation of junk littering the floor, then he went quickly to the ladder that reached to the hay loft. When he was halfway up, her head appeared suddenly over the edge. She was lying close to the opening; her greenish eyes stared at him hostilely.

'What are you doing here?'

'Damn you! I can come if I want to.' He had forgotten that he meant to be gentle with her. He climbed the last rungs, and knelt there, for the moment speechless with anger and emotion.

'Why can't you leave me in peace!' she said irritably. 'My head aches, and my legs ache, and in two minutes I'll have to be in the kitchen to help start the supper . . .'

He looked at her, and his rage made him want to slap that scornful little face. He made a vague, ineffectual gesture towards her; she behaved as if she didn't see it. Those strange green eyes of hers under dark upward-slanting brows, were fixed on him un-movingly. She was a beauty – they said she looked just like her mother, who had captivated one of the richest men in the country . . . like mother, like daughter. He wondered again, as he had often done, how she would be in bed. It was an image that stirred per-petually and pleasurably in his mind, and to see her now propped up in the hay evoked it strongly. It was always said that the red-headed ones were fierce. He hoped it was so.

Jane watched him carefully, watched his tongue flick over his lips. His blond, good-looking face was flushed; she could even see the pulse at the base of his heavy throat leaping. She had seen his gesture, and now he shook his head quickly from side to side, as if to thrust away her words.

'Jane . . .'

She hated the harsh sound of his breathing. She put her hands on the floor and pushed herself back a foot or two.

'Jane, they told me it was your birthday yesterday. I've brought you . . .' He thrust his hand into his pocket. 'Look what I've brought you!'

In spite of herself she craned a little, but he kept his fist closed. He saw her action at once, and some of the tension left him. This sign of interest from her put him in the position of superiority he should properly have held over her. He closed his fist more tightly. 'Do you want to see it, Jane – do you? Come here and I'll show you.'

She was immediately wary, and the look of indifference closed down on her face again. 'I don't care,' she said shortly. 'It's nothing to me.'

'Isn't it?' Suddenly he opened his hand. In it lay a tiny locket of blue stone that Jane imagined must be turquoise. He began to swing it on its fine gold chain.

'Pretty – isn't it pretty? Would you like it, Jane?'

She said nothing; her fascinated gaze rested enviously on the locket. Her small wardrobe held nothing in the way of adornment, and this was the first time in her life any had been offered to her. She pictured herself wearing it, and treasuring it. With all her heart she wanted to stretch out her hand and take it. Then she glanced from it to Harry's face, and recognized his air of confidence.

'No – I wouldn't like it.' She drew her knees up under her chin, and turned her head away with a gesture of finality.

The action was a last goad to Harry; he flung the locket into the hay. He felt that he hated her more than he had ever hated any thing or person in his whole life – because she scorned him, because she looked untouched, and yet her body was a passionate living thing, and her hands and lips were strong and exciting. He wanted to force himself on her, and then be finished with her; he wanted to tear down, violate, use, even destroy.

'Slut . . . little bitch.' Very deliberately he pronounced a string of obscenities.

She looked back at him, her head darting round in a swift movement. For the first time she felt fear. Her lips puckered in an attempt at a smile; it was a grimace which showed her teeth.

'Harry . . . don't take on so!' She attempted to placate him. 'You shouldn't have bought the locket – your father will be angry . . .' Her voice trailed off. He didn't even hear her words. She watched him begin to crawl towards her – slowly as if he didn't care how long it would take to reach her, because he was no longer uncertain.

She looked around her, and there was no escape, because already she was too close to the edge of the loft, and Harry was between herself and the ladder. The looming bulk of his body was full of menace; she knew she had made the mistake of treating him once too often as a fool who could be laughed away. He came on towards her with a kind of quiet purposefulness. At the last he moved swiftly. He threw her back on the hay as if she were a featherweight – angrily and cruelly.

The world seemed to slide towards darkness as she felt his great weight press upon her – her whole vision was filled by him, the sunlight blotted out, the sweet scent of the hay no longer in her nostrils. She could smell the male smell of him; her lips tasted of his. Then there was another taste; there was fresh blood in her mouth from the wound his teeth inflicted. A helpless rage swept over her, rage that she had so misjudged him, rage that all her foolish, impractical dreams had ended like this, and that she would be Harry's wife, married with haste and resentment because of the fear of having his child – or even if there were to be no child, Harry would only need to tell Tim Cooper what he had done to her and Tim would see her wed as soon as was decent. She tried to cry out, but only a harsh croak came past her lips; his weight made it nearly impossible to breathe. She poked at his eyes, tugged savagely at his hair, but he didn't seem even to notice it. Clumsily he grasped at the bodice of her gown, tearing it swiftly to expose her left breast; she felt his lips urgently against it; his thigh moved and pushed harder into hers. She fought to keep his hands from her skirts, but he shook her away, all the time plucking at her petticoats and stockings. Then she felt his fingernails against her bare flesh, and there was pain. Her breast also hurt, and she wondered if his teeth had cut her. She closed her eyes, and imagined a whole life-time of this – pictured herself gradually learning to respond because there was no satisfaction elsewhere, and because the future held nothing different.

His weight pressed on her unbearably. She opened her eyes again and gave a last, desperate heave sideways. Her movement was unexpected, and he rolled with it. For the space of a second or two his bulky frame seemed to be poised. Then he started to grab at her frantically; he lifted his arms, and grasped at her shoulders for support. She sensed what was happening, and flung herself swiftly backwards from the edge of the loft. His hands slipped off her. He thrashed wildly in the hay, but he had no agility to maintain balance, and he was already more than halfway over. A flurry of hay rose in the air as he disappeared, and she heard his body strike the ground below.

For a moment she lay where she was, drawing in great mouthfuls of air, feeling the sudden coolness of clammy sweat breaking all over her. Then she rolled over and peered down.

Harry was directly beneath her. The fall seemed to have stunned him; he had lifted his head a few inches from the ground, and was moving it slowly from side to side. His eyes were open, but there was no comprehension in them. He gazed about him stupidly; his

glance rested on Jane above him, but he gave no sign of recognizing her. She dropped back in the hay and revelled in the wonderful
relief of knowing that he was moving, and alive. Then she heard
him moan.

By the time she climbed down the ladder, he had managed to
raise himself on to one elbow. He still looked dazed, but now his
face wore the tightness of pain.

'Harry – are you hurt? – are you?'

She squatted beside him, but he didn't take any notice of her.
With cautious fingers he was feeling the upper part of his right
leg. Jane drew in her breath when his fingers touched his knee:
then the agony was quite plain on his face. She was nearly sick
when she heard the grating sound as he gingerly prodded his shin
bone. In sudden panic he tried to move, and the fractured bone
broke through the skin. They both stared at the blood which started
rapidly to stain his stocking.

The sight of the blood seemed to unnerve him; he had not
uttered a sound except for that single moan. Now he struggled
and tried to pull himself to a kneeling position on his uninjured
leg. His face blanched with the effort, and he collapsed again, the
sweat standing out on his face and neck.

Jane put her hands on his shoulders to press him down.

'Be still, Harry! – be still! I'll go and bring someone . . .'

He turned his head, and seemed to be aware of her for the first
time. His tight lips stretched back over his teeth.

'You!' He grabbed her arm savagely. '*You* did this!'

She tried to pull away. 'I didn't!'

'Look at it!' His tone rose almost to a shout. 'Look at my leg!
I'll be a cripple . . . I'll be on crutches – *me*!'

'No, Harry. No!' She was panic-stricken, struggling to tear his
fingers from her arm. 'You won't be a cripple! Doctor Crosby'll
mend it – he'll bind it up with two sticks, and it'll be straight.'

'No one ever walked rightly again on a leg snapped in two –
I'll be worse than the greatest weakling in the village. And it's your
fault – you bitch!'

Suddenly he swung out with the back of his hand. She ducked,
and the blow caught her fully across the left eye. Blinded, she
stumbled back out of reach.

She squinted down at him. 'I didn't do it – I didn't harm you,
Harry!' Her voice rose in a wail of despair.

'You did, you bitch . . . and it'll be a long day before you forget
it. There's more ways'n one to skin a cat, and even if *I* can't give
you what you deserve, you'll see what my father will do.'

Jane didn't miss his meaning. Everyone knew that Harry's

father had the ear of the local magistrate, Sir George Osgood. Suddenly she realized it was not Harry's rage alone that threatened her. He was only a young and dull-witted man; but his father wielded power – and she was a serving-girl at The Feathers, with only the doubtful protection of Tim Cooper, whom she suspected owed money to Tom Black, behind her. She looked fearfully at Harry's shattered knee, and the unnatural angle at which his leg lay. She had heard that the law could put you in gaol or even transport you for breaking another person's nose – what was the punishment for crippling a man? In his furious threats she suddenly felt the menace of prison-ships, and Botany Bay.

Harry was turning again, looking around him as if he was about to shout for help. Urgently she bent towards him.

'It wasn't my fault – I swear it wasn't! I didn't know we were so close to the edge. I swear to God I didn't!'

He looked at her with his face full of pain and rage. 'If *I* must go dragging my leg about for the rest of my days, I'll see *you* don't go easy, either, curse you! I'll see that you don't forget Harry Black. You think you can throw back the present I bring you? – I'll make you wish you'd crawled for it on your knees!'

He stopped, exhausted with the pain and effort.

She backed away from him, numbed with fright. Her shaking fingers tugged clumsily at the latch. She tried to mouth words to soften him, but she could say nothing. The late sun washed over her again, and she looked at it, bewildered and unbelieving that it should still be there. She clutched her torn bodice and started to run across the yard. Before she reached the kitchen she heard Harry's shouts.

As Jane entered, Sally paused in her task of basting the poultry on the spit. A look of alarm crossed her face.

'Why, child – what is it? What under Heaven has happened to you?' Her gaze took in the torn bodice, Jane's dishevelment. As she put down the basting ladle the noises in the storeroom reached her.

'Jane – what's going on?'

Already the two stable-boys had gone to answer his cries. Jane had a sense of pressures closing in about her; she felt the beginning of a frightening chain of events she had no way of stopping. Abruptly she seized Sally's plump hand and pulled her towards the pantry, then closed the door quickly behind them both.

'I have to tell you first. In a few minutes Harry will be in here screaming lies about me, and I want you to have the truth.'

Sally's florid face grew still more flushed as she listened. She made little clicking noises with her tongue while Jane talked. At the finish she shook her head despairingly.

'I'm not saying he can set the magistrates on you, Jane – but I'm not saying he *can't*, either. Tom Black's a powerful mean man when he's aroused, and there's no telling how he'll take it – Harry being his only son and all. And there's no witnesses to say that you didn't entice him up to the hay-loft . . . and that being the case, a man would be entitled to some . . .' A sharp look crossed her face. 'You *didn't* entice him up, did you?'

Jane gave an exclamation of disgust.

Sally held up her hand. 'All right, Miss High-and-Mighty. It might have been better for you if you had!'

Jane wrung her hands. 'But what am I to do? That's the story he'll put about, for certain, and when he does . . .'

Sally cut her short. 'There's only one thing to do. I'm not saying it's the right thing – but it's all I can think of.'

'What is it?' Jane demanded.

Sally hesitated, her broad, rough hands outstretched for just an instant in an uncharacteristic gesture of indecision. It wasn't one thing she was thinking of, but many. The first of them was Jane's safety, and Sally hadn't lived here all her life without learning how far and how powerfully in this district Tom Black's influence could stretch. But there was another aspect of the matter that troubled her, and which she didn't try to put into words for Jane. From this point onwards she knew that Jane would have no use for The Feathers, and The Feathers no use for her. Whatever the outcome of Harry's threats, Jane's life would be a misery in the village, and The Feathers would be housing someone who had suddenly become hostile to those about her. In this final and savage rejection of Harry Black, Jane had placed herself beyond the sympathies of the people who had accepted her as part of their world; she had rejected The Feathers as well as Harry. She had, as plainly as if she had spoken, told this small world that she had outgrown it. The alternatives to The Feathers were uncertain, and they might hold a more distasteful future than Jane had even now. Sally knew Jane thoroughly, knew her as wilful, proud, and as yet unchastened by life; she loved her also, perhaps even more than her own daughters because Jane demanded a different kind of love. Her heart ached at the thought of what she had to do.

'Come here with me.' Sally flung open the pantry door. She strode across the kitchen, and reached for her shawl which always hung behind the door. 'Where's yours? – well never mind that now! Quickly, put this on! It'll cover you up a little for the time being – you're such an indecent sight, you'll have everyone on the highway stopping you.'

'The highway?'

'You're terribly slow-witted, Jane, for someone who's in trouble.' Sally was already reaching down from the tall dresser the copper jug where she kept a little money, out of Tim's sight and knowledge. She bundled it into her handkerchief and thrust it into Jane's hand.

'You must go to your mother, of course. She'll surely have friends who'll help you if Tom Black brings charges. And Master Black'll not be so quick to act if he thinks you've someone behind you, by the same rule.'

'Oh, Sally . . . !'

'Quickly now, before Harry has the whole house listening to his woes. I want you out of the way before Tim starts arguing the whole thing.'

A brief kiss on Sally's cheek, a briefer glance at the open door of the storeroom where she could dimly make out the figures of the stable-boys bending over Harry; then she was on the village street, running and keeping the shawl wrapped well about her. The village was past – familiar houses she had known all her life. Then the open fields again, and the dip of the road southward.

She slowed her pace a little. She was on the road to London.

2

Jane spent the night in an abandoned barn, whose fourth side was open to the skies, and to the piercing cold showers which fell before dawn. Sally's money was too precious to be spent on lodgings, and even at the humble inns along the road she would be a suspicious figure arriving without baggage or decent clothes. There was always the possibility that Tom Black might have sent after her directly he had learned she was gone. With this in mind, she left the London road immediately she was past the village, cutting east-wards across the fields, and making wide detours of the hamlets, and even the isolated cottages. Just before dusk she judged that she was far enough beyond any immediate pursuit, and she turned south again along a narrow road; there seemed to be a fair amount of traffic here for the time of year – carts laden with market pro-duce, poultry and meat. There wasn't any doubt that they were making for the capital. She watched them for a time and then went back along the lane to the empty barn she had noticed. The

February night had turned raw and cold.

All night she lay in the dirty straw, miserably clutching her stomach, and listening to its empty rumblings; and the night seemed endless. She began to scratch at the lice which already crawled on her body and hair, ashamed to think that she would have to present herself to Anne tomorrow in this condition. She was frightened – frightened of many things . . . of Tom Black, of Anne who very likely would not welcome her, frightened of the thought of arriving in London with only a few coins in her pocket. The only thing that seemed worse than her present condition was the vision of herself married to Harry Black, enduring his coarse love-making, his infidelities, and his stupidity with a dull, impotent hatred. All the same she was hungry and frightened enough to weep a little, and then to dry her eyes angrily because tears were so little help; so she just lay in the straw, sleeping fitfully, and waiting for the morning.

She was on the road early, walking briskly, and trying to stop thinking of how hungry she was. By sunrise she could already see the outskirts of the city lying before her, the morning still grey with mist, though the sun was breaking through and just tipping the chimney tops. The sight of it tore down the depression of the long night; she gazed at it with mingled satisfaction and wonder, smiling suddenly to herself, and enjoying the sensation of a new confidence and excitement.

She decided, then, firstly that she was a fool to go hungry when she had money in her pocket – and after she had filled her stomach, she would find someone to give her a lift. She was still several miles from Anne's doorstep, and the road was crowded with carts and wagons. Among all of them, one of the drivers was going to respond to a smile from her.

The tavern she chose was a poor place by comparison with The Feathers, and the clientele was shabby and hungry. But before its door stood a number of carts, so she walked boldly in, and asked for buttermilk and bread. Grudgingly she paid for it, and as she ate, began to take stock of the inhabitants of the smoky room. She wasn't conspicuously dishevelled among them, she decided – and a great deal cleaner than most. Hurriedly she sifted them all – and finally fixed her gaze on a man whom she had seen tending an ancient equipage outside.

He responded almost right away; coming over confidently and dropping down beside her on the bench.

'That's a mighty fine eye y've got there, luv.' He had a dark, gipsy-like face, which looked as if it had been screwed up like a bit

of old paper, and stuffed under the battered hat. 'What happened?
– did someone 'it you?'

Inwardly she cursed Harry, and at the same time forced a bright
smile on to her lips.

'Looks as if I walked into the bedpost when the candle went
out, doesn't it?' She grinned impudently at him, and winked with
the good eye. He threw back his head and roared with laughter.
Everyone in the room turned to look at the pair, and some of them
laughed also. Suddenly Jane had a mental image of the sight she
must present – almost in spite of herself she joined in the laughter.

She could feel the laughter down inside of her – deep in her
throat and belly. After the miserable hours of the night it was a
good feeling to be laughing again; she was grateful to the grimy
little carter. She liked the twist of humour on his lips. Still laughing,
she turned to him.

'Heading into the city?'

He nodded. 'Aye, luv.'

'Got room for me?' She thrust a foot forward, making sure to
uncover and display her ankle. 'My shoe rubs, and I've no mind
to walk farther.'

He looked at the ankle, and then nudged her sharply in the ribs.
'Always got room for a spot o' company – specially when it's red-
headed!'

She gazed at him hoping she looked helpless, but not too demure.
'Going anywhere near Albemarle Street? I mean . . . well, I've
never been to London before, and I'm dead sure to get lost . . .'

His brow wrinkled. 'Well . . . I wasn't exactly going in that
direction. Got a call to make on the Oxford Road, and then I'm
'eadin' for Battersea. But seein' as yer foot 'urts . . .' Then he
brightened up, and nudged her again. 'Well . . . what the 'ell! The
master'll not know it, and what's an hour or so when it's t' oblige
a lady?' He slapped his thigh in satisfaction. 'What'd me ol' lady
say if she could see me with a red-head!'

So when Jane entered London at last, it was in the company of
a ragged carter, and seated behind his skinny horse. His dark little
eyes noted the wonder in hers as she gazed at the brightening
spectacle of the city, stared at the tall, crowded buildings. With a
gesture that indicated the jumble, he said :

'If yer the kind that takes t' city ways – then it's the fairest place
y' could wish t' see ! They got everythin' 'ere – just everythin' ! And
all y' need is money . . .' He turned and inclined his head towards
her with a grotesquely gallant bow . . . 'or a pretty face !'

They turned south off the Oxford Road, and made their way

through the great fashionable squares lined with the high, narrow houses. Servants with sleep still in their eyes polished the brass door-knobs and lanterns, and swept the refuse into the mud-filled streets. In one of the crowded lanes between the squares, a pail of slops, thrown energetically from an upstairs window, caught the horse squarely across the back; he was too weary and too old to be startled by it. The hem of Jane's gown was soaked. She stared back indignantly at the window, but there was no one there.

The carter, whose name was Mick, grinned cheerfully.

'All in a day's work, luv. Y've just got t' mind where yer goin' in this man's town!'

The city was like a confused dream to her – so many faces and people, and noise such as she had never heard before. The noise was everywhere; it seemed to come from the ground and the rooftops – raucous voices shouting at each other, tunes being whistled, and cries of anger as people stepped back out of the way of heavy coaches. The dirt was everywhere too – mud and refuse underfoot, the suffocating odours of rotting food, the smells from the fishmongers and the livery stables, the cloying smells of unwashed humanity, the smell of excrement.

Mick had spent a long time over his call in the Oxford Road, and the city was getting into the stride of its day. The shutters were down from the shop fronts, and she feasted her eyes on the displays, the milliners, the gun-shops, the wine-shops – but it was still far too early for fashionable folk to be astir, Mick told her. But she saw carriages and coachmen waiting before the doors of some of the great houses, and the coffee-shops were open, with the newspapers fresh on the racks.

Her senses drank in the excitement of it – the feeling that all the world was gathered here in this awakening city; here lived riches and fame and splendour. The sun burned away the early mists; it lay on the slanting roofs and gave brilliance to the suits of livery she saw all about her, the gold and silver braid shining as if they were polished. The heavy, pungent odours drifting from the bake-shop made her realize that she was hungry again. She sniffed the London air – the stench and perfume – and her teeth chattered with indefinable excitement and dread.

They came to Albemarle Street at last – Jane suspected that Mick had taken her there by a roundabout way. She glimpsed the clock on St James's Palace at the bottom of the slope on the other side of Piccadilly, just as Anne had described it to her, suddenly she knew that all of Anne's world was before her. They found Anne's house – elegant and in good repair, though Jane noticed the mud of several days caked on the doorstep.

Mick leapt down, and rapped on the knocker with his whip. He rapped twice again before the door opened; the sullen face of a young girl, bedraggled hair under an untidy cap, appeared. Her brows were knit sharply in a frown.

'Well? – what do you want?' She looked critically at them both.

Jane drew herself up stiffly. 'I wish to see Mistress Howard,' she said, with her best imitation of Anne's voice.

'Mistress Howard doesn't see anyone at this hour in the morning. Come back later.'

Jane began to climb down off the cart. 'I'll wait,' she said shortly. She stepped up to the door.

The girl half-closed it with a threatening motion. 'Look 'ere, you dirty baggage – you can't come in 'ere unless the mistress says so. So just come back at a decent hour.'

Mick waved his whip at her. 'You mind yer tongue – y' nasty bitch! This 'ere young lady'll wait . . . an' I'm 'ere to see she does!'

Jane put her hand on the door. 'Mistress Howard will see me. I'm her daughter.'

The girl's mouth dropped open in disbelief. 'G'on – don't give me none o' that . . .'

Then she screwed up her eyes, looking closely at Jane. Her brow furrowed again; she put her head on one side, studying the other's face intently.

'Well . . . I must say you do *look* like the mistress – that red hair an' all . . .'

Mick lowered the whip slowly; he stared wonderingly at Jane. 'Y' mean t' say yer mother's the *mistress* here!' His eyes ran significantly over her dirty gown and Sally's old shawl. He pushed his hat to the back of his head. 'Well – I dun' know. There's never any accountin' for 'ow folks'll act. Y'll be tellin' me next yer a bloody duchess!'

She shook her head. 'I'm not! . . . more's the pity!'

He was already backing away; the game between them was ending and he clearly indicated that he didn't expect to have further dealings with folk who lived in Albemarle Street.

'Well, Duchess . . . thanks for yer company.' The battered hat came off in a flourish. He climbed into the cart, and sat waiting to see her admitted.

Jane saluted him briefly. 'I enjoyed the ride – thank you. You saved my feet a lot of walking.'

He nodded, and winked. 'An' what use would yer pretty face be t' y', if it couldn't save yer feet.' He touched his hat with the whip. 'Good day t' y', Duchess! – and good luck!'

Jane turned from him, and the girl opened the door reluctantly. 'I suppose it's all right t' let y' in . . . though I ain't takin' the blame if yer not supposed t' be 'ere.'

She brushed past Jane, and started to walk towards the back of the house, with a sullen, lumpish gait.

'Just a minute!' Jane's voice was firm. 'Please tell Mistress Howard that I'm here.'

The girl spun round furiously. 'Tell 'er yerself! I ain't takin' no more orders in this 'ouse, believe me!'

'What do you mean?' Jane said. 'You work here, don't you?'

'Not any more, I don't! Not a penny piece of wages 'ave I seen in three months – 'n' I'm packin' me bag this very moment, an' I'll 've the law on 'er if she don't pay up!'

Jane looked at her for a moment in silence. This was as bad as any thing she had imagined – and yet there was no time to sit and lament about it now. She wasn't going to wait around down here, feeling her confidence ebb away with every minute. She had to see Anne now, while she could still use her tongue to convince her mother that Sally's idea had been the right one. To confront Anne now would give her the advantage : if she waited she would lose courage, and become the frightened servant girl from The Feathers.

She stiffened her neck, and looked at the girl coldly. 'Keep a civil tongue in your head!' She gestured towards the staircase. 'Where is my mother? – is she still abed? Where is her chamber?'

The girl shrugged indifferently. 'Y' figgerin' t' go up and see 'er . . . in that case y' can announce yerself!' Then she hesitated, and when she spoke again her tone was silky. 'Y'll find 'er abed, all right. It's the big chamber two floors above this . . . above the drawin'-room.' She indicated the way briefly, and then stood watching in silence while Jane moved past her to the staircase.

With the girl's hostile gaze still on her, Jane forced herself to assume a look of confidence as she mounted the stairs. Her hand trembled slightly on the balustrade. She caught a glimpse of the drawing-room as she passed – pale green, and gold and white, with mirrors reflecting the brilliance of crystal. The stairwell was panelled in light pine – the house was soft and feminine . . . Anne's house.

On the next floor she found the ante-room to Anne's bedroom – a prettily furnished apartment that made her more than ever conscious of her torn gown and matted hair, the lice on her body. She stiffened herself to approach the door and knock. With her hand poised, she heard Anne's voice – she had almost forgotten the peculiar beauty of that voice, its sweet, low pitch, and how it

sounded forever on the edge of laughter. While she stood there
Anne actually did laugh – that clear unabashed laugh, not now
with the charm of long ago when Anne had been in love, but
charming still.

It unnerved her a little to realize that her mother was not alone,
but Jane was determined that she would not return to the hall and
sit waiting meekly under the eyes of that sullen girl. She knocked
firmly.

'Come in!' Anne's tone was indifferent, as if she had been
expecting the knock.

The room had a warm, intimate kind of perfume which touched
Jane's senses even before she fully took in the scene. She entered
slowly, and had an instant impression of a frivolous kind of disorder, of luxurious things, of carelessness. There was a scatter of
clothes about, and an embroidered glove lay foolishly in the centre
of the carpet. A caged bird was singing in the sunshine by the
window.

Anne was naked, except for a shawl which lay across her
shoulders, propped up against pillows on a tumbled bed. The bed
was a huge one, with great carved legs, and hung with green silk.
Anne's breasts were firm; like a young girl's. She displayed her
body with a careless pride in its beauty.

Without turning she said, 'Patrick . . . I rang hours ago! What's
kept you?'

When she got no answer she glanced questioningly around. Her
features froze in an instant of disbelief.

'Jane! . . . Mercy upon us!' She half rose on the pillows, and
dropped back again, as if the breath had been knocked out of her.
She gestured helplessly towards Jane, then looked immediately
across at the window seat.

A lean, dark-haired man, who sprawled there in shirt and
dressing-gown, straightened as he became aware of Jane's presence.
Then unhurriedly he rose to his feet.

Jane looked from one to the other, and her cheeks burned a dull
red. The rumpled bed and her mother's nakedness were clear
enough signs, even without the presence of the man; probably
the bed was still warm from his body. It was too late now to efface
herself; she must appear to them both like a naïve little fool, who
knew no better than to blunder into the room where Anne lay
with her lover. She knew now the full extent of the malice of the
servant girl in sending her here unannounced. She was furious at
her own stupidity.

Neither of them seemed perturbed. Anne had recovered herself, and now she gestured imperiously.

'Jane! . . . what in the world are you doing here? Come here, child . . . how you've grown! . . . what a sight you look!'

Jane went towards her. Anne's voice had been warm and surprised, but not angry. In the next second she felt her mother's arms about her in a light hug, and her face brushed those firm breasts. Anne smelled of scents and powder – a smell that Jane recalled from a long time ago. There was another scent – the erotic scent of a woman whose flesh is desired and loved.

Anne released her, and carelessly drew the shawl over her bosom. For some seconds she gazed at her daughter's face in silence, then she put out her hand and swung her in the direction of the window.

'Look, Ted – my daughter, Jane. Grown up – and looking like a gipsy. Jane, this is Lord O'Neill.'

He bowed. 'I'm happy to know you, Miss Jane.'

His accent was soft. She had heard this voice in gentlemen who used the coaches to and from Liverpool – the Irish voices with music in them, and easy emotion. He spoke with polite gravity, as if she were a great lady, and entitled to his consideration. As she curtsied, she examined him more closely . . . a tall man, younger than her mother, a graceful, slender-hipped body, a fine linen shirt with costly lace ruffles. She saw this, and saw also, that with all the gravity of his deportment he was laughing just a little at her. It wasn't unkind laughter – he was too lazy, and, at the moment, too content, to be unkind. He was merely amused.

She didn't like his being amused. With deliberate hauteur she looked away from him.

Anne had been studying her. 'Jane, you've grown into a woman while my back was turned. How old you make me feel! . . . a hundred and two years, and toothless!'

Then she laughed, displaying for O'Neill's fascinated eyes her small, pretty teeth, and drawing her body up straight, so that her breasts pointed through the fine wool. O'Neill joined in the laughter, his gaze resting on her fondly.

Jane stood between them, feeling clumsy and gauche, feeling less than a woman because Anne was more of a woman than anyone she had ever laid eyes on. There were refinements in Anne's sensuality that she had never been conscious of before; it was easier now to see her as a man did. Like most other women placed beside her, Jane felt inadequate. She backed towards the door, preparing to excuse herself.

An agitated knocking halted her.

'Come in,' Anne called.

The door was flung open.

'Oh, ma'am! It wouldn't have happened if I'd just been there. I slipped out for a second to give the butcher a piece o' me mind about the joints he's been sendin' – and I get back an' what do I find but that stupid young piece has let a stranger in . . . An' upstairs, too, an' all . . .'

Jane stared in astonishment at the speaker, a young man whose dead white face was topped by a great shock of lank black hair. He was tall and angular, dressed in servant's clothes which fitted him, but seemed to hang limply on his thin frame. He couldn't have been more than thirty years old, judging by the way he moved, Jane thought, but he gave the impression of someone much older. His brow was furrowed with lines of worry, and his whole body seemed to be screwed up in a ferment of anxiety. He looked only at Anne; no one else mattered to him.

'Calm, Patrick! – be calm! There's nothing to get in a state about . . .'

'Well, saints in heaven, ma'am, I wouldn't have let anyone get past me . . .'

Anne held up her hand for silence. 'I know you wouldn't, Patrick, but this is one occasion when it's just as well you weren't there.' She gestured towards Jane. 'This is my daughter, Patrick.'

He swung his head slowly.

'You remember,' she prompted. 'My daughter . . . who lives at Hampstead.'

He gazed at her wonderingly, shaking his head. 'Heaven help us! It can't be true! Why, ma'am, she's the spittin' image of y' . . .' His face broadened into a kind of foolish grin. 'Why . . . I would have known her anywhere . . . so like you, she is, ma'am.'

'We're not as alike as all that, Patrick.'

'Well, now . . .' O'Neill drawled. 'I'm hardly telling the difference between you!'

Anne said firmly: 'There is a difference, and you all know it, so stop flattering me.' She looked across at Patrick. 'Miss Jane will be staying here . . . for the time being. We'll need the small room upstairs made ready . . . and . . . oh, yes – it will be breakfast for three instead of two.'

Patrick favoured Jane with a low, untidy bow. ''Twill be a pleasure to serve you now, Miss Jane. An' forgive me, miss, for the disturbance . . . it's so strange to be seein' y', an' all, after hearin' about y' all these years, and not really thinkin' y'd come t' life one o' these fine days . . .'

Anne clapped her hands together. 'Patrick, we're hungry. Talk to your heart's content when our bellies are full.'

He made his strange ducking bow again. ''T' be sure, ma'am. At once! Right away!' He left the room swiftly.

Anne flung aside the covers. 'Jane – reach me that gown, please.'

Jane watched while Anne discarded the shawl, and put on the green velvet robe. She slipped out of the high bed, tying the gown at her waist. Her limbs were beautifully formed; she seemed no older than Jane herself.

She looked across at her daughter.

'Child – you should eat before you talk. I won't ask you yet what brings you.' Then she gestured towards the end of the room. 'You'll find water in the pitcher behind the screen – and soap and comb and things . . . Later Patrick will leave some in your own room.'

Jane moved obediently towards the screen, wishing that Anne didn't have the effect of making her feel so coarse and dirty, wishing also, O'Neill didn't have to be present while she washed. She felt like a child being sent away in disgrace. And yet it wasn't, she decided, Anne's fault. There weren't any rules for dealing with a daughter who appeared from nowhere, looking like a bedraggled tramp – especially with a lover to witness the scene.

As she reached the screen, Anne's voice arrested her again. 'Just one question, Jane – only one.'

'Yes?'

'That black eye? . . . how did you get it?'

Jane didn't answer at once. She stood looking at the toilet table, abstractedly noting its dainty appointments. With O'Neill looking on, she didn't know what to say to Anne. She shifted from one foot to the other, fidgeting with the heavy brush, twisting it in her hand. Then turning, she caught sight of herself in the mirror. The bruise under her eye was puffed and ugly; there was dried blood on her lip. She looked hideous, slatternly, like a brawling street woman.

Abruptly then, she turned back to face Anne and O'Neill.

'I've worse things than a bruised eye.'

She let Sally's shawl drop to the floor. The torn gown and her bare bosom were fully visible to them now. On her left breast were the weals where Harry's teeth had bitten into her flesh.

'I got the black eye from the same man who tried to rape me. All *he* got for his pains was a broken leg.'

Calmly she picked up the shawl again and threw it across the chair. 'So that's why I am here – I'm running away.'

She stood there only long enough to see the expression change on both their faces. Anne had grown pale, and O'Neill looked as if he had suddenly seen a different person in the place of the one who had been there. It gave her a bleak kind of satisfaction to know that she had taken his attention from Anne.

Then she moved behind the screen, and one by one began to strip off her clothes until she was naked. As they dropped, each one, to the floor, she felt that she was shedding all of herself that belonged back at The Feathers. She washed every inch of her body, freely helping herself from all the toilet bottles to scent the water. Carefully she put on the dressing robe which Anne brought to her, an elegant, blue thing which was only a little worn at the wrists. Without tongs she couldn't achieve the fashionable curls she would have liked, but her hair combed down loosely on her shoulders looked even better, she thought.

A different and more calculating face stared out at her from the mirror. Whatever happened now, good or ill, she could never go back to being the girl who had climbed into the hay-loft less than a full day ago to watch the London coach depart.

2

They ate breakfast in the ante-room. Jane knew that she had the full attention of both Anne and O'Neill, and she savoured, not only their attention, but the luxury of the room, the fine china, the silk gown she wore. More than that, she was not a stranger at Anne's table; she sipped her chocolate slowly, and a sense of intimacy and ease began to flow through her. Patrick had lit a small fire in the grate. The sun and the rosy fire-light mingled on the faded carpet; Jane could feel the warmth and the peace as if they were things she could put her hands on.

Anne and O'Neill remained quiet to listen to her; as she relaxed she grew expansive, finding better and less clumsy phrases to explain her arrival, to tell of what had happened yesterday at The Feathers. It was important to her that they should feel the strength and the enraged despair of Harry Black; she sought words to tell them of the power and influence Harry's father wielded, of his arrogant pride in his own position and achievements. It was important to her own pride that they should know she hadn't come on any slight and foolish pretext.

She was also aware of the need to be brief, and not tearful. Anne was a woman of laughter, who wanted only to be amused; it would be fatal to make the mistake of boring her, or wearying her with a tale of trouble. Anne had always dismissed her woes with a shrug; Jane knew she must quickly learn to copy her.

O'Neill was full of noisy indignation. 'Damn it, Anne! – the fellow ought to be punished!'

Anne shook her head slowly. 'No, Ted – it can't be that way. Jane did the best possible thing to cut her losses and run for it.' She smiled wryly. 'She's a pretty woman – and there's always, I hope, a little danger in being pretty.' Then she spread her hands. 'If Black doesn't pursue her, that's the best we can hope for . . .'

'Nonsense!' O'Neill cut her short. 'There isn't a chance that he'll do anything about it. I'll warrant the man's not such a fool as his son. He'll know that once Jane's come to you, he wouldn't stand a chance. I know that kind – big men in their own little field, but scared as the devil to chance themselves beyond it. If Jane had stayed around he'd have to bring charges to save his face – now he'll have every excuse not to.'

'But if he should . . . ?' Jane asked.

O'Neill looked at her, his grey eyes softening. 'What are you thinking, my dear? . . . are you thinking that people go to the gallows or Botany Bay for less?' He shook his head. 'Don't trouble yourself about it – you'll not see the gallows or a prison ship – not while I can help you. If you'd stayed at The Feathers it might have happened – here with Anne you're safe. Black would know well enough that her influence matches his. He'll leave it alone, you'll see.'

Anne gave a short laugh, and shrugged. 'Would to God that my money matched his! Then I'd go into the court with the King himself and expect to win!'

They made it sound so easy, these two, Jane thought. They could joke, and shrug their shoulders, and the menace no longer existed. O'Neill could use the weight of a title, and a word spoken in the ear of a man belonging to his club, or with whom he passed the time in the coffee-houses. Anne could probably use influence in certain places also, if she had to. It was no harder than that. They had made their decisions and cleared their minds of the problem. Now they wanted to put it aside, find something to laugh at, as Anne had done over Tom Black's money. If they were going to forget about it, Jane decided that she could forget too, almost as easily. It was pleasanter to revel in luxurious rooms and silk gowns than worry about what might possibly happen tomorrow.

Anne yawned delicately, like a cat, and fell to talking with O'Neill about a party which a woman called Myra Burke would give that evening. '. . . They say she's used most of the money old Benson left her to decorate the new house. But just think – she has such frightful taste!' She gave a mournful little pout. 'All that beautiful money going to waste on Myra Burke, when I could use it so much better.'

O'Neill crumpled up his napkin. 'Well – I don't care if the woman hangs her walls with tapestry or old bags so long as I win some money this evening. Blanchard took a load off me last night.'

'Of course you'll get it back,' Anne said quickly. 'It always comes back somehow – if the luck's with you.'

O'Neill turned to Jane. 'Listen to her! – There was never a woman courted luck so faithfully. I'll swear she bows to it three times before she goes out in the evening.'

Anne shrugged. 'What if I do? – all the gods must have their offering. If I believe in luck hard enough . . .'

She glanced towards the door as it opened, and broke off her sentence. The half-defensive smile she had worn became tender and warm.

'And here's William come to bid us good morning,' she said softly.

Jane turned her head slowly; she almost didn't want to look. It was impossible not to hear the love and protectiveness in Anne's voice; she hadn't realized before that she was jealous of William.

William was tall for his age, and was every inch Anne's child – except that his eyes were dark and framed with heavier brows than hers. He had the same red hair, and features that were curiously strong and defined for a child; here also were Anne's graceful, easy movements. He wore a dark velvet jacket that made him look like a young prince. It was clear that he had known of Jane's arrival; he moved towards his mother immediately, but an inquisitive, eager smile had already started on his lips, and he looked directly towards Jane. He responded with a childish brevity to Anne's kiss.

'William – this is your sister, Jane. She's come down from Hampstead to stay with us.'

He nodded. 'Yes, I know. Patrick told me – he's in a bother about it. Betty packed her bags and went this morning – and he has no one to help him get the room ready.'

Anne's brow darkened. 'So Betty left! Well – there's one ungrateful baggage the less for us to trouble about.'

'She says she'll be back, Mamma – she wants her wages.' William said it as if servants' leaving with wages unpaid was nothing new to him. He moved around the table towards Jane. He held out his hand to her.

'I'm glad you've come,' he said. 'Patrick says you've come from Hampstead. Is that a long way?'

'Quite a long way,' Anne said, a trifle irritably. 'It's a long pull for the horses up to Hampstead.' It was the first time she had made

even the vaguest reference to the distance as a reason for her long
absence from The Feathers. Jane knew that Anne would never
make more of an excuse than this.

Jane held William's hand briefly. She felt no warmth towards
him, only a jealous suspicion. This good-looking little boy had no
business to be so self-possessed, so sure of Anne and of everything
about him. He spoke with Anne's clear tones, and her inflections
– he was everything that contact with Anne had made him. She
fiercely envied him the years he had spent in this house, and the
confidence they had bred in him. She was tongue-tied beside him
and angry because he had destroyed the mood of intimacy she had
revelled in.

'How do you do,' she said formally, and let his hand drop.

He wasn't to be put off. 'I want to show you General.'

He went back to the door quickly, and emerged again pulling
on the collar of a large black dog. The dog came with just enough
reluctance to assert himself; he went to Jane with almost as much
curiosity as William displayed.

'I've had General for two years. Mamma gave him to me on
my birthday, and so General and I always have our birthdays
together.'

Jane ran her hand over the curling black coat. 'He's very handsome,' she said lamely. She couldn't find anything else to say, and
yet it seemed to be expected, because Anne and O'Neill were
staring at her, and waiting on her words as much as William was.
She felt herself flush, and there were tears of annoyance and
frustration pricking the back of her eyes. She had been doing so
well – almost feeling that she belonged with Anne and her titled
lover, sipping chocolate daintily and feeling at home in a silk gown.
But William was obviously so much more at home here; by comparison she must seem once again the country girl, full of clumsi-
ness and unease.

Even the dog gave William an added advantage – standing
beside him William looked like a portrait child, straight and
elegant, his hand resting possessively on the collar. She wanted
to shake him; he was bred in the fashion of all the spoiled and
favoured children of the rich who had come to The Feathers – the
ones who had given orders, and expected service from her as their
due. And yet he was her half-brother; he had Anne's love, and so
much besides.

O'Neill spoke at last. The pause had become too lengthy, and
he was detached enough from the three to be able to sense Jane's
feelings. There had been an instant sympathy in him for this girl
with the bruised eye and marked breast who had, before his fas-

cinated gaze, this morning slipped into a new world.

'Aren't they alike now, William – did you ever see two so alike?'

William considered for a moment, giving Jane a careful and unselfconscious scrutiny – just as if she were a stuffed dummy, Jane thought angrily, with no eyes and ears.

'Well – I don't know . . . Patrick said that too. He said Jane was as pretty as Mamma, but I don't know. I don't think she's *quite* as pretty.'

'Indeed now – the pair of them would turn heads wherever they went. Indeed they would!' Suddenly O'Neill's face broke into a broad smile; he smacked his thigh appreciatively. 'I've got it, Anne – by God, that would set the town talking!'

Anne looked at him quickly. 'What are you talking about, Ted?'

'Why don't we take Jane to the reception this evening . . . you know, dress her up in one of your gowns, and let people think they were seeing your double. What a joke that'd be . . . why, it'd be around the town in no time.'

Anne's face was troubled as she turned towards Jane.

'Jane . . . I . . .'

Jane knew suddenly that this time was one time when she had to speak entirely from her own instinct – she must make a decision and override O'Neill without fully understanding why she did it. To go to a fashionable party wearing one of Anne's lovely gowns had been part of the dream she'd carried. Now the chance had come, and it was hers only to say yes, and there would be the gown and the slippers, the headdress and the carriage. And yet she knew she wasn't going to accept. There was no reason she could put into words even now why she should refuse, but she did.

Anne's gaze was fixed on her anxiously as she spoke to O'Neill.

'Oh, come, Lord O'Neill! – would you have me at a party with an eye like the black end of a pot! Why, I'd no more look like my mother, than I'd look like the queen! The truth is, sir, my bones ache sorely from the hard ground last night, and I'm in need of a little rest.'

She glanced across to Anne again – Anne who now cuddled William loosely in her arms as he leaned against her chair. In her eyes Jane read deep relief and satisfaction – and yet it was more than that, it was pleasure in her daughter, and commendation for a decision wisely made. She said nothing, but she nodded faintly, almost imperceptibly.

To Jane it was like a door being opened. William mattered now much less than he had two minutes before.

3

The gowns lay piled on the floor before Jane. She touched them with reverent and excited hands – the silk and velvet had the feel of enchantment beneath her fingers, and the colours spilled over the rose carpet in a mad and rich confusion. There were mostly greens – Anne looked best in green – with a blue and a cream and a white among them. There was a cloak with the trimming of fur, and a wide-brimmed hat. Anne had tossed them out of her wardrobe, and bundled them carelessly together.

'They all need a stitch somewhere – and I'm useless with a needle. You're a trifle taller, I fancy, but there are hems . . .' She examined the hems a little doubtfully, noticing the mud splashes from the London streets; then she tossed them aside with a shrug. 'Well . . . do the best you can with them. I'm sorry there's no money at the moment to buy you new ones. Perhaps later . . . perhaps when my luck stops being so parsimonious!'

She had said this on her way out to an afternoon drive in the Park with O'Neill. She had worn a fur wrap, and the brim of her hat dipped provocatively over one eye – but it was still possible to see that her eyes looked tired, and that when O'Neill or William weren't present, there was no zest in her voice. The soft perfume she wore lingered behind in the ante-room; Jane could smell it in the gowns piled on the floor.

One by one she tried them – startled to see, suddenly, how closely she resembled Anne. They were gowns meant to attract and hold attention; the low-cut necks, that revealed her breasts, were very deliberate. She would have to lace tighter to stay with the waists. They were the kind of clothes a woman like Anne would always wear.

The few hours she had been in Anne's household she had used to listen and observe, and she tried to settle her jumbled impressions. From the unending contact with people at The Feathers she had learned enough to be able to sum up the situation here without much difficulty. Jane knew the feeling and atmosphere of a household deeply in debt – but here they lived only as the rich did. Here was recklessness and extravagance at its height. Anne needed money badly, and yet she lived at a rate that would have frightened most people, forever trusting that luck would bring the cards right, and that she would ride home with money in her pocket.

In a strange way Patrick was behind most of the façade of splendour. He sped about, his long body poking at awkward and ungainly angles, getting through the work of five servants. He ran the household, and even doubled as coachman; he supervised William through most of the day and made it unnecessary to employ a tutor for more than a few hours. Jane wondered, had Patrick been any kind of a scholar, if Anne wouldn't have pressed him even to that extra duty. The man had a nervous, agitated thinness, and his eyes were red-rimmed from lack of sleep; yet he never halted in his tasks, or seemed to notice the appalling burden of his work. He was devoted to Anne, worshipping her with his eyes and tongue, treating her with a mixture of grave paternalism, and the reverence he would have given to a queen.

Jane fingered the rich stuff of the gowns, and decided that possibly one of them would have paid for her keep at The Feathers for a whole year. But in Anne's life, new gowns were vastly important, and Hampstead was a long way off, and easily put out of mind. Here, where servants were clamouring for wages, and the butcher to have his bills settled, it would be easier to pay those on hand than worry about a daughter who never showed herself, and never asked for money. Jane tacked an edging of lace in position, and thought, with a wry smile, that her mistake had been in not coming to Anne much sooner. Anne would always take care of whatever problems forced themselves on her; the rest could wait or be forgotten. As long as she had been prepared to fend for herself at The Feathers, Anne had been prepared to let her do it. Now she was here, and Anne would bestir herself, and be as energetic on her behalf as she was for most others.

It didn't occur to her to feel angry over Anne's treatment; that was the way Anne lived, and nothing would ever alter her.

In a way, Jane thought, it explained why William had remained here, instead of being sent off to be nursed as she had been. Anne had been passionately in love with William's father, and his child was loved for his sake. By the time William was of an age to be troublesome to Anne, he had been a fixture in her household, and there would have been no thought of sending him away. Besides that, Anne with the years slipping by her, had the need of love — and whatever men came or went, William was always with her, a perpetual reminder of the man she had loved unchangingly.

O'Neill's position, she felt, was impermanent. He would go when either he or Anne tired of the other. Jane guessed that he had no money — apart from Anne's complaints of the lack of it, O'Neill didn't have the air of a man who was contributing substantially to her support. There was no possessiveness about him. Rather, they appeared as two people who had come to an amicable arrangement which could be broken at any moment, whenever they desired. They were together because they needed company and amusement – possibly, Jane thought, because there was no one better in sight for either of them. They were affectionate to each other, but only the lightest kind of loyalty was involved. O'Neill kept rooms in a tavern in Crab Tree Yard, Anne had told her; so when the parting came there would be no sense of breaking up Anne's household or her routine of life. They would part affectionately, but with a shrug of the shoulders.

Without Anne's presence about which to pivot, the house seemed strangely quiet. Jane listened to the silence; she could no longer hear Patrick's brogue shouting orders at the cook, or hear the sounds of his feverish activity, the doors closing noisily, the dishes clattering in the basement. There was peace here at last – the rooms were dusted, the fires laid – upstairs William worked with his tutor. The absence of noise was unfamiliar; Jane had always lived in the midst of haste and bustle, and now, with tasks waiting to be done, as she knew there were, it was difficult to grow accustomed to the idea that she would not be asked, or expected, to help with them. She decided that she liked the silence and peace of this house; she liked sitting here with nothing more arduous to do than sewing a few ruffles, and lengthening some hems. She still wore Anne's silk robe, and felt comfortable in it; the memory of the lice-ridden clothes that Patrick had taken down to burn she put aside hastily. For the moment there seemed nothing out of joint – except the sight of her work-roughened hands against the rich material.

The door opened very quietly; it was only the sensation she had that someone was staring at her which made her turn. William stood half-shy in the door, a hopeful, expectant smile on his face.

'Would I disturb you if I came in? Patrick said I must ask first.'

She was tongue-tied and uneasy in William's presence, and she certainly didn't want him; but there was no way of indicating that without also letting him know her feelings. She had no alternative but to motion him in. The black dog was with him – his head thrust round the door just as William's was. They came in together, and William drew up a footstool close to her. He seated himself where he could watch what she was doing. The dog squatted beside him.

Jane glanced at him quickly, before bending over her work again. He seemed different from this morning – to start with his face was streaked with jam, and his hair was wild-looking. He had changed his jacket for an older one. He was still as self-possessed as before, but now he almost resembled the young children who had played in the village street at Hampstead. She felt herself warm a little to him.

'I thought you were having lessons,' she said quietly.

'Oh – they're finished,' he said happily. 'Mr Taylor goes to give lessons in mathematics to the daughters of Sir Sidney Stone at this time.'

'Math . . . mathematics? To girls?'

'Yes – it's funny, isn't it. But Sir Sidney is a sailor, and Mr Taylor says he makes the girls learn about mathematics and astronomy just as if they'd been boys, and were going to sea.'

'How strange,' Jane said, wonderingly. Her own aptitude with a column of figures was extremely sound, but she had once looked in Simon Garfield's book of Euclid, and the strange drawings and lines had seemed completely useless and bewildering. She began to wonder how much William knew of the subject; she hoped it wasn't much.

'What lessons do you take – can you read and write?'

'Oh, yes!' he said quickly, as if it were an accomplishment to be taken for granted. 'And I have lessons in geography and history and mathematics.'

'Oh – do you?' She was vaguely envious of his knowledge even though at his age it couldn't be very great. 'Is Mr Taylor old?' She had memories of Simon Garfield, crabby and impatient in his old age.

'Oh, no – he's young. He's only been down from Oxford for a year, and he's waiting now to go off on a botanical expedition to the South Seas. He likes to talk more than teach.'

'To talk? – to you? What does he talk about?'

'Oh – all kinds of things. He talks about plants and birds. And he talks about the Revolution in France. He's afraid if war breaks out they won't fit up a ship for the South Seas.' She nodded as he spoke. There had been so much talk at The Feathers of the Revolution and the chance of war; she had listened to the heated discussions, and always agreed with the speaker of the moment. She had never understood the aims of the Revolution, or what the people of France expected to gain by it. Now she felt ashamed of her ignorance. It was to be expected that London would buzz with news of it. This was the city where people made and lost money in wars and revolution. Among the poor folk and the country people it was a matter of going away to fight in wars they didn't

make, and didn't understand – and in which, perhaps, they would
die. She nodded again at William. In the future she would have
to listen, and remember.

'Does – does he expect there'll be war?'

William nodded emphatically. 'He says they're bound to find
an excuse to execute the King sooner or later, and England will
surely come into the war. Parliament talks about it all the time –
and a Jacobin doesn't hardly dare to open his mouth in this
country.'

'What else does he say?'

'That the brothers of the King of France are causing trouble
wherever they can – saying that everyone ought to go to war with
France. Mr Taylor says that they don't care what becomes of the
Royal Family. With the King and the Dauphin dead all of them
would be nearer to the crown themselves.'

'Can't they leave France? I've heard that a great many of
French people have.' It was all she knew about the present crisis,
and she repeated it rather desperately.

William's eyes opened wide. 'Don't you know? – the King and
Queen Marie Antionette and their children are shut up in a Palace
in Paris. They tried to escape and were sent back.'

Jane applied herself to her work again. William was only repeating parrot-fashion what he had heard, but still he made a better
showing of knowledge than she could. But somehow she didn't dislike him for being better informed than she; it was simpler to
accept the fact that William was a town child, brought up in the
society of adults. If he repeated what he heard it was useless to
resent it.

He watched her in silence for a time, his hands clasped over his
knees as he squatted on the low stool. Occasionally he put out his
hand to pat the dog, to pull gently at the long black curling ears.
Then, rather shyly, he touched the silk of the dress.

'This is my mother's gown,' he said. 'Are you going to wear it
now?'

She nodded. 'Yes – I'll wear it.'

'You'll look pretty in it,' he said matter-of-factly. Then his eyebrows shot up, as if he had just remembered something of importance. 'This morning . . .' he began quickly, '. . . you remember
this morning when I said you were not as pretty as Mamma?'

She took her eyes away from the green silk. His expression was
serious. 'Yes, I remember.'

'Well – I didn't mean it. I think you're just as pretty. But I had
to say that because Mamma worries over how she looks. I see her

staring in the looking-glass, and it seems to make her sad. But I knew that *you* knew you were pretty, so it wouldn't matter my saying that for once.'

Jane nodded. She didn't know what to answer; if William had already begun to notice Anne's concern over her looks, then he was not going to be fooled by any denial she would make. She began to feel vaguely sorry for William; to her way of thinking it was an unnatural life for a child. He was cut off from the companionship she had known in Hampstead, the sharing in the village activities – but here in London, Anne's way of living would automatically cut him off from the society of the children of conventional families. Probably he knew this well enough; he was a lonely child who played with his dog – who talked to Patrick of household matters and the gossip of the street, and to his tutor of wars and revolution. And he came in daily to greet Anne at breakfast with her lover. Suddenly she knew the richness of what she had shared with Pru and Lottie and Mary in the kitchen of The Feathers, things she had which William would never know. He had Anne's love and attention, but it had created a prison for him. The picture of the envied child in the velvet coat faded for Jane, and it was never to return again.

Then she also put out her hand and stroked the dog's head, and played with his ears as William was doing; the child glowed with pleasure.

'He's nice, isn't he? Feel how soft it is here – look, just in this underneath part of his ears.'

Jane's fingers followed his; the dog's skin had almost the texture of the fabric in her lap. 'Why do you call him General?'

'He's called General after great-great-grandfather Blake.'

'Great-great-grandfather Blake? . . . was he a general?'

William's fine eyebrows shot up. 'Why yes! Didn't you know that? I would have thought that Mamma would have told you!'

'But *who* was he?' Jane demanded impatiently.

'Why . . . he was a general, and he fought under the Duke of Marlborough. He fought with him at Blenheim . . . He's in all the old books about the wars. Mr Taylor has read some of them to me.' His smooth child's brows wrinkled in astonishment. 'Do you suppose Mamma *forgot* to tell you about him!'

'I expect so,' Jane answered dryly. Whatever Anne's motive for not telling her about the Blake background she didn't imagine it was forgetfulness. But she didn't want to waste thought any longer over Anne's motives; she wanted to revel in the knowledge of what was, suddenly, and incredibly, hers. It gave her an aware-

ness of identity to hear William group her with a family which
had existed before she was born; she wasn't accustomed to the
idea of belonging to someone. William had peopled that blankness
and made it alive; there had been a great-great-grandfather and
he had been a general – there were even history books to prove it.

Jane touched William's arm. 'What do you know about him? –
tell me!'

He shrugged. 'I don't remember all of it. Blenheim's somewhere
over in the Low Countries, isn't it?'

Jane didn't know, but nodded encouragingly. 'Yes – I think so.'

'Well, they won a great victory there, and great-great-grandfather Blake was there with Marlborough all through it. Mamma
said he brought back a lot of booty from the wars . . . gold and
tapestries . . . silver plate . . . things like that.'

Jane stared at him wide-eyed. 'What else?'

William cast back in his memory in an effort to satisfy her.
'Well . . . I can't remember much else. Except . . . except I re-
member Mamma telling me that great-great-grandfather was all
set to be made a lord – or something of the sort – and he offended
Marlborough's wife, the Duchess, Sarah. The Duchess was the
Queen's greatest friend, so of course he didn't get the title.'

Jane gave a little gasp. 'Is this true?'

William looked pained. 'Why yes – it says so, right in the books.
All except the part about the Duchess. I told Mr Taylor, and he
believes it – he says it's the only reason he could understand, why
great-great-grandfather wouldn't have had a title.'

'Well – imagine that!' Jane's tone was dreamy; she was wrapped
already in the wonder of discovering a past for herself, a past in
which great and famous names jostled one another. There had
been money as well – gold, William had said, and silver plate and
jewels, probably – and a family of whose blood she was. They had
been people of position and prominence – all dead now, and vanished, but it explained why Anne moved and talked with that
faint arrogance and authority. It explained many things – why
William was brushed with the same dignity, why she herself had
gropingly sought something beyond Harry Black. She knew that
her hunger over these years at The Feathers had not been only a
longing to be with Anne; she had wanted identity, had wanted
to know that there were people and a place from which she was
sprung. Her thoughts now were confused and excited; she reached
out greedily for all that William could give her.

'What else do you know . . . about *them*?'

'Them?'

'Yes – the family !'

'There isn't a family.'

'What? – *none*?' In the few minutes William had been talking she had brought to life a host of personalities centring round the General – a wife, children, a house and all its accoutrements . . . grandchildren, and their children, who would be cousins to William and herself. She had fashioned them in her mind because she wanted them. Now William had wiped them away.

'Only grandfather – that's all.'

'You mean Anne's father – no one else !' She was sadly disappointed; the phantom world narrowed down to only one man, and he, she thought, would be an old man.

'Mamma never spoke of anyone else – she had no sisters or brothers. She told me about a cousin, a little boy, who lived with them for a while. But he went away – to France, Mamma said.'

'Where did they live? – where does Anne's father live?'

William was becoming wearied by this questioning game. Anne's family had never troubled his thoughts greatly, except that he had had a child's pleasure in seeing the General's name in the history books. But there was too much happening all about him to leave time for speculation about people who were dead. He was puzzled by Jane's eagerness, and worried because she expected him to know so much.

'Some place in Kent, near the sea, I think. Mamma says they used to have sheep – I would have liked to have seen his lambs,' he added regretfully.

'What was the name of the place?'

William screwed up his face wearily, pushing his memory to one last effort. 'I don't . . .' Then his expression lightened. 'Why – yes, I do remember! They lived on the Romney Marsh, by the sea, in Kent. The house where Mamma grew up is called Blake's Reach. Yes! – that's it ! Blake's Reach!'

She was almost satisfied – she had enough for the present to think about, to savour. Quietly she took up the silk again, and began making her minute stitches in the edging of the fichu. Blake's Reach . . . near the sea; a place called the Romney Marsh, where there were sheep. She turned the few details over in her mind lovingly; they belonged to her now, as much a part of her, and belonging as much to her, as they did to William. She looked at the child's head, with its untidy red locks bent towards the dog. They shared something in common now – something neither of them had ever seen.

They were together only a few minutes more before Anne returned. Below they could hear the carriage stop, and the bustle that surrounded her entry. She called instructions to Patrick over her shoulder as she came into the room; her lovely face looked a little drawn and pale above the dark fur wrap, but her eyes glowed softly with pleasure as she saw Jane in the big chair and William on the stool close to her knee.

'Well, my loves.'

She held out her arms to William, but her glance included Jane. Again Jane was made acutely aware of the smell of her perfume, the rustle of many silk petticoats as she bent over her son. Anne's presence always seemed identified for Jane as much by smell and the rhythm of her movements, as by the sound of her voice.

She threw off her wrap and settled herself in the chair opposite Jane. William came forward with a stool to put under her feet. He dragged his own stool midway between the two women.

'Ah . . . William! You have two women now to fuss about. Have you been watching Jane sew?'

He nodded briefly; negligently stirring with his foot the pile of gowns on the floor. 'Jane sews so fast – like this!' He gave a comically swooping imitation of the needle flying in and out of the fabric.

Anne smiled; she bent down and examined one of the dresses closely, her fingers running critically over the hem, and a darn in the lace.

'How exquisitely you sew,' she said quietly. Her eyes met Jane's over William's head. 'I've rarely seen anything to equal this.'

Jane nodded. 'Sally was a beautiful needlewoman – when she had time away from the kitchen.'

'I suppose she taught you to cook as well?'

'Why, yes . . . You couldn't help learning . . . seeing it day after day. I've not such a light hand as Sally with pastry, but my sauces are good.'

Anne looked at her for a moment in silence. 'Well . . .' she said at last, 'you've learned things you'd never have glimpsed if you'd been living here.' She fingered the lace again. 'It's no mean accomplishment – Sally's taught you more than I know.'

Jane wanted to say that Sally hadn't taught her to move across a room gracefully, hadn't been able to teach her how to fill awkward moments with light chatter, how to sit in a chair with perfect stillness. These were Anne's gifts, precious things that Jane hungered for. Bending her head, she scowled a little at the sewing in her lap.

'Oh – it's well enough, I suppose,' she said dully.

William was picking through the gowns on the floor. 'You wore that to a ball once, didn't you, Mamma?' he said poking the cream silk.

She nodded. 'That was the last time I wore it – some fool spilt wine there on the side. Jane will have to take out that panel. That blue should look well on you, Jane.' She sighed a little. 'I thought it was a shade too bright for me last time I wore it.' With an almost unconscious gesture she passed her hand over her cheek, as if she felt the lines of age gathering there. She got to her feet, restlessly walked to the window to look out at nothing, then came back and looked over Jane's shoulder at her work. Jane had seen her hurried, nervous glance towards the mirror as she passed. Her white hands looked transparent as they gripped the chair-back.

Suddenly there was a little exclamation from William. He looked quickly and guiltily towards Anne. In his hand he held the wide-brimmed velvet hat; in the other hand, forlornly, lay the velvet rose that had trimmed it.

'Look . . . look what I've done!'

Before Anne could speak Jane reached out and took the rose and the hat from him. 'It's nothing, William! Just a stitch here . . . and one here . . . Looks better than it did in the beginning, doesn't it!'

Anne shrugged her shoulders helplessly. 'You see, William . . . we have someone now who can mend things. Jane's clever with her fingers . . . very clever. Much more than any woman we've ever had in to sew.' She paused. 'I wonder . . .'

Jane sensed the request that was coming; she guessed the pieces of mending waiting, the things that the maids who were never paid had refused to do, the underwear rolled in the drawers laid aside for the stitch they never got, the fraying cuffs on William's coat. Everyone who loved Anne served her; it was natural for her to ask it, and to expect an acceptance.

The request didn't come because Patrick interrupted them. His long neck poked around the door urgently.

'Ma'am, Lord O'Neill has just sent word that you're to dine an hour earlier – with Mr Richard Burgess.'

'Dick – why, Dick's back in town!' Anne's face was pleased and animated. 'Why, I wager he'll clean out Myra Burke's tables. Dick's always lucky – it's lucky just to be with him. I'll win tonight, my loves! I feel it in my bones that I'm going to win!'

Patrick had advanced into the room; he held a candle in his hand. 'And is it so poor we are that we can't afford to have a little light now! Sure 'tis wearing yer eyes down to the sockets ye'll be, Miss Jane.'

As he spoke he lit two candles on the table, and hastened to draw the long curtains. Jane was surprised to see how the dusk had gathered, how little shreds of mist had collected under the eaves of the house opposite. Without noticing it, she had been leaning towards the fire-light to see her work.

Now Patrick had gone into the bedroom – setting a taper to the fire laid there, lighting the candles. Jane saw the colours of the room leap into life, the soft green of the bed hangings, the sheen of rosewood.

'Isn't it time now, ma'am, for you to be getting ready? Lord O'Neill sent word that he'd be round on the stroke of the half-hour, and here you are without your hair curled, and not even a gown laid out . . .' He clicked his tongue. 'An' bad cess to that lump of a girl walking out this morning without even a word to a soul . . .'

As he talked he was busy about the room, taking out and arranging bottles on the toilet table, folding Anne's wrap, laying her hat away. He talked without self-consciousness, as if it was a habit of long standing; he knew Anne heard him, but he never expected an answer. His talk was a privilege that his devotion had earned for him. He enjoyed his monologue enormously.

'An' will you be wearing this white one again, ma'am? . . . sure, ye look like a queen in it, and there's many who'll be there this evening that I'd like to be gettin' an eyeful o' ye . . .'

Anne moved into the bedroom. 'Yes, Patrick, that one . . . though Heaven knows I'm tired enough of it. I saw a lovely thing – green – at Seiker's today. They wanted a young fortune for it, and I owe so much there already . . .' She wandered to the toilet table.

Patrick came close to her. 'An' it's yerself that's not lookin' too well, ma'am,' he said, peering solicitously at her reflection in the mirror. 'Yer not strong . . . I keep tellin' ye yer not strong, an' ye don't get enough rest, and there's all this comin' and goin' . . .'

Still clicking his tongue disapprovingly, he bent over Anne. As a matter of long habit, he began to loosen the hooks of her gown.

Patrick and William had gone, and Jane sat hunched on a stool watching Anne dress her hair. She was skilful, her hands moved swiftly, arranging, patting, pressing. The smell of the hot tongs invaded the room.

'Just as well I've learned to do it myself,' Anne said, looking at Jane in the mirror. 'So many of these wretched girls are careless and stupid – and before you know what's happened, they've burnt a piece off. I don't let anyone touch it now.'

Jane nodded. 'You're very quick.'

'You learn in time . . . it takes patience in the beginning.' She opened the drawer of the toilet table. 'I have a pair of tongs here I don't use. You can take them up to your room.'

'I don't know . . .' Jane began. Then she stopped, unable to voice her thoughts.

Anne laid down the tongs. 'You don't know . . . what?'

Jane gestured helplessly. 'So many things . . . my hair – that's just a beginning. How do I wear a hat like the one you wore this afternoon? How do I learn to say the right things . . .' She clapped her hand over her left eye. 'Why, look at me – I'm not even presentable!'

'Hush!' Anne said soothingly. 'There's much you don't know, but you're not a fool, and you'll learn. You'll learn very quickly, I promise you that.'

'How?'

'Soon – soon enough,' Anne said. 'Almost before you know what's happened. Or before I know . . .'

Jane straightened herself. 'I won't be round your neck long . . . you know that!'

'What are you talking about?'

Jane looked at her without wavering. 'I'm strong, you know. I haven't been bred like you . . . to all this.' Her hand indicated the room, the litter of the toilet table. 'I know how to work. That's all I know.'

Anne shook her head. 'Too late for that, Jane. Too late, my dear. You've gone past that now – very suddenly. If you had chosen to stay behind and marry Harry Black, you would have stayed within what you knew. You would have been safe there – your future settled, nothing more expected of you. But you went beyond that. You asked for something more. We don't know yet what that will be – better or worse than Harry Black. We've got to think, Jane – we've got to think about what's going to happen to you.'

Jane shook her head, bewildered. 'I get frightened when you talk like that. What is there for me? – what can I do? There's no money for me to stay on here . . . I can't earn a living as a governess or anything like that. There's nothing – unless I'm a nursemaid.'

'There has to be something! You'll have to marry!' She flung down the comb. 'But where? . . . where? And how? If I let you out as Ted wanted, you'd be as much of a sensation as he believed. You'd have men flocking about you, the fools! But would there be one to marry you? . . . I don't think so, somehow. That's some-

thing I've learned from all these years. Only it would be harder
for you. In two days the whole town would have named you your
mother's daughter. Do you see that, Jane? Do you know what
I'm talking about? If you had said "yes" when Ted asked you to go
to the party this evening, it would have been the end for you. In
a few weeks you'd have offers – in a few weeks you'd be the mistress
of some man, probably the one who could best afford you. It would
go on like that – and men never seem to marry their mistresses.'

'It happened once,' Jane said. 'Viscount Hindsley . . . surely
you . . . ?'

Anne gave a little shrug of resignation. 'But it didn't happen.
In the end it was just as if Johnny had never been . . . as if I'd
had no right to him. He was so madly in love with me he was
blind to everything else, but when he was drowned I felt it was
because he'd gone against the rules. It's perfectly natural to have
a mistress – but she isn't married and allowed to bear children who
succeed to the title and fortune. And it doesn't do William any
good to reflect that he might have been the heir of a rich man.'
Anne gave a little shudder; her face in the mirror looked haggard.

'I know . . . I know . . .' Jane said.

There was silence between them, and Anne began slowly to
draw the bottles and jars towards her. Carefully, patiently, she
began to apply the cosmetics, the orris root powder, the rouge, the
burnt cork for the eyelids. Jane's gaze never left her.

'It's money!' Anne said suddenly. 'It's always money. Don't let
anyone ever tell you it doesn't matter. It always matters!' She met
her daughter's eyes firmly. 'It wouldn't have made Johnny come
back to life for me – no matter how badly I wanted him – but it
would have made things different for me after he was dead. It's
always easier to bear sorrow when there are not bills waiting to be
paid.' She gave a short, nervous laugh. 'Well, at least it's more
dignified!'

She shrugged again. 'Well . . .' she added, 'I suppose I've had
my time, all the good years when it came to my hand whenever
I wanted it. That was the time when I couldn't go wrong at the
gaming-tables – I just couldn't go wrong! And the men were
generous in those days . . . and always the right ones seemed to
come along when I needed them. I was younger, of course. Men
are always more ready to open their purses to a young face. Well
. . . well, I suppose mine isn't young any more.'

She paused in her task, and craned to look into the mirror more
closely. She turned from side to side, her fingers stroking her white
throat.

'I'm glad now when it comes time to light the candles – I've grown afraid of the strong light. I don't want the sun to shine too brightly because it will show the lines.' She sighed. 'I used to love the strong sunshine.'

She leaned back, away from the mirror. 'I'm thirty-eight years old. That's not very old, Jane – but it's too old to find yourself without money, or any prospect of it. And without a husband to find money for you.

'I wonder if I've become foolish with age!' she added. 'I don't even seem to have the judgement about men I used to have. Once I used to pick and choose . . . I was cautious enough to make certain that he was worth choosing. When it came to parting we did it amiably. My bills were paid, and there was a gift or two thrown in – a necklace or a brooch. I used my head then . . . and planned. The pity of it is that I didn't use it enough to save a little of what I had in plenty. When you're young, you think you can never stop being young.

'It's a sorry thing to see a woman being a fool . . . and when you know it's your own self being foolish, then it's worse. I've watched myself making mistakes, and go on making the same ones again. I've picked the wrong men – or haven't even picked – just let them happen along. A charming smile and a dash of wit was enough. All I needed at times was someone to make me laugh. A woman in business ought to know that she can't afford luxuries like laughter. *I* can't afford it.

'Look at Ted O'Neill – he's another mistake. He's good company – he's gay, and has spirit. And he has no money! He's here in London trying to sell the last of the few acres of bog he's got left somewhere in Ireland. And he's barely got the price to take me to supper or to Vauxhall.

'And yet I keep him round . . . fool that I am! I don't know what else to do – I couldn't stand not having a man around me somewhere.'

She stood up. She was clever with her hands, and the artifice of the cosmetics looked almost natural. What she had said about the candle-light was true; now she looked no different from the woman who had come to The Feathers when Jane was a baby. She stepped into the white gown; her breasts, pushed up by the high tight corset, were almost completely revealed. It was the costume of the fashionable women of the town, and she wore it to perfection. There was a sensation of anticipation in her movements, a little colour in her cheeks now that the day was finished, and the evening was come again – she would laugh and be gay over supper, and afterwards there was the beckoning prospect of the gaming-tables.

Below they caught the sounds of O'Neill's arrival, Patrick's foot-steps on the stairs hurrying to announce him. Jane watched the slight half-smile of pleasure widen on Anne's lips. Everything she had said of herself was true – she couldn't stand not to have a man about her.

2

Anne's household settled down to sleep. In the basement, the cook slept heavily in the arms of the stable hand who worked at the tavern four doors down the street; the room reeked of the gin they had drunk together. Above, in his narrow slit of a room that had once been a pantry, Patrick slumbered lightly, his ears ready to catch the first sound of Anne's return. William lay with his legs curled up to make room for General who slept on the end of his bed.

Jane, with her hair washed and brushed, and wearing a night-gown of Anne's, sat before her fire struggling with a letter to Sally Cooper. The room was cosy against the chill of the spring night – – not a luxurious room like Anne's, plain curtains and a single rug before the hearth. But she found it oppressed her less than the costly and delicate beauty below – she enjoyed the linen sheets and the good china washset without being frightened by them. Most of all she enjoyed the sense of space and privacy – but all this was impossible to convey to Sally. She sharpened the quill again, and wrote a few more lines on the heavy, expensive paper Anne had given her. The words, written in her open, childish hand, looked stupid and ineffectual, she thought.

Earlier Patrick had brought her a toddy – hot and strongly spiced with rum. She fought against her closing eyelids, and wrote steadily on. It had been Patrick's last chore of the day – unless of course, Anne called for anything when she returned; he would then be ready, in nightshirt and tasselled cap, to do what she asked. But when he brought Jane's drink, he had a pleasant feeling of relaxation, and a need to talk. His homely face lightened with pleasure at the sight of Jane.

'Well – is it writin' y' are, now? That's grand – that's grand! Master William, now, he's a great hand with a pen too. Sure, learnin's a wonderful thing, for them that has it!'

He set the toddy before Jane, and backed reluctantly towards the door. 'Is there anythin' else y'll be needin', Miss Jane? Sure y'll not hesitate to call upon me, now, will y'?'

Jane smiled faintly at his anxious and eager expression. 'Thank you, Patrick. I have everything I want.' She gestured towards the room. 'You've made me very comfortable here.'

'Sure, 'tis a pleasure, Miss Jane – 'tis wonderful that y're here now. Master William – he's a mite lonely from time to time, poor wee soul. It's grand that y'll be company for him. And the mistress, too . . . maybe you could . . .'

'Maybe *what*, Patrick?'

'Well . . . she's not strong, Miss Jane, as you'll have noticed. So thin she is, and she'll take no rest at all. An' as for eatin' . . . why the sparrows do better! If you could just persuade her now an' then t' take a little more nourishment, t' sleep a little longer – maybe in the afternoon . . .'

'I'll try, Patrick . . . I don't know. My mother's not a woman who can be told to do things.'

'An' don't I know it, Miss Jane,' he sighed, with the look of one whose patience has been tried beyond the point of speech. 'I don't expect her to listen to an ignorant fella like myself, but I thought if y' just spoke t' her, tactful-like . . .' He spoke with a kind of agonized concern.

'You worry about her a great deal, Patrick . . .' she said gently.

'An' sure, who wouldn't . . . the precious soul that she is.' He looked at her solemnly. 'I don't need to tell y', Miss Jane, that yer mother's the greatest and the kindest lady 'twill ever be me privilege t' know. She had the goodness of an angel.'

Jane looked at him silently, her eyes urging him to go on.

'I have reason enough to remember her goodness . . . she took me in when I was dyin', Miss Jane. I came over from Ireland one terrible bad winter . . . the harvest had been worse than nothin', and there was terrible hunger through the land. There were too many of us already for the farm t' feed, so I took the few shillin' I'd got, and came to try me luck in London. Well, there was I, a raw Irish lad, green from the farm, and it wasn't long before me money was taken from me, and I was walkin' the streets hungry, like any other beggar. There was a terrible lot o' beggars on the streets that winter, Miss Jane. An' I was ill, too – a lung fever that came on so quickly I didn't know what hit me. The mistress found me on her doorstep, half dead, one morning when she was returnin' from a party. Nothin' would do her but that I must be taken into the house, and a doctor called – in the middle of the night, Miss Jane! – for a poor fella like meself! I tell y', that woman's an angel! The best foods I had until I was better – an' me so weak I couldn't stand on me two feet for long after that night. I swear to y', Miss Jane, that I would have been dead by mornin' if she hadn't taken me in. I was past knowin' what was happenin' to me then, but I knew it later, believe me.'

'And you've stayed with her since?'

'Could I think of leavin' her? – specially now when she needs me? I've been with her thirteen years – good years and bad ones. I was with her when Lord Hindsley was drowned, and when Master William was born. Oh, her grief over that was somethin' terrible. If I could have given my life to bring him back I would have done it, Miss Jane. The other servants – they've come and gone, but I've stayed because she needs me.'

'You haven't wanted to marry, Patrick? – to have your own life . . .'

He looked at her in wonderment. 'Sure, where among all the dirty trollops about here could there be anyone even a little like the mistress? Sure, it would sicken me stomach to have to look at another woman about me who wasn't like her – she's such a lovely lady, Miss Jane.'

'Yes . . .' she said softly. 'Yes, Patrick, she is.'

He left then, happy and complete because he had been permitted to talk about Anne. Jane went back to her letter thoughtfully. There were so many things to try to tell Sally apart from the bare fact that she was here, with Anne. There was this new side of Anne which Patrick had revealed, the compassionate woman behind the frivolity, the tender mother to William . . . there was this strange household itself, running on debt, and the whim of the cards. There was also the new experience of Blake's Reach, of the existence of a family back in Anne's past. There was too much to tell. In the end she wrote to Sally a self-conscious letter, telling her the details of the trip, and begging for news of Harry Black. She was dissatisfied and unhappy with it as she pressed down the wax with Anne's seal.

She fell asleep conscious that she was under Anne's roof. Patrick's toddy did its work even against the current of excitement which made her restless and wakeful. But she dreamed as she slept, and her dreams were not only of Anne, but of William also. She saw them both, walking by the sea, wrapped in the mists of the dream, and they entered together the house that William had called Blake's Reach. She herself stood by the gateway, and watched them enter; they didn't see or notice her, and she knew that she was an observer in the dream, and not part of it.

The grey dawn was breaking over the house tops when she woke briefly to hear Anne's subdued voice, and the deeper one which belonged to Lord O'Neill. Then she turned over and slept again, quietly this time, and dreamlessly. The noise of London's early morning began to stir about her.

4

Jane had to lift her skirts high above the mud. Jerome Taylor had tried to insist on her staying in the carriage until they reached the other side of the square where the arcade was; but, of the London she had so far seen, Covent Garden remained Jane's favourite place, and she had overridden his objections, and dismissed the hackney carriage, determined this time to walk among the stalls herself. It was her third visit here, and she looked about her, pleased by her growing sense of familiarity. Jerome held her anxiously by the elbow; William walked on her other side, his face bright in the midday sun. She found herself studying the porticoed entrance to the great church, which dominated the square, with interest, and some affection. It was a fine thing to be able to recognize a London landmark.

'Do you like it, Miss Jane?' Jerome Taylor murmured close by her ear. 'It was built by Inigo Jones.'

Jane had never heard of Inigo Jones, but obviously his work was something to admire, so she craned to look at the building through the almost solid masses of people and traffic, of carriages, carts and wagons. Strangely it did not seem at all aloof from the teeming activity surrounding it. She thought it joined with nice harmony into the arcaded shops that formed the side of the square. In the centre of the Garden were the wooden stalls of the vegetable sellers, the fruit sellers, the herb sellers – and overhead the pigeons wheeled and circled in endless monotony, their raucous cries mingled with the rapid voices of the humans who jammed the narrow alleys between the stalls. There was din and confusion – there were more people than Jane had ever seen together at one time. There was the strong odour of rotting food, and sweaty, unwashed bodies, of decaying clothes and grease. There was also the occasional whiff of scented hair pomade as some young man of fashion strolled by; there was the smell of London grit.

Jerome gripped her elbow more firmly as they stepped out into the stream of traffic to cross to the arcade; William also reached up, with an air of protectiveness, to take her other arm. Gradually they worked their way across. The ringing curses of hackney drivers, and the derisive laughter of the barefooted street urchins who dashed almost under their wheels were all about them. Underfoot, the cobbles were slimy with squashed, rotting vegetables and manure. In the arcade were the coffee-houses, the music and print shops, the open doorways where the prostitutes lounged, waiting for clients. Above almost every shop were the bagnios where a couple could remain undisturbed for an afternoon or a night. At the back of the arcade were the crowded lanes and alleys where the brothels and bawdy-houses flourished. It was an evil and noisy place, a hub for the city's teeming life. Jane's senses explored it wonderingly.

A tattered woman whose face was both young and old beneath its filthy cap, thrust a bunch of sweet-smelling herbs towards her; a peddler tried to sell her a brilliant blue bird in a cage; the bird was huddled miserably on the perch, shivering. William suddenly pulled his hand free and ran back to the woman. He fumbled in his pockets for a penny, and the woman favoured him with a grin which showed her broken teeth.

'Gor blessya, luv!' Her breath reeked of gin.

William gave the herbs to Jane, pleased that he, and not Jerome, had thought of buying them.

They entered The Bedford Coffee House. It was dark inside; and they felt rather than saw the sawdust under their feet. The day's newspapers were spread on the table they were given. Jane blinked rapidly in the dimness; there was almost as much noise here as in the Garden. Men argued furiously, and in the same breath called amiable greeting to acquaintances across the room. The waiters sped about in dirty aprons. Jane wrinkled her nose a little thinking of how Sally Cooper would have disapproved of the musty atmosphere. But when the chocolate was served it was delicious – sweet, hot, and as thick as syrup. They sipped it contentedly, making some cohesion now out of the din. At the table next to them a thin, middle-aged man sat writing at a steady pace, taking no notice at all of the traffic and the talk surrounding him.

Jerome leaned towards her. 'It's probably a pamphlet or gossip-sheet, Miss Jane. They sit in places like this and collect their information.'

There were only two other women in the room. It was too early for the fashionable women of the town. The Covent Garden coffee-houses were the last calls on the long way home to bed. When the more respectable places had closed their doors, the arcade and streets of this district sprang into dubious life. Often liveried coachmen and carters bringing the early produce to market crossed angry words in the grey dawn. The Bedford was one of the most famous of the shops – the wife of the proprietor ran the largest bawdy-house in the town. Jane knew that Anne came here sometimes to listen to the newest piece of scandal, lingering to read the latest pamphlets which thundered against the Jacobins until the light grew strong over the steeple of St Peter's. Jane remembered how often Anne had spoken of The Bedford in the past; it was the place where high life and vice rubbed shoulders with the greatest ease.

Jane turned from her scrutiny of the man at the next table, and began to examine the room again; a low red fire burned in the great hearth. Over the years the smoke from it had blackened the panelled walls, and dimmed the vivid colours of the lewd painting that hung over the mantel. Jane studied the picture – in Hampstead there had never been a painting like this one exhibited in public view. She turned and found Jerome's eyes on her. He reddened, and looked down at his cup.

She had been in Anne's house for over four weeks, and March had passed into April. From the first day, the ease and softness of life in Anne's household fitted Jane like the gowns she had made over for herself. She learned that it was possible to sleep after the sun came up, to expect hot water waiting when she did rise; she put goose grease on her rough hands and watched them grow soft and white, the bruise around her eye had vanished. Jane knew she enjoyed this sense of ease, but it never became wholly real to her; daily she expected it to end.

Jerome Taylor was a part of the new life. From the first day when they had passed each other on the stairs he had invented every kind of excuse to be in her company. She grew used to seeing his eyes follow her – but, without knowing the reason why, he irritated her vaguely. Perhaps it was because she had always imagined a scholar would have no thoughts to spare for women. But he was handsome in a quiet way, and had pleasing manners – and quite obviously he spared time to think of her. She needed friends in this new world, so she smiled on him, and accepted his stammered compliments. In return he gave her a gentle devotion.

The days passed and inevitably she began to grow restless. There was not enough occupation for her energies in the house – the gowns Anne had given her were all renovated, and she had finished all the mending that had piled up. With Patrick's help, she turned out cupboards all over the house, settling order into their chaos, and at the same time earning the hatred of Anne's slatternly cook.

The time began to pass heavily, because life at The Feathers had never trained her to sit in the white and gold drawing-room with a tapestry frame. Anne's round of activities was ceaseless; she was happy and lighthearted because the luck seemed to be with her and she gaily attributed this change to Jane's presence. She paid a few of the most pressing debts to get rid of the dunners, and ordered the gown she had admired from Seiker's – also one for Jane. Jane was pleased by Anne's good-humour, but a sense of guilt gnawed at her. There was no sign that Harry Black was going to make charges, and she worried less about the danger from that direction. With this gone, the days stretched before her idly.

At last, a little desperate, she went to Anne and suggested that she must find some employment. It would have to be somewhere away from London – Anne's reputation and her methods of getting money would make a situation in London nearly impossible. Her fine gowns and her hands that grew always softer were no help either. Anne shrugged her shoulders.

'Child, enjoy yourself while you're able! When the money's gone will be time enough to think about what you must do. Enjoy yourself . . .'

But where? . . . with whom? There was only William and Jerome Taylor; the whole teeming world of London waited beyond Anne's silken-curtained windows, and her only companions were the child and his tutor. She began to slip into the schoolroom, and listened to Jerome's pleasant voice as he read history with William; with faint wonder she studied the maps that recorded Captain Cook's voyages in the Pacific, and heard accounts of the settlement at Botany Bay in New South Wales. Jerome Taylor responded instantly to her need and loneliness. He went to Anne and asked if Miss Jane shouldn't be taken to see the sights of the town. William, of course, would go with them.

Anne had lain back in her bed chuckling over it when Jane entered the bedroom one morning.

'Oh, Jane, that poor young man! He's dazzled! And I was just about to forget to pay his salary this month – now I'll have to find it somewhere. I couldn't have it on my conscience.'

And she told it to Lord O'Neill with great relish.

Jerome's devotion made Jane uncomfortable. She wasn't used to being treated as if she hadn't seen a mud puddle in her life before. But she learned to play the part he expected from her reasonably well, knowing that he had mixed with gentlewomen all his life, and was impressing her with the pattern. She stifled her impatience and high spirits, and tried to remember the things he talked about. She followed him quietly round the city's churches which Christopher Wren had built. She learned to draw him out. He would talk on happily, and nothing was beyond him – the Revolution in France, the War of Independence that had cost England her American colonies, the root system of the dandelion growing at their feet in the churchyard, the science of botany, and what he hoped to record on the voyage in the South Seas. She listened to it all, and tried to remember. He knew more than she had believed was contained in one mind. He loved music and painting too – as his confidence grew he began to talk of visits to the playhouses, occasions when William could not be present. She was eager for the experience of learning the city by night. These excursions to Covent Garden and The Bedford were a step in that direction, a faint brush with the world that Anne inhabited.

William's head turned and twisted endlessly; he sipped his chocolate and let nothing go by him. He had all of Anne's restless curiosity. These past days with Jane and Jerome Taylor had been blissfully happy ones for him – free from lessons of a formal sort, and mingling with the crowds and bustle he loved. He approved of The Bedford completely, approved of Jane because she drew the glances of the men, approved of the packed, suffocating odours. He liked the world as he saw it.

Then he spoke suddenly. 'There's a man over there who keeps staring. I've stared back at him, and frowned, and I've shaken my head at him. But he just goes on staring.'

Jerome Taylor looked angry. 'Who? . . . where?'

'Over there, behind you.' Jerome turned round quickly as William indicated the man – a youngish man, with the aged, timeless look of a sailor, the faded eyes and the weathered skin. He wore a sailor's jersey and a tasselled cap.

'Who – *that* fellow?' Jerome looked back at Jane. 'Miss Jane, perhaps you would like to go. This is no place to have a scene. It would be all over the town in a day . . .'

'Oh, hush!' Jane broke in. 'Look – he's getting up! He's coming over here!' Jerome's eyes clouded, because she was visibly excited and expectant.

Without haste the sailor made his way through the crowd, never taking his eye off the group, staring at them unblinkingly and without embarrassment. He bent over the table a little. Indignantly, Jerome rose to his feet.

'Look here . . . !'

The sailor took no notice of him. 'You'll be a Blake,' he said to Jane.

'What?'

'You'll be a Blake,' he repeated. 'You'll be a child of Anne Blake, or I'm a dead man.'

Jane looked at him with rounded, astonished eyes. 'Yes . . . Yes, that's right! My name's Jane Howard. Anne Blake is my mother.'

He nodded, a wide grin splitting his face. He pulled his cap off his head.

'I seen y' 'ere once before, an' I said t' myself soon as I clapped eyes on y' were kin o' the Blake family . . . but this time I were sure.' His eyes examined her face again carefully, wonderingly. 'Well . . . so y'er Miss Anne's and Tom Howard's child! Miss Anne — she were about yer age when I seen her last. She were much of an age with meself.'

'You knew her when she was at Blake's Reach?' Jane said. It was strange to hear that name uttered like this to a man she had never seen before.

He nodded again. 'It were like I said — she were much of an age with meself, and she used t' come ridin' through Appledore most every day. Sometimes she'd stop by the cottage and talk with me mother. Why — the whole Marsh knew Miss Anne. Blake's Reach weren't big enough to hold her. She were out in all weathers, and she used t' talk t' every living soul she met on the road. The way she used to act — the folks used t' say the whole Marsh belonged t' her.'

He warmed to his own memories. 'Just you ask her if she don't remember riding into Appledore and talkin' with Mary Thomas . . . and young Adam hangin' round to catch a glimpse o' her. She were that pretty! There were so many Thomases around in them days y' couldn't hardly stir a step without y' fell over one o' them. Ask 'er if she remembers!'

'She remembers — I'm sure she remembers!' This was from William, who couldn't contain himself any longer. His face was flushed with excitement.

The sailor turned and regarded William carefully. 'An' this will be another Blake — same hair, same mouth.'

'My half-brother,' Jane said. After a slight hesitation, she added, 'Won't you take a seat?'

Jerome Taylor's expression was thunderous as the man slipped easily into the seat by Jane; he was outraged and ruffled. But a glance from Jane forbade any objection; stiffly he acknowledged the introduction Jane made.

Adam Thomas was not at all disturbed by Jerome's scowl. He

continued talking calmly. 'We did 'ear, down on the Marsh, that
Miss Anne had a child – maybe two or three. Just scraps o' news,
y' know – maybe picked up from one o' the folks from Rye, who'd
been t' London. But I come up 'ere to London meself a few weeks
back, an' I begin askin' about 'er. Was told she comes 'ere t' The
Bedford once in a while. I've been keepin' an eye skinned for 'er
– she always bein' so friendly-like, she'd never take offence at any
of the Marsh folk speakin' to 'er . . .' He looked pointedly across
at Jerome.

'Miss Anne ain't never been back t' the Marsh,' Adam observed
regretfully. 'We always did 'ope that maybe some day she would
make it up with the old man. But the Blakes – they always been
'igh-spirited and proud people. Weren't no way, really, that Miss
Anne could make amends, and the old man ain't the forgivin' type.
Proud as peacocks, the Blakes are! Always 'igh and mighty they've
been, and there's some o' the gentry about as 'asn't liked it – but I
say – and there's many a one as says it with me – that it'll be a bad
thing when the Blakes go from the Marsh. An' the time's comin'
pretty soon, ma'am, when there'll be none on the Marsh who's a
Blake, either by birth or name. As long as the Marsh folk remember, there's been a Blake . . . It'll seem wrong without them.'

'Without them?' Jane echoed. 'Why?'

Thomas shrugged. 'Why, ma'am . . . Well, it's plain old Spencer
can 'ardly last the year – 'e's drinkin' 'eavy. I do 'ear, and 'e's not
a young man any more. Seems like 'e don't care, neither . . . the
land's almost all gone, and the 'ouse be fallin' down about 'is ears.'

'The land's gone? *Why?*'

He shrugged again. 'That's 'ardly my business, is it, Miss Jane?
What the gentry do is their affair – and it's not for the likes o' me
t' 'ave anything to say about it. If Spencer Blake takes too much
t' drink when 'e's settled down with the cards . . . well, a man's got
the right to gamble with 'is own property. But once y' start slicin'
up a fine property like that was – sellin' a bit 'ere, a bit there –
well, it don't amount t' much, now. The tenant farmers 'ave most
of it – and old Spencer, 'e 'asn't troubled to improve the sheep,
and they're a pretty run down lot, not givin' anythin' like the yield
o' wool or mutton, or the fancy price the Blake's Reach stuff used
t' fetch. A pity like – that's what I say.'

'The land's gone . . .' Jane repeated it in a dazed fashion.

'Aye – it's gone, an' beggin' Miss Anne's pardon, there's no one
could really blame Spencer. There's the man all alone in the great
house, not kith or kin near 'im. 'Taint any wonder 'e takes a drop.
It seems 'e don't care what 'appens to 'im, or t' Blake's Reach.

There be no one t' leave it t' after 'e's gone – that is, no one who'll live on the Marsh. After Miss Anne ran away with Tom Howard, 'twas said 'e named the nephew, the dark little one who was half-French, in 'is will. But then 'e ran away back to France. But it don't matter whether Spencer left 'im in the will or cut 'im out, because 'e's dead.'

'Dead?'

'Aye . . . 'is 'ead cut off in this Revolution that's goin' on. I remember 'im almost as clear as Miss Anne – as dark as the devil, 'e was, and could ride a horse like I never seen before. Well, 'e's dead, now – and 'tain't likely there'll ever be Blakes on the Marsh again . . .'

'No . . . I expect not . . .'

He scratched his head slowly. 'Well – I was thinkin' that maybe I'd perhaps see Miss Anne about 'ere some place. I could 'a' told 'er about 'ow feeble old Spencer's gettin' . . . maybe she'd go and visit 'im. Guess even people as proud as the Blakes make it up sometimes. Would do the old man good if she went back and saw 'im – would kind o' lift 'im up if 'e saw 'is grandchildren. 'E's a touchy old devil, is Spencer – but there can't never be a man as won't feel like makin' friends when 'e's near to dyin'.'

Jane nodded. 'I'll tell my mother what you've said – maybe some time she'll be here, and you must say it all again to her. How long will you be in London?'

He scratched his head again. 'Can't rightly say. I get some work from time t' time. Was figgerin' I'd get t'gether a few shillin's and make me way to Liverpool, and ship out from there.' He grinned suddenly, and his face seemed full of an unholy glee. ''Ad a brush with the Customs men a few weeks back, so the Marsh ain't exactly 'ealthy for me right now. But I'll be back! – some day I'll be back! The pickin's are too good t' lose . . .'

He favoured Jane with a broad wink, and another grin, as if she shared some fantastic plot with him. He rose to his feet then.

'I'll bid y' good day, Miss Jane – and you'll please remember me kindly to Miss Anne. Just tell 'er what I've told you – and say it came from Adam Thomas. That's all.'

'Wouldn't you come and tell her yourself?'

He shook his head. ''Tain't for the likes o' me t' be callin' on Miss Anne. Just tell 'er the old man's slippin' – that's enough. No one tells Miss Anne what t' do – no one! An' this ain't none o' me business, see. Ain't none o' me business!'

He made an attempt at a clumsy bow, and strode out of the coffee-house, disappearing into the crowd in the Garden. Jane

watched his sailor's cap bobbing; when he was gone from sight she
turned quickly to Jerome. Her face was pale; two brilliant spots
of colour burned in her cheeks.

'I must go back now. I must speak with my mother.'

2

Anne sat once again before her mirror; she listened while Jane
talked. Her face, reflected in the pale oval, was thoughtful; she
nodded quietly at Jane's words.

'So . . . Charlie's dead! . . . And Father is dying! Well, that's
the end of the Blakes!' Her voice was curiously hollow and lifeless.

'Don't you care?'

'Care?' Anne stirred a little. 'I don't know – it's so long since
I've seen Father I can hardly feel what it will be like to know that
he's dead. And Charlie – he was a little boy when I left. He was
my first cousin, the only child of Spencer's brother, who married
a Frenchwoman. I can't think of him as a man who has lost his
head. All I remember of Charlie was the way he used to ride
across the Marsh as if he and the pony were one animal. He was
so dark, Charlie was – and so silent. It's as if you told me a shadow
was dead.'

'But you don't care? . . . about Blake's Reach?'

Now Anne's expression took form and meaning. 'Care about
Blake's Reach? You mean why don't I go and make it up with
Father and he will leave Blake's Reach to me? Well – I'll tell you
plainly. I hate Blake's Reach! And I'd rather die than have to go
back to live there!'

'But the inheritance?'

'What inheritance?' Anne snapped. 'Will it do me any good to
inherit a crumbling pile of bricks, and a mountain of debts? I have
enough debts of my own!'

'How do you know?' Jane persisted. 'How can you be sure that
Adam Thomas knows all the truth? Or that he knows any of it?
He may be wrong.'

'He's not wrong. The Marsh people always know everything
that whispers or breathes on the Marsh. Adam Thomas's father
was one of our shepherds, and his father before him. The mother
worked in our dairy. Don't you think they know? Believe me,
they know almost as much as Father does about Blake's Reach!
Didn't he say that the land was gone? Well, let me tell you – that
land is money. You need land for sheep, and sheep are all that
matter on the Romney Marsh.'

'But there must be something! – something that's worth saving!'
Jane's voice was anguished. She couldn't believe what her senses
were telling her – that Anne meant to do nothing about Blake's
Reach, that she wouldn't stir a finger to keep any part of it for
herself, that she could let it all be submerged in a tide of indifference.

'There's nothing worth saving – nothing! There was almost
nothing worth saving twenty years ago when I ran away with Tom.
Father had a match all made for me with a man who could have
put Blake's Reach back on its feet. Only he didn't take into account
the fact that I didn't care enough for Blake's Reach to save it at
the expense of myself.' She gave an angry toss of her head, and
her lovely voice grew a trifle shrill. 'He pretended he loved me –
worshipped me! But all it was was pride in the way I looked, and
how I sat a horse. He gave me everything I wanted, but all it
meant was that in the end I should be agreeable to marrying myself
to Roger Pym, and living on that God-forsaken Marsh for the rest
of my days.

'Do you think,' she demanded harshly, 'that I care to go back
now and drop on my knees to him, just so that I'll inherit the mess
he chose to make of his life? I'm in a mess too – but at least it's
one of my own making! Do you think I could go back there and
live? You don't know what it's like, Jane. Just flat – all of it, and
Blake's Reach standing on the cliff above the Marsh where the sea
winds cut you to pieces, and the roads so bad in winter that you
couldn't even travel the six miles to Rye for a little company and
gaiety. There's nothing but flat miles of sheep, and beyond them,
the sea. Just think of it! – sitting by the fire all winter long, and
listening to the gales sweeping up the Channel . . . and knowing
that there was nothing to do except struggle up the hill every third
Sunday, to sit in the Blake pew in the church great-grandfather
Blake built with money he had stolen in the Marlborough wars.
No news, no excitement – nothing except the whisper that runs
round the Marsh when a big run of smugglers' goods have been
safely landed. The only lights that show on the Marsh by night,
Jane, are the beacons and the lanterns that light the smugglers'
luggers into anchor. On the one hand you have murderers and
cut-throats for company – on the other there's the country squires,
with their dowdy wives and daughters.'

'Murderers? What do you mean – *murderers*?'

Anne said quietly, 'In all of England there's no district so
favourable to the smuggling fraternity. They're born seamen, Jane
– more brave and reckless than men have right to be. Tea and

brandy and tobacco – the whole country uses smuggled goods without thinking that they break the law by not paying Customs duty on them. And it's the men along the coast from Kent to Cornwall who bring it in. The Romney Marsh has an edge on all the other counties because it has the wool that the Flemish weavers need. They take wool instead of gold to pay for the tea and brandy. They make fortunes, Jane – real fortunes! Don't you think men will murder for such money? I can tell you that the life of the man who informs isn't worth a penny piece on the Marsh. He had best say his prayers.

'That's what the Marsh means, Jane – smugglers, sheep and clottish squires. Could you expect me to want to go running there now to a father I have never cared for, and who has never cared for me? Could you see me *living* there, even if the land and the money wasn't all gone? It's unthinkable!'

In those terms, it was unthinkable. Jane turned away slowly. 'Yes, it is,' she said.

Over by the window she stood for a long time pondering what Anne had said. It sounded bleak and sombre – the long winters of Channel storms and the slow pace of country life. She thought of the old man who was dying there alone, who had quarrelled with every living blood relation – and who, perhaps, was now regretting it. She thought of the long succession of Blakes who had been on the Marsh, the house and the family that Anne hated, but which symbolized part of the life of the Marsh itself to Adam Thomas. It seemed criminal to her that Anne should make no attempt to salvage some of it. The energies of a family for generations had gone into the making of this, the last one – and she was going to cast it aside like a gown out of fashion. The whole idea made Jane desperate and rebellious.

'The Blakes – they've been there a long time?' she asked. 'Even hundreds of years?'

'Three or four hundred years, for certain, Jane. They were there when the Marsh really *was* a marsh, with the tide waters sweeping in when the Channel ran high. They helped dig the ditches and the innings that drained it, and made it one of the most fertile lands in England. They are part of the Marsh, almost as old as it is. They're a proud name there – even now, when the power's gone from it, it's a name that's remembered. They've held titles and positions – Lords Proprietors of the Romney Marsh, and Barons of the Cinque Ports with the right to carry the canopy of the Sovereign as he goes to Coronation.

'Oh yes, it's an old and a proud name, Jane. But the Blakes are finished. Leave them in peace.'

Then she rose from the toilet table, and went downstairs to the drawing-room, her mouth folded in a bitter and angry line. The brisk rustle of her petticoat seemed crisp and determined. Soon the sound of her laughter floated up, the artificially gay laughter of a woman who was seething inside.

Jane stayed for a long time staring at nothing through the window.

'There has to be some way to convince her,' she whispered to herself. 'She has to go to Blake's Reach. *She has to go!*'

3

At The Theatre Royal *The Beggar's Opera* was playing. Jerome Taylor had shyly stammered an invitation to Jane, and managed to ignore William's pleading eyes. Now he moved, tongue-tied with pride and happiness, beside Jane through the foyer of the theatre. The first act was over, and the audience spilled out of the pit in a bewildering press, laughing, talking, humming airs from the opera which they had known all their lives. The people from the boxes came down to push their own way into the throng. The air was suffocating with the mingled smells of perfume and hair pomade.

Jane eyed the scene with delight, and Jerome with great contentment. He was quite certain that there was no other woman there to hold a candle to Jane. She wore a white gown, and Anne had loaned her a fur-trimmed wrap. He wondered how she managed to look like a woman of fashion well used to attending the theatre, and still retain some of the freshness that had so attracted him when she had first come from Hampstead. Seeing her now as she slowly swished her fan in an imitation of Anne's movements, it was an effort to recall her bruised eye and frightened manner on that first day. She had, he decided, used her five weeks in her mother's household to startling effect. It was only at this thought, and of the future, that his brow clouded a little.

Jane had been happily silent beside him, watching the crowd and storing up every detail against the time for recollection. Now she suddenly stared and snapped her fan shut.

'Look, there's Lord O'Neill! Oh! . . . he's seen us!'

Jerome turned and saw, and inwardly cursed. Lord O'Neill was shouldering his way through the crowd, obviously making towards them. He reached them, smiling good-humouredly at the crush, bowed to Jane and kissed her hand.

'My dear Miss Jane – how beautiful you look!'

She thanked him with a smile, conscious that beside her Jerome had greeted O'Neill in a tone that was barely civil. She broke in quickly. 'Is my mother here? – I believed she was not feeling well this evening. She said she would stay at home.'

O'Neill shrugged. 'That's what I was told – and she didn't appear to want my company, so I took myself off . . .' He turned his smile on Jerome now. 'She told me, Mr Taylor, that you had accompanied Miss Jane to the theatre, and I was wondering if I could prevail upon you to allow a lonely man to take you both to supper. It really would be a great kindness on your part . . .'

Jerome stiffened, and his face grew red. 'Why – I hardly think . . .'

O'Neill turned appealingly to Jane. 'You won't desert me, Miss Jane? Think how lost I am without your mother's company. Perhaps you can persuade Mr Taylor . . .'

'I . . . well . . .' She wanted desperately to go with him, to taste just once the sort of company that her mother knew night after night. She wondered where they would dine, and whom she might see there, what prominent figures from the political and social scene would be pointed out to her. Perhaps she might even be introduced to one or two of them . . . her thoughts ran on wildly. She was wearing a gown that was fit for any occasion, any company; just once she wanted to find out what it was like to dine with a titled man who was a part of the fashionable world of London, wanted to be treated as if she also belonged there. Only the thought of Jerome made her hesitate. If she wished she could pretend not to notice his discomfort; she knew he would submit to any decision she made. But she had seen the look of disappointment that had come over his face.

'Well, Miss Jane – what do you say? Will you come?'

She didn't have time to reply. O'Neill turned as he felt a hand fall on his shoulder. His face brightened with pleasure as he recognized the two men standing behind him.

'Gerald! When did you come back to Town? – I didn't know you were here.'

The other man, dark like O'Neill, and almost as tall, took his outstretched hand. 'Got back from the bogs today, Ted. And thanking Providence I have! – Ireland is no place to spend the winter. But my good lady wife will present me with an heir in two months, and is determined he shall be born on the estate. So I've left her to contemplate the bogs, and I've come to enjoy myself a little . . .' He was no longer interested in O'Neill, but was staring directly at Jane.

O'Neill turned. 'Forgive me, Miss Jane. May I present my cousin – Gerald Hickey . . .' His flourish indicated the second man. 'And my good friend, Sir Phillip Guest. Miss Jane Howard.' Then he added hurriedly, 'Oh . . . and this is Jerome Taylor.'

Jane found her hand being kissed by both men, while appraising eyes were run expertly over her.

The one O'Neill had called Phillip Guest spoke now. 'Charmed! . . . and charming!' Then his brow wrinkled a little. 'Howard! . . . isn't that . . .'

'Anne's daughter,' O'Neill said. 'Miss Jane has come from the country to visit her mother. Anne was indisposed tonight, and I was fortunate enough to find Miss Jane here with Mr Taylor. I was just trying to persuade them both to keep me company at supper.'

'That's splendid!' Hickey spoke now; he was smiling broadly at Jane, and still holding her hand. She had to give a little tug to free it. 'You'll allow us to join you, Ted?' He nodded to Jane. 'Your mother and I are friends of long standing . . . Sir Phillip has also known her for many years.'

Then he clapped O'Neill again on the shoulder. 'Where has Anne kept her all this time? London has far too few red-headed women, and none so lovely, Miss Jane. Anne Howard's daughter . . . well . . .'

Guest broke in then. 'Look here – do we have to stay to the end of this thing? Tony Cox is gathering some friends together at Drake's . . . why don't we all go there now? It would be an amusing evening . . . and Miss Jane would . . .'

Jane no longer hesitated. She laid her hand firmly on Jerome's arm. She smiled at them all demurely as she spoke. 'I'll have to beg you to excuse me, gentlemen. I'm feeling a trifle unwell myself, and I was about to ask Mr Taylor to take me home immediately.'

As she curtsied she caught the wondering and puzzled exchange of glances between the three, the shrugs and the raised eyebrows. She knew that they were not at all deceived by her pretence. She hadn't intended them to be.

No words passed between herself and Jerome until they were settled finally in the hackney carriage, but she felt the reassuring pressure of his hand under her elbow. At last, in the darkness of the coach, she spoke to him.

'I'm sorry, Jerome. I'm sorry to spoil your evening. I had to leave – you know that!' And then: 'I was getting beyond my depth.'

'I understand, Miss Jane.' There was more warmth than disappointment in his tone.

When they reached Albemarle Street she was still a little dazed by the shock of realizing how firmly she was labelled as Anne's daughter. Had she wished it, this evening could have been the beginning of a new episode, a whole career. It was there, ready and waiting for her; but if she were to repeat Anne's life, it would have to be because she chose to do it, not because it was expected of her. In those few moments she had felt her newly found identity threatened. In the minds of O'Neill and his friends she was not a person in her own right, but another Anne, and it was assumed that she would think and behave exactly as Anne did. She was discovering at last that she was not permitted to go into Anne's world on her own terms; the terms were already made for her.

Anne had heard them return, and she came out of the drawing-room, and stood at the top of the stairs.

'Jane!' Her voice was shrill and unnaturally loud. 'You're back early!' And then as Jerome closed the door she added, questioningly, 'Isn't Lord O'Neill with you?'

Jane shook her head. 'I wasn't feeling well. I asked Jerome to bring me back.'

'Did you meet Ted? Was he there?'

'Yes, we met him. He was going to supper with his cousin, Gerald Hickey, and Sir Phillip Guest.'

'Did he ask you to go?'

Jane hesitated, but Anne's eyes were on her firmly. 'Yes,' she said.

'Why didn't you?'

Jane had had enough of it. 'I thought I had already explained that. I'm not feeling well.' With great deliberation she turned her back on Anne, and began to pull off her gloves. But the gesture was wasted; Anne had already started up the stairs to her bedroom.

Later, when Jane was alone in her own room, she lay for a long time, fully dressed, on the bed, staring at the ceiling. It was cracked, and would soon need repair; she traced the line of cracks, her mind was busy with the new problem she had suddenly found tonight in this house.

'I can't stay here,' she whispered, twisting her face towards the pillow. 'I can't stay here!'

4

Jane knew that she had to go, and that it must be soon. But there was no time to speak to Anne, or to try to disentangle the currents of jealousy and resentment that had been so crudely revealed in that conversation on the stairs. What neither of them knew was that, by the next day, time had almost finished for Anne.

It had been strangely humid for April, and when the rain started in the early evening Jane and William watched it falling past the window with a feeling of relief. They thought only momentarily of Anne, who had said casually that she might take a boat down to Chelsea with O'Neill and some others. Jane and William were both in bed when she returned, and so they didn't know that her gown was still wet from the drenching she had had, or that even so soon there was the dampness of fever on her skin.

It was Patrick who called Jane from the schoolroom in the middle of the morning, at the time he usually gave Anne her chocolate. His sharp face was made sharper by panic.

'It's the mistress, Miss Jane – she's ill!'

For four days they watched the struggle – it was only a slight struggle on Anne's part. Death waited on her almost from the beginning. She lay propped up against high pillows making a small effort to breathe; the flesh seemed to drop off her frame with terrifying swiftness. With frightened eyes Jane saw the bluish lips, heard the soft bubbling liquid in her lungs. When she coughed, the mucus was blood-streaked.

The doctor would give a despairing shrug of his shoulders. 'Not strong enough to fight – she was worn out before it began.'

In the end, it seemed as if she drowned in that engulfing liquid; her eyes looked out helplessly from a face sunken into age, and she paid no heed to Patrick's imploring voice and gestures. When she died, William was almost the first to know it. After Patrick's instinctive movement towards Anne, he gave one sharp shriek of terror, and flung himself into Jane's arms. O'Neill stood transfixed at the bottom of the bed, not moving or saying anything for a long time; his face had the look of confusion and disbelief. Patrick was weeping.

Jane bent and put her arms about William, and took him away from the sight of Anne. At the same moment she consciously recognized that she was taking up what remained of Anne's life.

In comforting William she found distraction from a bewilderment almost as great as O'Neill's; when at last she was alone to face her own reaction to her mother's death, her grieving took the form of a protest, a desperate crying out because the time had been too short. Not too short for Anne herself, who had wanted no old age of faded looks and ailing body; it was she, Jane, who had been cheated. There hadn't been enough time to know Anne as more than a radiant but vague personality; there hadn't been enough time to learn from her all the things she wanted desperately to

know, there hadn't been time to plan with her any kind of future
for herself and William, or to make any move to consolidate it.
So when she wept for Anne they were tears to ease the lonely ache
in her heart, but they were also the selfish tears of youth, angry and
unforgiving.

It was Jane who made the choice of the place where Anne should
be buried. Of all the churches Jerome Taylor had shown her, she
remembered only one clearly.

'The one in Covent Garden,' she said.

When it was over she knew that they all waited on her expectantly – O'Neill, Jerome, Patrick and William. They waited for her
to speak as Anne had done, to make all the necessary plans and
decisions. O'Neill knew that he had no place any longer in the
household, but he waited still – waited for the woman he had seen
buried in Covent Garden where the endless rumble of the wheels,
and the nasal Cockney voices could reach her. He, like the others,
hovered about Jane, because it seemed that in her Anne still lived.

She was completely Anne's daughter when she did make up
her mind, prepared to face argument with stubbornness, and go
ahead with her plans. She had lived with Anne for less than six
weeks, but she knew all that Anne had been, and she knew what
was expected of her. Even if she shed tears at night into her pillow,
they weren't permitted to show next day in her face.

'We can't stay in London – William and I,' she said.

'Where will you go?'

'We will go to Blake's Reach.'

5

All of them had arguments against it – but none of them could
suggest any other plan. Already the bill-collectors were at the door,
more persistent than ever now that Anne was dead.

'We can't stay in London, that's plain,' Jane said firmly. 'Wherever we go in this town they'll be dunning me for money, and
there's nothing to pay them with. If I go to my grandfather perhaps
. . . well, there's a chance he'll take us in. If he doesn't . . .' She
shrugged her shoulders. 'We won't be any worse off than we are
now.'

Patrick spoke up desperately. 'Then I'll go with you, ma'am.'

They looked at him startled.

Jane shook her head slowly. 'I can't pay your wages.'

His face flushed painfully. 'Do you think I'll take wages from

you? . . . Miss Anne's child? She clothed me and fed me, and that
was all I required.'

'I couldn't, Patrick . . . it isn't fair.'

He set his lips stubbornly. 'I'll be a grand help t' y', ma'am. It'll
give y' some standin' t' arrive with a servant by y'. Y'll have me
when y' need me.'

He seemed to take it as settled, especially when O'Neill presented Jane with the beautiful pair of greys that drew Anne's
carriage. The carriage was the one Viscount Hindsley had given
her, and O'Neill had put his own pair of Irish thoroughbreds between the shafts. He made light of the gift.

'I always considered that they belonged to Anne,' he said. 'Besides, Patrick's right. The better impression you make, the bigger
your chances. If you go cap in hand you'll get nothing, and no
welcome.' Then he shrugged. 'Apart from that, those horses are
worth money. You may need them.'

Jane thought his graceful and light-hearted manner of giving
was impressive when one remembered he was almost penniless
himself.

Patrick, then, was to go as coachman. A period of desperate and
secret activity fell over the house. From the outside nothing must
appear unusual, for while Jane remained, the bill-collectors were
confident of their money. So Patrick told them stories of Jane being
prostrate with grief, and unable to attend to business. At the same
time the cook was given her wages and dismissed, so that her
tongue would not wag about the preparations for leaving. In his
market basket, Patrick took Anne's silver and sold it. The jewels
Viscount Hindsley had given her were sold long ago – she had been
wearing paste copies so that their absence wouldn't disturb her
creditors. Jane shook her head regretfully over the few inexpensive
trinkets that were left. The best of them Patrick took away to sell
– she kept the rest, because by now she had entered completely
into the idea that she must make the best impression possible. She
packed boxes and hampers with Anne's gowns, her fingers busy
half the night with alterations to them, and with the necessary
repairs to William's clothes. She packed some of the finest linen,
and the little soft lace-edged pillows without which Anne had
never travelled. The silver spoons and forks went into Patrick's
basket. O'Neill told her that some of the figurines in the drawing-
room and the china were valuable; they also went. A fever of
stripping and selling fell on them – Jane regretted that the crystal
chandelier in the drawing-room was too bulky to go into the market

basket. O'Neill took a small painting to a dealer in Bond Street, and came back with fifty guineas. They ransacked cupboards to find more to sell.

Jerome didn't hold himself aloof from this. The hours he was supposed to give William lessons he spent helping Jane, his eyes anguished and already lonely. As, one by one, Anne's lovely things disappeared from walls and cupboards and tables his face grew sadder and more dismayed. Unlike O'Neill, he had no grief for Anne to bury in the bustle and hurry, so the dismantling of the house hurt him, because it made Jane's departure certain. But he was clever with William, keeping him so busy that there was hardly time for him to wander disconsolately into Anne's empty room. Sometimes at night he would sit with Jane as she waited, her hand in William's, for the child to fall asleep. They would talk very softly in the dimness.

'It can't be more than three or four months before the ship is fitted up, Miss Jane. We'll be in the South Seas for two years – I don't suppose . . . well, I don't suppose I'll ever see you again.'

'Who can tell?' she murmured. 'Much can happen in two years. My grandfather may be dead . . . I may have come back to London. Anything can happen in two years. You'll enjoy the expedition . . . you've always said that . . .'

'Yes,' he agreed, but he said it distastefully.

The only unsaleable item was the house itself. O'Neill advised Jane against doing anything with it at the present. 'Once anyone finds out you want to sell, you'll never be allowed to leave here until every penny Anne owed has been paid up. You'll have lawyers' fees to prove you've the right to sell it – and agents' fees, and the Lord knows what. Besides, I know Anne mortgaged it . . . leave it until you see what way the wind lies with your grandfather. You may be glad to come back.'

Jane looked around her and knew that she would never be coming back to this house. This represented Anne's extravagance and irresponsibility; to come back would be to admit that she would need men like O'Neill and Hindsley to pay for it.

She gave a short little laugh. 'It's too late to give me notions of living in a house like this, Lord O'Neill! I'm not very handy at spending money I haven't got!'

He looked at her carefully, from her curled hair to the hem of the expensively simple gown she wore. 'You could learn . . . learning to spend money isn't difficult. And you'd find better men than myself, Jane – ones who had money enough to satisfy every wish.'

Jane bent over her sewing. 'Anne made her mistakes – and she told me I didn't have to make them too.'

O'Neill said nothing. He didn't think it was any notion of virtue that held Jane back – but rather a sense of thrift and good-management. But it was a waste, all the same, he thought. He looked at her, and knew that she was made for a man's bed, and in this city she could have been highly paid for the privilege. Because she wasn't careless like Anne, she would make her choices better, and for her there wouldn't be Anne's career of debts and extravagance. He had observed her carefully since her arrival, and he knew that she took to ease and luxury with the eagerness of someone who has longed for it. And she could have had it – just by allowing herself to be seen about on his arm, by letting herself be displayed and examined, by giving up this ridiculous independence she had. Instead she had chosen to scrape together a few pounds, and set off for the wilderness of Romney Marsh, and the doubtful welcome of an old man. And just for the hope of inheriting a ruin . . . it didn't make sense to him. He didn't want to think of all that beauty and excitement going to waste. It was worse than pouring gold into the Thames – he had thought she knew enough to know that.

He couldn't decide whether she was passing all this up because she hadn't fully realized the possibilities before her, or whether she was taking a bigger gamble in bidding for respectability, her family name, and the long chance of a good marriage. If that was the case, then he admired her courage and was doubtful of her chances. Above all, he hoped that she would have the good sense to show young Jerome Taylor the door, and that a moment of sentimentality wouldn't condemn her to a life of penny-pinching as the wife of an impecunious man of science. Besides that, Jerome deserved something softer and kinder than Jane – he didn't deserve to be ruined by a woman with ambition. They were wrong for each other, these two – totally wrong. But he guessed that Jane already knew it.

So he said nothing. He aided her with the preparations where he could, spent his time with her because he missed Anne so badly, and he continued to think his own thoughts – thoughts of the glittering success she could have been, of the jewels and money she could have had, the houses and the carriages, the notoriety. At the same time he was envious because she had the strength he didn't have to give it all up.

The rush of preparation was finished, and they were ready to go.

Patrick went to the livery stable, paid a little on account on the bill Anne owed there, and took the greys and the carriage. It remained outside the door until the streets were dark and quiet; Patrick carried the boxes out at intervals, and stowed them inside where they wouldn't attract attention. It was time for Jane and William to leave – O'Neill had agreed to stay in the house for some days so that the bill-collectors should not realize it was empty.

Jerome was there to say goodbye. He watched as Jane leaned from the carriage window, and O'Neill stretched up and kissed her softly. Jerome hesitated a second, and as his hand clasped Jane's, with sudden desperate courage, he also sought her lips. It was a clumsy kiss, and full of heartbreak.

'I'll never forget you, Miss Jane – I'll think of you always. It's only two years . . . I'll come to Kent to see you as soon as I'm back.'

She pressed his hand hard, and was astonished to find that there were tears in her eyes. Then Jerome stepped back and took his place beside O'Neill.

'As soon as I come back . . .' he repeated.

Jane waved, and the carriage moved forward. She and William strained from their seats to get the last glimpse of the pair. She held Jerome's words firmly in her mind against the terrible loneliness and panic which threatened to sweep over her. She tucked William's hand in her own.

'Did you hear that, William? Mr Taylor is coming to see us as soon as he gets back from the expedition.'

William stroked General's head, and said nothing. It was impossible to tell what he felt about leaving the house in Albemarle Street.

Jane didn't know, nor did Jerome, that war with France would be many months old when he returned, and that he would transfer immediately into His Majesty's Navy. He was to die under Nelson at the Battle of the Nile; he was never to see Jane again.

But none of them knew it that chill April night in 1792 when Jane and William set out for Blake's Reach.

PART TWO

I

The wind drove in hard from the sea, pushing heavy grey clouds across the grey March sky. The ancient town of Rye was behind them on the hill – the sloping terraces of roofs, the square-towered church and the crumbling fortress walls. From Rye, they had been told, the road ran straight by the edge of the Marsh to Appledore. On the heights above the Marsh, a mile this side of Appledore, was Blake's Reach.

It had been a journey of fear and doubt and self-questioning. As they made their way over the weary, bone-shaking miles of bad roads from London, Jane had lived with a sense of unease and disquiet – made worse by Patrick and William's dependence and their faith in her. They never questioned, as she did, the wisdom of what they were doing; they accepted her decisions without thought, blindly believing that what she did could never be wrong. William and General often sat with Patrick on the box, and, alone, during those hours, Jane wrestled with doubts and misgivings. Viewed in a cold, sober light, it was expecting much of Spencer to hope that he would welcome them without reservation. They were trusting in the slender chance of his loneliness being greater than his pride, and greater, too, than an old man's desire for peace and unchanging habit. Every mile that brought them closer to Rye the words of the sailor, Adam Thomas, grew fainter, and Anne's forthright rejection of Blake's Reach and its rundown inheritance louder and stronger. Anne had been a woman of the world – not a girl caught up in romantic impulse. More than that, she had known Blake's Reach, and she had known Spencer Blake. Suppose Spencer Blake should shut the door on all three of them, should refuse to receive them even for a night? What then? . . . William and Patrick would turn to her for the answer, and, as yet, she had none.

There had been too much time during the long, dragged-out days of fighting the mud and bogs of the spring roads, the delays of the tollhouses, the aggravating slowness of their progress, to wish that she had never seen William and Patrick, had never heard of Blake's Reach. A few weeks ago she had been responsible only for herself, and for herself she had been able to provide with no other aid but that of her strong body and capable hands. Now her hands were soft and encased in soft gloves, and she travelled like a lady and money flew from her purse into the eager palms of servants and lackeys. Now she had two mouths to feed besides her own, and shelter and security to find for them all. She sat in Anne's velvet-lined carriage as it bounced over ruts and pot-holes, and wondered if she had made a bad exchange.

Even the end of their journey was obscure. They knew only that they should go to the Romney Marsh in Kent, and that the ancient Cinque Port of Rye was their best goal. So they travelled slowly over the turnpikes, asking at all the tollhouses if they were heading in the direction of Rye. Most of the tollkeepers were as ignorant as themselves of what lay beyond the next ten miles of rutted road. They got lost several times, and there were delays which meant more nights spent in expensive inns – for it was obvious that a carriage and pair like this could not draw up before a modest tavern. Jane travelled with a purse containing some coins and a pair of paste earrings close at her hand; this was in case they were held up by one of the highwaymen who haunted the turnpikes. The rest of the money was sewn into the lining of William's coat. Patrick lived with a pistol on the seat beside him, which he swore he could use. For all three of them there was fear – and for Jane there was fear and uncertainty, and self-blame.

Last night they had slept at Tenterden, and this morning about noon had reached Rye.

They entered the Port through the great medieval gateway to the Old Town, and the greys had struggled to keep a footing on the steep, slippery cobbles. At Rye the air carried the tang of the sea – that's what Patrick had told them the smell was, for Jane and William had never seen the sea. The little silt-packed harbour lay below the town, and the Rother cut a sluggish course between mud banks to the sea a mile or more away. The host at The Mermaid Tavern where they stopped for dinner, was talkative. He put Jane and William in a private room and pointed to the crest over the chimney-piece.

'The crest of the Cinque Port, ma'am. Rye used to be the best and the greatest of them before they inned the Marsh, and the silt blocked up the harbour. This town used to stand on the cliffs overlooking the sea – can you imagine that, ma'am?'

Jane didn't welcome his talk, or the curious glances he kept giving her when he came himself to serve their dinner; she paid no attention to his hinting at the strangeness of a young woman travelling with only a servant and a child. But when he asked her if she would accept a glass of brandy with his compliments, she was forced, out of politeness, to comment on its excellence. She tasted and approved it; Tim Cooper's cellar had held nothing so fine as this.

The landlord shrugged carelessly. 'Oh – good brandy's one thing we have no lack of in these parts.'

For an inn in a declining seaport, she thought, it was an absurd extravagance to offer brandy like this to its patrons free. But she sipped gratefully, for it helped to delay the moment of departure. It was almost time to face Spencer, and she was nervous. The landlord handed her into the carriage, and she could no longer avoid giving him the information he had wanted. She had to ask directions to Blake's Reach.

'Blake's Reach, is it?' His eyes narrowed. 'Why – there ain't no one goes to Blake's Reach these days.'

Then an expression of dawning comprehension appeared. 'Why, you must be . . . Well, I was tryin' t' place y', and I should have know y' for a Blake! I've lived sixty-six years in this town with Blakes comin' and goin', an' I ought t' know a Blake face when I see one. But there ain't been none of them about these past years . . .'

'If you please!' Jane said primly. 'I am in a hurry!'

He made a half bow. 'Why, certainly, ma'am, certainly! You follow your nose t' the bottom of the hill here – the outskirts of the town it is – and you'll see the road forking to the right sign-posted to Appledore. It runs along the edge of the Marsh. And on the left 'bout four-five miles, you'll see Blake's Reach. Can't miss it. A big, old house stuck up on the rise, where the cliffs used to be.'

There was a flush of excitement on his pinkish, flabby face as he watched the carriage turn out of the courtyard. Without bothering to take off his apron he followed it to the end of Mermaid Street. Then, at the best pace he could manage, he set off for Watchbell Street, gasping a little for breath, and heedless of the stares of his business friends in the town who hadn't seen Dick Randell move with such speed since the days when he had been a slim ostler at The Mermaid.

But Randell was heading for Robert Turnbull's office in Watchbell Street. Of all the people in Rye, Robert Turnbull would be the one most interested in the news that a carriage had set out along the Appledore road to Blake's Reach.

2

The rain had started to fall when they came to Blake's Reach. For five miles they had followed the road over the Marsh – on one side were the miles of flat pasture lands, interlaced with countless winding dykes and ditches and banks. The wind bent and swayed the new spring grass and the tall rushes; the young lambs huddled close by the ewes for shelter. On their left was the broken line of low, Kent hills – the cliff face of past centuries – sweeping round in a wide arc to encircle the Marsh from east to west. Jane recalled the host at The Mermaid telling her that once the sea had lapped the base of those hills; now The Wall held back the sea – a frail, man-made thing which the Marshmen watched and guarded ceaselessly against tide and wind and storm. In the grey light the Marsh seemed to Jane a faintly sinister place, fertile and yet desolate, unnatural looking. The wild clouds came sweeping in from the sea. The farmhouses were tight and prosperous; they were also withdrawn and alone. Shut away from the rain and the wind in the snug carriage, she shivered momentarily, and could not have said why.

Suddenly William stirred and touched her hand. 'Look – yonder! That's Blake's Reach!'

'Blake's Reach ahead, Mistress!' Patrick called from the box.

She craned forward to look. It was on the left – as the innkeeper had said. The house stood halfway up a steep, sparsely wooded ridge which rose sharply from the level of the Marsh. Through the rain and the gathering mist they could see only the outline of the house. There were two wings, one of mellow rosy brick, and the other, older and smaller, was a jumble of sloping roofs and blackened oak and plaster. A few poplars and elms gathered about it. An orchard straggled down the hill to meet the dyke at the bottom.

The carriage wheels rumbled on the bridge that spanned the dyke, and the horses started the pull up the steep hill. The tall gates of Blake's Reach stood open to the world – gates of massive rusted iron, and stone walls overgrown with ivy. Patrick took the difficult turning on the hill without pause, and swept along the short drive to the space formed by the L-shaped buildings.

Jane's hand moved convulsively. 'Oh . . . oh, my lord!'

Against the racing clouds she saw the tall chimneys, and the cracked and broken chimney-pots. Over the porch were rose vines, grown to monstrous proportions and full of dead wood, like gnarled

old trees; someone had tried to cut the vine away from the crest
chiselled in the stonework over the door. Jane recognized some of
the heraldings she had seen in the crest of the Cinque Port. Ivy
covered these walls too – some of it overgrown so that it sealed
the casement windows. Nettles and weeds were high in the tangled
lawn; shrubs fought half-heartedly with the vines that weighed
them down. Midway down the slope was a broken stone wall
which might once have sheltered a rose garden. The wind tore at
the young buds on the vines, and splattered the rain against the
dirty casements. The leaves of last autumn, and the winter's mud
lay piled against the doorstep. There was an air of deadness over
the whole place.

'There's no one here,' Jane breathed, half to herself. 'There's
some mistake! – this isn't Blake's Reach!'

But she uttered the words hopelessly, knowing that nothing she
could say would make this spectacle of ruin disappear. This was
Blake's Reach, without a doubt. This was the ruin to which Anne
had refused to return, this was the decayed farm of Adam Thomas's
description. A feeling of doom and hopeless fatality was here like a
visible cloud.

Patrick jumped down from the box. He knocked loudly with
the whip handle on the door. There was no sound at all from
within. 'Open up there! Open up!'

William got down beside him; General sniffed and pawed a
little before the door, and then his ears cocked and he moved back
down the drive to the corner of the house. All three of them turned
and looked after him.

An old woman appeared there – an old woman wiping her hands
in her apron. She had thrown a shawl over her head against the
rain; grey wisps of hair had escaped it, and blew in the wind. She
stood and surveyed the group and the carriage warily.

'What do ye want? Who are ye?'

Jane got down from the carriage slowly. 'This is Blake's Reach?'
she said.

'Aye . . .' The answer was choked off as the old woman's gaze
came to rest fully on Jane. Her features contracted sharply; her
brow wrinkled, knit in close lines. She began to walk purposefully
towards Jane, ignoring the others. She stood and peered up into
the girl's face.

'Mercy on us!' Wonderingly she shook her head. 'Can it be? –
Miss Anne's child? Is *that* who ye are?'

Jane nodded. 'And William also.' She touched the child's
shoulder.

The woman gazed from one face to the other. With a hand that trembled slightly she reached out and touched William's red curls, brushed them back off his forehead in a gesture that she seemed to have been performing all her life.

'Mercy on us,' she said again, more gently. 'I never thought to see this day!' Her eyes were bright with fierce, unshed tears. She turned back to Jane. 'You'll be her child by Captain Howard?'

'My name's Jane – Jane Howard.'

The woman dropped a stiff, quick curtsey. 'I'm Kate Reeve, Mistress – an' I cared for Miss Anne from the day she was born, till the day she went away with Tom Howard. She'll have talked of me, perhaps?'

'Yes,' Jane lied. 'She talked of you.'

The old woman nodded, gratified. 'And Miss Anne? . . .' she hesitated. 'She's living . . . ?'

Jane shook her head. 'My mother is dead.'

Kate nodded, and there was no surprise or shock on her face. 'I never thought to see the day that would bring her to Blake's Reach again. She went away with no love in her heart for Blake's Reach and the Marsh. Glad to go, she were.'

A fierce gust of wind whipped her skirts about her thin frame. She clutched the shawl tighter. 'They do say, though, that blood be thicker than water.' Again she reached out and touched William's curls. 'You have come back – Miss Anne's children!'

'And my grandfather?' Jane prompted. 'Is he here? – is he well enough to see us?'

Kate's jaw dropped. 'Ye don't *know*?' she said in a thin whisper. 'Know *what*?'

She looked at them solemnly. 'Yer grandfather, Spencer Blake, has been dead this month an' more.'

'Dead!'

Jane echoed the word, hearing it on her tongue, knowing the finality of it. Spencer Blake was dead. More than a month he had been dead, and she and William were his only living descendants. She didn't feel grief and shock at the idea that an old man whom she had never seen was dead. His death was safety for herself and William; there would be no one now to deny them entrance to Blake's Reach, no one who had the right to send them away. Blake's Reach was a slight inheritance – but it was a roof, and a place to be. It was a purpose for existence, an identity. She was a Blake, and William was a Blake, and this decaying house was a refuge for them for as long as they had a mind to stay. Her eyes swept over the building again, and now she felt some affection for the crumbling walls.

'Aye . . . he's dead,' Kate said. 'An' I thought 'twas the news of it had brought ye here. I thought Mr Turnbull, the Blake solicitor in Rye, had found ye, and ye'd come to wait here with me for Charlie.'

'Wait for Charlie? What do you mean, Kate? Who is Charlie?'

'Why – Charlie Blake! Yer mother's first cousin – the one that ran off to France. He be the one Spencer named in his will. He be the heir to Blake's Reach.'

Jane gave a strangled gasp. 'Heir! That isn't true! Charles Blake is dead!'

Kate shook her head. 'That's what we first heard, but then the news came that 'twere a mistake, and he were still in prison in Paris. Robert Turnbull came out here to tell me about it. He told me that I were to bide here, and keep the house against the time when Charles should come back.'

'Come back . . . !' Jane echoed the words dully.

'Aye,' Kate nodded. ''Tain't a sure thing he'll ever come. Mor'an likely he'll lose his head in Paris. But until he does, Blake's Reach belongs to Charlie, and I must wait here for him.'

She surveyed the house in much the way Jane had just done; looked at the tall broken chimneys against the racing clouds, looked at the garden desolate in the rain.

'Aye – I must wait here until Charlie either loses his head, or comes to claim his own.'

2

So they were all waiting for Charlie . . . They were waiting for Charles Blake to come and claim his inheritance.

Jane sat with slumped shoulders before the fire Kate Reeve had lit hastily in the room that had been Spencer Blake's sitting-room; her stunned brain repeated the words over and over, trying to make herself grapple with the fact of this new disaster. Somewhere in a Paris prison Charlie Blake awaited trial, and if he should live, then she and William were again homeless and rootless. Her mind stirred sullenly in revolt at the thought; it seemed an overwhelming injustice that Charles Blake, who had cared for Blake's Reach no more than Anne, who had run away from it just as Anne had done, should be named in Spencer's will. It wasn't just, and its injustice spoke of Spencer's bitterness towards his daughter; the whip of an old anger and hurt had been meant to reach out and touch Anne. Jane shivered a little. If Spencer Blake had been alive when she and William had presented themselves at his door she now believed that he would have refused to see them.

Then, as she considered this chance, Jane shrugged her shoulders with a grim kind of resignation. With Spencer dead, things were difficult enough; had he been alive they might have been a great deal worse. The thought took hold. They said possession was nine points of the law. She was here at Blake's Reach; Charles Blake was shut away in a prison in Paris. For the moment she was decidedly better off than he. And one could only live for a moment at a time; the future was anyone's guess.

But the present was with her now, and she would have to tackle it. Whatever happened to Charles Blake, she would still have to get herself and William through the next day, and the next week. The present crowded upon her; with growing interest she began to look about the room.

She knew without being told that Spencer had used no other room at Blake's Reach but this and his bedchamber. This room had a look of wear as well as neglect about it – books tumbled haphazardly on the shelves, papers still littered the tables, there were mugs and glasses on a battered oak sideboard, and many candles about, and the spatters of candle grease on the floor and furniture. She knew what had happened here; this was the orbit of a man who had withdrawn to live within one room, to eat his meals here, to doze here before the fire, to seat what little company came to Blake's Reach in the great high-backed chair facing his own. He had drunk his brandy here in solitude; she wondered if he had invited neighbours here to gamble – or if he had lost his acres and money in the taverns and inns at Rye and Tenterden and Dover. She saw the dust on the bookcases, the threadbare rug, the curtains whose silk had rotted and was faded to dusty rose colour. There was apathy and bitterness in this room; perhaps, before he died, Spencer had hated Blake's Reach as much as Anne. She suddenly became impatient with the Blakes. It didn't take much skill to be unhappy, and to hate; it was too easy. She was impatient with Spencer and Anne, and even the unknown Charles because they had let themselves be defeated.

Now she looked about the room, and felt superior to the man who lived here with his brandy and his hate.

There was a sound outside, and she stirred, and looked expectantly towards the window. But it had been a distant sound carried

by the wind, and no one came. She was waiting now for Robert
Turnbull, the Blakes' solicitor, and executor of Spencer's will. Kate
had routed out a tow-headed youth – who was one of the only two
hands left on the farm – to take a message immediately to Turnbull. It was more than five miles to Rye, the rain was coming
down in torrents, and the boy's horse had been a miserable creature.
It would be after dark before Turnbull could arrive. Kate had
gone off towards the kitchen murmuring something about preparing food; Patrick and William were in the stable tending the
greys. Jane moved her feet restlessly. She wanted to see beyond
this room, and the dark panelled hall with the great staircase
where her boxes were now piled. But it needed Robert Turnbull's
arrival to sanction her presence here. It was too soon to go wandering towards the kitchen, or to open the heavy double doors that
led off the hall. As curious as she was, she must wait.

The sounds of his arrival came much sooner than she expected.
The dusk had come imperceptibly with a darkening in the rain
clouds over the Marsh. The shriek of the wind was high and strong.
She had grown accustomed to the absence of human sound in all
that clamour, and it almost startled her to hear voices and the
clopping of horses' hooves on the weed-choked gravel. She had a
quick glimpse of a man in a tall hat muffled in a heavy coat,
followed by the tow-haired boy, before there came the sounds of
his knocking. Instantly she rose, and was halfway to the window
before she recovered her sense of dignity. She returned to her chair,
and spread her skirts, taking deep breaths to calm the beating of
her heart.

She knew why Robert Turnbull had come before time. There
had been no need to send for him. She remembered the interest
of the host at The Mermaid, and knew that in the towns that
bordered the Marsh, a stranger did not enquire for Blake's Reach
without arousing curiosity, especially if the stranger's hair and face
called to mind too vividly the Anne Blake of twenty years ago.

She knew that Robert Turnbull had been told of the carriage
and pair heading towards Blake's Reach; he had set out of his
own accord without waiting for the summons. The tow-haired boy
had met him on the road to Rye.

She sat stiffly and waited for him to enter.

2

A little more than an hour after Jane had driven over the Marsh
road which led to Blake's Reach, Robert Turnbull also turned his

horse right at the fork signposted to Appledore. He carried a
strange, half-bitter ache in his heart.

For many years he had followed this road back and forth to
Blake's Reach – ever since he had entered his father's law firm in
Rye. Blake's Reach had always been important in the Turnbull
firm, because none of them were able to forget that their prosperity
dated from the time, early in the century, when John Blake, lately
back from serving with Marlborough, had placed the legal affairs
of Blake's Reach with the newly-founded firm of Turnbull & Son.
The prestige of the Blake name brought a flurry of business to the
offices in Watchbell Street – smaller squires and farmers hastened
to follow where the Blakes led, as well as the few more important
men who trusted John's recommendation because he was their
friend. It had been an easy matter to serve the Blakes when they
were in the full flood of riches which John's loot from the wars
had swollen; the rent roll was fat then, and sheep from Blake's
Reach fetched a high price in the market. John managed his farm
with a soldier's precision, making every quarter acre yield its share;
his wife had brought him a dowry of lands and money and at her
death his manipulations had doubled them in value. Then with the
extravagance which was lacking in none of the Blakes, he built
and endowed a church on the hill above his house; it didn't matter
to him that it was more than half a mile from the nearest village –
he had wanted his church on the highest point above the Marsh
and the inconvenience caused to the people in getting to the services
held every third Sunday only served to remind them that John
Blake was a man not swayed by the wishes of any clergyman or
bishop. John brought new lustre to a name that had been a power
on the Marsh for a long time; he built up a new fortune for his
descendants, and his descendants betrayed him.

His only son, George, wasted and spent and mortgaged with
a cheerful lavish hand; George's sons, Spencer and Richard, were
bent in the same direction until Richard removed himself by marrying a French heiress and going off to mismanage her estate in
Normandy. Spencer continued to indulge his passion for gambling
unchecked, believing that he was possessed of his grandfather's
genius for investment, and that if he were patient there were
fortunes to be made by the turn of the card, or from the tobacco
plantation he had bought, sight unseen, in Virginia. He woke one
day to the realization that his only child Anne was beautiful, and
that in her, not himself, lay the hope of lifting Blake's Reach free
of its debts.

The Turnbull firm had been with the Blakes through all the

changes; the memory of what John Blake had accomplished for
them by putting his business in their hands, was sufficient to make
it a tradition in the firm that the Blakes must be served, no matter
for how many years the services of the firm went unpaid.

For young Robert Turnbull it was something much more personal than a tradition of service. He was only two years older than
Anne, and he had watched the spoiled, imperious child grow into
a woman of startling beauty. It was not simply a matter of knowing that he loved Anne, that she was a bright flash of brilliance
and romance in his plodding existence. Along with loving her he
must recognize that loving her was all he could do. The Turnbulls
were servants to the Blakes, and Robert Turnbull was no more
than the young man she consented to chat to while she waited
impatiently for Spencer to be through with his business in the
Watchbell Street offices. Not only was a marriage for a Blake with
a Turnbull unthinkable, but Anne herself barely knew he existed.
Robert knew very well what Anne's marriage was supposed to
accomplish for Spencer and Blake's Reach; even in the unlikely
circumstance of Anne's loving him there would have been no hope
of marriage.

So Robert allowed himself only the indulgence of loving her,
and inventing excuses for going to Blake's Reach. It was no surprise
to him when the news came that Anne had got herself out of the
marriage Spencer had arranged for her to Roger Pym by running
away with Tom Howard. Tom Howard he knew only by sight –
a gay, laughing Captain of Dragoons without a penny to his name,
and only average luck with cards. They went to London, Tom
resigned his commission, and when Spencer tried to have the
marriage annulled on grounds of Anne being under age, she wrote
that she was already pregnant with Tom's child.

That closed the matter. Anne's name was never again mentioned
voluntarily by Spencer. His gambling continued, and now there
were stories of his heavy drinking to add to it. His affairs grew
more knotted and more complex for the Turnbulls to manage, with
I.O.U.s written in a drunken scrawl turning up for payment, and
lands being sold to meet them. The Virginia plantation hadn't
shown a profit for many years. Spencer was drinking too much and
refusing to listen to Robert's pleas to get rid of it. There was no
reasoning with him; a kind of mad obstinacy had fallen on him
now that Anne wasn't there to soften his moods.

Then two years after Anne had left, her cousin, Charles, who
was then thirteen, also ran away. He was Spencer's nephew, and
he had come unwillingly to England when his parents had died

during an epidemic of typhoid fever in Paris. Richard's will had appointed Spencer as Charles's guardian. He had come to Blake's Reach when he was nine years old, and he had clearly detested the place. He managed to make his way to France, where his mother's family took him in. Spencer retaliated by keeping the money Charles's estate paid him for the boy's upbringing until Charles was of age to inherit. Spencer had never cared for the slim, dark-haired boy who had rarely spoken to him, but his going was a deadly insult. He was now quite alone at Blake's Reach.

As best he could Robert Turnbull followed the events of Anne's life. He was not subtle about asking for news of her from the occasional inhabitant of the Marsh who happened to go to London. He heard about Tom Howard's death in the debtors' prison, and had flinched to hear the horrible derisive laughter of Spencer when he had been told. By one means and another Anne's career as the mistress of rich and fashionable men became known in Rye. The town buzzed comfortably with the scandal for years until it heard of Viscount Hindsley, whose prominence and wealth at once bathed Anne in respectability – which lasted only until he died. Anne never answered the letter Robert wrote her at that time, and the neglect hurt him more than he wanted to admit. It was then he gave up the struggle to make himself like some other woman well enough to marry.

It seemed to Robert that, even with the amount Spencer was drinking, it took him so long to die that he stood a good chance of gambling away the roof over his head before it could happen. Through the years Robert watched the Blake's Reach acres shrink, the land sold freehold to tenant farmers, and gone for ever. The Blake barns leaked, and one wing of the stables was burned down. Spencer's farming methods were a laughing stock right across the Marsh. But the ageing man, shut up in his sitting-room with the brandy decanter, cared for nothing that was said about him. No one was bidden to tend the garden, or fix the broken windows; few people came now to Blake's Reach, and those few were at pains not to notice the disorder and neglect. Sometimes Spencer was to be seen walking on the Marsh itself, his shabby stained coat blowing in the wind. The farmers who met him raised their hats and hurried on.

Robert came to dislike and even dread his necessary visits to Blake's Reach, and to resent the tradition of service to the Blakes handed down to him since the days of his great-grandfather. He gritted his teeth and endured Spencer's sneers and bitter hatred; he salvaged what he could of the wreck Spencer was bent on making of what remained to the family. Knowing that Anne had a legitimate child by Tom Howard he even ventured to protest Spencer's will which gave Blake's Reach to Charles. He had not been received at Blake's Reach for a year afterwards for his pains. Spencer, he knew, hated both Anne and Charles – it was a question of which one he hated more.

Now Spencer was dead at last, and Anne's child had come to Blake's Reach – a girl so like Anne that it had sent Dick Randell at The Mermaid scuttling along to tell him. Robert didn't know why the girl had come, but he sensed trouble, and he sensed that the complication of the Blake affairs had begun all over again.

But trouble or not, for the first time in almost twenty years he made the journey to Blake's Reach hopefully. Times and events were changing, he thought – the old things worn out and the new coming to take their place. A new and young Blake had come to the Marsh – maybe this time one with the blood of old John Blake, Marlborough's general, strong in her veins. Sometimes, just sometimes, miracles happened. The Blakes had need of a miracle now.

The wind blowing from the sea was like a knife in his back. Blake's Reach looked no different – slashed by the rain and showing its neglect painfully. Robert sighed. Anne's daughter would need all of old John's spirit and toughness.

When she rose to greet him, he knew that his premonition hadn't been wrong. He had seen the portrait of old John too many times not to know by what stick to measure his descendants. Here was old John's face in a feminine mould, the face of a young woman boldly drawn, with the family red hair curling crisply back, and greenish eyes that regarded him, not with apprehension, but a certain caution. She accepted his greeting with reserve.

He bowed. 'Your servant, ma'am. My name is Robert Turnbull.' She inclined her head. 'I am Jane Howard.'

He approved of her; not knowing whether he was friend or enemy, she didn't commit herself to any overtures. She met his stare firmly, not yielding an inch in confusion. She merely waited for him to speak.

'You're so like your mother,' he said gently.

It wasn't exactly true – Dick Randell had told him she was as beautiful as Anne, but he, Robert Turnbull, who had memorized every expression of Anne's face with the eager diligence of a lover, knew that she was not as beautiful. Anne's had been a more delicate face, a gayer face. This girl had a certain toughness and directness Anne had never known. She was modishly dressed in a travelling costume of blue velvet which became her skin and hair wonder-

fully; it was tightly fitted to her pointed young bosom. Her body
was provocative and arresting, and when she moved towards him
she managed herself with an instinctive, undeniable grace.

He instantly liked and respected what he saw. The thought
crossed his mind in those first few seconds, that perhaps, after all,
the Blakes were to have their miracle.

Their hands met briefly, and then Robert went to the chair
Jane indicated on the other side of the fire. They studied each
other carefully.

Jane saw a man of about her mother's age, with dark hair
turned almost completely grey, and weathered skin that told her
he spent much time in the sun and wind. He was not tall, but
broadly and powerfully built, with strong hands covered thickly
with hair; his eyes were remarkable, dark brown and deeply set,
almost too sensitive in that rugged face. He did not dress as she
imagined a country attorney would; his clothes were immaculate
and of excellent cut, though the colours were discreet. If he had
lived in London, she thought, he might have become a dandy. The
only thing out of fashion about him was the absence of a wig. His
might have been any one of those cosmopolitan faces she had
glimpsed in the coffee-houses or in Bond Street. It was a calm,
intelligent face that looked at her now, and waited.

3

Kate came and served them wine in smeared glasses, carelessly
set on a tarnished silver tray. Her old hands shook with excitement
as she poured from the decanter; a smile played on her lips each
time her gaze fell on Jane.

'This is a great day for Kate,' Robert said, when she had gone.
'To her you are Anne come back again. You and William are
young, and for the old, there is always hope in youth.'

Jane's eyes regarded him gratefully over the rim of the glass.

William was brought in then to be presented. Patrick stood
silently in the doorway watching as William made his bow to
Turnbull. Then, tugging at General's collar, the child went to
Jane's side quickly, and from that vantage point, viewed the
stranger eagerly. He answered Turnbull's questions about his
lessons, but he was watching to try to sense Jane's own reaction
to the man before giving himself too readily. Patrick's anxious
face softened a trifle; he glowed with pride as Jane described to
Turnbull his years of service to Anne.

Then the servant took William back to the kitchen. As the door
closed behind them, Robert spoke softly.

'A child of nine years is a burden for a young woman to take on ... And Anne's servant ...'

Jane shrugged. 'What else was there to do? When Anne died, Patrick was as helpless as William. Over the years he had grown to expect Anne to decide everything for him. Without her he was lost. As for William ... no one can turn out a child who's been gently reared to fend for himself. William's no baby, but he knows more about the fashionable life in London than he does about earning a shilling or two ...'

'And so you took them both?'

'I had no choice.'

The formalities were completed between them; they moved on to the business of understanding each other.

It was less difficult than they thought. Kate brought in supper; it was jugged hare, poorly cooked and served on chipped plates. With it she brought coarse, blackish bread and a large slice of stale Cheddar cheese. It was many years since Robert had taken a meal at Blake's Reach, and he was appalled by what he saw. But the wine, brought up from Spencer's cellar, was excellent. When the dishes were cleared away they lingered over the wine, and they grew comfortable with each other. Their talk became easy and unfettered; Jane realized quickly that if she was to remain at Blake's Reach she needed Robert Turnbull – among all these strangers she had to trust someone, and she decided to trust him. It was obvious that he knew Anne's history in some detail, and when he pressed for more information, she decided that it was safer to tell him everything than to play with half-truths. As her ally he could be invaluable, and already he was almost that. Without holding back, then, she told him of the years at The Feathers, and how she had come to London in a wild flight and been absorbed into Anne's strange household. She told him of how Anne had died, and how Patrick, O'Neill, Jerome Taylor and herself had schemed to take whatever could be taken from the creditors. She told it matter-of-factly, and was startled to see the distress in his face.

'I hate to think of Anne ... to die that way, in debt, troubled by creditors ...'

'Don't waste your pity, Mr Turnbull. Creditors never troubled Anne. She never spared a moment's thought for them. She died in a comfortable bed, with people who loved her all around her. She had soft and pretty things all her life, and gaiety. I don't think she even minded dying because it spared her the pain of growing old.'

'But leaving William to you and no provision made for him ... ?'

She shrugged. 'I see it this way. Today I have a trunkful of beautiful gowns, a carriage and two fine greys, and I have some gold to jingle in my purse. When I left The Feathers I had Sally's old shawl and a few pennies.' She spread her hands emphatically. 'If I also have William, then that's only to be expected. Fair exchange, Mr Turnbull!'

He smiled, half-reluctantly. 'Most people wouldn't call it fair exchange – but I applaud your spirit.'

'That's as you choose, Mr Turnbull – I'd rather fight to make my own way, than sit and wait for things to happen. I almost waited too long at The Feathers. No more of that for me! From now on I take every chance that comes – *every* one!'

He nodded. 'Then they'll come . . . or you will make your own chances.'

'I will – if I can.' She went on quickly. 'Living at The Feathers has taught me things gently-bred people don't know. You had to be sharp there, or you were taken in. An innkeeper on a busy road has to know more than two and two make four. I've learned things from him, and they've stuck with me.' She added, with a touch of pride: 'The idea of selling the things off quietly from Anne's house – that was mine.'

'I heard that Hindsley had given Anne jewels,' he said. 'Wouldn't they have fetched something?'

'The jewels were sold long ago. Anne had paste imitations made, because it wouldn't have done for the people she borrowed from to know that the jewels were gone.'

Again Robert gave a half-smile. 'It's an inherited talent with the Blakes to conceal the state of their finances. In the old days Spencer also was cunning in hiding his difficulties from his neighbours.' His face sharpened suddenly. 'He had a purpose, though. He had planned a good match for Anne from the time she was a child, and when she was fourteen he had the man picked out and ready. Roger Pym would have given half he possessed to have married Anne. He was a young man, just come into his father's estate, and he was more than ready to lend Spencer large sums on the understanding that Anne should marry him when she was eighteen. There wasn't any real wickedness in Roger Pym, I believe – but in Spencer's hands he was an inexperienced child, and he hadn't learned that his money couldn't buy everything he wanted.'

'Anne wouldn't have him?'

'Flatly refused to consider him! To marry Roger Pym would have meant burying herself in the country. It would have meant a life-time of paying a lip service to all the past glories of the Blakes. She was appalled at the thought of taking up the dull job of running the estate, and giving a child to Roger every year. None of that was for Anne. Tom Howard presented himself, and she ran off to London with him.'

'She could have stayed . . . ?' Jane said musingly.

He leaned towards her. 'You must realize that Anne didn't give a fig for position or family or almost anything else. She didn't care in the least for what the Blakes were then or had been. She was a creature of such gaiety – like a bright and improbable flame here among all these solid country squires. She was too lovely and too spirited to be tied down . . .'

Jane knew the familiar tones the attorney used. Ever since she could comprehend them, these were the tones the people who had loved Anne had spoken in. It was clear that Turnbull had loved her mother. She accepted the knowledge, not as something strange, but as a fact that was decidedly to her own advantage. Having loved Anne, Turnbull would feel nothing but warmth for a daughter who resembled her. She fixed her attention firmly on him, encouraging him with her eyes to continue talking.

'Spencer never recovered from the blow of her running away,' Turnbull said. 'She had hurt him financially, and she had wounded his pride beyond bearing. He grew old very quickly . . . and bitter. He didn't trouble any more to keep the Marsh from knowing what was happening to Blake's Reach. He hated Anne, and I think he took a fiendish delight in making sure that there should be nothing left for her to inherit. He grew to a stage of bitterness when he could laugh openly at Anne's misfortunes – Tom's death, and Viscount Hindsley's.' Turnbull's voice was sour at the memory of it.

'Then,' Jane said, 'if he were alive yet, William and myself would not have been received at Blake's Reach? . . . strange how certain I was that he would welcome us. Anne told me what to expect, but I wanted to believe what that sailor, Adam Thomas, had told me.'

'Most assuredly he would not have welcomed you,' Turnbull said dryly. 'And as for Adam Thomas . . . well, people about here feel for the Blake family. It's part of their tradition. They can't think of the Marsh without a Blake. Adam Thomas was loyal – but misguided.'

She stirred suddenly in her chair. The firelight caught the red of her hair, burnished it like copper. Her face had grown sharper and whiter.

'And you – *you*, Mr Turnbull – think that I was misguided to come here? Blake's Reach doesn't belong to me!'

'It's unfortunate,' he answered, 'that Spencer didn't know how good *you* would have been for Blake's Reach. The family have never needed one of the General's kind so badly . . . Spencer didn't know that you were one of the General's kind, Jane.'

She said quickly, jealously, 'And Charles? – what will *he* do for Blake's Reach?'

'Ah, Charles . . . let me tell you about Charles.'

She leaned back, her lips folded tightly.

'He was the only child of Richard, Spencer's brother – the one who married the Frenchwoman. Charles was born in France, and brought up there. For some strange reason, when his parents both died within days of each other from a fever, his father's wishes had been that he should come to Spencer to be cared for, instead of staying with his mother's family. She was related to the Poulac family, one of the oldest in France, and they were willing to have the child. Charles didn't want to go to England, but Spencer wasn't prepared to pamper a child's whim. Besides that, Spencer was to have an income from the French estate for Charles's education. He wasn't going to give that up! Charles came over to Blake's Reach – a very unwilling little boy, I recall. I fancy he was nine or ten years old then . . . about five years or so younger than Anne . . .'

'Yes, yes!' Jane said impatiently. 'But tell me *about* Charles? What sort of a person was he?'

'It's difficult to know. He spoke only French when he arrived . . . and I didn't quite know what to make of him. He was handsome, certainly – very handsome. And intelligent, too – quick to learn. After a time he spoke English very well. And I remember him on his pony. He could handle that, or even a horse, as well as a man. He was very dark . . . like his mother, they said. People thought he was sullen, but I think it was his shyness over the strange language in the beginning – and at the end because there was no one he cared to talk to.'

'And what did Anne think of him?'

He waved her to silence. 'I was coming to Anne. I think she was very important to Charles, but what she felt, I'm not sure. It was plain that he adored her. She must have seemed so light and gay among all these others – almost French, I suppose. She was kind to him when she remembered he was there . . . he was just a little boy, and she was growing into a young woman with thoughts and occupations of her own. But I remember they used to ride together on the Marsh. You'd see them in every kind of weather – he was such a splendid horseman, and he wanted her

admiration so badly. He'd dare her to jumps she shouldn't have
been allowed to take, just to show her how well he could manage
them.'

His tone grew reflective. 'It must have been terrible for him
when she ran away. Spencer had never taken much notice of
Charles before, but when Anne left, the child was forgotten completely. Spencer used his money shamelessly . . . and Charles grew
too tall for his coats and breeches, and he had holes in his stockings.
In the end he settled the matter for himself by riding his pony to
Dover, selling it, and paying for his passage to France. He went
to his mother's family. Spencer clung on to the money from the
estate until Charles was eighteen and could inherit. It was a bitter
and vicious wrangle over the money . . .'

They listened to the rain and the crackle of the fire, and Robert's
thoughts were back in those years. Jane looked about the room,
seeing it suddenly with the eyes of the little French boy whom
Spencer had ignored – the boy in his jacket grown too short and
worn at the elbows. This had been Spencer's room, and the boy
must have watched him here with fear and loathing.

Suddenly Robert spoke. 'I suppose he was the loneliest child
I've ever known . . . After Anne went he used to spend a great deal
of his time in the tower of the church up there on the hill. On a
clear day you can see the French coast from there. He was eating
his heart out.'

'And now he's eating his heart out in Paris – in prison!' she said.

He nodded slowly. 'I suppose that's true. He's been in prison
more than a year. I wonder if England seems a free and happy
place for him now that he has seen France overrun by Revolution . . .'

She interrupted sharply, 'Over a year! When does he come to
trial?'

He shrugged. 'Who can say? We've already had one report of
his trial and execution . . . and later found that it was false. I try
by every possible means to get news of him. Some English interests
are still functioning in Paris, but I've had no direct contact with
him. I still am not sure that the letters I've bribed certain people
to get to him have ever been received.' He began to shake his head.
'His cousin, the Marquis, is dead, and other members of the family,
so I'm told. If Charles ever comes to trial I have little hope for him.
The excesses of the Revolution grow worse daily . . .'

'What is his crime?'

'His connection by birth with a noble family – though I'm sure
the Revolutionary courts will find some other name to call it by.

I have very little hope,' he repeated, 'less and less as time goes on. I have a feeling that he will die.'

He stopped speaking, and a deep silence hung between them. Jane began to wish, vainly, that she had not questioned Turnbull about the unknown Charles. Before, he had been a phantom with no substance, demanding nothing of her. His only reality had been given him by Anne when she had called him 'Charlie'. Now he was clothed in flesh and blood, he was a shy, dark-haired boy, growing out of his jackets and breeches; he was a lonely child gazing towards the coast of France from the old cliff face. He was that child grown into a man, rotting in a Paris prison, waiting trial and almost certain death. Now he had become too real, a phantom no longer. Pity had stirred and awakened in her, and she could never be free again of the vision of Charles. By yielding to pity she had involved herself in him, in the question of whether he lived or died. Blake's Reach could be hers only by the death of Charles . . . and he was a stranger no more.

Turnbull spoke her thoughts. 'So . . . you will likely inherit after all . . .'

'He has no wife or child? No heir?'

He shook his head. 'There is no one, I am told. The new French Government has confiscated his estate . . . They would take Blake's Reach also if they could.'

Jane gripped the arms of the chair. 'And if I inherit . . . what is there for me? How much has escaped Spencer?'

'Very little. The inheritance is slight . . . almost nothing. Perhaps fifty acres, and some sheep. This house and the outbuildings . . . two horses and a few head of cattle . . .'

'Is there a kitchen garden? Are there some hogs?'

He looked startled. 'Why . . . yes, I believe so! But Kate is old and a poor gardener. There's been no one to care how things were done at Blake's Reach for so long. The hogs get swine fever, and Spencer couldn't keep a good shepherd, so at lambing time the flock has suffered. He hasn't bought a good ram for many years, and the quality of the sheep is poor . . .'

She cut him short. 'Cows, hogs, chickens . . . a kitchen garden . . . I could live on that, Mr Turnbull. To some people, that would be riches!'

'It's not riches to a Blake on the Romney Marsh.'

'But it would do!' She said eagerly, 'It would keep us going until I could build things up . . . until I could build up the flock, buy some rams. It would certainly do, Mr Turnbull!' Her face was alight, and glowing.

He looked grave. 'Those things aren't done in a week, or a year, Jane. And meanwhile the roofs leak, and the damp rots the wood . . . the mice take over all these unused rooms. Can you wait to build up a flock while the house tumbles about your ears? Do you want to give all your youth to a kitchen garden and a pigsty?'

The glow faded slowly, and was replaced by a look of stubbornness. 'What else can I do? There's William to think of . . . neither of us can live on air.'

He rose from his chair slowly, and went to stand before the fire. The moving light fell on his greying hair, and deepened the lines on his face. He stood there, with head bent, and hands clasped behind him for some minutes. Then he turned to her.

'If Charles dies and you inherit Blake's Reach, Jane, there *is* something beyond the value of this house and land which will be yours.'

'Something . . . ? What?'

'There's a ring . . . a black pearl set in a ring. The Blakes have always called it the King's Pearl.'

She gasped, and turned a little pale. 'A black pearl . . . !'

'Yes . . .' he said. He spoke with faint reluctance. 'It is reckoned to be worth a considerable sum of money.'

'But why didn't you tell me! This could make such a difference!' She drew in a long breath. 'The pearl could be sold, couldn't it, Mr Turnbull? It would fetch some money! . . . it could set things right here!'

'I would not like to see you sell the pearl if it were yours.'

'Why not? There's so much needing here that it would buy . . .'

He pursed his lips. 'What do you suppose kept Spencer from selling it? – only a tradition stronger than his need for money, his passion for gambling. Like all the Blakes he venerated it because more than a hundred years ago it was the personal gift of a king.'

Her face sobered. 'What do you mean?'

'You've heard about the Great Rebellion – the time when Cromwell took over and His Majesty, King Charles the First, was beheaded?'

She nodded. 'There were families in Hampstead who talked about it as if it were yesterday, and they had all ridden with Cromwell . . . or the King. They still hated each other for what happened all that time ago . . .'

'A country in civil war isn't an easy thing to forget . . . some gained by it, and some lost, Jane. The Blakes were Royalist, and Henry Blake fought by the King's side. He almost went into captivity with him. One of the last acts His Majesty did was to

take from his finger the Black Pearl, and entrust it to Henry for
safe delivery to Queen Henrietta. Henry nearly lost his life attempting to reach France with it, but eventually he put it in the Queen's
hands, and helped her find a buyer for it. The King's widow and
children were very short of money . . .'

Jane was leaning forward. 'And Henry . . . ?'

'He went to Amsterdam, and worked for a Dutch merchant.
Blake's Reach and the estate were confiscated. His family fled into
exile with him. Like all the other Royalists they were very poor. At
the Restoration they came back, of course . . . and eventually
Blake's Reach was theirs again. King Charles the Second was a
vain and pleasure-loving man, Jane . . . but people do say that he
never forgot a kindness, and he was the most generous soul alive.
He was hard-pressed for money himself, and there were demands
on all sides, but Henry was eventually called to Whitehall, and
another Black Pearl was given him. Not as fine as the first, but still
worth a good deal of money. Charles gave it to him as a remembrance of loyalty, and his service to the Queen. Henry cherished it
above everything he owned, and the Blakes have always felt their
luck rests in the Black Pearl. They feel that if it is sold, their luck
will go.'

He watched the struggle in her face between pride in the tradition, and the practicalities of her upbringing. At last she tossed
her head.

'Luck! As if the Blakes' luck hadn't flown out the window long
ago. Is it lucky to keep the pearl, and lose Blake's Reach?'

'Well . . . and what would you do if you had the Pearl, Jane?'

'Sell it!' she said without hesitation. 'The luck of the Blakes
couldn't be any worse than it is at the moment – and perhaps
Henry meant it to be kept for just such a time. I think he'd forgive
me!'

'What would you do with the money?'

'I'd set this place back on its feet. I haven't lived among farm
people all my life without learning a thing or two. I'd buy rams,
and I'd grow enough feed to hand feed the cattle through the
winter, and they'd go fat to market. I'd get land wherever it was
going hereabouts. I'd mend the roof and weed the drive. I'd plant
new roses, and sit in a silk gown and wait for the gentry to come
calling.' She laughed as she spoke the last words.

'Wait for the gentry . . . ! Why?'

She looked at him very pointedly. 'Are there none about here
to marry, Mr Turnbull? Are there no eldest sons that haven't been
snapped up? It's true I have no fortune, but I have the Blake

name . . . and if it were mine, Blake's Reach itself would soon be
no inconsiderable trifle.'

'You mean . . . you mean you want to *marry* here? You want
to marry some squire's son?' He looked at her in wonderment.
'But you'd be like Anne – you'd die of boredom within a year!'

'I expect boredom, Mr Turnbull – and it's not likely to kill me!
You forget that I've lived as a servant, and I didn't care for that.
I've also seen how Anne lived, and I could do without the excitement of the gambling table. If I have to die of boredom, it will be
with a full stomach, and in peace and security.'

Then she added : 'What energies I have would be well spent
on Blake's Reach. Will I die of boredom if I have this? . . . it would
be a game of patience to get back the acres Spencer lost. The man
who married me wouldn't be getting a bad bargain. I would be
ambitious for his good as much as my own.'

He considered her carefully. It was amazing how right she was
. . . it was a proposition as shrewd and calculating as anything he
had heard, and yet, he believed that she would be honest in her
bargain. She would give fair value – and more. He didn't believe
that she would cheat. The audacity of the plan was its strength
. . . she just might be lucky enough to pull it off. He looked at her
as dispassionately as he was able. She had beauty, and a certain
brash confidence which made it noticeable; he took in the rounded,
elegantly provocative figure, and the modish clothes, and found
himself comparing her with the rather solid ladies of indifferent
charm whose families held the wealth of the Marsh. Beside most of
them she would have the sharpness of a new flavour. He knew
she possessed none of the accomplishments ladies thought so desirable, and which, in the end, bored men. The women, he thought,
would see through her quickly enough – but all the men were
likely to see was the graceful curve of her neck, and the way she
moved her hips. She was clever, more clever than Anne had been;
she had prudence and an eye to what side her bread was buttered
on. It was possible . . . mad as it seemed now, it was all possible.
She might pull it off.

He looked at her and smiled. Suddenly he wanted to see it
happen. He wanted Anne's child living here on the Marsh, doing
successfully what Anne had refused to do; he wanted to see a
former serving-girl from The Feathers come and make fools of all
the families who prided themselves on their birth and who said
the Blakes were finished. This was a descendant that old John
Blake, Marlborough's general, would have delighted in – the best
the family had produced in nearly a hundred years. He savoured

and relished the thought.

She was encouraged by his smile.

'Give me time! Give me a little money to begin with, and I'll put Blake's Reach back where it should be. I could do it, Mr Turnbull! *I could do it!*'

Now he smiled more broadly. 'You could do it! Yes! . . . I believe you could do it!'

He took a step towards her. 'If Blake's Reach becomes yours, you shall have all the help I can give – in whatever way I can give it. And here's my hand on it!'

But even as his hand gripped hers he felt again the familiar sense of loss. For the second time in his life he was bidding goodbye to Anne Blake . . . the first time money and position had defeated him, and now, when he had accumulated money and when the Blakes could no longer bargain for titles or power, the years were against him. He studied the young face before him, and for a second wondered if, even now, it were too late.

She had reached eagerly for his outstretched hand, then abruptly the triumph and the glow was wiped from her face. Her hand dropped limply back into her lap.

'I'd forgotten,' she said dully. 'It isn't mine, is it? – it isn't mine yet.' She looked at him distractedly. 'To wish a man dead – God save us, that's murder! But I *want* Blake's Reach, and before it's mine, Charlie must die!'

Unconsciously she had used her mother's name for him; she had called him Charlie.

4

The hired boy, Jed, had brought Robert's horse to the front door. The hinges creaked as it swung stiffly open. Kate put up her hand to shield the candle flame from the wind that ripped in from the sea, and flung itself against the house. Outside the night was black; there was nothing to see, there was only the sensation of low thick clouds scudding across the sky. The rain had stopped.

Robert looked at Kate.

'Miss Jane will be staying here at Blake's Reach, Kate. She will be staying . . . until Master Charles comes back!' He leaned nearer the old woman. 'Care for her, Kate.'

Then he went swiftly and mounted the horse. The boy backed away respectfully.

As she saw him mounted, and about to turn towards Rye, Jane had a terrifying sense of her aloneness. She was here, with this

great echoing house behind her, and the vastness of the Marsh
lost in the black night; she had spoken brave and defiant words,
but now she felt small, and a little afraid. Impulsively she went to
Turnbull's side, her hand gripping the saddle.

'You'll come again?' she said urgently.

He nodded. 'I'll come this way from time to time. You'll find it
strange at first, Jane. These are seafaring people, as well as farmers,
and there are those with a touch of wildness. But many of them
knew and loved Anne – they'll welcome you back. I have only this
to say to you . . .'

He broke off, looking about him to see where Jed had gone. The
boy had vanished into the darkness. Kate still stood by the door.

'Yes . . . ?' Jane urged.

He leaned down, and spoke softly in her ear. 'Take no notice of
what seems strange to you in these parts, Jane. Close your eyes to
what you had best not see. Those who mind their own affairs come
to no harm.'

She looked up at him, startled. 'In heaven's name, what are you
saying?'

He answered her as quietly and calmly as before. 'This is a seafaring race, Jane. These men have gone to sea for hundreds of
years, and . . . well, times are hard, and a smuggler is paid a great
deal for one night's work.'

'Smu – !' She clamped her lips down before the word was
fully out. She glanced back at Kate anxiously, but the old woman
appeared to have heard nothing. The wind blew her hair into her
eyes; she strained on tiptoe to be closer to Turnbull.

'Anne told me a little – I'd forgotten what she said. She hated it.
She seemed to be afraid of it.'

'Well – there have been foul crimes done in the name of smuggling . . . murder among them. But that happens only when folk
get too talkative or too inquisitive of other folk's business. But
mostly it flourishes without hindrance because there don't begin
to be enough Customs men or ships to check it seriously. And the
art of bribery is not subtle when practised by determined men,
Jane. Even when a known smuggler is caught the magistrates don't
convict, either from fear for their own skins, or because there's no
one can be got who will give evidence against them.'

He straightened a little in the saddle. 'This is their land, Jane
– and never forget it! Deal, Dover, Rye – all along the coast as
far as Cornwall they rule the roost. It would be safe to bet that
there's hardly a fisherman along the coast that hasn't run a cargo in
his time – when weather and moon is right. When it's done on a big

scale, it can make men rich. And the rights and wrongs of it don't seem to matter against that. The Marsh is sheep country, and when the Government clap their stupid tax on the export of wool, and farmers are threatened with ruin, do you think they won't run their bales to Flanders, and be glad to take a contraband cargo in return? And for the labourers – they earn in one night what they'd get for six weeks' work in the fields. So there isn't any use expecting them to see it in any other light but as bread in their children's mouths, and boots on their feet.'

He looked towards Kate, who was staring at them curiously, her neck craned to try to catch the gist of that low-toned conversation. Then once again he bent closer to Jane's ear.

'Don't stand out against it, Jane. And don't talk of it – don't even see it! You'll find the whole countryside with the smugglers, and their hand against the excise men. And it isn't only the small people – there are rich and powerful men in these parts, Jane, who've grown fat on the profits they've had, who are always looking the other way when the Customs man asks for help. And as for the Church – well, every parson within miles of the coast enjoys his contraband brandy and tea, and the only price he pays for it is silence, and a blind eye. At least that's what the wiser ones do. Otherwise there's trouble in the parish, and in turn trouble with the Bishop . . .'

She nodded quickly, her teeth beginning to chatter in the cold wind, and the nameless chill that Turnbull's words had brought out. Now the blackness of the Marsh was a hostile thing that screened what she must never see or talk of. She remembered Adam Thomas who openly said that he had left the Marsh to avoid the Customs men; and there was Kate, standing there and perhaps guessing what it was they talked of so quietly. These people were your friends so long as you stood on their side, and closed your door to the riding-officers. Between the two the line was clearly marked.

She drew back a little, and her hand slipped off the bridle. 'I understand, Mr Turnbull. I understand.'

He raised his hat, and then she stood and listened to the sound of the hooves growing fainter, and finally ceasing. Then she went back to where Kate stood waiting patiently.

The old woman looked at her with happy eyes as she shot the bolts in the heavy door. The candle flickered wildly for a second in the draught, and then grew still.

'It's a happy day for us that you've come back, Miss Anne.'

Jane glanced at her, startled, and then realized that Kate's memory had slipped, and that for the moment it seemed that it really was Anne who had come back to Blake's Reach.

She reached and took a second candle from the chest, and lighting it from Kate's was a formal little ceremony.

'I'll light you to your chamber, Mistress.'

3

It wasn't, after all, Anne's room to which Kate led her.

'I've put Master William in the chamber beside yours, Mistress, and you'll be sleeping in Charlie's old chamber until I can get Miss Anne's room aired and ready. 'Tis smaller here, and the fire heats the place quicker than in that other great chamber.' She opened the door and stood aside. 'You'll be snug here, Mistress, and little Charlie won't mind you havin' his bed these few nights.'

Jane held the candle high, and looked about her. The room was still strewn with the things that Charlie had left, his lesson books with the battered covers, the model ships he had sailed on the dykes, some dusty butterflies pinned to a sheet of paper, a riding whip with a broken handle. A row of seashells was arranged carefully along the mantel. The four-poster bed took up most of the space; the bed curtains were limp and frayed. Charles's room was in the old part of the house, where the ceilings were lower, and laced with black oak beams. There was a knowledge of loneliness here, as if the walls had listened too frequently to a child's weeping, short cries that were choked back in shame and in fear that they might be heard.

Jane turned quickly to Kate. 'I will do very well here, Kate, until my mother's chamber is ready. Good night!'

'Good night, Mistress. Rest well.'

She listened to the old woman's footsteps moving carefully down the passage. This room would not do very well for her; she would be out of it by tomorrow. She looked around again, shaking her head. Her lips were grim as she tentatively touched the bed Charles had slept on, and the table he had used for his lessons. She opened the great oak cupboard, and there were his clothes, painfully worn, and smelling of dampness and rot. With a stirring of pity she fingered them, picturing the long, thin wrists that had shot out from the cuffs. She didn't want to feel any more pity for Charles; she didn't want to think of him again. Almost certainly Charles would die. At this moment his life stood between her and her possession of Blake's Reach; she did not want to feel anything at all about him. Yet here the presence of the child he had been was a real thing – something she could touch as she now touched his coat. Nervous and angry suddenly, she slammed the door shut. She set down the candle, and began to undress with cold clumsy fingers.

Kate had laid her nightgown across the pillow. She felt the scratch of the rough bed linen against her, then her feet touched the hot bricks Kate had put there. Raised on her elbow, she blew out the flame.

The moving light of the fire filled the room – a warm, intimate light that played on the carved surfaces of the bed posts, and gave a ruddy beauty to a little mirror hanging crookedly on the wall.

Jane lay and watched the glow on the bed canopy. The room was peaceful. She turned her face wearily on the pillow, and then with a detached wonder, she heard herself murmur, *'Good night, Charlie! Good night!'*

2

The sound that woke Jane was almost lost in a sudden high shriek of the wind. She lay quietly, struggling against sleep, but becoming aware of the stillness and peace in the room with her, and more certain that the sound had come from outside the house. She sat up, listening; there were red embers in the fireplace still, and she guessed that it couldn't be more than an hour since she had fallen asleep. It had begun raining again. She could hear no other noise, nothing to account for her waking, but she slipped from underneath the blankets, shivering as the chill of the night struck her. The casement was fastened tightly against the rain; she pressed her face against it, but could see nothing. There was no light from any of the windows below, nor in the wing of the house which jutted at right angles.

It came again – but this time a familiar and recognizable noise. It was the sound of horses' hooves on the driveway which led past the house and round the back to the stables. Quietly she opened the casement and leaned out; light needles of rain fell on her. In the blackness there was nothing to see, but the horses and their riders were now almost directly below her. She guessed that there were perhaps four of them. She waited for them to stop by the front door. But they swept straight on, moving at a quick trot. Then the sound diminished and changed as they rode through the gates, and started down the hill to the Marsh.

She gasped, and the explanation struck her coldly; it was their

own horses that had been ridden away with such complete boldness – the horses belonging to Blake's Reach, and the two beautiful
greys Lord O'Neill had given her.

The thieves were gone already – lost somewhere out there in that
blackness.

Savagely she banged the casement behind her, and scrambled to
find flint to light the candle. Then she flung a cloak about her
shoulders, and thrust her feet into icy shoes. Outside in the corridor
she paused, shielding the flame with her hand; the house was unfamiliar – the only thing she recognized was the head of the stairwell in the new wing. In outraged haste she made for it.

'*Kate! Patrick!* Wake up! Someone's stolen the horses! Patrick
– *wake up!*'

As she raced down the stairs she heard General barking – a
frenzied sound in the otherwise still house. Now the strangeness
of the house maddened her; in the hall downstairs she flung herself
futilely against two locked doors in her search for the kitchen. She
found it at last – a flagstone paved room with a huge fireplace
where the live embers still glowed. Leading directly from it was
a twisting narrow staircase. She stood at the bottom and called
loudly, '*Patrick! Kate!* The horses – someone's taken the horses!'

It took her several minutes to light one of the lanterns she found
ranged on the mantel, and more time went on struggling with the
bolts on the kitchen door. Above her she could hear noises now –
Kate and Patrick calling to her, and General still barking.

'*Mistress! . . . Wait!*'

Jane didn't wait. She ran across the rough paving to the stables,
the rain pelting down into her face, making her gasp and twist to
escape it. The wind struck cold right down to her bones. The stable
door was latched, but not locked. She flashed the lantern quickly
along the stalls; there was no answering movement of animals. The
stalls were quite empty. In fury she banged the stable door again,
and started back to the kitchen.

Her rage made her forget the cold. Angrily she faced Kate, who
waited beside the door. Patrick was behind Kate, with his thick
driving coat over his nightshirt, and a long expanse of bony ankle
showing above his shoes. By the light of the lantern he held, his
pale face looked thinner than ever, and the hair blacker. At the
doorway was William, barefooted and wild with excitement, straining on General's collar to hold him.

It was Kate who must bear the brunt of her wrath. 'What sort
of an idiot is Jed to go off and leave the stable unlocked! As if
things aren't bad enough without we lose the horses as well . . . !

Those greys – they were worth money! And the carriage . . . how can I use the carriage without horses?' Furiously she swept past Kate. 'Oh, the fool! – the blasted fool! Just wait until I lay my tongue about his ears – yes, and a whip about his stupid shoulders . . . !'

'Hush, Mistress . . . Hush you now! There's no need to be fretting.'

'No need!' Jane's irritation increased. 'Well, then, how are we to get them back? By morning they could be anywhere . . . Day after tomorrow they could be sold, and gone forever!' Her voice quivered at the thought of it.

Kate shook her head; she closed the door firmly behind Jane and reached out and took the lantern from the girl's tense fingers. Her wrinkled face was framed by two grey plaits hanging down across her shoulders.

'Easy, Miss Jane! They'll not be sold anywhere tomorrow, and you'll find them back there, safe and snug. And more than likely there'll be a little present of tea or brandy to go with them.'

Jane looked at her coldly, her anger dying in a second as the meaning of the words came to her.

'You mean, Kate,' she said, 'that this is the doing of the smugglers . . .'

'Yes, Mistress.'

'Why?'

With great deliberation Kate looked at Patrick. 'Yer man, there – shouldn't he be takin' Master William back to his bed now, Mistress.'

Jane nodded slowly. 'Yes . . . yes.' Then to William she said: 'You'll take your death of cold. Look, you have no shoes . . .'

He grimaced. 'But I want to go and look for the horses . . . Lord O'Neill wouldn't like to know that the horses are gone.'

'We are not going to look for the horses now, William. I . . . made a mistake. They're not stolen.'

He tugged irritably at General's collar. 'We're *not* cold, and we're *not* tired,' he said loudly as he turned away.

Patrick went with him, and he was about to close the door, Jane motioned him. 'Come back here – when William is settled.'

Kate looked after them doubtfully. 'Is it wise, Mistress – yer man, can he be trusted to hold his tongue?'

'My mother died with Patrick by her bedside,' Jane said sharply. 'His devotion is more to be trusted than any soul I know.'

When Patrick returned Kate had a brisk fire of kindling started. She had taken away Jane's wet cloak, and given her an old woollen shawl. The blackened kettle hanging on the firecrane had begun to steam. As Patrick eased his long body into the corner of the settle, Kate handed them mugs of strong sweet tea.

'Take it now, against the cold,' she urged. 'I've got a drop o' brandy in to warm yer insides.'

She settled herself in her own tall-backed chair, wrapping her soiled grey home-spun shift about her thin flanks.

'Well, Mistress,' she said, 'ye've lived inland until now, and you'd not be expected to know the ways of sea-going folks. But where there's an easy bit o' money to be picked up, there are always men to be found to do it. The French coast is very handy-like to the Marsh, and the tax on tea and brandy's high enough to make sure that a body would never get the taste of it.'

Patrick moved indignantly. 'That's all very well now – haven't we all been settling for contraband tea and stuff whenever we could get our hands on it. 'Tis only fools who pay the full price, whether they live inland or not. But look you, woman, this comes close to home – there's empty stables out there now, an' them two beautiful creatures that were the joy of Miss Anne's heart are gone. An' here's Miss Jane worryin' her head off about them . . .'

She held up her hand for silence. 'Will ye let me be? I've more to say, and I'll finish me piece in me own time.'

'Go on, Kate,' Jane urged.

The old woman swayed a little in her chair. 'Ah, I know well that the whole country gladly takes what our gallant lads can get past the Customs boys, and I dare say the folks on the Marsh would go on running the cargoes even if the other great injustice weren't here to ruin the farmers.'

'Injustice?' Patrick's aggressiveness rose to the bait.

'Aye – a foolish and cruel tax Parliament put on shipping wool from the country. They say 'tis to help the weavers – and the weavers pay as little as they like, and it's ruin for the farmers. What could you expect men to do with the prices they offer for English wool across the Channel? What fools they be in London if they think a man will see himself ruined when all he has to do is run his wool across to Holland to fetch a fancy price.

'All along this coast, Mistress – from here to Cornwall, the highest and the lowest – there's hardly a family it doesn't touch in some way. Even the small people on the Marsh have a hand in it on their own account. The Dutch ships heave-to off the shore, and the folks row out and buy the cargoes as free as you please. All it needs is a dark night, and some idea of where the Revenue cutter is likely to show up. And the Revenue men – being paid as miser-

ably as they are, and scared stiff, most o' them, to come up against
the smugglers – well, they're not always very slow to sell that kind
of information. In good weather yawls and little sloops slip across
to Jersey and Guernsey and fill up with as much as they can hold.
The Channel Islands, Mistress, are like big store houses for everything the English smuggler wants. 'Tis a profitable business, even
when it's done in a small way.'

'We've all known that for a long time, woman,' Patrick said.
'But in heaven's name will ye tell us where the horses are?'

'I'm gettin' to that,' Kate said crossly. 'I'm gettin' to that directly.
Now – what I've been talkin' about's small stuff, a side line, you'd
call it, for the smaller folk without much money. But for the big
men in the business it's a different thing. There are men on the
Marsh and hereabouts who've made themselves rich in a few years
on runnin' the tea and brandy. They're the ones who own the big
luggers – the Folkestone boat-builders make a fancy, handsome
craft, with fore and aft rig, that'll outsail anything the Revenue
people put on the seas. All along the coast – places like Rye, Deal
and Folkestone – they put out of harbour in the usual way with a
small crew on, like as they was goin' fishin'. Then they heave-to off
the coast somewheres, and wait until the darkness. Then the fisher
folk and the village people come out in their rowing-boats, and
leave a crew on the lugger of as many as forty to sixty men, Mistress
– depending on the size of the lugger. Then they're off to France
or Holland, and the people on that side be only too willing to give
them the sort of cargoes they want – why, in places like Flushing
and Roscoff, they leave a permanent man there to have their stuff
ready for loading, just like a regular business.'

She sipped her tea, nodding her head sagely at the thought of a
business well handled. 'When it's all stowed, then back the lugger
comes, and at night the boats come out again, unload the cargo
and the extra men and run it in shore. That's where the horses
come in, Miss Jane. It needs a powerful lot of horses – maybe as
much as a hundred – to carry a cargo like that any distance from
the sea before dawn.'

'And *that's* where our horses have gone!' Jane was shaken by
the audacity and simplicity of it.

'Heaven help us!' Patrick said impiously. 'T' think of them two
darlin's with a load on their beautiful backs – them that weren't
built for it. I'll sit up wid them for the future – and see that it don't
happen again.'

Kate looked at him coldly. ''Twould be a foolish person who
locked his stable when they thought their horses might be needed.

Mor'an likely they'd find it burned down for their trouble. But if they're obligin' – why, there'll be a present, tea or a couple o' half ankers o' brandy, nice as y' please, left back with the horses in the morning. Them fine gentlemen,' she said slowly, 'are easy to deal with as long as a body goes along with them. But it's a dangerous and foolish thing to cross them. There've been bad tales o' murder and beatin's. The smugglers are the law along the seacoast, and there's none that dare stand against them. Informers have a bad time of it, I can tell you . . .'

Jane frowned. 'But everyone must *know* . . . A hundred horses can't pass along a road unnoticed.'

Kate shrugged. 'They do when everyone's particular to draw their curtains tight, and close the shutters. And in the morning – why they've not heard a sound. It ain't healthy to have keen ears in these parts.'

'Well!' Patrick said with satisfaction, 'they'll not accomplish much on a night like this.' He was still thinking sadly of the greys.

'Unless the wind drops they'll not land anything this night. It means that the lugger will put out to sea for the day, and tomorrow night they'll try again. But it's a dangerous business, because by the second night the Preventive Officers may have got wind of it and have called out the Folkestone Dragoons. There's often a drop o' blood spilled on nights like those, let me tell ye.

'The smugglers usually have a few different places they can drop a cargo a bit inland if they're pressed – "hides" they call them. It depends on the information they get about the Revenue people which one they decide to use.'

She put down her cup and leaned forward to stir the logs. The light played over the gaunt hollows of her face; the thin plaits of hair looked curiously childish now.

'In the past years, Mistress, Blake's Reach has had a hand in that.'

Jane stirred in alarm. From Patrick there was a frightened gasp. 'Mother of God!' He looked expectantly round the dark kitchen.

'You don't mean they leave the cargo here, Kate!'

'No, Mistress! . . . No! They leave it at the church up on the old cliff face there. Likely you saw it as you came from Rye this afternoon? Aye . . . well, that's John's church. One way an' another they do say he made a lot o' money – this is what I hear, Mistress. It was all before my time. So he built this church that no one wanted in particular – St Saviour's-by-the-Marsh, it's called. Ain't in any useful position, not for church-goin' folks – stuck off by itself, away from the village, just because old John had a notion to build it where it looked right over the Marsh. He endowed it, and there's a service there one Sunday in three, just for the sake of the vicar earning his keep, so to speak. Though he doesn't much like riding over from St Giles. But he has to do it, like it or not. Not many of the villagers come to it, either – too far when the weather makes the roads mucky. As churches go, it ain't much use.

'It makes a good store, Mistress, seeing as they have upwards of two weeks to move the stuff before the church is opened for the service. I expect the vicar knows – but he don't dare say nothing. If truth be known, he's probably been paid to keep quiet. There's so much profit in a big run that any number of folks can be paid for services like that.'

'Did Spencer know?'

Kate permitted herself a faint grin. 'Why, bless you, Miss Jane . . . there's a key to the church kept in this house, and it's a privilege of the Blakes to walk in there whenever they've the notion! Your grandfather was paid handsomely for forgetting his privilege at times. Perhaps the smugglers might use the church only once in three or four months, but Spencer got his money regardless.'

'Money!' There was an eager catch in Jane's voice. 'Have they paid since he died?'

Kate shook her head. 'Well, they've not paid *me* – that much I can tell you. O' course, I ain't important, but I know what was goin' on because sometimes – well, yer grandfather wasn't up to seein' to things and he trusted me, Mistress. I don't think Mr Turnbull knows of it, so *he's* not got the money. Like as not they're glad to get out of paying.'

'Well, they *won't* get out of paying. Who else knows – Jed? or Lucas?'

'No, Mistress – if they've found out they've kept their mouths shut, as it's prudent to do. They've no call to go to the church – or no call to poke their noses in where they're not wanted.'

Jane looked firmly from Kate to Patrick as if daring a contradiction.

'It's money that belongs to the Blakes . . . and for the time being it belongs to *me*. If Charlie ever shows up I'll settle my debts with him. Now – who do I see to get it?'

Patrick looked at the ceiling wordlessly, his melancholy face expressed his outraged feelings. Kate's horror was plain.

'Lord, Miss Jane, you're thinkin' of goin' after 'em. 'Tain't wise, I tell ye! Ye don't know these kind o' folk. You're new to the Marsh . . . and the Marsh don't care for strangers pokin' into their business.'

'I'm not a stranger,' Jane said shortly. 'I'm a Blake! Now tell me – what's the name of the man I must see.'

Kate's voice wavered. 'Oh ... Miss Jane ...'

'What's the matter, Kate? Are you afraid I'll inform? What sort of a fool do you take me for? All I'm interested in is the money for Blake's Reach. After that they can all drown or hang, and it's no concern of mine.'

Kate shook her head. 'Aye, but you're young, Mistress, to have words like those on yer lips.'

'I have to have words and feelings like that or Blake's Reach will be sold over our heads. Now, tell me – what's the name of this man?'

'Mistress, I tell y' to stay clear of this business. Y've no idea where it may lead y' . . . Some bad things 'ave 'appened . . .'

'Kate, you'd better tell me. If you don't, I'll find other people to ask, and that could be worse.'

Kate sighed and shrugged. 'Then y'd best be seein' Paul Fletcher, over at Old Romney. I doubt he's the man behind it all, but he's the man to see. He's not long back on the Marsh after leavin' the Navy. But, Mistress, dear,' she added pleadingly, 'you'll mind what you have to say to him? I don't trust none o' them what mixes in the business, and Mr Fletcher being a gentleman makes it harder to judge.'

Jane felt a wave of anger and irritation sweep over her as she listened. She was tired, and the chill was beginning to creep into her bones. It seemed that everyone – Kate, Patrick, even Turnbull – was bent on putting only fear and frustration before her. At the same time they clung to her, and looked to her to provide the means and reasons for existence – somehow. She wrapped her nightgown more closely about her ankles; it was wet and dirty where it had dragged in the mud of the stable-yard. The wind had dropped while Kate talked, and she could no longer hear the sound of the rain. The smugglers would bring off the run, she thought, and someone – perhaps this Paul Fletcher – would be richer for it. She thought wearily and enviously of the gold that would be earned for this night's work, and of the frightening way the golden sovereigns in her own purse had dwindled since they had left London – frightened when she considered all that was needing at Blake's Reach, and the demands that would be made on her. And the only saleable possession left to her – the pair of greys – were out somewhere on the dark night, risking their precious hides to make someone else's gain. The thought enraged her; she felt young and ignorant, and the difficulties ahead were beyond counting.

She rose to her feet stiffly, gathering all the dignity and firmness that was left to her, because somehow, now, it mattered that Kate and Patrick should never sense her weakness.

'I've dealt with so-called gentlemen before, Kate. When the horses are rested, I'll drive over to Old Romney. Whatever sort of person Paul Fletcher is, he still must pay what he owes.'

As she flung herself once again into Charles's bed she suddenly realized the implication of what she had said.

'God help me,' she whispered, 'I've thrown my hand in with smugglers.'

She fell into an uneasy and dream-filled sleep, but when the sky over the Marsh was streaked green and faint purple in the dawn, she woke and heard them. She leaned far out over the open casement and listened as they went by. The greyness of the morning still hid them, but she knew the sounds well enough – the sounds of heavily-laden horses climbing the hill slowly, the sounds of men's voices kept low and hushed. When they were passed, she climbed back into Charles's bed and slept deeply and quietly.

She woke to a fair spring day, with the sun already high. When she went to the window the scene of the day before was gone. The Marsh was green and soft, the air as clear as polished glass, so that she could see the shipping in the Channel five miles away. Blossom was opening to its full in the tangled orchard; the warm air was alive with the hum of insects.

And then she remembered that it was hardly yet two months since she had left The Feathers.

4

All of them, Kate, Jed and Lucas recognized that this morning was different from others at Blake's Reach, and they hung around the kitchen waiting for Jane to appear. They expected orders from her, and she gave them as if she had been doing it all her life. A sense of urgency was upon her, and it made her shrewd and firm as she had never been before.

First of all she went with Lucas and Patrick to inspect the greys, to stroke their silken noses, and commend Lucas's grooming, to order the carriage washed and the stables swept. When that was done, Lucas would go to his usual duties of tending the sheep – there were new lambs in the flock, and she was sharply conscious of their worth. Grinning, Patrick helped Lucas move down to the cellar two half-ankers of brandy, which had nestled innocently in the straw near the greys. Lucas's movements were eager and swift, as if, after the years of apathy at Blake's Reach, he welcomed the crispness of the orders. Before him, Jane made no comment over the brandy; if the acceptance of brandy and smugglers was part of the life of the Marsh, she meant to show how completely she belonged here.

Next Jed was dispatched, with a clip on the ear from Kate to hasten him, to the village – to Appledore, which was nearly a mile away. There he was to round up as many women as could leave their children and the cooking for a few hours, or to bring with them any children old enough to wield a mop or a rake. Jane was counting heavily on their curiosity to bring them, and, in the first flush of their enthusiasm, to get work from their tough, country-bred bodies that would lift the air of grim neglect from Blake's Reach. There was no money for carpenters and masons, but women and children were cheap to hire. For the present she would have to be content with clean windows and clipped hedges, and shut her eyes to the leaking roof and the crumbling plaster.

'Some day,' she murmured, half under her breath, 'I'll do the job properly!'

'What was that, Mistress?' Kate asked.

'I said,' she repeated distinctly, 'that some day I'll do the job properly. Some day Blake's Reach will be the most respected house on the Marsh.'

And they believed her. There was an immediate scurry to carry out her orders, as if they expected, magically, to see the old house dissolve and re-emerge before their eyes – just because she had said so. She noticed, with a touch of satisfaction, that this morning there was no talk of 'Master Charlie'.

'Jane!' She turned at a tug on her skirt. 'Jane – what shall I do?' William's face looked up earnestly into hers.

'You? Why . . .' A gleam of mischief appeared in her eyes. 'Why, William, you can be useful, too. Here . . . !' And for the first time in his life William found that his hands held a broom. 'You can go and help Lucas sweep the stable.'

He went without a word.

It was then, when the men were busy, that Kate led her to the drawing-room.

'There was little a body could do to keep a great house like this in order, Mistress, with no help,' she said as she opened the door. 'But 'twould have been a crime to let this go. I've done what I could . . .'

She stepped inside, and Jane looked into the darkened room

without much hope. Dust flew out of the curtains as the old woman
drew them back. The spring sunlight came flooding in, revealing
the long, finely panelled room, hung with portraits. She quickly
took in the elaborately carved mantel and cornices, and the handsome high-backed chairs from which Kate was stripping the dust-
sheets. Her eyes lit with excitement; she walked rapidly down the
length of the room, lifting a cover from a marquetry table, bending
to examine the exquisite work on the tapestry-covered chairs. She
paused, and absently her hand cut a great swarth in the dust lying
on a rosewood harpsichord.

'The Master never used this room,' Kate said laconically. ' "Too
cold", he said. I think, myself, that he never fancied the company
of his family on the walls.'

Jane hardly heard what she was saying; she had begun pulling
at a rolled-up carpet lying along one wall. Its colour made her
gasp – a brilliant gold ana blue, with a texture like velvet.

'The Master said John Blake brought it back from Brussels when
he was at the wars.'

Jane was thinking that not even Anne's house in Albemarle
Street had had anything as fine as this. She fingered it reverently,
then looked around the room, and finally at Kate.

'We'll put it in order,' she announced. 'Some of the women
who come must help you put it in order. We must have a room fit
to receive guests in.'

'Guests? To Blake's Reach . . . ?'

'Certainly,' Jane said tartly. 'There will be guests here and we
must receive them fittingly. Now, I want the floor waxed, the
mirrors and windows cleaned, the curtains . . .'

Kate made a nodding acceptance of her instructions, believing
by now that whatever Jane said would somehow be so. It was all
too bewildering for her to take apart and question. The years since
Anne Blake had run away from Blake's Reach had been dragging
and weary ones, and her mind and her footsteps had showed in
acceptance of them. She had accepted the loneliness of this house,
and the feeling of doom. She had expected to die knowing it that
way. Now she was not fit to resist what Jane decreed, only knowing the joy of hearing a crisp young voice sounding in these rooms
again, and the light, impatient tap of a woman's heels on the
boards.

Jane moved from room to room this way, giving instructions,
listening to explanations from Kate. On the way she discovered a
chest of tarnished silver, and a stock of glasses begrimed with the
dust of years. Patrick rubbed one in his apron, and held it to the
light.

'From foreign parts, I'd say, Miss Jane. I've seen ones just such as these in Lord Ormby's house.' His eyes gleamed over the silver. 'Heavy as a bad conscience, Mistress,' he said, feeling it lovingly. 'I'll warrant they'll fetch a good price ...'

She shook her head, and laid her hand restrainingly on his. 'No more selling, Patrick, until we have no other choice. Clean it, and put it into use.'

'It were too much for me to keep up with,' Kate said in an aggrieved voice. 'The Master didn't care what he ate off ... so I stacked it away here ...'

The talk and the small discoveries went on until they heard the voices in the yard. Jed was triumphant at the head of his band; there were eight women, and about as many children, three of them boys of almost thirteen, and strong and big enough for the work Jane wanted. They looked at her with expectant, excited faces, and she reminded herself that she must take the time to give them the gracious salute they considered customary. There were curtsies, and even small gifts – eggs and pots of honey and preserves; there were little speeches of greeting, and expressions of sympathy over her mother's death. They talked of Anne as if she had been at Blake's Reach only yesterday; Jane realized that a number of them would have been about Anne's age – perhaps had worked here in the kitchen or dairy, and grown up with her. Even her arrogance they had forgiven her, and had loved her for her generosity and high spirits; Anne's laughter had been a gift to this house, and to everyone who had come under its roof.

Then they proceeded to the real business of the morning and they bargained a little over the price to be paid for their help. Everyone enjoyed it; it would have been a disappointment to them all if Jane had accepted their first price. But Sally Cooper had brought Jane up, and she was no one's fool. Finally the price was settled, and the mops and pails were brought out, the ancient gardening tools were oiled and scraped for rust.

Strange sounds which Blake's Reach had not heard in many years began to float out on the clear, bright morning – the sounds of mingled, good-humoured voices, of stiff windows opening, the sounds of shears in the overgrown hedges, and rakes crunching the gravel in the drive. Patrick was everywhere, shouting instructions, pulling ladders about, cleaning a window and then rushing to scrape the mud off the porch, to help a village child pluck weeds from the gravel. The acrid smell of soap and water meeting dust began to blend with the odours from the soup pot on the kitchen stove.

Clutching his broom, William ran about like a child in an excited dream, useless and unspeakably happy.

2

The morning was well on when Jane was free at last to get the
key from Spencer's desk, and start up the hill towards the church.
She was happier than she had been for many days, optimistic and
confident. She kept twisting her face to get the sun fully on it. The
stone church, St Saviour's-by-the-Marsh, crowned the edge of the
old cliff-face at its highest point. The sea that had once washed
beneath the cliff was now the flat Marsh land itself, rich and green,
dotted with the grazing sheep, and the curving dykes. She turned
off the road into the church lane, and then halted. The tracks left
by the horses and men were quite distinct in the soft mud.

She stood thoughtfully, fingering the key in her pocket, gazing
absently at the long waving grass in the graveyard, the motionless
hands of the black-faced clock in the church tower. The light over
the Marsh had a strange, intense quality. She listened to the birds
– plovers and a distant lark; there were two herons in the dyke
at the bottom of the cliff. Below her the sloping roofs of Blake's
Reach were touched with moss in places. It was a world suddenly
familiar to her, and growing dear.

She turned and followed the path to the side door; the key
slipped easily into the oiled lock, and she swung the door open,
letting a broad beam of sunlight fall across the grey stone floor.

The damp and chill struck her instantly – and the strange, pervading smell. She caught her breath in a gasp of astonishment. The
lovely, graceful church was piled high along each wall with bales
of wool. The greasy smell of wool dominated that musty air, and
with it was mingled faintly the woody smell of the brandy casks
and the tea boxes. Everywhere – in the aisles, on the pews, in the
carved choir stalls – were the bales and casks. She picked her way
among them, collecting dust and fluff on her gown as she went.
The delicate colonnade of three arches on each side of the nave was
disfigured with the costly litter of contraband. She looked around
with awe, trying to reckon what the cargo could be worth, and
how many men had risked their skins and liberty to land it somewhere down on the Marsh shore during last night's storm.

The brandy casks were ranged in rows almost up to the altar
itself. She stood at the bottom of the pulpit steps and tried to count
them – and gave up. She glanced over her shoulder, the thought
striking her suddenly that this was the first time she had ever been
in a church quite alone before. On an impulse she mounted the

steps, enjoying a sense of power as she stared down at the immovable, silent congregation of wool bales and brandy kegs.

She cleared her throat.

'John Blake built this church,' she said loudly, sonorously. The echo, sounding back, startled her. *'John . . . this church . . .'*

She went on, 'The smugglers own it now.' *'The smugglers . . . the smugglers . . .'* it repeated mockingly.

The next words died in her throat. Horrified she listened to the sound of a key being fitted to the lock. She looked around wildly for a retreat from her absurd position, but there was only time to drop down behind the marble front of the pulpit before the door opened. A man's heavy tread sounded through the church. She counted the footsteps, purposeful, and growing nearer. About the centre of the aisle he stopped.

At last he spoke, a calm, assured voice – unmistakably the voice of a gentleman.

'Well, preacher! . . . Is your sermon finished already? You don't save much for late-comers!'

Scarlet with embarrassment and rage, Jane rose slowly to her feet. Standing below her, legs thrust apart and arms folded, was a tall, blond man, whose careless, unpowdered hair was dragged back into a short pigtail. He wore dusty breeches, and his faded, water-stained jacket had been part of a naval officer's uniform. The markings of rank and insignia had been removed.

He was smiling at her – a friendly, quizzical grin.

She returned his stare coldly. 'Who are you?' she said, although she had already guessed his identity.

He dropped his arms and bowed.

'Paul Fletcher, at your service, ma'am.' He raised his eyes to her again. 'And you, of course, are the Blake of Blake's Reach.'

'I have a name!' she snapped. 'I'm Jane Howard!'

He shook his head. 'It matters not, dear Madam, what your name is. To the Marsh folk you are simply the Blake of Blake's Reach. And . . . while you look like Anne Blake come to life again, you can hardly expect to escape it.'

'*You* knew my mother.'

'I knew her, of course. I was a child when she went away, but even to the young savage I was then, she was unforgettable.'

Jane had nothing to say to this. The blue-eyed gaze of the man was disconcerting, and she was miserably conscious of all the things that were wrong with this meeting. She had had it planned – a carefully staged piece in which she would drive to visit Paul Fletcher in all her finery of silk and velvet, behind Lord O'Neill's greys. The advantage would have belonged entirely with her. Now he had caught her, dishevelled from the morning's work, shouting to this empty church, and must surely think her half-crazy. She had been made to look foolish – and with that had failed to uphold the prestige of the Blakes. She scowled at him.

'Would you please come down, Miss Howard?' he said politely. 'I find it difficult to talk to a ghost in a pulpit.'

She obeyed reluctantly. As she came towards him his eyes narrowed, and he cocked his head slightly.

'It's amazing,' he said softly, as if he hardly meant her to hear. 'The same walk even . . . almost the same voice . . . !' He spoke louder. 'You'll have to be patient with the stares you encounter, Miss Howard. Your mother was just about your age when we last saw her. No one here ever saw her grow fat, or her hair fade . . .'

She shrugged. 'Not you, or anyone else, Mr Fletcher. She didn't grow fat or faded.

'However,' she added, 'it was not my appearance you came to discuss – or my mother's.'

He was older than he had appeared from the pulpit. Now she could see the weathered lines in his face, and his eyes were alert and watchful – experienced; his body was strong and heavy-shouldered.

'I was on an errand at Appledore, and I learned that the Blake had come to Blake's Reach. I came to call, and bid you welcome.'

'*You came to call!*' She ran her eyes meaningly over his shabby coat and the stained breeches. He was unperturbed. With equal coolness he surveyed her dusty gown, her hair carelessly drawn back off her forehead.

'The informality of my call was not meant as an offence, Miss Howard. As you can see . . .' he indicated the piles of contraband, 'my business is pressing.'

'Yes, indeed. So is mine.'

He nodded. 'Naturally, Miss Howard – there are many things to discuss.' He gestured to the pew behind her. 'Please sit down – this may take some time.'

She sat down, perching herself on the edge of the pew. He dragged forward a brandy cask for his own seat.

'Of course, this isn't your rightful pew. The Blakes belong down there.' He pointed towards the front of the church. 'But it's already full.'

She looked towards the altar, and noticed for the first time a large, boxed-in pew, on whose front panel was emblazoned the coat of arms which she remembered over the porch at Blake's

Reach. It was set at right angles to the rest of the pews; on its faded blue velvet cushions were piled an assortment of odd-looking bundles, wrapped carefully in tarpaulin.

'Laces fit for a queen,' Paul Fletcher said. 'We're particular to put only the choicest merchandise there.'

Swiftly she turned back to him. 'Perhaps the Blakes are a laughing matter to you, Mr Fletcher, but you'll hardly expect me to join the mirth. My family might have been fools, but I am one member of it who isn't going to be laughed out of what is rightfully their property. There's a question of some money to be settled between us.'

He leaned towards her, both his hands resting on his knees. 'Let us understand each other,' he said carefully. 'The smuggling fraternity is tightly-knit, and we keep to our own rules. Certainly we make a living by not paying the King his revenue – but we *do* expect to pay for our privilege. Our business is highly organized, and it isn't run on debts. We use this church, and we pay for it.'

'There's been no money paid since Spencer Blake died.'

'Naturally not! Whom should we pay?'

With great deliberation she turned away from him and looked about her. She looked at the wool bales, the brandy casks, the tea-boxes, and at the bundles of lace in the front pew.

'There's a great deal of money in this cargo, Mr Fletcher.'

She pointed to the bales stacked against the far wall. 'You'll get a good price for that on the Continent. The weavers in Holland pay well, I hear. Of course, there's a rub in handling so much – you need a good, large store, don't you? Somewhere not too close to the sea, and not too far inland.'

'Yes?' he questioned.

'I mean,' she said, turning back to him, 'a store like this is a splendid one. You ought to be willing to pay handsomely for it.'

'I'll pay what I paid your grandfather – ten guineas on the first of each month.'

'Ten guineas . . .' She considered this carefully. 'Ten guineas . . . But after all, that's only your word.'

'There are no written contracts in our sort of business. Ten guineas was what we agreed upon.'

She shrugged. 'My grandfather's death ends all agreements and contracts he made. *I* have taken over now, and the new price is . . .' She paused, and considered. 'The new price is fifteen guinea pieces, to be paid on the first day of each month.'

He answered without hesitation. 'I won't pay it!'

'And that, sir, will undoubtedly be your loss. This place suits you very well. The village is nearly a mile away, and the vicar a little farther. A service is held only one Sunday in three, and the rest of the time everything's securely locked against Preventive Officers, who can't break into a church. It takes time – valuable time to you – for them to get permission to enter here. Oh, yes – all this is worth paying for.'

'But not worth what you seem to think. Spencer Blake was paid that much money only out of deference to his position. "Manorial Rights" I suppose you'd call it. That sum of money doesn't bear any relation to the value of the store.'

'Then if you're not prepared to pay what I ask, you must find some other place for your cargoes.'

He leaned towards her again, and spoke quietly and sharply. 'It distresses me to have to remind you of the fact, Miss Howard. But has it occurred to you that Blake's Reach can't afford to let go even the despised ten guineas?'

She shook her head. 'You're very wrong, Mr Fletcher. Blake's Reach needs money so badly that the miserable hundred and twenty guineas a year you offer is hardly worth thinking about.' With the tip of her finger she began idly to trace the grooves in the carving on the pew. 'Don't you see that once a certain stage of need is reached, a little money does practically nothing? Will a few extra pounds put a new roof on? Or buy a new flock? It wouldn't *save* Blake's Reach – it wouldn't even begin to patch it up!'

She was watching him carefully now, trying to feel how far she could go with the bluff. 'It's really very simple if you look at it my way. I *can* afford to do without your money because it's such a small part of what I need.'

His eyebrows had lifted a little – in amusement, Jane thought. 'Then why press for more if this is a matter of indifference to you? Why not give it freely . . . let's say, as a generous gift of the Manor? They say the poor are always the most gracious givers.'

'It's a virtue I'm not very practised in,' she retorted sharply. 'I'm asking a higher price because I don't like to be undervalued.'

He laughed outright. 'Undervalued! I've never known a woman more conscious of her price!'

'Price isn't value, Mr Fletcher.'

His expression grew sober, and he shook his head. 'I hope for your own sake, Jane Howard, that, in all you're getting yourself involved with here, you'll still be able to distinguish value from price. I mean, to know how much is worth . . . what!'

'I understand very well what you mean.' She tapped her nail

against the edge of the pew. 'What I want to *know* is will you pay what I'm asking?'

He shrugged, losing his air of seriousness and concern, becoming flippant again.

'How can I say?' Reaching behind him he caught his coat tails and spread them out for her inspection. 'Do I look like the man who owns that cargo? You surely must know the difference between a prosperous smuggler and his hireling? It's not for me to settle what shall be paid. I'll carry your message, of course . . .'

Jane pursed her lips. 'I thought a man of your . . . talents, Mr Fletcher, would hardly be content to labour for another man. I see you as a leader . . .'

'Of course you do,' he said, blandly ignoring her tones. 'Talents I undoubtedly have, but it takes time to acquire your own lugger. I left the Navy ten months ago.'

'The Navy regretted it?' Jane prompted.

'It would be idle to pretend they did – with a line of men ahead of me for promotion that would stretch from here to Rye. Too slow for me – too slow. What's the use of being made a Vice-Admiral the year you die of old age?' He shook his head. 'It was divorce by mutual consent. I can't really think the Navy grieves the loss of Lieutenant Paul Fletcher.'

'So . . . you're not rich enough to own the cargo? Then who does?'

'I'm paid so that *that* gentleman doesn't have to soil his hands with the illegal business of smuggling. The dirty nights waiting for the boats are not for him – or the unpleasant thought that you might have to kill a Preventive Officer to save the cargo. No, that's not for him at all! One of the many nice things about being rich is that when you want to break the law, you pay someone to do it for you.'

'You're not going to tell me his name?'

'I not only won't tell you – I'll even warn you it's not a question that's safely asked on the Marsh.'

She felt the coldness of his words touch her like ice. She wished she needn't be constantly reminded that this was a world of suspicion and chase, of quick and savage revenge on the informer. It was all much better when smuggling was made to seem a fairly light-hearted business of keeping out of the way of the Revenue men. She stirred restlessly, wanting to be free of the thought. All she had wanted was a few extra pounds from this bounty in which the whole sea coast appeared to share, but Paul Fletcher wanted her to feel the darkest fears of any of the men who walked the roads with contraband at night, or who sold information to the excise men, and spent the gold with terror in their hearts.

'You make the Marsh an evil place,' she said in a low tone. 'I'm afraid . . .'

His features relaxed. He was almost tender when he spoke.

'There's no need to fear when you belong to the Marsh as the Blakes do. They have been here as long as men have been recording its history. They belong here – not like the Fletchers, who were small farmers and newcomers hardly more than a hundred years ago. The Blakes . . .'

He stood up abruptly. 'Come with me!'

He held out his hand to her, and she took it without a thought, caught up in his force and energy. He led her back to the door, and stood aside to let her pass. They stepped out again into the sunlit world, and the damp smells of the church were gone. The light was so brilliant and solid-seeming that Jane wanted to put out her hands and feel it, like a living thing. The green miles of the Marsh were there, the flat shores, the sea like a blinding mirror.

Impatiently he pulled her around to the other side of the church, where the sweep of the view was much greater.

'Shade your eyes! Now look down there. That great dyke down there – in the break between the hills towards Rye – that used to be a tidal river, when the Marsh was still a marsh, and half covered with water in every high tide. And the smaller dyke branching from it – do you see where it goes? It runs from there right along here beside Blake's Reach!'

'Yes – I see.' And then impatiently: 'But what . . . ?'

'Wait! Try to think of a time, hundreds of years ago, when the river found its way out to the sea through mud-flats, and this dyke was a small creek flowing into it. A man called Blake came to settle on a reach of this creek, and gave it its name. Not an important man – just a very obscure cousin of a family who were prominent ship owners and merchants. In fact, they were barons of the Cinque Ports, and that was a title to be proud of in those days.

'This Blake,' he said, nodding towards the dyke and the house, 'had his chance when the Rother changed its course after a great storm some time, they say, about the 13th century. Then this side of the Marsh was flooded only at exceptionally high tides. The reclaiming of the Marsh had been going on since the Romans came to England, and after the river changed its course, the time was right to start on this part. The Blakes began making their innings – reclaiming, ditching and draining, and the acres of pasture for their sheep grew with each generation.'

He laughed suddenly, in amusement. 'As your grandfather told the story, one day the Blakes stopped working for a moment to draw breath, and found themselves rich – and bearing the title of Lords Proprietors of the Romney Marsh, to boot! And they weren't humble folk any longer.'

'That's a good story,' she said with satisfaction. 'I don't care if it isn't exactly true – it's still a good story. But what became of the other ones – the ship owners?'

He shrugged. 'I don't know. Died out, I suppose – or lost in poverty. This used to be a great sea trading area, but as the reclaiming of the Marsh went on, the harbours began to silt up. New Romney's a mile and a half from the sea now, and Rye harbour is a mile from the town itself. When the trade left the Ports, I imagine the ship-owning Blakes went with it.'

'It seems to me,' she said coolly, 'that you've too much information about the Blakes. How much of it have you made up?'

He laughed. 'None! I swear to you – none! I've heard it from your grandfather when he wished to impress on me the inferiority of the Fletchers by comparison to the Blakes.'

'You hated him, didn't you?'

'Hate him? Why should I? He was an old man, full of drink and despair. He was shamed, too, by the thought that he and his father had brought nothing but disaster to their family. At one time, he told me, the Blake land stretched to the great dyke in the south, and touched the fringe of Appledore.'

'And now,' Jane said, 'there's only a few fields, and hardly enough sheep to keep them cropped. Don't tell me, Mr Fletcher – I *know*.'

'There are ways to get land,' he said quietly. 'When times are bad, small farmers grow less careful of their inheritance. It needs patience . . .'

She broke in roughly. 'And money! Where do you think the money would come from?'

'The King's Pearl! Everyone knows that Spencer never sold the King's Pearl.'

'The Pearl belongs to Charles.' She pointed towards the house. 'Down there we're all waiting for Charles to come back.' Her voice shook with a scarcely controlled anger. 'I've been here less than a day, and already I've fallen into the pattern. This hour, or maybe the next hour, he might come back.' She looked away. 'No – the King's Pearl is not mine to sell.'

'Charlie Blake is as good as dead – if he's not dead already! You'll be mistress of Blake's Reach, and free to do what you please with the King's Pearl.'

She stood silently, fighting hope and enthusiasm, not wanting
Paul Fletcher to see them, but wanting to hear him say again that
she would be mistress of Blake's Reach. Once again she wanted to
hear that land could be won with money and patience. She
struggled to keep the excitement from her face and eyes, and it
wasn't possible. Paul Fletcher knew as well as she did what thoughts
were hers, how the fate of an unknown man in a Paris prison could
seem so little beside what lay under her hand. With a little money
she could live with dignity and honour at Blake's Reach – so that
by degrees she stepped completely and forever across the line that
had separated her from this family, so that there would come a
time on the Marsh when she and no one else would symbolize the
Blake family, when the memory of old scandals would die . . .
Paul Fletcher's voice, sure and firm, broke into her thoughts.

'And I know what you'll do. You'll put every penny you can
lay hands on into Blake's Reach – as careful and saving and
industrious as any of the first Blakes who settled on this creek.
You'll make a dull marriage to further your plans, and not to
anyone who will take you from this place. You'll sacrifice everything to it – and it'll be wrong! It will take everything, too – your
youth and all the good years there should be for you. It will take
your beauty, Jane.'

Vaguely she was aware that he had called her by her name, and
she didn't turn to rebuke him. Nor did she attempt a denial of his
words. 'You don't like the Marsh, Paul Fletcher,' was all she said.

'I'm unwilling to give my life to it! It's worked over – there's
nothing but these eternal sheep and the blasted winds. Its society
and people are stagnant, like all of England. I'll leave it behind
when I can.'

'Where will you go?'

'When I've gathered enough money from cheating the King's
Revenue I'll go and trade more or less honestly in the West Indies.
I'm a seaman. Not a porter of other men's brandy.'

'Why the West Indies? – why not one of the English ports?'

'Because I want to go where there's air to breathe, and sun on
your bones, and rum for the asking. Money isn't so important . . .
I could live like a king there for what I'd earn on the profit from
a single sloop. And if a man cares to exert himself, if he's got wits
and guts, and will take a risk, then he can be rich. I said money
wasn't important – well, it is! To me it's important. I like money
. . . and sunshine, and women who smile easily, and laugh. I'm
sick in my belly with these stiff-necked dames who wouldn't un-

6

bend to pass the time of day with disreputable Paul Fletcher.'

'Are you disreputable?'

'Never mind that,' he answered shortly. 'Ten years from now it won't matter.'

Suddenly he touched her arm.

'Think of it! Ten years from now you'll still be living here – working and scrimping for the honour of a name. And I'll be free of it all, in a place where names don't count.'

Her body stiffened, and she drew away from him. 'Why do you talk like this? What can it matter to either of us what the other does?'

'Of course I talk out of turn – I always have! I'm saying this because I think you're making a mistake, and it's a damn shame! You've come here out of the blue, and now you've seen Blake's Reach, and you think you want to be part of it. You don't understand that it's finished, and that someone like yourself can't be walled up in a tomb for the sake of a tradition which seems dazzling in its fashion, but will drain the life from you.'

She stirred, opened her mouth to speak, but he cut her short.

'Believe me, it isn't worth it, Jane,' he said. 'Get away before you're caught up in it all – before you forget there are such things as being young, and laughing whenever you feel like laughing. You're trading your youth and freedom for the empty game of playing a lady with a penny in your pocket. You don't know all the difficulties yet. But even in the few hours you've been here you must have felt doubts . . . You're even breaking the law. You're throwing your hand in with a bunch of dirty smugglers. And what for? You're doing it for a crumbling old ruin and its debts that aren't worth a thought in a young girl's head. Get away from it, Jane!'

There was no response in her face – the obstinate, stubborn Blake face, immobile with anger and wounded vanity and pride. He felt saddened as he watched its unchanging stare.

'Since when, Paul Fletcher, have women been able to decide which way their lives will go? Do you think I have any choice? *You fool!* – it's Blake's Reach, or nothing!'

She turned swiftly and walked away from him, the hem of her dusty blue gown swishing against the long grass. Her slight body was rigid, as if her anger and scorn were barely confined by good sense. When she reached the gravel path she looked back briefly.

'I'll expect you with the answer about the money tomorrow evening. *Without fail!*'

Only during his naval service had Paul Fletcher remained silent under a tone like this. He was moved to protest, and then dismissed the thought, shrugging. When a woman looked like Jane Howard you allowed her to say such things, especially when the sun was like fire in her red hair.

5

Jane walked swiftly down the road to Blake's Reach, her mood savage and tinged with bitterness and disenchantment. She examined the house critically in the light of Paul Fletcher's words, and now she saw only the broken roof tiles, and the rusted iron gates. Abruptly her plans became like a bright, romantic dream that had fallen in pieces at her feet.

Her feelings softened instantly she turned into the drive, and her shoes crunched on the raked, weedless gravel. The vines were cut away from the shining windows, and they were open to the April sun. The boys had attacked the hedges too eagerly – they were cut unevenly and too low. The effect was drastic, but at least clean. The nettles and dead leaves had been piled ready for burning. The tangled rose garden would be the next thing to set in order, she thought. It seemed suddenly very desirable to grow a rose that would be her own . . . roses were such beautiful, useless things. She wondered if the orchard was past bearing fruit, and if it would be possible to set out daffodils between the trees in time for next spring's blooming. She knew nothing of growing flowers – at The Feathers there had been a thriving vegetable garden, but nothing so frivolous as a flower. Daffodils, she remembered, multiplied of themselves, and five years from now . . . She checked her thoughts, and turned to go indoors.

The whole place smelled of soap and fresh wax polish. From the direction of the kitchen came the sound of many voices, and an occasional burst of riotous laughter – she had no doubt that the Appledore women appreciated Patrick's sallies, and his liberal hand with the ale. There was also the smell of broth and new-baked bread.

Patrick had already started in to clean what had been Spencer's sitting-room. It was still untidy, scattered with his books and the piles of old papers she would have to read and sort through. But the floor and windows shone; the curtains had been brushed and shaken. Patrick had lighted a small fire in the cleanly-swept hearth. The fire tools were polished. The table was set with two plates –

clean silver and glasses laid on a fine damask cloth that had belonged to Anne. Patrick's sense of the dramatic had led him to withdraw himself and his helpers, leaving the room ordered and waiting for Jane's return.

Looking about her, Jane brushed aside finally Paul Fletcher's warnings and prophecies; back here at Blake's Reach they lost their power. Triumphantly, she reached out and pulled the bell cord.

William was as changed as the house. He sat beside her at the table, eating with those precise and assured manners that had startled her at first, but in every other respect he was different. He wore a coat too tight and short for him; at Patrick's bidding he had washed his hands impatiently, but the sweat marks showed clearly in the dirt on his face. The red curls on his forehead had caught a thin cobweb. Except for his greeting, he was quiet – for once too hungry to talk.

Patrick came to attend them at the meal, his swift, swooping movements like a fly. He accepted Jane's praises calmly, and waited for Kate's entry with the tray of food to start his attack.

'Sure, it's a real cook you'll have to be gettin', Miss Jane. Wouldn't this stuff be lying in yer belly like a lump o' lead, and y' comin' to an untimely death wid the indigestion . . .'

Kate sniffed, and banged down the tray. 'The Irish are naught but a bag o' wind, and so needn't be troubling about their bellies.'

'In good time, Patrick – in good time,' Jane said. 'Kate does very well for our needs at present . . . which, Heaven knows, have to be simple enough to match my purse. Time for a cook when we have a full pantry.'

'Aye, Mistress, aye,' Kate muttered approvingly, casting a glance at Patrick's downcast face. She was delighted at this blow to his love of grandeur and ostentation. 'Ye've wisdom far greater than yer mother, poor lady,' she finished.

Jane held Kate back after Patrick had gone to supervise the vast meal spread in the kitchen. The old woman waited expectantly at the end of the table, her hands folded against her apron.

'I met Paul Fletcher this morning, Kate,' Jane said quietly, spooning her broth which she thought was surprisingly good.

'Aye, Mistress.' The tone was careful.

Jane looked directly at her. 'Tell me about him, Kate.'

Her head jerked nervously. 'What, in Heaven's good name, should I know about Paul Fletcher, Mistress. It's not for the likes o' me to have anything to say of him.'

Jane was impatient. 'Oh – Kate, don't be foolish! I'm not asking you to tell me anything the whole Marsh doesn't know. Where does he come from? . . . how long have the Fletchers lived here?'

'Oh . . .' Kate shrugged. 'Is that the all of it, now? Well . . . a bit of a wild one, is Mister Paul. He's one o' the Fletchers of Warefield. He's brother to Sir James Fletcher who lives at Warefield House over near Hythe. The family came to the Marsh some ways back – about my grandfather's time, I'd say, and they've done well out of it. Sir James is rich, Mistress. They say he has a lot of his money in some company way off in India – and that do make him twice as rich as he used to be.'

Jane raised her eyebrows. 'Rich, is he? Well . . . Paul doesn't look like a rich man's brother.'

'It doesn't follow, Mistress. Paul's the younger brother – and the estate be fixed on the elder. He had some share of his father's money, though. Not a fortune, they say. But whatever it was, he went off and bought a part of a plantation in the . . . West Indies . . . wherever that might be.'

Jane nodded. 'The West Indies . . . ? What happened to the plantation?'

Kate shrugged. 'I don't know the exact rights of it now, Mistress. Perhaps Paul hadn't much of a business head in those days. They do say his partner tricked him, and then the fever wiped out all the slaves. He lost whatever money he put into it.'

'And so he came back?'

Kate nodded. 'He came back and went into the Navy. He's a good sailor – the people from this shore have always been rare fine sailors – but he joined late, you understand. They say the Navy's a slow place to rise in, and young Paul has too much of a will to enjoy bowin' and scrapin'. He stuck it for a couple o' years, and then a year ago – more or less – he suddenly turned up on the Marsh again. He took Jim Rogers's cottage at Old Romney, and I hear he's makin' a book o' charts . . .'

She added, looking first at William's head bent over his food, and then at Jane, 'O'course, what he does with the rest of his time is his own business. He'll not make a fortune out o' any old book o' charts. He's quick and clever, Mistress, but there are those who must know what he's about – if you take my meaning . . .' She glanced again at William. 'They be waiting to catch him. But then – ' with a shrug, 'doubtless he'll get off lightly. He has influence, and he handles a pack o' men so big the magistrates be mortally scared o' them. He's Sir James's brother, t'boot – and Sir James is an important man on the Marsh.'

'Yes . . .' Absently Jane fed General a piece of bread soaked in gravy.

'Though, mind you,' Kate continued, 'they say the pair o' them don't get on too well. Sir James is a solid man, and he's no love for anyone as wastes his money. Paul doesn't go often to Warefield House. His brother's lady wife, Alice, can't abide him. There be some old quarrel between them.'

'Is Paul married?'

'Married? . . . not that the Marsh folks know of. With all them black women in the Indies he didn't need to have a regular wife, they tell me. He's a restless one, Mistress . . . A handful for any woman.'

William had finished eating, and he bent down and gave his plate to General to clean.

'*I* met Paul Fletcher this morning, too,' he said.

Both women turned on him instantly. Kate gave a wail. 'Master William, you didn't go . . .'

Jane cut her short. 'Where did you meet him? – *How?*'

William looked indignant. 'I didn't go *anywhere*! I was working there by the gate, and a man came up the hill leading his horse. He seemed to know about me – he knew that we'd come yesterday. He said his name was Paul Fletcher, and he promised to come back and bring me some white mice.'

'*Then* what did he do?'

'Why? nothing! He just stood there for a while, watching all the people work. He just laughed a little, and shook his head, and went on straight up the hill. Do you suppose he'll really bring the mice? I'd like to have them.'

'I wouldn't be at all surprised,' Jane said, ungraciously. She pushed back her chair and rose. 'I've no doubt he's plenty of time to collect white mice, as well as waste the morning standing laughing at other folks labour . . .'

William looked at her in astonishment. Kate said nothing, merely started to clean up the dishes. Jane waited for her comment, and when there was none, she turned away, irritably brushing the dust on her gown.

William and Kate could hear her voice trailing off as she walked down the hall.

'They must be finished eating now . . . I want them to understand I don't pay them to sit stuffing themselves . . . Patrick! . . . Patrick! . . .'

2

Paul Fletcher's cottage was at the lower end of the tree-lined lane that led to Old Romney Church. Every Sunday the bells tolled and the people walked and drove along this lane, and stared into this cottage, and shook their heads because he never showed himself at the church door. They said the wildness had got into him since he had sailed the Caribbean, and maybe – God save us – he had even brought back the taint of Popishness. Paul knew what they said, and didn't care.

He turned his eyes with relief away from the wearying distances of the Marsh, and fixed them on his own moss-touched roof. The landscape of the Marsh was oppressive to him – flat, dull, with the wind forever sighing in the elms and swishing the willow trees. It seemed to him that he had always hated the Marsh, but he knew that there must have been a time when he had loved it – perhaps long ago when he was a thin, sunburned boy hunting for birds' nests in the hedgerows, or being taught to sail by the Dymchurch fishermen. He knew the secret places of the Marsh, its twisting tracery of roads was etched on his memory; so often he had lain and watched the sky reflected in its thousand and one stretches of water. He might have loved it then, but it was a long time ago.

His horse headed down the lane towards the cottage, and the rooks in the trees over his head suddenly rose in a body, and filled the air with their unearthly screeching. His mind was closed against the sound because he could still hear the footsteps of the girl as she hurried away from him along the church path, with the sun on her wild red hair, and the dust on her blue gown. He smiled a little at the memory.

He unsaddled in the lean-to at the back of the timbered cottage. No smoke came from the chimney, and he knew as soon as he opened the kitchen door that this was yet another day on which Mary Bridges, the woman from the village who cooked for him, had neglected to show herself. Last night's supper and today's breakfast dishes still littered the table. He had let the porridge burn again this morning, and its acrid smell lingered in the untidy room. Although he was hungry, he turned away from it in disgust.

His sitting-room was a bare apartment – furnished for all his needs, and lacking any touch of warmth or ease. It was a functional room – a place to store his books and mariners' charts, his quadrant and compass; there were shelves for his wine and glasses, a peg on the door for his hat and coat. It was dusty; the red curtains

were still drawn across the windows as he had left them last night.
He jerked them back now, and the sunlight flooded in.

There were stiff, dead daffodils in a stone jar on the windowsill.
In a springtime burst of enthusiasm Mary Bridges had put them
there a week ago.

He poured himself brandy from a decanter, and dropped wearily
into a chair. He had had no sleep last night – and the rain had
soaked through to his skin. He felt the brandy flow easily to remove
the tenseness, and thought that six nights from now, if the weather
held he would spend another night waiting in the darkness on the
shore . . . another night waiting for the signal, waiting for the
shape of the lugger to emerge from the blackness as they rowed
with muffled oars towards the rendezvous . . . another night to
listen to the tramp of the porters' heavy boots, with the armed
boatmen at the front and rear of the column. Another night . . .
and another . . . until there was enough money to leave it all behind
him. Enough money to leave the Marsh forever.

He was tired to death of the comfortless round of his existence
– this dreary, sterile life that held none of the things he wanted,
only risk and danger, and their accompanying terrors. But daring
and courage of this sort commanded a high price. If the cargoes
were good, and the runs successful, he wouldn't be here very long
– not long enough to forget how to enjoy himself.

The sun beat warmly on the back of his neck. He closed his
eyes; the uncomfortable, dusty room receded, and now he was
crunching the sand of a soft-coloured Caribbean beach under his
boots, and the blue-green water beyond the surf line was strangely
like the eyes of the girl who walked beside him. She laughed, and
talked to him lightly, and the breeze blew her wild hair. It was red
hair, and the blue gown she wore was faded by the fierce sun.

Paul fell asleep with the glass still clutched in his hand.

3

On the evening of the day after her meeting with Paul at the
church, Jane ordered a fire to be lighted in the drawing-room at
Blake's Reach. She dressed herself in a gown that had been one of
Anne's favourites – a green silk with heavy cream lace – and settled
herself to wait for him. Responding to her lead, William also presented himself in the drawing-room, wearing one of his velvet
jackets, and his hair darkened with water. With General beside
him, he sprawled on the blue and gold carpet before the fire,
impatiently thumbing his way through a book he had taken from

Spencer's shelves; he talked hopefully about the white mice Paul had promised, and kept looking at the clock on the mantel.

Jane stifled her own impatience; finally Patrick came and took William, protesting, to bed. She added logs to the fire, and the ticking of the clock went on in the stillness. The fire threw shadows across the floor. In this light, Jane thought, the room looked handsome; the carved cornices and mantel took on depth and richness – the frayed edge of the carpet over by the windows was lost in the dimness. The Blake portraits, painted by provincial artists, made them look calm, almost dull, people, with no history to speak of. She could see her own reflection in the mirror on the far wall, – it should have pleased her because at this distance, the pointed white face might have been Anne's own. But instead she sat, with nervous hand plucking at the lace, wondering why she went to this trouble to receive Paul Fletcher, and why it now seemed important what he thought of Blake's Reach and herself. Yesterday she had thought him a meddlesome and impudent stranger. She knew she was looking at the clock as many times as William had done – and she couldn't stop it.

At last she had to tell herself that he would not come that night. She kicked the rug back from the hearth, and went slowly into the hall. Patrick was there, dozing in a big chair, with the candle ready to light her to bed.

During the day they had cleaned and aired Anne's old room. The fire was burning there, and her nightgown laid out. Patrick held the candle high.

'It doesn't look like Miss Anne's chamber,' he said softly. 'I miss the pretty things she kept about her – like toys they were in her little hands. I just can't think now, that Miss Anne grew up in this gloomy old hole.'

When he was gone, Jane crouched before the fire in her nightgown. The chamber was vast and chill; there was, as Patrick had said, none of the charm and warmth of Anne's London bedroom about it. Now, with Patrick gone, the silence was deep; she listened, remembering with faint regret the chatter of Mary in the small room they had shared at The Feathers, of the alert wakefulness of Lottie and Pru when Sally had imagined them asleep for hours. In this silence there was no companionship. Was this, she wondered, the solitude Paul had warned her of . . . was it possible that time and years could slip away in this quietness, as he said, and she would wake one day to find that she had missed too much. He had wanted her to leave Blake's Reach . . . perhaps he spoke from his own knowledge of the vast empty bed, the unshared seat by the fire. She rested her head on her drawn-up knees, thinking of him standing below her in the church yesterday, making a joke of his poverty and his unkempt clothes. Yesterday he had had a feeling for her, a notion to help her, a thought for her future. Perhaps that was all yesterday with Paul; tonight she had waited, and he had not come.

4

Kate was scandalized when Jane took the hoe and spade and set to work on the overgrown vegetable patch at the back of the stables. She worked with a frantic kind of energy, to try to rid herself of the fears of the night before. Without the women and children from Appledore, Blake's Reach was very empty and silent; she found herself listening for footsteps, for voices, but there were none. Jed and Lucas had gone to try to mend some fences down by the dyke; Patrick had taken it upon himself to turn out the great pantry storeroom; he and Kate had been in the midst of a fierce quarrel when Jane had passed through the kitchen. But even they had stopped shouting at each other now; there was nothing to hear but the cries of the birds, and the gentle droning of the insects in the spring sunshine. Jane tried not to acknowledge to herself that it was a lonely quiet.

Presently she heard footsteps on the brick walk, and looked up expectantly. William, hands in pockets, and wearing a shirt that was too tight for him and thin with age, came around the corner of the stables.

'I'll help,' he said.

She smiled at him. 'I wish that you would. But it needs three good men here, instead of one good man . . . and a woman.' She handed him the hoe. 'Here – you rake off all the weeds in the parts I've dug.'

The hoe was too large for him, and he was inexpert with it – raking the soil into uneven piles, or splattering it over both of them as he shook the weeds and nettles free. But they worked together with a comfortable sense of companionship; with William's presence the spectre of loneliness had dwindled. Jane began to hum under her breath as she thrust the spade into the soft damp earth; she was dirty and perspiring when Kate came hurrying to tell her that there was a messenger from Robert Turnbull waiting for her in the stable yard.

Robert Turnbull had sent her one of his own horses in the charge of a groom – a light roan mare whose coat had bronze tints as she moved. The note from Turnbull was brief, written in a quick, firm hand; its brevity gave Jane the feeling that he was writing to an intimate. *'I hope you will regard the mare as your own for the time you are with us here. Her name is Blonde Bess. You will find her willing and gentle, and her manners are excellent.'* It was signed simply, *Robert.*

In her pleasure and excitement, Jane didn't stop to consider all the implications either of the message, or the loan of the mare. The manner of the action was, she imagined, typical of Robert Turnbull, offhand and understated; his motives she didn't trouble to question. She directed Kate to give the groom from the livery stable some ale and cheese before he set off back to Rye; Patrick remained with her and William to admire and to touch, talking in soft voices to Blonde Bess, pronouncing her name over and over, stroking her shining coat, fingering the fine leather of the harness. Jane helped Patrick lift William into the saddle, and, watching the sudden delight in the child's face, she was immediately saddened at the thought that he did not have a pony of his own.

'She's beautiful . . . she's beautiful!' William chanted. Jane was struck by the sight of the red-headed child atop the red horse.

'Mr Turnbull's a good and generous gentleman, now,' Patrick said with conviction.

Jane glanced at him sharply, sensing that his statement was not meant innocently. 'Mr Turnbull has been a valued friend to the Blakes for many years. He . . . he grew up with my mother!'

'Oh, to be sure,' Patrick answered piously. 'He will continue to be a valuable friend, I trust, Miss Jane. There's always something to be said for a man that knows a good piece of horse flesh . . .'

'Patrick! . . . Blonde Bess is a *loan*! Nothing more! And Mr Turnbull intended nothing more! And you're not to gossip about what's not your concern!'

Patrick looked pained. 'I swear to Heaven, Miss Jane, that there's never a word out o' me mouth, I was only meanin' that all I hear of Mr Turnbull is that he's a fine gentleman . . .'

'Enough!' she said. 'Enough talk now! There has to be more work and less talk in this house. William and I will stable Bess . . .'

Patrick bobbed his head in assent, but she checked him again as he turned away.

'Understand, Patrick – *Mr Turnbull is not Lord O'Neill!*'

She helped William down from the saddle, and together they took the mare into the stable. William pumped some water into a pail, and struggled across the yard with it, standing quietly by to watch as Bess drank.

'Not too much,' Jane cautioned. 'Let her cool down . . .'

She put a few pitchforks of hay into Bess's stall, and William helped her with the unsaddling. The mare stood patiently, feeling their hands on her without protest or anxiety, as gentle as Robert Turnbull had said. And when they closed the door of her stall, she did not go immediately to the hay, but stood to watch them hang the saddle and bridle on the wooden pegs. Through the bars at the top of the stalls the pair of carriage greys regarded the mare with faint suspicion.

Jane and William went back to work on the vegetable patch. The sun was hotter now, and it beat down on the back of their necks. The fichu of Jane's gown grew damp with perspiration. The weeds seemed thicker than they had been before, and higher — the riotous growth of the ten or more years that had passed since the last gardener had departed from Blake's Reach. The enthusiasm of William's first attack on the weeds began to fade; he looked hot and weary. Jane bent her back stubbornly, but she paused often to wipe her forehead with a grimy hand. She toyed with the idea of sending once again to Appledore for help, and then recalled the hearty country appetites she would have to satisfy at her table, and the shrinking pile of coins in her purse. So she shrugged, and thrust the spade once more down among the weeds.

This second time she was too far gone in her own thoughts to notice the footsteps on the brick walk. He was standing above her, and speaking, before she raised her eyes.

'It's too warm a day . . . and you'll spoil those fine hands . . .'

Paul Fletcher smiled gently as he spoke. This was not the amused, mocking tone he had used two days ago in the church. He said the words simply, as if he was concerned for her.

She thrust the spade into the ground, and straightened. His presence here covered her with confusion, and yet she was aware of a great warmth of relief and pleasure sweeping through her. She was glad he had come; there was nothing more to do than admit it. She was conscious of only a second's regret for the silk gown and curled hair of last night, and then the regret died, and was finished.

'Necessity presses,' she said, jerking her head towards the weed-choked beds. 'I've a thrifty notion to eat my own produce and stop paying my neighbours to supply it. What happens to my hands,' she shrugged — 'I must bear with. You see I — '

William's patience had gone. He dropped the hoe, and moved towards Paul, breaking into Jane's speech.

'Did you bring them, Mr Fletcher, sir? — the mice? Did you bring them?'

Paul nodded back in the direction of the stables. 'I left them with the manservant – Patrick, is that his name?'

William immediately started along the path, then halted. 'Where? – in the stables?'

'Yes – Patrick seemed to think that that's where they should stay . . .' Paul found himself talking to empty air as William vanished around the corner of the building.

When William had gone a silence fell between them. Jane was amazed to find herself suddenly tongue-tied, even a little shy of the man who stood there. He looked different from the person in the church. His hair was powdered and caught back with fresh ribbon; he wore frilled shirt and sober, well-cut breeches and coat. He held his expensive, but not new, hat under his arm. The buckles on his shoes were silver.

'I came to beg your pardon for not appearing last evening, as you had ordered me to.' When she gestured to dismiss the words, he smiled. 'I regarded it as an order – just as you intended, and if I had possessed seven league boots I would have been here, and at your service. But the – er – trade which engages me is an unpredictable one. I was many miles from Blake's Reach last night.'

The hostility they had felt in the church seemed to have gone. She sensed that he was no longer here to criticize; he had come to accept her presence as Kate and Lucas, and the villagers of Appledore had done. The little time that had passed since they had seen each other had wrought a change in him also. Those blue eyes, with the sun-wrinkles etched in the skin about them, did not laugh and mock her now.

She spread her hands to indicate the dirt on her gown. 'You missed a fine sight by not being here last night. I put my prettiest silk gown on for your benefit, and curled my hair, and played the fine lady in my drawing-room. It's hard that you should come now when the fine lady has given place to the maid-of-all-work.'

'I suspect I'd be afraid of that fine lady in her drawing-room, and I like well enough what I see now. The dirt on your chin is a charming adornment, and you wear it with distinction.'

She put her hand to her face, self-consciously, and was silent. She was without words, and she felt that he knew it. What was the matter with her – she, who in the church had answered him with such great sureness? Wasn't it possible to take this compliment from him with ease – to let it warm her, and encourage her, as he had meant it to? He had been gentle, kindly, and didn't she have grace enough to lift her eyes to him, and smile her gratitude? There had been too much pretence in the last weeks of a poise and security she did not truly feel. It would be such a relief not to have to pretend with this man.

At last she did lift her eyes, and smile at him.

'Thank you.' His own smile answered her, broader, gayer. 'You know, you are pretty when you smile like that – the kind of prettiness that has nothing to do with being beautiful . . . Such a pity you don't smile more often. A woman should . . . it's softer. A man gives almost anything to a smile.'

And now she did smile broadly, teasing. 'And have you given often? You sound experienced in smiles.'

He shrugged. 'There's no nicer object of giving than a charming woman. And if the giving turns out to be a loss after all, then the memory generally has a pleasant tinge to it.'

Then he dismissed the subject with a wave of his hand. 'Well . . . I must tell you more of that philosophy later. I hoped to gladden your heart this morning by telling you that the extra money for the church would be forthcoming . . .'

Her lips drooped a little. 'No . . . ?'

'I don't know yet. I haven't been able to discuss the matter with my employer. I sent a message that I wanted to speak with him, and I find he's away from home these few days, and may not return for a week.'

'Well, then – it must wait. There's no help for it.' It was not possible, now that he had so far penetrated her stiff guard she had held up before her world, to keep the disconsolate note from her voice. 'I . . . I would like to know as soon as possible.'

'The other day you said the money hardly mattered to you.' It was spoken with the merest indication of a questioning note – to be taken up or not, as she chose.

She gestured slightly, taking in the hoe, her soiled gown and the wilderness of the vegetable plot. 'I can't pretend with you. The money matters – of course it does !'

He nodded. 'I understand this well enough. I don't like your mixing in this affair at all, but since you're determined to have it so, then I don't see why my employer shouldn't be parted from a little of the money I earn for him. I'll do my best . . . I promise you that.'

For a few seconds she studied him, smiling a little to acknowledge his promise; then she shrugged and shook her head.

'What is it?'

'You're different today,' she said, 'and it isn't just your fine coat. You made no promises of aid when we met before.'

He laughed at her reference to his dress, but he didn't seem inclined to give her an answer.

'Go on,' she prompted. 'You surely can tell me. Is it . . . ? Are you beginning to think, perhaps, that I'm not so mad, or so foolishly stubborn in deciding to stay on here?'

Leaning on the spade, she waited for him to speak. He frowned a little, and looked away from her, looked towards the two great oaks that raised themselves above the line of the roofs of Blake's Reach, and towards the hazy sky over the Marsh, whose stretching distance was broken by a swooping flight of seagulls. He seemed to be reaching for an answer, struggling for words which would not come easily.

'It really isn't my business,' he said at last, turning back to her. 'But I thought about something you said – up there in the church.'

'What did I say?'

'You said . . . "Since when have women been able to decide which way their lives will go? . . . It's Blake's Reach or nothing!"'

'Yes, I said that! So . . . ?'

'I began to feel I had done you an injustice. There must have been other ways open to you . . . in London. You're a beautiful young woman, and men open their purses to beauty and youth. Instead you choose to burden yourself with a young child, and a debt-ridden estate. I think your aims are mistaken, but I admire your courage. If I can get money for you, I will.'

He hadn't intended to say so much, and the knowledge that he had betrayed himself made him brusque. It was the first time he had realized how often she had been in his thoughts since their meeting. He spoke again, quickly, before she had time to frame a reply.

'And – you'd better give me that spade. So long as I'm here I could make myself useful.'

And then he tossed down his hat on the brick walk, and his fine coat followed it. Impatiently he rolled the sleeves of the frilled shirt, and then reached out and took the spade from Jane.

The hours that followed were the happiest Jane had known for a long time. She seated herself on an upturned pail, her gown bunched under her, and watched Paul as he worked. She took pleasure in the rhythmic, purposeful movements of his strong body, with no motion wasted or laboured. It was good to sit and rest, and to be with him. His shining boots were covered with the damp soil, and his shirt stuck wetly to him with sweat; the carefully tied hair began to drift loose. He dug systematically, and swiftly. As the sun reached its midday heat, she protested that he had worked long enough. Half the vegetable garden was now cleared.

He leaned back on the spade. 'The Navy puts callouses on your hands that never wear off. And as for this pale English sun – you wait till you've seen the noon sun in the tropics, then you'll know! But . . .' he conceded, 'I've a thirst you could cut with a knife.'

She planned to give him dinner in Spencer's room, with the fine linen and silver to distract him from the heaviness of Kate's cooking. Before they went indoors she took him first to the stable to look at Blonde Bess. Paul remembered seeing Turnbull ride her on the Marsh; they spent some time discussing her points. Paul was frankly curious about the loan of the mare, and, Jane thought, a little stung that it was not in his power to make a similar gesture. William was there also, squatting in the sun by the door, absorbed in watching the two white mice in the cage; his interest in Blonde Bess had faded a little. Paul went to join him, and they were both bent over the cage as Jane turned to go and give Patrick instructions about laying an extra place at table.

As she walked across the yard, Paul called to her.

'It's too good a day to be in the house . . . Why don't we take some food down into the orchard?'

William sucked in his breath quickly, his eyes widening with excitement and pleasure. It occurred to Jane, as she watched him, that he had probably never in his life eaten a meal out-of-doors.

And so it was Paul who accompanied her into the kitchen, who filled a pitcher with cider, selected the cheese, and directed Kate in cutting slices of bread and brawn. Kate and Patrick were disapproving – and speechless. Kate was afraid of Paul's presence at Blake's Reach; she did no more than glance towards the simmering pots on the stove which was the dinner Jane and William should have eaten. She obeyed Paul's orders with folded lips, and spoke only once, an aside to Patrick which Jane was meant to overhear.

'Well – it's to be hoped Lucas and Jed don't see them. A fine thing it will be to have talked about all over the Marsh!'

Jane pretended she didn't hear. Whatever regrets she would have later for the recklessness of this hour, it would not diminish her pleasure in the present. She took the pitcher firmly, and followed Paul from the kitchen. General was waiting for them in the yard; he closed in behind the small procession as they made for the orchard.

There the long grass was soft, and smelled sweetly. The trees, blossoms still upon them, and not yet in full leaf, let through the sunlight in soft dappled waves that stirred and moved as the breeze touched them. Bees droned among the blossoms, moving from

flower to flower; farther off and high up somewhere, a lark sang.
They looked for it, but it was invisible against the sun. When the
bread and cheese was finished, and they had drunk all the cider
they wanted, Paul lay back in the long grass, his hands clasped
behind his neck, his eyes closed. Jane leaned against a tree trunk,
idly stroking the long silken curls on General's ears. Peace and
acceptance was established between them, an unspoken thing.
William lay on his stomach, studying the ceaseless movement of
an ant; presently he grew bored with this, and called to General.
Together they moved off down towards the great dyke at the
bottom of the slope.

Paul opened his eyes.

'I shall not come here again like this, Jane.'

She turned to him, disturbed. 'Why not?'

'Need I say it to you? You saw how it was with Kate – and
she's a loyal Blake servant! There will be tongues less easy on you
if I appear again at Blake's Reach for no urgent reason. I'm held
in some suspicion hereabouts, and it can do you no good if it's
known I'm a visitor at Blake's Reach. Perhaps we shall meet sometimes – out on the Marsh, where there's fewer people to see. But
in Rye or Hythe or Folkestone, if we should meet, we will bow and
pass on – or else not see each other.'

She flushed, and was glad he was looking away from her, staring
straight up into the trees above him; it came like a blow to have
this said to her now, to have him destroy the peace she had believed
they had shared in these past hours. He could have spoken from
solicitude for her reputation – or perhaps out of boredom. She
tried to see this visit as it might appear to him. What man wanted
to come calling to have a spade and hoe thrust into his hand, to
ruin his fine clothes and his leisure hours in one stroke? Would he
stay away in future because he expected young women to entertain him, not put him to work, or to involve him in unwanted
problems? What did she know of Paul Fletcher, after all? – and
what kind of a naïve fool was she to suppose that there was no
other woman who waited for his visits. Suddenly the picnic in the
orchard seemed like a silly game, and he had probably suggested
it in preference to eating Kate's cooking. It seemed as if the best
entertainment Blake's Reach could offer him was bread and cheese.
Her face grew hot again at the thought of it.

'Just as you wish,' she said shortly. Then she got quickly to her
feet, and began gathering up the remains of their meal.

'If you'll excuse me, I have things to see to indoors.' She was
aware that he glanced round at her, startled. She bent to pick up

the cider pitcher.

'I won't detain you any longer,' she said. 'I'm sure you have many other claims on your time.'

5

Paul was gone, having taken leave of her with polite, impersonal words, which could have been the result of his bewilderment at her sudden change of attitude, but which she chose to interpret as indifference. His going left an emptiness, and she flung herself into the kitchen in a fury of suppressed rage. Her energy demanded an outlet, and found it in elbowing Kate out of the way, and starting in to bake a batch of bread. It would have to be rye bread, for Blake's Reach had not seen a sack of white flour for a long time; she would have to see to it that there was white bread to serve when guests came to the house – the fine grained white bread that had been a luxury item at The Feathers, but commonplace on Anne's table. Some of her anger against Paul spent itself as she kneaded the dough; she told herself she was a fool to care what he thought of herself or Blake's Reach, for he was no part of the future here. She would think about him no more. Then to absorb herself she tackled a complicated cake recipe, which she had watched Sally make for special occasions at The Feathers – an extravagant one calling for eggs and great quantities of sugar and spices. It was to be a surprise for William, and an act of defiance at the same time.

But the thought of Paul did not leave her; she spent a restless night, and next morning at breakfast snapped irritably at William, and ignored General's wordless pleadings for scraps from the table. Grimly she went back to digging in the vegetable patch, though today William kept clear of her. Dinner was a gloomy meal, rabbit pie and rice pudding which she and William ate as quickly as possible, and in silence. The afternoon was warm and still; her digging grew slower. To break the monotony she took up the hoe, and started working on the part already dug. Suddenly she flung the hoe down.

'I've had enough of it! I'll take Blonde Bess out and try her – maybe I'll even ride to the sea!'

But as she crossed the yard she slowed her walk. William sat in the sun on the wide flagstone doorstep of the kitchen; his face was turned in towards the kitchen, and he was talking. Jane could hear Patrick's voice replying to him. Between his knees he steadied a pewter jug, and he polished it vigorously. As she drew nearer,

Jane could see the table covered with the silver Patrick was cleaning. William looked up a trifle apprehensively as she approached;
it was then she changed her mind about riding alone on Blonde
Bess.

She spoke to William gently, but her motion included Patrick.
'Would you like to drive into Rye?' she said. 'We need supplies for
the pantry, and . . .'

Patrick got to his feet instantly. 'I'll harness up the greys,
Mistress. Sure it's a little breath of air you could both be doin'
with. It'll not take any time at all!'

The jug clattered against the flagstone as William scrambled up.
'I have nine shillings left from the sovereign Lord O'Neill gave
me . . .' He quickly put the jug back on the kitchen table, and was
shouting his plans for the purchases he would make as he dashed
up the back stairs to his room.

Jane looked at the suddenly emptied kitchen, realizing how
quickly in these few days the quiet routine of the country had
become their own, when a simple trip to buy kitchen supplies
could cause such excitement. Anne had spoken of boredom, of
monotonous routine, at Blake's Reach – and had dreaded having
to suffer them again. Was she much different from Anne, she wondered. The unpleasant memory of Paul's prediction thrust itself
back into her consciousness.

Rye looked almost familiar to her now – the square-towered church
on the steep hill, and the Rother curving sluggishly round the cliffs
that made the town-site. It was market-day in Rye, and farmers'
carts, with here and there a more elegant vehicle choked the streets
leading into the centre of the town. The cries of chicken, geese and
duck fattened for market filled the air, mingling with the thick
country accents, and the din that came from the open doors of the
ale-houses. Pretty, frightened calves looked with great eyes of non-
understanding at the throng. Jane's carriage moved slowly under
the great gate into the Old Town, and Patrick started asking
directions to the shop in George Street where Kate had told them
the supplies for Blake's Reach had been bought in Spencer's time.
When they drew up before it, Patrick looked at it in doubt.

'Don't seem to be much of an establishment, Miss Jane,' he
said as he opened the carriage door. 'Should we try somewhere
else?' He jerked his head towards the lower streets, where the
market-day crowd was mostly gathered.

'No – this is the place. We'll stay here.'

The shopkeeper had already opened the door, and was bowing

to her – a stout man, wrapped in a huge snowy apron, which
matched the colour of his shirt. Gossip about her arrival had done
its work well; he had been expecting a visit from her.

'Welcome, Miss Howard. I am Samuel Purdy, the proprietor.
I hope that we may have the honour of continuing to receive the
patronage of Blake's Reach.'

Jane didn't quite know what to make of the situation. As Purdy
bowed her into the shop with many expressions of pleasure, and
his wife bobbed a curtsy, Jane decided that his servility was due to
one of two reasons – either that Robert Turnbull had settled
Spencer's account here already, and Samuel Purdy had summed
up the impression given by her dress, the carriage and pair, and
he was hoping for further and lavish patronage, or – and this
seemed more likely to Jane – that the bill was still unpaid, and he
wanted settlement. She wished she had questioned Kate about it.

The interior of the shop was dim, but it had the rich, heavy
smell of good food. Purdy tempted her with many delicacies she
could not afford, and she put them aside briskly – ordering sugar
and white flour, honey, raisins, barley, salt, soap and candles. The
last two were items Sally had always made herself at The Feathers,
but at Blake's Reach there had been too few servants to make that
thrifty practice possible. As she went down her list Samuel Purdy
grew disappointed, and his manner showed it. He brightened a
trifle when she added at the end some small quantities of the
spices she needed for cooking, and which were so expensive.

Then she gathered up her reticule, and prepared to leave. Purdy
hurried to open the door. 'Doubtless you're hardly settled, Miss
Howard, and we shall see you more often when you know what
you lack at Blake's Reach.'

'Doubtless. Good afternoon, Mr Purdy.'

Patrick was loading the purchases into wicker baskets to stow
on the back of the carriage; Jane motioned to William that they
would walk down George Street, and leave Patrick to his task.
William had barely fallen into place beside her, when he suddenly
tugged frantically at her sleeve.

'Look! There's Mr Fletcher!'

Jane stopped dead. 'Where?'

'Across the street. Look, he's bowing!'

Jane managed to return the bow with no more warmth than
was barely civil. Beside her William said, 'Well – aren't you going
over?'

'Certainly not!' Jane dragged swiftly at his arm, and looked
away from the straight, blond figure once again dressed in the old

seaman's coat. She was conscious that Paul himself had not moved, but stood straight, hat under his arm, looking across at them. She started to walk briskly down the street.

'We've too much to do to stop and gossip . . .' In a wave of confusion, she swept straight into a draper's shop, pulling William with her, and found herself buying three yards of wide lace, and a length of printed cotton, neither of which she particularly wanted. In panic she took the money from her reticule and paid, leaving quickly before she committed any more folly.

And outside, directly across the street from the draper's, was Paul. He had been studying the bottles in the curved window of a wine merchant's shop, but he half-turned as Jane and William reached the pavement. His quick glance took them in, but no one in that crowd on the street could have had time to notice it, for he turned back to the window immediately. Jane took William's hand, and moved on to where the crowd was thicker.

They loitered before the stalls of vegetable produce, but bought none, because it was the end of the day, and the best was long since gone. They looked at some cages of birds for sale – brightly coloured foreign birds that Jane doubted would survive the dampness of an English winter. There were smooth, plump fantails, which she wanted to buy, but resisted. From a stall of odds and ends, William bought himself a magnifying glass, and Jane added a second-hand book of fables, printed in large characters with elaborate chapter-headings and tailpieces, because she was conscious that she ought to be more firm with William about lessons. And all the time, she kept glancing back – and always Paul was there, two or three stalls away from them, but steadily keeping pace with their progress. He never seemed to raise his head, or to look at them, but he was always ready to move when they did. Sometimes the crowd between them thickened, and she lost him. Then the crowd would fall apart, a farmer's cart move on, and there he would be again.

They were drawn, at last, by the smell from the baker's shop, the warm smell of spices and sugar and jam. Almost without thinking Jane found herself inside, the bell on the door bouncing and ringing loudly, and the woman, inevitably fat, coming forward with pink smiling cheeks. Here the smell was close, and nearly overwhelming; she was suddenly hungry. Instead of the modest purchase of a few muffins to eat at supper, she found herself pointing at a rich plum cake, and a sugary loaf sprinkled with cinnamon. For William there was a small almond custard pie, to eat in the carriage on the way home. As she paid for them she felt guilty – in view of her dwindling funds it seemed a scandalous indulgence, which she could not explain. And at the back of her head was a faint notion that Paul Fletcher's presence in the street outside had something to do with it.

But when she stepped down into the street, he was no longer there. The market had begun to dissolve; the people were fewer, and the sun was low on the roofs that overhung the cobbled streets. Animal droppings and vegetable refuse lay thick on the ground where the stalls had been, and a chill little wind had started to whine about the houses. Paul was nowhere in sight.

She drew her wrap about her, and hurried back towards George Street; William was tired, and he was thinking about the custard pie. Rather fretfully he protested her pace as she climbed the steep street to where the carriage waited. Patrick came to attention as he saw them; he sprang forward to open the door.

'I was thinkin' you were surely lost,' he said. 'There're some quare types about in a sea-coast town . . .'

'Oh, stop fussing, Patrick!' She suddenly found his solicitude irritating. 'What could happen to . . .'

She broke off, staring into the carriage. On the floor over by the opposite door was a basket of oranges, and beside it a glass jar containing dried figs and prunes; there was also a blue china bowl with a sealed lid, filled with preserved ginger – the same, she recognized, as she had rejected at Samuel Purdy's shop. She turned to Patrick.

'How did these get here? I didn't order them! . . . Patrick, *you* didn't . . . ?'

'An' I wish t' Heaven I had, Mistress . . . for yer deservin' of all such delicacies.' He shook his head. 'No, ma'am, 'tweren't meself . . . Mr Fletcher came, not three minutes ago, and left them for ye. Got them out of Purdy's place, he did. A present, he said.'

She scarcely heard any more of the chatter as Patrick settled her in the carriage with a light robe about her knees, and spread a handkerchief on William's lap to catch the crumbs from the pie. On the road back to Blake's Reach she answered William's questions absently but gently, and now and then, as the wheels jolted in the ruts, her foot touched the basket of oranges, and she smiled secretly and quietly.

Back at Blake's Reach she was mortified to find that, beside the lace on Anne's gowns, the stuff she had bought from the draper in Rye appeared cheap and coarse. She rolled it, and put it away sadly; perhaps it would do to trim some undergarments that no one would see. The length of cotton, when she held it against her, was a washed-out green, and made her skin sallow and her hair carroty-red. The printed pattern was old-fashioned, and too large for elegance. She gave it to Kate, with the promise that soon, when there was less to attend to in the house, she would make it into a gown for her.

She slept soundly that night – and curiously free from thoughts of Paul Fletcher.

She lay in bed, only half-awake, when Kate brought her the bunch of primroses and the note. She caught her breath a little at the sight of them – pale, soft little things, still wet with dew. Kate's lips were pursed in disapproval.

'Found these by the kitchen door. Fine friends – that don't dare come knocking at the front door at an hour that's respectable!'

When she was gone, Jane read the note. *'I have news for you, and Blonde Bess needs exercise. At Appledore take the road sign-posted to Snargate and Old Romney. I will wait at the willow grove a mile beyond Snargate.'*

6

They had been so still that a family of wild-duck clinging to the shadow of the tall reeds had ceased to listen for them. Jane, lying on the grass, slowly raised her head, turning her face to catch the sun fully on it. On the other side of the dyke a row of elms grew straight and tall; near the footbridge a wild apple tree was in full bloom. The warm breeze occasionally carried the scent and the falling petals towards them. Everything was quiet, save for the hum of the insects, and the faint plopping sound when one of the ducks broke the surface of the water.

'It's so peaceful,' she said softly. 'I haven't had such peace since . . . since I was a little girl.'

'I used to think the Marsh was peaceful, too,' he said. 'That seems a long time ago . . .'

She did not answer, tried not to hear the disillusionment and near-bitterness in his voice; she did not want to cloud one second of this golden day, nor give a particle of it to regret or unhappiness. It had begun like no other day had ever before begun – those pale, wet primroses, and the note, and then the meeting with Paul at the willow grove beyond Snargate. It had been so early then that the sun had not yet burned the dew off the pastures where the sheep cropped quietly. She had dressed herself in a habit that had belonged, of course, to Anne, and had enjoyed the sight of her own reflection in the mirror. Patrick had helped her to mount Blonde Bess, and for the first time she had ridden out on to the Marsh alone, feeling the strangeness and excitement, the small fear, of once again being on a horse. After the first few minutes her hands and body relaxed; she and Bess were no longer apart from one another. She allowed herself to respond to the steady, even motion of the mare. Bess was a perfect creature, she decided — full of breeding and good manners. With her gloved hand she patted the mare's neck softly.

Paul waited for her at the grove of six willow trees where two broad dykes joined each other. He and his horse were almost hidden by the long curtain of waving green, but as she approached he mounted and rode through to meet her.

His smile was gay; he swept off his hat with a gesture that had the lightness of this spring morning in it. Again he had discarded his seaman's coat for the well-cut clothes he had worn to Blake's Reach.

'Good morning!' he cried, when she was within earshot. 'What a sight you are! — no one but a London tailor cut that habit, or I'm a Dutchman! You ride well, Mistress Howard! Of course all the Blakes have ridden well . . .' He shrugged, and laughed. 'And here I've been thinking that you didn't appreciate or deserve anything so good as Blonde Bess!'

She laughed in return. 'See how wrong you are! I've been riding since I was a child, and I'll warrant when I choose to I can ride astride as well as any man.' Then she leaned forward and touched Bess's neck again. 'But it's mostly Bess . . . she'd make anyone look good.'

Then she looked at Paul. 'I hope it's good news that brings primroses to my door so early.'

'Good news! — wait till you hear! Twenty guineas a month for the church! Twenty guineas!' he repeated, in a tone that was almost a shout of triumph.

She gasped. 'How . . . ? How did you manage it? Twenty guineas . . . ?'

'I waited to see what was offered before I said your price. The offer was twenty guineas.'

'Twice as much,' she said slowly. 'But why, Paul . . . *why*?'

For an instant some of his good humour seemed to desert him; he frowned slightly. 'How should I know? I've learned never to question what good fortune comes my way. I'd advise you to do the same.'

Then abruptly he swung his horse's head towards the open spaces of the Marsh ahead of them. 'Come on – the morning's wasting! Riding in that stuffy carriage to Rye hasn't given you any idea of what this piece of country's like.' He looked back over his shoulder, smiling again. 'Come on! I've a mind to test that boast of yours that you're a rider . . .'

He dug in his heels, and his horse sprang forward; he urged it quickly down the steep bank of the dyke towards a spot where he knew from long experience that the water was shallow enough to be forded. Taken off her guard, Jane was left behind.

'Paul! Wait for me! . . . Wait for me!'

She would never forget this day. She lay in the sun now with Paul sprawled on the grass near by, and she closed her eyes for a second and lived the delight of it again. She had never been so free, so unfettered – she thought she had never before felt so young. Paul had been gay, easily matching her mood, and encouraging her to voice every stray thought that entered her head. There had been many things to share, and many things to laugh about; she had enjoyed the kind of frivolous relaxation she had not known since the old days when she and Sally's three daughters had shared an idle hour over the kitchen fire at The Feathers. But Paul had no resemblance to those three laughing girls : Paul was a man that many women would have called handsome; he was young, masculine and strong, his voice was firm and low-toned, and there was a touch of humour about his mouth and eyes. When they shared their simple lunch at an ale-house on the other side of Ivychurch, she found herself colouring as she looked up suddenly and caught his warm unabashed gaze on her; he was looking at her as a man looks at a woman he finds attractive and desirable. He didn't try to cover that look, or turn it into anything less than it was; he questioned her with his eyes, honestly and seriously. It was she who lowered her eyes, and looked away.

That moment had gone, but the memory of it stayed with them. They were acutely conscious of each other; they lay in the sun by the dyke, a yard or so of grass separating them, and found other things to talk about.

He glanced at her. 'Did you know you've got petals in your hair? You look like . . .'

'And so have you – it's like snow.' She twisted a little, resting her elbows on the grass, and cupping her chin in her hands. 'Oh, look at Blonde Bess there . . . Look at her, Paul! How lovely her coat is in the sunshine.'

'I can't think,' he said lazily, 'what possessed Turnbull to send you Blonde Bess, of all his horses. He loves horses – that I know – and he keeps a number of them at the stables in Rye. But Bess is the favourite, and the best of them.'

She glanced at him sideways. 'Are you sure you can't think why he sent Bess? He was very fond of my mother. I think perhaps he was in love with her.'

He shrugged, rolling over on his back, and squinting up at the sun. 'Turnbull . . . in love with Anne Blake. Well, why not? – stranger things have been. But I can never think of Turnbull allowing himself the luxury of such waywardness. Though, Heaven knows, Anne Blake was easy enough to fall in love with . . . when I think of her then . . .' He moved his head, and looked at her. 'Well, Jane, people will love you too, because of the memory of Anne.' He chuckled, a quiet, derisive sound. 'I can't think that it was anything but a romantic, sentimental memory that prompted my . . . my employer to increase the price on the church. Twenty guineas! – well, there are fools born every minute. *I* wouldn't have paid it!'

She chose not to take him seriously. 'Well! – I can see you think money is wasted on me. You'd rather have me receive you in the vegetable patch, than by the fire in my drawing-room – *and* wearing my green silk gown.'

'In the vegetable patch you looked beautiful. I shall cherish the picture, even more than the imagined image of the girl in the green silk gown.'

'Why? That's not as a woman wants to be remembered.'

He gestured helplessly. 'How do I tell you? – is it because I see you as something wild and free, wearing the look that courage wears? Even being here, as you are, with me now – riding out on the Marsh with me despite all they had to say against it at Blake's Reach – eating bread and cheese and ale with me in a tavern. And here you are, letting the sun freckle your white skin, and your hat has almost blown into the dyke, and you don't notice it. Oh, Jane – Jane, don't you see that it doesn't take much to sit by the fire in a green silk gown.'

'Hush! . . . hush, now!' she said, laughing and not able to be angry with him. 'Sitting by the fire was an accomplishment, too. Things have been done at Blake's Reach, Paul – and they're *my* doing. I'm responsible for the fact that the drawing-room is fit to receive guests in . . . and carriages can drive to the door now and I've no need for shame.'

'I know what you've done to Blake's Reach, Jane, even in these few days. At Appledore – and even farther than Appledore – they think you're some kind of miracle. They expect to see old John Blake pacing the drive with you some day, passing on advice. No one can decide whether you've no more money than Spencer, or whether you've inherited a fortune from Anne, and know how to be economical with it.'

Jane laughed outright at that; the sound was loud and unrestrained. The duck fled to cover in the reeds; farther along the dykes, two heron, startled, rose up quickly in lovely, graceful flight.

'Oh . . . !' She dabbed at the moisture in the corners of her eyes. 'That's funny – how Anne would have laughed! So Appledore thinks I'm an heiress . . . Well, let them think it! None of them have to know that I've spent the last hour lying here wondering how I can spend the twenty guineas to get the best from it. Which, I wonder, of the leaking spots in the roof most needs attention? – or would it be better to spend it where it would show most? Should it go on the garden or the kitchen? You see, Paul, I'm being strictly honest – every penny shall go on Blake's Reach, none into my pocket.'

'Well – I wish it were otherwise, Jane. I wish there was a shower of gold going into your pocket, and that there were green silk gowns without number.'

She opened her mouth to make a teasing reply, and then closed it again; Paul's face wore a look of repressed irritation and annoyance.

'What is it? – why do you look like that? I was only joking . . .'

'I wasn't joking! I'm disturbed because there *is* a way of sending a shower of gold into your pockets right at the moment, and I can't use it.'

'Why not?'

'Because it takes money to make money – and I haven't got enough to start.' He looked at her with enquiring eyes. 'Not incidentally, it would send a shower of gold into my pockets as well. How much money have you got, Jane?'

'How much do you need?'

'Five hundred pounds – thereabouts.'

'Well! You might as well look for five thousand from me! I haven't got that much, and if I did I don't think I'd want to risk all of it with . . .'

'Why? Because you've heard I once lost money you don't think I can be trusted. I tell you, Jane, this is as sure a thing as you'll ever hear of. It can't miss!'

'*What* can't miss?'

'It's this way.' He rolled over on his elbows until he was facing her directly. 'There's a man by the name of Wyatt in Folkestone who's in trouble for money. He built a lugger to certain specifications – the chief of them being that it could out-sail any Revenue ship on these seas. The man who ordered it has gone back on the order – got into money trouble himself – and he's cancelled. Wyatt is in debt, and looking for a buyer.'

'Are you suggesting we *buy* a smuggler's lugger?'

'Child! – you couldn't buy a lugger for a few hundred pounds. But Wyatt is desperate, and would be willing to take cash for the hire of the craft. You see it isn't just the matter of the lugger, Jane. You've got to have enough in hand to buy the cargo, pay the porters, a few pounds here and there as bribes . . . It adds up. But the profits! – three hundred per cent isn't unusual! Even a few months with the use of the lugger would pay us both handsomely. On the very first cargo we'd make enough to buy the second.'

She shrugged, unconvinced. 'Well, suppose – just suppose – we *could* hire the lugger. A few months wouldn't make us enough profit to buy it outright. What would happen when Wyatt found a buyer?'

'Well – ' He gestured briefly. 'We'd be back at the beginning, wouldn't we? – even if a little richer for our pains. Besides, many things can happen in a few months. Fortunes change . . .'

'What do you mean? . . . "Fortunes change"?'

'Exactly what I said. By the end of the summer news may have reached you of Charles Blake. By the end of the summer you might be able to sell the King's Pearl.'

Her mouth dropped open slightly; she gave a short gasp. 'Sell the King's Pearl to buy a smuggler's lugger! You must be out of your mind!'

'Some people wouldn't say I was – those who know the smuggling business. In a few seasons you could make the sort of money you haven't dreamed of, Jane.'

'Yes, and throw my hand in with a pack of murderers! It sounds like a poor way to invest the King's Pearl. I don't think I want any part of that side of it.'

'You've listened to too many exaggerations, Jane. The smuggler's band is as good or as bad as its leader. There are some men who'd think no more of murder than stealing a chicken from a cottage garden. But I don't happen to be one of them. Don't forget, it suits them to keep up all the old tales of murder and violence. The more frightened the people are, the less interference there'll be.

And don't pretend you aren't already a part of it, or that you can turn your head away from it. Every person who buys a half-pound of smuggled tea is part of it – which means about three-quarters of the whole of England.'

She didn't contest the point, knowing the truth of it far too well. 'All right – all right! But what's the use of talking? – I haven't that much money and the King's Pearl isn't mine. So there's an end of it.'

'I wish it didn't have to be the end – there won't be another chance like this one. Couldn't you borrow? Couldn't you borrow it from Turnbull? Any man who lends you Blonde Bess could be persuaded to lend you more.'

She sat up straight, two bright spots of colour burning her cheeks. 'I don't think I care to ask Robert Turnbull for money on *your* behalf. I don't want to have to hear him refuse. I don't want to guess what he thinks of me.'

'Does it matter to you what he thinks, Jane?'

'Of course it does! He believes me, and he trusts me – he'd want to know how I'd use the money, and he wouldn't be fooled by the answers I could think up. No! – not Robert Turnbull!'

'I didn't know you thought so highly of him,' Paul said slowly.

She turned on him. 'If you weren't so busy hating everything you see on the Marsh, you'd discover there *are* people here who know how to live . . .'

'Hush! Jane – I didn't mean to rouse you!' he said lightly. 'I should know better than to tease a Blake. They're famous for their lack of a sense of humour.'

'Well! – And I've known long ago that the salt-water dried up your sense of . . . of . . .' She struggled helplessly for a word.

'Proportion?' he suggested.

'That will do as well as any – and I won't be badgered by you any more. Loans! . . . money! I've only been a few days on the Marsh, and you expect me to raise money! Why can't *you* do it – you must know enough people. They say your brother's a rich man. Ask him!'

Paul sighed. 'Him last of all! I've just managed to pay off my debts, and I'd need to match your five hundred with five hundred of my own. It can't be done, Jane – hereabouts I'm reckoned to be a bad risk.'

'That wild Paul Fletcher?' she said softly. 'Do they expect you to run off with it?'

He grinned. '. . . or spend it on women.'

Suddenly she laughed. 'What a couple of paupers we are! No

possessions – and no money!' She glanced over at him slyly. 'Expensive clothes . . . fairly pleasing manners – but no money! What can we do?'

Abruptly his face darkened; his eyes lost their amused, teasing expression as completely as if he had pulled away a mask. He gazed at her intently, his brow furrowing. Then he leaned over and tugged at her arm, so that she collapsed on the grass; he pulled himself nearer.

'We can use what we have, Jane – we can enjoy what we have.'

He bent over and kissed her savagely, wildly – a frantic, searching kiss that carried overtones of despair. He rubbed his face against hers, cheek yielding to cheek, covering her with soft, biting kisses, that were passionate and yet protective. She murmured, and he covered her mouth again with his. Gently he kissed her ears, and her throat; his hand sought the swell of her breast under the habit. He could feel the tautening of her body as she responded.

'Oh, Jane . . . Jane,' his voice was low and troubled. 'You're so lovely, Jane . . . and if I had everything the world could give me, I'd still want you.'

Their heads were close together, red and blond, in the sun. The breeze stirred again, playing through the reeds where the wild duck hid, and lifting and scattering the blossoms over their two bodies, lying so still on the green spring grass, and aching with their need and longing.

They rode together on the Marsh until the approach of dusk – disturbed and wondering, hardly speaking to each other, or looking into the other's face – and yet there seemed no way to part that would not be painful and violent to them both. Jane followed Paul's lead on the winding roads mindlessly, without question, only wanting above all things in the world that the closeness between them should not be jarred or broken. She lent her body willingly to the rhythm of Blonde Bess's movements, feeling the wind in her face, hearing it thrust against the elms. Startled birds rose from the hedgerows at their approach; plovers shrieked from their nests in the fields. Jane looked about her and smiled, accepting the subtle magic of the spring afternoon and the presence of Paul at her side with equal sureness.

They rode westward under the great sea wall at Dymchurch where the level of the Marsh was lower than the sea itself. Paul led her off the road to paths among the sand dunes. They emerged from the dunes finally, and halted.

To Jane the sea was part of the afternoon – no more or no less strange and wonderful than everything that had preceded it. She stared at it until her eyes ached; the wind brought tears to them, and she saw the scene through a haze. It was a miracle of light and movement, a heaving, crashing thing, that deafened, fascinated and awed her. It was an immensity she was not able completely to grasp.

Paul reached out and took her hand gently.

'Out there is France, Jane – some day you'll come with me and see it. And over to the west there . . . that foreland is Dungeness. It's nothing but a huge shingle bar the sea has thrown up over hundreds of years. It's a natural barrier against the sea on this side of the Marsh, but it's helped, as much as anything else, to silt up Rye Harbour, and the mouth of the river.'

The long miles of shingle Paul had called Dungeness, were desolate save for the swooping gulls, but now, in the spring, it was cloaked in patches with the wild flowers that somehow managed to take root there – drifts of sea pinks and of broom, and starry stonecrop . . . inhospitable, frightening, with the sea booming endlessly, remorselessly against the rounded stones that formed its substance. Jane struggled to repress a shudder.

Paul leaned towards her. 'It frightens most people – those that bother to come and see it. They say there's nothing like it anywhere else in the world.' He shook his head, gesturing briefly. 'It'll be even less inviting if we linger here, Jane. See those clouds coming up along the coast? . . . That means rain within a half-hour, and we'd best be away from here. This is the devil's own place to be caught in a storm – nothing to break the wind over all those miles.'

He dropped her hand, and turned his horse swiftly. 'Come – there's nowhere hereabouts to shelter, and you'll be soaked.'

With a last look backwards to that desolate foreland, they turned their horses. Before they were clear of the sand dunes, the rain was falling lightly, the clouds racing ahead of them eastwards across the Marsh. It was the cold cheerless rain of spring. Jane turned up the collar of her habit. They rode another mile, and the rain was heavier; it had started to drip from the brim of her hat.

Paul leaned towards her. 'We'll have to shelter at my cottage – it's not much farther on.'

She nodded, looking at the darkening sky, and thinking without relish of the miles between her and Blake's Reach. When they entered the street of Old Romney it was deserted – not even a dog huddled in the shelter of a doorway. Smoke curled from the chimneys, and they heard the sounds of many voices from the alehouse. Through the uncurtained window of a cottage Jane caught the bright gleam of a fire, and suddenly she felt the chill of the rain in her bones, and was conscious of the long miles in the saddle.

'I'm stiff,' she said to Paul. 'I'm hungry, too – and I think that Blonde Bess is almost too much for me. It's been a long time since I've ridden so far.'

'We're almost there,' he answered. 'It's over yonder, in that belt of elms.'

At the end of the village the road forked – a left turn to the church, which stood, oddly, by itself, and was reached by the lane that followed the curve of a dyke. Sheep grazed in an open field between the village and the church. Paul's cottage stood midway along the lane.

The rooks rose from the elms at their approach, their harsh cawing deadened a little by the steadily falling rain. Together Jane and Paul went to the lean-to stable at the back. Paul dismounted, and reached up to help Jane; she rested in his arms briefly, her cheek brushing his wet coat. Then she raised her eyes to look at him deliberately, questioningly, and she found an answer there. They knew, both of them, as surely as if it had been put into solid-sounding words, that, whether the rain had come or not, they would still have taken the fork leading down to Paul's cottage.

2

Jane pulled off her wet jacket and skirt, huddling gratefully into the warmth of the shabby padded dressing-robe Paul had given her. Her boots and hat and gloves lay in a pile over by the door of the sitting-room. Paul had built a fire, lighted candles and drawn the curtains against the gathering darkness. He was out in the stable now, tending the horses; faintly she could hear him whistle as he moved about. She stripped off a petticoat whose hem was heavy with mud and wet, and flung it with the other garments, shivering a little as she loosened her hair, and bent towards the fire. The wind had risen, and moaned fitfully in the elms by the gate.

Paul came back, and she watched him silently as he busied himself with rum and some spice jars ranged on the shelf. He had taken off his coat, and under the fitted waistcoat of dark blue silk he wore a shirt of fine linen. It pleased her that he had taken trouble to dress in his best for their meeting, but Paul had none of the instincts of the fop and the dandy. The long day in the sun and wind had done its worst with his carefully powdered hair, but he appeared not to have thought of looking at himself in the mirror that hung in his bedroom. At most he would give only impatient and grudging attention to his appearance; the unkempt figure she had seen for the first time in the church was truer to Paul Fletcher than this handsomely dressed man, muttering to himself as he blended the spices.

'It's a mixture used in the West Indies,' he explained to her. He had heated a poker in the fire, and he plunged it now into the liquid. It hissed furiously, and he thrust it under her nose. The fumes brought tears to her eyes.

'Good, isn't it?' he demanded. 'Here, taste it! Best thing I know to drink when the rain gets down into your bones.'

The liquid slipped down easily, and the warmth started to spread through her. He knelt on the hearth rug beside her, and instinctively she moved closer to him, wanting the reassurance of nearness and contact. Gently he put up his hand and stroked her hair.

'It's strange, Jane, what you have made happen to this unlovely place. An hour ago it was simply a roof over my head – uncomfortable and lonely. Now there's a red-headed girl sitting before my fire . . .'

'Hush,' she said. 'It's I, Jane Howard! – remember it's the girl you quarrelled with not a week ago. I'm no different . . . though I believe you've mixed a little spell with your brew, because I think I've almost forgotten what it was we quarrelled over.'

'There was no quarrel,' he said. 'I spoke my mind too strongly about your mixing so closely with smuggling, or having knowledge that could be dangerous to you.' He sighed then. 'If I could, I'd remove you from everything that has even a taint of smuggling. Part of me doesn't want you here, sharing my rum and my vaguely shadowed reputation. I know I shouldn't have allowed you to come here, but I couldn't deny myself the delight of your coming to share even so little . . . From this moment on my hearth will never again be empty, because I shall be able to see you here, as you are now.'

'Paul . . . I wanted to come!' She spoke with difficulty, looking towards the fire. 'It's been lonely . . . and I've been afraid! I've needed to talk with someone who . . . who is my own kind.' She uttered the last words wonderingly, as if realizing the truth of them for the first time.

'Then you'll never be afraid any more as long as I am here – or lonely. Now you have Blonde Bess, and you know my door is never locked . . .'

She put her head against his shoulder, unaccountably finding tears again welling up; she swallowed hard against the lump in her throat. 'No one has ever said such a thing to me before. I feel safe here, as if nothing can touch me or hurt me, and I don't have to

pretend I'm stronger than I really am. I've never felt this way . . .'
She looked up. 'Paul, what does it mean?'

'You and I have to find out what it means, Jane. You and I . . .'
He paused, searching despairingly for words to make his meaning
true and clear. 'You and I have been thrown together by circumstances and by our own wills – as violently as any two people can
be. It isn't conventional and decorous, and it certainly isn't part
of any plan either of us had made for the future. But don't you
see, Jane . . . !' She could feel the calloused palms of his hands
against her shoulders eagerly, joyfully. 'Don't you see that this
could be better than mere plans! If you and I are for each other
then in Heaven's name let us have the courage to say it!' He
rushed on. 'Maybe in the eyes of the rest of the world Paul
Fletcher is not the best thing that could happen to Jane Howard –
but that's the rest of the world. It's in our own hands, Jane, to
make a different decision. Neither of our lives is so cut and dried,
so tied and bound down, that we can't face each other honestly
and say that we love . . .'

'And are we in love?' she asked slowly.

'Are we?' he repeated. 'Or did that moment of decision slip by
without our noticing? Did we fall in love out there on the Marsh,
or was it even so long ago as the first time we saw each other in
the church? Do you know when it was, Jane?'

She shook her head. 'I don't know . . . I don't even know that
it's happened.'

'Do you believe it could? Can you look at me – know what my
life is, and what I am – and believe that it could all be dedicated
to you? – that my life could be so dedicated that no moment of it
was not bent to the purpose of serving and loving you?'

He leaned forward and kissed her on the lips. '*Could* you love
me, Jane?'

She said softly, 'I could . . . I *do* . . .'

With quiet movements he pushed the robe back off her shoulders,
and plucked at the ribbons of her bodice.

'You have such beautiful breasts, Jane . . .' He touched her
briefly, and then his hand dropped as she pulled away, flinching.
Instantly she recovered herself, her cheeks colouring hotly.

'I'm sorry . . . sorry. For a second I forgot it was you . . .' Her
voice was muffled and low.

He gathered her into his arms. 'Someone hurt you, Jane . . . and
you still remember!' He rocked her gently, as if she were a child.
'I said you were never to be afraid . . . and you need never fear me.'

For answer she lifted her face to his, seeking his lips.

'I'm not afraid . . . and I want to be sure I'll never feel lonely again.'

He laid her down tenderly on the rug. 'You never shall . . . never!'

3

The rain had gone when Jane and Paul rode back to Blake's Reach. The wind was fresh, and the dark clouds scudded swiftly across the Marsh, parting sometimes to show them a glimpse of the pale young moon. Sometimes they saw its reflection in the pools of water on the road, and then the wind would stir and distort the water, and all they saw was starry points of light. The Marsh was dark and secret, and at this hour there showed from the cottage windows only an occasional light or the glow of a dying fire. The beat of the horses' hoofs was loud in the village streets; the clock struck the hour as they passed by the church at Appledore. In a cottage garden Jane could distinguish the ghostly outline of an apple tree in bloom. Briefly her senses were filled with the remembered fragrance of the hour they had spent by the dyke.

They spoke no words of farewell to each other as they rode up the hill and passed through the gates to Blake's Reach; they had all the confidence of time to spend together in the future. Gently, before he dismounted, Paul leaned across and touched her mouth with his lips.

'Remember, Jane . . . my door is never locked.'

They were engulfed then by a flood of light from the kitchen door; Kate and Patrick came hurrying out, lanterns held high and grave disapproval plain in their faces. Jane cut short their enquiries.

'I'll have you understand that I am mistress here,' she said. Her tone was very quiet. 'And when I come and go is no one's concern but my own.'

Then she gave her hand to Paul. He dropped a kiss on it, mounted without a word, and rode out of the yard. Patrick took Blonde Bess into the stable; Kate waited silently to light her to the kitchen.

'I'll make ye a toddy, Mistress,' Kate said. 'A little something to get the warmth back into yer bones. Folk do go down with terrible fever from riding the Marsh b' night. It's the mists in the dyke, Mistress.'

'I'm not cold, Kate — but I'll have the toddy, if it will please you.'

She sat on the settle by the fire, staring into the flames, and hearing nothing of Kate's vague mumblings in the background.

Dimly she understood that Kate was making dark hints of sickness and death and worse for those who didn't stay safely within their own walls when darkness fell, but she heard her as if the voice came from another world. So much had changed from the moment she had ridden away from here, so much was different, and could never be the same again. Her body and her mind had been stirred to a depth she couldn't as yet comprehend; she had been touched and altered and reshaped, and a deep peace and gentleness lay on her like a covering. The facts and personalities of her small world had not yet broken through it, nor did she want them. She sipped the toddy, and thought of Paul.

Patrick came back from tending to Bess, and he stood for a long time with his arm crooked over the corner of the settle opposite, his white bony face with its shock of dark hair on the forehead, meditative and wondering. She finished the toddy, and raised her head to look at him.

'Heaven help us!' he said. '. . . an' here she is with eyes in her head as bright as stars!'

She rose to her feet, picking up her hat and gloves.

'Patrick, do you remember what my mother looked like when she was in love?'

She took the lighted candle from Kate's hand, and left the kitchen. Patrick straightened, shaking his head. The old woman clasped her hands nervously; her face, when she turned to Patrick, was grey and strained.

'May Heaven help us, indeed! When a Blake falls in love there's no tellin' what things may come upon us. And here she's fastened her heart on a wild one, an' it'll bring ruin to us all.'

As Jane reached the head of the stairs she saw the light from William's candle under the edge of the door. She stood quite still, listened; she could hear his thin child's voice running on and on softly, like a trickle of water. In the empty silence of the house, the sound was eerie and disembodied. She went to the door and opened it.

The dog, General, raised his head, and William glanced up at the same moment. He sat propped up against the pillows, and the candle behind his rumpled hair gave it a fiery aura.

He grinned, and patted the edge of the narrow cot in invitation.

'William – you should have been asleep long hours ago.' It was beyond her ability then to make her voice stern. He sensed her mood and took advantage of it.

'I want to show you George and Washington.'

'George and Washington?' she said vaguely.

'Yes! – you remember!' he said, hurt by her forgetfulness. 'Mr Fletcher gave them to me. I thought they might get tired being shut up in their cage – you know – cramped.'

Jane sat down where he indicated. There was a tiny movement among the folds of the blanket, and William suddenly pounced with his right hand, and then his left. Each of his hands was pressed firmly against the mattress, and between the thumb and first finger of each, Jane could see the whiskers and small bright eyes of a white mouse. William looked at her expectantly.

'They're very handsome.'

He nodded. 'Yes – they are,' he said complacently. He indicated the cage on the floor. 'Would you pass that up? I'd better put them in – they're frightened of strangers, and they might run away. They might go down the holes in the floor, and the other mice would kill them.'

She opened the cage door, and watched him deposit the animals, and close it quickly. She took a crumb of cheese from his hand, and poked it through the bars.

'Why are they called George and Washington?'

'That's what Mr Fletcher called them. We gave them their names. The one called Washington is named after an American hero of the Revolution – though Mr Fletcher said it wasn't considered the right thing in England to say he's a hero. The other one's called George, after the King – though Washington's name is George, too.' He frowned. 'I can't remember exactly what he said . . . something about the times when they fought each other they were the King George and George Washington, but the rest of the times they were just George and Washington. Mr Taylor once explained to me about the American war of the Revolution – but I don't remember it all. Do you know much about it, Jane?'

She shook her head. 'No.'

The information seemed to please him. He bent his face towards the cage eagerly, tapping against the bars to attract the attention of the mice.

'Aren't they pretty, Jane! So quick and neat! . . . I wonder what my mother will say when she sees . . .' His voice faltered, and he gazed up at Jane with an agonized look of realization and loneliness. He drew his breath in quickly, and his whole body seemed to heave.

'Oh, Jane . . . I miss her so! *I miss her!* She always looked so pretty, and smelled so . . .'

She caught him into her arms, and he buried his face against

hers. At first his sobs were loud and violent, cries of outrage and
fear; then they came more softly, tired and whimpering. He held
himself close to her for the comfort and security of her living
presence. She stroked his head, hearing herself murmuring words
to him, saying things about Anne she had never known, but which
she knew now he wanted to hear. He grew quiet in her arms, and
finally he slept.

General lay at his feet on the bed; she placed the cage of white
mice where William would see it when he woke. She rested her
hand for a second on the dog's head; then she took the candle
quietly and left.

7

Early the next morning Jane sent Jed to Rye with a message for
Robert Turnbull, asking for him to come to Blake's Reach that
afternoon. There was only one thought in her mind as she carefully
penned the note – that Blake's Reach needed money desperately,
and Paul's plan to hire and use the lugger at Folkestone for carrying contraband was the only way to get it. But to hire the lugger
and buy the cargo too she must find five hundred pounds to match
what Paul could put up. And Robert Turnbull was the only one
who might lend her that much money; there was no one else.

It was a golden May day, and the sun fell across the mirror as
Jane dressed for his visit. She nodded to her own reflection as she
brushed her hair.

'You're about to be a smuggler, Jane Howard! Have you
thought what's going to happen to you if you're caught?'

Then she scowled, slamming the brush down, and reaching for
her gown that lay ready for her. She turned back to her image.
'Breaking the law, am I? Well, it's nothing more than thousands
of other people are doing. And there'll be no violence – Paul promised me that! I'll get into it and out of it quickly. And then I'll
forget it. Just as soon as I have some money to get things started
here again, I'll pull out and I'll forget it.'

She studied herself in the lilac gown, that had been chosen with
Robert Turnbull in mind. It gave her a look of calm and gentleness.

'But what of Paul?' she said suddenly. 'I love Paul – and I want
him. I want him and Blake's Reach both. There's got to be some
way I can have both . . . and Robert Turnbull's the first step.'

She chose to wait for Robert by the broken wall at the bottom of the garden, where the climbing roses had made their own wilderness. She began cutting out the dead wood, as she had seen the cottagers do in Hampstead, clipping and tying back, working at a leisurely pace, until she saw him coming down the garden towards her. The stocky, expensively-clad figure was a shade too eager, the brown eyes were expectant and waiting. She waved a greeting, and then bent and clipped the rose bud she had been saving for him.

She held it towards him. 'Welcome! This is for you – the first bud! It's early, and I don't expect it will open . . . but I thought you might wear it for me.'

He accepted it from her, smiling a little, and put it in his button-hole.

'Save me the last one, also, Jane. I'll come in the autumn to collect it.'

'But the autumn's a sad time in a rose garden,' she said. 'I don't want to think of the last bloom . . . it makes me afraid I'll be leaving Blake's Reach . . .'

'You won't be leaving Blake's Reach. I'll be here to collect the first bud of next spring as well.' He stepped back from her, head tilted a trifle, studying her.

'You know – I find it strange to see you here in the garden. Anne never cared to work in the garden. She said she had no under-standing of flowers.'

'She was made to look at flowers, not tend them,' Jane replied laying down the clippers. She smiled teasingly. 'You really must stop looking for Anne in me. I'm a woman in my own right, you know.'

He nodded. 'And I do you a grave injustice if I suggest any-thing different. Forgive me, Jane – it's the face that tricks me.'

'How well you remember her,' Jane observed softly. 'You re-member everything about her – everything she did and said.'

He shrugged. 'Why not? Life is too slow in the country not to make a personality and a face like Anne's exciting. It isn't likely I'd forget.'

'You never wanted to leave Rye? – to go to London perhaps?'

He shook his head. 'When I was young I saw no reason to – and then years later when I woke up to the fact that I was bored, the habit of prosperity and comfort had become ingrained. I chose to remain where I was bored, rather than risk the dubious excite-ment of starving. I like good horses, fine wine and rare books . . . I'm a dull man, Jane, and I've grown reconciled to it.'

'A dull man? – never that, Robert!' It was the first time she could recall speaking his name aloud. She bent down swiftly, and began piling the clippings and tall weeds into a flower basket; he stooped to help her, and their hands brushed, and then withdrew as if they had been stung. Jane smiled a little shakily, handing him the basket. At the same time she slipped her arm through his free one.

'I've really brought you out here to boast,' she said lightly. They began walking back towards the house. 'I wanted to show you what I've done. It was such a bright, wonderful day, and I have no conscience about bringing you away from piles of legal papers.'

'Nor I in coming. Besides, aren't the Blakes my clients? I'm here to serve them, and if it happens to be a beautiful spring day – all the better!'

She halted, pulling on his arm. 'I suppose . . . it's just occurred to me that *you* must have been one of the people who suffered most with Spencer's gambling. How long is it since you've had a bill to the Blakes paid?'

'Hush!' he said, urging her forward again. 'You don't know what you're talking about. Old John Blake, the general, put my great-grandfather into business, and made him prosperous. I don't think the Blakes have seen a bill from us in nearly a hundred years.'

'More fool you!' she said. 'But if that's how you choose to do business . . .' She tugged at his arm quickly. 'No, not there . . . I want you to come round to the vegetable garden. William and Patrick and I have worked on it – and we'll eat from it before the summer's out.' She gestured briefly. 'And over there – by the wall – I thought I'd start an herb garden. Sally Cooper taught me a little about herbs . . . she used to make herb tea for anyone who was sick in the village.'

'And you hope to do the same?'

She shook her head. 'Don't tease me! I need the herbs for the kitchen . . . besides, the village has grown so used to Blake's Reach in a state of beggary and ruin, I think they'd laugh to see me step out of a carriage bearing herb tea!'

They inspected the vegetable plot, and stopped to exchange greetings with Blonde Bess in her box. Robert spent ten minutes admiring the greys, discussing and praising their fine points; then Jane and Robert went through the kitchen, Kate curtsying and looking disapproving of Robert's presence there, Patrick bowing, with just the suggestion of a wink to Jane. She took Robert to see Spencer's sitting-room, and then in triumph, to show him the drawing-room. His pleasure in all the changes was real and out-spoken.

'Jane . . .' he said, shaking his head. 'Jane! it's incredible! The place hasn't looked like this since Anne – no, even before Anne left it was showing signs of Spencer's lack of money. He had got rid of most of the servants – the highest paid ones. How have you done it?'

'I have Patrick,' she said simply. 'And Patrick is young – and I am young. We believe in ourselves, and we don't think Blake's Reach is in a hopeless situation. Of course, I don't know when Patrick sleeps – if he ever does. He gets through the work of three men.'

Patrick had laid a tea-tray, and she made the tea from a spirit kettle, counting the tea from a rosewood caddy which had a tiny lock. She glanced at it, and smiled.

'I can't think why anyone who lived on the Marsh should trouble to lock up their tea. It isn't much of a luxury in this part of the world.'

'No it isn't – and there's many an old labourer's wife with an ache in her bones who thanks the Lord it isn't. If it weren't for the smugglers' runs most of the people in this fair kingdom would never taste tea.'

She handed him the cup. 'Are you feeling generous towards the smugglers today?'

'Not especially. I don't care what smugglers do as long as they keep out of my way. I enjoy cheap brandy and tea as much as anyone else.'

'I hoped you were feeling soft about everything today.' She faced him across the tea-tray, across the shining silver and the delicate cloth that had come from Anne's house. 'I hoped you were feeling soft because I have something to ask you.'

'What?' He fixed his gaze upon her firmly, his eyes were speculative.

'You've looked around here, Robert. You've seen what I'm doing. You've looked at the greys, and the carriage. There's some silver Spencer forgot about, and didn't sell. You've an idea how much it's all worth.'

'Yes.'

She drew a deep breath. 'Then I'm going to ask you for a loan – with these things as security.'

'How much?' His voice didn't betray either surprise or distaste. He was brisk – the legal and business man.

'Four or five hundred pounds. As much as I can get.'

'What would you do with the money?'

'Well . . .' Again she drew a deep breath. 'There's the farm first.

The stock is badly run down, and we need new rams. And with good rams we'd need better fencing, so that the strain remains pure. There's a chance I might be able to buy back a field adjoining our land on the Appledore side – good grazing, they say it is. I want to buy feed for the sheep to carry them through the winter better ...'

'Do you really know what you're talking about, Jane? – or is this just hearsay?'

'Mostly hearsay,' she admitted. 'But I was brought up in the country, you remember – and I've learned a great deal from listening to Lucas. He's been a shepherd – a "looker", I think he said they call him here – all his life, and I think he's not without some skill.'

'It's true,' Robert said. 'Lucas could have had better positions, but he's preferred to stay at Blake's Reach. Lord knows why – it wasn't for love of Spencer. But let us go on, Jane. That's the sheep – what else?'

'The roof,' she said. 'I went up to the attics to look at it yesterday. Another winter's rain might be serious. There are windows to be replaced, and in the old wing the plaster is cracked badly, and starting to fall off. There are some rooms where the ceiling's not safe ...'

'Nothing for yourself, Jane? No gowns or hats?'

'They're the only things I *don't* need. I've trunks full of gowns that once made London goggle, and will certainly keep a country district talking for years.' Then she shrugged. 'But there's always curtains – every pair in the house is rotting on the windows. But they'll hang for a while yet. Frivolous things – well, I'd like them in plenty. But they can all wait.'

They sat quite still, looking at each other. Robert's fingers drummed quietly on the arm of his chair; the sound made Jane nervous. She wondered if she had gone too far, if she had misjudged his feelings for Anne, and how far he was susceptible. Suddenly she felt a little afraid of him. He was not like other men; there was little one could guess for certain about Robert Turnbull's feelings. He lived a life whose inner core was known only to himself. His reserve was deep and close; she wondered if she had tried to make a friend of him too quickly, and now had blundered. He might despise her for the crudeness of her request. He might despise her, and still give her the money, disappointed in her, and unable to forgive her because she was not Anne. The silence dragged out. She held herself straight, determined not to show the nervousness that now swamped her. Everything she had said to Paul about

Robert Turnbull seemed true. She had made clumsy excuses for borrowing the money, and he had seen through them. Had he been mocking her about the gowns and hats? – she felt that she had been a fool, and she was about to apologize and take back her request, when he spoke at last.

'I can make you the loan, Jane – there's no trouble about that. But why do you risk your own possessions as security when the money would go into the farm and house? It should be a loan to the estate.'

Her head jerked back. 'Just suppose one fine day Charles Blake walks in here? What then? Have I got to tell him I've further mortgaged the place to try out a few ideas I have? I'd look a pretty fool.'

She rose from her chair, and began to pace the room. Then she swung around and looked at him.

'Can't you see what it's like – forever living with the thought that he may come back? I work here, and I scheme and think until my body and my head ache from it. And if he should walk in here it will all have gone for nothing. If you lend the money to me, and not to the estate, I will have a share in Blake's Reach . . . If *he* comes back I'll have some right here!'

Her voice was shaky. Suddenly she put her hands up to her forehead. 'If only I *knew*!'

'Knew what?'

'About Charles Blake – dead or alive!'

'Dead or alive doesn't matter, Jane. You shall have the money as soon as you want it. Only it pains me to see you expend yourself and your possessions like this. You're too young, Jane – there should be other things in life for you. Don't give *everything* to Blake's Reach . . . Keep a little of your life for living!'

She took her hands down from her head. 'Someone else said that!'

'Someone else? Who?' His tone was sharp.

She bit her lips, realizing that she had almost brought out Paul's name – and that Robert Turnbull would not have liked to hear it. 'Who?' she repeated. 'Oh . . . I don't remember. Perhaps Kate . . .'

He cut her short. 'There's just one stipulation I make . . . I will give you the money, but I don't want to hear what you do with it. I don't want it to stand continually between us. They say you can never make friends between borrower and lender – I don't want that to happen to us. Do you understand, Jane? Once it is done we won't talk of it. I'll collect my debt in say – five years. And that will be the end of it.'

'Very well,' she said slowly. 'That's how it will be.'

He stood up to take his leave. 'And the interest on it will be a rose delivered each spring. Agreed!' He smiled, and fingered his button-hole as he spoke.

'Yes! Agreed! A rose each spring.'

Jane was uneasy as she gave Patrick the order to bring Robert's horse around; Robert Turnbull puzzled and disturbed her. He had an air of power and knowledge that went past the simple function of a country attorney; his ordered bachelor's life didn't fit with his lack of concern over lending her the money – even more so because he could give it to her without enquiries or stipulations, or seemingly without a man's desire to manage the affairs of a woman. They stood at the doorway waiting, talking aimlessly of the work she had had done in the garden. She shot a glance sideways at him. The quiet eyes were faintly amused, and she had no idea why.

As Patrick brought his horse, suddenly there was a commotion. William dashed round the side of the house, gave them a brief look, and fled down the slope of the garden to the orchard. General followed him closely.

Robert laughed. 'Those are energetic playfellows William has conjured up for himself. I wonder if he fancies he's being pursued by smugglers – or is it the Preventive Officers?'

'He's never had so much space to do what he likes with,' Jane said. 'And no one has time to mind what he's at, either. After London it must be a paradise for him. In a few days he's grown into a little savage . . . he should have a tutor . . . or someone.'

Robert laid a restraining hand on her. 'Time enough. Let him have the summer to run wild . . . let him get to know the Marsh. For a boy it's a wonderful place. He ought to feel the Marsh in his bones . . . he's a Blake, too.'

William's red hair was lost among the budding leafiness of the trees. Turnbull swung himself up on his horse.

'The child should have a pony,' he said suddenly. 'It was stupid of me to overlook it. I'll see what I can find – ' he broke off. 'I think I may be able to suit him. There's a pony I have stabled at Rye – belongs to the child of a friend who's had to go abroad. William could borrow it – keep it exercised.'

'He would be glad of it,' Jane said. 'I know he'd be glad of it.'

Turnbull bent to make his farewell. 'Take care of yourself, my dear. Blake's Reach, I know, is in good hands . . . rather astonishing hands.' His eyes were no longer amused; his lips were tight and firm, as if he were keeping a check on his words.

There was something in the look that touched Jane strangely —
a lost, hesitant look, the look of someone wanting to ask for something, and not daring.

She gave him her hand.

'One other favour,' she said.

'Anything you want!'

'Invite me to supper!' she said firmly. 'Invite me into Rye to eat
supper with you!'

His tight line of his lips slackened. 'Would you do that, Jane?
Would you really do that!'

'Haven't I just invited myself? I'll come gladly if you'll have me.'

'Bless you, Jane — I'll be honoured. Tomorrow evening, then.'

She watched him ride along the drive, and turn out of sight on
the road, his broad square shoulders erect and jaunty. The clip-clop
of the horse's hoofs were loud in the still afternoon air. She leaned
against the stone pillars, gazing after him, wondering about this
quiet, powerful man, wondering at herself for what she had just
done. In the space of an hour she had moved much closer to
Robert, and yet was more puzzled by him than before. He seemed
aloof, but yet she could not say he was lonely; a solitary man, but
not one to invite pity. There was a strength in him that seemed as
if it had not met its test. She frowned, and shook her head.

As she turned to go indoors, Patrick moved nearer.

'You'll excuse me, Mistress — did I hear Mr Turnbull say he
stabled a pony for a friend that Master William could use?'

'Yes? — what about it?'

'Well, now — isn't that the strange thing! Sure wasn't that fine
fella from the livery stables in Rye — the same that brought Blonde
Bess, Mistress — wasn't he boastin' o' the string o' fine horses Mr
Turnbull stables with them, and there was never a mention of a
pony. Never a mention! Sure I'm thinkin' Mr Turnbull has only
to snap his fingers for a piece of fine horse-flesh to appear.'

She fixed her gaze on him coldly. 'And if he does, Patrick — is
that any concern of ours? We'll just be glad of what he's sent, and
not ask questions about it.'

'Yes, Mistress,' he concurred. 'We'll do that.'

2

Quite a large part of the people of Rye, drawn into the narrow,
cobbled streets by the mildness of the spring evening, saw the
carriage standing before Robert Turnbull's house at the top of
Mermaid Street. The carriage was handsome enough to attract

attention, and the pair of finely matched greys would have drawn a crowd anywhere. A small crowd did gather, in fact, and the two young boys who had been lavishly tipped to hold the horses' heads were puffed with pride. Patrick, decked in a coat of livery that dazzled the passers-by, leaned against the door, ready and willing to answer almost any question asked of him.

And so it was that one part of Rye's population learned that Anne Blake's daughter, Jane, was inside having supper with Robert Turnbull; and yet another part of the townspeople actually saw her when she came out on Turnbull's arm, and headed up the lane towards the church. It was a sight Rye would talk about for the next month.

They could see that she was tall, red-headed, and moved well, and those who could remember said she had more than a passing likeness to Anne Blake. But it was her costume that they would mostly talk of – the costume, the carriage and the horses. Which was just as Jane had planned it should be. She had thought out each detail of her dress, knowing well enough that she was over-dressed for the occasion, but knowing also that perfect taste was always too subdued to call for comment. So her gown was low cut enough for the women to say it was indecent, and the men to ogle; she wore a small fur piece about her shoulders, and ostrich feathers on the wide brim of her hat. It would have been a fashionable costume for Vauxhall – and she had worn it as much for Robert Turnbull as for the townspeople of Rye.

She had asked to see a little of the town before they ate supper, so with her hand in Robert's arm, she walked Rye's streets – passed the square-towered church to Rye's grim old fortress, the Ypres Tower, that had endured through five centuries of weather and attack from across the Channel. Robert pointed out his firm's offices in Watchbell Street, and took her to stand on Rye's cliff face, looking across the Camber Sands to the ruined Castle, and beyond it to the sea that washed over what had been the town of Old Winchelsea.

'Drowned, Jane,' he said. 'Drowned in one of the storms that silted up the harbours of the Cinque Ports, changed the course of the rivers, and helped make the Marsh as you see it now . . .

'It used to be a great town,' he said as they turned back. 'One of the greatest in the kingdom. Queen Elizabeth came here once . . . and of course Rye sent its quota of ships against the Armada. The beginning of the Navy, back in the days of Edward the First, came from these Ports. Great sailors, these men were – great men with ships!'

'So they are even now,' she said dryly. 'They make the run to France pretty quickly.'

He nodded. 'Yes – and they take risks to do it. You've heard, I suppose, that smugglers taken prisoner aren't sent to gaol? – as sailors they're much too valuable to rot in prisons. They're impressed into the Navy, and a bos'n counts himself lucky to get a Romney Marsh smuggler.'

'Your mind turns on smugglers, doesn't it,' she said, forcing herself to make the remark come lightly.

'So does the mind of everyone in these parts,' he answered. 'There isn't any escaping it.'

She found sharing a meal with Robert a fascinating and unique experience. He lived in a compact little house with a walled garden, from whose windows she could see The Mermaid Tavern. It was a house devoted entirely to the care and comfort of one man, and everything in it reflected taste, and a feeling for beauty. It was a man's world, richly but soberly furnished, smelling of expensive cigars and old, fine leather. His housekeeper was a silent, neat creature long ago trained to anticipate Robert's wants; she lived at the lower end of the town, and had learned that Robert Turnbull was a man who enjoyed his own company. After serving her excellently cooked meal, she left discreetly; they heard the door snap after her, and her footsteps on the cobbled street.

The contrast between the house and Blake's Reach was great, and Jane found herself responding to the atmosphere. They seemed to laugh together a great deal; Robert's attention was flattering and respectful – the wine was good, and it was potent. It was a relief to talk to Robert, and to know that from him there were no secrets kept; she could talk at will about The Feathers, about Anne in London, about her visits to Hampstead – even about Lord O'Neill. On only one subject did she keep silent; she never mentioned Paul Fletcher's name. Robert sat opposite her, the candlelight keeping his face a little in shadow, and he looked like a man well content.

During the evening he had given her five hundred pounds in bank notes, and she had insisted upon a form of receipt and acknowledgement of the loan which she could sign. She felt the bulkiness of the money in her reticule as she gathered up her things and prepared to leave; suddenly she was uneasy, the enormity of what she was doing breaking upon her coldly.

As he came forward with her wrap, Robert paused. 'Jane, what is it? What is the matter?'

She touched the reticule. 'This money . . . it frightens me! Two

months ago I wouldn't have known what to do with it. Am I like
Anne, do you think? — or Spencer? Perhaps I'll do nothing more
than add to the debts the Blakes have piled up.'

Gently he laid the wrap about her shoulders. 'Have courage,
Jane. Nothing is won except by the daring. And even I . . .'

For a startled second she felt his fingers on her bare throat, a
fleeting and sensitive caress, like the brush of a bird's wing against
her. She turned around. Robert held her by the shoulders. He
leaned towards her slightly, and she thought he was going to kiss
her. Her body went rigid in her effort not to show surprise.

Abruptly he dropped his hands and straightened.

'No . . .' He shook his head. 'No — nothing is won by those who
venture nothing.'

All the way back to Blake's Reach Jane clutched the reticule
tightly to her, gritting her teeth against the jolts of the carriage
and the pain that shot through her head. She had drunk too much
wine; the world swam before her in a mist in which the lights of
the cottages along the road were fiery blurs. But her anger and
contempt for herself were living things within her, fiercer than the
pain in her head, more real than the wad of money in her hands.

'Fool!' she told herself. 'Fool! . . . fool! What a little country
idiot you are that you don't know what can be done to a man . . .
Smile at him, listen to him, ask and take favours from him. Yes —
even bare your breasts for his eyes. And then you're surprised when
he wants to kiss you! You've made yourself into the image of the
woman he loved, and you're surprised at his caress . . . You thought
you could play Anne's game, but you don't know even the first rule
of it. Idiot! . . .'

The tears of anger and humiliation started to stream down her
face, falling unheeded, and spotting the bright silk. The carriage
jolted cruelly in the ruts, and she shivered and wept through the
miles to Blake's Reach.

3

When the first streak of dawn appeared across the eastern sky of
the Marsh, Jane had saddled Blonde Bess and started towards
Paul's cottage. The roads were lonely and unfriendly in the grey
light; the flush of the rising sun was low and small on the horizon;
but the mists of the night still lay over the dykes, and wrapped
like grey moss upon the trees. She would have taken to the fields,
but a countless number of dykes lay between her and Old Romney
— some narrow and weed-choked, others wide enough to halt

Blonde Bess. There were bridges, Paul had told her, but it needed years on the Marsh to remember all of them; to the stranger they were a nightmare maze. She hunched her shoulders to keep out a chill that was partly of her own imagining; it seemed to her that at this hour, between night and morning, the Marsh had slipped back to the times before its wastes had been reclaimed, when little boats carrying raiders from across the Channel had used its swampy creeks. It was eerie and silent, a land possessed of old secrets and old terrors.

She was shaking with nervous impatience by the time she slid down from Bess and hammered on Paul's kitchen door. The sounds echoed strangely through the house. For the first time she paused to wonder what she would do if he were not there. She tried the latch and it yielded.

Paul was still sleeping in the tumbled four-poster. She shook his bare shoulder violently.

'Paul! Wake up! . . . do you hear me? Wake up!'

His eyes flickered open, and closed immediately. Then they opened wide with an expression of startled surprise.

'Jane! What in the name of Heaven are you doing here?'

She drew back a little from the bed, frowning. 'You said I could come any time. Wasn't that what you said?'

He propped himself up on his elbow; the movement seemed to pain him. Under the covers his body was naked. He rubbed his hand wearily across his eyes. 'Of course I said it – and I meant it! But I didn't expect you today . . . now. What time is it? . . .' He closed his eyes briefly. 'My head feels as if it's still the middle of the night.'

She shook him again impatiently. 'It isn't the middle of the night for me! I've something to talk to you about – and I want you to pay attention. Here!'

She tossed the reticule on to the blanket. 'Look at that! – Five hundred pounds!' Her voice had an edge of triumph.

Abruptly he sat up; she watched his expression change. His features seemed to contract, and even darken under the rough sun-streaked hair. He didn't open the reticule; instead he poked at it, as if it were a strange and vicious animal.

'Where did you get this?' he demanded. 'What have you been doing?'

Her eyes grew cold. 'Where did I get it? . . . I went to the only source I have. The one you told me to go to.'

'Turnbull!' Suddenly he reached out and caught her arm in a tight ungentle grip, pulling her closer to the bed. 'Turnbull! –

that's who gave it to you, isn't it? *Answer me!*' He jerked at her arm again.

'Of course it was! Who else!'

Now he caught her by the shoulders, and dragged her down close to him.

'Last night you got it, didn't you? Last night when you went to his house?'

'How did you know that?'

'How could anyone who was in Rye last night not know it? I watched you – I watched you from the windows of The Mermaid. It was quite a show! . . . and don't think it wasn't appreciated. You were all the rage in the tap-room of The Mermaid – and every other ale-house in Rye, I'll wager! Every story they could remember about your mother was raked up – and some that never happened were thrown in for good measure. Oh, yes – I know about you, and inside of a week half the county will know!'

She tried to pull away from him, and couldn't.

'And so you got drunk!' she said. 'You were stupid enough to be jealous, and you got drunk!'

'Why shouldn't I be jealous? It was more than any man could stand to see . . .'

'Oh, hush! Like every man you're a fool – and a sentimental fool, at that! Didn't you guess why I would go to Robert Turnbull? – didn't you *ask* me to find the money?'

'You didn't have to make a spectacle of yourself! You didn't have to make it look as if you were paying a call on a man who was in love with you.'

'Perhaps he is in love with me! Does that matter to you? Didn't I bring the money, and isn't *that* all that matters to you?'

'Damn you! No! Four days ago perhaps it *was* all that mattered to me. Can't you see that things have changed since then. You must know . . .'

He released her shoulders, and she felt his broad hands cup her face. She could feel the callouses on his palms as he caressed her cheeks gently.

'Jane! – dear Jane! There is nothing now that matters except you – and Robert Turnbull can take his money back and go to hell! We don't want it, Jane.'

'Why?' She frowned, trying to push herself back to read his expression. 'Can't you get the lugger? Has something gone wrong?'

He sighed and dropped his hands. 'I want to talk to you, Jane. Come and sit here, by me.' He patted the blanket close to him. She obeyed with some reluctance, mistrusting the softness of his

C.G.O.–N

tone. He leaned back again on his elbow, one of his hands holding hers tightly.

'We don't want the money because I think we should clear out of this place.'

'What are you talking about? Leave here and go . . . where?'

'The West Indies.'

She stared at him unbelievingly, her mouth dropping open a trifle as the meaning of his words came fully to her. 'Have you gone mad, Paul Fletcher? Do you think I'm going to leave Blake's Reach?'

'Leaving Blake's Reach you'd be leaving nothing! I've told you — you can't put life back into a dead thing. And Blake's Reach *is* dead!'

She tossed the idea aside with a gesture, unable to give it any importance. 'I seem to remember you told me you hadn't got the money yet to set yourself up in the Indies. Has something happened to change that?'

'Nothing has happened except you! Nothing is changed — I still haven't the money to set myself up.'

She shrugged. 'Then why talk of it?'

'Because I must! Because this is an ugly and foul business you're about to get yourself into, and I'd rather a thousand times take you out of this than own the finest sloop in the Caribbean.'

Her eyes narrowed. 'But what would you do out there?'

'There are smaller ways to start. There are businesses I could manage, plantations that need overseers . . .'

'No!' The sound came from her throat as a shriek. She tried to pull away from him.

'You expect to take me to that! To be someone's servant! I've had enough of it, I tell you. Enough of it! A few months ago I didn't know Blake's Reach existed, but now I've found it, and I have position and respect, and soon I will have money. Do you expect me to leave what I've got now . . . and everything I hope for in the future?'

Then her tone dropped, and grew gentle and pleading. 'Please, Paul — try to understand.' She touched the reticule briefly. 'Neither of us can do anything without money. And this is the start of it. Why shouldn't we take it when everyone else does? Just a few runs, Paul — just a few cargoes to get us on our feet. This money belongs to Robert Turnbull, and I mean to pay it back. I can't if you won't help me.'

'But you still believe that you can make something of Blake's Reach?'

She was cautious. 'I can try. If I fail, that will be the only thing that convinces me.'

'And me? What becomes of me? Must I wait round here while you conduct your experiment? Or am I of interest to you only because I can be of service?'

Her mouth grew a trifle grim. 'I don't want you to say that!'

'I do say it because it may be true. I've seen better men than I wither in the clutch of an ambitious woman. I won't let it happen to me.'

'Nothing will happen to you that you don't want to happen. What difference can a few months make in your life? I've known you a few days – and you ask me to say I'll give up something that's in my blood. If Blake's Reach is no good I'll find out soon enough. But give me time . . .'

'And time for me to make enough contraband runs? That's the time you're thinking of, Jane, isn't it?'

She didn't answer him directly.

'Will you do it, Paul? Will you do it for both of us?'

A look of defeat and weariness settled on his face. He seemed to struggle against it for a few seconds, and knowing that the struggle was useless. He put his hand to his forehead.

'My head hurts,' he said. 'As if the boom swung round and hit me. Perhaps I have been hit, and I'm too dazed and stupid to know it.'

Then he shrugged. 'Yes, I'll do it.'

She leaned towards him. 'It won't be for long. Just a few months. That's all.'

'Will you be satisfied with a few months – or will you grow greedy like all the others?'

She put her face close to his. 'Do we have to fight? Do we have to talk of the Indies or Blake's Reach? Can't we just be happy with one another, and because of one another? Paul . . . I've wanted you so much.'

'Wanted me? . . . do you love me, Jane?'

'Heaven help me! Yes . . . yes, I love you. And I've wanted you close to me, near me.'

'Is this true?'

She put her arms about his bare body, resting her head against his shoulder.

'Why do we have to disbelieve? Let us just be happy as we know how to be. I want to forget all the other things . . . I just want you.'

The memory of the journey across the Marsh last night, weeping in the darkness of the carriage, and of her swift, lonely ride to Old Romney in the dawn was strongly upon her. She felt the strength of Paul's arms, and then felt them tighten about her, and the memory and the fear grew fainter. He was real and living, his head bent close to hers, his breathing in rhythm with her own. She could draw determination and confidence from him, and energy and a zest for living. Because he had strength, she also was stronger.

'Why is it,' she whispered, 'that I can find peace only with you?'

'Stay with me then,' he said. He pulled her backwards, and their heads were close together on the pillow.

8

Once Paul had committed himself to making the run, Jane's part in the matter was finished. She ran against a hard wall of determination when she tried to enter into the arrangements and plans.

'Stay out of this, Jane,' he said curtly. 'This is not something for a woman to dabble in – it's dangerous and it's ugly. Stay out!'

So he went his way, and kept his own counsel, as he had done before, and she had to contain her impatience and her desire to share his activities and his dangers in the only way she could. In the following weeks she settled to the day-to-day routine of Blake's Reach. The spring flush of the May days gave place to June; over the broad acres of the Marsh the lambs were growing fat, and the June roses were blooming in the hedges. The land lay peacefully under the bright summer sun, but it was a false sense of peace. Even to Blake's Reach, unconnected with the main highways to London or the ports, came the news from Paris, news of the growing tension and the powerless position of the King, of the daily executions. With each mention of the Revolution, Jane's heart stilled for a second – a little intake of breath; there was always the thought that the next packet to Dover might bring news of Charles Blake . . . Charles, dead or alive. As time went on she found it easier if she pretended that Charles Blake had never existed. That way there could be no guilt, and no pity.

But the fishermen of Kent and Sussex had a closer contact with the Revolution than the mere exchange of talk and gossip. France was now at war with Austria, and as the excesses of the Revolution grew, its victims grew more desperate; many of them crossed the Channel in a smuggler's lugger, paying their last gold for the privilege of sharing space with a contraband cargo, sometimes cowering among the brandy casks as the lugger ran from the guns of the Revenue cruiser, and landing on a lonely beach, thankful that the moon was hidden behind the clouds. For many of them their first knowledge of England was the sight of lamplight gleaming faintly on muskets and pistols.

At this stage of the Revolution, those who came were penniless. They could be met on the Dover road, frightened, bewildered, streaming towards London and the hope of help and shelter from the people they had called friends in the secure days of the court at Versailles. The fear in Jane's heart was that some day one of them would start out from Dover across the Marsh on roads he had known as a boy, moving with certainty towards Blake's Reach.

Robert Turnbull knew her fear, and he encouraged her to talk of it, to try to ease the load.

'One of my business associates at Dover enquires constantly among those who come across, Jane,' he said. 'I hear nothing fresh — some remember him in prison and most think he's dead. But they're frightened for themselves, and have no thought to spare for a man they scarcely knew.'

And her hand, passing the tea-cup, or the wine-glass, would tremble slightly, and her young face grew rigid and disciplined into an expression of indifference. He watched the struggle between pity and self-preservation.

'There will be war,' he would say. 'There will be war with England sooner or later, Jane. They will find a reason to execute King Louis...'

'War ... ? If there is war, will we ever have news of him? There will be no way to know ... your contacts will be cut off from news...'

He nodded. 'It could happen that you would have to wait out the war here at Blake's Reach...'

She shuddered. 'Waiting ... and never knowing. I don't think I could bear it...'

But her faith in herself was stronger than her belief that Charles Blake was still alive. Deliberately she went on with her plans for Blake's Reach, stretching into a future where Charles had no place. She spent some of her hoarded money to make further repairs to the house, to renew some window glass, to scythe the long grass in the orchard. Money had to be spent where it would be most noticed because it had to serve as evidence to Robert that she was directing his loan where she had said it would go. There was no possibility of buying rams until after Paul had brought a cargo across, and some gold flowed back into her pockets; but accompanied by

Lucas and Patrick, she made tours of inspection to the best farms
in the district, and afterwards filled Robert's ears with knowledgeable talk she had picked up. In the habits fashioned by London's
best tailor she was observed by many sharp-eyed farmers' wives,
and occasionally the occupant of a carriage, passing Jane and the
small entourage on the road, would bend forward to get a better
view. Jane was comfortably aware that her presence was known
and talked of in the houses of the gentry across the Marsh, and
she waited for the day when the first of those carriages should turn
in at the gates of Blake's Reach.

By now the vegetable garden was planted, and in immaculate
order; Kate went each day to stand and stare admiringly at the
sprouting crop; the beginnings of the herb garden were made. Two
lads from Appledore came to the kitchen asking for odd jobs, and
Jane used this cheap labour to whitewash the dairy and the old
cow stalls; the vegetable plot was fenced in, and the poultry
rigorously kept away. Two carpenters from St Mary's – the village
to which the Blake church officially belonged – came and did some
work on the stables, at the same time appraising the quality of the
greys, Blonde Bess, and the pony which Robert had sent for
William. Patrick and Kate kept their mouths closed, and the report
went round, neither confirmed nor denied, that the new mistress of
Blake's Reach might not be a great heiress, but she was not a
pauper. Jane stitched away at the faint signs of wear in the table
damask she had brought from London, added lace to a selected
few dresses whose necks were too low for day wear, and kept her
own counsel. She sensed the change in Blake's Reach, and was
happy because of it. She saw Luke and Jed and Kate take pride
in the new dignity that had come to them, saw them go to their
work with will and energy, comfortable because Blake's Reach and
its occupant were no longer a subject for laughter and scorn in the
village. She was beginning to taste the satisfaction of her accomplishment. The days went on, and Charles Blake's name was heard
less and less.

She rode on the Marsh often with only William beside her,
discovering its variety and its sameness, struggling to memorize
the tricks of its winding roads and its bridges. William's face now
wore a heavy pattern of freckles, and his hair was bleached with
the sun. His clothes were often dirty, torn and mismatched; his
hands and fingernails were grimy from weeding in the vegetable
patch. But even in these few weeks his child's body and temperament had taken on a certain toughness that made him unafraid to
walk the mile to Appledore, and join the village children in the

rough-and-tumble games they played. He came back one day bloody from a fight with the boy who had called him 'The Bastard'. In a fashion he understood that this would be his name always, but he would accept it only from those he knew were his friends and had earned the right to call him that with affection. The day after the fight he returned to Appledore as usual to join the games, and among the women watching from the cottage doors there were raised eyebrows, and the opinion in the ale-house that evening was that the young 'un at Blake's Reach was tarred with the same brush as the mistress. In the village there was a kind of inverted pride in William because he had been beaten and had come back to the possibility of more.

The school books he had brought from London gathered dust, but he was learning other things. He developed an eye almost as sharp as Jane's for a bargain – telling her at which farm the eggs were cheapest, and whose honey was the best, and at what prices. It was he who brought the news of the widow at Snargate who was selling up, and whose sow Jane bought cheaply. General was, as always, close by him wherever he moved, smelling of the stable and the saddle-soap and oil William handled constantly. Looking at them, Jane found it difficult to recall the first time she had seen these two – the child in the blue velvet coat, with the delicate features, the silken dog posed at his side. William seemed years older, and the London child was gone. He had the run of Blake's Reach, and beyond it, from sunrise until he grudgingly gave up his struggle against weariness at night. He went out to meet his new world with the ardour of someone who has been, unknowingly, in prison. Never again did Jane hear him weep at night for Anne.

But Jane forced William to return to the blue velvet coat on the Sunday they decorously climbed the hill to attend service at the Blake church. Neither of them wanted to go – in Jane's life there had been little time for church services, and they were something quite new for William – but they both knew what was expected of them now. And so they took their places in the carved pew with the faded blue cushions, emptied now of the tarpaulin-wrapped bundles of lace, and the brandy kegs. The church, Jane noticed, still smelled strongly of tobacco and wool.

No Blake had occupied the family pew since Charles had come, a boy of thirteen, reluctant and alone, to sit shyly in its shadows. The village of St Mary's had turned out almost in a body in the hope of Jane and William attending. No detail of their behaviour or appearance was missed – not from the exquisite lace that filled the neck of Jane's rose-coloured gown and the slippers made of green silk, to the fact that neither of them was familiar with the hymn book. But it was conceded that they were a fine-looking pair, red-headed and spirited in the traditional fashion of the family. No one voiced the thought, but they would all have been disappointed if these new Blakes had lacked the touch of wildness that was expected.

For Jane this was remembered as the morning she discovered that she was proud of William. She was proud of the straight shoulders which now strained the seams of the blue coat, of the high intelligent forehead and his bright, quick eyes. Behind his back they might call him 'The Bastard', but it was plain to anyone's eyes that he was the bastard of the nobleman – there was the evidence of good breeding in every line of his body. His clear young voice bellowed the words from the hymn book with magnificent unconcern for the tune; during the long sermon he kept his hands still and his back straight. Jane knew that he entered with her into a sense of the occasion, and after the service they were like a pair of conspirators going through the ritual of hand-shaking and greeting, William executing his formal bow that could only have been learned in London drawing-rooms. It was almost, Jane thought, too good a performance to be wasted on so small a parish as St Mary's. Perhaps if they had gone to Rye . . .

But there were other things Jane had to learn during those weeks of waiting, of the life of the Marsh and the lands on its borders. Some of the knowledge was bitter and unpalatable.

It was not enough, it seemed, to parade London-cut clothes, and a fine carriage and pair. Nor was it enough to put Blake's Reach into a semblance of order, and walk to church services up on the hill. Much more was needed before the first of those carriages bearing the wives of the local gentry would turn into the driveway. They had to make sure that she was not Anne Blake all over again – and on the Marsh it took years to make sure.

Anne Blake's reputation, heightened and coloured, had spread during the twenty years since she had left. In gossip she had been the mistress of half the famous rakes in London, and her only husband had been a commonplace captain of Dragoons from the Folkestone station. True, she had borne a son to the scion of one of England's oldest and richest families, but since the child possessed neither his father's name nor money, where was the advantage in that? Nothing was known about Jane . . . but there was enough speculation. She might possess the family failing of a weakness towards gambling, and set up gambling-tables at Blake's Reach – such as Anne was supposed to have done in London.

Without having seen her they already knew how she was looked at by men – and the low-cut gowns and tightly corseted waist, apart from the famous Blake red hair, were altogether too much competition for marriageable daughters. So Jane waited vainly for the carriages, and gradually she began to understand why they did not come.

There were two which did come. The first brought Roger Pym to her door, and when Kate rushed upstairs to tell Jane of her visitor her old eyes were bright with excitement and remembrance.

'He's the one yer mother was t' marry . . . the one the Old Master had picked for her . . .'

Roger Pym was some years older than Anne, a shy, gentle man, clumsy and tongue-tied, wearing expensive, dowdy clothes. His face wore a wistful expression as his gaze rested on Jane. He played nervously with the silver knob of his cane.

'You're so like her . . . your mother. She was very beautiful, too.'

Jane thanked him with a smile, and looked away from his regretful eyes to engross herself deliberately with the tea-tray Patrick had brought in. Pym was in an agony of embarrassment and shyness, and Jane had the impression that he had needed to gather considerable courage to make the visit. But he managed to talk a little of Anne, and even speaking her name was a relief to him. He said nothing more than any other person across the Marsh might have said of her, but his voice betrayed the years of hoping and disappointment.

'I have children too,' he said. 'Some of them round about your age . . . five daughters and two sons . . .' Then he was overcome with embarrassment again as he realized that they would be Jane's natural companions in other circumstances. He could not offer the invitation which he knew should have been forthcoming. There had been too much talk at home about Anne Blake's daughter . . .

'No doubt my wife and daughters will be calling shortly . . .' he said unhappily. 'They've been busy lately . . . summer is a busy time . . .'

He went reluctantly, wanting to stay on and indulge the desire to talk about Anne, and yet uncomfortably aware that to stay longer might involve or commit his family. He stumbled off, a shy man with sad eyes, who for thirty minutes had lived blissfully in the past. He would probably never dare to come again, Jane thought.

The second visitor was Paul's brother, Sir James Fletcher. This time there was no carriage, but a thoroughbred horse which brought warm glances from Patrick. Jane quickly changed her gown before going to greet him.

Immediately she sensed curiosity of a different kind from Roger Pym's. It was cold curiosity – cold and examining. He looked like Paul; he was older, with blond hair turning pepper-and-salt, bulkier in frame, a good body going a little to fat. In a rigid, controlled way he was handsome; his clothes were well cut, and looked as if they had come from London.

He never once mentioned Paul's name, behaving exactly as if he had come on an ordinary social call. And yet he made a few slips – let fall small pieces of information about her that could only have come from Paul. She began to dislike him, sensing patronage in his remarks about the work she had done at Blake's Reach, and he referred too openly for politeness to the poverty of the estate.

'You've opened this room, I see – well, it's about time. Haven't been in here for years. Spencer didn't like this room . . .'

He crumbled, but did not eat Kate's plum cake, as if to point up the heaviness Jane already knew too well; he drank two cups of tea, put his cup down and started to pace the room. He paused deliberately on the frayed edge of the carpet, flicked at it with his polished boot as if it had tripped him. Then he looked across at John Blake's portrait. He looked at it as if he had seen it many times before, and it was an old enemy.

'Spencer used to wish he had the money the family spent to build and endow that church up there . . . Well, I suppose nothing else was good enough for them after John had covered himself in glory at the wars. Strange, wasn't it, that he didn't get a title at the same time?'

He looked back at her quickly, seeming to realize now that his words had been insulting.

'I've always thought,' she said evenly, 'that titles only went to those who asked for them. John Blake would have been a viscount or an earl, but there's some story about him falling out with the Duchess of Marlborough. It takes courage of a kind not to care what happens to a title . . . And who knows? . . . perhaps he was right not to take it. After all, the Blakes are simple people, and this is a modest house . . .'

She said this with full knowledge that he had been made a baronet only seven years ago; she knew she took a risk in snubbing him, but it was important that James Fletcher should never be allowed to think she was a spineless ninny, too overwhelmed by his aggressiveness to claim for the Blakes what was their due. She waited for his reaction.

It was as she hoped. He came back to his chair, and settled to talk, more respectful now, attending to her carefully when she chose to speak. He was arrogant and overbearing, but he was a rich and successful man, the owner of many acres on the Marsh itself, and several large farms around Warefield on its border, where he lived. On farming matters he was worth listening to. He told her where to buy stock, and when the time came, where to sell it, which dealers to go to, which farmers she could trust.

He rose to go. 'You'll do all right,' he said heavily. 'Yes – you'll do all right. I'll confess I laughed when I heard a female had come back here to take over – specially a Blake, for they've not been noted for their common sense in the past. But you'll be all right because you know how to take advice. Now . . . you come to me when you want anything, you hear? I'll tell you what you want to know. Robert Turnbull's well enough in his way, but he doesn't know about farming. Just you send a message, and I'll come along and set you straight on things . . .'

Walking with him to the door, Jane tried to hold her rage in check. He had patronized her, snubbed her, and not once mentioned his wife, Lady Alice, or said that he expected to see Jane at Warefield House. He accepted Patrick's assistance in mounting without thanks. He fixed his eyes on Jane thoughtfully.

'You know,' he said, 'Paul didn't tell me the half of all this . . . you . . . the house . . . No, not even the half of it!' He raised his hat briefly. 'I'll drop in from time to time . . . see how things are with you.'

Jane watched him go, her expression angry and distasteful. 'Pig!' she said. 'You overdressed pig! . . . and I wish you didn't look so much like Paul!'

Her brows knit together as she turned to go indoors. 'And there's something here that's not right . . . he knows more about me than he should, and yet he and Paul pretend they hardly see each other . . .'

The answer occurred to her suddenly, and her eyes widened with comprehension. The pieces fell into place with startling precision. She pondered the possibilities, and they carried too much weight to seem untrue. Was it, she wondered, James Fletcher who was putting up the money to finance Paul's smuggling runs, and that this was the reason Paul had come back to the Marsh? James Fletcher had known his whole financial situation, and when the plantation in the Indies had been lost, and the years in the Navy passed without promotion, had he been the one to wave the money before Paul's eyes, and promise him enough of the spoils of the game to compel him back here even though he hated it? He knew

588   BLAKE'S REACH

Paul's seamanship, his ability to organize – and his crying need
for money to start in trade again. Among the seafaring men of
the Marsh, only Paul could appear at his brother's house without
question or suspicion. He would be the perfect front for a man
who had looked for a way to operate in the smuggling game on a
large scale.

'It's possible,' Jane said aloud. 'It's possible . . . and it may be
true. And that's why the money on the church was raised to
twenty guineas without a fuss – he just couldn't miss the chance
to patronize the Blakes! I wonder did he enjoy sitting here thinking that he was paying the wages of my servants . . . or the cake
he didn't eat! Oh, damn him! . . . the pig!'

She started to gather up the tea-cups, rattling them irritably and
then was annoyed to see that she had managed to chip one of
them. She scowled at the Blake portraits on the wall, the calm
unanswering faces which belonged to her family; for the first time
the sight of them gave her no pleasure.

2

She was not subtle when she took the story of his brother's visit to
Paul. She questioned him bluntly about things she had already
half-guessed.

'So he talked too much, and you could fill in what he didn't say?
Well . . . he always was a fool in dealing with people who weren't
his inferiors, and I suppose coming to Blake's Reach was almost
too much for him, and he had to talk . . .'

'What do you mean?'

Paul shrugged. 'It's an old story . . . some snub Spencer gave
him long ago, and people got to know about it. James looked
like a fool, and he's never forgotten. He's always disliked any
mention of the Blake family – they've been here too long, they've
held too many offices and posts, they've had time to become gentle-
folk, and would have been aristocracy if they'd used their heads
. . . Oh, yes, he thinks about it all, and it rankles. He's even jealous
of that church, and the endowment, and the fact that the Blakes
have the right of presenting a parson to the living there.'

Jane smiled wryly. 'How he must enjoy paying for it as a storeroom for his contraband . . .'

'Of course he does!' Paul snapped. 'He wouldn't give it up if
it cost twice the money . . . it's the kind of stupid joke he enjoys.'

'You dislike him very much, don't you?'

'I could hate him if he were worth sparing the thought and

effort to. We've always been like this – he the elder son with the estate to inherit, and I the poor fool who had to earn his way. He didn't like it when I cleared off to the West Indies . . .'

'But you came back . . . you came back to work for him!'

'Only a greater fool than James himself would have let his feelings stand in the way there. I was in debt, and James knew that. He believed that somehow if he could get me back here, working for him, no matter how much money I earned, I'd never keep it. He believed I'd always be in debt, and that I'd never be able to get back to the Indies. In his mind he saw me here forever – being paid by him, listening to his damn-fool instructions, tipping my hat to him and clicking my heels. The few times he's visited me here he can't believe his eyes . . . he doesn't know what happened to the old Paul, the one who spent money on fourteen silk waistcoats, and Brussels lace for his shirts. He suspects, of course, that I squander it on a fancy woman I keep somewhere – Dover, maybe.

'Most of the time I manage to ignore the fact that he's my brother. I try to think of him as the man who provides the money, and whose commission I take because I've earned it. In seven months here I've paid my debts, and I've put nearly six hundred pounds towards our cargo . . . does that sound as if he's generous! – well, he's not! He knows what he has to pay in commission for my risking my freedom, and perhaps my neck five or six times in the month. He's bought the finest luggers, and he pays the top price for porters . . . and he makes a sweet profit. If I make two runs in a week he can land upwards of two thousand half-ankers of brandy, and seven or eight tons of tea. There's money in that, Jane – money for me, as well as him.'

He ran his hand through his hair, pulling the loose ends from the pigtail. He looked worn and desperate as he talked, and his hands were tense.

'He doesn't know, of course, that I'll go as soon as there's enough money. It's a dirty, ugly business, and I've no mind to go on with it at another man's bidding – least of all my brother's!'

He threw his hands up suddenly. 'Oh, Jane, you don't know what sweet relief it will be to be free of him, to breathe the air again knowing I'm my own master. I walk the decks of his ships, and I hate even the smell of them – *I*, who've loved the sea for longer years than I can remember. For me, there's an odour about my brother James and all his dealings that befouls even the ships he owns . . .'

He brought his clenched fist down into his palm. 'I'll be free,

Jane! . . . just wait a little longer and I'll kick myself free of this
bog he has me in! There's a whole world out there in the Indies
you don't know of yet – there's freedom for a man to be what he
can make himself, self-respect – gold if you've the skill to take it
. . . I mean to get back there if I have to land every one of my
brother's blasted brandy kegs with my own hands!'

3

The daily round of Jane's life was open for the whole Marsh to
see, for Appledore and St Mary's to gossip about over their ale-
pots. The other side of it, secret and hidden, concealed from
curious eyes, was known to herself and Paul Fletcher. It was known
also to Patrick – and it was guessed by Kate Reeve.

Before dawn broke she would leave the house silently, saddle
Blonde Bess, and take the now-familiar route to Old Romney, the
route which Paul had shown her, across the fields and dykes, away
from the roads and cottages and farms, away from the chance of
gossip or speculation. The meetings with Paul were violent with
an ecstasy that was heightened because they were brief and stolen.
Here she entered a world completely apart from the planned
routine of Blake's Reach; this was a world of love and pleasure
and pain, to be lived only in the racing moments between dawn
and the time when the Marsh folk began to stir abroad.

The rides were lonely, and sometimes dangerous as she set off
in the half-dark. But it seemed to Jane that only for the space of
time she spent in Paul's arms did she escape from the sense of
loneliness and struggle; his presence banished consciousness of fear
or time or danger. The memory of being with him sustained her
through each succeeding hour of the day.

At first Paul made an effort to keep her away – and found that
he was weak and powerless to forbid her to come. Long before
dawn he was awake and listening for her. The days she did not
come he counted as lost. He raged against the furtiveness of their
meetings, and yet he knew there was no other way he might see
her. Too many people suspected him of involvement in some way
in smuggling – his solitary existence, the irregularity of his comings
and goings, and above all his knowledge of the Channel and its
ports, of ships and seafaring, of the Marsh itself, were suspect. He
knew there was danger to Jane in an open friendship with him. He
dared to do no more than stand in the stable yard at Blake's
Reach from time to time, ostensibly talking to William and Patrick,
or to bow formally if he and Jane happened to meet in the streets
of Rye. He tried to deny himself the sight of her, and was not able.

She had become an obsession, and he could not discipline himself to stay away from her; he was swept towards her with a fierceness of passion that gave him no peace. Jane was not peace or finality to him; she was pleasure and joy and torment. She was love and she was also despair. She was a volatile, elusive creature, whose body was given to him, whom he did not yet possess; his rival was a crumbling house on the edge of the Marsh, and a worn tradition in which he had no faith. They quarrelled and they loved with equal violence; for neither of them was there victory or defeat.

She came to know that chart-strewn room at Paul's cottage as if it were a territory mapped on her own soul; she knew its dust and untidiness, the books stacked upon its shelves. She watched Paul spin the globe and his fingers trace the names of the Caribbean Islands, while his excited words spun a dream for her of blue-green seas, and a lush vegetation. Paul's clothes carried the smell of salt-water; there was sand in all his pockets, and the cuffs of his sleeves. She rested her face against his shoulder and heard him talk of trade in the Indies, of fortunes won in trade, and how they could be won, and lost again. She smelled the sea-water on his coat, and wanted fiercely to make him look at her, and to forget his dream. For a space of time she could succeed, and he was bound to her closely and strongly; the bright dream faded, and she possessed him and Blake's Reach as well.

But there was bitterness in knowing that she could hold him only with her body; she would cradle his head against her breasts, feel his roughened seaman's hands caress her flat belly and firm thighs, and she knew with all this he was hers only for these moments – a short time of forgetfulness when his will was bent to hers, and that time was limited, and gradually he would awaken and become aware. And in awareness he would draw back from her, resenting the hold she had taken on him, resenting her domination.

'Stay with me,' she would whisper when they were close together, spent and still, a little at peace. 'Stay with me here . . . together we could do so much . . . so much, Paul.'

She could feel the tension of his limbs, and his fingers would bite her flesh with his rejection. 'With you I could build a kingdom . . . anywhere but here!'

And they would draw apart, angry with each other, wanting to deny their love, and yet sick at the thought of a parting. Bitterness and desire grew swiftly for them both, and the strange knowledge that beyond desire there was love.

4

'She's called the *Dolphin*, Jane, and as sweet a craft as I've ever laid eyes on . . . trim and smooth, and as fast as a bird.'

Paul smiled at the recollection; his tone was soft and honeyed, as if he spoke of a woman. They were drinking tea before the fire in Paul's sitting-room; the kettle was steaming gently on the fire-crane. They both knew that in a short time Jane would have to leave, and they were pretending to ignore the fact.

'You've sailed in her?'

He nodded. 'I've put her to sea under Andy Smith. She's on legitimate fishing business, and the Revenue men can board and search her any time they like. All the better if they do, because I've put her out in the Channel to establish an identity as a fishing craft. Let the Revenue men get used to the sight of her . . . but if it ever comes to a chase, she's faster than anything on these seas.'

'I want to see her, Paul!'

He frowned, taking her hand in his and rubbing it gently. 'You know how I feel about that, Jane. You must have no part in all this . . . it's bad enough that you even come to this cottage.'

'But there must be some way to see the *Dolphin* – she must come into port somewhere.'

'Folkestone's her port – and anywhere else along the coast that the Revenue cutters aren't.' He shrugged. 'I don't see why you couldn't get a look at her . . . somewhere hereabouts. I'll think about it . . .'

'If she's at sea, why are you waiting?' Jane demanded. 'Why don't you bring a cargo over now?'

'Easy!' he cautioned. 'Easy . . . these things take time. There have to be contacts, a whole new organization. I'm using a different agent in Flushing, different men as porters here – and have to arrange other landing places and hides for the cargo. The bribes have to be passed out with some discretion. There are a hundred details, and this time I can't afford a slip. This time it's my own money . . .'

'You mean your brother doesn't know!' Her eyebrows shot up. 'You're not using the same men? . . . not buying from the same agent . . . ?'

'He'll smell it out, sooner or later, but I'll keep it from him as long as it's possible. I'll go on doing his work for him, taking the commission until my own operations are big enough so that I can throw his orders back in his face.' He grinned a little. 'Of course,

I won't get much sleep between the two operations, but what's sleep compared to money?'

The time had come for her to go; she rose slowly. 'Why does it matter if he knows? What can he do?'

'He will try to buy out the lugger – demand a slice in the cargo. James is as eager for money as I am, and if he lays eyes on the *Dolphin* – especially if he knows I'm running her – then he will have her. Even for the pleasure of taking her away from me he would have her. He's greedy, is my brother James – and different from the way you and I are greedy, my love.'

She squinted in the cracked and spotted mirror to adjust her hat. Then she turned to him.

'Paul, I want to come with you!'

'Where?'

'When the *Dolphin* makes the run – when they bring the cargo in.'

His face darkened. 'Have you gone mad, Jane? That's no place for you!'

'I've as much right to my place there as you! I want to help – I could act as lookout ... or hold a lamp ...'

He whistled through his teeth. 'You little fool! Do you realize you'd be recognized by the men? If anything went wrong you'd be caught and charged as a common smuggler. This is the most dangerous time of the year, when the twilight is long, and the dawn comes early. It's madness to even think of it.'

'You suppose I'd let myself get caught? – not with Blonde Bess! Your men wouldn't recognize me. I'll borrow Patrick's clothes, and ride astride ...'

'No, Jane!' He caught her roughly by the arm, and hustled her out to the stable; she struggled irritably to shake him off, but he held her, his fingers pinching her skin through the cloth of her habit. He helped her to mount, and then looked up into her angry face.

'Don't forget that I'm master of this operation – and my orders are obeyed! Just don't forget it, Jane!'

He gave Blonde Bess a smack on the rump, and the chestnut moved off smartly. He stood and watched as Jane, all sense of caution and discretion gone, dug her heels in and headed for the fence. In full view of anyone who might have been looking from the village in the direction of Paul's cottage, she put Blonde Bess over the jump. It should have been scrambled and ill-prepared, but somehow it managed not to be. Bess took it with confidence and grace.

'Well,' Paul muttered, looking after her, 'if you don't get yourself hung as a smuggler, you'll surely *break* your neck! You little fool!' He slammed the kitchen door behind him.

'And sweet heaven why did I have to love you!'

She made no attempt to hold Blonde Bess in check after the first jump; the animal became the expression of her rage against Paul. Speed and movement were needed. She wanted to leave the memory of his dictates, wanted to tire herself and exhaust the emotion that she knew was childish and dangerous, and which she could not control. She put Bess recklessly over fences and dykes she could never attempt before, feeling the mare respond instantly to her touch, rejoicing in the way she gathered herself up for each obstacle, and took it without a change of rhythm.

Robert Turnbull was waiting where the road forked to Blake's Reach. He was riding his bay, Roger, a powerful horse, sixteen hands high, and broad in the chest. Robert sat astride him calmly; it was impossible to guess how long he might have been waiting. He raised his hat.

'You jump well, Jane,' he said as she came up beside him.

She was breathing heavily, not pleased to see him and trying to hide it. 'Bess likes it,' she said shortly. 'I have to hold her in . . .'

He smiled. 'Well . . . she's young, too.'

Jane jerked her head abruptly. 'Will you come and have breakfast? – it's only a mile from here . . . ?' She tried to make her tone gracious, and didn't succeed.

'I'd be delighted to,' he said. It wasn't the answer she expected, and she almost betrayed her surprise.

'We'd better hurry, then,' she said. 'Kate's food is bad enough at the best of times, but uneatable when it gets cold.' She urged Bess forward.

He turned Roger and hurried to catch up with her. 'I would ride with you some morning if I knew where you were,' he said. 'Do you come by here often?'

She spurred Bess to a canter. 'I'm here often enough . . . you can ride with me if you find me,' she called back over her shoulder.

With a stifled curse, Robert followed her.

It wasn't the first time they had met on the Marsh early in the morning. She knew it had been Robert's habit for many years to ride before he started the day's business in Watchbell Street. At first she had encountered him in places she expected he would be – generally on a road that led directly to Rye. Then it seemed as if he had started a game of hide and seek with her, appearing in places he would never normally go. And now, today, here he was well past Blake's Reach and on this little-used road that led directly from the house to Old Romney. She was suddenly fearful, dreading to feel these brilliant dark eyes fixed on hers again, fearful of reading in them what he knew.

Robert Turnbull, without appearing to ask for information, seemed to know what went on behind every closed door across the Marsh. It was very possible, she thought, that he also knew she went to see Paul at Old Romney. There was no getting away from the man. Wherever she turned, there he was . . . polite, helpful, kindly. And he seemed to know the thoughts in her head before she had time to form them.

Patrick brewed the chocolate that morning, and it was good. Kate's bread was still warm from the oven, and not yet lumpy. Jane piled honey on it, and her mood began to soften. Robert had been talking of nothing in particular, and her suspicion and tension left her.

Then suddenly he put his cup down; the action, unnecessarily sharp, made her look at him questioningly.

'There's been a great deal of activity on the coast lately . . . and it's late in the season for it.'

'You mean shipping?' she said carefully. 'I thought summer was the best time . . .'

'No, my dear, I mean smuggling. It tapers off, you know, during the summer. These calm clear nights with long twilights give the captains very little time to make their rendezvous on the coast and land the cargo before they're sighted by Revenue cruisers. The Revenue cruisers grow a little more daring, too, with the shorter nights, and besides, there's less excuse for them to lay up in port for bad weather or repairs.'

'Oh . . .' she said faintly, nodding, and striving to hold down the wave of apprehension that swept through her.

'Yes . . .' He gestured to her for permission to use his pipe. Then he began to fill it, deliberately concentrating on it, and looking away from her. 'Yes . . .' he repeated, ' – and the Dragoons become more co-operative with the Riding Officers during this season. On a winter's night they don't enjoy the discomfort of chasing smugglers they're not sure are there at all. But of course, if they capture a cargo they share the proceeds, and it's not a bad sport for a summer's night. They'd be a great deal more use to the Revenue if only the poor fools would realize that it's in their own interest to make sure the Dragoons always got their fair share of the spoils. There's discontent over that question . . . which, of course, is an aid to the smugglers.'

He looked at her from behind the light haze of smoke.

'Do you see much of Paul Fletcher, Jane?' It was lightly spoken.

She shrugged, not so much afraid now that the question had come into the open, but she wondered how much Robert knew, and how much he should be answered.

'Oh . . .' she said, '. . . I see him now and then. He has rather an attachment to William. He brought him some white mice when we first came. When he's passing he sometimes comes into the stable. He tried to give me advice on the vegetable plot . . .' She added quickly, 'I told you, I think, that Sir James Fletcher came here . . .'

He waved the last aside. 'Sir James being here isn't important. Whatever he is or isn't behind that bombast, he's a respected man in these parts – I should know, because I handle his affairs. But Paul – that's another matter . . .'

She drummed the table with her finger tips. 'Yes . . . ?'

'Let's look at it as people like myself see it, Jane. Paul Fletcher lost money in the Indies, and comes back here, penniless and in debt, to a place that he's known to dislike. He gave it out that he was making charts of the Caribbean . . . well, and good, except that we know he can't make any money from that.'

'So . . . ?'

'So he has all the qualities needed to make an extremely successful smuggler! He's learned organization and discipline from the Navy, he's intelligent and – I imagine – brave. He's a good sailor, and knows every inch of this coast. And from a small boy he's been a leader . . . he's made even his brother seem slow and a trifle dull . . . for which, of course, Sir James hasn't forgiven him!'

'So . . .' she measured her words carefully. '. . . So you think Paul Fletcher is responsible for the increased smuggling this season?'

He shrugged. 'A guess, my dear . . . only a guess, but I've shown you the reasons why I think as I do. He's daring . . . not reckless, but daring . . . and I'm afraid he'll be caught.'

'And do you tell this to everyone?' she said sharply. 'Do you tell enough people so that however lazy or frightened the Preventive Officers are they'll have to make some effort to catch him? Is that what you do, Robert?'

He shook his head. 'My thoughts and deductions are only for you, Jane. You're so new here . . . and rumour and gossip take little account of the truth, as Anne learned. I would not like to see the Blake name involved . . .'

She stood up. 'Are you the conscience of this family? Are you its guardian . . . or are you waiting to see the final end of it?'

'Jane!'

'Do I understand you? Are you saying that Sir James, who's a bully and a braggart, may come into my drawing-room, but that Paul may not stand in the stable yard for fear the sacred Blake name might be contaminated?'

He rose also, shrugging again. 'Make of it what you will! There's nothing more for me to say!'

They looked at each other, silently. There was a challenge now between them, and even this, strangely, drew them closer.

5

Behind them Jane and Paul could hear the horses pulling at the sparse grass that grew on the sand dunes; compact grey clouds had closed in overhead and the Channel was flecked with white-caps. They crouched in the shelter of a steep bank, and Jane reached out to take the glass from Paul.

'There she is, Jane – the *Dolphin*! And as pretty a thing as I've seen . . .'

Jane swung the heavy glass, and could see nothing but the suddenly magnified grey swell; then there was the horizon and the darkening sky. She dropped it briefly, sighted the distant lugger again, then put it back to her eye. Suddenly the light, graceful lines of the vessel sprang up to meet her. She watched the slow plunge and dip; the sails seemed curiously white against the grey backdrop. Her hull was painted black, and the long bowsprit was red. She tried to count the gunports, then the glass tilted and focused on the name lettered in gold – *Dolphin*.

She gave a short gasp of excitement.

'One hundred and thirteen tons burthen,' Paul said. 'Twelve guns, not counting the swivels, and thirty hands. I'll take on thirty or forty more men for the passage to Flushing. That should be enough to handle the cargo quickly, and with good weather the *Dolphin* will be back here in two – maybe three – days.'

'Where will the extra men come from?' she said, flexing her arms to ease the weight of the glass.

'Swing over landwards to the right. That village there – got it? – that's Barham-in-the-Marsh. Most of the extra men will come from there, and that's where I'll unload the cargo . . . unless the Preventive Officers are waiting for it too.'

She moved the glass over it carefully. It was a village of grey stone, grey slate roofs touched in places with moss, whitewashed doors, and nets the colours of seaweed spread to dry. It lay in a crescent around a shallow indent, and upturned fishing boats were drawn in on the shingle. Wooden breakwaters ran downwards from high watermark across the shingle and disappeared into the surf. Broad-winged gulls wheeled over the roof tops and around the grey square-towered church. The cottages, the church walls, the cobblestoned street had been pitted by a thousand storms sweeping in from the Channel. Here no trees could survive the winds; over to the west she saw the finger of the Dungeness foreland poking out into the sea.

'I've got labourers coming from some of the farms round Lydd – over there to the west. They'll help unload the small boats and lead the horses. The hide is over by Ivychurch, or if that road isn't safe, we'll make for a place just this side of Hythe.

'The *Dolphin*'s been fishing this water now for a couple of days,' he added. 'There shouldn't be anything new for the Revenue cruisers in the sight of her hove-to off this shore.'

'How close in will she come?'

'I can't risk her closer than a half-mile off shore. She draws too much to make it safe. The shingle bars build up around here, and keep shifting.'

'How many boats from the village will you use?'

'All of them. Practically the whole village will help – even the women. We'll signal the *Dolphin* from the church tower.'

She put down the glass, turning to him. 'Aren't you afraid someone will inform? If the whole village knows . . . ?'

He looked at her sideways, faintly amused. 'There are hundreds of villages along this coast-line that support themselves on smuggling, and an informer has a pretty sorry time. Those among them who don't like it, take care to keep their windows shut tight and the blankets over their ears.'

He laughed then, at the concern in her face. 'Don't worry, Jane – it's a discreet little village. It's been handling contraband cargoes for as long as it's stood there.'

He got to his feet, and put out his hand to help her.

'You must be on your way now. I'll guide you back to the road, but I won't come farther than that. There's no sense in us being seen riding together – besides, I should turn back to Barham. There are one or two people I must see again before the *Dolphin* leaves for Flushing.'

Jane rose reluctantly, handing back the telescope. 'Will she leave soon?'

He scanned the sea and the heavy grey sky. 'Just pray that this weather holds on – as dark as it can. It's any time now, Jane. As soon as I have news of the plans of the Revenue cruisers the *Dolphin* will be on her way.'

She turned back to look once more at the small spread of canvas, which was all she could now see of the *Dolphin*. She gestured briefly with her hand, a half-wave, half-salute.

'There goes my luck and my fortune – well may she ride !'

9

The streets of Folkestone were beginning to empty, and the long shadows were reaching across the cobblestones. People were hurrying now, where they had strolled an hour earlier. Most of them were making towards home and supper, and those who weren't, like herself, had an idle, purposeless air. Reluctantly Jane turned away from the display of discreetly trimmed hats in a milliner's window; Patrick would be waiting with the carriage at The Wool Pack, and there was no further excuse to keep her in the town.

Sheer restlessness had drawn her away from Blake's Reach this afternoon to visit this port, where the shipping packed into the harbour and the bright coats of the Dragoons flecked the crowd. She could see the line of mast-heads down by the harbour, with the gulls wheeling above them; the smell of fish and salt water was strong. Mingling with the crowds had stifled her restlessness for a time, as she responded to the noise and the movement about her. But her few purchases had been made long ago; the sun was dropping behind the chimneys and the tempo had slowed. Now the shops were emptying, and the ale-houses came into their own, their windows lighted, their doors open to the summer twilight and the passers-by.

It was four days since she had been on the sand dunes near Barham-in-the-Marsh with Paul – and she had not seen him since then. Twice in the early morning she had gone to Old Romney, to wait hopefully until the sun was high and full before returning to Blake's Reach. She reasoned that Paul's increased activity could mean only one thing – that the *Dolphin* had at last turned and headed for Flushing, and that almost at any hour now she could be expected back off the English coast. The full meaning of Paul's refusal to allow her any active part in the run came home to her now; it was hard to bear the knowledge of her own helplessness, to realize how little she mattered now to success or failure. She

faced the thought unwillingly, and Kate and Patrick had had to
bear the brunt of her displeasure. Even William sensed her mood
and kept out of the way – making a vague excuse when she
suggested driving into Folkestone. She had gone by herself – aloof
and lonely in the carriage, missing William's talk, and haughtily
refusing to let Patrick come with her as she made her tour of the
town. She was slightly ashamed and ill at ease now as she made
her way back to The Wool Pack, and obsessed with the feeling
that every other person but herself had somewhere to go. Her
footsteps lagged, although she kept her head held stiffly and erect.

It was a relief to see Robert Turnbull standing beside the carriage
outside The Wool Pack. He was chatting amiably with Patrick,
and he broke off as he saw her.

'My dear Jane . . . !' Now he was smiling broadly. 'It was such
a pleasant surprise when I recognized the carriage . . .'

'Yes, I had some shopping . . .' The sight of him had never
been so welcome before. She found herself smiling unrestrainedly
back at him.

'I was going to have supper here before starting back to Rye,'
he said. 'Could you stay and share it with me? The food here is
good . . .'

'Why, yes!' she said at once, beaming at him. 'There's nothing
I'd like more.' And it was true – except for the fact that she
wanted to know above anything what was happening to the
Dolphin. A grin immediately appeared on Patrick's face; it pleased
him to know he would have a few hours of ale and gossip in the
tap-room; but for him the best thing was to see the smile return
to Jane's face.

The inn was crowded. But Robert Turnbull was well known
there, and he hailed the innkeeper confidently. The man shook
his head apologetically as he explained there were no private rooms
left. With lips pursed in annoyance, Robert took Jane's arm and
was about to turn away. It was unthinkable to him that Jane would
eat in a public room.

'Your pardon, sir!'

Robert halted. 'Well – what is it?'

'There is a small dining-room, Mr Turnbull, that has only one
other party in it. I'm sorry I can't offer you better, sir – but the
other party are very quiet. All ladies and gentlemen, they are.'

'Oh, well . . . in that case.' Robert turned to Jane, who nodded
quickly. Not for good reason would she be cheated now of dining
at the inn with the sound of people's voices pleasantly about her,
and a blessed escape from Kate's cooking. She urged him forward
firmly.

'It will do very well,' she said crisply.

The innkeeper seated them at a table that gave a view of the crowded masts of the harbour; the sun was rosy on the still waters. But their attention went immediately to the group who sat about the table before the fireplace. Even though they had fallen silent, there was no mistaking the foreignness of those faces; they were wary and strained, but in every gesture as they ate they proclaimed that they were not English. Robert bowed to them formally before pouring wine for Jane. But his eyes flickered over to them many times as he sipped his first glass.

The innkeeper came himself to carve the duck and a side of mutton. Jane's lips twitched hungrily as she smelled the applesauce and the mint jelly; she held her glass towards Robert again, preparing to enjoy the wine and food; pleasantly aware that the *Dolphin* and Paul were slipping to the back of her mind.

It was annoying then, to hear Robert softly question the innkeeper about the strange group, six of them, who sat at the second table.

'Frenchies, sir!' the innkeeper said, pausing with the carvers held high. Then he leaned closer to them. '*Emigrés*,' he added in a whisper that was too loud. 'Just got in. Making for London by tomorrow's coach.'

At this single word uttered in their own tongue, the heads of all six immediately turned. They regarded Jane and Robert firmly, their faces showing a mixture of apprehension and fear. Robert set down his wine and rose, bowing again.

'Mesdames . . . Messieurs.'

In response the men of the party, four of them, also rose, executing bows that for nicety and precision were wildly out of place in that simply furnished room of an English seaport inn. Jane caught her breath sharply, and she was aware of sudden pain in her chest. With hostile eyes she examined in turn those foreign faces that were even now dissolving into smiles as they listened to Robert Turnbull. She looked at each of them minutely, carefully, as if daring one of them to assume the recognizable features of a Blake.

When she was satisfied she turned her attention, with growing wonder, to Robert. Not for the first time she was surprised by the extent of his knowledge. The phrases that came quite readily to his tongue were French. She didn't know that the people opposite shuddered privately at the horrors of their language as spoken by an Englishman; once again she was filled with the sense that the full extent of Robert Turnbull's personality, the quiet and modest country attorney of Rye, would never be known to her.

Now the strangers were talking, breaking in upon each other in their eagerness. From their sighs and despairingly raised eyebrows, their elaborate shrugs, Jane knew that they were describing their experiences – though it wasn't clear to her whether they were complaining of seasickness or imprisonment. She inclined her head frigidly as Robert presented her, '. . . *Madame la Comtesse . . . Madame de . . . Monsieur de . . .*' acknowledging the introduction to each in turn, conscious as she did so that the eyes of the two women rested on her gown and hat with frank curiosity. She was irritated with Robert for continuing the talk – she didn't want to hear, even in a tongue she didn't understand, of revolution and flight and death. Then at last she heard the words her ears had been straining for. Robert spoke Charles Blake's name.

Now her eyes darted from one to the other frantically, waiting for an expression to change, a look of recognition to come. One by one they shook their heads. She breathed easily again.

Then one of the women suddenly broke into animated talk, her sallow, handsome face wrinkled with an effort of concentration.

'*Lentement, Madame . . .*' Robert gestured for her to slow her pace to allow him to follow. Jane lived the next moments in an agony of suspense. Charles Blake's name was used many times. Then came the last expressive shrug, the final shake of the head.

Jane tugged at Robert's sleeve imploringly. 'Tell me . . .!'

He looked at her, and now he also shook his head. 'Nothing . . . nothing we didn't know before. They don't remember him at Court, but they knew his kinsman, the Marquis. The lady who spoke . . . the Countess . . . recalls him in prison. She says she remembers that he had an English name. She was in Paris in prison at the same time.'

'What's she doing here?'

'She was released – over a year ago, I think she said. It is difficult for me to follow exactly. She went south to the château of her friend, Madame de Marney, and posed as her child's nurse until they learned that the de Marneys were about to be denounced and imprisoned. Then they had to flee with whatever they could carry with them . . . the child died on the journey.'

'And the others . . . ?' Jane said.

'*Emigrés* they met up with in Dunkirk.'

'Do they know what has happened to Charles?'

Again he shook his head. 'More than a year since she's heard of him – and even there he was one among many. She described him, though – dark and tall, as I fancy he must be now. Handsome, she said . . .' Then Robert smiled a trifle. 'She says he does not look like an Englishman.'

The conversation seemed to be exhausted; Robert turned his attention back to Jane. In subdued voices the other group began to talk among themselves. Jane picked through her food dully, and drank the wine with complete indifference; the sound of those French voices across the room unnerved her. She was aware of nothing except that Charles seemed very near – a stranger full of menace.

Then one single word of Robert's penetrated her daze. 'What?' she said suddenly, lifting her head. 'What was that?'

'The Dragoons, my dear,' he said patiently. 'I was speaking about the Dragoons.'

'Yes? . . . what about them?'

'Their commander, Leslie, is a good friend of mine. He's a man from these parts – I have handled some affairs for his family . . . and so, whenever we meet we generally take some time to share a glass of wine or ale.'

'Yes . . . yes,' she said impatiently.

Turnbull shrugged. 'Nothing of importance, my dear . . . I was just talking so that you might remember that I'm here.'

'I'm sorry . . . it's those people . . .'

He smiled, and went on. 'Leslie was grumbling because he'd have to turn out tonight. They're expecting trouble . . . smuggling trouble, I would guess, from the sound of it. Of course Leslie didn't say exactly . . . even he could hardly be so indiscreet. But I judge from his lack of enthusiasm that he's expecting an all-night affair, and the Dragoons have never looked on chasing smugglers with much enthusiasm. The Revenue people frequently find it convenient not to pay them their split of the cargo when it's captured. After a time the Dragoons don't make very willing helpers.'

'But it *is* tonight?' she insisted.

He laid down his glass. 'Yes . . . why?'

She shrugged weakly, the corner of her mouth twitching even with her effort at control.

'Oh . . . nothing. I must remember to draw my curtains tight, and not hear anything on the road.'

He said lightly, 'If the Dragoons are out, I wouldn't advise you to ride too early on the Marsh tomorrow morning. You may meet the stragglers – from either side.' From then onwards it seemed that the meal dragged to an interminable length.

2

Robert even insisted upon riding back to Blake's Reach with her,
although the sea-road to Rye was much shorter than circling the
Marsh as he would have to do. He barely listened to her protests
– just hitched Roger to the back of the carriage, and then joined
her inside.

'It's purely selfish, Jane,' he said as he settled himself. 'The fact
that the Dragoons anticipate trouble tonight gives me the pleasure
of riding with you, and at the same time imagining that I'm
protecting you.' He laughed as he spoke.

'Protecting me!' Jane shrugged. 'These days I have so much
protection I hardly know what to do with it. It's not like the old
days at The Feathers – nobody fussed much about me then, but I
never came to any harm.'

He nodded. Lights from the open windows they passed fell
across his face briefly, highlighting the firm, broad bones; now it
was a sardonic and amused face.

'You'll forgive me speaking so, Jane – but these are some of the
disadvantages of being a lady. She's expected to be as delicate as
air, and yet strong enough to bear the pain of childbirth, to manage
and run a house with skill and economy, but not intelligent enough
to bother her husband – and she has to ride in a stuffy carriage
on a summer's night flanked by men putting irksome restrictions
on her, when her feet may be itching to get out and walk . . .'

'She can also lie abed on a winter's morning,' Jane broke in.
'And she needn't soil her hands from one day to the next.'

'And what about yours, Jane – don't they get stiff with the dirt
of the vegetable plot, and scratched with the rose thorns?'

'And they'll be scratched for as long as they have to be,' she
answered shortly. 'Blake's Reach can't afford a lady yet.'

He did not reply, and they rode in silence for some time. The
summer's night was fine, with a light wind blowing that whispered
in the trees and the hedgerows. They left the lights of Folkestone
behind; there was a faint moon, a waning moon which deepened
the shadows. Low on the horizon was a mass of clouds, and Jane
watched them carefully as they rode. There seemed no movement
there, no sign that they would slip forward to hide the moon. If
the *Dolphin* were to land tonight there was danger in that pale
light. She was thankful for the silence and the darkness within
the carriage, which made it unnecessary to keep the anxiety from
her face and voice. She leaned farther back into the shadows and

hoped that Robert would have nothing more to say.

Their peace was shattered on the outskirts of Hythe. Here the roads divided — one led to Appledore, the other cut across the Marsh to the coast. Outside the first ale-house in Hythe's main street they were hailed.

'Hold there! Hold in the name of His Majesty!'

Robert muttered something under his breath, and lowered the window. They could hear Patrick curse, and his voice rose loudly in complaint. '. . . nothin' but a bloody edjit to be lepin' out at the horses this way . . .'

Robert cut in. 'Who is it? . . . what does this mean?'

Two men came forward, the first of them carrying a lantern which he raised above his head to examine the occupants of the carriage.

'His Majesty's Customs.' Then the lamp held near to Robert's face. 'Why, it's Mr Turnbull! . . . Jack, it's Mr Turnbull!'

'I can see that,' the other man growled. 'An' you'd best let me handle the lamp in future if you don't want us both run down.'

Robert looked from one to the other. 'What's the trouble?'

'Nothin's the trouble, sir . . . leastways not yet.'

'Well, then . . . ?' he prompted.

'Well, Mr Turnbull, we were stoppin' the carriage to ask if you'd seen any movement on the road out of Folkestone. The Dragoons, I mean, sir.'

'No . . . none. Are you waiting for them?'

The man swore softly. 'All of three hours, sir . . . with it gettin' darker by the minute.' He swayed a little as he spoke, and clutched the arm of his companion. 'We're stuck here and darsant move for fear we'll miss the soldiers, and they'll go to the wrong place.'

Robert's manner became relaxed. He opened the door of the carriage, and leaned out. He gave the first man a light tap on the shoulder. 'Now look, George . . . I've known you long enough to know that you think strange things with a drop inside you. Are you sure the Dragoons were meeting you here? I was speaking earlier to Major Leslie . . .'

The man broke in with protests of injured dignity. 'This *is* the place, sir, and we can't go on by ourselves because the landing place's been changed . . . leastways we've picked up information which makes us think it has. We heard of a cargo coming in at Barham, and now we think it's been changed to Langley, this side of Dymchurch . . .'

'Is it really tonight, George . . . are you sure that's not a mistake, also? From what I hear there's a cargo run in most nights of the week along here.'

George spat on the ground in disgust. 'Not this time o' year, there ain't. This one's in a hurry – an' it's a big cargo. An' if those perishin' fools what call themselves soldiers don't show up, we'll miss the lot.' His voice took on a tone of wailing complaint. 'There's only two of us . . . and I reckon there could be mor'an a hundred owlers. We darsant go near 'em if the Dragoons don't show.'

'They'll be along in due course,' Robert said. 'They're not likely to set out so early as to give the lugger and the captain warning and a chance to clear off.' He closed the door again. 'Just you stay out of the ale-house until they come. After all, you can't expect a landing for a few hours yet.'

'Tide'll turn early enough, sir – if she's a big lugger she'll need to keep it with her.'

Turnbull shrugged. 'Well, these are things I've no experience of. I'll bid you good night now, and advise you to be more cautious with that lantern. You might have frightened the horses badly.'

They shifted about apologetically. 'We didn't recognize the carriage or pair, sir. 'Tain't usual to see a strange carriage here-abouts travellin' as late as this . . .'

'This carriage belongs to Miss Howard,' Turnbull said briefly. 'Miss Howard is the granddaughter of Spencer Blake, and is now living at Blake's Reach. I'm sure you'll recognize it in future and give Miss Howard any assistance she may need.'

The lantern went high again. Two hats were pulled off sheep-ishly, as they ducked in semblance of awkward bows. 'To be sure, Miss Howard . . .' and, 'Welcome to the Marsh, Mistress . . . I remember your mother. Most folk on the Marsh remember her.'

As they drove on again, Jane could hear Robert's tongue click disapprovingly; he shook his head.

'No wonder smuggling has such an easy time of it when they're the sort who go into the Revenue service . . . the pay's wretched, and most of the time they know they're against hopeless odds. I imagine in their place I'd stick to the ale-house, too.'

'Do you think the Dragoons will come?' she said faintly.

'In time, I suppose. Then they'll argue and finally decide where they'll go and look for the lugger. And by this time everyone in the ale-house knows their plans, and I'm certain the smugglers do as well.'

'You think so?'

'Almost certain – most people on the Marsh would rather hinder a Revenue man than help him, and they can pass the word along with greater speed than you'd believe. This game is hundreds of years old, Jane, and so far the smugglers have managed to stay ahead of the Revenue.'

She licked her lips, feeling the sweat break all over her body. She thought of Paul gathering his men quietly to await the lugger, watching and cursing the moon. She imagined the forms of men stumbling in the darkness under the weight of brandy casks, and then the faint jingle of harness as the soldiers rode, with the moon striking on their muskets. Robert was certain that the word had been passed along – but had it been passed? If the cargo was captured she was not only penniless, but in debt, condemned to fighting a hopeless battle against the ruin of Blake's Reach, and with it, herself. And for Paul it was the end of the dream of escape. Did he know that? – *did he know?*

She looked across at Robert. 'How do you know so much of what goes on on the Marsh – those Revenue men, you knew them, didn't you? And the Captain of Dragoons . . . and everyone else, I think.'

He shrugged. 'I have time to know them, Jane. I've been here for many years, and many people have come to me in trouble. But it's not only those who sit in my office I know. I like to ride, and a man alone out here on the Marsh observes a great deal, and makes many acquaintances – some of them strange ones. I see a labourer's wife with a swollen belly, and pretty soon I can lean over the garden gate and admire the new baby – and maybe I have some toy for it to play with. I travel constantly between these towns all over the fringe of the Marsh, and I eat where my fancy takes me – I don't care whether it's The Wool Pack with Johnson's best wine, or bread and cheese at an ale-house. People know that a man without wife or child of his own can spare time for them and their problems. They know there's nothing waiting for me in Rye but a housekeeper who daren't open her mouth against the irregular hours I keep. And if the dinner she cooks is spoiled, then it's spoiled – and as long as I pay for it, I'm the one who'll say how it's to be disposed of.'

'A free man . . .' Jane murmured.

He shrugged. 'As free as man can be . . . and as empty.'

After that they sat through the miles to Blake's Reach and did not speak, each completely wrapped in thoughts that were their own, and not to be shared. The heavy clouds crept slowly on the horizon; sometimes a light wisp darkened the moon. The willows along the dykes swayed and sighed. Out on the Marsh somewhere a dog howled. At Appledore the elms were stiff against the moon; the scents of summer were in the air, the heavy smell of flowers, and sweat, and dry crops in the fields. For Jane, the scene was touched with melancholy, a strange static feeling of deadness before some momentous action. She found herself at times holding her breath; it would have been a comfort, she thought, to reach out and touch Robert's hand, but she did not. Mostly she thought about Paul. If the lugger they talked of was the *Dolphin*, Paul was a few miles from here, and in danger. Perhaps it was danger he knew of, and had deliberately counted and calculated the risk. She considered all the other nights he had been in danger, and realized that only this one seemed real to her; always before it had been an anonymous, unknown danger in which she could not share. Now she had seen the *Dolphin*, lovely and built for a purpose; she had seen the village where the boats would land. Danger now had a shape, an identity, and a place.

She was frightened, badly frightened – and for the moment, quite helpless. The carriage turned up the hill to Blake's Reach.

Robert lingered to share a glass of wine with her. They sat in Spencer's sitting-room – altered now, somewhat, neater, but still his room, a frowning place. It was while she sat twisting the glass, drinking little, that the idea came to her. She wondered why she had not thought of it before, and then knew how strongly Paul's wishes had rested on her. The feel of life began to flow through her again, a tingling in her veins, a heightened sense of time passing.

She shifted impatiently in her seat.

Robert looked at her, and then rose. 'Yes, Jane – I'll go now. I'm quite well aware that for the past five minutes I've not been here at all as far as you knew or cared.'

Then suddenly he leaned over and kissed her fully on the mouth, a firm, hard kiss with no tenderness in it.

'I can kiss you now because it doesn't matter to you. When you slip off into your own thoughts, Jane, don't forget that I'm a man, and you are a very desirable woman.'

Then he turned and left her.

3

When Robert left her, Jane sat for some moments, even though each minute was important to her. She pressed her fingers to her lips feeling Robert's hard, angry kiss again. There wasn't time to think of all he had meant to convey in the kiss and his words, but she felt ashamed, and sad that he should have had to say these things to her. Then she rose, trying to pull her wits about her, and called to Patrick.

'Is Kate in bed?'

'Ay, she is – and snorin' fit to shake the rafters.'

'Good! – then . . .' She broke off. 'Patrick, pay attention to everything I have to say, and remember it! First of all, I think the Revenue men have caught up with Paul Fletcher. They've got wind of a cargo coming in tonight, and I'm certain Paul is landing it. I have to warn him. I have to go to him.'

A look of horror froze on Patrick's features. 'Blessed saints, you might get caught yourself!'

'Not with Blonde Bess.' She moved closer to him. 'I have to go! . . . I've put five hundred pounds of Robert Turnbull's money in that cargo, and I've no thought to see the man I love dragged off to prison.' She gripped his arm. 'Patrick, this night is everything for us – you, as well as myself. If it comes off we stay at Blake's Reach, we start to live, with real gold jingling in our pockets, and no bills unpaid. If we lose, we're worse off than we've ever been, and I've no skill at a card table.'

'Mistress, dear,' he said in a low tone, 'I'll not have you expose yourself like this. I'll go, Mistress – I'll take the message.'

She shook her head. 'You don't know the Marsh well enough – you'd be lost, and might be captured. You don't know the place where they're bringing the cargo ashore. It would be madness, and a waste for you to go. Now, quickly, saddle up Blonde Bess!'

A pleading frown came to his face. 'Mistress, just stop a little. If you go there – to wherever the landing is – you'll be in danger you haven't looked to yet. You'll be seen by more than Mr Fletcher. Some of the men will see you, even dark as it is. There aren't many ladies hereabouts that ride alone on the Marsh, and they'll start to guess. Would you have it known among a gang of smugglers that you were one of them?'

'I am one of them,' she said soberly, 'and tonight I'll earn my place there – but they won't know it! I'm going to wear your breeches and shirt, Patrick, and bind my hair up. With any luck they'll never see me in the light, and they'll never know who the strange boy was.'

He shook his head. 'And if the dawn comes, Mistress – what then?'

'I'll plan for that when the time comes. If I'm not back here when the house starts stirring, you're to tell Kate I'm indisposed, and lying abed, and be sure you leave a window open for me at the front of the house . . .' She ran her hand distractedly across her forehead. 'Heaven help me, there's a hundred details . . . you'll

have to think your way around them if anything goes wrong.' Then
she gripped his arm. 'Wish me luck, Patrick – and I'll be lying safe
abed by the time the sun touches our roof.'

He saddled Blonde Bess, and watched her go, cold and sick
with fear for her. She had looked surprisingly slight in his old
breeches and stockings, and the shirt with the sleeves rolled to
the elbows. Her hair was bound up in a cloth in the way sailors
wore it, and she had darkened her face and hands with soot from
the chimney. Over all that she had wrapped the ragged cloak
Kate wore outdoors in the yard in bad weather. Only the tips of
her boots showed beneath it. When she was finished she looked a
fearful sight; she didn't in any way, he thought, resemble her
mother now. Now she looked like some sexless spawn of the
London gutter, an evil and desperate creature for whom he could
feel no love. Miserably he saw her disappear into the darkness.

She headed towards Barham-in-the-Marsh riding astride on Jed's
saddle. It was a relief to feel the strong rhythm of Blonde Bess's
frame under her, to know the time of inaction was past. She wasn't
sure that she would find Paul or the *Dolphin* at Barham, but it was
nearer than Langley. At the back of her mind was the question
of what she would do if Barham was deserted – Langley lay somewhere over beyond Dymchurch; she had never seen it, and never
been there. There was also the thought that Langley was much
nearer to Folkestone, and that perhaps the Dragoons were already
there. She touched her heels smartly to Bess's sides.

She rode with head bent, making the best pace she dared on
those roads. The clouds had moved up from the horizon; heavy
drifts blotted out the moon intermittently.

'Paul will welcome it,' she muttered, watching the faint light
on the road ahead fade as a cloud with a heavy underside of rain
moved across it . . . 'But it could mean a broken neck for me!'

She pushed on, surprised to feel her body cold, although the
wind did not seem strong. The road that forked to Rye was left
behind, and vaguely, in short spells of moonlight, she could see the
tower of Lydd church ahead.

'Move, Bess! . . . move, sweetheart!' she whispered, leaning low
to the mare's ear.

Lydd was silent and shuttered, the church dark behind the
screen of elms. She listened fearfully to the clatter Bess's hoofs
made against the cobbles; she urged Bess to greater speed to carry
them away from the menace of those still houses. They were free
of the town at last, and Barham lay ahead. Soon she caught the

smell of the sea, the smell and tang that conveyed a sense and a memory of Paul to her; soon she would hear it – and hearing it remember that for Paul it was the sound of freedom. As her straining ears caught the vague, distant murmur, a new thought came. Abruptly she slowed Bess to a walk.

If the *Dolphin* lay off Barham and Paul intended to unload it here, there would be look-outs posted. It was possible that there would be a road-barrier, or if warning of the Dragoons had reached Paul, there might even be a trip wire stretched across the road. The thought of what it could do to Bess's legs frightened her; she slipped down and took the bridle to lead the mare.

The deep quiet remained unbroken; there were no lights and nothing seemed to move in the town ahead. The thickening clouds parted for a moment. She scrambled up on a stony dune to get a vantage point from which she might catch a glimpse of the *Dolphin*. Briefly she saw the empty expanse of the moonlit Channel, before the clouds closed up once more. It was then she heard the sound she had been waiting for – the crunch of heavy boots against the hard ground.

Except for that one sound they were silent – and speedy. Bess's reins were pulled from her hand at the same moment that a strong pair of arms pinioned her own. Her short cry was stifled by a hand clapped over her mouth – a hand that had the ageless smell of the sea worn into it. She could feel them looming above her in the darkness; there were two of them, and a third who held Bess. She knew then the first moment of true fear that night. There seemed nothing that would stop the blow that would knock her unconscious so that they could bind her wrists and ankles with ease and speed.

She took the only way of saving herself. Wriggling desperately, she half turned so that the free hand of the man who held her encountered the full roundness of her breasts under Patrick's thin shirt. He paused in only an instant's hesitation; then he ripped the shirt open to the waist and she felt the calloused palms explore her bare skin.

She heard his swift intake of breath. 'Fer Christ's sake . . . Hold it, Tim! Bring the lantern!'

The man who held Bess brought out a lantern from the folds of his cloak. Three sides of the glass were blackened, so that the light could be cut off by holding the fourth side against his body.

"Ere! You feel this 'ere, Tim!' And then another hand was on her, a hand that after a second of surprise, began to fondle her with rough eagerness, so that even in her fear she felt her nipples rise and harden.

"Old the lantern up! . . . No! – turn it away from the sea, y'
fool!'

They lifted the lantern cautiously, and she felt the cloth pulled
off her head. Her hair fell heavily about her shoulder.

'A girl! Fer Christ's sake! – a girl!'

'Well, watdidya think, with them two pointin' at yer. Or meby
y' was thinkin' t' look further. Meby down here . . .' He put his
hand on the belt Jane had hitched around Patrick's trousers.

'Cut it out, y' fool. This ain't no whorehouse – this 'ere's business.'

'I wouldn't mind doin' a bit o' business with this one right now.
I'll be bound she wouldn't be unwillin' too long. Not from wot I
felt . . . and these red-heads get wild.'

'Shut yer mouth! We don't even know 'oo she is – or wat she's
doin' 'ere.'

'Well, ask 'er! Take yer big paw away, an' ask 'er!'

He removed his hand from her mouth, though he still held both
her arms tightly behind her back.

'Co-mon, now. Spit it out! – whyarya 'ere?'

She took a deep breath and pitched her voice to the slower
sing-song tone heard in the kitchen of The Feathers.

'Take yer filthy big mitts off o' me, and take me to Paul Fletcher.
I'll 'ave a thing or two t' say about the way the men he hires do
their jobs, y' no-good bunch o' slobs . . .' She followed it with a
string of obscenities that the stable-hands at The Feathers would
have admired.

"Ere! You shut yer mouth, y' filthy little bitch. 'Oo says we can
take y' to Paul Fletcher! 'E ain't 'ereabouts!'

'Aw, come orf it,' she said. 'I know 'e's 'ere, an' I've got a
message t' deliver to 'im!'

"Oo sent y'?'

She had her answer ready. 'Adam Thomas – y' know Adam
Thomas, of Appledore!'

'Then y' ain't speakin' the truth! Adam Thomas ain't been in
these parts fer months past.'

'D'ya think *I* don't know that! I'm a cousin o' his – Liza
Thomas's me name. I live beyond the Marsh, up towards Tenterden a bit, and when 'e cleared out a few months back, I took a
notion t' go with 'im. We been in London – together. An' now
Adam's all fixed to slip across the Channel to Roscoff as an agent
for a gentleman as I won't mention now. 'E and me – we're goin'
together. An' 'e picked up this information, and I'm carryin' it t'
Paul Fletcher. An' y'll kindly get out o' me way, or Mr Fletcher'll
likely pin yer ears back when 'e knows what I've t' tell 'im.'

She looked at them challengingly, daring them to defy her confidence. They looked uncertainly from one to the other, then she felt the grip on her arms slacken.

'There! That's more like it!' she said, looking at the circle of wary faces. She drew the shirt back across her bosom, fumbling for the missing buttons.

'An' y' can just lower that lantern now, because y've all looked yer fill. That sight's only for those as 'as gold to jingle in their pockets. An' if y'll just lead me now to Mr Fletcher, I'll say nothin' more about what y' done t' me.'

They exchanged glances. 'Well, can't do no 'arm – an' she's better under our eye than lettin' 'er go . . .'

'Seems fishy t' me. Ain't never 'eard of Adam Thomas an' Paul Fletcher gettin' together . . .'

'An' why should y'!' she retorted. 'Since when 'as Mr Paul Fletcher taken to discussin' his affairs with the likes o' you three?' She wrapped her cloak about her. 'Come now – git movin'. I'm not a patient woman, as y'll find out if y' delay me any longer.'

Mistrustful, sullen, they yielded then. 'Well – com'on, then! Tim, y'd best stay to keep look-out, and we'll take the girl and the 'orse along.'

They moved in single file. The man with the lantern was first; it was held low, and its beam carefully directed away from the sea. Jane was next, and the second man followed her closely, leading Bess. Without a word they entered the outskirts of the village, past the small shuttered cottages, and the single inn. The white shingle was in sight now, gleaming faintly as the small waves lapped it. She had expected that they would go straight towards the beach, but instead the leading man turned aside abruptly to follow a white pebble path that wound through tall grass. The high building that loomed suddenly in the darkness she recognized as the square-towered church Paul had pointed out from the sand dunes. They ignored the great main door, and followed the path to the side of the building. Then the man in the lead started down a flight of stone steps that led to the crypt. She guessed that it also led to the entrance to the tower.

4

The stairwell to the tower was steep and dusty, and the light from the lantern was dim. Jane groped for hand-holds in the rough walls, then finally the density of the darkness lessened; they came through a trapdoor on to the roof of the square tower. The figure of a man, leaning against the parapet, turned swiftly.

'We found her headin' this way on the Lydd road, Mr Fletcher. Leadin' an 'orse.'

'We've brought 'er to speak for 'erself. Says she's got a message for you . . . 'er name's Liza Thomas.'

'Liza Thomas? . . .' His tone was speculative.

Jane stepped forward. 'You ain't never 'eard o' me, Mr Fletcher. I'm cousin t' Adam Thomas from Appledore. He sent me.'

There was a perceptible stiffening of Paul's body, but he said nothing for a moment. For Jane it was a moment to wonder whether he would recognize her voice before she was forced to begin explanations in the presence of the other men.

He spoke quietly. 'All right, Harry . . . John. You can leave her. Hitch the horse by the south door. I'll be down directly there's any sign of movement out there.'

They waited in silence for the men to leave. Paul made a warning gesture towards her; he stood by the trapdoor watching the lantern light grow fainter. Then he stooped and closed it.

'Big ears!' he said softly.

She moved close to him, taking his arm. 'Paul, I had to come –'

He shook off her hold impatiently. 'Damn you, Jane! Don't you know the meaning of discipline? How do you think this operation is run. We're not here to play games! . . . you've disobeyed orders!'

His tone, stern and unfriendly, stung her to retort. 'Just wait before you have too much to say!'

He ignored her, sweeping on. '. . . And you've exposed yourself to these men. How long did you think you'd go unnoticed in that ridiculous costume? – and riding Blonde Bess, I'll be bound!'

'Wait!' There was a period of cold silence between them. 'I'll leave when I've said what I have to say. I'm aware we're not here to play games . . . and don't imagine it was a game for me to find my way here across the Marsh tonight. Or to have those men pawing me!'

'Did they touch you . . . ?'

'It took them overly long to decide by feel whether I was a boy or a woman . . . they were ready for a little sport. It's a good job they're afraid of you, Paul.'

'Well, what did you expect?' he said shortly. 'These aren't gentlemen with pretty manners. They take a woman when they want her, and in whatever circumstances they can get her. And a woman wearing breeches is an open invitation. In their minds you were just asking them to put you on the ground and have their sport . . .'

He went on. 'Two of those men were impressed into the Navy, and served their term. You know what happens on the lower deck, Jane, when the Navy's in home port? . . . the men have three feet of space to lie with their women. And those who want a woman take her there with all the others, or go without. It doesn't make for reticence or consideration of the woman they use . . .'

'Oh, hush!' she said angrily. 'I haven't come all this way to have you preach to me about the wenching habits of sailors. That was a risk I took . . . along with breaking my neck if Blonde Bess stumbled. I've got five hundred pounds at stake tonight . . . and a good deal more. If we lose the cargo tonight, I lose Blake's Reach.'

'I didn't know it was yours to lose . . .'

Her voice was tense and slow. 'It is mine – make no mistake about that! And unless you lose this cargo it has a chance of being something I might be proud of . . .'

'Lose the cargo?' he said. 'I've never lost a cargo!'

'You could – tonight. The Preventive Officers know you'll try to land it and the Dragoons have been called out.'

He was silent for a time; she strained to see his face in the darkness but there was nothing to see. There was no movement of surprise or alarm; nothing but stillness and silence. She had never imagined such coldness in Paul, and she began to know, suddenly, his qualities as a leader.

'How did you hear this?'

She told him quickly of the meeting outside the ale-house at Hythe, repeating as well as she remembered everything the two excise men had said. Between them the hostility dropped away; she had the feeling that Paul had forgotten her as a person, forgotten his own anger with her. He was completely and impersonally absorbed in her words.

'So they'll go to Langley – it's as I hoped.'

'Then you knew?'

'Yes, I knew. The word leaked out. Perhaps an informer – or perhaps carelessness. One of the women, maybe. Time enough to deal with that after we're through tonight's work.'

'Couldn't you have stopped the *Dolphin*? – sent her back?'

'If you want profits, Jane, there's no time to wait around on the movements of the Customs men. *You* have to set the pace! The *Dolphin* could make another trip to Flushing for a cargo in the time we would have wasted letting her cool her heels outside the legal limit. Organizing a run costs money, and I've no money to waste. So I let the *Dolphin* come on, and let the word get back to the Preventive men that we had learned they were planning a raid, and we'd switched the operation to Langley. It's near enough not to rouse suspicion, and if the *Dolphin*'s sighted in the Channel, she could be making to either place.'

'If she's sighted, won't they send a Revenue cutter out?'

'They would, if they had one. The cutter, *Falcon*, whose station this is, suddenly developed a mysterious leak in Folkestone today, and she's unfit for duty.'

'You did it?' she whispered.

'I arranged it – and it cost plenty. But I had to be sure the *Falcon* wouldn't interrupt the unloading tonight. She doesn't have the *Dolphin*'s speed, but she could either force us to pull out to sea, or fight it out. At any cost I want to avoid doing either – the *Dolphin*'s loaded with a cargo that'd make your heart sing just to see it, Jane. I managed to borrow some more money, and this cargo's worth more than a little risk.'

Suddenly he gripped her arm, the even control of his tone breaking. 'For the first time, Jane, I'm not being paid to take a risk! – this time it's for myself, and the profit's mine! Nothing's going to stop me making that landing tonight!'

'The Dragoons . . .'

'Ah . . . !' The sound was contemptuous. 'I'll take my chances on the Dragoons. They've no liking for chasing smugglers, and no heart in it. If they're clever enough to come back here after drawing a blank at Langley, then we'll have warning of it and clear out. Just an hour or two's all I need, and I've planted false scents at Langley that should keep them busy for that length of time.'

'Just an hour or two . . .' she said. 'Then could I stay? . . . Paul, let me stay!'

'Stay! . . . why?'

'Surely there's something I could do . . . you need to hurry, don't you? Then why shouldn't I be of some use, even if it's just staying with the horses. I'll reckon there's not an able-bodied woman in this village tonight that's not lending a hand somewhere.' Her tone warmed and grew persuasive. 'Don't you see, Paul – it's *my* cargo too that's coming in tonight. It's my luck that's riding on the *Dolphin*. I want to be here . . . As soon as they start unloading they'll all be so busy they'll never notice me, or stop to wonder who I am . . .'

Her voice trailed off indecisively, and she stood beside him at the parapet waiting for his answer. He said nothing. The minutes dragged out, and still he didn't stir or speak. The moon was gone, completely blanketed now by the clouds that had built up solidly in the west. In the silence and darkness there was only the sea, not seen, but heard in the lapping against the shingle bars, and felt in the sharp wet smell in her nostrils. Gently Paul's arm came about her shoulders; he held her lightly against him, almost absently, seeming to draw comfort from her presence, but not surrendering his watchfulness to her. At this moment she was a companion, nothing more. Her eyes strained in the darkness to catch the signal at the same moment that he would. She was calm, knowing fully the danger in which she stood, and also aware with another part of her mind, of the strange joy of sharing it with Paul; of feeling each second go with a heightened sense of its passing. She knew that there might never have been another moment like this in her life again. Her senses were sharpened to perceive and to remember; there was sadness in knowing that the memory of this might have to serve many evenings of dozing by the fire. Her body grew taut with stillness, so that she hardly seemed to breathe.

It came at last. A blue light flashing twice from the Channel. Paul uncovered the lantern that stood at his feet, and flashed it above his head once – twice.

He spoke softly. 'Down to the beach . . . quickly!'

Confidently and surefooted now, she followed him down the winding staircase.

The beach was crowded with people who seemed to move with ease by the dim light of the masked lanterns. Low voices were heard, speaking briefly with a pitch of urgency; she caught the sound of boats scraping against the shingle, the subdued splash of oars. Her ears were assailed with all the unfamiliar sounds of the sea and the people who lived by it. Occasionally there was a woman's voice, not authoritative, just part of the background, because it was recognized that speed was needed, and that a woman was no more than a strong back and a pair of hands. Jane could only vaguely make out the forms moving among the boats, the outlines of the boats themselves, the small swirl of foam where the water broke against the shingle. There was a string of horses waiting – some of them were harnessed to carts. The shingle made heavy walking; the rounded stones rolling under her feet; several times she half fell, and Paul didn't notice. Once again he seemed to have forgotten her identity, and even her presence. She hurried after him, and humbly kept silent, suddenly aware of her ignorance and uselessness in the midst of this orderly speed.

He gave one or two swift commands in passing along the boats, stopping a moment to watch one of the craft being pushed off. But for the most part his orders were unnecessary. The people along this sea coast had been going out to meet the smugglers' luggers for many years and many generations.

But he assigned no duty to her, and gave her no order. She followed him closely, and in silence, trying to efface herself, and merge into the bustle about her. Then the last of the boats was gone, and a quiet fell on the group left behind. A soft murmur in a woman's voice now and then was all she heard – that, and the stirring of the horses, and the impatient stamp of their feet. She wondered why Paul did not go with the boats, and then immediately answered the question for herself by realizing that in a crisis the leader must be on the shore. The skipper of the *Dolphin* and Paul were the only two that night who counted for more than their ability to lift a keg of brandy.

She grew nervous in the silence and the waiting. Around her, some of the dark forms sat down on the shingle; she stayed close by Paul's shoulder, wishing for the easing of tension that would come when the boats returned. There was no sign of a break in the clouds, and she realized that she would not get even a glimpse of the outline of the *Dolphin*. The monotonous slap of the tide on the shingle grew oppressive. She stood with her chin huddled into the collar of Kate's old cloak.

It seemed a small age of time before again she heard the faint swish of oars, and the first boats showed through the darkness. Suddenly Paul was by her side no longer; he moved first towards the string of waiting horses giving orders in a low, tense voice, then he brushed past her hurriedly, wading out into the surf to meet the first boat.

After that there was no time to wonder where he was, or what he was doing. She found herself surrounded by people pressing forward to unload the cargo. A young woman moved beside her, and started to hitch up skirts and petticoats and move out into the water – a deep-bosomed young woman with the strong supple body of a hard worker. Jane followed her, feeling the shock of the cold water as it rose above her boots and swished about her legs. She found herself next to the young woman as they both grasped the gunwale of the boat, and started to drag it ashore. It scraped with unusual loudness on the shingle. Jane was half soaked with water as the crew jumped out; for the first time in her life she tasted the salt spray on her lips. Suddenly she could feel herself laughing inside with excitement and nervous expectancy. She became one of the group; she fell into line beside the young woman, forming part of a chain that extended to the waiting horses. A large package was dumped into her arms, and she passed it to the next woman; from the feel of the oilskin she knew it was tea. Moving past them were the line of men carrying the tobacco bales. Out at the *Dolphin* she knew they would be loading the wool bales which the boats had brought out – the wool which would pay for their next cargo in Flushing or Roscoff. Her body fell into the rhythm of the movement; she began to glow with a sense of exhilaration and triumph. It was difficult to keep from laughing out aloud now. Suddenly and incredibly she knew that she liked being here for the sake of the excitement alone; that she was also securing the future of Blake's Reach was a thing quite apart. She knew that she was consciously enjoying the swirl of the water about her legs, and the knowledge that a few miles along the coast the Dragoons were searching for them. She found herself grinning at the young woman, and receiving an answering grin as she turned to pass on the next bundle.

They finished unloading, and helped push the boat again. Then they moved to the next boat; the line fell into place, and the movement was set up once more. After a while her arms and shoulders began to ache and twice she nearly lost her footing in the water when she leaned forward out of balance to take an oilskin package. But the sense of excitement did not leave her; she knew her nerves were at a pitch where she could have gone on working to the point of collapse. She knew that time was passing; her feet grew cold in the water; her arms and shoulders felt as if they were on fire.

Now the first boat carrying the brandy kegs had touched the shingle. She paused briefly to watch the ease with which the men slung the half-ankers on their shoulders, and waded out of the surf towards the horses. Then she felt a tug at her arm; the young woman beside her gestured towards the carts. Quickly she scrambled to catch up with the others. The women were waiting patiently, bundles in arms, to help load the carts and the pack-horses. Here Jane was more at ease, and she slipped round to hold the head of each horse as it was loaded; most of them were work horses, heavy and strong, but others were of lighter build, borrowed from the stables of the neighbouring farms. The tea and tobacco was all loaded, and they had started tying the kegs in place when the alarm came.

'Light in New Romney tower, Mr Fletcher!'

A sudden stillness descended on the whole group; action was frozen for a second – arms upraised with kegs, fingers buckling harness. A low, uneasy murmur rose in a few throats. Over to the east they could all see it – a light that blinked and disappeared, and blinked again. Someone was waving a lantern from the tower of New Romney church.

Then Paul's voice was heard, dry, matter-of-fact, carrying along the line of waiting men and animals.

'All right! . . . you all know what you have to do! There's time yet. That light means they've only got to the edge of New Romney. The kegs still in the boats are to stay there. Row them out and drop them overside. We'll pick them up tomorrow. Get the stuff that's been landed into the carts – and move yourselves or you'll all have the privilege of serving in His Majesty's Navy.'

He turned and called to the end of the line. 'Jerry! – start the potato carts moving! You've plenty of time to get to the turn-off by Carter's place before they do. Smartly, now! *Move, boys!*'

He strode along the line, checking the loaded carts. The head of the procession was ready to move; at the end two carts detached themselves and started off in the direction of New Romney.

Jane plucked at Paul's arm as he passed. 'What's happening?' she said softly.

'Came before their time, damn them!' He was poised, ready to move on. 'I've two carts loaded with potatoes as a blind. They'll wait by the turn-off to Carter's farm, and when the Dragoons come up, they'll think they're part of the cargo making towards the hide. If Joe can lead them a bit of a chase, then it's extra time in our hands.'

Then his tone dropped. 'Now you get out of here! – do you understand me! Go and get Bess, and by the time the Dragoons touch Barham, you should be the other side of Lydd. I'd send a man with you but I'll need every hand for unloading at the other end.'

'Where are you taking the cargo?'

'It's better if you don't know that. But it's not far from here, and we'll all be under cover before the Dragoons start nosing round.'

He put his hand on her shoulder and spun her round. *'Now, go! – quickly!'*

Without a word she started moving down the line, heading in the direction of the church. She ducked in between two carts, and started helping with the loading on the off-side, out of Paul's sight. There was haste but no confusion; the loading went on in an orderly fashion. The boats had already pushed off from the shingle, and out farther in the bay she heard the first splashes as the kegs started to go overside. Although she knew it was common practice to dump kegs in an emergency, and retrieve them later, each separate splash was like a blow to her. Suddenly she was conscious of her water-logged boots, and the weight of the wet cloak pulling at her shoulders.

The loading was finished. The women stood by watching as the men tightened the last ropes, and the head of the procession started to move. It was heading towards Lydd. The hide Paul had selected would be an emergency one; no one wanted to leave the cargo close to the coast or to the place where it came ashore. But there was no choice. Mounted Dragoons could easily overtake the cavalcade, and the cargo was rich enough for them to risk an armed clash with the smugglers. Paul had to get it hidden as soon as possible, and move it when he could.

They were dragging the boats up on the shingle now. Out in the darkness she knew the *Dolphin* would be preparing to stand out to sea. The women were withdrawing silently to the cottages. She remembered Paul's orders to get away from Barham, and she turned and marched with the procession until she came to the gate of the churchyard. She slipped inside and stood pressed against the rough stone pillars until the last of the carts had passed. Quiet fell on Barham then. Only a few sounds – retreating footsteps on the shingle and the cobbles, doors closing, low voices fading into nothing.

By the time the single street rang again with the beat of the Dragoons' horses, Barham-in-the-Marsh would present the appearance of a sleeping village.

To Jane the strange new quiet was suddenly sinister and she wanted to leave it behind. She hurried along the path to the great main door of the church, and past it around the corner to the crypt entrance.

'Bess!' she called softly. 'Bess!' There was answering movement in the darkness as the mare stirred. Bess meant for Jane familiarity and a means of escape; a warm sense of relief flooded her, and she quickened her pace almost to a run. It was already too late to stop when she remembered the steps leading to the crypt. Poised on the edge of them, she clawed the air frantically for a second before she started falling.

She woke to full consciousness with a gasp as the cold, evil-smelling water hit her face. For some time she had a sensation of nothing beyond darkness and the pain, and then she became aware of a warm hand cradled under her head. She could hear a voice – a woman's voice, but the words ran together in a blur.

She sighed, and turned her head to try to shut out the voice; she wanted to slip back into the ease of unconsciousness, where the pain didn't trouble her.

'Com'on now! – com'on! You'll 'ave t' wake up quick-like because there ain't no time . . .'

Jane, more awake now, remembered the voice. It belonged to the young woman who had worked beside her unloading the boats. She struggled to respond to the urgency in it now. She made an effort to sit up, and found the other woman's strong arms supporting her back.

'There – that's right now. Y'll be yerself in just a minute . . .'

The gloom lightened a little as Jane's eyes grew accustomed to it. She was sitting on the stone flagging at the bottom of the steps leading to the crypt door. The woman knelt beside her. Jane put her hand to her forehead, gingerly, feeling the grazed skin and the blood slowly oozing through.

'I dunno wat 'appened,' she said, slipping back into the broad accent.

'Y' just forgot them steps were there,' the woman said. 'Gave y' a nasty bump. Sorry I 'ad t' wake y' so sudden-like, but them Dragoons are 'ere.'

Jane started. 'Already?'

'Y've been out t' it a long time. I 'ad t' get one o' them vases orf a grave t' throw the water over y'. Stinks, don't it?'

'The Dragoons . . .' Jane repeated. 'My God, we gotta get outta 'ere.'

'Y'r dead right!' the woman said laconically. 'First thing y' know they'll be bustin' in here lookin' t' see if we've put the cargo 'ere. If they find y' yer a dead duck – y' bein' a stranger. An' dressed like that . . .'

Leaning on the other woman, Jane got slowly to her feet. A terrible weakening pain shot through her ankle when she put her weight on it, but she didn't say anything about it because there was nothing either of them could do. They started up the steps, Jane supported by the young woman.

By the time she got to the top, Jane was breathing heavily. Beads of sweat stood out on her face and neck. But the light breeze blew coldly on her. She discovered that she had lost her head scarf, and her hair was soaking from the douche of stagnant water. It smiled vilely.

"Ow did y' find me?' she managed to say between pinched lips.

'That's easy! I followed y'.'

'Why?'

'Why – because I'm the curious type, and yer a stranger. An' . . . an' because I never 'eard of Paul Fletcher takin' up with one o' the local girls . . .'

'I ain't local!' Jane said curtly. 'An' I ain't 'is girl, neither . . . more's the pity! T'morrow I'm crossin' to Roscoff, and I ain't never goin' t' see 'im again.'

'Then wat are y' doin' 'ere?'

They had reached Bess's side, Jane hobbling painfully. The mare began to nuzzle her enquiringly, and Jane could have sobbed with relief to feel Bess's great, patient strength under her hands.

'I'm 'ere because I brought a message to 'im – and 'e don't like t' see a pair of 'ands go idle.'

She put her uninjured foot in the stirrup and with a grim effort swung herself up, pushed and half lifted by her companion. Up there she felt safe – almost independent of help. She looked down.

'I been told the Marsh folk never asks questions – it ain't 'ealthy!' Then she added, 'But I'm grateful t' y' . . . would 'ave lain there waitin' for the Dragoons t' pick me up if y' 'adn't been nosy . . .'

'Ain't nothin',' the woman said briefly. 'Glad t' 'elp . . . an' I didn't mean t' . . . Y' wouldn't tell Mr Fletcher, would y'?' she said in alarm.

'Told y' ain't never goin' t' see Mr Fletcher again,' Jane said. 'But I'm obliged t' y' . . . much obliged. Watsyer name?'

'Rose!'

She put her hand down to the woman. 'Thanks . . .' Then abruptly she stiffened. 'Wat's that?'

'It's them – the Dragoons! Y' gotta go!' At the farther end of the village they could hear the steady beat of horses' hoofs, and rough irritable voices raised.

'Wat about yerself?' Jane said. "Ow y' goin' t' get 'ome?'

Rose broke in. 'I'm all right, I'll cut along the fields 'ere and get in the back door. Y'd best go the same way.'

'Can't!' Jane said. 'I only know the road from Lydd, an' if they chase me into the fields and with all them dykes . . .'

'Yer right!' Rose agreed. 'Well – get goin' then. Y'll stay ahead o' them if y' get movin' now!'

They were too close. She knew that as soon as she drew close to the village street. Down near the beach she could hear them, hammering on the cottage doors, shouting questions and orders to the villagers. The main body of the Dragoons were still down there, but only a few houses separated her from the head of the

column. But there was equal danger in turning back and attempting to find her way through the maze of dykes where she could
be cut off with ease. Better to trust to Bess's speed. She knew if she
were caught there was no kind of explanation that would cover
her presence here in these water-soaked clothes.

She leaned low to the mare's ear. 'Bess! – sweetheart, it's up to
you!'

Then she dug in her heels and Bess sprang forward. The sudden
clatter of her iron-shod hoofs on the cobbles seemed in Jane's ears
like the thunder of a thousand tiles sliding off one of the cottage
roofs. She turned Bess's head towards Lydd, praying that by this
time Paul would have cleared the carts off the main road, and that
she would not be leading her pursuers directly to him.

The shout went up immediately.

'Halt! Halt in the name of the King!'

She did not waste time turning back to look – it was still too
dark to see anything clearly, and while it made the road ahead
full of unseen pot-holes for Bess, at least it covered her identity.
Bess was too well known on the Marsh to allow her to be seen in
broad daylight. Grimly, Jane remembered her own red hair
streaming behind her like a banner that anyone could read.

She had overlooked the possibility that the Dragoons would
send one man to the Lydd end of the village to stop anyone leaving
it while they searched. She couldn't see him, but he was there –
mounted, and directly in her path.

'Halt! – in the name of His Majesty!'

She rode straight on, and the dark shape of the other horse
seemed to spring like an apparition out of the darkness. She tugged
at Bess's head sharply to avoid a collision. Startled, Bess reared,
and Jane was nearly thrown. She was too frightened and occupied
trying to keep her seat – clinging wildly with her knees and thankful that she was astride – to be able to do anything about the
soldier. He was reaching out to take the bridle when she slammed
her heels hard into Bess's side. The mare started forward with a
jerk, and carried her beyond the reach of the man's hand.

She had gone a few yards when she heard the sharp whine of
the bullet over her head.

She had reason then to be thankful for Robert Turnbull's love
of good horseflesh. Out on the open road Bess had her head. She
responded to Jane's touch with a burst of speed that made the
wind sing past Jane's ears, and left the sounds of the soldier's
pursuit behind. She bent low over Bess's neck, not demanding any
more of the mare, knowing that she now had as much as Bess

could give. The mare had endurance and courage far beyond her own, and she needed no urging.

At the outskirts of Lydd she checked Bess's pace to listen. There was no sound of anyone on the road behind her. At a more sober pace she rode through Lydd, and turned on the Appledore road towards Blake's Reach. She felt very much alone, and lonely. The light grew rapidly.

By the time Blake's Reach came into sight it was full dawn. It had been a journey of acute discomfort – the weight of her wet clothes, and the chafing where they rubbed against the saddle, the stiffness she was beginning to feel from riding astride. Apart from that her head ached violently where she had hit it in her fall, and her ankle was swelling inside her boot. She eased herself in the saddle to try to take the weight off her ankle, but it was necessary to keep Bess to a fair pace because the danger of her situation increased with the growing light. She gave a long sigh of relief and weariness as she crossed the dyke and began to climb the hill to Blake's Reach.

The gates stood open as always. The house looked gentle in the dawn – and welcoming. She looked at it with satisfaction, remembering the rich cargo and what it would do for Blake's Reach. It was hers – and safe.

Nothing seemed to be stirring, and nothing seemed amiss. She began to wonder if Patrick had stayed awake, and if he would come to meet her. Her ankle now pained her badly enough to make her want help to dismount.

But no one came, and she couldn't risk calling out. So with infinite effort she pulled herself out of the saddle, and slid to the ground, almost crying out as her weight came on her ankle. She saw that Bess had water and oats before leaving her, and then braced herself for the walk across the yard to the kitchen.

But the door opened before she reached it. And it wasn't Patrick or Kate who stood there. Jane saw a tall, lean man, whose black hair was pulled roughly back with a ribbon, and whose dark eyes in his sallow, handsome face, regarded her with calm intentness. He wore an old, faded jacket, and his stockings were badly torn. His complexion had the pallor of prison upon it.

There was no mistaking his air of belonging here at Blake's Reach.

She felt the blood drain from her face.

'Charlie! You've come back!'

C.G.O.–O

5

Afterwards she was to remember, through the shock and the fear, how he cut her boot away from her swollen ankle with gentle, almost tender hands. He spoke hardly at all, except to murmur swift instructions to Kate and Patrick to bring him water and clean cloths to tear into strips. They obeyed him in silence, too much in awe of his presence and his authority to offer suggestions or comments.

After her ankle was bound up, he took fresh water and started to bathe the dirt and blood from her face. He put his hand under her chin, and turned her face towards the candle as he worked.

'Smuggling?' he said, looking down at her.

She nodded.

'How did this happen?' He indicated her ankle and the cut forehead.

'The Dragoons were coming. I fell down the church steps . . .'

'Everyone safe? Is the cargo safe?'

She nodded again.

'Good!'

He waited, silent, in the settle by the fire, while she drank the toddy that Patrick had prepared. It was impossible any longer for her to fight the weariness which swept over her; even the shock of Charles's return was numbed. She couldn't hold her confused thoughts in place – thoughts of Charles, and of Paul and the cargo, and of what the future would be now that the heir had come back to Blake's Reach. Her hands grasping the pewter mug began to tremble.

Charles was on his feet instantly, and took the mug from her. Then his tall frame bent over her, and she felt herself being lifted bodily. The room swam dizzily before her eyes. Patrick sprang to open the door, and go before them with a candle.

'Anne's chamber?' she heard Charles say.

And she was conscious of him waiting beyond the drawn bed-curtain while Kate struggled to get off her clothes. She waved Kate away when the old woman brought her bed-gown.

'Can't! . . . not now!'

She closed her eyes and sank gratefully into the softness of the down mattress. Someone had drawn the curtains and the room was hushed, but still she could hear, as if far off, the sounds of the summer morning – the birds and the harsh cries of the sheep. She breathed in the peace and safety of it, the knowledge that she was home.

Then the memory of Charles intruded. She opened her eyes heavily. He had pulled back the bed-curtains, and was standing quite close, looking down at her; even in the dimness she could see his dark straight brows knotted in a reflective frown.

'So you came,' she said drowsily. 'You came after all, Charles. Well, I should have known that some day you'd come. I have no luck. I always lose – like Anne . . .'

'Anne was a good loser, Jane.'

She turned swiftly on her side, away from him, wanting to sink into sleep, and feeling only the sheer physical pleasure of stretching her naked limbs, freed from wet, chafing clothes, in the great bed. The weight of her hair dragged on the pillow. Suddenly she was aware of a question she had struggled with, and which had now formulated in her mind. She turned back to him, opening her eyes and half propping herself up on her elbow.

'But you were in prison,' she said. 'How did you get out? Did they set you free?'

He shook his head. 'Some of the money Turnbull's been sending over found its place. I came out of La Force in a coffin, and the dead man is buried in the courtyard. I got to Dunkirk, and a lugger – a smuggler's lugger, Jane – took me to Rye. They were Rye townsmen, and they trusted my pledge of Robert Turnbull's name to pay them for the passage. He gave them the money – and gave me a meal and a horse to bring me here.'

She dropped back on the pillow.

'And so you knew about me? . . . you knew I was here . . . ?'

'Robert Turnbull described you well – with great feeling – but he omitted some aspects.'

'Or he doesn't know them,' she said drowsily. 'Perhaps even Robert didn't guess it all. But what does that matter? . . . he'll know soon enough. We'll talk later, Charlie . . . later.'

'Yes – later.'

She fell asleep under his gaze. Standing motionless, he watched her for some time, watched her features relax as her sleep grew deeper, and her movements less wild. Almost involuntarily the name came to his lips as he bent to pull the blankets higher on her shoulders.

'Anne . . . !'

Then he drew the bed-curtains tightly, and left her to sleep.

PART THREE

I

It was a fair day, with light, inconspicuous clouds moving across the Marsh sky, and the warmth of the sun came pleasantly through Paul's coat as he rode. But he had no thoughts to spare for the leafy greenness of the countryside, or the brilliant colours of the wild fowl in the dykes that beat to cover at his approach. Since yesterday, Charles Blake had occupied the centre of his thoughts.

He had dressed with unusual care for the meeting ahead of him, and at the same time despised himself for doing so. He had no patience with the niceties of fine dressing, and no aptitude for them, but he wore his best shirt, and he had tied his hair back with some care. Even with all this, he felt that, beside Charles Blake, he cut no very elegant figure.

Yesterday, Charles had dismounted at his door, and had taken a glass of brandy in his sitting-room. With dismay Paul tried to contain, he had heard the story of Charles's return to Blake's Reach the night before, and of Jane's arrival in the dawn with a wrenched ankle, and the bruises and dishevelment of the night still upon her. Paul felt his face grow hot with shame as he realized that, while he had got his cargo safely to the hide, Jane had been left behind, and had nearly been taken. For Paul it was bad enough that she should have been in danger, but the knowledge had an added sting that Charles Blake should know how completely he had failed to protect her.

Irritably he had gone to pour himself more brandy, conscious of the other man's dark eyes upon him in quiet appraisal. Charles still wore the thin faded coat in which he had arrived, and coarse stockings borrowed from Patrick, but he looked, and was, a man of great authority. Paul didn't like the French, and was reluctant to praise them; but this point he had to concede to Charles.

Charles had come with something to say, and Paul gave his full attention as the other talked. Jane, he heard, had awakened about noon, and Charles had sipped a glass of wine in her bed-chamber with her as she had hungrily eaten the food Kate had brought up. Paul recognized that there had been no point in Jane trying to hold back any of the truth from Charles, when he had already seen so much; Charles had been brought up on the Marsh, and he was

no fool. She had to trust him, whether she liked it or not – and
trust the fact that nine out of ten bystanders were sympathetic to
the smuggler rather than the King's import duties. So she had told
him about Paul, and about the *Dolphin*, and in the course of telling
him that, much more was revealed. Charles had heard, grudgingly
at first, and then with more ease, how she had borrowed money
from Turnbull, and why; he learned what she had struggled to do
at Blake's Reach since she had come there.

It was a story Charles had heard the night before from Robert
Turnbull, but on Jane's lips it had reality.

'An amazing woman!' he said to Paul as he finished the retelling.

'Yes . . . amazing,' Paul echoed, and there was a twist of pain
in his heart to have to discuss Jane in this way with a man who
fifteen minutes earlier, had been dead to him.

Charles accepted more brandy, and sniffed and rolled it on his
tongue appreciatively. He was silent for a little time, as if weighing
up the man in whose house he sat. He examined, with minute
detail, everything he saw – the jumble of books, the charts spread
in seeming confusion, the mariner's instruments, and lastly, the
work-hardened hands of the man himself.

He put aside the glass. 'So then,' he said, 'after Jane told me
all this, I rode into Rye to see Turnbull again.' He paused, looking
at Paul. 'From him I came directly here.'

'So . . . ?' Paul said.

'So . . . you must guess why I've come. I want to join you and
Jane. I want a part of the *Dolphin*.'

Paul's gathering resentment broke out then. He spoke quickly.
'And what the devil makes you think you can just walk in here
out of the blue and say "I want part of the *Dolphin*"? What makes
you think you've any chance of getting it?'

Charles waved him to silence. 'I'm sorry if I offend you – but
my own need is urgent to force me to be blunt. It's quite simple.
The Government of the Revolution has taken every sou I owned,
every hectare of land. I come here and find that my uncle, Spencer
Blake, didn't weaken with age in his determination to leave nothing
of Blake's Reach for his heirs.' He spread his hands. 'What am I
to do? – I need money.'

'And do you think you can join us without contributing your
share?' Paul said coldly. 'Or is that your price for allowing Jane
to remain at Blake's Reach? – if so, then she doesn't need to
remain. There are other doors open to her . . .'

'You go too fast, Mr Fletcher. And too far.' Charles quite

deliberately waited to take a leisurely sip of his brandy before he picked up again.

'As I said – I need money. And I haven't forgotten that here the quickest way to make money is in smuggling. For that I'm prepared to do more than contribute my share. I want to buy the *Dolphin* outright.'

'Buy it! I don't see . . .'

'Unlike Jane, Mr Fletcher, I, being the heir, have the right to sell the King's Pearl.'

It was true, of course, Paul thought. For the first time he stopped to wonder if his words to Charles had been too hasty, and spoken clumsily. Possession of the Pearl implied a great many things, among them the fact that if Charles had wanted to take the *Dolphin* from him, he need not be here talking about it. The boat-builder at Folkestone was ready to sell it to whomever came with the purchase price in his hand. Charles could have had it without consulting either himself or Jane. Even in the light of this thought Paul wasn't prepared to like the French any better, but now he reminded himself that Charles Blake was half-English, and also that he had been brought up on the Marsh.

He tried to cover his apprehension with unconcern. He shrugged. 'I see . . . then I'm in your hands, Mr Blake . . . as far as the *Dolphin* is concerned.'

'Quite the contrary!' Charles answered. 'Do you think I could run this operation without you, or someone as skilled as you are? Do I look like a seaman to you? – or do you imagine these people would follow me as they do you? It's obvious that I shall need your services and your help.'

He smiled a little. 'No less an authority than Robert Turnbull assures me that for this job there's no better man on the whole coast than Paul Fletcher.'

'*Turnbull* assures you? How the hell does he know what kind of a man I am?'

Charles's eyebrows shot up. 'I assumed that you would know . . .'

'Know *what*?' He almost shouted the words.

' – that Turnbull has money invested with almost every smuggling operation of size between here and Dover !'

Afterwards Paul thought that he must have made some vague reply to Charles's statement, but he had no recollection of it. He got to his feet slowly, fumbling for the glass, and walked over to the table where he had put the decanter. He poured brandy into his empty glass, not because he wanted it, but because he suddenly found himself standing there, and he needed to give his hands

something to do. Then he wandered to the window, and gazed
out without seeing anything. Turnbull involved in smuggling . . .
the thought needed getting used to . . . And not just involved in
it in a small way, as many people were, but up to his neck in it!
What shocked Paul was that he, who was so deeply in the
smuggling trade himself, had not guessed where it was that a
country attorney would get the money to live in such style, or what
kind of clients Turnbull had who kept him riding back and forth
across the Marsh, instead of sitting solidly at his desk in Watchbell
Street. He played with the picture of Robert Turnbull in this new
role for a minute, fitting together the pieces, seeing the advantages
the attorney would have. There were few people who had such a
close knowledge of this whole area, or who could talk privately
with so many different types of people without the slightest suspicion resting on him. He made friends easily, and he was trusted,
and since an attorney's business was always private, no one would
question his comings and goings. His alert mind would store
information as he plied his acquaintances with ale or wine, and
what would be easier than to pass it on to the quarter where it
could be most helpful. A man without an enemy, was Robert
Turnbull, and the whole Marsh tumbled its problems and its
gossip into his ready ear. The enigma now made sense, and Paul
was conscious of a dawning feeling of admiration for Turnbull,
who could play the role of the bystander with such ease. It
annoyed him to recall how many times he himself had been
deceived – not so much deceived, as simply unaware. He began
to feel foolish because he had never before seen or suspected what
was now so plain; at the same time he could admire the discipline
that had kept Turnbull firmly in the background. Few men could
have been in his position of power, and never succumb to the urge
to use it.

Or had he used it? – suddenly Paul remembered that Turnbull
was his brother's attorney, and he remembered how James had
always seemed unwilling to give direct answers to Paul's questions,
had delayed giving instructions, had seemed to wait on the word
and command of someone else. If James was connected with
Turnbull in smuggling operations it explained many things . . .
how James had got his contacts, how he had information about
the movements of the Revenue cruisers and Preventive Officers
up and down the countryside, how he had had plans laid, and a
ready-formed group of men to carry them out when Paul had
come back to the Marsh. Turnbull had been, no doubt, the source
of all this.

Abruptly he turned back to Charles. 'And how long have *you* known about Turnbull?' he demanded roughly.

'How can I remember? – it's a very long time ago. It was Turnbull who first asked Spencer to agree to rent the church on the cliff as a hide . . . more than twenty years ago, that must be. Turnbull was a young man then.'

'All that time – !' Paul shrugged again, trying to dismiss his irritation. 'Then he's devilish clever!'

Then he added, quickly, 'What I don't understand is why he gave Jane the loan of that money . . . of course he must have guessed what she wanted to do with it. He must have known she would find out about the church, and not stop until she knew the rest of the story. He must also have known that, if our venture together was successful, I'd refuse to work for my brother any longer. He cut off one of his own sources of profit – why?'

'Probably because a woman asked him, and that woman was Jane,' Charles said. 'Turnbull has given a lifetime of service to the Blakes, and for Anne or Jane I feel that he would give much more than service. Even for me, who during these years has grown almost a stranger to him, he did more than could possibly be expected of him. He was the only man I trusted when I lived here on the Marsh . . . Did you know he has been sending money all the time I've been in prison to try and buy my freedom? Is it surprising that he should find himself unable to refuse Jane? Even if it meant a loss to himself?'

He added, quietly, 'So I've asked him if he will join us – if he would like to have a share in the cargoes of the *Dolphin*. Do you have any objections?'

'Objections?' Paul repeated dryly. 'I'm not giving the orders any more. And it seems that I'm back working for my old employer . . .' He leaned back in his chair, and looked at the ceiling, a quizzical, half-defensive grin on his face. 'What luck I have! Just time for one cargo from the *Dolphin*, and already Jane has been in danger, the Dragoons have been at my heels, and now *you* land on the beach. It's a wonder we didn't have the good fortune to bring you over from France as well. Under the circumstances, that would have been entirely fitting.'

Charles rose to his feet, laughing a little, and shaking his head. 'Ah, my friend . . . I'm too lately delivered from prison to wish to put my foot on another man's neck. You'll be master of your ship, that I promise you. And as for Turnbull – he has long since learned the skill of remaining in the background, and, as you know, he can sometimes be of very great value. We each of us need the other . . . it's as well to bear that in mind.'

He put out his hand to Paul. 'Turnbull will come to Blake's Reach tomorrow afternoon. May I expect you then also? I thought it only fair to Jane that she should hear what final arrangements we make between us. You agree . . . ?'

Paul nodded, taking the other's hand firmly. Then he stood by the cottage door and watched Charles ride away towards Blake's Reach, noting his relaxed air and his splendid seat on the horse. He was hatless, and his unpowdered black hair gave him a jaunty, nonchalant look, almost gipsy-like if one did not see the face beneath it – the sensitive, rather weary face with the dark eyes that had stared at death for a long time. Paul had searched for qualities in this man that his talk with the French merchants and fishermen had led him to expect in the despised aristocrat of their description. As different as the French and English court and society were, so he had looked to find those differences in Charles Blake. He had looked for the airs and manners of the nobles who had gossiped and flirted the days away at Versailles, whose refinements and fopperies were imitated by Europe, and whose perversions gave scandal to the world.

As usual, Paul thought, rumour had been coloured and exaggerated, or else Charles Blake had not been touched by the reeking stench of decay that had hung over all French institutions. Charles had been less than a day in England, and already he was firmly gathering up the threads of his inheritance, weaving the strands closer and stronger, making the best that he could of its texture. Even with the effects of prison and the voyage from France still on him, he had set about taking his affairs in hand with a firmness and confidence that Paul could not help but admire. There was boldness and purpose in Charles Blake; it remained to see whether there was also staying power.

After Charles had left him, he had gone, more from a sense of restlessness than for a real purpose, into Rye. There, as he had expected, the place buzzed with the news of Charles's return. He sat moodily over his brandy in The George and listened to the comments and speculations passed on every side of him. They ranged from predictions of final and complete ruin for Blake's Reach, to the rosiest dreams of future prosperity; almost in the same minute he heard opinions that the touch of Charles's effete aristocracy was all the estate needed to finish it, or that he would revive and restore it with the money he had inherited from his mother. The opinions varied according to whether or not the speaker had approved of Jane; now that she was deposed some were regretful, others were slyly glad. Silently Paul cursed their busy tongues, and wondered why he had come to hear what he knew quite certainly would be said.

And they were saying it. As the unspoken thoughts had formed in his heart, he heard the words uttered aloud. They said that Jane would have Blake's Reach in any case – that she had always meant to have it, and there was one sure way. Charles had come without a wife to Blake's Reach, and Jane would see he did not stay that way for long. She had a better head for business than her mother, and would never allow things to drift as Anne had done. Jane and William would never leave Blake's Reach.

Close to Paul, a man stretched out for his replenished tankard and said confidently, 'It weren't no light-minded thing that red-head did – coming all the way from London to Blake's Reach and spending good money on it. She has her heart fixed on it, and she'll have it, one way or t'other.'

Paul wanted to stand up and shout to the crowded room that it was not so, to deny it with all his strength – but that was impossible because he was himself unable to stifle the doubt that had come to occupy and possess his heart. She said she loved him, and he wanted to believe it; but there was no telling how strong her attachment to the ideal of family and tradition had become. To him it was a false ideal, but to Jane it was new and exciting, and there was a chance that it might prove stronger than whatever she felt for him. Now Charles had returned, the real and legitimate heir to Blake's Reach, and he was no weakling fool, but a man who appeared to have combined some of the best results of good birth and character, a sharp-witted man willing to take a risk, a man with no illusions, but a dangerous charm.

Not even the repeated brandies Paul drank, as the evening wore on, would still the doubt. He had to face the worst danger he had yet known – and he could take no action against a formless untouchable enemy.

He still carried his fear and apprehension as he rode towards Blake's Reach to keep his appointment with Charles – that, and the headache the brandy had left him. He was afraid of what he would see that afternoon; he was afraid to have his fears confirmed.

As he turned up the hill towards the house he saw a horseman by the gates. It was Robert Turnbull, and he had dismounted and stood talking to William; the heads of William and the attorney were close together. At Paul's approach Turnbull straightened.

'Good afternoon,' he said pleasantly. His lips were slightly smiling.

It was a shock for Paul to look closely at Turnbull and to realize that, unconsciously, he had been expecting a change in the man's appearance. It was strange to know suddenly some of the things that had been hidden beneath the façade of the busy, respectable legal business in Watchbell Street, and to see that Turnbull himself betrayed none of these things. He was discreet and affable, as always, dressed in his usual expensive, quiet clothes. The glance he turned on William was kindly and warm.

Paul began to feel that it would be easier to command the *Dolphin* for Turnbull directly, than to do it through the agency of his brother. His features relaxed. 'Good afternoon,' he replied.

Then he looked at William. 'How are you? How are George and Washington?'

'They're well,' William said hastily. But his mind was on something more exciting. 'My Cousin Charles has come back,' he said. 'He escaped from prison in a coffin. He escaped from the Frenchies.'

'Yes – I know.'

'And he's going to live here now,' William went on. 'He's going to live here with Jane and me. Jane said he really owns Blake's Reach . . . but we don't have to go! We can stay here . . . and Charles took me riding with him this morning. We went clear across to Saltwood Castle. I've never seen anyone ride as well as my Cousin Charles . . .'

Paul felt the dismay rising in his heart again as he looked at the bright, eager face of the child.

2

Already Blake's Reach was different. Following Turnbull into Spencer's old sitting-room, Paul felt the difference. Jane had cleaned and put this room into order, but she had never been able to dent the masculine stamp Spencer had put upon it. Now Charles had come, and he had made this room his own – in a subtle fashion, without changing it visibly. There was no doubt who would be master in this house.

Paul's eyes went immediately to Jane, who sat on a high-backed chair with her bandaged leg resting on a footstool. He examined her face carefully, and felt the difference there, too; Jane was not sure of herself. She was wary of Charles, and feeling her way. But, Paul noticed, she didn't appear to draw any sense of comfort or support either from his own presence. She smiled at him, but it was a brief smile. It was the first time he had seen her since they had stood together on the shingle at Barham, but there seemed to be no acknowledgement of that in the rather reserved look she gave him. She put up her hand uncertainly to toy with the curls that lay on her forehead. He realized she must have arranged them that way to hide the cut Charles had told him about; she was pale, and her body seemed tense. He moved to go and take a seat near her, but she had started to talk to Turnbull. Disheartened, he stood where he was.

Then Charles came in, and they looked at him expectantly. In a quiet voice he greeted them, and poured wine for Paul and Turnbull. Jane declined it, and he took none for himself. Paul found himself, even in Jane's presence, unable to take his eyes off the tall figure in the same threadbare coat of yesterday, who had taken his stance, his legs astride, before the mantel. He came to the business of the afternoon without preliminaries.

Tomorrow, he said, he was going to London, and he would offer the King's Pearl as security against a loan. He would bargain for the highest price he could get, and trust to luck to pay it back before the Pearl should be forfeited.

'I agree with Jane,' he said, looking from one face to the other, 'that if the Pearl has to go, it has to go – because Blake's Reach has never stood in such need of what it can bring.'

They discussed then the details of using the money. Paul was to negotiate the purchase of the *Dolphin* from the Folkestone boat-builder, but Charles was to be the outright owner. All four of them were to share equally in the costs of the cargo, but Charles, as owner, would take two-fifths of the profits.

Jane, who had been silent until then, spoke. 'I will, of course, now start repaying Robert's loan from my share of the cargoes. I imagine Charles will prefer to make improvements to Blake's Reach in his own time, and Robert's money needn't be used for that . . .'

Turnbull cut in: 'With the interest . . . you haven't forgotten the interest!'

Charles looked across at him, his eyebrows shooting up.

Jane gestured quickly. 'It was a . . . a pleasantry! I was to give Robert the first rose from the garden here each spring until the loan was repaid.' She didn't let her eyes go to Paul as she said this.

Now Charles smiled. 'It's most certainly an interest I should insist on being paid were I in Robert's place.'

Paul moved restlessly in his chair. 'The *Dolphin* . . .' he said sharply.

'Yes . . . ?' They had all turned towards him.

He drummed his fingers thoughtfully a moment, as if he had not been fully prepared to speak his mind, and the words had come too quickly. But they were waiting on him. He frowned. 'It seems to me from all I've heard about the value of the Pearl, that it will fetch more than's needed to buy the *Dolphin*. And with us all sharing the cargo, the individual contribution is smaller, and the profits less.' Now he looked directly at Charles. 'Why not use the rest to buy or hire another vessel? – you can't put Blake's Reach back to what it was overnight, and in the meantime the money could be earning you round about five times your investment.'

Turnbull gave a little exclamation. 'Fletcher's right! As long as you're going to borrow on the Pearl, you must get as much as you can and let it earn for you . . .'

Charles waved them to silence. 'I have plans for the rest of the money. At the moment they don't include spending much on Blake's Reach . . . and I'm not sure even in the end Blake's Reach will have anything spent on it.'

'*Other* plans?' It was Jane who spoke, the words forced from her in a gasp. She hadn't wanted to question Charles, but his rejection of Blake's Reach had touched her rawly. Two spots of colour flamed suddenly in her cheeks. Paul wanted to turn away from the sight of her distress.

Charles nodded. '. . . A private matter.' But then he looked once more at Jane, and suddenly he threw up his hands. 'Ah, *Mon Dieu*, why should it be private from my friends? I keep forgetting that I am free – and in England. I know that I may speak to you, and you will respect my confidence.'

They nodded in agreement, Jane with them, but her hands gripped the arms of the chair tensely as she waited for him to go on.

Charles clasped his hands behind his back.

'It takes less money to buy a strong man out of prison than a sick woman. I will need every penny I can lay hands on – gold to buy the silence of many people, not just a few – gold to buy the service and the help she will need to reach a port. She cannot walk or run, or sleep in the open, as a man can. Nor can she ride out of La Force in a coffin.'

Jane was deadly pale. 'Who . . . who is it?' she said in a whisper.

'Her name is Louise de Montignot. She is the widow of the man who was my greatest friend, Phillipe de Montignot, Comte de Labrit. He died on the guillotine a year ago, and Louise has lately been brought to La Force. If the guillotine does not have her, she will cough her lungs out in La Force.'

No one said anything; their eyes were fixed on Charles's face.

It had become hard and tight, the cheek bones prominent, and his eyes bright with anger.

'Phillipe was with me in La Force, and before he was murdered he learned that Louise had also been charged and imprisoned. I swore to him that while I lived I would not cease trying to aid and comfort her. I cannot consider myself free of that promise. She still lives, and I must send gold until there is enough to buy her out.'

'Is it possible?' Paul asked quietly.

'The concierge is human, and, like most humans, greedy. As in my case, it is possible that, if the danger to himself is not too great, he can be bought. But from there on the difficulty begins. A sick woman cannot travel easily, or without attracting notice. She must have places to rest on the way, and someone to travel with her. I have friends still in Paris, but it takes time, and there is much danger . . . for Louise and for them.'

'And if . . . when she escapes, what then?' Jane's lips were pinched.

'Then?' Charles repeated. 'Then she will come here – to Blake's Reach.'

3

It had been a relief to Jane that the talk between Charles, Paul and Robert Turnbull had continued until the supper hour; hardly listening she had let it flow over her, and her own thoughts had gone on, thoughts that spiralled forever round Charles's statement that he would bring Louise de Montignot to Blake's Reach.

The three men had eaten supper heartily, absorbed in ever more detailed planning for running cargoes on the *Dolphin*. There was to be more money available, so there could be richer cargoes, more porters, more batmen, larger bribes and better protection. An atmosphere of confidence grew up between them, each adding suggestions and a little argument, but in the end always deferring to Paul's opinion. To Jane's confused mind there seemed to be many toasts to their mutual success, in which she joined, and she repeated the words of the toasts automatically. For some reason Kate's food was better that evening; she had either been inspired by Charles's presence to make extraordinary efforts, or she had been frightened into accepting a few of the hints Patrick poured into her constantly. The best china and glass and silver were set out, and Anne's good linen was on the table. Patrick had even placed some roses from the vine over the porch and placed them in a silver bowl in the centre of the table. Looking at it, Jane paused to wonder how many years it was since Blake's Reach had known such a festive evening.

After supper they had gone to the drawing-room where Patrick had lighted a small fire – more to brighten the hearth than for any other reason. Patrick also had responded to the occasion, sensing that whatever plans had put the three men into such fine good humour could hardly bode ill for Jane or William. He left brandy and glasses on the marquetry table. This time it was Paul who lifted Jane and carried her to a seat by the fire. Robert went before them with her footstool. The brandy glasses were filled, and there was yet another toast; Jane responded with stiff lips.

Charles had been in this room before, but only for a cursory glance. Now he wandered about, glass in hand, examining the portraits and the pieces of china displayed in the corner cabinet. He opened the harpsichord, and pressed a few keys lightly, wincing at the jangling sound they made. Then he came back to stand by the fire. Jane saw him looking at the carpet closely. He felt her gaze on him, for he turned to her.

'Aubusson,' he murmured, nodding towards the carpet. 'It's valuable . . . pity that end is so badly frayed.'

'Could it be repaired?' she said.

He shrugged. 'Probably . . . but I wonder if it's worth troubling.'

She looked away, staring into the fire and sick inside at the implication of his words. She felt the tears prick her eyelids, and once again the thread of talk slipped away from her. This room was familiar to her now – she didn't have to turn to see the colours of beautiful wood surfaces lovingly polished back into life, or the richness of the gold leaf on the china, or the texture and depth of the carpet. She had made this room come to life again. But Charles did not seem to care whether it lived or stayed mouldering under its dust. She leaned her head back wearily, and her eyes half-closed. Suddenly she was very conscious of the throbbing of her ankle.

At last they went, Paul and Robert, bidding her good night with a briskness that was part of their high satisfaction. Paul's face had undergone a change during the evening – no longer unhappy and full of suspicion. He was once again firmly master of the *Dolphin*, and he, like Jane, had been strongly affected by the news that if Louise de Montignot reached England, Charles would bring her to Blake's Reach.

Jane didn't want to be left alone with Charles. She wanted her bed, and solitude. But she raised her eyes, and found Charles staring at her thoughtfully.

'Paul,' he said quietly, 'he is your lover?'

She nodded, not troubling to deny it. It began to seem that Charles knew or made a shrewd guess at everything that happened at Blake's Reach. 'Yes – he's my lover,' she said.

'Why aren't you married? – he wants to marry you, doesn't he?'

'I – I don't know. We haven't talked about it.'

'You mean you don't allow him to talk about it, Jane. I know a man in love when I see one. He has run away from women before now, but you he would marry tomorrow. You're partners in everything else – why not in this also?'

She shrugged. 'Paul isn't a partner in Blake's Reach. He'll go back to the West Indies as soon as there's enough money.'

'And he wants you to go with him?'

'Yes.'

'And you – you prefer Blake's Reach, Jane? You want him here, don't you? You want him and Blake's Reach both. You have a dream of seeing it back as it used to be, and Paul at your feet, adoring you. Isn't that so?'

'I didn't say it was so. Why do you twist things . . . ?'

He gestured back to the portraits. 'You're the first real Blake they've had in a hundred years – strong enough and determined enough to do everything you think should be done for this house and this family. Of course . . . you may destroy yourself, but you don't think it would be destruction. You don't see it that way at all.'

She was silent. He paced the length of the room, and swung round abruptly, speaking in a louder tone.

'But I came back, Jane, and now you think the dream is finished. I'm a usurper under this roof, aren't I? – not as good for them . . .' he nodded back towards the portraits, 'as you would have been. Well, I'm not as good, and it's unfortunate for Blake's Reach that I didn't die as I was meant to. You're thinking that, Jane – and it's true! And you've heard me say that I'll bring Louise here, and you're thinking that this house may not have two mistresses . . .'

Suddenly he flung out his hands in a gesture of dismissal. 'Well, Blake's Reach was intended for you, and I'm not sure in the end that it won't be yours, after all. But take care you don't lose your happiness, your youth, and Paul Fletcher to it!'

She could feel the room move around her crazily and there seemed no blood left in her body, no will to deny his words, or oppose him. She pressed her lips together, but she wasn't able to stop the tears that began to slide down her face. But she still was too proud to put up her hands and brush them away.

Charles was gone from Blake's Reach almost two weeks, but even with him away, life did not fall back into the pattern Jane had established. It was true that her orders were taken, and attended to as before, but a feeling of impending change hung over the place. Her rule was temporary, and it was coming to an end.

With her ankle still bandaged she sat in the garden through tedious, impatient hours, and her thoughts were uneasy and confused. The time hung upon her heavily; she longed for the relief from thought and speculation which riding the Marsh on Blonde Bess would have brought. The days grew warmer, and the countryside lost its fresh green. The bright red of the roses on the vine began to fade in the sun, while Jane twisted restlessly in her chair, her thoughts forever on Charles.

Robert Turnbull rode out to Blake's Reach several times during Charles's absence. Not once did he refer to the last time he and Jane had seen each other alone, the night they had dined at The Wool Pack in Folkestone. He talked without any sign of constraint — their plans for the *Dolphin*, Charles's return, the details of Charles's escape — all in his usual calm manner, and Jane began to wonder if perhaps she had imagined his firm, passionate kiss as he left her that night. But other things recalled it, if not Robert's words. He had withdrawn a little from her, no longer so eager or spontaneous; she began to be conscious of the difference in their ages. Now when he talked to her, he was once again the man who had loved her mother and was kind to her, Jane, only for the sake of the memories he carried. She knew that he would never again kiss her.

But to Robert, at least, she could talk about Louise de Montignot, and find some relief in that. Endlessly she speculated about Charles saying he would bring Louise to Blake's Reach, and she wondered aloud about what he had meant by the statement that, in the end, Blake's Reach might be hers. Robert had no answers for these questionings; Louise de Montignot was still in La Force, and it seemed probable to him that she would never come out.

Paul also came to Blake's Reach. He came at night, and discreetly, but he was full of good humour, and an aggressive jubilation. Firstly he liked Charles's absence more than his presence at Blake's Reach, and he would have preferred it if Charles had

stayed in London altogether. But apart from that, in these two
weeks, the *Dolphin* had completed two trips to Flushing and was
already on her way back there. The runs had gone off without
delay or danger, and the cargoes had been large and profitable.
Because of the long twilights fewer vessels were making the runs
from France and Holland, and there were more men available as
crew and porters. The added danger of these runs did not seem
to trouble Paul. On his second visit, he brought Jane two hundred
guineas in gold pieces. It lay heavily in her lap as she sat and
listened to him.

He paced the length of the room, his excitement and impatience
revealed in every movement. 'Do you see it, Jane?' he said,
gesturing towards the leather pouch she held. 'Do you see it? —
and that's just the beginning! From now on it will be profit . . .
and more profit! A few more months like this and we'd have
enough to go.' Then he frowned. 'At least we'd have enough if
we didn't have to split the profits with Charles and Turnbull,' he
shrugged. 'Well . . . the one good thing in this arrangement is that
I know the *Dolphin* won't be lifted from under my nose. And my
brother James can't get his hands on it either.'

Then the excitement would die a little, and his voice grow
softer. He would sit on the floor by her footstool, leaning back
against her chair, taking her hand and pressing it gently against his
lips and cheek. He would talk then about the Indies, his tone
filled with longing and regret; he would try to describe to her
how the beaches looked in the dawn; and the strange violence of
a tropical thunderstorm. Her fingers would stroke his face lightly,
and he would talk on. Mostly the talk was soft — to match his mood.
But once his longing flared suddenly to something stronger, an
anger at the days and weeks slipping by, a protest against the
frustration of his love.

'Damn it! — what am I doing here, when I could be out in the
Indies where I want to be! What's the use of piling up money
when it brings no pleasure with it? Sometimes I think I must be
out of my mind to agree to the life I live now . . . only seeing you
at times when it's discreet, denying myself the sight of the only
person who means anything to me. I think I *am* mad!'

He looked up at her desperately. 'Without you the money is
nothing — you know that, don't you, Jane? I love you . . . I love
you foolishly and completely, as if I were a boy in love for the first
time. I love you tenderly and reverently, and if you have flaws
my eyes don't see them any more. This is I — Paul Fletcher — saying
things to a woman I never thought to hear myself say. Have you

any idea how much it hurts to love this way? — and not be able
to shout my love to the world? Marry me, Jane! Soon! . . .
quickly! As quickly as possible.'

'Marry . . . ?'

'Yes! Marry! Is that such a strange thought? Don't you love
me? Isn't that the reason we're here together now?'

She bent her face to his in a sudden upsurge of fear that he
might withdraw from her. 'Oh, Paul — my love, my dear love . . .'
Her voice trembled. 'I do love you, and you must know it! If you
left me . . .' She struggled now against terror at the thought. 'I
would be empty without you — useless! It would be like a dark
night . . .' She shook her head, closing her eyes for a second. 'Don't
ever leave me, Paul, because without you there is nothing in this
whole world for me. There's no peace, no trust, no confidence . . .
there's no love any more.'

He grasped both her hands in a rush of triumph. 'Then we must
leave here! Why should we wait any longer? If each is all the
other wants, why do we waste time? In London they could tell
us what port the next ship for the Indies sails from . . . We could
take William with us, if you wanted that . . . We could be together,
Jane! — together and free!'

'So soon . . . ?'

'Why not? What is there to keep us? The money? . . . well,
we're not penniless, I've energy and skill to sell, and they fetch a
good price out there. Why do we wait about here just to see the
money pile up? When you're young, gold isn't worth time . . .
Come with me, Jane!'

'It isn't the money . . .' She stopped then, because she couldn't
face him and say what she felt. She was torn between his urgent
pleading, the love in his eyes, her own need of him — torn between
these things and a longing in her own heart that she could not
name to him. But it was there, and he recognized it.

'I don't believe it,' he said slowly. 'I *can't* believe it . . . And
yet it's there so plain a blind man could see it. You still want
Blake's Reach, don't you? . . . you've *still* got some strange, un-
reasoning belief that somehow it will be yours. It's obsessed you,
hasn't it? What in Heaven's name . . . ? What does this place have
that you cannot give it up?'

She gestured, panic-stricken. 'No! . . . there's no way it could
be mine now that Charles has come back.'

He pushed aside her groping hands on his arm, and rose abruptly. 'Yes . . . there is a way. If you married Charles you could keep
Blake's Reach. Is that what you're waiting for? Are you waiting

for Louise de Montignot to die, so that Charles will turn to you?'

Shaking and weak, she also rose to her feet, supporting herself on the arm of the chair. Diffidently she put out her hand towards him, then, frightened by his look, she dropped it back to her side. 'No! . . . no, that's not true! It's you I love, Paul. You! . . . *you!*'

He started towards the door. 'A man in love has little patience, Jane. I won't wait long, because if I do, there'll be little in you worth having. I want your love, freely given – no reservations, and no second thoughts. I'll have you that way, wholly and completely – or not at all.'

He left her with no other words, and she sank down on the footstool before the fire. She was alone, her face buried in her hands, left by him to regret that she had not thrust everything aside, had not gone with him, this very night, if he had demanded it. Why did she feel any hesitation about leaving this house where she might expect to see another woman installed as mistress? What kind of spell had this place, this family, put upon her? Was there no peace for her, no escape from it, even in loving Paul? What had happened to the peaceful moments of love?

In these weeks the news of Charles's return had gone far beyond Rye, and the near neighbourhood of Blake's Reach. Robert and Paul both reported comments they had heard, and she guessed bitterly that what they neglected to tell her were the questions and the gossip they had listened to about the probable future of herself and William. She thought of all the women of the prominent families who had refused to call on her here; and she knew what they would be saying.

It was Robert who brought her the Dover newspaper which reported Charles's presence at the reception given by the Prince of Wales. The Prince was not popular, but he was still Royalty, and would be Regent at any moment his father's madness took a turn for the worse; the Dover newspaper lifted Charles's name from the list of guests, and printed the item eagerly. Jane read it, and thought of how the Marsh would enjoy this piece of news. Charles had been in England only a few weeks, and already he rubbed shoulders with the highest in the land. Jane flung the newspaper away from her in savage humour. Now that Charles had come back, the Blake family would return to the place it had held in the affairs of the Marsh, and she, Jane, would remain the outsider.

2

When Charles returned from London the house awoke to a life that was subtly different from the reawakening it had had on Jane's arrival. He came, riding a new horse whose lines bespoke fine breeding, with clothes tailored by London's most expensive firm and with gold in his saddle bags. The day after his return the carpenters and plasterers were called in and Blake's Reach rang with the sound of hammers and saws, and men's voices. Two new men were hired, one for the horses, one for the garden; a man came down from London to tune the harpsichord. The household watched these changes, and regarded Charles with awe and excitement. This was traditionally how the Blakes should behave; this kind of behaviour was understood and approved.

Charles did only one thing that met with protest, though no one dared at first to voice it before him. In London he had hired a Frenchman called Henri, and he announced to Patrick and Kate that in future the preparation of the food would be solely Henri's task, and his word within the kitchen was to be law. Patrick was to wait on tables as usual, and Kate to attend to the household; a young girl was to be engaged in Appledore to help both herself and Henri. The arrival of Henri threw Patrick and Kate into a strange alliance; they both cordially detested the small, energetic Frenchman. Henri spoke no English, and the kitchen was constantly in a turmoil because of the misunderstandings which arose.

'You must do the best you can. Mend your own quarrels in the kitchen, and see that Miss Jane and myself are not disturbed by them.'

'A cook could have been found . . .' Jane said acidly. 'Even if we had to have one from London. But this Henri . . .'

This also Charles brushed aside. 'Why should I trust to the doubtful ministrations of an English cook, when I can have one of the finest French chefs? I found Henri in London; he had just made his way over here, and had no money. He had been cook to the Comte de Barzac, and committed the crime of remaining loyal to his master. I was very lucky to find Henri – I have tasted his food many times . . .'

And so a foreign despot came to rule in the kitchen at Blake's Reach, and there was no more peace for Patrick and Kate, but, Jane admitted, the food was delicious. So also, she reckoned, would the food bills be enormous. Several times a week Henri sent the farm cart as far even as Dover to get the choicest fish and meat and game for his cooking pots and oven. He looked with some scorn on Jane's vegetable and herb garden, and pronounced it totally inadequate. With a wave of his hand Charles sanctioned the planning of anything Henri demanded.

Robert Turnbull commented wryly on the changes. 'You see what the King's Pearl can do, Jane? – we shall yet see a miniature Versailles at Blake's Reach. I wonder, though,' he added, 'how much of this Charles has actually paid for? He may be more of a Blake than he seems.'

Since Robert would not question Charles about money, Jane herself did not have the courage to do so. Charles merely said that the Pearl had brought a very good price. The details of the transaction seemed to bore him.

Jane had not been forgotten during the London visit. Or perhaps, she thought, it was merely that he regarded her as a part of Blake's Reach. The evening of his return he sent Patrick to his room for three specially wrapped boxes, which he put into Jane's arms – two pairs of fine kid gloves, a length of blue silk, and a wide hat elaborately trimmed. Jane put it on, and turned from the mirror anxiously for his inspection.

'No! No!' He jerked the hat impatiently to a deeper angle over her face. 'There – now walk away, and come back to me.'

Meekly she did as he told her. As she wheeled he was shaking his head. 'Keep your back straight, and – *Mon Dieu* – pull your chin in. You're a lady, not a soldier!'

She coloured, snatching the hat off, and flinging it into a chair. 'Why do you bother? – why do you try to make a lady of me? Does it matter how I wear the hat? And that – ' she pointed at the yards of shimmering silk. 'I have gowns aplenty, and what need have I of one more? Where am I to wear it? Who's to see it?'

'There'll be plenty to see it – and you also! I fancy we'll not lack company at Blake's Reach.'

'No, I suppose not,' she replied, with an edge to her voice. 'Not since the Dover paper reported that you were at a reception given by the Prince of Wales.'

He raised his eyebrows. 'So they picked up that, did they? Well, it won't do my credit on the Marsh any harm.'

'Tell me about it,' she demanded. 'How did you get there?'

'Can't you imagine? – London is swarming with titled French *émigrés*, some of them cultured and talented men, whom the Prince admires. The Marquis d'Orbec presented me to the Prince. It was nothing very grand – quite informal.'

She shrugged. 'Whatever it was, it will satisfy the gentry hereabouts. Now that they know you're back, they'll come in flocks like silly sheep!'

He appeared not to have heard her; he was fingering the frayed edges of the gold curtains thoughtfully, and whistling half under his breath.

Jane's prediction was right; within a few days the first of the carriages came rolling along the freshly raked drive, and a liveried footman sprang down to open the door. Jane, watching from the window of her chamber, saw Roger Pym alight, and turn to help a woman whose face was hidden from Jane's view beneath a plumed hat. She caught the sound of high-pitched voices, and two younger, slighter women followed their mother.

A few minutes later came Kate's agitated knocking on her door. 'The Master bids you come down, Miss Jane,' she said. 'Mr and Mrs Roger Pym have come . . . and Miss Elizabeth and Miss Sarah.'

'The fish to the bait!' she said softly. And then, 'Oh, damn the Pyms!' But she changed into one of her most becoming gowns — one which Anne had worn for afternoon drives in the Park — and brushed her hair smooth before going downstairs. She sucked in her breath a little with nervousness as she entered the room. She felt the sharp scrutiny of three pairs of feminine eyes, and of Roger Pym's kindly ones. Then Charles rose from his seat and moved towards her.

'And here is my cousin, Jane . . .' She hoped it was not her imagination which made her fancy that in his eyes there was approval. She went through the exchange of greetings with stiff lips, angry with herself because she cared that these people would call at Blake's Reach for Charles's sake, but not for hers. Roger Pym she favoured with a particularly brilliant smile, at the same time swallowing hard at the obstinate lump in her throat.

She had no way of judging what kind of impression she made on the ladies of the Pym family, but this was, as she had guessed, the first of many times she was called to the drawing-room in the weeks that followed.

After the Pyms came the rest . . . Lady Stockton from Saltwood Castle, Sir Anthony Burroughs from Meade House, the Berkeleys from Ham Street, and the Wests from Ebeney. Sir James Fletcher also came; this time his wife, Lady Alice, was with him. Charles treated them all with friendliness, but somehow remained aloof. He refused completely to discuss the details of his escape. They went away curious and disappointed.

Inevitably there were questions put to Jane about her plans for the future, some of them mere insinuations, others completely blunt. Always Charles spoke for her.

'There's much to be done here, and my Cousin Jane has kindly consented to remain on to attend to the housekeeping for me. The recent death of her mother . . . you understand we Blakes have a need of each other at present.'

And after they had gone he chuckled lightly. 'We can't prevent them talking, Jane, so better we put the words into their mouths than have them invent their own. Do you mind very much being compromised by me . . . ?'

White in the face she snapped at him. 'If you want me to go, I'll pack my boxes at once!'

A look of laughing bewilderment came into his face. 'But why, Jane? . . . this is your home! I'd be devastated if you went!'

And hearing the teasing quality of his voice, she turned and left the room.

In one matter he was prompt and ready with payment. Within three days of his return the lugger, *Dolphin*, was bought from Wyatt at Folkestone, and the papers passed into Charles's hands. From that moment onwards, Paul turned his energies with grim earnestness to the task of running cargoes and making profits as quickly as possible. After the transfer of the *Dolphin* to Charles, Paul came to dine at Blake's Reach. He was in high good humour. He raised his glass to Jane and Charles.

'Will you drink with me? This is the day of freedom! I have told my brother I am his servant no longer.'

'Then we'll drink to freedom and prosperity,' Charles said gravely, 'for each of us!'

Paul's eyes, bright with hope and excitement, were on Jane. Her heart warmed as she responded to the emotion she read there; she echoed the toast eagerly.

'James was furious, of course,' Paul said, 'and half sick to think he hadn't got me to order about any more. I didn't, of course, tell him that Turnbull was still involved. Turnbull can keep his own counsel on that. He was mightily suspicious of you, Charles. He knows well enough I haven't the money to buy the lugger, and your return falls in too happily with my sudden prosperity. It only needs you to tell him he may no longer use the church, and he will be certain.'

'I think, though,' Charles said thoughtfully, 'that I'll let him go on paying rent until he puts together another organization. It might be foolish to store Blake cargoes so near the house . . . we'll think on it a little.'

After that night Jane saw Paul very rarely, and almost never alone. Three times she rode over to Old Romney, and each time he was absent. She learned that he was pushing the *Dolphin* to make more runs than ever before, finding extra men for the crews so that they could work in relays. The *Dolphin* was making use of the fair summer weather, and remained no longer in port than was strictly necessary. Paul took on some Dutchmen as crew from Flushing, registered the *Dolphin* in that port, and made arrangements to water and provision the lugger there, so as to remain out of the sight of the English port authorities.

Flushing was not her only port; she made trips to Guernsey and Roscoff, and slipped briefly into Le Havre and Dunkirk, though Paul said nothing of these visits to Charles or Jane. Whenever the *Dolphin* sighted a vessel flying the Revenue stripes she put on as much sail as she could carry and slipped away, herself flying the Dutch flag. Paul himself made the trip to Holland a number of times, not skippering the vessel himself, but in order to help expedite the buying of the cargoes at the other end. The times he was not aboard the *Dolphin* he spent riding between the various rendezvous picked to land the contraband along the Marsh shore. He ate carelessly, and seemed never to sleep. Jane saw that he grew thinner, and his eyes were weary, though they never lost their look of feverish excitement.

With Paul absent so often, the time began to hang heavily upon Jane's hands. She was unsure of her position at Blake's Reach, and there was no telling, from one day to the next, what plans Charles would make for work on the house or outbuildings – plans which he seemed to forget to tell her about until the workmen arrived to carry them out. She was confused and uncertain of what to do, conscious that her help was unnecessary now that so many people came from the villages about to do Charles's bidding. Blake's Reach began to wear a clean fresh air; men were hammering on the roof, and stripping away panelling where the damp had rotted it, an upholsterer came from Dover to measure for new curtains for the drawing-room. Charles also ordered a small army of village women in to clean the dining-room which had not been used in the past twenty years; new curtains were made for there, as well. Jane thought its splendour, the first evening they dined there, was decidedly cold. The candles in shining silver candlesticks cast pools of light in the centre of the long table; Charles seemed far away from her and the corners of the room were shadowy. Even Henri's food tasted different here; Patrick moved about silently on soft-soled shoes. Jane shivered a little, and wished they were back in Spencer's old room.

It should have pleased her to see Blake's Reach begin to re-
emerge as the house of charm and beauty it had once been. But
she looked at it with a sick heart, counting the gold it was costing
to make these restorations, and knowing, that for all their spending,
not a single acre of land, or an extra sheep was being bought. There
were new horses in the stables, but no new cows were bought;
there was a new gardener, but not a shepherd. She made a faint
protest about the bill from the upholsterer for bedhangings and
curtains.

Charles looked at her coldly, with raised eyebrows. 'I've lived
in prison long enough to want these things about me.' He appeared
to have forgotten that once he had said he did not intend to spend
money on Blake's Reach.

'But . . . but how to pay?' she faltered.

'Let the *Dolphin* pay for it all — it's well able to !'

She was filled with rage as she watched him go. He was driving
Paul to almost superhuman efforts in order that all his whims
could be indulged, so that his cellar should be well stocked, and
his kitchen boast a French chef. Paul's long hours on the shore
at night, and on the deck of the *Dolphin* were paying for the silk
coat on Charles's back, and the gold-buckled shoes he wore, for
the thoroughbred horse and the new dinner service of fine china.
And beyond the orchard the Blake lands had not received a foot
of new fencing, nor was there any labour expended on digging the
weed-choked dykes, or replacing the rotting footbridges. The profits
of Paul's work would go on trifles, and Blake's Reach would be
just as impoverished as Spencer had left it.

'And what,' she asked herself, 'will Charles do when Paul has
enough money to go?'

But during these weeks she wouldn't allow herself to examine too
closely the change that was slowly being worked in Paul. Charles
and Turnbull had turned the running of the operation completely
over to him, with authority to buy and to sell where he pleased,
to hire what men he wanted, to send the bribes where he thought
they were needed. The steady flow of profit that came back was
his justification. He was left alone to do what he pleased with the
Dolphin, and he revelled in his freedom. Jane saw that he was
beginning to enjoy his work; he came to Blake's Reach more often
now, still discreetly arriving and leaving by night, and always in
the same exultant mood of success. He laughed as he spoke of the
brushes with the Revenue cutters, and boasted of how easily the
Dolphin left them behind. Only once had they ever been near
enough to a Revenue cutter to be challenged, and even then they

had simply ignored her signal to heave-to, and had been out of gun range within a few minutes.

Smacking his knee with satisfaction at the memory, he gestured towards Charles. 'We should have a sister-ship to the *Dolphin*. When we have half the purchase money I could get Wyatt to lay the keel . . . I've an excellent man who'd do as skipper . . .'

Charles nodded his agreement. 'A good idea . . .'

Jane could have cried out in despair. Charles was chaining Paul to him as James had never been able. He was intoxicated by his mastery of the *Dolphin*, by the efficiency of his plans, and their smooth, quick operation. He no longer talked of the ugly business of smuggling, but found it, instead, a fascinating game.

Sometimes, as he laughed, he reminded her unpleasantly of his brother, James.

So there was a murderous rage in her heart against Charles during the long hot days of August when there was so little rain, and the dust rose chokingly from the Marsh roads and fields as the livestock moved across them. Charles insisted that she accompany him to repay the calls on the neighbouring gentry; she sat beside him stiffly in the carriage, and just as stiffly in the drawing-rooms of Meade House, Ebeney and Warefield House. She did all the correct things, faithfully copying the customs and habits of the womenfolk, joined the dull conversations which were no more than local gossip repeated and retold at each place they visited. She found herself irritated and bored with it, and the image of Paul was with her all the time – Paul, confident and boastful, Paul growing a little greedy for the spoils of the game, and caring for them for their own sake, Paul, who saw her now only at Blake's Reach, and for short periods of time.

But worst of all was the realization that these days Paul talked very little of the Indies.

Jane performed the social round as Charles expected her, without protest, and sat at the head of the table when he bade people to dine with them. She found the business of entertaining grow easier with each occasion, and once the challenge of learning and mastering the niceties of it were past, it also began to bore her. She had none of the accomplishments that were admired in the drawing-room, and she soon began to accept the admiring attention of the men with the same calm as she took the icy politeness of the women. She recalled longingly the dawn rides to Old Romney, and the eager embrace of Paul's arms.

In spite of her hostility, Jane recognized that when Charles chose to exert himself, he was a charming and interesting com-

panion. She learned many things from him in their daily contacts;
his conversation was full of references to events and ideas she had
never heard before, and when she found that he did not despise her
ignorance, she learned also to question him, and then to listen.
He held up to her a mirror of a culture she had not known existed.
For the first time she heard the names of Rousseau and Voltaire,
and the *Encyclopédie* and learned that the Revolution was not an
idea brought into existence in a single day by the National
Assembly. It was difficult to reconcile the fact that Charles, an
aristocrat, knew and sympathized with the ideals of liberty. Sometimes when they were alone together he would read to her. In the
cool of the orchard he would lie on the grass and read to her from
the treasonable Tom Paine's *Rights of Man*, and solemnly intone
the clauses of the American Declaration of Independence. She
gazed at him in awe and admiration, and would spend long hours
staring unseeingly across the Marsh, puzzling the things he had
said to her.

Paul, who because of his knowledge of Louise de Montignot in
Paris could afford to ignore the gossip that Charles would marry
Jane, was still jealous of Charles's learning and scholarship.

'I'm a simple Englishman,' he said bluntly to Jane, 'and I don't
pretend to be a match for some fancy French philosopher.'

'I understand only simple Englishmen,' Jane replied. 'And I
don't think Charles supposes himself a philosopher.'

But it was one thing to hear Charles execute the graceful little
minuets and gavottes on the harpsichord, and quite another to try
to follow him as he put his horse to jump the dykes and fences of
the Marsh. On a horse he was matchless, as if he and the animal
had only one identity; William was lost in wonder and reverence
of him. The three of them – Jane, Charles and William – became a
familiar sight on the roads and in the hamlets across the Marsh.
Wherever they went the labourers and the village women knew
them, and acknowledged them with lifted caps and curtseys. A
great many of them came forward to congratulate Charles on his
escape; Jane was touched by the obvious sincerity of their words,
and she also began to think of the escape as something miraculous.
William began to identify himself closely with Charles, beaming
with pleasure during these encounters, and taking the congratulations as being meant for him also. With the working people
Charles unbent to a degree he never did in the drawing-rooms of
the gentry; he was kind and leisurely in his speech, and talked
with the children as well as their parents. After a short time there
was nowhere they could ride on the Marsh that some 'looker'

would not pause from his task of herding the sheep to wave to
them, or the carpenter's apprentice look up from his tools to smile.

This Charles was familiar to her – a companion, almost a
friend, a hero to William, a master for Blake's Reach, and someone
to restore honour and dignity to the Blake name. The other side
of Charles was known to her only by what she could observe and
guess.

At least twice a week he rode to Dover, sometimes more frequently. On occasion he would bid Turnbull come with him, and
once Jane dared to question Robert about these visits.

He shrugged, a weary gesture that already had the look of defeat
about it. 'Always the same object – Louise de Montignot. He is
pouring gold into the pockets of anyone who has even half-
promised him some information or aid. But so far as we know she's
still in La Force, and he's growing desperate . . . the news from
France is bad . . .'

Jane knew well enough what the news from France was; the
whole of Europe was watching, unbelievingly, the events in Paris
where the Reign of Terror was gathering force. When the news
reached them at Blake's Reach of the second storming of the
Tuileries and the massacre of the Swiss Guard, Jane saw Charles
come as close to desperation as he would ever be. In a frenzied
need for action he saddled his horse and rode to Dover. When he
returned next day it was with the news that the royal authority
had been suspended, and the Royal Family imprisoned in the
Temple.

His face was haggard, his eyes dull from lack of sleep; at night
Jane heard his ceaseless pacing in his chamber. He left his food
almost untouched. The long August days moved on slowly, and
they gave up talking of the awaited storm that would freshen the
still air, and lay the dust. Jane found what tasks she could to
occupy her, but there were never enough to absorb her energies.
Charles's tortured face was always present to remind her of what
hung in the balance across the Channel, and her own thoughts
were never far from Louise de Montignot, and that strange, inexplicable statement of Charles's that perhaps, in the end, Blake's
Reach would belong to her, Jane.

3

Charles nodded at Jane down the length of the dining-table, and
for a moment the look of tight weariness his face had worn all day
lifted. His smile was cynically amused.

'I had a visit from the vicar of St Mary's this afternoon. I
believe you know him – the Reverend Sharpe who takes the service
at St Saviour's?'

'Yes . . . ?'

His long fingers plucked at the grapes on his plate. 'He thinks
it's high time I proved to the parish that I've not succumbed to
the wicked influences of my despised French relatives, and turned
Papist.'

She shrugged. 'Laugh if you like, but to the people on the
Marsh you are English, and you had best show yourself in an
English church. The vicar's right about that. No one expects the
Blakes to be religious people, but they expect them to do what all
the other Blakes have done before them.'

'How stern you are, Jane!' he mocked her. 'And what a tyrant!
You should be the mother of a large brood, and bring them all up
to be good Blakes!'

She hated him when he laughed at her. She glanced at his dark,
lean face almost lost in the wavering candlelight, and thought that,
with his thin mouth and black hooked eyebrows, he had a devilish
quality about him. But afterwards, in the drawing-room, when
he sat at the harpsichord and played the chorales he loved, his
expression was peaceful and at rest. Jane's heart was touched when
she thought of the long months in prison, and the horrors he had
seen and did not speak of, and she was glad that sometimes he
could be at peace. They would sit wordlessly there for an hour and
more, with only the thin plucking sounds of the harpsichord between them.

On the next Sunday morning, wearing his finest coat and gold-
buckled shoes, he walked up the hill to St Saviour's-by-the-Marsh.
Jane and William sat beside him in the Blake pew, stiff and conscious of every eye fixed upon them. The word had gone around
that Charles would attend this morning's service and apart from
the villagers who packed the church, people from two parishes
away had made excuses to visit cousins in St Mary's, and had come
to stare at the man who had escaped from the hands of those
Frenchies, and, as they believed, the jaws of death. Robert Turnbull, who had been bidden to take dinner at Blake's Reach with
them, had come early, and slipped into a pew at the back of the
church.

At the appointed moment Charles rose and went to the pulpit,
and in his beautiful, sensitive voice, read the Lesson; he was a
splendid figure standing there in wig and silk coat, his hands
resting on the Bible that bore the Blake crest on its leather binding.

His demeanour was perfect, humble and yet dignified.

The vicar offered prayers of thanksgiving for Charles's deliverance from the anti-Christs across the Channel, making it seem as if the God he prayed to was also an Englishman. Then, before he began his sermon, he made the announcement that, in thanksgiving, Charles would present St Saviour's with a rose window for the south transept.

For Jane it should have been a great moment, a moment of complete identification with a family and a way of life that had continued here for hundreds of years. Instead it was almost a moment of imprisonment; she felt the heaviness of those years upon her like a load. For an instant she caught a glimpse of her own self as she had been the first Sunday she had attended service here, saw the puppet she had been, playing the game that Charles now played. But he had gone much further. He would give a rose window to the church in thanksgiving for a return he felt no joy in. She glanced out over the approving congregation, and their red-cheeked country faces dissolved before her eyes. Instead she had a second's vision of the congregation of wool bales and brandy casks she had herself addressed from the pulpit. But now she saw the softly coloured light from Charles's new rose window streaming down on the smugglers' congregation. She closed her eyes to shut out the vision.

After the service Charles lingered just as she had done, playing out the ritual of the handshakes and the greetings, accepting the congratulations. William was close by his side, enjoying the occasion, performing his same courtly little bow; Jane joined them, but her smile was set as if she were a wax doll, and her hand resting in the vicar's was like lead.

Robert Turnbull was with them as they set off down the hill. After the meal he walked with Jane among the rosebeds, where the blooms were dusty and faded, turning brown at the edges.

Jane paused, and nodded up towards the church. She said bitterly, 'Well – we'll yet see the King's Pearl spent on silk bedhangings and a window for the church. Was it for this the Blakes have kept it all these years?'

Robert shrugged. 'I wonder how Charles intends to pay for it? However – it was a nice gesture and it makes the people happy even if it never comes into being. Well . . .' he glanced across at Jane, 'it was a great sight to see all three Blakes at service this morning. You're making the family respectable, Jane!'

'Respectable . . . !'

'Once,' he went on, 'they were full of adventure and spirit –

BLAKE'S REACH

even perhaps, nobility. Now they're merely respectable! Not a bad change!'

Abruptly, to avoid replying, she bent and put her face close to a crimson rose, breathing in its dusty fragrance, which meant the end of the summer.

3

Paul stood on the shingle at Barham on a night early in September, and blessed his good fortune. The night was calm, but dark, so dark that although he could hear the creak of the rowlocks, he could not see the boats that were pulling away from the *Dolphin's* side. The first of the cargo was coming ashore, and from all the information he had gathered, he knew that no Preventive Officers or Dragoons would bother him this night. The cargo was a rich one, the biggest he had so far brought across, and he had chosen Barham for the landing because of the speed with which the cargo could be handled here. He smiled to himself in the darkness; along with the contraband goods the *Dolphin* had also brought two passengers, who had not only paid handsomely for their passage, but once they touched the shingle, would be no further responsibility of his. Refugees fleeing from the Terror in France were the best kind of cargo to carry; they gave no trouble and their passage money didn't need to be reported to Charles or Turnbull. They were always worth the risk involved in taking them aboard in a French port.

He heard the scrape as the first boat touched the shingle. With a swift order to the waiting cart-driver, and the eager crowd of women, he moved forward.

As he expected, the first boat carried, among the kegs and the oilskin packages, the two passengers. Paul wasn't in the least interested in their identities or their persons; the captain of the *Dolphin*, Joe Shore, would have collected their passage money before the vessel weighed anchor in Le Havre. All Paul wanted now was to get them on their way, so that their presence wouldn't hinder the loading-party.

He watched them, two dark figures climbing stiffly from the boat, moving with the timid movements of people unaccustomed to the sea. When they reached the shingle they stood close together, staring about them in a kind of helpless bewilderment.

He spoke to them in clipped tones. '*Messieurs . . . !*' They turned

expectantly. 'I have a cart waiting to take you to Folkestone. From
there you may easily arrange transportation to wherever you wish
to go.'

'*Merci . . . merci beaucoup!*' The words were spoken dully, as if
the ordeal of escape and the sea voyage had left the speaker unnaturally submissive. The second man, however, gestured to hold
Paul's attention.

'*Monsieur . . .* I beg you . . .' His English was heavily accented,
but understandable. 'I have to reach a town called Rye . . . The
captain, he told me it is near here.'

'It will be possible to arrange your journey from Folkestone to
Rye tomorrow,' Paul said coldly. 'I have only one cart and it must
take you both to the same place. Now if you will . . .'

'One moment, Monsieur! It is of extreme urgency that I reach
Rye as quickly as possible – a matter of life and death.'

'Whom do you wish to see in Rye?' Paul said.

The man gestured violently. 'From there I must seek a gentleman called Charles Blake . . . lately arrived here from France. I
am instructed that he lives close by that town. I must reach him!
I repeat, Monsieur, it is a matter of life and death!'

Tonight the lights of Warefield House were visible far beyond the
park that surrounded it. Of all nights this was the one on which
Paul had least wanted to approach the house where he had been
born. Tonight all the families of the gentry living in or on the
fringes of the Marsh were gathering here to celebrate the coming-of-
age of James Fletcher's eldest son and heir, Harry. From the bonfires that blazed in the grounds, and the smell of roasting pork and
the garbled shouts that carried to him on the wind, Paul knew
that James's tenants were also making the most of the occasion.
There were precious few times, Paul thought, that his brother's
tenants ever got a free glass of ale from their landlord.

But the very fact that this was a night of celebration had made
it impossible to send anyone else. There was a message to be
delivered to Charles Blake, and he was here, somewhere among
the guests who thronged James's hall and drawing-room, and
spilled into the garden outside, and even went to mingle with the
tenants round the roasting-pits. As little as he wanted to appear
on James's estate tonight, where he was most certainly an uninvited guest, Paul could think of no one who would be less conspicuous here than himself. He knew the back passages and staircases of the house intimately, and two of the menservants here gave
him occasional service as porters when there was a cargo coming

in – this, of course, being regarded as none of Sir James's business. If he could find one of these men, it would be simple to get a message to Charles to meet him in an upstairs room. Paul knew that all the local magistrates and the military officers of the surrounding countryside would be among the guests; it would have been extreme folly to have allowed an emotional Frenchman, who had been robbed of all discretion by his anxiety and exhaustion, to appear in this assembly. There was no telling what the Frenchman would have blurted out, and perhaps not only the landing-place and the name of the vessel he had come over on be revealed, but Charles's name linked, even indirectly with the smuggling trade. And where Charles's name was linked, so inevitably must Jane's be.

As he approached the back of the house, Paul slipped from his horse, and stood waiting within the heavy shadow of the trees. For some minutes he studied the activity in the kitchens and servants' quarters, which were clearly visible through the lighted open windows. One by one he identified the servants, and watched their movements as they hurried back and forth between kitchen and dining-room. He grimaced with distaste as he plotted how he would creep, like a thief, into his brother's house.

Down on the shingle at Barham he had struggled with himself before making the decision to come here. It would have been simple to pretend not to hear the urgency in the Frenchman's plea, and tell himself that tomorrow would have been soon enough for Charles to know what news had come for him from France. He would have to admit now to Charles that he had been bringing over refugees, and receiving payment for them without Charles's knowledge, and it would have been much easier to do this anywhere but here under these circumstances.

But the Frenchman had said 'a matter of life and death', and the name he had whispered to Paul on the shingle at Barham had been that of Louise de Montignot.

2

The music and the laughter and the voices had been too much for Paul, and almost without a choice in the matter he found himself walking softly along the upstairs passage towards the gallery and the great staircase. He knew he was drawn here by only one thought; with good luck it was possible he might catch a glimpse of Jane.

Once the fireworks display had started on the terrace, entering the house had been easy enough. He had waylaid Shelby, the man-servant, in the stone passage between the kitchen and dining-room, and had despatched him to find Charles, and conduct him discreetly to one of the disused nursery rooms. But for Paul the wait in that bare, dusty room had been too long. When the fireworks were over, and still Charles had not come, he had succumbed to his own desires. One sight of Jane would be enough – just one, he told himself.

He crouched in the corner of the gallery where the shadows were deepest, and searched the lighted hall below. The guests were streaming back in from the terrace now; they made a moving mosaic of textures and colours – silks, velvets and satins in every colour he could name. And there was Jane at last, in blue silk, with her brilliant hair like a flame above it. He saw her white shoulders and bosom which the gown revealed, the sway of her body as she moved, and he knew that there were many other men down there who looked at her as he did. He pressed his face against the wooden balustrade, sick with the knowledge of his love and desire, sick with the frustration of being unable to walk down those stairs and claim her before this whole company. He tried to look away, tried not to hear her laugh or to see the movement of her hands as she opened her fan. On one side of her walked his nephew, Harry, on the other a man he did not recognize, in the uniform of a captain of the Royal Navy.

He risked discovery when he stood up and leaned over the balustrade to watch her as she disappeared through the open doors into the drawing-room.

Charles waited until the hall was almost deserted before coming upstairs. Wordlessly Paul motioned him to follow, as he led the way back to the nursery.

'What has happened?' Charles said as he closed the door behind him.

'You know a man called Pierre Latour?'

'Latour!' Charles exclaimed. 'Pierre Latour was Phillipe de Montignot's secretary. Is there news . . . ?'

Paul nodded. 'Not good news, Charles. Latour landed tonight from Le Havre. He needed to see you urgently, but I could not let him come here . . .'

'Quickly . . . tell me! What has happened to Louise?'

'Still in Le Havre,' Paul said. 'Latour brought her down from Paris by barge, and they lodged at the house of friends of Latour, whom he swears are loyal. Then he looked around for a ship to

take them to England. They had to wait . . . you understand the
tension has been growing this past month, and everyone is suspicious . . .'

'For God's sake, *tell me*!'

'He contacted Joe Shore, the skipper of the *Dolphin*, and
arranged passage for them both. But before he could get back to
the Countess he learned that he was under suspicion himself. He
dared not go back to the house where she was, because it would
have led to a search, and her description is circulated in every
port in France. She would have been recognized and taken. There
was nothing to do but slip back to the *Dolphin*, and bring the news
to you. He says someone else must be sent to get her.'

Charles's thin lips tightened. 'And Louise herself . . . ? What
did he say of her?'

'She's very ill. How ill, he's not sure – they couldn't risk calling
a physician. He says . . . he says that even when he was making
the arrangements he doubted that she would have the strength to
make the journey across . . .'

Charles was silent; he clasped his hands behind his back and
paced the length of the room. As he turned back Paul saw his face
was drained of colour, the skin pinched tightly on the high cheek
bones.

'She will die!' he said distractedly. 'If she is left there, she will
die! *Mon Dieu* – think of it! She is there all alone . . .'

Paul shook his head. 'Latour assures me she is in good hands,
and that his friends will care for her . . .'

Charles waved his words aside. 'But she believes she is deserted!
– and she will die!'

A burst of laughter from the kitchen yard below seemed suddenly to mock his words. Then there were drunken, ribald whistles,
and a girl's high-pitched voice, laughing also, and protesting.
Someone gave a faint cheer, and there was more laughter. James's
tenants, Paul thought, were making good use of his free cider and
ale.

'We will find someone to go over,' Paul said. 'There are plenty
who will do that for payment . . . there are some I know in
Folkestone and Dover who speak French tolerably and may come
and go without . . .'

'It would take too much time,' Charles cut him short. 'We cannot
afford the days – even the hours! It grows worse in France all the
time. Since the royal authority has been suspended, and the King
a prisoner in the Temple, every hour a royalist stays alive is an
hour of grace . . .'

Abruptly he broke off, looking now directly at Paul. 'You say the *Dolphin* brought Latour over?'

Paul stiffened, preparing now to face Charles's accusations of double-dealing. 'Yes, it did – Joe Shore brings over anyone he can give passage to on my authority, and if you think I've no right . . .'

Charles gestured impatiently. 'What does it matter! That's your affair. I want to know where the *Dolphin* is now.'

'Lying off Barham. She's waiting for me to come back – I'm captaining her to Flushing this trip . . .'

'Good!' Charles exclaimed. 'Then ride to Barham and hold her there. Don't let her move! I'll join you as soon as I can break away from here.'

'What do you mean – hold her? The *Dolphin* leaves for Flushing as soon as I go aboard!'

Charles laid his hand quietly on the other's sleeve. 'Ah, no, my friend! The *Dolphin* will sail for Le Havre as soon as *I* go aboard!'

Paul's expression darkened. 'I'm captain of the *Dolphin*, and I say she'll go to Flushing, as arranged. There's plenty in Dover who'll go for the Countess, and in the meantime she'll come to no harm. She'll be more rested, and better able to undertake the journey . . .'

'Every day she stays in France the danger grows worse,' Charles said calmly. 'The *Dolphin* will sail tonight for Le Havre!'

'But I have a cargo of wool loading that's due in Flushing . . .'

Charles's grip tightened on Paul's arm. 'I'm not asking you for the *Dolphin*, Mr Fletcher. I'm commandeering her!'

3

The group who waited in Joe Shore's cottage at Barham turned their heads expectantly as they caught the rumble of the carriage wheels on the cobbles at the end of the village street. Paul rose, took the candle and went quickly to the door; he had posted Joe's son, Matt, to watch for the coach and direct it to the cottage. It stopped before the door, but Paul waited, his hand on the latch, listening to the low-toned conversation outside. Then he heard Patrick's voice as he urged the greys forward again, and the carriage moved off towards Lydd. Shielding the candle with his body, Paul opened the door.

But it was not Charles who entered first. There was a tap of high-heeled slippers on the cobbles, and the brush of heavy silk against the door frame. Startled, Paul fell back a step, and Jane moved past him; she was followed closely by Charles and Matt

Shore. Matt dropped the latch into place, and leaned back against
it.

'Jane!' Paul's tone was a shocked protest. 'Why are you here?
Why have you sent the carriage away?'

She turned back to him. The billowing silk seemed to fill all the
space in the small room, and her perfume was heavy on the air.

'I'm coming to France with you,' she said simply. Then she
glanced to Charles for support before she went on. 'I'm coming
because the Countess is ill, and will need a woman on the journey
back . . .' Her voice faltered a little as she encountered Paul's
thunderous scowl.

'This is madness!' he said. 'Utter madness!' He turned furiously
towards Charles. 'Have you gone out of your mind to permit this?
There's danger – you said yourself there's danger! If anything
goes wrong there'll be no leniency for Jane.'

He swung back to Jane appealingly. 'Jane, have a thought
before you do this! I beg you, have a thought!'

'Why should there be danger for me? I'm not wanted in France.'

'You'll be aiding the escape of a royalist . . .' He looked back
at Charles. 'Why don't you stop her? – since you seem to be commanding this expedition!'

Charles shrugged. 'I don't stop her because I don't believe she'll
be in danger. And . . . and I was profoundly grateful to her for
offering her help. Louise may be dying, and a woman alone on
this sea voyage . . .'

Paul threw out his hands. 'Oh! – this wretched Frenchwoman!
So long as she is served it doesn't count what danger Jane is
exposed to . . .'

Charles held up his hand. 'I think we've talked enough. I have
pointed out to Jane what risks she will run, and she is still willing
to come. Is that enough for you, Fletcher? The time is going, and
we stand here and make talk . . .'

He looked carefully around the group – from Paul to Joe Shore,
the *Dolphin*'s captain, to Matt, to a man he had never seen before,
sitting wearily hunched over the table, and finally to Pierre
Latour. He held out his hand.

'Latour! It's good to see you here in freedom!'

Emotion crossed the other man's face swiftly as he gripped
Charles's hand; he held on tightly for a moment, struggling for
control.

'I do not feel as if this is freedom, Monsieur. I have saved
myself and failed my master, and Madame la Comtesse . . .'

'You have not failed, Latour. She is out of La Force, and only

a few hours by ship from England. We shall have her safe here
. . .' He broke off, as the other shook his head.

'Monsieur . . . I fear for Madame's life. The time in prison has
weakened her greatly. We only made Le Havre because it was
possible to come directly from Paris down the Seine by barge. And
getting her out of La Force . . . I tell you, Monsieur, it was
genius! And it cost a fortune!' For an instant his melancholy
face lit up. 'Such a beautiful plan, Monsieur . . .'

'I'm sure it was, Latour, and you deserve great credit . . . your
skill and loyalty have earned Madame's unending gratitude, and
mine also . . .' He broke off, and put his hand on the other man's
shoulder as he saw the tears well up in those tired, bloodshot eyes.

'Oh, Monsieur,' Latour whispered, 'go to her! She needs help
so badly, and she may be dying. So brave she has been, and so
helpless . . . and since Monsieur le Comte was so foully murdered
by those fiends she has no one but yourself. All the family dispersed, or dead . . . living in exile and poverty. Her son is dead,
and her brother – there is only you, Monsieur! You will take care
of her?'

Charles nodded. 'I will take care of her.'

Then he motioned the other to a chair, and he drew one up for
himself. 'Now, Latour, you must remember every single detail we'll
need to know to reach her . . .'

Their talk went into French then, rapid questions and explanations, and finally Latour produced a piece of paper on which he
had drawn a crude map. To this he added a name, and an
address. As he wrote, Charles looked up at Paul.

'Is everything ready to sail on the *Dolphin*?'

Paul nodded curtly. 'Yes – I shall captain her myself. Joe here
has made six trips without a break, and, in any case, there's only
one cabin, and we shall need that for the Countess – and Jane,'
he added grimly.

Charles's gaze slowly turned on Jane. 'My dear, I'm afraid to
ask you if you've reconsidered your decision. You heard what
Latour has said . . . Louise needs kindness, and a woman's care . . .'

'I'm coming!' Jane said brusquely. 'Let's have no more talk
about it!'

Charles nodded. 'Very well – I'm glad to hear it.' Then he
gestured towards her gown. 'Couldn't you find something –' he
appealed to Joe Shore. 'She'll be in more danger from that gown
as she goes up the side of the *Dolphin* than from the Frenchies.'

Shore nodded. 'That she will! There should be something about
the place to borrow.' He moved towards the passage leading to

the back of the cottage. 'I'll fetch my daughter – I sent her packin'
t' bed when I knew Mr Fletcher an' the two others was comin' . . .'

He opened a door at the end of the passage, and they could
hear a low murmur of voices. Then a woman's figure appeared,
wearing a nightgown and wrapper. But by the smoothness of her
lustrous dark curls and the fetching angle of her cap, it was plain
she hadn't been in bed. She held a candle, and it shone directly on
her pretty lively face.

'Well, quite a company we have 'ere!' She gave a little gasp
as her eyes fell on Jane. 'Didn't know the Queen o' France 'ad
escaped.'

Jane remembered the voice, the warm, rough voice in the
Barham churchyard on the night of the run. She held out her hand.
'Rose!'

4

The hull of the *Dolphin* seemed to tower above Jane, the masts
and rigging lost in the blackness of the sky; she had crouched
stiffly in the boat as they were rowed towards the *Dolphin*, afraid
to move in this strange new world where everything was damp
and smelled of old fish, afraid of catching her feet in the tackle at
the bottom of the boat, afraid of losing her balance – afraid, most
of all, of earning a rebuke from Paul. She felt lost and forlorn, and
she had a moment to wonder if she had been in her right mind in
agreeing to go, before Paul motioned her to start on the ladder up
the side.

Matt Shore's shoes, which she had borrowed from Rose, were
too big for her, and she was clumsy. It seemed an incredible labour
to haul herself up the rope. The ladder was a treacherous thing –
giving and swaying with each movement from her. Her face was
wet with sweat when she drew level with the deck, and rough
hands pulled her the rest of the way. She found herself set on her
feet with less care than a bundle of cargo. Charles's head had
appeared at the top of the ladder, and soon he also was on the
deck. She took another hitch in the belt that held Matt's breeches
loosely about her waist, and waited for Paul. He was the only one
reassuring thing in this bewildering scene, and she needed him.

But he would come to her only after he had given detailed
orders to the hands, and consulted in low tones with his mate. She
stayed away from Charles, feeling humble and unsure of herself,
and not wanting to betray it. As she stood there, questioning her
own sanity for offering to make the journey, she tried to fix in her

mind Rose's words, and the expression on the girl's face as she had helped Jane change into her brother's clothes.

'If Paul Fletcher was my man I'd go with 'im, too! I'd follow 'im wherever 'e went.'

She could hear the rattle of the cable as the anchor came up, and the quick movements among the crew as an order from Paul sent the hands aloft. She watched the mainsail unfurl, and the sight as the breeze slowly filled it was one of new, unbelievable beauty to her. A slight shudder ran through the *Dolphin* as the vessel lifted to the breeze. Her bow swung slowly about, and she set course on a tack that would take her clear of the tip of Dungeness.

Jane squeezed herself in against the bulwark, and hoped she would get in no one's way until she was told what to do. The breeze caught the ends of the cloth Rose had bound about her hair, and they flipped across her face. She could feel the heave and drop of the *Dolphin*, and the motion, not yet too strong, pleased her. At her feet on the deck was the cloth bundle containing the old gown and petticoats Rose had given her to wear in Le Havre. In the box under Rose's bed lay her own silk ball gown.

At last Paul came to her; he stood beside her staring up at the starless sky, listening, she thought, to the steady thrumming of the wind in the rigging. He leaned back, his back and elbows against the bulwark, feeling the rhythm of his ship.

'Well, Jane,' he said. 'Here you are, aboard the *Dolphin*, and there's a woman lying over there in Le Havre, who'll take Blake's Reach from you!'

In the darkness she moved and pressed herself close to him, standing on her toes and reaching up to put her arms about him, to put her hands behind his neck and pull his face down to her.

'Forget that woman lying over there,' she whispered. She opened her lips to meet his kiss, and pushed her body firmly against his, feeling her breasts hard against his body, feeling him tighten and respond to her urging. They rocked together with the motion of the vessel.

'Yes, I'm here aboard the *Dolphin*,' she said softly. 'And you promised me that one day I would see France!'

5

Jane lay wakeful and restless in the narrow cot, huddling naked under the thin blankets that smelled of sea-water. She occupied the tiny stern cabin, the only one on the lugger; at the end of the companionway Charles had tried to stretch his length in a hammock slung between two beams. She wondered if he also lay awake, listening to the creak of the timbers, the wind that now shrieked high in the rigging. The weather had worsened steadily, and for more than an hour the *Dolphin* had been rolling in high seas. Sometimes the wind brought flurries of rain against the stern ports; Jane shivered and pulled the blankets higher about her shoulders, wishing that the morning would come, so that at least she might see how rough it was, instead of imagining mountains of water beating against the small vessel. She lay with her hands on her queasy stomach, and a kind of respect began to dawn in her for the men whose livelihood was the sea, for Paul, on deck now since they had left Dungeness, and for the hands who had swarmed up the rigging.

She sat up and fumbled in the darkness to find her shirt; after she had put it on she slid out of the cot, easing her way along the bulwark until her groping hands encountered an oilskin she had seen hanging there. She brought this back and spread it over the cot, and once more crept down between the blankets, wishing she now had the biscuits Paul had offered, and which she had declined.

The *Dolphin* suddenly gave a much more violent pitch, and she grabbed the side of the cot to save herself from rolling out. The *Dolphin* might be a thing of beauty and joy to Paul, but to her it was damp and cold, and possessed of sly, ungracious little tricks to trap the unwary. The night seemed endless.

Still clutching the side of the cot, she closed her eyes, and kept them closed firmly; after a time she seemed to drift towards sleep. The *Dolphin* settled back to the steady pitch of the past hour.

She was brought to complete wakefulness by the boom of a cannon. The sound was close by, and loud, even in the wind. She sat bolt upright, frantically trying to make out some shape in the blackness beyond the stern ports.

Above she could hear orders being shouted; she distinguished Paul's voice, but could not hear the words. The orders were followed by the rush of horny, bare feet drumming on the deckhead above her cot. She could feel the swing as the *Dolphin* went about a different tack. Then, for an instant, through the ports, she caught sight of the riding-lights of a vessel. Then the *Dolphin* gathered way, and the lights fell astern.

She sat there, shivering and frightened, straining to try to hear what was going on about her. In the passage she heard a muttered curse in French as Charles struggled to find his shoes in the darkness. Then she heard his steps on the companion ladder. She too wondered if she should dress and go on deck; she remembered

Paul's orders, and that crowded deck space where every inch seemed to be given over to equipment and gear. She slid down between the blankets once more, and decided that, unless a cannon shot came through the stern ports, she was better where she was.

There was no hope of sleep now. She listened, but she could hear nothing more. There was no further fire from the other vessel, and the *Dolphin* did not return the shot. She sensed the increased speed of the *Dolphin*, as if Paul had risked putting on more sail. There were no more shouted orders from the deck, and Charles did not return, either.

She lay there still, watching the ports for the first light of dawn, wondering how long it would be before the storm blew itself out. It was September already, she thought, and this was the first storm of autumn.

A watery sun rose, breaking through the racing grey clouds. Except where the sun touched it, the sea was also grey, with a heavy swell running. The *Dolphin* seemed to be all alone in the Channel; Jane lay listening to the cries of the gulls who followed in the wake of the ship.

At last Paul came down to the cabin, his eyes dull-looking, the lines of fatigue set hard on his face. He wore a sou'wester, but no oilskins and his clothes were wet. He dropped into the seat under the ports, flinging his arms and legs wide in a mighty stretch and a yawn.

'Lord, Jane, I'm tired! No sleep since . . . since days ago!' He closed his eyes for a moment, moving his head from side to side to stretch his neck. Then he looked at her again. 'We'll be in Le Havre by afternoon. Got blown off course last night.'

'Is that all you can say,' she asked. 'Or didn't you notice the cannon shot?'

He grinned. 'I wondered if it woke you!' Then the smile faded; he shrugged. 'We came near to it, Jane! – Lord, it got so dark when that weather blew up that you could hardly see your hand in front of you. Then suddenly I got a sight of the riding lights on this craft, and we went so close I could see she was flying the Revenue Stripes. We weren't flying anything at all, and I'm hoping she'll still be trying to guess who we were.'

'But the shot . . . ?'

'She fired a blank to signal us to heave-to, but we weren't stopping for courtesies like that! We went about as quickly as we could make it, and got to hell away from her. The *Dolphin* was built to run, not to stay and fight . . . well, there wasn't a sight of them this morning.'

'I was frightened,' Jane said. 'I was scared stiff!'

'That's the most sensible thing I've heard you say for a long time. Anyone but a fool would have been scared . . . we've got a load of wool aboard I was supposed to ship to Flushing, and we have no export licence to show if we'd been searched.'

'Charles went on deck,' she said. 'I heard him go up.'

Paul nodded. 'He stayed there right through it, and, for a landsman, he managed not to get too much in the way.'

'He's still there?'

'Yes – stayed there all night. Hardly spoke a word, either. Didn't seem to be afraid – didn't even ask if we'd lost the Revenue cruiser. Just stood all night on the deck, and didn't say a word! Wouldn't even go to the galley with me to get something to eat. He's still there . . . just looking at the empty sea.'

Jane shivered. 'I don't understand Charles.'

'Nor do I! – don't even understand myself for doing what he tells me to! This trip to Le Havre . . . it's madness! Even though he owns the *Dolphin*. I'm her master and I could have refused to do as he said. Why does he have to go himself? . . . he could have sent someone for this Frenchwoman, and he wouldn't have endangered his own life. To escape once is enough . . . Doesn't he know he's asking too much of his luck to do it again? Doesn't he know that, Jane?'

'I think he knows it,' she said soberly. 'And perhaps that's why we do as he says, and go where he tells us. He has great courage, Paul, and somehow he carries you along with it. Look at me! – I lie here and wonder why in Heaven's name I ever said I'd come along. I don't feel brave, and I don't love Louise de Montignot. But Charles has such courage and he's so direct and determined about what he has to do for that woman – and I found myself saying I'd go.'

Paul rubbed his hand wearily across his eyelids. 'You admire him, don't you, Jane?'

'I think he is brave,' she said frowning, 'but he is cold! It is almost as if he doesn't know what it would feel like to be afraid. He looks at you with those cold, black eyes . . . and he drinks and he rides and he spends money – perhaps he even makes love – and I don't think his heart ever beats faster for it! Can you think how he looks now? – as cold as the sea!'

She pulled the blankets close about her chin, and rolled on her side, facing Paul. 'I wonder,' she said musingly, '. . . I wonder if he loves Louise. I wonder if it will make him happy to have her at Blake's Reach?' She looked at him questioningly, and yet did not expect an answer. 'Or does he think of it only as a promise he gave, and must keep, no matter what he thinks or feels about Louise . . .'

'I don't care what Charles feels about the Frenchwoman,' Paul said. His tone was dull, as if he were repeating something he had decided a long time ago, and now it was an established fact. 'All I care about is that you are here, on the *Dolphin*, and I must be here also to see that nothing happens to you. I will go ashore at Le Havre and get this de Montignot woman, and I will use whatever cunning and skill and speed I have in doing it. And it won't be for her sake, or for Charles's, but for you, Jane. He has taken you into danger simply by lifting his finger and beckoning. If I love you I have to save you from Charles's obsession and his ruthlessness – I have to take you out of danger.'

His eyes had closed again; his lips looked thin and pinched.

'You're very tired, Paul,' she said softly.

'Yes . . .'

'Could you sleep if you came in here with me? If I lay very still, could you sleep?'

His eyes flickered open. 'Not even you could keep me awake now, Jane.'

He sat on the edge of the cot, and she helped him strip off the sodden clothes. They lay in a pile on the deck; he kicked his boots aside and they slid across the deck and collapsed against the door. She squeezed herself against the bulkhead to make room for him in the cot, then she put her arm under his head, and covered his shoulders with the blanket.

He lay still for a few moments, breathing heavily; she began to think he was already asleep. Then suddenly he spoke, in a low, dull voice. 'What will you do, Jane, when she takes Blake's Reach from you? Are you going to come with me?'

Softly she pressed a kiss on his temple. 'Sweetheart, we'll talk about that when the time comes,' she murmured.

Then she gathered his chilled, weary body close to her, holding him against her to give him warmth. He seemed to yield himself to her then, not protesting or making any further effort to talk. His wet blond hair had fallen down across his forehead. He slept, with his head cradled against her breasts, a heavy, exhausted sleep that lasted until the sun was high.

4

All through the hours of the afternoon and the coming of dusk Jane and Charles waited for Paul to return. It had been a golden September day, warm, with only a hint of freshness in the breeze to carry the premonition of winter. And even that slight chill had gone once they passed the entry to the port of Le Havre, passed the round battlemented tower that had dominated the fortifications since the days of Francis the First. Jane watched the grey granite walls of the *quais* slide by them, and tried to hold back the shiver that touched her, in spite of the sun warm on her back. Charles looked unconcerned, as if he was not aware that the menace of an enemy now lay all about them.

'That is *La Citadelle*,' he said, gesturing over to the right of the entry. She turned and looked, and the sight of it was not reassuring. It was a high, square pile of masonry, facing both to the estuary and to the town itself, with fortified lookout towers at intervals along the walls. Not even the green of the trees within the enclosure softened its lines. Jane turned away quickly.

The Basin du Roi was more cheerful. The town clustered close about the shipping docked here; the bustle of people going about their everyday affairs had a normal look to Jane's eyes. It was a town not so very different from Folkestone, and she could almost persuade herself that this was England, peaceful and safe. And while she looked, her hands clutched the bulwark tightly to conceal from Charles their trembling.

The houses were of plaster and timber and tile, many different colours, whose top storeys overhung the cobbled streets. Washing was hanging from the windows, brightly coloured clothes flapping in the breeze like a great flock of birds on the move . . . or banners, Jane thought, yes, banners for a celebration day. She wondered why she thought these things, why she tried to persuade herself that this was a happy place, that no danger for them existed here. Behind one of these windows Louise de Montignot lay, and perhaps she even heard the harsh voices of the *blanchisseuses* Charles pointed out to her, calling and gossiping to each other over their wash tubs gathered about the fountain. The tubs were coloured also – blue and green.

During the afternoon the crew of the *Dolphin* had made an exaggerated show of discharging and consigning to a warehouse the cargo Paul had carried aboard at Barham. The bales of English wool had, after all, served their purpose in providing a pretext for being in the port.

Paul memorized the map Latour had drawn; from where they had dropped anchor in the Basin du Roi they could see the stream of traffic moving along the Rue de Paris. In the Rue de Paris Paul was to look for a wine shop, which also sold bread; there he would enquire for Albert Cornand.

Jane and Charles watched while Matt Shore rowed him to the steps of the *quai*. Then he was lost from sight among the crowds. They settled to wait.

The dusk came down slowly on the town. Jane had tried to sleep down in the cabin, but without the wind on the open sea it was stuffy and oppressive. Charles was still on deck when she came up, and it seemed as if he had not moved from his position by the bulwark. He turned as she paused beside him.

'A boat has just put off from the *quai*,' he said briefly. 'I think it is Paul, but there are two other people with him. One of them is a woman.'

In the gathering darkness it was difficult to see the boat, but as it drew nearer she recognized Paul in the stern. Matt Shore had stationed himself by the steps of the *quai* throughout the afternoon; Paul had wanted to remain as inconspicuous as possible, and had avoided using one of the small craft which waited there to serve as a ferry. The boat pulled in to the *Dolphin*'s side; it carried, as Charles had said, two passengers beside Paul. The first, a man, and a stranger to Jane, began to climb the ladder; Paul tried to steady it as the other climbed. Timidly the woman followed.

It was not Louise de Montignot; Jane knew this as soon as the woman stepped on to the deck. She was middle-aged, heavy with a pasty fleshiness; she wore a grey gown with a fraying, dirty fichu and a soiled cap on her grey hair. She looked weary and afraid, her brown eyes regarding them suspiciously. Jane had had many different ideas of what Louise de Montignot would look like, but she knew certainly that this was not she. Charles said nothing.

Paul joined them, and wordlessly motioned them all towards the companion-ladder leading to the cabin. Jane opened her mouth to speak to him, but his face was set with an anxious preoccupation she knew could not break with a casual word; she let her hand rest in his for a moment as he helped her on the ladder and he smiled in response, a smile that briefly warmed her, and let her share his anxiety. Charles was the last to come down the stairs;

he stood by the open doorway while Jane, Paul, and the two strangers tried to find space for themselves inside.

Paul gestured towards the pair, who had settled themselves side by side on the seat under the ports. The man, Jane guessed, was near sixty, with straggling, scant hair. His eyes looked out of his lined face with a desperate appeal.

'Monsieur and Madame Duval,' Paul said. 'I found them in hiding at Albert Cornand's shop, and they asked me for passage from France.'

'You will be going soon?' the man asked. 'It is imperative, Monsieur, that we leave quickly.' With a kind of shock Jane realized that he was speaking English, and in passing she wondered how he had learned it.

From the doorway Charles spoke. 'We will leave Le Havre as soon as our business here is completed – not before.'

'Completed!' The woman spoke, a deep voice that carried the tones of disgust and bitterness. 'If it's the Comtesse you've come for, then your business is completed. I know a dead woman when I see one, and she's as good as dead.'

Charles said coldly, 'But she still lives?'

'She lives, yes . . .' The woman shrugged. 'But for how long? A few hours – a day at the most!' She nudged her husband, and nodded towards Paul savagely. 'You've paid good money for this passage! You must demand that we leave immediately. I have no use for this waiting about for a dead woman!' She heaved her plump shoulders as she spoke. Beside her husband Jane noticed that she appeared strong and muscular, despite her fatigue; in her fierce way she was protective of him.

The man gestured apologetically to Charles. 'Forgive her, Monsieur! It is not usually Marie's way to be so – so harsh. But we have had an unfortunate experience trying to help a lady who was sought by the Commune . . . most unfortunate! I had a business in Paris, you understand. I am a violin maker with a high reputation . . .'

'Ah!' Marie Duval exclaimed contemptuously. 'A sentimental fool, that's what he is! Involving himself with the escape of an old patroness of our firm – one who should have taken her chance of justice before the courts as all good citizens do! But no! – he must meddle, and now we are ruined! Lucky to get out with our lives, and what gold we had in the house. We are ruined! . . . ruined!'

'Then be thankful you're not dead!' Charles said, dismissing the Duvals, and turning to Paul. 'What news is there? What of Louise?'

6

'It is as they say,' Paul answered. 'I have seen her, and she still lives.' Then he shook his head. 'But as for getting her aboard the *Dolphin* . . .'

'You have spoken with her?' Charles said eagerly. 'Have you told her I have come, and soon she will be in England?'

'I told her,' Paul said, 'and she was glad to know you were here. But when I told her you were coming, and that tonight we would take her aboard the *Dolphin*, she said nothing.'

'Nothing?'

'She said only that she would be happy to see you, but nothing else.'

Charles brushed his words aside. 'It is only her weakness – she must have time to get used to the idea that we have come to take her away.' He frowned as Paul began to shake his head. 'What is wrong with you! Have you turned into a miserable coward like everyone else – like this pair here?' He indicated the Duvals. 'Are you doing to desert her when we are so close?'

'I think,' Paul said quietly, 'that the Countess hasn't the strength to reach the *Dolphin*.'

'We will *make* her reach it! It can be done – a carriage or a sedan chair to the *quai*, and then we will carry her into the boat. Matt Shore must rig up some kind of sling to get her aboard. Damn you, why are you shaking your head? Are you defeated before we have begun?'

'Not defeated! Not yet! But things have been happening in France in the past few days that make even the short trip between Cornand's shop and the *quai* dangerous for a woman who must be helped every step of the way.'

'What has happened?' he demanded impatiently.

'Has Monsieur not heard?' Duval said. 'The news came from Paris this morning, and the town is in a fever.'

'What are you talking about?'

'Since the affair at the Tuileries last month, when the Swiss Guard was overthrown and the Royal Family taken to the Temple . . .'

'You mean when the Swiss Guard was murdered,' Charles said tersely.

The man shrugged. 'As you wish, Monsieur. Others have a different way of looking at it. Towards the end of August the citizens of Paris saw the funerals of the patriots which *they* claim were murdered by the aristocrats during the same attack on the Tuileries. All through the month the arrests have been countless, and the temper of the people so inflamed it was not safe to open

one's mouth unless to denounce a neighbour or a brother to the
Revolutionary Tribunal. It was necessary, you understand, to
prove that one was a loyal patriot. It was then we fled . . .'

'Yes – what more?'

'Terrible rumours have been spreading about Paris . . . the
Prussians were at the gates, the National Volunteers had gone to
the front and Paris was unprotected. The word went around that
the attack on the city was to be the signal for a counter-revolution.
The prisons were to be thrown open, and the women and children
would be at the mercy of the aristocrats and their paid assassins.
I thank God we got away . . .'

He shuddered, closing his eyes for a second. 'Today the news
reached here from Paris. An order was issued two days ago –
September the second, that would have been – by the Commune
that all the prisoners in L'Abbaye and La Force were to be tried
immediately – it was an order for execution or release. At midday
the same day an alarm gun was fired from the Pont-Neuf, and a
black flag was flown at Hotel de Ville. They say already hundreds
have died, hacked to pieces by the mob who wait only the few
minutes given to the mockery of a trial. It is the same for them
all – criminals, priests, prostitutes, royalists. It is release or death!
A massacre, Monsieur!'

'And it continues?'

'So far as we know, Monsieur. The news reached here today,
with orders for a special watch to be set for persons attempting
to escape, the Seine being one of the best ways to leave Paris . . .'

'This morning we were nearly caught,' Marie Duval said. 'We
left the house in which we spent the night but a few minutes before
it was searched by the National Guard. You know now why we
have no wish to wait here like sitting ducks until they decide to
search all the vessels in the port. I tell you every citizen has suddenly two pairs of eyes – one for himself, and another for any
action or word he thinks suspicious. It is a time when patriotism
cannot be taken for granted. It must be proved!'

She looked fiercely at Charles. 'And this Comtesse . . . the de
Montignot woman . . . her description is circulated to every port
and border in France. If I had guessed she was lodged in Cornand's
house I wouldn't have set foot in it! This town is not Paris, I tell
you. This is a small place, and everyone knows the other's business.
A strange, sick woman will not go long undiscovered, even hidden
away in the back room!'

'Keep your tongue still!' Charles said roughly.

Her face reddened. 'I'll not be quiet. We have paid good money
for this passage, and we demand to leave immediately. There isn't

a hope for that woman, and while we stay here the lives of all of us are in danger!'

'There are other foreign vessels in port,' Charles said. 'You are at perfect liberty to find a passage with any captain who will take you. Or else – ' he paused – 'or else get down on your knees and pray that Louise de Montignot lives to board this ship.'

He turned slowly to Jane. 'You have heard all this, and now the task is more difficult than we believed when we left England. Are you still willing to come ashore and help us with Louise?'

Jane nodded. 'I'll come!'

Paul got to his feet, his face wearing a look of irritated resignation. 'I've always believed that this whole venture was a piece of folly committed without thought. *You*,' he said, looking at Charles, 'should never have set foot in France while the present madness is on them, and you already know what I think about Jane being here.' He gestured briefly. 'However we are here, and every hour we remain increases the danger, so let us go and be done with it.'

Duval's delicate hands gripped his knees convulsively. 'Monsieur . . . as things are at present, the National Guard is likely to search all ships in the port . . . I implore you, Monsieur . . .'

'We will return as speedily as possible,' Paul said.

The Duvals sat in grim, unwilling silence as the three left the cabin.

2

Matt Shore and another hand from the *Dolphin* rowed them to the *quai*. They already had their instructions from Paul; they were to wait by the steps of the *quai* until the next morning, if necessary, and if they were questioned they were to say the Master of the *Dolphin* was ashore negotiating the purchase of a cargo. Nothing was to be said of the passengers who had gone aboard the *Dolphin*.

The evening was mild, and there was still a great deal of activity in the streets, with doors and windows flung open, and the sound of rapid voices everywhere. The stern lights of the ships riding at anchor in the Basin made broad gleaming paths across the water; the tide was running high, and the stench from the rotting garbage and debris tossed into the Basin was not so strong as it had been through the afternoon. The boat nosed the granite steps of the *quai* gently, and Paul stepped ashore, turning to give his hand to Jane. She found it was a miserable business trying to scramble from the boat to the slippery steps, hampered by her skirt and petticoats. As soon as Charles was ashore, Matt used his hands to pull the boat along to a mooring ring on the dock wall; the oars were shipped, and the two men settled themselves for their watch.

There was the usual number of idlers on the dock, sitting about on the bales and crates, enjoying the warm evening, chewing tobacco and spitting with relish as they discussed the day's news from Paris. Charles began to mount the steps; Jane followed, with her arm through Paul's; Charles was wearing the oldest coat he could find among the crew of the *Dolphin*, and a battered, stained hat. In his hand he held a lantern. Jane's eyes were on him as he climbed to the level of the *quai*, and she wished that he would carry himself with less pride. With his height and his head erect, even in those deplorable clothes, he was a figure to turn and look at. It was a mistake, she decided, and one that Paul had spoken against from the beginning, to allow Charles to come ashore. Even so soon two groups at the top of the steps had fallen silent, their gaze fixed curiously on Charles. He stood very still, holding the lantern low to light the steps.

Under his breath Paul muttered a restrained curse. 'Why does he have to look like that — even here !'

Jane looked beyond Charles as she reached the *quai*, and she sensed that what happened was not as accidental as it was made to appear. A man detached himself from the group nearest Charles, making some remark in French she could not understand. He stepped backwards and cannoned into Charles with considerable force. With an exclamation of annoyance, Charles spun round. Instantly his body went limp, and she saw him sway a little as he stood. The lantern, she noticed, he held well down at his side.

They exchanged a few words; even in the unfamiliar tongue Charles's voice was slurred and thickened, the stranger's apologetic. The man, however, did not step away from Charles; he was shorter than Charles, and he stared up intently into his face. Then Charles turned, still swaying, and caught Jane's arm. He leaned on it heavily. Quickly Paul reached over and took the lantern from his hand. Suddenly Jane felt herself caught roughly in Charles's arms; he tipped her head back and the hood of her cloak slipped off. Then Charles's lips were on her mouth, and he was kissing her. She stayed in his arms obediently, numb with astonishment. She could feel his hands in her hair, pulling it free of the cloak so that it spread about her shoulders. He went on kissing her, and from one of the groups there came a little chorus of appreciative whistles and cries.

Charles said softly, his mouth still pressed against hers, 'I'm drunk, and so are you ! Understand !'

Then he pulled himself away from her a little and looked in the

direction of the whistles. He held his arm about her shoulder, and
sketched a grotesque, clumsy bow, swaying as he did so. He called
something to the men in French, and there were some answering
comments, and laughter, and someone shouted – 'Une Anglaise!'
Jane could feel the pressure of Charles's hand on her shoulder
forcing her down in a rough curtsey. She smiled as she did it, and
knew that Charles was laughing too. A small round of applause
greeted her action; standing on tiptoe she managed to place a kiss
on Charles's cheek, at the same time reaching up to tweak his ear.

All this time the man who had cannoned into Charles stood
silent, his eyes moving rapidly over the three of them. Suddenly
he put out his hand to detain Charles. Paul stepped in beside
Charles and brushed roughly against the stranger.

'*Pardon, Monsieur,*' he said amiably. He spoke with an exaggerated English accent. This seemed to amuse the men standing
about; there was more laughter. By the time Paul had recovered
from his stiff foolish bow, and replaced his hat, Charles and Jane
had already moved down the *quai*, Charles walking with the
absurd erectness of a drunken man.

'Hey! Hey! wait for me!' Paul cried, starting to run after
them. He waved his hand with a flourish to the men by the steps.
When he reached the others he slipped an arm about Jane's waist.
They walked as rapidly as they dared towards the Rue de Paris.

Suddenly, as her mind cleared a little from the bewilderment
of those moments by the *quai*, Jane found herself afraid. She did
not dare to question Charles yet about the stranger who had
cannoned into him; there was nothing to say, and nothing to do
but imitate his slightly lurching walk. In the emptiness, fear touched
her with its reality for the first time. A faint shudder ran through
her body. Instantly she felt Paul's arm tighten about her, comforting, reassuring.

He bent close to her ear. 'Don't be afraid, sweetheart. Nothing
will happen to you – nothing.'

She knew well enough that he was making an uncertain prediction, but there was no uncertainty about his tone. His words
were clear and bold, and she believed, irrationally, that somehow
he would see to it that nothing did happen to her. It was easy to
believe whatever Paul said. She raised her head, and entered with
more spirit into the part Charles had assigned to her.

In the Rue de Paris there were more people, and more noise. There
was also more light from the taverns and shops, as well as the
upper storeys of the close-packed houses. The doors of the brothels
were wide open, the half-naked prostitutes soliciting briskly among

the seamen and townspeople who passed by. Charles pulled his
hat forward on his head, tipping it at an angle so that it partly
shadowed his face.

'Who was it?' Jane said in a low voice. She stopped by the doorway of a shop to poke at a great hoop of cheese displayed there.

Charles crumbled the edge of the cheese with his forefinger.
'Has he followed us? Is he anywhere near?'

Paul glanced casually back. 'I can't see him.' He leaned closer
to Charles.

'His name is Bouchet,' Charles said. 'He used to be a steward
on Phillipe de Montignot's estate. It was he who denounced
Phillipe and gave evidence against him at the trial. As a reward
for his display of patriotism he was given a position serving the
Commune. I imagine he's grown fat on bribes during the last year.'

'What is he doing here?'

'I can think of only one reason. They must know in Paris that
Louise is believed hiding here, and they have sent him to stir up
the authorities, and to identify her. It must have been he who
saw Pierre Latour, and hoped he would lead them back to Louise.
He must have been waiting here in Le Havre hoping that she
would be forced to show herself. Maybe he knew that Latour got
away on the *Dolphin* and he is having a watch kept on all the
quais in case the *Dolphin* should return. He must be certain that
Louise did not escape with Latour, or he wouldn't still be in Le
Havre.'

'But *you* . . .' Jane said. 'Did he recognize you?'

'I think he did,' Charles answered. 'He isn't quite certain – it
was dark enough there to make him doubtful, and he's only seen
me a very few times some years ago. Either he was confused by
what we did there at the *quai*, and believes we're no more than
smugglers taking a lady on a joy-ride to France, or else he knows
that Latour left on the *Dolphin*, he has recognized me, and now
he waits for us to take him to Louise.'

Then he suddenly shouted to the shopkeeper, and demanded that
he come and cut some cheese immediately. Charles paid for it,
counting the coins with drunken solemnity into the man's hand.
Then he broke it in three, and handed a piece each to Jane and
Paul. They nibbled it as they continued on down the street.

Paul began to hum softly, unmusically, waving his hand to
match the rhythm of the beat; suddenly, to the air of *Greensleeves*
Jane heard him sing : *Cornand's shop is on the corner over there
. . . Cornand's shop . . .'* Jane nudged Charles. '*Cornand's . . .
Cornand's . . .'*

They marked it with only the briefest glance; it was a triangular
building, commanding a view of two streets; and it didn't seem
to lack customers to sit at the tables in its dimly lighted interior.
Paul had continued to hum, now he broke into a whistle. Under
cover of it, Charles spoke.

'We'll go to a tavern where you're known, Paul,' Charles said.
'We'll have to find someone you can talk to about buying a cargo.'

'I know only a few people in Le Havre,' Paul answered. 'It
isn't one of my regular ports . . . We could try the Three Brothers
in the Rue d'Ingouville. Will Bouchet follow us?'

'Of course he will! That's why you've got to behave exactly
as you would if you were here to get a cargo.'

'We'll have to separate if we're to get rid of him. He can't
follow each of us. The one he follows should go back to the
Dolphin – that will keep him away from Cornand's.'

'Supposing he has other people helping him?' Jane said.

'He hasn't had time to get help yet, and if we keep moving he
won't dare let us out of sight . . . We'll make the Three Brothers
first, then move on before he has time to send a note or message
to the Guard . . .'

Les Trois Frères was a dim little shop, heavy with the odours
of stale sweat and tobacco. It sold good brandy and was a recognized meeting-place for seamen. The proprietor nodded to Paul
with a half-familiar gesture, and came to serve them immediately.
As he placed the glasses before them, Bouchet entered. He did it
quite openly, without trying to efface himself. Charles had carefully seated himself with his back to the door. Paul spoke to the
proprietor, using slow precise English, loud enough for Bouchet
to hear.

'Have you seen Monsieur Bordillet this evening?'

'*Monsieur Bordillet? – ce soir? Non, Monsieur.*' He shook his
head.

'Damn!' Paul said. 'Swallow your drink, and let's move on.
He'll be about somewhere.' The shopkeeper shrugged uncomprehendingly, and pocketed the coin Paul gave him. Paul helped Jane
to her feet; Charles caught her arm as before, and they walked
out to the street. Behind they could hear the scrape of the chair as
Bouchet stood up.

At four other taverns they did the same thing. At each Bouchet
either entered boldly, or stayed within sight of the door. At the
fifth one a large moustached man suddenly rose as they entered,
calling cheerfully to Paul.

'Oh – my friend! They tell me you've been enquiring for me!'

'Every blasted place in the town,' Paul said. 'Drinking too much of your bad French brandy.'

'My friend, you cannot insult our brandy – they pay too much for it back in England . . .'

He seated himself at their table, and called for brandy. Jane didn't even attempt to drink it when it came; she merely smiled in acknowledgement when Bordillet raised his glass to her. Suddenly she felt Charles's arm round her shoulder again; he spoke softly in her ear.

'Can't you do better than that? – you're supposed to be gay!'

Obediently she reached for the glass, forcing it to her lips, turning to toast Charles smilingly. The brandy was like fire to her throat and her protesting stomach. It was a long time since the scrappy meal one of the hands had thrown together on the *Dolphin*, even a long time since that bit of cheese they had eaten in the Rue de Paris. She wondered how many more taverns there would be, and how many more glasses of brandy . . . The room was growing hazy before her eyes; in a little while she would be too stupid to be of any help to Charles. A kind of despair entered her then, recognition of the possibility of failure. She wanted to put her head on that stained battered table and weep.

Suddenly, under cover of the table she felt Paul's hand seek hers, and finding it, grip it firmly; with his thumb he stroked the back of her hand. All the time he talked on to Bordillet, but she knew what the gesture meant. With that pressure on her hand he was saying to her all the things of which his love and concern for her gave him intuitive knowledge. He knew her misery and near-defeat, he knew even her hunger and the nauseous burning of the brandy in her stomach, he knew the closeness of despair; he was placing himself between her and the spectre of fear, telling her that she had not been lost from mind even in the heat of danger. And all the time he kept up the loud, aggressive talk with Bordillet appearing even to enjoy the drawn-out haggle over the price he would pay for tobacco. He shouted his scorn and contempt of the other, and had the same insults hurled back at him; both men seemed to be equally engrossed in the matter. This was one cargo that Paul would never take aboard, but certainly Bordillet could not have guessed it, nor did she think could Bouchet, seated two tables away. She half-turned her head, and took a long look at Bouchet's intelligent, bitter face; he returned her stare unblinkingly. She hated the mocking falseness of this chase where pursuer and pursued remained only a few feet apart.

She leaned towards Charles, smiling at him for the benefit of Bouchet.

'How long do we go on this way?' she whispered. 'We're no nearer to Louise!' Her hand tightened on his arm. 'Why does he just follow you? Why doesn't he arrest you and be done with it?'

'This phase of our play is coming to an end now,' he said. 'It is important that Bouchet believes you and Paul are genuine, even if he suspects me. Now he has seen you here with Bordillet, I think he won't trouble you.'

'But *you* . . .'

'He may not be sure that I'm the same person he knew as Charles Blake, who was a friend of Phillipe de Montignot, though I'm sure he knows that Charles Blake was imprisoned and escaped. Prison changes a man's appearance, and it's some years since he's seen me.'

'But he follows you, just the same.'

'What else can he do? He has no other clue. When Latour escaped from Le Havre Bouchet lost the trail to Louise, and now he is sticking with me because he hopes that I'll lead him to her.'

'Why doesn't he have you arrested on suspicion?'

'What good would it do him? Even to prove that I was Charles Blake? He knows I wouldn't tell him where Louise is – and to the Commune, and for Bouchet's own future, she is a much more important capture than I. Besides, with luck, he might get us both!'

'So . . . what do we do?'

He drained his glass and set it down firmly. 'I will leave here, and Bouchet will follow me. When you see that he is gone, take Paul and go to the Cornands' shop. If necessary, you must take Louise to the *Dolphin* without my help.'

'She will find more strength for the journey if you are there,' Jane said slowly.

He nodded. 'I know that, but if I can't shake off Bouchet, you and Paul must manage it alone.'

'How long are we to wait?'

'No longer than an hour. The streets are quieter and it grows more dangerous.' He dropped his hand on to hers, lying on the table. 'At all costs you must get her to the *Dolphin* – and Paul is to sail as soon as he can make ready.'

'To *sail*! But what about you!'

'Don't wait for me.'

He pushed back his stool and prepared to stand up. 'Don't wait for me, do you understand? If the *Dolphin* sails without me, I'll make my own way back to England.'

'And if you don't . . . ?'

'If I don't get back to England, Jane, then I know *you* will welcome Louise to Blake's Reach in my place, and care for her.'

He stood up then and began to make amiable, careless farewells to Paul, calling the tavern-keeper to refill Bordillet's empty glass. Jane watched his stumbling exit, and watched Bouchet also rise and follow him to the door. She was startled to discover that it was not brandy, but tears, that blurred her last sight of him.

5

The streets were emptying, as Charles had said, and their footsteps were too noisy on the cobbles. Jane had never before known the kind of fear that gripped her now – not even those moments when the Dragoons had entered Barham had been like these. This was a fear of something unknown, a betrayal, a false word, a moment of time lost, and the hope of safety with it. She held her cloak tightly to her body, and paced her steps to Paul's quick ones. The dark streets were no longer friendly.

Albert Cornand's shop in the Rue de Paris was locked and shuttered; it had a sad, deserted look – grey plaster peeling off the walls, and no lights visible anywhere. Paul's knock seemed thunderously loud, echoing in the canyon of those overhanging houses. To Jane it seemed as if everyone in the street must hear that knock, and come to stare at them, and to question.

'*Qui est là?*' The urgent whisper on the other side of the door startled her.

'Fletcher! – Captain of the *Dolphin*!'

The bolts were pulled back softly, and the door swung open just enough to admit them.

'Quickly!' Then the door closed behind them, and they were in total darkness.

'For Heaven's sake bring a light!' Paul said. 'What's the matter with you?'

'Pardon, Monsieur, but I did not want anyone who might be watching to see who it was came in.'

'Is someone watching?'

'I don't know, Monsieur, but one can't be too careful.' As he spoke a door at the other side of the room opened and a woman stood there holding a candle. Jane glanced about her quickly, and recognized the room she had seen from the street earlier in the evening, the room that had been packed with Cornand's patrons. There was the smell of wine characteristic of each place they had visited while searching for Bordillet, but here there was also the smell of bread and sweet pastries.

The woman was tall, and had a frail appearance; it was hard to imagine her living with the sweet pastries and the wine.

'Monsieur Fletcher! Thank God you have come!' Her voice was a soft whisper as she moved towards them.

'What is wrong, Madame?'

'The Comtesse, she is going to die! We thought that you would not come back . . .'

'How do you know she is going to die?'

'Ah, Monsieur . . . !' The light of the candle fell on Albert Cornand's worn face; he had the pallor of someone who spends his life indoors, but his body was stocky and well-built. 'She is worse!' he said, shaking his head. 'I fear it is but a few hours now.'

Madame Cornand spoke quietly. 'What are we to do, Monsieur? She must leave here, or she will die on our hands – and how are we to explain the body of a dead woman? Before God we have been loyal, Monsieur, but this is asking too much!'

'Dying . . .' Paul looked at Jane. 'All of this – and she will die, after all.'

'Yes, Monsieur, she will die – and very likely we will die also for harbouring an enemy of the People. It is cruel . . .' Jane had the feeling that Madame Cornand had been brave for a long time, and now, at last, the control was beginning to slip.

'Courage, Cecile!' her husband whispered. 'We are not taken yet, and perhaps Monsieur will devise some – ' He broke off. They had all heard the quick footsteps in the street outside, and had paid no attention except to lower their voices still further. Now the footsteps had stopped outside. Someone rapped lightly on the door.

'*Qui est là?*'

'*Un ami – an ami de Paul Fletcher!*'

'It's Charles!' Paul said. 'Quickly, open the door! Get him inside before he's seen!'

Charles slipped inside like a shadow. He was panting, and drops of sweat stood out on his forehead. He leaned back against the door.

'I got away from him! He followed me to the *quai*, so I went into a wine shop and had some brandy. Then I went into the brothel next door. He didn't follow me there – he waited outside. As long as you have enough gold they don't ask questions in those places, and they helped me through a sky-light, and showed me a passage into the next street. I told them it was my brother-in-law. They were most sympathetic.'

He stood upright then, taking a deep breath. 'Forgive me – I stand here talking, while there's so much to be done.' He looked at Cecile Cornand. 'Madame, is she up there?' he said, nodding towards the stairs.

'A moment, Charles!' Paul said. 'It's more serious than we thought. The Comtesse is dying – Cornand says only a few hours now.'

Jane watched his face as he listened; instead of shock or grief there seemed to be anger there. He was angry with Paul for speaking the words.

'I don't believe it!' he said. 'I don't believe it! She can't die now that she is so close to freedom! Louise has more courage than that!'

'It isn't a question of courage, Monsieur,' Cecile Cornand said gently. 'I think the Comtesse thought of herself as dead when she knew Pierre Latour would not return. She is worn out – there is nothing she can do for herself.'

Charles scowled. 'I don't believe this talk,' he said. 'Let me see her.' He motioned Madame Cornand towards the stairs. She moved to go ahead of him with the candle, but on the bottom step she paused, and turned back.

'Monsieur, you understand the position? If the Comtesse dies here Albert and I, we are lost! There is no way we can take her body from here . . .'

He cut her short. 'She will leave here alive, and you will not be troubled, Madame! Now – please take me to her!'

Jane climbed the stairs behind him, her eyes fixed on his erect shoulders and back. He was a strong man, and a courageous one, and she wondered if he had, perhaps, the strength to will Louise to live – if he could breathe into her his own spirit of defiance. He was so stubborn in his belief, and single-minded in his determination to get her to freedom that, for the moment, no other life but hers was of any importance. Paul and herself, Albert and Cecile Cornand, the Duvals waiting on the *Dolphin*, they were all helpless before him, doing what he bid them like puppets, bending before his formidable purpose. Perhaps Charles knew that with Louise it would be the same, and from him she would gather the strength to go with them. Whatever happened, they were all in Charles's hands, compelled to do as he instructed them.

Jane looked at the face of the woman in the bed, and she wondered how she could ever have feared her. Louise de Montignot could have been any age; her face was not wrinkled, but it was drawn and haggard, so that she appeared, at first, to be an old woman. Her hair, which might have been blonde once, was almost white. But there were traces of beauty in the features – delicately fashioned chin and brows; her eyes were light blue. She wore a plain, coarse bedgown; the clumsy material stood away from her thin bones. Her hands were blue veined and transparent.

She had spoken to Charles briefly when he entered. Now she closed her eyes, and seemed to rest for a time, with long intervals between drawing each breath, as if she were trying to save her strength to speak again. Her eyelids flickered open heavily; she moved her hand in a slight gesture that motioned Jane closer to her bedside.

'Monsieur Fletcher told me you had come over from England to be with me,' she said slowly. 'It is most generous – I am grateful. But you must go now, while there is yet time.' Her hand touched Jane's briefly, then it fell back on to the bed cover. She closed her eyes again, and the difficult, slow rhythm of her breathing was resumed.

'Charles!' Paul called softly from the shadows over by the window. 'Come here!'

Charles rose stiffly from his seat by Louise. Jane caught a glimpse of his face, rigid and sober, his lips folded in a tight line. Albert and Cecile Cornand stood by the open door, and as Paul spoke there was a slight movement from them, a stirring of alarm. Albert took a step farther into the room, as if he meant to join them. But then he paused, shaking his head.

Cecile Cornand had hung blankets before the two windows to make sure none of the damp night air would reach Louise. While Charles had sat by the bedside, Paul had moved between the two windows, each on a different side of the triangular-shaped room, and parted the blankets cautiously, just enough to give him a view of the streets below. Now he stepped back and gave place to Charles.

'Down there!' he said.

Charles stood by the window, looking down into the Rue de Paris. The seconds slipped away, and an unspeakable suspense gripped the people in the room. It even communicated itself to Louise, through the isolation of her weakness. Her eyelids moved.

'What is it?' she whispered to Jane.

Jane touched her hand reassuringly. 'Nothing – nothing at all.' Louise didn't seem to hear her.

Charles stirred, and dropped the blanket back into place.

'It's he . . .' he said wearily. 'It's Bouchet – he has more cunning and more tenacity than I gave him credit for.'

From Louise there was suddenly a sharp cry, a much louder and stronger tone than she had used before.

'Who is it? Have you been followed?'

Charles spun round. 'Keep her quiet!' The words rang out harshly, cruelly.

Then, as he realized that it was Louise who had spoken, his face underwent a swift change. It had the stricken, contrite look of one who has sinned unforgivably. For the first time Jane saw self-accusation and dismay in Charles's face. He strode across the room to Louise's side, bending low over the bed. His hand groped wildly for hers; but his voice was very firm and strong when he spoke.

'Louise, I love you! I have always loved you!'

'I know.'

The listeners barely heard her. The words were a whisper, a sigh. Charles straightened, and laid her hand gently back on the bed cover. Then he motioned them all to follow him from the room; they went without question, feeling that they ought never to have been there; and yet they knew that Charles didn't care that his words had belonged to them all. Nothing mattered to him but that Louise should hear them.

They grouped together on the landing at the head of the stairs. Charles closed the door softly, and then turned to meet their questioning gaze. He looked firmly at each face in turn, not shrinking from what he saw there.

'I am sorry,' he said. 'I regret I've brought this trouble on all of you. The man out there in the street is Bouchet, an agent of the Paris Commune.'

Madame Cornand covered her face quickly, in a gesture of distress.

He went on, 'I believed I had shaken him off. I came here only because I thought my presence would give the Comtesse better heart and strength for the journey.'

He shrugged, but not casually, as was his custom; it was a gesture eloquent of the inevitability of fate, and his acceptance of it. They had the feeling that he spoke the words because he had to, because it was owing to them that he should speak. But his thoughts and needs were back behind the closed door.

Slowly Madame Cornand's hand came down from her face. 'Monsieur, we cannot blame you for mistakes made from compassion. But –' she tried to hold her voice steady – 'but what are we to do?'

'Bouchet has only one concern,' Charles said. 'He has been sent to find Louise, and because he recognized me, he *has* found her. He has never heard the name Cornand, and the Commune expects no arrests of such people. Neither will he risk his quarry to follow you, Jane – or Paul. So long as this house is watched only by Bouchet, you are able to go. If you go immediately, Bouchet can do nothing. He is helpless. He has followed me here, and here he will stay until the National Guard can be called out to take the house, and whomever they should find inside it. When they come they must find only Louise and myself. She will not live to be moved from that room, and for myself . . . I may not leave her.'

6

It was all finished; by now Louise was dead, and Charles taken.

All day, while the *Dolphin* beat her way against perverse winds towards the English coast, they had lived with the knowledge that this must happen. But while the day had been young, with the sun hot and strong on the white sails and reflected blindingly off the surface of the water, they had not quite believed it. They had heard Charles's words, and knew that he was committing himself to his own death, but they had clung to some slight hope of his escape. They didn't speak of this to each other – none but the most necessary words passed between them – but they had kept the thought stubbornly. Then, as the shadows of the masts and the bulwarks grew long on the deck, and the white chalk cliffs came into view, they began to admit secretly the foolishness of this hope. There was no possible escape for Charles and he, better than anyone, had known it.

As if drawn by a common thought they had come together in one place at the bulwark, watching the coastline as the *Dolphin* slowly inched her way to Folkestone. Paul had taken on no cargo in Le Havre, and for once the *Dolphin* had no need to fear a Revenue cruiser coming into sight. The sun lay gently and pleasantly on the low hills of Kent; to the watchers on board the *Dolphin* the land looked safe and peaceful.

Suddenly Albert Cornand spoke : 'It will be all over by now – yes, by now it is all finished, and he is perhaps even on his way to Paris.'

'He was a brave man,' his wife said gently.

'He was a rash fool,' Marie Duval commented.

Auguste Duval sighed, 'He was a man in love.' His tone was low, but for the first time since he had come aboard the *Dolphin* it seemed that he was prepared to hold to something on his own conviction.

'Never will I forget it,' Cecile Cornand said. 'I hope I never again have to live through minutes as long as those when we were getting to the *quai*. That man, Bouchet, staring at us . . . and not knowing if he'd let us go, or if there'd be a guard on the *quai* when we got there.' Her voice trembled. All day she had been waiting to say these things, and she couldn't hold them any longer.

Marie Duval looked at her hostilely. 'How do you think we felt? Trapped like rats on this ship, and waiting every second to hear the Guard come on board searching? And not knowing what had happened to those three . . . going off like that and leaving us . . . I tell you, Madame, *they* were long hours.'

'Not so long as the time he spent waiting for them to come,' Cornand said. 'Though, for him and the Comtesse I suppose it was short. Strange to think of them alone there in our shop, Cecile. I wonder if she died before the Guard came. I hope so . . . It must have been a very bad time for him . . .'

Jane turned suddenly and faced them.

'Can't you stop talking about it?' she demanded fiercely. 'He made his own choice . . . and if he wanted to be with the woman he loved, then he had what he wanted. There was no "bad time" for Charles. There would only have been a bad time for him if she had died alone, before she knew that he had come for her. Don't you see — as long as she knew that, he didn't care!'

'It's well for the rich, who can afford to be romantic,' Madame Duval said. 'For us it is different . . . we are still alive, and have to go on living. And what with? And how? Everything we had is gone, Mademoiselle! We are ruined . . . ruined!'

'I've heard you say that before,' Jane answered, 'and I don't believe it. You have your lives, and you have a future. England is a strange country to you, but to make a living and to have a future is not any more difficult there than in Paris. People are much the same wherever you go — as greedy or as kind. There's love and there's hate. There are people who'll help you, and those who won't.'

She nodded to Auguste Duval. 'You take your talent with you, Monsieur, and your wife has shrewdness enough for six people.'

Marie Duval shrugged. 'You talk easily, Mademoiselle!'

Jane was not listening to her. Her gaze had shifted to the Cornands, still leaning against the bulwark gazing at the land where they would be alone and without resources. What was there to say to them, she wondered. They had no talents, and no gold. They were ordinary people with only the virtue of the courage that had kept them loyal to the dead Royalist cause; now their courage would have to see them through loneliness and perhaps poverty. They might later decide it had been too high a price to pay. There was nothing to say to them, she decided – nothing they didn't already know, and they would not thank her for platitudes. They had each other, and they knew that also. Each counted on the courage and loyalty of the other. There was no need to point out that to them. So there was nothing to say; they knew well enough what was ahead of them.

She slipped away from the group and moved aft, where Paul was taking his turn at the wheel.

She had spent no time alone with him since they had left Le Havre. She knew that he had been on deck most of the night, and this morning had flung himself into the hammock Albert Cornand had vacated to snatch a few hours of sleep. All through the day he had been preoccupied, as if he hardly knew she was there. But now he smiled at her, and his eyes came to life.

'A few hours and we'll berth in Folkestone, Jane. It seems wrong to be heading back this way in broad daylight, without a cargo and without a worry about a Revenue cruiser.'

She leaned back against the bulwark, slightly behind him. He had to look back over his shoulder to see her.

'That's not what you're really thinking, Paul.'

'No,' he admitted. 'I'm thinking of him – and so are you.'

'Yes . . .' she said. 'I'm thinking of him.'

Charles would stay with them all of their lives. They would never be able to forget Charles, not they, nor the Cornands, nor the Duvals. For her and Paul he was someone they would remember, not at intervals, with faint surprise that he had gone so long unthought of, but he would be with them constantly. Jane knew that he had had many things to teach her, and that she would not be finished realizing and learning them for a long time. She wondered if he had ever known or cared how much she would learn from him.

For one thing, she had learned that the tradition and pride of a family like the Blakes did not lie in such things as building and endowing a church, or presenting it with a rose window, but in loving, and giving one's life in proof of love. She would remember Charles as a self-centred man, proud and cold, indifferent to the feelings of those about him, and sacrificing everything, even to his life, for Louise. He had given his life carelessly to serve his own sense of honour, and it was in such gestures that the greatness of a family, as well as an individual, lay. Perhaps he had tried to tell her this when he had clothed Blake's Reach with the trappings of position and importance, when he had hung silk curtains and bidden his neighbours to eat with him in the chill splendour of the dining-room. He had shown her a cold house, without love.

Now she looked at Paul, looked at his profile against the sky, the short blond ends of hair blowing in the wind. His strong hands were at ease on the wheel, and his feet planted on a familiar deck. Here was a man in his own element, a man she loved. And Charles had warned her not to lose him.

Suddenly she knew that it did not matter now that she owned the deck he stood on, that she owned the *Dolphin*, she owned the Pearl, and she owned Blake's Reach. She could not fully possess these things without the wisdom to use them in the right way, and the right way was not in fashioning them into a chain to bind Paul. He would always have more energy than discretion, more will to make money than skill in keeping it. But he had a dream, a vision, and his eyes were happily blinded by it. He wanted no fetters, and no burden of convention or tradition. She did not know if his dream of a kingdom to be won in the West Indies was something he would always keep, or whether he would attempt to turn it into a reality. Whatever he chose – to stay on the Marsh where he had been born, and to live out his life with her at Blake's Reach, or to seek the source of the dream in the West Indies – she would be with him. She had glimpsed the dream and the vision in Charles when he had elected to stay with Louise; it was this same shining thing she could never permit herself to destroy in Paul. If Blake's Reach had to be sacrificed to it, then it would be, and she would hold her peace.

And now she had to try to tell him this.

She called softly, 'Paul . . .'

He looked back at her, wearing the slight, familiar smile that warmed her.

Epilogue

In the grass-grown graveyard of St Saviour's-by-the-Marsh are the headstones that mark the graves of Jane and Paul Fletcher; the tall grey slabs, weathering in the rains that sweep across the Marsh from the Channel, record no more than the bare facts of their names and ages. Beside them are the graves of those of their children who, being born on the Marsh, chose to live out their lives there. In the church itself a plain tablet, not a rose window, records the name of Charles Blake.

For Charles there is no marked grave. His headless body lies in quicklime, along with the others who perished during The Terror, in the cemetery of the Madelaine in Paris.

Nor is William's grave marked. He was lost when the *Raven*, largest vessel of the merchant fleet he had gathered together for trade between London and the West Indies, was wrecked off the island of Jamaica.

FIONA

Prologue

The Scots call it 'the sight'; some think of it as a curse, to others it seems a kind of gift of grace. I have it, and in my own heart I hold it a curse – undeserved, perhaps, but there, like a birthmark, or a twisted body.

From the time I first knew of it, when I was nineteen, until now, at twenty-three, it has cost me my peace of mind, and three positions as a governess – positions hard to come by for the daughter of an impoverished Scottish clergyman. So that was why I tramped the hills above my father's little parish of Silkirk, on the Ayrshire coast in the late spring of 1833, unemployed, impelled by a restless energy, wondering what was to become of me, and what other crisis this unwanted gift of fate would bring to me.

I thought about it often now as I sat among the heather to rest on these long walks, watching the grey sea that swept down the North Channel from the Atlantic, past the top of Ireland and the Mull of Kintyre, watching the ebb of the tide and the shining miles of strand exposed, and then its slow return to the inlet of Silkirk. I kept telling myself that there would be a return from the ebb for me also. This could not be the end, here at Silkirk, with the journey hardly begun.

From the first two positions I had left with excellent references and there had been no problem about a new position – just a matter of answering advertisements and waiting. That was because the ability to see into the future was an uncertain thing, not to be called up at will, not to be conjured up for one's own good or gain – it was just a flash of a coming event, and a warning, with no reason behind it. It had not then brought me into trouble.

I had been governess to a small boy when the first sight had come – and it could, charitably, have been dismissed as sharp hearing, or a kind of animal instinct of things not being right. But it had saved a coach with my employers and their son, as well as myself, from plunging into a river from which the bridge had already been swept away by the rushing water of a cloudburst. The coachman had been pushing his team against the slashing rain, one lamp extinguished by water, racing to get home to a warm kitchen and his supper. Suddenly I had screamed for him to stop, had pounded like a madwoman against the carriage roof, striving to make him hear, and finally lowering the window and letting the rain pour in upon us all to reach around and somehow grasp his coat. We stopped in time; but the bridge had been at the other side of a sharp bend, and no one could have seen in that blackness that it was gone. They didn't believe, either, although to make it seem right, they said they did, that anyone could have heard the changed sound of the water as it crashed over the debris of the bridge. My employers were grateful to me, but they didn't talk about it, and I knew that from then on a sense of unease rested on them about me; but the coachman talked, and in the village the locals turned to look at me. There was something not quite right. I was an excellent teacher, my reference said, and good with children. But they sent their son to a preparatory school sooner than they had planned, and I think they knew a kind of relief when I was gone from their roof.

The next pupil had been a girl, Charlotte, a spoiled and pampered darling, saved by a sense of humour and a sweetness that no one, least of all myself, could resist. I was with her two years, mostly in the big house in Edinburgh, with summers spent at the family's lonely retreat among the hills and hidden lochs and islands of the far Highlands. Many of the family came to that distant summer house, cousins, in-laws, grandmothers. It was a young cousin, seventeen, called Bruce, who had got out the boat for the sail he made on their own private loch whenever the weather would permit. This day, I remember, seemed made in heaven — golden, calm, with soft clouds drifting before a barely perceptible breeze. Charlotte had waited impatiently, skipping from one foot to another, as Bruce readied that small craft moored at the dock. That was how I saw them from the windows of the drawing-room. Charlotte's mother sat sewing and gossiping with Bruce's mother, her sister. I remember I suddenly cried out, 'No – no, they mustn't go! Something is going to happen! There's going to be . . .' I stopped. I didn't know. I had the sight, but I saw imperfectly.

I remember also the sharpness of the tone that answered me. 'Nonsense, Miss McIntyre! What can possibly happen? Bruce has been sailing all his life and on a day like this . . . They are quite safe. Calm yourself!'

But I didn't. I remember running from the room, and the slam of the front door behind me, and the rush down the slope of the path slippery with pine needles. I remember, too, with awful clarity, the raising of the sail, and the way the playful breeze took it, and the gaily painted little craft standing out from the jetty. I remember my cries and shouts, and the breeze blowing them back at me, and Charlotte's saucy wave, and the sun on her golden hair. The little waves lapped the shores and the pines sighed above me, and it was a happy, lazy, gentle day for sailing.

It stayed that way for an hour, and stubbornly I sat on the jetty and waited until the little boat should round the bend of the island, set secret and mysterious, in the middle of the loch. I was there on the jetty when the squall came, as it does so often in the Highlands, rough rain and wind sweeping in suddenly. They found the capsized boat quite soon, but it was a week before the bodies of Charlotte and Bruce were found at distant parts along the shore.

Charlotte's mother wrote my reference, again an excellent one, but her face was turned away from me, as if she strove, in charity, not to let me see that in some way she held me responsible – as if my vision of tragedy had somehow caused it to happen. Her hands and voice were cold in parting as she said goodbye, and made herself wish me good fortune. I had brought, she seemed to say, no good fortune to that house.

From the third position I was dismissed without a reference, and, I suppose, in justice, I deserved none. I had done no wrong to the family, but I had behaved in a way that no respectable young woman ever should. But I had been compelled by that same force that had occurred on the other occasions – something so strong that I had had to act upon it. Something I could not explain, and which could not be proved. So I was back home in Silkirk, answering advertisements for GOVERNESS WANTED, but getting no replies because that vital reference from my last employer could not be supplied. I walked, and waited, and fretted, and wondered why I had had the bad luck to be born as I was, with those terrifying flashes of the future, which threatened to destroy those they concerned, and perhaps me. Three times I had looked into the face of the future, and I hated the power of this awesome gift.

I

Suddenly the rain was not the fine drifting mist that had veiled
the hillside all afternoon, blotting out the sweep of the higher
mountains and the distant glimpse of the peak of the Nerrick;
now it was a torrent that came in sheets. I felt the weariness of
tired limbs and wet skirts clinging about me, and the cottage was
there, at hand – an almost ruinous cottage, the thatch ancient
and the whitewash peeling, the little enclosed yard a pool of mud
with stepping-stones to the door, and a few hens crouching close to
the wall for shelter. A thin smoke drifted from the chimney, and
no dog barked to challenge my entry. It was a struggle to open
and prop back in place the dead tree limbs that served to keep
out the wandering mountain cattle. By the time I had done it I
expected the door to have opened, and the woman to be standing there. But it remained shut blankly, the rain beating against
it.

It took a time too, even after my knock, for her to come, although I knew she must have watched me from the single tiny
window. Finally the door opened grudgingly.

'Will you let me take shelter for a moment? I've a mile or two
to walk before I'm home, and I've no thought to take a drenching.' I said it confidently enough, because the tradition of hospitality among these people was as deep as their poverty. And she
and I were not strangers to each other. On finer days when the
cottage door had stood open and she had sat by it at her spinning,
we had exchanged nods as I passed. Or rather she had returned
my greeting with a long, vaguely hostile stare.

She said nothing now in return, just jerked her head to a stool
before the smoky peat fire. But when I seated myself, and tried to
shake a little of the wet off my cloak without spreading it about the
room, she came to the fire herself and swung the black pot on its
hook over the embers. Then she went back to her spinning wheel
close to the window, and bent about her task again in the wan
afternoon light. The rest of the room was dark, and it was cold,
despite the fire. There was nothing much in it – a single table and a
few stools, a row of blackened pots on the mantel, a pallet of straw
on the hard-trodden earth floor, with a bundle of rags as bed-
covers. I remembered that a few years ago, when I had sometimes
walked this way, there had been a boy, her son, I supposed, who

had tended the few sheep which provided the wool the woman spun and wove. There had been a barley patch and a few potatoes. The remains of a poor garden were still there, but there was no man about the place – it had the look of it. The boy would be grown and gone, gone to Glasgow probably in the hope of work and wages, exchanging one poverty for another. The woman looked old, but she may not have been so old; need and hardship lay in every line of her face.

It was an embarrassment, then, to see her take down from the mantel a pewter caddy, and measure with careful hand, the tea into the earthenware pot. For her, tea would be an almost unthought-of luxury, something she permitted herself a few times a year.

I made a gesture of protest. 'No . . . please, no . . .'

She made a clicking sound with her tongue, slightingly, as if to remind me that she knew the ways of those better off than herself. 'Dinna ye be the minister's daughter?'

I nodded, shamed to think of the poverty that seemed to us to sit on the manse so heavily, and yet it was only the poverty of lacking new dresses and bonnets, and my father wanting books he could not buy. This woman seemed to put me in my place; I took the black brew in a tankard from her meekly. 'Thank you, mistress.'

She took no tea herself but retreated again to the wheel, bent over it, her face turned away from me. For a time I felt uncomfortable sitting there while the silence grew thick between us. Even through the thatch I could hear the rain, and there was no excuse for going; I sipped the tea, not enjoying it, but knowing I had to drink it to the end. Hospitality had been offered, and must now be endured, no matter the cost. I only wished that her hostility had seemed less personal – more against the world than against me. But in her few glances in my direction it was me she saw, not merely someone from a more fortunate world. I waited, but still the rain came down, and there was no decent escape.

After a while though, I retreated to my own thoughts, those useless and wearisome companions of these last months; I seemed imprisoned in the black hopelessness of them, and was tired of their repetition. The questioning never yielded an answer. My father just said: 'Wait – something will come.' I hadn't his patience, and his belief. For me, waiting was hard.

There was a reason, more subtle and never spoken of, other than the need to unburden my father of my support, for having to leave the manse at Silkirk. I was now, at twenty-three, already regarded by some as an old maid, and I had three pretty young stepsisters coming along, the eldest, Mary, being courted by an eligible young man from Ayr. For some reason, since I had come home, the courtship hadn't been progressing very well. It wasn't to be believed, of course, that he found me more attractive than that Dresden doll, Mary. I wasn't the kind of woman that eligible young men paid much attention to – hair too red, and apt to be wild, as was my tongue at times. It was true I had had, until last autumn, suitors of sorts, a rather solemn professor at Edinburgh University who wrote scholarly letters, but hadn't seemed able to make up his mind whether or not I would be a suitable wife for him. I know I was said by some to be too large, and certainly I towered over my stepmother and sisters. But my father said I had my mother's eyes, the tilt of her chin and head; that seemed for him to make up for any other deficiency. But it still was no reason for a young man like James Killian to listen to me with more attention than he gave Mary; and to suggest that everyone should go walking on Saturdays when I said I was going alone. So now, on Saturdays when he was expected, I left the house before he arrived, and came back when he could be reckoned safely to have left. I was growing tired of my lonely meal of sandwiches eaten on the mountainside while my stepmother invented tales of my gay social life that took me elsewhere. I don't think James Killian believed those tales. Each time he asked about me, and each time more searchingly, as Flora, our all-purpose maid eagerly related to me from what she overheard. All of us knew it would be better if I could leave Silkirk, and leave James Killian to Mary.

I thought now longingly of that last position, governess to the three rough-and-tumble little sons of a Glasgow merchant. I had enjoyed it while it lasted, and the family had been good to me. It was cruel it had to end, by my own doing, that day last autumn in Kelvingrove Gardens.

It had been such a fair day, a day suddenly given back from summer, a Sunday afternoon with the sun warm, and still there was the scent of damp, rotting leaves. The sun had brought out thousands to stroll in the gardens, for the most part a fashionable crowd, with the light striking the velvet bonnets and the tall silk hats. The man who had set up his little rough-hewn platform at the junction of several promenades didn't belong to the well-dressed crowd; his clothes were shabby and careless, his accent was working-class with the overlay of some learning upon it. I don't know how long he had been speaking to the crowd that had gathered about him when I came – there was no policeman in sight, but I supposed it was against the by-laws to hold meetings like this one in the park. But he was the kind who would never pay attention to by-laws. And what he had to say wasn't for the ears of the Glasgow tenement dwellers either, from whom he was probably sprung, and who could do nothing about his cause even if they had wanted to try, which was doubtful. His audience was here, among the prosperous who did the trading and the money-making, who built the ships and made the contracts. As I remember every detail of that afternoon, I remember that man's face — pale and thin, and burning fire-like with his passion.

'And will you not, my brothers, set them free? Will you not end this traffic in human misery — end this shame set upon a great nation like a running sore? Who can expect the blessing of serenity when men and women are still born into a lifetime of slavery, still branded and sold from one man to another like cattle...'

A speaker in a park can never expect to have it all his own way; inevitably there are the hecklers, and he knew to expect them. Men who build ships, who deal in trade of any kind, go pale at the thought of anything interfering with that trade; I think there were some there who simply cried out in anger because one of this kind had come to disturb their comfortable, well-fed Sunday afternoon.

'You are behind the times, friend. The slave trade was abolished long ago.'

A pointing finger from the speaker on the platform. '*You're* behind the times! Don't you know that a pirate trade still plies from the African shores to the Indies, with conditions worse now than ever before. And have you no pity for those who are already in bondage, born to it, condemned forever to it, the outright property of their masters, who have the power of punishment, even of life or death over them?'

'And haven't we,' he was answered, 'taken them from their own brothers who sold them into slavery? Taken them from the darkness of their ignorance and shown them the light of the Christian God?'

'Under the lash we have given them the Christian God. Who of them may not accept Him?'

'Don't the plantations feed and clothe them?'

'In rags, and feed them on what they can raise on the Christian Sunday in their own garden patch. *That's* how we feed and clothe them. Try it, my friend — try just one day working the cane under that sun and under a whip, and you will know what a damnation slavery is. You will rise up in your thousands and demand that Parliament pass the Emancipation Act – '

'And who will pay for it, my friend? Who will put the sugar in your tea – or shall we do without it?'

Another voice, 'And who will pay the indemnities? Or shall we send our own to work the plantations?'

With horrible humour someone shouted back : 'That would be a good way to get rid of a few undesirables from these shores – the over-breeding rats of the slums – '

Suddenly it seemed to involve them all, all of that once good-humoured crowd that had paused to hear some madman rant on about a question that everyone knew he could not solve, and what's more, in its solution, would dig hard into the pocket of the taxpayer. The question of money had been raised against the question of the freedom of unknown ignorant blacks. Money will always involve a Scotsman, one way or another. A dozen voices shouted at the speaker; some argued back and forth with each other. For the moment I didn't think about what was being said, slavery or not; I stared fascinated, at that tired, strained face, a face with the look of hunger upon it, and eyes that seemed to consume him with their own fire. It seemed to sway and hover above that jostling mass of people, disembodied almost. I began to hear the rising menace in the low murmur of anger that had come to join the indignation and outrage. The sacredness of property had been questioned. The first, quick reaction seemed to be the urge to strike down the one who had dared to question – except that it was impossible that such a thing would happen on a Sunday afternoon in Kelvingrove Gardens. No, such a thing would never happen.

And yet it was then I felt it – or rather, I saw it. I saw it with the most fearful intensity of any one thing I had yet experienced in my whole life. This was not like the other times – this I *knew*. I saw a crowd, I saw this man standing above them as he did now, shouting at them with his passion-choked voice. I saw a sudden surge, and he was pulled down. I saw blood, and the man lying still, and the blood in pools upon the ground, the silent, terrible witness. I tell you, in God's name, *I saw it*. And yet it did not happen. The man still stood there, striving to make just one person among them understand and feel what so stirred him. And what I saw was his danger – I saw his death, and there was no power in me to stop me doing what I did then.

I pushed my way through the people, some of them giving way sheerly in surprise that it was a woman who thrust through them

so wildly. When I reached the little platform there was no choice
about what I must do. In a second I was up there beside him,
almost pushing him off, his surprise more than anything making
him give way. All I knew was his mortal danger, and I had to
avert it.

'Listen . . .' My voice hardly reached the first rank of the crowd,
but the sight of a woman there beside him silenced some simply
from curiosity. 'Listen . . . you must stop. You must stop this! Let
him go; – I say let him go his way. Or terrible things will happen . . .'

I was mad, of course. Even as I heard my own words I knew
how they must have sounded. The man didn't want me there beside him; he didn't want any woman to fight his battles. 'Miss,' he
said, 'get down! I thank you – but get down!' What he didn't
know was that he needed me. He hadn't seen the vision of the
crowd and the blood and his own still form. But suddenly I knew
that even if he had seen it he would not care. The man was born
to die by whatever caused him to live. And he lived now for the
issue of slavery. He did not want the presence of some hysterical
woman to detract from his martyrdom. Almost roughly he tried
to push me from the platform; I clung to his coat sleeve for a
moment, unwilling. And then the focus of the crowd changed to
me. I heard the sounds of disapproval, the words and catcalls
'Shameless . . . Brazen . . .' I did this man no good – no good at
all. I was a wretched embarrassment to him, unwanted. It was
then I felt a tug on my own arm.

It was a woman who touched me, a middle-aged woman whose
gentle face was puckered with disapproval. 'Come down at once,'
she said, in a tone that was accustomed to being obeyed. 'You do
this unfortunate man no good – and you make a spectacle of yourself.' Beside her stood a man, her husband, shaking his head, regretting that someone like me, who might have been a daughter
to him, should so far forget herself, should do this inexplicably mad
thing.

'You don't understand,' I said. 'Something terrible will happen
if I don't stop it . . .'

But it was then I knew that the vision I had seen was not something that was certain to happen now; there was a time for it to
happen, and a place. And if the time was not now, then there
was nothing in all God's world I could do to stop it. It lay somewhere, waiting, in the future; it was in time to come. I was suddenly cold with shock and fear; I felt my body go limp, and
meekly I stepped down and permitted myself to be escorted

through the crowd by this unknown man and woman. The people parted before me, perhaps sensing that I was someone set apart, wanting nothing to do with my act of madness. Afterwards, I thought of the act of kindliness and courage performed by those two to take me from this place of spiritual hell. But I was not aware of it then, only of my own agony. I turned and looked once at the man on the platform; as we walked away down one of the paths towards the gates of the gardens he had begun to speak again, and once more the jeers and the heckling had begun. How did I tell him that one day he would face a crowd, and then he would lie still upon the ground in his own blood. I shook and trembled, and wished I did not have to bear the knowledge, but it was with me. I had seen it, and there was no way to wipe it out.

I remembered afterwards that I had not thought to thank the man and woman who had delivered me back to the merchant's house. I did though, still haunted by the man in the park, manage to ask if they knew who he was. 'Scobie, his name is,' was the reply. 'Thomas Scobie – a well-known radical. A rabble-rouser. He'll come to a bad end, I've no doubt.'

I didn't have any doubt, either.

Of course it was inevitable that news of what was called my escapade should reach my employer. And of course it was embroidered until it seemed that I had stood there and harangued the crowd in a violent anti-slavery speech. I did not deny it; I probably was against slavery, except that it had always seemed a remote thing and beyond my power to change. What I could not do was to explain the real reason that had compelled me towards that platform; I could not bring myself to tell of the vision of destruction; better be branded wild and indecorous than as one who had that dreaded gift, 'the sight'. So I said nothing, and packed my bags, as asked to. There were tearful farewells with the little boys, but plainly it was unthinkable to keep me on.

I made one more effort for Thomas Scobie's sake. On the way to the inn where I would get the coach to Ayr at which place my father was to meet me with the trap, I stopped the cabbie.

'Would you know of a Thomas Scobie – a man who holds meetings – addresses crowds? He's anti-slavery . . .'

'I've heard the name. He's agin many things, that one.'

'Would you know where he lived?'

'The Trongate, somewheres. Wouldna doubt if we went there we could ask, and find him. But it's nae place for someone like you to be going . . .'

'Go,' I said. 'We'll try.'

We went, and I was regretting it from the moment we turned in among the warren of the tenements. The cab itself was a sensation among those high, swarming buildings, the narrow alleys between, the stench and dirt and noise. We inquired many times, and found the place where Thomas Scobie lived. 'I'd go with you, miss,' the driver said, 'but I daren't leave the cab. There'd not be a piece of your luggage left, or even the cab itself if I trusted it to one o' these. Here, get away there, you rotten scum . . .'

I pushed through the teeming gutter urchins, shaking off their plucking hands, refusing their pleas for money. I walked up the six flights of stinking stairs to where they said Scobie lived. I knocked three times at the door that was pointed out, and there was no answer. It yielded, though, when I turned the knob.

That remembered face, white, strained, hungry, looked up from a table littered with papers; he frowned. 'Dinna I tell you . . .' He stopped, and the frown grew deeper. 'It's you! What the devil do *you* want? Haven't you done enough? – you nearly caused a riot the other day. And no one would listen to me any more.'

'I came because I couldn't leave without telling you . . .' He made a difficult audience. He just sat there, not offering me a chair, nor any encouragement. I stumbled through what I had to say; it sounded ridiculous, and at the end of it he gave a kind of snort of derision.

'You mean you came here to tell me *that*. A piece of foolishness like that!'

'I *had* to. My conscience wouldn't let me go without . . . You see, it's not the first time.'

He pointed his pen at me. 'Get out, woman. Do you think I've time to waste listening to this foolishness? All right – you've done your duty, and I suppose I should thank you, but you're wasting your time, *and* mine. I'll tell you, it takes no great prophet of the future to predict what will happen to me. Up and down the country men like me will die before the injustices of the people are righted. Slavery isn't the only issue that must be fought. In one place or another I *know* I'll die. Do you think the memory of Peterloo isn't in the hearts of all of us? Of course I'll die, and most likely by violence. It is something all of us know. *Now* will you leave me be . . .'

I went, and it had been a waste of time, just as he had said. He had not seen it exactly as I had, but he knew his chances, and he accepted them. Miserably I pushed my way through the children once more, and the crowd of women who had come to join them, some of them shrieking insults at the woman who visited the like of Thomas Scobie. The cabbie whipped up, and we charged through the crowd. At the public coach I had to give him an extra large tip because he complained so bitterly at the danger to his cab and horse in going into such a place. I couldn't blame him; I had only the consolation that I had done what I could. Thomas Scobie knew what was coming.

Back at Silkirk I attempted to tell only my father of what had happened. It was one of his rare failures in understanding; he turned his face from what I described as if it were a blasphemy. Only God knew the future, he said, and only the devil could have induced such madness in me. He told me to pray on it, and after that he never mentioned it. Some closeness that had been between us diminished then; my stepmother and sisters knew only that I had made a spectacle of myself, and had been discharged; bewilderment and a kind of pitying worry settled on them. Clearly I had become a great liability to the family. Only my little half-brother, Duncan, the only child of my father's second marriage, the beloved pet of the household, didn't understand or care that I was in a kind of limbo. I delighted in him, played with him, taught him, and he was the only joy of those sombre days.

When I was not with Duncan, I walked the hills and chafed against the bonds of being a woman and unable to strike out for myself, at the bonds of convention and family. My father grieved for my impatience and my stepmother worried for my future — and the worry turned to hostility when James Killian, even knowing the madness I had committed in Kelvingrove Gardens, took to speaking admiringly of me. 'Shows great spirit, Miss Fiona,' he kept saying. 'Not many young ladies would have dared.' After he said that for the third time, rather too warmly, I began to stay away from home on Saturdays.

I think I must have sighed then, as the weight of the whole thing pressed upon me too strongly. Suddenly the woman sitting by the window spoke.

'Ye've trouble for one so young . . .'

I didn't bother to ask how she knew. The village knew everything.

'I have,' I answered flatly. 'Who hasn't?' I was selfish, and young, and I didn't stop to think that my troubles were trifling compared to what hers must be.

'Aye – precious few,' she answered, but not rebuking me.

And then the silence fell again. It seemed that silence was the habit of years with this woman; she might almost have forgotten how to speak. But I had grown uncomfortable again, impatient for the rain to ease, so that I could, with decency, leave. But it still continued steadily, sheets of a wet curtain. It fell, hissing, into the low fire, and threatened its extinction.

'Yer mither used to walk this way too – I mind her, often, walking here among the hills.'

'She did?' I couldn't remember. I wondered why this woman would break her silence to speak of such a thing, except to imply that my mother had had reasons also for unhappiness, for restlessness, that drove her from the house. But this couldn't have been so; there could have been no really deep troubles for a woman as loved as I knew my mother to have been; I had been brought up in the sounds of my father's adoring recollection of her, and once I heard him say, in a kind of agony, 'Perhaps I loved her too well. Does God mean us to love a human creature in that way? Was it His judgement . . .?' I had been too young to deny that doubt, and wouldn't have known how. In my father's eyes and memory she had been always young, always beautiful. They had been young together, and there had been hope, and promise for the future. William McIntyre had been a young minister to watch, and with a wife such as Elizabeth McIntyre, kind, tactful, good with the poor of the parish as well as the elders of the kirk, everyone knew that he soon would be leaving his country parish for a calling of wider importance. But Elizabeth McIntyre had died – a terrible death, and with her had died their second child, my brother. Ambition and concern for the future alike both left my father that day; he never moved on from his country manse, and he didn't care.

It had been many years before he had married again, and this time it was to the widow of a distant cousin of my mother. Her husband's death had been fairly recent, and she was utterly helpless in her new position. She had three daughters, and a tiny pension. My father had gone to Edinburgh to try to help her with some legal matters, to ease her burden, and had returned married to her. I didn't blame him; she was pretty still, with a delicate, winning air which called out the protector in a man. But I sensed almost at once that my father regretted the marriage, acknowledging, as time went by, that it might have been a hasty mistake, something undertaken out of a feeling of duty to my mother's family. I thought my stepmother, though pretty, was a rather stupid woman; or perhaps this opinion was only my jealousy finding another name, for my father never said a word against her. The marriage, though, had brought the great joy of this other son, Duncan, now six years old – a beautiful, intelligent golden child whom the whole household worshipped, myself, I think, most of all. For this gift alone the marriage must have seemed worthwhile to William McIntyre.

'Ye've the look o' her.'

I was wrenched back to this room and this woman. 'Who? – Who have I the look of?'

'Yer mither – though she were more delicate-lookin'. Finer, ye might say.'

Blunt she was, but at least it was something to be compared to my mother in any way.

'I mind her once, settin' where ye are now. It was rainin' that day, too.' Some of the rigid self-control faded from that cracked voice, as if memories of happier times softened her. 'I mind I had ma husband then, still. And ma own child was underfoot. Playing there by the fire, he was, and the golden head of him puttin' yer mither in mind o' her own wee bairn. She said she would bring him to play next time – though it were a long way for a wee lad's legs to carry him, and he had not yet got her fondness for climbing on the hills. But she brought him, as she said. A bit worn out, he were, fra' the walk, but it were like an adventure for him to be sa far fra' the village. He got a liking for ma own son, Keith. It were strange, a lady like yer mither t' come sa far t' sit in a humble place like this. For her sake I persuaded ma husband to make the journey to the kirk a few times, though he dinna approve much o' the minister. Too fancy-like, he thought him. She brought me wee things – home-baked bread, and the jams she had put by in the season, and such things. A good woman – and it wasna her fault that the curse was upon her. She herself were fra' the Highlands, and they do say there be many there that have it so.'

I swung on the stool to look at the woman. The spinning wheel had stopped, though she still bent over it, holding it, as if to call up from it the memories of things just as they had been then.

'The curse?' In Scotland that meant only the one thing, and the very sound of it filled me with fear; 'You are wrong!' I cried at her. 'There was no curse.'

She lifted her head. 'Is it nae a curse t' see the future? For that was what she saw. I will never forget the day or the hour – a day when it rained like this, and she sat before the fire with the two wee boys playin' about her feet. It was the last time she ever came, and ye dinna wonder I wasna at the door to welcome ye this day, for I never wanted kith nor kin o' hers across this threshold again. Bad luck is bad luck, I say, and the sight is bad luck to most.'

I hadn't the strength to deny it now. 'What happened?'

'I dinna ken. I was workin' here – probably here at the wheel, as I did most afternoons. Then at a sudden there were a cry fra' her, as if she had been hit. I turned an' looked at her, an' I never saw sich a look on the face o' mortal woman. Afeared, she was, an' stricken terrible. "The child," she called out. "The wee child!" An' then on a sudden she were snatching up her boy and dragging him away fra' ma son. I asked her what frightened her, and she wouldna say. She took him at once an' reached for her cloak, and would ha' been gone on the instant if I hadna caught her by the arm an' held her. "In God's name," I said, "wha' did ye see? Wha' did ye see that so frightened ye?"

'She pulled her bairn fra' the house, as if the plague ha' come on us asudden. "Death! was wha'," she answered me. "Death! I saw a golden-haired little boy lying dead. It was . . ." I remember she moaned and cried. "Dead, he was. Your son was lying dead."

'An' she broke fra' me, and took the bairn wi' her, runnin' an' me runnin' after her, followin' her a good way down the hill-side, pleadin' wi' her, beggin' her ta say in wha' way it would come. But never a word she said, an' never again she came.'

For a time I could say or do nothing, just sitting there frozen in a kind of agony of soul and body. At last I made myself stir and gather my cloak about me; it still rained, but that didn't matter. I had not been welcomed here in the first place, and now we both knew why I could not stay.

At the door I said to her: 'Was it soon after that it happened?'

She nodded. 'I had waited wi' this terrible fear in ma heart, not darin' ta speak it to ma husband, lest speakin' bring it to come about. I waited, and I watched my bairn, an' wouldna let him fra' ma sight. But then one day I heard it – when the wind is right ye can hear the tollin' o' the kirk bell fra' here. An' then I knew it wasna my son she had seen lying dead. I sent my husband to find out what was the trouble. But before he were gone even I knew in some way that the wee bairn were dead. She had seen it, but she hadna been able t' believe it were her own son, and she hadna been able t' keep him fra' it.'

I nodded, and she stood at the door and watched me make my way through the rain-sodden yard, and struggle again with the gate of logs. Of course I knew how my brother had come to die. My father would not speak of it, but in a village like ours, and from kitchen gossip, a child learns such things. My mother had been driving the little governess cart along the sea front, along the part where the thick, high wall protects the village from the waves of the winter storms. No one had ever noticed what caused the pony to shy, and to break from her control, but the racing, swaying cart had gone the length of the front, faster and faster, as if the animal had been maddened by the shrieks and cries of those who witnessed the wild dash, and by the man who had tried to grasp the bridle and had been thrown to the ground. My mother had clutched my brother, the reins gone from her hands; they say the cart hit the sea wall three times in that terrible run before it finally splintered, and the two were thrown from it. They were horribly injured; they say my brother lived only a few minutes after the blow on his head. But my mother survived for some hours, carried to the nearest cottage across the road. But she was conscious, and she lived long enough to look on the face of her own dead son, and perhaps realize, in that final horror, which of those golden-haired children she had seen lying dead that day, as they played together in the crofter's cottage on the hill.

But at the gate I suddenly stopped, and I don't know what made me do it. 'And your son?' I called to her.

Even through the rain I saw her face darken. 'What's it t' ye?'

'He's not here now?'

'Nae – he's gone. He's good an' safe. Gone to Canada.'

'You've heard from him?'

'There's nae been time. A few months only he's been gone. I'll hear fra' him as soon as there's news o' a job t' be tellin' me. In a few weeks I'll be hearing fra' him.'

I said it. God, what made me say it – why didn't I keep my mouth closed on what I seemed to know? 'You'll not hear from him.'

Then a wild stream of curses fell upon me, curses in the ancient Gaelic tongue, fearful-sounding, and scarifying. I was grateful for my ignorance of what she was saying, and wishing I had left her in the same ignorance, wishing I had left her her peace for as long as she might have it.

I turned and stumbled down the hillside, slipping and sliding in the wet earth, through the heather and the cow pats, her cries growing fainter and fainter, but never quite lost to my hearing, because they went with me, and never ever afterwards could be erased.

2

My clothes were sodden and mud-grimed by the time I reached the manse. I went round by the back through the stables to avoid the stares I would have encountered from the windows along the sea road; even in the distress I felt there was always the obligation to keep up my father's position in the village. And this way I stood a better chance of avoiding James Killian – though perhaps it would have been a good thing if he could have seen me then, wild and distraught, my wet hair streaked across my face, my clothes like a peasant's, a creature, almost, from another world. But the trap he hired each Saturday was gone from the stables.

I stood there thankfully in the shelter of the archway, trying to draw breath, struggling to gain a little composure before going into the house, planning my way up the back stairs, and how I would have Flora dry my clothes before the kitchen fire. I was deadly cold, and yet I could not bring myself to go in; how could I encounter any member of the family normally with the stream of that woman's unintelligible curses still swirling about me? And why had I said, against all knowledge and pity, that she would never hear from her son again? Well, I said it, and there was no taking it back. The worst of the afternoon was the knowledge that this terrible thing in me had its seed in my mother; until now I could have believed in coincidence and chance, but no longer.

It was then, just as I was gathering myself up to make the final dash across the yard, that the kitchen door opened. Duncan's small, bright face looked out, scanning the yard. He seemed to have been waiting; his expression lit up as if patience had been rewarded. 'Fiona!' And then, bareheaded in the rain, he was racing towards me.

I put out my arms to him, to the innocence and warmth, but this was a day that was to be blackened forever in my memory. As he came towards me, and as I leaned to embrace him, I had another vision of him – of this small, eager-faced child. But now he was fleeing from a building that burned furiously. Behind him I could see the flames, leaping high, lightening the darkness of the dreary evening. His expression seemed to change to terror, and a kind of madness. He was mortally afraid, and then, so was I. I didn't know at that moment whether I saw him dead or not, because the vision went no further. He was pursued, but not only by fire.

As he reached me I pulled back my arms that had meant to welcome him, and he cannoned into me.

'Fiona!' It was an expression of pained reproach. Never before had I treated him this way.

'Duncan, laddie . . . oh, Duncan!' The vision was gone, and though its horror remained he was there, safe, well, unafraid, beside me. I swept him into my arms as I had meant to, and prayed that my touch was not some kind of contamination to him, that contact with me would not mean the fulfilment of that dreadful sight that I had seen.

'I've been waiting,' he said, the reproach melting, but he was still aggrieved.

'Waiting? For what? – you knew I would be back.'

'Yes – yes. I knew. But I wanted to be the first to see you. To tell you the news.'

'Is it Mr Killian, Duncan? Has he spoken for Mary?' I felt a great sense of relief.

'Oh, *that*. No – not that! He's just been here all afternoon. They've been doing silly things like singing in the parlour. No – I wasn't waiting to tell you that. It's the letter. The letter that's come.'

'What letter?' A kind of desperate hope sprang in me. Someone had offered me a position. I would soon be off their hands at Silkirk.

'A letter from a long way off – Mama says from the relations out in the West Indies. I didn't know about the West Indies, but Father has promised to show me in the atlas after supper.'

'Yes?' I urged impatiently. 'Yes – what about the letter? What did it say?'

'Well, it says for Mary to come. There's some little boy they want her to look after and teach. But of course Mama won't let her go. She says there's Mr Killian to think of, and Mary mustn't go.'

I knew at once what was to be. 'So I'm to go in her place? That's it, isn't it?'

He wrapped his arms tightly about me, squeezing the wetness of the cloak to my body, heedless of the rain as we swayed a little out of the shelter of the arch.

'But Fiona, you won't go! You won't go, will you? They say it's a fearsome way off, and when will I see you ever? Fiona, don't go! You'll stay here – won't you? I don't want you to go!'

But I knew if there was the least chance, I would go. I clung to Duncan, and the pain of the thought of going was a physical thing. But I would go, not mainly because it was a position to go to, a reason to leave Silkirk, though much farther and more irrevocably distant than I had ever been before. I would leave because I was now afraid of what my very presence would do to this precious child. It was possible, as perhaps my mother had done, that I carried some cursed seed of tragedy within me, innocently, but like some disease. If I were not here perhaps the vision of Duncan running terror-stricken, pursued, with the flames leaping behind him would never come to pass. Perhaps it was my presence that would bring these things, and my absence would deny them.

'We'll see, my pet,' I said, stroking his wet hair, and trying to comfort him. 'We'll see – the West Indies isn't so very far away.' It was the other end of the earth, and if what they said of the fevers and the sicknesses were truth, I might never see Duncan again. But by that single fact I might spare him. So I would go.

3

'They say they are very rich.'

'*Who* says, my dear?' my father asked patiently of my stepmother, trying to calm the excited nervousness behind the words.

'The family – the family, of course. One hears these things. Oh –' a toss of her pretty head – 'I *know* we are just the poor Scottish branch and the London family only ever paid a courtesy call whenever they happened to be in Edinburgh. But then they *did* very kindly invite Mary for that lovely visit to London last year, so we know how well *they* live. But the West Indian place was mentioned – wasn't it, Mary? – and the London family have some interest in it . . . And even so – aren't all West Indian planters rich? All that sugar . . . ?'

'On slave labour,' my father said, but no one paid any attention to him. I saw his glance go quickly to me, and away again; were we both thinking of what I had tried to describe to him of that day in Kelvingrove Gardens? But we would not talk about slavery here among the family.

We were seated around the big table in the dining-room, Duncan had gone to bed, and the youngest of the little girls, Sarah. The supper dishes had been cleared, and the door to the kitchen passage firmly closed; the fire had been built up, and we were there, plainly, for as long as it took to reach a decision. As far as I was concerned, the decision was made. I knew clearly that in the minds of my stepmother and Mary it also was made. Now it needed my father to go through the motions. Emily, the middle girl, was there only because she was of an age now to be included in family councils, not because she was old enough to be sent in Mary's place. The fact that we, the children, were consulted at all, was rare indeed; in every other family we knew the father alone would have made the decision.

'Of course Mary may not go,' my stepmother said. 'Mr Killian is on the verge of a declaration, and if Mary were even to indicate that she thought so little of him as to even consider leaving here, why he would be offended to the point where he would be justified in giving up any thought of making an offer.'

'That is as may be,' my father answered. 'But why must Fiona go in her place? Fiona was not the one asked for. Why not simply write and say that Mary is about to announce her engagement, and that will be that.'

Why did I feel so grateful to him, so warmed? Just to know that in all the difficulties I had brought on him, in the impossible position in which I had placed myself, he still did not grab at this opportunity to see me gone, and off his hands. Some of the closeness we had known came back with those words. I wanted to grasp his hand, to let him know that I would bless him for ever for what he had said, but that would have stiffened his attitude. It would have made him fight to keep me here.

'But it is a *marvellous* opportunity,' I said. 'I should love to go.' I watched my stepmother's eyes light with pleasure and approval. 'The Indies are so romantic, aren't they? Sunshine every day – and those exotic flowers and birds . . .' I was desperately reaching for whatever I could remember, leaving out the darker side – the illnesses, the miscegenations, the whispers of witchcraft, the strange tales that filtered back of the Creole families. Let my father not be reminded of all of this side of the picture.

'Of course, Fiona is *trained*,' my stepmother went on. 'They will be getting a real governess instead of Mary, who hardly could cope with a growing boy . . . Doubtless they have no notion that Fiona is free of her last position, or they would have asked for her. Perhaps it is just as *well* they don't know. The reason was awkward . . . And they do say they are rich,' she repeated, as if that should finish the argument. 'There would be many servants – '

'Slaves,' my father corrected.

'Oh, you know very well that the house slaves are just like ordinary servants here! Fiona would be well looked after. And who knows . . .' She brightened still further. 'They say young ladies are scarce out there. Fiona may make a good marriage.

They say the planters are very rich ...'

'Who says?' my father insisted. 'I beg you, Dorothy, not to make these generalizations. *Who* says all these things? – and why should it be so desirable for Fiona to be married so far away from home?'

Her head came up. 'As to that! – the farther from home the better! Fiona has *ruined* herself here. She has no chance of marriage at all. Out there – well, they'll just never hear of her escapade, and I *do* know they are rich, William McIntyre. At least, the Maxwells are rich, and that's all that counts.' She pointed to the letter lying on the table. 'If Fiona does not take her chance now, I think she will regret it for the rest of her life. There is not time to write and suggest that she come in Mary's place. We will, of course, inform the London Maxwells at once. But out there they need a governess at once. When Fiona arrives they will be so pleased to have her, a young lady from a good family, with training, that they won't ask any questions about how she came to be available. That is – ' she looked pointedly at me – 'unless she takes it into her head to harangue them on slavery. *Then* I should think her stay would be very short indeed.'

'Dorothy – that is enough.' On a very few occasions my father's authority was exerted, and he was obeyed. 'It is for Fiona to decide. After all, what do we know of what she is going to? What do any of us know of the Maxwells except that they are reputed to be rich?'

My stepmother was sobered. 'What do we know of anyone?' she asked, in truth. 'We just have to trust. Andrew Maxwell, the boy's father, is getting on in years. It was a late marriage. He has heard through the London Maxwells that I have three daughters, and the oldest is of an age to go out and help to take care of the son, and to teach him. The salary is handsome – and Mary – Fiona, that is – is to be treated as one of the family, since she is so. A nice change, I would think, from dinner on a tray in the school-room.'

Put that way, it sounded like a fairy-tale that governesses some-times dream, and there was nothing in the letter that lay between us on the dining-room table to shatter the dream. I reached for it, and studied it yet again. The tone was polite, even appealing, *'My husband, you must know, is advancing in years, and I must help him a great deal with the business of the plantation. This leaves me less time than I would like to spend with our young son. It would be esteemed a great favour by my husband and myself if one of the Maxwell family could come to help with his teaching*

and training. We hear from our London cousins that your daughter Mary is of admirable temperament and suitable age ...'
There was more like it, and it sounded too good to be true. To begin with, women who wrote in a hand so thick and bold and black were not apt to be so polite. And there was the slightly foreign flavour to it, as if she had once been taught how to write polite English letters. And all the unspoken authority of a woman who was used to running things, who was used to being obeyed, and did not for a moment expect these poor Scottish relations to refuse her offer was to be seen in the arrogant pride and assurance of that elaborately penned signature : *Maria Medina y Palma de Maxwell.*
I stared at it, fascinated, mistrusting the writer, somewhat afraid of her already, but knowing that I would do what she asked.

4

I went almost before there was time for second thoughts. The London Maxwells were written to, as Maria Maxwell's letter had instructed, to advance the passage money. 'Merchants – and something in banking in the City' was how my stepmother described them. She said only of me that I was free to go, whereas her own daughter was not, and how fortunate it was that I had already had some training in the charge of small boys. I was described fulsomely in terms that my stepmother had never used of me before; Andrew Maxwell was getting a paragon to take care of his son if the letter were to be believed. The reply came at once. The firm of Maxwell, Maxwell, Maxwell & Grimmond – which Maxwell it was we could never decide from the signature – were sure that Miss Fiona McIntyre would make an entirely satisfactory substitute for her stepsister, and the writer would be pleased if she would find it convenient to embark on the *Clyde Queen*, leaving shortly from Glasgow. Passage had already been secured. The shock came when the sailing date was mentioned. It was in ten days' time.
My stomach turned as I thought of the long voyage, and so little time to prepare, so little time to be sure that I was doing the right thing. But the surety came whenever I looked at Duncan. And I learned to shrug my shoulders; when was one ever sure what was the right thing? In that, at least, my stepmother had not been stupid.
So a trunk was brought from the attic and I packed my clothes; there was little among them suitable for the climate I was going

to, but there was neither time nor money for new ones. On the last day Mary came to me with a pin-cushion she had made, and an embroidered ribbon fashioned into a bow for my heavy knot of hair. The gifts were offered without words, but with a look of thanks whose meaning I understood. I packed some books for this new young charge whose name I didn't even know, and tried to brush aside Duncan's tears and protests.

It was hard when the time finally came. My father had hired a carriage to take us all the way to Glasgow, and would come with me to see me aboard the *Clyde Queen*. Duncan clung to me then, and I tried to calm his sobs and howls of outrage; he had consulted the atlas, and he knew that the Indies were much farther away than London, which was the farthest his imagination yet reached. I was fighting my own tears when my father touched my arm.

'There's a woman there, Fiona – she has come and asked to speak to you.' He seemed puzzled, but he was invariably courteous to anyone to make a request of him.

I turned, and there, standing by the arch of the yard, where I had seen my vision of Duncan on that terrible day, stood the woman from the crofter's cottage. Very slowly I released myself from Duncan's embrace, and went towards her, a sense of dread growing in me. I still heard those ancient curses that had followed me down the hillside.

She gave me no greeting, but her voice was low. What was said was to be between us only. 'They say ye are goin' – they say ye are goin' a long way, and some never come back fra' those parts. So I thought I would come an' tell ye, so that ye would know.'

'Know what?'

'Ma son, Keith – ye asked if I hadna heard fra' him, an' I said nae. I telled ye he were in Canada, an' soon I would ha' news o' him. An' ye answered that I never would hear. Well, I came t' tell ye that ye were right. Ma son is dead. He never reached Canada. Some sickness on the ship, and he lies buried out there in the sea. So ye knew it, an' I have come t' tell ye that. Bad luck ye bring wi' yer cursed gift o' what is not yet known. So leave wi' that gift fra' me, and remember this lonely woman.'

Then she turned, that gaunt figure wrapped in her ancient ragged plaid, and started along the road that led from the village.

'Fiona – ' my stepmother called, perhaps startled by what I knew was plainly upon my face. 'Who was that woman? – extraordinary!'

I did not dare look at Duncan. 'Come, Father, it's getting late. The ship will not wait on the tide . . .' A hasty embrace, the quickest for Duncan, who clung hardest, and then I was in the carriage, and we were moving. I turned my face to the window, and my father, with understanding I sometimes did not give him enough credit for, asked no questions.

There was no real hurry, and we made the *Clyde Queen* three hours before the tide. As we cast off my father stood on the dock, his hat raised, and the freshening wind fanning his long, silvering hair. Although there were miles of the Clyde yet to come, and the Isle of Arran and Ailsa Craig and all the other islands standing off the coast, he was truly the last sight of Scotland for me. I passionately willed that with my going would go that threat to Duncan, that the end of Scotland would be the end of the curses and the visions that are legend among our history. Deliberately I turned my face towards the yet unfelt sun of the Indies, welcoming it, wanting it. I turned my face and my future towards a mansion called Landfall.

2

'It will be the first thing ye sight as the sun rises. Be here at dawn, before the clouds have cleared off Kronberg. We will be hove-to all night. I'll not risk rounding the Serpent Rocks after nightfall.'

The quick tropic dusk had come down just as the outline of the island had appeared. There had been the call from the lookout, and the half-smile of pleasure which Captain Stewart had permitted himself at the exactitude of his navigation, and my wild rush to the bulwark. But the swiftness of the dark defeated me; the island was there, hilly, rolling, sweeping in the southern end to the sharp outline of the volcanic peak, Kronberg. The sea purpled suddenly as the light rushed away, and the island was gone – a dark land-mass that disappeared as the stars already blazed in the light-blue sky. It was too late even for Captain Stewart's glass to help me. The trade winds that had driven at our backs most of the way across the Atlantic had died, as they did at night.

'Do ye not smell the land?' he said. Yes, I smelled the land.

I smelled it too before dawn as I crept up the companion ladder and once more stationed myself at the bulwark. The light was rushing in as it had ebbed last night, a swift tide. The stars grew paler, the sea lightened; the coolness of dawn still lay on us, but my palms sweated slightly as they gripped the taffrail. My mind was crowded with the few things I had been able to gather to myself during the long weeks of the voyage, the snippets of information, the words half-said. The *Clyde Queen* was an island ship, delivering and taking on her cargo from all over the Indies. Any officer who had made the voyage a few times had already gathered the stories of the islands, heard the names of those who mattered, could embroider the histories and the legends. But it was the third mate, young Mr McPherson, this only his fourth voyage, who had told me most about the Maxwells, and about Landfall, and that wasn't much. I had often walked until late at night on deck, savouring the coolness after the heat of the day, knowing I would not sleep well in the stuffiness of the cabin that had not seemed to have a whisper of fresh air since we had passed the Azores. Once or twice we had stood together by the rail, watching the stars swing with the gentle roll of the ship, and he had told me his little knowledge of the Indies, and had ventured a question or two about my own journey. After we had left the Clyde the thrust of the North Atlantic had produced the expected seasickness in the four passengers the *Clyde Queen* carried, a man and wife, and another woman, going, like myself, as governess, but to a family on Barbados. We were some days at sea before all four passengers were gathered about the captain's table, and the questions were asked. 'I,' I said, 'am going to take care of a little boy on San Cristóbal. The family is kin to my mother.'

'And which family is that?' Young Mr McPherson blushed as he spoke. The third mate did not speak often in the presence of his captain, but he seemed eager to talk to me. I remember, though, the instant expression of grim dishumour that had crossed the captain's face, and he glanced sharply down the table at his officer.

'Maxwell,' I said quickly. 'Maxwell, of the Landfall plantation. Do you know of them?'

The captain answered for him, and silenced his third mate. I don't recall that Mr McPherson ever spoke directly to me at table again.

'Aye, Miss McIntyre, the Maxwells are known. Anyone who knows San Cristóbal and the islands thereabouts knows Andrew Maxwell.'

And there was what had been said to me in Mr McPherson's low voice at the rail those few evenings when his watch had per-

6

mitted him time to talk, or his captain's eye had not been upon
him. When I had tried to question him, he had shrugged ruefully,
and smiled. 'I've been told, Miss McIntyre, that I'm not to discuss
the Maxwells with you.'

'Why ever not?'

'Because I found out – or was told, very bluntly – that the London firm of Maxwell are part-owners of this vessel, and one doesn't
discuss one's employers.'

'But one also can't be so rude as to refuse to answer a lady's
natural questions, can one?'

He chuckled in the darkness. 'No, Miss McIntyre, one couldna
be *that* rude. I don't know much, mind you . . .'

'Maria Maxwell?' Why did she interest me, I wondered, more
than her husband.

'A great beauty, they say. I've never seen her. Spanish – almost
purely Spanish, although the island has been British for so long.
The Dutch had it for a while in between the Spanish and the
English. All these islands have a checker-board history – prizes of
war, and pieces of paper signed in Paris or Vienna. But a good
many of the old Spanish aristocracy lingered, and are as clannish
as we Scots. There are a good many Scots on the island, I know.
Where the English settle, the Scots come to do the hard work.
Andrew Maxwell is a big landowner, Miss McIntyre, but I wouldna
doubt he worked hard enough in his time. It wasna given to him
on a plate.'

'He married late . . .'

'Aye . . .' A hesitation. 'He married late.' I was not so innocent I didn't know his embarrassment. He didn't mean me to suppose that Andrew Maxwell had been some crabbed bachelor.

It might have been two weeks later before we had our next
conversation. Maria Maxwell, what little he knew of her, obviously
fascinated him also. 'They say she is magnificent – and almost
runs the plantation single-handed now. They say no woman
has ever been able to control the slaves the way she does. They
say . . .'

'You are keeping Miss McIntyre from her rest, Mr McPherson.'
It was Stewart's voice behind us; the rebuke was very clear. I was
neither to be spoken to, nor was gossip to be related to me. It was
the last time Mr McPherson ever sought my company alone, or
spoke to me privately. But I felt him watching me; often I felt his
gaze on me as he stood his daytime watch on the poop deck. But
that was all.

Now it was Captain Stewart who joined me at the bulwark.

The first tip of the sun was appearing, and the island was abruptly
bathed in an unearthly light, the water suddenly brilliant aqua-
marine, shading to sapphire where it ran to the shallows, the land-
mass itself purple, with the top of Kronberg still in mist, but the
long ridges of its sides brightening to green as I watched. The
coast stretched long and far out of sight, the bays indented, this
north side rocky and wind-driven.

'Maxwell's kingdom.' The captain's voice sounded more than
usually acid and burred. 'Everything stretching from Kronberg to
the Serpent Rocks on this side is his, and much more on the other
side of the mountain – no, you dinna see much of the cane fields
this side – too wet and steep. But the house is there, on the ridge.
There was a time when it was the first thing you saw of San
Cristóbal – that and Kronberg and the Serpents. Landfall House,
and well named. You can see it there, white, though the garden
grows close. And I've no doubt Andrew Maxwell's glass is trained
on us at this very moment. Old men don't sleep late.'

I don't know what loosened his usually taciturn tongue; perhaps he forgot, in his memories of the many voyages at which
he had made this landfall, his usual habit of discretion; perhaps he
was moved to give me the information I had sought from McPherson. 'It's never been a lucky place,' he added suddenly. 'I couldna
pretend to know all its history, but it was built long before Andrew
Maxwell was born. Been left to go derelict several times, I think
– absentee owners. I did hear some tale that when it was being
built there was some trouble between a female slave and her
mistress – some white women are particularly savage with slaves,
Miss McIntyre. It was said that before she was done to death,
the slave put a curse upon the house. Well, I don't know why I
repeat such things – the islands are full of fanciful stories of curses
and spells and witchcraft. It follows wherever the African goes
. . . And Andrew Maxwell has had his share of trouble.'

Since I was to leave the *Clyde Queen* so soon, I risked his
displeasure. 'You don't seem to care for Andrew Maxwell, Captain
Stewart.'

'Ah.' I had the feeling that if I had not been there he would
have spat into the water below us. 'It's not ma business, Miss
McIntyre, to care or not to care for Andrew Maxwell. I have
other things to think about. I neither care nor don't care for
Negroes, either, but I have never touched the trade, in all my
years sailing these seas. Men make fortunes from other men's
backs, Miss McIntyre. That's legal and permissible, but a Christian
doesn't have to admire it. Slaving's a dirty business, no matter which

end of it you're on. Oh, I know, the transportation of slaves from Africa was supposed to have ended years ago, but the illegal cargoes have been making three times the money they did before it was forbidden, so it still goes on. Well, you'll see – and you'll probably accept what you must in the life you see lived here on these islands. *You* can do nothing to change it. Females do best to mind their own business, and especially where you're going. Good morning, Miss McIntyre. We should be docked by ten.'

And then he turned from my side and bellowed an order to the brigade of hands who had appeared with brushes and buckets for the morning ritual of deck-cleaning. The captain ran a tight ship, and it would arrive in Santa Marta, San Cristóbal's harbour and main town, with its decks holystoned white, and every piece of brass gleaming.

And I would go below and pack my trunk, giving my last glance to that partly obscured white house on the ridge, not able to stand still any longer under the spyglass of an old man who woke early.

They had sent an elegant light carriage for me – shining black with yellow-spoked wheels and gold tassels on its cushions; its Negro driver was clad in white duck with yellow epaulets, a black tricorned hat bound with gold, and he wore a look of massive imperturbability; a young boy, dressed much as he was, but without the dignity of the hat, held the horses while he inquired at the gangplank for the lady to be taken to Landfall. No one of the household had come to welcome me; perhaps that was too much to expect. The big Negro was silent and unsmiling as he helped me to my seat, and strapped my trunk to the back of the carriage. Captain Stewart had bade me goodbye at the top of the gangplank. Without knowing why, now that the ties to the *Clyde Queen*, never strong or affectionate, were cut, I felt alone and almost afraid in the midst of all that bright bustle of the ships at anchor, the carrying of bales and barrels, the sing-song voices of the slaves speaking in their gulla language what they didn't care for the white man to know. There would be a sudden burst of laughter, and then nearly always the irate voice of an overseer checking it. There was movement and colour and sound all about me; and most of all there was the brilliant sun, the sun that reached everywhere, hurting the eyes and blackening into shadow any place it could reach; there was the splash of shocking colours in unexpected places, vines spilling over walls, coloured cloths bound around the heads of the Negro women, the warehouses along the dockside painted in fading pinks and blues and greens. It was a cheerful chaos of movement and colour and light, and yet even while the sweat ran off me as I waited, I felt the strange, cold undercurrent of fear. It might have been Captain Stewart's speculative eye still on me from the ship, or it could have been the frozen attitude of the driver, or one of the many, quick, but blank glances that went to me from the Negroes who passed the carriage, the sideways glance under heavy lids, that neither welcomed nor cheered me. Relief from it came at the last moment; the driver was gathering the reins into his hands, and reaching for the whip when there was a sudden clatter down the gangplank.

Under Captain Stewart's eye, Mr McPherson ran towards the carriage. I felt his hand, moist as mine was; his brow was beaded in perspiration.

'Good luck, Miss McIntyre. Good luck at Landfall.'

I pressed his hand. 'Thank you . . . thank you very much.'

'Perhaps . . . perhaps when the *Clyde Queen*'s next in Santa Marta. Oh, well . . .' He shrugged.

I said something in reply, heaven knows what it was. But his act of defiance of his captain had served to raise my own spirits. I drew myself up straighter as the carriage slipped at a smart rate through the business section of the town, the warehouses and the streets arcaded against the sun and the rain; then we came to the big houses with the gardens enclosed by high walls, the shutters already closed against the sun, the tangle of blossoming vines cascading over wall and arched gateways. Down the lane between, and at the back of the houses, were the unpainted shacks, with sagging shutters and lifted off the ground on rotting wooden stumps. A breeze blew now in my face, and the sweat began to dry. We came to the outskirts of the town; the houses gave way completely to shacks, and then the start of the cane fields. There were long, rolling hills of tall cane, endlessly tossing and waving in the wind, so that the colour changed as if one watched the shadows racing across a field of unripe corn. But this was gold that the planters set into the ground, and with the sun and the rain it grew gold for them. There were sometimes little clusters of wooden huts where dirt roads bisected; there were signposts which I realized pointed not to villages, but to plantations – Barrow's End, Montrose Hall, Mary's Fancy. Now what caught the eye were the greathouses themselves, always set upon the ridge of a hill to catch the breeze, and sometimes Spanish-looking bell towers outlined against the hard blue sky, the conical shape of the stone windmills that served the sugar factories. Kronberg, my own particular landmark, grew nearer, but it took a long time for us to reach the rather severe whitewashed archway and the sign post that said LANDFALL. The cane fields went on, then a group of palm-thatched shacks, and a faded sign that was lettered WINTERSLO. At this junction was the stump of a crumbling stone pillar with the chiselled words SAN FRANCI. They were worn by time, almost obliterated, and hardly registered. More and more cane fields – the roof line of a house, very spare, against the dry side of the mountain. Then Kronberg was upon us; the carriage climbed a little about its base, a narrow road; the cane fields were behind us, an almost rank tropical growth had begun. Deep shadow, tall trees, huge thick vines like languorous snakes twined about them, strange, unknown flowers, and the flash of coloured birds; we had come to the windward side of Kronberg, the side where the rain spilled down, too steep for cane, magnificent in its dark beauty.

And then there were tall stone pillars, and great iron gates and a tracery of iron archway set with a lantern, grander than anything I had ever seen. Suddenly the small boy who up to now had copied the silence and dignity of his senior could bear his solemnity no longer. He turned and there was a quick flash of an unexpectedly cheerful, prideful smile. He might be a slave, it told me, but he belonged to a rich master.

'This Landfall,' he announced.

2

As the drive wound towards the house there were glimpses of the sea, the sapphire flash, the fleck of white curling over the rocks. The trees were tall, and within their shade the huge-leaved tropical plants; in the spaces between the sun was fierce to the eye, and the bright green grass grew, hot and brittle-looking, as if it were razor-edged, and would not be kind or cool to bare feet. Everything was immaculate, and yet I sensed that a year's neglect – even a month's, perhaps – would bring the vines rampaging, and the grass waist-high.

We swept up smartly before the high white stone house, the drive circling about an enormous, grey-trunked tree, perhaps the biggest I have ever seen. The driver checked the horses expertly; our arrival was accompanied by the clamour of dogs, who darted from around both sides of the house, and by the children, dark-skinned children in faded cotton who seemed to come from no-where – they had not been there, and suddenly they were there, soundless, shy, keeping well back, ready to disappear once again, and yet with children's eagerness to witness what was going on.

Half their attention was on me, and half directed towards the steps that led up to the house. They held themselves in readiness to go when someone should appear.

At first there was no one. Once the driver had shouted the dogs to silence, the quiet was painful, just the steady stir of the wind through the branches and vines. As if he knew the awkwardness, the driver took his time getting down and handing over the bridle to the boy. His slowness increased as he opened the door and let down the little folding step. For a moment he hesitated, as if he feared to offer his black hand to my white, as if his should not be the instrument of welcome to the house of Andrew Maxwell.

His action was halted by the boy. 'Here is Master.' He was not smiling now, and it was said almost in a whisper.

The house was surrounded on all sides with a deep, two-storeyed, veranda supported by vine-thickened pillars – later I learned to call it the gallery. Its depth matched the great height of the mahogany shutters that framed each of the many french doors – all of them standing open to the breeze. So intense was the shadow cast by the gallery that for a moment I had difficulty seeing past the glare of the white stone to the man who stood in the doorway opposite the steps. Then I took in the hugeness of the figure, the white clothes he wore, and the flamboyance of the red silk sash bound about his waist. We stared at each other for moments, my hand still extended towards the driver, but his was no longer there to help me alight. Then I saw the silver-topped cane in the hand of the white-clad figure, and the sure movement with which it was discarded – not thrown to the floor or leaned against the door frame, but just simply put away from him, and received by another hand, a slave whose presence there he took for granted. I saw the effort to straighten the great height and bulk, the effort to pace the wide veranda with some youthfulness of movement. But as he stepped out into the sunlight, his hand went to the hot iron railing for support, and it was an ageing, and possibly ailing man who came carefully towards me. He did not flinch at the burning kiss of that intricately wrought rail; the steps curved outward in a graceful sweep, and he held the rail all the way down to the end posts, which supported two great lamps like that above the gateway.

But the expected words of welcome were not the first which came as he started towards the carriage.

'Fergus – Goddammit, Fergus! Where is Fergus?'

The strength and power of the voice fought the wind, and seemed to echo back through the whole house; the dark-skinned children vanished, the dogs crept back to the shade, or towards the stables. No word was said to me. In the stillness of the moment I was suddenly aware of a quick flash of colour, as a huge bird, scarlet and yellow plumaged, swept by with a harsh shrieking cry, like mocking laughter.

Now Andrew Maxwell addressed the driver, whose own stillness seemed part fear.

'Where is my son? Was he not on the dock?'

'Master Fergus not there, sir.'

'Goddammit!' For a second I thought one of those giant hands might rise to strike the man. But the fist unclenched, and instead the hand went at last towards me.

'Miss Mary Maxwell – welcome to Landfall.' The big, puffy lips parted in a smile that showed tobacco-stained teeth; but I had the odd sensation that the smile was genuine. I was not included in the general anger. 'Forgive the seeming churlishness, Miss Mary. I had instructed my son to be on the dock to meet the *Clyde Queen*. You must think us a strange, unmannerly lot here at Landfall.'

He could be charming; a pointed beard hid the fleshiness of chin and neck, and he had somehow the look of a rogue; but he could be a charming rogue. At last I was out of the carriage, and tall as I was for a woman, I still had to stare up at his face. I squinted against the glare; the sun burned and the sweat bathed my whole body again. It was no place for explanations, but I could not, even for a moment, assume Mary's identity.

'Thank you for your welcome. I hope I will be just as welcome when you know that I'm not Mary Maxwell, but her stepsister, Fiona McIntyre.'

The thick lips tightened just a trifle and the eyes narrowed. He looked at me closely, my face, and then a careful up and downward sweep that took in all of me. There was no subtlety in that look; it was as frank as anything I had ever been subjected to.

'I think,' he said finally, 'that we had better go inside.' And then he took my arm; it was not a gentle touch, but rather as if he had taken me unto himself in place of the cane he had discarded; the pressure of his fingers on my arm hurt, and he meant them to, as if he tested me, and must make me know how much strength still remained in him. This way we climbed the stairs, his hand again on the rail, the other pressing, leaning, cruel. Having shown his own strength, he seemed to want to gauge mine, to find out how long it would be before I would pause, or try to shift the burden. I did neither. We continued on into the blessed

shade of the gallery, across its checkered marble floor and then
entered an inner gallery, as wide as the first, furnished along its
whole length like an informal sitting-room, and running, as the
outer one seemed to, around the whole house. I felt the cooler air
here, and relief to the eyes. Then we passed through the core of
the house – a hall whose beautiful staircase split to branch in two
directions, the open doorways to a great salon on one side and to
the dining-room on the other. The pressure on my arm directed me
towards the salon, much as the pull on a bridle. Compared to the
glare outside, it was almost dark here. There was mahogany,
floors and massive furniture, there was silver and paintings, and
crystal chandeliers whose prisms tinkled gently together in the
tropic breeze. Here, at the centre of the house, with the breeze
following straight through, untouched by the sun, it was as cool as
a summer's day in Scotland. Again I felt the perspiration drying on
me, and the strange chill of the tropics struck at me.

'Sit there.' He indicated a chair in which I must sit upright, a
chair for a tall man rather than a woman. He himself went to a
sofa, big, heavy, red, whose sagging springs told me that it was his
own special place. As he sat he clicked his fingers and a servant
appeared – I reminded myself that I would have to get used to
the idea that these people were slaves, not servants, with no choice
to disobey, without the chance to leave to find some other work.
This was their life – the beginning and end of it. At this moment
the black faces seemed anonymous to me, featureless, indistinguishable, the carefully downcast eyes without identity or will. The
plain cotton dress of the house slaves furthered this illusion that
all were the same person, forever reappearing in a different role.

'This is Dougal,' Andrew Maxwell said. 'He oversees the house.'
A Scottish name; I wondered if they had their own private names,
the names that came from Africa, or were they also lost in the
generations of slavery. Perhaps I shivered a little at the thought,
and Andrew Maxwell saw it.

'You'll take this little drink now,' he said, as Dougal laid a tall
glass on the table beside me, and another, together with a jug,
beside his master. 'I know what's on you – it's hot as hell, and yet
you're cold. You're wearing the wrong clothes, of course. We'll
have to see about that. But you must guard against the chill. Watch
for it at night . . .'

I sipped and felt a fiery sweetness against my tongue and throat,
and a burning within me. It was not unpleasant – too sweet perhaps, but pervasive; there was the scent of spices, cinnamon and
nutmeg.

'In Scotland, Mr Maxwell, ladies rarely drink spirits. Especially ministers' daughters.'

He slapped his hand against his bulging thigh as if challenged. 'And here, miss, you will do as I say. And I say that a little rum to burn out the chill will do no hurt. I've lived in this climate all my life. I *know* how a white man survives. And so we'll have no namby-pamby notions about what ladies do or don't. *Here* they do!'

'Perhaps you're right,' I answered coolly, 'but that is surely something I'll have to discover for myself. *I* haven't lived here all my life, but I've been wet a thousand times up on the mountains in Scotland with no more when I got home than a cup of tea to take away the chill. Scotland makes hardy women, Mr Maxwell. My blood isn't thin yet.'

For some reason this defiance pleased him. He threw back his great head, and the chuckle of appreciation was rich and long. 'Then you *are* no namby-pamby, miss. Not a bit of it! No thin blood in you.'

I looked down at my glass with mock demureness. 'Don't you want to know, Mr Maxwell, why I am here in place of my step-sister?'

He sighed. 'I suppose so – but you suit me, I know that already. I was expecting a Miss Pink-and-Pretty, described to me by old Jeremy Maxwell when he wrote about someone coming out for the boy. I suppose she couldn't come for some reason, and they sent you instead. That's it, isn't it? Well enough, then. I would say we've done well in the exchange . . .'

'I *insist*, Mr Maxwell, on presenting my qualifications. I am quite experienced as a governess. My references – '

'You insist, do you.' He laughed at me. 'I can *see* your qualifications, Miss Fiona McIntyre. I like redheaded women, and all the better if they're big and shapely. You're a fine woman, Miss Fiona. The women used to be like you when they first came out to these islands – like my mother, a strong, handsome woman, and if her husband hadn't been killed she would have borne him a dozen sons. But in a generation or two the blood thins out in more ways than one. I'm sick of looking at sallow Spanish complexions on women who haven't the strength to lift a child. The Spanish blood here, Miss Fiona, has run to seed . . .'

Was he drunk already, I wondered? – at this hour? I had smelled the rum from him as we had walked together, that and a strangely sweetish tobacco smell that seemed now to cling even to my own clothes. Did he always speak to women in this way? His gaze upon me was so frank that I wanted to turn away, or look down, but would not give way before him. He was complimenting me, flirting with me almost in a way that was shameless and high-handed, since I was almost as bound as his slaves. He said he liked women big and redheaded, and despised the thin blood and sallow skins of the Spanish. And yet he was married to a woman whose beauty was a legend even to those who had not seen her. And where was that woman? – and where was the child I had come to care for, and teach? Why did I sit here, near noon, drinking rum with a man with a lecherous eye and a rough tongue? The answer was as it had been all of my adult life; I had, at this moment, no other choice. You stay where you are when there is no other place to go.

'There wasn't time to write, you understand,' I said. 'It would have taken months for letters to be exchanged, and Mrs Maxwell's need seemed urgent. Since I had had experience, and my sister none, we thought . . .'

He cut me off with a wave of the hand. 'Oh, they wrote us about the other one – Miss Pink-and-Pretty. I didn't care for the sound of her. Too young. Too . . .' he weighed his word '. . . inno-cent. She might not have stood the test. I've a feeling you will. *I* would have chosen you – '

'Was anyone else doing the choosing, Mr Maxwell? Is there someone else? And who are *they*?'

'They? – damn them! The London Maxwells, of course! Every-thing arranged through them. Poking and prying, and saying do this and do that. Just because they have a small interest in Land-fall. Merchants, Miss Fiona – bankers and merchants, not men. Is there a percentage in it? – they'll take it. That's all they go by! One of their kind here at Landfall now. A Maxwell – one of the clever young men of the firm. Old Jeremy's youngest. But old enough to be a pryer and a snooper. He's got a game leg – hunting accident. Supposed to be a crack shot. But he's one of your cold-fish type. Shoots and rides because a man has to do those kind of things, not because he likes them. Careful with his drink and his talk. And what's worse, a reformer. Wants to change everything. Damn near to being a radical. I keep telling him he'll reform him-self right out of his fortune if he's not careful. I'm so damn tired of hearing about Wilberforce and Wesley. Busybody, that's what he is . . . Wish he'd go home. Only been here this two weeks and I'm sick to death of him. Supposed to be recuperating after an illness . . . he's in better health than most men will ever see. Excuse to be here, that's all. Busybody . . .'

'Mr Maxwell – have a care. You say too much! You forget I'm
a stranger, and governesses aren't supposed to gossip.'

'A stranger?' He looked puzzled, confused and abruptly, even
in the dimness of that inner room, his age was more apparent.
'Yes, a stranger, I suppose. Brought here. Brought here like Miss
Pink-and-Pretty would have been. Forget the governess part . . .
But a Maxwell, still. Your mother was a Maxwell. The Maxwell
part counts. That's what counts . . .'

He took up his glass and drank, and for a time I had vanished
for him, like the dark-skinned children he never saw, like the silent
slaves whose presence one didn't acknowledge. He sat and brooded,
an old man, massive, seeming ill, loaded with a life behind him
and little ahead. I might almost be sorry for him, but no one could
ever be sorry for Andrew Maxwell. I was forgotten; when he spoke
it was as if it were for himself alone, a reassurance, a prop, a
reminder. 'You have to watch what is done to you.' He was remembering something out of his own experience, something that
this first remark about Mary Maxwell being brought to this place
had evoked. 'You have to fight for what should be yours, or they'll
take it. They'll take it all . . .'

'Women don't often have the chance to fight, Mr Maxwell.' I
recalled my presence to him; he saw me again with a start of
recognition; his eyes alert again, and wary.

'Women have their own ways. What is it in the Bible about the
little foxes and tender grapes? . . . come, you know the Bible!
You're a minister's daughter, aren't you?'

I chose not to supply the words for him. 'I take and remember
what parts of the Bible I want to, Mr Maxwell. I am not sure
yet whether I'm a Martha or a Mary. Life is hard . . .' Why was
I saying this to him, who would be expected to have little sympathy
with the trials of governesses? 'Life is hard, and a woman learns to
take it as she finds it.'

'Aye, and it's well you should know it,' he answered, with
no consolation for me. 'Well that you should know it and act upon
it. But women who suck the heart and spirit from a man . . . they're
the devils who walk the earth. The dark devils . . .'

He drank again, deeply, and once again I also sipped the fiery
drink, and he was right about it; it was strangely comforting. I
felt the stiffness leave my body, the chill all gone. I waited for a
time that seemed polite, but Andrew Maxwell appeared to have
nothing more to say to me. He could, if he wished, exercise his
prerogative to make talk or keep silent, but the drink had made
me bolder.

'Mr Maxwell – might I be shown my room? And when may I meet my charge?'

'Your charge?' He looked bewildered again, and then light broke on him. 'You talk like a governess, Miss Fiona. You mean my son. No – no, you can't meet him yet. He's out with his mother. They ride together every morning. She is teaching him, you see, how to care for the plantation.' The words tumbled together in a burr of anger and resentment.

'Teaching him to . . .?' I leaned forward. 'But he is only – how old, Mr Maxwell?'

'Seven!' He almost shouted the word at me. 'Seven years old and his mother thinks it time he learned to take charge of the plantation. Speak to me now of little foxes . . .'

'Foxes?' It was strange how both of us froze at the sound of that voice, I, who had never heard it before, as well as the old man. He was gazing towards one of the doorways that led from the front galleries, and I saw his free hand tightly grasp the cane that had once again been placed beside him. For myself I had to turn.

'There are no foxes on San Cristóbal.'

I rose to my feet. They stood there, as beautiful a pair as ever I had seen, this mother and her child. The woman was dark, with the classic, rich beauty of Spain in her face, in the dark magnificence of her eyes and hair, in the high cheekbones and the smooth complexion like warm ivory. She was not tall, but seemed so, in the perfection of her body, closely outlined by the dove-grey riding habit. In place of the high black hat that would have gone with the costume, she wore the broad-brimmed Cordoban knotted beneath her chin. There was style and grace and an arrogant sureness in every line of her. I knew that only this kind of woman could have penned the black, confident, aristocratic script of the letter which had come to Silkirk, and now that I saw her, I knew that every word of that letter had been a lie. This woman needed help from no one, least of all a governess from a Scottish country rectory.

At last she conceded to the ritual. She came towards me, peeling off her white cotton gloves, which were then thrown with her riding crop on to a table. 'I expected to welcome Miss Mary Maxwell – but surely you cannot be she?'

She was quicker than her husband had been; I was not the one she had written for, not the one described. I was older, I had not Mary's air of gentle docility; at that instant I was glad Mary was not here. She could not have stood for a moment against this woman. But somehow I knew that Maria Maxwell would have preferred my stepsister.

I explained, as I had to her husband, the reason why I had come in place of Mary. 'We wrote to the Maxwell firm in London, of course, as you instructed, and they assured us that my coming, since Mary was not able to, would be in order. I have their letter to you . . . I have had experience . . .' I stumbled over references and such things. Her detached gaze disconcerted me; she seemed determined that nothing should be made easy.

'The Maxwells – ah, yes, they would approve. It only needs their approval. Well, you are here . . .' The rest was left unsaid. Belatedly, almost as a gesture of contempt, her hand was extended. 'Welcome to Landfall, Miss McIntyre.' We touched for the minimal time that courtesy demanded. 'We are surely fortunate, are we not, Andrew, to have the services of such an experienced lady. I had expected to welcome Mary Maxwell, of whom we had heard such good reports, but one is lucky under any circumstances to induce a Scottish lady of good family to come here . . . especially a Maxwell.'

I at once felt old and big and awkward, and a poor substitute for the one expected. I murmured something in reply; all of it was false, and we all knew it. Whatever the reason, I was not welcome at Landfall by this woman.

And now she beckoned the child towards me. There was no doubt in her mind, as had existed with her husband, what role I was there to play. 'And this is to be your charge. This is my son, Duncan, Miss McIntyre.'

Her son, not our son. The boy came towards me confidently, though having waited until his mother had finished speaking. And what had been the mere outline of a golden-haired child against the greater brightness of the gallery, fresh-skinned and pink-cheeked, now assumed features and a personality. My hand, instead of going towards him, instead clutched at my skirt, as the perspiration of shock struck at me. I could hardly believe what I saw. I wondered if the strength of the rum had hit me as I rose, or the nostalgia for home and the familiar things had gathered force to deceive me. Before me seemed to stand my own Duncan, my little half-brother, the adored only son of my father. Of course there were some differences – slightly higher cheekbones and a more pointed chin which he took from his mother; but otherwise the Maxwell blood had repeated this extraordinary replica of that other Duncan, growing up in the Scottish rectory. I glanced back to his father, the big man whose grey hair would once have been the same red-

blond, whose beard and heavy jowls hid what once would have been
a face like this one. The Scottish strain had won over the Spanish.
It would not have troubled me – I would have been glad except
for the terrible memory of a golden-haired child racing towards me
from a burning building, racing in terror – and terror not only of
fire. I had crossed an ocean and come to a strange life in order to
place distance between myself and my own little Duncan. And now
I was confronted by this other one, and the danger must still be
faced. I remembered the words of the woman from the mountainside cottage. 'Bad luck ye bring wi' yer cursed sight o' what is not
yet known. So leave wi' that gift fra' me, and remember this lonely
woman.' I was remembering, and I was terrified.

The silence had become too much; I must move – must say something. The child stared at me with unabashed wonder, not used
to having his advances spurned. Maria Maxwell's voice broke the
spell.

'There is something wrong, Miss McIntyre?'

Desperately I ran my hand down my skirt to remove the sweat,
and held it towards him. 'No ! – no, nothing wrong. It is just, Mrs
Maxwell, that your son so much resembles my half-brother. Extraordinary . . .'

She was not pleased. 'Yes – visually the Maxwell strain is strong.
But for the rest – '

I didn't hear what she said. I had gripped hands with this
Duncan, and for a child it was a hold of astonishing strength and
firmness. I could feel the muscles of my face relax, and I must
have smiled, because he suddenly smiled. The kind of radiance and
beauty that had blessed my little half-brother's face was there, the
winning grace, the eager pleasure.

'I'm glad you've come,' he said, the only real welcome I had
had at Landfall. 'We'll be doing all kinds of things together, won't
we?'

It was childish and normal. I put the terror and shock from me.
If I had to come just to be here for this child to run to, then this
was reason enough. 'Yes, we're going to do all kinds of things.
We'll teach each other things . . .'

I had one friend at Landfall, and he was a seven-year-old
child.

It wasn't until I was upstairs, sponging myself all over with lemon-
scented water, that I remembered when Andrew Maxwell had
struggled down the stairs to the carriage, the name of the son
he had called for, the one he had cursed for not being on the

dock to meet me had been Fergus, not Duncan. I remembered, too, the words of the third mate of the *Clyde Queen*. 'He married late . . .'

I lunched alone with Duncan, in an upstairs corner room that was to be our schoolroom. It was like no schoolroom I had ever known before; two sets of french doors opened to the upper gallery in two directions – one to the mountain, the other view through the garden, beautiful, slightly mysterious with its winding paths and unfamiliar plants, vines smothered with blossoms which were almost unreal in their size, gave tantalizing glimpses of the sea; there was the sound of waves against the Serpent Rocks, always diffused and broken by the wind that occasionally grew to the strength of gusts. Duncan talked – mostly I listened. He was accustomed to being listened to, as had the Duncan at Silkirk. He talked of his pony, Ginger, and the coves along the two shores of Landfall – the wild Atlantic side, the dead-calm bays of the lee shore. He talked of the sea creatures he saw there; he pointed out the tiny lizards that ran freely through the house, and we laughed at their curious *geko-geko* cry. They caught the insects, he explained, and he watched me closely, testing me like his father to make sure that I showed no fear of them. Often in his talk there was mention of Fergus, but I did not ask him about Fergus. Children have a way of knowing which question is meant to lead them on. He warned me, in a way his father would have, of the sun that could make you ill if you went out in it hatless; he talked of the rains that came sweeping suddenly and drenched you right through, and were gone within minutes, leaving the earth steaming. But such soakings didn't trouble him; always there were fresh, dry clothes, and the comforting black hands, and all was effortless. He didn't have to ask for anything; it was there, like the thin, black woman, Juanita, who came to lead him away.

'The siesta,' he pronounced to me. 'Everyone rests now.'

Even for me, even for a governess, there were the hours of the siesta, because no one else in the house stirred. But I noticed, as I walked the gallery from the schoolroom to my bedroom, that the gardeners still worked, the sun blazing upon their ragged straw hats. In my room a woman waited, impatient with my seemingly aimless lingering, to close the louvred shutters against the light. She said her name was Charity, and she was to look after me; I could have laughed, but she wouldn't have understood why. My stepmother had been right about my having things that no governess dreams of. I rather liked the look of this woman, plump, young enough still, her skin a pleasant, shining brown. She didn't avert her eyes from mine quite as swiftly as most of the other house slaves had done, and her head did not go down automatically when I appeared. She had been unpacking my trunk, and she went back to the task, clucking in a forthright way over the heavy clothes she brought out.

'What kind of place this, mistress – where you wear such things?' She touched them with slightly disdainful fingers, and they did look ugly and rather sad in the white, lofty room, with its mahogany dressers and wardrobe, with the large bed dressed with a white spotted Swiss muslin canopy and fine linen sheets. No room for a governess this one, and no place for my old grey alpaca and plaid shawl.

'Very cold,' I answered. 'Not like this at all. There is much snow where I come from.'

Her expert hands loosened the strings of my stays. 'I hear about this snow thing, mistress, but I no believe it. No thing like that happen here.' We were standing before the oval pier mirror, and I saw her dark eyes examining me closely as I stood there in my loose shift with its low neck – a summer one, the lightest I owned. There was something in the look that reminded me of the way Andrew Maxwell had examined me, almost a summing-up.

'You damn fine woman,' she pronounced at last. 'You got fine breasts and hips, like the men want. It pity you wear such ugly clothes.' And then as my own hand had gone automatically to take the pins from my hair, her own had brushed them aside, as if even this slight task must be too much for any white woman. My hair came down, the whole, full length of it, past my waist, and I heard her give a little gasp; her fingers ran through it slowly, finally crushing its thickness. 'It like fire and silk,' she said, in a hushed voice.

I turned away and went towards the bed, unable to answer her. In Scotland such things are rarely said, not with that implication of sensuality. I had never lain down to sleep in the afternoon in my life before, but now it seemed my senses craved the dimness, the impression of coolness. The linen sheets and soft mattress received me as if I had known them always. I heard the soft shuffling of Charity's bare feet for a few moments longer, then stillness. I sensed her near me, and opened my eyes. She was standing quite close, gazing down at me. Even in that plump and pleasant face there was a knowledge of hardness and pain. Again her eyes assessed me. 'Yes, mistress – it good thing you come to Landfall. A woman like you. Maybe you ease the trouble of this house.' Then the slap-slap of her feet on the polished floor and the repeated whisper as the door closed. 'Like fire and silk . . .'

Perhaps it was the voices which woke me, or just the sense that the heat of the day was passing. I lay still in the dimness, unused to the surroundings, feeling the strange wideness of the bed after the narrow bunk of those weeks of the sea passage. And then the voices, not close to me, not the sing-song of the slaves. I recognized Andrew Maxwell's tones, the rumble and the burr, rising suddenly, as if he could not contain himself.

'Damn you, Fergus! – I told you . . . !'

I rose and went barefooted to the shuttered doors and swung them wide. The afternoon sun was low enough to have begun to probe the depth of the gallery. I went to the railing, not bothering to conceal myself, just driven by curiosity about this Fergus who had failed to meet me at the dock that morning. I possessed no light wrapper, and in the warmth of the afternoon it had not occurred to me to reach for my plaid. I stood beside one of the great pillars of the house, which dripped with a vine whose flowers were enormous golden cups. The sun caressed my bare neck and arms, but did not bite as it would have done at noon. The full languor and beauty of the waning tropic afternoon was on Landfall, and the effects of sleep were heavy on me, making me careless.

I leaned far over the rail to see them. Andrew Maxwell stood on the lowest step as if he had followed his son down to emphasize what he was saying. There were no slaves in sight, though probably they listened, just as I did.

'. . . you think I am too old now to be obeyed? – that you know everything? I still give orders here. I am still obeyed!'

The other man, face screened by the wide straw hat he wore, was mounted on a good chestnut horse. He sat it well and held its impatient movement with ease and sureness. 'And I tell you, Father, that while there are more important things to attend to, I'll leave the meeting and escorting of little Scottish governesses to those who have the time. And God knows, if there were a dozen of me working at Winterslo there still wouldn't be time for fripperies. Can't you ever get the notion into your head that a man can change? And if you've still any notion to force me into something I don't want, then, my father, you had best put it from your mind. The woman I –'

I must have leaned too far, absorbed, unabashedly listening and craning to see this man. First he looked up, his talk suddenly checked; then the old man turned slowly, his neck bending upwards stiffly.

At once the hat of the young man came off; he was his father's son, as Duncan was. He was as Duncan would one day be. I was suddenly aware of the size of him on the horse, the red-blond hair, the fair skin that somehow accommodated itself to the sun and was deeply browned. Even at this distance I was aware of the blueness of his eyes, like Duncan's, but these with sun wrinkles about the corners. He was beautiful, in the way a man can be, and never more beautiful than I saw him that afternoon, before I knew him, before I loved him.

And then it came. The sudden awareness of something wrong, the chill of the soul that was not part of this tropic warmth. Why did I seem to see, back there, deep in the shade of the giant cotton-wood tree that guarded the house, the shadow of another horse-man? – this all black, and vague, without form, but charged with a terrible threat? It was like seeing this young man mirrored back there, a double-image, but the dark side of the mirror. One instant only, and it was gone. An illusion perhaps, a shred of my un-easy dream. But the shape had seemed to me like the horseman of violence.

The illusion was fully gone as I heard the raw, licentious chuckle that broke from the old man's lips; I was made aware of my-self – of my hair, tumbled from sleep, falling about me, of the loose, low-necked shift, of my whole abandonment to the sun and the languor, and my rooted fascination with the young man below me.

'There's your little Scottish governess, Fergus. It's a pity you chose not to obey me and be at the dockside this morning.' The laugh that followed was wild, and I turned and fled back to the shadow of the room.

And as I went I saw her, Maria Maxwell. She stood in the door-way of what must be her own room, for all the bedrooms opened on to the common gallery. She, too, must have been wakened by the voices. Her wrapper was of the finest lawn and laced with red ribbon; her feet were in tiny red satin slippers. She was smiling oddly, and I saw the contempt in her smile. She said no word, and there was no reproach. There was no need; I knew what I looked like, dishevelled, loose, frowzy – a woman with no sense of decency. She made me feel like some bawd – and I was an eavesdropper as well. I felt my face burn with shame, and I could stand her gaze no longer. I crashed the shutters closed behind me and fell on to the bed, weeping the first of the tears I was to weep at Land-fall.

3

I did lessons with Duncan until it was time for his supper and
bed. It seemed strange to begin work again almost at twilight, but
the dusk came early, and the hours of siesta made it necessary to
divide the day in this way.

He was a strange child – oddly precocious in some matters, shockingly ignorant in others; he knew some of the history of Spain.
Cortes and the conquistadors were his heroes, rather than Columbus.
He knew the life of the plantation, and he was conscious of money
in a way my own half-brother never would be. He knew about
the West Indies, about London, Bristol and Liverpool, and nothing
else. 'They sent the slave ships from Bristol and Liverpool to the
Gold Coast,' was his explanation. 'Then they didn't let anyone take
slaves from Africa any more, and everyone thought that was the
end. But the slaves kept coming. They always do.'

There was a kind of cruel indifference in the way he said it;
slaves were not people, just objects. That was what he had been
taught, and he had never heard any other opinion. For the beginning I would have to let it go; you did not change a child in an
hour, and I still must find my way at Landfall. We did arithmetic
and a little Latin; he was intelligent, but opposed to anything that
did not bear directly on the business of the estate.

'Won't you have to count your barrels of sugar?' I asked. 'And
calculate how much they will earn on the London market?'

'Yes, but I won't be doing it in Latin.'

I applied the chalk firmly to the blackboard. 'Nevertheless, we
will learn Latin. Do you want to look like an ignorant fool when
you visit your Maxwell cousins and go into London society?'

The Maxwell pride was touched. 'No,' he said. 'No – I never
want to be a fool.'

'Then learn,' I said. 'The Scots have made their way only by
fighting, working and learning. In Scotland a scholar is an honoured
man.'

He wasn't quite sure whether to believe me. His world was quite
secure. 'My father – Fergus – I don't think they're scholars, Miss
Fiona, but I don't think . . .' But he did think. 'My cousin, Alister,
I suppose he knows a lot. I suppose he knows Latin and all those
things.' He was suddenly aware of a wider world. I had challenged
him, and the soft little child's mouth was set. 'We will learn then,
even if it's Greek.'

'Greek you'll not get from me, my laddie. I'm only a woman,
after all. But before I leave you'll at least know there's such a

place as Greece.'

He looked astonished. 'Why, will you be going, then? I thought if you had come all this way, you would be staying forever.'

'Nothing lasts forever, lad,' I said. 'You'll grow up . . .' But I really meant that already I saw in Maria Maxwell's attitude that my time here was limited. One day would come the clash that could never be forgiven. As if aware that it might come soon, I hurried him on. 'Now, let's move along. Time is going.'

He bent over his slate, but in a moment or two his head was up again, the puzzled, winning, utterly irresistible look upon his face that my own little Duncan had often worn. 'You know what, Miss Fiona . . .'

'What . . . ?'

'You're quicker than all the other ladies I know.' His brow wrinkled. 'I don't know what it is. You talk so quickly . . . and move . . .' With a cheeky gesture his fingers walked across the slate. 'One, two, three, four. Quick – quick !'

'Impudence !' And yet I couldn't help laughing. 'Well, then, we'll make the best of it while it lasts. A few weeks of the siesta and I'll hardly be able to move across the room.'

'No, not you,' he said, and he bent once again to copy the Latin declension. Before it was finished, the lean, saturnine Juanita, the slave who had taken him to his siesta, entered with a tray of food. It was set for one only.

'Mistress Fiona to eat downstairs with the master and mistress,' was her curt explanation. At least that part of Maria Maxwell's letter had been the truth.

While Duncan ate I began to read to him from a history of Scotland that had come with me in my trunk. It was time he had other heroes besides the gold-seeking Spaniards.

I wore my best summer gown that evening, the one reserved in Scotland for the very occasional garden party I had attended, the summer church festival. Charity clucked with disappointment as the dress was put on. It was a pale green sprigged muslin, fine enough in Silkirk, but looking terribly old-fashioned, limp and prim here. Why did the constant crying of the cicadas, the scent of the jasmine, the soft warmth of the night induce such discontent? Why did I long, passionately, for the first time in my life, to be beautiful, to wear the plumage of the peacock?

'Why you wear that silly dress right to the neck, mistress? Why you not show yourself off – fine woman like you ?'

But still she piled my hair up, her fingers handling it with pleasure and skill; the candles were set in hurricane glasses to protect them from the breeze; in their gentle light I thought I looked better than I had ever done before. But I had to stop Charity placing a camellia above my ear.

'Governesses don't wear flowers, Charity.'

She snorted. 'You damn fine woman waste yourself.' I laid down the camellia with some regret; there were just a few times when I felt life wasn't quite fair.

I thought I was the first downstairs; the candles in the chandelier were lighted in the hall, through the open doors to the dining-room I caught a glimpse of the long table and the gleam of silver and crystal. But no one moved there, and no voices came from the salon. From the back of the house I could hear the sounds of the kitchen, the chatter of the kitchen slaves, the occasional sharp command from Dougal. Strange how the openness of these West Indian houses distorted sound – brought close what was distant, while the breeze carried away that which was near. Perhaps that was why Maria Maxwell did not hear my approach. The cicadas thundered their night-time chorus, the air was filled with the fragrance of the flowers that spilled everywhere, from heaped bowls on polished tables, from the perfumed garden itself. I felt that same mad discontent swell in me. It made me long – for what? For what?

I experienced a sharp upsurge of this unfamiliar state of being when finally I did look upon Maria Maxwell. I paused in the open doors of the salon, and she was there. At the far end of this great room stood a chimney and an elaborate marble mantel – this same feature appeared in balance in the drawing-room, surely an immigrant architect's nostalgia for the centrepiece of the great drawing-rooms of European houses, for this climate could have no need of such things. Above it was a large mirror, framed in scrolled silver-gilt. On the mantel were the only two candles that were yet lighted in that vast room. Just that one pool of light, and what I saw in it made me draw in my breath, and something as close to real envy as I had ever known shot through me.

The fact or the thought of jewels had never entered my consciousness before – perhaps because I had never seen any such as these, just the garnet brooches and gold chains of my employers' wives. I had never imagined such as I saw now. Maria Maxwell's back was to me, and in that mirror I saw the unforgettable fire of diamonds about her throat, the great green glow of the huge emerald star in her hair, the long green cataract of the emeralds hanging from her ears. She studied her own image intently, perhaps as fascinated as I was, and then she raised both hands to her face, fingers spread on her cheeks and the mirror seemed to explode into a thousand colours as the candlelight flashed back the burning torches of sapphire and ruby. The bevelled mirror edge caught the leaping colours also, and for a moment Maria Maxwell stood there ringed with the fire that lived within the depths of those stones. I was transfixed. I felt as if I had unwittingly stepped into some other time, some other place, that in a moment wigged footmen would bring candelabra, and there would be laughter and music and other such bedecked women in some fairy-tale palace in a world dreamed by a child.

The dream, like the vision in the mirror, was shattered by the hoarse, growling voice from the dark place where the red sofa stood.

'Maria! – can't we have any damned light in here? Here's Miss Fiona, and she can't see her way across the room.'

She turned. 'It *is* dark. How careless of me.'

She faced me fully now. There were no jewels. There was no play of fire about her. Her throat and ears and hands were bare. There was no glowing warmth of emerald in her dark hair, just the perfect symmetry of her perfect body outlined by the close fit of the emerald silk gown she wore, its low bodice revealing her up-thrust breasts. The only glow was the ivory sheen of her skin.

A clap of her hands, and Dougal was there, and lamps were springing into life.

I blinked stupidly as the familiar objects were revealed. It was all as it had been at noon, when Andrew and I had sat there. But what had I seen in the mirror? Was it a chance and freak reflection of the colour of the gown in the bevelled edges of mirror and silver frame? Was it . . .? Did the spirit of some woman who had once inhabited this house come sometimes back to peer wistfully through Maria's eyes at the reflection of what no longer existed? Did Maria herself long to see her own reflection decked in such jewels, and had I caught an instant's manifestation of that longing? Was the discontent I had experienced not all born in my own soul, but communicated through some unwanted bond with this woman? Had this been what Maria *wanted* to see in the mirror?

I thrust my fright and bewilderment from me as best I might and stumbled towards the nearest chair. Maria gave me a tight smile, a smile that seemed to take in the limp, prim gown, my awkward movements, the lack of social ease. Andrew Maxwell

acknowledged my presence with a wave of his glass; he made no
motion to rise, just looked at me with a vague indifference, as if
the spark of lewdness that had leapt in him at the sight of my
dishevelment that afternoon had died.

'Miss McIntyre, may I introduce your kinsman, Alister Maxwell?'

I hadn't seen him; I had no notion of his presence there either.
He was leaning against the doorway that led to the outer gallery, as
if he must catch the breath of the night, as if this inner room
bound and confined him too closely. I thought it extraordinary that
three people had been in this room as I entered, and each had been
alone, in silence and, except Maria, in darkness.

He came forward at once, and took my hand, as if glad of the
release from his solitary state. He was not what I had expected.
The limp was there, yes – as Andrew had said. What else had I
imagined? – the reformer dressed in sober blacks, the horseman
and expert shot watered down to some palid stick with the Maxwell
blond hair gone pale and sleeked down by the weight of piety?
What I saw was a gentleman of fashion, tall, slender, immaculately
dressed and tailored, though there was nothing of the dandy about
him – just the impeccable fastidiousness of the silk shirt and waistcoat, the fine leather of the closely fitting boot, the cut of the buff-
coloured coat. The drawing-room seemed his place, not the dreary
meeting halls of the reform leaders. I could not imagine that immaculate coat ever spattered by rotten vegetables, not that hand
raised to quote the Bible to curse another.

'Miss McIntyre, I'm delighted to meet you. I remember meeting
your mother once on a visit to Edinburgh as a child. The family
always considered her a great beauty, I do recall.'

In that case, I thought, I was probably a sorry disappointment.
Well, what did it matter? I was grateful for his presence, for his
smile, a rather grave smile; I began to feel that I would like him.
He certainly didn't make me feel like a disappointment, and – this
was unexpectedly welcome – he didn't look like a Maxwell, either.
At least he was not blond and handsome in their fashion. Dark,
rather sharp features, thick eyebrows, a long face. In a moment of
wicked relief that here was not yet another of the blond beauties, I
thought it was just as well he had not been born a woman. That
face, in a woman, would have resembled a rather intelligent,
thoughtful, elegant horse.

'Some wine, Miss McIntyre?' Maria Maxwell gestured towards
the decanters. I saw that she had no glass herself, so I declined.
And then I wished I had had the courage to take it because it

might have helped me through the pause that followed. I was still
shaken by the sight in the mirror. With half my mind still upon it,
I must have seemed raw and ill-at-ease. But then who would not
have been? This room had contained three people, and the atmosphere that hung on it was that of some violent quarrel, though no
word had been spoken. Or perhaps it was that whatever quarrel
existed at Landfall was of such long duration that it had settled
upon the place, like fungus growing steadily on the walls. I remembered then Captain Stewart's comment . . .'It has never been
a lucky place . . .'

Movement and pretence of ease were made by Alister Maxwell,
and I blessed him for it. There are some men gifted with manners,
with concern, and he seemed to be one of them. He drew a chair
towards mine and sat down.

'I'm in Scotland far too seldom these days, Miss McIntyre, and
the Maxwell cousins are so numerous . . . It has been shameful on
my part that I have never been to pay my respects to Cousin
Dorothy – and your good father, of course. It's a remote parish, is it
not . . .?'

I lost myself for a moment in telling him – the sea, the hills behind, the summer visitors, the long winters. He knew it all, of
course; he had been in Scotland enough times to know. But at least
there was talk to relieve the deadly silence between Andrew Maxwell and his wife.

'Your stepsister, Mary, came to visit an aunt in London a little
time ago. I remember her well. A pretty little girl . . .' He sounded
as if he knew what we all acknowledged about Mary – she was as
pretty as a doll, and in time grew just as boring.

Abruptly Andrew Maxwell's glass was raised, thrust out towards us. 'Ah – Miss Pink-and-Pretty. Come now, Maxwell –
you remember her better than that. At least your father does, from
his letters. She was being looked over. Not good enough for a
London Maxwell – but all right to send out here. Good enough for
my son –'

'Andrew –

Maria Maxwell's voice was a whisper, but he turned quickly in
her direction, and her look had the same power over his as it
did me. He was silenced; but he signalled to have his glass refilled
once more. Now, because politeness demanded it, Alister Maxwell
gave his attention to Maria. There was some discussion about a
horse that had gone lame, how it should be treated, what had
caused it. I did not feel left out; Alister had helped me over my
first difficulty, and I expected no more of him. I felt free now to

let my eyes wander about the room, since Andrew was disinclined to talk. I saw more things than I had seen at noon, when he had commanded all my attention. It was as richly furnished as I remembered, but rather heavy in feeling. There was much plush and heavy gold-tipped frames on age-darkened pictures of people in stiff dress that I imagined might have been of the Spanish court. The piece that drew the attention, after the white marble mantel, was the huge cabinet, reaching almost to the ceiling, with long glass doors two-thirds of its length, and drawers beneath. It could have come from some palace in Spain; magnificently carved, with thin, elongated figures of what I imagined to be the twelve apostles forming the divisions between the glass doors, and surmounted in pediment fashion by a host of child angels. The whole was topped over the centre doors by a carved cross which looked as if it had once been broken off and replaced slightly askew. It gave the massive cabinet the look of being about to fall forward. It was a gloomy piece, but its contents were of a different order. It contained books, as one might have expected, but one whole shelf was given over to a collection of dolls. Maria and Alister were still talking horses, and I felt free to rise and go to it. They were not ordinary books, nor ordinary dolls. Each volume was bound in vellum, the titles inscribed in faded manuscript in an ancient style. The dolls, though, riveted my attention. Exquisitely dressed, all of them, they seemed to represent the regional dress of different parts of Spain – among them even the Moorish dress of Andalusia, and one with the wide panniered skirts and tight curls of the Velásquez portraits. The wax faces were fashioned with great artistry, not blank and staring, but with the expressions of real people. They seemed old; some of the fabrics were starting to rot; they each had their appointed place, the rag bodies held to a wooden rack. I would not have dared to touch them, but instinctively my hand went up towards the glass as I leaned to get a better view.

'It is locked, Miss McIntyre.' Maria had been watching me, for all her apparent interest in the subject of the horses. 'I dare not allow the hands of any of the slaves upon those things – even Duncan might be tempted. They are very old, and very precious. The manuscripts, some of them, are illuminated, and one or two are believed to have come from the library of the sainted Philip the Second . . .'

'I must persuade you, some day, Cousin Maria,' Alister said, 'to allow me to look at them. In a very humble fashion I am also a collector of books.'

She swept the statement away. 'And the dolls – they were made especially for the Infanta Catalina, and given to a cousin of my great-great-grandmother, who had been a lady-in-waiting . . .'

A roar of derisive laughter came from Andrew. 'And a lot of good they do you, that pile of junk. My wife's only dowry – that cabinet and its contents, and I am tired to death of the sainted Philip and his books mouldering away with mildew there, and those stupid dolls. No wonder the Infanta got rid of them – if they ever belonged to an Infanta. Probably gave them to the washerwoman.'

'*Hombre!* Despicable liar – !'

Dougal's soft voice. 'Dinna, mistress.'

In an awful parody of normalcy, Alister took Maria's arm as they moved through the hall to the dining-room. Andrew was helped to his feet by Dougal. He leaned heavily on his cane as he started, and was about to reach for the arm of the slave for support. Then he remembered me. His head jerked around, and a strange light came to his face, as if he were recalling something of long ago. The ugliness of his ill-humour with his wife disappeared.

'Come, my dear. It's a long time since I've had the pleasure of escorting a real woman to dinner . . .' But his hand did not take my arm. Instead I felt his own arm about my waist, his weight heavy and dragging. 'You must forgive an old man his infirmities.' But I felt no infirmity in the way he clutched my waist behind his wife's back, nor the press of his fingers into my flesh.

4

Dinner was a little better. The wine that was served to all of us seemed to stimulate Maria Maxwell; she talked – though exclusively to Alister, demanding gossip of London, of fashion, of the theatre. The controlled face grew animated; she flirted harmlessly with the practised ease of a born beauty. Her mouth pulled down at the corners in an enchantingly provocative pout. 'We are so dull here – of course, my husband does not permit us to entertain at Landfall. But when one goes into society – only little parties, little race meetings. No real *ton* – is that not the word, Alister?'

He smiled indulgently. 'The exact one, Cousin Maria. But I would dispute your contention of dullness. Life is dull in most places – it isn't all one long party. People work in London just as they do everywhere else. *I* work – I go to my offices every day and sit over my dull accounts –'

She cut him short. 'But nevertheless, I would like to go to London. Since those wretched Bonapartes ruined Spain, there is no place to go but England.'

'That isn't what I hear from you, Maria,' Andrew said, stuffing his mouth with bread. 'All I hear is those two years you spent in Madrid and your noble relations. How grand everything was – how high class. Apparently the Bonapartes didn't ruin *them.*'

She shrugged. 'The aristocracy survived even the Bonapartes. But they kept to themselves. Life was not . . . gay. Some fortunes were ruined. You do not have the French and the English fighting across a country for all those years without life being affected. No – if I had my choice it is to London I would go now. But my husband will not be budged –'

'No – and well you know it, Maria.' The undercurrent of anger seemed always present in Andrew Maxwell's voice. 'And you know yourself you're talking a lot of nonsense. If I said tomorrow that you must pay a long visit to London – that you must take Duncan to see the sights and give him an idea of how life is lived elsewhere, you know you wouldn't leave. After all' – and now his tone became sneering – 'who would run the place? Who would see that we were not being cheated? Who would see that the slaves were kept properly in order? Not *this* old man – not this poor wretch who was only fit to build up Landfall, but not to . . .'

She replied with swift cruelty. 'You are quite right, my dear husband. Who would do all these things?' Now she looked at Alister. 'You see, I also have my dull accounts to attend to.' She gave a little sigh and a shrug. 'And London is so far away. No – it is better to stay. One must be content . . .'

'Content!' The voice was harsh and low, and came from the darkness of the gallery beyond the dining-room. We had heard no noise of his horse, so he must have walked from the stables. No slave had announced his arrival. He stepped into the light, Fergus Maxwell, big, handsome, carelessly dressed in the shirt he had worn that afternoon, neck loose, even a rip in one sleeve. His hair was tumbled and untidy. I might almost have thought him drunk, if the voice and the stance had not been so firm, so sure.

'My dear Maria . . .' He advanced a little into the room towards her. 'What is this about contentment? *You* will never be content until you own the whole island. My father, for once, is quite right. You will never leave Landfall for London. After all, the money's at Landfall, isn't it? And in London there is only all this nonsensical talk of emancipation.'

She chose to ignore his words. 'Good evening, Fergus. I did not

expect the pleasure of your company for dinner but, of course, do
sit down . . .' She snapped her fingers, but it was unnecessary. A
place was already being laid, and three slaves waited by the big
silver serving dishes until Fergus should be ready for them. He
went to the sideboard and poured himself wine. He was about to
put the glass to his lips, and then he paused.

'Thank you for your welcome, Maria. And my father. It is
always good to know that one is welcome in one's home.' He raised
his glass to them.

'Sit down and stop making a fool of yourself,' Andrew Maxwell
growled.

He seemed not to hear his father's words, nor to see the chair
held for him by Dougal. Instead, he walked down the long table
to me.

'And this, of course, is the little Scottish governess. Not quite
what we were led to expect. But welcome to Landfall. My name is
Fergus Maxwell. Everyone seems to have forgotten to introduce
us. Fiona McIntyre, isn't it? Well, it's a nice change from having
another Maxwell — '

'And what's wrong with being a Maxwell?' I said. I heard my
own voice, and it sounded tart and sour, like a governess's. I had
spoken like that because I hated his mockery, because I feared to
reveal the kind of strange warmth the sight of him gave me. His
manners were atrocious; he seemed to want to hurt each person
in that room, and perhaps all beyond it. And yet I couldn't dismiss
it as mere bad manners; in that marvellously handsome man whose
grace should have won him friends effortlessly, there was an air
of defensiveness. The blue eyes, with their sun-wrinkles radiating
from them, were wary. I could remember seeing dogs and horses
like that — some that had been treated harshly and never again
would respond to a friendly overture, and yet whose pride would
never permit them to grovel or beg a favour, no matter how badly
needed. He could have been twenty-six years old, and for a man
of that age, the son of his father, he looked tired and confused and
reckless, as if he didn't know what to do next, nor did he much care.
Like a child he wanted to provoke and annoy, and yet the adult
knew all the play acting was nonsense. He was too young to have
begun to despair. This was what I felt about Fergus Maxwell, and
I wished with all my heart that our first meeting might have been
more private, without the eyes and attention of the whole room,
white and black slave, upon us.

And then I added, more softly, perhaps with the hope that my
words would not reach the others, perhaps with the thought that

I could erase the image of the acid-tongued governess, 'One accepts what one is, Mr Maxwell. I hope I have not suffered from being my mother's daughter.'

It took him a very long time to reply. I thought I saw a flicker of regret in his expression; but Fergus Maxwell would not be accustomed to a polite apology. He looked at me carefully, and the appraising stare was like his father's; I was forcefully reminded of Charity's words as she had gazed at me as I had undressed. 'I would say you had not suffered from that cause at all, Miss Fiona. No – not suffered in the least.'

He gave a little bow, the best he could do, I thought. And then he went to his place at the table. The talk flowed on as before and, as before, it was only between Maria Maxwell and Alister. Sometimes a sardonic, derisive comment came from Andrew, but his son said nothing. He said nothing at all while the dishes were passed around and the wine continued to be poured. But I saw how often, almost an involuntary action, his eyes went to Maria; it made me almost sick to see it, that look of mingled longing and hate. He seemed unable to help himself, and I – I was no better, since I could not myself turn my eyes from him. He said nothing at all until Maria rose to indicate that the meal was ended. I knew that I would not be expected to sit with her in the drawing-room, and the men probably would sit over port. I said my good-nights quietly.

As Maria reached the door Fergus, only half-risen from his seat, called loudly to her.

'I suppose it's all right if I stay the night? The roof of my room at Winterslo is leaking like a bucket full of holes, and my well-trained servants have managed to get my bed stuck nicely in the doorway. I thought I might take shelter with you until we either take the door down or cut the bed in half. I suppose that would be the solution, since a bachelor needs only half a bed – '

I wished that something, just once, would have shaken her coolness. 'There is always a bed for my husband's son at Landfall. Gentlemen – good-night.'

I followed her, my steps dragging. As I passed Alister Maxwell, I looked at him fully, frankly appealing to him for some support, some sense of normalcy in this house full of mockery and contempt and tension. I sought light in my bewilderment and confusion. As if I had spoken my need he answered at once. 'Let me fetch your candle, Miss Fiona.'

Andrew said sharply, 'There's half a dozen housemen to do those kind of things, Alister. Pass the port – '

His way of disregarding Andrew was not so pointed as Fergus's
had been; he simply indicated without rudeness that he would do
what he wanted to do. He even took my arm as we went to the
long table in the hall where the candles in their glasses were lined
up. With a wave of his hand as practised as Maria's he dismissed
the slave who had lighted one at our approach. He came only to
the foot of the staircase with me. I stood on the first step, and
we were poised there in full view of both the drawing-room and
the dining-room. Andrew Maxwell and his son had both turned
to watch us, and Maria had resumed her stance before the mirror,
but this time facing the door. Alister and I were a little tableau
motionless for their gaze.

I forgot decorum and the newness of our acquaintance in my
desperation. I spoke very softly, and I hoped to the watchers it
appeared to be the conventional phrases of thanks and leave-
taking.

'For God's sake – who is Fergus Maxwell? I was told there was
only one son. And his father married late. Was there another
marriage – a first wife?'

'No first wife. But Fergus Maxwell is the son of one of the
island's celebrated scandals.'

We could say no more. Charity had appeared at the head of
the staircase, waiting. I took the candle from Alister Maxwell's
hand and turned and started up in obedience to the unspoken
command that had seemed to come from each one of those who
watched us.

5

The tropic night is not a silent one; the cicadas sing, the lizards
give out their strange cry, sometimes the rustling of bat wings
is heard, and distantly the surf pounds against the Serpent Rocks.
But the wind dies, only to rise again with the strengthening of the
sun in the morning. So the night was hot and airless, the fine
linen sheets damp beneath my body, the pillow wet with the sweat
of my neck. A dozen times that night I felt that I must chop off
the weight and length of my hair; later I learned to braid it.

So wearily, with little sleep to help me, I got up when the first
light began to penetrate the downslanted louvers; I seemed unsteady on my feet as I threw back the shutters and saw the
beginning of that most precious of times on a West Indian island,
the beginning of the day. I walked out to the edge of the gallery;
everything was calm about me, no wind stirred, no leaf moved.

The distant sea was the pale, pale blue it had only before sunrise; I heard the first crow of a cock. I knew that the time of peace would be of short duration. But it still was the time of enchantment; everything at that moment looked as if it were freshly born. It was as if I were there, at the beginning of all things, at the beginning of time, of creation itself. My father would have recognized this moment; it was all unspoiled, unsullied, innocent.

I went to one of the low cane chairs that stood about the gallery, feeling sure that no one else of the household would be astir at this time. I was filled with a sense of futility, almost despair. I felt I would not stay long at Landfall; everything was against it. Even though a kind of vision had brought me here, I began to recognize that I might see what should be done, what role I should play, and yet be prevented from playing it. I had not been able to do anything for that young man, Thomas Scobie, who had spoken to the crowd in Kelvingrove Gardens; he would go on to whatever his fate was, quite regardless of my warning. I had a terrible presentiment that all here at Landfall were headed for destruction. There was already a kind of moral rot, but their ruin would be total. It would come in some physical form. But what could I, a stranger, an outsider, ignorant of every single factor of their lives and histories, do about it? Perhaps I was merely sent to witness the destruction, powerless to prevent it, knowing my impotence beforehand. Perhaps I was to share in the destruction. These are the thoughts that gather after a sleepless night.

'You, too, are awake early.' I hardly recognized his voice; it was different, hushed, weary. Perhaps his night had been like mine; perhaps the vast quantities of rum did not bring sleep; I remembered what Captain Stewart had said about old men not sleeping late. Andrew Maxwell stood at the corner of the gallery; perhaps he had been looking at me for some time. But now it didn't matter about my nightgown, and the plaid thrown loosely about me, my bare feet; it didn't matter about the tangled and sweat-soaked hair. There was none of the posture of the lascivious man who had gazed up at me from below yesterday, the one who had squeezed my waist last night. This was just a tired old man, subdued in the aftermath of an uneasy night. He wore a long silk robe, rumpled, frayed about the sleeves and neck, and his feet, like mine, were bare.

'One usually does not sleep well in strange places the first night. And then, I am not used to the tropics . . .'

'None of us gets used to the tropics,' he replied. 'Our bodies aren't made for it, even if we're born here.' He went to the railing as I had done, just standing, watching the light grow, the outline of the coast appear, the clouds begin to lift off Kronberg.

'The best time of the day,' he said. 'Always has been – just these bare few minutes – fresh, still. Now – and late at night. I used to walk late at night, when I was able. I used to swim early in the mornings. At night the stars are so close even an old man can dream of reaching to touch them. And the sky is blue, not black . . . you will get to know these things, Miss Fiona. But I doubt you'll ever get used to them. There are too many contrasts – the violence of the rain at night, and then this stillness in the morning. I love to hear the rain pounding on the roof at night – do you know that? I love this peace at dawn. And then the heat of the day comes, and you long for the dark again.'

He came and slumped into a chair near mine. 'Well, what do you think of Landfall?'

'What can I think of it? It's a fine house, Mr Maxwell. A very grand house – but I haven't seen anything else, have I?'

'Don't be a fool, girl! Landfall isn't just the house. What do you think of us? Landfall is a house anyone can admire – anyone who comes here does. But we make it. I want to know what you think of us.'

I faced him quickly. 'It isn't fair to ask such questions of me – and I don't pretend to try to answer. What do I know about you?'

But he pressed. 'What do you think of my son, Fergus?'

'He is a handsome, bad-mannered young man. That's all I know about him. I didn't even know he existed . . .'

'Well, did you think it was something my wife would write in a letter to invite a Miss Pink-and-Pretty out here? Would she say that a sometime member of our household was her husband's illegitimate son? Well – would she write such a letter to the wife of a Scottish preacher?'

'It would have been more honest to do so.' I was growing angry. 'Perhaps my father would have looked more kindly upon such an admission than upon its concealment. What did you expect me to do, Mr Maxwell? Throw up my hands and weep? Pack my trunks? Governesses don't enjoy the luxury of such displays. And don't you think my father has tried to help many a girl in our village "in trouble" as they say? He's a human being . . . a good, kindly man.' And then I added, I don't know why, except that it seemed suddenly important to remind myself of the fact, to hold it to me as a defence against what I saw here. 'He loved my mother. He knows what it is to love.'

'It's strange he didn't know about Fergus. Perhaps he did, but he didn't talk about it. It might have made you decide against a good position – '

'He didn't *want* me to leave Scotland. I didn't have to come.'

'The London Maxwells knew about Fergus,' he persisted.

'We never see the London Maxwells. Only the time Mary went . . .'

'Ah, yes, Miss Pink-and-Pretty. Well, old Jeremy wouldn't have told her. Ears too delicate.'

I gathered the plaid about me and started to rise. 'I think there's no point in continuing to talk now, Mr Maxwell. I will say things I would rather not – should better not – say. I don't like to hear my stepsister referred to as Miss Pink-and-Pretty. There's a deal more to her than that. I can hardly instruct you in manners, but you need instruction as badly as your son.'

He waved his hand. 'Hush, hush, girl! Yes, I go too far, I know. You will have to try to forgive my crudities. I've not had anyone worth practising manners on for some time – not really ever. I could like you, girl. For that I'll try to mind my tongue. So sit easy and enjoy what's left to us of time before the bell.'

It seemed churlish to reject his offer of peace, and besides, I was awash in a sea of ignorance. If he was in a mood to talk, before there was too much rum in him, it might help me.

'You've wondered about Fergus, of course.'

'Of course,' I answered.

'Well, better hear it from me than some mumbled half-truths from Charity, and snippets from our Cousin Maxwell. He'll only have what was told at secondhand, in any case. After all, Fergus is my son. I'm the one who knows.'

I saw his fingers flex and unflex on the arms of the cane chair; it was almost as if he were counting back the years, ticking them off to arrive at the time when the story had begun. It mattered what was important to him, and it did not begin with Fergus.

'I said you reminded me of my mother. She was your type of woman – a fine, handsome, strong woman, with more strength in her soul even than in her body. As I said, she would have borne a dozen like me, if my father hadn't been killed. He had brought her out here as a bride, and they were carving a small estate out of uncleared land – land no one had bothered with before – they were building Winterslo. It was fierce, hard work. He had very little capital, and that meant fewer slaves than he needed for the work. He couldn't afford a white overseer, and so he mostly acted as his own driver – that's the man who moves the slaves in line through

the canefields. They have to be kept moving, you know – and often
the whip is needed. All of them are lazy rascals. It happened then
as it happens still. The black man rose up with his machete against
his master; they say my father died with one stroke. Well, the slave
was flogged to death – or hanged. I don't know – my mother refused to talk about it.'

Suddenly his tone changed to impatience. 'Oh, don't look
like that, girl! Men die violent deaths. It has always been that way.
Slaves are a tricky business. Never trust a slave. They will steal your
food and your secrets and, if they can, your life. Better to flog
and be sure, than trust and be dead. Don't try to make them
grateful to you for favours. They have long memories – their
memories go back to Africa, and there is no forgetting. Just be
warned.'

I took what he said, and knew I could not protest. I had known
what I was coming to. Had I expected it to be pretty? Hadn't I
known that humans in bondage forced the making of rules and
that life on a plantation would be lived according to them? I
might as well have expected to walk and see innocence among the
stews of Glasgow, as expect to find slaves happy in their plight here
in the islands of the sun.

'What did she do, your mother?'

'She went on. She was that kind. She had more courage than
six men. With Winterslo half-built, she made a few rooms habitable
for us both, and no slave slept within the house at night. She
learned how to handle a pistol, and she carried it with her, as well
as a whip. She carried me with her also into the fields, holding me
before her on the saddle, and when I was old enough I rode my own
pony. But I suppose I was hardly ever beyond her sight until I
proved I could take care of myself. She taught me what I know of
books – mostly it was accounts that mattered. There was no money
for such luxuries as a governess. It was a hard life we both knew,
Miss Fiona – acre by acre slowly cleared, a room at a time completed at Winterslo. She had to learn it all, and then teach it to
me.'

'Did she ever think of remarrying? White women must have
...?'

'Perhaps she had some romantic fancy that no man she ever met
came up to my father. Perhaps she was too engrossed in the plantation, too busy, to affect the idle airs that might have made her
attractive to other men. You age quickly in a life as hard as hers.
It's even possible, Miss Fiona, that she frightened men off. They
don't like to know that a woman can do a job better than they can.

She would have made a difficult wife for any man who didn't measure up to her standards. Who would expect such a woman to sit idle in the drawing-room of some plantation greathouse? In any case, for whatever reason, that was how it was. She didn't marry again.'

'And you didn't marry?'

He shrugged. 'I hardly had time to notice. Oh, let us not be delicate about it. Of course there were women. Where there are slaves there are always women to be had. And there were others – others I came across in Santa Marta – quadroons, octoroons, women who never expect to marry a white man, but don't want a black one, either. As long as you have a few gifts for them . . . well, I was no saint. I was a young man, and I took what I needed. My mother didn't expect otherwise. She just ignored it, as all white women do out here.'

'Then what? – Fergus had a white mother.' He was talking now, and nothing could stop him. I could ask him anything, and the answers would come tumbling from memory, perhaps from nostalgia. He needed to speak it again.

'I must have been thirty-six – yes, I must have been all of that. Can you imagine that I fell in love for the first time? She was white – of course she was white. And she was seventeen years old – a child almost. I met her at a ball in Santa Marta. I wasn't eligible, you know, but bachelors were always invited. She was the most beautiful thing I had ever seen – and no one since then to touch her. She was soft, and yet like porcelain – great green eyes shining. Enough to drive a man out of his mind. I remember I knocked a man unconscious out in the garden so that I could have his dance with her. And I made her – I *made* her – promise to come riding with me the next day. I half-expected her not to appear, but she did. Of course there was a groom with her, but he was a slave and he did what he was told. We met often after that – an old ruined greathouse in the hills. She would have been whipped and locked up if her parents had known.'

He added, 'It was the first time I had been in love. I didn't pay attention to the rules. I didn't even know them.'

He sighed; it was the sound of a man who has almost begun to regret the looking-back, the pain, the confrontation of old memories best left dormant. 'I wondered why she kept putting off the time when I would go and speak to her father. I wanted to marry her. God knows, I was probably the least eligible, in terms of material goods, of any man on the island, but no man could have loved her more. Then she told me – in the end she told me.

She was engaged to marry the heir to one of the richest and highest-born names in England – let's not talk of the name, Miss Fiona. You would know it, but it no longer matters. He had come out on a visit to one of the family's plantations on San Cristóbal, and had merely seen her. He hardly knew her at all – she was still in the schoolroom. But connoisseurs as well as rough men like myself know something unique when they see it. She was spoken for, and she was to be married by her eighteenth birthday.'

He gave a harsh, wild laugh, that seemed too loud for the stillness that yet surrounded us. 'But it was too late, you see. Those meetings at the greathouse, and the slave who was too frightened of me to speak to her parents. I was mad for her, and she was only seventeen. Yes, I suppose you'd say I had seduced her, but I'll swear to this day that she loved me, and it seemed no wilful violation, but just the only thing that could have happened between two people who felt as we did.

'Then suddenly she stopped coming. I went to her parents' house, and no one would admit me. I inquired after the slave who had always ridden with her. He was dead, Miss Fiona – he was dead. Never trust a slave.

'No one saw her in Santa Marta, and there were rumours that she was ill with fever. Her noble fiancé was expected back at any time. I was frantic, and yet I couldn't get in to her. Short of shouting her name in the streets of Santa Marta, there was no way I could force her parents to see me. It went this way for several months. Oh, yes, I got a note – one of those little schoolgirl notes dictated by a mother with that rubbish about my attentions being unwelcome. I didn't believe a word of it. I even heard she had been shipped off the island, back to England. And then there was the day the man she was to marry arrived. It was some months before he was expected, I remember. No letter to announce him – nothing. Just his arrival, and his natural demand to see his future bride. They tried to stop him – they told him, I think, she had a contagious fever. They had hoped, you see, to have it all over before he came, but he came too soon. He persisted – perhaps he loved her, too, as much as one could without knowing her. Well, he saw her finally, and he saw that she was carrying another man's child. He said nothing to her, I'm told – no words of love or reproach. He put his hands about her throat and choked out of her the name of the child's father. And then he turned his back on her and left. An hour later, in the presence of several witnesses, he swore to kill me.

'He did it, of course, in the proper English fashion. He sent his seconds, and I rounded up a couple of real friends I had, and we met as arranged. I shot him through the heart. And my poor little girl – my little love – gave premature birth to my son, and died. I never saw her before she died.'

His voice now was a hoarse whisper. 'Perhaps I never would have seen my son, but the slave entrusted with getting rid of him – drowning him, probably, or throwing him where he would never be found – preferred the risk of telling me that he had been born and still lived. I went to the house that night and demanded him. They made very little trouble over giving him over to me – who wanted such a child? But how much better if they had given me his mother.'

After all these years the pain was still there, the sense of loss, of being cheated. 'So I brought him back to Winterslo, more dead than alive – a tiny, half-breathing, seven-month infant. I gave him to my mother and she took him. She saved his life – found a wet nurse for him, constant watching, keeping him warm, keeping him cool. He was strong, for all that he had come too soon. But he survived those first weeks, and I had my son. What I wanted was his mother.'

It had been the beginning of the hurt in Fergus, of course, the child there at Winterslo instead of the mother, the child brought up by an ageing woman. There would have been little softness in Fergus Maxwell's childhood.

'There was an inquiry, naturally,' Andrew went on. 'Duelling is illegal, but a man has the right to defend himself. There was a fuss in England, but the courts here didn't touch me. But it was the beginning of isolation at Winterslo. We had never had much time or money for social life, but after that we went nowhere and were asked nowhere. And I didn't care to go, either. I turned my back on the whole island, and I gave everything I had to making them regret that the mother of my child hadn't been permitted to marry me.'

'But Landfall . . .?'

'I'd been watching Landfall – coveting it, probably. Some of the best sugar land on the whole island. What was wrong was an absentee landlord – and a series of mishaps and unlucky chances ever since the house had been built. The best overseer you can get isn't enough to counteract the absentee owner – you have to be there yourself and know what you're doing. I knew the state it was in – it adjoins the Winterslo lands, though Winterslo doesn't produce half the crop by acre. I knew that Landfall's overseer was drunk half the time, and I made it my business to come over here regularly – drink with him, though never half as much as he did. I saw to it that he always had a good supply of rum, and I made up from my own store what he took from the Landfall barrels. Within two years Landfall was showing so little profit that it was ready for anyone who would take it. So that was when I went to London – to the Maxwells. I mortgaged Winterslo for everything it was worth, and with it went my own record of working it up to that point. They lent me the money and kept themselves an interest in the place, and I came back here, and Landfall was mine. It was mine – under a staggering load of debt, but it was mine.

'That was the only time I ever left the island – and I didn't stay a week in London. Give it to the Maxwells – old Jeremy didn't keep me hanging about for an answer. While I was there I used another name. Because of the man I'd killed – his family was very powerful . . .

'One other thing I did, though. Mostly for my mother's sake, but partly for my own, I travelled up north, far into the High-lands, to the village that both she and my father had come from. I did not say who I was, contacted none of the families. I just looked, and climbed those hills, and knew a different kind of rain than I'd ever known before. I saw how they lived. And then I began to understand what made them as they were – that streak most Scots have in them. Stubborn, independent, prideful, damned obstinate, and able to take what life hands to them. I came back knowing better who and what I was . . .

'The rest was hard work, and the refurbishing of this house. My mother was against ever coming here; she wanted no part of it. It was half in ruins, and she would have let it go. But it was first the garden that caught me – it had been planted more than a hundred years before that, when the house was first started. I cleared the vines and the undergrowth, and the pattern of the garden came to life. I learned about plants, because there were some plants here I had never seen before. I sent to London for books – how Santa Marta would have laughed if they'd known that rough, uncouth Andrew Maxwell was sitting up of nights over botany books. And then the house began to fascinate me, as the centre of this garden. I set some men to work on it – it was half-unroofed, but its interior had been built of mahogany, and the termites don't take hold in that too easily. My mother opposed it all the way, and probably she was right. I was in no hurry, but room by room it was restored, and I began to pick up furniture and bits and pieces. And the stories got about Santa Marta, and everyone thought that one day I would break out of my cocoon and Landfall would be a great place for visiting and parties. Perhaps they were nearly right. I didn't realize it until the place was finished, until the gardens were restored to what they once had been, that probably at the back of my mind I had been preparing a home that the parents of the girl I had loved so much would have been proud to see her mistress of. And when it was done I closed the gates; those eager to see it were never invited. My mother was dead; Fergus and I lived here alone – that is, until eight years ago.'

'And Winterslo?'

'That belongs to Fergus now.' His voice rasped on the words. 'It was good enough for my mother and me. He complains, but it is *his* turn to work to get what he can from that land now. It doesn't yield like Landfall, but a man can live from it. An estate can't be cut up, Miss Fiona – that's how you make peasants of landowners. There can be only one heir to Landfall.'

'And that will be Duncan.'

'That one will be Duncan.'

From the back of the house, somewhere, a bell began to toll. It was a mournful sound on the morning air, like a lament, slow, reluctant. Andrew Maxwell began to heave himself out of his chair. He was without his cane, and the movement was painful.

'That's the bell to get the slaves into the fields. They do a few hours' work before breakfast is brought to them. Charity will be bringing your water up. It's time to get ready. We work early here, before the heat of the day.' Then, as if it were all part of the same thought, he added, 'Teach him well, Miss Fiona – if you can, teach him quickly, and teach him some Scottish good sense. There could be troubles coming for us here all over the Indies, and he's very young yet.'

Very slowly he left me, bare feet shuffling more heavily than the slaves, his hand occasionally going to the wall to support himself. I sat for a while longer, pondering what I had been told, listening to the sounds of Landfall coming to life. Mostly I was thinking of Fergus, the child that Andrew Maxwell's conscience had saved from death, who had been willed to life by the care of an ageing grandmother, the child gradually learning these things about himself in the isolation of Winterslo, and thereafter hating the world for what it had not given him. Was that the darkness I had seen behind him yesterday like a second rider in the shadow of the great cottonwood? – the black bitterness, the dark past? There were things at Landfall I did not understand, perhaps never would. Did they come from the past, like the vision of the jewel-bedecked woman I had seen last night? – were they the future? Did they exist in this time now? I could not tell. The solid walls about me seemed to breathe of things to come – or were they past? My weary mind could not accept it all; I shook myself as if to wake from a sleep of many years. My very limbs felt old as I gathered myself up and began to make my way back to my room. I turned the corner of the gallery dreamily, hardly distinguishing the figure who leaned back against one of the pillars, the red-blond head crushed back into a tangle of honeysuckle, perched on the railing itself, one foot touching the floor for balance, the other drawn up, his knee clasped by both hands.

'As he said, Miss Fiona, the best time of the day – almost gone now.'

Now he turned his face fully towards me. 'I should be back there at Winterslo now, beginning the day with my hands in the fields. But I was remembering too – just as he was.' The tone was gentle, without mockery. I just stood rooted, staring at him; the face was strangely naked, vulnerable. He would not quip with me as he had done last night. He must have listened to the whole recital, the story retold.

'I'm glad you know it all, now,' he said. 'And best it came from my father. You know, you look at him now – gross, half the time drunk, smoking that rotten weed, that Indian hemp, and it's hard to believe he could have loved so romantically – with that kind of delicacy and absolute loyalty – and such a creature as he describes. Could it have lasted, I wonder, if she had lived? But for him she lives forever – just as she was. But as he said, he wanted her, and he got me. I was remembering . . . I was remembering Winterslo, and my grandmother. I was remembering being young here at Landfall without her. I hated it – this grand big house, and just the two of us. You heard how it was. He prepared this house for a woman who was already dead. A house made ready for a ghost – a bride who never came. No carriages came driving up, no champagne was drunk under those chandeliers. There were just the two of us, staring at each other down that long table. Is it any wonder we hated each other?'

'Hate . . .' I said slowly, shaking my head trying to say clearly what I meant, but the words were leaden on my tongue. 'It was here before you – it goes on.'

'I know.' He put his other foot on the floor and straightened. 'We met it here, and it goes on. What can one do?' Then his tone changed. 'But he said one thing to remember. Duncan! – try with Duncan. He needs it. None of us can give him what he needs. Perhaps you can. Goodbye, Miss Fiona. I don't come often to Landfall. I don't know when I'll see you again.'

I almost put my hand towards him. 'Perhaps . . . No, it is nothing.'

He may not have heard; in a way I hoped he hadn't. Did I want to be even more vulnerable? He was almost at the corner of the gallery when he turned and looked back. He didn't even smile as he said it.

'You know, you're really quite beautiful when you're not all tidied up.'

3

Slowly, with a care that I had never practised before, I began to find my way at Landfall. The first day set the pattern of the day-to-day happenings; the times of rising and going to bed, the times of meals and lessons with Duncan. But that was only the outward rhythm, the set time pieces by which any household runs. There were a thousand things I did not know about Landfall, but the key lay in the people who inhabited it, and there never was again a session so frank and open as I had that first morning with Andrew Maxwell.

It was true that I still woke when the first light fell across the louvers; before sunrise the cocks crowed, but now the sound signified something more to me than the break of day. After the first day, after my first walk beyond the house itself, following the paths that led through the garden, I found the slave quarters. I did not inspect them closely; hostile dark eyes told me that these wretched places were private and that no stranger was welcome. They invited no scrutiny; least of all they invited pity. I left the dank and crumbling huts almost as abruptly as I had come upon them – they were closer to the greathouse than one thought, but in the tropics the eternal cloak of greenery hides many things. But I knew now that as soon as the cocks crowed, those quarters, still in darkness, were astir, the black forms stumbling forth from sleep so as to be ready for the bell that called them to the fields. I learned to dread the toll of that bell. Always, just after it sounded, Charity would appear with my scented water and I would wash and dress. But I never did it without thinking of my little labours that lay ahead, and of those who went to the field under the sun and the plaited bull-thong lash of the driver.

Almost every morning, after I woke, I heard the bare-footed shuffle of Andrew Maxwell on the gallery as he paced; sometimes there was that awful sweet smell of the hemp, as I now knew it to be. But not again did I open the shutters and go to the railing to watch the swiftly passing moments of the dawn. The first morning had been an accidental meeting; now it would seem to be an attempt towards intimacy, and I would not give Maria Maxwell cause ever again to view my dishevelment with her contemptuous amusement, the suggestion in her glance that I offered myself regularly to the gaze of a man clad only in a nightshift. I had only the weapon of dignity against Maria Maxwell; I could not afford to blunt it.

Breakfast was in the schoolroom with Duncan – an early breakfast. As Andrew had said, work began early here against the heat of the day, the dead part of the afternoon that no white person seemed to be able to go through without seeking the relief of the darkened bedroom, the uneasy doze. It seemed a strange breakfast to me – fruit, papaya, mango, bananas, the juice of oranges, little bread rolls and butter already soft even though it was stored in the cool cellars of the house. Always a few blossoms lay on the tray as it came – hibiscus, frangipani, a sprig of bougainvillaea. It was as if all white people must begin their day with the offerings of the Indies, the fruit and the flowers. The meal was made gay by the visits of what Duncan called the sugar-stealer, the banana-quit, a tiny, sparrow-like thing, black with a yellow belly, who came boldly to take the sugar from the bowl and to peck at the bananas as we peeled them. And always, at the vines, the humming-birds danced on the air with the myriad stirrings of their wings, seeking the sweetness buried in the blossoms, seeming to stand still before one's eyes so fast was the movements of their wings. And there were the others, particularly the glossy black grackle who came fearlessly to the gallery to wait for the crumbs that Duncan spread. I had to stop Duncan crumbling whole rolls for them, knowing that whatever was not eaten from our breakfast tray would go into Charity's pocket on the way downstairs. I was still too Scottish to see the birds, although Duncan's playfellows, fed before the people. I was beginning to find the Scottish habits of economy and diligence more than a little difficult to make sense of to Duncan. There was food, plenty of it, and always someone else to do the work. What other kind of life was there? Why should he be put to the trouble of finding out about it, of practising its ways? He was intelligent, wilful, more given to talking than to learning. It was hard to be stern with him; he was too much like my half-brother; in the waves of homesickness and nostalgia that swept over me, all I saw was the face of that other child, the face of my father, also. In the midst of all the exotic comforts of Landfall I found myself sometimes longing for the chill of the Scottish manse, and the cold wind that drove in on that other side of the Atlantic.

Our lessons were interrupted midmorning when Maria Maxwell came to call her son to her side to accompany her for her ride through the plantation. He would go quickly for his riding-boots and hat, and a miniature riding crop to match his mother's, his very eagerness a part of the dismay I felt at the task of trying to change what was born in him. When they went my time was my own. On my first day, feeling that the hours of idleness were not justified, I asked Maria Maxwell if there was something I could do for her during this time.

'I know a little about accounts,' I said, faltering under her amusement at the offer. 'And I can do a little plain sewing . . .'

She almost laughed. 'Really, you must not trouble yourself, Miss McIntyre. There are those who already attend to such things. And besides . . . the accounts of the plantation are hardly simple arithmetic.' Her tone quite clearly implied that that was all I might be trusted with.

She swept from the room in her dove-grey habit and Cordoban hat, Duncan running beside her, his face upturned with admiration and the desire to please and interest her. They rode away, and often I watched them from the gallery – she on a grey horse, with a white mane and tail, which she sat superbly, Duncan on a blond-red pony, a frisky, difficult animal, almost too much for a child to manage. But he permitted himself no sign of doubt or fear; if his mother expected him to ride Ginger, he would ride him.

'She could kill them both one day.' I spun round at the sound of Andrew's voice. 'She will egg the boy on to something that's beyond him, and they both will come to grief.' It was difficult, when Andrew knew I was freed from the schoolroom at this time, to avoid him. 'She won't even take a groom with her. It isn't right. No white woman should go alone . . .'

Usually by this time of the morning he carried his glass of rum with him, or a slave was at hand to place it where it was wanted. It must have been a deprivation for him, in those first days I was there, for him to leave it behind, to bestir himself to take me through the gardens of Landfall, naming the trees and plants for me – sometimes stumbling over them, annoyed when his memory betrayed him. The marvellous flamboyant trees were in bloom, but he dismissed them as common stuff, preferring the scarlet upthrust of the magnificent African tulip tree. The names were magic: Showers of Gold, Chinaberry, Pride of Burma, Cordia, the Geranium tree, the great Lignum Vitae, the heaviest wood in the world. 'I could make a fortune by selling a few of those trees to shipbuilders,' Andrew remarked. There were sweet-sop trees, West Indian almond and pomegranate. There was the Immortelle. 'Poison,' Andrew said. 'There are a lot of poisonous trees in the tropics. The natives use the leaves and seeds to stun the fish. And the oleanders – watch for them. Even something cooked over the wood of oleander is poisoned.' He showed me the precious cacao trees, always planted under the shade of the pinkish-flowered 'Madre de Cacao'. There were the pink and yellow pouis, the Jacaranda, and even the rare Napoleon's Button. 'It's only seeded once in twenty years,' Andrew growled at it. 'A botanist's curiosity.' Cup of Gold, Alamander, Petrea – strangely like lilac – twined themselves wherever they would find space. 'We are in the rainy season,' Andrew said. 'They like it – the heat and the wet. There will be less wind from now on. Hurricane weather is still. November will see us through it. The cane grows and ripens now, and in January we will start to harvest. Don't be deceived by this garden, girl. The heart of Landfall is those cane fields out there . . .'

He took me for a cursory tour of the sugar factory, where the cane was fed into huge pressing machines and the juice extracted. He showed me the vats where the juice was boiled up, the scum taken off, the boiling process being ever refined until the rum or sugar or molasses was ready. 'Landfall's rum is good,' Andrew said. 'Good soil . . .'

He chuckled grimly as he pointed to the huge axe that hung on the wall of the factory. 'That's for any slave who's foolish enough to fall asleep feeding the cane into the rollers. The only way to save them then is to cut off the arm – some do. We work long hours when the harvest is coming in . . .'

It seemed a grim place, imbued with the weariness and sweat of those who had toiled here, curiously ramshackle by comparison to the rest of Landfall. Andrew didn't seem to notice. He pointed out to me the paths of the garden that led to the wild coves of the Serpent Rocks and those that led over to the lee shore, where, he said, I would find the bays like glass.

'I don't go down to those places any more,' he said. 'It's too much to climb back. I could always take a horse, I suppose, and go over to the lee shore – but I don't swim any more. I used to be a strong swimmer. Good enough, even for the Serpents. I don't want to flop about like a jelly-fish over there in those warm bays and remember what it was like when I could breast the surf of the Serpents. And the heat of the day is too much. I don't care for it at other times. I've never liked shadows in the water – can be sharks or barracuda. I like the sun now in the water; I need the warmth. At one time I didn't care. That is why an old man takes a young woman to his bed – he hopes for warmth . . .'

In those first days I saw nothing more of Fergus, and in a way I was glad. He disconcerted me as even Maria Maxwell could not, and I had enough strange and new things to learn without trying to fathom Fergus, his silences, the light that just might be contempt for himself that came and went in his eyes. And yet I kept watching for him; I know I did. When we sat at lessons, and I heard the sound of a horse on the gravel paving before the house, it needed as much discipline as I possessed to sit still in my chair and not to go to the railings to see if it was he who had come. But I would hear the voices, and it was always Alister; no visitors ever came to Landfall. Duncan talked often of Fergus; he seemed to have a deep attachment to his half-brother, strange in that they were so far apart in age, and Fergus saw him so seldom. But Duncan had a child's sure knowledge of those who liked him. Perhaps out of his loneliness he was striving to establish a camaraderie, an identi-fication with another male creature, someone not worn out and dis-interested like his father.

'Can you ride, Miss Fiona?'

'A little – but I've no habit. Why?' I thought of the old walking boots and the serge skirt that would have to serve me. I had grown out of the habit that had been one of the extravagances of my teenage years, and now Mary wore it.

'Because I want to ride over to Winterslo and see Fergus.'

'You may do nothing without asking your Mama first.'

'Well, then, I shall ask her. She lets me do anything I want.'

He didn't tell me that the request had been refused, but I knew it was, because for a day he sulked and went petulantly to fetch his hat and riding crop when his mother came for him the next morning.

It was Alister who was my prop in those first days; the one figure of normalcy in that household. Without him I don't know how I could have endured those dinners, when Maria Maxwell blazed in the full brilliance of her beauty and talked and laughed and flirted with a falsity that was like ice in the heart. Without Alister there I imagine the meals might have gone forward in silence and that I might have readily blown out the candles at

my end of the table and simply have vanished. But Alister talked
to me as if I existed; as if I were a person and not just a figure –
a governess. He was tactful beyond belief; there were amusing
stories dragged up from his childhood when the Prince Regent
had been at the height of his follies. 'My father's bank never lent
money to the Prince. He preferred to forgo the Baronetcy and save
his money.' He spoke of how twice he had seen the young Princess
Victoria driving in Hyde Park, the very young lady who would
be Queen. 'Not exactly a beauty, but sweet-looking,' he said. 'I
would wish for more spirit – but they say her mother, the Duchess,
permits her no liberty. Poor child . . .'

He was the first I had ever heard to express pity for someone
who would be a monarch; somehow it made me feel that he saw
greater equality in women than most men did.

Judiciously he urged Maria to talk – especially when she had
had enough wine she might bring forth one of the old island stories.
Who had married who and why, and why this estate or that had
been lost or won. There were stories of week-long card games from
which men had emerged beggars or had climbed nearly to the top
just by the winning of some hundreds of acres of cane fields or a
consignment of slaves. But there were never stories of the slaves
themselves; there seemed to be an unspoken agreement among
whites that the evil and danger they lived with must not be spoken
of too openly, as if the fears that possessed one must somehow
be held down. There were no stories, even when no slave was
present to listen, of such things as had happened to Andrew Maxwell's father; there were no tales told of the night that certain
greathouses that I saw outlined on the ridges of ruins had been
burned. And yet there was always the sense of looking over one's
shoulder.

There were the times, also, a little further gone in wine, when
Maria boasted of her ancestry, giving, without words, her opinion
of the lowliness of the Maxwells. 'The Medinas are grandees of
Spain,' she said. 'The San Francisco holding is an original land
grant from Isabella and Ferdinand.' San Francisco was her family's
estate.

'San Francisco is three acres and a chicken run,' Andrew said,
taking his wine with relish.

She flashed him a look that would silence any man. 'San Francisco was once half the island of San Cristóbal. Stolen – stolen by
the English.'

'Your men were too weak to hold it, my dear. The Spanish
blood gone to seed. They'd been in the Indies too long without

ever accepting them as their home. They lived as exiles, without ever embracing what was theirs, clinging to a worn-out tradition. What was it about those card parties . . . wasn't that how San Francisco went . . . a hundred acres here, fifty there . . .'

Her eyes flashed pure hatred. 'Sometimes a generation comes where there is not weakness . . . someone who knows how to win back . . .'

He wasn't paying attention. 'What a pity Columbus was an Italian,' he rambled on. 'Or we should never hear the end of this Spanish business.'

'But the Spanish had the wisdom to put up the money for Columbus's voyages,' Alister put in quickly, dampening the spark that flared. 'The Genovese bankers didn't have the vision of Isabella. Thoughts like that serve to keep bankers humble.' He bowed his head in mock penitence. Maria was a little appeased, and I marvelled again at his adroitness.

But Alister was busy in other ways than just that of enlivening the evening meal. He seemed to come and go a lot, riding to Santa Marta on business he never talked about. Whatever it was, it was business that seemed to disturb Maria. Often she would refer to these journeys – teasingly asking him what the gossip of the town was, as if she hoped to find out just where he had been. And he was always ready with some story for her, a morsel picked up at Lawrence's club or on the gallery of the Royal. He wasn't quite successful in giving the impression that he spent his whole time at those two hotbeds of island gossip, but he made a good try. And there often was a little present for Maria from Santa Marta's best shop, Rodriguiz – a fan, a gossamer length of silk for a stole, the latest London magazines which, naturally, were months out of date. But I knew he did these things not because he had time to spend in Rodriguiz, but because he wished Maria to think he did. I don't suppose any of us were deceived; Alister Maxwell had never wasted time in his life.

But when Alister rode it was not only to Santa Marta. 'I need the exercise,' was all he ever said about it. But quite early in the mornings, and in the late afternoons when the shadows had begun to gather, I would see him go off along the paths and bridle trails that led from Landfall. Sometimes he would take food with him, and stay away the whole day. Maria never got much return to her questionings about how he spent those days. 'I just ride – I look at the estates. Sometimes I find a cove and bathe. That's what the doctors told me to come here for . . .' He added, with a wry touch of humour, 'People are beginning to get used to seeing me riding in all kinds of odd places – that madman from London who doesn't know enough to stay in out of the sun. Sometimes I fear I trespass, but no one seems to mind. Sometimes I'm invited into one of the greathouses for a drink. I don't know whether it's need for company, or sheer curiosity, but the ladies of San Cristóbal love to talk . . .'

'*Them* – gossips, all of them,' Maria pronounced. 'They just want to find out what goes on at Landfall. No one comes here, so they must make a mystery of it. They have all the time to just sit and gossip. An idle lot . . .'

'Your mother, Donna Isabella, is not among that number, then,' Alister said, obviously amused by her vehemence. 'I thought the other day it was high time I paid my respects to Donna Isabella, so I rode over to San Francisco – mind you, I've passed it many a time, but I didn't think it an advantageous hour . . .'

'You *went* to San Francisco!' Maria looked startled. 'You should have told me. I would have sent a message. I would have taken you there myself . . .'

Again Alister's wry smile that said nothing. 'It might have been just as well if you had. I never did meet your good lady mother. She's very adept with a musket – or rifle – or whatever firing piece she had. I didn't wait to find out. She judged the range to a nicety – not to hit but just to warn, I imagine.'

Maria's cheeks flushed. 'A thousand pardons, Alister. She would never have done such a thing if she had known it was you. But they are three women alone there at San Francisco, she and my sisters. There are very few slaves, and none worth the having . . . She lives in the past, sometimes, my mother. As if there were still things to protect there. She is old – her mind wanders a little.'

Alister shrugged. 'Her aim doesn't. But no matter – I had no business calling without prior notice. I hope you will convey my apologies . . .'

Andrew laughed loudly at the story. 'She's still a fire-eating old bitch. A dab hand with a gun and a whip and her tongue, that one.'

And then, too, there were the mornings when Maria was out with Duncan that I heard Alister's voice coming from the office where the estate business was managed, a sectioned portion of the inner gallery at the back of the house, a room lined with ledgers and journals. Some, which Andrew himself showed me proudly, were the ledgers of Winterslo, kept by his mother. The place was the workroom of a young, nondescript man, Fellowes by name, who seemed on a perpetual seesaw of hate and fear towards his mistress. Maria went there every afternoon after the siesta; sometimes their voices, his low and, I thought, abject, hers reaching a shrillness not heard in the salon, would rise to us in the schoolroom. Often I heard him called a fool and an idiot; his stooped figure over the ledgers was another symbol for me at Landfall. He seemed to work irrational hours – sometimes absent, sometimes burning the lamp late into the night; but never was he invited to the table or to a glass of wine. And yet, like a dog's, his gaze would follow his mistress with a kind of hopeless adoration; she knew it, of course, and received it with her own kind of tantalizing contempt. Fellowes seemed to me one of the typical tragedies of the Indies – the young Englishman without money who comes in hope of a fortune, comes much too late and is doomed to the two-room house with the tiny veranda not too far from the slave quarters, who eats his meals alone in the room next to the kitchen and whom no white woman will marry because, unless he has luck with cards, and entré to the clubs, he will stay in that tiny house, on one estate or another, for all of his life. His life is likely to be short in the Indies. There are no companions but the flask of rum and one of the lighter-coloured slaves.

What interested me was Alister's apparent right to enter the estate office at any time, whether Fellowes was present or not, and open up the books. He did this most often when Fellowes was away – during the siesta, or at the time when Fellowes went to check stores and equipment, or into Santa Marta to give the orders for the plantation's needs. I found that Alister took to the siesta no more readily than I – and sometimes, in the walk I took after lunch, before I would give in to the temptation of that darkened bedroom, I would pass on the outer gallery, and he would be there, seated at the desk. Sometimes he heard my footsteps and turned from the books to nod towards me; sometimes he was too intent and I passed unnoticed. There were times, also, when Maria herself broke the sacred custom and stayed with him after lunch in the office. But at those times her voice was not the one she used to Fellowes – I heard it soft and slow, explaining, laughing off some item of expenditure, almost cajoling. I would go to my room, and later there would be her footsteps on the stairs, and much later, Alister's. I had begun to notice that on the evenings after these sessions in the office she took more than usual trouble to be charming to him. And all the time Andrew Maxwell did nothing, said nothing. He asked no questions about the management of Landfall, did not turn even a page of the current ledgers. Will and energy was gone from him; he seemed to drift, simply to wait upon the arrival of each new day.

There are some things that governesses learn, and I thought I had learned them all – to hold my tongue, to bide my time, like Andrew, just to wait. In theory I knew them all; at Landfall I transgressed the rules. It is a risk which leads to victory and a certain ascendancy, or to being sent home. In those early days I didn't really care if I were sent away from Landfall; I didn't care except for Duncan.

Perhaps it was because the evening seemed exceptionally warm. '– hurricane weather,' Andrew pronounced as he slumped into his chair for the evening meal. The dimity dress, my best, had been handed over to Charity to be washed and had come back a limp survivor, and I had by now gone through the second best summer dress – one never needs more than two 'best' summer dresses in Scotland. And so that evening I suffered through a meal of curried meat in a dress tight to the neck of wool. I could feel the perspiration standing on my forehead, once or twice I wiped it from my eyes. The wine kept coming, and out of desperation I drank it, and it made me all the hotter. I listened to Maria flirt with Alister, and I hadn't the spirit to try to salvage any of the conversation for myself. At the end I could stand no more. As Maria rose, I came to my feet with a speed that took the slave, who had been waiting to draw back my chair, by surprise. It slid across the polished floor and crashed against the wall. I had not meant such violence, but there it was; it always happened that way with me.

'Mrs Maxwell . . .' Andrew's apathy was broken by my tone. 'Mr Maxwell, I would like to talk to you both . . .'

Instantly Alister rose. 'Permit me – I'll leave you alone.'

'No!'

With a jerk of her head Maria had signalled to Dougal to remove all the slaves. They went silently; at least they were beyond our sight, but one knew that they waited in the hall, listening, they stood within the shadows of the shutters in the hall. They knew how to wait silently and listen. They were beyond our sight, but we knew they were there.

Maria resumed her seat; the calmness of her movement made mine seem exaggerated and absurd. 'Please do not leave, Alister. As a member of the family, I am sure there is nothing that Miss McIntyre has to say that may not be heard by you.'

'It's just that . . .' I was lost and foolish; how stupid to make a scene at dinner just because one was hot, when a few words to Maria any morning would probably have achieved the same results.

But still I was conscious of her face-saving concern before the men.

'Very well, then – I'm sorry it has to be before Alister, because it is of such small importance. It is simply that I need to have my quarter's salary advanced. I need it at once.'

Maria's eyebrows shot up. 'Indeed? I wonder why? Are you not catered for at Landfall? Is there some complaint? If you have been neglected in any way, you may be sure Charity shall be punished . . .'

I threw back my head and laughed – a laugh I would not have believed of myself; was it true that the wine and the tropics and the heat did something to one's head? I heard this stranger laugh.

'What is the use of punishing Charity for what she cannot help? Look at me – just look at me!' I tugged at the high neck of my gown. 'I'm dying,' I said. 'I'm stifling. I came out here at two weeks' notice with clothes suited to a Scottish winter and no money for others. I must have some dresses – some cotton. I'll make them myself – even if the result will hardly do credit to Landfall and its standards. Or perhaps – ' and now I overreached myself, looking directly at Andrew. 'Perhaps you would rather I came down in my shift.'

It was the end; of course it was the end. I would leave Landfall tomorrow. I had opened my mouth wide and said the first thing that came. I had done myself in, and perhaps I was not sorry. Perhaps it would be no bad thing to be leaving Landfall.

'God's blood!' The shout came from Andrew. 'Girl, are you such a fool you couldn't have spoken before this? I mentioned it to you – when did I mention it to you? – about wearing lighter clothes.' He pointed at me. 'I've meant to speak of it – every day I've meant to speak of it, and I keep forgetting. Another week in things like that you've got on and you could be dead. Cotton – Lord, girl, you must have clean cotton every day in this climate. Maria, why have you not done something about it? She should have silks, too. You're supposed to pretty yourself up. Silks – ah, yes, that's it. Silks – light as a firefly. Blue silk and green silk, for your eyes, girl – and orange silk, for your hair . . .'

He was drunk, of course. I stared at him, stunned, my hands gripping the table because of the weakness in my knees. Suddenly he was on his feet, his chair sliding back just as mine had done, and there was a great running stain of wine on the lace frill of his shirt. He was beside me, grabbing my arm painfully. I was reminded, through all the chaos of this scene, of the way he had held me in the first moments of our encounter.

Now I was hustled from the dining-room; I heard a kind of hiss of protest from Maria, but she seemed as bewildered as I. As one would have expected, the doors of the dining-room opened as Andrew dragged me towards them. No need to guess that the slaves had heard every word of what had been said.

'Up here – up here.' Andrew was hauling himself up the stairs, leaning heavily on me for support. When we reached the landing and turned, I saw that Maria and Alister had come to the foot of the stairs and were staring up at us. For once the coolness of the woman seemed to have deserted her. Her eyes burned with fury.

'Andrew – what are you about? Have you taken leave of your senses?' The English so perfect, the strength of her passion so Spanish.

'Oh, for pity's sake, woman, be quiet! I am still master at Landfall, aren't I?'

We had reached the tall presses where the household linen was stored. I would not have thought that Andrew carried keys to such places, but the habit of ownership had not yet completely died in him. He went to the end press, fumbling terribly with a ring of keys, trying many before he found the right one, as if he had not used them for a long time. While he did this I saw that Maria and Alister had come to the landing of the staircase, holding back, but ready, as if they expected that Andrew might do himself or me some harm.

Now the doors of the press were flung wide. Rolls of cloth lay folded neatly on the shelves, plain cloths, printed cottons, Swiss muslins – cloths for a lady, these; nothing here for the household slaves. But there, to the side, lay the silks, bolts of them, it seemed, glowing with richness and texture in the dimness of the evening. Andrew's hands reached for them with the wildness of a drunken man; they tumbled on the floor, all about us, spilling like some rainbow fountain, a mad glory of colour and sensuous delight. One he clutched and draped about my shoulders. 'There's silk for you, girl! There's silk for you. More than one woman could ever wear. Here – take your pick. It was bought by Landfall. It belongs to Landfall!'

I had only the strength to make the token gesture. I picked up and refolded one of the rolls, hurriedly, not well, but at least it was done. I placed it back on the shelf.

'It belongs to the woman for whom it was bought. No other.'

Then I turned and left him. I did not go to my room – the rooms at Landfall are too accessible. Instead I found my way back along

to the stairs and to the landing where Maria and Alister stood. I
brushed past them without a word. My shoes clattered on the
stairs. The slaves parted automatically as I reached the hall below.
As I stumbled towards the door and the steps to the garden I
heard Andrew's bellow, loud and pained, shocked into a kind of
sobriety.

'Girl – I'm sorry. Come back. Come back . . .'

When I paid no heed he must himself have hurried to the top
gallery overlooking the darkness of the garden. He could not see
me as I ran along the first path that presented itself. But he knew
I was out there, and he was startled that an apology from him
had not brought me instantly to heel. His voice strained above the
chorus of the cicadas as he called into the darkness.

'Girl – come back! I'm sorry. God damn it – *I'm sorry*!'

2

Alister found me perched on a rock above a path that led down
to one of the coves of the Serpent Rocks. I don't know how I had
come so far, but suddenly I had been there, the pounding of the
surf in my ears, the curl of the white water tumbling dangerously
below me. It seemed the end of a journey; I could go no farther,
and all the Atlantic stretched before me, reaching away to home
and familiar things. It was here, with the thunder of the surf at odds
with the calm brilliance of the tropic night and the stars, that I
clutched my knees with my arms and put my face down and wept
my tears into the wretched wool dress. I wept, and the sound of
the surf drowned my tears, and the scurrying noises of the lizards
and land crabs, and the thousand things that inhabit the tropical
undergrowth. I wept, and forgot to be afraid of those scurrying
creatures about me; it seemed easy to weep at Landfall, I who
had shed so few tears in my life. And when the tears were done,
there was just the sitting and the dumb misery. I hated Andrew
Maxwell for the crudity of what he had done – I hated myself
for having been part of it, for having allowed it to begin. I hated
all of Landfall, and that really didn't matter because I would be
leaving tomorrow. No, it didn't matter. Hate is a corroding thing,
and I would forever look back on this night with shame.

Alister was almost beside me, and because of the crash of the surf
I did not hear him come. 'Fiona . . .?' I could see the blur of his
face, and my shame was thicker than ever. But I was glad it was he
who had come – that they had not sent a slave to fetch me back
ignominiously.

'I've been searching for you,' he said. 'They were going to send out slaves, but I thought that might . . .' He didn't quite know how to say it. 'I thought you might be frightened.'

'It was good of you.' I made myself turn back to face him, made myself say what had to be said and get it over with. 'I've been such a fool. I'm ashamed of myself. It was a dreadful scene – '

'Enough of that, now.' He scrambled up on the rock beside me and established himself there, knees drawn up as mine were, as if it were the most natural thing for a fashionably clad man to be settling down in this hot thicket above the cove to talk with a stupid weeping governess. 'You've nothing to reproach yourself with. It was natural. I'm ashamed of myself, indeed, that I didn't stop that fool, Andrew Maxwell. To have placed you in that position . . . unforgiveable. But between that stuff he smokes and the rum, I sometimes wonder if he's sane. But it was unforgivable of me to let it happen.'

I felt my hands clench tighter about my knees. 'But I was so wrong to choose that time. I should have spoken to Mrs Maxwell privately. It was just so hot . . . and the curry. But that's no excuse. I should have more control.'

'And Mrs Maxwell should have seen your need the second you arrived at Landfall. In fact, my partners should have known that in London and made an appropriate allowance. It was shaming for you to have to speak of it at all. I should have done something myself, but a man hesitates to butt into women's affairs, and I had hoped that Maria might have already started someone to work on things for you. Poor Fiona . . . one gets desperate, doesn't one? Is it the heat? – hurricane weather, as Andrew says. Or is it just Landfall?'

'Well, I'll know soon enough, because of course now I must leave Landfall. I'll leave tomorrow. There must be some place in Santa Marta I can stay, and I suppose there's *some* employment I can take until I have enough money for the fare back home. Perhaps you could . . . you must know some people in Santa Marta . . .?'

His hand was upon me. 'You cannot leave Landfall. You *must* not.' I had never heard that urbane voice so intense.

I shrugged. 'What choice is there? How can I stay? Mrs Maxwell will see that I'm well gone by midday.'

'Maria will do no such thing. It will not be permitted. It *is* not permitted. Don't you think that has already been decided? Do you think we said nothing to each other back there? You will stay.'

'It doesn't much matter whether or not I am *permitted* to stay. I cannot stay. I have been embarrassed and have made a fool of myself. I have my own pride, you know. What is left for me but to go?' I turned to him; his face was grave, intent, brows drawn together with concern, all revealed to me in the brilliance of the night, and the light thrown upwards by the crashing surf. 'It is an impossible situation.'

'Nothing is impossible if you have the will to survive it. You are needed at Landfall.'

'Nonsense! – no one needs me.'

'Duncan needs you.'

In spite of the warmth, did he feel my shiver? – how could he know, how could he have touched on my spot of secret vulnerability? He could not even guess of that moment under the arch of the stable-yard at Silkirk, the vision I had sought to flee only to be confronted again by it here. I saw Duncan again, and I was cold, despite the warmth and the wool dress.

He knew what my silence tokened. 'If you go, who is there at Landfall to help Duncan? Knowing what he needs, how can you go?'

There was nothing to reply. He did not know the exact reason why I would stay; he knew only that I would.

I felt my hand grasped as he pulled me to my feet. 'Come now, we must go back. You would be less than I think you are if you do not go back – and stay.'

I let him lead me along the twisting path back to the gardens and the house; he led my footsteps now where before they had found their own way; I was weak and exhausted and unresistant. And when we came in sight of the house there were no slaves to mark our coming. Alister still led me, my hair slipped from its knot, my body and dress soaked with sweat, up the stairs to the gallery. Only one light burned there. Beyond it, on the inner gallery, almost lost in the darkness, Andrew Maxwell sat. He said no word, but his head bowed slightly as we passed. If this were an apology, it was as much as I would get. In the hall one of the row of candles was lighted. Alister lighted another from it and held it high as he helped me up the stairs. As we approached my room the door opened and Charity stood there.

'Come, mistress . . . you need rest.'

And for the first time I knew the experience of falling into the skilful, ministering arms of a black woman.

3

My exhaustion lasted beyond the first light, beyond the crow of
the cock. It lasted even beyond the ring of the plantation bell, because I did not hear it that morning. I didn't hear the shuffling of
Andrew Maxwell's bare feet on the gallery; what I woke up to
was the pounding of his fist on the shutters. 'Wake up, girl – wake
up! We've got to be stirring early. Have to get to Santa Marta
before the heat. Get up . . .'

Charity was there with the water, and she opened the shutters
a half inch to hiss at her master, 'Mistress getting up. You go
about yor business.'

And only a raucous laugh greeted her impudence.

There were no lessons with Duncan that morning. Before we had
finished breakfast I heard the sound of the carriage on the drive;
Andrew stood before us, immaculate in his white clothes, resplen-
dent in a fresh red silk sash, his beard trimmed and combed, his
hair scented.

'Come now,' he said, 'no time to dawdle.' And instantly he
was frowning. 'Where's the thing I told them to have ready for you
this morning? You can't go into Santa Marta in *that*.' I was wearing a flannelette blouse, thin, shrunken from washing, tight under
the arms and seeming ready to break its buttons. '*Charity* . . .
God damn you, Charity! I'll have you flogged within an inch – '

'Here, master, here.' Her dignity under provocation was impressive. 'Jus' finished. Things not made in five minutes. But ready,
like you say.' She held a garment in her hand, held it towards me.
It was a blouse of exquisite *broderie Anglaise* as light as a puff
of wind, frilled, shirred, tucked. There was no way to know how
many women had sat up all night over its creation while I had
slept.

'There, girl, go and put it on. And let's get on our way. It's
getting hot already.'

As I went with Charity, I heard Duncan's argument begin. 'But
I'm coming, too, aren't I, Papa?'

'No – no, son. This is a woman's day. We have things to get for
Miss Fiona.'

'But, Papa, I want to come. Just once, can't I come with
you?'

In the walk to my room I measured the long pause. Then
Andrew's voice, muffled, as if he choked a little. 'Son . . .' Another long hesitation. 'No, there's no reason why she should have

you *all* the time. Go – go and get your hat. Go – and hurry up.'

4

It was such a day as I had never known in my life before. Chaos,
excitement, talk, argument, and the final exhaustion – all this
combined with the fierce heat of the busy town as the sun moved
higher, where one welcomed the breeze that sometimes blew up
the streets from the waterfront, and the deep shade of the arched
galleries that protected the pavements from the sun and the swift,
passing showers. Alister had ridden with us in the carriage into
Santa Marta, but he had little to say during the journey and went
his own way as soon as we reached the town.

'What's the matter, Alister? Are you afraid of women's things? –
don't like to be seen buying with a woman?'

Alister smiled lazily. 'Indeed I'm not. But I'm too much of a
politician to get involved in choices. No, let Miss Fiona have her
own enjoyment. Too many cooks, you know, Cousin Andrew . . .
Shall we meet at the Royal for some lunch?'

But whatever Alister thought, I wasn't having too much my
own way. We drove on to Rodriguiz when we had set Alister
down at Lawrence's. Andrew simply stood in the doorway, blinking after the glare outside, and thumped his stick. At once the
manager and a clerk were at his side.

'Ah, so good to see you here, Mr Maxwell. You don't often
venture from Landfall these days. Rodriguiz isn't often honoured
by your presence, though we *do* see Mr Alister Maxwell . . .'

Andrew ignored the courtesies. 'Enough of the talk, Alvarez.
We've things to do. First some chairs, man. Do you expect me to
stand about in this heat? This is my kinswoman, Miss McIntyre.
We'll have something to drink, if you please. And see that there's
something worth the drinking in mine . . .'

'Of course, Mr Maxwell – at once, sir.' Alvarez clapped his hands
agitatedly. 'Oh, and – er, welcome to San Cristóbal, Miss McIntyre.
I *did* hear that a relation had arrived at Landfall . . .'

Andrew dropped into a cane chair and thumped his stick in
earnest. 'Alvarez, I said enough of the talking! We need things,
and we've not got all day. Now my kinswoman, Miss Fiona, didn't
have time to prepare for her journey here and arrived without
proper clothes for this climate. She needs everything – *everything*,
you understand. Now start – and bring the drink!'

Alvarez, with a shop manager's acumen, knew what my station
at Landfall was and that governesses did not dress to compete with

their employers. So with quick Spanish gestures assistants were summoned, drinks laid before us, Duncan was greeted and inquiries made for the health of Mrs Maxwell, and with clicks of his long snapping fingers the appropriate rolls of cloth were indicated and brought for inspection. They were what one would have expected, the sensible things, the dull cottons, the serviceable linens, the hard-wearing carefully chosen fabrics of my calling. Andrew rejected them without consulting me. 'God's blood, man, she's not a nun! Look at her!' He jabbed his stick violently at the magentas and dark greens and several rolls of cloth went tumbling to the ground. Duncan burst into a child's hysterical giggle.

'And what are *you* laughing at, damn you?' Andrew snapped, already out of patience. 'I only brought you on condition you didn't make a nuisance of yourself. Do you want to see Miss Fiona dressed in *those* drabs!'

'No – they're ugly.' His face screwed up in distaste; he wriggled off the chair and solemnly walked the length of the counter, Alvarez and an assistant now following him with intense seriousness. 'I like that – and that – and that. And that thing there – the one like the inside of a shell . . .'

It was beyond my imaginings, the old man and the child together picking the daintily printed cottons, the sprigged and dotted muslins, the fine lawns and batistes. It could have been a trousseau for a bride and was completely incongruous for my position at Landfall.

While Alvarez was directing one of the assistants up on a ladder to pull down yet another roll of cloth, I leaned close to Andrew and whispered, 'Mr Maxwell, I *can't* allow it. It's preposterous! Who ever saw a governess tricked out in things like these? I'd have to work ten years to pay for them. Have you forgotten who I am? Are you trying to turn me into some kind of peacock?'

'And what if I am?' He shouted the words at me, and I fell back in my chair in shock. 'And who said anything about payment?' His third glass of rum was on the counter beside him; he was almost sulky, the way Duncan sometimes was when he was thwarted in some desire. 'Can't a man have some pleasure in his life? I don't like looking at drabs . . .' He broke off, looking up sharply at a thin, elderly man with a stylishly waxed beard and moustache who had approached and was bowing to me. 'Well, Rodriguiz,' Andrew said grumpily, 'still overpricing everything, I see.'

'Ah, Mr Maxwell, still with your little joke. Miss McIntyre, welcome to our establishment. And as for our prices, Mr Maxwell, you know well that quality has never been cheap. Value for money, always, as your good lady wife knows through her dealings here over the years.'

'You talk too much, Rodriguiz. Well – I suppose it's business.' Andrew waved his stick to indicate the whole shop. 'You're carrying some pretty fancy lines. There must be some who are still spending, despite all this talk of emancipation. We'll all be paupers then . . .'

'You're doing some spending yourself, Mr Maxwell. You can't believe much in emancipation. And yes, there's still money on San Cristóbal, praise be. We've been trading for two hundred years on rum and sugar, and I don't believe it will all come to an end tomorrow.'

'We've traded out of those black skins,' Andrew said, pointing at a young Negro woman who was dusting counters and carrying glasses used by other customers to the back of the shop. 'When that stops – when they've the right to turn their backs on us except for pay, then we're all finished.'

Rodriguiz bowed again, a faint, unbelieving smile trying to stretch his thin lips. 'Then may that day be far off, both for Rodriguiz and for Landfall.' He turned to me, cutting off the discussion. 'Any assistance you need, Miss McIntyre, I am entirely at your disposal.' And then he sauntered to one of the many arched doorways that gave on to the street, hands behind his back, bowing and nodding to almost every white person who passed, a man as dependent as any on all the black ones whose presence he didn't even seem to see.

I turned back from my study of him because Andrew once more was violently rejecting something which a young woman was offering. She was a handsome, haughty young thing, in her early twenties I guessed, with a skin that was almost white and hair that was a lustrous and straight black. Because of her skin colour – an octoroon, I thought – she qualified to wait on white customers, and might have been used by Rodriguiz to tempt his male customers to purchases they wouldn't have thought of making. Rodriguiz seemed that kind.

But now Andrew was waving his stick in violent rejection of what she was offering us – an array of corsets, all ribboned and embroidered. 'No, she doesn't want any of that kind of thing. Doesn't need 'em. For God's sake, *look* at her, woman. You want to bundle her into those stupid things, so she'll have the vapours.'

'I *am* looking, Mr Maxwell,' the girl replied, with a cheeky toss of her head. 'I can't imagine Miss McIntyre wearing an evening gown without something of this kind . . .'

Andrew saw the picture at once, perhaps remembered his wife in the evenings, her high-pointed breasts thrust up by the lightly boned bodices. 'Yes – yes, I understand. Well, go ahead . . .'

'It will be necessary to try them, sir . . .' Andrew was still grumbling over the waste of time as I was escorted upstairs by the young woman to one of the fitting rooms that opened on to the upper gallery of Rodriguiz. No customers sat up here; the louver doors were open for air and a large screen protected the modesty of the customers should one of the assistants happen to pass.

The girl knew as well as Alvarez what my position was at Landfall; except for colour, I had fewer advantages than she as far as money was concerned. She dealt with me with a kind of realistic arrogance that acknowledged both her position and mine.

'A lucky one, you,' she said, as she tried the first of the corsets. 'Mr Maxwell's in a buying mood.' She nodded towards me in the mirror. 'Well, at least you've got something to put into a corset . . . You should see some of the ones that come here expecting us to make them sprout bosoms by magic. Mr Maxwell, he'd appreciate that kind of thing. Lucky for you Mrs Maxwell didn't come. Lucky for me, too. She looks at the cost of everything three times and expects her discount, and then there's no commission for me.'

'I can't discuss my employers,' I said, an angry flush mounting in my face. And yet I was helpless before the girl's insouciant humour. We were both dealing with the whim of an old man, and she wasn't unfriendly. She just knew who I was and what I counted for.

'No, wiser you don't,' she answered, and laughed with a flash of marvellous teeth against the café-au-lait skin. 'You play it well, Miss McIntyre. No talk – no trouble.' She frowned critically into the mirror. 'Look, I've something that will suit you better than this even. Might as well have the most. Wait – I won't be long. Shall I send something to drink up here?'

'No . . .' She was gone swiftly, with a rustle of skirts, a young beauty helplessly trapped in her colour and making the most of what there was. I guessed that Rodriguiz wasn't her only source of commission.

She took longer than she had promised, and I sat on a cane chair behind the screen and closed my eyes for relief from the excitement and chaos of the last hour, the varying emotions, the shock of knowing that here I was treated as some kind of upper servant to whom an ageing employer had taken a fancy and to whom everything in the shop was available. I had an uneasy feel-

ing that they half-believed that I was Andrew Maxwell's mistress; I
was grateful for the first time that Maria was a beauty, and therefore the idea less likely.

The door opened softly and the young black woman who had
been dusting downstairs was suddenly before me, a tall glass of
lime juice on a tray. 'Miss Charlotte, who wait on you, she say
bring drink. And gentleman downstairs, he send this note.'

'Gentleman – you mean Mr Maxwell?'

I sipped the drink, and she shrugged, her expression blank and
vacant, as if, like most of her kind, she took refuge behind feigned
ignorance. 'I don't know name – he just put it on tray as I come upstairs . . . He ask if only one lady up here.'

I reached for the note, puzzled. It was written on a Rodriguiz
sales slip, as if it had been scribbled at the counter in a great hurry.
There was no signature, just an indecipherable jumble of initials. I
read it and knew at once that it was not meant for me.

'*Savanna Trader stands off S.F. tomorrow night.*'

I refolded the note and laid it back on the tray. Before I could
explain to the girl that there had been a mistake, the door was
flung open violently, with no preliminary knock. Rodriguiz himself
burst in, his face under the waxed beard and moustache was tight
with fury. He took no notice of my state of half-undress, as if there
was something of far greater importance to him that simply blanked
out what I looked like.

'A thousand pardons, Miss McIntyre. I'm afraid you've been
bothered by this stupid girl here, who has instructions never to
approach any customers. Stupid, all of them.' Almost as a reflex
he gave her a blow across the face that sent her reeling back and
seemed to leave an imprint even on that dark skin.

'Really, Mr Rodriguiz!' I protested. I was playing now at an
instinctive game of holding him off. Something was much more
wrong than the fact that a slave had come into my presence without
permission. 'The girl was simply bringing me a drink which apparently Miss Charlotte had instructed her to bring. There can be
no harm, surely . . .'

'The note,' he said, his hand reaching to snatch it from the
tray. I was quicker. I held the slip of paper there and smiled innocently.

'Why? – is this some message from Mr Maxwell? He must
be growing impatient. As a matter of fact, I didn't notice it and
the girl didn't say anything.' I lifted it and started to unfold
it.

'You have not read it?' Rodriguiz demanded. He was desperately striving for his composure, the urbane air he affected.

I smiled again, looking vague and blinking, as if I couldn't imagine what the fuss might be about. 'Why, no – I only just had time to sip the drink, which was most welcome – it grows very hot doesn't it, Mr Rodriguiz, in the town towards midday. Was the note not for me, then? In that case, you must certainly take it to whomever it was intended for.' I relinquished my hold, smiling, and then as if remembering that I was sitting there in a corset and shift, made a movement to throw my blouse about my shoulders. All the time I looked beyond Rodriguiz to the black girl who had brought the drink and the note. We both knew I had lied; I wasn't sure why I had done it myself, except that I had the feeling that I now knew something that I or any other outsider was not supposed to know. I could see the face of the black girl melt in a kind of relief. It would not be she, either, who told that I had read the note; she was already in enough trouble for having brought it to me without permission.

Rodriguiz was bowing, his expression relaxed somewhat, but I wasn't absolutely sure he believed me.

'A mistake,' he said. 'Simply a customer who believed it was some other lady upstairs.' He warmed to his explanation. 'Rodriguiz is something of a hub for town business, you understand. Many people make appointments to meet here, or discuss business that has nothing to do with us. Of course we don't mind – ' He spread his hands. 'The more people come into the shop, the more goods I sell. Forgive the intrusion, Miss McIntyre. You are most gracious. And, yes, I believe you are quite right. Mr Maxwell does seem to be growing impatient. I'll send Miss Charlotte up at once.' He bowed himself out, and I was left sipping the drink and thinking about what had happened. I was startled again by the sudden appearance of the black girl, who had come along the outside gallery and paused fleetingly in the doorway.

'Psst!' She was dark as a shadow against the glare outside. 'No mistake. The man ask if there is lady upstairs. I say only one. He give me the note to take. I didn't know it not for you. Good thing you say Mr Rodriguiz you not read it. I get more beating. He beat if I do something – he beat if I not do it. You good to keep your mouth shut – '

She suddenly vanished from the doorway on silent feet, as if her ears, keener than mine, had heard Miss Charlotte's step. The young woman bustled in, her arms piled with more corsets.

'I'm sorry,' she said. She was panting, as if she had run up the stairs, and her own stays were far too tightly laced. 'Mr Maxwell is putting on a turn down there. Hurry . . . hurry . . . He wants everything done in five minutes . . .'

'You've become busy down there, then?' I said. 'There are a lot of customers?'

She snorted. 'Here, slip this on. I think it's the kind for you.' Then as she laced me she answered my question. 'Busy? – we haven't had such a quiet day for weeks. Mr Maxwell is still the only customer on the drapery side. My commissions are going to be small enough today. Over next door – the provision side, is packed with men, buying whatever they buy – bolts, screws, flour. Nothing in that for me. The little boy's gone over there and he keeps bringing his papa things he wants to buy, but Mr Maxwell, he isn't moving from his chair . . .'

Her chatter continued as we raced through the business of selecting what we thought the best. But my mind wasn't on the business and I let her make the final selection. If Andrew Maxwell and Duncan were still the only customers in the drapery side, then whoever had sent the note had assumed that it could only have been Maria Maxwell upstairs. The note had been meant for her, and somehow Rodriguiz had found out the mistake and come running, ready to cover both for Maria and whomever had sent it. I worried the question as I dressed again quickly. I was sweating, but not because of the heat, as I ran down the stairs again to Andrew.

His humour, as Miss Charlotte had warned me, had suffered a reverse. Before he had been jovial in his rudeness, but now he had tired of the whole thing. He had bought Duncan a model ship and a silver studded harness for his pony that was an absurd luxury for a child. He had visibly wearied, and I saw that a whole jug of rum now stood beside him. I was told to give the size of shoes and riding boots I needed, and a selection of bonnets was to be sent with the rest of the purchases. I was not permitted time now to try any.

'Just send a lot,' Andrew ordered. 'What we don't like we'll just send back. And have the whole lot waiting at the Royal by the time we have finished lunch. See that it's there, Alvarez. I won't wait.'

'But, of course, Mr Maxwell.'

Andrew began to heave himself from the chair. 'There's just one other thing,' I said.

Irritably, 'Well, what is it?'

'Oatmeal,' I said.

Alvarez clasped his hands together as if the thought were ecstasy.

'Oatmeal – but of course. If you would just step next door into the provisions department . . . there are many things that might interest you, Mr Maxwell. New delicacies we are importing all the time, as well as, of course, the general rations for the slaves . . .'

But Andrew was staring at me in wonder. 'God's blood, girl, what in the world do you want oatmeal for? Is this some foolish cosmetic fad? Leave your complexion alone – it's white enough for any man's taste.'

'It isn't a cosmetic I'm thinking of, Mr Maxwell. It's Duncan's breakfast. Have you ever heard of a Scot growing up without oatmeal for his breakfast?'

Momentarily his good humour returned. 'Oatmeal? Of course – oatmeal! Don't know if it's ever been cooked at Landfall. My mother must have cooked it last when Fergus was young. Yes – oatmeal. The child needs it!'

'I don't want it,' Duncan wailed. 'I don't like the sound of it.'

'Alvarez – send oatmeal.' Andrew struggled to his feet, aided by Alvarez and an assistant. Rodriguiz had not reappeared. 'And you,' he said to Duncan, 'will do as you are told. You will mind what Miss Fiona says, and you will have oatmeal for breakfast.'

Alvarez helped Andrew into the carriage, and me, with considerably less deference. I glanced back as we drove off, and Alvarez was standing in the sun watching us, wiping the perspiration from his forehead, with the desperate air of a man who doesn't know whether to smile for the business he has done or shake his fist for the insults he has endured. I felt almost the same way about the treasures that had tumbled into my lap that morning, and knew the growing conviction that some price, not money, would be exacted for them.

Alister was waiting dutifully at the Royal for us, and we lunched on the upstairs gallery, which gave directly on to the town square and the whole line of the waterfront, with the vessels riding at anchor, some of the bigger ones out in the harbour, others moored to the piers themselves, taking in and discharging cargo. The gallery of the Royal was as near to a club as anything I had ever experienced; everyone knew everyone else. There were few women, and I felt the many glances, and in some cases the frank stares, directed at me. Andrew grumpily returned a few greetings and didn't encourage anyone to linger by our table; there was one exception though – a grizzled man, older than Andrew, a retired sea captain who was now a ships' chandler in Santa Marta. Mal-

colm Gordon was his name, and his knowledge of Andrew seemed
to run far into the past. They had that sort of unwordy acceptance
of each other. He was invited to join us.

'Well, ye've turned a head or two, Miss McIntyre,' was his
greeting to me. 'A young and handsome female new in Santa
Marta has all us old coots fidgeting in our chairs. Dinna have
much else to do these days. This middle of the day lot – we're all
past much less but looking. 'Tis in the evening the young ones
come, and then no ladies will be here.'

'If you've a notion, Gordon, you're talking to a lady – and
you're right about that – then keep a decent tongue in your head.
Or I'll be telling you to find your own table,' Andrew said.

'Aye, Maxwell – pleasant as always. And right, too. I forget
how to talk to ladies these days.'

Andrew ordered lunch without consulting any of us, and a jug
of rum. 'Quit the cackle, Gordon, and stick to what you know.
What's in the harbour? How's business? Is anyone making any
money?'

'Aye, money's still being made, and everyone looking for a good
harvest. There's lots o' talk about this emancipation business, but
most think it's only talk.' He made a sweeping gesture at the
harbour. 'Well, look for yourself, man! Look at that line of craft –
does it look like there's business? Busy as any time I've known. Bigger ships coming in too. There's the *Lady Beatrice* loading these
two days by tender and full to the decks – she'll go with this evening's tide. This is the fifth time this year the *Josephine* has been in.
She and the Yankee ship out there, *Savannah Trader*, will go with
the morning tide . . .'

I spent my lunch hour absently attending to the conversation,
keeping Duncan in order, but staring mostly at the graceful vessel
that rode well out from the piers in the deep water. She would leave
with the morning's tide, Captain Gordon said. But the scrawled
note had said she would stand off – where? – tomorrow night S.F.
If the note had been intended for Maria then I knew. Tomorrow
night the *Savannah Trader* would stand off San Francisco. Why?
There was no answer in the faces about me. Rodriguiz knew,
but Andrew did not; I would have been ready to swear that he did
not.

5

The spirit of gaiety and adventure was gone, and we drove back
to Landfall in a mood of irritability that bordered on depression. All

Andrew's store of strength had been used; he had eaten a huge lunch unwisely in the heat, and drank heavily, but I thought it was not merely the discomfort of the meal and the drink that showed, but actual pain; for the first time, as I covertly studied his face as we jounced over the island's roads, I saw the pallor of grey beneath the weather-beaten and burned skin. Often he shifted his bulk uncomfortably; beside me, Duncan had lost interest in the model ship and had fallen asleep, leaning heavily against me; once he opened his eyes as we hit a particularly deep rut. Then his hand stole into mine as if seeking some comfort he could not ask for; I kept it there, our palms moist against each other. I sat upright, supporting Duncan's weight, looking out of the window at the endless cane fields that seemed to blur before my eyes. It was very hot; the fine *broderie Anglaise* was crushed and rumpled, and it stuck to my back wetly where I leaned against the leather cushions. The journey back seemed longer than I remembered. I stiffened my body against the desire to slump, to succumb to the weariness. Then finally I turned to the two other occupants of the carriage. Alister, who had taken the sunny side, had tilted his hat to relieve the glare on his eyes; under the shadow cast by the brim, I found his eyes fixed on me. intent, thoughtful, speculative. Quickly I looked from him to Andrew. His gaze, too, was rooted on me and Duncan, the crumpled mass of we two together; for a moment his lips twitched, but there was no way to tell if it had been the beginning of a smile or a grimace of pain. I turned back to the cane fields, and Duncan's head fell forward against my breast. I held him there, letting him sleep on in this attitude of babyhood again, letting him dream his dream until this seemingly interminable journey should be over.

The only thing that marked any stage of the journey was the sight of a solitary horseman at a point on the road where we had passed the junctions that led to any of the plantations except Landfall, San Francisco and Winterslo. The man put his hand to his hat in the barest gesture of recognizing a fellow-traveller on a lonely road. He said nothing. Andrew gave no sign of recognition at all; he stared at him with glazed eyes, as if he were no more important than a thousand men he might have seen on the streets of Santa Marta. But strangers did not come this way. Only the three isolated plantations lay beyond.

It was then I began to wonder if Maria had received her message after all.

It was long past the hour of siesta when we reached Landfall, but gratefully I obeyed Andrew's orders to retire until dinner.

There was no sign of Maria. Duncan's voice echoed plaintively
through the rooms as he called for her to come and see his silver
harness. But she was not there to answer, and his lip drooped. He
was taken by Juanita, and I heard his voice, petulant and complaining, as his sweat-soaked clothes were removed and he was prepared for his rest. Another thing I heard as Andrew pulled himself
up the stairs on Dougal's arm. It was a whisper of pain, as if he
did not mean to give it utterance, but it escaped him. 'God damn
her – oh, God damn that she-devil.' And then, 'Dougal, bring my
medicine. The strong one.'

I slept heavily, and it was Charity who shook me awake. 'Come
now, mistress. It late already.'

I bathed in the midst of what should have been the happy
chaos of the day's purchases. Charity purred with pleasure over
the things, and I wondered at her – she in her coarse cotton, her
wiry hair bound in the white handkerchief, fingering with un-
feigned delight what she could herself never possess, relishing them
in a kind of triumph.

'You sure set that ole man on his ear, mistress. Now you be
fine – like her. Now I be proud when you go downstairs. The
mistress not the only one now . . .' The plump brown face beamed
with satisfaction. 'Here, you put on one o' des new corset . . .'

Then she brought out the green dimity dress, freshly laundered,
limper than ever. But it had changed. In place of the high neck
with the little tight collar, the whole top had been cut away almost
as far back as the shoulders. It was cut very low, and a trimming
of ruffled lace gave a bare sense of decency.

'Charity, what has happened? I didn't tell you to do this.' But
she had it over my head and my protest was muffled.

'It wear out,' she answered, with half truth. 'When it washed it
all come apart. Best we could do with it.'

I was angry, wondering by whose orders this had been done,
feeling the outrage of being manipulated by an old man's spite
against his wife. 'And the lace. Where did the lace come from?'

'The mistress give it.' Yes, I thought, as she must have been
forced by Andrew to 'give' the *broderie Anglaise* last night. Then
I turned back to the mirror and saw my reflection. It could have
been that I had never seen myself before. The cleverly cut corset
gave all the advantages it had been intended to; the low cut of
the dress was almost indecent to my eyes unused to the sight of
myself this way. Charity's quick hands were already at work on
my hair.

'Charity, I can't wear this! It's – it's shameful!'

'It's all you got to wear,' she answered cheerfully. My hair was going higher, pulled and twisted and puffed. What was nearly a lady of fashion looked back at me. 'You got something to fill a bodice like that, you wear it,' she added fiercely, tugging at my hair. 'What you afraid of? You white, mistress – you beautiful to a white man. Everything here to take. You put your hand out for nothin', you get nothin'. So you wear yor pretty dress and you put out yor hand. 'Cause you get nothin' settin' like a mouse . . .'

But it was like a mouse I crept downstairs, hoping to be the first in the salon, hoping to find the seat farthest from the light and the gaze of the others. I thought I had done it; I was halfway across the room before Andrew spoke. He was seated as if he also wanted to avoid the light, away at the far end of the room, near the open doors and the smell of the garden.

'Splendid!' he said. His voice sounded oddly weak. 'Come sit here by me, girl. It's been a hard day.' And then when I came to the chair he had indicated, he nodded slowly, with satisfaction, almost like Charity's. His look was quite without the half-leer I had expected; it was dispassionate, detached. The pupils of his eyes were dilated. He did not seem drunk, but the customary glass was close at hand.

He said a strange thing then. 'We will have company now. Now Fergus will come.'

I accepted the drink he offered, because I had to have courage to face the others. And I sat silently there in the growing darkness with him, experiencing almost a sense of comradeship and yet wondering why he had said that now Fergus would come.

4

The next morning, as soon as Maria had taken Duncan for the usual ride, he quivering with excitement over using the new harness, I walked with a purpose for the first time towards the coves that lay on the lee shore, past the Serpent Rocks. I wasn't sure where I was going, or how I would know if I ever reached the place, but I was going to find a bay belonging to the plantation of San Francisco where a ship might lie. I followed the paths that Andrew had indicated; they grew wilder and more overgrown as I went. I could not use Kronberg now as my guide, because the sight of it was lost by the trees crowding here. I did not want to take the road that led out of Landfall, the one where the signposts pointed to Winterslo and San Francisco. That might have been, in the end, the easier way. But I had no excuse to be there on that hot dusty road by myself, among the cane fields; I would not risk skirting the greathouse of San Francisco itself. I had too vivid a memory of Alister's description of a sharp-eyed old woman with a gun who sat on the gallery and did not welcome strangers. So I went on in the heat in the direction Andrew had indicated, and the jungle-like growth gave way to drier, more scrubby land, and Kronberg once again appeared. I did not know whose land this was, or if it had ever been thought worth cultivating. I emerged at a kind of a headland that seemed to form the last of the Serpents, and there, below me, was the first of the coves.

It was unexpected; I had only Andrew's description and it had not prepared me for the sheer perfection of the place. Suddenly from the headland I looked down on the dazzle of the almost white sand, lined with sea grapes and almond trees; the sapphire shallows were like glass, wavelets, a bare inch high, lapped the shore. Few strong tides would ever touch this place; a line of sea debris marked their farthest reach – pieces of wood, seaweed, coconut shells. There were tracks across the sand, the webbed feetmarks of birds, long trailing lines that could have been made by crabs. But it seemed to me then that no human foot had ever touched this virgin sand. It was enchantment – it was primitive, lost paradise. Huge-mouthed pelicans swooped for fish, gulls cried, overhead a hawk hovered, waiting, watching, the 'John Crow' scavenger bird of the islands. For a few minutes I stood still, entranced, given over to the magic of it, to the peace in the midst of its teeming life of bird and fish and lizard and lowly ant. I, who had lived by the sea all my life, for the first time knew the feeling that it would have been a heady intoxication to tear off my clothes and plunge my body into that warmly receiving water. I knew why Andrew did not come this way any more. It was a place of innocence, and youth and strength — all lost to him now.

After a while I remembered why I had come. I had to plough across the sand and then climb to the next small headland – another cove, much as the one I had left, and the water more inviting as the sun grew hotter. Yet another scramble, this time making my way around comparatively level rocks; another cove, and there at the far end a massive headland, and something – at this distance I could not see very clearly through the scrub that overgrew it – the semblance of some buildings.

My breath was labouring, and I was tired by the time I gained the top of the headland and the first signs of the buildings. Here, under the sprawl of vine and thorny scrub springing from pockets of wind-blown soil, I could see the traces of level, man-made floors. But I didn't go on at once, because from here, also, for the first time, I glimpsed two houses. They were set back, on the slopes above cane fields, the farther one hardly visible, the nearer one so massive that even at this far distance I could feel its overwhelming presence. It could only be San Francisco, and that dusty white speck set on a far ridge, several bays over, would be Winterslo.

The headland where I stood narrowed to a long spit of land that hooked around its bay like a long, protective boom. Beneath the scraggle of the pervasive growth I could just discern the outline of what must once have been the ramparts of a fort-like building. And everything about me declared that this had once been the outpost of the first protection of Santa Marta harbour. Any ship approaching from the east would have had to round the Serpents and fall into line of the guns that must have been mounted here, and those from the south and west could not make the harbour without being seen and the signal sent. San Cristóbal had been a way-station on the treasure route from Central America to Spain. This warren of crumbling lava-rock beneath my feet had served its purpose to guard and protect, and the mansion on the hill behind had been part of the great Spanish presence in these islands – shrunken and all but gone.

Like the grandeur of Spain, this too had gone. Sea grapes grew in roofless rooms, vines smothered the crumbled walls, walls that were so covered with lichen they were nearly indiscernible from the sea rock itself. Lizards scurried from my path as I scrambled over the broken walls, birds started up before me, shrieking. I saw places where iron had fallen – gates, window bars, even huge cannon, and were now mere rust stains on the white sand. I stared down into rooms deep in the ground that must once have been dungeons. I felt the impress of the Spaniards here, striving to hold the land against the many invaders; even under that burning sun it was gloomy, with the indefinable stench of decay, almost the smell of things that had happened here, men dying, or being put to death, and the rampant vegetation taking it all back, remorseless, unstoppable. I did not like the place, but before I left it I believed I had found what I had come seeking.

There was one room that would once have faced upon the beach itself, but now was almost screened by the sea grapes. It was the first floor of what had been a taller building; the higher walls were nearly gone, but the stone floor which formed the roof of the lower room was still sound. Nothing marked it from the rest except that through the sea grapes I caught the glimmer of new metal, and when I had pushed my way through, instead of the open, gaping doorways that had greeted me everywhere, here was a stout, good wooden door, with new heavy hinges and locks; high up in the wall was a single air hole, and there, too, the bars had been renewed, not the rusted stumps I had seen elsewhere. There was no sound from within – no movement. But everywhere here in the sand I could see the footprints; there were those who wore boots, and those, as always, who were barefooted. I looked back at the perfect calm of the bay, the hooking headland that guarded it, the narrow passage with no ripples to mark hidden rocks, and I thought that if the *Savannah Trader* had a rendezvous here, there was no place more fitting. It was the first time I had a premonition of danger, and I turned and scrambled across those perilously rotting walls, over the farthest ramparts, and slithered, panting, back into the bay by which I had approached the fortifications. When I had gained my breath I took the first path that led back in the direction of Landfall and the Serpents. I no longer had the time to scramble from cove to cove, nor would I now, after what I had seen, expose myself at each headland to a possible watcher on the gallery of the San Francisco greathouse. I felt I must now be on San Francisco land; tracks led through fields of thin cane, weeds growing almost as high as the cane itself, the scrub starting to invade. But there were no slaves at work in the fields here; I saw no one. I kept heading towards Landfall at a stumbling run, and I was near exhaustion by the time the welcome shade of the great trees came, and then the cleared paths and the cultivated gardens.

I went around past the stable yard, up the back way, hoping that Maria would not be in the office. Juanita saw me from the kitchen, but I was past and round the bend of the back stairs before she could do more than come to the doorway to get a better look. Duncan was halfway through his lunch in the schoolroom, his mouth drooping because he had been left alone.

'I went for a walk and got lost,' I said, as I gulped a glass of water. It wasn't right to be making explanations to a pupil, but Juanita would ask him when she took him to his siesta.

'You've been over on the bays on the other side,' he said.

'How do you know?'

'Sand,' he answered. 'The Serpent bays are all rocks. Your clothes are full of sand.'

I sighed and nodded, knowing that soon every slave in the household, and Maria also, would know that I had sand in my clothes.

But it was Andrew who brought it up at dinner that evening. 'So you got over to the lee shore, did you?'

'I hardly meant to go so far – I was curious, after what you had told me. But I got lost on the way back . . .'

'Should have asked for a horse,' he grunted. 'Don't go wandering about in the heat. The sun is more deadly than you know, Miss Fiona. But the bays . . . what did you think?'

I sighed, and made myself remember only the first of them, recalling the enchantment, the peace, the beauty. 'I think it was the first round the point from the Serpents,' I answered dreamily. 'It was so beautiful I couldn't believe it. I just sat there under the trees. I kept very quiet, and watched the birds . . .'

'It was a long walk,' Maria observed, with her usual cool civility.

'Not for a Scottish governess,' I answered, forcing a smile: 'In Scotland most families expect governesses to walk with their charges at least two hours every day. It's called "hardening them up" or "getting plenty of fresh air". Most times it's just cold, wet air, Mrs Maxwell. Yes, I'm used to walking . . . I've done it all my life. It's natural to me now. Just as the siesta is here.'

'Next time take a horse,' Andrew said. 'The heat can be a killer, girl. And don't ride alone. You don't know what you can run into. I'll send for Fergus –'

'Fergus has his own concerns,' Maria observed. 'As he keeps saying, Winterslo is very demanding of his time.'

'I don't want to cause any inconvenience,' I mumbled, feeling my face blaze. 'It's much easier to just go down to the Serpent side . . .'

'Much easier,' Maria agreed.

Alister broke in with his cool drawl. 'I'll be delighted to escort you any time you wish to ride, Miss Fiona.' And then with a quizzical look at Maria. 'But we will remember not to intrude on Donna Isabella's peace.'

Now Maria's eyes flashed. 'Forgive me for my seeming neglect of your entertainment, Alister. A visit to San Francisco must certainly be arranged. Any time . . . but I, like Fergus, have my duties . . .'

'Oh, enough!' Andrew said impatiently. 'San Francisco isn't worth a visit. That old witch over there and the scarecrow daughters aren't worth any man's time . . .'

I sighed and leaned back in my chair, away from the light of the candles. Andrew was showing his drink, and the smell of the sweet tobacco was all about the room; it was the usual night at Landfall.

But it was not quite the usual night. Sleep had never come easily at Landfall; the tropical night is not a peaceful one, and now, as the days grew hotter and the air stiller, the heat stayed trapped even within those high, shaded rooms. But this night I waited, not for sleep, but for some sound that might tell me that indeed it was San Francisco bay to which the *Savannah Trader* would come, and that it was Maria who would go to unlock that strong new door in the ruins of the fortifications.

But one does not go through the whole night without sleep; many times I slipped into an uneasy doze and woke with a start. But what did I listen for? – what did I expect to hear? I didn't know; and I should also have known that it wasn't my concern.

But after these weeks I knew now the approach of dawn long before the first cries of the cocks. By then I could stand my sweat-soaked bed no longer. It was still dark when I went out on to the gallery. My bare feet made no sound; in the darkness there is the instinct to walk on tiptoe. I kept close to the railing to avoid the chairs scattered about. The scents of the jasmine and honeysuckle were strong. As I passed Andrew's room I heard the sound of his heavy snoring; had this been one of his times for 'the strong medicine' as he called it, or had the heavy rum drinking of the night before carried him long past the time of his usual waking? I went round to the back of the house, the side of the stables and the way to the lee shore. What did I wait for? I didn't know. But I leaned against one of the pillars, half-seated on the railing, as Fergus had been. The dark blue started to drain from the night sky, and the paler, predawn colour came to replace it. A little while longer and that mystical moment of the dawn in the tropics would be upon us. I closed my eyes, and for a few seconds the whole still universe about me seemed to hold its breath.

In that time I almost missed her. With nerves raw and taut, perhaps I sensed rather than heard any sound. She moved with the lightness of a cat from the deep shadows of the trees across the open space of the driveway to the back steps of the house. I pressed back against the pillar and I had only those few seconds to be sure that a figure actually moved there. A slim young boy she looked like, in tight black Spanish trousers and jacket. The brim of the Cordoban hat kept her face completely hidden until one brief moment when she looked up. No one but Maria had those perfect, chiselled cheekbones, that long sweep of neck, that particular set of the head upon the shoulders.

Did she check for a second, as if she saw me? – or was it my own sudden intake of breath? But noiselessly she moved on and up the steps and was lost on the gallery below me.

I remained frozen there, pressed against the pillar. And then abruptly I woke to my own situation. Already Maria would be making her way into the house and towards the stairs. In a kind of agony of deliberately slow movement, I felt my way back along the railing; turned the corner, heard once more Andrew's snores. The jasmine and honeysuckle crushed wetly between my groping fingers, giving off their strong perfume. I blessed the change in the light in these last minutes; I could now see the outlines of the chairs and, more important, the half-open door to my own room. I was there at last, gasping, shutting it with shaking fingers and not daring to push home the bolts lest the sound be heard by Maria. Inside it was still dark. I caught my toe in the edge of the woven grass matting, and almost fell. The bed received me like a haven. I turned my face into the pillows and spread my arms as though at the end of a night of restless dreams. And with every nerve I listened; there, on the other side of the landing, in the second of cessation between Andrew's snores, I heard what I had waited for, the faintest click of a door opening and closing. Either she had not seen me in that one brief upward glance, or she knew that I must already have abandoned my post. Maria would never betray herself by making a scene.

The beating of my heart slowed at last. Then the sleep that my outraged nerves and brain demanded fell upon me; I woke to Charity's hand on my shoulder and the bright sun streaming in at the slatted louvers.

'You sleep like you was dead, mistress.'

2

If, indeed, Fergus had been bidden by Andrew to come to Landfall, he, as he had done on the day of my arrival about the command to come to the dockside, chose not to obey. I did not hear any more from Andrew about Fergus coming. I just knew, without reason, that I wanted him to come. After the expedition to Santa Marta a quietness settled on the household, but for me there was no serenity in it. It was like the stillness of a cease-fire; we were quiet, but not at peace. The days passed, and Maria gave no hint that she knew that I had seen her return to Landfall in that dawn; she was civil to me when she encountered me, but most of the time she seemed not to notice me. I never made up my mind whether this was a genuine preoccupation with other things or a studied insult. For her, I almost was not there. Alister continued his comings and goings, either riding the roads around the estate or making the day-long trip into Santa Marta; he also continued his sessions in the estate office, alone or with Maria or Fellowes. His good manners preserved a pretence of normalcy at dinner each evening. A few times, quietly, beyond Maria's hearing, he complimented me on my appearance. I would smile and thank him, knowing it was simply part of his effort to make me happy at Landfall, but what he said didn't bring the glow of pleasure it had been meant to do. I knew what I wanted, and it was to hear those words from Fergus; but he did not come. So I grew bored with the endless trying on of the new dresses made by the Landfall seamstress from the materials that had come in such quantities from Rodriguiz. I stopped protesting about the low necks of the gowns for the evening. I accepted anything and everything because none of it was part of me. I would leave them all behind when I left Landfall.

Andrew seemed less evident than before. Not often now was there a return to the vigour of some of our first exchanges; less often did I hear him pace the gallery in the moments before sunrise. 'Master not well,' was all that Charity would answer to my inquiries. I could not ask Maria about her husband; this was many of the things not said between us.

Despite her shrug and laugh, though, I asked, and received permission to go into the kitchen to instruct in the making of oatmeal. At first Duncan refused it, and then I began to mix a little honey with it as it was served, and he accepted it. Andrew, often at a loss for something to say to a child so removed in years from him, would tweak his ear in passing, 'Having your oatmeal, eh, boy? That's good – that's good!' and would shuffle on, not waiting for an answer.

I saw him roused, though, to attention one day as he sat on the outer gallery. Duncan had just returned from his morning ride with his mother, and we waited for the call to lunch in the schoolroom. Duncan was hopping from one square of black and white marble to another, chanting softly to himself, 'Fulodden – Cuflodden – Glencoe . . .'

Andrew stirred, as if some lost-past memory had returned to him. 'Flodden – Culloden,' he corrected automatically. 'You're learning about your people at last, laddie. I know all those names – the way my mother taught them to me. You come from a strong, hardy people, boy, and never you forget it. When I'm gone, you've to remember, always, that you're a Maxwell.'

During lunch Duncan stared at me apprehensively, stammering a little over the question, apprehensive, wondering.

'Do you think Papa is going to die? I heard Juanita say to Flora that he – '

'We are all going to die, Duncan, some day. Never listen to gossip.'

'But *soon*,' he persisted. 'They think he will die soon.'

'Your papa is getting old, Duncan, even though you are still young.' I had learned the folly of telling half-truths to children, the cruelty of it, the way they always found you out and held it against you.

'But if he died, you'll stay here, won't you?'

'When your papa dies – and that could be a long time from now – you will still have your mama.'

'But *you*?'

'I might be old then myself. I might want to go back to Scotland.'

He scowled. 'I *hate* Scotland. I hate oatmeal, too!'

I walked every morning while Duncan rode with his mother, determined, somehow, to keep the lassitude of the tropics at bay. There was the sense of a struggle between me and the elements; if I softened or gave in, I would be lost. I clung to old habits with a kind of desperation, and Andrew kept telling me not to walk in the sun. But sometimes I was drenched in the sudden rain, too, and watched the steam rising from the baked earth, and I thought of the workers in the cane fields, endlessly moved forward under the lash of the driver, soaked six times a day at this time of year, and drying off under the pitiless sun. I saw them, and more often heard them singing in the fields when I walked, and they were the saddest songs I ever heard, sadder even than the ballads of Scotland, because they were without hope.

Sometimes, though not often, I walked through the slave quarters, empty during the day because fieldhands were away, and noisy only with the sounds of the children. The very young ones were friendly, curious, still smiling when they saw me; the older ones, already set to tasks about the house and garden, depending on their ability, had begun to display the sullen indifference of their parents. They would look at me with blank, impassive gazes, dropping their lids over dark eyes, and it was impossible to do more than offer the morning greeting. This would be answered with the tipping of the ragged straw hat and some slurred response, which could have meant anything. Those children lucky enough to have shown some aptitude were put to work in the house; they were the envy of their brothers and sisters, who were doomed to the endless hoeing and cutting in the cane fields, the endless sun, the endless fear of the lash. Not that the house slaves were exempt from the lash, but they were quicker and cleverer and knew how to conceal their failings. In the fields the weaker dropped behind the line of workers, and the punishment was inevitable.

'Mind you,' Alister once said to me, 'Maria runs a good plantation. It's probable that the slaves are better off under her than they were under Andrew. But that is because she knows their value. When Andrew began, you could always buy more slaves from Africa when yours had been worked to death. It was legal. Now you have to go round the law, buy them from the illicit traders or breed them. Maria, you've noticed, is very careful of her slaves who are with child – gives them privileges that encourage them to become mothers, to keep their children to full term. She excuses them from field work for the last months, and for the first month after the birth. I suppose to most of them here bearing a child must be like a great long gift of rest. Other plantations I've seen . . . well, pregnancy is a curse as well as a burden. Many children are lost. The mothers risk their own lives to get rid of the child . . . There's no marriage of course. Just the offspring of one of the few joys they know . . .'

There was something still rudimentary and essentially Scottish in Alister which showed through the politeness and London veneer at times. We were talking now on a subject that few men of his background would discuss with an unmarried woman, and he did it without embarrassment or fuss. Oddly, we had grown to be friends, and I thought with a little dismay of the time when he would leave Landfall.

'But the children here at Landfall? – do they all stay?'

'They are Maria's by law. They are hers to do with as she wishes.'

'To sell them?'

He answered reluctantly. 'To sell them. To keep them. Whatever suits the economics of the plantation.'

'It's monstrous! It's wrong! *You* can't believe –'

'I didn't say what I believed, Fiona.' It was a mild reproach. 'What I'm telling you *is*. But it is all coming to an end. It will all soon be finished. Wilberforce is old, but his movement is far stronger than one old man. Parliament will finally pass its act – this year, next – some time soon. Emancipation will come to the British colonies. There will be no more holding, or buying, or selling of slaves. No man will own another man, body and soul. Slavery will be dead.'

'And Landfall?'

'Landfall will die too. No plantation owner can afford to *pay* these people to grow sugar cane, now that the British monopoly is dead. Year by year money has to be poured back into the plantations. They do not sustain themselves, even if they pay nothing for the labour. They must meet the price of sugar on the world market. Without slaves they cannot do it. No – Landfall and all its kind will die.'

'Are you sorry?'

'Sorry? – no. Why should I be? My grandfather made a fortune from sugar on estates all over the Indies – a piece here, a piece there, never giving himself the trouble of managing any of them himself, but never financing absentee ownership. The man to whom he lent money had always to be here, watching the cane grow, seeing that the rum and sugar and molasses got on to the first ships available. No Maxwell ever dealt with an overseer. Yes, he made a fortune. I'm not going to deny that fortune or its origin in slavery. But everything comes to an end in its time.'

'And the time is soon?'

'I think the time is very soon. There will be no more Landfalls built – except in the American South. When the slaves are free each will try to cultivate their own little patch, will try to buy the few acres from their former masters. And their masters, lacking every other means to get money, will sell it to them acre by acre. The whole system will crumble. No one knows what will happen to the price of sugar then. All I know, Fiona, is that all this is finished. It is finished.'

'They don't act as if it is finished. Santa Marta – Rodriguiz. No one seems afraid.'

'Because they do not believe that the stroke of midnight is at hand.' It was high noon when Alister said this to me; we had paced a garden walk together, and finally sat on the bench beneath the great cottonwood that faced the house. I looked to its white, dazzling splendour, the dark, cool inner recesses, the distant figure of Andrew on the inner gallery with his rum. It did not seem possible that it was all over. Alister recognized the disbelief in my face.

'Because they can't accept that emancipation is more than a bad dream to disturb their slumbers. They can't believe that a British parliament will set out to kill them, but it will. The moral movement is there, in England, and the profit is going out of sugar. When the two forces combine in sufficient strength, there will be the end of slavery, and the end of Landfall.'

'You don't seem disturbed. You – the Maxwells stand to lose a great deal? Or do I presume?'

'Presume as you wish, Fiona. We have had our time, and our profit. Can we press more blood from these black skins? Can we take more from a man than his life and his soul? I – I for one will see the end of the whole business without regret.'

And then, abruptly, without excuse or farewell, he left me. I remember the tall, elegant figure, marred by his limp, pacing off along the path away from the house. I did not know why he was here, except to preside over a death. I looked back at the house, at the old man there, and thought of the young child riding out with his mother, riding out into a way of life that he thought would last forever. And I was charged, in whatever way I could, with preparing him for the knowledge that it would not be. Alister had charged me with this task without actually speaking the words; Andrew also had said it when, on that first morning at Landfall, he had told me to teach him well. Andrew might close his eyes to it, in every way he could, but he knew, as well as Alister did, that the end was coming.

But I knew what Duncan saw each morning, the row of black, sweating bodies moving ever forward, the rhythm never to be broken, the sting of the lash to give them strength and energy. The task laid upon me seemed more urgent and nearly impossible.

A few times I took again the long walk to the first of the coves beyond the Serpents, on the lee shore; it was, as before, languid, utterly beguiling, with only the glare of the sun on the white powder sand to strike the eyes. Sometimes I took off my boots, hitched up

my skirts and joyously walked the shallows of that blue-green bay;
then I would sit hunched beneath the shade of the sea grapes,
watching the birds, and pondering what was happening at Landfall. Most often I thought of Maria; I thought of the note that
had come to Rodriguiz, of that slender figure passing in the shadows
before dawn into the house. What was I to make of it? Was it an
assignation which was none of my business? I could not imagine
the fastidious Maria making a rendezvous in the humid cellar behind that locked door in San Francisco bay. But then, what did I
know of the passions of a woman like Maria? The exterior was a
careful mask; would I do any good to rip part of it away to expose worse? And what right had I? My first duty was Duncan –
to preserve, to protect, to arm him. For this reason I never spoke
of what I had seen and witnessed to the only person I could have
spoken to, Alister. I believed he would be no part of it; one does
not prematurely topple the structure that one knows is bound to
crash. I clung to the thought that I was here for some purpose,
something to do with Duncan. For this reason I had to survive
and endure, and I would.

More often, on the morning walks, I went to the Atlantic side
– the side that faced on the Serpents. I went, perhaps because it
was closer to the house, perhaps homesick for the wild surge that
reminded me a little of the pound of the waves against the sea wall
at Silkirk. Here, in the wild, wave-dashed cove below the rock where
I had sat with Alister on the night of my humiliation, I seemed to
hear more clearly the voices of home. Here I was not lulled by the
tropical languor, this was not the lotus-land of the dead-calm sea.
Here the final strength of the long Atlantic rollers tumbled into
rocky pools, and my feet felt the sharp sting of the cuts inflicted
by their roughness. I tasted the salt spray on my lips, the dash of
salt to cut through the soggy-sweet veneer that lay on everything
at Landfall. I learned to love the endless swell and crash of the
waves, the backward suck and once again the swell. I learned to
observe the minute things of the sea that inhabited these sun-
warmed pools, the tiny fish, the myriad life that swarmed and
teemed; I grew used to the sight of the hairy leeches clinging to
their rocks, and I even found a pool that was the home of a small
octopus. Once, as I pried and poked with a stick, I saw the slow,
waving tentacles rise – baby tentacles, yet full of menace. Like the
cove on the other side of the Serpents, the San Francisco cove where
the crumbling fortifications held their own sense of horror, I
learned to stay away from this pool also.

It was to this Atlantic cove I came after I heard the news of

Thomas Scobie. I walked on to the outer gallery one day after Duncan had left with Maria, and Alister was seated in a chair near the steps. In his hands he held a letter – that was not unusual. Many letters came to Alister, following him faithfully across the sea as if he were someone that the correspondents could not let go of, even for a brief time. But now he was not reading, just staring ahead at the massed green foliage of the garden, a look of abstraction and doubt on his face that seemed wholly foreign.

'Alister?' I made no attempt to phrase my inquiry discreetly; we had passed that stage with each other. 'Alister – is there something wrong?'

He turned to me slowly, and he was frowning, as if he didn't know how to answer the question. 'Wrong – no, nothing more wrong than is ever wrong.'

I took a chair beside him. 'And what does that mean?'

He touched the letter. 'A friend, Peter Jenkins – he was fighting a by-election near Bristol. Of course the emancipation issue was a big one – Bristol grew rich from the slave trade when it was legal, and there are plenty of pirate ships that bring slaves over still owned by the Bristol men. Well, it wasn't a pretty fight and my friend lost. Oh, we expected to lose, but one must fight these battles regardless of the chances. But that wasn't the tragedy. One of his helpers, someone who went around the villages speaking for him, was killed. It was a mob killing – stoned and kicked to death, and no one to hold responsible for it. No one to bring to justice.' He looked down at the letter again. 'He was a Scot. Thomas Scobie by name. From Glasgow. No education or money – he wasn't well known in the movement. But he puts the rest of us to shame by giving his life for it.'

There was a cold misery in my heart. I wanted to shriek, to cry out that I had known, and I had told him. But I also had known that he would go on to whatever was determined for him, the end that I had already seen. But I could not tell Alister. It was past, and the warning had been useless, as I knew it would, and by malevolent chance the knowledge had followed me all the way to this place and this hour. I wished I had never known what happened to Thomas Scobie. I wished I had never heard his name again. But I had; I had been meant to know about Thomas Scobie. One does not escape.

But I said something. Thomas Scobie had at least the right to the memorial of having his name spoken. 'I once heard Thomas Scobie speak,' I said. 'By chance – in Glasgow. He was the kind who would be . . .' I hesitated. 'A martyr.'

Alister nodded, as if the coincidence didn't seem strange to him. He tapped the letter with impatient fingers. 'I'll be leaving Landfall soon, Fiona. I can't sit here much longer, going over accounts, trying to find the ways, large or petty, that Maria is cheating. I've had enough of endless arguments about slaves and food allowances, and how many yards of cotton the women need each year. There's too much work waiting in England. What's wrong at Landfall is only a tiny part of what's wrong everywhere. And there are men dying to put right what's wrong, and I'm sitting here. Well, a month will see me gone.'

'You'll go back into the family business?'

He sighed. 'Yes – I have to. One needs money to fight battles. One needs influence, and that's all that money is – all it's worth.'

I gave a half-laugh to try to cover my dismay that he would be gone so soon and I would be alone here, facing Maria. 'You'll have other responsibilities, I'm thinking, Alister. You'll not remain a bachelor forever.'

He shrugged. 'You know, one can stay a bachelor too long, looking for the right woman. And then suddenly you find no one will have you – that is, no one you want. I haven't seen my chances when they've come, and I don't know them until they're gone. I'm a very plain man, Fiona, and, with women, sometimes a shy man. I've always been apprehensive of great beauties – they demand so much, as if beauty was all they needed to give. What I want to do in life needs a certain kind of woman. She would have to be someone who knew what I was about, and believed in it. Someone who would understand neglect, and long hours, and sometimes a boring social life cultivating people who don't interest her for what they may do to help. Your little misses of seventeen bore *me*, and the ones who might know better also know what they could be getting into.'

'Getting into – ?'

'When I get back to England I'm going into politics. Not just with money this time, but with my own person. If other men can stand on platforms and face hostile crowds, so can I. I'm going to stand for Parliament whenever there's a chance, and I'll get there, if it takes me ten years. And I'll do it on my own terms, without compromise.'

I shook my head. 'Then you'll have women clamouring for your attentions. A Member of Parliament – a position of honour. What woman wouldn't be delighted –'

'There aren't many who'd be delighted by what I'd be going to Parliament for. I'm going to be one of those damned reformers

Andrew's always cursing at. Oh, emancipation will have come by
then, I've no doubt of that, but there are more things than you
can think of that need changing. We have to clear the children out
of the factories and lower the working hours – we have to get the
poor decently housed. We have to do something – if, God help us,
anything can ever be done for that wretched country – about the
Irish question. These are the things that concern me. Oh, I know
I sound like a prig, a pompous prig, at that. But I can't help it.
I've come to the time of my life where I either have to fight or I'll
lose whatever soul I've got still. So you see a wife, Fiona . . . Well,
woman don't like having a perpetual fight on their hands. They
don't like seeing the money their children should inherit going on
nameless brats in the mill towns and the mines. But that is how
it will be.'

I looked down at my hands clenched tightly together in my
lap. 'You make me ashamed, Alister. I've never thought to do
such things in my whole life. I'm a minister's daughter and yet I
don't seem to have taken in the first part of what it means to love
and to work for something not immediately touching me . . . Yes,
I'm ashamed.'

'Women haven't the weapons of men,' he reminded me. 'They
sustain and comfort and succour. But as for loving . . . you have
the gift. It shines from you . . .'

He rose abruptly, and the last words were almost lost in the
scraping of his chair on the marble floor. Perhaps he hadn't meant
me to hear them. 'I must go and answer this. There's a vessel leaving Santa Marta for London tomorrow . . .' He left me, and I
wished he had stayed, because he left me with only the thought of
Thomas Scobie for company.

So I took my hat and went out into the sun, taking one of the
paths that led to the Atlantic coves. But Thomas Scobie marched
there beside me, that pale face and the eyes of a man in fever. He
was with me still as I found my boulder down in the first cove, just
clear of the dash of the high-flung spray. I crouched there, knees
drawn up, under the shade of the big hat, my boots and stockings
beside me, my bare feet drying quickly in the sun, and the salt
caking on them. I had plucked at a hibiscus as I came through the
garden; I don't know why, except that they were there in their
thousands for the taking. I saw it, already wilting in my hand, and
I let it go. The wind carried it backwards, but the next wave
reached the pool where it had fallen and it was sucked away and
gone. It was the only tribute I could offer to Thomas Scobie –
that and my memory of him.

I sat on, careless of the time slipping away from me, knowing only the sun and the crashing rhythm of the waves. And it was here that Fergus came upon me. I was glad it was not as Andrew had planned; I was wild and wind-blown, clad in a high-necked, long-sleeved blouse and an old skirt I still wore on these morning walks. I was just what I was – no silk-decked lady seated in a candlelit salon; I was plain Fiona McIntyre, Scottish governess. I didn't have to try to be anything else.

I simply looked up, and he was there, barefooted himself, boots thrust under his arm, swinging across the rock pool towards me, the quickness of his stride telling me how hard his feet were, how used to the bite of the rock and the tiny shells, the sting of the salt.

'Well . . .' he said.

'Well . . .?' I questioned. It was neutral ground. Neither had the advantage; neither owned the sea nor the scene, the grandeur, the splendour.

'May I sit with you?' he said.

I moved my boots and stockings to make room on the rock, and the ghost of Thomas Scobie rode out on that Atlantic wind to give way to this most living man. Fergus sprang up beside me, sitting closer than I thought he would, not looking at me, but out across the cove to the Serpents. The sea is a great equalizer; if we had been back at Landfall I would have been nervous, flustered. Here the tension was all in the crash of the waves, not between us.

'I see,' I said, 'that someone once taught you manners – taught you to ask for things politely. I was afraid, perhaps, you were just like your father.'

He laughed. 'You see through him, don't you? He's mostly humbug – especially with women. All that rudeness – it's just a show. He has to cover up because he's getting old now and he feels he's losing his power. But you're right, of course. Someone did teach me manners – the same woman who taught him. It's a pity neither of us remembers those lessons better. My grandmother was a little like you. A bit of a stickler for the right thing – not necessarily the proper thing. Just the right thing. The plain Scottish virtues. I'm sorry I seemed to laugh at them. In my way I'm as bad as my father. All humbug. But I hope you can teach a few of these things to young Duncan. God knows, he'll have need of them.'

'I do my best,' I said quietly. They all demanded this thing of me, as if all else were helpless, as if some evil threatened Duncan

that they already knew of other than that he would see great change
and must be prepared to meet it. What none of them knew was
what I had seen of this child in that brief, terrible vision on the
other side of the world. 'But I have no power – governesses don't.
And little influence. And far too little time. Duncan is a strong-
willed boy and he has been terribly indulged.'

Fergus leaned in closer to hear me over the sound of the waves.
'Indulged . . . yes, I know. Fought over. Spoiled . . . But perhaps
not yet beyond redemption. A pity you didn't come sooner.'

'His mother . . .' I said.

'His mother – yes, there's his mother.' It was answered with a
kind of bitter finality. 'There's no way around that woman. She is
stronger than six men. Yes, I suppose all the plain Scottish virtues
– even if you had had him from birth – would have small chance
against that diabolical Spanish greed, that obsession to get back
the things of the past. Oh, yes, I'm sure you've heard her boast.
But in part she's right. San Francisco *was* an original land grant
from Isabella and Ferdinand, and it was almost half the island of
San Cristóbal. The Medinas are grandees of Spain. Probably these
were poor country cousins, but there's a nut of truth in all her
talk. No one would care if that was the end of it. But she pours all
that rubbish into Duncan's ears, when all need or use for it is gone.
The Spanish side is better dead in him, but Spanish pride doesn't
permit of such things.'

'Scottish pride is a wee bit stiff-necked too,' I reminded him. 'But
you might do your share if you really are concerned for him. He
admires you . . . he talks of you constantly.'

'My father won't let me near him – nor will Maria. No – Duncan
won't learn from me. Better he shouldn't. There's too much you
don't know about Landfall, Miss Fiona.'

I didn't want to drive him away, and yet I had to risk further;
it had come to me that these moments were incredibly precious.
We had come so suddenly together; we were talking as if no barrier
of space or ignorance had ever stood between us. It was hard now
for me to credit that there had been a time when I had not known
Fergus. Somehow the whole world had changed since he had
pulled himself up on the rock beside me. We were two people, not
strangers. We were a man and a woman; the elaborate ritual of
formality was dispensed with. There had been no intermediate
stage, no drawing-room play, no polite invitations to walk, to
fetch wine, to turn the pages on a music stand. We would never
have any of these things. A whole chapter in the book had been
skipped and neither of us missed it. The story went on.

I said, 'What was it like at Landfall in the early days – when you were a child? You began to tell me that morning . . .'

'There wasn't much. All of the things that are good were there at Winterslo. It was my grandmother, really. She was the soul of the place. She was a Bible-reading Christian who still could defend her husband's tolerance of slavery, who forgave her son *his* bastard son and brought that grandchild up with love and dignity. She was rigid and stern, but she believed in the commandment of love. She was just there, like a tall tree for me to cling to. My father clung to her too. She ruled us both, but there was no cruelty in her. I remember how completely she disapproved of my father attempting to rebuild Landfall – grandeur was no part of her ambitions and, in any case, she knew that we were destined to be no ordinary plantation family – giving parties and going to parties. You know she died before Landfall was ready, and I remember . . . well, I remember it just as if my shelter from a hurricane had suddenly been taken away. My father knew only two things – he was just as he is with Duncan today. A shower of presents, and utter neglect. I came to the stage, I remember, when I would have gone back gladly to the nightly Bible-readings of my grandmother in preference to the things he showered on me. It was his time I needed, not his presents. And it was like that with the plantation too – the times when he worked all day in the fields and half the night over his books, and the times when he almost forgot that Landfall existed. These . . . these were the times when he was occupied with some woman.' He suddenly gestured to dismiss any idea I might have formed. 'Oh, make no mistake – none were brought to Landfall. I knew only what I learned from the slaves. They knew everything. I never knew who the women were – perhaps quadroons or octoroons. There may even have been a white woman or two in Santa Marta whose family was poor enough to let her think of marrying Andrew Maxwell. But nothing came of any of it, and he never let things get completely out of hand. Landfall prospered, in spite of slaves being expensive and hard to come by. Before he was ill – before Maria and that rotten weed she gave him to smoke – that, and the rum – he was a clever manager. I think he made a lot of money. He didn't tell me such things and I wasn't allowed any part in the management. Then he gave me Winterslo, and they are the same hard, infertile acres that my grandfather worked, though every crop that comes from them they grow poorer and meaner.'

'I'd like to see Winterslo.'

'You wouldn't like it,' he said quickly. 'It isn't Landfall.'

'I would like to see it.' Then I halted. I didn't know who else
lived at Winterslo. I kept blundering and stumbling between
one piece of ignorance and another. 'Well, perhaps . . .'
He turned swiftly. 'All right, then. Come. Come tomorrow.
Can you ride?'
'I'm not a horsewoman like Mrs Maxwell. Something gentle
and old.'
'I'll come for you tomorrow – when Duncan has gone with
Maria. Come to the stable yard.'
He went back across the rocks to the path that led to Landfall.
He didn't wait for me; didn't ask my company. He just went.
He had dispensed with so much, and yet some of the lacks were
painful. I was reminded of what Alister had said about a woman
having to stand neglect. Beyond the reach of the waters, I put on
my stockings and boots and climbed up towards the path. The
sun was unbearably hot and I was weary and my senses drained.
My head ached fiercely; I was conscious of a terrible loneliness in
his absence.

3

I went to the stable yard the next morning as soon as Duncan
and Maria had left. I was nervous, hoping I would not be too
early, hoping not to have to wait about while the slaves stared at
me, yet afraid to waste a moment of the few hours that were mine
to be with Fergus. I remember I even worried, as I ran to change
into my old skirt, that Fergus would choose this time again to
assert his independence and simply not appear. But he was there,
waiting, none of the arrogance of the usual manner apparent,
and I – I was like a schoolgirl, shy, tongue-tied.
Maria's particular groom was there also, holding, though that
didn't seem necessary, an old mare who wore a side-saddle. This was
the slave Samuel, a massive silent man, woolly hair going grey at
the temples, whom Andrew ordered to accompany Maria and
Duncan each morning and whom, just as firmly, Maria usually
ordered to stay behind. He was said to be devoted to her; I had
heard Maria herself boast, 'That man – he will die for me.' But this
morning, for some reason, he seemed pleased to be a party to a
meeting that Maria knew nothing about.
'Ready then?' Fergus said. 'I thought women always kept a
man waiting.'
'That can't have been among the list of Scottish virtues your
grandmother admired.' I looked at the mare; her head drooped

and she stood perfectly still in the sun. 'You were making sure, weren't you? I think even I can manage this one.' I felt the gentle strength of Samuel's hands as he helped me from the mounting block to the saddle. I looked down into the black face upturned to mine, and for once the eyes did not shift away, the confrontation was not evaded. 'Mistress be all right on old Rosa. Jus' try her firs'. Nes time, perhaps something better . . .' For some reason he seemed to wish me well, and when I smiled my thanks an answering smile came, not the mechanical response that he was bound to make.

I had to urge Rosa forward. Fergus on his chestnut moved off from the stable yard and along one of the back trails that led away from the house. There was not room for us to ride abreast, so we were silent as we went through the deep shade, sometimes ducking under vines as the way grew rougher. We took a fork in the trail that I had not ever noticed on my wanderings. The vegetation was wild and rampant on either side, but the single trail was well-marked, as if used frequently, by a horse and rider. It was a track actually carved into the side of Kronberg, but much higher up than the carriage road that led to Landfall.

'I've never been here before,' I called ahead to Fergus.

'It's the quickest way to Winterslo. This part gets the most rain — a real forest, isn't it? Never been cultivated. You couldn't clear it. Once we're round the next corner, though, it's like the desert again. Kronberg takes all the rain on the weather side. There's nothing left for the lee slope. That's where Winterslo is.'

It was, as he said, a sudden and startling change. The breeze fell off, the trees grew scattered and we were in sight of the lee shore of the island. From this height we could look down on the sparkling green of Landfall's wide acres of cane. There was the greathouse I had seen from the headlands of the coves, the hook bay where the fortifications were. And then, farther along, and higher up towards Kronberg's slope, was the dusty white house I had taken to be Winterslo. We had started to descend, and rode now abreast, on a dusty track between cane fields. The cane wasn't as tall as that on the Landfall fields, nor the ground as well tended.

'I don't have enough slaves to work it properly,' Fergus said. 'Most of this is ratoon cane. It means you just let it come back from its own roots for a third and fourth year instead of replanting every second year. Doesn't yield such a good crop — each year the cane is smaller. Each year I replant a few acres, but it's never enough. I do what I can, but the place needs money and more labour. My father neglected this land after my grandmother died

– said the soil wasn't worth the effort when Landfall produced much better.' He pulled his hat more firmly over his eyes. 'But I'm supposed to work it somehow, and make it pay. It's an inheritance, he keeps telling me – something my grandfather and he toiled over. Somehow that is supposed to inspire me.'

We were descending now a much gentler slope between the cane fields; the road was deeply rutted with ancient wheel marks. I could see no slaves working in the fields. In this same stretch at Landfall there would have been several gangs, the air would have been full of their voices, the oddly melancholy songs they sang that made the rhythm of their movements among the cane. Here was silence, not the sound of birds even.

Then suddenly, involuntarily, I checked Rosa. I looked from side to side among the cane, but could see nothing. But something had caused me to stop. In the midst of the fierce heat of the sun there was a coldness here; I couldn't repress the shiver that went through me. I turned back to Fergus to find him staring at me strangely, a puzzled and somehow shocked expression on his face.

'What is it, Fiona?'

'Nothing – nothing at all.'

'But you stopped! – you look . . . strange.'

I tried to shrug and smile. 'I don't know why. I thought there was someone here. It's ridiculous, I know – but I suddenly felt cold.'

He edged his horse close to mine, our legs rubbing as the horses came together. 'You feel it? You know?'

'Know?' I wished we might move on. 'What is there to know?'

He knew that I hated the place; he urged the horses forward again before he answered. 'It was just about that place, my father tells me, that my grandfather was murdered. There, just out of sight of the house. It was about the first thing I can remember, being brought here and being told about it. My grandmother didn't like him doing it, and he defended himself to her by saying that I had to be impressed early never to trust a slave – if possible, never even to turn your back on one.' He paused, and then added, 'Well, it's something that comes to you. You get used to learning to live with the feeling. I suppose every white person is afraid most of the time, even if we do forget about it. It's always there, somewhere at the back of your mind. But we try to put it away from us, or we'd go insane – or never go to sleep. Most, I think, sleep with pistols beside their beds – there, that's Winterslo.'

We had turned from the cart track on to what must be the dirt

road that joined the Landfall road farther down. We approached it
from the side, but I had been right when I had recognized it from
the headland, this straggle of buildings. There was an avenue of
sorts, almost as rutted as the cart tracks, lined with thin casuarina
trees, planted long ago with Scottish carefulness as a windbreak
rather than for their beauty. The sugar mill was close to the house,
loosely joined by a line of stables and outbuildings. The house itself
was smallish, symmetrical, only the necessary gallery around it to
distinguish it from the four-square house that fairly prosperous
farmers in Scotland built. There was no striving for presence or
grandeur here; it was simply the house that a hard-working Scot
had built for his wife and child and then had been murdered at a
spot on the ridge above it, out of sight. I said nothing; there was
nothing I might say about Winterslo that Fergus would not have
called humbug. As we came nearer the shabbiness became more
evident. There was no garden to speak of – just the bare place in
front of the house partially shaded by a few clumps of mampoo
trees which leaned away from the wind. The earth seemed dry
and cracked; hens scratched without enthusiasm. Where the
windows would have been in a Scottish house were the french
doors – the heavy hurricane shutters hung on the outside, the
louvered inner ones for closing at night. All of them sagged and
leaned, needing paint. Fergus had to shout before a slave came
from the direction of the stables to take our horses. He did not
come at a run as those at Landfall would have, but shuffled forward, in dirty white clothes, with a kind of lazy indifference that
told me he had little fear of his master.

'Damn you, Daniel, can't you move yourself once in a while?'

The man shrugged. 'I no hear master come.' It told me something I had wondered about, as I was bound to. Fergus obviously
did not use a whip – or very seldom. The man led the horses away,
chanting something to himself; there was no backward look. He
had no fear of later reprisal. Fergus had forgotten about him; he
took my arm with all the solicitous politeness that Alister might
have used as he led me up the few steps to the gallery – not here
the wrought-iron rail, the curving stairs at Landfall. The gallery
was furnished with a few sagging cane chairs. But he led me farther
into the dimness of what was the main living-room and staircase
hall at Winterslo.

It was dusty, even dirty. Balls of fluff raced across the floor at
our advance; dust lay on everything, save on one end of a big
mahogany table – one good enough to have graced Landfall.
Everything else was cane – chairs whose supports were crisscrossed

with cobwebs, a few small tables. There was an elaborate sewing
table whose silk had rotted almost to nothing; there was one age-
spotted mirror. In places the heel of my boot seemed to crunch into
the rotten wood of the floor.

'Welcome to Winterslo.' Fergus said it with no conscious irony;
he was used to the place. He clapped his hands. 'Hannah –
Hannah! Where the devil are you?'

It took some time for the woman to come from the back premises;
the kitchen would be out there, separate from the main house. She
was thin, laconic, middle-aged.

'You call, master?'

'You know damn well I call. Bring us some lime juice, with
rum for me.'

She shrugged. 'No limes, master.'

'Then *something* – and try to be quick!'

Fergus shook his head, as if knowing he was being made a fool
of. 'It's no use. I have no hand with them. They do as they like.
Well, here it is. Sit down.'

'Am I not to see the rest of it? Upstairs? I haven't much time,
you know. Duncan comes back and I am expected to be there.'

'Upstairs? – upstairs is what you'd expect. Worse than this.
Leaking roof. Spiders. Termites in the stairs and floors. Well – I
invited you to Winterslo. You can't see the kitchen. You'd probably be sick. Well, then – come upstairs. It will certainly take
Hannah her own good time to bring two drinks.'

I followed him up the stairs – not a grand staircase like Landfall's, but the narrow, wallhung one of a Scottish house. The
railing was dusty under my hand, and the sweat made the dust
stick. A corridor at the top divided the bedrooms. Six, there were,
I think.

'My grandfather hoped for many children, I suppose. This house
would have done for a time.'

He led me from room to room, flinging open the doors, showing the rooms empty except for a chest or a wardrobe, too plain
to be moved to Landfall. He came to the end room, the corner
room with two long windows that opened on different aspects.
'This is where I sleep now. It used to be my grandmother's room.'

It was barren, unswept. Whatever embarrassment I might have
feared, there was none here. If Fergus had a mistress, if he had had
many mistresses in the past, none were here at Winterslo. The
four-poster bed was roughly made. Two worn silver-backed brushes
lay on a bureau which had one drawer missing; a clothes press with
an open door swinging on one hinge revealed a jumble of clothes.

There was a kind of awful bleakness about it that had nothing to
do with poverty. No one cared. No woman lived here – a flower or
two would have helped, a picture on the wall, even one of the
shells that lay strewn on the beaches. But there was nothing. I
could make no comment; I just went to the window that gave the
view of the sea. Unlike Landfall, Winterslo did not possess the
luxury of an upper gallery, so the sun blazed directly through the
open shutters. Even with the breeze that moved between the two
windows it was very warm. The shutters reached down to the
floor and a little railing stretched across each window.

'Don't lean on it,' Fergus cautioned. 'Everything is rotten with
termites. The whole place needs to be gutted. Perhaps,' he added,
and I felt that he wasn't joking, 'perhaps there will be a revolt
one day and the slaves will oblige by burning it down.'

I turned back to him. 'Do you expect a revolt?'

He shrugged. 'They threaten at times, like hurricanes. Sometimes they strike – mostly not. But they are part of what we live
with, like the pistol by the bed.'

Instinctively my eyes went to the table by the bedside. Its dust
was undisturbed, but it had a drawer with a keyhole. He knew what
I was looking for, and he nodded. 'No slave sleeps in this house
at night. I bring one of the dogs in. It can't be helped. It is the way
we grow up out here.'

'Alister says that . . .'

He cut me short. 'I'm not interested in what Alister says. He's
full of what London thinks the West Indies are all about, but he
doesn't know the reality. He's read the books, but he's never known
how it feels to see the cane flattened by a hurricane. He will spout
Wilberforce at you, but he doesn't know how much better off these
people are than they were in Africa. They were slaves there, too.
One tribe selling another tribe, and it's a damn shame the trade
was ever stopped. We're dying out here for need of slaves, and in
Africa they're eating one another. No – don't talk to me about
Alister. The man's a pompous ass!'

As if he were afraid of my rebuttal, he turned swiftly and started
from the room. 'We'll go down. It's damned hot up here in the
middle of the day – and even Hannah must have produced something to drink by now.'

I took another swift look about before I left, impressing the
cheerless quality of this room upon my memory; I knew that I
would think often of Fergus here. One other thing I noted. From the
window that faced towards the shoreline, the ridge that ran between these lands and San Francisco's was too high to permit a

view of the hooking bay below the greathouse; a vessel riding there would be seen by no one except those at San Francisco itself.

There was a sickly sweet drink waiting for us below on a table on the gallery, and Hannah had added rum to both. 'She doesn't know any different,' Fergus said. 'I can't teach her – haven't the patience. She doesn't want to be taught. She likes things the way they are. When I want to frighten her I threaten her with bringing a wife to Winterslo – there's a lash still hanging in the kitchen from my grandmother's time. But she only laughs at me. She doesn't expect a white woman at Winterslo very soon. She isn't so stupid, either. What woman would want to come here . . . ?'

I didn't know what to say; I just stared out to sea and sipped, and was strangely glad of the rum to ease my nervousness. But if I had any more I might talk, and I might say things that should not be said. I wanted to lean over and touch this man's arm; I wanted to feel his hand rest on mine. We were as different as two people could be – he rough and prickly, of no intellect and little education, holding views on slavery I found hard now to accept. I saw no books in this house, and I had lived all my life with books. But he had a curious sensitivity; he seemed to know what was in people's minds, and when one was past the brusqueness he was a gentle man. No slave at Winterslo feared the lash. He attracted children as well as women – I knew Duncan's devotion to him even though the two rarely saw each other. He was a man who could appreciate the wild grandeur of the Serpent coves, and went there alone just for the beauty of it; and yet I knew the stories of his often having been involved in brawls in drinking places in Santa Marta. But one could forgive him that when one knew the cheerless state of Winterslo and the grudging, tension-laden welcome he received at Landfall. He was a man disinherited, and yet he did not hate the child who was the cause of it.

My thoughts grew dangerous. I was suddenly swept with a desire to have him myself; it is a terrible thing when this happens in a woman. In these awful moments I knew that my desire was as strong as any man's could ever have been. It was not supposed to happen, but it did. I could make no move and I was choking on my own need. There is an awful knowledge that comes to one at such times. All at once I understood why people acted in the madness of passion – why lives were swept away, ruined; I understood now the meetings between Andrew and Fergus's mother, the girl of only seventeen in the deserted greathouse in the hills. I understood why Fergus had been born – but now it was the difference between merely knowing and understanding. I had not believed before in the flood of need and longing; now every nerve in me stretched and strained towards him. If he had made the least move in my direction I would have clutched at him and my soul would never again know freedom. Was I to call this love? – it was absurd. How could I love what I didn't know? The trouble was that I hadn't experienced the sickness of love before; I hadn't known its irrational power.

My hand was shaking as I put down the glass, half-full still. 'I must go.' How had I managed to say it?

He looked at me fully in the face. 'Do you want to go?'

Did he know, as he seemed to know many other things? I thought I could not bear it if he knew my torment now, and yet, if he never were to know, what a waste it was, what a lack of honesty. If he knew, would he hold the knowledge like some weapon? I had put myself at his mercy – but then he was not an ungenerous man.

'It isn't what *I* want, is it? I have to go back to Landfall. I'm not paid to . . . Well, I must go.' The cane chair creaked violently as I pulled myself out of it, and held it a moment for support.

'I know . . . I know.'

It seemed an interminable time until the horses were brought around, and all that time we said nothing, just stood by the steps, waiting. But something in Fergus's expression warned the slave who brought the horses, because I saw the grin, that had seemed to be habitual, suddenly wiped away. He, too, said nothing as they both helped me mount. We rode off down the dusty avenue; a quick glance back, and Winterslo was less inspiring even than before I had seen inside it. And yet I wanted back there; I yearned towards it, and dreaded the return to Landfall.

At that same place, just over the rise on the way to the Kronberg forest, Fergus checked his horse. He looked back at me. 'Fiona – how did you know? How did you know it was here?'

I shook my head, refusing to meet his gaze. 'I just had a feeling . . . How was I to know?' I appealed to him.

'All right.' With that strange knowingness of his, he did not press me further, did not seek to probe the sore point of my existence. He urged his horse forward, speaking back to me over his shoulder. 'I think of it myself each time I pass here. But you *knew*. I would never have known where it happened if I hadn't been told. There's the difference, you see . . .'

He knew about me, I thought, and yet he did not shrink from the knowledge, nor fear it. He accepted something in me that he did not understand, but he demanded no explanation. We went on, and did not speak again until the trail cut into the slope of the mountain joined the fork that led to Landfall.

'You can leave me here. I know the way now.'

'You don't want me to come?'

'It's probably better if you don't.'

He nodded, half-turned his horse, then checked again. 'If you know the way back, then you also know the way to Winterslo.'

'Yes – I know it.'

'Perhaps you'll come.'

'Perhaps.'

He hesitated. 'Just tell Samuel . . . he's a friend. He'll see you have a horse.'

'It isn't usual,' I reminded him. 'A woman to come visiting alone . . .' How mean and pitiful the words sounded; I was ashamed.

'Not to a bachelor's house . . .?' He had said it for me. 'Not to the house of a man like me?' He edged the chestnut back closer and leaned in the saddle towards me.

'Do you care, Fiona? Do you care about what's the usual thing and what isn't? Or should I say the proper thing?' Now he leaned so that his face almost touched mine, but both hands stayed on the reins. 'Fiona, you're not like other women – we both know that. I have the feeling – I know – you've seen things that other people have not seen. Somewhere, in some place, you've been in a kind of hell. Each of us has our own. Most of us never admit they exist. But you and I – we know they do. There's at least that much honesty. So if you come on this trail again, you will know what you're doing. And if I see you come up the avenue at Winterslo again I will know that you have admitted that you don't give a damn about what is the usual thing. You know the way – and I will look to see you coming.'

I held Rosa, and watched him until the green tangle had absorbed the form of the horse and rider. Then I moved Rosa forward, back to Landfall. I had never known anything like this wildness of joy, and at the same time the fear of committal. I was coming to recognize that no love that carried this burden and this reward could ever be a peaceful one.

4

I made myself wait. I told myself that I must wait at least three days – five days – not so much that pride had to be satisfied, but that I could not trust my own senses because of the tumult within me. Everything that was reasonable told me that to love Fergus

Maxwell was folly – to think of marriage to him was madness, even if he had wanted it. But marriage – I was going too far. Good sense would tell anyone that for the woman who married Fergus Maxwell there would be no future; if Landfall had no future, then even less so did Winterslo. But the coldness of my reasoning shamed me, and the heat of my own passion hardly let it have expression. In all my moments, the best and the worst, I could only think that to marry Fergus Maxwell would be pain and pleasure; pain I already had – would I not also reach for the pleasure – try for it? And then I called myself a fool. All he had asked of me was to come again to Winterslo. This was not the fashion in which a man courted a woman he thought to marry. He had said: 'Do you care, Fiona – do you care for what is the usual thing?' Was this an oblique invitation to take his bed but not his name? And I was just mad enough to do it.

So I made myself wait. In a kind of agony I made myself wait. And finally he came.

He did all the correct things. I heard the argument that raged between the connecting bedrooms of Andrew and Maria when his note came very early one morning asking permission to come that evening to dine. He also, it seemed, asked if Duncan might be permitted to come downstairs to dine with them, as it was so long since he had seen him. 'Goddammit, he's still my son!' I heard the angry bull-voice announce. 'And Duncan is his kin . . .' And Maria's tones, rising too shrilly, dropping into Spanish when her emotion became too intense. But Duncan himself won.

'I am to dine downstairs,' he said to me as breakfast was brought in.

'Then mind you be credit to Miss Fiona,' Charity said, determinedly shouldering Juanita out of the way as they served dishes.

I seemed to be in a fever all day. I did not take my usual morning walk when Duncan left with his mother; the hours of the siesta were sleepless. I deliberately stayed indoors, not wanting to bear the stigmata of the sun in freckles and reddened skin. He had seen me at my worst in the sun-baked cove and in the dust of the cane fields. Now let him see me as Andrew had thought to contrive it – cool, silk-clad, a creature of the salon. But in the end I was afraid. I dressed early and did not let Charity fuss too much with my hair; the dress was the simplest that the seamstress had fashioned, though still with the low-cut neckline that seemed to be her forte.

I crept downstairs and sat on the inner gallery, far in the shadows. But Fergus was early too, and it was here he found me. He was as

well-dressed as his household could contrive, the shirt ironed,
though none too well, the jacket of indifferent cut, dusted and
sponged. He had left his horse in the stable yard and came walking
quietly in the dusk. The slaves were just beginning to light the
candles in the salon and dining-room. He came up the front steps
unheralded, blinking a little in the light that came up from the
hall; but before he moved on, he looked carefully up and down
the length of the inner gallery.

'Fiona?'

I stirred slightly, and he came towards me, his step quick now.

'You didn't come!' It was an accusation, a cry of wounded
pride, of disbelief.

'Must I come every day? I have other things . . .'

He leaned down, gripping the arms of my chair so that his
face was very close to mine, intense, passionate, so startlingly like
Duncan's when he was disturbed.

'I would have you come every day, I waited.' Again it was a
reproach. 'And what other things have you to do? Is it Alister?
Does that fool take your time? If I knew . . .'

And then he straightened, and stepped back, and the look of
reproach changed to a puzzled frown. 'You're different! Why are
you all tricked out like that? Who gave you that dress? Why are
you wearing it? – is it for Alister to ogle you? Dammit . . .! Why
have you changed? I liked you the way you were!'

I grew angry. 'What I wear is my own business. And for whom.
What right have you – '

'None,' he said. 'No right at all. I apologize.' His tone was very
stiff, cold. 'I might have known you would not come. It was too
much to expect.'

Then he turned and strode back along the gallery to the hall. I
heard him say something to Dougal, and soon there was the tinkle
of crystal against crystal. Then silence. I sat there in the darkness
of that far corner of the gallery until I heard voices from the salon
– Andrew's loud burr, Maria's laugh, Duncan's excited shrillness. Then I made sure to enter from the hall, as if I had just come
down.

Andrew turned to me with an air of triumph. 'Miss Fiona – my
son Fergus has given us his company tonight. I'm sure you can't
have forgotten him, although we see him so seldom. Fergus's manners always make such an impression.'

'Good evening, Mr Maxwell.' It was as coolly said as if I had
never seen him before. And I had the wry satisfaction of seeing
the blackness of the look Fergus directed towards Alister as he

went to take from Dougal the wine he knew I preferred. As Alister bent over me with the glass, Fergus deliberately turned his back and gave his whole attention to Maria.

Dinner was livelier that evening. For the first time I saw Alister provoked to some passion by the taunts that Fergus threw to him.

'Wilberforce is old – spent. The English know that slavery has to survive or the West Indies is dead.'

'Then the West Indies is dead, my friend – Cousin.'

'It will never happen. What about the Americans?'

'The slave states in America will come to it in their own time – it will be a dreadful time. But as soon as sugar and cotton and tobacco cease to be so profitable, you will see the moralists taking over. The moral attitude will prevail when the commercial has ceased to have force.'

'You are a cynic, Alister.' Maria's smooth voice, unbelieving.

A slight bow towards her. 'A realist, Cousin Maria. Moral fervour flourishes when a man's pocket can't be hurt any more than it has been.'

Maria shrugged. 'Words! – I do not believe it!' I was listening to her voice, but mostly I was looking at her. Had she ever been more beautiful? – was it just the dress, one of her more elaborate ones, or was it the company of three men, none of whom could possibly ignore her, which added the essential spark to her beauty, gave it purpose, the sometimes missing radiance?

'It will happen,' Alister said, unshakable.

'Then times have changed. But I do not believe it. The whole of the Indies are founded on this institution. Can a whole region be left to die because of some old Englishman mouthing in the English Parliament? We all know it must go on. After all, it comes from antiquity. We did not begin it. We did not invent it. My family had known it from the beginning in this island.'

Were any of them aware, I wondered, of the slaves who stood about? – did they imagine them deaf or too ignorant to understand? What was behind the blankness of those faces, the features themselves lost in the dimness behind the candles? They were not quite children, no matter how much Maria wanted to believe it.

'Then your family,' Fergus said, 'were among the Spaniards who worked the Arawaks to death.'

'They had never worked!' Maria retorted. 'They did not know

what it meant. So they died. So others were brought from Africa.'

Suddenly Fergus spoke to Duncan. 'Spanish gold!' It was almost a shout. 'Duncan, never believe other than that. It was gold the Spaniards came for, not land, not work, not sugar and rum. Gold and silver. They were bad colonists. The worst! A land must be cherished, not for what it will give by force, but what can be coaxed from it. Never believe in gold and silver, Duncan – never, never!' It was as if he had known that the time would be short. The words tumbled out, nearly incoherent, oddly at variance with the way Fergus himself lived.

He had known he must be quick. Already Maria had given a signal and Duncan's chair was being drawn back from the table. A black hand reached to take his.

'Mama . . . you promised!'

'It is late, Duncan. Long past time you were in bed. This was a favour, remember? Not a promise.'

He offered no further protest. But when his mother moved her chair sideways so that he might come to kiss her good-night, he still clung to the black hand that led him. He deliberately turned his head.

'Duncan!' Maria's tone was sharp, furious. He kept on walking. I almost saw, as well as sensed, the pressure tighten on the hand that held his. The message was plain; she had delivered him into these hands, expelled him from this company; he would stay where he had been assigned. I could have cheered his action, and yet I knew I would have trouble with him in the next few days. He had heard the rights of slavery disputed, and yet he was entrusted to the hands of a slave. The confusion created in his mind would appear in sullen imperiousness. I would be caught halfway; both the servant, and yet white.

When the doors had closed on Duncan, Maria wheeled back to Fergus. 'And where would England be in the Indies without Spain? Was it not Spain – Isabella and Ferdinand – who sent Columbus? Who paid good Spanish gold for his venture? And what did the English do? They waited until the stream of gold and silver was coming back from Mexico and Peru to send their pirates into the Spanish Main. We were plundered and robbed and wrecked. Talk to me of your Drake and Hawkins! Pirates – all of them! And your English soldiers who came to take San Cristóbal when they knew it was vital to protect the treasure routes – when they knew we had done the work of colonization, of bringing the Christian faith –'

'Of bringing the African slaves when you had exhausted the

Arawaks in the search for gold.'

Instead of the explosive retort I expected, the cool smile returned to Maria's lips. She was in control again. 'Need is always filled from whatever source available.' She nodded slightly towards Alister. 'Of all men, a merchant banker must appreciate this. And the search for gold – or silver – or the riches of the earth will continue as long as man is on earth. We Spaniards did not begin it, we will not end it. We are all its servants.' She looked around the table. 'Who here can claim to be free of it? I shall challenge that one, and call him – or her – a liar.'

The meal broke up then. There was no formal end. The men did not stay for port. We just stood, and each went his way, to the hall, the salon, the gallery. But not one of us cared to deny what Maria had said. Greed or lust was in the very bones of all of us. Only she had the strength to call and name it for what it was.

I sat on the gallery for a while alone, hoping, I suppose, that Fergus would come to me there, but he seemed to have gone. I could see Maria sitting over embroidery in the salon. Alister went to the office, and I heard him asking for lamps to be brought. After a time Maria joined him; then began one of those continuing dialogues of commerce they seemed to hold – rum, molasses, sugar, yards of cloth, sacks of corn – on and on it went. I should have gone upstairs, but I was too restless yet. I moved to go down into the garden, and as I neared the dining-room I was surprised to see Andrew still at the table. I had to pass where the light must strike me, and he saw me and called.

'Well, girl! – had a good evening?' And then laughed raucously at his bad joke. The port decanter had been pushed aside and a jug of rum stood beside his hand. Dougal had his patient, endless position near his master, waiting, I suppose, for him to be ready for the ascent of the stairs.

I just stood there, not trying to reply. He scowled at me. 'Well, evenings at Landfall have never been noted for their gaiety. Not even after I married Maria. Too late . . .' He raised his head and surveyed the whole lofty room. 'Don't know why I built the place. Better to have stayed at Winterslo.' He was very drunk, I thought. It would need more than Dougal to get him to bed.

'But there's Duncan,' he added suddenly. 'There's Duncan. He'll make things right. Pity is, I'll not see him a grown man. Pity . . .' He had forgotten my presence. He bowed down now over the table.

'Good-night, Mr Maxwell,' I said softly, and moved on. He was not aware of my going.

After the house, the garden seemed friendly; even the night creatures that scurried and scuttled were less hostile than the humans. I walked towards the back of the house, drawn by the dying fires at the doors of the slave quarters and the soft cadence of their voices. I stayed within the shadow of the great baobab that grew there, and none saw me. They soon would sleep, perhaps a less-troubled sleep, for all their wretchedness, than the inhabitants of the greathouse. I turned at last to go back to that lighted splendour.

'Fiona!' Fergus's voice was low; he came along the path from the stables.

'I thought you'd gone.'

'Wished me gone?'

'I didn't say that! Why must you twist and invent things . . .?'

'Well – I'll tell you the truth. I was halfway to Winterslo. But I had to come back to see you.'

'I usually go to my room after dinner.'

'I would have sent Charity for you. I would have gone myself.'

'Perhaps you wouldn't have been welcome. After the things you said to me . . .'

'Oh, for God's sake, Fiona!' he gave a low, almost a moaning sound. 'Must we go on this way? I'm no good at playing this game. Never have been. Like my father, I've got no drawing-room manners.' He reached and took both my arms. 'Fiona, I came back just to tell you I didn't mean those things I said – and yet I did mean them. I'm jealous – I admit it. You didn't come to Winterslo, and I've never spent such long days in my life. I have never waited like that before. Do you understand?'

'I'm not sure.'

'Of course you're sure! A woman always knows when she has a man in torment. I didn't think you were the sort who teases.'

'I never prom –' I couldn't finish; he had suddenly taken me in close to him as if he meant to make me part of him; I had never been kissed like this, as if I were being dragged across the threshold of some place of passion I had never known existed. But I found, once the entrance was made, that I might be there forever. This was the reply to the longing I had felt for him as we had sat together on the gallery at Winterslo. This was drawing close to something I had sensed in the second I had first seen him, seen the splendour of his beauty and strength, felt the stirring in me that had not been entirely stilled since that moment. I was helpless to prevent the response that surged through me; I could no more have left my lips cold and closed against his than I could have physically wrenched myself from his arms. Our bodies seemed to mould together, and then, knowing that the complete fulfilment was denied us now, stiffened and hardened and finally suffered the agony of withdrawal. I was weak, and almost sobbed as we drew apart.

'Tomorrow. Tomorrow I'll come for you,' he said. 'I have something to show you. No – we won't go to Winterslo. You have to see something else – something that may make you bear with Landfall until . . . until . . . Oh, God knows what will happen to us. I have nothing to offer you, but yet I can't let you go in peace. But tomorrow I'll come, and you'll be waiting.'

I stood for a long time beneath the shadow of the great tree after he left, until my senses had cleared, until the shaking and weakness had nearly gone. I was wild with joy, and yet bereft. I had told myself I would suffer the pain for the pleasure; well, now it was mine, and it was scarcely to be borne. I saw the lights in the house had begun to be extinguished, and so I began to make my way back. I went straight in by the kitchen. I think I stumbled on the steps, because the noise caused both Maria and Alister to look around from the desk where they sat.

I must have been a sight to disturb them, because Alister stood quickly and came to the door of the office. Behind him, Maria's face, for one unguarded moment, lost its cool control; was it rage I saw there? – hatred for the first time plain and unmixed with contempt. She wasn't amused by me any more.

'Fiona? – are you all right?' Alister said.

I suppose my hair was dishevelled, probably there were deep creases in the silk gown, and it was stained with sweat. Probably the wildness of my emotion showed as if I had spoken it. I lied, very badly.

'Perfectly all right, thank you. Good-night.' I imagine my walk must have looked a little drunken as I went in towards the hall; I remember trying to hold myself very erect, and think that it must have looked strange, because things seemed to be spinning about me. I was sure of it when Maria, jolted out of character, suddenly called after me.

'Fergus – has he gone?'

I didn't look back at her. 'I expect so,' I answered, and floated on as if I dwelt in some magic place of secret access. I knew that she guessed it had been Fergus who had caused this disarray, this indifference to what they thought. I couldn't help it. I couldn't help it. If I lost everything I could not lose whatever there was of Fergus for me to have. I took my candle and made the slow ascent of the stairs. At the top I looked down again. Alister had come to the hall and was staring up after me. And I thought that he also knew. But his expression, inscrutable, calm, unlike Maria's, told me nothing. I felt a faint regret that I might have earned his disapproval; he had been my friend at Landfall, and for that he was precious; but I could not weigh this beside my need for Fergus.

I went softly into Duncan's room. He lay asleep, hot and tumbled in the big bed, his face in the candlelight so like the little half-brother who had always wrapped the blankets cocoon-like about him against the chill of that unheated Scottish manse. I put the candle on the table and bent lower; it was then I saw the tear stains on his cheeks, the aftermath, of course, of his being dismissed so abruptly from the dinner table. I was shamed by the sight; it was here I should have come directly myself, to comfort, to help him. But I had thought only of myself, and Fergus. I brushed the sweat-soaked hair back from his forehead; the touch half-wakened him. His eyelids fluttered open. 'Miss Fiona . . .?' Suddenly his arms came up and clutched me, clung about my neck.

'Hush, now. Sleep . . . ssh . . .'

'You'll stay?'

I put my lips, bruised and warm from Fergus's, to his forehead.

'I'll stay.'

I sat with him, lightly holding his hand, long past the time when he slept again. It was strangely calming, to sit with this sleeping child, to feel the life of Landfall go quiet about me, the last closing of the other bedroom doors, the dusty shuffle of the slaves' feet, the extinguishing of the gallery lamps. Only the unceasing cry of the cicadas kept up. The whole house was still as I went to my room; I pulled myself quickly out of my clothes and fell into bed. I slept at once, waking only when Charity brought the water next morning. The sun was already sliding past the edge of the gallery, the sounds were of the household well on the move. Despite the turmoil of my whole being, it was the best night's sleep I had had since coming to Landfall.

5

Fergus was waiting when I went to the stable yard. A horse also was waiting, saddled, not the drooping-headed Rosa, but a small, light-footed animal who regarded me with some suspicion as Samuel led him to the mounting block. 'This is Fidelito,' Fergus said. 'He'll carry you better than Rosa, and I'm certain you can manage him.'

Samuel's smile now was open as he helped me mount. 'He will go well for you, mistress. I have spoken with him.'

I regarded the slave seriously. 'You can make horses understand you, Samuel?'

'Of course.'

I did not doubt him, and somehow I felt more secure on this animal because of what he had told me. We made good headway through the forest path that led from Landfall. At the point where the foliage thinned and we had taken the road to Winterslo a week ago, Fergus pointed us on a road that led, it seemed to me, through cane fields that must yet be on the Landfall plantation.

'Push him on,' Fergus said, slapping his hand down on Fidelito's rump. 'This is Landfall territory, and I've no wish to meet Maria and Duncan. At least not yet. On the way back it doesn't matter.'

I had to put all my wits and strength to holding Fidelito in those first moments when we broke into a canter. It was a long time since I had ridden a horse at this pace, a horse remotely as lively as this one. But the magic of Samuel's words persisted. 'He will carry you well,' Fergus had said, and he did, accepting me, knowing my limitations, but not despising me for them. Fergus kept just perceptibly ahead of me, his right hand free to reach for the bridle if Fidelito should get beyond my control. But it wasn't necessary; Samuel had spoken well to him. As we settled into a steady pace I grew confident enough to relax a little and call to Fergus.

'Where are we going? Why does it matter about meeting Maria now?'

'Because if she met us now she would guess where we were going. She'd try to stop us – or insist on going with us.'

'Then where are we going?'

'To visit Duncan's grandmother.'

It was a second before it sank home. 'Maria's mother!'

'Yes – now we'll get on. Maria may possibly see the dust we're kicking up. She has eyes for things like that.'

It was neither Landfall nor Winterslo. San Francisco announced itself in the ruin of stone pillars that fronted a road which would eventually join the main one to Santa Marta. Pieces of rusted metal lay about the pillars, the remnants of lamp standards or of gates – it was now impossible to tell. The butchered stumps of a once-magnificent double row of trees exposed the rutted avenue to the merciless beating of the sun. At the gate Fergus checked. 'We may go easier now.' I wondered if he was giving the old woman time to recognize him, and hold her fire.

He halted and wheeled his horse sideways, looking back over the cane fields we had ridden. 'It all once belonged to San Francisco. Landfall – Winterslo, this land all about us, and much farther on towards Santa Marta than you can see. You once could have ridden half a day and still be on San Francisco land. But at the time when the islands were first settled, when San Cristóbal was a way-station for treasure ships from Mexico and the Isthmus, land that didn't yield silver or gold was hardly worth bothering about – or so the Spaniards thought. The Medinas didn't bother – in those days it gave them sugar effortlessly, and the supply of slaves was cheap and easy. They took it all for granted and sent their children, as long as they could afford it, to be educated in Spain. But they were fools, or weakened by indulgence. Bit by bit it all went. The place can't sustain itself any longer. They have only a few slaves and just the acres down to the bay there. Yields just about enough rum for the old woman, it seems to me – rum and the patch of Indian hemp she grows. They live off the few bits of vegetables and fruit they can grow – and handouts from Landfall's kitchen. There aren't any men left, you see. Just Donna Isabella and Maria's two sisters, older than she, who will never marry.'

His voice broke harshly. 'Sometimes I suspect that Maria would like to cut off even the little she gives them – really starve them out. Then what remains of San Francisco would be hers, as well as Landfall.'

We were riding slowly up the avenue as he talked. Already I could see the figure seated on the gallery of the greathouse. The land about us was desolate, unhoed, and therefore baked hard. Trees and shrubs struggled for their own life about the house, but no hand had tended them for many years and the stronger had taken over. It had not the feeling of Winterslo – that simplicity which might, with care, show dignity; it had been built on a far grander scale than Landfall, but the grandeur was fallen to ruins.

As we drew nearer I began to wonder if the house itself could stand the vibration of the horses' hoofs; the massive columns were crumbling, remnants of their carved capitals lay among the vines and weeds. To give it added height and scale once a balustrade parapet had topped the building; now the gaps were stark and bare to the hard blue sky. An arched cloister had once joined greathouse and outbuildings; a few columns still remained in their broken beauty, the line of arches was smothered in the rampant growth.

The figure on the gallery had watched our approach intently, but without moving. No warning shots had greeted us, as with Alister. She knew Fergus and possibly respected his anger. As we came to the foot of the steps the figure stirred to action; the thump of a massive fist upon the table seemed to echo through the emptiness of a dead house. It brought no immediate response. I knew that the figure was that of a woman, but she seemed barely that. She was grotesquely fat, clad in a soiled white gown that hung loosely from her shoulders, of no particular style, simply a garment to cover her body. Except for the pendulous breasts it might have been hard to tell that she was a woman; she wore her hair pulled severely back, greased into place, screwed into a thin knot that was not visible as one faced her. The features themselves were sexless, lost in fat, the eyes black slits, the fingers thickened stumps of wrinkled olive skin.

Eventually a slave appeared in one of the doorways in answer to her shout. It took a long time then for someone to come and take our horses. I had difficulty holding Fidelito quiet, and I somehow had the impression that the great hulking figure in the chair enjoyed my discomfort. But at last a man came, and Fergus bade him simply to hold the horses within the shade of one of the trees. Then he led me up the steps to the woman in the chair.

'Donna Isabella – may I present Miss Fiona McIntyre. No doubt you know that Miss McIntyre has come to Landfall to – '

She cut him short. 'I know – I know. My grandson, the little blond boy who can't even speak Spanish, is being schooled by one from Scotland. One of the Maxwells.' She gave a fierce, horrible laugh. 'Old Maxwell. He keeps his own to his own.'

She seemed to scowl at me through the dark slits. 'Well, sit down.' She waved to a dilapidated chair. It was placed so that I had my back to the view and the sea, but it also faced directly into the main salon of San Francisco. In proportion it was far more splendid than any of Landfall's rooms, but it was a scene of almost unbelievable decay and squalor. Every piece of furniture – there seemed not to be many of them – appeared to be broken, perhaps by the weight of this enormous creature. Upholstery was torn and looked as if it had mice, or even worse; empty glasses and cups stood about, smeared, flies swarming for the dregs of sugar in them. A torn mattress lay near the foot of the stairs, perhaps bedding for a slave, perhaps for the old woman who could no longer mount them. There was a central fireplace to this huge room; ashes lay thick in it, and even a fire-blackened pot hung there, as if this were a crofter's hut in Scotland. From the back regions came the heavy smell of something cooking; but the whole place also bore the smell of a thousand greasy, burned meals; the very walls seemed saturated with dust and neglect and despair.

The old woman thumped her fist again. 'Katarina! – Joanna! Come! We have guests.' Her manner was somehow triumphant over the filth and decay; thus she might have bidden her daughters to welcome guests to the most splendid mansion in the Indies. And while she called to them I studied her more closely, the stained, sack-like gown, the grime caked beneath the long fingernails; I smelled the odours of an unwashed body, of rum and the same pervasive smell of the hemp that Andrew smoked. Somehow I knew then that Maria had introduced the weed to Andrew, and with the purpose that it would reduce him to the same kind of hulk that faced me now.

The sisters came at last, at once reluctant and yet eager, as if they hated this public display of their poverty and yet were starved for the sight of a different face, to hear another tongue. They had probably watched us ride up the avenue. One of them came bearing a tray with hastily washed glasses on it, still wet and smeared.

It didn't matter which was which – they were both the same. They were Maria's sisters, with her features which somehow had gone wrong, the nose hooked, the jaw too pointed, the brows too black and heavy – her body again, but thin to the point of emaciation, flat-breasted, long, dark, sinewy necks. They wore cotton gowns, faded and limp, but clean enough. Their hair was greased back like their mother's, the same tight knot. It was almost impossible to believe that the beauty of Maria had flowered from this stock.

But their manners still carried the mark of generations of stiff Spanish ladies who had been schooled in Spain, though I knew Maria was the only one who had ever been there. Tonelessly, but politely, they welcomed me to San Francisco and San Cristóbal; in the same manner I was asked about the voyage out, how I liked Landfall and the climate. Had I ever visited Spain? Did I speak any Spanish? When I answered no to this last, the old woman suddenly shrieked with hard laughter.

'I would have thought that the English spent so much time trying to chase Napoleon's soldiers from Spain that by now Spanish was their mother tongue.'

'That was a long time ago, Donna Isabella. And the English are notoriously resistant to foreign innovation – so foolish of them, don't you think, to have refused Philip's Armada the chance to teach them a few civilized things.'

The old woman scowled; I didn't feel repentant, but I had made more of an enemy than I need have done. 'Philip was once England's king through his wife, Mary Tudor.'

'I think the English, and even the Scots, would dispute that England ever had a Spanish king. But I will endeavour to tell both sides to my pupil, so that in time Duncan will judge that question for himself.'

'In time, when the old one is gone, my grandson – his real name is Ferdinand – will go himself to Spain to be educated. There he will learn the true story, as well as the true faith. Now he is being brought up in this heretic religion . . .' The words were final, and chilling, and I said no more. I suddenly realized that only Andrew's unsteady health and age stood between Duncan and the total influence of his mother, and of this family from which she sprang. I understood now many things that had not been clear before – Maria's taste for show, her care for business, what Fergus and Alister called her greed. She only of these four had escaped the island heritage of indolence in women. But she had escaped more than that. These pathetic women, her sisters, were the last relics of the workings of the tragedy of a long decline. I thought of Maria, only eight years removed from this, and I understood at once her cruelty and the coldness. The stiff pride she displayed was still evident in these dried-out women; it seemed all that was left to them.

Some sickly drink was finally brought, though not to Donna Isabella, who had a jug beside her, just as Andrew did. The talk drifted on. Donna Isabella – I wondered if it were a courtesy title only – demanded gossip of Santa Marta from Fergus, and when he shrugged and said he had none, she seemed to grow annoyed.

'What? You never go? You don't try to tell me that? We all know how Fergus Maxwell keeps the tongues wagging with his fights, and his gaming, and that whisky they bring from Scotland . . .'

He sighed wearily. 'That was some time ago, Donna Isabella. May a man never live down the foolishness of his youth? Winterslo occupies every minute of my time. I have no money for gaming and Scotch whisky.'

'So you live like a monk?' she demanded scornfully. 'Ah – *that* I do not believe.' Her tone was rising. She had refilled her glass from the jug a number of times, and she did so once more before she spoke again. She turned fiercely in my direction. 'Well, there is a reason now for him to stay nearer home – more reason than to be near my daughter, Maria. Oh, I hear about it – I hear it all. I hear how old Maxwell goes and dresses you like some doll at Rodriguiz. For what reason? He's not capable of crawling into a woman's bed any longer. It wasn't for himself, for his own pleasure all those things bought from Rodriguiz – the silks and laces and all the rest. Look at you now, in a finer blouse than my daughters possess between them, wearing boots that would clothe them for a year! Why does he do this? You – some sort of servant brought from Scotland! Because you are Maxwell, and he sees a way – '

Fergus had seized me by the arm and pulled me to my feet. 'Come, Fiona. I brought you for a purpose. Now it's been accomplished. There's no need to stay for the abuse of a drunken old woman.'

He was pulling me along the gallery to the steps. The two younger women were on their feet, outraged. But the rage of the old woman was much fiercer, her tongue looser from the rum. A stream of vilifications in Spanish followed us; Fergus thrust me into the saddle and shouted at the slave to hold his horse while he mounted; but the man was slow and muddled, and perhaps understood better than we did what his mistress shouted. By this time Donna Isabella had managed to haul herself from her chair. Struggling to hold Fidelito, I was suddenly confronted with the unforgettable sight of her vast bulk at the top of the steps, one arm clinging to a pillar, the other raised with a clenched fist at us.

'I'll tell you, you Scotch slave, why the old man does these things. He thinks to marry you to his son, Fergus, and get Fergus away from my daughter's skirts. I know – I know! I hear everything and I know. There was to be another Maxwell girl to come – younger and prettier than you. She was to be for Fergus. But you came, but you are Maxwell too, so you will do as well. I hear it all – how much money Andrew has promised Fergus to make the marriage to the other one. Money for Winterslo. Money to be a gentleman again. All he had to do was to marry and keep away from Maria. Because everyone knows that Fergus is crazy for Maria. The whole island knows that he is crazy for Maria – even before she married the father. And he will keep on being crazy in love with Maria, even if the old man has tricked you out like a –'

Fergus yelled at her. 'For God's sake, shut your mouth, you indecent old bitch! Fiona, don't listen! It's not the truth. *Not the truth*, you hear!'

But the anguish in his face was there to be read; guilt, shame, anger. There was some truth in the obscene ravings of the old woman, and all of us knew it. In a kind of madness of distress I suddenly brought the crop down on Fidelito's flank and he leapt forward from the limp hand of the slave. Down the rutted avenue he plunged, beyond my control now, but the thunder of his hoofs was like the breaking of something within me. I hardly tried to check him, just sat there, not even gripping hard with my knees. If I fell, there might be the saving grace of a broken neck, and it seemed easier than having to accept the pain of the old woman's revelations. So I let Fidelito have his head, to go like the wind of fury. I didn't care. In those moments I wanted to die.

I could hear Fergus coming after me, hear his cries, But Fidelito was swift and had the start of him. We pounded on down through the cane breaks, and at last the straggling trees that marked the beginning of the Kronberg forest appeared. I had lost my hat, my hair streamed behind me, the wind blew cold through my sweat-soaked blouse; but Fidelito's sweat was working through my skirt and he was beginning to slow. I knew the danger of the approaching trees, but still I did not try to halt him. Let it be. But he also knew the danger, and he had had his wild dash. As we entered the area of the scattered trees the gallop dropped to a canter, and then as the forest loomed he slowed almost entirely. I still had no control of him; it was his own will. The wonder was that I had remained in the saddle.

Almost at once Fergus was beside me; he reached for the bridle to check Fidelito completely, and the horse accepted it.

'Fiona – what on earth possessed you to do that? You know how easily you could have been killed?'

I swung in the saddle, furious, trembling. 'Would it have mattered? Yes – I suppose it might have mattered. I would not have been here for you to marry, and there would have been no money from your father. And still you would have lusted for Maria!'

'Fiona – '

I couldn't stand the pain any longer. I had to act, to make him feel something of what I had suffered. I raised my crop and hit him directly across the cheek.

Before the crop fell I knew what I had done. He sat as if he were frozen in the saddle, and small beads of blood oozed from the welt. For a moment I closed my eyes at the sight of it, wondering by what devil I was possessed that had caused me to take an action I would have despised and condemned in another. It was added humiliation to know that I was no better, no different from the shrieking Donna Isabella, no less savage than Maria with her slaves.

I pressed the crop, and the hand that had wielded it, to my mouth. 'Forgive me,' I said, and choked on the words. 'Forgive me.'

'Perhaps it is as well,' he said. He seemed tired, almost resigned. 'They say that punishment releases guilt. It is easier for me if you strike me than if you wept.'

'But I do weep inside.'

'All courage weeps inside. Yes – you know there was some truth in what the old woman ranted. But it was not all the truth. I would have told you, but without those drunken obscenities she shouted. Can you bear to hear it? You know I took you there this morning for Duncan's sake, knowing what you would learn of what he faced in the future, to help you prepare him. But she is further gone than I believed. She drinks – all the time, constantly – and smokes that wretched stuff that Maria brings to my father. She is mad – mad!'

'But how much truth is there in madness?' I demanded. More blood seeped from the cut and some had started to trickle down his face. The sight of it unnerved me.

'We have to talk, Fiona. We *must*. You'll have the truth. All of it!'

The blood flowed more freely, and I was helpless before the evidence of what I had done. He got down from his own horse, tethered it, and came to help me dismount. I was weak with fatigue and emotion, and I clung to the pommel for a moment. Then he led me to a place beneath a tree festooned with vines. The deep shade engulfed us. The wind touched the branches high above our heads, but did not reach us. The tethered horses stretched for the greenery within reach.

The final thing was the way Fergus laid his hand on mine. I tried to make myself snatch it away, but I could not. I was his, held faster than the horses.

'I saw her first,' he said, 'when she was about nineteen – a little older than I was. You can't imagine what she was like then – hush,

Fiona! – I don't say this to hurt you, but to try to make you see it as a boy would see it. Life wasn't good at Landfall. I was lonely. I still missed my grandmother, and I had grown too old for the friends I had among the slaves. Of course, there were the female slaves, but they were always there and mine for the having. They never could be companions.

'Even with a house like Landfall, we didn't entertain – well, you know that. It seemed to amuse my father to let the rumours of its splendour spread about the island, then invite no one to visit. We rarely went to Santa Marta, and then only for short times. My father worked like a slave himself. The only companion I had was the young fellow who kept the books. He was also supposed to be my tutor. It isn't much wonder I grew up ignorant and unmannerly – but that's all past, and one can't go back. Andrew is trying not to make the same mistake with Duncan.'

'But Maria,' I urged, impatient. Without thinking, I put up my handkerchief to wipe the blood from his cheek. He smiled, and held my hand there for a second.

'I'm coming to Maria. I had never seen her before. Of course I knew about San Francisco – but there had been a falling out between Andrew and Donna Isabella. Not surprising. Both of them, at one time or another, have probably quarrelled with everyone on the island. So we didn't visit, even though they were the closest plantation. I knew about the three sisters – the youngest a beauty, everyone said, and sent to Spain to get a husband when she was seventeen. But she was back – desperate, probably to make good the failure in Spain. She came to Landfall uninvited. She said she never meant to present herself at the house at all, but just to walk through the garden to see it. She had walked from San Francisco. Her horse was lame, she said, but I don't think she had a horse. Of course she meant to be discovered. In any case, it was I who found her in the garden, just standing and staring at the house. I'm sorry, Fiona – I have to say it. She was so lovely then . . . fresh, with a kind of innocent beauty. Knowing her now, and what kind of hell she grew up in at San Francisco, she never could have been the guileless child I thought her. But it was as if my wish for friend and lover and wife were suddenly there in one person. I suppose I fell in love with her from the first moment I saw her.

'My father was in the fields, so I asked her into the house. It was the first time I had ever shown Landfall to anyone. I could see she was impressed, but not admitting it. That damnable pride they have – but then, at one time, San Francisco had been far

grander than Landfall. But she seemed sweet then – gentle, smiling,
and more beautiful in dresses that were cast-offs from her sisters
than she is now in her silks. Do you understand this, Fiona? – how
it was possible? How it seemed to me then?'

I nodded. I knew very well how it was possible.

'For some reason I sensed that I should keep her away from
Landfall. I was afraid, I think. We used to meet at Winterslo,
which was closed up – except that I got the key. For the first few
weeks it seemed a sort of paradise. I had her all to myself. I was
madly in love with her and yet I didn't lay a finger on her. We
talked for hours – she was very amusing, and she was much better
educated than I was.'

He was silent then for a while. 'It seems impossible now to believe
that I could have been so innocent that I thought she was too. I
didn't dare to touch her. I meant to marry her, but I wanted her
for just that little time to have for myself. I knew as soon as I
spoke to my father and Donna Isabella it would all be finished.
From then on we would be in the middle of people – forever,
probably. We would never have a time like that, all to ourselves,
again.

'But of course my father got to hear of it – in time, the slaves
tell everything. I think he was rather glad I wanted to marry and
settle with someone, but he wished it wasn't with one of the
Medinas. "Degenerate", he called them. "Worn out". But in any
case he told me to bring her to Landfall one afternoon and he
would make a point of staying in from the fields to meet her.

'Well – it was the end. I should have known it, but my senses
just didn't take it in at the time. All I knew was that my own father
was as blinded by her as I was. I sat there, dumb, between the
two of them, and listened to them talk, and it was like listening
to two people I had never met before. She had all the tricks –
you'd think she'd been in a London salon all her life and that she
was forty years old at least. And yet still this shining, wonderful
young beauty. He was captivated – worse, infatuated. And at an
age dangerous in a man. I never felt so miserable as on that ride
back to San Francisco. I remember she talked all the way, about
nothing – to stop *me* from talking, I suppose. She made excuses
about meeting me the next day at Winterslo. It was only when I
accused her of not caring for me that she gave in. I suppose at
that time she wasn't sure of my father, and she was afraid of losing
me.

'Well, she came the next afternoon to Winterslo, but the spell was
broken. I still wanted her more than I had ever wanted anything

in my life, but she was no longer untouchable. She was no better than my father, since she could match him so well. I took her that afternoon, Fiona – no, I'll never believe that it was force, although she might say so. I think she already had made up her mind what she was going to do, but she wasn't going to miss the taste of me if she could help it. She is capable of all the passion that you sense under that controlled surface, even now, and when she was aroused she wanted it as much as I did. At times, when I can hardly credit now that that afternoon happened at all, I make myself remember her hands, those passionate, greedy hands ripping at my shirt. She is like that – she was. I make myself remember, Fiona. And I hate her the more . . .'

'But you didn't marry her.'

'I wasn't given the chance. Perhaps what happened that afternoon frightened her – when some sanity had returned to us both. Perhaps I was to blame. But whatever happened, I think I would have lost her, and it's just as well I did.'

'*What* happened?'

'To this day I don't know exactly – I never stayed to hear the details. I left Landfall the morning I found out and spent a month between the taverns and brothels of Santa Marta. Finally, my father came and pulled me back to Landfall. I should never have gone back – but I was a lot younger then and my father had always told me what to do.'

'Fergus – *what* happened?'

'Slut! – she came to Landfall alone one night and went up to his room. Don't ask me how – I never wanted to know. I was too sickened by it. Perhaps she made her own way up while we were at dinner. You know how easy it would be to come in by the back stairs. Perhaps it was all arranged between them. Whether she came by invitation to my father's bed, or just presented herself, in those days he wasn't a man to refuse. There she was, and the first inkling I had of it was her presence there in the house the next morning. The slaves were told that they had married – but I knew they went to Santa Marta to be married that very day. It is on some registry somewhere, but I have never wanted to find it.'

I knew there was no lie here; I felt the cold horror of it; I knew she was capable of it. 'But *why*? – you were young, her own age, already her lover, wanting to be her husband. A . . . a beautiful young man.' I could not stop those words coming. 'And he was already beginning to be old. You would have inherited Landfall . . .'

'That was it, I think. Perhaps I would not have inherited Landfall. I am called Maxwell, but my father has never attempted to legitimize my birth, to make me legally his son. I've always thought he blamed me for my mother's death and sometimes he couldn't stand the sight of me. You heard him say it, Fiona . . . "I got my son, but it was the mother I wanted." Who knows what was in Maria's greedy mind? Perhaps she thought the claim could be disputed by other Maxwells. That was a risk she was willing to take — anything was better than San Francisco, and she had no dowry to attract other planters' sons. All she had was her beauty and her wits. But when she saw that my father was infatuated, she took the supreme risk. She must have known — how could she not? — that no man would resist the sight of her naked in his bed. Perhaps she even had him believe she was still a virgin. In any case, she won. He was still infatuated with her when she bore his son, his first legitimate child. She knew she was secure then. Rights were established. She would be his widow, and her son would have Landfall.'

The words were like a cold breath in the warm, tropic dampness of the forest. I listened to the birds, to the wind above us, to the gentle tearing sounds the horses made as they grazed. These were the beautiful things of the forest; there was also the scorpion, with the deadly lash of its tail. I was suddenly suffused with the wretched knowledge that under the beauty of this island was the evil that greed had cost. I was aware, in a way I had never been before, that each acre under cane was at the price of blood and that when people were hardened to suffering they did not notice how it was inflicted, nor count the cost. I was moved one stage forward in this story of Maria's greed, of Andrew's passion to pass on what he had acquired, of the whole tormented cycle of love and hate.

I had to ask the question; we had gone too far now to let me have peace until it was asked and answered. 'Is it possible . . .?' I turned and faced him fully. 'Is it possible, then, that Duncan is your son?'

The question was answered in his face; the misery had been lived with for a long time. 'No one can be sure — not even Maria — that Duncan is not my son. My father has never spoken of it — not to me. But he had to wonder, as I do. Once he learned what she was, he had to wonder.' His hand gripped mine as if he sought strength. 'That is what is at the heart of the rot at Landfall.'

We remounted and rode back towards Landfall. I was surprised to find the sun only a little past its noon position. Too much had happened; a very long time must have passed. Only as we neared the stable yard did Fergus turn to me again.

'Fiona – believe in me a while. It's been a long, lonely passage, these years, and at times I haven't wanted to live through any more of them. But now I do – I want very much to live. Don't refuse to see me again. Don't leave Landfall.'

I couldn't reply; there was a blur of tears before my eyes, making hazy the bright noonday. I half-nodded, and we moved on.

Maria waited in the centre of the blazing square of the stable yard, erect, her face deeply shadowed by the Cordoban hat, the symmetery of her figure heightened by the way she held her crop with a hand at each end. Slightly behind her stood Samuel. They looked as if they had been standing there, still as statues, for a long time.

She waited until we were close, then her words, low, furious, were directed at me.

'*You* – who gave you permission to ride my horse? You are a servant in this house, not its mistress!'

I would not say I was sorry. 'I didn't know Fidelito was your particular horse, Mrs Maxwell.'

'*I* arranged for Fiona to ride Fidelito, Maria,' Fergus said. 'I take the responsibility.'

'You *have* no responsibility at Landfall! Nothing here belongs to you.' Until now her wrath and her attention had been focused on me, but now she looked directly at Fergus, and saw the wound across his face. Suddenly a bitter, harsh laugh rang out, reminding me of the drunken old woman on the gallery at San Francisco shouting her obscenities.

'So you – you have had it! What did you try? Did you make an attempt on the virtue of the little Scottish governess? And did she give in, after an honourable struggle? You – you both are like rutting peasants!'

I could take no more of it; I tried, without assistance, to dismount, and Maria, seeing that, was abruptly moved to action by her fury. I felt her clawing hands upon my legs, reaching for my arms to pull me down, as if she must actually see me in the dust at her feet before she would be satisfied.

Then an extraordinary thing happened. Suddenly, from behind, those raised arms were pinioned by Samuel's dark ones. Shock froze Maria; she did not struggle or attempt to escape.

'Master Fergus help you dismount, mistress,' he said.

I half fell into Fergus's arms. 'Go!' he said. 'Go inside, quickly!'
I knew better than to disobey. I ran. But I could not outrun
Maria's scream of rage. The enormity of what had happened had
finally broken on her.

'*You have put your hands on a white woman!*'

The slaves were called early from the fields that evening to witness
Samuel's flogging. Alister and I had both gone to Andrew where
he sat on the front gallery and asked him to forbid it.

'It's my fault,' I said. 'I should not have ridden Fidelito without
your wife's permission.'

'Be quiet, girl,' he grunted. 'You don't know what you're getting
mixed into. It is nothing to do with you. No slave may strike or
interfere in any way with a white man. And should he dare to touch
a woman . . .' He shrugged. 'Samuel is lucky to have his life. Maria
doesn't flog for no reason – good slaves are hard to come by, but
our lives wouldn't be worth tuppence if we let anything like this
go. So leave it be, and keep out of what's not your business.'

I walked away; Alister stayed – perhaps to reason further. I
was sickened and desolate, and thought of going to Winterslo to see
if Fergus might not be able to stop it, and knew it was useless. He
would have already tried to excuse Samuel, and it was already
plain that Maria's fury was more against Fergus and myself than
against the man who had tried to intervene. She was punishing us
through him. When the bell tolled to call in the fieldhands, I took
Duncan and hustled him from the house lest Maria might send
for him. We took the walk to the cove near the Serpents; I had
a feeling that Samuel would bear what he had to without outcry,
but I could not let Duncan hear the sounds of the whip. And then
I told myself I was a fool; it was something to which Maria daily
exposed him during the morning rides. But we sat on the rock above
the cove and I told him about the way the sea swept at the wall at
Silkirk, and then he told me about the great winds that flattened
the crops and shredded all but the best-built greathouses. He
talked from hearsay; he had never himself known a hurricane.

'But we're safe now. It's too late in the year.' And he repeated
the jingle :

> 'June too soon,
> July stand by,
> August you must,
> Remember September,
> October all over.'

I thought as he talked he forgot about Samuel, but he had not. As it grew dark, and I judged the terrible ritual would be over, we started back towards the house. It was saddening then, the way he sought to comfort me. His hand went into mine.

'You know, slaves don't feel like you and I do, Miss Fiona. You have to be hard because they don't feel the pain so much.'

I jerked him to a halt. 'They are men and women, just like you and I. They feel the same way.' Suddenly I reached and as hard as I could I pinched the tender skin of his arm.

'Ouch!' It was a howl of outrage.

'Did you feel that, Duncan?'

'Yes.' He was stunned with shock.

'Then Samuel feels what the whip does to him. He *feels* it, Duncan.'

He was silent all the way back to the house; not sulking, just quiet. As we parted, he to his supper and I to prepare for dinner, he lifted a puzzled face to me. 'You mean he really feels it the same way?'

'He feels it. I promise you that. When you say your prayers tonight, pray for him. And pray you never have to feel such pain.'

I wished I could have avoided dinner downstairs that evening, but it had to be faced. So I dressed in the most flamboyant of the gowns Andrew had provided, and even sent Charity for the camellia that I had not dared to wear before. There was open war now between Maria and myself, and if I had to be dismissed from Landfall, I would go leaving with them a remembrance of some spirit. For none of them would I ever again be 'the little Scottish governess' – I who was not even small in build. I would not creep about any longer and pretend I was not there. Before I left Landfall, Maria would have cause to remember that I had existed.

Charity was approving. 'You look like a great lady,' she said. And then as she studied my shadowed face in the glass she bent forward and said softly. 'Don't grieve, mistress. Samuel suffer for other things beside what he did today. He has shown pride to her before this, and he would not see you pulled to the ground at her feet. We are not fools – we know what is.'

Then she straightened. 'I have child by Samuel – a boy of ten years who will be as strong as his father and bear pain as he does. So go down, now, mistress, and hold your head high. You have done no wrong at Landfall.'

I deliberately delayed going downstairs until I thought they would all be assembled. Never again would I hurry to hide in the shadows of the farthest end of the salon. All three turned at my entrance. Alister was on his feet at once, pouring the wine even before Dougal had reached the decanter. He brought it to me.

'Will you sit here?'

'No,' Maria said. 'We will go in to dinner.'

'Dinner isn't ready,' Andrew interrupted. 'Let her sit.'

I had taken only the first sip of the wine when Fergus appeared in the doorway. He was neatly dressed, brushed, combed; his face wore the wound of my despair as an ugly swelling all about the welt, which he made no attempt to conceal. His expression was sober, colder, more contained than I had ever seen it.

'Good evening,' he said, and his bow was more towards me than Maria. 'May I dine with you?'

Without hesitation Maria answered him. 'Get out! Get out and stay away from Landfall!'

Andrew said nothing to his wife. He simply lifted his hand and signalled to Dougal. 'Lay a place for my son.'

And then in a few minutes, 'Come, Miss Fiona. May I have your arm? I believe we are ready to dine now . . .' This time there was no lascivious squeeze at the waist as we went in, but a solemn, almost stately procession. It was all ruined by Fergus's harsh chuckle as he brought up the rear.

'You'd almost think we were society here at Landfall.'

The meal went badly, as it was bound to. But the teaming-up was different this time. Alister and Fergus talked together and somehow managed to exclude Maria; it was the first time I had seen them co-operate to the same end, whatever their feelings were about each other. And the snub to Maria was painfully evident. Andrew seemed to enjoy it.

As Maria rose, and I followed her example, the men drew together for port. It was then I asked my question, loudly, before Maria could leave the room.

'Fergus, you have been most recently through the slave quarters. How does it go with Samuel?'

'He's hurt – but he'll recover. Maria would never do away with a good slave.'

A kind of hissing sound came from her; at times she seemed very much Donna Isabella's daughter. Fergus turned his head with slow insolence and looked at her. 'But a very unfortunate accident has occurred. Fidelito is dead – poisoned, they are saying, by berries he must have eaten in the forest.'

Maria's scream of rage echoed through the house. And for a

moment, watching, I saw the faintest flicker of emotion, of satisfaction, race across the faces of the slaves who stood about to attend to us. They had their own weapons against the whip, it seemed.

5

All pretence of peace was gone from Landfall. It was not merely that the hostility between Maria and myself was now plain and open for everyone to see, but that all the tensions that had lain half-buried were stripped naked. Each time I looked at Duncan the question of which man had fathered him rose again, and was unanswered, and I thought of the nearly eight years that it had festered in the hearts of the three people who made his triangle of love and hate. Even with the memory of Fergus's kiss, his arms about me, his plea of his need for me to stay, I could still hear the obscene shouts of the old woman on the gallery at San Francisco. 'He think to marry you to his son, Fergus, and get Fergus away from my daughter's skirts.' I could still remember how Fergus's eyes had devoured Maria that first evening he had appeared at Landfall, the time when I had sat silent and unnoticed. The question I had not asked Fergus kept coming, and at last I asked Andrew if I might sometimes ride Rosa, and he answered, 'Ride any horse in the stable. They are all still mine – whatever she says.'

So I asked Samuel, whose wounds were healing – though still breaking open if he strained too much, and the blood would ooze through his shirt – if he would have Rosa saddled; and I rode to Winterslo. Fergus was there. A slave must have seen me coming and had run to tell him, because he was waiting to help me dismount.

'Finally – you've come.'

'I haven't come to stay. No, I won't get down. I just have one question to ask you. I want the answer – plain and honest. Don't lie to me, – and don't talk around it.'

'What is the question, Fiona?'

'Has your father offered you money to marry me? – money for Winterslo, as that old woman said? *Am* I to be your part of the bargain to keep away from Maria?'

His face was wracked with a kind of agony, but it was anger as well as shame. 'How can you expect me to answer such a question in a situation like this? I have things to explain. You *must* come into the house.'

From the advantage Rosa's height gave me, I looked down at him coldly. 'The truth will be no different out here or in there. Well, is it so?'

'Oh, God – you're so much the Scotswoman, Fiona. So blunt!'

'If you mean I'm not full of Spanish wiles, then *that's* the truth. I *am* plain and blunt. That's the way I was brought up to be. And the lack of truth is what is wrong with Landfall. If . . . *if* I should marry with you – if I should marry with you, Fergus Maxwell, I would want to know exactly what the marriage meant. I would want to know where love lay and where truth lay. I would want to know where loyalty lay.'

He stared up at me, his eyes squinting narrowly against the glare of the sky. 'I have not asked you to marry me, Fiona.'

'And well I'm aware of it,' I said. 'But that old woman shouted something and my ears heard it. I want to know if there's truth in it.'

It took a long time; I thought he might walk away. But finally he nodded. 'You could say there is some truth in it.'

'I don't want *some* truth. I want all of it!'

Now he himself was cool. 'That, my dear Fiona, you will never have this side of paradise, if such a place exists. You must be content with what part of the truth I possess. We are all humans, Fiona. Why do you set yourself above sin, and greed, and loving in the wrong place?'

'Do I?' I was taken aback, as if one of my father's congregation had suddenly stood in the kirk and called into account my father's own life. More thoughtfully I answered him. 'Perhaps I do. Then tell me – and let me think.'

'Then think hard. You know my father – you know Maria. My father gave me Winterslo when I was barely twenty, and nothing to run it on. He told me to ask Maria for what slaves she could spare. She could spare only her sick and her old. So Winterslo stands today almost as it did then. And then Andrew thought to have me married – oh, yes, there was the thought to get me away from Maria. A man can hate, and lust, after the same woman. Perhaps I should say that for both of us. So he thought to have me married, but there was no woman on the island – no suitable woman – who would have me. After all – what do I have to offer? A rundown plantation, and no claim on my father's estate. After some years, and some highly coloured tales of the kind of woman I was associating with, he began to think of a Maxwell – a little miss, fresh from Scotland, too innocent to know what she would be caught in. First a governess for Duncan, and then, if things went well, a wife for Fergus. Oh, yes, Fiona – there was money mentioned. But do you believe for one moment that Maria would let slip any money from her hands – to give to *me*? Even if there is money. I begin to doubt it. My father talks money, but he hasn't opened a ledger for years. Why do you think Alister is staying on so long, if not to find out where the money has gone? *I* don't know if there is money to spare at Landfall, all I know is that I'll see none of it. And as for the other . . . What the hell did I care for what they sent out from Scotland – Maxwell or not? They could do what they liked. But I would make my choice. And all there would be to offer would be Winterslo, nothing more.'

'That is the truth?'

'That is the truth, Fiona.'

'Well enough, then,' I answered.

We gazed at each other a long moment as if the will and the passion and the desire must find its match. We were as near equal in those seconds as man and woman would ever be, sizing up, weighing; it was the final hesitation before every commodity – life, trust, hope, love – was thrown into the scale. It was the moment before committal; we were hard with each other, like two merchants across a counter. I might have been saying to him, 'For my love – what will you give me? For my loyalty, my faith, my children, what will you offer?' Without a word I could almost believe he answered silently, 'My love.' But I wasn't sure.

'Well enough, then,' I said, again.

And then I turned and rode away.

But it was not only within the household itself, but also beyond it that the tension gathered. Maria's flogging of Samuel had seemed to mark a point. The slaves on Landfall had been well-treated, they were not so ignorant as not to know that healthy slaves were more in the interest of the owner than those half-starved and worked to death. But Samuel had been Maria's special slave, said to be her guardian. And now the muttering was that he had only guarded her from herself, and the ignominy of his punishment was worse than the pain. So no smiles, even forced or feigned ones, greeted us in the house. The blank, impassive faces now took on the expression of real sullenness. Small difficulties arose. Meals were late, or overcooked. New sheets were torn in the wash, dishes were broken. Harnesses snapped, horseshoes were cast, the windmills were clogged with debris, but Maria could not order a hundred slaves flogged. The faults were never pinpointed; no one in particular would be blamed. The lash began to fall indiscriminately, but a flick on the shoulder was not a flogging at the post. Two expected babies were still-born. But when Maria went in the morning to see the tiny bodies, there were none.

'Buried, mistress, buried, where the spirits cannot find them.' I did not believe it. But I felt that those proud mothers might have sent their children beyond even their own sight rather than deliver them to Maria's ownership. God only knew where they were, but they did not belong to Maria.

'Wilberforce is dead,' Alister announced one morning. He had ridden early to Santa Marta on business, and back immediately to Landfall with the news.

'Good! – let's drink to it,' Andrew shouted. 'Now perhaps all this stupid agitation – this nonsense they talk of emancipation – will die with him.'

'It will not die,' Alister answered. 'Prepare yourself for it.' His face was terribly drawn, pale under the suntan he was beginning to acquire. I thought he trembled as he stood, and he had come back to Landfall, unwelcoming as it was, as his only place of privacy in which to bear a grief. Contrary to his rule of never taking spirits in the heat of the day, he went, uninvited, to Andrew's jug of rum and poured for himself.

'Alister?' I went to his side. 'It grieves you – this news.'

'I knew him,' he said. 'I met him several times. I could not call him my friend. He was too old, and too many people claimed friendship with him. But he was a voice of conscience. I admired him.'

We sat together on the gallery, in silence, until Maria returned with Duncan, and I went with him upstairs. It was the first time I had observed a period of mourning for someone I had never met.

But there was other news that disturbed the household, and every other household through the island. The news drifted in from Santa Marta; it was talked of in the clubs and shops, and no one could say if it was the truth. The tale grew. It was that a Negro – said to be a former slave in the Indies and taken to England and freed by his master – some even said bought by Wilberforce or Tom Clarkeson and trained just for this purpose – had come to San Cristóbal and was making the rounds of the plantations in secret, coming to the slave huts at the dead hours of the night and telling them of what was going forward in the English Parliament

and that one day they would be set free by law, and must prepare. Such a man was never seen – no one ever claimed that; but
the rumour spread. There was more than one man, some plantations maintained. And the ships docking at Santa Marta carried
tales of the same man being active on all the British islands. It
became an apocryphal story – within the space of a few weeks a
legend.

'But Wilberforce is dead,' Andrew kept saying. 'And all that
nonsense goes with him.'

But the tale of the nameless, formless man, secreted from slave
hut to slave hut, persisted, and loomed like a shadow.

Whatever ailed Andrew grew worse; a doctor now came regularly
from Santa Marta; I noticed the pupils of his eyes were huge and
dilated; the drugs prescribed must have been very strong. He did
not sleep unless the strongest drug was administered, and that
was not always. In my own periods of sleeplessness, I would hear
him grunting and cursing – the sound carried through the open
louvers of the shutters. Then he would sit, bad-tempered, all
through the day on the gallery – not often now with the energy even
to lift the spyglass on the ships that rounded the Serpent Rocks towards the harbour of Santa Marta. Often he would fall into a
doze of exhaustion and then awake, as if stabbed by pain, and
reach for his rum.

'Can nothing be done?' I asked Alister. 'He's dying, isn't he?'

'Yes – by slow degrees. Maria always seems to prevent me from
talking to the doctor. From the look of him I would say some
disease of the liver – and the breathlessness. His heart is not strong.
The doctor is a reputable man – I've made inquiries.'

As if spurred by the thought of Andrew's death, Alister began to
spend more and more time in the estate office. Sometimes his tone
with Fellowes and Maria grew loud and impatient with frustration.
Snatches of talk would reach me. 'But *why* did it cost so much? I
know the price at that time from our other plantations – why pay
these prices?'

There would be some murmured explanation, but sometimes
Maria's own voice rose in angry defence. 'What did you expect?
I was very young at the time – very inexperienced. My husband
– well, you know how he drinks. He began to drink heavily about
that time and I had to take over. One does what one must, and I
had no experience . . .'

'But you have gone on paying these prices.'

'Prices rise. Haven't you noticed? And one gets less and less
for sugar.'

'Landfall is living beyond its purse according to these books. Our other plantations do better, even with the price of sugar as it is.'

'Then they are fortunate in having a competent man to run them. What can one woman do . . . ?'

He would persist. 'And here – this huge item for the replacement of the entire machinery of the factory – the crushers, new vats, all these things . . . I have looked at the machinery of the sugar mill myself and none of it is new.'

'That was very unfortunate. We built the new mill – for greater production, you know, and to be ready when the present machinery wore out. I bought more slaves to run it; we cleared more land for the extra harvest. The mill burned down. I didn't need the slaves and couldn't afford to feed them, so I sold them. I had to let them go at a loss. There was a drought at the time and an oversupply of slaves to be fed. No one wanted more slaves.'

'The books show the purchase of slaves, but not their sale.'

'Well' – the tone sulky – 'I have never been trained as a book-keeper. Our overseers come and go. Some of them stole from us. No one can keep overseers. *You* must know that. Ask! – on every plantation it is the same. "Rich as a Creole" is an expression that has no meaning any more, Alister. The only ones who grow rich from the Indies are people like the London Maxwells – those with money to lend and interest to collect.'

The arguments between Alister and Maria were now becoming part of the general tension at Landfall; dinner in the evening becoming intolerable because there was no longer a pretence that had been maintained of cordial relations. I wondered how long it would be before Alister made stronger accusations than just those of bad management. How long could he himself stay at Landfall? He had said a month more, but that time had almost gone. And yet everything bore on the person of the dying old man; how much longer had he, and how much would he defend his wife? Any accusation in law had to be made against him, and I knew that Andrew would not live to be held to a final accounting.

Every day I expected my own dismissal from Landfall by Maria, but it did not come. Perhaps in that matter, also, Andrew was the key. But I knew I would be gone as soon as he ceased to live. My anxiety was for Duncan; one could not grieve for the old man, too far gone in indifferent cruelty to those about him, his whole nature warped by the death of a girl twenty-six years ago, and the birth of an unwanted son.

I did not go again to Winterslo, although my heart and soul yearned for it. It was a testing time; I waited, and three times

Fergus presented himself for dinner at Landfall, and only made
the tension more intolerable. We had no private conversation, and
each time that Maria spoke and Fergus looked in her direction, I
would think again of what had once been between them and if a
man ever recovered from such a love. I knew I could not share
a particle of Fergus with another woman – not a thought, not a
look. It was my first knowledge of jealousy. I often saw Alister's
eyes upon me during these times, and I wondered how much he
guessed of my feelings. Probably he had himself been part of the
plan to bring out the 'little Scottish governess', but that was to
have been my stepsister, and a more biddable, perhaps a more
easily won wife for Fergus. Of me, not even Alister, with his cool,
knowing temperament, was sure. Least of all was I sure of myself.

Once as I took my candle to go upstairs after dinner – I had
never changed my habit of avoiding the salon once the meal was
ended – Fergus actually left the dining table to come to the stairs
as I started up.

'Fiona – won't you stay a while? It's cooler outside – won't
you walk a little?' And then, in a much lower tone, 'I have waited
at Winterslo for you. I've gone to the cove at Serpent Rocks. I've
waited, Fiona – I've waited.'

'Then wait longer, and learn, if you can, how a woman must
be wooed. Pride is a foolish thing, Fergus, but I have it. Only
when I am sure . . .'

'You fool,' he hissed in anger. 'As if there is any such thing as
being sure. You either trust or you don't. Being sure is for those
willing to take no risks. If you are that kind – I know you are *not*
that kind – best forget me.'

'Perhaps better to. Perhaps you misjudged me – it may be that
risks aren't in my nature.' I added, 'Wait – wait a little longer.
Something will happen soon at Landfall and we will all know what
we have to do.'

He turned away, furious, humiliated, perhaps, because although
our words had not been heard by the onlookers, the tones, my
rebuff of Fergus, must have been plain. Instead of returning to
the two men and the port, he simply stalked out of the hall. Before
even he had passed the kitchen quarters, I heard him calling
loudly for his horse.

It was one more night I sat for hours on the darkened upstairs
gallery cursing myself for a fool that I was alone when I might
have been with Fergus.

Andrew himself cornered me the next evening when I went

to the salon before dinner. We were alone, and he beckoned me sharply.

'Come here, girl. Sit where I can see you.' I did as I was told, and he leaned forward from the red sofa to peer closely at me.

'Well, are you going to marry my son?'

'That's a very odd question to ask, Mr Maxwell – when he hasn't asked it himself.'

'Then blast his God-rotting soul! What's he about? And what are you about? You think I'm so blind I can't see – couldn't see what happened last night. You sent him away.'

'I didn't send him away. He went.'

'You didn't encourage him to stay.'

'Should I? Is that why I'm here? I thought it was to be governess to Duncan.'

'You know damn well why you're here. So blast you too – but all women are cheats and teasers. Greedy, soulless teasers. Or are you looking somewhere else? Is it Alister you're after? Well, don't look there. Take my son. He may be the last one who offers.'

'In that case, I may do without. And he hasn't offered.'

'Well, Goddammit, what do you want? A written declaration. My son isn't like that.'

'And I, Mr Maxwell, am not part of any bargain not of my own making. In time – if Fergus asks me – I will make up my own mind.'

'Then be sure you don't run out of time!'

I got up and left him. The dinner hour seemed more unendurable than I had ever known it.

And so the leaden days of heat dragged on at Landfall; the trade winds some days were entirely stilled, and the heat sat on one like a tangible weight. Clothes were soaked with sweat; tempers were short.

'Hurricane weather,' Andrew would mutter as he woke from one of his dozes on the gallery. 'Too still. Hurricane weather.'

2

The nights had never been easy at Landfall; with the trade winds still, the heat seemed trapped even in these lofty rooms, and I tossed and lay wakeful on a sweat-soaked pillow. I dreaded the night, and yet dreaded more the coming of the day which had to be met with the exhaustion of drooping eyelids. I went back to the practice of walking, barefooted for quiet, on the gallery, trying to tire myself to the point where sleep would defeat the heat.

It seldom worked. I often considered going down into the garden to walk when sleep eluded me in this way, not with much hope that it would be cooler there, but I would have greater space to walk, and could do it with less care. Finally the night came when I did go down. Things had now reached the stage at Landfall where any further transgression of the normal rules – even if it should be known that I left the house at night – could make no difference. It lacked a few hours to dawn, the moon was still high, when I threw a cotton wrapper about my nightgown and went downstairs. Dougal and two other house slaves slept. Landfall was a well-maintained house – the catch slipped back silently; I propped a doorstop against it in the unlikely event that a breeze would spring up strong enough to slam it. In seconds I was down among the sheltering darkness of the trees.

The sense of escape from the house was relief, even though here it was hardly cooler. In the time at Landfall the garden had become a friend, the garden and all the beauty beyond it, even the dusty, rolling cane fields. I trod the garden paths now with confidence, and even the wider areas beyond it. The trees began to break, and I was on the edge of the rich Landfall cane fields. The moon made it hardly less bright than day, but there was the absence of the burning heat. It was so still not even the tall ripening cane stalks moved; they shone silver now, not green. It was a land transformed. It was strange how the fear of such things as spiders and scorpions did not disturb me as did the tension lying entrapped within the walls of Landfall. I walked on and on, those dusty cane breaks seeming now as familiar to me as the hills I had walked behind Silkirk. I walked on, like one spellbound, wondering how I could have gone all this time without daring to come out at night beyond the region of the house. This was a different land I saw, moon-haunted, star-struck. There was only the brilliant sky, and the tall cane, and I walked like a sleeper in a dream, and there came to me catharsis, release, and the final, blessed soothing of the spirit.

I could not tell at what point I became aware of different sounds – not the sounds of the night, the cicadas, the rustle of the lizards disturbed by my passage, the occasional call of the night birds back in the forest. There were human sounds, indistinct, muffled, but definitely human. Without much thought I headed for the first of the coves on the lee shore, already now glimpsing from the top of each rise, its silvered-mirror surface. But these sounds came from over on the right – several bays along from the first. Standing on the highest point of a cart track among the cane, I took my bearings from the gaunt outline of the crumbled balustrade that surmounted the greathouse of San Francisco. Farther off I could see the dim speck that was Winterslo. I stood very still, and listened. The sounds were hardly there, but they were there. The ridges of these small valleys that led inevitably to each sandy cove had the effect of an amphitheatre; sounds were magnified beyond their normal strength. It is odd how memory flashes back irrelevantly, but I remembered suddenly my stepmother once saying I had the ears of a fox. I knew now that something was taking place in the bay below San Francisco. I stood rooted, one fear only holding me – that I might inadvertently stumble on some ritual of the slaves, some place where they practised the ancient rites of Africa forbidden to them now. The old fortifications at San Francisco might be that place. And then another thought took me. Perhaps this was one of the meetings arranged for the black man of legend who travelled from plantation to plantation, giving the news of freedom to come. Did I dare to face that? Did I dare to try to know what the plans were when that time, dreaded by the whites, longed for by the blacks, arrived? But I had seen a vision of terror at Landfall; perhaps this night I had been sent to know its time and place.

I licked my suddenly dry lips and thought of going back for Alister, but it was too far and it would take too long. Long before dawn whoever moved in that cove down there would be gone.

So I went on, thankful that I had chosen a fairly dark-printed wrapper to throw over my nightgown, but the thin slippers which served well enough for the garden walks and the tracks would be treacherous on the loose lava-rock of the fortifications. The night whose brilliance I had delighted in was now, all at once, a menace and a curse.

I moved steadily towards the San Francisco bay, and the doubt was growing that this could be any planned meeting of slaves, or a landing place for the mysterious black leader. Even though it was sheltered from view of the sea by its jutting headland, from San Francisco itself, any vessel, however small, could be seen entering, and the noises would rise to the greathouse, just as they did to me.

I had reached the end of San Francisco's poor cane fields and come into the stretch of territory too sandy for cultivation. Again I hesitated, knowing I could turn back at this point but perhaps not later. There was the dull sound of movement – human movement. Though I could hear them, the voices were hushed and low-toned; but I heard a command, a smothered threat and, just once, the unmistakable crack of a whip. Then I knew beyond doubt that this was no meeting organized to greet the nameless black man of legend. Wherever the whip cracked, there were white men, and I was going to see.

The path led directly to the cove and the beach, but I could not take that way. I lost track of time, almost lost direction, as I pushed and squirmed through the underbrush towards the fortifications, cursing the slippers that kept falling off, and the long, clinging wrapper that seemed to clasp each thorny bush. Once, in a hollow of darkness, I was stabbed in the arm by the point of some plant; I wondered if, ironically, I had fallen victim to the point of the formidable plant that could take out a man's eyes, or worse — known locally as Spanish bayonet. But finally I was there, at the first outcrop of the crumbling walls, and now the light was welcome — I was remembering those roofless dungeons yawning ready for the plunging fall. I lay along the edge of one of these walls and let the scrubby growth shelter me; then I watched and concentrated on what was happening in the bay.

It was bigger and deeper than I had supposed — with nothing to give it perspective before, I had thought it only a little larger than the others. But the vessel that rode out there, sheltered well within the hook of the headland, was no island schooner, but something as big, bigger perhaps, than the *Clyde Queen*, something that could ride the rough seas of the Atlantic. As I watched, a longboat moved from the shadow of its hull, coming to shore, catching the glint of the moonlight on wet oars, giving out the dull sound of muffled rowlocks. Several figures — black or white, I couldn't tell — stood waiting for its arrival at the water's edge. I watched it for a moment, and then another sound broke on me, a dreadful sound, a sort of keening, moaning cry that was an African's expression of despair and fear and pain. I remembered the room with the barred windows and the lock on the stout new wooden door. I knew then what this whole business was about. Slaves were being brought ashore. The vessel out there, so beautiful in the calm brilliance of the bay, was an illegal slaver, probably at the end of its voyage from Africa. Illegal, I knew, because any normal transfer of slaves from island to island would dock and do its business openly in Santa Marta harbour. The closer human sounds I heard were most likely of those already brought ashore and locked in the dungeon room.

I kept still, and waited. The longboat finally touched the beach, and all but one of the figures went to drag it ashore. And then I heard the sound that one need hear only once and may never forget – the sound of chains being dragged by a human body. Sharp cries went up as men and women were hauled bodily from the boat and set on their feet, lined up and forced to begin to march up towards the fortifications. They were chained by the ankles, a long row of perhaps twenty. Once again came the crack of the whip as one of that dreadful line stumbled and fell and was dragged by the weight of the others.

I began to put the pieces of the pattern together. Maria was using this bay, with the knowledge of Donna Isabella, if not of Andrew, as the off-loading point for the illicit ships that plied the slave trade from Africa. I couldn't be sure where all of them went from here, but the *Savannah Trader* would have been carrying a cargo to no other place than the southern states of America. It was possible other smaller, island vessels came here also, picking up their illegal cargo and slipping off down-island with it. Perhaps slaves from other islands were themselves brought here. For the American captains it would make good sense. They were spared the long voyage to Africa and back – the infamous Middle Passage – with the wait on the fever-ridden coast at the old slaving forts for enough bodies to fill their holds. They were spared the disease, death, the threat of insurrection of the voyage itself. Here they would have only those who landed alive, and if others were sent from different islands to this gathering point, they could be reasonably sure of fit, healthy slaves, used to plantation life, perhaps already bred for generations to the ways of the white man, inured to the life and knowing what was expected of them.

With a kind of horror I saw that several of the females in the line carried babies, and other, older children, clung desperately to the rags of their mothers' skirts. I remembered then Maria's care for her pregnant slaves, the better feeding and rest given them to encourage them to bear more children. The result of this policy should have been that Landfall would teem and swarm with children – but it did not. There were a dozen or so about the slave huts and garden, too young yet for the fields; were the others gone, sold, like this lot here? Did Maria really sell small children away from their mothers? I suddenly remembered the two still-born babies of these recent weeks and the failure to produce their bodies for Maria's inspection. Had the certain knowledge that they, once they were old enough, would be sold away from Landfall caused the mothers to hide them, even risking death for it? They must believe that the day of freedom was very close at hand to have dared such a thing – to cling to their children, hidden, with the desperate hope that one day they would live to see freedom. All at once I, too, began to believe in the legend of the messianic Negro, travelling with his message of faith in freedom to come.

This seemed to have been the last shipment of slaves from the vessel. The longboat returned and was taken aboard; I heard the rattle of the anchor chain and watched the raising of the sails, in readiness for the slightest breeze that would blow from the land. I heard more of the dreadful sound of the chains, the orders, the hiss and crack of the whip, but I could see nothing of what was taking place. All of this was on the beach below the line of the fortifications, and I would have had to go too near to see any of it. Instead I began to squirm and wriggle my way back towards the path they must take if they were bound for San Francisco; it didn't seem possible that the new line of slaves just landed could be packed into that barred room with those already there.

I stayed back from the path, in the underbrush, and I heard the chains long before the column drew level. I thought it was a white man who led them – I could see boots, highly polished, in the light of the lantern he carried. One or two more booted figures passed with the column, whips trailing; sometimes the moonlight reflected palely on a white face. I could also, from my low level, see the bare, sometimes bloodied feet with the manacles about the ankles. I did not dare risk raising my head more than a few times, knowing that my own face would show as theirs did, that my hair in the moonlight could look nearly blonde. I stayed crouched and still until the procession was well past me. I did not hear the whip again; the slaves were now accustomed to the rhythm of the march and were moving with the terrible resignation of their kind.

I began to ease myself to a nearly upright position, my cramped limbs trembling after the effort of staying so still. But I had misjudged the end of the procession; I had not heard the footfalls on the sandy trail. What reached me first was the whisper – low but sharp. Maria's voice.

'Wait! – did something move there? Did you see?'

There came the murmured answer saying something I couldn't understand.

'Go and look – here, fool, take the lantern.'

I had not seen the light because the door that masked its side had been closed down to a slit. Now it was opened back and the tall figure of a man began to thrust his way through the undergrowth. I flung myself face downward, but he must have heard the movement, for he came steadily in my direction; I could see the light of the lamp swinging on the ground as he came close. Very close to me he stood, and I could see his broad black feet. I knew the scrubby brush could never give me enough concealment, that the lamp shone directly on me. I turned my head sideways and looked up.

The light did not reach his own face; all I knew was that he was black – no features showed themselves in the moonlight. I moved to a squatting position, unwilling, until it was absolutely inevitable, to give my identity to Maria. The man must have realized that I did not recognize him, but he could see the fear and apprehension in my face. So with a single quick swinging movement he raised the lantern high, and I saw that it was Samuel. He gave the faintest shake of his head, and one of his hands made the gesture for me to keep down. At once he turned and plunged on through the brush, as if following some further sound he heard. He went on and on, and finally Maria's voice called urgently to him.

'Stop wasting time. If there is nothing, come.'

Obediently he returned to her, passing the place where I crouched with the lantern well-shielded on my side.

'Nothing, mistress. Maybe some cat – many cats from the stables go wild over here. They go quick – you never catch them.'

'Well, then, come on ...'

I risked raising myself up to watch them go and wondered how I had failed to recognize that slender figure, in the tight Spanish trousers and jacket, with the Cordoban hat, among the group on the beach. But she would be there, of course; nothing with which Maria concerned herself would be left to the direction of others. I thought of the white men who had accompanied the column; one of them, or the man who paid him, had scribbled that note that had come mistakenly into my hands that day at Rodriguiz's. And Rodriguiz himself would be part of it, because he had known what that note contained. But only his money or his organization would have aided tonight's operation; not for him the long rides to Landfall, the wait for the vessel, the chivying of the captives to wherever they were put to wait the next ship. He would do none of these things while someone as competent and ruthless as Maria was here to command. And I had no doubt that she did command, and I knew also where the money from Landfall filtered, the reason for the deliberate chaos of the books that Alister argued over. Maria had made an investment that she dared not show on paper; where the profits lay probably only she knew.

And with this knowledge a shiver of fear possessed my body

like a fever. If Maria knew I had witnessed her in this criminal act I was in much greater danger than merely being dismissed from Landfall. It was too easy to imagine the ways she could find to make sure I would be silent forever. What did I do now? — how did I go? Did Andrew know? — if he did, then I had no protection. I had no place to turn, no one but Alister — or Fergus. Or should I just pack my trunk tomorrow and go? Should I take the life-saving chance that Samuel's silence had offered me. But I had come, I thought, because of the vision of Duncan running towards me, needing my help. If the vision had been a true one, then I still had a role to play at Landfall. And by going, I must also leave Fergus. Would I take the swift, easy path away from danger and trouble and spend the rest of my life a Scottish spinster growing old teaching children that were not my own? — or did I live for my own supreme moment and take the chances that must accompany it?

Chances? — I never seemed to make a choice. Somehow the safe and sensible way never opened itself before me; I seemed to have been born to live in turmoil. As much as I didn't want it, it was my natural place. Unless Maria forced me to, I knew I would not pack my trunk that day and leave Landfall.

It was at that moment that I remembered that I had left the door propped open. Maria would find it on her return and the hunt would be on. She would know at once that only Alister or myself would be gone, and it would be a simple matter to find out which. I forgot what might be coming on that day, and the next day. The thing now was somehow to get as far away from this cove as I could and to invent some excuse for being away from the house.

The dawn was almost upon the land, and it comes as swiftly as the night in the tropics. Already, over towards Winterslo, I heard the first cock crow; I wanted desperately to go towards the house, and to Fergus, but it was too far away and San Francisco lay between us. It would be nonsense to say to Maria that I had walked as far as Winterslo alone at night. So I turned my back on it and the trail that led to San Francisco. What I must do was push my way through the scrub and over the little headlands to the first cove past the Serpents, the one they knew I had visited before. I ran, as much as that rough terrain would let me, and I blessed the lifelong habit of tramping the Scottish hills, the good strong legs that now had to carry me past the point where I thought I could go no farther. I had to be in that cove before sunrise, and I was, the breath tearing in my chest like a knife, my knees trembling under me. I was there — this, the most beautiful, the calmest cove, where the shallows were most lucid, the sand whitest. I raced down to the water's edge, shed my ruined slippers, my wrapper and nightgown, and ran on straight into the water.

Oh, God, what heaven it was; its warm soothing balm, its salty buoyancy which bore my tired body like gentle, uplifting hands. For long minutes I forgot the danger, the fear, the horror of the night. I could not swim, but the calm shallows let me lie, and turn and twist, in a kind of ecstasy of sensual delight; the sand was fine powder beneath me when I touched it, like a great easing down bed beneath my whole body when I came and lay at the edge, where the tiny wavelets lapped against me. My hair streamed all about me, gritty with sand, my face and limbs that were above the lap of the water already beginning to dry with a film of salt upon them. I lay there, my face on my folded arms, feeling the sun gently warm on my skin, letting the fear and fatigue slip away from me. My dawn swim would explain my absence, my excuse would be the heat and my inability to sleep; it would explain the open door. Let Maria, if she could, prove that I had been anywhere else. For the moment I was safe here, and reluctant to go, and my strength and courage restored by the blissful ease of the water and sun. Perhaps for a few moments I even slept as I lay there, my senses unconsciously girding me for what I knew must greet me back at Landfall.

I shook myself awake, and the sun seemed hotter, and there was a sound in the cove. Not the sound of someone coming along the path, the crashing sound of the undergrowth, but the sound of water — the thrashing of the water that a swimmer makes.

I turned on my side and half-sat up. The swimmer came towards me, long powerful arms beating through the water, cutting diagonally across the bay, as if he had dived from the rocks at the point. I remained quite still, making no foolish, coy movement towards my wrapper. He reached the shallows, and stood up, as naked as I, and I saw the splendour of him, with the morning sun shining on his body and the wet blond-red hair. There are moments in life that make the pain of the rest of it worth the living; this one I was to hold forever. Some things are as natural in their time and place as breathing is to our every second; our coupling now was as if it had been intended from all time. There was no fumbling, no undue haste. We loved each other. There was to be no stain of virginal blood on a bedsheet to remind me of the exquisite pain of his entry; the gentle wavelets washed it away, and the sand was clean and white.

Fergus had his horse tethered on the other side of the cove and I

rode before him on the saddle, his arm circling my waist to hold
me. My wet hair streamed about me; from time to time he would
nuzzle it back across my shoulder and lean and kiss my cheek.
'You are a disgrace!' he laughed. 'You are wonderful! You never
have been so beautiful!' And I laughed too, because it was suddenly funny and joyous that I looked so terrible. He had finally
noticed my torn wrapper and the ruined slippers, and once, as I
raised my arm, and the sleeve fell back, he saw the cut from the
cactus.

'What happened?'

I shrugged. 'I ran into something in the dark. It doesn't hurt.
The salt water washed it clean – see, it doesn't even bleed.'

'Have Charity put something on it. Some of the slave remedies
are better than anything our doctors have thought up.' Then his
arm tightened about me. 'I have to keep you safe, don't I? I think
you must be a little mad, Fiona – the way you ride horses and go
walking about the island at night dressed like that. Weren't you
afraid? Do you never think about things like snakes and spiders?'

'Your father told me all the snakes were gone – they imported
the mongoose to get rid of the eggs.'

'*Most* of them are gone, but you can get an unpleasant surprise once in a while. Oh, my mad, wild girl – if only I'd known
you went to that cove to swim early in the mornings . . .'

'I never have before. But last night the heat – well, I don't think
I had any sleep at all. I just meant to walk a little in the garden,
but I kept on going. I know the way there – but I don't swim.
Can't! The most daring thing I've done so far is to take off my
boots and stockings and wade.'

'Well, it's the best cove,' he conceded. 'I don't often get so far
myself, but last night, as you say, the heat was fierce. Winterslo's
too close in under Kronberg for comfort. Most mornings I swim in
the bay closest to the house. But I was awake half the night too,
and with the moon so bright I just saddled up and timed it to be at
that cove at sunrise. It's one of the places I like best – I used to go
over there when I lived at Landfall . . .'

He had ridden, and yet not crossed the path of the chained
column of slaves heading away from the San Francisco cove? He
had heard nothing? Had not seen the vessel stand out to sea
from the San Francisco bay? All of it was possible – there were a
dozen different ways he could have come to the cove, and the time
that had lapsed between my encounter with Samuel and that final
waking on the edge of the water with the sun already warm on my
body had been considerable. I remembered the booted white men

who had moved with the procession, but it never occurred to me until this moment that Fergus might have been among them. Would he do such a thing? Would he join forces with Maria if money was involved? I did not believe it. I believed all the other stories of him – gambling, drinking, the women he had had, but I did not think him capable of the kind of deviousness that this morning's action would need. Fergus couldn't lie that well. I didn't think he could lie with his body; could I, myself, be so gullible and so savagely deceived? Had Maria sent him to find me when she found the open door? – had he been ordered to find out if indeed I had seen any of the happenings at San Francisco cove? Would I not have poured out the tale to the man who had just made love to me? Every woman would, so reasoning said; and was that why I had said nothing? Because the doubt was there – had always been there about Fergus. He had demanded answers of me, and I had given him none. But this morning I had made an answer with my own body. Once again I was aware of the cruel capriciousness of the gift that would let me see certain things that were to come, to sense some things that were buried in the past, but could not be summoned at will to tell me what I needed most in my life to know with certainty.

So I leaned back against Fergus and closed my eyes, and willed with all my strength to believe in him, to banish the doubts. Because now I was committed to him. For good or ill. I had loved with instinct, not reason. We came close to the house, and as if he sensed my thoughts, he checked his horse and leaned and kissed me on the mouth, a very gentle kiss, without passion, as if he sought to soothe and reassure.

'Leave everything to me,' he said.

Why did I doubt? Those were the words of a man assuming a responsibility, beginning to pay in love and support for what he had taken. I slid down off the horse, and he dismounted at the entrance to the stable yard. Although the path led to the kitchen entry, he led me round the building so that we might enter in the sight of everyone by the front steps. How could I doubt? – this was the action of a man proud of what was his.

They were all three in the hall – Maria dressed in a long wrapper, looking as fresh as if she had slept the night through. Andrew must have been told I was missing from the house, because he had dragged himself downstairs in his robe and sat with his jug beside him, bare-footed. Alister was dressed, impeccable and correct as always; he made it a habit to breakfast downstairs.

The doubt faded as I watched Maria's face. She had not ex-

pected this. The faces of all three registered, for brief seconds,
their private emotions. The faint look of shock that Alister permitted himself was immediately tightened out of existence. As
Andrew took in my appearance, a sly, knowing smile appeared; he
almost chuckled in triumph.

'We were getting a little anxious,' Alister said. Maria said
nothing, but that fact spoke most. Her features twisted as she
looked from me to Fergus, and I saw a kind of fear come into her
eyes that already held hatred. But I thought the fear had nothing
to do with the thought that I might have witnessed the events
in San Francisco cove. She stood rock-still, gripping the edge of
the long hall table. Then I saw that her eyes left me and seemed
to devour Fergus.

Fergus led me to his father.

'I want you to know that Fiona and I will be married – quite
soon.'

It was done. He never had asked me. I had told him to wait,
and still he had not asked me. But no asking had been done this
morning, either. And I had made no condition of acceptance,
either. We had not discussed, nor bargained nor planned. In those
few words, spoken now before them all, the questioning in my
mind was stilled.

It was as if in assuming responsibility for me, Fergus had also
gained authority in his father's house. He did not even glance
towards Maria. 'Go upstairs now, Fiona, and rest. You've had no
sleep. Duncan can do without you this morning. I will come
back. There will be things to discuss.'

3

I bathed, and Charity's hands had never seemed so gentle. She
seemed to chuckle several times while she tended me, a kind of
half-suggestive laugh. 'You and Master Fergus – you all fixed
now.' How quickly the news went among them. 'And that other
one – the mistress – she want to kill you for jealousy.'

I roused myself from the kind of half-doze I was in. 'Mistress
Maxwell has nothing to be jealous of. She has her husband and
her plantation.'

'Those things not enough for a woman like her, mistress. You
watch and take care. She not give up Master Fergus so easy – '

'Give up?' I grabbed at her arm and jerked her about to face
me. 'Give up! What is there to give up?'

'She never let go, that one. Not all these years. Why you think he never marry until now? She hold him, and make him wait. And her old husband, he drinks, and she help him to drink, and soon he be alive no longer, and then she have Master Fergus.'

'That isn't true, Charity! Why would Master Fergus wait so long? He's free . . .' My voice trailed off.

'That one use Obeah woman. Her woman, Juanita, what she bring from San Francisco with her, she very skilled with magic. Mistress make her use spells to keep Master Fergus alone there, waiting at Winterslo.'

'But she didn't keep him.' I was triumphant, sure. 'That's wrong. Now he's mine!'

Charity shrugged. 'But Mistress Fiona has magic of her own. Obeah woman see it and know it. A different kind. She tell Mistress Maria about you. So you take Master Fergus quickly, and you marry. And then it too late for the mistress.'

I sank back on the pillows. 'You're wrong, Charity – very wrong. There's no such thing as magic. White people don't have magic.'

There was a kind of contemptuous rumble in her throat. 'That what white people always say, but if they find Obeah, they punish those who make talk with the gods. So if there is no magic, why they afraid of it? I see white people die of black man's magic. I see their hearts dry up, and no white doctor able to save them. Maybe Mistress Maria already use it against her old husband since you come. She afraid now, because of you. But I think maybe your magic very strong too. You have not sickened. I watch. I see no signs.'

'I have no magic, Charity.'

'You *see* things, mistress. And because you see things you are strong against them. Now sleep and be rested, because there will be much trouble with the mistress.'

I closed my eyes, not able to argue, and she turned the louvers against the light, leaving the room on tiptoe. But she left no peace behind. It was nonsense – everything was nonsense that she spoke. One heard, of course, the tales of the dark powers that had come from Africa with the slaves, the secret knowledge passed on to the gifted. But one never believed them. And yet – and yet somehow they had known of my own wretched glimpses of the future. How had they known that? The happiness of the morning was destroyed. Not just this warning troubled me, but the terrible knowing words, 'She not give up Master Fergus so easy . . .' But it had all happened so long ago, and he was past the fever of his young, first love. He said he hated Maria. But did he still belong to her? I turned my face on the pillow and tried to shut out the thought. But a thousand doubts now repossessed me and I was reminded, horribly, of the first time I had seen Fergus, of that strong young shining beauty, laughing up at me, and the nameless, formless shadow I had seemed to glimpse in the deep shade of the trees behind him, the black rider of violence. There was no peace or rest.

I dozed fitfully, and when I rose again in time to meet Duncan when he returned from his morning ride, it was not Charity who came to the room to attend me, but instead a young woman, Flora, Juanita's daughter. She had always been Maria's second attendant, a faithful obeyer of her mother's instructions. I had never had any conversation with her. She was the kind who hung her head and pressed against the wall whenever a white person passed her. I had never cared much for the look of her, either – very thin, with a sharp face and claw-like hands.

'Where is Charity?'

She shook her head. 'Charity sick. Mistress say I look after you.'

'Nonsense! – Charity can't be sick! She was perfectly well a few hours ago.'

The girl hung her head and would not meet my gaze; I saw the faint shrug which suggested it wasn't her business to question orders. 'Mistress say Charity sick, and I to look after you,' she insisted.

I submitted. There was nothing I could do about it at this moment, but I hated the touch of those thin hands; even in the heat they seemed cold. I dismissed her as soon as possible, but she hung about stubbornly, folding clothes, tidying drawers, making clucking sounds of contemptuous disapproval that made her opinion of Charity's work clear. At last I had to go to Duncan and leave her alone in the room. I hated leaving her there to poke and pry among the few very personal things I had brought from Scotland, the cherished mementoes, those little presents pressed into my hand – the little book of my half-brother's drawings of the world of Silkirk as he saw it, the worn Bible from my father, a locket of my mother which I had never worn because the gold chain seemed too thin for safety – I think it must have been hard for my father to part with this. And there was the little velvet pincushion embroidered with my name that had been Mary's gift, a sort of thank-offering for my departure from Silkirk and leaving James Killian to her. I hated the cold, claw hands touching these things, the dark eyes studying them. I began to understand better why whites kept saying that the slaves knew everything, and in time they told everything.

When Duncan went to his siesta I went in search of Alister; he was not in the office, nor on any of the galleries. Andrew dozed with bent head on the red sofa. I beckoned Dougal to the hall.

'Master Alister – have you seen him? Is he riding?'

The man shook his head. 'Master Alister gone.'

'Gone? – gone where? To Santa Marta?' I was dismayed; it was to Alister I meant to tell my story of last night's happenings. He would know what to do, how to advise me. He would take it all out of my hands, and I would not have to face the problem of telling Fergus and wondering how he would act against his own father and Maria. I would not have to place the burden on him, because Alister would shoulder it; I didn't doubt that Fergus would be angry that I had first confided in Alister, but I couldn't help that. I was shielding him; it was what one did for the man one loved.

'Yes, to Santa Marta. In big hurry. But for good.'

'For good! You mean he's *left* Landfall!'

Dougal nodded. 'Left. Letter come this morning, and he say he must go back to England. He say ship leaving Santa Marta on morning tide, and he still have business to finish there. So he pack and go while Mistress Fiona sleep. But he leave letter – here.' He moved to the drawer of the long hall table and took out an envelope. 'He give it to me for you.'

I wondered if Maria had had it first – these were the kind of thoughts that came to me at Landfall. But when I turned it over I saw that Alister had also known the same thought, and it was heavily sealed and stamped with his own personal seal. I went to the bench out under the cottonwood where we had often sat and talked, and my hand trembled a little as I broke the seal.

My dear Fiona. News has come this morning from London that I am needed as soon as I can be there. There was not opportunity for a farewell; you were sleeping and, in any case, in this house, only the most formal words can be said without rousing the passions of those who hear them. I am sorry to leave at this stage, when perhaps my presence might make things easier for you. But my time here is up, and I have been able to accomplish little. You know I wish you happiness, always. Take your Fergus, and love and cherish him, as you know well how to. Do what you can for

Duncan. There may not be much time. I have a feeling there is very little time.

And so Alister went from me. I thought of how often I had watched that elegantly clad figure limp away from me down one of the garden walks, the head slightly bent, the hands clasped behind him, and the face, when one saw it, with its thoughtful, almost melancholy cast. He was gone; I could barely realize the fact. He had been part of Landfall since I had come, and unconsciously I had thought of him as being always here. A prop was gone from my existence. I looked back at that gleaming white house and I knew it held no friend. For the first time I was truly frightened.

4

After the siesta hours, all of which I had spent on the bench under the cottonwood as if the house were too hostile to enter, I went to the schoolroom to find Duncan in a perky, cheeky mood, and grinning with delight over the news that Fergus and I were to marry. He did not mention Alister, and I thought it probable that no one had bothered to tell him that Alister had gone. It would have happened during the morning ride, and perhaps Alister had never been more than a rather vague figure to Duncan, someone who had come to sit long hours in the office and who took solitary rides and walks. He could not have known the concern Alister felt for him and the helplessness in the face of it. I did not speak of his going now; I had not the courage for it. For me it was supposed to be a happy day.

'Now you'll always stay?' Duncan demanded of me. 'I'll always have you.'

'I'll be living at Winterslo,' I said quietly. 'I can't be with you all the time. And then' – why be coy with him? – 'Fergus and I will probably have little boys of our own – girls too.'

'But I'll be *first*,' he said. 'I'll still be the first.'

I nodded. 'Yes, I suppose you will always be the first.' And I conceded that indeed he might stay first in my heart, even with the always intrusive knowledge that he could be Fergus's son. 'Perhaps,' I said, to give him hope, 'your mama will let you come to Winterslo for lessons.'

He scowled, looking terribly like Fergus as he did. 'My mama says that some day I must go to Spain to be educated. That's why she always speaks Spanish to me when we ride each morning. I pretend not to understand, and that makes her angry, but it

pleases my father. I know *he* won't let me go to Spain. But when
he's dead mama will be able to do as she likes.' The childish voice
trembled; he had accepted already the thought of his father's
death, but the changes it would bring were harder to imagine. 'But
if she tries to send me, I'll run away to Winterslo.'

'I don't think we would be allowed to keep you, Duncan.' Why
build false hopes in him? 'Try not to worry about it. You are too
young to send anywhere yet, and by the time you are grown perhaps your mama will have changed her mind. Perhaps you may
even want to go – to travel off the island.'

'I will *never* want to go to Spain,' he answered firmly. 'I think
Spain is filled with ugly, dirty old women like my grandmother,
Donna Isabella. My aunts aren't so bad – but they don't count at
San Francisco. They do everything Donna Isabella says.'

'She is an old lady, Duncan. Often old people don't understand young boys – they've forgotten what it was like when they
were young.'

'She was cruel to me,' he said bitterly. 'One time my mother
took me over to San Francisco, and they talked, and told me to go
to play. There was nothing to do – no one to play with. I went
over to the stables, but there was no one there, either. So I started
exploring those ruins at the back – San Francisco is the oldest greathouse on the island and had the most land. They had big store-
rooms and slave quarters – and places like that. They've all fallen
down now, but I had a good time exploring them. Then my mother
and Donna Isabella came looking for me, and when they discovered where I was Donna Isabella whipped me. Across the
breeches and on my shoulders – not the bare skin, like the slaves.
But she *did* whip me and I hadn't done anything wrong. So now
when my mother takes me to San Francisco on the morning ride,
I just sit out there under the big tree and hold my pony, and I
don't even take a drink when one of my aunts brings it to me.
Donna Isabella would like to whip me for *that* too, but my mother
won't let her.'

I felt his fear and bitterness; I also had known the whip of
Donna Isabella's tongue. I did not dare say openly that his sense
of grievance was justified – that would have stiffened it and led
to more trouble.

'You will soon be grown up, Duncan, and no one will whip
you, ever. That is why you must never whip a slave – they feel it
just as you did then. And they hate you for it. And one day the
whip may turn around, and be in *their* hands.'

'It couldn't be,' he said, incredulous. 'The law won't let them have things like that. We are their masters. We own them!'

'Oh, Duncan – Duncan, it can't always stay this way! One day it will change. You have to be ready for the day the law says you must drop the whip, and the black man will be free.'

'If that ever happens I will come running to Winterslo. Winterslo will be safer. Fergus never beats his slaves, so you see, they will go on letting Fergus be their master.'

It was a childish, simplistic solution to the woes that might be to come; and yet it seemed to represent about the only answer the white man in the Indies had so far prepared for himself against the day when the whole structure of his world would tumble about him.

The shock of Alister's going had driven the thought of Charity from my mind; I was struck with a strong sense of guilt and annoyance to find that Flora was once again waiting to help me dress for dinner. She stood there, sullen, with her eyes on the ground, waiting with the towels and the scented water.

'Charity is ill?' I asked her. 'What is it – a fever?'

She shook her white-turbaned head. 'Don't know, mistress. I not ask about Charity. Mistress Maria jus' say look after you, and I do it until she tell me stop.'

There was nothing to be got from her; the whole washing and dressing ritual was an aggravation at her hands. I submitted with as good grace as I could, but I shrunk from her touch. The final assault on my nerves came when she was brushing my hair, before tying it into its knot. It was something I disliked even Charity doing, but with this woman it became intolerable. I closed my eyes for a time, trying to calm myself, knowing it would soon be over; but the cessation of her movement, and the sudden reaching past me to the dressing table, roused me. I started as I saw the pair of scissors in her hand.

With a movement as sharp as Maria might have made, I struck her arm, and the fingers, nerveless with fright, released the scissors and they went flying across the polished floor.

'What are you up to?' I turned away from the mirror to face her directly. 'What are you trying to do?'

In answer, rolling frightened eyes, she held up a handful of hair from the back of my head. 'It longer than the other parts, mistress. Jus' tryin' to fix it. It not go in properly with other parts.'

I stood up. 'I will tell you when to cut my hair. Never dare to do such a thing. Now go – go. I will manage very well by myself.'

6

She cringed. 'But mistress say I look after you. She beat me if she know I don't do it.'

'Out!' I said. 'I will tell the mistress I won't want any help. I will tell her I told you to go.'

'Please, mistress . . . please. Mistress Maria beat me.'

'The mistress will not beat you when I tell her I sent you away.'

She submitted, and the smooth glide of her bare feet announced her going. She was frightened because she was stupid, I told myself; no one would beat her if I said I preferred to wait until Charity could attend me herself – as if I needed attending! With hands that trembled with rage, I bundled my hair into a clumsy knot, buttoned my own buttons as I had done all my life, and then ran, in the gathering darkness, down through the house and out by the back way towards the stables and the slave quarters.

I wasn't welcome there, as I had known. The slaves were gathered about their fires and their cooking pots, the only time of day they were free of their master, the only time to gossip and sing the songs that had not the melancholy rhythm of the cane fields, the only time to revert to the African life that was for most of them not even a vague memory, but only a tradition.

'Charity?' I demanded of the first group. 'Where is Charity?' They shook their heads dumbly.

'Is she sick? Does she have a fever?'

Again no reply. 'Which is her hut?' They pointed, several pointed, but no one would speak a word. I went to it and looked inside. It was dark; there was no fire before its door. Even in the darkness I knew its emptiness; there was the sound of emptiness about it. I knew that not a thing remained there.

'Where's Samuel?'

Someone pointed towards the stables; I raced back there, leaving behind me a deathly silence at each of the cooking fires. They would not be at ease again, they would not sing again, tonight, I thought.

Samuel was at his last task of rubbing down a horse. He halted as I came to him.

'Samuel – where's Charity?'

He didn't attempt the policy of silence the others had given me. He had saved me the night before; a bond existed and we both recognized it. Mutual trust existed; it had been forged by this black man; it was no gift of mine, from whom it should first have come.

'Charity is gone,' he said.

'Gone! What do you mean? Run away?'

C.G.O.–T

'Not run away. Nowhere to run away to all alone. No – Charity sold. Sold to a man on the other side of the island. Very sudden. Mistress says she to be house slave to a man who is getting married and have no other house slave yet.' His voice jerked, but his clever, gentle, strong hands on the animal were still.

'Sold!' I couldn't believe it. 'Sold! – but she belongs to Landfall.'

'Charity was born at Landfall – same as I was. But she sold away from it. Her son – he go with her. But he *my* son, Mistress Fiona. Charity have two other children – but they sold away long ago. But this one *my* son. I have to find out where he gone. I have to get him back. I think I know, and if I know, I get them back.'

'But if they are just the other side of the island . . .?'

He shook his head, and the dark face was suddenly twisted with rage. 'Mistress Fiona saw las' night. She know what happen. Slaves come – slaves go. I think Charity and my son be sold off the island. I have to stop it, mistress – I don't know how I do it, but somehow I do it.'

'Why should she be sold now? – *now*?'

He shook his head. 'How I know what goes on in Mistress Maria's mind?' For a moment he went back to brushing the horse, as if to calm himself, to gain control. At last he spoke, hesitantly. A slave was not used to offering opinions to his masters, or to being asked for them. 'I think . . .'

'Yes?'

'I think maybe Charity become too close to Mistress Fiona – she grow fond of her like she belong with her. She say these things to me. And Mistress Maria don't like that. Charity not tell her things she want to know. Maybe she not do things Mistress Maria bid her about Mistress Fiona. Mistress Maria will not stand for anyone to oppose her.'

I was stunned. 'Because of *me*! And you think she's being sold off the island? Where to – America? How can we stop it, Samuel? What can we do?'

His despair was in his action as he leaned his dark head against the horse's neck. The deep voice was muffled; he had begun with confidence, but the confidence was false. 'What is there to do? It is death to run away. But even death be sometimes better – but Charity and my son would suffer too. Maybe they can't stand the pain so well. And if we try, where to go? No boat, no money, no place for the black man to go. No place but back to Africa, and we never get back there. No way to get back there. Even the wind

blow the wrong way for any black man to get back to Africa. Only
the soul of the black man get back there after the white man has
squeezed all the work from his body. Only the soul can go against
the wind, mistress.'

I turned and ran back to the house, and I felt the tears that
Samuel would not shed running down my face. What had we
done? – what had we wrought on this earth, all of us? – those who
knew what they did, and those, like myself, who had been guilty
of never caring until it struck at our own persons, our own hearts.
I had spoken more truly than I knew to Duncan that afternoon –
some day the whip would turn around and be in their hands.
And our own souls would know the wind that blew the wrong
way.

I was late to dinner; they were already seated, and Fergus was
there. Somehow I had not expected him to come for the meal, but
he was there, and his presence comforted me. It was strange to
look across at where Alister had always sat and to miss him. I did
not offer any apology or explanation to Maria; things had moved
past that.

'So Alister is gone,' I said.

'Yes, and good riddance! Damned nuisance,' Andrew responded.
'Perhaps now we'll have some peace from reforming this and
changing that.'

'It is a time of change,' I said. 'Everywhere. Alister means to be
part of it. Alister is simply a man of his age.'

'Oh,' Fergus said, a little ruffled, 'you're becoming a politician
now, are you?'

I smiled at him. 'Rest easy. It will be a long time before women
are politicians. I have no ambitions to change things in too much of
a hurry. But I just hope I recognize change when it comes. I am
sorry, though, I did not see Alister before he left. I might have
hoped that next time he was in Scotland he would call on my
father and tell him – '

Maria cut me off. 'I would not let him disturb you. I assumed
you needed rest – after your morning's exertions.'

I managed to smile at the barb, both the inference of what
had happened between Fergus and myself and the suspicion that I
had in fact seen something of what had taken place in San Francisco cove. 'I was quite rested, thank you – but I sorely missed
Charity's help. Is it true she has been sold?'

'And what if it is?' Maria challenged directly my right to question any arrangement made by the mistress of the house.

'It was sudden.'

'Sudden? – no, I don't think so. Charity has not given satisfaction for some time. She has grown careless. The other day she broke several crystal glasses. She was fortunate she received no more than a reprimand. On other plantations . . .' Maria shrugged.

'But she was born at Landfall.'

'So now she goes elsewhere. Perhaps to a mistress who will not be so lenient. And Landfall will do with two less slaves. Her son went with her. What a pity Alister is not here to know about the new economy rule instituted at Landfall. Two less mouths to feed, and a handsome sale entered in the books. He would have commended me for once, would Alister. But he is gone – and so is Charity.' She actually smiled at me, or it seemed like a smile – gloating, perhaps, a little, that two props of my existence had been removed. I looked around the table; there were just the four of us left, dangerously cross-tangled.

After dinner I waited for Fergus on the gallery and we went into the garden together. The first moments of our embrace felt to me like a return from a long journey – and yet I had waited only since that morning. It was the beloved feel of the familiar, the longed-for, the well-known, and yet I knew only what my heart and senses told me of him. If my senses were wrong now, then they had been wrong all my life, and would be for the rest of it. Our bargaining had been swift and unspoken, and we were committed. I abandoned myself to the feel and the touch and the excitement of him, the pleasure of his hands, his lips. How did one live for so long without knowing such pleasure existed?

Once again I held back the information of what I had discovered that morning at San Francisco. I would not yet shatter the happiness of these first hours in which we knew we were bound to each other. Now that Alister was gone, the urgency was gone also. It occurred to me that Fergus might already know of what went on at San Francisco and kept silent, because if he were to make any accusation his own father would be involved – Andrew Maxwell would be held responsible for his wife's actions. Perhaps he had already talked with Maria about it and had been reminded of the public scandal it would cause, and again his father's responsibility. It was clear that Maria did not run the operation without help from others in Santa Marta – other interests too powerful for a young man like Fergus, without money or influence, to fight. It could be that he was inured to it, just the way he and all the rest of the planters accepted slavery itself. Duncan wasn't the only one who needed re-education. I wondered, with a shade of unease, what my father would think when I wrote that I was going to marry a man who owned slaves, who believed in slavery? And then I thought wryly that emancipation, if it came soon enough, might save me that problem. We would have other problems then.

I deferred also talking to him about Charity. Samuel would find out if indeed she and his son were intended for sale off the island, and if he came to me with that news then I would speak out. I would speak out to Fergus, to Andrew – and mostly to Maria. I would threaten in whatever way I could, even if it were the fairly impotent threat of making her activities public knowledge. This was where my own responsibility lay. If Charity were sold into the American states now, then her chance of freedom was gone, probably forever. Tomorrow I would find out from Samuel what he had discovered. If she had really been sold to a planter on the island, then she was safe. If she had not, then I would have to act. I dreaded it, and this was a moment again when I missed Alister. He would have had so much more authority and weight than I possessed.

And then I missed nothing, because Fergus had laid his head down on my shoulder, his lips against my neck. 'It will have to be soon, Fiona. I'm not going to wait – I can't wait.'

'There's no need to wait,' I answered. 'No need to wait – if you're sure.'

'Sure!' He raised his head, and his strong, rough hand tilted back my chin painfully to make me look up at him. 'It's been like coming out of some wilderness. Since . . . since Maria I've been drifting. She may be savage, but she is strong. God, how strong she is! You are the only thing I have found stronger than Maria, the balance that outweighs her. Some of the things that have been in my life between haven't been pretty – things that have happened in Santa Marta. But I kept hoping for an end – a reason to end it. Oh, it hasn't all been bad. I've been slowly coming to my senses and I've worked hard at Winterslo. But the wine of my leisure has been bitter as gall. I've had enough – I've done with it. I want only you.'

'And I – ' I said. 'I have to have you. I want to have children with you. To work with you. Anything, anywhere – just so long as I am with you.'

His grip relaxed a little; he let my chin drop. 'You believe me that there's no money, don't you? All that talk about my father promising me money to settle down and marry the right sort of woman is just so much talk. My father can say what he likes, but when the time comes, it won't be there to give – and I don't look for it. You've seen Winterslo – there's just me and that.'

'I know it,' I said. 'I told you I was prepared to work. I've never had luxuries – not until Landfall, and everything at Landfall is unreal. What will I miss? Your grandmother and your father made enough out of Winterslo. Can't we do the same?'

'Suppose . . .' he said the words grudgingly. 'Suppose all this talk of emancipation comes to something? What then?'

'You'll have to pay the slaves to work, that's what. They'll be free to leave you and go elsewhere. But there'll be compensation. There'll be something, Fergus.' Now it was I who gripped him hard and tried to shake that bulk of man. 'We can do *something*. So what if we're poor and there isn't silver on the table? We will have Winterslo, and the rain will fall, and the sun will shine, and the cane will still grow. There'll be less money – but we won't starve. You've never been in Scotland, Fergus, so you don't know how we feel about land. Just own the land, and have shelter from the rain, and you're already a king.'

'A king?' He smiled, and I realized then how rarely he did it, how seldom it was not the sardonic smile that attempted to conceal bitterness and hurt. 'Would you make me a king, Fiona? A king of a little worn-out strip of territory where too little rain falls, and when it does the roof leaks?'

'To me, you are a king. No less – do you want more?'

He gathered me again into his arms. 'You know,' he said, his lips against my hair, 'I almost want to weep. Me! – a grown man. I have not wept since my grandmother died. Why do you unnerve me – unman me?'

'I did not unman you this morning.'

Now he laughed, loudly, a laugh that would be heard by those within the house, a joyous laugh of triumph and pleasure and mastery.

'No – nor shall you! There will be many other mornings, Fiona.'

5

Counting the candles on the long table, it seemed that I was the last to go upstairs. Only one remained – an oversight, I thought, because Alister had been so long a guest in the house. The sight of it made me feel again my vulnerability, now that Fergus was not here and the stabilizing presence of Alister gone. I wished there had

been a chance to say good-bye, but then it would have been, as he
said, no more than formal words uttered before the others. I looked
into Duncan's room to see that he was sleeping, and then went to
my own. It was an unpleasant shock to see Flora seated cross-
legged on the floor by the open louver doors, her head nodding
in sleep. She sprang to her feet as I entered.

'What are you doing here?' I demanded. I heard my own
voice, sharp and rasping. I had had too much this day, and I did
not want this woman now.

She hung her head. 'I help mistress . . .'

'I told you, Flora, I don't need help. Now go, please.'

'Mistress Maria say I am to help you.'

I made myself take her bony shoulder and I gave her a slight
shake to emphasize what I said. 'Now understand, Flora. You won't
be punished – but I don't care what Mistress Maria says, I prefer
to take care of myself. Go now – go !'

There was no pleading from her as there had been before.
Perhaps I was also growing hard in the crucible of Landfall. But I
caught her last direct look at me before the head went down into
the customary position; I saw the eyes, black, passive no longer,
blazing momentarily as if a fire had been lighted there. And
I knew for myself what most white people must sooner or later learn
in these places – the absolute and unrelenting hatred of the black.
I remembered something I had once heard about needing to
grow up and to make enemies. I had truly come of age at Landfall.

Sleep fell on me like a blanket that night. Even with the consciousness of both love and hate earned on this, the most momentous day of my life, I fell into a sleep that was part exhaustion. I hadn't bothered to braid my hair – even though I would not
admit it consciously, I did miss Charity's ministrations. So I spread
it like a fan about me on the pillow, and I slept within seconds
of lying down.

I don't know why I woke from such a sleep, except that in an
atmosphere such as Landfall's, one's senses are never fully deadened. I struggled out of sleep, my eyelids still weighted. I heard
no movement, saw nothing. But I had the choking knowledge
of danger; I felt it, as I had felt other things, not to be explained
reasonably. I opened my eyes wide and let them grow accustomed
to the darkness, lying quite still on my side and trying to keep my
breathing rhythmical and deep. Then abruptly I flung myself
round in the bed, sitting up in the one movement. I looked then

straight into the face of Flora; even in the darkness I knew it – its shape, the glow and intensity of the eyes.

My own hand flew to my lips to suppress the scream I wanted to let out.

'You! What are you doing? What are you about?'

I flung back the sheet and dropped to the floor; she was forced to retreat before me. 'What?' I demanded. 'What? – *what*?' With each word a violent shake of her shoulder.

'Nothing – nothing. Jus' to see you all right. Mistress tell me –'

I slapped her face, hard. My fear and rage were undoing me; I was scarcely able to control myself. In those terrible seconds I wondered what Landfall was doing to me – to hit Fergus as I had with the riding crop, to strike this woman who dared not strike back. And yet some powerful premonition told me that I must be done with her forever.

'Go!' I said. 'Go! Never come back into this room. *Never!*' I was holding up my hand and she was retreating before me all the time I spoke. 'It is bad for you to come back . . .' If this primitive ritual was all she would listen to or understand, then she would have it. 'I see things . . . bad things for you.'

She was visibly frightened. She backed away from me to the door and, still facing me, attempted to open it with one hand. Something dropped from her other hand and slid across the floor. The downward slanted moonlight from the louvers caught its gleam. I went and picked it up; Flora stood as if frozen. It was the scissors with which she had tried to cut my hair the evening before.

I went straight to her, brandishing them in her face; she leaned away from me, terrified. 'Why do you steal this? Why?'

'Not steal, mistress. Jus' come to look after you. Come to cut the spells that gather at the full of the moon. Mistress not understand these things. I take care . . .'

'No! You do not take care!' I held them between our two faces like a talisman. 'Do not come near me again. I make spells far more powerful than scissors can cut – more powerful than your gods make. So keep away!'

Her hands scrabbled at the door handle like a frightened animal; a soft click, and she was gone. Very slowly I went back and replaced the scissors on the bureau and returned to bed. I was trembling and soaked in sweat. There was no more sleep. I was made wretched by what I had done. To strike her was bad enough, but I had done worse. By those who know it – and the unfortunate few who possess it, the gift of 'the sight', or the curse of it – is never taken lightly, nor spoken of, nor invoked without truth. It cannot be called up at will. I had used the threat of it fraudulently to frighten that poor, ignorant girl. I had misused its power. In each of the few instances when I had known its presence before it had been involuntary, and I had spoken without calculation. Tonight I had felt no such compulsion, merely used the sensations I had known before to frighten, and to protect myself. I had begun to know power, and that was dangerous. I had begun to know corruption.

6

It was earlier than ever before when I heard Andrew's pacing on the gallery outside – before even the first glimmer of light had touched the sky. Something had changed in the sound of that pacing, too – it was not the slow shuffle of a man with nothing to do, but someone with a purpose. Up and down, up and down – a pause, as if he stopped to see or to listen, and then the pacing resumed. I got out of bed and put on my wrapper, and went and opened the long doors to the gallery.

'Fiona?' It was no greeting. I could just distinguish his bulky outline as he leaned against the railing, staring outward, as if he strove to see what was yet hidden. The moon was down, and the first light of the dawn had not yet come.

'Come here!' I joined him at the railing; he smelled of rum and tobacco and sweat; a sleepless night for him also, I thought.

'Do you hear it?'

'What?'

'The wind, girl – the wind.'

'There is always the wind – except at night and these summer months.'

'Not from this quarter. It's coming from the wrong quarter, the lee shore, damn it!'

'What does it mean?'

'A storm – that's what it means. Perhaps a big one. We may have a hurricane coming at us, Fiona.'

' "October all over," ' I quoted him, from Duncan's rhyme.

'I wish I could believe it. The worst hurricane I ever knew on San Cristóbal came in early October. I remember it – when I was about Duncan's age. It took two days to pass completely over the island – and there was this great calm suddenly in the middle of it, and then the wind again. We harvested no crop at Winterslo that year, I'll tell you – nor did any other plantation on the island. And we all pulled our belts tighter, whites as well as slaves.'

I felt a kind of excited fear tug at me. 'You think this is one of the great winds?'

'Listen to it, girl – listen to it!'

It had a low eerie moaning sound, with sudden, sharp gusts that blew my hair wildly; and it did come from the wrong quarter – it was not the north-easterly trade that blew the ships across from the African coast. Even the air smelled different, as if it were charged with some power. In the gusts I could taste the salt, driven on it, driven right across the island from the wrong direction.

'It's dark,' I said. 'Why doesn't it get lighter? It's past the time – surely it's past the time.'

'It may stay dark. This may be one day you don't see the sun on San Cristóbal, Fiona.' He leaned farther out on the rail, his eyes fixed on the horizon, where now, just the first sullen streak of grey was beginning to show. His white hair blew about him, his beard and chin jutted forward as if he were trying to smell something, like an animal.

'It's out there – it's out there. A big one, I think. But who knows how big? – how it will turn? I've heard them coming, and then going, and then twisting back again in two days to the same place. I wish I knew – God, I wish I knew what this one was to be! We may decide it will be a big blow, and it may pass by harmlessly, and all we will get is an hour or two of heavy rain. Or it may come straight at us and we could be flattened. Well, I'm going down to look at the barometer . . .' He shuffled off, and I was left standing at the railing, watching the ominous grey that crept into the sky, feeling the sudden slash of rain on my face, and something that clung there wetly – the shredded petal of a blossom.

I turned and went to Duncan's room to wake him. If the great wind of legend was to come, it would be the first for both of us. I knew I had to keep him close.

The roars of Andrew from the outer gallery below roused any in the household who might still have slept through the rising wind. 'Barometer's near bottom! Everyone up! – everyone start getting ready!'

I bundled Duncan into his clothes and rushed to my own room to dress myself. The wind was increasing. I could hear the scurry of slaves all over the house. It was very strange not to be washing and dressing in the radiant, sharp beauty of the tropic dawn. Except that it was oppressively hot, it seemed more like the dark mornings when the winter storms had raged in from the Atlantic at Silkirk. The rain was almost continuous; through the house I could hear the banging of any of the louver doors that no one had yet had time to fasten. I took Duncan downstairs with me; we ate breakfast standing around the sideboard – just bread and butter, and hot tea. We stood there, because there was no time for any of the slaves to wait on us. Duncan giggled and nudged me. 'No oatmeal,' he said. I thought it was lucky Andrew didn't hear him laugh. He seemed in a mood to clip his ear for levity.

Andrew appeared suddenly to have come into his own; he still staggered about, still needing his cane and Dougal's arm for support, but for the first time since I had come to Landfall, no one thought to look to other than he for orders. Maria was quiet, and seemed strangely preoccupied, as if the coming storm was a threat to more than Landfall; she obeyed Andrew without question, as we all did.

The shock of those early hours was the appearance of Alister, riding alone, drenched to the skin, a bundle of clothing wrapped in tarpaulin strapped to the saddle before him. He slipped off his horse and hitched it to the stair rails. Andrew, moving through the hall on Dougal's arm, stopped.

'What the devil are you back for?'

Alister shrugged wearily. 'I had some idea I might be of more use here than sitting it out in Santa Marta. I went on board late last night, but they began to feel the swell from the wrong quarter long before dawn. The captain said he'd not take a chance on putting out into it until he saw how it blew. If it was going to be a bad one, I thought I might help you here ...'

Andrew just grunted. 'Are you able to ride farther? There's some hours before it will reach its height, if I'm any judge. Never know, though, how quickly these things are moving. Well, will you ride out again?'

Alister's head jerked back, and a flood of crimson came to his face. 'I'm able, at least, to do that!'

'All right – all right! Don't start getting touchy now. We may all be cooped up here for days, and we'll need what patience we've got. Well then, here's what I want you to do. Get Samuel to saddle you up a fresh mount, and get one or two of the cane carts harnessed up. Throw in a cushion or two if you think it's necessary. Take Samuel with you. Then get over to San Francisco and get that fat old she-devil and her two daughters over here. And all the slaves . . .'

It was then Maria made her only protest. 'No – no! My mother will never come. She will never leave San Francisco!'

'Well then, if the storm grows worse, San Francisco will be her burial mound. That old heap won't stand a blow like the one we had sixteen years ago. Half of Santa Marta went with that one.'

'*I* was at San Francisco sixteen years ago. It held up. My fore-fathers on this island built well.'

'Don't give me any damn nonsense now about your forefathers. *I'm* responsible for the women they left behind. I don't care what you do, Alister, but make her come.'

He turned and went back down the steps and unhitched the horse to lead it around to the stables. I had just a moment to run to the edge of the gallery, the rain slashing at me. I reached a hand towards him, and for an instant only we touched. 'Thank God you've come back,' I said. And his weary smile was my answer.

I stopped Andrew in the hall to ask about Fergus.

'Fergus? He's the least of my worries. Fergus knows what to do.'

He paid me no more attention, and I was left to worry about what he meant by those words as he set me my own tasks. Firstly I was to supervise the removal of all the furniture from both the inner and outer galleries into the centre core of the house. 'If it hits us directly,' he said tersely, 'the rain will come at us almost horizontally. The hurricane shutters will keep most of it out, but some will come under the doors and in at the sides. Anything valu-able will have to be moved out of its reach. Anything that can move – or fly – with the wind will go. Remember that. And when that's done, go upstairs and see that every piece of furniture is moved up against the inner walls. The lighter pieces can be moved on to the landing. We will see to closing the shutters. My wife will see to the food . . .'

The kitchen quarters were on the outer gallery at the back, and therefore vulnerable to the wind. They could not be used so long as a hurricane blew; ever since the first word had been given by Andrew there had been a flurry of cooking – the ovens brought up to heat and the sides of meat brought in from the outbuildings to be cooked and made ready, the dough pounded for bread, as if we prepared for a siege. The fires were to be put out before the wind blew too strongly. 'Seen places burned down from a spark left in the kitchen when the wind blew too fierce,' Andrew grumbled.

There was a convoy of slaves set to carrying water into the house, filling every receptacle that anyone could find – vases, glasses, pitchers, bowls and buckets. 'But with all this rain . . .?' I questioned Andrew, 'won't there be plenty of water?'

He glared at me. 'Don't tell me you really *are* stupid, girl? Do you think you're going to stand out there with a bucket and collect it as it falls? We can't get to the cisterns – couldn't think of opening one of those shutters at the height of it if we are hit directly. Stupid . . . didn't think you were that stupid.' And he went off.

Perhaps I was stupid; it seemed to me many times that morning as I went about the tasks allotted to me, that a kind of mist would come before my eyes, and I had to keep repeating to myself the instructions that Andrew had given me, and I found my tongue seemed to stick over certain words as I gave the orders. I had never seen the slaves move as quickly as they did then – or was I that much slower? The pace that preserves one against the heat was dropped. Everyone moved with speed and surprising agility; it was as if they moved to the rhythm of a new order, a new dance. Perhaps it was fear, perhaps it was simply the stimulus of change in those unchanging lives. Duncan came with me everywhere, moving his own most cherished possessions on to the gallery around the staircase, where they would be safest from the rain. I found it sometimes hard to keep up with this new pace; I was clutching doorways and banisters as I watched the furniture lined up against the inner walls, the cane chairs piled, the rush-matting rolled and placed safely. I did it against the crushing grip of the worst headache I had ever known, the kind of headache that made it a small agony to turn my head or bend my neck. I told myself that it was the storm – wasn't there something about atmospheric pressure? But whatever it was, I had to go on. Everyone had their tasks to see to, and mine must be done. Sometimes, though, through the haze of pain, I saw Duncan looking at me with puzzlement, but he said nothing. I found as I made my rounds that I was leaning on him. He seemed to understand, with his precious knowledge, that I needed him. He stayed close and didn't ask questions.

As this went on Andrew himself was overseer for the more serious preparations. As the outer galleries were cleared, the shutter doors were closed, as they were every night; then, outside them, the great stout hurricane doors were closed – those that I had thought of as largely ornamental now moved on their massive black hinges. Huge cradles of metal were ready to receive the iron bars placed horizon-

tally into them, to lock the shutters tight against the wind. It was
almost like the sound of doom as each of the big doors was swung
into place, and the bars came down with a crash – the feeling
returned that we were closing ourselves into a medieval fortress
against a siege. I could hear Andrew swearing as some of the shutters resisted, the hinges creaking. 'I'll have the hide flogged off
those responsible for letting these things go. Look at this – rust!
One good gust and it could go. Lazy bastards!' And then more
cursing as he saw that some of the shutters had warped, and it
took several slaves with hammers to pound them into place. 'Fellowes!' Andrew roared. 'Where's that idiot? – why isn't he here
helping?'

'I sent him yesterday to Santa Marta,' Maria answered. 'I expect he stayed overnight.'

'Hmm . . . but Alister came back, didn't he? *He* got himself
here. Must say I never expected him to have the guts. Could have
sat it out nicely in Lawrence's. Santa Marta would slide into the
sea before *that* place would go. Well, Fellowes always was worthless . . .'

'Are any of them any different?' Maria retorted. 'Alister blames
me, but –'

'All right. We'll have plenty of time to argue the merits of overseers later on. How are they doing in the kitchen . . .?'

The centre of the house grew darker and darker as each shutter
was closed against the slashing grey rain. Within, it was like night –
like no night I had ever known at Landfall. But we were permitted
few candles or lamps.

'Save the candles – save the oil. It may be all we have for the
next three days.'

Finally, exhausted, Andrew fell back into his red sofa; Dougal
hastily topped a glass with rum. 'I remember the last time we did
this – before you were born, Duncan. No – not before you were
born. You were a year old, and didn't care what was happening.
It was a day just like this. Started with this kind of wind and rain.
We made all the same preparations. Cooked up everything –
turned the house upside down. It must have been the tail of it we
caught. The wind died that same afternoon – a little rain misted
over, for all the world like the sort of thing I remember from
London. One of the quietest days I remember on the island. We
waited, in case it came back at us, but finally we undid it all and
put everything back in place, and ate cooked meat for two weeks.
And then the ships started coming into Santa Marta – those that
were in fit shape for the voyage and not on the rocks. Down the

island they caught it – Martinique, St Lucia – torn apart. Hundreds drowned. Buildings gone, plantations ruined. That's the way of the big winds. They circle and sweep, and it takes you months – if you ever do – to find out exactly where they began and where they went to. If you pray, Miss Fiona, pray that today we are doing all this for nothing, and that we'll eat cooked meat for two weeks.'

It came to the time when he roared the order. 'Maria – tell them to douse the fires. I don't like the sound of the wind.'

It had been rising steadily – so much so that it became difficult to hear what was said against its howl and the drumming of the rain against the roof and outside shutters; some of the gusts rose to shrieks, and seemed to claw at the house as if it would pull its bones apart. All the storm shutters save the last one leading to the kitchen quarters, and one other, on the side away from the direction of the wind – ironically the Atlantic side – were closed. I heard them closing up the kitchen one.

'How?' I said, my voice sounding to me oddly slurred as I tried to focus more clearly on the things around me. 'How will Alister get in? How will anyone get in? Once that last door is closed we'll never hear them.'

'We don't close the last door,' Andrew answered. 'We keep a tight hook on it to stop it slamming about, but it is still open a little. It's important to remember in a big wind always to leave an escape hatch on the side away from the wind. Some wind always forces itself in – you must give it somewhere to go or you could burst your own shutters. But you've got to watch it – every minute you've got to watch it. If you should get into that calm that sometimes comes in the middle of a big wind, then you have to be ready to close that side and open up on the other the second the wind starts again, because it can be coming from the other direction. At least, that is what they tell us, those who've been through the calm. Of course, from others we never get any information, because they're dead.'

He chuckled grimly, and applied himself to the rum again, and it suddenly struck me, through the growing obtuseness that the headache had brought, that he had actually enjoyed the whole performance of this ritual. He had taken all precautions, but he didn't really care what happened now. He soon would die himself, and he knew it; he didn't really care if he and all this should be swept away in the wind that blew from the direction that no man could foretell.

2

At last Alister came, his clothes plastered to his frame, his hair beaten down about his cheeks. The two sisters, Katarina and Joanna, were in the same state, the clinging wet dresses only serving to emphasize the thinness of their bodies, the dark hair hanging down gave them a strangely crow-like appearance. They stood there, pools of water forming about them, with a beaten look of exhaustion and fear. Five pathetic-looking slaves had followed them. They huddled together as near to the still-open door as they could, round, frightened eyes gazing apprehensively at Andrew.

Alister only came to the edge of the gallery; the horse and the mule had still to be stabled.

'The old woman,' Andrew shouted. 'Where is she?'

'Wouldn't come,' Alister yelled back.

'I told you to make her come, no matter what.'

'You neglected to remind me to take a gun. I rounded up the slaves – all hiding in the outbuildings, with the two women doing all the work to get the place ready. I tried to get the slaves to force her into the cart – she's not a woman you can pick up in one hand, remember. She threatened to blow my head off if I came near her. I told her she was in danger – she laughed at me. "Just leave me a good supply of San Francisco rum," was all she said. "I'll sit it out, as I've sat out all the others, and in no other house than the Medinas'." '

'I told you . . . !' Maria cried. 'I told you!' And then she turned on her sisters. 'And you left her. Fine ones you are! Well, you will suffer for it!'

Katarina wiped back hair from her forehead with a gesture of infinite weariness. Then she spread both hands so that we could see them – scratched, bleeding, blood welling at the knuckles. 'Suffer! – as if we haven't already! How long is it, my fine sister, since you have tried to hammer a storm shutter into place, with the wood cracking and splintering before your eyes? One, on an upstairs room, came off its hinges and struck me.' She made a jerking notion of her head towards her left shoulder. The rain had washed all their garments so thoroughly that it wasn't until now that we were aware of the blood that was soaking the wet sleeve. Her arm dangled limp and awkwardly.

Alister had had enough of it. His horse, held by a stable boy, was restive as the boughs of the trees near it slashed and moaned.

'I did what I could,' he said tersely. 'If the old woman wants to die there, perhaps that should be her choice. I'm off to the stable. Will there be some men staying there with the horses?'

'Yes,' Andrew answered. 'The best ones I have. We try to keep the horses quiet. The stables are well built. They'll not go in the wind, unless it's worse than it's ever been.'

'Samuel will stay there,' Maria said. 'He is best with the horses.'

'Samuel isn't here. He's gone.'

Shock registered even on Andrew's face. 'Gone! – gone! How do you know?'

'He insisted on driving the cart over to San Francisco while I rode. I said I would need help with Donna Isabella. He waited until he knew the ladies would come, and helped me find the slaves. Then he – ' Alister shrugged. 'Well, he just disappeared.'

'The fool! There's no use in him running. There's no safer place than here now. No ships will be leaving harbour – he couldn't take a boat out. Well, he'll come back again. They always do when they get frightened enough.' He waved his hand. 'All right then, get along. We'll do well enough without the old she-devil.'

When Alister was gone Maria turned on her sisters with a torrent of Spanish, wild, abusive, her cheeks flaming with un-accustomed colour. At the end of it Katarina merely shrugged and answered, deliberately, I thought, in English.

'Words, sister – words! It is not you who have any longer to deal with our sainted mother. As your esteemed kinsman pointed out – if she chooses to die at San Francisco, *that* is her right. But we – Joanna and I – prefer to live, at least a little longer. So we have taken your good husband's hospitality and left her her supply of the best San Francisco rum – and her other necessities – and she will live or not, as God wills.' She gave a long, deep sigh. 'And now, my dear sister, would it be too much to ask of your hospitality that we might have dry clothes? Anything will do,' she added with deep sarcasm. 'No doubt there are wornout clothing of the slaves . . . nothing too splendid, you understand, lest we get notions above our pockets. And would it be too much to ask for water and salve for our hands? – and perhaps a bit of old sheet to bind my shoulder?'

Before Maria could reply there came a bellow from Andrew. 'Juanita – Juanita!' After a while the old woman shuffled up from the cellars. 'Don't take so long to answer my call.' He jerked his head. 'Attend to the señoritas. See that they have whatever they need of Mrs Maxwell's clothes. And bring some of your

ointments – the right ones, mind. None of your witch's brew.
Have Flora help you . . .'

The last task Andrew gave me was to see to bringing down
mattresses and bedding and laying them out wherever they would
fit in the hall, and the salon and the dining-room. 'Safer down
here,' he said. 'You can never tell when the roof might go. We
would be safer still in the cellars, but that's where the slaves will
go, and you'd never stand the stink. In any case, we have to show
ourselves superior to them even when we're all in the same boat.
Believe me, if that old woman at San Francisco survives, the tale
will go to every slave on the island that she is a witch, and braver
than the bravest man. They're frightened of her now, but that
will be nothing to what she will enjoy if she lives through this.
And she does enjoy it – by God, *how* that old woman enjoys
them being afraid of her!'

And Andrew would also have enjoyed that, I thought, if he
had possessed it. But the passion was gone, and the power had
passed to his wife. In this show he had put on since early morning
I had seen a faint echo of the man who must once have been.
But he was fading; he still was bellowing orders, but the spring
was running down; I had the feeling that he would not, from now
on, very often leave the red sofa.

One thing I asked again, as the last of the mattresses was laid
in place. 'Fergus?' I said. I was clinging to the door-frame of
the salon, wondering why nothing would stay still before my eyes.
'You sent to bring them from San Francisco. But you leave Fergus
in that place that's falling apart. You talk of *this* roof going.
That one could fly!'

He took the pipe from his mouth. 'That I can leave to Fergus.
He will come or not, as he decides. I don't have to give him
orders or instructions.'

'You might have given him an invitation.'

'Invitation!' That roar of forced laughter came. 'You ought
to know what happens when I *invite* Fergus. It is the one way
to be sure he will not come. So leave it – and stop fussing. *All* you
damn women stop fussing!'

He went back to his tobacco, and his figure slumped.

Then Alister came back from the stables; he came through the
dining-room, his arms loaded with the bound ledgers and journals
from the office. 'Is there any help?' he said peremptorily. I noticed
that his limp was now very pronounced and that he was near
exhaustion. 'I would like every book and paper taken from the
office – it is very exposed there on the outer gallery. We can't do

much with water-soaked books. It's very odd that you've taken
so much trouble about everything else, and neglected this.'
'So . . . ?' Maria said. 'So now you are master of the books at
Landfall, Alister?'
'I'm master of them to the extent that I have a right to see
them preserved. We also have interests at Landfall, Maria.'
Andrew stirred. 'The books – the books! Goddammit, why
didn't you think of the books, Maria? Idiot! Why, my mother's
books from Winterslo are there. Bring them all – every last one
of them! Go – set them to it!'
Alister waited long enough to see the start of a chain of slaves
that were set to bringing in the rows of ledgers from the office,
and then he also went, slowly and with some pain, up the stairs
to seek dry clothes.

Fergus did come; he came when it was almost too late, when the
wind had reached a force that made me believe what Andrew
had said – that no man could stand upright in it. He brought
with him the ten slaves that Winterslo possessed, and with each
of them was a bundle, wrapped in straw matting to protect it
as much as could be done from the rain.
'Fergus!' I raced forward and threw myself into his arms. I felt
his embrace, eager but swift, and he was looking over my shoulder
to his father and Maria.
'I tied down everything that could be tied. I nailed shutters in
place, and the nailing only showed me what the termites had
really done to the place. There was no way to tie the roof on.
I did what I could, and in the end I decided it was better to live,
if one could, to go back there, even if it was ruined, than to die
with it. We have brought our own food. All we ask is the shelter
of your roof, my father.'
Andrew gestured broadly. 'Welcome once more to Landfall,
my son. You see, we are now complete. Alister returned from
Santa Marta and performed the service of bringing the Señoritas
Medina from San Francisco. He also has his books for company.
Fiona has you. The house is well stocked with food and drink, our
slaves are thankful for shelter from the storm and are therefore
docile. All we lack is the old lady of San Francisco, who refused
to come, and for which we may be thankful. Make yourself at
home, my son. We should be a happy, spritely little party to sit
out the storm. Yes, fill your glass with rum, Fergus, and make
yourself at ease. It will be as if we celebrated a great happening,
instead of facing the due date of repayment that the sugar islands

exact every so often from those who win her riches. So take your glass, my son, and put a good face on it. My bones tell me that this time it will be repayment in full.'

It was then, still holding Fergus, that I was no longer able to control the whirling of the room about me, the gathering mist before my eyes; it was then the full blackness came.

3

There was no single part of the remainder of that day or of the night that distinguished itself from the rest in my mind; people seemed to come and go as I lay on one of the mattresses in the salon; there was talk, but I understood little of it. I sometimes felt those who bent over me, but other times I woke from the blackness of a kind of unconscious sleep to find that Fergus's hand was holding mine, that it was he who wiped the sweat from my face, but I had not known of his being there. Sometimes Flora's face was there, and I would close my eyes upon it, because she brought a strange fear; sometimes Alister was there, and I took comfort from his presence, as one does from those of good sense and purpose. Once I was aware of some greater presence, slow and heavy, over me, and it was Andrew, with Dougal holding a lamp. The sweating, but strangely expert fingers felt for my pulse.

'Some sort of fever. But I don't know – she doesn't seem the sort to go like this. Don't like the look of it. Not a bit. If we could get a doctor . . . Well, it's beyond me . . .'

All that was constant through that night, constant through the burning that seemed to consume me, and the dizzying whirl of light and dark about me whenever I opened my eyes, was the sound of the wind and the rain. Sometimes gusts came that roused me, and I would find myself sitting up, waiting for the moment of final destruction, waiting until the walls would give before its power. Nothing could stand against the wind, I thought. We would all go with the house, buried beneath its falling walls, buried down where the slaves were, in the cellars, equal, finally, in that common grave.

But the walls held, and the roof held, and all that we felt, locked in our darkness, was the draughts and eddies of wind that forced themselves through chinks in the great storm shutters. As each new gust rose, I could hear the accompanying moan of fear that came from the cellars; the slaves could give utterance to their fears, but we, the whites, could not. For us, the release came in the kind of bickering that accompanies those who are locked up together against their will. Once they had become accustomed to the fact that I was ill, and began to accept it, the hushed tone of the voices gradually became normal. They were not afraid to wake me, because it was no natural sleep I slept. Sometimes the voices came in Spanish – often Andrew's hoarse bellow would trumpet out. I heard Duncan's voice, querulous, bored, demanding. Sometimes I was aware of the activities of this ill-assorted lot. The sisters, Katarina and Joanna, brought out the gaming table and shuffled their cards, and carried on with some game that seemed to have occupied them for years – they had won and lost vast sums to each other, all on paper. Alister sat under Maria's frowning gaze and kept turning the pages of the ledgers. He hardly ever spoke. Maria had little occupation – her needlework was denied her for lack of light; she seemed unable to bear either the sight of Fergus so closely beside me, nor of Alister's patient scrutiny of the books. I had the impression that most of the time she paced the hall – but her footfalls, as always, were very light; there was just the suggestion of her presence. She came back and forth, a restless, hovering spirit, waiting, as we all did.

But in the end, exhaustion came to everyone. We even grew so used to the shriek of the wind that only the worst gusts would cause us now to pause and listen. One by one, because the clocks said midnight, all lay down on the mattresses spread around and took what sleep was possible. We had worked since dawn; even the tumult could not deny sleep finally. Quietness fell over the house itself, while the storm outside had its way. Andrew slept fitfully on his red sofa, always the rum beside him, and the sweetish smell of the tobacco staling the rooms. There came that moment during the night when all of us must have believed that the climax had come, and the final end. There was a great tearing, shrieking sound, almost as of an animal in pain, and then a long series of crashing noises that went on and on, for minutes. All of us there in the room were silent, until, at last, the crashing sound stopped.

'A tree,' Andrew pronounced. 'One near the house – probably the big cottonwood. Torn out by its roots. It's probably damaged the foundations of the house. We shall all be torn out by the roots if it lasts at this strength much longer.'

All I knew then was that the pressure of Fergus's hand in mine seemed to increase, as if he would will some strength back into me. There was a moment, though, when the touch was relinquished. I heard Fergus's and Alister's voices in whispers very close.

'I'll stay with her now,' Alister said. 'You'll have to get a few hours' sleep.'

The offer was roughly rejected. 'Mind your own business! She's mine – I'm taking care of her.'

'Don't talk rubbish, man! You'll have to get some sleep or you'll be useless when this is over. Perhaps by morning it may be possible for someone to ride for a doctor – or at least to bring back some medicine. If you can't keep awake, how can you do it? Besides, there is the watch to keep. We can't afford, all of us, to fall asleep. You might doze off. Who knows when the slaves may come up from the cellars? Can you be sure they haven't taken knives down there with their bundles?'

It was only then, dimly, that I comprehended our danger. Alister sat on a cane chair beside me, occasionally leaning down to give me water when I asked it, performing the tasks that one would not have thought possible of that fastidious man of bathing my face, neck and hands with a cloth wrung in water; and all the time he faced the entrance to the salon, watching, his gaze going from me to it constantly. When he put down the cloth he would take up again the pistol that he had held for all these hours. It was not permitted for all to sleep at once, for fear of the bare feet coming silently across the floor, and the machetes that could end a life before the sleeper woke. I was glad that, as the party sought their mattresses, Flora had been sent to the cellars again; her presence was almost worse than the fear of the storm.

Then it was morning, though the blackness was the same. There was a stirring; voices again. There was a movement towards the dining-room, where the food was laid out on the sideboard. The wind was still with us. Was the cry of it, though, a little less shrill, the gusts a little less in force? Or was it just that our ears now were so attuned to the tumult that we no longer heard it with such fear?

Flora had been permitted up from the cellars again, and with her came Juanita. Between them I staggered to that primitive arrangement in one of the store rooms where women could use the buckets. Even after one night, the smell was noxious. They both held me, their hands seeming to crush my flesh. I broke into a sweat again, nearly fainting as they supported me back to my mattress. As I lay down again Andrew roused himself and came close, leaning over me.

'Don't like it,' he said. 'She should be showing signs of coming through it now if it were an ordinary fever. Wish to God we could get a doctor – not that those quacks know any more than

we do about what ails a person in this climate. But at least it
would be *something*. But we can't send yet. Wind's dropped a
bit, but it's still too much for a man and a horse. And no doctor
would come – cowards, the lot of them.'

I felt Juanita's hand thrust back the damp hair from my forehead, and I shrunk from her touch, pressing myself into the mattress.
'White doctor no good, master. This spell come from the wind,
and Mistress Fiona's spirit fly away with it. No white doctor know
about these things.'

'God rot you!' I heard a crack, and I thought that Andrew had
struck the woman. But I was no longer sure of anything that was
happening. 'I'll have none of that damned nonsense here! Are you
trying to frighten her to death? Mistress Fiona is strong. She will
get well. Hers is no spirit to fly with the wind. She will live and
bear many children for my son. To hell with your witchcraft. Go
and tell your gods that she will live.' He turned heavily, in fury,
to his wife. 'Maria, why do you let this rag-bag near Fiona? Why
do you let her say these things? Are *you* trying to frighten the girl
too?'

The voice answered behind me. 'You know yourself, Andrew,
how skilful Juanita is with her herbal remedies. How many sick
slaves has she brought back to health for us? Send for the doctor,
by all means. In the meantime, who better have I to offer than my
own Juanita?'

'There must be *something* to do! Haven't we anything to give
her, Maria? – why the hell don't you help? You and your precious
sisters . . .'

It ran on, a stream of abuse against everyone, hardly distinguishable to my dulled ears; I seemed now to be listening to sounds
other than those close at hand. I seemed to hear the gurgling sound
of water. The scene about me faded and I was following the tide
as it ebbed on the strand of Silkirk, leaving miles of shining sand.
I felt that tide, the silvery line receding, the sand left firm and hard
beneath my feet. I wanted to go with it, to catch up with it; it was
then I began to feel cold. I felt my body contract against the cold,
but nothing could hold it out. At that moment I began not to feel
Fergus's hand in mine; I knew it was there, but I could not feel it.
From somewhere, from chests long stored, at Andrew's command,
came blankets. They were piled upon me, but the essential body
heat was gone. There was the moment when I felt Fergus's body
clamped to mine to attempt to infuse warmth into it. I passed in
and out of consciousness, sometimes knowing what went on about
me, sometimes not. And all the time my mind followed that silver

line of sea as it receded across the sands and out into the Atlantic.

I felt something else; hands that tried to appear gentle, but instead were sharp, hands that seemed to bite into me, rather than support me as they raised me to a sitting position.

'Drink – it will do you good.'

'No !' Fergus's voice.

I knew nothing but that liquid splashed across my face, and some ran down between the blankets. Then Maria said, 'You asked me for help. It is an old island remedy. The best we can do now.'

'I wouldn't trust a glass of water from your hands to her. Now leave her to me. After all – I am the one who loses most. If she goes – oh, my God . . .'

Did I hear him sob, or was it the cry of the wind? Did a man like Fergus weep; could he care that much? I don't know; I never will. The wind went on, and the household moved about me, and still I was cold, as was the water on the strand when I finally caught up with its foaming edge, and touched it. It was icy cold.

In my clear moments I could feel the restlessness that gripped all those there growing by the hour. Katarina and Joanna had gone back to their cards, but they muttered sourly, without interest. Alister still looked at the books, but from the impatient flick of the pages I knew that he no longer studied them with any concentration. Maria moved about – sometimes ordering Dougal to tidy the sideboard – but there was nowhere to wash dishes. I heard the buzz of flies between the gusts of wind. Maria was the most restless of them all. She paced constantly between salon and hall, a disturbing figure who moved in and out of my line of vision. Finally Andrew could stand it no longer.

'For God's sake, woman, will you be still! You know how to be quiet enough when it suits you.'

She didn't answer him, but her footsteps retreated towards the dining-room, and I supposed she sat there alone. I heard Andrew heave himself off the sofa and stump into the hall.

'Duncan – where's Duncan ?'

The piping voice floated down from the upper landing. 'I'm here, Papa.'

'What are you doing?'

'Just getting some of my soldiers, Papa.'

'Well, get them, and come down. I don't trust you up there. If you open one of those doors into the bedrooms the pressure could burst open a shutter. So get your things and bring them down.'

The unusually docile reply : 'Yes, Papa.'

I could hear his slow, careful steps as he came down. And then there was a crash, and a rolling of small objects over the floor of the hall. The tiny vibrations hit into my head like blows. Maria must have left her place in the dining-room.

'Duncan!'

'Well – I dropped them, Mama. I couldn't help it.'

'And look! – you have taken my little rosewood chest without permission. See – look! The hinge is damaged. You are a very bad child . . .'

'I had nothing to carry them down in.' He was sullen, on the defensive, awaiting his punishment.

Andrew shouted from his sofa, to which he had returned. 'Leave him be, Maria. He is cooped up. He has to do *something*. The hinge can be mended, for God's sake. Leave the child alone. Bring your things in here, son . . .'

'That box came from Spain more than two hundred years ago.'

'So – it's time it had a knock or two. It's not sacred. Come – bring your things here, son. You can play with your soldiers here.'

It was seldom that Andrew interfered with any direction Maria gave to Duncan, but at the times he did, the boy knew he had complete licence. He seemed to know now that he was the instrument of his mother's anger against her husband. He knew that he had just escaped a box on the ear, and was gleeful over it. He chattered happily to Andrew as he came in, the toy soldiers restored to Maria's damaged little chest. Maria herself now said nothing; she must have retired again to the dining-room. Duncan, having been encouraged by Andrew, sought to exploit his interest, bringing the chest of soldiers close to the sofa and beginning to play about his father's feet. But Andrew could never for long suffer Duncan's endless questionings, his demands for attention. He wanted to be left to drink his rum in peace, and the child bored and annoyed him.

'Duncan – take your things over there. And be quiet. Stop your chatter.'

I saw that Duncan crept away, hurt, bewildered. He knew he was under threat of punishment from his mother, and now Andrew had dismissed him. It was part of the constant see-saw of his life, the reason why he clung to me with such tenaciousness. He glanced reproachfully towards my mattress, as if to chide me for not being able to help him; but he kept away, as he had been told to.

890 FIONA

The hours passed, with numbing ennui settling on everyone –
hours or minutes, I couldn't seem to tell. The wind appeared
to die a little, and the stronger gusts were fewer. Or perhaps I no
longer heard them.

I was roused, though, by Andrew's sudden great bellow of
triumph.

'The glass is beginning to rise! – *the glass is rising.* We may be
through the worst of it.'

Now, at this moment, it was Alister's cool hand I felt on my
face. 'Hold on, Fiona – hold on!'

'Take your hands off her, Goddammit!' Fergus's nerves were
raw, and for a moment I thought he would strike Alister. 'She's
my responsibility – mine! mine!' Once again I felt his whole
body pressed against me, trying to will warmth into it, uncaring
of those about us. But how different it was now than our time together on the sunlit beach when we had moved with each other
in a radiance of joy at the edge of the water. The tide was cold,
and I was in much deeper.

Fergus began to talk of being able, in an hour or two, to ride
for a doctor. Andrew grunted, and wondered aloud if any doctor
would consent to come to Landfall when so many in Santa Marta
would need help. I heard him order Flora to bring rum from the
sideboard decanter – always the best rum in the house. With his
own hands Andrew mixed rum and several spices and bade Flora
build a fire in the long-unused fireplace to heat it. He also ordered
my mattress to be carried close to the fire. But the wind backed the
smoke down the chimney and the room was filled. Furious, Andrew
threw water on the kindling, and we choked on the smoke and
the acrid stench. His failure to help disturbed him; he watched
critically as Fergus made me drink the rum – its warmth was only
momentary. Juanita hovered, and the sight of her black, glowering
face behind Andrew's frightened me. I turned away.

'Mistress Fiona die,' Juanita said. 'Master not let Juanita use
her remedies, mistress surely die.'

'Shut your foul mouth and get out of here,' Andrew shouted.
'I told you to keep away.' He went back to his sofa, as though
discouraged; I could hear his heavy breathing across the room.

Maria's voice was next – how long after I don't know. She had
come to the door of the salon. 'The wind is dropping. It is passing.
When can we go out?'

'Not yet,' Andrew replied ' – and you won't much like what you
see when you do go out. There's nothing much left out there to
hurry to.'

'My mother at San Francisco? – she is nothing?'

'That worn-out old hulk!' Andrew snorted. 'You would do better to have a care for this young woman here among us. *She* is worth saving – '

He was cut short by a cry from Maria. 'Duncan! What are you at *now*? Haven't you done enough damage? Put those back at once!'

Everyone looked to where Duncan, seated before the great cabinet that had come from San Francisco, was playing with his soldiers. But he had progressed, perhaps from boredom, from the familiar pattern of lining them up in rows and knocking them down. He had removed the two low drawers beneath the glass doors of the cabinet and had stood them on their sides, making a fort for a detachment of his troops. With the contents of the drawers – little boxes, needlework frames, a set of dominoes, a group of small framed cameos – the flotsam of a household – he had constructed outer ramparts to his fort for the storming troops to attack.

'Leave him be, Maria,' Andrew said again. 'He's doing no harm – he must have *something* to occupy him. If you had any thought you might read to him for a while . . .' Then his own tone changed sharply. 'What do you have there, Duncan? Is that one of the dolls? You shouldn't have that.'

'I didn't *take* it,' Duncan answered sullenly. 'It was there – in one of the drawers. I haven't *done* anything to it.'

'In one of the drawers? Why was it there?' He turned to Maria. 'Why would it be there? The cabinet is always locked. How would it have come there?'

I shifted my gaze painfully over to where she stood, but her features were indistinct.

'It is nothing,' she answered sharply. 'Nothing – just that I noticed some of the lace was ripped the other day and took it down to mend it. Something interrupted me and I just laid it in the drawer. Duncan has no cause to be rummaging in those drawers.'

'Well, then, put it back where it was,' Andrew said, exasperated. 'Then the boy can't be blamed for any damage.'

She seemed first to hesitate, and then she moved swiftly as if to forestall anyone else. I could hear the jingle of the keys as she brought them out, the rattling sound as she struggled to fit the right one to the lock.

A grumbling mutter came from Joanna. 'All *our* childhood we were never permitted to handle those dolls . . .'

The doors of the cabinet swung open; Maria reached down for

the doll, but Duncan was there before her. 'Let me put it back, Mama – let me!' He moved eagerly along the crowded rack, seeking the place from which the doll had come. At the end he stopped, puzzled. 'Where . . . ?'

'Give it to me, Duncan! Give it to me.'

She snatched the doll from him and attempted to thrust it into line with the others; but there was no place for it – no empty space on the rack which supported all the others. In the dimness, the eyes of everyone in the room strained to see, to watch the frantic effort Maria made to find room for it, to make it stand in line with the others. It kept falling, and in the meantime Duncan had made a slow inspection of that whole long shelf. The shout of triumph he gave reminded me of Andrew.

'There's a new doll! – a different doll! That's why there's no place – '

Maria cut him off, her cry much more fear than annoyance. 'Duncan, leave it to me! Don't touch . . .'

But he had it down off the rack and held up for us all to see. 'Look, a new doll!' All we could see clearly was a whitish, shapeless thing, and a flame of red. 'It's not like the others, though.' His tone dropped from excitement to a kind of distaste. 'It's ugly.'

Andrew leaned forward. 'Give it here to me, boy.'

Maria made a snatch at it, but Duncan slipped past her and ran to Andrew. 'It's an ugly doll, Papa – not a bit like the other ones.'

Andrew sat for a long moment staring at the thing that Duncan placed in his hands. 'Good Christ!' he said. 'A doll of Fiona! A stinking filthy voodoo doll.'

There was a terrible silence in the room; even the wind for that time seemed to be still. No one moved or spoke, frozen in their attitudes by the thing that Andrew held. It was I, in the end, who finally made the first movement, spoke the first words.

I lifted my hand in the strongest gesture I was capable of, and flung a hoarse whisper into the stillness.

'Let me see it.'

He was wise enough not to thwart me; he heaved himself once more from the sofa and, leaning on Duncan's shoulder, came to the edge of the mattress. All this time Maria stood, still and erect in that way she had, before the gaping doors of the cabinet.

It was Fergus who reached for it, and held it up so that I could see it. By now the others, Alister, Katarina and Joanna, had moved closer, drawn by the horrible fascination of the thing. Fergus held it where it caught the light from the lamp on the floor behind my head.

It was a white thing – a white rag doll, utterly unlike the waxen beauties in the cabinet. This had no shaped features on its round, monstrous head, but they were indicated by crude smears of red – lips, eyes, brows, nostrils. It was, as Duncan had said, ugly – dreadfully ugly, and dressed in a shoddy little garment made from one of the old print dresses I had brought to Landfall and which had fallen apart in the wash, I had been told. So bad all this was, but there was worse. Stitched to its calico head, in a terrible matted tangle, was human hair, bright red hair smeared with some dried substance.

'Fiona! Fiona's hair!' The horrified whisper came from Fergus.

But when I reached up for it he let me have it, perhaps knowing that I needed to see all of it in order to combat it. I put up an unsteady hand to grasp it, to bring it closer to my blurring vision so that I might examine its frightfulness. I touched and felt it.

'Blood,' I said. 'The red stuff is blood.' And as I squeezed the clumsy body, I felt the sharpness prick me through the gown it wore. Then I recognized the pearly heads of the pins that pierced the rag body at the place where the heart and liver would be in a human; I squeezed the horrible hair and found pins there also. 'Pins from my little pincushion,' I said. 'The pincushion Mary gave me.' I let it drop.

From far back in the room, because she had retreated once again into the shadows, Joanna spoke in a whisper. 'They say the spell is more powerful the more of the things they can get that belong to the person who is to die. Fiona's hair – the pins. And setting it in a place where it could look at her . . .'

'Obscenity!' It was Alister's voice. 'This is an unthinkable obscenity. Burn it! Burn it at once! To think that *you* people believe these things . . .'

Joanna replied with sullen obstinacy. 'I only know what I have seen before. They have spells we don't know anything about – how they work, or why. Fiona will probably die. She is too far gone now – and that thing has looked at her all night and day.'

'Die!' There was a fearful howl from Duncan. 'No! – No! Fiona can't die!' He was kneeling by the mattress, his arms wrapped frantically about Fergus, his head buried imploringly against him. 'You won't let her die, Fergus! She promised she would stay forever.'

I brought up my hand to touch him, and he pulled back from

Fergus, half-afraid to look at me in case his fear should be realized. 'No,' I said, 'I'm not going to die.'

The water around me was terribly cold, but I knew I would not die. I had something yet to do; something that concerned Duncan. My befuddled brain had no precise memory of what I had to do for him, but it had to be done. I knew it because I had once seen it; so I would not die yet. 'No,' I said to him and to Fergus. 'I'm not going to die. It isn't finished yet. I haven't done what I came to do yet.'

His pressure on my hand was swift. 'Quiet then, my love. You know it?'

'Yes, I saw it – once. I can't remember . . .'

His pressure on my hand was swift. 'Quiet then, my love. You will not die.'

From behind came Alister's voice, barely restraining his fury. 'Can we be rid of it now – this unspeakable thing! Will you burn it *now*?'

'Wait.' Andrew grunted as he bent over to pick it up. 'Wait. You must be careful how these things are done.'

'You surely don't believe in any of this nonsense?'

'I've lived here long enough not to be surprised at anything that comes out of Africa.' He faced Alister. 'After all, are things so much more civilized in England? Do churchmen still not struggle and pray all night against the devil as if he were an evil shape with horns and a tail? That is all these people have done – they have put horns and a tail on the devil. Do English churchmen still not preach the fire of hell that burns forever, but never consumes? Do they believe in the saving grace of the soul? Well, then, what right have we to deny some power to a belief far stronger than any of us possess? They *believe* that they can kill by the ritual murder of this stupid rag doll. The damage must be undone by the one who created it.' He turned to Flora, cowering back in the shadows behind Maria, crouching down, her face buried in her hands.

'Flora – bring up your mother. Quickly!'

She scampered away, bent, as if she were a terrified animal.

'I have to protest,' Alister said. 'To go along with any of these beliefs is a blasphemy. Burn it, and be done with it.'

'And perhaps watch Fiona's life burn up with it!' Fergus cried. 'Don't be such a bloody fool! Do it as my father says. He has a lifetime of experience and a knowledge of these things that you will never have. Leave it to him.'

'It's monstrous – monstrous!' Alister protested again.

'Monstrous, I agree,' Andrew answered. 'And I am dealing with this monstrosity the best way I can. Ah – '

Juanita and Flora had come – Juanita standing silent, defiant, upright before Andrew. Flora's head hung, and she seemed to shiver.

'It was your doing, Juanita, wasn't it? Even though you have been forbidden to practise these things?'

'Mistress bid me,' she said flatly.

'I *know* that. And Flora helped by getting Mistress Fiona's hair after Charity had been sent away?'

The older woman did not answer, but from Flora came a wailing cry. 'I am afraid, master. I afraid not to do as I told. Mistress say she send me someplace far away . . .'

'You'll be more afraid when you know what is going to happen to you now.' Andrew raised his hand and pointed at them both, as if uttering judgement. 'Burned,' he said, his big voice rising to its full force and assuming a quality of power one seldom heard there now. 'Burned, as you would finally have burned this doll. But before that happens I will myself drive a nail through your heart like the pins in the doll – '

Alister broke in. 'For God's sake, stop this at once! You make matters worse by going along with the pagan beliefs of these people. Just get rid of that *unspeakable* thing. Get rid of it!'

'My son has said it. Be quiet, my friend, and don't meddle with what you don't understand. Juanita will die instead of Fiona – and Flora along with her, so that the gods will have two instead of the one promised them. It will be a much worse death than that Mistress Fiona would have died, I promise you that, Juanita.'

From Flora the wailing became louder; Juanita still remained silent, eyes blazing with hatred and contempt, but not fear.

'Or . . .' Andrew went on. 'Or there is another way, and perhaps I will be merciful. Perhaps I will not even send you to the judges at Santa Marta, who would certainly hang you. Perhaps all will yet live. But the spell must be removed.'

Juanita stood for some moments longer, her arms folded, as if she thought carefully about her final submission to the white man. Then she turned and went close to Maria, and deliberately spat at her feet.

'I die for no white woman,' she said. 'I take away *this* spell, but the old one, the curse put on Landfall long ago by black woman, that still stay. The one who did it is gone, and never will the spell go. So you rot here forever.' Then she came back to the mattress, reaching for the doll. Instinctively, I shrank back from her closeness, and she looked at me with venom.

'You tell Flora your magic greater than ours, but now you know it not the truth. If doll not been found, when I should have placed more pins at the right time, you die for sure.'

'Enough of that,' Andrew ordered. 'Now begin.'

Juanita squatted down on the floor, the doll lying before her. Then she began a strange chant in her own language; it began and then broke. She looked up at Andrew. 'No good,' she said. 'Must be done at the middle of night, when the moon will shine.'

'The gods sent the great wind because you had done wrong. There will be no moon – no middle of the night. Now get on!'

She began again, the weird chant; on and on it went, like the shriek of the wind itself. Then she broke off, and the lower pin was removed. The chant started again, sonorous, rising and falling. Another pause, and the second pin, the one in the place of the heart, was removed. In the same way, three pins came from the head. I wanted to turn away, to see no more of it, but I couldn't, as none could, not even Alister. She clicked her thin black fingers, and at once Flora produced the little scissors I had brandished in her face. With great care then, totally absorbed, Juanita began to remove the rough stitches that held the strands of my hair to the body. That done, she removed every stitch which bound together the crudely sewn body of the doll. The stuffing flowed out, as if it were my own life blood; tiny, cut-up ribbons of cloth from all the garments that I had had to discard since coming to Landfall. It all lay there in the end, an indistinguishable mass, a conglomerate of me, Fiona, shredded.

The black eyes looked at Andrew. 'Now it be sent to the wind.'

'Then do so.'

She gathered up the heap, and I saw everyone, except Maria and Alister, move to the hall where they could watch her go to the door that was partly open and secured on the hook. It must have been Fergus who held it open; I heard him say something to Juanita. There was a moment of that strange chanting again, and then they all returned, all except Juanita and Flora, whom Andrew ordered back to the cellar.

'An abomination!' Alister said. 'I never witnessed anything so barbaric in my life. To think that you subscribe to these beliefs! . . . To think you let a child stand here and watch them. You must be mad!'

'So would you be mad, or respectful, in the same way if you lived here long enough. And as for barbaric – is there not still a law in England against witchcraft? If it does not exist, why is there a law against it?' Andrew collapsed back into his sofa. 'I meant Duncan to witness this. *He* will have to live with it. Better let him know how to deal with it. What matters is that the corrective be carried out according to the manner *they* believe in. Our tendency is to deal with everything our way. It doesn't always have the desired effect. But I think we may now expect Fiona to get well.'

'It was a fever,' I croaked. 'That's all. A fever. It broke and I got cold. But I am getting warmer now. It was the wind . . .'

'It was anything you care to call it. But it was when you got cold that I feared you were going. It is not the normal course of fevers here. But I will not try to convince you. Believe as you wish. Dougal, where is the jug?'

The jug was brought and placed beside him. He looked around the room, surveying all of us, once more in command. He seemed to brood for a while, then he pointed at Duncan.

'Time for you to rest, my son. Dougal will go up on the landing with you – lie down there.'

Duncan had to make his usual protest. 'But it is not yet time. We have not had lunch. It is not siesta.'

'The clock does not matter while the wind blows, Duncan. In a little time the wind will be down and we will need your strength to help clear up like the strength of a grown man. So go and rest, and be ready for it.'

Reluctantly Duncan turned towards Dougal, but again Andrew called him. 'Come here, my son.' Duncan went to his side, and Andrew leaned forward and with a rare gesture of affection he kissed the frown on that young brow. 'Be at peace, my son. Remember this old man cares for your welfare.'

I glimpsed Duncan's face as he went off. It shone with a kind of joy I had never seen there before. Andrew had provided in that single gesture the antidote to the horror the boy had witnessed, the reassurance that the world would soon assume its proper rhythm; he had even given him the gift least bestowed by Andrew, the evidence of love. In that moment I forgave Andrew many things.

'Well, my wife,' he said at last, when Duncan and Dougal had gone. 'Well, it was an attempt. You could no longer wait for the old man to die, because Fiona would have had Fergus before that would happen. To try to kill me with too much speed would have been too obvious. I know as much as you about the poisons and their spells. So it had to be Fiona.'

Maria had taken her usual seat, her face quite unchanging as Andrew spoke, her eyes half-shut as if she must endure with patience the ramblings of an old drunken man. 'Your talk is foolish, Andrew.

You know that Juanita has lied. You know I have no belief – '

He thumped the arm of the sofa. 'By God, you *do* believe, and would practise it yourself if you could! And you still lust after him – you lust after my son, Fergus, and you cannot bear the thought that he will marry and be beyond your reach when this sick old man finally dies.'

'Would I then have married you – not him? I *could* have married him.'

A grim smile played across Andrew's features, the acknowledgment of some pyrrhic victory gained. 'Yes, indeed, you could have married him, and known a life not much better than you had at San Francisco. You knew that Winterslo was all that was really promised him, and there was always the chance that with him married to you, and you both at Winterslo, I myself might finally have taken a wife and Landfall would be lost to both of you. But you didn't think it would take so long, did you? I wasn't so old – I'm not so old now – but you thought I had less in me and that both Landfall and Fergus would be yours much sooner. It has been my only pleasure, these last years, to live on in spite of you.'

'If you knew all this, why then *did* you marry me? I had no way to compel you.'

'Only the time honoured way. And I was fool enough to honour it. Mistresses I had had, but never had I taken a woman from my son, nor believed, in my madness, that she actually preferred me. Ah, what a fool I was then, and what a woman in bed you were, my wife. My madness is hardly to be wondered at. You made me feel like a boy again, and I was a man past my middle-years. I had laughed at such foolishness in other men, and didn't know it in myself . . .' Abruptly he jerked his head around. 'No' – pointing at Katarina and Joanna – 'no, don't you start creeping away as if all this earthy talk was too much for your maidenly ears. You are the same clay as she and, for all I know, you knew as well as she did what was schemed. It probably all came from the old she-devil at San Francisco. After all, with me and a child, Maria could secure Landfall. With my son, Fergus, not legitimate, who knew what might happen? Who could say what Maxwell might not come forward to dispute his claim – '

'Stop!' It was a cry of anguish from Fergus. 'Must you go all through this again – and now, before Fiona? Haven't we all lived in our own hells because of this business? What good does it do to rake it all over again? We all make our mistakes – '

'Mistakes we made. You are right, Fergus. And regretted them – day after bitter day. Most of all, myself. Most of all, myself. I don't want to dwell on the evil and greed she was capable of – my own are enough. But it is one thing to be greedy and ambitious – are any of us free of these kinds of things? Attempting to murder is something else. *That* is what I speak of now, and before Fiona, who nearly was the victim.'

Alister broke in : 'But Fiona does not believe in such things! It was, as she says, a fever, which now has broken.'

'But those who made the attempt *did* believe. That makes them guilty. That girl was coming-close to death, and you know it. Look at the change in her since that accursed thing was done away with! Look at the colour come back to her face. Whether you believe it or not, it almost happened. It was attempted – and by my wife. Shall we pass it over as if it had never been? It is not possible, and well you know it.'

'But I deny your accusations,' Maria said quietly. 'I deny them. You have only the word of an ignorant, frightened old slave, seeking to save her own skin, as a charge against me. You know that is not admissible in law. How can you say Fiona has not angered Juanita in some way that earned her hate? How can you *prove* all that you say?'

'Didn't you send Charity away – without a word to anyone, to replace her with that skinny wretch who was too frightened to do anything but what you and her mother bade her? Was Charity Fiona's protection? Was that why you got rid of her?'

'I have sold other slaves off this estate. You have left all that in my hand these past five years. Why should this prove anything? You make some nonsense in your head, Andrew. You are older than I thought and,' she added cruelly, 'sicker. You should have a care about what you say.'

'No house slave ever left Landfall before Charity. And when did she leave? The very day you knew you would finally lose Fergus. The day you knew that very soon he would marry Fiona and be lost to you, no matter how quickly after that I died. And, my wife – this most of all – who but you has the key to the cabinet? Who but you has ever put a hand inside it since you brought it to Landfall? Haven't I seen you a hundred times dust the whole contents yourself, not trusting anyone else to handle those things you treasure so? And who but you, Maria, my clever, capable wife, would have taken time and thought yesterday morning, in the midst of our preparations, to place the voodoo doll where it would be most likely to be within sight of Fiona and yet unnoticed? Oh, no, this is not the work of an ignorant slave, as you call her.'

She shrugged. 'Say what you please. I may carry my keys at most times, but they are not forever in my hands. Juanita comes and goes in my room at all times. It is too easy to borrow a key – it is Juanita you should be asking all this of, not me. And,' she added, 'if I am guilty of attempting such things as you charge, why did I not tell Juanita to work her spells against you, Andrew?' The tone was deadly quiet, difficult to hear against the wind that still thrust against the house. 'After all, you are already unwell. Easier – far easier to kill you than a strong young woman.'

Now he pointed a gloating finger at her. 'Because I watched you, Maria, when Fergus and Fiona came that morning and told us they would be married. You were shaken as I had never seen you before. For the first time you were not absolutely sure that Fergus would choose you, once you were free. If I had dropped dead at your feet at that moment, you couldn't have been sure that he wouldn't still have wanted Fiona above what you could offer him. It was a different Fergus you saw that morning, wasn't it, Maria? A man liberated – happy. You were frightened. You had to hurry. And so it had to be Fiona, not your husband.'

'You still make nonsense. Fergus and I have quarrelled for years. If I have desired him, as you say, why did I not cause your death long ago?'

'And for how long has quarrelling not been used to mask desire? You quarrelled with Fergus for his visits to Santa Marta, his lack of attendance on you. And for the rest of it – patience and fear. You know how to wait for what you want, I'll give you that. Just feed your husband enough rum and Indian hemp and his spirit will give up in time. And fear – one does not place oneself in the hands of a witch like Juanita without good reason. Even *you* were afraid of that. You could wait, just so long as Fergus continued his fooling about with the ladies of Santa Marta. You didn't even worry about the proposals to invite Mary Maxwell to be Duncan's governess. You knew Fergus. He likes – forgive me, Fiona – stronger stuff than the descriptions of the kind of girl Mary Maxwell seemed to be, even if she were pretty as sugar icing. If Mary Maxwell had come there was every chance that Fergus would have taken no more notice of her than a schoolgirl, which is hardly less than she is. But instead Fiona came, and with her your trouble.'

Again she shrugged as if growing weary of the whole tiresome discussion. 'Conjecture, Andrew – all of it conjecture. You have no proof. Nothing real that you can charge me with. No court will accept the evidence of a slave, or of ritual murder. Even the stupid rag doll does not exist. *You* saw to that!'

He took a long, thoughtful drink from his rum. 'Who said anything about charges? I'm too well aware that no court would entertain any such thing I cared to say about you, and I've no reason to give this island a scandal that would surpass anything they've had to gossip about since I provided the last great topic for them. No – it will not pass beyond this room. But there's a law that runs between man and wife – a natural justice that has nothing to do with courts or judgements. It is here that *I* am judge. I still live. I still have the strength to carry out what punishment I deem fit.'

'What?' Maria's tone was fainter. 'What?'

'I still live, Maria. I still may dispose of my possessions. I still may order what is to happen after I die.'

'And what will happen?'

'Fergus shall have Landfall, as it should have been right from the beginning. I shall disown you – a pittance only, so that you have no complaint before the courts. You will not dare to contest because too many witnesses now sit in this room to hear what I am saying.'

'And so to have vengeance on me for some imagined crime you will disinherit your own son?'

'Duncan? *Is* he my son, Maria – or is he Fergus's son?' The wild, drunken laughter rang out, the laughter of hurt and loneliness, the laughter of ugly triumph after the years of sitting on that red sofa brooding on age and impotence.

'Neither son will be dispossessed. Fergus will inherit jointly with Duncan, and be trustee for him until he comes of age. I will indicate that I then leave it to my son, Fergus, to see to a just distribution of whatever the joint estates of Landfall and Winterslo can command. And if he *is* Fergus's son, not his half-brother – or whichever it be – I think I may safely leave a natural justice to work itself out. It has a way of doing so.'

'And me?'

'Why, my widow will, of course, be entitled to remain on at her home. Though Landfall will have a new mistress. Will you like living under Fiona's direction, Maria? I fancy not, my wife. I think you will return to San Francisco – mouldering there, like your wretched sisters. Eight years older than you left it, and the lines beginning to come in your perfect face and a reputation earned across the length and breadth of San Cristóbal as a hard woman. What man will come riding to San Francisco to court a widow without an inheritance? Not a woman such as you, Maria – not from such a family.'

At this came a shriek, almost more tortured than the wind, from Katarina – or Joanna – who could tell? It was Katarina who spoke.

'No!' she said. 'No – it cannot be! It must not be! We have not worked all these years – '

'Katarina, be quiet! I order you!'

'Order me!' Katarina flashed back at her sister. 'You order me. How can you dare – *now*! I – ' And then her words choked back; she seemed to strangle on them. Her hand flew to her mouth as if to stifle a new sound of fear. We all turned to look to the doorway to the hall, where she stared. I half-raised myself on the pillows to see.

He stood with water still streaming from the wretched rags of his clothes. As I grew used to the sight of him I could see more, the pink streaks growing redder of blood that began staining the soaked shirt, the blood that trickled from his thick mat of hair, the cut over the eye that had closed it and gave him an oddly maniacal appearance.

'I have come, master,' Samuel said.

He must have found and let himself in at the storm shutter that was still on its hook; Samuel would know the preparation for hurricanes at Landfall as well as Andrew. He had come home and had known how to make his entrance.

Andrew grunted, but it was Maria who sprang to her feet. 'So – you have come back! There was no way to escape, after all, as I have always told you. So you have taken your beating out there in the storm and come crawling back like a dog. Well, you have been punished, and will be punished further.'

There was a long, painful smile twisting those thick lips. He balanced himself lightly on the soles of those bloody feet, uncaring, defiant.

'I will be more than punished, mistress. I will die. I know what happens to slaves who disobey. But I have brought back Charity and my son with me – and I ask the master, while he is still master, to spare them.'

'Charity . . .?' Maria took a few paces towards Samuel. 'You will say nothing about Charity. She is my concern. You have done wrong, but you will be spared. Now go down below, with the rest.'

But still he stood there, rocking back and forth, soles to heels, defiant still. 'No good, mistress. No more bargains that you do not keep. You have promised me that one day there would be freedom for me if I did as you say, but when you send Charity away

I know that promise never be kept. Some of my people, coming over on the slave ships, jump to the sharks rather than go on in their chains. It would have been better, I think, if my father had done that thing. But I am here, and I have disobeyed you. I know the punishment. I know what I know about the mistress. I have come only to ask that the master will spare Charity and my son – because there is talk that soon freedom will come here in these islands, and I want them here so that they have it.'

'What are you talking about?' Andrew demanded. 'Doesn't make sense. Charity would have her freedom like everyone else on this island if such a foolish measure should come to pass – which it will not!'

Fergus left my side and was standing beside Samuel, shaking that huge shoulder, and I saw, sickeningly, that his own hands became reddened. 'What does it mean, Samuel? *Where* did you find Charity and your son?'

The massive black head turned to Fergus, and even he seemed smaller. 'You don't know that, Master Fergus? I always wonder . . . though I never see you there those nights the ships come. I always wonder how much help this little woman has – whether you help her. The men who come, those I do not know. I think maybe you . . .'

He looked at Andrew. 'Master does not know? He not know what his woman is about? He let her roam the country at night, and dress like a man, and he not know. But I tell myself that even if master know about San Francisco, he not know that Charity and my son sent there. He would never let them go like that, I think. So I bring them back, and I ask him to protect them. Jus' keep them at Landfall, master. We have lived through the great wind, Charity, he and myself. It is a sign of life for them.'

Andrew waved his hand. 'Never mind that. Where did you find Charity?'

'At San Francisco, where I think they be.'

'San Francisco? Why?'

'Master not know?' A mocking, wholly knowledgeable smile twisted Samuel's lips again. 'I think I give the master old news. He must know all these things.'

'I'll tell you when to stop answering my questions, Goddammit.'

Samuel made a slight shrug. 'I go to San Francisco because that is where the mistress gather slaves from other islands and from the ships that come from Africa. She sell them – to America. Ships come. Small ships from other island. Big ships from Africa.

This is not the only stopping place for the ships from Africa. Too many come for such a place. She gather the slaves to wait for the ships that come from America. In America, they say, there is no talk of slaves being free. Still pay good prices for slaves. I know it against the law for British to carry slaves from Africa, but still they come, master. She gather slaves at San Francisco, master. Once a ship in that bay, no ship passing see it. Safe from the Serpents, and no one see who come or go. Sometimes ships stop at night there, leave slaves, and next morning in Santa Marta with ordinary cargo. No one ask questions. But I speak old things, master — you know this.'

'Go on!' It was neither Andrew nor Fergus who spoke, but Alister. He limped towards Samuel, and now the two white men confronted the slave. In an odd way, Samuel still seemed to dominate.

'You want to know, master? Well, they all say you own Landfall, even if you don't say so yourself.'

'Never mind that. Just tell me.'

'They come in and go out at San Francisco bay. But between the times the ships come, the slaves are locked in the old dungeons at San Francisco — the ones away from the greathouse. I know about it for years, master, because mistress, she say if I help her, one day she let me be free. So I do it — what it to me? Just more black men, same as me. Going to other masters. Once this side of the ocean, they never get back, so what difference it make to me whether they stay here or go someplace else. They go to America. Perhaps America different. Perhaps things better there. I not know. I jus' do what mistress tell me, because she favour me, and because of that Charity and my son get favours also. You would do the same, master. But now with the talk of freedom, I not want them sent to America . . .'

'All right — all right!' Alister had had enough; he turned from that bloody figure and paced the length of the room, hands behind his back in that characteristic attitude. I looked at Samuel again and began to wonder, then, how those three had lived through yesterday and the night and the passage of this long day without shelter. Even now, with the wind and rain still slashing, they had made their way back to the only shelter they had ever known, to Landfall. Samuel had probably carried his son and supported Charity, but still had fought his way here, willing to offer himself as victim, but to find respite, and perhaps, if the predictions were true, freedom in the end for the two he cared about. And yet we called these people uncivilized.

'Punished you will be,' Maria said in a low tone. 'And just to make you know what you have done, Charity and your son will suffer along with you.'

Andrew turned upon her. 'Quiet – be quiet! Have you forgotten what has happened this day? Have you forgotten what will be your position in the future?'

But Samuel did not know what had happened this day; he still addressed himself to Maria. 'Better they suffer pain than they drown, mistress.'

'What?' Alister spun around. Samuel looked between them all, Andrew, Maria and Alister, in confusion. In the end he spoke to Alister.

'Master, I went to San Francisco with you because I not believe what the mistress say about Charity and my son being sold to a man on the other side of the island. It happen too quickly. She decide too quickly. No house slaves ever sold from Landfall. I think she need Charity away from Mistress Fiona, so she send her to wait with the other slaves for the next ship that come from America. I know the place where the slaves are locked until the ship come. In the dungeon of a very old place that have no top left to it any more – only the floor of the old rooms to hold them in. But that floor is stone, master. And the place is right there beside the ghut where the water streams down from Kronberg. In the hurricane that become a great river. It rise and rise – I know it. All inside that place will drown. They will drown in their chains, master.'

'What did you do, Samuel, when you left me?'

'You remember, master, that I took the great axe from the sugar factory with me when I go with you? I say it in case any trees fall across our path with the cart and the donkey. Well, when I know the old lady not go with you, I know you could walk if trees come down on the way back. So I leave you and go to the place where the slaves are. I chop and chop – it the only good piece of wood left at San Francisco because the mistress herself see to it being made new and strong. And all the time the water rising. It come about my feet already as I chop at the door. But then I am through at last, and the slaves come out. But they in chains, master. Cannot move through the hurricane in chains. One fall – all fall. In chains they have no chance. So I have to chop at the chains, and the axe break. Then I have to search through all the old things at San Francisco. I find the great hammer in the blacksmith's place. I hurt many of the slaves breaking the chains – they all so close together. But at last all of them done, and free. I say I can do no more. They must shelter for themselves. For Charity and my son and myself I find a place in the stables where it not too bad, if the roof stays on. Water come in to the stables all night, but walls hold up, and the roof, where we are. When the wind die a bit I decide to bring Charity and my son back here to Landfall. For me – I know I die. But they do no wrong. They would have drown, master. I think perhaps Master Fergus' – but more hopefully he looked towards Alister – 'might give mistress the money she would have for them. And then they stay. That is what I have come to say.'

Behind him now appeared Charity and the boy; I remembered that I had seen him about the house; he was being trained for inside duties. They both were cut much as Samuel was, by the slashing of the trees as they had come through the forest, by the falls they had taken; they looked exhausted and beaten, as if the stables had been but little shelter from the storm; they must have been famished too, I thought. Bare-footed they stood there, and around the ankle of each was the manacle, with its short length of chain dangling; there were deep gashes in the skin around the manacle, and the boy balanced himself on one foot, as if he could not put the other to the floor.

'I come back, master,' Charity spoke to Andrew. 'We have lived through the storm, and you not send us away again!' It was more a statement than a plea, as if their escape and return to Landfall was a miracle that no one could deny.

But Andrew grunted and made no direct reply. 'Go below now and feed yourselves, and bathe those cuts. See to the boy, Charity – his ankle looks bad.'

She had her arm protectively about her son, but now her gaze was upon me. 'Mistress Fiona need me? She sick?'

'She's better again,' Fergus said. 'Now do as my father says. There is plenty of food. Eat and rest. We will need you all when it is safe to go out again.'

The three began to turn away. 'One moment!' Maria's voice stopped them. 'San Francisco? Donna Isabella?'

Samuel turned back reluctantly, as if he wished she had not asked. 'I don't know, mistress. Roof gone from greathouse. The rain pour in. Some shutters banging open. It stood many winds, that ole house, but this the last.'

'Donna Isabella?'

'I don't know, mistress. Before I leave I go and call. Some of the roof fallen in upon the place – some fly with the wind. The wind still great and maybe she in cellars and not hear. They say there are places in San Francisco that no one know about. Perhaps she gone in one of those places . . . I not see her.'

'Liar! You didn't even look! Donna Isabella is not one to hide in the cellars. She would have stayed where you left her.'

'The wind blew through that place, mistress. Everything torn about. Soaked with rain. How can I tell where she be?'

With a wave of her hand Maria dismissed him finally, and the three limped out into the darkness of the hall again. From Joanna came a soft whisper, not a sound of grief, but of fear.

'The slaves are loose! They will have found her. She is dead, and Samuel did not have the courage to admit it. The place is torn about – the roof gone.' The tones rose to a wail. 'She's dead! We all will be dead with those savages roaming free. San Francisco's gone. It is an end – an end!'

'Be quiet!' Maria ordered. 'You make me sick with your endless moaning. You tremble for your own miserable skin when it is our mother you should mourn. Those slaves will have broken in. She will have been killed, and the house plundered for food and rum and anything else they fancy.'

'And your doing, my wife. So it's been illegal slave-running that's occupied your spare time and thoughts these last years, has it? It has been that which has taken you from this house at night when you thought I was sleeping. I've watched you go, and thought – God and Fergus forgive me – that it was to him you sneaked away. Well, you have done what you did alone, and you have brought this, and possibly your mother's death, upon your own head. What *are* the penalties for importing and exporting slaves illegally, Alister? You know all that kind of thing . . .'

Alister gave a shrug of deep disgust. 'Why didn't you inquire about that before you let your wife carry on with her activities?'

'Dear Cousin, I didn't *know*. What have I to do with San Francisco? She comes and goes as she pleases, my wife, and no one can say her nay.'

'And yet you've just confessed that you knew she went somewhere – and believed it was to the arms of your own son? What kind of rottenness is this? Believing that of Fergus, you still could push Fiona at him – or Mary Maxwell, or whoever had come to Landfall?'

'Yes, whoever had come. I made my wife write for Mary Maxwell because your father, Jeremy, put forward her name in a letter. But I had little hope about the kind of girl he described. When I saw Fiona, though, I knew at once that she would be the instrument of my vengeance against this scheming little wench I married. Yes, I thrust Fiona at Fergus, just to see my wife

burn in a torment of jealousy and rage. It was the old man's last
joke.'

'Filthy! And I don't believe it,' Alister said. 'I just don't believe
that Andrew Maxwell – the Andrew Maxwell who once was,
didn't know what his wife was about. Or that you made no effort
to intervene if you believed that your son and your wife were
lovers? Not even *you* could care so little! If the details of this
come out – and with illegal slaves who belong to no one loose on
the island it is bound to be known – will you stand up in court and
say you didn't know what your wife was about? What court will
believe that of Andrew Maxwell? That he couldn't keep his
own wife under control? They will laugh. You would make me
laugh now – except that you make me sick! This whole stinking
business makes me sick. Whether you knew the details or not,
you knew she was up to something more complex than arranging
lovers' illicit meetings. What was it – you just took the profits and
never asked where they came from? You *never* asked where the
extra money came from, the money that was never entered in any
of the ledgers? I'm not the only one who will not believe you,
Andrew Maxwell.'

Andrew reached for the jug of rum, and in pouring it, it clattered noisily against the glass, some spilling about him, on to the
sofa and down his shirt front. It made me aware that the wind
was dying steadily and that my senses were growing sharper. I
struggled to get another pillow under me, to raise my head, but
Fergus's hand was there before me. I looked at him fully in those
moments of silence. In his face was an expression I had never seen
there before – tenderness, despair, hurt – a kind of plea for understanding and for forgiveness of the sort of world that was being
unfolded before my eyes. I knew then what was the truth – a truth
I had made myself believe and yet until now had not truly believed. That he had possessed Maria only once – long ago. I had
been prepared to take the half-truth from him, because I was mad
with a passion for him as great as Maria's must have been. And
yet his look at me was a gift of the whole truth. I could rest,
and there would be no more doubting. His hand stroked my cheek
gently.

'Profit –' Andrew waved his glass. 'Profit, you say? I knew
of no profit! Don't try to pin *that* on me. The Maxwells were
repaid their debt, weren't they? – and a profit commensurate with
their investment? Once that was done what came and went at
Landfall was my business alone.' Then he put down the glass. 'No
– that's not really how it was. The debt was out of the way, and I

was married to Maria. After that, the money that came and went from Landfall was no longer my business. I didn't care to make it so. *She* managed, and I let her. As for not caring . . . you're quite right, my cousin. I haven't cared a damn what she has done almost since the day I married her. Not since the time when I finally saw past that look of innocence and knew to what sort of woman I had given my name and what little remained of my honour. Yes, you're right. I don't care a damn!'

There was a terrible finality about it. It was true; he simply didn't care. No one could really reach this man, behind his rum and the fumes of the hemp. No one could imagine him being made to answer for anything from that place on the red sofa.

'You realize,' Alister said, 'that when the news gets about the island that the loose slaves were held at San Francisco, and shipped from there, you will be held responsible. After all – you are Maria's husband.'

Andrew waved his hand contemptuously. 'Let them try! See how far they get! Let us first see how many others were involved and who will first make the charge. If my wife has been shipping slaves from this island, there were many others besides herself who were involved. If you delved you'd find, I have no doubt, some very influential names connected with this affair. No one person – a woman – could organize and capitalize such a scheme. Oh, I don't at all put it past her to have thought of it all – and the use of San Francisco was perfect. She must have been dipping into the Landfall money to put up her share. But I would wager you anything I have that there will be no inquiry. These things have a way of being hushed up. Everyone knows, and no one says anything. If there was trouble, no one would come forward to stand as Maria's protector – but then I doubt anyone will come forward to accuse her either. Self-protection, my dear cousin. We all have made our mistakes.'

Alister turned to Maria. 'There *were* others involved, I suppose? And the American captains came gladly, knowing that those they got here had survived the Atlantic crossing and were rested and fed up before being put on the block, or else they were slaves from other islands – healthy, strong, used to the kind of work expected of them. After all, *you* took the risk of those who died on the way – the Americans just took those who survived. They pay premiums for that kind and are spared the expense of the whole voyage to the Gold Coast and back, and the risks that go with it. It was a nice trade for you, Maria – profitable, and well organized. You could not have done it by yourself.'

She shrugged. 'I will admit nothing. Do what you like.'

'You don't admit knowledge of the voodoo doll, either. And can you deny the manacles on Charity's ankle? Come, don't try to make a fool of me! It was profitable, and you hid the profit somewhere. You took what could be stolen from Landfall and put it into this venture, didn't you? Where are these profits, Maria? – buried under the sands somewhere down there in one of the bays? Or in one of those places Samuel says no one but Donna Isabella knows of at San Francisco?'

'Profits? Are you mad!' Maria's tone woke to fury. 'Do you think this miserable plantation runs itself? What do you suppose has happened to the price of sugar in these last years since the British monopoly was ended? Everything I have put back into Landfall, and you, Alister Maxwell, so pious and full of feeling for the lot of the slaves, you have had your share – '

'My share! I've never shared – '

'You have! What do you think paid you the return on the capital you Maxwells invested here? Just because it appeared as nice clean money in a London bank doesn't mean it wasn't earned out of this soil. I have paid you your money. Nothing but me and my efforts have given you your profits, and yet you come out here and rant to me about the emancipation of the slaves that have added sugar to your bank accounts? No less than any of us you are guilty. There *is* no gold buried under the sands of any of these bays – there is nothing but what you see about you. There is Landfall, and its possessions, including the slaves, and there is a ruined crop outside our doors at this moment. Make what you like of it. It is all there is!'

Alister shook his head. 'If that is all there is – then you *have* run the plantation as badly as the books say.' He looked at Andrew. 'There's nothing here in assets, and despite all the inquiries I've made on the authority of being a shareholder in Landfall, can I find anything in any of the banks in Santa Marta. The estate is living hand-to-mouth, and there's no capital anywhere *I* can discover. Your wife is either a very poor manager or an extremely clever embezzler.'

Andrew just laughed. 'Well, that will be *your* problem, Alister. Yours and Fergus's. I won't be here to worry about it. I told you I don't give a damn any more. I've worked all my life for nothing, it seems. When everything should have been bringing its reward to me, it all suddenly tasted sour. Nothing has been worth the struggle. But I'll not stand up to defend myself in any court, or try to untangle this mess, because I'll not last this six-month, and we all know it. You're going to be left to fight it out alone. You'll not harvest a crop after this storm for at least eighteen months. If there is nothing here, as you say, Landfall will be done for by then. There'll be nothing . . . nothing. But I won't be here to see it, and I don't care.'

'But I *do* care.' The note of hysteria in Katarina's voice was ominous. '*I* care. My sister, what have you done with it? Ever since you came to Landfall you promised that one day there should be ease and plenty. You were putting everything back into Land-fall – the profits from the slaves – everything. And when the old man was dead we should come to live here. Where is the money now? What have we worked for, Joanna and I? We have worked for you, kept our wretched mother alive, fed your stinking slaves in their hole, and every night trembled for our lives lest they break loose and murder us in our beds! And for what? For noth-ing! – this Alister says there is nothing!'

'I kept you alive, didn't I?' Maria answered. 'You ate. You wore clothes. You kept what little there was left of San Francisco. I could do no more. Alister is right. There *is* nothing else.'

'But *this* – Landfall – was to be everything! And now your hus-band is dispossessing you. And why? – because you still were greedy for the son of the man you married. And Fergus – he now gives his love to another woman, and you try to kill her. So – you have been no cleverer or wiser than we.' Her face was glistening – with sweat or tears of frustration. 'You! – for whom the last good things at San Francisco were sold, for whom more acres were mortgaged and lost so that you could have two years in Madrid and capture a rich husband. Well, you were not clever enough for that, but you made us believe you had achieved some-thing almost as good. But now, you, the clever, the beautiful Maria, the favoured of our mother – you end up no better than we. And not even San Francisco still stands. Its roof is open to the skies. Will you stay here on the charity of Fergus's wife, or will you come back to share our existence? Will we, my sister, spend the rest of our lives together huddled like animals in our own stables? Is that the future you promised us?'

Maria shrugged, as if weary of it all. 'You talk too much – you fear too much. The future will be what it is. There is no money – I have either managed badly, as Alister says, or this plantation costs more than anyone realizes. Have it whichever way you wish. The crops are ruined, and the coffers are empty. Fergus will take anything that is left. Now cry about it if you wish, for all the good it will do, but leave me in peace.'

'Peace, is it?' It was a cry of outrage from Fergus. 'Peace, she says! What peace have you given anyone these last eight years? What have you ever brought to this house but shame and rottenness? When you came it was thriving, even if it had yet to taste happiness. Now you leave it bankrupted . . .'

I made a gesture with my hand to stop them talking, to try to gather strength to say what I must; but no one took any notice. Fergus's hand was still on me, but he was looking at Maria, as was everyone else. She sat in her chair with a kind of regal stillness, an unassailable strength in her that could not be beaten down with words or threats or any stirring of regret in her own heart. One knew, looking at her, that she would accept good fortune or misery, even death, in exactly the same way. In that slight, beautiful form, for the first time, I saw the stoic determination and patience of Donna Isabella. Maria also was capable of sitting out a hurricane in solitude.

'I will go away,' she said. 'I will bother no one. There will be no one brought to court. There will be no scandal. You can say I have gone to Spain . . . Duncan I leave to you, Andrew – or to you, Fergus. In either case, he will be with his father.'

'And us?' Katarina screamed. 'What of us?'

'You? – you and Joanna will manage for yourselves, as best you might all these years if I had not kept you going from whatever Landfall could spare. Learn to work – learn to work as I will have to. But I will not do it at San Francisco. I will never go back to San Francisco except to bury my mother.'

'Very impressive, Maria,' Alister said. 'But I don't believe you. What will you do? How will you live?'

A sudden fire came into her coolness. 'Why should you trouble about that? I am not yet old – nor undesirable. There are ways a woman can live, if she must. It shall not, however, be done on San Cristóbal. I have some respect for my mother's memory and name. You, yourself, Alister, may escort me to the first ship that's fit to leave Santa Marta harbour, bound for no matter where. And I tell you there will be no chests of gold dug up from the sands to go with me. And you may spend the rest of your life setting spies to find moneys deposited with some bank, somewhere, and you will find none. Because there is none. You will see. I ask just for enough money to leave. After that . . .' She shrugged, and then paused. 'So how does that seem to you, my husband, as an alternative to the fate you planned for me, living here under the rule of a Scottish governess, or grubbing out an existence at San Francisco like my two spiritless, witless sisters? Oh, no – that is not for me! I

6

still shall wear silk and who knows, perhaps one day I shall at
last wear diamonds . . .'

It was then my plucking hand finally caught at Fergus's sleeve.
'Diamonds . . .' I said.

He bent lower. 'Diamonds,' I repeated, trying to make my
voice heard by them all. 'What about the diamonds?'

By now the magic of the word had captured them; they all were
looking and straining to hear.

'It's nothing, Fiona. Just Maria dreaming her dreams. No one
must ever be sorry for Maria – don't you know that? She has no
pity and she cannot accept it from anyone else. The talk of diamonds is a dream.'

'It was no dream. I know it now!' My anger made me stronger.
She was going; she was going and leaving her son, leaving behind
a dying husband and a house, a plantation wrecked, her sisters
snivelling with fear and hatred at the knowledge that they must
fend for themselves.

'They *were* diamonds I saw. Jewels . . . A great fire of jewels!'

'Jewels? – where?' Katarina demanded. It was the first time
she had spoken directly to me since she had come to Landfall.
Then she looked at Maria. 'Jewels!' Her tone rose with excitement.

I struggled to raise myself higher, and Fergus thrust another
pillow behind me. I was much stronger; the ache and weakness
had almost left my bones. I was sweating again, but it was the
usual sweat of the tropics, not of fever.

'I thought I saw once . . .' My burst of courage and confidence
was quickly running out. 'Once, as I entered the salon I thought
I saw Maria –' Then I shook my head. 'Oh, no. It does not
matter. It could not have been, because when she turned from
the mirror . . .' I lay back against the pillows. I could not make
myself speak. I could not reveal to them all, to their scorn and
their fear and their questionings, that second part of my life that
I tried to keep hidden from everyone. I could not speak the vision
that I had believed to be some reconstruction of the past and
reveal it as a fantasy. 'It is nothing,' I said faintly. 'Just something
I thought I saw, but I was mistaken. Because when she turned
she wore no jewels.'

'Go on,' Alister urged me.

I turned my head stubbornly away. 'I have said all I saw. It
was a mistake – some trick of the chandelier prisms reflected in
the mirror. It was nothing – I tell you, it was nothing!'

A thin, tired tone came from Andrew. 'Listen to her . . . Listen to her! She sees – and senses. Some of the Scots have that sight. Some see what is not there, but hidden . . .' His voice faded, as if the effort was too much.

'Jewels?' Alister had caught at the thought, but I felt Fergus's hand press mine more closely, and I knew he was remembering the day that I had checked my horse at the place where his grandfather had died. It was the thing I had not wanted, to puzzle, frighten, bewilder. I had not wanted to set myself apart. Better that she should have gone with all she could lay hands on than that I should have to live the rest of my life here having given this knowledge of me into their keeping. Never afterward would I live as a normal, ordinary woman in the sight of any of them here in this room.

'Jewels!' Alister nodded, as if something was coming clear to him. He looked at Maria. 'Of course you were willing to leave by the first ship and without any chests of gold. The gold has already been translated into something much more portable, easier to hide, and with no tiresome banks to give up your secret. Clever of you, Maria. Even if I had set someone to follow you, the jewels could always have been the gifts of some admirer, couldn't they, and not the product of Landfall's robbing?'

Maria ignored him; she was looking at me, quite calmly. 'You have been an ill wind in this house. Ever since you came nothing has been the same. You have stolen my child and the man I would have had as my husband. You have spied on me – here and at San Francisco. In time you would have gathered it all to yourself. It is a pity that Juanita's spell did not have time to work fully. We would have been better rid of you. But I can see that the fever is still in your brain. There are no jewels – there *never* were any. You saw nothing.'

I did not answer her. She was right. I had seen nothing, nothing that was tangible. Perhaps a fever of jealousy had possessed me even from that first night. I *was* jealous of Maria. Had the gift been thwarted by an unworthy thought, a desire to pull down the one whom I feared and envied? No, there was no answer.

But Alister would not let it go. 'Jewels? – but how would you know you got your money's worth? Weren't you taking a great risk? It is easy to be tricked – one must be an expert.'

'As to that,' Katarina spat out, 'I can answer that. Maria does know the value of what she sees. There have been jewels in the family. We have not always lived like peasants at San Francisco. My mother knew jewels. She had some in her young days. Our grandmother had many more. All gone now. But what was left

was looked at many times, and the knowledge comes. Maria had
the names of many jewellers in Madrid when she went there with
the last of our little hoard, and she bargained with them all – and
learned all the time. She was patient, and she got a better price
even than our mother had been offered here. In those days she
was truthful enough to tell us. Today she would have told us only
half as much, and kept the rest.'

'But how were they come by? How does one get jewels here
on San Cristóbal?' Now Alister was asking the questions of
Katarina, who could hardly wait to pour out what she knew. It
was plain now that she cherished no further thought that Maria
might have shared anything she had put away with them. She,
like all of us, had heard all that Maria wanted was to be gone
from San Cristóbal as quickly as ship could take her. There was
no hope now to silence her. Like Samuel, she knew now that her
sister's promises had been worthless, and the Spanish sense of a
wrong to be avenged had been roused in her. There was to be
nothing for herself and Joanna; there would be nothing for Maria,
either.

I made one more attempt, but I don't think anyone but Fergus
heard my words, and even he was hardly attending. 'But I tell
you I saw nothing that was *real* . . . When she turned, there was
nothing.' I ended with a kind of sob; it was no use. They were
all off following their own routes of revenge, enjoying the hound-
ing of the woman whom, for one reason or another, they hated.
They were like a pack in full cry, and I had provided the false
scent.

'How does one get jewels on San Cristóbal? – how has one ever
got them? Oh, yes, I know the saying now goes "Poor as a West
Indian planter," but do not forget the days when they used to say
"Rich as a Creole." Those were the great days of the islands, and
the women vied with one another in their homes and their carriages
and their dress. Jewels were part of it – part of a man's fortune.
The jewellers used to come – private visits to greathouses, tempting
the women. The best known was the family of Greene. English.
Generations of them. Grandfather, father, son. Honest – you got
your value. If times were bad – a bad harvest, he would always
buy back. They came to the island once or twice a year. Less often
now, because the money has gone from sugar and the estates are
already mortgaged. They go now to the new rich in America,
but there still are some clients left, still some who trust jewels more
than gold.' She gave a bitter, sobbing laugh. 'Do not worry – the
value will be there in whatever she has bought. She has both the

knowledge and a trusted source.'

Alister said, 'Then where are they, Maria? Not in the safe — we've already emptied that.'

She shrugged. 'Since you have dreamed up these jewels you can all play the game of searching for them — after all, it will pass the time, won't it, and we're all sorely in need of some occupation.' She turned to Andrew. 'You know the house best. Where would you suggest they all begin? There can be no secret places here as there are supposed to be at San Francisco. You rebuilt it — you know it all. Go on, my husband — play their game. What do the English call it — hunt the slipper?' Then she pointed at me. 'Or better still — ask her. If she sees so much that isn't in anyone else's sight, then most certainly she will know where these jewels are that do not exist. Ask her — ask her!'

I was silent. They all looked at me, and there was nothing to say. They didn't know it was not something to be summoned at will, and I had already said too much. At last, desperately, I burst out, 'I only *thought* I saw them . . .'

'Leave her be,' Andrew said softly. 'Leave her in peace.' He sipped his rum, and the liquid moved violently in the glass; he needed both hands to set it down. His facial muscles seemed to have stiffened into a mask of indifference and pain; his lips twisted sideways. The last words seemed to have been spoken with difficulty.

Joanna, though, had no thought for Andrew; she spoke, forging ahead of her sister. 'The Scottish one saw her with jewels in this room. She says she *thought* she saw them — perhaps she did. Then don't trouble looking in safes and secret places in the cellars. Maria's wealth — if it exists — will be in the only thing she brought with her from San Francisco. Her only dowry. The one thing that only she may open, whose contents only she may touch. Look in the cabinet.'

'The cabinet?' Katarina's face grew longer as her mouth dropped. 'Of course! The place where the treasures at San Francisco were always kept.'

'No!' Maria's composure was shattered at last. She sprang from the chair and towards the cabinet, but Katarina had dodged between her and Alister, as Alister had stepped to block Maria's path. The doors still stood wide, as they had done from the moment of the discovery of the doll. Feverishly now, Katarina ran her hand along the shelf that contained the vellum-bound manuscripts, the ones that were too precious to handle, that only Maria could dust. Katarina came finally to the one she sought.

'Here!' she dragged it out with shaking, clumsy hands and hurried with it to the centre table of the salon.

'Leave it be,' Maria ordered. She seemed shocked and surprised to find her arm held firmly by Alister and she was unable to free herself – as if suddenly an ant had stood up and blocked her path. 'Let your sister show us, Maria. You have long promised me a sight of some of the illuminated manuscripts.' The mockery in his tone was heavy. 'It's a pity it took a hurricane to bring that time about.'

Katarina was fumbling with the heavy brass clasp of the volume, but it did not yield. Without any further words she went straight to Maria, still held by Alister, and took the ring of keys that Maria had replaced in the pocket of her gown. 'Here,' she said, 'this small brass one. I would know it anywhere. You do not forget the things you grow up with.'

'Katarina, I warn you – you are making a mistake, and you will regret it. There will be nothing more from me . . .'

'Regret?' her sister answered. 'What is there to regret now? What is there to lose? Have you not told us to look to ourselves? Perhaps Joanna and I now have something to gain.'

The lock yielded easily; what had seemed a volume was a vellum-covered box, with edges ridged as if they were hand-cut paper. From it, not clumsily now, but with care, Katarina brought out a folded bundle of white cloth. This in turn gave way to many layers of dark velvet. Joanna came forward to join her sister, walking almost on tiptoe. Piece by piece the jewels came out – I could not see them all; the table was above my line of vision. I hardly wanted to see them. Some were unset – single stones, green, red, the flash of many colours at the heart of whiteness. I was glad Fergus had not gone to look, nor had Alister moved. The sisters' long fingers handled those stones for a while; the wind had dropped now so that in the lulls we could hear the little gasps which were the only sounds they made. The great piece was the necklace, diamonds, I supposed. There was nothing I had ever seen to gauge it by. For a long moment Katarina held it up. She did not, as many another woman might have done, go to the mirror to try what the precious thing would do for her. Instead, after studying it for a time, she laid it back gently among its velvet folds.

'There – there is for so many nights to live with those savages so near – so many days to see that they were fed, so many times to see that their stinking place was cleaned out after the ships had gone. There is for so many years of taking care of our mother, of taking orders from our cheating sister. There is for so many hopes that withered . . .'

Was she crying? – did rage then give way to self-pity? Was it too much to see their years of subjugation to a younger sister represented by the cold fire of the gems? With dark heads bent over the contents of the box, the two long sallow faces contemplated the fruits of the struggle.

'There, also, is so much stolen from Landfall,' Alister said. 'It is stolen from Duncan – from Fergus.'

He had released the grip on Maria; there was no further need to hold her. She rubbed her wrist where he had held her as she looked at me, but the rigid discipline of her bearing suggested the control that had returned, and that, once more, she was untouchable by the lash of fortune. There certainly was no self-pity in her tone. 'You – you!' she said to me, the tone very quiet, as if she were pondering, rather than lashing out. 'I should have listened to Juanita the day you arrived and sent you packing. She knew. Perhaps like recognizes like. That was my mistake – not to believe what Juanita told me about you. I don't know *how* you saw these things. I rarely permitted even myself to look on them. But you did see them. Not even Juanita knew about them, but she warned me that your magic was very strong . . . How strange I should have harboured you in this house for a single hour. If I had obeyed instinct and Juanita I would have sent you back on the *Clyde Queen*. If it had not been for my husband I should have done so – but I knew he could not last and you would have gone then. Well, it is done . . .'

'Yes, it is done, Maria,' Alister said. 'But why? – why, Maria? was there need? What were you afraid of? That Andrew would turn you out? That he would change his mind and Landfall might still go to Fergus? You had to steal and squirrel away against the future you were not certain of?'

She answered him calmly. 'You often are stupid and pompous, Alister – but sometimes you are shrewd and guess right. What is certain in this world? I learned to ask that question very young. I learned to ask it after enduring the snubs of those who thought themselves leaders in San Cristóbal when ours was the oldest blood on the island. I learned to ask it in Madrid when possessing beauty counted for nothing, nor even the illustrious name I bore, if there was no fortune to go with it. I learned to set no store by anything I could not hold in my hands and count. And so I began to put away against the day when anything might come to pass – if Andrew should tire of me, if Fergus would not have me, if the hurricane should come, if, even, as they kept saying, the slaves would be freed and we would have no labour for the cane fields. Against the inevitable day when I would look in the mirror and know it was all over. The small bundle in velvet was my protection against the storm, from whichever way it blew. And now, at this moment, it is again my protection, because once more the wind has changed.'

'Changed?' Fergus questioned. 'It hasn't changed, Maria. It's almost spent. It hardly blows any more.'

'You never were very subtle, Fergus – always taking things exactly as they are said. Perhaps, after all, I would have tired of you, when your beauty was gone, as mine would be.' She paused, and then her voice rang out clearly as she pointed, not towards the box on the table that had held our attention, but to the red sofa in the shadows.

'You see, once again, the wind has changed. My husband is dead.'

I felt Fergus's grip on me tighten and heard the sucking in of his breath. It seemed a very long time before Alister made himself move to that still figure, slumped, as always, against the end of the sofa. He looked no different except that his stillness had a terrible kind of permanence to it. I realized that Maria must have been the only one watching him in those last moments, the moments when the jewels had flashed in the fingers of her sisters. She must have watched the final twist of pain of the lips, perhaps the slightest movement, the silent cry for help. She must have watched the stillness descend, and she had stood and watched as he died as untended as if he had been all alone.

Alister was feeling for pulse, and with swift fingers unbuttoning the rum- and sweat-soaked shirt and bending to listen for a heartbeat. Fergus went, with a slight reluctance, I thought, to join Alister. I wondered how, at that distance, in the dim light, Maria had been so certain that life had passed from Andrew's body in the final spasm. Why had I not felt it – I, who was supposed to feel these things? But she had spoken the truth. Fergus brought a lamp close, and for five minutes the two men bent over him; the rum was useless – probably the only time that Andrew's lips had ever rejected it. There was no pulse; the heart did not beat. Finally they closed the eyelids over the little slit of vision that had remained to him in those last minutes.

Maria spoke. 'I am right? He is dead?'

Fergus answered. 'He is dead. My father is dead.' And then with great gentleness he swung his heavy legs up on to the sofa and laid his arms out straight; then he took the rumpled silk handkerchief from Andrew's pocket and spread it across the still face.

'Don't let Duncan come in here,' was all he said.

I fell back against my pillow, and heard the little moans from Joanna and Katarina. For a moment there was no further sound in the room, and then I heard the tap of Maria's heels, a deliberate, firm tread. First she went to the table and wrapped again the jewels in their velvet and white cloth, and locked the vellum box. She carried it with her as she walked, but she did not approach the dead figure on the sofa. Instead she went into the hall, and I could hear her calling to some of the slaves to come from the cellars. There was the familiar slap of bare feet, and Maria's voice, low, giving some order. And then we heard it, the sound we had waited and prayed for through two days and a night – the sound as the shutters to the inner gallery were unlatched on the side away from the wind, the great hammering sound as the first of the iron bars was pried out of its place, the final crash as the first of the huge outer storm shutters was thrown open.

Light and air suddenly flooded in. A rush of wind stirred through the whole house. Only one door on the windward side was opened, but it was enough. The darkness fled. Gone with the rush of the wind were the scents of our fear and bitterness, of rum and sweat and the hemp. The sounds now were not of our voices raised in accusation, contempt and hatred; the sad cries of lives ruined and choked. What we heard now was the tossing of the trees in that high, but no longer destroying wind.

7

In the tropics, burials are swift. With the carnage of the cane fields, the roads washed out and trees laid across them, there was no possibility of burial for Andrew at Santa Marta.

'It doesn't matter,' Fergus said. 'It doesn't matter where he lies now. He would probably want to be at Landfall.'

'Or Winterslo,' I said.

He seized upon it. 'Yes – at Winterslo. That is the place he really belongs to.'

The plantation carpenter was set to work on the coffin, and then Maria summoned Fergus and Alister to her. 'Now we will go to San Francisco – to my mother. We will take what is necessary to make another coffin, and the slaves to carry it.'

Katarina and Joanna refused to leave Landfall. 'What is there to go to? And what is there between Landfall and San Francisco but those savages that Samuel has set loose?'

'There is our mother – alive or dead.'

Katarina shrugged. 'She didn't care for us – dead or alive. We were her slaves as much as that wretched herd. If she is dead, then our absence will not trouble her. If she is alive, then we are no better or worse than before. For me – it can wait a few hours. Until the wind has died completely. Until the way to San Francisco has been cleared. I have come through the forest once in the wind. I will not again.'

Fergus carried me upstairs to my bed, and Charity, the manacle removed, and her wounds bathed, came to stay with me. In a more solemn procession, Andrew's body was carried upstairs to lie once more on his bed, and await burial. I made sure Duncan was in my room with me before this happened. There had been enough grim spectacles this day to haunt his memory. There was no reason for him to look upon the pain-twisted face of Andrew, to smell, as the last thing, the smell of rum.

I told him about his father, and he lay curled against me on the bed, clinging fiercely, with the tears only slow to come; the fears were greater. 'What will happen now, Fiona? What will happen to *me* now?'

'I will take care of you,' I said, holding him closely. It was a rash promise; one I had little idea how I would keep. I felt the tremble of his body, and heard the ring of the axes and the crash of the machetes as the party set out for San Francisco.

It moved on to the early hours of the morning, and still they had not returned. By then I was out of bed and dressed; Duncan refused to stay in bed and followed on my heels like a hound. Suddenly the house was mine, and I had to organize and command and plan. Katarina and Joanna stayed upstairs; when I sent Charity to tell them that a hot meal had been prepared, she brought back the message that the ladies would have it on trays in their room. I was both relieved and angry, and took care to show neither to Duncan.

I took on the task of seeing that Andrew's body was washed and prepared, since Maria seemed to have left no instructions for it; while this went on, Samuel took Duncan to the stables to help feed and groom his pony. The stables had survived; the slave quarters and their vegetable gardens were wrecked. With Duncan gone and Charity's help I did what was necessary for Andrew – bound his chin until the *rigor* of death should hold it firmly, did what I could to compose his features, washed his body with scented water. Charity cleaned and dusted the room, and with Dougal to help, we laid him on clean sheets. I sent Charity to see if any blossoms remained in the garden. She came back empty handed, save for some ferns plucked from the base of the great trees. I slanted down the louvered shutters and lighted a lamp at each side of the bed. These things I remembered from Silkirk, and I thought they might have pleased Andrew.

When it was all done I paused, all alone there, and just as if I had been at home in Silkirk, I found myself on my knees beside the bed. What was I to pray for – for the salvation of a soul that Andrew hardly believed existed? – for the return of honour to a name that he cared about? I tried to think of things my father would have said of him. All I could think was that life had been hard for Andrew Maxwell, and the last years had brought the worst unhappiness and pain. It was indeed better that he should be returned to Winterslo for burial; those days had been his best, when he had worked with his Bible-reading mother to make the soil yield its precious crop, when he had laboured with hopefulness before the tragedy that had brought Fergus to him.

While I knelt there the door opened and Duncan came to me. He came and stood beside me in the half-darkness, staring solemnly at the figure of Andrew. 'Are you praying, Miss Fiona?'

'Yes, Duncan. Do you want to pray with me?'

His answer was to kneel. Before he buried his face in the coverlet he said to me, 'I don't know what to say. What shall I say?'

I hadn't known myself. 'Just pray in your heart. Just bid him good-bye and ask for peace for him. Peace is all that's needed in the end, Duncan.'

We stayed silent there for some time, heads bowed, the last of the great wind still tossing in the trees beyond the gallery. Then finally I touched Duncan gently, and seeing his tear-wet face I bent and kissed him. 'We have done what we can. Pray for him – and never forget him. The dead still live when they are remembered.'

To ease the waiting, I set about the task of trying to get the house in order again. The slaves were subdued, talking little and with muted voices. They did not like the presence of Andrew's body in the house, and worked swiftly so that they might be released from the place of death – even if it were only to try to construct some shelter from the tangled rubble of their huts. They would not stay in the cellars. Juanita and Flora had disappeared. I didn't even ask about them. I would have been thankful never to have set eyes on either again. I could find no slave willing to sit with

Andrew's body, nor would Katarina or Joanna.

'We have prayers to say for our mother,' was the reply I got. 'And not by the bedside of that godless man.'

So Andrew waited in the final loneliness of death even before burial.

It was dawn, and Duncan had finally given in to his weariness and allowed me to put him to bed; I stayed beside him, holding his hand, even, despite the presence of death, singing to him the old Scottish songs that were like a foreign tongue to him. When he slept at last, I went for a few minutes to the gallery, and the growing light revealed the wreckage of the garden below me. It was almost calm now; the wind seemed hardly more than what normally began to blow as the sun reached strength each day. I looked with a kind of horror at the scene; the great cottonwood tree uprooted, its huge spread filled the whole circle of the drive in front of the house, its highest limbs lying just feet away from the bottom of the steps. Other trees had also gone, smaller ones that we had not heard in the whole hideous tumult. Oleander and hibiscus, bottomless, lay flattened, frangipani stripped bare of leaves and branches, naked and gaunt to the sky; and as the light grew I could see on past the ruin of the garden, to the wilder parts and to the sea, where huge swells flung foam high into the air about the Serpents. And yet it was itself, a dawn of unsurpassed beauty – the peculiar intensity of the light, the moment of coolness, almost peace. The rain and wind-battered earth seemed to be settling once more into its fertile sleep. As I quietly walked the full square of the gallery I noted the tightly closed louvers of the room where Katarina and Joanna slept – or lay awake, in fear, waiting for the attack they feared from the freed slaves; I saw, too, in the dawn, the breakfast fires before the remains of the slave huts. I could hear their voices – the chanting, infinitely melancholy songs they sang. I didn't know if they offered thanks for deliverance from the storm, or a dirge for a dead master. Would I ever know these people? I wondered – in the lifetime I would spend here with Fergus would I ever know what lay behind the blank masks of even those who grew closest to me? I doubted that I ever would. Suddenly I wanted very much to be gone from Landfall, to remove to the simpler style of Winterslo, to minimize the gap between these unknowable dark people and the way we lived. But then, for the first time, came the agonizing thought that perhaps Winterslo itself no longer was habitable; that it, like San Francisco, had given up to the storm, its rotting timbers letting its roof fly and opening it to the skies and the rain. It was ironic to think that Fergus and I, like the Medina sisters, might begin our life together in a made-over stable.

But somehow it didn't matter. I also had a reason for a song of thankfulness. I also had been delivered from the storm and had survived an attack from a force of evil I had no real knowledge to fight. I went back then, more willingly, to a chair in Andrew's room, believing that he had the right to even this small vigil. I fell asleep in the chair, thinking that I would ask no more grace or bounty than to have Fergus for myself and, somehow, to carry out my promise to take care of Duncan.

Within the hour they were back. I heard the sounds below, the voices, and sprang out of the chair and ran down.

'Fiona!' Fergus cried, concern marked on his mud-splattered face. 'What the devil are you doing up – and dressed! You should be abed – you should rest!'

'I'm well,' I answered. 'Quite well. Everything has gone now. Just be quiet and don't wake Duncan. He *would* stay up with me most of the night . . .' I stopped because Fergus was holding me, not closely or passionately, but in a kind of calm of wonder, as if he had never believed to do it again. His lips brushed my forehead.

'You're sure?' he demanded. 'You seemed to travel so far from me – almost slipped beyond me. I thought I had lost you.'

I heard my own laugh, and was rather shocked to hear it in this house of mourning. I answered in a broad Scottish accent. 'Ye'll no find it sa easy t' lose me in the future, mon. I'm wi' ye noo, and ye'll no be shut o' me fra' this day.'

Now his embrace tightened to one of joy and strength. 'Go on wi' ye, woman. Ha' ye no shame?'

'I dinna know the word, Fergus Maxwell.'

We broke from our embrace to find that Alister and Maria had entered the hall. Once again I was impressed, as I always had been, by the unyielding strength of the woman. Her gown was covered in the red mud of the island's earth, her hair hung in tails about her face and her hands were cut, and still bleeding. Beside her, Alister was in the same state, as was Fergus, but it seemed natural to a man, and in her a further proof of her invulnerability.

'Donna Isabella?' I was forced to ask, with lips suddenly gone dry.

Alister answered. 'We found her dead where Maria said she would be. One of the slaves . . . It could have happened no other way. Probably a machete.' His face was very white and strained. He had stood the ordeal less well than either Fergus or Maria. Without further questions, I was suddenly sickeningly aware of the fate the old woman had met, the savage reprisal of a slave gone mad with hate and terror, the kind of death that Andrew's father had known in the cane field. Maria had been right; Samuel must have seen her, and would not be the bearer of such news – or feared that he himself would be blamed.

I bowed my head slightly to Maria. 'I am sorry.'

She nodded wearily and then shrugged. 'She was old,' was what she answered, this extraordinary woman, 'and very tired. She wanted no more of life.' And yet in the face of the seeming indifference I knew that a rock of Maria's existence had rolled away from her. She derived her strength and her temperament from the domineering old woman; probably many times in their lives they had done battle against each other, and enjoyed the clash of arms.

'She is at rest,' Alister concluded. 'Maria helped dig the grave by lamplight. We waited till dawn to come back through the forest.' I thought of those two women cowering over their beads in the room above, and of the woman before me, and in spite of myself my admiration and awe of her grew. On every level she was formidable. If ever I should be able to carry out my promise to take care of Duncan, I knew that any son sprung from this woman would challenge all my strength.

I waited a moment, then I said: 'There is hot food – I had them make a stew from the cooked meats. The ovens are lighted again. Your husband, Mrs Maxwell, is upstairs. I did the best I could . . . I'm sorry I could not force any of the slaves to sit with him. They seem to be afraid . . .'

'They would be,' she answered, her tone contemptuous and tired. 'And of course my sisters have done nothing . . .' Her glance took in the hall and salon cleared of the mattresses and swept, the dining-room cleared of the used dishes.

'They were tired and . . . afraid, also, I think. They seem to fear an attack on the house by the slaves that Samuel set free.'

'They always find something to be afraid of!' Maria spat out the words. Then she half-sighed. 'Well, let us eat, since there is hot food. Then we will bathe and rest an hour. We must send slaves to dig a grave – you, Fergus, must tell them where. And then, before the sun is too high, Andrew must be buried.'

She might have been the conventional, though strong, grieving widow. It was difficult to remember the acts of treachery, the misery that Andrew had suffered, so great now was her dignity. I found myself in the kitchen with her, putting food on to plates and trays and carrying it to the men; it did not occur to me to disregard any direction she gave, to disobey an order. She did not summon any slaves from the quarters, and none came near the house. I poured rum for the men, and wine for Maria. The food and drink brought a little colour to each face, though they did not once speak except what was necessary about the burial arrangements for Andrew. I myself took the dishes back to the kitchen, and Fergus went to the slave huts, looking for his own slaves to send them to Winterslo to make the preparations. When I came back to the hall, Maria was already on her way upstairs; she did not go to her sisters' room, and they did not emerge to question her. A terrible, deadly quality of weariness and silence had descended on the whole house. I heard a door open and close, and knew it was Andrew's room; Maria had gone to look upon him. No one would ever know if it were with hatred or remorse or indifference, for she would certainly never speak of it.

Alister stood there, half-supported by the newel post; I had never seen him look as he did now. The momentary revivant of food and drink had faded; just a weariness and despair was left.

'It was terrible,' he said. 'It was the worst sight I ever saw, that old woman. I wish to God . . .' Then he stopped and seemed about to turn and go upstairs.

'You wish what?'

His tone became suddenly strong. 'I wish with all my powers that you were not staying here. Oh – not just at Landfall. I wish you out of these islands forever. The black people – I think their time has come, and who can blame them if they show no more pity than we have done. I think we are just starting to pay the price . . . just starting.'

His limp was very pronounced as he climbed the stairs.

2

The noon sun was high before they had managed to clear the road from Landfall to Winterslo for the passage of the cane cart which carried Andrew's coffin. Fergus walked, leading the mule, and the rest of us rode, most of the Landfall slaves on foot behind us.

From somewhere, perhaps a relic of her wardrobe from Madrid all those years ago, Maria had found a black dress and mantilla; she rode regally behind the cart as if she were the consort following the bier of a king. She kept Duncan close to her, he on the pony with the silver-studded harness, which had been Andrew's last, wildly extravagant gift. The rest of us just wore the clothes that came to hand, the most comfortable for the heat and ride. Alister had borrowed a shirt from Fergus, but his trousers were still the mud-stained ones of the night's digging; he wore a ragged slave's hat to shield him from the sun. Except for the devastation about us, there was no telling of the passage of the hurricane. The same blue sky above us, the same burning sun, the same cooling wafts of the trade winds to dry the sweat as it soaked our clothes. The trades would begin to blow again, and the days would be cooler. 'October, all over.'

Fergus had not slept, but had gone to Winterslo with the slaves to select the site. It was on the slope below the house, in a grove of mampoo trees that somehow had survived the onslaught. As we breasted the last rise, I lifted my eyes to the house, not having dared to ask Fergus, when he had returned for his father's body, the question that had haunted me. It was like a miracle to see Winterslo still intact; the roof was there – some shutters hung off their hinges, but it was still a house, and would be a home. Alister urged his horse up beside me.

'Did it worry you? – I thought of it myself. But it must have been sheltered a little by the height of Kronberg. It's not so exposed as San Francisco.'

'It was good of you to think of us . . .' I murmured, 'in the middle of everything else.'

'I am always thinking of you,' he said, and his tone was edgy. He let his horse drop back, and I rode on alone.

Alister held the Book before him, but he spoke the words from memory, just as my father would have done.

'. . . He that believeth in me, though he were dead, yet shall he live . . .'

I knew now that this grove also contained the graves of Andrew's mother and father; it was natural he should have returned here. We had a plantation, then, Fergus and I, a true one, of toil and tragedy given to this red earth. I thought that when I came to live at Winterslo I would somehow make a garden of this bare, henpecked place. I would bring my children here, and Duncan, and they would cherish, not shun it.

And then the psalm. '. . . He maketh me to lie down in green pastures.' The awful irony of the words that followed struck me and made me wonder at the wisdom of the choice. 'Thou preparest

a table before me in the presence of mine enemies . . . Surely goodness and mercy shall follow me all the days of my life; and I will
dwell in the house of the Lord forever.'

We murmured, 'Amen' – all except Maria and her sisters, whom
she had forced to follow to the graveside and witness what they
considered a heretic service. I could not help thinking, as we remounted, that a table had indeed been prepared in the presence of
Andrew's enemies. We rode back now, to the pickings.

3

On the return to Landfall, Maria was fully in possession. She presided over an almost silent meal, and then the siesta was observed,
though it was impossible to sleep with the ringing of the axes all
about the house, chopping at the fallen trees, clearing some of
the debris from the garden, beginning the reconstruction of the
slave quarters. Fergus had remained at Winterslo to begin the
work there; I missed him desperately. Without him, without
Andrew, I had no shield against Maria, and I knew that my days,
even my hours, at Landfall were numbered. Very soon, also,
Alister would go. The end had come with savage abruptness, and
none had been prepared for it, except, possibly, Maria.

It was no surprise, then, to be summoned from lessons with
Duncan as dusk began to approach, to come to the salon. 'I am
to stay with Master Duncan,' Charity said. 'And he is to go on
with his books.'

'How will Charity know that I'm reading?' Duncan said sullenly.
He didn't like my being summoned away from him; he, too, felt the
insecurity of Andrew's absence. 'She can't read herself.'

'That the truth, master. But my son learn to read.'

'How?'

'I have spoken with Master Fergus. He try to buy us both for
Winterslo, and Mistress Fiona teach my son to read.' She had never
spoken of such a thing to me, but simply took it for granted that
I would not refuse. 'My son not spend his life in the cane fields. I
am sure of it now.'

And how many others, I thought, as I went downstairs, believed the same thing? We had taken them from the simpler ways
of Africa and they had learned that books and writing were the
keys to the prosperity of the white man. Not all of them would forever be tillers of the soil. If emancipation should come, money,
however little, would have to pass from the hands of the white into
the black, and with it would be the beginning of the turn-about.

By slow degrees, one or two would creep up and onward from his fellows. So very likely Charity was right, I would teach her son to read.

They were assembled in the salon – Maria, Alister, Katarina and Joanna. I missed the figure on the red sofa. Fergus had also been sent for, and he came at last, protesting. 'Look, Maria, there's fully as much work to do at Winterslo as here, and I haven't anything like the number of slaves . . . I've no time for social gatherings.'

He had not changed his clothes, and they were mud-stained from the still-wet earth, the old clothes he habitually wore on the plantation. It was strange to see Alister similarly dressed; only the perfect fit of the mud-caked boots were a reminder of his usual elegance. But he still bore the scratches on his face and hands, as did Fergus, as reminders of the wreckage and the journeys to San Francisco.

'It is of some importance, I think, Fergus,' Maria replied. 'I intend to say these things only once. All of us might as well know them at the same time. I do not want days and weeks of argument, or secondhand reports of what I said. Let us be finished with it now. We all have work to do.'

Alister crossed his legs and leaned back in his chair. 'Well, Maria?' I drew confidence from his tone. Alister would not be stampeded by Maria. And yet I was wondering, without Andrew, what he could do to change what was now the order of things at Landfall.

'First of all,' Maria said, 'the will that my late husband made is still valid. Whatever he said in this room before he died does not matter. What matters is what is written in the will that lies in the safe of the solicitor in Santa Marta, and I *know* that has not been recently changed. And that gives Landfall, its contents, its assets as well as its liabilities, to me as trustee for Duncan until he is twenty-one. From that point on, I still retain a one-third share of the estate. Is that clear to you all?'

'Is *that* what you dragged me over here to listen to?' Fergus burst out. 'I knew what was to be! I expect nothing of Landfall, as I expected nothing of my father once you had twisted your way into his life. I want nothing. I want nothing but Fiona . . .'

'Take her then!' Maria flashed back at him. 'Take her! I see you are mad to saddle yourself with a dowerless wife, and soon you will have a brood of children under your feet. Take her, then – and look back to this time and regret it all the days of your life.'

'Regret? – regret what? That I wanted Fiona and not you? The difference is like smelling honeysuckle – if you ever took time to do such a thing – and taking a scorpion to your bed. Thanks – if that's all I came to hear, I'll be off. Fiona, you must pack and we'll find you somewhere to stay until we can be married. They'll be dispensing with quite a lot of the formalities in Santa Marta just now. I imagine we can arrange it very quickly.'

'Duncan?' I said faintly. I was haunted by my promise, by the knowledge that what I had come to do was still not yet done, and things were slipping past our control; without Andrew there was no appeal.

'And why should you concern yourself with my son?' Maria demanded. 'He is no one's business but my own. He will probably go to Spain when he is older, and learn what he never could learn here. Whatever happens, my son is finished with the Maxwells.'

I watched Fergus's face as this was said, and it worked strangely, anger, the flash of self-accusation again, and the half-closing of his eyes in a kind of despair were there for me to see. He was unable to do what his father had done in his time; he was unable to claim a child who might be his son. He looked at me as if begging forgiveness; I nodded, just slightly, but I could give him no hope. Maria had everything now.

'And us?' Katarina said, with her sardonic, twisted smile. 'What disposition have you made for us, my sister? Are we to be allowed the crumbs from the table?'

Maria shrugged, as if their fate were of little concern to her. 'You will live, I expect – but not here at Landfall. Do you think I want to spend my days cooped up with two quarrelling spinsters? We shall see what can be made habitable for you at San Francisco . . .'

'Ah, good of you, I'm sure,' Joanna cried. 'After all, it is still our home!'

'You are wrong, Joanna. It is now *mine* – solely. You do not think that our mother was so improvident as to leave it among the three of us to have what little remains wasted and torn apart? She made her will, and showed it to me, and it also waits in Santa Marta. You will live their at my discretion, and I shall work the two estates together – thus the small acreage of San Francisco will be added to Landfall and brought back to fertility. Its cane will come to the factory here, and we shall have a more economic usage.'

'You are suddenly businesslike, Maria,' Alister observed drily. 'Showing more sense for proper management than you have professed all these years. But the Maxwells aren't finished at Landfall, even if you take your son from their sphere of influence. Before you start bringing San Francisco sugar to the Landfall mill, and sharing its slaves, remember that the Maxwells still own a share of Landfall – does that also mean you are willing for them to have part of San Francisco?'

'Never – *never*! No more of San Francisco goes into strangers' hands, least of all to Maxwells'. The loan was paid off – It was my husband's life work to do that.'

'Not in full – remember that! Not in full. We still retain our interest for forgiveness of the last part of the loan. That is why I came here. To look into all of this. But this is not new to you. You know this very well.'

'Yes – well I know it. A seemingly magnanimous gesture that had only Maxwell interests to prompt it. Why give up part of a good estate? But that same document also gave my husband or his heirs the right to buy outright from the Maxwells at the sum stated then, plus the interest on the money that would have accumulated in these five or six years.'

'And you are willing to meet that price?'

She nodded, and her tongue flicked eagerly over her lips. 'Yes, I will meet that price. Jewels are good for more than wearing by frivolous women.'

'Those jewels were bought with money taken from Landfall in order to finance your part in illegal slave-trading.'

She sighed. 'Alister – you are not stupid. Do not act this way. You heard what my husband said. There are those on this island who would never stand to see the charge of illegal slave-trading brought against me. They will unite against the outsider, and there are powerful people involved. We know how to take care of our own on this island. We can get any number to swear that they were merely selling off the natural increase of their own slave population. Why dwell on this? – you know, as well as Andrew knew – that it is useless. After all, he himself, many years ago, when Fergus was the subject of a great quarrel, was protected by the island courts against the might of a great and powerful English family.'

She rapped her nails against the arm of her chair as she considered the rest of the matter. 'And as to taking the money from Landfall, you yourself have sat night after night over the books trying to find some way I have been cheating, and you have not succeeded.'

'I could go on. I have not the time or the will to pursue it myself, but I could send men from London with all the time in the world. The least we could charge you with was gross mismanagement.'

'You will charge *me* with nothing! Legally a husband is responsible for the financial matters of a household. It is only twenty-four hours since my husband died, and that responsibility ceased.'

'*You* personally may not be held responsible, but the estate may be made to pay more. I will have a court order made to secure the books – '

'Then you will be lucky, my friend. Much vanished in the hurricane. The books no longer exist.'

Alister stiffened in his chair, looking about the room that I had ordered cleaned after they had set out for San Francisco. I was certain the books had not been here when I had come down, which could only mean that Maria had made her own disposition of them before she had left the house. She had remembered them, as she had remembered the jewels and every other thing that was important to her future. Were there no weaknesses in this woman?

She was completely triumphant, but the iron discipline still was maintained; she did not permit herself to swagger. She reminded me then of the man in Silkirk who sometimes came to play chess with my father. My father, emotional and excitable, had never been able to restrain his pleasure when he had a move building up to trap his opponent, and thus had always alerted him. My father had anticipated triumph, and usually given way to defeat. With Maria it was the opposite; she showed no joys or triumphs, no sorrows or griefs. There seemed no point at which she was vulnerable. Fergus would not try to find that point; he wanted away and out and to be done with it; he would cut his losses, even the loss of his own son, if Duncan were indeed his son. Alister might try to fight, but he faced a battle of almost impossible odds. If the books were gone, Maria would make certain that they were never seen again. Alister would have to go to a hostile court with no evidence in hand. I doubted that he would; he was not the kind to make a fool of himself, nor to waste time and money on a hopeless cause. He would know it would be hopeless; and he would also know to the last penny the sum agreed upon in the document which gave the Maxwells their continuing interest in Landfall. He would calculate the interest due. He would get what he could, or send someone else to get it. Then the Maxwells would be gone – except for Fergus and myself. Suddenly the brood of children that Maria had predicted became a promise. The Maxwells would flourish again; Duncan would have cousins – they would be called cousins. There would be meetings. The Maxwell influence would not give way entirely before that of long-ago Spain.

It seemed to be over. If Alister was going to fight, he was not wasting his energy now on argument. It was Katarina who spoke for us all. 'If we might prevail upon your hospitality, my sister, for just one more night . . . It is difficult to set out for Santa Marta at this hour.'

'Santa Marta? Why would you want to go to Santa Marta?'

'And where else have we to go? There are still a few old friends there who will give us shelter out of regard for our mother – until there is a roof over our heads at San Francisco. Until it seems safe to return there. Of course, they will wonder at us not staying on at Landfall, but then, my sister, you must accept conjecture and gossip as the price of our removal.'

Maria showed a rare impatience. 'Oh – stay then! Stay. Just keep out of my sight. I've more to think of than your worries.'

Fergus rose. 'Fiona, I shall come for you in the morning. You will be ready?'

'Yes, I'll be ready.'

Did the last flicker of hope die then in Maria? – there was no telling. She showed nothing. Alister sipped his wine. 'I also shall be returning to Santa Marta in the morning, Maria. I shall inform the authorities that slaves are loose in this area. I'm sure they will send what assistance they can.'

'It isn't needed. I have never been afraid of a few ignorant blacks.'

'Nor was Donna Isabella.'

A frightened whimper came from Joanna, but a gesture from Maria silenced her. 'No doubt,' she said, 'I shall have communication from you as regards the transfer of the rest of the property?'

'No doubt,' was all he answered.

I could not believe that it was all ending; the Landfall adventure was done and over with. Fergus came and kissed me briefly on the forehead. 'Tomorrow,' he said, and then he was gone. Katarina and Joanna made their exit, asking for trays to be sent to their room. They were clearly going to be troublesome guests. I wondered if Maria, Alister and myself would sit to a silent meal, the whole fabric of Landfall having been rent since last we sat to dinner by candlelight at that long polished table. This was the last time.

8

But it was not a silent meal to which we gathered that evening. There was a tumult all about Landfall that was nothing like the shriek of the storm, but in its way it seemed no less menacing – perhaps it was even more so, since we did not know or understand its meaning. From the slave quarters, where usually the silence of weariness brought an early quiet, the voices came loud; sudden laughter when there seemed no cause for it, and sudden bursts of song that were wild and careless – nothing like the songs of the cane fields. The cooking fires were not allowed to die, but were heaped high. I walked with Duncan around to the back of the upstairs gallery before I took him down to dinner, and we saw the dark figures silhouetted against the flames, and one or two actually leaped in the air as if in some ritual dance of joy or exaltation.

Duncan had come down to dinner because Juanita and Flora still were missing since the storm had died, and there was no one to stay with him and put him to bed. I myself had suggested it; it seemed a heartless thing to leave him alone so soon after he had seen the man he had called his father buried. Maria had simply shrugged her assent. Her attention was more on the missing slaves.

But it was Duncan who voiced all our misgivings at the table. 'Mama – why are the slaves so excited tonight? I've never heard them like this. And after a hurricane – with all their huts smashed and the gardens lost. Is it – is it because of my father?'

'Not your father, Duncan. But we will find out why. I think they may have found some of the rum in the San Francisco cellars. It is nothing – they will exhaust themselves soon and go to sleep. I will go myself and see later. It is nothing . . .'

The food itself was the strangest I had ever eaten at Landfall – scraps of the cooked meats that had served us through the storm tossed together in a dish that lacked the subtle flavour of the spices we were used to, watery and tasteless. It was served by Dougal alone, without the assistance of the two other slaves who usually helped him. There was nothing to accompany the dish except the stale bread baked before the storm, and some almost raw yams.

Maria thrust her plate away in disgust. 'Dougal – what does this mean? Why are we given this filth to eat?'

He only half-turned from his task at the sideboard, his head low. 'Cook not here, mistress. No girls to help. I try to make this myself, but I not cook.'

'And Pitt and Randolph?'

'The same, mistress. Gone. Not come in to help with the table. I cannot go look for them – I have not time. And the mistresses upstairs not been served yet. I call Charity to take a tray, but she not come. I think she gone off to find Samuel.'

Maria half-rose from her chair, and then dropped back. 'It has to be rum they have got hold of. Well, we shall see about that. Dougal, serve the cheese and some more wine, and take away this mess. And bring some fruit.'

He shook his head. 'All fruit eaten during the storm. Bananas not ripe – and what was coming in the garden all destroyed.'

'There are crocks of mango and papaya laid down. Why did you not bring them?'

'I look, mistress. All gone. Shelves in the cellar are bare . . .'

I saw Maria's face tighten, and an expression that might have been the beginning of apprehension came upon it. She controlled it, as always, but her reaction was not as it had been in more secure moments, a cry of anger. She asked no more questions of Dougal. 'Very well, then. You may go. And when you go to those thieving savages by the fires let it be known that the mistress is very angry and that she will punish the offenders. No slave is to stay within the house tonight. Before you go, take wine and bread and cheese to the señoritas. And leave the keys . . .'

He was gone before the pounding of the drums began – from somewhere far off, beyond Winterslo, it seemed to be. When they first started they were greeted with silence from the noisy fires in the slave quarters. Then, after some minutes, during which none of us spoke, either, the drums were suddenly answered by a wild shout – more of a howl than a shout that broke from the throats of those about the fires. But no drum came from Landfall to answer the one over the mountain.

'The drums!' Maria was frowning. 'It has been a long time since they were heard. It is forbidden – something they brought with them from Africa, but they have gradually lost the art. It was their way to talk to each other from one estate to another. But not many know how to read them. Juanita can . . .'

'It means something more than rum and deliverance from the hurricane,' Alister said. Suddenly all of us were looking at the blackness beyond the open louver doors and wishing, I think, as I was, that the storm shutters were still closed against the din and whatever it signified.

'We will lock up securely tonight,' Maria said. 'You and I will do it, Alister. In the morning they will hardly be able to stir. It will need a whip to get those dull heads awake tomorrow.'

'Listen! – do you hear it, Mama?' Duncan paused with bread and cheese half-crammed into his mouth.

'What? – hear what?'

'Bells – do you hear bells?' Faintly, between breaks in the drumming, even farther off, the sound of bells, the great estate bells that were heard morning and night to call the slaves. But never this wild, unrhythmical crash, as if several men swung together on the rope and would not let go.

Alister thrust back his chair and went on to the outer gallery. 'Something is wrong! They are never rung after sunset, Maria?'

Her face was pale, more strained than I had seen it at any time during the hours of inquisition she had endured during the storm. 'Never – except for an emergency! That is the bell of Harford Hall – I know its sound. And there, that thinner one, that is Drake's Bay.' She had gone to join Alister, her voice drifting back to Duncan and me. 'Why did they not ring directly after the storm? Why now? There is no more danger now?'

Alister jerked his head towards the back of the house, and the howls and shouts, the thud of bare feet slapping the hard-packed earth of the yards. 'There is a danger we don't understand yet.'

'Then we soon will.' Maria strode back into the room. 'I am going to find out what this nonsense is about. Duncan, fetch Mama the whip from the office.'

'Stay where you are, Duncan . . .' Alister rapped out the order. 'You also, Maria. Fiona – quickly run up and bring the pistol from the drawer in my bedside table. No, Maria – stay! I forbid you to move. Quickly, Fiona – and bring the shot.'

As I sped to the stairs I could hear the argument begin – Maria claiming a proprietor's right to decide what should be done. Alister calmly stating a man's responsibility to a household of women. As I rushed down from Alister's room, which was lighted only by the glare from the slaves' leaping fires, I was joined on the landing by Katarina and Joanna.

'What is it?' they demanded, clutching hands reaching to detain me.

I shrugged them off. 'Better come down and find out.' They huddled over the candle, heads together like black crows.

'We have not yet been offered anything to eat . . .' were the last wailing words I caught. I left them to their own concerns.

They were all still in the dining-room, but Alister was moving very quietly around, closing and bolting the louver doors. 'Can you handle a pistol, Maria?' he said, almost casually, as I returned.

'Yes – I once was taught. I think I still have some skill.'

'I guessed you might. Well, then – load it and release the safety catch. Now come with me and cover me while I close the doors. First snuff the candles so that I am not outlined for them . . . We will do the inner ones first. Leave only the hall one open, and be ready to run if I tell you. That means all of you – the señoritas also.' They had slowly crept down the stairs and joined us. 'Where are the bars stored that secure the storm shutters?'

'Inside – Andrew always kept them inside in case . . . The place under the stairs. I myself saw to them being stacked back there before we left for San Francisco. Andrew always felt – my God, it has not come to this, Alister?' It was the first time since the storm began that she had spoken to him as a woman to a man, a woman in need, suddenly, of help. The new posture sat oddly upon her. 'It cannot be that they will try something? Why now? Because Andrew is dead? Most of them have barely laid eyes on Andrew for these last two years – but it would not explain the drums and the bells from the other estates. What is it, Alister?'

'We will talk later,' he said tersely. 'Just come and follow me – try to keep me covered with the pistol. Where are the other guns we had here during the storm . . . ?'

They went off together, suddenly allies in this common threat that none of us understood. Katarina and Joanna were now in the dining-room, standing by the sideboard, lumping wedges of cheese on bread and eating it with a haste and lack of dignity they would normally have scorned; from Joanna's hand dangled a rosary. Between bites she murmured to her sister, 'God preserve us – has it come here too? Will we have the same fate as our mother?'

Katarina was more realistic. 'For us it will be worse, sister. We are not sodden with rum.'

'Better meet it on full bellies, then,' I said. I caught Duncan's hand as we followed, discreetly, Alister and Maria. But being a watcher fretted me, as it did Duncan. 'The bars!' I said. 'We could start to bring out the bars to secure the storm shutters.'

It was heavy work, between a woman and a small boy; we managed only a few. As the doors were closed the ringing of the bells was gradually blotted out, the sounds of the drums fainter. But the shouts from the slave quarters seemed to grow louder. Unconsciously, we all began to hurry, working almost in rhythm to the chant outside. We made our way around the whole house, two women at each side of a bar, lifting and holding, while Alister hammered it into place with a poker from the fireplace.

As we moved from one to the other, Duncan once pulled at my arm. 'Why are we doing this, Fiona? What has happened?'

'No one knows,' I said. And it was true.

It was as well the messenger came in those minutes before the last shutter was secured, otherwise the hysteria of Joanna might have made Alister decide against opening up. The man must have left his horse tethered a long way down the avenue and come on foot, for we heard no sound; he simply slipped around the hall door and stood there, panting, trembling, I thought.

'Mrs Maxwell – '

'Luiz!' She stood for a moment as if rooted; then she hurried forward. 'What is it? Have they sent you?'

'Mr Maxwell? – where is he?' The man was very tired; he swayed a little as he stood, dressed in a shirt and thin trousers unsuitable for riding. I thought I recognized him, but I could not remember from where.

'Mr Maxwell is dead.' Maria's tone was almost reassuring, as if to tell the man he had nothing to fear; but he looked about all of us gathered in the hall as if he wished we were not there. Particularly he looked at Alister, and there was no doubt of the recognition between them.

'My sympathy, señora. Señor Rodriguiz will be grieved . . .'

'What brings you?' Alister rapped out.

'I was sent from Santa Marta, to bring the news. The town has been badly hit, half the buildings in ruins – only a little water damage, though the tide came high into the streets. I helped carry the goods from the cellars – they say there are many drowned, swept away out to sea, but as yet no way of counting . . .'

'No one sent you all this way to tell us this. We might have guessed it for ourselves,' Alister said.

The man gestured with his hands, as if to wipe out the inconsequential nature of what he had been talking about. It was then, suddenly, that Duncan proved that he had recognized a need before any of his elders. While the man had stood there gasping out his words, Duncan had gone back to the sideboard and filled a large glass of wine. Now he offered it silently. The man took it in three gulps, closing his eyes and breathing in heavily. For a moment his hand fumblingly fell on Duncan's head. '*Muchas gracias, señor.*'

'Now – quickly,' Maria demanded. 'What is it?'

'You hear the bells – the drums?'

'Of course we hear them.'

'Except for the storm and the conditions in Santa Marta and on the roads you would have had this news sooner. But I came when it was possible.'

'What for – for God's sake – why?' Alister shouted.

'The final news, señor. The news we have waited for and refused to believe. A British vessel managed to beat her way past the Serpent Rocks and into Santa Marta harbour before the storm grew too fierce. But no one could come ashore until long after it was over and the swells had died a little. But the news was through the town in an hour, and the bells were tolling and the people were loading their guns.'

Alister heaved a great sigh, and briefly a weary half-smile came to his face; there was no exuberance, just a quiet thankfulness.

'Emancipation? Is that it? The British Parliament have finally passed the bill?'

The man took the last dregs of the wine. 'Emancipation – yes, señor. All slave children under six years of age are automatically freed. Those older, more gradually, according to age.'

'God!' That single word from Maria – disbelief, resignation in one. And then quickly, 'Compensation?'

'Twenty million pounds sterling voted by the British Parliament to slave owners in all the British colonies.'

There was silence. Maria moved across the hall and sat down, as if she needed quiet, and a place to think. We might not have been there. Her words were hardly for us, but for herself. 'Twenty million pounds – to be shared among all of us. It is nothing! It is nothing when it means the end of a way of life. We cannot work the cane fields and pay for the labour – sugar and rum do not bring that sort of money any more.' She continued, softly, as if musing. 'These islands . . . what is to become of them? Every plantation will end like San Francisco. Can you imagine us selling to get money to pay labour? . . . and who will there be to sell to? To *that* lot of savages out there? No white man in his right mind will buy land now. Twenty million parcelled out among so many . . . so little . . . so little. *They* will not work without the lash. They will work only to eat – a mango tree, a banana tree, a hen or two to scratch the ground. The bush will take back the cane fields. All our work here will disappear, and sugar mills rot and fall apart. Oh, I know them – they will lie under the trees all day and make sport of their former masters. And no slave will work with another for their common good. A long night is coming now on these islands. They will fall into a sleep, and the world will forget about them . . .'

Her tone quickened, and she turned on Alister. '*That* is what

your Wilberforce and his like have brought upon us. *All* now will
be poor, not just the slaves. That is what they think to pay off
with their wretched twenty million pounds. I will make you a prediction. Twenty years from now not one greathouse on this island
will still be tenanted, except by the remnants of a family who can
find no other place to go – as it was at San Francisco. Who simply
wait for the next hurricane to take the roof, and hope for, or expect, nothing else.'

She clenched and unclenched her hands on the arms of the
chair, her features suddenly bearing a strong resemblance to her
sisters', all at once a dark, brooding Spanish face, proud, vengeful,
pessimistic. And yet it seemed to me she spoke the truth. I, too,
was going to pay the price of the liberation of those whose lot I
had sighed over; I was going to pay with more than words. I wondered if Fergus and I would be among those who waited in a
plantation greathouse with no hope, and nothing to expect except
the inevitable coming of the next hurricane. Would we stand, he
and I, and our children, and watch the cane fields go back to
brush and spindly second-growth trees? But we would stay – I had
no doubt of it. I had come late to the islands, and now their
economic flowering was over. But I had found Fergus and my life,
and I would never have to go to sleep at night with the weight of
owning another human being upon my soul. In a sense it was a
relief. The worst they had expected had happened, and there would
be no more time spent uselessly fearing it. It was now my task to
make good to Fergus, to make him believe what the Scots, driven
from their lands, believed – that he who had land, any land, to
cultivate and make fruitful, no matter how poor, was still a king.
If poverty was our future, then I would make it a proud one for
him and our children. It was a task my father would not have
thought an unworthy one.

We were all silent for a time, thinking our separate thoughts.
In the last days we had lived through momentous events – almost
too much for my crowded and weary mind to recall. Death and
destruction had touched us harshly, and humans had pitted themselves, one against one, in ugly and mortal struggle. But this new
happening was far beyond all these smaller events. It was the end
of a way of life, the closing of an era that had lasted more than
three hundred years. The long twilight since the prohibition of
the slave trade from Africa had finally ended in the night.

'They knew before we did,' Alister said. 'That was the message
of the drums and the bells, but it had reached them here even
before that. They would not tell us . . .'

I had gone back to the dining-room and refilled the man's glass, and brought a plate of bread and cheese. He came to eat it at the hall table with murmured words of thanks, and bolted it as if he had not eaten in many hours. I remembered him then, prompted by the name of Rodriguiz. He was a clerk in the shop and, I believed, the man whom I had seen riding back from Landfall the day that the message had been wrongly delivered into my hands. I understood then some of the important and influential people with whom Maria had joined in her slaving activities. No wonder she, and Andrew himself, had known that no one would come forward to accuse her. I began to think that the Rodriguiz emporium was the convenient centre for all their activities. And believing there still were captive slaves at San Francisco, Rodriguiz had sent one of his badly needed help to this far end of the island to warn her.

'They think they are *all* free,' Maria said. 'That is why they all deserted and will obey no order . . .'

'God defend us,' Joanna wailed. 'What will we do? . . . what is to become of us?'

Luiz crammed the last of the bread into his mouth and spoke urgently to Maria. 'Señora – could I have a private word with you? From Señor Rodriguiz . . .'

'We don't have to be private any more, Luiz. *They* know,' she said, jerking her head towards Alister and myself. 'And in any case, there is nothing to be done – no precautions to be taken. My slave, Samuel – you remember, the big one – released them all before the storm. They are loose – and now think they are free! They have already murdered Donna Isabella.'

'Mother of God!' Luiz crossed himself. 'Two deaths, and now this! I bring bad news upon bad news.'

Maria waved aside his concern. 'Have you a gun?'

'A pistol.'

'Then you will stay here tonight. A second man will be a help.'

He shook his head. 'That I cannot do, señora. Señor Rodriguiz has sent me at considerable cost to himself. There is much talk of a slave revolt in the town, and he has to guard both the shop and the warehouses. We are very thinly spread. His instructions to me were to return immediately I had given you the news and urged . . .' His voice trailed off; he did not want to admit before Alister his knowledge of the slaves who were hidden at San Francisco. 'But would it not be wiser if all of you here came to Santa Marta? Those out there' – he jerked his head in the direction of the slave quarters – 'could prove more than one single man and a household of women could manage. That is what you should do, señora. We should all go back to Santa Marta together.'

'When I need advice, I will ask you for it,' Maria said coldly, putting him back in his place. 'Do you think for a moment that I would leave Landfall to the hands of those savages? Tell Señor Rodriguiz I am indebted – and that we have not faint hearts here at Landfall.'

Little whimpering sounds came from Joanna. 'Please, sister – would that not be the better plan? There would be more security in Santa Marta.'

'If you think so – go then! You will be one less we shall have to worry about. Go out to the stables now and saddle up, and try the ride through the darkness with Luiz – he will protect you, I'm sure, past all those plantations where the bonfires burn, and the bells ring, and they beat the drums.'

Joanna shrank back. 'I would not dare to go to the stables the way the slaves are now. Alister . . .'

'I would not risk Alister, my sister, to save your skin. He is the only man we have, and a good shot. So long as they know he is here they will keep their distance.'

Joanna lowered her head and said nothing more. Luiz took a final look around and then bowed to Maria. 'I go now, señora, and I wish you well. Señor Rodriguiz will send news again when it is possible.'

Before he slipped around the half-closed shutter, I plucked at his arm. 'You know Winterslo?'

He nodded, impatient to be off. 'I know it. Where Fergus Maxwell is.'

'Go there,' I said. 'Please! Just give him the news you have given us. He will make ready to defend himself if he has to.'

'Señorita, I cannot. There is no time.'

'Please – please! It is not out of your way. Just the distance of the avenue off the back road to Santa Marta. Please – not five minutes of your time. Just to warn him.'

'Much more than five minutes, since I will have to leave my horse and go up the avenue by foot if I am not to let every slave on the place know I have come. It is too much . . .' Then he shrugged. 'Well, since you ask it, señorita.' Then, unexpectedly, he added, 'I like Fergus Maxwell. He and I once had a good fight, and neither could down the other. We made it up by getting drunk together. Yes, it was a good fight. I'll go. Good-night.'

Luiz had been gone for more than an hour, and I had put Duncan to bed and seen him asleep before the pounding began on the shutters that guarded the main hall door.

'Pay no attention,' Maria commanded, 'and they will soon tire of it. They are drunk and crazy.'

But the pounding went on, and faintly, through the din from the slave quarters, I heard Fergus's voice.

'Quickly, open up,' I said to Alister. 'It's Fergus.'

But when he squeezed through the half-opened door he carried the blood-soaked body of Luiz in his arms. A scream, quickly stifled by her sister, came from Joanna. My hand, holding the candle, trembled violently, so that the shadows rocked across the shocking sigh of the two men, one covered with the blood of the other.

'He's still alive,' Fergus said. Alister had slammed the door and was bolting it into place. 'I found him on the road between here and Winterslo.'

Maria quickly explained his visit, and the news he had brought, as Fergus carried him through and laid him, without thought, on the red sofa that had been Andrew's. 'His horse was gone,' Fergus said. 'And there was no pistol. I suppose they thought him dead. He was thrown among the cane, but he moaned, and I heard him . . .' A lantern, held close to him, revealed a machete wound cut deep into his shoulder. A few inches higher and his neck would have taken the blow. He bled terribly.

Maria sped to her store room and was back with a box of medicaments and bandages, strips of linen torn and rolled ready for such emergencies. I brought what was left of the hot water from the pantry – with the shutters closed, the kitchen and its fires were once more barred to us. 'I heard about it,' Fergus answered. 'My slaves tell me more than yours do, Maria. I didn't know whether to believe it or not, but when I heard the drums and the bells . . . well, I thought you might need help. My lot are chanting around the fire, but I had a feeling that the ones Samuel let loose from San Francisco would follow him here.' As he talked he bathed the wound, and started to bind it up. 'If he lies quiet it may stop bleeding. If the bleeding continues he will die before the night's out.'

It was said with a certain matter-of-factness. We were all growing calloused by the events of these last days, and the weariness was almost more than one could bear. And yet we faced another night of sitting and waiting, of listening. Another night to be afraid to sleep. Another man was dying – might die, on that red sofa.

Fergus straightened and stretched his limbs, cramped from carry-

ing the weight of Luiz. 'I slipped the saddle off my horse out there
and sent him home. I hope he runs down any of those black devils
who come near him.' And then, 'Alister, I'll borrow a shirt from
you.'

Alister gave a weary smile of acknowledgement. 'You forget – I'm
already wearing *your* shirt. I took one or two of Andrew's into my
room – they'll fit you like a nightshirt, but at least they're clean.'
While he spoke his eyes kept moving from one end of the room
to the other. He crossed now into the dining-room to check there.

'Fiona will show you where,' he called back.

I waited there in the room with Fergus while he stripped off
the blood-soaked rag and used the water in Alister's jug to wash. In
the flickering glow of the candlelight I watched with fascination
the ripple of the muscles in that broad, lean back; and yet I saw
that his movements were slow, and strangely clumsy. I thought we
all must be slower and less nimble than two days ago, fighting the
desire to close eyelids on stinging eyes, the desire just to lie and be
still. But outside they were not still; they leaped high before the
flames and shouted their songs of victory, songs almost forgotten,
so seldom had they been heard in the lifetime of any of these
who now seemed to learn them anew as they chanted them over
and over.

Fergus came to me, and his embrace had the feeling of desperation in it, as if he must try to shut out the sounds that would
destroy our pleasure in each other. For the first time, in the strength
of his arms, I sensed the anxiety that his words would not express;
in the way he clutched at me, trying to absorb my own body in a
single embrace, I knew that he wondered if we would live to finish
what we had begun. He put his head down on my shoulder, in the
final gesture of a weary man.

'Fiona, love – I need you. My God, how I need you! Will
it ever be over, do you think? Fiona, you're wiser than I – and
better. Will we ever be alone together again, and quiet, and at
peace? Will we ever be able to love each other again?'

'Soon, my love – very soon.' But I was not sure. I was frightened,
and it sounded like the promise I had made to Duncan that I
would be there to take care of him.

We went downstairs, and Fergus set about loading the guns
that had been put away after the storm. Then he took his own
pistol and rifle and made his station in the dining-room; Alister
took his place in the hall. Maria sat with her sister, pistol in hand,
near the red sofa with Luiz. To keep himself from falling asleep,
Fergus taught me how to load the rifle and the pistol, making

me practise the movements again and again. 'Don't wait for me
to tell you,' he said. 'You have to do it immediately I pass each
one to you.' This was another art I had not thought of learning
for the years to come, but I supposed it would be part of it, like
the baking and the sewing, and the rearing of children. Along
with things like teaching Charity's son to read. I thought it ironic
that we might perish on this, the night of freedom, the night when
we were no longer the masters of those outside – like the soldier
killed at the instant of cease-fire.

9

It came by the means we had most feared, the one from which
we had no protection. Towards dawn, when the need for sleep
was almost insupportable, the slaves seemed to grow quieter. 'The
rum has done its work,' Maria said. 'They will sleep soon, and the
fight will be gone from them.'
  'I hope you are right,' Alister said. But he didn't sound hopeful.
'How goes it with Luiz?'
  'He is unconscious still. But there does not seem to be fever.
And the bleeding has stopped. When it is light – ' She stopped
and spun around. I had come to the doorway of the dining-room
to listen to their talk, and now I motioned Fergus to come too.
  We all heard it now, a faint sound against the big outer storm
shutters of the doors directly behind the staircase. We pressed
against the louvers of the inner gallery, trying to interpret the
sounds, the width of the gallery and the thickness of two doors
separating us from whoever or whatever made the sound. From here
it sounded feeble, like nails scratching against the wood in the
vain hope of entry.
  'Don't be fools! Get back and watch the other places,' Fergus
called from the hall. 'It could be a trick . . .'
  We stepped back, but the sounds went on, slow, gentle. We
could hear no voices. 'It is nothing,' Maria decided. 'Just one of
the women wanting in. She is tired – drunk, probably. Perhaps she
has been raped by one of the strange slaves. They always come
back to their masters when there is trouble, when things get beyond them . . .'
  But she was wrong, and we knew it when the first faint tendrils
of smoke curled under the door that we watched and forced their
way through cracks where the louvers did not close tightly. But by

this time the smoke must have filled the whole of the inner gallery, because it was coming under all the doors around the whole inside core of the house. Now the sound became real and identifiable, the ominous crackling of burning wood. Those outside must have built the heart of the fire from the remains of slave huts and piled brush on it. The old, well-seasoned wood of the storm shutters, dry now that the rain had not touched them for more than a day, was ripe for burning; patience, and the supply from their own bonfires, had kept the brush alight until the shutters themselves caught. From then on, their victory was certain.

'Try not to panic,' Fergus said quietly. 'They may not mean to kill us. They are probably after more rum – or food. They know they are not owned by us any longer. Perhaps they think they will take everything that is ours. Tomorrow . . . ' he added wryly, 'Santa Marta will be full of rum-filled blacks trying to sell silverplate.'

'We are dead,' Joanna sobbed.

'We are if we stay here,' Alister said. 'We'll have to break out. Leave them the house, if that's what they want.'

'No – no, I won't. I won't have them . . .'

'You have no choice, Maria. Don't be foolish. There's no way to fight a fire once it takes hold here – no pumps, no equipment or men to do it. You don't think *they* will help put it out!'

I heard the last as I sped up the stairs to Duncan's room. He wakened slowly, but so used he was by now to the extraordinary events of these days that he didn't question my snatching him from the bed. I thrust him into a chair and began lacing on his boots, remembering, even in my panic, that we probably would have to run through brush and, barefooted, he would be a handicap. He was querulous as he came out of sleep. 'I don't want to go – I *won't* go in my nightshirt.' His outraged masculinity was another prod to my imagination; I thought of him hampered, as we women were, by skirts, and I caught up breeches and a shirt as I dragged him from the room. I half-lifted him down the stairs, fearing the nightshirt would trip him. 'Now do whatever you're told, Duncan. I'll take care of you.'

Alister had hammered the iron bar off the main door, the one directly opposite the staircase. Maria stood by him with a pistol ready, and a gun on the floor beside her. Katarina and Joanna crowded about them. As Duncan and I descended into the acrid pall of the smoke he began to choke.

'Are you ready, Fergus?' Alister shouted.

In answer, Fergus appeared from the salon with Luiz in his arms, his pistol thrust in his belt. Luiz's head hung limply. They joined the group by the door. Alister glanced over us all, his arm poised to pull back the shutter. 'Stay together,' he said. 'It's the best chance we have. Remember the fallen tree is only feet from the bottom of the steps, and don't blunder into it. We can't go too far until it gets lighter. We'll never get to Winterslo in the darkness, and you can't waste shot firing at shadows. Remember' – this was mainly addressed to Joanna to calm her – 'they may not hinder us at all. They may only want what's in the house.'

Maria leaned towards her sister, brandishing the butt of the pistol. 'And if you scream, I'll break your jaw with this.'

We extinguished the last candle, and Alister eased open the door. We moved out, going cautiously, slowly, because of Fergus carrying Luiz. We felt the scrape of the branches of the cottonwood at the bottom of the steps, but there was no sound, no flash of a machete to challenge us. We eased our way gently through the tangle of brush left after the storm, going deeper and deeper into the shadow; the way was painful and slow. Luiz came briefly to consciousness and moaned. But the sound didn't matter, because the crackle of the flames was beginning to drown all else.

When we were a distance from the house, Fergus had to lay down his burden to rest; we turned back to look.

It was a fearful sight. We had heard the terrible crash of the storm shutter going down, and had known that with it the slaves would be swarming within the house. But none of us, least of all they, had anticipated the spread of the fire. Firing the storm shutter had ignited the floor beams of the upper gallery and the flames were already running through, on those dry, seasoned timbers, to the bedrooms and the staircase hall. They ran like liquid along to the beams. As we stared, every window and doorframe at the back of the house caught; the night sky was brilliant with the glow, the whole dark frame of the house silhouetted before us. Frustrated by the heat and flames at the back, the slaves had run to the front, the more daring among them dashing through the one open door we had left and on into the dining-room and salon to snatch what they could – silver, glass, pictures they fancied were framed in gold. But they were quickly driven back by the heat and smoke, and the loot was small. What none of us had reckoned on was the draught created by that single open door at the front of the house acting like a chimney, and pulling the flames forward inexorably to engulf the whole structure.

'It's gone,' Fergus said. 'There's no saving anything. We'd best try to move on farther while they're still enjoying their show.' He bent again to pick up Luiz.

FIONA

Alister's voice came from the darkness. 'Right, then – let's go.'

'I can't!' A wail from Duncan. I looked down at him. 'I'm getting into my breeches.' In those seconds, while Duncan and I struggled with unseen buttons, and tried to tuck in the nightshirt, Alister had time to check the pale light reflected from the faces about him.

'Maria – where's Maria?'

'Ma – Maria . . .?' Joanna stuttered. 'I don't know. I thought she was going ahead with you. When we came to the bottom of the steps and past the tree she suddenly put this thing in my hand. I don't know how to use it.' She waved the rifle Maria had carried wildly, and Alister slapped down her arm smartly and pushed on the safety catch. 'After all – she *told* me to be quiet.'

'God in heaven – where is she?'

Katarina's voice might have been Maria's, so deadly cool it was. 'Did anyone see her bring the jewels with her?'

There was no answer from any of us. Katarina continued. 'Then you can assume that she went back for them. It was unlike her to forget about them even when the fire first began. But they never would leave her mind completely – never. Like the slaves, she thought she could race the fire.'

A race it was; the fire now had turned the corners of both the upper and lower galleries; through the cracks in the shutters we could see the lower rooms illuminated, as if by some magic candle. 'She couldn't have gone back! She *couldn't* have been so mad!'

'She could – she *is*!'

We could all see her now, the slight figure on the front upper gallery, long skirt fanned by the draught of the flames. From one hand dangled a small bundle – the white cloth that had wrapped the jewels, tied and knotted to hold them. With the other hand she gripped one of the great brick pillars. She did not look outward, towards us, and a possible salvation, but down, at the slaves who swarmed and ran below her in a frenzy of excitement and hostility. Once she looked backward, and we knew the danger was equal – try the burning staircase or jump. In either case, in the end she would face the knives and machetes below.

It was Duncan who broke the spell of inaction upon us. 'Mama!' The hold she possessed on him was strong; his short lifetime had belonged only to her. He feared her danger; he feared her loss. He had lost Andrew, and he could not bear the thought of his entire world being taken in one stroke. He broke from my hands in a sudden start of terror, racing, mad, hysterical, back towards the burning house and the mob before it. 'Mama!'

It was as if, in all the roar of the flames about her, she heard the cry, because she turned towards us. At that instant, the dark figure appeared on the gallery behind her, naked, shiny with sweat, one of the slaves newly shipped from Africa, crazed with rum, hunger and the desire for revenge on these white tormentors.

As Duncan had started to run, Fergus dropped Luiz once more and plunged through the tangle of brush after him. Without thinking, without pause, I followed him.

I stumbled many times on that run, crashing into fallen trees and debris because my eyes were dragged ever upward to the scene on the gallery. Maria had backed away from the terrible figure, her hands and bundle held behind her as if to shield it. Before he reached her, though, she retreated to the doorway of the smoke-filled room from which she had come and tossed the bundle inside. Then she braced herself against the doorway in some mad attempt to stop his entrance. But he had no interest in whatever the small insignificant bundle contained. Now beside her, he towered over her – a black giant. First he pulled her back to the railing so that no one should miss the sight. Then, in a single wrenching movement, he took the neck of her gown and ripped it between his hands – bodice, petticoat, stays – almost the whole length of the gown gave before the strength of those maniac hands. Then, with her arms held tightly behind her back, he turned and exposed her to the eyes of the crowd below. Howls of derision and triumph greeted the sight of her gleaming white nakedness.

Then I dragged my eyes down. I had reached the edge of the crowd that milled before the house. The Landfall slaves were there, as well as the naked black captives of San Francisco. I could hear Fergus's voice – he had thrust his way through. Duncan seemed to have vanished into the maelstrom of jostling, swirling, jumping bodies. And then I saw him coming towards me, held high over the heads of the crowd, borne, not in Fergus's arms, but Samuel's. The Landfall slaves were nearest me, and they did not menace – they parted as if to give Samuel passage with his young, screaming, kicking burden. He was almost through the central mob of the African slaves when the blow – a knife, a machete, I never saw which – hit him. But he kept on coming, propelled by a great momentum, towards me. At the edge of the crowd, where the Landfall slaves hung back, he set Duncan, with infinite gentleness, on his feet. Then Samuel crumpled slowly to the ground. Duncan, seeing me, ran to me, his nightshirt trailing from his breeches. I received him then into my arms, as I had known I would. I squatted down and held his face against my breast, the halo of sweat-damp curls outlined like a young angel's against the fierce glow of the fire. With his head pressed there hard against my breast, my other arm holding him with cruel tightness so that he could not turn, I looked up and saw the part of the vision that had been denied me. As always, the sight had been incomplete.

Fergus was gone, past and through the slaves.

'Oh, God – please! No – no. Fergus . . .!' I heard my own cry, but I could not stop looking. Fergus had vanished into the house, and the fire now had reached the front of the building, the beams beneath the feet of Maria and the slave were ignited, and every door and window frame behind them. The giant black figure now lifted her in his arms and tossed her like a baby, up and down, a plaything. Nothing was visible of his features but the broad white line of his teeth as he laughed. I could not hear Maria scream, the roar of the flames was now too loud. But I saw her mouth working, the contorted agony of her face, a woman in mortal fear. In another moment, I knew, the slave would throw her down among the crowd below.

But in another moment the black shining form had toppled, and Maria fell from his arms. Through the smoke I could only dimly see Fergus; he had taken the risk of hitting Maria as well as the slave with the single shot he could fire. The risk had been small; she would have been just as dead down there among the machetes.

I saw him scoop her up and run back through the blazing door-frame of her bedroom. That was the last sight I ever had of him, cradling Maria's limp form in his arms. A moment later came the terrible sound that tore into my being like a knife as the staircase came crashing down.

The first flames started up through the roof.

I knelt there, Duncan still clutched to me, and I saw it as it would be when there was no more of Landfall the fire could consume. I saw it as it would be in the future; as it had been in the past – blackened walls and chimneys, skeletal to the hard blue sky, to the morning radiance, to the evening glow. I saw it as it must have been when Andrew Maxwell had first looked upon it and coveted it.

The slaves knew our presence there, but none came near us. Perhaps fear of Alister's gun kept them away; perhaps the Landfall slaves now knew the enormity of what had happened and contained the Africans. But I thought that the fire and deaths they had witnessed had been the catharsis they had sought. The first light of dawn brought the sobering memory of the white man's justice that still ruled the island, even though the black man was free.

Alister came and touched my shoulder. 'Come, Fiona.'

He shouldered Fergus's burden of Luiz, and we began the trek to Winterslo. No one spoke on that long march in the growing light, no one, except Katarina. 'He was a fool to have entered the house. No man could have saved her.'

I did not dispute it; it was perhaps something Fergus had had to do, compelled, as I had been, by an extraordinary force beyond reason. I would not try to reason it; but I could not yet accept its fact. I was dumb, not able to speak, even if there had been anything to say. I clung to Duncan, and he to me; neither was there a sound from him. We sought comfort in the touch of each other's bodies, like animals. That was all we could do.

2

By sunset two more graves had been opened at the grove of mampoos at Winterslo; Alister had brought back from Landfall two more rough boxes with the bones of Fergus and Maria. Several heavy showers during the day had cooled the still smoking ruins. He had taken the Winterslo slaves with him for the task, but those at Landfall, subdued now, hungry, bewildered by the sudden lack of authority to impose a regime and provide food, had come willingly to help with the search. The bodies – what remained of them – were in the cellars, among the charred remnants of the heaviest beams, all that had survived the fire.

For decency's sake, and to spare my suffering, I thought, Alister had provided two boxes. But for all I knew the bones of both, indistinguishable, lay in one coffin, locked in that eternal last embrace.

The light was almost gone as Alister once more recited the burial service, this time from memory – those parts of it he could remember, since a search of Winterslo had turned up no Bible or Book of Common Prayer. The lanterns were lighted before we finished. 'Dust to dust, ashes . . .' The numbness still possessed me; I seemed to feel nothing. I could not weep. The only sensation I seemed to experience was a deep resentment that it was Maria who lay there now with Fergus. I had thought to lay my own bones there and to possess him forever. But he was lost to me. Somehow, in the end, she had won.

We did not try to sing a hymn, nor do anything but what was barely necessary; I think all our hearts were as dry as the bones laid there. But the slaves took up a dirge of their own as we walked back up the slope to the house. Alister, I knew, would see to it that the graves were marked in granite – he would put on the names but no one but he would know what lay in each box. Very soon the vines that twisted from tree to tree would cover that raw earth. Perhaps I was the only living creature who would hold Fergus in my heart forever. This place would live so long as I remembered it. Even for Duncan, his hand clamped wetly in mine now, the memory would grow dim. Only I would live in it as if my life had stuck fast at this spot.

A meal was made; we sat down at the table. I suppose we ate, but I remember none of it. Fergus's two house slaves hurried about, making up beds with patched mildewed sheets. Alister distributed some of Fergus's stores to the Landfall slaves so that they might eat. There was a sense of unreality about our movements. We did what we had to do now, but no one seemed to have any idea of how life would carry on tomorrow or the day after. No one knew how the devastated cane fields would be restored or replanted; no one knew of a way to pay the former slaves for work they had done in exchange for food. No one knew, since there was no harvest, how there would be any money to pay. The Landfall slaves seemed reluctant to go back to the plantation now that no white man was there to tell them what to do; a slow realization seemed to be breaking upon them that the freedom suddenly conferred might be the freedom to starve. I thought that in time they would come out of their trance, and some would begin to plant their gardens again and re-thatch their huts. Others would wait for a while, waiting to share what they thought was the white man's wealth; and when it did not come, they would drift towards Santa Marta and make a living from the streets of the town in any way they could. They would become the crowd on the street corner of any town I had ever known.

It was during the meal that the future of Katarina and Joanna was decided.

Alister suddenly said, speaking only to Katarina, recognizing that it was she who would make the decisions for both, 'Have you plans – for the future?'

She shrugged, the gesture one of anger at the futility of the question. 'What plans could we have? We have no money. We will have to return to San Francisco and do what we can to keep body and soul together. I suppose we are no less stupid than the slaves — we can make a few things grow. But we will have to become tillers of our own soil.' She laughed harshly. 'The Medinas have come a long way since Queen Isabella's land grant of half the island of San Cristóbal.'

'Oh, sister, do not — ' Joanna wailed.

'I will buy San Francisco,' Alister said flatly.

There was a long silence. 'Why?' Katarina asked finally, deep suspicion in her tone. 'Why would you do that?'

Alister shrugged. 'Perhaps I feel a responsibility to Maria's sisters — to Duncan's aunts.'

'You carry family feeling far, my friend.'

He glanced over at me. 'The Scots always do.'

'If so,' Katarina said crisply, 'it is one of the few things about the Scots the Spanish would understand. But this is not the answer for us. You will give us a certain sum, and within a certain number of years we will have exhausted it, What are we to do then? Beg on the streets of Santa Marta? Poverty coupled with pride demands obscurity, señor.'

'You haven't heard my offer,' he answered drily. 'Perhaps pride is another thing the Scots and the Spanish have in common. I would make you an outright bid — generous in the circumstances. Part of it, I suggest, would go to the purchase of a small house in Santa Marta — they will be going cheaply now, I would wager, since there will be an exodus of merchants from the British islands. The remainder I would invest for you in London. As part of the purchase agreement you and your sister would receive an annual income from that investment — enough, I estimate, to allow you modest comfort — a servant or two. *They* also would be cheap once the former slaves learn that it takes money to buy bread.'

'Ah . . .' Joanna gave a long sigh. 'To live in Santa Marta! To hear Mass every day, sister — to entertain old friends occasionally, to pay visits. Could it be . . .?' She looked longingly at Katarina.

'You will have the initial payment and the agreement for an annual income before you part with the deeds of San Francisco. I will not repeat the offer. It is accepted now or it is rejected.'

Katarina's harsh laugh again. 'What choice is there? As little as before. One has to trust you, and hope the trust lies more worthily than with Maria. It is accepted.'

'Ah . . .' Again a long sigh from Joanna, as if a promise of a kind of earthly bliss had been held before her. Fergus's house possessed no such refinements as table napkins; she brushed tears from beneath her eyes with her fingers.

'And then,' Katarina said, 'there are the jewels. You must begin at once to recover the jewels. They are rightfully ours.'

Alister sighed. 'For that, you must have patience. They lie somewhere in the ashes of Landfall, and it will be a long time before labour can be spared to make a search. If any of the slaves know of them, you may be sure many will not be recovered at once. But they cannot eat diamonds. For a while they will bury them, and then they will take them to Santa Marta to try to sell them. Piece by piece, they may come to light, but only if the buyer is honest. I will leave instructions. I will tell the authorities. Every possible source will be informed. But always remember that Duncan is the only child of Andrew and Maria Maxwell, and their sole heir. You may make your claims before the courts, and no doubt justice will be done. But justice will also demand that the reason for your claim to share in any jewels recovered will also require that the source be revealed. You have abetted illegal slave-trading . . .'

Katarina put down her knife and rose from the table. 'You are clever, señor. Yes, we will make our claims. That is the least we will do. Come, Joanna . . .'

Her sister followed limply, in mute protest against leaving the first real food she had eaten in more than a day. She trailed up the stairs after Katarina, murmuring complaints about the roof having leaked severely during the hurricane, and no doubt their beds were still damp.

Neither had inquired as to Duncan's future.

Charity helped me wash and put Duncan to bed; she had simply stayed on in the house at Winterslo as a matter of course. I had had the cot he would sleep on put in my own room, and now he wore one of Fergus's shirts as a nightshirt, the sleeves rolled many times. He was silent and very tired, his face pale. He asked no questions of me, as if he dreaded answers. It almost seemed that, like myself, he wanted no part of tomorrow. As she helped with the preparations for bed, Charity's eyes pleaded mutely with me to tell her what was going to happen, what was to become of us all, but I had no answer, no more than anyone did.

I sat with Duncan, holding his hand, until he slept, and then Charity whispered to me that she would stay until I came back upstairs, lest he woke again and was frightened. 'Father and mother both he has lost — and yet he does not weep. It is not right.'

'The weeping will come,' I said. 'It is too much. Children are wiser than we know, and will not believe more than they can bear.' It was so with me. My mind still struggled against acceptance of what my heart would not bear.

'Go down, mistress, and walk, and take some air. And perhaps tears will come for you. I know. I bury a man also this day.'

I went down slowly, wondering if I could walk myself to tiredness beyond this numbness I already felt, and perhaps, finally, to sleep. But the face of Duncan haunted me. It was one thing to grieve for that which was dead, and would never be mine, but now I must take up the burden of a living promise. I had told Duncan I would take care of him. Somehow the promise had to be kept. I had very little idea of how it was to be done. But an image of Silkirk was beginning to reappear, the memory of my father's kindness, his solicitude for children. Poor man, I would load him heavily, and he would take it up with a certain joy. Perhaps there would be two Duncans growing up at Silkirk. My father would take both to his heart, and somehow, in whatever way, I must earn enough to make this possible.

A single lamp now burned in the main room. The table was cleared, but the chairs were left just as we had pushed them back, and the crumbs remained; during the night cockroaches would scurry over them. I knew all these things now about the tropics. And yet beyond the doors that led to the gallery the night was beautiful, soft and sweet-scented, a few faint wisps of white cloud moved slowly before the brilliance of the stars. The cicadas sang; the whole earth seemed to hum of its fertility. No breeze stirred, but there was a coolness against hot eyelids and burning eyes. I went to the edge of the gallery and sat on the steps, and my gaze was drawn instinctively towards the clump of mampoos outlined darkly against the star-bright sky.

Alister's step was soft as he came to sit beside me. From the back of the house I could hear the voices of the blacks – one could call them slaves no longer. Sometimes a voice was raised in song, as was their habit, but now they had reverted to the songs of the cane fields. There were no more shouts of triumph. They feared now, like all of us, with a different kind of fear, for their future. Freedom was not gold, only the licence to earn it.

I said to Alister, 'You have been generous to the sisters. It was madness, that offer you made for San Francisco. Anyone can tell it is not worth a life income for those two. No one in his senses will want land here any more.'

'Perhaps I am not in my senses, and perhaps my partners will tell me so plainly. In that case, I shall pay out of my own pocket. But I want those two wretched women off my mind. I don't want to wake up and wonder if they are starving. Remember . . . I saw their mother. Let them have their court tussle over the jewels, as they turn up – if they do. It will keep them occupied. It will keep them fighting and hating. Fighting keeps people alive. But I also intend to see Duncan's interests protected.'

'But the land? San Francisco – Landfall – Winterslo. What is to become of it?'

'Most of it belongs to Duncan, and I will advise him never to sell. Land will go a-begging here, in a very short time. We will work a crop, if it is economically possible, but that I doubt, without slave labour. But as he grows older, I will advise him never to sell – never! Even if land here is worthless and someone offers him the price of a good horse, he must never sell.'

'Why not?'

He half-turned to me. 'Do I have to tell you, a Scot, what land is? It is the only commodity that never devalues over the long term, never wears out, never ages. It may seem worthless, but it is not. It is there, and it stays. The landlords knew it as they spread out and bought from simple farmers the fields that surrounded London and Manchester and Bristol. The great English nobles knew it when they fought one another to death for it, and some went and dispossessed the Irish for the sake of their bogs . . .'

'But here you said without slave labour the land is virtually worthless. Perhaps the price of a good horse.'

'Someday, Fiona – it could be a hundred, two hundred years from now – they will find a crop that needs the sun that I have grown to hate. I haven't a notion what it will be, but these islands will wait. Something will be found that needs this sun – and perhaps machines instead of men. Whatever it is, the land will pay heavily again. So let it sit and wait. There will be more fortunes for the Maxwells from these lands. For Duncan's heirs.'

I looked once more towards the mampoo grove, and my heart and eyes and lips were dry.

'And Duncan himself . . .?'

'He will stay with us, of course.'

'Us?'

'With us. With you and me, Fiona. He will come back to England with us. You are going to marry me.' It was a statement, not a question.

I jerked upright, and pulled back from him. 'You are mad! You are trying to set the whole world in order, and it can't be done. Oh, you are very kind – too kind, but you only hurt us both. I loved Fergus – I loved him with every shred of my being, a love that sometimes seemed unreasonable, but it was there. I still love him. You *know* it. You must not talk this nonsense of marrying me. It mocks me, and what I feel for another man.'

'I never meant to mock you – or your love for Fergus. I *know* you love him still, and always will. The lover taken at the moment of love goes on living forever. I know you will never cease to love and remember him. But still, you and I will be married.'

'But why? *Why?* Knowing this, why, in God's name!'

'If I ask you, isn't that enough?'

'No!' I cried. 'No – it isn't enough! You pity me. You feel responsible for me, the way you do for those two greedy, pitiful wretches upstairs. You solved the problem of what to do about them. Is this your way of taking care of *me*? Spare me that! Spare yourself! Pity can go too far. Beware of its tyranny, Alister.'

'Not pity, Fiona – envy.'

'You *are* mad! No one can have envied me in all my life. What do I have? – what can I give?'

'I envied what another man had won. But I can't tell you that now. You have too lately listened to his words of love. You buried him today. What can I say in the face of that? I would wound and hurt you beyond forgiving. I only ask for time – but time in marriage.'

'It can never be,' I said, as harshly as Maria ever could. 'I thank you – and you do me great honour. But I have to tell you that Fergus and I were lovers – once. Just once. There never was a second time. Never a second chance. But I also have to tell you that we would have continued to be lovers until the marriage was performed, and forever after that. Now, can you say you still want me? You would shame yourself.'

'I knew that – of course I knew it.'

'You *knew* it?'

'Oh, Fiona . . . Fiona! Do you think me quite blind? Do you forget I saw you that morning as you came back from the cove with Fergus? Until that moment I never saw a woman clothed in glory. You wore love with a radiance I had never imagined could exist. It was then I envied Fergus with all my soul.'

'Envied . . . ?'

'It's very simple, isn't it? And not at all extraordinary. I *wanted* you. Until that moment I didn't know the fullness of what I couldn't have, of what I'd let go unnoticed in my own heart. I don't know that I could have won you from Fergus before that, but I didn't even try, did I? Then it was too late. Fergus possessed you, body and soul, and I was closed out. Why do you think I left Landfall that same day? – why I wrote you that pompous note that

said nothing? There was no particular urgency about my return to
England. I just couldn't stay within the sight of you and Fergus.'

'But you – Alister – there must have been many women who
would gladly have married *you*. Women with names and fortunes
– with beauty. You haven't waited all this time for someone like
me.'

'Not someone like you – for you. Fergus waited, didn't he?
Fergus gave up what Maria blatantly offered – for you. And as for
what I have to offer . . . I offer nothing but the kind of life I once
told you I am going to try for. It won't be an easy life, though
you'll have physical comforts. You will have to make friends with
people you would rather not be friends with, so that others can be
helped. People with influence in the right places. You will have to
curb pride and temper and independence. I will demand loyalty
to my causes – absolute and uncompromising loyalty, no matter
if you think they are sheer madness and hopeless. I don't have to
ask for fidelity. I *know* you. You were born with courage and
fidelity in your soul. If I am patient, if I wait, perhaps once again
I will see that radiance. If not . . .' He shrugged. 'If not, I still will
have the woman I have wanted most.'

'It cannot be,' I said slowly. 'Even on these conditions, as incredibly generous as they are, it cannot be. You would be cheated.'
I looked at him fully. In the brightness of the night I could see
his features very clearly, strained, weary, hollow-cheeked. I wondered if the events of these days, the lack of sleep, had not un-
hinged him a little so that he talked the kind of madness I had
accused him of. Was he also sucked dry, as I was, and could only
cling to that which was familiar, not daring to envisage the future?
But no, he had the future very clear, as he always had. He had
already pointed the way – hard work, effort, endless speaking,
travelling, talking, persuading. He knew what he was about. His
direction and purpose had not changed in the slightest degree. He
knew what I was about too. He had seen Fergus and me together,
and he knew, as fully as any man could have done.

'It cannot be,' I said again. 'Do you realize – have you thought,
Alister – that it is possible – it is just barely possible that already I
am carrying Fergus's child?'

'I have thought of it,' he replied. 'I have thought of it all – everything that it implies. If I waited to find out if that possibility were
a fact, any offer I made then would be false, bogus. Good God,
woman! – what you did, you did in good faith! Will I condenm you
for that? It isn't untouched, untroubled virtue I want! It is *you*!
You *are* virtue, whether you have loved out of wedlock or not.

Don't you understand that?'

'You would be willing . . . ?' I said, incredulous.

'Of course I am willing. We will be married tomorrow in Santa Marta. It can be arranged. And you will suffer and indulge me for a while until your grief slackens its bonds a little. You will grow used to accepting me, because you have the courage to do it. So that if there is a child, by the time he is born in England, neither of us will know if he is my child or Fergus's.'

'That is – that was how it was with Duncan,' I said. 'No one truly knew whose child he was. And it poisoned three lives. They lived in hell, those three.'

'It is not the same. I don't try to steal you from another man. I can never take you from Fergus. You do not come to me from greed, but because I need and want you. Leave it to me, Fiona. Trust me. Leave it to me, and let peace come into your soul. Grieve for him, and never try to hide it from me. We need never suffer dishonesty between each other. We are gone long past that. I can offer you protection, love, honour . . . a place for your children in my heart, and for Duncan, whom you love. I've gambled many times in my life. This will not be the last gamble, but it is the greatest. If I bring it off, it will be the greatest prize.'

'I am no prize. I never have been.' But I leaned against him, and he pulled my head towards his shoulder, his hand stroking my hair. The grove of mampoos was very still in the night air, against the radiant sky.

'Weep, my love,' he said. 'Weep.'

I did, and it was the beginning of healing.

A FALCON FOR A QUEEN

C.G.O.–X

THE CLANS · THE MOTTOS

MACDONALD OF CLANRANALD
My hope is constant in thee

CAMPBELL OF CAWDOR
Be mindful

SINCLAIR
Commit thy work to God

MACPHERSON
Touch not the cat bot a glove

(MAC)LACHLAN
Brave and Trusty

FERGUSON
Sweeter after difficulties

Prologue

There are places in the valley where I will never go again; there are paths up its glens where I will never direct my pony's steps. The faces, the voices, the names meet me there, and they do not go away. Regularly, of course, I must cross the path through the graveyard to the kirk, where those names are chiselled into the stone. But the spirits do not lie there; for me, they do not lie there. They are the restless ghosts – those who loved – wrongly, wilfully, with passion, without reason. They all wait for me, everywhere in that valley, but especially in some places to which I do not go. Ballochtorra begins to crumble on its height; the rains and the snows take their toll of the roof, the ice creeps in to break chinks in the walls. The ivy is taking possession; very soon it will need the knowing eye to distinguish what was newly built, in the pride of wealth and ambition, from the very old. The rooks gather in the ivy-grown trees and on the battlements. And forever, ceaselessly, my eyes search the skies for the sight of a falcon.

I

It is a long way to come from China to the depths of the Scottish Highlands, for the sake of a few words splashed in confused Mandarin script, down the side of a scroll, with a drawing of a bird perched on a bare willow bough. But I had come, unbidden, unexpected, and for all I knew, unwelcome. I had come because my brother, William, lay buried in a churchyard in the heart of the Highlands, and before he had died had scratched those few words. Yes, a long way to come.

I had sent no message, no telegram, perhaps for fear that I could be turned back – from what I knew of Angus Macdonald he was capable of doing that. So I stood with my trunk and my father's leather bag on the tiny station of Ballinaclash, and there was no one to meet me, and, so far as I could judge, no way to get where I wanted to go.

The stationmaster shook his head. 'Cluain, is it? Well, that will be a good six miles and more. They are not expecting you . . . they did not send the gig.' The curiosity was evident; only an innate kind of courtesy held back the open questions the man longed to ask. 'I'm very sorry, mistress, there will be no conveyance for hire about here. As you can see, it is not even a village. Just a halt when there's a passenger, and to collect the post, and such.'

'There has to be some way . . .' I shivered; it was chill, and it was going to rain. Who would have expected to be dropped here in the middle of a seeming wilderness, pine and larch lining the steep railway cutting, and the sound of the train already lost in the distance as it had rounded the bend? There were no houses, no smoke curling from chimneys; there was nothing but the promise of rain, and the anxious, bewildered stare of the station-master. Clearly no one came to Ballinaclash unheralded – not even from Inverness, much less from China. Clearly, also, I must be mad to have done it.

But there was something, beside the sigh of the wind through the pines, and the automatic clicking of the railway telegraph in the little office, there was the sound of footsteps behind me, and out in front of the station, tucked into the shelter of the building, was a small, one-horse landau, the horse's head held by a man in a long tweed coat. He too was staring at me, and past me, and at that moment he took off his hat; but the action wasn't for me.

'I see your bags there.' I turned; the man who had evidently got off one of the end carriages of the train and walked along the track with his single bag in his hand, had also raised his hat, but he put it back on. A long, quizzical face, under blond streaked hair; his eyes were an intense, light blue which might have seemed innocent and even childlike if it hadn't been for the lines cut deeply at the corners, lines that almost exactly paralleled those at the corners of his mouth. It was a youngish face, and yet weary – or was it the face of a young man, disenchanted.

He continued, with no trace of shyness. 'No one has come to meet you? My name is Campbell.'

He was so cool, so matter-of-fact, that he would have flustered me if I hadn't been so tired, and had so much else to think of.

'How do you do,' I said automatically. Didn't one say that in polite society, however absurd the place and the meeting? The forms were always observed. 'No – no one has come to meet me. I'm not expected. I thought I could perhaps hire . . .'

He was already shaking his head, and I thought I detected a half shrug of the shoulders, as if in wonderment at the foolishness of some people. 'Well, now you see you can't, Miss . . . ? Is it miss?'

'Howard,' I said.

For a second the detachment fell away. 'Howard? You're William Howard's sister? Yes – yes, I should have known. You look like him.'

The sound of the name was comfort. It was so long since anyone had spoken it. No one, since I had left China, had spoken William's name. 'You knew William?' I clutched at the thought.

'Yes . . . yes, I knew him. Not well, but then he wasn't here that long.'

'No – not long. Just those visits from Edinburgh, and then last summer . . .'

He did not let me dwell on it. Already he had taken my arm, and at the same time was beckoning the man who stood by the horse. 'Stevens, give Mr McBane here a hand with the luggage. All of it. We'll be taking Miss Howard to Cluain.'

'Cluain, sir? *Cluain* – ' But then he stopped abruptly, as if there had been some authoritative signal from the man who held my arm. I felt I was being rushed, my decisions made for me. And yet, why not? My immediate problem was solved; I was grateful, as well as tired.

'I like to drive,' the man said. 'Do you mind coming up front with me, or will the wind be too much for you? Stevens can sit with the baggage.'

I nodded; what was a little wind? The man had spoken William's name, and seemed to call him back to life. I let myself be helped up on to the seat, and then the man swung himself up beside me, taking the reins from Stevens. Then we waited as the bags were brought, carried by the stationmaster and Stevens, and stowed in the passenger space. Everyone seemed to move swiftly to Campbell's orders, yet there was an odd comradeship between them all; there was no sign of servility cloaking resentment. The stationmaster was relieved to have me off his hands – but yet he had shown a concern for me. He raised his cap as we prepared to move off.

'Well, then now, mistress. You'll be grand now, and like as not there'll be no rain before you reach Cluain . . .'

Campbell made a vague salute of thanks with the whip, and we were off. The vehicle was well sprung, the horse strong and good, even the road between the pines and larches seemed smooth. It didn't even seem cold any longer.

'I hope I'm not – ' I began.

'Oh, now,' he cut me short. 'Please, I beg you, don't start all those politenesses. Would I have left you standing there on Ballinaclash station? If you're silly enough not to have warned them that you were coming, then the least I can do is save you from some of the consequences of your folly. I don't think,' he added, without emphasis, 'that Angus Macdonald likes surprises.'

'Perhaps not. We'll see. All he can do is turn me away.'

'He'll not turn you away. The world may think us barbarians here in the Highlands – oh, romantic barbarians, perhaps, but still barbarians. But somehow, in all our poverty we still have our traditions of hospitality, which we keep. And I suspect that Angus Macdonald is a believer in blood's being thicker than water. You're the only grandchild he has left.' Then, with devastating candour came the thrust. 'It was William he wanted, of course. A girl will hardly be of much use to him.'

'No,' I answered flatly. 'I hardly expect to be of much use.'

He glanced at me quickly, and then back to the road, his rather austere face softening a little, as if he regretted his words. 'So . . . you decided to come here, after your father died?'

'You knew that my father was killed?'

'The whole kingdom knew it. Perhaps you don't realize how good the British newspapers are at whipping themselves into a frenzy over a tragic and bloody happening far away – most especially when it concerns a bishop of the Established Church. For a couple of days they were in a fever over it. There was talk of sending gun-boats. Imperial dignity had been gravely insulted. I wonder if anyone thought of what you must have suffered then – with William so recently dead.'

'Perhaps it was merciful that I didn't know William was dead at the time. My grandfather's letter had not reached me. He doesn't seem to believe in telegrams, either.'

'Good God!' He looked at me again, for longer this time. 'You were quite alone, then, when the news of William came. I'm very sorry, Miss Howard. You've had . . .' Now his voice dropped so that it was hard to hear above the sound of the hooves, the rush of the wind through the trees. 'You've had a very bad time.'

'My father had many friends . . . they helped very much. Yes, we knew about the talk of gun-boats, but no one in England seemed to realize that my father was killed in a local uprising two hundred miles from the point at which the Great River – the Yangtse – is navigable by a gun-boat. And what use would it have been – I knew it was the last thing my father would have wished. It was senseless, hysterical talk. These things are dealt with in their own way in China. But people in England seem to have some very odd ideas about China. When I prayed in those days, I prayed that the Foreign Secretary was better informed than the journalists.'

They were plain, sensible words, calm words, ones I had long ago reasoned myself into, to try to stop the hurt. But yes, he was right, it had been a bad time. Very bad. But China was often cruel, and violent death was common. The hardest thing to bear had been the thought that it need not have been my father; there were many others he could have sent on that journey. But he never excused himself from what he conceived to be his duties – never sought to, because he loved them. Even when visitation literally meant journeys of a thousand miles, and he would often be cold and hungry, his clothes sodden, or his skin burned with the fierce heat of those summers. No, the progress of a bishop in China had little in common with the stately procession from one parish to another he had described to me, with a kind of a laugh, as being the custom in England. To be fair, the Church paid for a greater dignity than my father ever maintained, he saying that there was so much else to spend the money on in China than keeping up episcopal state. He travelled usually only with one curate, who acted as his secretary. There could have been few bishops who had the frightful distinction of ending their lives with their heads on one of the ever-present bamboo poles of the Chinese. He had been unlucky. He could hardly even have consoled himself in those last horrible moments that he was dying in the cause of bringing the light of the faith to the heathen hordes. He had been unfortunate enough to have been caught unwittingly in a rising against a local war-lord in the remote Szechwan province – he and the curate and two engineers travelling with him to prospect the route of a future railway into the interior. The forces of the war-lord had not come quickly enough to save the foreign devils. It was all the more sport for the faceless mass of peasants that one of their victims had been a high priest serving the foreign god. Some of the leaders of the rising had been punished with the usual refinements of public torture and execution by the war-lord. We had all known in Peking that no gun-boats or expedition would be necessary. And my father's body had been sent back for burial. They had tried not to let me know how brutally he had died. But I did know; one always knew these things in China.

It had not been enough. Their gods, or my God, had decided it had not been enough. Less than a month after the burial came a letter and a chest which buried the last I had in the world. There was a letter, addressed to my father, in Angus Macdonald's formal script and phrases. 'Your son, my grandson, William Howard, has died as the result of a hunting accident in the lands above Cluain. He is buried among his forebears in the kirkyard of St Andrew in the parish of Ballochtorra, according to the rites of the Established Church of Scotland. Should you wish . . . ' My father had no more wishes; he too was buried, according to the rites of the Anglican Church, in the British Legation compound in Peking. And I was in possession of William's personal effects, dispatched to Peking along with the letter. And they included the scroll, the line drawing of the bird on the bare branch, with the confused, inaccurate characters in Mandarin splashed down its edge.

And to what, and for what, had I journeyed? From Peking to Tientsin, by river to the coast, by larger boat to Hong Kong, then by British steamer through the Red Sea and Suez to the smoke and soot of London. Then by train on to Scotland, heading towards the heart of the Highlands, to Inverness, and then, by branch line to Ballinaclash, and from there . . . well, this man, Campbell, was taking me where I had decided to go – to Cluain.

How little I knew of it. How little I had cared to ask. Of course, all the English-speaking world has some fanciful notion of the Highlands. Hadn't we all seen those formalized sketches of the Queen and her Consort, and the castle they had built at Balmoral? – and from a later date there were those sad daguerreotypes of the dumpy little Queen in her widow's weeds seated on a pony held by her gillie in his Highland dress. Pictures of stags and misty glens, tales of feuds and rebellions, and brave, hardy men – the novels of Walter Scott. But the Diamond Jubilee had been celebrated the year before, and Victoria was now very old, and had to be in the last years of her reign; Edward, the Prince of Wales, had waited almost beyond a man's patience to assume the responsibilities for which he had been a figurehead so long. The century was dying, as the old Queen was; and I knew very well that the reality of the Highlands must be quite different from those misty pictures. There had to be winter here, and people who did not live in castles. Why hadn't I asked more about Cluain? In the letters written in answer to William's I had hardly mentioned it, much less questioned him about it. Had I resented his inexplicable attachment to it, the place he had not even wanted to visit? He had gone to Edinburgh University to study engineering, and he had been expecting, in time, that he too would be planning and building China's railways, competing, as all the foreign interests did, for the concessions of its rich trade. But Angus Macdonald had known he was in Edinburgh, and letters had passed between them. William had at first gone to Cluain unwillingly. 'I suspect this old man is possessive,' he had written to me before the first visit, 'and I have to be free to do what I have always dreamed of doing. I have to belong to myself.' There had not been any more written about being free. He had returned to Cluain at Christmas, and at Easter, and then the whole of the following summer. But it had been the onset of winter at Cluain again when he had died, and now it was the early days of June. My father had died in the middle of a Chinese winter without knowing his son was already dead. It has been the frozen earth for both of them, so far apart. I wondered now why, since I had not asked William, I had not thought to ask my father about Cluain; was it because I sensed that he felt a guilt about it, and it was cruel to probe it? I knew it was a breach that had never mended. He had married the only child of Cluain, and had taken her far away; she too lay in the Legation compound in Peking. He had known Cluain only for one summer – one summer's idyll in the Highlands, and he had been deeply in love. So I asked nothing, did not care to remind him, and he did not speak of it. I had let myself be absorbed in the life of China – the life that foreigners knew, that is, because no outsider could truthfully claim to know it fully. I had thought I would probably marry there – and yet I had fixed my thoughts on none of the young men who came and went at the Legations.

I had wanted someone who would stay in China. Unconsciously, perhaps, I had waited for William's return. I would have wanted his good opinion of any man I would marry. I had thought to make China my life, as it was my father's and would be William's. But now it was all behind me, the silken luxuries and savage cruelties, and I was headed towards Cluain, forearmed with so little knowledge, open to the wind. Perhaps, then, I shivered.

'You're cold,' the man said. 'I'm sorry. It was thoughtless of me to have put you up here on the box. I could have ridden down there with you. But I've been a week in Edinburgh and when I've been away from here I have a terrible longing to be back. And when I'm back I have to sit up high, and see it all again. I know I'm home then.'

'I'm not cold,' I answered. 'Perhaps just tired. And I know what you mean – about seeing it all . . .' There was so much to see, to try to know. It was beautiful; even my tired, bewildered gaze could appreciate that. Beautiful, but not soft. We passed from clumps of trees to vistas of open meadows, and beyond them boggy moorland. The wind raced through the young green crops; we seemed to climb and descend endlessly – sometimes through open expanses of moor, sometimes the road wound down and up a glen so narrow that the very light seemed to be shut out. As the clouds scudded before the wind, from time to time I saw the mountains – I knew they had to be part of the Cairngorm range. I had studied the map of Scotland so many times since Angus Macdonald's letter. We passed little cottages huddled where they could find a vestige of shelter – I knew the snows would come here, as they did in China. It was strange and wild, and it exhilarated me in a way I had not expected. My mother's blood was in me also, I thought. Suddenly I began to understand the feeling of recognition which must have stirred in William.

Then I saw it – a great place perched on a craggy outcrop above a river, a river whose white water tumbled and sparkled even on this grey afternoon. The place itself was high and old, turreted and battlemented. The centre building was of a great age, and had once been a fortress dominating the narrow pass through the glen. But obviously when times had grown more peaceful, portions had been added to it, and gardens laid out in broad terraces that descended to the river. Despite the gardens, its splendour had still a kind of grimness about it.

'What is that?'

'Ballochtorra.'

It was a name already in my heart; William would lie buried

somewhere near.

'Who lives there?'

'A Campbell.' Then he added, turning and half-smiling at me – the first time I had seen a smile, 'I do.'

'Then why did you say it like that? – a Campbell?'

'Because you, Miss Howard, are a Macdonald, whether you're called that or not. In Scottish history, ever since the massacre at Glencoe – oh, and before that, even – the Macdonalds and the Campbells are thought to be implacable enemies. It wasn't always true, of course. Often they had fought on the same side – just as often they've faced each other with drawn swords. As have most clans in Scotland. They've raided each other's cattle and castles. They've taken each other's women. Sometimes they've even arranged peaceful marriages. But you and I – we're supposed by outsiders to be hereditary enemies, but in fact it was different septs of our clans who were involved at Glencoe. You are a Macdonald of Clanranald, and I'm a Campbell of Cawdor. But still it was Campbells who were quartered on Macdonalds at Glencoe, and who took their hospitality, and who slew them that morning in the February snow – all from seven to seventy years old. Five o'clock in the morning, and many of them tumbling out of their beds, and ending dying naked and dead in the snow. It isn't forgiven or forgotten – even if the Macdonalds were rebels against King William of Orange – and the Campbells were said merely to be carrying out orders. That it was done by stealth by men living in the houses of their victims is what is not forgiven. It happened more than two hundred years ago, but we're still supposed to hate each other. Scotland's been peaceful for a long time now, and it's only fanatics who keep bringing up the Stuarts and Bonnie Prince Charlie. We have our old Hanoverian queen living here among us, and none would think of harming her, or her son. But it's a romantic, foolish game we Scots play that all the clans still share ties of brotherhood and blood. We've been as cruel to each other as men could be – Ballochtorra there would tell its tales, and its dungeons were there for other reasons than storing wines. But your name is Macdonald and my name is Campbell, and we're supposed never to let the memory of Glencoe die. Even though you and I are distant cousins.'

I sat upright. 'Cousins? How?'

He shrugged. 'It does happen. Oh, it's an odd story, and your grandfather would like to keep its memory bright, because he won himself a great personal victory from it. He won the best that Ballochtorra owned. He won the dower house of Ballochtorra, which is Cluain. With it he won the best lands in the strath, the lands that in the old days gave Ballochtorra its grain and cattle – gave it the lands to rent out to tenant farmers, who in turn gave service to the Campbells in times of trouble, so that the chief of the Campbells would protect *their* lands and houses, their women and children. Most would take the name of Campbell – or Macdonald or Frazer or Grant – whatever was the name of the chief they served. That's how the clan system worked then, when it was a real need, not a decoration. They clung together for mutual protection, as families do. And as families do, they often quarrelled. It was a system. It worked in its time. But that time is over now. On the order of the English, after the Stuarts' last hope vanished with Prince Charlie at Culloden, the clan system was broken. For many years no Highlander could wear the tartan, or bear arms. But we would do better to forget it, or at least understand where it belongs. It would be better if you and I were not expected to mistrust and dislike each other just because of our names.'

'Montague and Capulet...'

He sighed, a sound I heard even above the wind. 'Yes, Montague and Capulet, if you like. Forgive me for indulging in all this lecturing on something you perhaps already know – but you will perhaps be happier here if you remember a few of these things.' We were crossing a graceful arched stone bridge, and he glanced up at the heights of Ballochtorra. 'That was one of the things so attractive about William – he had many qualities we all liked. He was like a clean wind blowing through all this nonsense. He hadn't come with any preconceived ideas. He didn't hate Campbells because of their name. And he went against everything your grandfather believed in when he came to visit at Ballochtorra.'

'He always said he would be his own man.'

'He was. I never believed he would do anything he didn't want to do. You were very fond of William.' It was said in the same matter-of-fact tone.

'I had only one brother. In China one is isolated. There are fewer of one's own kind. I hardly know how other brothers and sisters feel about each other – if they are as close as we were. He was the elder – he led me everywhere. For a long time I didn't know what to think before asking William. He was like Father – but so much nearer my age.'

'And he led you here?'

'Perhaps.'

We had started on the steep ascent again, the road winding up around the castle to take the bend along the shelf of the crag. We came to a gatehouse, stone-built, but quite new, I thought –

turreted in the fashion of the castle; splendid iron gates were embellished with a gold-tipped shield, the armorial bearings a bird of some sort, with long arched neck, like a hissing swan. The gold leaf was so fresh I could read the motto above the bird. *Be mindful.* I wondered if it were meant as advice or warning.

I could not help the touch of acid. 'For those who have lost their best lands to another clan, you appear to be very prosperous.'

He nodded. 'Oh, yes – our good farming lands are gone. What we still have are the moors for rich men to shoot on.'

'Then you are rich.'

'Let us say my wife is rich.'

I was too tired; I couldn't take in any more of it. So I let the remark slide past me. I knew that soon I would face Cluain, and whatever waited for me there. I felt my shoulders sag, and it was then I truly began to feel the cold. The trees that had been cleared to give the castle its prominence were appearing again, an ancient planting of oak and beech. We were rounding the bend and coming out into a broad meadowland beside the river when I saw him. It would have been easy to miss him. He stood within the shadow of a beech, and the leaves above him were the only things that moved; the dog at his side was just as motionless. The man was dark – I could barely see his face in the shadow; he wore a kilt, some faded red pattern it was, and a ragged sheepskin jerkin above it. He looked at us steadily; his hand was raised, but not in greeting. We were almost past before I saw the bird perched on that raised gloved hand. A large bird, what kind I didn't know, but with intensely dark eyes, as still and unblinking as the man and the dog. Perhaps they all moved their eyes to watch us, but none turned a head. Oddly, though, Campbell, beside me, raised his whip in brief, rather curt, salute; the man did not respond. Then they were behind us, that strange trio, and somehow I managed not to turn my own head to look back at them.

'What will you do at Cluain?'

'Who knows. Perhaps I won't stay.'

We went on in silence for some time. Then he said: 'Angus Macdonald was bitterly grieved by William's death. William must have seemed an answer to all his hopes. I have only glimpsed him once in the months since then. He seemed to me very aged. Perhaps it would be a kindness if you made yourself stay, whatever happens.'

'Does that mean you believe I will not be welcome? I told you I was not expected.'

'Who's to say? Cluain is not an ordinary household. If you

should need a friend . . . if you should need somewhere to come, Ballochtorra is close by.'

'And your wife – will she welcome me?'

'She will welcome whomever I do. She welcomes a lot that I don't. That is no reflection on her, but on me. I'm not . . . very sociable.'

'You have done *me* a service for which I'm sure my grandfather would wish to thank you. I'm sure Cluain will not fail in the Highland hospitality you were speaking of. After all – as you said – I am his only grandchild.' And then quickly added, to cover myself, 'Most likely I will not stay long.'

'Not stay? A pity . . .' A pity for whom, I wondered. But now he was gesturing again with his whip, and the reins urged the horse to a quicker gait. 'There it is now – Cluain.'

It stood there alone in the broad meadows that rose gently from the river; the wind riffled through the young green grain; the cattle grazed the early summer grasses on the higher pastures, and those down towards the river. The cloud had lifted, and the mountains were clear and sharp, the wind blowing straight off them. I could not easily pick out the dwelling-house of Cluain, because the other buildings dominated it. There were not just the usual outbuildings of a good farm, but a long series of identical stone sheds, adjoining one another, which must be used for warehousing, I thought. Then there was the old stone pile with chimneys that ended in pagoda-like domes that might have come there straight from China. It was a strange sight – the grouping of buildings in the midst of a rural scene, like some factory pile lifted from the industrial North through which the train had taken me, but with these stones cleansed of soot and grime by the slashing rain from the mountains. I had not known what to expect a whisky distillery to look like, but this had not been in my mind.

'Angus Macdonald claims,' Campbell said, 'that he makes the finest malt whisky in the whole Highlands, and I've never heard anyone seriously dispute that claim. Now he is old, and William had become his great hope. I'm afraid he is a very sad and angry man . . .'

2

The road down from Ballochtorra's crag had taken such a wide curve to bring it to the level of the river meadows that now it had to wind back on itself to approach Cluain; the whole group of buildings faced us on a diagonal, so that we looked into the very

centre of it. The house I could now identify – the first building
we would reach, the smallest and the oldest. There was a stable
block, and a cobbled yard that served stables and house and
distillery. Across the road, beginning in a line with the distillery,
began the long row of warehouse buildings. These were low –
one storey only, but with roofs of dark slate. Although the pagoda
chimneys of the distillery dominated the scene, the brooding bulk
of the warehouses – stretching along the road like a great gabled
terrace – had a compelling quality about them, a sense of permanence. From the height of Ballochtorra I had seen the roofs
of farm buildings behind the distillery, and strung out along the
road past the warehouses, some cottages with garden plots. A town
all to itself, it seemed, and yet strangely quiet, as if everyone had
gone and left it.

But it did not remain quiet. A dog barked, and as the landau
drew near to the house a great flock of geese came at a wild run
from the direction of the warehouses, hissing and shrieking. Behind
me I heard Stevens's half-stifled oath, and Campbell had to hold
the horse in tighter to prevent it shying. Stevens slipped out of his
seat and went to the horse's head; we moved on at a slow walk,
and Campbell tossed the whip to Stevens, who used it to gesture
the geese away. Finally, even the big gander in charge of the flock
began reluctantly to accept our presence; he gave a honking
signal, and the whole white stream of birds turned and waddled
back to the warehouses, delighted, I guessed, with the fuss they had
caused.

'Damned animals,' Stevens grumbled. 'They should not be
allowed. This is a public highway.'

Campbell did not answer him. The flurry of geese seemed to
have brought no one to mark our arrival. The landau now stood
before the house. In the confusion, I had not had time to look at
it closely, but now it took on its overwhelming importance, as the
very heart of Cluain. It was not, as we stood beside it, after all,
so small. It was simply that the other buildings were bigger. They
all shared the same, almost painful, neatness. The house was much
the oldest of the group – the dower house of Ballochtorra, it would
have stood for perhaps two centuries before the distillery. It was
L-shaped, built about two sides of a courtyard. The high stone wall
of this courtyard was flush to the wall of the house itself, and an
ancient studded door, like the door of the house, faced directly on
to the road. Despite the noise of our arrival, both remained un-
yieldingly closed. The whole structure was built of massive, ir-
regularly cut stone, two-storeyed, with gabled windows in the

steep-pitched roof. What lifted it from the mere dignity of its age and good lines was a piece of sheer fantasy. Where the two wings of the building joined, a tower rose, its slightly inward-inclining walls reaching well above the rest of the house, and capped with a perfect rondel of slate, and a magnificently ornate weather vane. Its total proportions were so perfect that it seemed almost like a child's toy piece. My eye had long been educated to the studied delicacy of the Chinese houses, their walls and courtyards, the exquisite sense of detail that was not absent from anything they fashioned, so I responded to this place as if I had been born to it – as William must also have done. He had written that Cluain was beautiful; how beautiful, and in what way, he had not said.

Stevens went and banged the knocker on the door; it seemed to be minutes before we caught a glimpse of a figure near the window of one of the front rooms, and almost as long before the door at last opened. The woman who stood there wasted no effort on taking in the details of the scene; her gaze went at once to me, and eyes – brilliant, dark, deeply set, and shadowed with black brows and lashes, seemed to scour me with their examination. She was dressed in servant's dress, completely black, even to the apron, severe, unadorned. Black hair, streaked with silver, was drawn sharply to the back of her head; it was a handsome face. Tall, slender, she had an unassailable dignity, standing there, just looking at me.

Even the man beside me, so cool and self-assured until now, seemed struck with the same feeling as I. I could feel my throat dry. So, in the end, it was the woman who spoke first.

'If you had sent a telegram, we would have sent the trap. You are William Howard's sister.'

How had she known? I was not much like him. But she gave the impression that she knew things most people did not.

I struggled for composure; I was not going to be put out by a servant. But she was like no servant I had ever encountered. I made a movement, and Campbell came to life, leaping down off the seat, and hurrying round to help me down. Stevens had returned to hold the horse. I advanced towards the woman. 'Mr Macdonald is at home?'

'And why would Mr Macdonald be at home at this time of day? We work at Cluain.'

The insult was deliberate, telling me that if I expected to put her in her place I must know that I first had to find it. As I came closer I saw that she was older than she had seemed. There were fine lines in her pale skin, many lines; and then I saw her hands. They were shockingly red and worn with work, the skin broken at the knuckles as if caustic soap had bitten into it. But she held them before her like a badge of virtue, despising all who could not boast of gainful toil.

'I may wait then?'

She held the door a little wider. 'Aye, certainly you may. I see you have brought your bags . . .' She did not pause to see the effect of the remark, but turned and called over her shoulder, as if she knew someone would be close by. 'Morag . . . you are needed.'

From the back of the hall a girl came at once, and indeed she had been waiting and listening. She rushed forward, like a sudden flaring of light beside that dark figure; red curling hair spilled without discipline from her cap; she had red, soft, full lips and golden amber eyes. It was a perfect little heart-shaped face with white skin that flushed to apricot with excitement. No more than the woman beside her did she look like a servant, but she wore a white apron, and she bobbed me a slight curtsy.

'Welcome to Cluain, Mistress Howard. Och, it will do your grandfather's heart good to set eyes on you.' And she lifted her own glowing eyes to mine, and smiled.

There was a bustle as she ran forward to get the bags; Campbell helped her with them, for the woman in black would not step across the threshold. Silently she indicated where they might be placed inside the hall, as if Campbell were her servant also. I felt the hot blood of embarrassment rush to my face. I turned to the woman directly.

'You have the advantage of me, since you know my name. May I know yours?'

'I am Mairi Sinclair, housekeeper at Cluain.'

'Then, Mistress Sinclair, may I, on my grandfather's behalf, offer this gentleman, Mr Campbell, a cup of tea? He has been kind enough to bring me — '

But she was looking past me, and her wintery lips twitched.

'Sir Gavin, perhaps you will accept the hospitality of Cluain?' She knew he would not.

He didn't even look at her, knowing better than to play her game, it seemed. He returned to the doorway, and raised his hat to me. 'I hope all goes well. If I can be of assistance . . . You saw I live not far away.'

'Thank you — '

But the words were cut short by Mairi Sinclair. 'We all know it's but a short step to Ballochtorra, Sir Gavin. Master William was not long in finding that out.'

And then to my horror she closed the door in his face, and I was left there in the sudden dimness of the hall, for a moment helpless between this dark wraith of a figure and this radiant sprite of a girl. Then a sentence from one of William's letters flashed into my brain, yet one other thing I had passed over, not wanting to question, perhaps jealous again. *'There is a dragon-lady whom I believe the Chinese would respect and admire – and there is also an enchantress.'*

My eyes grew used to the dimmer light. What the stationmaster had predicted had come true; the rain, now it had come, slashed fiercely against the panes. There seemed a sudden massing of cloud across the valley – the strath, Gavin Campbell had called it. I repressed the shiver that rose, and cursed myself for an impetuous fool. Why had I not sent at least a telegram from London? Even more, why had I ever left those many friends in China who had offered homes to me, certain, as we all were, that young English-women always found husbands among the superfluity of men who came to reap the pickings of the rich trade. I had been a bishop's daughter, and there had been many who loved my father. There had been little money – even bishops do not grow rich on mission-ary work. But we had been rich in friends and goodwill; where servants and food are cheap, guests are a pleasure, not a burden. I could have made a slow progression from Peking to Shanghai, and even to Hong Kong, and I would have been welcome in a dozen houses. But I had chosen to come here, with no certain knowledge that I would stay, that I would even be asked to stay. And I had come all because of those nightmarish Mandarin characters scrawled down the length of William's scroll.

Remembering them, I lifted my head and looked carefully about me.

Approaching in the landau the house had seemed miniature; inside it had space and depth, and a kind of grandeur, possibly the grandeur of antiquity. It was spare and high and severe; the thought came that it was a little like the woman who ruled over it. There was a great stone fireplace here in the hall, and two carved oak chairs set stiffly before it. There was a dark refectory table with silver candlesticks upon it. The hall ran the whole length of this front wing of the building; I could see where the staircase curved outward around the tower. It was a stone stair-case, floating, seeming without support except for the massive slabs set into the wall of the tower. It had no banister, only a rope handrail attached to the wall. Narrow windows gave light fitfully. But there was other light; everything that hand could polish gave back the outside light — the planked oak floors, the candlesticks, the dark carved furniture. There was no flower, no rug, no picture. Even in the beautiful severity of the Chinese houses I had come to admire, there would have been a single flower or a dried reed in a vase. Here there were no concessions to human delight, or pleasure — nothing. But no denying hand could take away this beauty. It had been shaped by unknown masters of their craft hundreds of years ago. Having stripped it down to its bare bones, it was only the more beautiful.

Then something brushed against me, and in the silence I almost shrieked.

It was a cat. With difficulty I stood still as it investigated the unfamiliar smell of my skirt and boots. I had known cats before — the house in Peking had always had cats, plump, striped creatures, or black and white, one or other always sitting on my father's desk, or on a chair on the veranda, stalking among the bamboo brakes in the garden. But there had been no cats like this one. It was all white, immaculately white, as if it often walked in the rain, and preened itself daily. Finding no comfort from my skirts it went to Mairi Sinclair, as to someone well trusted, and from the shelter of her skirt, it raised its eyes to me. They were without colour; no green or blue in them, a pinkish tinge in that grey — an albino cat staring up at me, an elegant slim white shape against the black folds. It occurred to me that here also was a thing without colour or adornment, and Mairi Sinclair's creature as much as a cat will ever be. She did not put a hand down to pat or fondle it. I began to feel that for both such an action would have been unnecessary.

'I take it you will be staying the night?'

'Possibly.' We both knew there was no place else to go, and that obviously I had come with the thought to stay for many nights. 'That is,' I thrust at her, 'if you have room for me.'

'Room, aye — and beds aplenty. All dry and well-aired. We have few guests at Cluain, but you'll find nothing amiss in the arrangements. Come, Morag.'

With a quick, jerking movement she seized the trunk by one handle, and indicated to Morag to take the other. They set off along the hall. I was left standing beside the leather bag, and there was nothing to do but grasp it and hurry after them. It was a large bag, and almost too long for me to carry, so that it bumped against each step as I climbed. I found myself panting; the two women ahead of me were so quick, and I had a sudden awful fear of plunging sideways over that unprotected stair. I was too tired. I longed for hot water, and food, and a warm bed. I longed not to have to face my grandfather this night.

When I reached the hall upstairs the two women seemed to have vanished; the stairs ended there, and two passages opened to follow the L-shape of the house. I stopped, bewildered. I could hear the quick words that passed between them, but they were nowhere in sight. Then I looked and saw that the tower itself had an arched opening – and a further spiral of stairs led on upwards within the walls themselves. It was still wide; the steps were broad wedged. They ended at the top of the tower in the most extraordinary room I had ever seen. It was surprisingly large, following the curve of its outer walls, with three windows that gave a view of the valley – past the distillery and along the river, across the gradually rising lands to the mountains, and up to the crag on which Ballochtorra was perched. There was a stone floor, and the centre of the room contained a raised platform piled with split logs, a long copper hood reached up to form a chimney flue, ending where the sloping curved ceiling came to its point. The ornate weather vane I had noticed must have capped the chimney-pot. There was a fourposter bed, just fitted within two windows, hung with tartan curtains and covered with a wool spread of the same pattern. There was a tall hanging-cupboard with a drawer at the bottom set against the next space between the windows; beside it was a washstand. The third space was given to a desk that could only have been made especially for this room – it took the curve of the wall, and its ends were cut on the slant. The dark carved oak chair set before it was its match. There was an oak bench before the fire, and a standing sconce with two candles. Tartan curtains hung on wooden poles at each window, straight, without fringe or tie; they were a great splotch of colour against the white walls. The last space left between the windows was the doorway in which I stood.

The room was austere and plain – and quite magnificent.

'Was this? – Did my brother use this room?'

Mairi Sinclair turned from her task of stowing the chest as neatly as it would fit beneath one of the windows; she was frowning, and I thought for a moment that it irked her because the curved walls must forever defeat the straight lines of most objects. 'This room? – yes, the Master directed it.'

Morag took the bag from my hand. "Tis high and lonely up here, and when the wind blows and the snow falls, you could feel you were lost on a mountain.'

And high and mighty, I thought. Whoever lived in this room and saw Cluain's treasures spread before him would be tempted.

Who would not feel the lonely splendour of this place, who might not ache to possess it? My grandfather had wanted William.

'Fanciful thoughts, Morag,' Mairi Sinclair said. 'The tower room is the pride of Cluain.' Her tone almost suggested that she thought me not worthy of it, but at the same time she had sought to isolate me here. Whoever lived in this room must also be able to live with their own company.

I went close to one of the windows now and looked down on Cluain's two wings, and into the courtyard that was screened from the road by its high wall. Even from this height I could tell it was a garden that the Chinese might have delighted in – filled with the herbs of their wonderful cooking, and their healing medicines. The straight paths that met precisely in the middle at the sundial were encroached by the sprawl of lavender and thyme, sage and chamomile, fennel and parsley. The pervading neatness of Cluain was here defeated. The plants went their own wild, sweet way. I hoped I saw the hand of my grandfather here.

'The garden . . .' I began. There had to be some way to make contact with Mairi Sinclair.

'The garden is mine.'

I repressed a sigh, and turned back to face her; for a moment her expression seemed unguarded, and she was not so much fierce, as pitiful, defending what she thought of as her own. But I could have been mistaken. Her tone was absolutely unrelenting as she spoke again.

'I'll be getting down, then. Morag shall bring you some water to wash. The Master will be here directly.'

'You'll send for him?'

She shook her head. 'No one sends for Angus Macdonald. It is almost time for him to be in for his supper. He is very punctual. You will oblige him by not keeping him waiting, Miss Howard.'

Then they were both gone, with a backward look that contained a nod of encouragement from Morag. The rain came more strongly now, beginning to blot out Cluain's world, the mountains disappearing in the cloud, the mist boiling up until it almost veiled Ballochtorra. I was left alone, to make what I would of it – alone, except for the cat, which had settled itself upon the bed, paws folded in against its chest, staring at me with its wide colourless eyes. I tried to stare it down, but it was I, of course, who lost that contest.

Morag was back; I had heard the murmur of some song as she mounted the tower stairs, and she swept into the room with her blazing hair like some cheerful light. 'There now, it's nice and hot,' she announced as she set the jug down and a pile of snowy towels on the washstand. 'And I'll just be giving you a wee bit of a fire. It's a little comfort you're needing now.' As I watched, she rearranged the kindling with deft fingers, and put a match to a screw of paper. The dry wood caught at once; it was impossible not to know that Morag was one of those creatures for whom things always went right – quick, neat, clever in her movements, wasting no effort. She was as superior to her tasks as her face and hair were to her plain servant's dress.

'Do you live here, Morag?'

'Aye. I have my own room down there along the passage from Mistress Sinclair. The Master sleeps in the other wing. I have my own fire, and 'tis nice and cosy. The wages are fair, and the food is good – everyone eats well at Cluain.'

'Is that why you came?'

She laughed. 'I had not much choice, had I? I was born at Cluain. Mistress Sinclair delivered me. My father worked in the distillery, and we had our own house then. But he was killed when I was a wee thing – one of the drays overturned on the ice on that steep bit beyond the bridge at Ballochtorra, taking the whisky to the railhead. So then my mother came here to help Mistress Sinclair in the house. She stayed until I was eight, and then she was away to her sister in Inverness. She could not stick the loneliness any more – or Mistress Sinclair, she said – and I was welcome to come with her if I wanted.'

'But you stayed . . .'

'I did. I had been to Inverness, and seen it, and the place where my aunt has her dressmaking business, and I did not like it – not one bit. Besides, the Master's wife was alive then, and she favoured me – her wee girl, she used to call me. My mother knew what she was about, leaving me at Cluain. I had my tasks to do, of course, but I had a better time of it than my mother could hope to give me. Lessons I had from Mistress Macdonald, and advantages that were beyond my mother. And Mistress Sinclair is not so bad when you know her ways – we rub along, and I am not such a fool that I have not learned from her, too. Where else would it be like this? – me with my own room, and the right to be private when I please. I've seen those skivvys in those town places, and I have no wish to be like them. No one even knows their names . . . No, 'tis not for Morag MacPherson. And Mistress Sinclair, she knows it. You think she's fierce? – Well, she's proud, but what's wrong with that? Terrible skilful she is, at everything she sets her hand to. And a wonder with her herbs and remedies. People around here would far rather have her than a doctor – they come for miles to have her treat their ailments, and never a penny does she take. She says that the herbs and wild plants of the hedgerows grow free, and God put them there, and gave her the knowledge to use them, so she has no right to charge. A great Bible-reading woman she is. The doctor would like to see her stopped, of course, but she makes no claims, and takes no money. If people come to her, that's their business. Besides, the doctor's a great one for his dram, and none too clean . . .'

She rose from her crouching position before the fire, the flames now leaping high towards the metal hood. 'There now, I am chattering again. Mistress Sinclair says my tongue is my great fault. I'll leave you, mistress. The Master will be in directly – ' She paused. 'I think he will be glad to see you. This past winter he has not had an easy time of it. Ill, he's been, with a cough – and at times he seems very tired. He will not have the doctor near him. Since Master William died . . . ah, well, perhaps the sight of you will lighten that sorrow, mistress.' She dusted her hands together. 'You'll find him in the dining-room. 'Tis the only room he ever uses at Cluain. 'Tis the door on the right of the hall as you go down . . .'

She was turning to go, and then her gaze fell on the cat. Suddenly her voice took a strange edge, almost ugly. 'Devil take that thing! Isn't he always where he should not be, and never a finger to be laid on him, because he's Mistress Sinclair's!' She made a threatening motion towards the cat, but I saw that she did not attempt to touch it.

'Leave him, Morag.' I don't know why I said it. The cat had made me uncomfortable before, but now I sensed that it had often taken that place on the bed. 'He seems to like it here.'

'Och, he likes it fine. He knows he's not supposed to be up here – does a body ever know what damage a cat will be doing? But he took to coming here when Master William was here – and you're the first that used this room since then. I do not care to touch him, myself.'

Backing towards the door, her eyes were less friendly as she looked at the cat. 'I must be away. Mistress Sinclair will know I've been gossiping. She knows everything, that one. But a body has a right to a little information about a strange place – and it's precious little you'll get from Mairi Sinclair . . .'

She was gone, and now I approached the cat; I put my hand tentatively on his head. He did not stir. 'Were you William's friend, Cat? Did you know him well?' He answered nothing, of course, and no welcoming purr rewarded my gesture. He merely stared at the fire. I shrugged, and turned away. He had not come here for my company, that was certain. Perhaps he liked the lonely grandeur of this room. He seemed hardly a cat to sit cosily by a kitchen fire.

I took my toilet articles from the leather bag, my fingers stiff with a chill and tension that the hot water did nothing to help. When I picked up my brush I was suddenly aware of staring at the blank white wall before me where one would have expected a mirror. Then I became conscious of something odd about this room — something that I recognized now as being common to the other parts of the house I had seen. The furniture was old and rich, and it shone with the polishing of careful hands. The curtains were in good repair, but apart from their tartan pattern, utterly plain. I searched for something here that was not essential, and there was nothing, no ornament, no vase, no picture. One book only lay on the desk, and I knew without looking at it that it was the Bible. Surely William would not have suffered this — the clutter of his possessions must have disturbed this austere order. Angrily I turned back to where my reflection should have met me in a mirror, and there was nothing. It was as if in this room Mairi Sinclair strove to make the occupant feel as if he or she did not exist.

Anger drove out the sense of desolation that had been creeping upon me. Feverishly I brushed at my hair, and my fingers arranged the knot without aid of a mirror. I did remember what I looked like — I *would* remember. I did exist.

Defiantly I tied a red ribbon about the knot of hair, and found the red kid fur-lined slippers that I wore in the Peking winters. I found the cashmere shawl that William had brought me back from a visit to Canton, riotously glowing with the rich embroideries that the Chinese loved, and touched here and there with a thread of gold. I, at least, would not be forced into Mairi Sinclair's mould.

'Come, Cat,' I said, as I went towards the door. Surprisingly, he obeyed. He was out of the door before me, a swift white streak, and then, quicker than I, he was off down the broad spiral. When I reached the floor below, he had disappeared.

I went on then, unaccompanied, to my meeting with the Master of Cluain.

2

He stood there – a powerfully built man in whom the strength
seemed too suddenly to have wasted. He was not so tall, but the
breadth of the shoulders was great, only now they appeared bent
forward unnaturally, hunched. His distinguishing feature was
massive eyebrows hooked over deep-set eyes. There was a strong
thrust of jawline, but most of the face was lost in the gathering
furrows of age, and the dim light of the room. He stood, legs apart,
facing out from the fireplace, and he half-turned at my entrance.

'So – you have come. William's sister.'

'My mother's child.'

Why did I always have to make the tart rejoinder? Could I not
have greeted him without provocation in these first words? 'Learn
to curb your tongue, Little Sister,' William had once said to me,
using the name the Chinese had bestowed on me, 'and you'll have
the men at your feet – that is, if you want those kinds of men!'
I looked at this big ageing man, and I knew that he would never
be at my feet. I hoped I would never be at his.

He gestured irritably. 'Well, come in, come in! And close the
door. There's draught enough with this wind.'

I did as he bade me, and then went and stood near the fireplace. His voice was deep and strongly accented. 'You've come a
long way. Are you staying?'

'A while. If you'll have me.'

He shrugged. 'If it pleases you. You've a right to the roof of
Cluain.' It wasn't much of a welcome, but then he hadn't asked
me to come in the first place. A silence fell between us, which I
left him to break.

'Why *did* you come? You could not find anyone to marry you
out there?'

I flushed. 'There were some. That's unimportant. My father was
killed and –'

'Aye – I read of it. I was going to write . . .' The tone softened
a little. 'But I never got to it. In any case, the letter would have
missed you as it happens.' It was said with some relief, as if this
absolved him of any fault. 'I never did like him – your father. I'll
not pretend any different. He came here just for one summer, and
took away my only child – and she still so young. He was English,
and a minister of a different church. And he took her not just to

England where I might have seen her from time to time, and might have come to know my grandson. Och, no – he must carry her all the way to China, that miserable cesspool of pagans, where she died of one of their stinking fevers. No, there was no love lost, and I cannot deny it.'

'*I* loved him.' I had to say it.

Surprisingly, he nodded. 'That's as well. I like to see respect in a child – '

'*Love*,' I insisted. 'I loved him – and William too.'

Perhaps the outright declaration of love was too much for this taciturn Scot; his tongue would not come easily to such a word, nor hear it too readily from others. He half turned away from me, as if in embarrassment. '*That's* why I came.' Then I stopped. I could not tell him about the scroll. Some time, but not now. 'I had to see where William . . . Well, I knew he was growing attached to Cluain.'

As if I had wounded him and he could bear no more of it, he left the fire abruptly, and went to the sideboard. For a moment he bent over it, both hands placed there as if to steady himself. The voice was muffled and choked when he spoke again.

'Aye – and well I knew it. He would have been grand for Cluain, and Cluain for him. But he's dead now – and there's an end to it.' He cleared his throat thunderously, and his body straightened; the big head with its brush of white hair came up. 'Sit down, then, and welcome.' But still he did not look at me. 'You'll take a dram with me?'

'A dram?'

Now he turned back. 'Are you stupid, Gurrl? Have they taught you nothing of your heritage? A dram – *whisky!* Cluain's whisky!'

'I – I've never drunk whisky.'

'Then you are sadly ill-educated. Or perhaps you drank only brandy or champagne out there in the bishop's palace.'

'It was no palace. We were quite poor.'

This seemed to irritate him also. 'He didn't only take my child, but he could not even leave his own children decently provided for. Well, we'll not fret it. Doubtless you'll find someone to marry you. But if it's to be a Scot, then you'd better learn fine soon what his national drink is. Some women drink it – some don't. But here at Cluain at least you'll know what it is.'

He was unlocking a cupboard in the sideboard with a key he selected from a ring he carried. Glasses stood waiting ready on a silver tray. He poured from an engraved decanter into two glasses and came back and placed one in my hand. I had not sat down, as he had bidden me, so we faced each other, standing, across the breadth of the fireplace. The firelight caught the glow of the amber liquid in the good crystal glass. He raised his slightly towards me.

'Well, there it is, miss. *Uisge beatha* we call it in the old Gaelic tongue. *Aqua vitae,* the Latin scholars say. Water of life. Cluain's distilling – and your heritage. Well, miss, here's to us!'

He tossed his own glass back, and incautiously, I was too hasty in following his example. It was in my throat before I felt the fire of it, an aged smoke that seemed to pour into my lungs; I gasped for breath, and struggled not to choke. I was certain he could see the tears that came to my eyes, but I would not allow the cough and the splutter to come. He had been expecting that, I thought, and with a certain malicious pleasure.

I had to wait until my breath was even enough to speak. The whisky had an extraordinary aftertaste on my tongue, and although I knew the alcohol couldn't have affected my legs so quickly, I sat down without ceremony on one of the broad oak settles placed at each end of the fireplace. I knew he was waiting for a verdict, and I had my own satisfaction in withholding it.

'I'm not miss, you know – nor Gurrl. My name is Kirsty.' But I had the feeling the name 'Gurrl' had come to stay.

The words disturbed him. His big features twisted with a look of bitterness. He sat down opposite me, and the movement was that of an old man.

'Kirsty – Christina. Well, my daughter gave you *that* name but she could not give you the spirit and great heart of the woman she called you for. You'd have to be bred here in the Highlands to be her kind. But then my grandson came, and it was as if he had been to the place born. Now he's dead, and there's no one for Cluain but an ignorant girl, God help us! No one for Cluain . . .'

And then he drained the last of his glass. In desperation, with no words of comfort to offer him, I took another sip of my own. This time it wasn't so bad. At least it was warm; I could feel its glow move subtly through my veins. *Uisge beatha* – whisky – water of life. Cluain . . .

2

The hot dishes were brought in wordlessly by Mairi Sinclair, and left on the sideboard. My grandfather cut the meat, and we helped ourselves from the other dishes. As Morag had said, the food was good – it was excellent. I had been hungry, but the whisky had made me ravenous. I noted the plates we ate off, the silver utensils one would not have expected in what I had thought of as a farmhouse. But it was also the dower house of Ballochtorra, and judging from the furniture, must have shared some of Ballochtorra's riches. But here, also, while we ate off fine china, there was no single thing that was superfluous. The windows of the dining-room looked on to the enclosed garden, and there the plants waved and nodded in their own cheerful disorder. But no rose such as climbed those old walls perfumed this room; instead there was the smell of beeswax, and the peat and wood burning in the fire. Everything shone, and was set with mathematical precision. The great sideboard and the long table with stretchers, joining its magnificently carved legs, were precisely parallel. The two settles were at exact right angles to the fireplace, with no cushion or footstool to ease the sitter. Under the window opposite them was a smaller table – still of the same carved dark oak – it must all be about the Jacobean period, I thought, though I was hazy about such things. On the table was set a huge book bound in faded, though polished, brown leather, with brass trimmings on the corners, and an ornately fashioned brass hinged clasp which fastened and held the pages together. There were such ones on display in the richer homes of the residents of the British Legation in Peking, though it was characteristic that my father, a bishop, had never thought of declaring his faith in any such obvious manner; the small, thin-paged book he carried in his pocket had been sufficient. Beside the Bible, and more interesting to me, was the one note of individuality that the room contained. A chess set was there, the board and pieces polished, as everything was, but with the look of use about them. But no unfinished game was set up. The pieces waited, their four solid ranks opposing. Whoever dusted and polished them had learned in what order to replace them. But by now I was beginning to believe that the two women of this house, the older and the young, between them were capable of learning all they put their minds to. It could not be true that all Scots were as intelligent as the engineers and scientists they exported to the rest of the world; but quite certainly the stupid would not have lasted long at Cluain.

My grandfather ate in silence. I thought there might have been a prayer, but there was none. All, apparently, were not like Mairi Sinclair. Then, after a while, my grandfather laid down his knife and fork, and stared at me, as if he had suddenly, once again, become aware of my presence. I realized that he was totally unused to eating at this table with anyone else – he had forgotten that one could talk at meals. William, I thought, would have changed that. No one had ever been able to stop William talking.

The words came in fits and starts. 'You know what Cluain means in the old tongue, lass? Did your mother talk to you of things like that? – about Cluain, and such?'

'She died when I was four,' I reminded him.

'Aye, she did. So she did. Killed by the foulness of that savage place he took her to. Well, it's done now. But Cluain – Cluain means a broad, green meadow – a pasture. Och, we use a fancy name to call the whisky by, because the old words aren't understood. Royal Spey, we call it – because of the river. But Cluain's it is, and made from Cluain's own barley, and dried over peat cut from Cluain's bog, up there on the mountain, and most of all, brewed with the water from Cluain's own well – not river water, mind you, but from our own well. The water's a great part of it – Christina's Well, it is called, and it is the most precious thing on Cluain.'

He forgot who I was. He had a new listener – a new pupil. So he must have talked to William on that first night, seeing the one who would carry on Cluain for him, seeing the longed-for grandson.

'It must age, you know. And it must age *here*. Whisky that's new-distilled can boil your eyeballs out – send you daft. But here the climate is right. Don't ask me why. As soon ask how a good whisky is made, and you'll get a hundred answers, and a hundred different distillings. Some think the climate here is damnable, though it suits me, you see. It suits the whisky, too. Aye, it lies there in its oak cask – best if you can get casks that have been used for storing sherry – gives it colour, in time. Three years is the youngest whisky you can sell by law. But those who buy for blending know Cluain. They come up here from Glasgow and Edinburgh and they bargain and they buy just as the new spirit is distilled. They are content to leave it to age here, untasted, because they know they are buying the finest malt whisky the Highlands make. They ask no questions of Cluain any more. Some leave it only the legal three years, and then take it away to blend with their grain spirits – that's blended whisky, Gurrl, and if it weren't for the malt in it, it would not be even as good as your rot-gut gin. And then some – those who can afford to wait – they wait, and they leave it here, and it grows better with the years. Och, mind you, most of it ends up in a blend, but we all know that without the pure malt distilling, there would be no such thing as the Scotch whisky they sell all over the world these days. There's few that will pay the price, and wait the years to drink a pure malt brew. Perhaps there's few that have the head for it, except those that are brought up to it, here in the Highlands. But never mistake it. Malt is the heart and essence of it. It gives it the flavour and warmth. No whisky without malt, Gurrl – no whisky at all . . .'

Almost without noticing it, we were back at the fire again, seated on those opposite settles. Mairi Sinclair had come to clear the dishes silently, and I noticed that my grandfather was silent also while she was in the room. But we were alone again, and he held another glass in his hand, and again he seemed to have forgotten my real identity. He had taken out a pipe without troubling to ask me if I minded him smoking it. But I could not stand in William's shadow forever, and finally his eyes snapped alive. He seemed to come out of a dream.

'Och, why do I bother? What's it to you? 'Tis God's will, but 'tis hard when a man's worked all his life and there's no one to pass on his knowledge to – no one to care how a good malt whisky is made.'

'Cluain is a farm as well as a distillery.' Why did I seem to bargain for a place here, when I didn't even know that I wanted to stay? It was not the reason I had come.

'The farm is all right. It is a very good farm. But the glory is the whisky. Cluain is famous for it. What can a wee gurrl be taught about it? There's no woman I know who could run a distillery.'

'I'm useless to you, then?'

His words were brutal. 'Useless – yes. Just about useless. Unless you can find and wed a man that's fit to take over from Angus Macdonald. And that man will not be easy to find.'

'You place a high value on yourself, Grandfather.'

'I do that! Any man that's fought and worked as I have *must* place a high value on himself. He has proved that value.'

In the dim light that came from the fire, and the gathering twilight, I knew he would not see my faint, rueful smile. And I didn't much care if he did. I had come rashly, on impulse, fleeing from a China that no longer held anything I loved, coming here because of that scroll, and the scarlet characters splashed on it. What could I prove? – what could I do? I could stand beside William's grave, but that would not bring him back, nor answer my questioning. And then what? Cling on here at Cluain, knowing my grandfather would hardly turn me away; but stay on un-wanted – useless, as he put it. William had been fond of the Chinese philosophy that observed the bamboo bending before the wind and surviving, while the great oak was uprooted. 'It is easier, Little Sister, to go where the wind blows at one's back, than lean against it.' But he had never really practised that himself, nor could I. So in time I would leave Cluain, I thought. I would then take that road that so many of my kind did. A bishop's daughter, I would have references enough from his friends in the Church; but what waited would be no better than the position occupied by so many other women of small education, and less money. I would make a wretched governess, I knew. I did not know my place well enough; my quick impulses and sharp tongue would be no asset. And yet, that was all there was—that, and Cluain. If only, I thought, this old man sitting here had once held out a hand to me. But I would not beg, nor would he. We both were lonely, and alone. But what gigantic pride stood between that fact, and either of us admitting it.

I rose. 'I'll go up now.'

He nodded above his pipe, as if he didn't care. 'Aye. As you wish. You'll find a candle in the hall.'

There was no good night, as there had been no words of welcome. I took the candle, as he had said, placed ready in its pewter holder. But I didn't need it. In this far latitude the light still lingered. The narrow slits of windows gave little aid on the staircase, but when I reached the tower room it was still washed with the grey light of the evening. But the heart of the room was alive with the fire; Morag, I supposed, had laid turf on the glowing wood, and a bed of coals was forming a powdery ash. I crouched for a moment before it. William must often have assumed this posture here, and now I followed him. But suddenly the image of William receded, and unbidden, the thought came to me that this was not a room for a young woman alone. It invited another presence—a young man, not one's brother. It was a room to be alone with a lover. How large that bed looked, and how large the world beyond the three windows. How wonderful to be here with a man one loved, lost, as Morag had said, as if in the snows of the mountains. How, then, the fire would glow; how warm the bed. I felt the heat rush to my cheeks. I was alone, I reminded myself. There was no man—no man I loved. There was only the fire and the rain slashing against the windows. I got up quickly. Useless to dream.

On the washstand something new had appeared. It was a small swivel mirror with a drawer beneath, such as a man used. It would only let me see my face, not the back of my hair, or the hang of my dress—but it would do. And beside it a half-page torn from a notebook, well-formed but somewhat laboured handwriting, and with correct spelling. *I thought you would need the mirror. I have*

set a hot water jar in the bed. Be careful lest you burn your toes.
Morag MacPherson.

I smiled, grateful, wondering what I would have done in these first hours at Cluain without Morag. And smiling, I caught sight of my own face in the mirror. Did I look so much like William that the man Mairi Sinclair had called Sir Gavin had recognized me? – or had he simply made the association afterwards? We both were dark-haired and white-skinned; we both had eyes that were more grey than blue. Were mine as deep-set as William's? – as heavily lashed in black? I suddenly thought of my grandfather's eyes; had both William and I inherited from him that smudged darkness? It was strange, but I had never really thought until now about how I looked; I had somehow taken it for granted that I would do quite well. In Peking, every young European girl was paid compliments, called pretty, even if she were just passably so. I had been called pretty, but I knew it wasn't quite true. Not *pretty*. But William had been almost formidably handsome – and now I was said to look like William. I sighed, and turned away from my image in the glass. What did it matter? If I left Cluain to go South in search of a position the fact that I might be called pretty, or handsome, or whatever else, was a positive disadvantage. Who wanted a good-looking governess who wore red ribbons and slippers?

I went to the window and through the gathering twilight I saw the lights of Ballochtorra. It looked strangely far away now, and far beyond my reach. Lights burned at many windows – they had not yet drawn the curtains against the coming night, but they were prodigal of their lamps. There even seemed to be a few windows on the lower level which glowed with the brighter light of electricity. It was exciting and extravagant in this remote place – like the lights and the voices, the sense of company, and a place shared. Was there a large family at Ballochtorra? Cluain was so silent, except for the rain. One of the turves burned through then, and quickly folded into the bed of coals. The gentle sound came like a crash.

But there was someone else as alone as I was. On the road beyond the walled garden I heard, very faintly, the sound of the pony's hooves. At first the rider was indistinguishable in the grey light; he came out of the mist on the road leading from Ballochtorra, and I thought then that I recognized him. His long legs were thrust forward on a big, tough-looking Highland pony. He rode bareheaded in the rain, without the traditional Highland bonnet to match his kilt. He had been in the rain a long time;

even his sheepskin jerkin seemed to be sodden. The dog followed closely at the pony's flanks. The man held the pony with one hand; on the other, gloved, was perched the bird. Now the bird was not so still as it had been in the beech wood. It turned its head from side to side; but it made no attempt to fly up from its master's hand, hardly seeming to need the bright red streamers that attached it. I pressed closer to the glass, straining to see the strange procession. The bird danced a little on the glove, and I had the sensation that its bright hawk's eyes noted me; but the man did not look up. They moved on past the house and the distillery building, along the road that led up the strath. I followed their progress for as long as I could, longer than it took for the pony's light tread to fade into silence. Then the mist shut them off. I was alone again.

Now, to close out the mist and the emptiness I drew the curtains and lighted my candle. Then I turned to the task of unpacking. But even with the opening of the trunk I gave up the idea. Fatigue had been fought too long, and the whisky was almost drug-like in its effect. I fumbled among my clothes and found my night shift. I washed, and gave my hair a perfunctory brush; would I ever be convinced that it was worth the hundred strokes at night? A strong sense of depression was settling on me, in the way the mist had crept down from the heights of Ballochtorra. I laid more turf on the fire just for the comfort of seeing the flames leap up, and was ready to climb into bed when the notion came suddenly to me. I think it was born of the loneliness engulfing me – the frightening conviction that I had come all this way for nothing – without real purpose. I needed now urgently to touch someone or something that was familiar and loved, to drive away the sense of loss. I went back to the trunk and felt about in its depths until I found the box laid so carefully among the layers of my clothes. It came out, and in the candlelight the rich polish of the inlaid wood seemed more beautiful than ever before. I took the contents out tenderly; the figures lay securely each in their carved and padded niches within the box. When they were all out I turned the box over and opened the hinges wide; the chessboard was not flat, the hinges sunk so that they were out of sight, and the box itself was the playing surface. Then I laid the pieces on their squares – lining up the Queens and Knights, the Castles and the Kings, the Pawns forming their protective ranks before them. There was comfort just to hold these things, a feeling of order restored. It brought back to me sharply the thought that whatever happened, the game of life was still there, and the strongest game was always played by the attacker.

It was a chess set of great beauty and rarity – certainly, I believed, the most valuable thing I owned. It had been given to me by William, who had received it in thanks for a favour done by him for one of the Mandarin class. Neither of us could have put a price on it, and I had never asked William what he had done to have such a reward. It was one of the rarities of China – the 'rat' chess set, carved of Indian ivory, with all of the pieces having the bodies and faces of rats, but clothed in the costume of medieval China, the long gowns, the fans, the Knights mounted on richly caparisoned horses. Amber and ruby eyes gave them an astonishingly lifelike appearance. It had been made, William said, more than a hundred years ago. 'Take it, Little Sister,' he had said lightly. 'It may be the only dowry you ever have.' We made jokes about being poor; clearly William did not believe he would remain poor. He was clever and quick; he would come back to China with an engineering degree and help build her railways; we had seen too many fortunes made in China trade not to be infected with the belief that William might do it also. We were children of a clergyman, but we were realists.

With the pieces set up in their ranks, my hands grew restless. I began taking them off and setting them aside. It was madness what I was doing, but I couldn't help it. My fingers traced the moves of that last game with William – for some reason they seemed burned into my memory. Piece by piece, as the game progressed, my forces had fallen to William's. And then we reached the last move – it had been bold, and I had not seen it coming. Swiftly, William's hand with the Knight, and a little, triumphant laugh. 'Check to the Queen, Kirsty! Now puzzle that one out, Little Sister.' And he had gone off, chuckling, to some appointment. This had been shortly before he left Peking to begin the long journey to Edinburgh. There never had been time for another game, and in the weeks after he had gone I had not disturbed the pieces, and I had known there was no way out of the check. With the Queen taken, the King must fall. The check was complete.

The time had passed, and I had played with my father, or practised moves by myself, solved chess problems from books, determined to show William how I had improved when he returned. And it had all been wiped out. First my father's death, and then the letter from Cluain. The sympathetic voices of friends had murmured, 'Stay here, Kirsty. China is all you have ever known. In time you'll marry here . . . Stay, Kirsty . . .'

But I knew I would go. With the letter about William's death had come the scroll. I saw the crimson characters scrawled along its length – not much like William's careful rendering. And yet they could only have been made by William. I had translated them in my own rough fashion, and then, not believing my senses, had carried the scroll to my father's translator, a scholar of both Chinese and Manchu. He had shaken his head. 'It does not make true sense – your brother's thoughts were not concentrated.' Truth, or imagination, once the doubt had been aroused, I knew I must go. The wind was blowing away from China. My time there was over. I bent, as he said I should before the wind. 'Check to the Queen, Kirsty.' The game was done.

I was tired almost beyond thinking, but rest would not come. I went to the window that overlooked the garden, and drew back the curtain. The light from a candle in the dining-room cast the faintest glow beyond the window. My grandfather was still there. Perhaps tonight, in the desperation of fatigue, was the only time I would have the courage to ask what I had come to know. I let the curtain fall, and then I went back to the chest. For a moment my fingers closed over the box that held the scroll, and other things of William's which had been sent back to me – papers belonging to him, draftsman's instruments in their velvet-lined case, a silver watch, a collar stud. Not much else. William had still been poor. And then I released my hold. Time enough – the characters on the scroll would mean nothing to Angus Macdonald. First I would hear his own account of how William had died.

I pulled out my robe. It struck me again that it was also red – that favourite Chinese colour. A red silk robe, padded with layers of cotton against the Peking winters, high-necked, in the Chinese style with bands of embroidery at the neck and wide sleeves. Such garments had been cheap for Westerners to buy in China; in this setting it seemed outlandishly rich and foreign. I could not help it. This was all I had. My grandfather would have to accept it, as I must accept so much about Cluain I did not yet understand.

The soft-soled slippers made no sound upon the stairs. When I lifted the latch of the dining-room door his head was still bent over what absorbed him at the table. His eyebrows came together in a frown of enquiry – almost annoyance.

'Well?' Again there was no welcome in his tone, I was an intruder into the solitude of his years, the thousands of nights he had sat here alone.

Slowly now I advanced towards him. He had only a single candle beside him, and it flickered subtly over the polish of the chessboard which he had moved here to the centre of the big table. Here was no reflection of the richness of the one I had left upstairs; it was a plain board, and the pieces upon it were plain, with no decoration but the shape needed to identify each one; I recognized the classic Staunton set, the sturdy, weighted pieces of boxwood and ebony that the fingers could grip firmly, and the player could hear the decisive, satisfying rap of wood upon wood as he moved his piece. It was on such a set as this that William had taught me to play.

I laid my candle on the other side of the board and the shadows cast by the chessmen raced together and joined. The fierce old eyes looked at me across them. Unbidden, I drew out a chair and seated myself opposite him.

'You played with William?'

'I did.'

'Did he win?'

'Aye – he had a head on him, my grandson. A head I could have used for Cluain.'

'I would like to know how William died. I came here to learn that – to hear it from you.'

'I told in my letter how he died. What does it matter – since he is dead? All men must, in their time. His was before his time – when I had need of him.'

That, almost more than anything, was what made him bitter. He could not forgive William for dying because he had needed him; he had begun to believe that William was seduced away from China, away from my father and myself, and it might have been true. And then William had died and had cheated him. Had he ever loved William, or merely needed him?

The silence between us was heavy. The true darkness had come now, and the light of our separate candles and the glow of the dying fire was the only thing that warmed Cluain. And then, as my eyes dropped from the old man's, lest he should see my yearning for William, and for some comfort and companionship, I looked closely at the chessboard, taking in for the first time the disposition of the pieces – those that were set to the side of the board, and those that still remained. The familiarity I had sought asserted itself, the pattern I knew too well. Only one move remained.

I reached out and took up the Knight and placed it swiftly. 'Check to the Queen.'

Now our eyes met again in a look of dawning wonderment, of recognition.

'He played that game with you?' I said.

He nodded.

It was as if a wind had stirred in that quiet room, a cold draught had swirled about us. Somewhere, from back in time and beyond death, William had reached to us. He had played this game with us both, and both had reached the impasse which must acknowledge his victory.

'Was it the last game he played with you?'

'Aye.'

'With me, also.'

And now the silence was more than before; in it we knew we shared a bond, and for the first time we felt we shared our blood. William was there between us, strong, living. Who could believe he was dead when he was so forcibly with us? It was as if he himself had drawn me here, to be his instrument, his tool, to play the game as he had taught it to me, to attack, to dare, to seize and use what came in life. What he had not said, but what his life implied, was that when one went before the wind, one also used the wind. I was here because of him. His life was over, but mine was not.

'I would like a dram, Grandfather.'

For a moment I saw the lids close on those faded, but still burning eyes. I thought a shudder racked that strong body, and then the shoulders seemed to say even more. It was as if he were touched by a force he did not fully comprehend, but could not now withstand. Wordlessly he rose from his chair and went to the sideboard. He poured a good measure into two glasses and returned and set them each beside the candles. Then he raised his glass to me in slight salute.

'You were sent. I did not perceive it, but now I know. William has sent you. Welcome to Cluain.'

I returned his gesture, and we both drank. This time it was not strange, or burning; the peaty taste was only the essence of the smell of the peat fire burning here and in my room. The comfort I had sought was in his words, spoken at last, and in the warmth that slid through me with the liquid. I allowed it to carry away my fatigue and my loneliness. I thought of how many times William must have sat where I sat now, the candles burning the chessmen set out before them both, and the glass of whisky to each hand. Was it right to believe that someone could reach from beyond death to bring two people together like this? – was it tampering with forces that neither of us understood to try to invoke his name and his spirit? Was it an evil or a benign contact that we made? Were not such things forbidden? Forbidden or not, we both believed it was William who had drawn me here – inexplicably drawn together this old man with hunger in his eyes, and myself, hungry in my own fashion. The instrument of the contact had been the chessmen. William's hand had lain on these pieces, as it had done on those upstairs. He seemed to move them at his will – as he had surely brought me to this meeting. Strangely, I did not feel afraid. If William, though dead, was our bond, then let it be. There could be no evil where there had been love.

I looked at the old man and knew that the veil of indifference had been removed. He seemed to see me for the first time, and yet he was also looking at something, or someone, beyond me.

'Aye – you have the look of him, even. And I did not see it. It was as though I were blind. All I saw was a wee lass. I did not look . . . I didn't see.'

'Then tell me how he died.'

'Died? – he died. I wrote that in the letter.'

'You did not say how.'

'A hunting accident. I wrote it . . .'

'You did not write it. William had never been hunting in his life.'

'Och, I did not mean the English kind of hunting. Did you imagine this is country to set a horse at a gallop after a fox? No, he went with a gun after birds, or rabbits, or some such thing. A young man out for a walk with a gun.'

'We do not carry guns in China – no one who is not military. We are careful to try not to give offence – we are the Foreign Devils, and William had the peculiar position of being a bishop's son. I doubt that he had handled a gun in his life . . .'

'Here it is different. Every man will snare or trap or shoot to add to his family larder. Most will poach when they can. They must. Life is hard. And if you are rich you do it for sport. The Prince of Wales comes here to shoot . . .'

'William was not the Prince of Wales. Who was with him?'

The big head sagged as if with the weight of guilt. 'That was it. There was no one with him. He did not know it was a foolish thing to do. He did not tell anyone that he was going with a gun. He used often to take long walks. But only the most experienced here go with a gun. There was no time for him to learn.'

'You didn't warn him?' I accused.

His reply was submissive, as though in accepting me, he would deny me nothing now, not even the price of his own conscience. 'Perhaps not enough. It is hard, when you are old, to remember that a young man does not know all the terrain, cannot find his way in mist and rain. He was foolhardy to go so much alone, but

could I hold back a young man of spirit? Would I question him as
to his comings and goings?'

'No – you could not. Not William. Then how did he die?'

He sighed. 'That visit he intended only staying a few days – it
was all the time he could spare from the university. On the second
evening he was missing. He did not return when he usually came.
It was early November, and the evenings were very short then.
But I did not worry too much – he had made himself welcome in
a number of places up and down the strath, and he often tarried
in one or the other. But by the time supper was finished I knew
something was amiss. And then I checked the guns. He had taken
one. I was not sure he even knew how to use it. We could not set
out to search in the dark, but by dawn – and dawn comes late in
November – every man on the place, every household along the
strath – and aye, even every servant at Ballochtorra who had the
sense to keep upright on the moor had turned out to search for
him.'

'How long?' I could dispense with the details of the search.

'Two nights he was out. For one not bred to wrap himself in a
plaid, and make a bed from the heather and bracken, it was bitter
suffering. It was cold, lass. Even for us, it was cold. The second
night there was some snow. And he had the gun-shot wound in
his knee. He could never have walked.'

'You found him – where?'

'Close by. That was what near killed me. He had somehow
crawled into a rock opening in the crag up there by Ballochtorra.
Only a slight shelter from the cold and snow – and he had gone
unconscious. Not able to cry for help. We had believed he had
gone farther afield, and were searching up on the mountain.
Indeed, it was a wee bit of kitchen boy from Ballochtorra that
found him, trying to help with the search, but not daring to be
away from his post too long – not strong enough to go with the
men sent out by Campbell. We brought him back and I got a
surgeon from Inverness to remove the bullet – I did not trust the
man here not to bungle it. But we could all see that the fever did
not go down. I sent for a man from Edinburgh. By the time he
came, William was dead.'

I was relentless, even though I could see that each word seemed
to scar him as it came. 'How long?'

'Three or four days. He was nursed devotedly. Mistress Sinclair
did not sleep in all that time – as I did not, even though I went to
my bed. But the wound, and the exposure . . . Stronger men than
William have gone down before such things.'

'But the wounding? How did it happen?'

'He could not talk when we found him. His gun had been fired. He did not know about guns – how to treat them, how to handle them when walking in rough places. He shot himself.'

'He shot himself!'

He sighed. "Tis too easy to do when a man walks with a loaded gun in rough places. Those who should know better have done it. Could I blame him too much? But I did blame him. Folly, it was! A life wasted . . . my grandson's life.'

I held tightly to the glass. 'Did he recover consciousness at all? Did he ever speak of how it happened?'

'There were periods when he talked – but they were wild words, not to be understood. And Mistress Sinclair told us not to encourage him to talk, for it took his strength. What was the use to question him, or blame him – then? It was better to leave him in peace.'

In peace. The words on the scroll gave no impression of peace. 'It was up there he died? In the tower room?'

'Aye. I had had him put there when he first came to Cluain. I wanted him to know the feeling of being master of it – to be able to look over lands that he could call his own. And when Mistress Sinclair suggested preparing another room on the lower floor while the search was going on, so that it should be easier to nurse him, I would not permit it. I did not want him to wake up to some strange place. He had his few things there – I would not let her touch or tidy them. All the time the search was on she kept a fire high, and the bed warm and ready. She had her medicines ready, and she is better than any doctor in that way. But it was not to be. He came, and he was gone, so quickly. I had come to believe that the dearest desire of my heart was to be given to me. Vengeance is mine, sayeth the Lord. I knew then that I would have no joy in my old age.'

'Why vengeance?'

He rubbed his hand wearily over his eyes. 'Do not ask, Gurrl. Is there any man who has not done that on which judgement will be passed? Who shall not pay in the end?'

'God is merciful. He is a God of love as well as vengeance. My father always taught us that.'

His lips twisted in a bitter disclaimer. 'A comfortable philosophy for those who can let themselves believe it. For those who think they are without sin. The past is not undone. It is forever.'

My hand went forward and I let my fingers play over the figure of the Queen on the board, held frozen, it seemed, by that perpetual check from the Knight, held forever.

'There is the future, too,' I said quietly. 'The future is not yet written. It lies with us.'

'When William went I knew there would be no future. I did not care.'

'*I* care. I am William's sister, and a part of him still lives with me,' I cried. 'He would never have let me believe that there is no future.'

'There, Gurrl, do not take on so. Perhaps you're right – perhaps so. But finish up your dram with me, and take yourself off to bed. It's rest you need. And do not be afraid of your room and your bed because it was the place where William died. I would not have put you there myself, but Mistress Sinclair had made the arrangements . . .'

I finished the last of the whisky in a quick, angry swallow, and did not choke on it. 'I will never be afraid of any place where William was. And if he died there, then I am that much closer to him. My father also taught us that. Love is stronger than fear.' I thrust my chair back from the table, and reached for the candle. He almost let me go, but as I lifted the latch, the commanding words came.

'Wait, Gurrl!'

'What is it?'

'Do not be in such a hurry. Perhaps you are right. Perhaps there is a future, though I cannot see it myself. It is not in my ken.' Now his tone altered to a persuasive pitch it had never possessed before. 'Kirsty . . .' My name for the first time. 'Kirsty, find and wed a man that I can feel would have been William's equal. Find that man, Kirsty, and Cluain shall be yours.'

My hand trembled violently; the shadows darted all over the room. 'That is an impossible bargain! You are asking something of me I have no way of knowing that I can fulfil. A man! – *what* man? And why should the man I marry have to be measured against William? Every man has a right to be himself, not another man's shadow. No – there can be no such bargain, Grandfather.'

But he did not believe me. 'Go to your bed. In the morning you will see. In the morning you will see that Cluain is worth the having.'

'In the morning – in the morning I may leave!'

He merely shrugged. 'Please yourself.'

In the quiet of the house the sound was very loud as I pulled the door closed, and let the latch fall.

She was waiting for me. She stood on the first step of the spiral stair within the tower. She had probably been watching through the slit window the pale light that had come from our candles into the garden. She held her own lighted candle, and she must have stood there for a long time, for it was burned nearly to its end, as mine was. I went towards her, and she did not step down, so that I was forced to raise my face to hers.

'Mistress Sinclair . . . ?'

She did not wear her black to bed. A plain white shift, severely buttoned to the throat, was partly covered by a long red plaid. Her hair was unbound, the black streaked with shining silver; it softened the stark good looks, made her seem younger – no, not younger, but without age. The roughened hand clenched and unclenched the plaid across her breast.

'You have been speaking together for a long time,' she said at last. And then, as if she could not hold the words back. 'What about? – *what about?*'

'My business, Mistress Sinclair.'

'*What* business?' Her eyes were wild, anguished.

'Please step aside, Mistress Sinclair. I wish to go to my room.'

Her hand let go the plaid, and reached out and clutched my wrist with fierce strength. '*Tell me* – what business?' The candle jerked with her pull, and the hot grease splattered down on my hand. I smothered the exclamation of pain.

'Step aside!'

She had not anticipated my own strength. Now my hand reached up and caught her shoulder, and pulled her down off that first step. The way ahead was clear, and I went quickly, gathering my robe so I would not trip. Still she would not leave me. When she recovered I could hear her coming after me, a few steps behind, but at least the twist of one spiral away. The candlelight pursued me, and told me how close she was. I reached the door of my room and flung it open. But she was there before I could close it properly. I put the weight of my shoulder against it as she grasped at the latch.

The haunted, staring face was almost witch-like now, the beauty gone in a look of madness. For a moment longer she pushed against the door, and the insane, silent struggle continued. Then at last she seemed to crumble, as if some force had deserted her. She stepped back; the pressure came off my shoulder, and the door crashed against its frame. It was held open just by the thickness of the massive iron latch. Through the tiny space I heard her whisper, a plaintive, almost pleading sigh.

'It is not yours . . .'

I should have slammed the door shut and found safety. But I needed answers. 'What? – what is not mine?'

'Cluain. Cluain is not yours!' It was a wailing, sobbing protest.

She was mad – quite mad. I lifted the latch and it fell into place. Then I slid the bolt home with trembling fingers. I turned and leaned against the door, and breathed a sigh of thankfulness that for the moment I was beyond her reach. My body sagged as I waited for my heart to cease its pounding. Then, when I did not hear her steps retreating, I listened more intently. The whisper reached me through the stout planks of the door, and the words were accompanied by an eerie scratching, as if her nails clawed at the wood.

'*Cluain is not yours.*'

The intensity of the words struck me with terror. I gasped, and my body slid down the door until I was crouched on the floor. I laid down the shrunken stub of the candle, and rubbed my hand where the grease had burned, and her terrible, plucking fingers had dug into my flesh. But she heard me, and she must have bent also. The whisper came again, close to my ear. '*It is not yours!*'

I stayed there, unable to move. I did not know how long. I watched the candle begin to drown in the pool of its own grease . . . slowly, slowly. The wild hammering of my heart would not shut out that horrible whisper. '*It is not yours!*'

Then the flame flickered erratically, and died. At last I heard the soft footsteps in retreat down the stairs. But the words would not leave me.

I was stiff and cramped before I had the strength to gather myself up and find my way by the light of the last embers of the fire to the desk where a new candle stood ready. When it flared up and steadied, I went back to the chest and once more sought the box in which I had brought William's few things. I carried the scroll and the candle and went to the bench before the fire; I took time to lay a few sticks of kindling on the embers, and I huddled there for some time, listening – listening and hearing nothing. The smell of peat was the smell of Cluain, its fires and the essence of its golden, smoky whisky. I held my hand before that small blaze, but it seemed to have no warmth.

At last I made myself turn and take up the scroll. It had a slender bamboo rod at each end, and a red silk ribbon with which to hang it. Every knot of the bamboo, every fine line of the drawing was now more familiar to me than any other thing I had ever owned. How many hundreds – perhaps thousands – of times had I searched and examined and studied it. Its message had always been unclear, but now I thought I knew the terrible, desperate urgency with which William had sought to communicate. His mind had been clouded with fever and drugs. How had he managed to escape her surveillance long enough to stroke these characters with his brush? How had he managed, on that injured leg, even to drag himself as far as the desk? In a moment of lucidity – or in a fevered return to the lessons of his childhood, he had gone back to the language he had struggled to master in preparation for a lifetime in China. What William did, I also had always to follow, and I had tried to learn it as well. Had his wits been sharper than they had supposed, his strength greater, so that he had written it deliberately in a language that no one in this household could read? But he had known, when he dipped the brush in the vermilion ink – and the pain of this seared me as if I had thrust my hand into the fire – he had known by then that this would be his last message. And he had written it with the hope that my father and I would read it. It was a message he had never been able to complete.

I had puzzled over it so long, convinced that it was my own lack of scholarship that defeated me. But the translator had done nothing to help my bewilderment. He had shaken his head. 'Young Master has forgotten his lessons. He does not take trouble any more. The characters are untidy – mean little.' I had known my first frustration all over again. There are thousands of characters in the Mandarin language – and a thousand implications contained within each character. Chinese etiquette demands that nothing shall be said directly. How impossible to set down a simple, urgent message. We puzzled over it, the translator and I – he so much more expert, and yet so much more inhibited because of that. He had hardly dared say the words that had been my first reading of the characters.

'Your esteemed brother – he can hardly have been well.'

'How do you know?'

He shrugged. 'Untidy – not like him. Confused. The reading is not clear.'

'Tell me – tell me what you think he says!'

His elegant scholar's finger followed down the characters splashed on the edge of the stiff parchment; his anxious eyes had looked sideways at me.

'I think he says . . .'

'He says *what*?'

'I think he says . . . *"She has killed –"*'

3

The morning had an overwhelming normality about it. Morag woke me bringing the jug of hot water. Impossible, except for the splatter of candlegrease around the door, to believe what had happened the night before. I came up from sleep as if it had been a comfortable womb – slowly, with reluctance. Only the fact that I had to get out of bed to slide back the bolt brought Mairi Sinclair to mind.

'Och,' Morag greeted me, 'there's no need to be bolting doors around here. Who's to come in?'

She must consider me foolish and silly. 'I – I didn't think.'

'It's that heathen place you've come from. Well, let me tell you, there's nothing at Cluain to be afraid of. Well, now, there's your water. Mistress Sinclair said to let you sleep a mite longer this morning, because you would be tired after your journey. But she doesn't like to be kept waiting too long with washing the dishes, so I'd hurry if I were you ...'

The cheerful patter continued while she stripped back the bed-clothes with quick, competent movements; obviously everything was performed with great thoroughness at Cluain. Morag was well trained, but her chores didn't interfere with her talk. She talked of everything that came to mind – the red Chinese robe, exclaiming at its beauty, and how strangely it was fashioned; the fineness of the day, the sun already high and beginning to have warmth; the sky was washed a clear blue. 'A great growing day, it is, mistress ...' And then she added, with a touch of wistfulness as if with memories of a summer childhood when household duties had not pressed so urgently, 'A day to be running in the meadows. Mistress Sinclair will be out in the hedgerows gathering her wild flowers ...' With her words I heard the soft sigh of the breeze, the cries of the birds, the river in full spate after last night's rain. The world of Cluain about me was fair and beautiful; it was as my grand-father had said it would be. There was no mist and no mystery. As I washed, even the sight of Ballochtorra perched on its crag seemed a part of memory, a sort of drawing of a fairy-tale castle in a child's picture book ... there would be a princess with golden hair. I dressed, and kept telling myself that last night had been a dream, the confusion of fatigue and whisky. But as I went again to the door, the spots of grease declared quite plainly that it had

6

been no dream. On the spiral stair, though, they had been removed. There was no evidence now of that insane struggle.

The dining-room was empty, but my place was laid. There was hot porridge in a tureen, fish cakes, rashers of bacon, fried eggs – all kept hot over spirit lamps. Angus Macdonald ate a hearty breakfast, if this was his usual fare, and for a lone man he lived in some style. But I was not hungry; I took some fresh brown bread and a pot of honey, and tea. As I ate, I thought about Mairi Sinclair. What gifts the woman had, and how perversely she displayed them. The bread would be of her baking; she must supervise the dairy which provided the sweet, rich goodness of the butter. The honey was the best I had ever tasted – I thought of the bees droning lazily over the herb garden, giving the honey its wild, aromatic flavour. I thought of the lean herds of China, and the sleek cattle I had seen yesterday; I thought of the spiced, exotic dishes the Chinese ate, and the plain goodness of the food here. It should have come from the hands of a plump, comfortable, house-proud woman, gossiping as Morag did. And I kept remembering the haunted, anguished face of the woman the night before, afraid of something much more than the invasion of her kingdom by another female. She did not fear just for her place here, but for Cluain itself.

But whatever graces and gifts she had, she had another side, and I must both face it and ignore it. I would have to go in to her in the kitchen now, and wait to see how she reacted to me. Was last night some aberration she would prefer forgotten? – or would we continue as we had left off? And between us, forever, stood those unforgettable words on William's scroll. One day I would charge her with them – with them, and nothing else. And she might shrug her shoulders, indifferent and calm, and claim it was the ramblings of a fevered brain. And what did they mean, after all, and who was accused? I sighed, now more puzzled than at any time since I had first deciphered the characters. Knowing Cluain and the woman had made nothing easier or more clear.

For a while after I had eaten I wandered uncertainly about the room, lingering over the small task of loading the breakfast dishes on the tray, trying to spin out the time before I dared to face her in the kitchen – her own, indisputable domain. But there was so little in this room – so bare, so stark. The last century and a half might not have been, if one could believe one's eyes. No picture of my grandfather, or my mother; no sewing basket, no writing table, no animal by the hearth. Outside the birds sang and the herbs waved; inside it was static, a set piece. I paused before the

table which held the chess set. Last night's game, and its moment
of revelation, might never have been. I fingered the White Queen
in a moment of disbelief; but it had happened – it had. Then my
hands moved on to the Bible. It probably was very old; the leather
was drying out, even with the polishing. The brass corners and
clasp shone. Then I tried to open it. It was, as I should have
known, locked.

It was then I took up the big silver tray and started for the
kitchen.

The dining-room opened into a passage, and the kitchen door
was opposite. Close by was a door that led to the garden, and on
the other side the passage twisted out of sight around the curve
of the tower. A door back there would lead down to the river, and
the path I had seen from my window going around to the stables
and the distillery. On the stone floor, beside a bench, was ranged
a neat row of boots. Tweed coats and capes hung in a line above
them. As in all farms, few of the household entered by the front
door and crossed that shining wood surface. I steadied the tray
on one hand, and reached for the latch on the kitchen door.
Instinctively I had drawn in my breath, making myself ready to
look into Mairi Sinclair's face.

But it was her voice I heard. And it was raised to a pitch of
intensity I knew too well – not a tone she would have used to
Morag in giving her instructions, or chiding her about the day's
tasks. This was something deeply felt, and important.

'Och, it sickens me to see you hang about like this! Here it is
gone late in the day, and the Master's been at work since early.
Don't you *care* – now more than ever?'

The answer was slow, heavy with scorn. A man's voice, deep,
hardly concerned with the answer he gave her. 'Och, hush you.
Everything's in good order, and will be when we start distilling
again. What's there to do at this time? God Almighty, we've only
just finished after a long winter's work. You know right well we'll
not be distilling again until the barley's harvested and the weather
settles colder. From now on, my time's my own.'

Her furious voice cut him short. 'And what kind of farmer are
you that there's nothing to be attended to? The cattle are up in
the shielings to look to, the tackroom's full of harness to be mended,
the fences to be inspected. Does a farmer ever have time to call his
own? You and your roaming ways – will you never have done
with them? Never showing yourself near the farmyard. What does
the Master think of you . . . ?'

His exasperation was plain. 'Och, enough! *You* go and gather your eggs or make your butter or whatever else it is that you must next do for Cluain. *I've* earned my days to myself, and earned them right well, and he knows it. If I've a mind, on a day like this, to take some bread and ale and time to myself to walk where I want, then I'll do it, and no man will tell me else. He knows what I do for Cluain – well he knows it, and he doesn't dare question what I choose to do when there's no need for me about the place. He has other men who can mend the fences, and herd the cattle on the shielings – and plenty of that I've done in my time. Let him whistle to the wind for me, and I'll come when I'm right and ready.'

'It is not wise. Only a fool neglects his opportunities . . .'

'Wisdom, is it? Oh, God, your head's stuffed full of knowledge, and not an ounce of wisdom in it. When you walk along the roads and watch for your herbs and flowers, do you ever think to raise your eyes to see what's above you? Do you ever stop to listen to the birds, to watch their flight? Or do you only look to see where they've left their eggs? Well, if that's so, I'm sorry for you. I've no intention in the world of spending my life serving one man. I'll serve myself first, and then see what comes – '

'Tis Cluain will suffer . . .'

'Let it.' The words were final, and measured.

'Have you lost your senses?'

'Perhaps, but no great loss.'

The silence fell between them, as if she had heard more than she could answer. I listened to the banging of iron pans, a mark of speechless fury. I used the noise as a chance to rattle the china a little on the tray, and fumble at the latch. Mairi Sinclair was there in an instant; the door was flung open as she confronted me. She made a swift movement to take the tray from my hand, but I swept past her as if I had not seen the gesture.

'You have some magic with the bees, Mistress Sinclair. It is the best honey I have ever tasted.'

'I was coming to take the dishes – '

'No need, surely. Are you so grand at Cluain that I may not come into the kitchen? After all, you have the right to *my* room.'

She met my thrust in silence. I went on past her, to the big scrubbed table in the middle of the flagstoned room, putting down the tray with exaggerated gentleness. It was only then that I allowed myself to look around.

He stood leaning against the mantel, but his shoulders came higher than the shelf; it was not the face I recognized, because it had been nearly lost to me in the dimness under the beeches, and last evening he had bent his head before the rain. But the figure was unmistakable; even in the heat of the dispute with Mairi Sinclair his body had yet retained its quality of stillness, of being contained within itself – the same as when he had stood with the dog and the bird on his gloved hand, the self-containment of the man alone in the rain. He wore the faded red kilt – or perhaps another one, for this seemed dry – a shabby, almost ragged garment, and long socks knitted in the same pattern; I was startled to see a dagger – I would later learn to call it a dirk – thrust into the band of the sock by his right hand. The sheepskin jerkin was slung across a chair, the shoulders still dark with moisture. He was holding a tankard with both hands, which he lowered slowly from his lips. It was the same kind of prideful indifference I had seen displayed in so many small ways since I had come. Clearly this man was not in the habit of springing to attention.

I returned his stare without letting my eyelids flicker. If he thought he could stare me down, let him try. He was more than ordinarily handsome; he must have known it – but from his attitude and his dress he didn't seem to care if anyone else should be impressed with the fact. He seemed too rigorously bent on telling all the world that he was free of its opinion. Was there some lingering thought in his mind that anyone would doubt it? His skin was oddly white for a man who was used to the outdoors – a natural whiteness, not a pallor. Everything else was black – the tumble of rough hair, the straight hard black line of his brows – from this distance it seemed that even his eyes were black. The line of his mouth matched his brows, a face cut deeply by the horizontals of brows and eyes and mouth. There was no softness to be discovered in body or face.

And then, with great deliberation, with me looking at him, he set the tankard on the mantelshelf, and picked up the sheepskin. He nodded, not to me, but to Mairi Sinclair.

'I'll be away, then.'

I watched in a kind of stunned disbelief at the studied rudeness of the gesture as he went to the kitchen door, opened it, and closed it, not with a bang, but not gently, either. He must have known who I was; obviously he was an intimate of Cluain. This was not just an absence of welcome, but a complete rejection.

I had to ask her, though my lips were stiff with fury and outraged pride.

'Who – who was that?'

I thought she took some pleasure in the insult he had offered, and her own pride came thrusting up. I knew from that moment

I would likely never speak of what had happened last night. In the broad light of day, this woman was not weak, and would not be intimidated.

'Who? That was Callum Sinclair. My son.'

And then, with no more concern than her son had displayed, she went to the door and took down a black shawl from its hook. She went out, as he had done, without a further sign to me, but she was not hurrying after him. A moment later, from the windows of the kitchen, I saw her in a leisurely but purposeful stroll along the flagged path of the garden. She walked a few paces, paused, bent to touch or smell; for a moment I thought I saw her lips move as if she spoke to those plants, and their nodding in the breeze was their answer. In those minutes she seemed to me to become a different creature. Her body lost its rigidness; her waist and neck and head seemed to bend and sway with the grace of a beautiful woman; she moved as the plants did. And, it seemed natural, the cat was there also, running before her, the white body disappearing into the grey of the lavender, the colourless eyes peering from the tall thyme. She paid no attention to the cat, nor he to her, but they were a pair, a company. They were supreme in a kind of splendid isolation.

'Well, then – that's Callum Sinclair for you.'

Morag stood in a doorway that led, I guessed, to a scullery beyond. She was wiping her hands in her apron.

'And his mother,' I added. How easily I had slipped into the role of friend with this girl, her manner so easy, frank, without servility, but without presumption. Did this natural dignity belong here to this people, to this country?

'Och, aye – his mother. 'Tis his father they'll never be knowing.'

'Dead?'

She shrugged. 'Who knows? They do tell me that when Callum Sinclair was born here at Cluain – here, in this kitchen, I think – his mother seemed near to death, and Mistress Macdonald, who had taken her in at Cluain out of charity when no one else would, urged her to say who was the father, so that her child could have a name, and a claim on some kin. But she never spoke, and she lived, and no one has ever known, or dared guess – before her face, that is – who is the father of Callum Sinclair. And it is my own opinion that whoever they might have guessed and riddled then, none of them ever did know the answer. It was nearly thirty years ago, and since then Mairi Sinclair has become a much respected woman in these parts. No one ever talks about it any more. For sure, there has been no other man, for all have observed her like hawks. Let once a woman fall, and she is never free of the eyes and the tongues again.'

'Did she have no family, then? – at that time?'

'Mistress Howard, I was not born then, and by the time I had grown in curiosity, people were already forgetting – save the odd old woman who will be forever talking about things past. I have not much time for those kind of people myself, but my mother was a great one for collecting stories, and since she did not care for Mistress Sinclair, she made it her business to know all that could be known of this one.'

'So . . . ?'

Morag lifted her shoulders. 'Well, they do say that she lived alone with her father, the only child still left to him. A terrible hard man, they said, very close with his money, and never giving company or a dram to anyone. They were poor – or so he made out to be. Mairi Sinclair worked very hard, but he sent her to the little school down here in the strath. A long trudge it was – and work to do on the croft in the evenings, and a cow to milk before setting out in the mornings. Very prideful, her father was, and he could not abide the disgrace of his daughter being with child and unwed. They say he beat her until she was like to have died. The wonder is that she did not miscarry of the child – perhaps that's what he intended. That's the way some men are, mistress – too many of them. He put her from his door, and for a time she stayed with neighbours until she got her strength again. But they were a big poor family, sending children off to Canada and Australia, and it was no place for her to stay. She was bound for Inverness herself when Mistress Macdonald invited her to stay at Cluain. She was a very kind woman, your grandmother. There was something said at the time that the Master did not want her here, but your grandmother overruled him. I suppose Mistress Sinclair was a strange woman, even then, and her father was not liked. But she came, having no place else to go, and she stayed, and Callum Sinclair was born at Cluain. Och, she kept herself to herself after that and tended her child, and gave herself to Cluain as if she could never do enough for it. There were never any complaints about Mairi Sinclair. She read her Bible and soon there was Mistress Macdonald sending off to Edinburgh for books about herbs for her, because she seemed to have a natural skill with them. The Mistress encouraged Mairi Sinclair to write down her own records – how much of this and that she used in brews. They say she had a grandmother who was gifted in that way, but she was an unlettered woman, so the recipes were never set down. The boy – Callum – was clever too, and Mistress Macdonald could not be stopped from sending off for special books for him also, as he grew. Remember, it would not have been long after Mairi Sinclair came to Cluain that your own mother was up and off to China, and perhaps your grandmother was lonely. And as the Mistress was poorly in health, in time she began to pass more and more of the running of Cluain into Mairi Sinclair's hands. At the time the Mistress died, there was no change at Cluain – it went on as it had done before. There never was a better run household in the whole of Speyside, and the people were coming for years past to Mairi Sinclair for her skill with the herbs. They would even send for her when there was difficulty with a cow in calf, and the like. Stronger than a man, they said, and more gentle. She can soothe beasts with her very words – a soft tongue she has with anything that is dumb. No one ever questioned her staying on here after your grandmother died. Angus Macdonald would have been mad to let her go. People had long ago been saying that Andrew Sinclair had done himself a great disservice by sending her from his house. He had lost a rare woman.'

'Were they never reconciled?'

'Never, mistress, never. He could never bring himself to speak to her again, and, indeed, in time, I thought she would not have wanted it. So bitter he was – probably more bitter because she had turned out so well – that he did not even leave his wee bit of land to her or his grandson. It was left to some far cousin off in London, or some such place, who never bothered even to come and sell it. 'Twas only a poor bit of land, after all, with the gorse growing in on it, and fit only for a few sheep. But poor as it was, Mairi Sinclair was not to have it. The wee house on it fell into ruin, and the land was left go wild. They do say the cousin wanted to sell it, but none about here would buy – out of respect for Mistress Sinclair. They do say, also – though I can't tell if it is true – that to this day Mairi Sinclair has never set foot on her father's land again. And could you wonder at it?'

Absently, Morag moved to the range, and took a teapot off the hob. 'Will you be having more tea, mistress? Och no – ' as I held my cup from the tray towards her, 'I'll bring you a fresh one. Mistress Sinclair is a great one for doing things right. No sloppy ways in her kitchen.' Her eyes widened as I refused milk and sugar. 'That's a very strange way to drink tea.'

'Most people in China drink it that way,' I replied, as absently as she had begun her own action. She stood by the range with her thick kitchen cup stirring the sugar vigorously, and I had my fresh cup of fine china, but there hardly seemed to be any difference between us. I was finding a kind of democracy of independent spirits át Cluain.

'They say,' Morag continued, nodding towards the dark figure pacing the garden, 'that the Master offered to pay for Callum Sinclair's schooling, when he had outgrown what the local dominie could offer, for he was a very bright lad. But Mistress Sinclair would take nothing she had not earned herself, and it was she who paid when he went to school in Inverness, and even to Edinburgh for a year. I can tell you none ever expected to see him back here again. Who would suppose he would come back to a place where all knew his story, and none knew his father's name? At nineteen he went into the distillery full-time, and when he had reached twenty-four, or thereabouts, he was running the place, almost. Och, not the business side, though he knows enough about that. He is not present when the buyers come to make their price. But he knows it right enough. He knows all there is to know about the business. He has some uncanny knack with the whisky – he has the nose and the eye for it, and he seems to know just exactly the moment when the foreshots become true whisky, and when the spirit itself runs into the feints. It is a gift as well as an art, mistress, and he has it.'

'Then my grandfather values him highly?'

Morag shrugged. 'He does – and he doesn't. Callum is fierce independent. He demands his rights – and mostly gets them. There's no great closeness between the two, though the Master has taught Callum all he knows. Callum comes and goes as he pleases – never neglecting the distillery, mind, but never letting it have all his life or his interest. Anything less than that, of course, does not please the Master. I suspect that was what the trouble was about. Four years ago there was a great quarrel between them – Callum went back to Edinburgh and took some work there. But it was not long before the Master was sending for him to come back. And when Callum did, they struck their bargain. Callum lives now in a wee house up off the road, that he repaired and put in order himself. Not very often will he come and eat at his mother's kitchen table, and he has never spent a night under Cluain's roof since he came back. Before that – I remember when I was a wee thing, he moved himself out of the house and had a room over the stables. Always independent he was – and nearly always getting his own way. In the silent season when they can't distil, then he's off and away, and no man owns his time. He has his mother's gifts in a way . . . he knows every fowl and creature that moves. He walks the moors in all weathers, and no harm ever comes to him. He has never had an ill day in his life, Mistress Sinclair says. 'Tis my own opinion . . . well, who am I to say what is what with Callum Sinclair? There's not many he would be giving any information to about himself.'

'What is your opinion, Morag?' I pressed.

She shrugged again. 'I think that was why he came back from Edinburgh. He was born here, and he cannot abide the crampiness of the towns. He puts in his time at the distillery, and works like three men, and then is free. He would owe the Master nothing – nor any man, I think.'

Morag was nodding, as if she were striving to grasp the meaning of Callum Sinclair's life, her eyes on the figure of Mairi Sinclair as she bent to pinch back a bud, or pull a weed.

'They do fight something terrible at times. But mother and son, they're two of a kind. They walk their own way.'

2

I found my own way out by the passage that curved around the tower to the back door of Cluain. On this side of the house it was pasture down to the river bank – again, a parklike planting of oak and beech that told the many years that Cluain had stood upon this land. I noticed the churned-up mud of the path that the cows took to the dairy, but the stone path that skirted the house itself seemed, as everything else at Cluain, freshly swept. I paused for a time looking down at the tumble of the river, but irresistibly the buildings of the distillery drew me. I wondered if I would find my grandfather there, or was he elsewhere about the farm? And what was the 'silent season' they talked of, when the distillery did not operate? I was crossing the cobbled yard (that was bounded) when I heard the same terrible shrieking, hissing noise that had greeted my arrival yesterday.

I stopped, and then around the corner of the distillery the flock of geese came in a swirling tide. They came straight at me, their cries raucous, big white wings flapped awkwardly, long necks and beaks thrust forward. I had no time now to consider which door might lead to my grandfather's offices. I ran for the nearest one, the whole horrible tribe following me. It might be locked, and then I would have to go the whole length of the building to the next one. I turned and faced them, waving my arms and shouting, but they retreated just a foot or two, and that only for a moment. Then they were all around me again, and as I struggled with the

knob of the door I felt two quick pecks at my leg. Even through
the thickness of my skirt it was sharp and painful. As the door
opened on oiled catch and hinge, I turned once again and made
a vengeful lunging kick at the big gander who led the flock. For a
moment he was taken aback; I could nearly have laughed at the
almost human surprise he displayed in the way he reared back –
laughed, that is, if my leg hadn't hurt so much. But he was coming
at me again.

'Go on, devil! – go on,' I shouted, and slammed the door.

Outside, the screaming went on for a time, and then gradually
died down. I stood with my back to the door rubbing my leg, and
trying to get my bearings in the jumble of doors, passageways and
iron staircases. The windows were high up, round, and gave little
light.

'Are you hurt?' It was Callum Sinclair.

I didn't know where he had come from. Perhaps he had been
there all alone enjoying my discomfort, knowing what must have
happened. Then I saw his face more clearly. No, he hadn't been
enjoying anything. His face was still clouded and grim, as I had
seen it in the kitchen, but it showed concern.

'Not badly . . . I don't think.' I pulled up my skirt, not caring
what he thought about that, and examined my calf. The stocking
was torn, but that angry beak had only pinched me, not broken
the flesh.

Callum Sinclair nodded. 'You'll do. But you wouldn't have been
the first one Big Billy's drawn blood from.'

'The gander? Why does my grandfather have such a vicious
animal around?'

'It's not his choice. The whole stupid flock belongs to the
gauger – the exciseman – who lives in that cottage by the warehouses. He claims his geese go with him wherever he does, and
when he has them, he doesn't need any other watchman. He could
almost be right. Of course, since he's been at Cluain more than
twenty years, neither he nor his flock is likely to move on.'

I noticed while we talked that Callum Sinclair impatiently
weighed the spanner he held in his hand; then it wasn't quite
true, all that he had said in the kitchen about not caring what
went on at the distillery now that his agreed time there was
finished. Did he only say such things to worry and anger his
mother, to display his independence from Angus Macdonald? It
seemed as if he had been occupied with some maintenance task in
the building when the geese had alerted him to my presence. It
was with such care as this, of course, that he had won his bargain

with my grandfather; the indifferent gained no such privileges.

'What is the watchman needed for? In a remote place like this must one guard everything so carefully?'

For a moment he nearly smiled. 'Miss Howard – forgive me – you have a great deal to learn about the whisky business. There's a fortune in government excise taxes lying in those casks in the warehouses. If your grandfather had as much money as the government is owed in excise on the whisky he's holding for those he's sold it to, he'd be a rich man.'

'Does my grandfather let the gau – ' I stumbled over the unfamiliar word, 'the exciseman do what he wants at Cluain?'

Sinclair shrugged. 'And who's to say him nay? Cluain doesn't pay Neil Smith – Her Majesty's Customs and Excise does. Cluain provides his house, and he takes whatever measures he thinks necessary to guard the warehouses. And Big Billy's about the best there is. At night Smith shuts the whole flock in a pen that's built hard by the warehouse door there – so the foxes won't have a feast. No one could get inside without the whole world knowing it. In theory, a man is supposed to come from Grantown several days a week to relieve Smith – in practice it hardly ever happens. The Excise has long turned a blind eye to it. They know that Neil Smith has nothing else in his life but watching over Cluain. And Cluain is considered very secure. A small, compact distillery – the warehouses a continuous building, only one door that can be opened from the outside. Neil Smith always on duty. And with Big Billy, you hardly need locks. Beside the guard duty Big Billy performs, there's a nice profit at Christmas from the young birds that Neil Smith fattens up. Both ways, Smith does very nicely out of Big Billy.'

'Big Billy nearly did very nicely out of me. If this Mr Smith is such a great guardian of Cluain, why didn't he come out and investigate what I was doing here?'

'Oh, he undoubtedly saw the whole thing from his window, and is laughing his head off, the sour old man. He knows well enough who you are, and if it had been to the warehouses you had gone running, he'd have taken the greatest pleasure in telling you you had no business there. Besides, you couldn't have got in. And he would have let Big Billy torment you a little longer just to bring home the fact.'

'But it's all right to come here?'

'We're not distilling now. You couldn't even get a dram of newly distilled spirits drawn off now. So he's no care of who comes and goes here. But of the warehouses, only the exciseman and the owner have the keys. If anything is missing, the owner pays.'

'Don't you have a key? I've been told you're the most important man at Cluain.'

'Who told you that?'

'Not your mother.'

He shrugged again. 'It doesn't matter. I am not the Master of Cluain. I do not hold the keys.'

I rubbed my leg more fiercely. I had the strange impression if propriety had not forbidden it, Callum Sinclair would have done it for me. It wasn't that he was at all interested in me as a woman, but just that the thought of any wound or hurt aroused his sympathy. I continued to rub.

'Why were you so rude to me?'

'I didn't know I had been.'

I waved my hand impatiently. 'Oh, I have no time for this game you all play here. You know when. There, in the kitchen.'

'How could I have been rude to you? We hadn't been introduced.'

'And have we now? – except by Big Billy?'

And now his face actually creased in a genuine smile, and was incredibly altered by it. I began from that moment, I think, to wish I could draw it often from him. He laughed, and then his face came to rest again. The horizontals I had noted before were all back there – the straight brows, the eyes, the mouth; but not grim any longer.

'You're quite like your brother, William,' he offered.

'I'm pleased you think so. But did you like him?'

He nodded. 'William was all right. He had a lot to learn.'

I bristled with resentment. '*You* say that! William was always counted very intelligent – clever.'

'Clever, yes. That doesn't mean a man has nothing left to learn. William was young – '

'And I suppose you are old?'

He made a slight gesture of acquiescence, waving the spanner. 'Very well then. I give you the point. I am not so old. But I have not been protected. I am not the son of a bishop – ' And then he stopped, as if the inadvertent words had burned his lips. No one must enquire – no one could – whose son he was.

I gave my leg a final vigorous rub. 'Well, then, I am here now. I've run the gauntlet of Neil Smith and Big Billy. Has it been worth it?'

He seemed suddenly at a loss. 'I can take you back to the house. Big Billy keeps his distance of me. He will get to know you very soon . . .'

'Never mind Big Billy. Next time I'll flap a shawl at him – or something. But I can't have gone through this for nothing. You will show me the distillery?'

At once all the friendliness, the concern was gone. His face seemed to freeze over, not with deference, but in withdrawal. 'You will have to excuse me, Miss Howard. It is not my province. It is your grandfather's privilege – and he is not in the distillery. I am not the Master of Cluain.'

I clenched my fists, and for a moment my eyes closed in frustration. When I looked at him again those mud-grey eyes were staring at me in cold concentration. 'I,' I said, 'am tired of hearing of the Master of Cluain. There are other people in the world. Were you my brother's friend? A friend could show me about the distillery.'

'Friend? – I don't know that I was a friend. Would he have counted me that?'

'How would I know?'

'He didn't tell you of Cluain in letters? – talk about the people here?'

'It takes a long time for letters to get to China. He hadn't much time to get used to Cluain. Oh, he talked of it . . . in a general way.' Then I stopped pretending, to myself and to this man. 'Oh, it's no use! He *didn't* have much to say about Cluain. I think he was afraid of disappointing us. You know, he always intended to come back to China . . .'

'And he changed his mind? He meant to stay on at Cluain after he had finished with the university, didn't he?'

I gestured impatiently. 'How am I to know? He never *said* so. It's just what he didn't say. One began to guess.' Then I didn't want to talk about it any more. 'Well, will you show me the distillery?' I was looking about me, trying to dismiss the subject.

But Callum Sinclair persisted. 'So you guessed you were losing William – but he died without you knowing for sure. And then your father was killed. There was a lot written about it in the papers. A lot of talk – gun-boat talk. Everyone very upset. And then they said those responsible had been punished, and that was the end of it. We heard nothing more. I knew, of course, that William had a sister, I thought of you . . .'

Two men now had said this to me, in their different ways. They had thought of me, whom they didn't know. But no word had come from my grandfather. The first anger rose again, the sense of being unwanted. More than ever I was determined that Callum Sinclair would show me about the distillery. I would prove to my grandfather I had friends. I would win the same rights as William.

'Talk! Yes, there was a lot of talk! There would have been a lot more talk if one of their precious warehouses had been burned, or an opium shipment taken by bandits. But a man of God – well, there are always more of *them*! That's the way they think.'

I sighed, and very slowly shook my head. 'No – I didn't want that, even at the very worst moments. I know it was the last thing my father would have prayed for before he died – that there would be no slaughter of innocent or misled people to pay for his life. I think he always expected to die in some such way in China. No, there would have been no wish for vengeance.'

He nodded, and looked unblinkingly at me for a long time. 'I think I might have respected your father very much if he was really as you say. And you might hope William would have become like him.'

'Why?'

'He seems to have had no sense of power. I hate the weight of power and respect – and what is owed to people, and demanded by them because of the position they hold. So many feel the need to possess – and hold on. What is theirs, is theirs. Their pound of flesh!'

I shook my head wonderingly. 'What a strange man you are, Callum Sinclair. You should be out organizing workers' unions. Do you always talk like this? In the kitchen you wouldn't say a word.'

'In the kitchen I would have had to say useless, false words. Did you expect me to touch my forelock, and bid you welcome to Cluain? I leave that to other people. There are enough around to bow and scrape.'

Now I laughed. 'If you could know the lack of *that* I've had. No one has bid me welcome to Cluain. Will you do it now?'

He shook his head. 'No – I couldn't. I don't know that it's right that you've come. Perhaps you'll regret it – perhaps you won't. Your grandfather is one for his pound of flesh . . . remember that. One thing I'll tell you. The first morning your brother was here he wasn't left to find his way to the distillery alone, chased by Big Billy's tribe. No – the prodigal never had a warmer welcome. Hours spent showing him how it all worked. He couldn't possibly have understood a quarter of it that first day. And then the tasting session in the Master's office. Your fine young man was half tipsy by the time dinner hour came around. Angus Macdonald tried so hard he almost ruined it all – trying to pack into William's head in a few hours what it would, in a natural way, take him years to learn. And trying to educate his tongue to the niceties and qualities of Cluain's whisky at all its stages of maturing until William, I believe, could hardly see straight. The old man made it too obvious, and I thought it was in the balance, whether or not he would ever come back to Cluain. Your grandfather saw his heart's desire, and he was stretching out his big paws to grab it before it slipped from him. Power – power and greed.

'So now, Miss Howard, after what I've said, are you sure you still want me to show you the distillery?'

I nodded, humbly. 'Yes – yes, please. I think I trust you, Callum Sinclair. You're outrageously honest – and yet I'll trust you not to laugh at me because I'm a woman, and I'll seem stupid about things most men have some knowledge of.'

He rocked back on his heels. 'Stupid you're not, or you wouldn't be talking like this. Neither was William stupid. A woman, yes – but women can be the very devil, because they can hide their cleverness so well. They take a man unawares. So, all right then – I'm not the Master of Cluain, but I will try to do what he should be doing now.'

My mind was weary before we were half through with it. I said 'Yes – yes . . .' to each thing Callum Sinclair said, and in the first half-hour, even tried to ask questions. But in a little while I found I was just accepting, trying desperately to store what I could, and knowing I was making a miserable mess of it. And I suppose that Callum Sinclair knew it also.

But he was patient. He talked slowly, and as he talked, his voice grew more gentle, the words and phrases less clipped. He dropped his stride to my pace as we walked all through those vast soundless spaces of the distillery. I almost could see that this was how he had trained his setter dog to move obediently at his heels, with soft words and easy, patient movements. But he also had trained a wild, fierce hawk, a creature of the skies, and how had he done that?

Almost before we had begun I asked the one question I had prepared, the one that had puzzled me: 'Why do they call this "the silent season"? Why is the place empty? – no one working?'

'You're a little ahead of me. But no matter. Not much of it will make sense, the first time through. Later on, when the weather gets colder, you'll see the whole thing. We "go silent" as they say because the weather is too warm and humid now for malting the barley. Visitors to the Highlands think that's something of a joke, because for them the weather here is always cool, if not downright cold. But if we brought the barley in now, supposing we had any left in the stores, after screening it off for impurities, and steeping it in our own water for about two or three days, we would bring it to the malting floors – here, this way. Mind your dress. We keep the place clean, but it's becoming an old building, and not meant for long skirts . . .'

'The malting . . .' I prompted.

'Yes, the malting. After the barley's been steeped it's brought here – ' He opened a door, and a huge, completely empty room faced us, the stone floors clean-swept, but the whole place having a smell which seemed almost like a warm mouldiness. 'It's stacked about a depth of three feet here, and it begins to germinate. You could almost call it breathing. It takes in oxygen, and gives off carbon dioxide. It starts to give off a fair amount of heat, too, and we have to keep the temperature down at about sixty degrees – and that means the men must keep turning it with these shovels here – ' He reached beside me to a row of long wooden shovels stacked along the wall. 'We call these "sheils" and this whole process is called "turning the pieces". So you see, in these few months, when the weather's warm and humid, we stop altogether, because the barley will germinate too quickly – it grows little rootlets and these would tangle up, and all you'd get is a matted mess. So, we "go silent" about this time. This is a chance, too, to repair what needs repairing about the distillery, seeing everything's in good order for the next season. Breakdowns cost money. We're very careful with our maintenance. And when you have a farm and your own barley to harvest, then the silent season is a necessary thing. There's talk of some distilleries bringing in barley already malted from outside, but he would never hear of using any but Cluain's barley . . . the product has to be Cluain's from start to finish. But you must know that already.' He gave a quick sideways glance at me as he said that.

'But the silent season's a good thing. It gives a man a chance to get the smell of the barley out of his nose – barley in all its stages, dry and dusty, the wet smell of germinating, the reek of the peat when we dry it in the kilns, the smell of beer when it's halfway through its journey, and then that final smell that's spirits. A man needs to forget it. He needs to remember that there's another world outside these walls. I sometimes wondered if William . . . well . . .'

'What about William?'

'We never talked about it. But he took to walking, I noticed. He didn't spend all day here. And those were the times when Angus Macdonald could scarcely contain himself. He didn't want

William out of his sight, and William would not have it that way. Well, Angus Macdonald never did have his own son – and he too often made the mistake of treating William like a little boy. So William used to go off without telling him where, or when he would be back . . .' Then he stopped. 'And you must be thinking that it would have been so much better if William *had* told him – that last time. If he had, William would not have lain for two nights –'

'Please, no more. I've had enough of death.'

'I know. But it's something I blame myself for as well. *I* should have found him. I know every part of this country better than any man around. And I have a dog who lives by his nose. And we failed . . .'

'Please,' I said, 'could we go on? It is useless to talk of what might have been. My father need never have made that last journey into Szechwan, either. William need never have come to Cluain. For that matter, I need not have come. But I am here. Shall we go on?'

'As you wish.'

Had it created a coldness, this refusal to allow him to speak of this unfounded guilt he felt? But I could not bear it for him, and for my grandfather as well; they would feel as they must. I had my own thoughts to live with. We went on in silence to the great drying kilns, and his explanations were brisk and precise – that is, if anyone could be precise about what began to appear a very complicated process. How was it, I wondered, that they talked about illegal stills in the mountain country that could be dismantled and carried away, when it seemed that all this great plant was needed to make that warm glowing liquid I had tasted for the first time the night before. I asked Callum Sinclair this.

'What's made in those little illegal stills isn't brewed for the pleasure of tasting it, but to knock a man insensible.' He pointed to the drying kiln. 'That's what's at the bottom of those odd chimneys you see in every distillery.'

'They reminded me of Chinese pagodas . . .'

'We dry it over peat fires to give it its flavour – that, and the barley, makes Scotch different from the American whiskies, their Bourbon and rye. There's no particular mystery about making Scotch. It needs skills – traditional and ancient skills. Perhaps it needs a climate like ours – not just to mature it, but because the climate breeds the *need* for it. Those illegal brews are made, I think, just to help men forget what sort of winter they have to live through here . . .'

As we walked we came on two men bent over the task of re-soldering the joint of a pipe. I guessed Callum Sinclair had been with them when the noise of Big Billy had called him away. He punctiliously introduced both men to me, and both stood up and offered a murmured welcome. 'James Macfarlane, Miss Howard. John Murray . . .' As we moved out of earshot, he added, 'A distillery man is a very special breed. You won't find too much need of workers' unions here. They know their value – and so does Angus Macdonald.'

He continued on, and I tried to remember, and most of it went over my head. After drying in the kiln the malt was left for about six weeks, screened for impurities, and separated from the dried-up rootlets. 'The rootlets we call malt culms, and feed them to the cattle. After we're rid of all that we grind it up – it's called grist then – and it goes into the mash tuns.' He led me on to another room, containing four huge circular vessels. 'Three thousand gallons,' he said laconically. 'The grist is extracted four times with hot water – each lot of water higher in temperature until we reach about eighty degrees for the last. Only the first two extractions go on to the fermentation stage – we keep back the third and the fourth to form the extractions of the next batch of grist. All this mashing here is to reactivate the ferments which were stopped during the drying. Have you ever heard of enzymes – ?"

'I'm not a chemist.'

He nodded. 'The old man will be asking you questions. Even if you don't have any answers, at least it helps if you've heard the words. Well . . . let's keep on. The first two extractions from the mash tuns are called worts. Once we have the worts we haven't any more need for the barley, and that goes to the cattle, too. We cool down the worts to about seventy to eighty degrees by passing it through this heat exchange. Cooled down to this temperature, we run it into the washback, and add the yeast. Through here . . .'

I scrambled after him, ducking under pipes and stepping over some, the ends of my skirts getting damp from the little uneven places in the floor where water – or was it some of the products of the distillations – had collected. No, it would be water. Angus Macdonald – and, I thought, Callum Sinclair – would never have tolerated a sloppily cleaned floor. Big wooden circular vessels again ' – made of larch,' Callum Sinclair said. 'Perhaps it's just as well you've come in the silent season. It's a pretty violent affair when the yeast begins to work on the worts – it keeps bubbling all the time, and the men have to keep stirring it with birch sticks to keep it from boiling over. Maybe you wouldn't like the smell, either. It gives off carbon dioxide. The whole business takes about thirty-six hours – which is why I think we all need our time out of the distillery to get our lungs cleaned out. If you were a chemist now . . .' It was growing to be a joke. '. . . I would tell you about the enzymes first producing dextrose from the maltose, and then converting dextrose into alcohol and carbon dioxide. But you're not a chemist.'

'When will it be *whisky*?' I demanded.

'Patience. This is where we begin dealing with Neil Smith, as an excise officer. With me, or Angus Macdonald, he's calculated about the amount of spirit that the worts should yield, from the specific gravity of the liquid at the beginning of the fermentation, and at the end. The liquid at the end of the process is a clear mixture of water, yeast and a bit over five per cent volume of alcohol – that's about ten per cent proof. We call it the wash. This is what the pot stills have been waiting for.'

'Whisky,' I said faintly. No matter how they scoured and cleaned, the smell would forever be there, locked deep into the wooden containers, the roof beams, the cracks in the stone floors. I wanted to be done.

'Not quite,' he said. And he led me through a doorway and out on to a kind of gallery that looked down at two huge copper vessels, pear-shaped, almost, with long necks curved at odd angles. 'These are the pot stills,' he said. 'These are the heart of malt whisky. Let Angus Macdonald tell you about the patent stills – that's the spirit they mix with the pure malt to make a blend. But when someone says a pot distilled whisky, they mean what comes out of these two beauties here. Distilling is just turning liquid into vapour – the wash in this case – and condensing the vapour back into liquid. This is where it's done. The first one, the one with the big neck, is the wash still, and the other is the low-wines still. All distillers have their fantasies about their own pot stills. When Angus Macdonald has to have a part of one of these replaced because the copper is wearing thin, he will personally go and see that every small dent that might have been banged into the first still by accident over the years is reproduced – he does it with his own hands. There are some distilleries where they won't even disturb the cobwebs in case it somehow alters the kind of brew they finally get. We're not quite that daft at Cluain.

'We heat the wash by coals, and there's a copper mesh called a rummager dragged around the bottom of the still to keep the insoluble stuff in the wash from burning. The distillate is driven up the neck of the still, and into a coiled copper pipe – it's called a worm – that's buried in a tank of cold water. The alcohol is driven off first because it boils at a lower temperature than water – when it's all driven off what's left in the still is called pot ale or burnt ale, and we just run it to waste. The distillate is called low wines . . .'

'No whisky yet?'

He shook his head. 'The low wines pass through the spirit safe – the Excise has locks before and after on *that*. We check thermometers and hydrometers to see when all the alcohol has been driven off the wash still. When the distillate leaves the spirit safe it goes into that tank there, the low-wines charger, where it's mixed with what we call the foreshots and the feints – I know, I know . . .' He sought to soothe my bewilderment with a gesture. 'It's hard to put this in order, but the foreshots and the feints are the rejects of the second still, the spirits still, so I've jumped ahead of you here. Can't help it – whisky is a sort of backwards and forwards thing at this stage. The mix of the low wines, the foreshots and the feints all go into the spirit still – that's always smaller than the wash still. Then it's heated again, and the whole process of the distillate is repeated – up the neck of the still, and down through the worm to cool it. This time we run it off in three sections. The first part, the foreshots, is highly impure whisky – the middle running is what we want, and we send this into the spirits receiver. This comes over at twenty-five over proof, and we keep collecting it until it's down in strength to about five over proof. What's left is the feints, and that's impure whisky, too – so that's how the foreshots and the feints are waiting in the low-wines charger to mix with the next batch from the wash still.'

'How can you tell what's the real whisky, and what's the foreshots and the . . . the feints?'

'Over here.' He led me along the gallery and down more stairs – what a warren the place was, almost without logic, as if bins and kilns and washback and stills had all been fitted into the buildings as best they could. We seemed to have doubled back on ourselves several times. How William's engineering mind would have hated the jumble, have longed for a smooth, orderly progression.

'This is the spirit safe, here – and we control what goes into the spirits receiver by using these taps. It comes down to the simple – and difficult – fact, that it's here we decide what's acceptable whisky.'

It was something like a brass trunk with glass sides and top, fitted with measuring vessels and hydrometers. There were large brass padlocks on each end of it.

'We don't taste it, you see. The Excise doesn't permit that. They know every drop that goes through this safe, and we have to account for it. There's no hard and fast rule for deciding when we turn the distillate into the spirits receiver – when it stops being foreshots and becomes whisky, and then when it turns into feints. It comes out as colourless liquid, of course, and when water is added, the foreshots will become cloudy. When it is clear, we judge it to be true whisky.'

'Who judges?'

'Angus Macdonald used to do it. Now I do.'

'You're responsible then . . .'

He nodded. 'It's something of a nicety to decide when the liquid is a true potable whisky. An error – running the foreshots into the spirits receiver too soon, or letting it run on until some of the feints get into it – isn't anything you find out about immediately. With a good whisky like Cluain's, you'll maybe find out a dozen years later when you compare one batch with another, that it's not quite as it should be. It hasn't maybe got quite the flavour and character and bouquet that Cluain's distilling should give it. But Angus Macdonald doesn't seem to have made mistakes in his time. We've yet to find out how many I have made.'

'Why would one whisky be different from another? . . . aren't all malts made the same way?'

'No one has ever answered that, I suppose it starts with the water. The shape and size of the stills have something to do with it – some say the higher the still the better, because fewer impurities will get through. The angle of the lyne arm connecting the head of the still to the condensing unit has a lot to do with it – or so they say. But you'll not find a chemist anywhere who can tell you precisely what makes a good malt. They haven't turned it into a science yet – and I don't think they ever will. The knowledge, the way of doing it all, is passed on. You often get generations of families working in distilleries.'

'That was why my grandfather wanted William – '

Then I was sorry I had said it. Callum Sinclair's face hardened; he had, after all, told me that he was responsible for the judgement of what was good enough to be called Cluain's whisky. I had offended him – in more ways than one. I had to keep reminding myself that no one knew if, in his case, the skill was something he had as an inheritance, or merely learned. Did he ever, I thought, look around the faces at the distillery and wonder if it was from one of them his hand and eye had learned the knack?

'William,' he replied, 'knew something about chemistry and he was nearly qualified as an engineer. It would have been a whole new career, and many years, before he could be called a distiller. But, yes – your grandfather wanted him. Was it so strange? William was . . .'

He never told me what he believed William had been. Instead he turned abruptly away from the spirit safe. 'I don't hold the key to the warehouses, and I won't ask Neil Smith to open up for us. He'll follow you around like Big Billy. Ask Angus Macdonald to show you what's there. Is there anything else you want to know?'

He was back to the man he had been in the kitchen. Deliberately rude, determined to show me how little I mattered.

I put out my hand and plucked angrily at his sleeve. 'You haven't finished. I'm sorry if I've said the wrong thing – but you told me I'd never understand it all in the beginning, and it isn't just distilling one needs to understand in a place like this. You know well enough what I'm talking about. And then, you said yourself that my grandfather will be asking questions. Am I to say you stopped short . . . ?'

He sighed, and his shoulders seemed to relax a trifle. He looked at me with faint indulgence, as if I might have been an importunate child. 'Very well, Miss Howard. There's hardly anything left, so you might as well have the rest of it, and don't blame me if your head is spinning, and you can't remember any of what I've said. But now – you've got your whisky at last – true Cluain whisky, distilled with care – you could say love – in its traditional manner. What you get into the spirits receiver is about one hundred and twenty proof. It's colourless, extremely pungent, and would lift your head off to drink it. Though it's also a tradition that the Excise turns a blind eye to the men having their dram of unmatured, unbonded whisky every day. It *should* kill them, but it doesn't. They grow to ripe old age in the trade, and you'd never think of laying off a distillery worker just because he's an old man. I think myself they're like herrings in brine. They'd dry up without it.'

'Do you drink it like that?' I was thinking of the potent, but marvellously smooth distillate I had tasted the night before.

'Are you asking if I have the tastes of a gentleman? Well, I couldn't answer that. But I don't drink immature whisky.'

'Why do you twist things . . . ?'

He gestured. 'Oh, let us not go on! You're nearly finished with the distillery – and with me. Let's get to the end of it, and we needn't worry about what my habits or tastes are. Your grandfather wouldn't encourage it.'

'I don't care what my grandfather – '

'Miss Howard, you are keeping me. I have other things to do. Now, shall we go on?'

I nodded, clamping my mouth down on words I wanted to spill out. 'We add our spring water now before running the spirit into casks, which brings it down to about one hundred and ten proof. The casks are made of oak, and by preference they will have been used for storing sherry. This, over the years, gives a smoothness and a colour to the whisky. The size of the cask is a matter of choice – the smaller the cask, the faster the maturing. But there's a catch to that, though. The smaller the cask, the more whisky you'll lose through absorption by porosity. The oak has to be porous, to a degree, because the whisky has to breathe, without actually leaking. So you will lose something, whether you store it in thirty-gallon casks, or hogsheads of fifty-five or sixty-five gallons. You'll mature more quickly in smaller casks, but you'll lose more. You'll not only get a loss of volume during maturing, but you'll lose strength too. The humidity in the warehouse affects both the volume and the strength. The drier the place the more you lose in volume. That's why the blenders come and buy it here at Cluain and leave it with us. There's nothing quite like the dampness of a Highland warehouse. Then to bring it down to whatever proof is required, water is added at the boiling stage. But here at the distillery, when you are offered a dram it will always be of high proof, and our own spring water added to cut it to your taste. Another of the little mystiques of the art.'

He half turned and began to walk away from me. 'I think that's all I can tell you. Angus Macdonald will fill in the romance and the tradition of it all. Things he fed to your brother . . . But whisky is business, Miss Howard. Big business. Those who make it had better know what they're about.'

I followed him silently through the warren of passages and stairs to the door at which I had entered. It seemed a long time ago; he was right; I would not remember much of what he had told me about the distilling of whisky, but I had learned more than I had come to find out. I had learned about William and my grandfather. I had learned a little about Callum Sinclair.

As if he had made a sudden decision, he almost flung the spanner on to a bench beside the door, and took up his sheepskin. He opened the door for me, and at once I heard that familiar hissing sound. But now, when Big Billy and his flock rounded the corner of the warehouses and dashed across the road, the gander seemed suddenly to come to a sliding halt on the cobblestones. With one gesture of his hand Callum silenced them, and Big Billy turned haughtily and drove his way back through the flock, all of them falling in behind him, only little gobbling murmurs coming from their throats.

'Will Big Billy remember me?'

'I think so. He'll try to see how far he can go in frightening you. But he'll learn soon enough that you belong here, and after that it's a matter of facing him down. Neil Smith would probably enjoy seeing you too terrified to step outside the garden – but you must try not to give him and Big Billy that satisfaction. You have to show both of them that you have the right to be here.'

'Do you think I have?'

He pulled the door closed with a bang. 'I wonder why you bother to ask me? It's none of my business. But since you *have* asked . . . Like William, you have a right here so long as you don't give it away, or have it taken from you. His went by accident – almost by default. I wonder what you will do with your chance?'

The words tumbled out before I could stop them; he seemed the only link to William that was not mired in suspicion and doubt and greed. I had a terrible sense that very soon I might be given my chance, and might fail it.

'What would *you* do? – if you were I? *No!* – I don't mean that! What would you do if Cluain were yours?'

He stared at me, his features tightening into something I was beginning to recognize as the shell erected by a man who appeared to want little of anyone, and wanted to be asked for little. 'You ask foolish questions, Miss Howard. Indiscreet, childish questions. If Cluain were mine . . . I don't bother my head with such ideas.'

'Someone must. My grandfather is old. He says a woman cannot run a distillery. Now – *now* I've seen it, listened to you, I almost believe he is right. You've told me so much. Now tell me what you would do if Cluain were yours.'

I seemed to have touched a part of him which even his careful indifference could not hide. His eyes changed oddly, grew thoughtful and questioning. He stepped back and turned and looked over the whole length of the stone building, the two pagoda chimneys, even beyond it to the river and then across towards the mountains, over all of Cluain's land.

'If it were mine . . . If Cluain were mine I'd mortgage my soul to gut this distillery – use it as another warehouse. I'd build a new one. Build it as it should be. There would be logic and order in it. The distilling would be an even flow from the storage for the barley to the final casking and weighing – not this mad back-tracking and overlapping, fitting things in where there is space for them, not where they ought to be. How many times in there did we cross our own path to get to the next stage of the production? That's how wrong it is. It should be a quiet, orderly process, ticking away like a good machine. Instead there is wastage and double effort, and men tripping over each other. They're good workers, these men. They like what they're doing. I would like to see them have a place where they could double the output for no extra work.'

'And my grandfather doesn't know these things? Surely he must ... ?'

'Very likely he does. He doesn't ask my opinion. But I know him. Every stone of Cluain is his work – except the house, of course. He began in a very small way, with no money but what he could borrow, I'm told. He was geared for small production runs – remember, whisky has only fairly recently become a drink of the upper classes. Until the production of cognac was brought almost to a standstill by the Phylloxera blight, no English gentleman could be persuaded to drink whisky. Now, of course, it's respectable, and sought after. Cluain could sell four times as much as it produces. But your grandfather has his own ways. He has built Cluain and its reputation – and that's no small thing to have done. But he grows timid in his old age, I think – or tired. He could take Cluain's reputation to the bank now and build himself a new distillery with it. But he won't. The old feeling that you must reproduce every dent in the stills, and not dare to sweep away a cobweb hangs on. Cluain has served Angus Macdonald well, and he it.'

Then he shrugged. 'And who can blame him? At the end of a man's life does he start to build for the next generation when there is none? I know what *I* should do, but I'll not speak for what Angus Macdonald should do.'

He turned, and it was finished. 'You'll be all right now, going back to the house. I'll see Big Billy doesn't start after you.'

'You? – you're not coming to the house?'

He shook his head. 'I have my own house, and anyway it's too good a day to spend within four walls. I've given Cluain its due for the day – more than that. I hadn't intended to go near the distillery . . . but I knew Macfarlane and Murray would be working and I thought . . .'

'Where will you go?' I couldn't help it; it was an impertinence to ask it of him, but I couldn't help it.

Once again his gaze swept away from the immediate vicinity of Cluain, once again down to the river, over the barley fields to the mountains, up to Ballochtorra's heights. 'Where my nose leads me. I have a pony and a dog . . . and a bird.'

'Yes, I know.' I was giving so much of myself away to him. There seemed no pride in me. But lately pride had begun to seem such a useless, stupid possession, keeping one person from another. There was too much of it at Cluain.

'Then you know enough. A man with a dog, and a bird to fly . . . we will just go, that's all.'

I tried to keep him, even for a minute longer. 'It's some sort of a hawk, isn't it?'

It was as if I had struck a spark off him; his eagerness spilled out, transforming him. 'A peregrine falcon. Giorsal is her name. I found her as an eyas up there on the far side of Ballochtorra's crag, and she has been with me for three years. We hunt these lands together. She is the freest, wildest thing I know, and yet she returns to my glove each time, and seems content. She cares nothing for distilleries or whisky or whatever we do down here. Her element is the sky, faster than any living creature when she stoops in her dive. There's no compliment greater to a man than when such a creature comes back willingly to his hand. Mind you, on the days I cannot fly her, I will happily raid Cluain's meat-house to bring her food, and Angus Macdonald can think what he likes. The time I give to the distillery is time taken from Giorsal. She is demanding – and wonderful. Her name means Grace in the Gaelic.'

His face abruptly now took a wry, slightly bitter twist, as if a black humour had come to take the place of his exaltation. 'Do you know the ancient rule, Miss Howard, which lays down precisely the social order among falconers of who shall have what, who may fly which among hawks?'

'No – is there one?'

'There is. Precise and definite. It goes so . . . "*An Eagle for an Emperor, a Gyrfalcon for a King; a Peregrine for a Prince, a Saker for a Knight, a Merlin for a Lady; a Goshawk for a Yeoman, a Sparrowhawk for a Priest, a Musket for a Holy-water Clerk, a Kestrel for a Knave.*" '

Now he laughed aloud, as if he enjoyed what he had done to such orders and definitions. 'So you see, by those rulings I would be flying a humble kestrel. So when I fly a peregrine falcon, I am no less than a prince. Good day, Miss Howard.'

I watched him as he walked the length of the building – walked

away from me. The shabby kilt was swinging above his knees, and
I wondered why I never had seen before how it could become a
man, how light and free it made him seem. The sheepskin was
slung over one shoulder. Before he rounded the corner of the
distillery, I heard him whistle, some lilting, marching melody that
belonged to these hills and heaths. The world was wide about him,
and he and his falcon would lose themselves in its heart. I looked
up at the blue sky of this wondrous, soft summer day, and I
seemed already to see the distant speck vanishing into the sun that
would be his Giorsal in free flight.

I wanted to be with him – with him and Giorsal, and the dog
and the pony. The whisper rose inside me, unrepressed. 'Take me
– take me with you !'

But he had not asked.

4

That afternoon I followed Morag's directions and climbed up to
the kirk and the graveyard on the hill on the other side of the
river. I had to pass Ballochtorra, and cross the bridge below it. As
I gained height on the road opposite, the road which forked to go
to Ballinaclash, or to the kirk and on to Grantown, I kept looking
across at it. Seen from here, viewed straight on, not at the angle I
saw it from the tower room, it was a strangely unharmonious
building. The central fortress retained its old, rather grim beauty;
the rest, the new additions, seemed a tasteless clutter. Too much
building had been piled into too little space – the crag had no
room for broad sweeps, or matching proportions. Wings were
tacked on at different levels, like a lopsided cake. It was strange
how ill the mass of it suited the mood of the day. Yesterday, the
wind-driven rain, and later the mist that had boiled up about it,
had lent it dignity. On this blue-golden day that character had
been lost, and it lacked the quality of fantasy. Even this early in
the day, one side of it was already in shadow, because of the
steepness of the glen. By contrast, all of Cluain would bask in the
sun until the last of the Northern twilight. Seen close to, the
building was massive, overbearing. Its flamboyant style did not
seem to fit with the reserve of Gavin Campbell's manner.

Once I was beyond the glen that Ballochtorra dominated, my
eyes swept the sky for a sight of Callum Sinclair's hawk, Giorsal.
I had little hope of seeing her – how could I tell one bird among

so many, when most of them were unfamiliar? And did not
falcons climb so high that they were lost to sight? But I wanted to
pretend I had glimpsed her; it brought Callum Sinclair closer to
me, drew him back from his independent, self-sufficient journey,
the journey on which he had not, and would not, I thought, ask
for my company.

I had been late to the midday meal at Cluain. My grandfather had been in, had eaten, and had left again. 'The Master
is very busy, always,' Morag had said when she brought the cold
sliced beef, pickles, and the first delicate strawberries from Mairi
Sinclair's garden.

'Did he ask for me?'

'He did that, and none of us could say where you were. He did
not enquire any further. It is not his way. Were you at the distillery
then?'

Something in her tone disturbed me. 'Would it have mattered
to my grandfather if I had been there?'

'If you had been? Och – there's no saying. It was Callum
Sinclair then who showed you about?'

'Yes.'

She said nothing more, and finished quickly with the dishes on
the sideboard. I had to ring the small brass bell to summon her
at the end of the meal. Not again today was I going to enter Mairi
Sinclair's kitchen. I asked her then how I would find the kirk. She
nodded, knowing my mission. 'Should I send word to the Master?
He would have the trap harnessed up. He might have a mind to go
with you.'

'I prefer to go alone.'

I had a sense that she, or Mairi Sinclair, watched from one of
the upstairs windows as I set off along the road to Ballochtorra
and the bridge. And with as much determination as I could summon
I shook off the thought of Mairi Sinclair. If I let her obsess me she
would become a dark shadow on my life, and her insidious power
would grow. If I was ever to resist the woman, that anguished
haunted animal who had scratched upon the door of the tower
room last night, I must hold myself detached from her. But how
detached, and for how long? William's words came back to me,
'. . . there is a Dragon Lady here . . .' I was glad then, when I
was over the bridge, and the road twisted away from the sight of
Ballochtorra and Cluain. The land opened out, and the sun
seemed warmer. I began then to raise my eyes to look for the
birds, with only the faint, but persistent, hope that I would see
Giorsal. Giorsal meant Callum Sinclair. But how did one pick a

hawk from the sky? I felt depressed suddenly. The land and the people seemed more foreign than China. I would know only as much as I was permitted to know. I would never see the hawk in flight, stooping for her prey. I would only see the tamed, acquiescent creature on the glove — as if that was all there was to reveal.

The outline of the kirk was obscured by the ridge of a hill, but I recognized the dark shapes of the yews that Morag had described. It was not far from Ballochtorra, but out of sight. It stood alone, a tiny church with a square tower, without a village, or even a single cottage near it. It seemed so forsaken, as if no one ever came there, or had ever been there. And yet, it was in good repair, the stonework well mortared, the plain windows intact, the latch of the gate lifted silently and easily under my hand. A good stone wall kept at bay the cattle that grazed the hillside; only one or two bothered to lift a head. They were sleek with summer grass. Farther down were fields of barley and oats: somewhere, a meadow lark sang. There was utter peace here. Suddenly I was reminded of my father's grave within the British Legation wall in Peking. Some day, I thought, those alien feet would trample it in some new rising against the Foreign Devils. It was far better that William lay here.

I found his grave easily enough — there were not so many of recent years, few whose headstones were not weathered beyond reading, or toppled and half buried in earth and grass. There were several rows, though, whose headstones looked newly placed; they were polished marble slabs, but some of them bearing dates that went back several hundred years. The names were the same — Campbell . . . Campbell . . . Sir Andrew Campbell, his wife, Catriona . . . Mary Campbell . . . Sir Robert; three rows of Campbells, all lying in long-tenanted graves, with newly placed markers. Then, directly across the gravel path, I found William. It pleased me that here was no polished marble slab; the headstone was a piece of granite, barely cut to fit its place, the words chiselled deeply in it: WILLIAM MACDONALD HOWARD, and the dates his life had spanned. I was glad that no Bible text followed it; I was grateful to my grandfather that he had sought to give William the dignity of this simple memorial, the very roughness of the stone almost signifying that his life had not been finished, nor worn by time. There was no flowery text to extol his virtue — young people have not had time to establish that. The granite, by contrast to the polished marble, told another tale — my grandfather's belief in work and toil and simplicity decrying the formal splendour of the establishment at Ballochtorra. There was more than a hint of scorn for the polished niceties of the gentry.

The grass grew long on William's grave already, though this was its first summer. I wondered if I should bring tools one day to cut it; the Chinese every spring made a ceremony, called Ching Ming, of the cleaning of the ancestral graves. The siting of the graves was important to them; a well-placed grave could bring good fortune on the surviving family. 'William . . .' I whispered. I wondered if I would be here next spring to perform the ceremony of Ching Ming. Why did one come to talk to the dead where they lay buried? William was more present in the tower room of Cluain than he ever would be in this grave. But he lay in a fair place, and the free winds blew over him, and the clean winter snows would blanket him. The Chinese would probably have considered this a good siting. I was more than ever glad that it was not the British Legation compound in Peking, bitterly cold, stiflingly hot, dirty, always. I sat down in the long grass still wet from yesterday's rain, and leaned against the granite stone. 'William . . . why did you tell me so little? What does it *mean*? – what did you expect me to do?' No answer came, of course. No answer. There was nothing but the words scrawled with fevered hand on the scroll. William could tell me nothing more.

Then came the music. It was a great burst of sound, the sudden releasing of spirit in the mighty first notes of the Bach fugue. I stood up, electrified, frightened almost, by the great, unexpected thunder of it, and at the same time a sense of passion that a highly skilled musician was holding in tight discipline. It went on, the wonderful, remembered cadences of it. The chances of hearing such music in China were few, but I remembered this. In Hong Kong there was a church with an organ good enough to permit its great harmonies to come through. One did not forget such sounds. Now here again, in this tiny church in the Highlands, too small, I would have thought, for a pipe organ, with too small a congregation to warrant such an instrument or such an organist. The music simply did not belong here. This was no doleful tune of sin and repentance, not the austerity I had expected in the Church of Scotland. It was a great song of praise and exultation and joy. I stood in awe, my hand resting on William's stone; I hardly dared to draw my breath.

It ended, and I did not move, hoping, perhaps, for more of it. But nothing came. I waited, and finally there was the sound of the side door opening, and the lock being turned. The man stood on the step for a moment, accustoming his eyes, I guessed, to the stronger light, pausing to lift his face to the sky, and possibly to listen to the high, thin song of the lark. I knew him and without thinking, I raised my hand. He caught the movement, and looked towards me. Then he began to make his way among the long grass and the graves.

'Miss Howard – you're here alone!' His brow was wrinkled. But I thought he was glad enough to see me.

'Yes, Mr Campbell – I'm sorry, it's Sir Gavin Campbell, isn't it?'

'I seem to make a habit of finding you alone in places no one would expect a young lady to be.'

'Why not?' I glanced down at William's grave.

He shook his head, the brusqueness of yesterday's meeting gone. 'I'm sorry. Of course you would come. But somehow – well, one always expects nicely brought-up young ladies to do the expected things. But you – you don't wear black crêpe and lament in public. You merely come all the way from China alone, without so much as a telegram. I suppose I was so amazed yesterday it didn't really strike me until afterwards. Standing there at Ballinaclash halt with your bags, no mourning veil, no tears, no one to meet you . . . If I hadn't been there, I almost think you would have *walked* to Cluain.'

'I would have had to,' I said. 'Without the bags, of course.' Then I added, 'I'm really not all that different. I think I was just so frightened of coming, I simply came. If I had told my grand-father – if I had waited to be invited, I probably wouldn't have had the courage. As it turns out – I don't think he would ever have asked me. I think he had just not registered the fact that I existed. You see . . . I am not another grandson. It didn't actually shock me. I'm used to it, I suppose. The Chinese think that way about girls. No one wants them. China teaches one a lot of things, Sir Gavin. To survive, for one thing. To hold on to life – and all I have left is here. So I don't wear mourning, or a veil. All that seems rather useless to me. My father believed in life, and to him death was nothing. William believed in life too – though he didn't say it the way a clergyman does. And you – *you* believe, don't you?'

'How do you know?'

'The music. That was you at the organ, wasn't it?'

'Yes.'

I looked at him directly. 'It was the best thing that had hap-pened to me since the news came about William. It was life . . . and joy. No one plays like that – *that* music – unless the belief in life is in his very soul. You could even tell me now that you don't believe in God, and I *know* you believe in life. My father often said it was the same thing.'

'Are you a musician, Miss Howard?' He was not affirming or denying what I had said.

'No – not at all. One hears little but drawing-room ballads in China. Not very well sung or played. It was the merest chance I had heard the Bach before, and remembered it. It was Bach, wasn't it?'

'Yes – '

'But why was that all? I would have stayed here all afternoon if only you had gone on. Why did you stop?'

'It was the end, really. I'd finished, and I was just sorting through some music, getting hymns ready for next Sunday. But before I left I suddenly felt like flexing . . . well, perhaps your father might have said flexing my soul. No one in this place is supposed to hear that sort of thing – hardly anyone ever does. It would be a trifle suspect. This is a very stern God they worship here. But I play the organ for the few hymns they sing on Sundays – I find that duty easier and less hypocritical than reading the Lesson. The laird is expected to do something. If it weren't for the fact that people around here know I can manage a horse and a gun about as well as the next man, they might think that playing the organ was a rather odd occupation. The hymns are elementary. The village schoolmistress could do very well with them. I sometimes think I cheat her of a pleasurable task.'

'But the organ – that wasn't built just for simple hymns. Even I know that.'

He leaned against one of the Campbell stones and looked back at the church. 'No – the organ is far better than a church of this size should have. It's an absurdity, really, to have it here. It is too big for the space, for one thing. But it was paid for by my father-in-law, and he doesn't know how to deal on a small scale – with anything. The whole church was restored by him. The roof leaked, the tower was tottering, the choir loft was about to crash down. The congregation is so small the minister only comes over to hold a service every third Sunday. It could have been left to its final ruin, and hardly anyone would have noticed. But now you see what it is – with an organ far better than it warrants, and a large brass plate to make sure the Almighty knows who paid for it all.'

'You're rather unkind to your father-in-law.'

He shrugged. 'It would be difficult to be unkind to him. He wouldn't notice. You see, when the restoration was carried out he thought that his daughter would be buried here with all the other Campbells of this branch of the family. Now he couldn't have her lying beside a ruined church with the sheep and cattle grazing her grave, could he?'

'You're asking my opinion? I think you talk entirely too much, Sir Gavin. I'm a stranger – I don't know your father-in-law. You may play the organ like an angel, but your tongue is sharpened with more than a little malice.'

He looked at me, and actually laughed. 'Bless you, girl. Do I hear your father talking? Don't worry, I beg you. You'll hear at least that much of my father-in-law – and far more, probably – before you've been here very long. My father-in-law is James Ferguson.'

'Who?'

'Oh, yes – I'd forgotten the name wouldn't mean anything to you. You haven't been in whisky long enough. He is one of the whisky magnates – *blended* whisky, which I'm sure is never permitted near Cluain. He has as many blends as there are letters to his name, and if the way he spends money is anything to go by, he has a fortune made from all of them. He has – like all shrewd merchants – all qualities, all prices. All things to all tastes. I imagine your grandfather would disapprove of him utterly, and yet he sells to him. *All* the malt distillers sell to Ferguson. He needs the leavening of a whisky as fine as Cluain's to give *something* to some of the rubbish he buys elsewhere, or distils himself. A good malt can be cut very thin, you know, and made to go very far in blending. Ferguson was one of the first to invest heavily in patent-still grain whisky. He let the others make the expensive stuff, and merely bought their product. But whatever he touches, whatever he does, everything turns to gold, and the public have come to know it. They rush to invest with him, and he's in a great hurry to spend the profits. Witness the church and the organ – and Ballochtorra itself.'

'He couldn't have *built* Ballochtorra!'

'No – he restored the old tower, and added the rest. A suitable home for his only child. Mind you – if he had been quite so famous eleven years ago, or had known he was going to be quite so rich, he might have looked higher than a mere baronet for her. But still . . . I believe she wanted to marry me, and that's always a help.'

'And you?' I asked coldly. It was outrageous, what he was saying, and yet I couldn't bring myself to break away from him, as I should have done.

'Me? Good God! I was madly in love. She was eighteen, and so beautiful I could hardly believe that she would even look in my direction. Now, eleven years later, and a mother, she is matured, and London society is beginning to say she is the most beautiful woman in the kingdom. Myself, I'm not much accustomed to London society, so I'm no arbiter – but to me she is beautiful. You will see, though – you will meet her very soon.'

I felt ashamed; he had loved her, he most probably still loved her. If a man chose to deride his father-in-law, then it might be just that this place – this lonely graveyard and playing an organ that is a gift from such a man – had brought out more than he meant to say.

'It was even a good laugh in those days. I could still make a joke of being poor.' He seemed determined to go on. 'You see, I had fallen into the baronetcy simply because my father was a distant cousin unexpectedly next in line. I hadn't grown up with that in prospect. My father had scraped to send me to Cambridge, and from there I had thought I might be lucky enough to get an organist's post in some cathedral. I loved horses, as well as the organ. I couldn't afford either, really – except that the organ could be made to pay my way in life. And then, my father was suddenly Sir Bruce Campbell, because a young, unmarried second cousin had tumbled into the river – dead drunk, they say – and two months later my father died, and I was Sir Gavin. I'd visited Ballochtorra once in my life, and I didn't want either it or the title. It was almost in ruins even when I was a child. All at once I had a title, a castle, and no money. And a position as an organist was going to be much harder to find. Deans usually don't engage young men whom they think the congregation might suspect of looking down on them. I went back to Edinburgh, where my father had his law practice, hoping for some recommendation for a post – and almost at once I met Margaret – my wife.'

'The meeting turned out well.' I wished my tone hadn't been so tart.

He looked back at the church. 'Yes, you could say it turned out well. I hardly remember those days clearly. When you are so much in love, nothing has any sequence. I can hardly sort out what happened. I just know Margaret's father was suddenly present – and in charge. I suppose I was young for my age – we were both very young. And we were married.'

'And went to Ballochtorra and rebuilt it?'

'Before any of the rebuilding could begin we had our time there – just Margaret and I. The architects and James Ferguson were planning, and we were enjoying ourselves. We had one wonderful summer almost camping under open roofs. When you are young, and the fire is warm, and the wine is good, you barely notice such things. I suppose I should have thought about who was paying for the fire and the wine, but I didn't. It didn't seem to matter, then. It matters, though. In the end, it matters.

'You haven't met James Ferguson, but you undoubtedly will. He is a man who makes it his business to meet people. That you are a bishop's daughter will recommend you as much as the fact that you are Angus Macdonald's granddaughter. Though a Chinese bishopric doesn't count in the House of Lords.'

'You're very bitter.'

'Am I? Perhaps it's simply that I am no longer so young. I know now who pays for the fire and the wine.'

'Should you be saying this to me?'

'Why not? You came from China all alone. You don't act like a miss just out of school – you're William's sister, and if I'm not mistaken, you're just as knowing as he was. You'll see it for yourself. Is it so terrible that I should speak it? I don't run about crying it to the earth.'

'You play the organ – when you think no one hears. It speaks for itself.'

'Only to those who know already. So I'm talking to you. I'm giving the words to what you will guess – and perhaps come to understand. Without James Ferguson there would be no Ballochtorra now – just a vine-covered ruin. There would be no church, no organ, nor horses in the stables. There would be no gamekeepers, and no game preserved on the moors. Gavin Campbell would be scratching for a living somewhere, and the sheep would be clipping the graveyard now.'

'You said Mr Ferguson had expected his daughter to be buried here. Why wouldn't she?'

He looked at me with a sideways glance, and then at the neat row of graves. 'You don't miss much. Yes, we had thought that we both would lie here – and hence the restoration. But since then – I hope I haven't some dark genius for bringing such things on my relations – two cousins have died. One with his regiment in India, the other of typhoid in the Congo – *that* one was a mercenary of Leopold of the Belgians. It happens that they both in turn were next in line to the Marquis of Rossmuir. The solicitors have had to scramble about to find the heir, and it seems I am the one.' He made a gesture of dismissal. 'Oh, there's no riches with it. Rossmuir is an ancient title, but there's nothing left of the family lands but a few hundred acres of overgrazed grass up in Ross, and a much smaller castle than Ballochtorra was, even in the beginning, and which no one has lived in for more than a hundred years. The present Marquis is nearly ninety, bed-ridden, living in a few rooms in Edinburgh on the small income the land brings in. There doesn't seem any possibility that he will beget an heir to prevent my assuming the title. So you see, my father-in-law is torn between leaving things as they are here – or taking on the really challenging task of restoring an ancient ruin, and the traditional burial place of the Marquises of Rossmuir. What prevents him beginning now is that it's not in good taste until I have actually inherited the title – and the old man could stop him. And then, it's so far away in the wilderness up North, who would ever see it? No use splashing money about if it's only to be seen by a few crofters and sheep, now is it?'

I turned on him angrily. 'I think you're despicable! Why do you take this man's money when you so despise him? And if you do, haven't *you* the good taste to keep quiet about it!'

He sighed. 'You're right. I'm behaving like a vulgarian. And a smug one, into the bargain. I can't stop a father spending money on his daughter and grandson – it does give him pleasure. But for myself – as you say, the least I might do is accept it with grace. But what is it about you? – have you inherited a gift from your father of making people spill out their souls? I've said things that should decently be left unsaid. And yet I know if I don't say them, they'll be said to you by others – your grandfather for one. Perhaps I care that you hear my version of it – though why I should I don't know. Perhaps it's just that a man has a need to talk, sometimes – and I have the conviction that you don't repeat gossip.'

'The children of clergymen are brought up not to. We learn very early on never to notice who comes to our father's study for counsel or advice, and never to repeat any little piece of information a tired man lets slip. No – I don't think I gossip very much. And I'll be interested to meet Mr James Ferguson. We weren't wrapped in a silkworm's cocoon in China, you know. After all, the great powers were in there for trade – and the biggest part of it was to sell opium. Whisky seems infinitely preferable. If a man makes a fortune out of whisky – well, it's only what my grandfather would *like* to do.'

'Your grandfather's a different breed. He's a stubborn, prejudiced, rather narrow-minded old man, but his heart and soul is in making the best whisky this country can produce. He cares more for the quality of his product than for money – and always has. If you could choose your ancestors, then Angus Macdonald might not be a bad choice. Nor is the ancestor we have in common.'

'You said we were cousins – distant cousins. Who was the

ancestor?' But I was still thinking of what he had said about my grandfather. It pleased me that he did not appear to begrudge the respect that Angus Macdonald himself had claimed as his due. It made up for some of the things he had said about James Ferguson.

'She was Angus Macdonald's mother, and a Campbell of Ballochtorra. She lies there.' He was nodding to the ground beyond me.

It was an overgrown grave beside William's with the same rough granite marker, though smaller and worn with the weather of the years. I thought it significant that my grandfather had buried William in the plot where one would have expected he himself would lie. The ground beside William was empty, and unmarked, as though waiting. Beyond that was another similar marker, probably Angus Macdonald's wife, my grandmother. The long grass waved about the stones obscuring the names. I swept aside the grass near the marker Gavin Campbell had indicated and read the name lettered there – CHRISTINA CAMPBELL MAC-DONALD. My eyes went back to him, questioning.

'Why not over there? – with all the other Campbells?'

'Her father forbade her to marry John Macdonald, Angus's father. He had other ambitions for his daughter and Ballochtorra than the son of the laird of a small, poor island in the Hebrides – and a Macdonald into the bargain. Ballochtorra had fallen on hard times even then, and it needed a good marriage to restore it. She met her Macdonald in Glasgow, I believe, and came back to Ballochtorra for permission to marry him. When it was refused, she simply took off for that far island with her man, and never came back. Not that she was welcome at Ballochtorra. She was all that her father had left, the youngest child, his only hope. Both sons had been killed in the Napoleonic wars. His other daughter married a Grant, and went to Canada; there were no male children of that marriage. Christina's father had inherited a place in debt, and he got it further into debt. Gambling was his vice, not drink. He never forgave Christina for not saving him. That, at least, is how they tell me the story.'

'But she is here – buried at the church at Ballochtorra. So she did return.'

'She returned because Angus Macdonald insisted on it. They say that mother and son were very close – she lost her other sons in infancy. So her pride and ambition rested in Angus. We're an unlucky family, on both sides, when it comes to offspring. To lose one's children is not such an unfamiliar thing to the Scots – it's a poor country, and made poorer by bad landlords, and the breaking of the clans. Sons leave – go into the British Army to earn their keep, emigrate because they've been driven from their ancient clans' homes to make room for sheep. But usually there are enough of them – the women have been strong and prolific breeders – for a father to have sons and daughters about him in his old age. But Ballochtorra has not been lucky. There have been too few sons. For the Macdonalds it has been the same. Angus was Christina's only surviving child. He brought her to Ballochtorra when she died – it must have been a fearful journey for a young man to arrange in those days, with no help and no money. He came to Ballochtorra, and he insisted that this was where his mother would be buried. He had some notion, they say, that she had been homesick all her life for these glens and burns – that the Western Isles had never been her home, although she gave her husband and family and her new kinsmen her whole devotion. Her father, as laird of Ballochtorra, tried to refuse the right of burial here, and just as strongly Angus Macdonald insisted, pointing to the fact that she had been a member of the kirk when she was a girl. In the end even Sir Graeme Campbell's tame minister had to agree. But still Sir Graeme refused her a place in the family plots. In the kirkyard she might lie, but not beside her family. That is why she is there – with the path between them. But at least she had been spared the fate of being nicely cleaned and polished up like all the other Campbells. I sometimes wonder if some of these shiny headstones mightn't hide a darker reputation.'

'Then how does my grandfather come to be on Ballochtorra's land – at Cluain? If Sir Graeme would not forgive his daughter, how does the grandson come to be here?'

'He hasn't told you that part yet? I would have imagined his old triumph would have been one of the first subjects he would have talked of.'

'We had other things . . .'

'Yes – I expect so. As they tell it, Sir Graeme was old at the time, and sick. He had quarrelled with every member of his family, distant as they were. There were none who would have anything to do with him. Angus asked nothing of him but that his mother should be buried there, and insisted over his objections. Somehow, it got into the old man's head, after Angus had gone back to his island, that the young man had shown a proper filial respect, and a sense of duty, even if he was a Macdonald. This was something Sir Graeme hadn't experienced from his own family. He couldn't break the entail on the title or on Ballochtorra's lands, but Cluain had been split from it by some legal quirk a hundred years before. He had let the farm run down, but he had held off enough of his creditors to save it from them. Cluain was still in his gift. In a fit of what the Campbells called sheer perversity, but what I like to think of as a late attempt at making amends to his daughter and to a grandson he should have been proud of, he left Cluain to Angus Macdonald. And he lived only six months longer than his daughter. So Angus Macdonald left his island, from which his own people had already dispersed, mostly to emigrate, and he came to Cluain to claim it. There was a fierce legal fight. The Campbells claimed undue influence over a man they said was senile – and yet, of course, the row that everyone knew about over Christina's burial proved there could have been no influence from Angus – quite the opposite. Angus had no money for lawyers – just the merit of his case. The story goes that he marched into Samuel Lachlan's office in Inverness one day, told him why he had come, asked him to take the case, and if he won he would be paid from the profits of Cluain, and if he lost – well, Samuel Lachlan might wait a long time for that debt to be settled. You'll be meeting Samuel Lachlan – he's a part of Cluain's history now. Even in those days when he was still quite a young man, he was becoming known as one of the cleverest solicitors in Scotland, and very near with money – not the kind to take a case with so little prospect of payment at the end. And yet he did take it – who knows why? Perhaps he was tired of ordinary sorts of law suits. They say he came down to inspect Cluain before he would agree. Well, for whatever reason, he took it, and he won. It took almost a year before the appeals were through. In that time Angus Macdonald lived in a crofter's cottage on Cluain's property – the Campbells claimed he was in illegal possession but no one cared to face Angus and his gun. In the end Samuel Lachlan persuaded the Campbells it was useless to carry the claim to the High Court in Edinburgh. They gave in. There is a famous local story of the day the top-hatted Campbell solicitor came down from Inverness in his carriage – the railway wasn't there in those days – followed closely by Samuel Lachlan in a dirty hackney cab, wearing the shiny black suit which was the only one he possessed – myself, I think he's still wearing the same suit. The deeds and keys to Cluain were handed over to Angus Macdonald. Cluain, in quite good repair, and fully furnished, with the best lands in the strath, was his. Ballochtorra, with the roof starting to fall in, and only grouse moors and mountain bog to its name, belonged to the Campbells. It must have been a bitter sight for the new baronet in those days – he was the one my father inherited from – to look down from Ballochtorra at Cluain. Most especially when Angus Macdonald began to build his distillery. And even the distillery was almost an inheritance from Christina.'

'How so?'

'When she was widowed out there on her island, she grew desperate for something to employ the people. The land was very poor, and the salt spray from the Atlantic would hardly let a seed stay in the ground, much less grow and flourish. Sheep had been introduced in a last attempt to make the land pay. And of course, where you have sheep, the people must make way for them. But the sheep were in too small numbers to pay, and a few crofters still survived – her tenants, her family, now her clan. She thought of what had gone on here as she grew up, and she built herself a small distillery. But it was the sea that defeated her. She couldn't grow the right quality of barley, so it had to be brought from the mainland, and then the finished product had to be shipped back – all at much more cost than those closer to the cities and the new railways that were just starting to come. It was a very small distillery, mind you, and her output was tiny. And then one year the entire product of her warehouses – that is, all that was legally old enough to be sold as whisky, went down when a vessel foundered. It was the end of the distillery. She couldn't borrow any more, she couldn't hold out any longer. It was then, they say, that she sent Angus to Islay to work in a distillery. She couldn't give him the life of a gentleman, nor could she pay for a commission in a regiment – and she must have seen too many leave the Highlands to go off and die in England's wars. So she sent him to learn a craft and a trade, one that she believed in. When Angus Macdonald inherited Cluain, he inherited the perfect place to make malt whisky. There were his barley fields, his streams, the peat, the climate. There were literally dozens of distillers within a very few miles of his door. He was not an innovator – just carrying on with an ancient skill that had always been carried on in these glens. He believed, like Christina Campbell, that there was money in whisky, and he wasn't too much of a gentleman to soil his hands in the trade. Those men of the Western Isles are a tough lot – they have had to be to survive over the centuries. There's no softness in the living there. What poor soil and sheep haven't taken, the sea has. So Angus Macdonald came here afraid of nothing – least of all hard work. When he was secure in the title to Cluain, he went back and married one of his kinswomen, and he gathered together a few distillery workers and their families from Islay. He was making his own island race here among us. The farm was run on a shoestring, and the distillery built on money borrowed from Samuel Lachlan. It was a huge gamble that paid off. Angus Macdonald has taken in about forty harvests at Cluain, but his golden harvest is maturing now in those warehouses.' He looked down at the granite marker. 'I don't know if he's ever come to admitting to himself that he loved William. But one thing I'm certain of – he wanted him.'

'You know a lot about my grandfather.'

'I've made it my business to find out. I've pieced together the story of Christina and her father, and Angus Macdonald bringing her home here. No doubt your grandfather would tell it much better and I would have liked to have heard it in his words. But he and I have never been on those kind of terms. The barest civility passes between us. I'm sorry for it, but he's not to be moved. He can't forget that the Campbells tried to dispossess him of Cluain, and every time I look down on that place I know why they tried so hard. I've seen what he's built, and I admire him. But he's a man like that granite there – hard and enduring. You'll find very few chinks in that face he turns to the world.

'It was William who began to build a bridge between Cluain and Ballochtorra. He came quite often – and why not? It is the only place around here to visit, and he wasn't much occupied at Cluain. Angus Macdonald didn't approve, but William kept coming.' Then his voice dropped until it was almost a whisper, words forcing their way out that he may have tried too long to keep buried in his own mind, words like the swift rush of the wind past my ears. 'And again – why would he stay away? He was more than half in love with my wife.'

I wasn't really aware of when he left me. I suppose I stood there for a long time, staring down at the grass waving on the graves of William and Christina, side by side. When I looked up, Gavin Campbell was gone, as I hoped he would be. There was only the gentle tugging sound of the cattle grazing near the kirk-yard wall, and far above, the same lark. I lifted my face and scanned the whole wide sky; there was no far, high-flying speck that I could see. If Giorsal, the falcon, hovered up there somewhere, she was beyond my gaze and reach.

My eyes went back to the grave, to the freshly chiselled name in the granite. 'Did you love her, William? Did you love her – and not tell me of it? Was *she* the enchantress you found here?'

The breeze that blew through the small plantation of larches in the corner of the kirkyard was my answer.

2

My grandfather was waiting, and terse. He had his stance, as before, in front of the fire in the dining-room, but this evening a long shaft of sunlight struck across his face, and he seemed older than in the greyer light of last evening.

'I hear you've been through the distillery with Callum Sinclair.' The words greeted me as I came through the door; I jerked around to face him, and the door slammed.

'Yes. Have you some objection, Grandfather?'

'I do. I'll not have you being familiar with the distillery workers.'

'Familiar!' I came towards him, feeling my face flush with anger. 'Familiar! That is the last thing I can imagine anyone being with Callum Sinclair. It was hardly my choice, though. He simply doesn't permit familiarity.'

'He kept his place, then?'

'What *is* his place, Grandfather? He seemed to be everything – to know everything. And if he hasn't a place at Cluain – a real place, then I don't know who could.'

'He's too independent – and he does not know everything, in spite of what he may claim. He's bad for discipline among the other men. He goes off on his own while they work . . .'

'But he works for Cluain as no other man does, isn't that so? And they all know it? – and accept it? So what might be a privilege for them is a right for him. After all, you keep him on at Cluain.'

I seemed to have won my small argument, and rather wished I had not. My grandfather moved with irritated haste to the sideboard. Would it always be like this between us, I wondered? But then he turned back, and the two glasses were in his hands; he held one towards me. 'There – there's your dram. Health to you.' And he tipped back his glass without another look at me, as if we had been doing this for a long time, and there was no need for ceremony. Perhaps the arguing and the confrontation were to be part of our life together, a signal of acceptance. I sipped slowly, and now the whisky was familiar, and rather pleasing.

I sat down on the settle. 'Well, then, if you had given me time I would have told you that I was looking for you to take me through the distillery – I'd just heard Callum Sinclair telling his mother he wasn't going near the place today. And as I was crossing the yard that gander, Big Billy, came chasing me. I have his bite to prove it. I just ran in the nearest door, and Callum

Sinclair was there. Perhaps he spends more time working than you think.'

'Perhaps. So you've met Big Billy, have you?' His face creased in a near-smile. 'Well, he's the real boss of Cluain. Once you know Big Billy you can fairly claim to be on your way at Cluain. I suppose you know all about distilling now?'

'No. I don't think I ever will. Callum Sinclair told me it takes years – it was all the chemical things I didn't understand. I'll never remember which part of the process follows the next.'

'Perhaps you shouldn't bother. William was more confused than he pretended to be. You don't become a distiller overnight by studying the textbooks.'

I sighed. 'That was rather heavily impressed on me. Perhaps I *won't* bother.'

The big eyebrows lowered. 'Please yourself.' I watched his body sag into his chair. What a cross-grained pair we were. And I should be for his comfort, not his irritation.

So I said, in a softer tone, 'I went to William's grave.'

He nodded. 'So they told me.'

'They tell you everything.'

'The Master expects to be told. Morag knows most things that happen here, and she is a good wee girl. A level head on her for all her chatter. It would have been well for us all if she had known where William was bound that day . . .' His voice trailed off, the regret and pain blurring to silence.

'I liked the granite stone,' I said. 'I was glad you gave William the same kind as your mother's – and laid him beside her.'

'How did you know it is my mother's grave?' The words were sharp again, suspicious.

'I read the headstone – Sir Gavin Campbell pointed it out to me. He was there at the kirk – practising the organ.' I finished lamely. Perhaps I should not be telling this part of it. Gavin Campbell might cherish the privacy of those organ sessions, not wanting them talked of through the countryside.

'Campbell was there, was he? And fine well he knows where Christina Campbell is buried. It was she who brought Cluain to me.'

'He told me so. He told me as much as he knew about the story.' I suddenly burst out, wishing for once I could cut through this man's prejudice and layers of remembered enmities, 'He admires you, Grandfather.'

'Let him admire,' he answered, as if admiration was his right. 'Let him envy, too. The Campbells lost Cluain, and they've never forgiven that. Justice was done.'

'Oh,' I gestured wearily with my glass. 'How does it affect *him*? He was only a second cousin, or something of the sort. He never expected to inherit Ballochtorra. Cluain had been in your hands for a long time before he ever laid eyes on the place.'

'The Campbells were always greedy.'

'What need does he have to be greedy? Ballochtorra doesn't appear to need money.'

'No. His lady wife has enough of it. Or rather her slum-bred father. Out of the Glasgow slums James Ferguson came, and made a fortune on cheap whisky. He spends like a madman. And Campbell lets him spend. But Ferguson hangs on to his daughter's skirts, and is a noose around Campbell's neck. Where's the sense in being a gentleman, and having fine horses, and playing the organ, when your father-in-law can scarcely speak the Queen's English?'

'Is that Gavin Campbell's fault . . . he seems to love his wife.'

'Seems to!' He tossed his huge head back. 'Och, once they were young fools together, and it appeared the genuine thing. But tell me how a man can stand by and watch his wife change from a nice, simple, well-enough educated young gurrl – aye, James Ferguson is aware of his own deficiencies in that direction, and he bought the best teachers for his daughter. And she changed from being the simple wife of a local baronet into a London social butterfly. There's been a house rented for them in London these past five years, and I hear now that Ferguson has bought a grand big affair there, and is refurbishing it from top to bottom. There is always a room ready for James Ferguson wherever his daughter is. She knows who has the purse strings.'

'You seem to know a lot about James Ferguson's doings, Grandfather.'

'Och, Morag chatters . . .' He seemed not to realize what he revealed of himself. 'They say he is getting the London house ready in time for the Coronation. And that can't be too far off.'

'The Queen is not dead yet.'

'She hasn't many more years . . . But before she is dead, Ferguson is hoping that the old Marquis of Rossmuir will be dead, and Campbell will have the title. It would be his greatest dream realized if his daughter were to sit with all the other peeresses in the Abbey wearing a marchioness's coronet when the new King is crowned. I think he would like it almost as much as a knighthood for himself. Who knows – he might even get that. Whisky has created more than one baron . . . Money talks.'

'But still and all,' he added as he went again to the sideboard to refill his glass. 'Ferguson has yet only one grandson. She has given him only one grandchild.'

After supper he brought out the chessboard. 'A game?' he said, and I knew it was not a game, but a challenge. I nodded, and we sat opposite each other, as we had the night before. Mairi Sinclair came in to ask if there was anything else needed. Her features worked strangely as she took in the scene, but when she met my eyes, her own at once became blank, as if she had determined that never again should I glimpse what had been uncovered by that wild, unrecognizable creature on the stairs. That woman, she seemed to be telling me, did not exist. I had imagined her.

But this day, like yesterday, had contained too much, had had too many encounters. Angus Macdonald's eyes were on me sharply, and each move I made on the board scrutinized for what it told him. Did I play an attacking game, or a defensive one? Would I attempt to lure him into a gambit, sacrificing a Pawn or even a more important piece to trap him? Had I got the nerve for it? That night, I had not. I played badly, weakly, not anticipating even the ordinary moves I knew by heart, letting myself fall into too obvious traps he set for me. But there was too much else in my head, and emotions do not make good pieces on a chessboard. The old man won too easily; I thought I saw a dawning contempt in his eyes, disappointment, too. He was not even suspicious that I might have allowed him to win in order to flatter him. If I had, I would have been more skilful about it.

After he had won the second game I didn't wait for him to dismiss me. 'I'll go up now, Grandfather. I'm tired.' If it sounded like an excuse, I didn't care.

It was not chill as it had been the night before, but I set a match to the fire laid ready in my room, just for the pleasure of seeing that room glow with its light as the light outside began to fade. I sat for a while beside it, slumped on the bench, unwilling to begin the effort of washing and making ready for bed. My thoughts flickered erratically like the flames; the names I spoke to myself were William's, and Gavin Campbell's – and Callum Sinclair's.

Then I heard it, clearer this night because it was unmuffled by rain or mist. I went to the window at once, and they were there again, that odd quartet – the pony too short for the man's long legs, the dog, sleek today, his coat free of mud, the unblinking falcon on the raised gloved hand. The man must have seen the

smoke rise from this tower chimney, but not by the slightest movement that I could detect did he acknowledge my presence at the
window. Pride could not keep me from standing there, hoping,
waiting for a turn of his head, the faintest nod. Callum Sinclair
gave none. I watched him out of sight. Tonight there was a
difference. I had believed, yesterday, that he shared my sense of
loneliness, and I had experienced a kindred feeling with him. Now
I knew that Callum Sinclair would admit to no such thing. If he
were lonely it was a state he had dwelt in so long that he would
not be aware of its existence. He seemed to want nothing – and no
one.

I went then, back to look at the scroll again. I would not forget
it, must not. I would not let them lull me here into forgetting why
I had come. That strange woman, Mairi Sinclair, was the mother
of a strange son, and the fevered words on William's scroll might
well have truth in them. The slow fire of my anger and grief was
kindled again, and now there was a kind of jealousy as well – of
Gavin Campbell's wife. William had not told me. Of all the
omissions of his letters, it was this I found hardest to accept.

3

When Morag came to tell me that she had come, I could see the
curiosity alive in the girl's face, the faint apricot blush staining
her cheeks, and the shining red curls almost crackling with excitement at the uniqueness of the happening.

'It's herself! Lady Campbell has come to call!'

I rose from the desk in the tower room where I had been trying
to write a letter to Peking. It was a morning of discontent – the
sun strong and golden, but in this whole lovely world I surveyed
from these windows there seemed no place I could say was my
own to venture. The distillery was my grandfather's and Callum
Sinclair's, the garden belonged to his mother – beyond was Ballochtorra and the kirkyard, but that was where I did not want to go
again so soon. The fields and the pastures were beautiful in the
morning light, but a kind of tiredness of spirit was on me. They
would all wait.

But I did give the stray ends of my hair a little attention, and
put on more elegant shoes before I followed Morag down the
stairs. In the hall I automatically turned to go to the dining-room,
but an agonized whisper from Morag halted me. 'No – no, the
parlour! She's in the parlour! I've lighted the fire, and Mistress
Sinclair is brewing tea . . .' She was pointing to a door opposite

the dining-room.

The parlour. How strange I had not been tempted to try this door, to look inside – for all I knew it might have opened on an empty room. Why did I suppose that at Cluain all the doors must be locked? Was it Mairi Sinclair's hovering presence that deterred me; had I already so much given way to her possessiveness that I did not dare to open a door, or go and sit on a garden bench? If that was true, then I had come from China for nothing, and she would succeed in driving me from Cluain.

So I lifted my head and straightened my shoulders, assuming the air of the mistress of the establishment, as I opened the parlour door.

I had expected to dislike her on sight, but that was impossible. She had been staring towards the window, and as I entered she turned her head slowly with a movement of supreme grace, and rose to her feet.

Her voice was gentle, soft, almost childlike. 'Miss Howard – I hope I have not come at an inappropriate time. I wanted to welcome you among us. And, of course, to offer my sympathy on your father's death. And William – dear William. Gavin and I were both so fond of him. It is so sad for you . . .'

They were ordinary enough words, but when she said them, no one could have believed she did not mean them. I went forward to offer my hand, and she came to meet me. Yes, it could be true – it was just possibly true, what Gavin Campbell had said; she might have been considered the most beautiful woman in the kingdom. She was a golden creature – golden hair swept up under her hard riding hat, golden eyes with darker flecks in them, and a fringe of dark lashes, incredibly white skin. I couldn't help thinking, in those first moments, that she reminded me of a kitten not quite grown into a cat, a golden striped kitten, with a kitten's delicate grace, a kitten's velvet paws in little white gloves, a kitten's unconscious ability to charm and delight, no matter what she did. Her tan riding habit, accentuating her tiny waist, and the creamy lace at her throat were all part of a superbly organized design. Only a very beautiful woman in this age of overdressing could have worn clothes so simple – simplicity that must also have been outrageously expensive.

'And may I present my son, James – Jamie, we call him. I hope he does not bother you, but he was very anxious to come. He and William were friends.'

I had not noticed the child. He had been standing over near a high-backed chair, waiting with still solemnity until his mother

had finished speaking. Now he came forward and shook hands.
A fair-haired, beautiful child, but he had the intense blue eyes
of his father. One day he would be very much like Gavin Campbell. And one day soon, when that old man died in Edinburgh, he
would be the earl of somewhere. For some reason the thought
made me want to laugh, and so when I took his hand my smile
was broad, and it was answered by a flashing smile from him,
which utterly changed and irradiated that solemn little face.

'How do you do, Miss Howard,' he said, bowing. And then,
quickly : 'You look very like William.'

'It was kind of you both to call,' I said. 'Won't you please sit
down.'

'Thank you,' Lady Campbell said. 'Jamie and I have just been
admiring this room. It *is* very splendid, isn't it? One doesn't see
much like it these days. Now it is all frills and bows and sashes,
like a little girl's dress. This furniture must be *very* old.' She said
it with a kind of breathless reverence, as if she had not the means
herself to command such things. I found later it was a habit of
hers to admire other people's possessions extravagantly, as if she
had none of her own.

I looked around the room, and did not say I had never been in
it before. The furniture was the dark, carved oak that was in the
other rooms, as sparse, as devotedly polished. There was a long
table, a tall press, stiff chairs softened only by faded red silk
cushions. This room was grander than the others with its linenfold
panelling and carvings on the mantel. There was a central brass
chandelier, and wrought-iron fire-dogs. It also had the only carpet
I had seen in the house – a silken, worn, fragile thing, in fading
reds and golds. Instead of the inevitable Clanranald tartan at the
windows there was red brocade, very old, and fraying at its long
folds.

'Perhaps it should be *your* furniture, Lady Campbell. It probably
came from Ballochtorra in the first place and was brought here
to furnish Cluain, as the dower house.'

'Do you think so?' Her red lips twisted in a smile. 'I'm rather
glad it's not mine. I don't think I could live up to it – and I do
so like to curl up on a sofa. Perhaps I *do* like the frills and bows,
after all.'

'Those are ours,' Jamie said suddenly, pointing at the fire-dogs.
'They have our crest. The Campbells of Cawdor.'

I leaned forward and looked closely, and saw the shields embossed with the swan with the arched neck. They reminded me
uncomfortably of Big Billy. 'So they are,' I said. 'But my great-

38

grandmother was a Campbell of Cawdor – and in any case, I don't think my grandfather would give them back.' I heard myself with amazement. Was this the same person, two days in the Highlands and already falling into the romantic notions Gavin Campbell had warned me of?

'I *know* he wouldn't,' Jamie replied. 'He wouldn't sell *my* grand-father a part of Cluain – even though he offered a great deal of money for it.'

'Oh, hush, Jamie!' his mother said. 'You talk too much. We all know Mr Macdonald would never sell Cluain.'

'Grandfather didn't. He still thinks it should be part of Balloch-torra – as it once was.'

'Greedy little boy. You can't have everything.'

For once I was thankful for the appearance of Mairi Sinclair. She opened the door for Morag, who now wore an even more stiffly starched apron and cap than before, her hair severely tucked in, but her high colour and excitement unquenched. She bore a large silver tray set with cups and a silver tea service. In silence, as Mairi Sinclair stood by the door, she laid it gently on the table, and then went to the hall and brought a second tray, this one set with plates of scones and bread and butter, tiny griddle cakes, two kinds of jam, thinly sliced ham, little golden cup cakes. All this at eleven o'clock in the morning, and all presented as if Lady Camp-bell's visit had been expected for a week. I looked with respect at Mairi Sinclair; she had even brought the scents of her herb garden in the fresh parsley and watercress. She did not acknowledge my glance with a look of her own; just stood with the rough hands folded before her, seeing that Morag did each thing correctly, and then both withdrew, the door closing soundlessly.

'So!' Lady Campbell said. 'That's the wonder-woman of Cluain! I've never had a chance to study her before. Oh, she's in the kirk every Sunday there's a service, but always in the back pew, and always the first out of the door when the service is ended. Before the last of the gossipers are off the steps, you can see her striding down the road towards home. They say . . . they say that in any weather she refuses to ride in the trap to kirk when Angus Macdonald attends. How many times has Gavin stopped to offer to take her even as far on her way as Ballochtorra, and all we've had is a shake of that head, half-hidden in the folds of a plaid? She will keep that plaid when every other woman in Scotland is wearing a hat. And yet . . . if only I had her for Ballochtorra. *My* lazy lot couldn't produce this – ' she indicated the splendidly spread trays, 'if I'd given them a month's warning. And how she keeps

this place! Do you suppose . . .' She gave a little, childish laugh
as she accepted a cup of tea from my hands. 'Do you suppose a
speck of dust is ever *allowed* into this house? – or is it all frightened
away by the sight of her? No – perhaps I don't want her for
Ballochtorra, after all. She rather frightens me. She would think
me a silly, useless thing – which I am. But one doesn't like to *know*
that servants know it too well.'

'You are a fairy, Mama . . . and she is a witch! A witch all
dressed in black.'

'That's wicked of you to say such a thing, Jamie! Mistress
Sinclair does nothing but good. She is a good woman.'

'Some people say she is a witch,' the boy insisted.

'What a baby you are! There's no such thing as a witch.'

'She must be a witch, or she would have saved William. But
William died.'

I thought that white skin turned whiter. She shot an anguished
look at me, and then turned to her son. 'Never let me hear you
talk such nonsense again, Jamie. Wicked nonsense. It is cruel,
and unkind – and untrue! You know what your father says – it
would be better to have Mistress Sinclair nurse one than half the
doctors in Edinburgh. Now hush, child, and remember that
Mistress Sinclair is a good woman . . . Here, Jamie, have a griddle
cake. They are much lighter than the ones at home.'

She distracted the child, and he munched happily. The dark
presence of Mairi Sinclair seemed altered by the good things
she presented. We talked for a few minutes of nothing of consequence. The weather – what I might expect of a Highland summer.
'You will need your woollens *all* the time,' Lady Campbell warned.
'Thank heaven Papa will have the London house ready this winter.
But it will take a lot of persuasion to get Gavin there. I almost
think he loves it best here when the snow is thick. Oh, but the
wind from the mountains . . .' The fresh scone crumbled between
those delicate fingers, and she left it unfinished on the plate.

She rose to go. 'You will come to Ballochtorra, won't you? It's
so dull here – no company. Of course, when the shooting opens
we will have almost more company than we want. The Prince of
Wales has consented to pay us a visit . . .' She tried to say it as if
it were nothing, but a look of pleased triumph lighted her face. It
was the supreme accolade for such a young hostess. Again the little
laugh. 'Of course it is most kind of His Royal Highness, but it still
frightens me a little. So much to prepare. Papa is sending lots of
extra servants from London, but still so much can go wrong. All
the guests bring their own personal servants, of course, but I must

fit them all in somewhere. And all according to the rank of the master. I expect there will be anarchy in the servants' hall. It will be a simple affair, but we must give *one* entertainment apart from the shooting. A small dinner, with dancing afterwards – just the local people who would expect to be invited to meet the Prince. *You* will come, won't you? The Prince likes pretty women . . .'

I murmured something, a little awestruck, and already wondering, as women always do, what I would wear.

'Do you ride, Miss Howard?'

'Not very well. There were some tough little ponies in Peking, and one just learned to hold on.'

'I'm sure Gavin will be pleased to mount you from the stables if there is nothing suitable here. William used to use our horses.' The light little laugh again. 'I don't think Mr Macdonald liked that, but William always did what he wanted.' She took a last look around the room. 'I'm glad I've been here at last. Cluain has always fascinated me. How strange your coming here has given me the first chance to pay a visit. One could hardly pay a call on William. You *will* come to Ballochtorra, won't you?' she pressed again. 'I am at home every day, except when I ride. It would be nice to have a friend close by. You *will* call me Margaret, won't you . . . ?' It spilled on, the needless, almost guileless generosity, as if she must make an enormous effort to please, she who pleased with no effort but just looking as she did. It was as if a great uncertainty possessed her, as if she must gather everyone into her fold, so that there would be no enemies, only friends.

We went to the front door. Mairi Sinclair was there before us, waiting by the open door; a man, probably summoned from the stables, was standing holding a fine bay mare and an almost cream-coloured pony. Morag stood beside the mare, and she was feeding her from a bunch of young carrots. She offered a shy smile to Margaret Campbell, and the answering smile was radiant. I noted the carrots and thought that Mairi Sinclair was oddly indulgent of Morag at times – or was it that she simply liked animals, but could not unbend to feed the mare herself?

Margaret Campbell's light, graceful form sprang up to the side-saddle with only the semblance of assistance from the stableman. Jamie managed to mount by himself, proud of the fact. The woman's beautiful young face looked down at me. For the first time I saw the faintest hint of shadow upon it. 'Thank you for receiving me. I've enjoyed myself. It's lovely here. William and I used to ride together . . .'

And then she wheeled the mare, and the child followed eagerly.

They headed down the strath away from Ballochtorra. Big Billy and his flock came towards the pair, but somehow were halted by the faintly imperious wave from Lady Campbell's riding crop. Could she charm even that surly brute, I wondered? I was conscious of Mairi Sinclair staring after them, just as I was, that lovely couple, graced by beauty and wealth.

But it was Morag's voice that came from the doorway. 'Hardly a thing did she eat – and all that fuss! Well, a body can't stay a slip of a thing and eat your fill and do no work. True enough that Master William rode with her . . . I'm thinking she's looking for another company now.'

Mairi Sinclair turned on her fiercely. 'Hold your tongue, girl! Hold it, I say! We'll not have evil gossip here – '

I could not face them. I let them go back into the house, and I stood there watching as the riders continued on down the road. I was hearing again Gavin Campbell's words. 'He was more than half in love with my wife.' His voice so toneless, as if it were something he had come to expect. *'An enchantress . . .'* But somehow my jealousy was dissipated. Even I could not help falling under her spell; if she beguiled and bewitched, it seemed hardly more fair to blame her than if she had been a child, innocent, unknowing. I stood there until they were out of sight.

When I went back into the house the door to the drawing-room was closed. I opened it and looked inside. It was as still, as silent and waiting as if no one had entered here. There was not a crumb of the many Jamie had shed to betray his presence, the rug he had rumpled was straightened, the faded silk cushions plumped up. Only the fire spoke of people having been here. I was sure that Mairi Sinclair was only waiting for it to die, and Morag would be here clearing out the still-warm ashes, and laying a fresh one. A beautiful, sad, unused room, that should have been full of life. Had one of my ancestors stitched the tapestry firescreen – yes, that also bore the Campbell arms. Christina Campbell had locked us together – Cluain and Ballochtorra.

That afternoon, after a mostly silent and hurried lunch with my grandfather, I took out the old serge skirt and the boots I had worn when I rode those Peking ponies. Without permission I borrowed the Inverness tweed cape I found hanging with the various plaids and walking sticks in the kitchen passage. I took a stick that seemed to fit my height. And then I walked all afternoon. I walked along the way Margaret Campbell had ridden, past the distillery and the warehouses, over the small humpback bridge that crossed a burn which had been diverted and channelled around the warehouses, past the small houses that must be tenanted by the distillery workers, the houses with their neat garden plots. Children played there, young children, sometimes tended by older children, hardy, barefoot, rosy children, with shy, engaging smiles. The women did not seem to be about – except for one old woman sitting in the sun by her doorway, who waved her pipe cheerfully at me. Did the women work in the summer on the farm? I supposed it was so. Work was part of these people's lives, inescapable, unless you were Angus Macdonald's granddaughter, or as free of toil or worry as Margaret Campbell. I turned off on a track that led upwards through Cluain's pastures, and bent to follow roughly the twists of a small, fiercely-running burn, whose water was icily cold. The track threaded away from the pasture and into a shadowed glen. A little farther on, stepping-stones led across the burn to a neat stone cottage, with a stout paling fence about it, and a well-thatched stable. But its door was shut, and no smoke came from the chimney. Did my sense tell me right that this was where Callum Sinclair lived? It would not be among the other workers – and there seemed no other place this side of the river. It somehow resembled him, this place – the clear-running burn separating him from the rest of the world, the closed door, the air of aloofness and self-sufficiency. This was his manner, and this could well be his place.

Beyond here, the track grew rougher and the glen steeper; I turned back to the high pastures of Cluain. All the time as I walked I kept scanning the sky for the sight of the falcon. If she were in flight would she note and mark me with her hawk's eye, not something to interest her, and pass on overhead, unseen, unheard, as aloof as her master? I walked until I was tired, until the pasture gave way to heather. I flung myself down on its rough cushion, listening to the bees drone about me. William had described to me how these heather moors of Scotland turned a mauvish haze in the autumn, how the long shafts of sun would suddenly light a spot and turn it to royal purple. But he had not told me how Cluain's world looked from up here. I could still see the distillery buildings – not handsome but no longer ugly to my eyes. I could see the far glint of the river, and the rich green meadows. Ballochtorra was out of sight – from here one saw only the back of the massive crag. This was wholly Cluain's world. It was no wonder my grandfather loved and possessed it with such fierce passion.

I returned with a muddy skirt and a raging hunger. I was waiting, changed, with brushed hair, before the fire when my grandfather came in. 'You've been walking, I hear.'

'Yes.'

'Then have a care. We'll not want to send men to be pulling you from the bog.'

'Will you trust me not to go into a bog? I do not carry a gun, Grandfather, and I cannot be kept on a rein.'

'I thought women had other things . . .'

I held out my empty hands. 'What does Mairi Sinclair leave to me? Would you have me disturb –'

'No – no,' he said quickly. 'Do not disturb anything. Go – but go safely.'

He handed me my dram of whisky without question. How good it tasted as it was meant to be drunk, with my stomach rumbling with hunger, and my cheeks flushed from the sharp air and the long walk. I looked up from the fire and found Angus Macdonald's gaze on me, as if he also knew that I was beginning to feel Cluain's world. But he said nothing. I knew for a long time it would be something felt, not spoken.

We played chess again. I was tired, and yet stimulated. We played two games, and with the second, I won.

The big eyebrows came closer. 'Are you fighting, then?'

'Does one always have to fight?' The tiredness was swamping in. I didn't want to have to fence with him.

'Always,' he answered. 'Always.'

The white cat was on the bench before the fire when I went up to the tower room. He raised his pale eyes to me, and then lay blinking in somnolence. Before I was ready for bed, he went and sat by the door, appealing with nothing but his gesture to be let out. The white shape slipped down the stairs. That night I did not even glance up towards Ballochtorra, nor look down into the garden to see if my grandfather's candle burned. I did not wait for darkness, or the sound of the pony's hooves on the road. I simply slept.

5

The life of Cluain flowed about me, and like a stone in its stream I felt myself rubbed and harried by it, soothed and lulled. The rocks were there, bigger than I, immovable, the weights and counterweights of its whole structure were the customs and habits established over my grandfather's lifetime, a part of Cluain as he had fashioned it, and as the years had fashioned him. Against these rocks I was sometimes dashed and bruised, but I was part, then, of the flow of its life, and such things were accepted. But I also accepted, gratefully, the soothing regularity of its ways, the sense that I was becoming part of the established pattern. I, too, was being accepted. Not in all ways, not by all those here, not always without reservations, but I began to see, in the manner and the gestures of those about me that perhaps – just perhaps – the time would come when I too would be one of the rocks of Cluain.

The tower room both held me remote from it, and yet let me learn its world. From there I saw much and learned much, and a kind of humility came to me at times, because, in fact, it was all so much more complex than the first superficial glance would have revealed. Slowly, I began to forgive William for what he had not written to me. As I grew more absorbed, the details became more intricate, and how did one write to far-off China of a life like this? – especially if he had begun, as I did, to experience its fascination, and if he had not wanted to tell a waiting father and sister that he might never return to the dream of his Chinese railways. How could we have been told that the focus could have shifted from that huge, still mechanically unconquered land, to this green strath, to the lonely glens, to this seemingly narrow world, where all was already settled in its seasonably rhythmical pattern? No, we would not have understood. We would have thought his vision had shrunk, and been disappointed. And then, perhaps he had never meant it to be so. Perhaps he had not cared even to speak to himself of capitulation, lest it make it too irrevocable. It could not have been easy for a young man to allow his dreams to change shape, to alter, and to admit the dominance of Angus Macdonald. And the predominance of Angus Macdonald was the biggest rock of Cluain's world.

So I looked from the tower room, and I saw the ways of Cluain. I saw the passage of the days, the times and the events. I saw the

milking herd brought in in the early morning, and again in the
evening, I saw the changeless, routine work of the farm go on, I
saw Mairi Sinclair's lean body at work in her garden, the white
cat skipping beside her, or playing its own game of hide and seek
with the butterflies among the herbs. I saw, too, and respected, the
thin but never-ending procession of people, mostly women, but with
a number of men among them, who came along the back path to
the kitchen passage door. I saw them come, the women in plaids,
often with babies wrapped within the folds, and I saw them leave.
It was a silent procession, hardly in evidence if one went downstairs, but almost always, I saw, there was someone about the
place patiently waiting to consult Mairi Sinclair about some ail-
ment, asking for some salve or herbal medicine. There was a special
room in which she made these things. Often at night I saw the
light from her lamp cast out on the path beside the window. At
times I would pass people seated on the bench in the kitchen
passage, waiting; we would pass words of greeting, but it was
understood that I never asked the reason for the visit. I saw some
of them leave, faces lighted a little with relief, or at least a sense
of hope imparted. And then I would look at that black-clad figure
with new respect, but looking was as far as it went. Never again
was there a repetition of that first night's encounter on the stairs;
never again did she unveil the emotions that had distorted her
features, nor give that anguished cry. We were acutely aware of
each other, and yet our lives hardly seemed to touch. I left her
domain entirely to her, did not question or interfere with her
routine; I behaved, in that, entirely as if I were a guest with the
freedom of the house, and still respecting the fact that there were
places to which I would not presume. And she – she left me
strictly alone. We passed no words that were not necessary. I never
went to her kitchen; the room where she prepared and stored her
herbs was kept locked. I rarely even went to sit in the garden –
'her garden' I thought of it as being. Certainly, the few times I
was there, she never ventured out. A line of neutrality had been
drawn. Some day, if I stayed at Cluain, I knew it must be crossed,
but the time was not now.

Morag was our messenger between the two territories. It was
she who brought the hot water, the clean towels, my freshly
laundered clothes, she who turned down the bed at night, and
warmed it with a hot jar; she who fussed over me a little, and
asked me questions about China, insatiable to learn of a world
she did not know. She had no inhibitions, like Mairi Sinclair, no
bitternesses, like my grandfather. She wanted both to learn and

to tell. Her tongue rattled on regardless of what her hands did. Without Morag, there was so much of Cluain I might never have known, which would have come to me more slowly. Once as we made my bed together, I commented on the lack of pictures in the house, the absence of ornaments, the little touches that a woman might leave on a house. My mother had grown up here, my grandmother was not so many years dead. Had they lived with this starkness all their lives? And where had the mirror come from that Morag had produced so swiftly that first evening? So far, it was the only one I had seen at Cluain.

'Och, mistress, come now – I'll show you. Mistress Sinclair is in the dairy, and will be busy there this next hour. She does not leave it to the woman who comes to help to see that the churns are properly scalded, ready for the new milk . . .' And I was following her down the tower steps, unable to resist her beckoning voice.

'Wait there, mistress – first I must get the keys.' She was gone before I could stop her, and back again in half a minute. 'Quickly, now, mistress – I'll just unlock, and then I must put the keys back. I will lock up again later. Keys have always to be in their place at Cluain.' She unlocked the door of a room I had never before entered, and rushed down again to replace the keys on the board outside the kitchen door. It was a strange part of the simplicity of the ways of this country. Everything was locked, and yet all keys were displayed where any of those passing could have them to hand. The order was in locking; the trust was in leaving the keys on full view. It was the same with my grandfather, who made a ritual of unlocking the cupboard which contained the whisky each evening with the key from his chain, and yet he had shown me where the second key lay in an unlocked drawer directly above.

While Morag was gone I opened the door, and it revealed the most unexpected room of all at Cluain. Here was all that I had missed. Here were the pictures, many of them stacked against the walls, here were the little ornaments, some of them valuable, that might have graced the mantels of the rooms below, here were the family portraits, and the little painted miniatures of years ago.

'It was your grandmother's bedroom,' Morag said, coming close behind me. 'I almost grew up here. She was often ailing – always delicate. She needed things brought to her, and a child is good at fetching and carrying. Och – not that I minded. She was so good to me. Always sweets for me, and explaining whatever it was she was doing. She gave me most of my lessons here. She was a book-reader, your grandmother. The long winter days, when it was too harsh for her to be about, she would be here in bed, with a big fire going, and her books about her, and always an hour or two to spare of teaching me something from them. See, mistress, even the bookcases were brought up here because she did not, in the last years, very often go downstairs.'

Unspeaking, I wandered about. It was a confusion such as no other room at Cluain displayed. The books, yes – the pictures upon the walls. These I understood. But what of this indiscriminate jumbling of ornaments – Meissen bowls and plates, a Prunus vase my mother must have sent from China, silver vases, delf pitchers, engraved glass goblets. So much of this must have been part of the furnishings of Cluain the day Angus Macdonald took title to it. Laid face-down on the writing table were some framed daguer-reotypes; when I turned them over I saw faces more familiar than my own was now. These same likenesses had been the only adorn-ments of my father's study in Peking – the likeness of my mother, with myself as an infant on her knee, William standing by her side; my father as he held his first-born child after the christening, the four of us together after I had been able to stand on my own feet to face the camera. My grandfather must have looked at them often. They had not always lain face-downwards on the table.

I moved along, stopping to lift away from the walls some of the pictures stacked against them. Nothing distinguished, that I could judge, but the ordinary rural scenes that might once have hung on the walls of the rooms below – a portrait or two – which ancestor I didn't know. There were rolled-up carpets and rugs. There were four mirrors, of various sizes, one of them exquisitely framed in silver-gilt, and, I guessed, rare.

I went to one of the two big gable windows. The room was on the south-facing wing of the house, overlooking the herb garden, and giving a lower, not so awesome view of the Cairngorms as the tower room. It was large and lofty – with the fourposter bed it was quite a grand room, but without the intimidating quality that the tower room could sometimes possess. From here, the sight of Bal-lochtorra was blotted out.

I turned back from the window. 'Why this, Morag? Why are all these things here?'

'It is not so easy to understand, mistress. When Mistress Mac-donald died, gradually the things were brought here – the orna-ments and pictures and such. Mistress Sinclair said it was for safe-keeping. She did not want them broken, or worn out. And the Master, he did not seem to notice, or care. He never comes in here. Mistress Sinclair seems to think it is sinful to have ornaments about – though I think myself there cannot be much sin in a picture or a carpet. But she thinks life should not be too easy. She has her ways, mistress, and a body gets used to them. I tell you, though, I missed your grandmother sorely when she was gone. More than my own mother she was to me. I was ten then – almost eight years ago, it was. But Mistress Sinclair has not been unkind, you understand. She let me have a few little things for my room – a small mirror, some flower pictures. She lets me take one book at a time from the bookcases. But I have read them all now, and I am going through a second time. I have to come here to dust every week, and I think of your grandmother very often . . . a good lady, she was, Mistress Kirsty, and sad that she never saw Master William or yourself . . .'

So Morag's voice ran on, as constant a sound of Cluain as the river, explaining and telling. I stood before the window again, thinking of a different Cluain that my grandmother had presided over, a softer, gentler house. Yes, Morag must miss her, as I would have done. I turned back, and Morag was gone, leaving me alone to look once again at the pictures, to read the titles of the books – the Brontës, Jane Austen, Sir Walter Scott, Wordsworth, Tennyson, Coleridge. The idealized porcelain figurines of the shepherdesses on the mantel did not represent the real world as Mairi Sinclair had experienced it. And Morag, with her innate sense of tact and discretion, was leaving me to discover this other side of Cluain for myself. After that, I went back to the tower room and unpacked the pictures I had taken from my father's study – the same ones that lay in my grandmother's room, and I set them up on the desk. I knew I was staking my first claim on Cluain with that action, and Mairi Sinclair could make what she liked of it.

I continued to walk Cluain's world, and beyond it. I would follow the tracks wherever they led, sometimes through the gently sloping barley fields, sometimes to the higher meadows where the cattle cropped the summer grass, sometimes going farther into difficult country, rough and steep, where the tracks led to the moors on the slopes of the mountains, and would end in the peat diggings. The rich brown sediment was cut to the depth of several spades, and the water ran from the bog into the channels left by the cuttings; at intervals the peat was stacked to dry, piled neatly on end, waiting to be carted down to Cluain – or to whomever owned the bog. I was not always sure when I went beyond Cluain's land. Much of the moors, I knew, belonged to Ballochtorra, and so did the belts of forest. I wandered there, and sat on the film of pine needles, listening to the wind in the high branches; occasionally, then, I would catch sight of the red deer which roamed the moors and forests, some of them with their fawns, peacefully grazing, living through the days of their respite, their growing days, before the guns of the autumn would come. And finally I found the courage to explore the craggy area beyond Ballochtorra, the place where my grandfather said William had lain. There were massive outcroppings of granite, and some tall trees clinging precariously to the thin soil, oaks and beeches that had survived the feeling of poorer times when fuel had been short; but mostly here it was slender, dense, second growth, birch and larch and fir which must have seeded themselves, the cover lavish and beautiful in the summer months. And there were places where the rock was so sheer that no cover at all could find a hold there, and birds were its only inhabitants. It would have been from some such ledge that Callum Sinclair had brought down the eyas peregrine he had called Giorsal. There were many places among these rocks where William might have fallen, many places where he might have dragged himself to find a little shelter. I thought of these places whipped by wind and flying snow, as they had been at that time. I did not ask my grandfather the precise place where William had been found; that much I did not want to know.

But Angus Macdonald himself was not unaware of my wanderings. Sometimes I was back to the midday meal after he himself had come in. He never waited the meal for me, nor got up to serve me if I were late.

'I'm sorry,' I would apologize. 'I went farther than I intended.'

'One day you'll go too far.' He nodded towards the sideboard. 'Your meal is there.'

And the day came when Morag brought the summons from him to come to the stableyard. I found him there, and a man I had never seen before – not one of the farm or distillery workers – who jerked his bonnet towards me. He was holding the bridle of a Highland pony, a grey, plump creature, who looked at me with sure, calm eyes.

'Think you can ride her, Gurrl?' my grandfather asked.

'I can try.'

'Try her about the yard. See how you suit her.' It was obvious that he intended the pony to be suited by me, not me by the pony. She was short, and I swung myself up to the sidesaddle before either man could extend a hand. My legs seemed to trail, but she had such a broad back, I felt as if I couldn't be shaken off my perch. And that awkward-seeming animal had a surprisingly even gait, and a good mouth. She was not nervous, nor tense, just knowing. I felt, as I rode about the stableyard, that she would tolerate me, and do her duty by me as long as I treated her with equal respect.

'She'll carry you well, mistress,' the man said. 'She's not young, but she's stronger than many I've known, and sure-footed as a goat. She'll not lead you into any mischief.'

'What do you call her?'

'She is called Ailis. But if you – if Mr Macdonald – well, you may call her what you please. She'll not mind.'

'She should be called what she's always been called – Ailis.' I stroked the grey mane; she stood, quiet and patient, tolerating my long legs, my stranger's hand. 'Are you selling her, then?'

'I must, mistress. My wife and I, we're bound to Canada – to relatives. Ailis has been with us these thirteen years. We would leave her with a good master in a place she's used to.'

'Used to it, she is,' my grandfather said. 'She must know every road and track and path in this country – eh, Mr Ross.'

'All of it, Mr Macdonald. The garron of an exciseman goes everywhere. She's carried me safe and sound since she was a three-year-old, over every kind of country, and never put a foot wrong. You'll get no speed from her, mind, but she's the stamina of a dray-horse, and six times the sense.'

'Well, then, it's settled. You'll take her to the end box, Kirsty, and rub her down, and water and feed her. She'll be yours to take care of, mind, and I'll tolerate no neglect . . . Now, Mr Ross, if you'll kindly come to the office we'll finish our business, and you'll take a dram with me. Duty paid, of course,' he added, a rare attempt at a joke. The exciseman paused for a moment, laid a hand lingeringly on Ailis, and then moved off.

I slid down from the saddle, and looked at my gift horse. She returned my look, and then she slowly turned her head towards the stable, as if she knew exactly where she would be housed, and how plentiful the oats would be – a broad, inelegant-looking creature whose presence here spoke for him what my grandfather would not say. She would carry me well and safely, knowing this whole countryside; there would be no repetition of what had befallen William. Ailis was to be my companion and my guide.

So I led her to her box, and the stableman, John Farquharson, came to help me unsaddle, and showed me which pegs in the tack-room would be for Ailis's harness. He helped me rub her down, and feed her, and he evidently enjoyed working with that comfortable, plump little creature. 'Aye, she's a fine wee lass,' he said. 'A nice change, mistress, from the big lads I'm dealing with all the time.' He nodded towards the stalls of the huge Clydesdales that pulled the distillery drays loaded with the whisky casks to the rail-head at Ballinaclash — and to the empty boxes of the farm work-horses, those that pulled the plough, and the grain wagons at the harvest. There was only one other animal in the stable at Cluain — 'The Sunday Lad' he was jokingly called, an undistinguished-looking horse which drew the hooded trap when Angus Macdonald left his farm. The stable and smithy's shop reflected the house. Everything that was necessary was there, all clean, oiled, painted, well fed, well cared for. The Clydesdales were magnificent in their strength; The Sunday Lad would never be given a second glance, nor would the trap he pulled. They were decent, and more than adequate for their purpose, but they would rouse no envy in anyone's heart. It was precisely that effect that my grandfather sought. 'It's a fool,' he once said to me, 'who shows the world all he's got.' So in this age of display, my grandfather drove a modest horse and trap, and there was no way of telling if he could have afforded more.

The Sunday Lad did not so often come out on Sunday. The first Sunday I was there Angus Macdonald made his gesture to the curiosity of the community, and he drove me to the kirk. 'Och, they'll want to have their look at you, but they know fine well that your father was an Anglican bishop, and they'll not be expecting his daughter to be a prop of the Presbyterian establishment. They hold no brief for bishops in Scotland, you know. It's for the sake of your mother, and for your brother lying there in the kirkyard that you must occasionally show yourself. Myself, I've little time for the kirk. I would not say I was not a God-fearing man, but I'm not in agreement with the kind of God I get served up by this minister, and his sermons are too long, by a long way. And then, I've reason to remember that the ministers of the Church were often on the side of the lairds during the years of the Highland clearances, when the landlords wanted the people out, and the whole country turned into a sheep-walk. Too few of them stood by their human flocks, and too many instructed them that it was God's will that they obey their lairds, and remove themselves from the straths where their families and clans had lived for hundreds of years. They sent those poor bewildered creatures off on those rotten hulks to die of cholera and typhoid on the way to Canada, and they sent them with a sermon, saying it was God's will. And the people were meek, and obeyed, because it had always been the clan system to obey the chieftain. But I cannot forgive the men who helped make it easy for the lairds.'

'Your father was a laird.'

'Aye, he was that. The laird of a poor, small little island and *he* owed allegiance to the Clanranald chief. The people left Inishfare because the land could not support their numbers. It was not the sheep that drove them out, but the potato famines, and the poorness of the soil. It needed no minister to tell them to go. We were so small we had no minister of our own – just one who was rowed to us a few times a year for marryings, and christenings, and churchings, and such. Our dead we buried ourselves, and said the prayers over them, and the minister added his bit when he chose to come. But we mostly lived without him, and were not the less godly for it.'

'So you have one more reason not to care for my father?'

'Aye – you might say that,' he admitted calmly, as if his judgement could not be questioned. 'They're all cut from the same cloth, whatever kind of God they say they represent. I never saw a starving clergyman yet.'

And I would hotly deny that, and tell him of my father's labour in China – the burning heat of summer, the bitter cold of the winters when he worked among the poor, and was ill among them, and often received no respect or thanks for his pains. But my grandfather took no notice. 'More fool he, then. If they laughed at his Christian God, then he would have done better to expend his labours elsewhere. There's enough lying in ignorance and want in the slums of Glasgow without wasting men among the heathens and "rice Christians".' And I never found an answer to that.

So I was presented for all to look at in the kirk of Ballochtorra. Mairi Sinclair, as Lady Campbell had predicted, declined to ride with us in the trap, nor had my grandfather even invited her. 'She's already more than halfway there,' he said, when the trap was brought to the front door, and I murmured her name. 'In the winter snows, and the hot summer mornings, she's the first in kirk, and the first to leave, and no thank you to man nor beast for carrying her there. Leave it alone, Gurrl.'

We did, and I was embarrassed to find myself in the front pew, opposite Margaret Campbell and Jamie. Jamie waved, and smiled at me, and the minister frowned at him; Margaret Campbell turned at Jamie's nudging and bowed her head, more, I thought, towards Angus Macdonald than myself. My grandfather did not appear to see her. It might have been one of the few times in her life that Margaret Campbell had had the experience of not being seen.

And Gavin Campbell was in the organ loft, playing the simple

hymn tunes on the organ far too powerful for them. As I listened
to the homily, I understood better why he preferred to be there,
and not in the front pew. But it was over at last, and the congregation had their chance to examine me in detail. There was
a rather frigid handshake from the minister, and a moment's conversation with Margaret Campbell and Jamie as they waited for
Gavin to come down from the organ loft. It seemed to me that
he made an unnecessary delay. My grandfather did nothing more
than remove his hat while Margaret Campbell spoke. He nodded
to her, and made his way down the path to where he had tied
The Sunday Lad, and I was up on the seat beside him before
Gavin Campbell made his appearance.

About half a mile along the road we came abreast of Mairi
Sinclair. My grandfather did not even check the pace of The
Sunday Lad as he went by! By the barest tip of his fingers to his
hat he acknowledged her presence, the tall slender black figure
wrapped in the red Sinclair plaid. 'Nay, Gurrl,' he said to me, as
I laid my hand upon his arm. 'Leave it . . . leave it be.'

I ventured then one of my questions. 'Does Callum Sinclair come
to kirk?'

'Callum Sinclair?' My grandfather flicked the reins lightly over
The Sunday Lad. 'What should I know of what Callum Sinclair
does or does not do? It is not my business – nor yours, either.'

It was my grandfather's gift of Ailis which made me much freer
in the world of Cluain. The sturdy little creature carried me over
the miles of ground my own legs could never have walked; she
would follow without direction trails at which I had hesitated
before; with her I reached mountain slopes that seemed impossibly
distant, and she was sure-footed as a mule in the steep places of
the glens. I cut no very fine figure on her, I knew; I wore the old
serge skirt with the Clanranald plaid about my shoulders, or to
cover my head when the showers passed over. But I was free –
wonderfully free, and the pony seemed to understand my joy in it,
and even to share it. She was not quick, but she never seemed to
tire, and when I went to her box in the morning she accepted my
gift of sugar calmly, and showed no resentment at the sight of the
saddle. Perhaps she also enjoyed the lack of routine of our days.
When we set out we took whatever direction seemed to offer itself
that morning; sometimes I even let her do the choosing, and I
think her pride was flattered by this. We became a pair, the garron
and I, and it was she who led me to Callum Sinclair.

I saw him very seldom about the distillery yard, and he would pass me with a murmured greeting, tossed to me, I sometimes thought, as if I were a child; he never stopped to talk, and I never had an excuse to detain him. I would see him often on the pony, with Giorsal and the dog on the road that led past Cluain and Ballochtorra. Since I did not go to Mairi Sinclair's kitchen, I never again encountered him there, but occasionally the pony would be tied up in the stableyard, and I would know he was inside. It was hard to imagine that Giorsal accompanied him there, and the dog, but harder to imagine him without them. Did Giorsal perch on the kitchen mantel, and the dog lie before the range? Did he come as a duty to see his mother? – or to eat, as so many seemed to do, at that table? He would not be the only one to leave Cluain's kitchen with fresh-baked bread, and slices of ham. My grandfather must have known that no one of the many who came to consult Mairi Sinclair went away empty-handed, and he did nothing to prevent it. All that would have been settled between them long ago. Mairi Sinclair scorned to hide the giving, perhaps taking quite literally the biblical injunction to heal the sick and feed the hungry. But her son did not linger very long in the kitchen of Cluain; he was like his falcon, bound by the long red streamers, but impatient to be free.

After a time I had to acknowledge to myself that I was indeed searching for Callum Sinclair on those journeys with Ailis. I knew now that it was his small house, set off by itself, that I had discovered on one of my first walks. Shamelessly now, I turned Ailis's head in that direction. For almost two weeks I went that way, and always the door of the cottage stood closed, and I heard no movement of the pony in the stable; when I was early enough the chimney still smoked from the morning's fire, but the silence over the place was absolute.

And then the morning came when I rode that way early enough to hear the ring of the axe right across the strath. He was engrossed enough at the work that he didn't even hear our approach – only the dog set up a fierce barking, and he turned and looked towards us as we came up the track by the burn. He stood, then, resting on the axe beside the pile of timber he was splitting, breathing heavily, and with a gesture motioning the dog to silence. I faced him across the rushing water.

'Well – aren't you going to ask me in?'

For a moment he didn't move. Then with a slight shrug he came and opened the gate, and Ailis moved through the water on her own accord. 'If it amuses you.'

'Amuses me? Why should it amuse me?'

'Well – aren't you paying a call on the tenantry? I expect you
any moment to command my honest toil. Or have you come with
a message from Angus Macdonald telling me I've been away from
the distillery too long?'

Avoiding his outstretched hand, I slid down off the pony. 'You
know very well I don't carry messages for my grandfather. Nor
would he send me.'

'You're right about that – he wouldn't. Why have you come then
– curiosity?'

'Probably,' I admitted. 'You keep to yourself, Callum Sinclair.'

'And how else could it be? I'm hardly welcome in the front
parlour of Cluain.'

'Have you tried?' I tossed the words over my shoulder, not giving
him time to reply. 'Well, do you invite me into *your* parlour? I *am*
curious.'

'And I'm expected to satisfy your curiosity? A man's home is
his own, you know, and he's a right to keep to himself if he fancies
it.' Then he shrugged again. 'Well – why not? You're here now.
And I was just finishing up the wood. It's time for a cup of tea.
You can make it for us while I stack this lot.'

So I entered Callum Sinclair's house alone. He went back to his
log pile, and I was left, again like an inquisitive child, to do as I
liked. On the outside it was not like the houses of other distillery
workers, which were built of stone and slate, as the warehouses.
This was much older. It had probably been here as long as Cluain
itself. The thatch was new, and the windows seemed bigger than
most – I guessed that Callum had enlarged them. Also missing
were the inevitable hens that scratched about the doors of other
households. There was a tidy, almost painfully constrained look
about the place, as if no one really lived here.

But when I opened the door the kitchen-living-room was more
comfortable than I had expected. Callum Sinclair's hard-boned
austerity did not extend too far; I was surprised at the sight of the
shabby but still good leather sofa before the fire, the big roll-top
desk over against the opposite wall near the window, the bright
red curtains and cushions, a fairly new Turkish carpet that covered
most of the wooden floor. I didn't know what I had been expecting;
not the bare-earthed poverty of many Highland cottages, but,
unconsciously, perhaps, a repetition of Mairi Sinclair's painfully
ordered environment. It was a relief to see an open book flung
across the broad arm of the sofa, to see the untidy jumble of them
that spilled from the deal shelves running along one wall. There
was another open book beside the unwashed breakfast dishes on

the big table, and a scatter of crumbs over its surface. I lifted the kettle and put it in place on the range.

'I didn't really mean it.' I turned at the sound of his voice. 'I am not so inhospitable as you think. I was coming to make it.'

'You think I don't know how to?'

He went over to the sink and pumped water to wash his hands. 'I don't know what to expect. One doesn't know much about a bishop's daughter. Here in Scotland we don't know much about bishops – we think of them living in palaces, and their families.'

'Their families have no more money than the diocese can afford. My father's diocese was thousands of square miles, and his converts so poor he had to try to feed *them* – with money subscribed in England. There wasn't much left for himself. The only luxury William ever got was the promise of an education – and he didn't even have time to finish that.'

'And you? – what were your luxuries?' He had dried his hands, and was putting on a tweed jacket. Somehow, here in his own house, he seemed suddenly less withdrawn, less on the defensive – the tweed jacket instead of the sheepskin, the buttoning of his shirt collar, the way he carried the used dishes from the table and swept off the crumbs with a flick of a cloth. He brought fresh cups on a wooden tray to a table near the range, and made the tea with swift, efficient movements. His movements were part of the attraction of the man – nothing wasted, everything quite sure and un-hesitating. And when there was no more to do, he was still.

'Luxuries? I had my father and William. That is more than most have. We were a close family. We had books, and good Chinese food. We had servants – but in China it is impossible not to have servants. I was probably the least fashionably dressed female among the Europeans, but it hardly mattered. My father was often shabby, but no one seemed to mind that.'

He rose and poured the tea. 'It doesn't matter with you, either.' And his eyes took in the old shirt and the muddied boots, the plaid that I was coming to wear as Highland women did, serving as a garment for every purpose. His gaze was quiet and steady; I could take his words to mean what I pleased.

'Have a scone. They come from Cluain, so I suppose they're yours.'

I shook my head, and looked at him over the cup. 'Can't we stop this nonsense? You're an educated man, Callum Sinclair. All this game about being subservient at Cluain is unbecoming – worse than that, it's foolish. Cluain isn't mine – and you are not a servant. Can we have that settled?'

He actually smiled – a faint motion, like light breaking grudgingly through winter clouds, and then being covered too quickly. Like my grandfather, he didn't seem to have had much practice in smiling. 'And you're no fool. Well, all right – it's settled. I'll try to remember. Or at least I'll try to forget that you're Angus Macdonald's granddaughter.'

'If you feel that way about him, why did you come back to Cluain? There must have been other positions open to you – places where you wouldn't have had to . . .'

He raised his eyebrows. 'Wouldn't have had to work with my hands? Well, I suppose I could have found something. But that's just it. I *like* working with my hands. Most of all, I like being in the country – *this* country. I've known it all my life, and if there's any place I've loved, it's here. The only way I could have this and my independence as well was to work for Angus Macdonald. I could have worked for another distillery, but Cluain is . . . different. I thought about Canada or Australia, as so many of we Highlanders are forced to do. I probably would have herded sheep in Australia, or hunted for fur in Canada. Oh, I might have escaped some of the master and servant tradition. But I would not have been in the place I wanted to be. And no man is a servant who does not feel himself to be one. So I have stayed . . . for one reason or another I have stayed.'

'You didn't just stay,' I pointed out. 'You came back.'

'I came back only when Angus Macdonald asked me to. The head stillman was killed when a cask fell off a dray and crushed him. There were others here – but none Angus Macdonald thought would do as well for Cluain as I. Whatever it is that whisky needs – the nose, the eye, the sense – apparently in your grandfather's opinion I have it. If he could have done without me, he would have. We have no great liking for each other. But he sent for me, and we struck our bargain. I would work whatever hours the distillery required as long as it was required. In the summer I would be free of farm work – I would not harvest his barley, or herd his cattle. As long as the distillery was served, I was my own man. If I choose to work past midnight when we are in production, then it is because I am needed. And I will wade through any snow to get down there by six the next morning. But here, in this house, in the hours and the months that are mine, he has no rights. I do as I please. That is what we agreed. That is how it has been for the past three years.'

'But can't be forever.'

'Why not?'

'Most men marry. They take wives. They have children . . .'

He made a gesture of impatience. 'When the time is right. I have not yet found the woman worth giving up what I have – '

'They marry,' I repeated. 'They give their hostages to fortune.'

'Marry!' It was as if I had let loose a storm. He rose abruptly, the fluid body suddenly now tensed. 'Marry – and put fetters on myself.' The cup crashed down against the hob. 'With a mother like mine who never needed to clothe herself in the respectability of marriage, how would you expect me to feel? If she could stand her solitary state, and bear her son alone, and nameless, what need do I have to rush into those kinds of bonds . . . ?'

I was strangely touched that he should in this way refer to his birth. He was sensitive and irascible, and I knew that every minute he was acting as the son of Mairi Sinclair would act. I liked it that he felt no need to make apologies for her, and was proud of her courage. They might quarrel, those two, but they were the same breed, as Morag had said.

'And yet – most women give themselves into the bondage of marriage. They do as they are told. They bear children and nurse sick husbands. They accept – '

'What else can they do?' he said, with the maddening complacency of a man. 'What else is open to them?'

'Some choose to give themselves. Freely.' Was I mad? Would he think I was referring to his mother?

But his expression changed to a thoughtful regard. 'Yes – there are those who choose. Those who give freely. And they are the only ones worth having. Come – I'll show you something.'

Completely unselfconsciously he seized my hand and jerked me to my feet. My cup was banged down on the tray, and I was being pulled after him. The door was opened and slammed after us. Then I was thrust up against the end wall of the cottage.

'Stay there, and be still. She is accustomed to strangers, and will not bate off, but very few ever come here, and she may not like it in the beginning. Just be still. She will see you, and grow used to you.'

And then he went on, quietly now, into the shed that adjoined the stable. I waited, flattening myself against the wall, trying to keep in the shadow cast by the overhang of the thatch. I was very still, as he had commanded, but I couldn't still the endless hammer of my pulse, the dryness of my throat against which I couldn't even swallow.

He came finally, and the falcon was on his gloved hand, the bird wearing a red, plumed hood, as I had not seen her before. He stood in the open space, the red streamers wound through his fingers, and gently, with his right hand, loosened the leather thongs that held the hood in place, and slipped it off. The hawk saw me at once, and for a moment I thought she would start up; but she simply moved a little on the glove, and flexed those fierce hind talons. Then her head turned, scanning the whole horizon, taking in any new facts of her world. And then, sure that all was as it had been, the huge dark eyes focused on me. I instantly knew, not from any foreknowledge of hawks, but from the sensation those eyes produced in me, that this was truly a bird of prey. She lived by killing. She did not kill, except to eat, and even knowing that it was wrong to let her sense my fear, still I felt fear. I longed to twist and turn as her prey must do to escape those terrible sharp eyes, those great, powerful hind talons.

And now Callum's hand was upon her, stroking her with his forefinger, preening that shining healthy plumage. And still I was transfixed by those dark encircled eyes – the darkness that would permit no light to refract into them, that made the hawk's eye as great a weapon as those talons.

She seemed a big bird, almost as long as Callum's arm from elbow to fingers, feathers blue-black above, whitish below, barred crosswise with grey. There was a look of great power to her, power known and understood, power in control to be used as it was needed.

'She is very beautiful.' My voice was a whisper. 'Giorsal . . .' I took my tone from the way Callum spoke to her, and he talked constantly to her.

She turned her eyes upon me again as I spoke her name, moved again a little on Callum's glove, accustoming herself to the strange voice.

'Yes,' he said quietly. 'She is more than beautiful.' And then, gently, he released the red streamers from his fist. For a moment longer the bird remained there, moving slightly, so that the little bells attached to her legs jingled above the sound of the burn. Then with one great spreading of her wings – effortless to her, but which rocked Callum's arm – she rose. It was a swift climb but not too high; for a time she circled the cottage and its surrounding area, hovered, as if undecided about what she would do. Then she used all the power of the long wings to make her climb, up . . . up. I strained to see her, but finally she was beyond my gaze, a speck that vanished into the sun.

'See now – the valley,' Callum said. He was tense with excitement. 'See the birds rise. If they are wise they are going for cover –

the partridge and the grouse, the jays and the rooks. You know what she is to them – she is the shadow of death. They must try to evade her – they can't outfly her, any of them. She is the swiftest thing that lives on this earth. When she stoops to her prey – dives – some say she reaches nearly two hundred miles an hour. How they pretend to measure it, I wouldn't know. It doesn't matter what the speed is – she is the swiftest thing that lives.'

'And you have let her go!'

He looked at me wonderingly, and then remembered that I had everything to learn. 'That is the joy of it. She will come back. She is tame. This is her home – as this whole wide strath is her home. In the winter when the days are short and game is scarce, she would sometimes go hungry if she were in the wild. But here she knows she will be fed. You see, that is the true freedom. Now she is free, she could choose never to return. She could go south when the winter comes, as her kind have always done, down to the estuaries in England where the ice does not form, and other birds winter. In the summer she could go much farther north – to Sweden and Finland, the tundra country. But she was born here, and like me, this place is in her heart and her consciousness. She returns, always – freely!

'She is an eyas falcon – one taken from the nest. I found her, the first summer I was back here, three years ago. One of the gamekeepers from Ballochtorra shot her mother – I know, because I was watching the peregrine fly the strath, hunting for food, and I knew she had nestlings she had to feed. Where the male was I don't know – shot also, I suppose. Gamekeepers don't like them because they take the grouse. I watched the mother for weeks and I saw how often she flew to the crag beyond Ballochtorra, and knew the nest must be somewhere there. They like to nest on cliffs or mountain sides where they are safe under an overhang. When I knew the mother was shot I went to find the nest. There's some fierce climbing about Ballochtorra, and I couldn't see the nest. But finally I heard the shrieks – the cries of hunger and alarm. When I reached the nest her two brothers were dead – the male falcon, the tiercel, is smaller and lighter than the peregrine by about a third. Giorsal had eaten what meat was on them, and she was near to dying also. She was still unable to fly, unable to hunt, even lowly things like mice, the sort of thing they would despise when they are grown. So I carried her down, this weak little thing, in a satchel, wrapping her in cloth so that she couldn't spread her wings and damage them. She would need them all perfect if she were to fly as she should. But she was so weak she hardly struggled at all. I had meat for her, and she needed food and warmth. I brought her here, and it was days before she got enough strength to even try to challenge me. Then the great trial came. Before that she didn't care how she got the food, so long as she got it, but with strength, her confidence came. She would be tamed then, or not at all. I put her on the gloved hand, and I had to teach her to eat what came from my hand. That meant staying awake as long as she does, until she eats what's offered from the hand, and falls asleep herself. Two nights and three days it was. I was half dead. I carried her everywhere, within the house. I spent those two nights with her on the glove, resting my arm along the arm of the sofa, reading aloud – both to keep myself awake, and to get her used to the sound of my voice. She gave in, in the end, and our comradeship was begun. When you have fought out a battle like that, you prize nothing that comes easily.

'I was lucky. Giorsal was a good bird. Often an eyas will be no good – screamers all their lives. Like some women. I had so much to learn. I made her a perch there in the shed at the back of the stable, her own room, which I could darken, so she could be quiet and happy. I had the jesses ready when I went to get her, but the rest had to come piece by piece. I had to learn myself. I stayed up more nights learning to tie a falconer's knot, learning to tie the hood on with my right hand and my teeth. But after that first struggle, she took to it all as if she had been born to it. From the beginning, then, I represented food and shelter to her. She became so tame that I knew the problem would be to give her the confidence and the need to go and to make her kill as she should. A peregrine is a . . . a noble bird. It would do her – or me – no good to have her live her life as a tame bird on a perch. She had to experience the other side of her nature. I wanted to see her in her own element, ranging this whole country, hovering and stooping, making her own killing. Even if I lost her, once she did experience that freedom, I had to take the chance.

'I was glad of the long evenings, that summer. I knew she must be trained to make her killing before the summer was ended, as she would have in the wild state, or she would be ruined. She had taken to the jesses and swivel and leash so well – the jesses are the leather straps, and the brass swivel links the jesses to the leash. The swivel lets her move freely on her block, or the perch, without getting tangled up. I had her out on her block in the yard here every day that it was fair – You see how it has a hook in it to tie the leash into. There is another block out there beside the burn, so that she can bathe and preen and dry off in her natural place, which is a stony, running stream.' He grimaced faintly. 'Naturally, she loved it. To her it was the best of all worlds. She had companionship, food, protection, shelter. She took to the hood well. When you put a hood on a hawk she is calmed. She ceases to see – and I suppose, to care – about the world around her. She learned to be carried on the glove, hooded, when she was quite young. I used to take her down to the distillery to get her used to the noises and the different voices, and finally I could take her there even without the hood, and she would not bate off unless something very unusual happened. She was very well-mannered, as trained hawks are expected to be. But still she did not seem to want to fly on her own. She was growing fat and lazy. So I had to let her go hungry, and when she was hungry enough I would swing the lure, baited with fresh meat, so that she had to come to me for it – always on the leash of course. When the leash is long enough to let the bird fly to the lure, falconers call it a creance. I made the leash longer and longer. She grew angry at me when I left her hungry, and then she began to understand that she must fly for her food, must learn to take it as it whirled in the air before her. I had her coming a long distance to the lure, and then the final day arrived – by now I was praying because the bird and I, we seemed like one. I had given her life, and she had given me – well, I don't think I could name quite what she had given to me. There was a richness of experience I had never known before. But I knew we had to come to this climax, or it all would be worthless. That day I took off the leash and the swivel and she flew to that far tree there. I could hardly see her among the foliage. All I could see was the red jesses – and hear the bells. She might be gone forever. I swung the lure, and I prayed. I don't often pray. She came to the lure, and snatched the meat, and went to her tree to eat it. And then I held the meat in the glove. It was a long way to see such a scrap, but hawks can see anything. Once they have fixed their object, their eyes focus like the lenses of a telescope. She knew the meat was there, but she also knew that she was free. She came then, swooping. I will never forget the sight of her wings, nor the sound of them. She came and ate on the glove, and she stayed. I have never known a moment like it in my whole life.'

His pale skin was flushed; the dark eyes seemed to shine like his falcon's. '*That* is what I mean by something given freely.' Triumph and exultation flooded into him in that memory. He was recounting the story of a love. Of a creature sought and won, like a woman wooed. Perhaps it was at that moment that I began to love him, to wish myself that creature.

There was more he told me that day, but I do not remember all

of it. What I was hearing about the hawk was mixed with what I
was feeling about the man. I witnessed in that recounting the pride
and power of a lover, and my thoughts and emotions were mixed
wildly between the two. I was glad when the falcon had returned,
because now his attention was all on her, and he did not look into
my face as he talked.

The peregrine roamed the sky above us – not so high now that
we could not see the great gliding grace of the wingspread, the
feinted stoops, the playful dives. The whole strath was stilled. The
falcon roamed her territory, and all now had taken cover. All knew
that she was there – the beautiful, deadly shadow of death.

'She is playing,' Callum said. 'She has killed this morning, and
eaten well. She has no need for food. Now she is flying for the love
of it. She learned her own element, you see. But still she comes
back to me.'

And she did come back. She tired of her games, and came down
near the cottage. She hovered for long minutes, watching the new
outline of my shape against the cottage wall. But I had not moved,
nor had Callum. Then for a longer time she perched in a tree
nearby. But the bond between them seemed complete, and she
knew that Callum would have warned her if I had been a threat.
So then, with a final glide, she came back to Callum's gauntlet,
outstretched to receive her. Now she stood very quietly as he
gathered in the jesses, and gently drew the hood over her head.
I saw how he had to use his teeth as well as his free hand to draw
the thongs of the hood tight enough to stay in place. Blinded now,
Giorsal was at rest. He carried her back to the outbuilding of the
stable.

Even then I did not move. I was as transfixed by those thoughts
of Callum, as I had been by the brooding stare of the hawk. When
at last he reappeared I felt drained and weary. I did not want to
go back into the cottage. I had to be alone with this new thought,
alone where my face and voice would not betray my weakness.
Callum brought Ailis from her hitching ring beside the stable, and
before I was even aware of his gesture he was swinging me up into
the saddle as if I were the weight of a child.

'Is it possible . . .' My voice faded into a whisper. I felt my
hands shake as I took up the reins.

'Is what possible?'

'Do you think – could I – could I ever see her kill? So free and
wild, as you said she was – and still coming back to your hand. I
would like to see . . .'

'You want to see that? It means quite a ride. We have to go up on the moors, where it's very open, or you'll see nothing. But if you like . . .'

'I will go anywhere.'

'Then I will take you. Goodbye, Kirsty.'

I must have crossed the burn, must have made my way down the track to where it joined the road. I returned to Cluain, early for lunch. I do not remember the journey. In my brain was burned the image of the falcon, and of Callum. What was between those two, I wanted for myself.

6

In much the way that I was drawn into the life of Cluain, so I also drifted towards Ballochtorra. I knew my grandfather did not want me to go there, but I went, following where William had been before me. If I was slightly diffident the first time, it was also the last time I felt that way. Margaret Campbell welcomed me with an almost humble gratitude. As I waited in the grand and formal drawing-room into which the butler had shown me, I could hear her voice on the stairs, and the sound of her feet as if she were running. The door opened quickly.

'Oh, you've come! I thought you never would! I hear you've been riding all over the countryside on a fat little garron, and I was beginning to feel hurt that you never stopped at my door.'

'It's a little difficult to decide just which door one should come to. Ballochtorra is rather formidable – and your butler even more so! And then my fat little garron doesn't cut much of a figure in the stableyard beside your thoroughbreds.'

'Oh, you're *not* going to be like your grandfather, are you? Was there ever such a proud, stiff man? I know Ballochtorra is a little intimidating until one knows the way, but you see, you did find it. And *I* am just as much afraid of my butler as you will ever be – and *more*, because I have to do what he tells me. What it is to be mistress of a big house when they all know you weren't born to it! I'm really not mistress at all. I can only speak to the housekeeper, and the butler and the head gardener, and if they don't like what I am suggesting, I'm told it can't be done. Why, I can't even plant a rose bush where I want it. How William used to laugh at that! Oh, let's not stay in here. This room depresses me if it's not filled with people. Come into my own little sitting-room – it's so much cosier. We'll have some tea there.'

It wasn't a small room at all, except by comparison to the drawing-room. But it was Margaret Campbell's room — full of the charm, the soft colours, the air of restrained elegance which was essentially her own. It was scattered with silver-framed photographs — house-party photographs, shooting-party photographs; in the front row of one I saw the stout, bearded figure of the Queen's heir. Some day there would be the photograph that my grandfather said James Ferguson longed for, Margaret Campbell in the ermine-trimmed robes and coronet of the marchioness. The photos were mostly displayed on a silk-draped grand piano.

'Does — does your husband play here?'

'No — not very often. Gavin doesn't use this room very much. He gives Jamie his lessons at his own piano in his study — that's up in one of the towers. We had to take a window out to get the piano hoisted in. I was terrified it would drop.'

'Does it look down on Cluain?'

'No — that's what's strange. It looks straight across the glen at the narrowest part. The dark side of Ballochtorra, I call it. But Gavin likes it.'

The tea was brought, and Margaret laughed at how meagre it seemed beside what Mairi Sinclair had served. But the silver tray was laid with delicate sandwiches, and a dish of tiny, marzipan-coated cakes; at Ballochtorra the cook strove to tempt the jaded appetites of ladies, not to fill the hungry stomachs of countryfolk.

Margaret ran her finger along the bevelled edge of the table from which she served. A minute trace of dust was revealed. 'Oh, I shall have to speak to Mrs Macgregor again. Not that she can help it, poor thing. How can you hope to keep things clean with building going on? The place is nothing but dust.'

'Yes, I heard the hammering.'

'The whole valley hears the hammering. It is terrible. It should be done when we are away, but my father has taken it into his head that we must convert two rooms which weren't being used into one large billiard room for when the Prince visits. Can you imagine it? Workmen brought from London, even — cabinetmakers for panelling, all that sort of thing. And all in a rush. And Father thought the library was too shabby, and so all the furniture must be re-upholstered, and most of the books rebound. Except those that Gavin refused to let him have — he took them all up to his study. The silly thing is, of course, that the Prince never reads a book, even on a wet day. But the new leather bindings are *beautiful* colours . . .'

It sounded silly, and light-minded, and perhaps it was. But whatever she said and did was with such apparent desire to please, that very few could have resisted it. And after all, if there was money to be spent, she would enjoy spending it. Then too, there was for me the novelty of the change from Cluain. Here there was no austerity, little sign of the earnest drive that sparked my grandfather's life, and the passion for hard work that seemed to be part of Mairi Sinclair's religion. I relaxed against the silken cushions, I listened to the flow of light gossip and easy laughter that came from Margaret Campbell, and I was charmed all over again. In the midst of all this, the enjoyment, the thought struck me that at Cluain I never heard anyone laugh – not even Morag. My grandfather might have replied to that thought that there was little to laugh at.

'Do you play, Kirsty?' Margaret Campbell indicated the piano.

'No.' I said it outright, at last escaping from the fact that I played very badly. Here, no one need know that I had tried to play at all, and the childhood nightmare of stumbling through my pieces would be gone forever. It was not even a lie.

'Oh – I'm sorry. I used to have such an amusing time with William. We used to try duets together. He was quite good – not serious, though. Gavin thought we were a pair of fools. Gavin's music is so – so *intense*. He would rather no one heard him play. He spends so much time in that bleak church up there, playing for himself. Even in winter, when it's almost too cold to bear. Gavin thinks I'm . . . silly.'

'I'm sure he doesn't.' I said it gently.

'Perhaps he doesn't consciously think it. But when he goes off to that church alone I know he would rather have been what he wanted to be – an organist in some cathedral town. Working all day, training a choir, perhaps, with a good, quiet wife waiting at home. He doesn't really like Ballochtorra. Not the way it is now. And to tell you the truth, neither do I. It was good in the beginning, when we were just married. A ruin of a fortress, really, but it was beautiful in a wild sort of way.' Her tone altered, the faint regret changing to a kind of determined optimism. 'Well, perhaps one thinks that way when one is young – and it doesn't last for anyone. My father began to build and build, and it has become so big, Gavin seems lost here. He loves the moors and the mountains, but really, I think he would be happier in a cottage. When we are alone here, and I see him down the length of that big dining table, I almost think he wishes I were not here. And then he could just play his music and read his books – and forget about having to find something to say to me.'

She was actually smiling as she said it, and those flecked amber eyes were glowing as if she were not tolling the knell of a marriage. Only the slight plucking at the lace of her handkerchief betrayed her. 'It isn't his fault. He didn't ask to be saddled with Ballochtorra, and with my father. And now this other title coming, and things will be even more so. He loved me, you know – he *did* love me. But all this has built up like a wall between us – I can feel all the things he loves, his music and books, walking on the moors, on one side of the wall, and on the other side there's my father's money. We can hardly see each other over it all – or speak. The truth is, Gavin would like to *work* – and my father does not think it fitting for his daughter's husband to be involved in business. He must be a gentleman, and wait for his title, and then that little boy from the Glasgow slums that used to be my father will be buried forever. Jamie will probably never see the inside of a distillery, and it is driving Gavin wild that he can teach him nothing about the world that's coming to him. My father says the business will just grow and grow, that whisky will go on expanding, and there will be competent people to manage it. Jamie's name will go on the company directors' list, but he will never be in the management of the business. It's money, you see. It has made my father. And me – I love spending it. But it is ruining Gavin. When the house is built in London I doubt that Gavin will come for more than a few weeks a year – only when he must make an appearance. He will stay at Ballochtorra – and I, I will be the gayest, brightest hostess in London, and the Prince of Wales will come to my dinner parties. And my husband will be that awkward Scottish peer that everyone is glad isn't there to spoil the fun.'

Her tone wavered. 'The odd thing is, I suspect Gavin might be very good at business – if anyone ever gave him the chance.

'Well – I've talked too much – but I've needed to so badly. People misjudge me – or I make them misjudge me. They think I'm such a fool I don't know how Gavin feels. But do they know how I feel? I can't help it about my father. I can't help it that having all the money has made me so lonely here. No wonder I want to escape to London, to fill the house with guests. I must have distraction, or sometimes I think I'll go a little mad. I loved the times William came. He made me laugh, and forget it all. He was so good at so many things . . . he was so clever . . .'

'Did you talk to him like this – I mean about your husband?'

'You mean William was younger than I, and might have been shocked? But you see, William *knew*. He could see it at once. He was older than he seemed. That's why I'm talking like a fool to

you, because it seems almost like having William back again. I
don't babble like this to everyone. Oh . . . my father would be
furious if he heard me. He knows what goes on in the lives of the
people I mix with, all the careful arranging of bedrooms when
there's a house party. But he doesn't care just so long as the
façade of the marriage is kept up, and the guest list is fashionable,
and no divorces ever come of it all. It sounds wicked, doesn't it –
and it is. But he is ambitious – so terribly ambitious. He would not
approve of that behaviour for himself – and probably not for me,
because Gavin would not stand for it. But he wants me to be a
great hostess, and so I must know these people. If there are
rumours . . . well, that can't be helped. That is part of the game.'

Suddenly the long delicate fingers shredded the lace handkerchief with surprising strength and violence. 'Oh, you must despise
me!'

'Why should I despise you? What have I got to feel superior
about?'

Her eyes widened. 'You're a bishop's daughter!'

'I grew up in China. I've seen too many young girls sold and
used to feel surprised that it might happen in other places – in
other ways. Didn't William explain any of this to you?'

'He did – in a way. But I never talked like this to William. He
was a man. It might have been . . .'

'Misunderstood?'

'Perhaps. I valued William . . . as a friend. He knew I was
lonely. It wasn't necessary to say any more. I've said too much
now. I've put too much on you. And I don't want you to hate my
father. He can't help it. I've seen the sort of place he grew up in.'
A faint shudder went through her body. 'I would do anything –
anything – to get out of such a place. I can't blame him. He gave
me a different sort of education, and I'm supposed to be free of
all the need to fight people for what one wants. What he doesn't
understand, and never will, is that the world he's pushed me into
is just as scheming and full of competition as the one he came out
of. And dear God . . . the worst of it . . .'

'What is the worst of it?' She was going to say it, even if I tried
to hold her back.

'Gavin doesn't know to this day that my father made very careful
enquiries about his whole family before he let me marry him. Of
course Gavin was already a baronet, but I doubt seriously if he'd
even more than heard of the Marquis of Rossmuir. My father
knew all along that there was a very good chance that Gavin would
eventually have the title, even though there were two other men

to succeed in between. But he knew one was sick in India, and the other had been mixed up in some gambling scandal here, and was drinking himself to death in the Congo. *That* is why he let me marry Gavin. It was a gamble – and it has paid off. My father loves to gamble. This has been his greatest win yet. Ten years ago my father wasn't so successful or so rich – and there were not titles to be picked up for the asking for his daughter. Titles demanded *solid* money. It sounds so rotten and corrupt, doesn't it? But it wasn't meant to be. I loved Gavin – yes, I did love him.'

She got up, and the swish of the silk of her gown as she paced was all I heard in the room for a full minute. Then she turned back and faced me. 'There – I've said it all. Everything. I've never talked like this in my life. I don't know what has possessed me. Perhaps I've never been willing to admit it before – but my father is visiting us now, and because of the Prince coming, he seems more – oh, how do I say it? – more *pushing* than he's ever been. Gavin is feeling the strain, and so am I. I had to talk . . . do you mind so much? You – I think you like me. You have no reason to like me, but I think you do.'

'I do like you. Rather more than that.'

'William liked me, too.'

'Of course William liked you. Who could help it?'

We both swung to face the door. Gavin Campbell stood there, and he was smiling – a smile that told us nothing. There was no way of knowing how much he had heard, and I guessed he was never likely to say. Like William, he knew more than he had to be told. Now he was moving towards us.

'There's some tea left, I hope.'

Strangely Margaret Campbell was flustered. 'Why – of course! I'll ring for some fresh –'

'No, don't! I don't want the fuss. There must be some left. I don't mind it strong.'

'There isn't a cup for you. I never thought – well, you never come in to tea, here, Gavin.'

'Don't I? I forget to have it, I suppose. Never mind. They told me Miss Howard had come. I thought I'd come to find out what has taken her so long to visit. It isn't very friendly. Has that old man, Angus Macdonald, told you you shouldn't come?'

'Not in so many words. He leaves me much to myself. I expect I was just . . . shy.'

'Why! – William's sister shy! The girl who came all the way from China without an invitation is *shy*.' He laughed. 'You'll never convince me of it – no, Margaret, *don't ring*! I can't stand all the fuss. There'll be six maids as well as Wilson hovering.' Still on his feet he took up a sandwich and ate it.

'Oh, Gavin, please . . .' Margaret looked at him pleadingly. 'You so seldom come in here, and I can't even give you a cup of tea.'

He didn't reply to her. 'Mairi Sinclair does things rather differently, I should imagine.'

'Arrangements are simpler at Cluain,' I answered. 'It's only a step from the kitchen to the dining-room. And there's only Morag . . .'

'Yes – simpler. That's how it should be. Margaret and I are trapped by the people who are paid to wait on us. And there's Jamie, growing up hardly knowing how to tie his own boot-laces.'

'Gavin! – that's not fair! He does his best.'

'He does more than his best. It's a minor miracle that he hasn't as yet turned into a spoiled little prig. And I know you won't let that happen, Margaret.' He looked at me. 'You see, Margaret has that rare gift of being able to laugh at herself, and she's passed it on to her son, I think. She never allows him to forget where his grandfather started. And Jamie knows I only tumbled into my position. And I give Margaret credit for that.'

Then he walked to the piano, quite abruptly, and sat down. The music that came was not as I expected it to be. The melody was so well known, almost hackneyed, not the sort of thing a serious musician would play.

'I have a feeling Kirsty can sing. William had a good voice.' He spoke across the music to me.

I had always been told I had a 'pretty voice', and I'd never paid any attention to that. But now suddenly I felt that I wanted to sing – and yes, I could sing. I walked across to the piano, and stood slightly behind Gavin, glancing quickly at the music, but having no real need of it.

> 'If a body meet a body
> Comin' through the rye . . .'

He was singing also, a strong, good voice, a dark voice, almost, that seemed at odds with his fair hair and light eyes. Across the room from us I could see Margaret Campbell, handkerchief twisting again in her lovely hands. 'Why, Gavin . . . I never heard you play anything like this.'

He shook his head, as if to indicate that she was not to interrupt. I found myself singing alone.

'. . . all the lads, they smile at me
Comin' through the rye.'

He had turned and was staring at me, that peculiar, straight
stare I had first encountered on Ballinaclash station, a stare that
seemed to lock out everything else in the world. 'Yes, I thought so.
You have a voice.' The laugh was loud, triumphant. 'My God, you
have a voice!'

I don't know why it should have mattered to him; but in the
moments of that stare and those words, even Margaret Campbell
was shut out. We might easily have been alone.

Gavin escorted me to the stables that first time, leading me through
the back passages of Ballochtorra, the noise of the hammering
about us, but the age of the place revealed in these winding,
twisting ways. I felt I was back at Cluain. And then Gavin opened
the door that led directly on to the stableyard, and here the
building was so new that the ivy had not yet had time to take hold.
A great overweight clock tower dominated a quadrangle of thea-
trically fashioned horse boxes, and the entrance to the smith's shop
was the traditional shape of a horseshoe. 'A bad opera setting,'
Gavin murmured to me as he slammed the door. 'Enough thoroughbreds to satisfy a king's taste, and I keep wondering when the
prince-in-disguise-as-stable-lad will appear.'

'They are your horses.'

'Nominally, they're my horses, and I have to confess that I
haven't the strength to say no to any one of the beauties. Why
should I? – some other way would be found to spend the money.
It pleases Mr Ferguson. Give him his due, he does know good
horseflesh, and loves it. I just wish horses pleased us both for the
same reasons. At least we would have one thing we could talk about
together.'

'It rarely happens that the same things please people for the
same reasons.'

'William was always making remarks like that. It sometimes
gave me the odd feeling that I was talking to someone older than
myself.'

I laughed, refusing to let him make anything more serious of it.
The episode in Margaret Campbell's sitting-room had frightened
me a little; I wanted to brush aside what both of them seemed to
be thrusting upon me. 'That's because William and I were brought
up on Confucian sayings. The Chinese live by proverbs . . . We
used to play games of making up our own, the more ridiculous
the better. Like . . . "the shortest line between two points is the

longest way home." '

'And there's more wisdom in that than perhaps you know, Miss Howard.'

We had been standing watching as little Ailis was brought out by a groom, and the voice came to us from the shadow of the smithy's door. We turned and looked, and the rounded, shortish shape of a man in brown tweeds and a matching cap emerged; he was powerfully built for his height, but running to fat, with reddish whiskers and eyebrows over eyes flecked with amber, which was the only way he resembled his daughter.

'Miss Howard, may I present Mr James Ferguson, my father-in-law.'

He swept off the cap. He was expensively dressed, clothes probably from Savile Row, and boots from Lobb, but there was an indefinable air of vulgarity about him, the thrusting red face, the glimmer of the eyes under those sandy brows. He was exaggerated, like the clock tower. He looked what he was, and seemed pleased about it.

'Well – Angus Macdonald's granddaughter. You bear the stamp of the old man, the way your brother did. I wonder if you're his match.'

'Perhaps time will tell that, Mr Ferguson. Perhaps we'll never know. It isn't a woman's world yet, is it? – and we're really not able to compare.'

'Well, you've as sharp a tongue as Macdonald. Your brother, now, he was all charm. All charm and talk.'

I almost choked on my anger. 'Perhaps I'll improve, Mr Ferguson. At the time you knew William, life was happier for us all.'

I saw Gavin's hand as he held the bridle, the fist clenched into a tight ball. It was as well Ailis wasn't nervous.

'Mr Ferguson – please remember that Miss Howard has lost both William and her father recently. They *were* happier times . . .'

'Och, aye – aye. I know it well. I've a rough tongue on me, Miss Howard. Yes, you've had sorrow, and I can tell you would sorrow for a fine young brother as William was. Bright, he was, and full of promise, and Angus Macdonald was dreaming again of a future. But you can take your knocks, I can tell. You're probably as tough as old boots, and it will stand you in good stead. A pity you're not a boy. Angus Macdonald would have a second chance. But still, a bishop's daughter . . . you'll probably make a good enough match. Someone anxious to have their hands on Cluain –'

'For God's sake!' Gavin burst out. 'Will you leave it alone! You

may own Ballochtorra, but at least you'll treat its guests with
civility.'

'Miss Howard will not swoon, Gavin. She knows well enough
what I'm talking about. I've never had time in my life to waste
on pretty speeches – never learned to make them. She knows –
and so do you. I've a call to make on Angus Macdonald before
I leave. Perhaps Miss Howard will give me a cup of tea at Cluain.
I haven't a doubt we'll talk well enough then. Ballochtorra is a
mite over-refined, wouldn't you say, Miss Howard?'

'You're leaving then?' Gavin said.

'Day after tomorrow. I'll be back before the Prince's visit to
check that all is in order. Can't be away from Glasgow too long.
Things move in a man's absence. Mustn't give them the impression
I've too much time to play up here in the Highlands. People might
think I'm slipping . . .'

'Grandpapa, there's nothing slipping.' Jamie came running from
the box that Ailis had occupied. 'McClintoch made me check all
the buckles myself, just to make sure. He said we couldn't have
Miss Howard falling off . . .'

The face of the man altered quite visibly. There was no subtlety
in the expression. The rough vulgarity seemed to fall away in the
glow of tender pride that spread upon his face. He didn't care who
knew that he doted upon his grandson.

'Och, she'll not fall off that broad back, laddie. She's the
heftiest wee pony I ever saw. You'd not compare her, now, would
you, to your own Milky?'

'No – but I'd rather have Ailis. Ailis is famous. She carried Mr
Douglas Ross back home one night when the worst blizzard anyone could remember was raging, and he had a fever that nearly
killed him. She found her way all alone for near ten miles when
you couldn't see your hand in front of you . . . Everyone wanted
to have Ailis. But Mr Ross offered her first to Mr Macdonald.'

Ferguson looked at the pony with real dislike. 'There's no breeding in her, Jamie, lad. If you look at her closely now, she's about
the ugliest wee pony you'd see in a long day.'

'I don't think you should say that in front of her, Grandpapa.
She understands, you know.'

'To hell with what she understands! Am I surrounded by a lot
of fools here! A damned ungainly piece of horseflesh, she is, and
I'll see no grandson of mine mounted on such.'

'I'd still like her.'

'If you don't mind,' I said, 'Ailis belongs to Cluain.' And while
the three stood there, glowering at one another, I swung myself

up into the saddle without assistance. Ailis moved willingly, as if she were glad to be free of the place. She moved in her plodding, unconcerned, tranquil gait, not caring in the least for the turmoil she left behind her, not caring, I thought, for what she must have sensed in me. Without direction she turned on the road to Cluain as we passed through the iron gates embossed with the hissing swan. She was heading for her stable, and I also knew where I belonged.

I went many times to Ballochtorra after that. Margaret was not always there, nor Gavin, nor Jamie. They were out riding, Gavin and Margaret always separately, it seemed, and I did not wait on their return. But Wilson, the butler, had his instructions, and I was always offered tea, and a place to wait in Margaret's sitting-room. I never stayed unless she was there; Ballochtorra depressed me. For all the newness of the furniture, the curtains, the uphol-steries, the graceful trailing of ferns and plants at the windows, for all the well-kept splendour, it was a place that had lost itself. It had lost the stark beauty of Cluain, which would once have been its own; it had gained nothing by the fussiness of its new additions and decorations. I wondered how the spare elegance of Margaret Campbell's own person had been submerged under this sea of lace and trimmings and heavy velvets. It was, I thought, as if she had long ago given up caring — as if she allowed whatever fur-nisher her father instructed to come in and have his way with Ballochtorra. She had her presence marked only upon one room that I knew, her own sitting-room. Here we sat and talked, and ate those tiny cakes, and she played the piano. There was a kind of desperate gaiety about her at times, as if she were holding off the size and bulk of the house, the retinue of servants who stood ready to answer the bells, the whole ritual of her life. 'It is so different here from London,' she once said to me. 'Here everyone in the whole valley knows who comes and goes, and talks about it if it pleases them. In a city one can be more private. Here I feel I'm . . . watched. I wasn't made for places like Ballochtorra. I don't even sleep very well here — it's the quiet, and then every quarter hour that stable clock that Father put in tolling away. Sometimes I get up just after dawn and saddle up for myself, and ride out, just to feel I can really be by myself. I ride until I'm tired, and then I come back and sleep. I wish there were more noise. I like city streets, and bustle, and shops. I like to see carriages stopping next door, or on the other side of the square — better still if they come to one's own door. I like people coming and going . . .

friends, acquaintances . . . even strangers.'

And Jamie would sometimes come bursting in. 'Mother, today Father and I rode up beyond Ben Carden. You can't think how tiny Ballochtorra looks from there.' And again, 'Today we had to shelter from the rain under that crag over by Drumnoch . . . Father gave me his coat.' And another day, his face petulant with disappointment, he would report that his father had gone by himself. 'He rode off . . . I don't know where he's gone . . .'

But never again did Gavin come and join us in Margaret's sitting-room; he never again came to drink tea with us, demand sandwiches, never played the light, easy melodies for me to sing the words to.

And Ballochtorra continued to depress me, and especially I disliked the stableyard, where I had to go to get Ailis. This was wholly the creation of James Ferguson, heavy, overdone, the horses too pampered, the grooms too much their servants. And often as I left I found myself giving a swift, upward glance to the room where Gavin Campbell might have been, his own tower room. But his figure was never at the window where I could see him; I never heard the sound of the piano; I never was really sure which one of the towers and turrets of Ballochtorra, spanning the five centuries of its building, was the one he inhabited.

Riding, in those weeks, I came on Gavin only once away from the kirk, though Margaret said he was often on the moors. It had been a dry day, though overcast, the mountains lost in the clouds. Not a day to venture too far. I turned Ailis across the bridge at Ballochtorra, and instead of going towards the kirk, she had headed, almost at her own wish, in the other direction, up the steep hill on the road to the station at Ballinaclash. She had as strong a streak of curiosity as I, and I think it was she who first heard the sound from an unaccustomed direction. They were above us still, as we climbed up the glen, sounds that reached us from some place in the plantation of Scots pine and larch that hugged both sides of the slope. We found the track – very rough it was, and soft with leaf mould; we made very little noise, and it was covered by the cries and the sounds that came to us.

It was a clearing where a burn pitched headlong down from some spring above, rushing to join the river below. Over the centuries it had worn its own narrow path, and now the trees pressed about its edges, defining its course, as did the boulders that lined it. A small croft stood here, the usual one of the Highlands, two rooms, thatched, a smoking chimney, a single door, and hens pecking the ground all about it. There was a lean-to stable, and a sty to fatten a pig.

There were two men, a woman, and a boy of about sixteen in the clearing – and Gavin and Jamie. I checked Ailis and held her close, watching the scene. Gavin and Jamie were both wearing the kilt, the green Cawdor kilt, and Gavin was in the stream up to his knees. He had just finished attaching a chain about a boulder that stood squarely in the middle of the burn, forcing the water to flow each side of it, and raising the level almost beyond the banks. The chain was attached to a kind of pole harness I had seen used for dragging felled trees about the Cluain lands, and I thought I recognized one of Cluain's huge Clydesdales in the harness. One of the men stood beside Gavin in the burn, fixing the chain, testing it against slipping; the other man and the boy were at the horse's head, holding him. As I saw the second man in profile, I knew him as one of the farm workers from Cluain, Bruce Bain. Jamie was moving excitedly from one group to the other, until at a word from Gavin he abruptly changed his place so that he was on the uphill side of the horse and harness. Then Gavin signalled Bruce Bain, and he began to urge the Clydesdale forward. At first the big animal could get little grip in the soft ground; I could see the big body straining. The boulder rocked a little on its base, seemed about to move, then slipped back. Bruce Bain rested the Clydesdale a few moments; I could see the coat already beginning to darken with sweat. Gavin shifted one of the chains a little, to get a more secure purchase on the boulder. Then he signalled again. Again Bain began to pull on the halter. 'Ho! – come now lad! – come now!' The Clydesdale managed a step forward, the slack of the chain was taken up. Even from where I was I could see the ripple of the great muscles across the horse's chest. Another step; the boulder rocked, poised. The horse was forward two feet more, and the boulder was now shifted from the hole where it had bedded itself in the burn. Gavin was there, beside it, watching to see that the chains did not slip. I had to suppose he knew the danger he was in of the chains slipping, or of the horse being dragged backwards by the weight. He seemed foolhardy, but someone had to check the downhill side of the boulder, and it was Gavin. As I watched I saw him take a heavy iron bar, and use it as a lever to help the boulder out of its position. On the uphill side, the man did the same. The real danger came when Gavin called to Bain to hold the Clydesdale there, and he himself moved forward and plunged his arms down into that icy water, fixing a smaller rock under the boulder to hold its new level. It was an anxious moment, wondering if Gavin would be quick enough, if the horse could hold his position against the weight, if the lever of the other man would give Gavin's hands enough room for his task. Then Gavin stepped back, and called to Bain. The Clydesdale moved on – a mighty heave this time, as if he were thankful not to be asked to hold any longer. Then the boulder moved up the incline of the burn, teetered there a moment – another use of the bars from Gavin and the other man, another rock to hold the boulder secure, another heave, and the boulder was on firm, almost level ground. From there it was nothing for the Clydesdale to move it a few feet farther into the clearing – the hens dashing screaming away from the monster suddenly in their midst. Gavin scrambled up the bank, his boots and stockings wet, the edge of the kilt, and his shirt sticking to his back with sweat.

His voice reached me. 'Right now, Bain. We'll rest the horse, and then we'll move the thing off where it will be out of harm's way.'

I slipped off Ailis, and came forward. 'Gavin – Jamie!'

'Kirsty! How did you come here?' And from Jamie, 'Miss Howard, did you see it? The Clydesdale was wonderful, wasn't he?'

'He was, Jamie. I'm glad I came in time to see it. I was riding on the road below . . .'

The woman made a sketchy, but warm gesture to me. 'Och, welcome now, mistress. I'll be giving everyone some tea, now the great part's done. Everyone needs a wee rest.' She seemed to know very well who I was. 'And that great horse – a marvel, he is. And Sir Gavin so kind . . . We've been plagued with that terrible great thing . . .'

'Thank you. I'd like some tea . . .' I was following Gavin and Jamie to the edge of the burn. 'Look, Miss Howard. You see, the boulder crashed down here during a winter storm – it was just held by a tree above.' Jamie was skipping about in excitement. 'And it bedded itself in the burn, and every time there was a thunderstorm, or the snow thawed, the water would come spilling over, and washing into the McInneses' cottage. And so Father . . .'

'Jamie, Mrs McInnes has cake for you, I think,' Gavin said. He watched his son run towards the cottage. 'An adventure for him, Kirsty,' he said. 'He would not be left when he learned this morning where I was going.'

'That's Bruce Bain, from Cluain – and that's a Cluain Clydesdale,' I said. We sat on rocks by the burn, and Mrs McInnes brought us tea in battered pewter mugs, and oatcakes. Gavin began to strip off his boots and stockings. 'Will you not come to the fire, Sir Gavin? It's wet through you are.'

'I'm all right here, Mrs McInnes. And make sure, please, that Jamie doesn't eat too much of your good things. I'll be in trouble if he doesn't eat his dinner when he gets home.'

'Och, now, Sir Gavin, don't we all know that a wee lad has the appetite of three . . .' And she went off happily to feed Jamie all he would eat.

'Was it as Jamie said – the boulder . . . ?'

'Just about. The tree that was holding it crashed down last winter, and every heavy rain since has sent the water from the burn lapping past the McInneses' threshold. I walked up here one day and saw it myself. God knows, these crofts are damp enough. So I thought that when the burn was low in summer, I would have a try at moving it. Robert McInnes, you know, helps look after the kirk – as does Mrs McInnes. They kept my secret well. The minister has yet to hear about the strange, ungodly music the laird sometimes plays in the house of the Lord.'

'They're your tenants?'

'No – this is on MacKenzie Grant's land. McInnes just earns a few extra shillings looking after the kirk, and trying to coax some heat out of that stove in winter. Mrs McInnes cleans the windows and dusts – that kind of thing.'

'Grant land? – then why doesn't Mr Grant take care of the matter himself? You do know, Gavin – well, you must have known that the chains might have slipped. The Clydesdale might not have been able to hold the weight.'

'The horse I couldn't help. Perhaps I should have had two, but I didn't really think the boulder was that big – it was deeper in the burn than I thought. And if the chains had slipped, it would have been my own fault for placing them badly. If I'd been killed, it would have been my own carelessness. But I'd no intention of getting myself killed in front of my own son's eyes. I haven't such a taste for bad melodrama as that. It wasn't as dangerous as it might have looked.'

'But why do it? – since it's Mr Grant's estate?'

'Oh – I don't know. The McInneses are such decent people, and old MacKenzie Grant hasn't been on the estate for more than a year – he's sick in England, they say. His bailiff's useless – drunk half the time. The McInneses have asked, but they had no hope of getting anything done until Grant got up here himself, if he ever does again. It could have been years. Robert McInnes doesn't have much to live on – just this place here, on the estate, the right to cut a tree or two for fuel. He helps on the Grant farm, and digs the bog when work is slack. It isn't much of a living, but he's a good man.'

'But Bruce Bain, and my grandfather's horse?'

Gavin laughed. 'Do you think Ballochtorra's stables could produce anything like that Clydesdale? Oh, I made my arrangements formally with your grandfather. He offered the horse free – he also has a regard for Robert McInnes – but he said I would have to pay for Bain's time. That's your grandfather, Kirsty. He always manages to temper any generosity with a practical bite. I will probably never be given a bill for the services of Bain. But he warned me, did your grandfather, that the horse, if he were hurt or damaged in any way, would cost me a fortune. I believe it.' He suddenly lowered the mug from his lips. 'Lord, I wish this tea had a drop of Cluain's whisky in it. We make cold water up here in the Highlands, Kirsty. Be sure you never tumble into a burn. You might freeze in the same second.'

It was then I saw the blood ooze between his fingers as he held the mug. 'Gavin – your hands!'

He didn't even look down at them. 'Oh, it's good clean water, Kirsty. I won't be poisoned. That rock had a bit of a bite to it – but no fingers crushed, and nothing that won't mend.'

'But your *hands* – how can you risk them? The organ . . .'

He shook his head. 'You don't really understand, Kirsty. Because you see me at the kirk, you hear me play, you think that's really what I live for. Yes – I'm a musician of sorts. I used to be a much better one. And if I'd never seen this strath, and Ballochtorra and Cluain, I'd be perfectly happy as organist in some quite humble place, as long as it was a living. But these mountains and moors get into one's blood, even if one wasn't born to them, as I wasn't. Playing the organ isn't everything I want to do, Kirsty. It only helps fill the time – the emptiness.'

His low, musing tone helped me to ask the next question, one I thought, I might not have a right to ask. 'What else do you want to do, Gavin?'

'You'll not tell him, I know – perhaps he already suspects. But I envy your grandfather. I wish I had my fields of barley, and my fat cattle. I wouldn't mind hill sheep, difficult though they are. Forget the distillery – I would like to farm the land.'

'You can't? – isn't there any part of Ballochtorra's land you could use?'

'There's some – around the bend of the river past the crag. But it's boggy, and needs draining. It's subject to flooding but that can be an advantage, as it leaves you with some good soil, and you'll lose nothing if you're careful to move your cattle in time. I've seen stretches of peat-moorland reclaimed to clover pasture. There are places on Ballochtorra where it could be done. A man could make a living from it, Kirsty. Not a fortune – just a living.'

'Why don't you . . .' I hesitated. 'Why don't you try?'

'I'd need money in the beginning – not a lot of money, but *some*. That would mean James Ferguson again.'

'But he would help – surely – for his own son-in-law.'

He put down the mug. 'That's just it. James Ferguson owns enough of his son-in-law. He can't have my dreams also. He would laugh at such small ambitions – a few acres here, a few acres there. What need does a gentleman have for such petty concerns? His wife's husband worry about grazing for a few cows when he has thousands of acres of grouse moors? No. James Ferguson would never understand, and I've no need to try to explain. He must do things big, or not at all. So I leave it be just what it is – a dream. No more.'

I looked at him, his hair clamped to his scalp with sweat, his kilt sodden, his hands gashed and bleeding, and I thought that, yes, it did lie in Gavin Campbell, baronet and soon to be marquis, to turn out in the snow before a March dawn to help with the lambing, to move his cattle to higher ground when the river was in spate, to turn some of his bog-acres up there on the mountain into clover-grass. It was not a great ambition – but it was a dream.

I got to my feet. 'I must go, Gavin. I'm glad I was here this morning.'

'So am I, Kirsty. So am I.'

And each evening there was the return to Cluain. Often I had to hurry to be washed and changed before my grandfather came to the dining-room. It was very soon after my arrival that I noticed that he minded my absence; I did not know whether it was that he actually wanted my company, or that he demanded my attention. But I tried not to be late – to be waiting with my Chinese shawl and the red slippers, waiting for the invitation 'to take a dram with me'.

He did not like my going to Ballochtorra, but he never actually tried to prevent it. 'Come back from *that* place?' he would say to me, seeming to look at me through his whisky glass. 'Well, this must seem humble enough after all the frippery and finery they tell me they have up there.'

'Cluain can stand by any, Grandfather, and you know it. Besides,'

I added, watching my opportunity now, as he always did, to score my point. 'I'm surprised you listen to gossip about what goes on at Ballochtorra. I thought such things didn't interest you.'

'Och, who can help hearing it? Doesn't everything that Ferguson does cause talk? My own workers, who ought to know better, remembering that they make the best whisky in the Highlands, do pratter on about him like women. Just because he's made a fortune in a few years with the cheap rot-gut stuff.'

'But you sell Cluain's whisky to him.'

'And why not? He needs *something* to make his poison palatable. And believe me, Cluain's whisky is the heart of his most expensive blend. What Cluain distils here is what makes it respectable to have a Ferguson whisky in a gentleman's decanter. That is, for those who think they *must* have the blended stuff.'

'I don't understand about blended whiskies. Why can James Ferguson make a fortune in a short time when it takes so long to mature Cluain's whisky? I've never tasted the other sort . . .'

'And may you never. It's hardly fit to be called whisky when it's stood beside Cluain's – and, aye, maybe a few other Highland malts. What a blend is, Kirsty, is the mixing of the product of the pot still, the malt, like Cluain's, if they're lucky enough to have it, with the much cheaper, quicker product of the grain or patent still whisky. Most patent stills are of the type invented by an Irishman called Coffey, and they're known as the Coffey still. They make a spirit, you might say, but it can't stand on its own as a single spirit – you couldn't drink it by itself, as you do a pot still whisky – and that's a fact, not just my prejudice. It's simply a *fillings*, something to give volume to the blends of the malts you add to it. You might call grain whisky a silent spirit – without the malts, it simply isn't there, not drinkable.

'The patent still is a continuously working unit, while our pot still whisky is an interrupted process, as I hope our knowledgeable Callum Sinclair made quite clear to you. It costs about half the price to distil as does your malt whisky, and if you set up a big enough production unit, as our fine rich Mr Ferguson has done, with distilleries all over the Lowlands, and people rushing to invest with him, then you *can* make a fortune. But never forget that he has to come himself, or send his buyers, into these Highlands to find the whisky that will make his silent spirit a palatable drink. He makes a dozen blends at least – a little of this, a little of that – a dash of Cluain with a dash of the Glenlivet with a dash of Glen Grant. Infinite variations, they tell me, with infinite blends, and all priced according to the price he had to pay for the original malts that made the blends. There's no merit to a grain spirit by itself—it's what he adds to it. And the price and reputation of Cluain come high.

'Mind you, though, even the grain distillers can't get away completely from malted barley—they use about twenty per cent of it, and the rest can be anything you want, maize, wheat, rye or oats. But whatever they use, they can't do without the barley—they have to cook their grain until its starch cells are burst open, so that the malt can get into the heart of it. There's many that think malt is brought into grain distilling to give some life and colour and character to the stuff even at that early stage, but the plain fact is that the malt is necessary to bring about the chemical change that will start the fermentation. You cannot do without the malt, Gurrl, no matter what. And you cannot do without the malt whisky. The grain spirit does not need the ageing, nor the care in distilling, but it is simply not there without the malt. And never forget it. Malt can stand alone, be drunk alone, as it has been drunk in the Highlands for centuries. Grain spirit by itself is a useless, unsaleable thing. It will bring as little comfort or pleasure to a man's soul as something drunk straight from a chemist's bottle. As long as man needs solace for his grief, but no drunkenness, ease for his tired body, warmth for his blood, he will need the product of Cluain, and its like. Yes, Kirsty—Cluain will go on forever.'

'Cluain will go on forever, Grandfather. But you can't—nor I. Will there always be men skilful enough—caring enough—to make sure that it does?'

'They have to care, Kirsty. They have to care—and they are hard to find. That is the whole trouble with James Ferguson. He might as well be making boots or bricks, for all he cares. But we won't worry about him and his like. His day will come and go—and Cluain will still be here. Now let us eat our supper, and then we'll take out the board, and we'll see if the old brain or the young brain will win this night. In chess as well as whisky, experience counts. Experience counts, Kirsty.'

And nightly I was battling him over that board, sometimes winning, sometimes losing, but never again did our hands stray into the moves of William's game.

Very slowly, and only by dint of pushing, I was being admitted into the life of Cluain—the life of the distillery and the farm. Every day my grandfather was at his rounds of the farm, checking with the workers, watching the barley stand a little higher, the heads grow a little heavier, scanning the sky and sniffing the wind, like an animal, for rain. He watched for weak places in the fences, lest the cattle and sheep should break through to the precious crop, he gave orders about replacing the missing tiles on the barns and byres, he saw that the sheepfolds and cattle pens were in order and waiting for the snows of the winter, watched the meadows for the moment when he could cut the hay for winter livestock feeding. He would mount a horse who seemed as old and broad as himself, and ride up to the shielings, the small huts built up on the mountain slopes as living quarters for the men and young women who tended the cattle in their summer pasture – they spent their summer watching that the cattle did not stray too far, did not cross into the bog and be lost. There was something that reminded me of the frugal care of the Chinese for their animals in this ancient practice – each animal so precious that it could command this constant vigil. 'Ah, well,' my grandfather said, 'it will not be long we have it so. The people are leaving. There will be few young ones to send up into the shielings. They go to the cities, looking for work, and end crowded into one room in some filthy wynd, with buckets of slop thrown on their heads in the streets. And cattle breeding is becoming more scientific – we will soon have only Aberdeen Angus, and Cluain's herd is becoming famous. We will not risk the necks of the cattle up here in the shielings. We will have only as many sheep as we need for our own eating – pesky things, they are, forever straying, eating the grasses to nothing, eating the crops, breaking into the vegetable plots of the workers. No, soon the farm will become a showplace, the barley and the Angus will be its function. The distillery workers must be well taken care of – well housed. A distillery does not need many men, but good ones we must have. But the young ones that are surplus, the sons who have grown up at Cluain, will be on their way, for I will not have the jobs to offer them, and the agricultural wage is low. But I must stay in business, and I cannot pay more than the going rate – I am no gentleman farmer who breeds his cattle only to have something to point to when his guests come. The barley will provide the whisky, and the cattle bring always higher and higher prices at market – with now and then a blue ribbon for a Cluain breeding bull. That is how it has always been at Cluain. More than forty years I have been here, and each year something added. The big harvests have provided against the years of the lean ones. We have grown our own food, and we have been beholden to no one. Since the day I paid back the loan that set up the distillery, there has never been a penny borrowed for Cluain.

It stands alone – it will stand.'

'And the shielings,' I said. 'What will happen to the land when you no longer pasture animals up here – when there is no one to herd and shepherd them?'

'Och, the land will probably go back to the heather from which I first reclaimed it. The grouse will come in, and I will rent it to some rich Englishman who will come with his fine guns and dogs to shoot it over. Land is money, Kirsty. Never let go of land.'

'And yet,' I said, as we rode among the livestock, my grandfather's head always twisting and turning, expertly inspecting each animal to watch for signs of sickness, 'it will be a pity when that happens. Some more life gone from the Highlands . . . fewer people in the strath.'

His old face crumpled in a kind of scowl. 'Yes and no – the people have come here for hundreds of years, to the summer shielings. It used to be a good time – a time of release from the harshness of winter. There were special songs they sung at those times, and the lassies would flirt with the young men in the long evenings. There was whisky taken – to keep out the chill. It was beautiful . . . the twilights were long, and the shadows purple on the heather . . . Yes, there were good and bad times, and they are passing. Perhaps it will be no bad thing when it is gone completely. It is a sign of a poor people . . . you took your joys when you could and the summer nights were one of them, with a drop of whisky and a fire, and the stories told in the old tongue. No one speaks that any more, and this is the last generation of lads and lassies who will go to the shielings of Cluain . . .'

All the way back to the house that time he was silent, and his face wore its heavy, brooding look, as he remembered the past, perhaps, when life had been harder, but had held its joys – perhaps not wanting to look to the future when both he and the boys and girls would be gone. I did not dare interrupt his thoughts. It was only after we had dismounted and led the horse and Ailis to their boxes, and carried our own harness to the tackroom, which was the practice at Cluain, since no one could escape the careful and frugal rules laid down by its master, that I attempted to speak to him. We were standing by the pump, and I pumped water for both buckets.

'Grandfather . . .' I panted a little; the pump was well oiled and in good repair, as was everything at Cluain, but a heavy old thing. 'Grandfather, is there not some way I could help you a little . . .'

'Help?' He was instantly suspicious, on the defensive. 'What kind of help could I need from you?'

I sighed as I picked up my bucket and turned away from him. At times we seemed to go back to our first evening, as if the weeks in between had never been. 'I only meant in the office. You work there every afternoon on your papers and letters. I used to help my father with such things. I wondered if I could do anything . . .' I banged down the bucket while I wrestled with the door of Ailis's box, and half the water slopped over. 'After all, you keep telling me that everyone works at Cluain.'

'Why do you want to come spying into my affairs?'

'*Spying!* – is that what you think?' I picked up the bucket and more water spilled over my boots. It would have been a relief to have hurled the rest at him. 'Then you may forget I ever made the suggestion. I thought there might be a few unimportant letters I could take at your dictation. I don't expect to be *trusted* with anything . . . I am not the granddaughter of Cluain, nor its hired help. I am just a guest, left to be idle all day – '

'Hush, Gurrl, you're hasty. You're very hasty. Yes – if I think of it there might be a few letters you might do – a few accounts you might send out, and such. The men's wage packets have to be made up weekly. Samuel Lachlan comes down from Inverness once or twice a month to go over the books – there are some things in between that could be done. Nothing too important, but all of it taking time. And I'm not one to encourage idleness in any . . . Well . . .' grudgingly. 'We'll see. We'll see.'

I didn't know whether I was supposed to thank him, but I said nothing, just turned away to offer Ailis her water. The energy of my anger and resentment was eased as I rubbed her down. There was something, at least, to be proud of, in the healthy sheen of her coat. 'Aren't you a good wee thing,' I said to her, standing off to admire the clean legs and hooves, the shining back, and unconsciously, falling into an imitation of the accent I heard around me. And I gave her an extra measure of oats. She was fat already; let her be happy as well.

Very gradually, then, I was admitted to my grandfather's office, a cold, narrow room, crowded into a corner of the main distillery building, and smelling of the forty years of the malting and the fermentation, an oddly sour smell of old beer, despite the fact that everything was swept and scrubbed meticulously. Even the paper and dockets, particularly the leather-bound ledgers, smelt of it. 'It is only fitting,' my grandfather answered, when once I remarked on it. 'A thing should smell of what supports it. We do not pretend we are a sweet shop.'

It was dull enough, the work I did for him, and little enough.

'Dear Sirs . . . we beg to draw to your attention . . . Dear Sirs . . .
in answer to your esteemed communication of the fifteenth instant
. . . We remain, dear Sirs, your humble servants . . .' Humble –
not at all, I thought, as I carefully penned the words. My grandfather was a proud man, and he made and sold a proud product.
I began to think that it eased him to be free of this ritual formula,
by which he might seem to lessen himself. Of course, we could not
change the wording, which was time-honoured established, but at
least he had only to glance over it, and affix his signature; and it
pleased him now that the signature was in a different hand from
the letter. His had never been a clerkish script. 'You write a fair
enough hand,' he allowed me. 'At least, you cannot tell at a glance
that it is a *woman's* hand. Though some would guess it,' he added
doubtfully. 'Perhaps it is not a good thing to let them know that
there is a woman –'

'You could have a typewriter, Grandfather. And then no one
could tell who had written it.'

'A *typewriter!* No good modern thing! Next you'll be suggesting that we distil our own patent grain spirits! – set up blending,
perhaps?'

'Oh – I don't know,' I answered demurely, looking back to my
papers. 'It wouldn't do to go *too* far, would it?'

'You'll not laugh at me, miss, I'll tell you! Cluain managed
before you came, and can manage after you're gone.' And he
roared out, the draught from the slammed door lifting the papers
on the roll-top desk at which I worked. At first I smiled to myself,
and then I stopped smiling. Suddenly I thought of the world
beyond Cluain – of the time before I had known Cluain, of the
time when I might not be here. It was a cold thought. I applied
myself quickly to what needed attention, as much to distract myself
from the thought of leaving, as to get through the work itself.

Samuel Lachlan did not at first welcome my presence in my
grandfather's office, and on the day he came, I was excluded. Over
the years, firstly because he had to protect his investment, and then
because Cluain had become an absorbing interest in his life, he
had become accountant as well as solicitor; keeping Cluain's books
was a kind of relaxation for him, and he resented even the slightest
infringement of his domain. The ledgers were his, almost forty years
of them. He had grown old with Cluain, and with Angus Macdonald, putting to order the rough notations my grandfather had
made of the business transacted since Lachlan's last visit, setting
it all out in his neat, eminently legible figures. I was an innovation,
and he was too old to care for the new – and besides that, I was

a female with no place in an office of business. But I sensed that behind his sallow, thin face, and the perpetually stooped shoulders in the shiny black suit, there lived a passion for the welfare of Cluain almost as great as my grandfather's. This I had to respect, and to try to understand the man who harboured it. When first we had been introduced he had avoided my eyes and muttered, 'A pity about your brother – yes, a great pity about William.' But the pity was for himself and Cluain, not for me.

The day came when I was careless of the time, and had not left the office before his arrival. My grandfather had been called away to inspect a sick bullock, and I was alone when Samuel Lachlan opened the door of the office. He frowned when he saw the account books open. These were his property.

'Your grandfather lets you do some of this?'

'A very little. I only try to tidy up his notes, really. And just write a few letters about accounts – sending them out – writing to confirm appointments for buyers to come here – helping with the wages. Very simple, really.' I felt I had to defend my grandfather.

He came and bent over me; I could smell the age of that black suit. 'You understand this sort of thing?'

'Naturally I haven't done exactly this kind of thing before. But I used to help my father with the accounts of the diocese. It released one of his curates for other work.'

'Did the Chinese cheat you?'

It was useless to pretend; he would know. 'In the beginning they did. And when I found out, and tried to stop it, the system wouldn't work any more. It was like dealing with the Chinese cook – but on a much bigger scale. In a way, it was agreeing to ignore a certain proportion of stealing. It is the way things have always worked in China. If it got above the limit, then there were great rows – discussions, really – and all based on making an allowance for face-saving on both sides. Very important. But I learned – I actually began to enjoy it. I think I saved my father some money – we were always stretched so thin for money. The Chinese thought it was very funny to have a woman sitting in my father's office – but then they laugh at everything the Foreign Devils do. They think we are all very ugly, especially the women – big hands and feet, long sharp faces. It's one of the things you have to get used to in China – whenever you go out, there's always a crowd about you, just pointing and laughing . . .'

He forgot his suspicion for a moment, and seated himself close to me. 'Interesting . . . did they sell concessions for the contracts – supplying the mission stations?'

'Oh yes – that had always to be allowed for in the bargaining.'

'Did you speak the language?'

'Mandarin – the official language. I spoke it – I wrote it far less well. It is very difficult – complicated. I often had to use my father's chief clerk – it was he who tutored William and me in the language. But I learned to deal with the people who came to ask for the contracts myself – it was a system of agreeing how much cheating there could be. My father was glad not to have to do it. He wasn't . . . well, he wasn't a businessman. I don't think he would have been made a bishop if he had stayed in England. He wasn't good at asking people for money. I don't think he could have built any cathedrals . . .'

'Don't approve of cathedrals,' Samuel Lachlan said. 'A lot of show, and waste of money . . . And what else did you do in China – what else did you learn?'

I talked, quite forgetting to whom I talked. It was freer talk than I could have with my grandfather. This lonely man soaked it up with an eagerness he did not know he betrayed. 'China . . .' he mused. 'Well, it's a very long way. They say there are great fortunes made there. I once went to London – when the railway was finished to Inverness. Only stayed two days. Very expensive. China is too far.'

We were still talking when Morag came to summon us to the midday meal. I saw Samuel Lachlan's embarrassment, and Morag's disbelief. I was glad my grandfather was late for the meal; there was a weakness discovered in Samuel Lachlan's façade, and it would have been cruel to show that I had seen it.

He was always an honoured guest at Cluain. The meals were always especially lavish when he came, the fire heaped high, as if to try to warm those fragile bones. There were always his favourite dishes – large cuts of roast beef or lamb, fragrant herb gravy, inevitably apple tart and cream. He always carried back to Inverness a basket full of food from Mairi Sinclair's kitchen – 'it's shocking what they charge in Inverness for a scone.' He said her food relieved his dyspepsia, as did the tonic she gave him. 'Samuel's life is very narrow,' my grandfather said, seemingly unaware that his own was not much different. 'We try to give him some ease when he comes here. There is nothing in his life but work. He has never married. He has only one relation I know of – a great-nephew who used to live in London, and who has now gone to America. Samuel didn't approve of him . . . Cluain is his child. We have built it together. It is his pride to be associated with the greatest whisky to come out of the Highlands. Money alone could not buy him what he gets from Cluain.'

Morag sniffed, and shrugged when I went to help her make up the room Samuel Lachlan always occupied at Cluain, and I suggested that I might put a few flowers on the mantel.

'Och, don't be fussing yourself, mistress. He'd never notice them, that old man. Doesn't he live on the smell of an oil rag there in Inverness? He has a wee house on the quay there by the bridge – three articled clerks he has working in the downstairs rooms, short of space and candles they are. And Mr Lachlan lives in the rooms above – he's at work by six in the morning, they say, winter and summer. I've seen the place. The Master once sent me to Inverness with an urgent paper for Mr Lachlan. I wouldn't care to sleep there, myself – so dirty you can hardly see out of the windows. He has all his meals sent round from a chophouse close by. Slops, they are, by comparison with Cluain food. And yet they say he could buy and sell half Inverness, so much money he's made. He underpays and overworks his clerks, and still they tumble over each other to be articled to him. Each will learn the business so thoroughly with him that they will all look to make their own fortunes when they leave him. Och, he has the pick of them. Only the brightest, quickest lads will ever see the inside of Mr Lachlan's office, you may believe me, mistress. Reminded me of the way Mr Dickens described that old man – that miser – in one of his books . . .'

I did not believe her, and pitied him more. The history of Cluain was there in his neat hand; the first small production figures, the loan and interest paid to build the distillery, the charges for the sherry casks to store the first runs, the price of the fence that was all that had protected Cluain's precious product in those far-off days. 'We called it a bonded warehouse,' my grandfather said, 'but all that guarded it was a pair of dogs, and my gun beside my bed. I didn't sleep soundly in those days – the Excise would have had their price on every cask, stolen or not. And when I built my warehouses, one at a time, as they could be paid for, I built them strong and good, with a house for the gauger tight against the wall. I slept more easily the first night my casks were safe behind bars, with good stout walls, and under a roof.'

The scraps of Cluain's history came to me fitfully, and I was never allowed the full picture. The post that came daily was left for my grandfather to open, and there were still many letters that were answered by him, and then locked in the drawers of his desk, away from all other eyes except Samuel Lachlan's. The early ledgers, in their faded red leather bindings, were available, but the later ones, the last twenty years of Cluain's production and

profits, were locked in tall oak cupboards. 'Why should I leave
my business lying around for the world to see?' my grandfather
asked of me when I remarked on the security of locking the cupboards, and then locking the office itself. 'Shall I have every man
from here to Inverness gossiping about what is in Cluain's warehouses, and what-is sold to what blender at what price? The
Excise know right well – it is only a fool who would try to hide
anything from them, but they are paid because they are men who
keep their mouths shut. They would not stay in the service else.
Shall I let one blender know what another paid the year before? –
not every run of whisky turns out to be of the same quality,
though all of Cluain's is good. So they come and they taste, and
we make a price, and they pay – the Excise have the revenue
fixed, and we cannot afford to give away our product. But I keep
my samples locked up, as I am bound by law to do, and I see no
reason why I should not keep my information locked up as well. All
that is known of Cluain is that it makes a fine whisky and it pays
its wages and bills at the right time, not sooner, not later, than the
due date. Chatter is for fools like James Ferguson. Cluain has to
impress no one.'

I had my visit to the bonded warehouses, as Callum Sinclair
had predicted I should, and in the company of my grandfather,
attended by Neil Smith. Big Billy was there by the door, surrounded by his flock, but we had long ago come to terms; I was
accepted by Big Billy in the same way as everyone who belonged
to Cluain – we reserved a distance on both sides. My grandfather
observed the courtesy of asking Neil Smith if we might go into the
warehouses and the little man nodded, and produced his keys,
cackling a little with pleasure, as if he were showing off something
he owned.

'And I suppose you might say the Excise does own it – or a
goodly part of it – until the duty is paid. They'd hardly stand,
these days, for the way it was stored in the beginning. But it was
hard enough in the early days of this country to stop the smuggling
traffic in the Highlands. Just to get a man to take on a licence to
distil, and then to pay the tax was an accomplishment. In the
first years after licences were issued, the distiller himself often had
to ride with his casks strapped on the ponies and guns at his side
to bring it to his buyers – so bitter was the feeling here in the
Highlands against those who they said had thrown in their lot
with the Excise. Ever since the first tax was put to whisky it was
considered an honourable thing to distil illicitly, and slip your
whisky past the gaugers. It isn't done now, except for the odd bit

of rot-gut distilled in a hurry up in the mountains – you see smoke in an odd place, and you may know someone is brewing their few gallons. But if an exciseman goes to investigate, there'll usually be nothing for him to find. No, it's an ordinary, dull enough business now – except that every time the government wants a few more millions, up goes the tax on whisky. All we distillers would be millionaires if we saw anything like the price that whisky fetches when it's sold over the counter.'

He didn't seem to care if Neil Smith heard this. Both men might have respected each other, but they had their roles to play. I thought there would be little companionship for the exciseman among the distillery workers. He would have to like his own company, would Neil Smith, given a lonely place like Cluain. Perhaps Big Billy and his dog, a big yellow mongrel called Rover, were enough.

Inside the warehouses were beamed, earthen-floored caverns, bigger than they seemed from outside. The smell was of sour dampness. The casks were laid in rows, with racks made of huge wooden beams which had been fashioned to take the weight of the filled casks. There were high barred windows in the stone walls. Whatever chemistry or magic was happening to the whisky as it waited out its maturing phase, there was no beauty in the place it waited. We passed by the racks – row upon row of them. One warehouse opened into the other, with great oak double doors, very high – high enough to take horses and a loaded dray. Neil Smith was there at each door with his keys. We hardly spoke – what was there to say? The whisky stood in its kind of sombre, grim majesty, the casks lettered with the names of those who had come and bought, and had left it here in Cluain's climate to reach the age they desired before blending. The dates were there, the names, and Cluain's own burned into the oak of the casks. They would eventually come back to Cluain to be refilled. What stood in those casks, I thought, must have represented a small fortune, and never had a fortune worn such a plain cover.

The silence, as we walked through to the last warehouse, was broken by a dull, tapping sound – a measured tap, deliberate, with a steady pause between each stroke.

'What's that?'

'That will be Andrew Maclay,' my grandfather said, nodding towards Neil Smith for confirmation. 'Each day he makes his round. He has grown old, Andrew has, listening to that sound. He is tapping the casks, you see. Each day he taps and he looks, lest there be one that leaks – you will tell from the sound of it very soon how much is in it. He gets through a certain number each day. We cannot take them down all the time to keep weighing them, and the Excise allows for two per cent evaporation each year. If there is less in volume in the cask as it leaves the ware-houses than there should be, calculated on the size of the cask and the amount of evaporation that should have taken place in the number of years it's been stored here, then we must pay the duty. So a leaking cask can cost us dear. No distiller can afford to let his product run into the ground.'

I was glad we were through. Cluain's wealth might lie there waiting, but its heart was in the distillery. I did not envy the un-known Andrew Maclay his job.

As we crossed the yard again my grandfather pointed out the pipes that ran from the distillery to the building where the casks were filled, and weighed by the Excise. 'Nothing that holds spirits may run underground,' he said. 'And anywhere it passes through a wall, the wall must be broken into a hole so that the gauger can see that the pipe is whole and untouched on each side. Smuggling has been tried in many ways, and most of them discovered. You'll hear plenty of tales of the distillery with the pipe underground to some other building – even into the home of the distiller himself. But you need not be believing very much of it. Those are tales of a long time ago. We live by the law now, don't we, Mr Smith?'

'Aye.' The wizened little face split into a grin, and the keys jangled loudly in his hand. 'Aye – and must. The law is the law.'

I wondered why he made the law sound so unattractive. Or was it just the presence of Big Billy, who escorted us triumphantly out of his domain?

Morag was hurrying towards us across the yard, her white apron whipped by the wind, the tendrils of shining hair lighted by the morning sun.

'The gentlemen have arrived, Master. Mistress Sinclair has them in the dining-room. The office was locked.'

'So – we are late.' It seemed to disturb my grandfather. 'Ask them kindly to step over to the office now, Morag.' He made a little chuckling noise. 'I have never been late to meet my buyers before. They will say Angus Macdonald is getting old.' He turned away towards the distillery, leaving me to linger by the back kitchen walk, watching the procession of three tweed-suited men, who somehow managed still to look as if they were in the city, cross the yard, accompanied by Morag, who flapped her apron to keep Big Billy at bay. A trap stood in the stableyard, and the horse was munching oats. The buyers had arrived, and there would be more entries in my grandfather's ledgers, and more names placed on the casks buried in the warehouses. I went upstairs reflecting on the strangeness of the business – the samples taken from small, plain labelled bottles locked in the cupboards of my grandfather's office, the tasting, the bargaining – though there was little enough of that; the price of Cluain's whisky was almost as fixed as what the Excise would take in its turn. The decisions would probably be made now as to how long they would leave what quantities to mature at Cluain. A strange business, where one bought so far into the future. Some of these men might not live to receive the product they now bought – perhaps my grandfather would not live to see it leave his warehouses. They bought and sold the future. Whisky men were a strange breed.

And then came Morag's quick tread on the stairs to the tower room, the opening of the door without ceremony. 'Quickly, mistress – the Master has brought the gentlemen back to the dining-room. I've never known him do *that* before, and it almost the dinner-hour. They've always taken their dram in the office, and been off. And he says for you to come down at once . . .'

She was flustered; perhaps that accounted for the near-sharpness of her tone. I decided to take no notice of the fact that she had not knocked before coming in; it was not often that the routine of Cluain was disturbed.

I tidied my hair and went down. I never did remember the names of the three men who came that day – they were but the first of a series of buyers and heads of distillers' groups who came to Cluain to sample and taste and leave their order – or, in some cases, to plead with my grandfather for more of Cluain's whisky than he had to sell. 'I never have been able, in the last ten years, to distil enough to meet the demand.'

'Expand, Mr Macdonald. Expand. Cluain's name would bring you credit from any bank – '

My grandfather's face crumpled with scorn, but he held back the words that rose immediately. Instead he went and poured more whisky, and took his time about answering.

'We have no need for banks at Cluain. And we have no need for expansion. You may carry the word back to your friends that Angus Macdonald will not wake up in his bed one morning and find that he is owned by another. We make what we want at Cluain, as much as we want – and it will stay that way.'

I said I did not remember the names of those men, but I remember the remark of one of them as he took his leave, thanking me, as if I were the lady of the house, for the hospitality.

'My sister's son, Douglas MacAdam, will be touring in the Highlands this summer, Miss Macd – Miss Howard. A walking tour, I believe – he works with us in Glasgow. May I say that he has your permission to call if he should find himself on Speyside?'

The question was addressed to me, but I looked to my grandfather to answer; I could make no assumption about who might and might not call at Cluain. My grandfather nodded. 'We shall be pleased to see your nephew if he should come this way, Mr Hamilton.'

And when he had seen them to the trap in the yard, he came back to his belated dinner, and there was a kind of grim triumph about him as he went to the sideboard to carve the meat.

'And *that* word will pass along too. There is a granddaughter at Cluain. The wasps are gathering to the jam . . .'

It was what any girl might have heard, and my grandfather had made the conditions of my staying at Cluain clear enough. But he could not make me like them; I did not like them at all. I could hardly choke down the generous slices of meat placed before me. It was a silent, and, on my side, a dispirited meal. I felt as if I were being sampled and sold, like Cluain's whisky.

The little restored kirk across the river from Ballochtorra continued to draw me; so many times on the rides I took with Ailis, when we crossed the bridge, we would go there. Her reins slipped over the post of the kirkyard gate, and I would wander along the path that led me to the two granite stones. I did not think it morbid that I went there so often; I would spread that all-useful plaid on the grass by William's grave, and there was peace and companionship there. I sometimes wondered if I came because the ancient Chinese custom of reporting to the ancestors had unconsciously become part of me also. If I talked to William sometimes, it did not seem strange – I had always talked to William. I expected no answer from the wind that blew through the long grass in the kirkyard, and swayed the tops of the trees. There were no answers which I would not have to find for myself. But I talked aloud of Cluain, of my grandfather, of the life that flowed about the distillery, the herb garden, of Mairi Sinclair and Margaret Campbell, of Ballochtorra and Gavin Campbell. I talked of Callum Sinclair as my eyes scanned the sky for a sight of Giorsal, the falcon. I dreamed, and I wondered, in the way that I did when I lay wakeful in the big bed in the tower room of Cluain, seeking, searching, the firelight leaping under the copper hood, and William's Chinese scroll an unanswered message. William's presence was in

that room, here where he lay; it was also an imagined figure in all
the places of that world, on the close-cropped slopes of the
shielings, and the rocks of the glen of Ballochtorra, in Margaret
Campbell's sitting-room, and a third presence when my grandfather
and I sat with the candles lighted beside the chessboard at night.
The wind played in the long grasses, and there was music in it.

There was other music, and I admitted to myself, by William's
grave, that I also came for that. I was not rewarded as many
times as I went, but there must have been times Gavin Campbell
was there when I was not. Sometimes I could hear the organ as
I drew near the church, and I would just sit by William's grave
and listen, not to the fancied music of the wind, and the birdsongs,
but the thunder and the delicacy of the anthems and fugues, the
cantatas and chorales which were never heard on a Sunday in that
kirk. On occasions I was there some time before I heard the first
notes, as if Gavin sat studying and thinking about what he would
play. Then once, as I sat in the warm sunshine with my head
resting against the rough granite, I must have slept as the soft
notes of a piece I had never before heard had drifted into the air.
There was a kind of hush that day, no wind, no sound of cattle,
hardly a bird anywhere. Gavin's fingers went back, over and over,
one gentle little melodic pattern – trying it at different tempos,
with different emphasis. I listened, content; I didn't mind the
repetition. I could hum the notes myself by then. My eyelids
drooped, and I slept.

I woke and he was looking down at me. His face wore an
amused expression. 'I found Ailis distinctly annoyed because she
has cropped all the grass within reach. Do you come here often –
like this?'

I wouldn't tell him how often. 'Sometimes. I've heard you play
before. I like it.'

He squatted down beside me. 'It puts you to sleep, though.'

'Only today. And what's wrong with falling asleep? For all I
know, that might have been a rather special lullaby you were
playing. I don't know anything about music, you know.'

'You don't have to. It's enough that you listen. Next time, come
up into the choir loft.'

'I like it out here.'

'And I would like you there. I could tell you what I was playing,
if it interests you. You wouldn't have to guess . . .'

Next time I heard the organ as I approached the church, and
I went directly along the path to the side door. I glanced upward
to Gavin's figure in the choir loft, but I stayed in the back pew

of the church where he could not see me. Within the plainness of the Scottish church the grandeur of the music was almost over-powering. No wonder they did not want him to play such things when the congregation was present; the God of that music could be felt to be a God of love as well as vengeance. It would go down ill with the sermon. It had nothing to do with cold virtue for its own sake, or the fires of damnation. It was rich and sumptuous and very human. I crept up the stairs of the organ loft, and folded myself into a corner, well behind Gavin's vision. But when he was finished he turned to me at once.

'How did you know I was here?'

'I knew. The sound changes.' He laughed. 'I always know when I have an audience. Did you like it ... ?'

'It was wonderful – warm. It didn't sound like church music.'

'I'm trying to make my own transcription of some of the Verdi *Requiem* ... to give the organ some of the voice parts. The minister wouldn't approve. An Italian Catholic ... Come here now, and sing something for me.'

'Me? Sing with an organ? With you?'

'Why not? You've been singing hymns and psalms all your life, haven't you?'

'Yes, but not ... oh, well ... I can't.'

'Come ... You know it so well ...' And his fingers moved quickly, adjusting the stops, and the sound that came was soft, like a child's whisper. Yes, I had been singing it all my life, and perhaps he was thinking of William there in the churchyard, and I absent when he was buried; perhaps he was thinking of my father killed so far away from me, and his body carried back for burial, so that I never saw the face of either of them in death. He repeated the same introduction three times before I was able to open my mouth, but when I did the sound came surprisingly strong, as I had needed the healing grace of it. *'The Lord is my Shepherd; I shall not want ...'*

When it was finished I turned and looked directly at him, and it was then the tears started down my face. He didn't seem shocked or perturbed; he didn't even say anything. I just took up the plaid, and went back down the stairs, and closed the side door softly behind me. Ailis stood quietly by the gate, lifting her blunt unaristocratic face to greet me. I slipped up on to her back, and she carried me down the strath at her own unhurried pace. I had long ago stopped weeping by the time we began the steep descent to the Ballochtorra bridge. I felt fresh, like the day, but in some way, older. And just before we passed into the steepness of the glen, looking up, I thought, for a few seconds, that I glimpsed Giorsal's soaring, gliding flight far above me, the hovering, the downward swoop on the wind. Was it Giorsal, or a strange falcon coming into her territory? Perhaps, finally, a mate for the peregrine, I thought, and Callum might lose her. And then we were too far into the glen, and she was gone.

I never went to the kirk by arrangement; we left it as it had always been. Sometimes Gavin was there, sometimes not. I would sit in the choir loft, and he would play, explaining a little to me, occasionally coaxing me to sing one of the simple hymn tunes I knew by heart. 'Here – can you read these notes? – try it!' I tried more than I meant to, music far above my head. But I enjoyed it. I would leave when I wanted to, and not even say goodbye. But there was one other thing added to the thoughts that flowed through me as I lay waiting for sleep in the tower room, watching the reflections of the firelight on the curving ceiling. It was not so much Gavin himself, but phrases from the music he made, and the feel of it, gentle as the breeze, and then crashing like thunder. When a summer storm swept through the valley, the wind riffling through the ripening barley, I thought of Gavin's music, and sometimes I wakened sleepily to the thought of it when the first sound of the birds began at dawn.

And over all of this, of all the things that made up those weeks of the summer at Cluain, there was the image and the presence of Callum Sinclair. More absent than present. Even after the morning when he had shown me the flight of the falcon, when he had said I might come with him and see her leave his hand and go for her prey, still he eluded me. I still had to ride up from Cluain to seek him out, and often I thought he was not over pleased to see me – civil enough, but not encouraging. Many times his cottage was as empty as the first time I saw it; I could never arrange a meeting. I always had to take my chances – and luck wasn't always with me. It was not pride that kept me from it – I was beginning to believe that possibly I had no pride where Callum Sinclair was concerned; it was the fact that he seemed to sense that I was on the point of asking to meet him, even ride with him on a specific day, and he would somehow manage to cut me off, a kind of freezing static moment when the words would die on my lips. It was almost as if he was trying to stop me from breaking the bounds of pride, as if he tried to avoid for me the humiliation of a refusal. I encountered him sometimes about the distillery – he would appear there without notice, and some repair or maintenance work would go ahead; my grandfather did not summon him, because that was their agreement, and it seemed that Callum filled his duties, and Angus Macdonald had no legitimate cause for complaint; at these times, crossing the yard, or at the stables, he spoke to me as if I were a virtual stranger, always polite, and apparently quite indifferent. I wondered if he knew the hurt it caused, or was he more concerned to save my face before those that watched me.

I could not reconcile that creature with the man who sometimes consented to take me out riding with him in the hills, letting me follow where he led, Giorsal on his hand, the dog at his heels. I thought wryly at times that I was almost like the dog, happy when he would even look in my direction, and having to accept it when he would not. Like a dog I waited for him, I waited for a nod, a gesture, a word. At times I could not believe it was I, Kirsty, who acted this way; no pride, no independence – no shame, even. All he had to do was lift his hand, and I was there. I had been far more easily tamed than his falcon, and perhaps he valued me that much the less because of it.

He had promised me long treks when he had agreed that I might watch the hawk hunting, and they were long. There were those mornings, too few, when I appeared at the cottage on Ailis, and Callum, looking at the sky, would nod and make a motion towards the stable. 'I don't think we'll have much rain, if any – you won't get too wet. And the wind isn't too high. You can ride with us, if you want.'

I didn't try to keep the pleasure out of my face; I would never be good at lying to Callum. 'Yes . . . please. Does it matter about the wind?'

He shrugged. 'I suppose it doesn't. But I get a little nervous when the wind is high. Even after all this time I can still hardly believe that Giorsal will come back to me. If the wind is strong she may not want to turn and beat back against it – she may just feel like flying on and on with it – letting it carry her. A free creature like that – cousin to an eagle. Who can really expect her to come to a lure, to return always to the glove?'

'It is the hand that feeds her.'

'Giorsal can feed herself. And do we always love the hand that feeds us?'

'No – not always.'

He took food with him on these treks, enough for both of us. Once, recklessly, I followed him so far on to the moors that I knew I could never be back at Cluain in time for the midday meal. I didn't care. I would risk anything my grandfather had to say for the fierce joy of sitting beside Callum in the damp heather, and eating the rough pieces of bread, the cheese and apples and sharing the flask of ale he carried in the pouch he wore at his waist. That morning, dismounted and waiting, we had watched the supreme moment of the peregrine's life; we had watched Callum's setter, Dougal, among the heather, suddenly 'on the point', motionless. The hawk, at a great height above, 'waiting on', in Callum's phrase. A step forward from Callum, a rush of wings, a shout of '*Hoo . . . hoo.*' Giorsal did not choose the grouse that was immediately under her, nor the youngest and weakest. The leader of the covey was her prey. She was a swift blue-back cloud across the sky; we had the brief instant glimpse of her turning upside down with the deadly talons stretched – a miss, as the two birds battled for position. Then Giorsal was above, in pursuit for only seconds more. The talon struck from above now, and the spinal cord was severed in that instant. There was a small puff of feathers in the air. The grouse dropped, and on Callum's command, his setter held back.

'It is Giorsal's kill,' he said. 'I do not often use Dougal to retrieve. Just to flush the game from cover.'

I was wild with the excitement of it, and yet an innate caution made me wonder.

'Aren't we on Ballochtorra's land?'

He hardly bothered to look at me. 'Of course it's Ballochtorra's land – if that matters. What are you afraid of – gamekeepers? Do you see a gun? Do you see me carrying home a grouse for my supper? It is Giorsal's kill – she will preen and eat it. Show me the gamekeeper on earth who can prevent a bird from taking its natural prey – or fine it, or put it in prison. It might be Gavin Campbell's land, but he doesn't own Giorsal.'

'No one owns Giorsal,' I said quietly.

Now his gaze had more awareness of me in it. 'You are right. No one owns Giorsal.'

She brought her prey to Callum as a kind of token signal, but they both understood the game was hers. She withdrew to clean and eat it, and afterwards, Callum said, she would be full and sleepy, and readily come back to the glove, and go home to her perch at the cottage. As we ate our bread and cheese we talked. 'It's when she's failed to kill that I have to be certain to have something on hand for her to lure her back – a fresh-killed pigeon or rabbit. I cannot leave her hungry, or she may leave me.'

'And yet – the hand that feeds us . . .' I reminded him.

'She is gracious enough not to mind my hand when she is hungry. She has all the charm of the wild who have been tamed. No one can ever be quite certain of them. Shakespeare says it through Petruchio as he tames his wife . . . "My falcon now is sharp and passing empty. And till she stoop, she must not be full-forg'd. For then she never looks upon her lure." '

'How well do you know Shakespeare?' I was thinking that of all those I had known, only my father had quoted a writer with such ease.

'Passingly.' He shrugged. 'They tried to din a bit into our thick heads in that place my mother sent me. We Scots make a fetish of grabbing at any bit of learning that comes our way. In a land so poor, all we've had to live on is our wits. Brain and muscle have been our largest export. So I, like most others, took what I could when it was offered. It was worth it for some things, not for others. They did not teach me, for one thing, to be a distiller – nor a falconer. For that, I had to do for myself.'

'You could be so many things, Callum,' I said. 'It should be you who sits with my grandfather in the room when he talks about the merits of each distilling, each year of the whisky. And yet you choose not to – deliberately, it seems to me. You will not put yourself out to please my grandfather in the least way. And yet you might do so well for yourself if you did.' I knew at that moment what I was urging on him, and why.

'Perhaps it is the last freedom a man has left – to be what he wants, and do what he wants.'

I tried to let it go. 'And wear what he wants?' I said lightly. 'You are the only man I have seen hereabouts who wears the kilt constantly, and that pouch.'

He laughed. 'Wait until the shooting season starts. You'll see them all out, fancier than a lot of peacocks. So you wonder why I wear this ragged old thing? – and it is called a sporran, not a pouch, if you please. Well, let me tell you. The kilt is the best and most comfortable garment ever devised for walking across terrain like this. It does not get wet from brushing the heather, or when you ford a stream, the way trousers do. Until you have felt the friction of the wool swinging against your thighs, you can't know how warm it keeps you when the mist is rising. It is not like a long skirt on a woman – it gives warmth without hampering and dragging. In the old days, when all the Highlander had was his kilt, it was a single long run of cloth, woven by his mother or his wife, and he gathered it about his waist with a belt, and draped the end over his shoulders to keep off the weather. When he lay down at night, in his nakedness, he wrapped himself in it, feet to the fire. He had to be inventive, and thrifty in all things, even the clothes he wore. There were some clans, when they were charging into battle, who even stripped off their shirts for better freedom to swing the claymores. Well that . . .' He suddenly plucked savagely at the heather, 'is all finished. We were beaten – all of us, even those Highlanders who fought on Butcher Cumberland's side, at the battle of Culloden. That was the end of the Highlander. It was the breaking of the clans. Now we are a picture postcard. If I seem to dress like some sorry remnant from a Walter Scott novel, it's not because I admire the man's books. It's because the kilt is still the most practical and comfortable garment for the kind of life I live.'

'And how long will you live this life, Callum? The days are passing at Cluain – my grandfather's days. Will you stay when another man is master here?'

He shrugged. 'I don't live for the future. At times I believe I have none, and it doesn't worry me. I let myself see nothing farther than this year, this summer – '

'This *day*?'

He was sitting with his weight balanced on one arm, staring away from me to the place where Giorsal had withdrawn to eat her kill; so he was unprepared, and he fell sideways when I jerked quickly on his arm. He fell against me, as I had intended, and we crashed down into the heather, his body against mine. I put my arms about his neck and my lips found his.

'This day, Callum . . . *this* day!'

For an instant he responded; his body relaxed against mine, and his kiss answered mine. I could feel the communication between us as a living thing. I swear it was there – yes, I swear it. It was not only my longing fancy. For an instant, an unforgotten instant, he was mine. And then it was over. He straightened, and broke from my grasp, his face contorted with a kind of anguished shame.

'Why did you do that?'

I was in no hurry to get up. I felt no shame for myself. I had simply offered and given what I thought his stiff pride would never allow him to take. I wanted Callum Sinclair, and he must be made to know it.

'Why not? Do I have to sit beside you, ride beside you, do anything with you and pretend I don't want to kiss you – don't want you to kiss me. Well, I *do*!' I was getting to my feet now, standing to face him. 'And I want more than that. I want you to love me. And if you think that no well-brought up young woman ever says that, then you've still a lot to learn, for all your learning.'

I was looking into his face as I spoke, and in those seconds a terrible fear grew in me. There was no way to describe how I felt, or what it was that I sensed. It had no basis in reason. All at once I knew what I could not put words to. There was some kind of darkness between us, that found in me the mirror of what I saw in his features, the horrible, contorted agony of a man which had nothing to do with shame. This was something far more, and I did not know or understand it.

And still my stiff lips went on framing the fatal, stupid words. I felt I was driving him from me forever, and yet I went on. 'I want you, Callum. Not to tease – not to play with. I want you for myself, always. I want to see you the master of Cluain. I want to marry you.'

'Woman . . .' His voice was a raging shout. 'For God's sake keep away from me! *Keep away.* There is nothing for you and me. Nothing! There never will be.'

'You love someone else? *Who?* – who is it?'

'Who? If I love someone, it is not your right to know.'

'Perhaps not. But I will know. I will know, and I will wait. I know how to wait. I'm good at it. And I shall have you – '

He cut me off as he turned towards the pony. 'Do not wait. Don't waste your days, your years. It will be to no purpose. There will never be anything for you and me. Not now – not ever.'

'But you kissed me – I *know* you kissed me.'

'Yes. I kissed you, and I liked it. I admit that. But I will never kiss you again.'

'Don't you want me, Callum?'

'There's no answer to that. No answer . . .' He was walking away from me, across the heather to where the ponies were tethered. And I was running after him, my skirt dragging and catching, and once I stumbled and fell, and the breath was almost knocked from me. And then I was on my feet again. I was shouting into the wind.

'No answer but pride, is that it? You could not be seen to take anything from Angus Macdonald – even if it is his granddaughter, who loves you. You would not take me and Cluain as a gift . . . Callum, stop! Listen . . . please . . .'

But he had flung himself into the saddle and slipped the glove on his hand. At the sight of that, Giorsal came at once as if to a command – a swift black shadow across my blurred vision, and then she was back on his fist, and the dog already trotting at the pony's heels.

He turned his head at last. 'Forget it, Kirsty. Forget it. For your

own soul's sake, forget what you have said. Forget this day . . .'
The rest of the words were lost as he kicked the pony into a canter,
and they went down that slope at a dangerous speed. The falcon
swayed and jerked upon his hand, but clung there, not needing
the jesses to restrain her, or the hood to calm her. She clung to
Callum as if he were her life.

As he was mine. I would never forget this day. I would push
away the kind of blackness that had descended between us; that
I would forget. But I would wait, as I had said I would. To love
is something; it is something more than most would ever have.
I would love, and I would wait, no matter what. I would outwait
him, and time, and whatever other love it was that possessed him.
After the darkness that had fallen on me with my father's and
William's death, I was now experiencing a rekindling of spirit and
life. I told myself then that I would wait forever, if that were
necessary.

And then, quite calmly, I went to untether Ailis. I was patient
and gentle, and made my way carefully, noting the landmarks,
taking care not to be lost – and knowing that Ailis would never
let me be lost. What possessed me on the ride back to Cluain was
the sense of time to come. I had made a declaration to Callum,
and I would wait to see the truth of it proved. In the end he
would know that I loved him. In the end he would know that I
could wait. Cluain would wait; everything would wait. Despite the
awfulness of the way he had rejected me, confidence was there,
and it was growing. I came of an enduring race; Christina Campbell, lying in her grave beside my brother, was the proof of that.
We knew how to wait, and how to love – to love someone, or
something, with a passion. What I could not begin to imagine then
was how long the waiting was to be.

Perhaps my grandfather had seen me ride, late, weary, and wet
from one of the Highlands' fierce showers, across the stableyard
that afternoon; perhaps my absence at the midday meal had
angered him. Whatever it was, he barely spoke to me through the
meal that evening. He waited for a time after the last dishes had
been taken away by Morag, then he turned on me with a kind of
smouldering fury.

'They say you ride with Callum Sinclair.'

'They say . . . who are "they"?'

'Don't be impertinent, miss. I know what I hear.'

'Yes – I ride with Callum Sinclair when I can find him. He's no
more readily available to me than to you.'

'Then you will do it no more.'

'Why not?'

'Because it is not fitting, that is why not. Do you think I want to hear tales of my granddaughter running after a distillery worker.'

'My grandfather was – still is – a distillery worker. Are you looking to match me the way James Ferguson did *his* daughter? Are you looking for a title – or money – for Cluain? You won't get them through me.'

'I'm looking for nothing for Cluain but what it deserves. And Callum Sinclair is not for you.'

'But you keep him here – you have need of his services. You grant him privileges no other worker has because of his worth to Cluain.'

'What arrangements I have with Callum Sinclair are my own business, and no concern of yours. And Callum Sinclair shall be no concern, either. I forbid you to see him again. I shall speak to him, and if I – '

'*No!*' I thrust back my chair and stood up, leaning across the table to look into his old face; I could read little there – the eyes had veiled themselves behind squinting folds of flesh. Was it trouble, or fear, or just the obstinate snobbery of a man whose pride would not admit into his future the son of an unknown man, the son of the woman who ruled the kitchen of his home? And yet, that first night he had told me to find a man fit to follow him at Cluain. And there was none more so than Callum. And Callum was the man I wanted. Was it too much for him to face that?

'You will *not* speak to Callum Sinclair about me. You will *not* humiliate him so – '

'I will do whatever is necessary. I will even send him away from here.'

'Send him . . .' The thought made me freeze. My voice was deliberately quiet and controlled when I was finally able to utter the words. 'That will not be necessary. I assure you that will not be necessary. Callum Sinclair does not want me. Don't ask me how I know that – just believe it! To him, I hardly exist. I swear to you – *he does not want me!*'

The old head nodded. The eyes opened a little wider, and there might have been relief there, or was it just the satisfaction of feeling himself unthreatened, once more, unchallenged.

'It is as it should be. He is wise. He knows his place . . .'

'Then you are a fool!' I could hear my tone rising again, and knew it was perilous. 'Callum Sinclair's place is nowhere – and everywhere. He is fit for the company of kings, if he chose it. But he does make his choices – they are not forced on him. He is like his falcon. He only stays – he only returns – because he chooses to. And he does not choose *me* !'

I left him then, quickly, so that he could not witness the hurt, and the tears. It was strange; as I had ridden back that day I had known confidence, and I had believed I could wait for as long as was needed. Now I had heard myself speak what Callum Sinclair had tried to tell me, and somewhere now the doubt had begun, the anxiety, creeping in like shadows thrown down on the strath from the crag of Ballochtorra. I had not wept then, but I did now. I wept in a kind of despair before the fire in the tower room. For all its blaze and its glow, there seemed so little warmth in it. I shivered, and held my hands towards it, and there was no comfort in it. All I could see was Callum's retreat; all I could hear were his shouted words : *'Forget this day, Kirsty.'*

Callum tried to elude me, and I pursued him. It was a physical pursuit; it had to be. He never placed himself where I could find him easily, and so it became a matter of my placing myself where I thought he would have to come, of searching and finding the places where he was likely to go. I ceased even to make excuses for lingering around the yard between the distillery and the stables; I rubbed Ailis down so often, groomed and curried her, that she began to be sceptical of the whole game – she would look at me enquiringly, as if to establish that once a day was enough for a little nondescript pony. But she was also good-tempered, and put up with my sudden rush for the saddle when I thought Callum might be leaving the distillery – if I were even certain that he was there. There were so many times we rode out furiously on that road, waiting for the sight of that dark figure with the pony and dog. I even tried, and successfully, to pretend that I was riding sidesaddle, but using an ordinary saddle, and when I was out of sight of the farm buildings and the distillery, I slipped my leg over Ailis's back. It made the going easier, and for that few minutes on leaving I was able to balance sideways on her broad back, and spread my skirt so that the lack of the pommel did not show. She needed only one hand on the reins, and scarcely even that; with the free hand I held up the second dangling stirrup, and covered it partly with my skirt. So long as no one looked closely – and no one did any more – the pretence worked. But once we left the road, and I flung the other foot into the stirrup, I was free to follow the trails that Callum might have taken, to go into the steep and uneven places, and to let Ailis have her head. She led me into parts of the strath I had never seen before, never imagined. She would turn aside from the trail on to a narrow track that followed the run of a plunging burn, and she was like a goat picking her way up and down among the tumbled boulders, deep in the shadows of the overhanging ledges. She had no fear, no uncertainty, and she knew this land, with all its changing faces, as if it were her own pasture. She led me on to the open moorland, and on the pasture slopes, and she knew always where the bog began, and which path would lead us higher and farther in the shortest time. Had she learned all this in the years of searching for the illicit stills with Mr Ross? If she had not been a dumb animal, supposedly without understanding, I would have sworn that she knew my purpose. I talked to her constantly as we rode. 'Shall we find him today, Ailis? Shall we see Giorsal and find him when we watch where she returns after she has stooped?' And there was never the nervous, sensitive snort to answer my words. Ailis was a very matter-of-fact, a very intelligent, animal.

And a few times we did find him. He seemed to greet us with no pleasure, but neither did he send us away. But now I always stayed mounted; we would watch the falcon fly, marvel at the grace and speed, then the lazy hovering, the glide on the wind as she surveyed her terrain. Sometimes there was the excitement of the incredibly swift stoop, the burst of feathers in the air, the instant kill. Callum would let me watch, would give Giorsal some time to preen and eat her kill, and then suddenly, without a word of farewell, he would kick the pony into motion, and Dougal would fall in at his heels. Once or twice I tried to follow, but he was faster than Ailis; it was too easy to lose me once he wished it. A slight rise of the moor would take him beyond my sight, the twist of the glen would hide him. When I reached that point, he would be gone, and a half-dozen tracks would lead on from there. Unless the ground was very muddy, and the hoofmarks clear, I could never follow, and the few times I did, he still outpaced us. After a time I learned not to hope for too much; then I would let Ailis turn her head towards Cluain and the stable. She seemed to know as well as I did when the quarry was lost. We were never again late for the midday meal. There was never any reason.

'Don't do it, Kirsty,' Callum once said to me. 'You are wrong to follow me – to come after me this way.'

'Has anyone said I have followed you?' It was pitiful, the little effort I made to cloak my longing. 'Can I not ride where I please?

And if I sight Giorsal . . . ?'

'Those who sight Giorsal are looking for her. They have very keen and watching eyes. Forget about me, Kirsty. Forget Giorsal.'

'And what shall I do with my days?' I tried to make it sound mocking, as if I really didn't care. But I was not good at covering myself.

He lost patience with me. 'Oh, for God's sake! – do whatever it is that women do with their days. It is no concern of mine. But you must not come where I go. I will not be followed and watched, I will not be . . . hunted.'

I knew my mistake. He was right. If he were hunted he would disappear. I would never have him by naked pursuit. He might come only to the lure. And would I ever be lure enough? I watched him ride away that day, and the doubt was growing, large and hard within me, like a stone. What was it Callum Sinclair wanted? What would he take as the lure?

And once, on the return to Cluain, on a trail so little used that the bracken grew high about the pony's flanks, I suddenly came on Mairi Sinclair. It would have been easy to miss her; I was gazing ahead, trusting Ailis as always to watch her own footing, when the pony's head turned abruptly, and she checked. There, watching me, the Sinclair plaid twisted about her head, was the lean, once-beautiful face that I now looked at so seldom. I realized in that moment how many weeks had passed since our gaze had met in this way, how many times we had passed in the kitchen passage, and only a nod acknowledged my presence. But now the stare was frank and open. It was one of the times I had managed to find and snatch a few minutes' conversation with Callum. He could have passed this way; he could have passed his mother and not seen her, though that would be unlikely; Callum had eyes like his hawk. But the bracken was tall, and without Ailis, I would have missed her.

She lifted her face and looked up at me; the plaid slipped back, revealing the streaked black hair. How like Callum she was – and how different. And then there was another recognition. Her eyes looked at mine in the same way they had done on that first night at Cluain – the eyes of a woman desperate, and haunted – but always, except that time, controlled. I knew then for certain that Callum had passed her, and that she knew we had been together, however briefly, however unsatisfactorily for me. For a second her lips moved, as if she would speak, but no words came. She did not need to say them. They were the same as that first night.

'Cluain is not yours — it is not yours.'

I urged Ailis forward into movement. We were a mile nearer Cluain when I realized what Mairi Sinclair had been doing — what had been her reason for being where she was, if indeed she had not followed me deliberately, and not actually watched my meeting with Callum. In her hand she had held a long, roughly woven basket, and the flowers and herbs and berries of the field and wayside were there. I was suddenly aware, as the Chinese always had been, that what lay in that basket could have been for poison as well as for cure. The foxglove — digitalis — dead men's thimbles it was sometimes called, could mean healing as well as death. And among the bracken grew the tall, death-giving hemlock, and the belladonna — deadly nightshade. And who but Mairi Sinclair would know which was the edible mushroom, and which the poisonous toadstool? She could carry both life and death in that innocent basket.

And William's uncertain characters splashed on the scroll came back, every line traced on my memory. *'She has killed . . .'*

And so many nights of that summer Morag would come, some kindling and turfs in a basket, the hot-water jar in her hand. Often this task was done before I left my grandfather, but just as often I sat before the fire, or by the window, reading in the long twilight of the Highlands.

'Books, is it?' she would say. 'Yes — your father must have been a scholar . . . I remember Master William was forever at his books — that is, when nothing else offered. But then, it is to be expected of a man. He was near to having his degree as an engineer. They make it easier for men, do they not, Mistress Kirsty?' As she talked, she would move about the room, turning down the bed, placing the hot-water jar, taking any pieces of clothing I had left about and folding or hanging them. She always was busy with her hands; her tongue also was busy, but soft. It was hardly necessary to listen to her, except that the words came through. 'He spent a deal of time at Ballochtorra, though, did Master William. And yet, I would not have said that he and Sir Gavin were very close friends. The Master did not like it, of course. He likes nothing that brings Cluain and Ballochtorra together.' Then a clicking sound from her tongue. 'Och, mistress, this skirt of yours is getting to be a disgrace. I mean . . . Well, look you! It is so shiny and worn. You ride so much, and I'm having trouble now sponging the mud off it. Could I not send away to my aunt — the one my mother stays with in Inverness — to have another made?

I could take the measurements, and it would come back fitting perfectly – in the finest serge. And a few shirtwaists, while she was about it. These are washed very thin. I'm sure the Master would not mind the expense . . . After all, they are not silks and satins.'

'I would be very grateful if you would do it, Morag, but there is no need to speak to my grandfather. I have some money of my own – '

'Och, well, yes. A bishop's daughter. Mr Lachlan says great fortunes were made in China.'

I felt my anger rise. There was too much supposition; all the talk of the opium trade, the barter in railway shares, the great indemnities exacted from the Manchus. Everyone supposed that all in China had had their cut. I thought of the relative poverty in which we had lived, and I choked on the thought of riches. 'Morag, that is not so! I can't explain, but it is not so – not for all. And, please, put that back in the trunk – '

She was holding up the long loose coat of monkey fur which I had used during the bitter Peking winters, when the cold dust from the desert had blown hard against one's body. 'It should not be hanging, then?'

'The cedar-lined trunk is made to keep the moths out. Please put it back.'

'Certainly, mistress.' She was respectfully humble again. 'It is just that I have never handled a fur piece before. Och, and yes, it will be useful *here* in the winter, make no mistake. You will need more than the old plaid you wear now.'

'The plaid serves well enough.'

'It's a Highlander you're becoming? Well, you will wear it thin on your days of riding before you've done.'

'Done – done what?'

'Do you not go seeking Callum Sinclair?' She turned to me with a gesture of appeal. 'Och, mistress – 'tis no business of mine, and I ask your pardon. I have no right . . . But Callum Sinclair follows his own way – always has done, and does to this day. And the woman *he* seeks now is as high above him as that bird of his that he flies. High and mighty. Swooping and teasing, she is, and poor fool that he is, he does not see that. Och, a man he is, for all his education – and they all have their times of foolishness. He will come to his senses, perhaps, when the summer is gone, and she is gone.'

'Morag – ?'

'Och, mistress, I should have a lock on my tongue. Who am I to be gossiping about my betters? – though it seems to me sometimes that those they say are my betters can do what I would be in trouble for. But Callum Sinclair may seek her in the glens and on the moors, and she may be his for a time, but she will not be his forever. He will have to come down to earth, will Callum Sinclair. And he will crash like a stone, not soft-lighting, like his bird. He will fall heavy and hard. And he will lie there, ready for the hand that picks him up.'

'Whose hand?'

She shrugged, her back turned to me. 'Who knows? But, mistress, do not wear out your pony and your skirt riding after him. There is a season for everything. All comes right in its time. Those who have waited can wait a little longer.' She folded the monkey fur carefully back into the trunk. 'Then I will send to Inverness for the skirt and some shirtwaists, shall I, mistress? They will be quite inexpensive. And I see that you have a fine gown that will do excellently when His Royal Highness comes to Ballochtorra. They say it is to be a very grand evening, with all the gentry of the country coming to bow and scrape. Yes, you will look very well in this gown, mistress . . .'

'How do you know I'm invited?'

She laughed. 'Does not *everyone* know? There is little enough to talk of in the strath. What is said in the drawing-room at Ballochtorra is soon repeated in the servants' hall. From there, it belongs to the winds. We all know you and the Master are invited. We all know that *he* will not attend, and we are all waiting to hear what he will have to say about you going.'

'He has no say in it! I do as I please.'

She turned from the hanging press, and her face, usually pert and confident, was now softened and faintly wistful. 'It is well for those who can say it, mistress. May it always be so. But for freedom we must always pay. All of us . . . all that you see ride through this strath on their separate ways . . . some of the ways coming together, and some going apart. Freedom and power is always paid for, mistress . . . Now I'll just take the skirt with me, and make a note of the measurements to send my aunt. You shall have it back in the morning.'

She was gone, and I was left standing by the window, wondering about what she had said, wondering if this was one of the evenings that Callum would pass Cluain without ever raising his eyes to the tower window, without turning his head sideways. Were his thoughts always so much with the woman at Ballochtorra, for that was the only meaning Morag's words could have had? Did he ride out to meet Margaret Campbell? — and did the glens and

moors hide their meetings? No — it could not be so. It was not
Margaret Campbell's style. And yet fixed in my mind was the
imprint of Callum, motionless astride the pony, falcon on the gloved
hand, that dark and striking figure. If the imprint was there for
me, then why not for her? In her restless, seeking ways, had she
also fallen on the image of Callum that I forever carried? — and
would it go, as Morag said, when she went to London with the
first snows of the autumn? Did she play with him, to ease her
boredom, and did he believe that the game was no game at all,
but real?

Then the thought came to me for the first time. I went quickly
to where I kept the small box in the bottom of the wardrobe which
held William's scroll. Once again, my finger traced that shaky
brushwork, splashed, I had always thought, by the fingers of a
sick man. But in what way had he been sick then? *'She has killed
. . .'* Did I read not, as I had believed, the death of the body, but
of the heart? And had Margaret Campbell been the cause?

7

The Prince was coming. All up and down the strath the knowledge
of it was there, heard and felt. It seemed that every hour or so
another trap or cart or carriage rumbled over the bridge at
Ballochtorra — servants came from Edinburgh, and some special
ones, chefs and ladies' maids, and extra footmen came from
London, hunching their shoulders against the chill of the Highland
summer, and scornful of the lack of amenities, the lack of a village
or a town where they could spend their spare hours. They viewed
the whole terrain with distaste and hostility, and stayed within
the confines of Ballochtorra. They thought it shocking, the report
came, that the best view from the seat of a baronet — soon to be
a marquis — was spoiled by the ugly heap of the distillery. No
place for the Prince, they said. No place for them. They would
be gone, thankfully, as soon as he was, and well paid by James
Ferguson's money.

I did not see Margaret Campbell in those last days before the
arrival. I did not want to present myself at Ballochtorra — there
would be too much confusion, and no time for talk. And now, I
had grown reluctant to talk alone with Margaret, almost for fear
of what I would discover. I did not want to believe what I thought
I knew. And yet, in those last frantic days before the Prince's

coming, I saw her, late one afternoon, pass on the road that cut through Cluain, riding alone, looking straight ahead down the strath; it was as if she hoped I would not be there, would not see her pass, nor expect her to stop. She rode in a way I had not seen her ride before – as if she wished to make herself small and inconspicuous – as if she ever could, mounted on that wonderful horse, dressed as she was, with her back as ramrod straight as ever, and her head high. It was her expression, not her presence, that she seemed to try to hide. How could a creature like Margaret Campbell hide? – she could never be unobtrusive, unnoticed. Women like her had been born to be noticed. But she did not stop at Cluain's door, and from the tower room I watched her progress along the road, until she turned off upon a sidetrack, so rough not even a cart could have gone that way. Even without Morag's voice saying it for me, I was asking myself what a woman, with a household turned upside down to receive the heir to the Sovereign, was doing riding alone in the last hours before his arrival.

The engraved invitation had lain in the drawer of the writing-table in my room for several weeks. I had answered formally, although it was known that I would come; it was also known that my grandfather would not accompany me. It had been a courtesy gesture on Margaret's part to invite him. I had taken out the dress that Morag had said would do very well for the evening a dozen times – shaken it, tried to push some life into its rather tired ruffles. It would do well enough, I supposed, but it did not excite me. It belonged to the Peking of three years ago, when I had been younger, and had had more taste for ribbons and bows. It was low cut – I had thought at the time my father might have been displeased, but he was not – and it showed off my shoulders and bust, and even I knew they could stand showing. The silver slippers that went with it were a little dulled, but they were all I had. And over it, the monkey fur, of all ridiculous things. But again, there was no choice. And who would see, except the long-nosed servant who took it from me? And Cluain's trap, with The Sunday Lad to carry me, was what I would ride to Ballochtorra in. My grandfather had been fairly disgusted when one of the distillery workers, Ross MacKinnon, had come forward and asked if he might drive me, and wait to take me back. His wife would come also, he said. They just wanted to stand about the stableyard and listen to the music, take their share of what was handed out from the servants' hall, perhaps even catch a glimpse of the Prince.

'Have they no pride?' Angus Macdonald demanded of me at the supper table. 'Have they turned themselves into servants? – into gaping street fools watching a circus – and if it were a Stuart prince, not that fat Hanoverian! Who would suppose that they are independent working people, free to come and go at their will, bowing their head to no man?'

'Perhaps they are just kind – and ordinary,' I said. 'Should I drive The Sunday Lad myself, and enter by the stable door? Perhaps they don't want *that* for Cluain. They are more proud than you think – and life can be a little dull doing the same thing year in year out.'

'It has never been dull for me. *I* have never found life in this strath dull.'

'You are the Master of Cluain. As long as you can count your barrels of whisky growing year by year, life is never dull. For them it could be just season after season . . . and just growing older.'

'Och!' He turned from me in disgust. 'You're too soft, Gurrl. They have a good life, and should know it. And no need for frivolity. Waste of time. Waste of money. But then, James Ferguson seemed to have plenty of money to waste.'

'Waste – or spend? If he gives happiness . . .'

He looked back at me sharply. 'Happiness! What do you know of happiness?'

'Very little, Grandfather. Very little. I am trying to learn.'

He grunted, and was silent for a long time, as if he did not care to question in what ways I was trying to learn. Finally he motioned with his hand. 'If you can get your mind off the fripperies up there at Ballochtorra, perhaps you'd be good enough to favour me with your attention for a game of chess. Bring the board, please. And try to concentrate your mind. I do not care for too easy a victory.'

But I could not concentrate my mind, and that night his victory was a very easy one indeed.

It had not rained all day – not even a passing shower to dampen the road, or wet the heather on the moor where the shooting party had been all day. From Cluain we had heard them set off, and I had sped to the tower room, trying to see which of the distant tweed-clad figures might be the Prince. But there was more than one stout man in the company. They did not pass Cluain, but turned towards the other side of Ballochtorra's lands. It was said that tomorrow they would shoot over the moors above Cluain, and I think the only satisfaction my grandfather had in the Prince's presence in the strath was the fact that he would have to pass by the distillery, would have to see it, and ask about it, and be told that Cluain's was the greatest malt whisky in the Highlands. Whether this would actually be said or not I didn't know – or whether the grander members of the party would merely commiserate with Gavin on the fact that he had such an eyesore on his doorstep. But I guessed that my grandfather firmly believed that the whole story of Cluain would be related to the Prince, and he took a sour pride in it. And I knew he would take care to be well out of the way before the procession of gigs and traps went by, following the earlier ones that carried the food for lunch. It was not in Angus Macdonald's blood to stand, cap in hand, to watch the progress of a prince.

Nor, I thought, would Callum come down to the roadside to see them go by; Giorsal's fierce bright eyes would not look on that famous bearded face – and for the days that the guns roared up on the moors, and the cries of the beaters sounded, she would only be flown in the early hours, and later, when they had departed. Callum would never risk one of the fancier shots in the party trying his skill on matching the flight of a falcon should Giorsal be tempted by the game driven up by the beaters. No, she would stand, safe and calm, hooded, with the jesses and swivel firmly attached to the perch, in her little hut. Perhaps for these days she would eat rabbit that Callum had snared, but she would be no prize for a sportsman to boast of over dinner.

The day passed, and the shadows started slowly down the strath; the pale transparency of a moon rose while the northern sky was still bright as day; my grandfather noted with satisfaction that a few clouds drifted across its surface. 'Och, there'll be rain before the night's out.'

'Nonsense,' Morag said, when I repeated my grandfather's opinion; she was taking away the white dress with the ruffles to see what a hot iron would do for it. 'It will be as fine a night as you ever saw, and half the people in the strath will be creeping in by Ballochtorra to see the festivities.'

'And will you, Morag?'

In an instant I knew I offended. 'I, mistress? No, not I.' Her chin had come up sharply. 'I have an imagination. I *know* what will go on there tonight. And I've no mind to be of those peeking in at windows. It is not my way.'

'But there must be plenty of young men who would want you to go with them . . .'

She handled the latch on the door heavily. 'None of my choosing, mistress. I will go and do the dress now.'

I ate very lightly with my grandfather; we had supper unfashionably early at Cluain, at the end of a workingman's day, rather than the hour when the gentry began to feel hungry again. So, for the sake of form, I sat with him at the table, and ate as little as I could. He noticed.

'Better eat while you can, Gurrl. There'll be so many courses and so many flunkeys to pick up just the second His Royal Highness sets his fork down, and so much talk – first to the right, then to the left – that you'll scarcely get a bite in. And finish up your dram before you go. It will put heart into you. And don't touch the wine. Spirits and wines have never mixed. Have your dram here at Cluain, and touch nothing else but lemonade all evening. Tonight – although I wish you did not go at all – you are Cluain. It behoves you to do us credit.'

I thought of his words as I went back upstairs. 'You are Cluain.' He was investing his pride in me. I knew, for his sake, for William's sake, for my father's sake, that I could allow no fault, no gaucherie to mar my behaviour. I would have to be all that they might want of me. And yet, on the way up the stairs my limbs seemed to drag. I had never learned to dance – it was not the kind of thing we spent much time on in Peking.

It was still early, but the slanting sunlight was casting shadows in the tower room. I wandered first to the fire, a small fire, lighted, I thought, by Morag, to give me cheer; and then I went to the washstand, and looked at myself in the mirror. A lot to do on my hair, yet. A lot to do, everywhere. Then I sensed something amiss, something out of place. I turned and looked around the room, and there was nothing immediately out of order, nothing obvious to see. I looked up, and there, instead of his usual place, when he visited the tower room, on the bench before the fire, or curled on the bed, Mairi Sinclair's white cat was hunched, in an attitude of hostility and defiance on top of the tall wardrobe. The colourless eyes looked down at me balefully, as if he were blaming me for something. Never before had he looked at me that way.

At once, then, my own eyes went to the bed. It lay in shadow, and at first I had seen nothing except the dress, freshly ironed, that Morag had laid out. I had paid no attention to it when I entered. That dress had begun to bore me long ago. But now I saw what had been done to it.

The disturbance was first evident in the bed-cover, the rumpling of it, in that house where everything was forever in order. I moved closer, very slowly, not wanting to see what my senses already told me. The dress lay there, yes, where Morag must have placed it while I sat at table with my grandfather. What had been then a simple thing, a girl's white ball dress of ruffles and ribbons, was now a shredded mess. Fierce claws had raked across its innocent silk and lace, and the fabric had given before the onslaught. The bodice was mutilated beyond repair; the scratch marks even extended halfway down the skirt. A spirit of malevolent vicious fury had attacked it. I would never, nor would anyone else, wear that dress again.

I walked slowly across the room, stunned, disbelieving, and yet already knowing that the evening had ended for me. I would not be going to Ballochtorra.

I stood beneath the wardrobe, looking up at the cat. 'Why did you do it, Cat? Do you hate me so much? Did it disturb you? But you have never touched anything else – ever. You have been so peaceful . . . Why, Cat?'

I sucked in my breath with fear as he leapt. But instead of the digging cruel claws I had expected, only the roughened surfaces of his pads met my shoulder. He clung there, and hesitantly, reluctantly, I made my hand come up to support him. I turned my face to look into his, and what I saw was not the baleful stare I had imagined in the half light, but a fear, and a frenzy to be comforted. Before I had realized my action, my hand was stroking his head, and then, for the first time, he gave me recognition. He rolled his head against my neck, and I heard him purr. It was like hearing the dumb speak. He had never spoken to me before.

I stroked him for a while longer. There was no hurry now. I would not be sitting at that grand long dinner table at Ballochtorra – one of the favoured ones invited to dine with the Prince instead of merely invited to come and dance and take supper later. I thought absently that I would have to send a message of indisposition; Margaret Campbell would have to alter her table arrangements.

I suddenly thought of it – the last gift of my father's oldest servant, a woman who had taken care of his needs for more than twenty years in China, moving where he did, away from her family, which was a great sacrifice, caring for his children when he had been away on his duties; a woman who had known my mother. She had given me a parting gift – heaven knows what it had cost her of her savings. It was not fashioned on Western lines – her mind could not conceive of why we wore such desperately uncomfortable clothes, or why they should be cut so immodestly.

So of a precious, costly roll of white silk, embossed with prunes blossom whose pink was only to be discerned with the second, close look, she had had made for me a ceremonial robe in the Mandarin style – the high collar, the wide sleeves, the slight indentation to the waist, and the flare to the skirt. She reported that the Old Empress, Tz'u-hsi, wore such a robe, fashioned so, and I had to believe her. How she knew it, I did not question. Very few people had seen the Empress.

And tonight I would wear that Mandarin robe, before the man who was to be my own King, and it might remind him that others gave their lives in distant and hard places, for the establishment of which he would be head.

Still cradling the cat, I went to the door, and halfway down the spiral stair. 'Morag – Morag, quickly!'

I had to call several times before she heard me. She came running. By that time I had found the robe, hung with my other clothes, but neglected. I was still holding the cat when she came into the room.

'Is the range still hot?'

'The range is always hot. But why –' Her gaze fell on the dress on the bed. 'God Almighty! – what has happened? I laid it here fresh and lovely, mistress – och, that dratted cat! He has sneaked in here when I was not paying attention. He is forever sneaking in here, damn him! – get him out of here, mistress! He was probably taken about because something was lain on the bed, where he usually sleeps. Och, the lovely dress – the dress! What shall we do? It cannot be worn. And you have nothing else to wear. You cannot go . . . Och, the shame. You cannot go!'

'I will go. Will you iron this, Morag. Can you heat the iron and press the skirt and the sleeves. Very gently. The silk is the finest. It must be handled very gently . . . a warm iron, only.'

She took it, held it up, and her face registered her disgust. 'You mean, mistress, that you will wear this heathen garment before His Royal Highness. It isn't fitting. It is outlandish – almost an insult.'

'I will wear it, Morag. Will you iron it for me, or will I do it myself? Either way, I mean to wear it.'

'Very well, then, but it is a disgrace . . .'

'Morag!'

She turned her head away slowly. 'Yes, mistress.'

As she reached the door I called to her, 'Morag, do you want to take the cat? If he has done damage –'

She flung the words over her shoulder. 'I would not touch the dratted animal. He is a fiend!'

And she was gone, her heels making an unaccustomed noisy clatter on the stair. I continued to stroke the cat. I knew he had had nothing to do with the dress upon the bed.

I went downstairs when I heard the trap come to the front door. A strange calm had descended upon me; the worst had happened now. After this, the rest of the evening would seem anti-climactic. Here I was, going off to be presented to the Prince in what surely must be the strangest dress he would ever see worn within the whole country. How different my face had looked above the high collar – I had brushed my hair very smooth, and had not bothered with the curling tongs; it was straight and shining, dark, and caught into a low knot at the back. I had done it that way so that my hair would not offend the gown, nor one make the other absurd. An ivory Chinese fan with a red ribbon hung from my wrist; the long white gloves that were meant to cover bare arms were lost in the wide falling sleeves. I thought of the worn old lady who had given this glittering silk as a present, and wished that she could have known in whose presence it would be worn.

They knew downstairs – all of them. Oddly, the cat had stayed with me all the time I had dressed and had actually sat upon the table while I had done my hair, as if he did not want to leave the comfort of my presence. I set him down now outside the door, and he went before me down the stairs. They were waiting below in the big hall – my grandfather, Mairi Sinclair, and Morag – those two standing by the archway that led to the kitchen passage.

Mairi Sinclair spoke first. 'If the cat has done damage he shall be punished. And I shall refund the money for the gown.' The words came in a nervous rush, as if she had rehearsed them, and that was all she would say.

'It would be senseless to punish him, Mistress Sinclair. If he did damage it, it could only be because he was upset by something, or frightened. He has been many times in the room, and never before touched anything. And as for the dress – I don't care about it. I was almost a child when it was made. I am not a child any longer and don't care for little girls' dressed-up clothes.'

Mairi Sinclair did not answer. In the dimness of the heavy archway I could see no change in her expression – only the clenching red hands before the black gown. The cat rubbed against her legs.

I had come near to my grandfather now; he was scrutinizing my face. 'No tears?'

'I save my tears for things that matter. I am decently dressed
– if strangely. His Royal Highness can be shocked – or amused
– as he pleases. He can't possibly know what it cost a peasant
woman in China to give me this gown. I am proud to wear it.'

His old face creased along its seams. It was impossible to know
what his thoughts were, if he cared at all for the destroyed gown
or for the tiny Chinese woman who had given me this one. But
he nodded, suddenly, as if he had made a decision.

'There is something else which I hope you will be proud to
wear.'

He moved to the long hall table. 'Come here, lass.'

I went to him, and he had taken in his hands a very finely
woven long piece of silk tartan of the Macdonalds of Clanranald.
He handled it with great care as he hung it about my body,
looping it under my right arm, and arranging it so that it was
gathered on the left shoulder, and fell in a long swath down my
back. 'It was woven by your great-grandmother, Christina, and
worn by her on a very few occasions. And here – ' He was pinning
it in place on my left shoulder with a silver brooch which looked
as if it had just come from being polished by Morag or Mairi
Sinclair. He showed it to me before he thrust it into the cloth.
'The Clanranald crest badge, Kirsty.' He translated the motto
from the Gaelic. *'My Hope is Constant in Thee.'* And now he was
bringing a second, and this one I recognized. 'This was her own,
and she brought it to Inishfare with her. The badge of the
Campbells of Cawdor – you have the right to wear both. And if
the Hanoverian prince has any knowledge of his kingdom, he will
know the Clanranald tartan, and he might remember that it was
on Clanranald land that Bonnie Prince Charlie first raised his
standard in Scotland, and it was on Clanranald land in the Isles
he had his last refuge before leaving Scotland forever. I wonder
will this foreign prince know so much? – I doubt it. But you may
wear these with pride and honour, and know that you are as good
as any in that company.'

It was then for the first time I felt the prick of tears behind my
eyes as he escorted me to the trap where Ross MacKinnon and
his wife waited, and handed me into it. But he did not stand by
the door of Cluain to watch us go. That was not his way.

The candles were glowing, and the electric light was putting on
its show in the rooms at Ballochtorra when I arrived, although
the northern twilight was hours away. The Sunday Lad disgraced
himself at the door as I went, unescorted, up the steps. Wilson,

the butler, ushered me in, harassed, I thought, by all those strange faces of the footmen behind him, those who had never been at Ballochtorra before. As The Sunday Lad moved off around to the stables, a stable-lad rushed out to sweep up his leavings. I gave the monkey fur, sniffed at, into the hands of a woman I had never seen before, and for a moment lingered in front of a mirror in the vastly enlarged and transformed cloakroom. I smoothed my hair automatically, but for the first time I saw myself full length in the pier glass. How absurd it looked – that shining, luxuriant Chinese robe, with the tartan sash woven in its sombre Clanranald colours. But when I moved the prunes blossom embroidered on the gown caught the light, as did the silver of the two brooches. I could see the shock, near outrage, in the face of the woman who attended the room.

In the drawing-room there were perhaps thirty people already gathered. My name was announced, and Gavin came hurrying forward. He took my hand. 'Pay no attention to it all,' he said. 'It's all a joke. We'll laugh about it some day.' And then, almost as an afterthought, he added quickly, 'How lovely you look . . .'

But he had to turn away, as the names of the next arrivals were announced. I was alone, except that a footman was immediately at my side, with a silver tray. It looked like champagne, the pale, straw-coloured liquid that I had never tasted. 'Thank you – no . . .' And then the need for experiment went beyond my grand-father's cautionings. 'Well, yes . . .' He lowered the tray slightly, so that I might take a glass. Then I looked around, and saw that very few other women held a glass, and those who did were mostly elderly, seated, and heavily surrounded by men. I stood alone, glass in hand, and there was no one to talk to, no one who looked as if they would ever talk to me.

A few more people arrived. I had left it rather late, I thought. 'Lord and Lady . . .' They looked at home, familiar, Scottish probably, but already acquainted with the Prince. 'Major James McCulloch-Johnstone . . .' Perhaps that was the odd man invited to balance my presence. How Margaret must have searched to find a single man who was acceptable. Still no one came and spoke to me.

Without any words there was a kind of tremble suddenly through the company. The footmen disappeared, and the glasses as well – at least for the time being. As if at a command, the company rose to its feet, the elderly ladies helped, but once there, assuming attitudes of such rigidity that I thought they might never be able to let go. There I stood, with the glass still in my hand,

no footman in sight, no tray to receive it. People were forming
in a line down one side of the long room. I found myself squeezed
out, and hurried along behind them searching for a space. And
then I remembered the glass in my hand. I left it on a table, that
slowly bubbling champagne, still untasted. Then, almost two-thirds
down the room I found a space in the line. The door had not
yet opened, but everyone was ready.

'His Royal Highness, the Prince of Wales!'

I was craning forward to see him, perhaps the only one of that
whole line, who all seemed frozen. Was it protocol to pretend
that he had not yet arrived until he was level with one? The ladies
first in the line were curtseying, and the men bowing. There came
at that moment into my mind all the thousand forms of Chinese
etiquette which I had never mastered. That stout, august figure
was moving slowly along the line, nodding to those who were
already known to him, and members of the house party, pausing
to acknowledge the introduction by Margaret Campbell of those
invited to meet him that evening. She moved beside him in a kind
of haze of gold, the gown, the skin, the hair – no other colour
but the fire of emeralds at her throat and ears; but she could
have done without jewels completely – she was a kind of shimmer
of beauty herself. They were almost level, Gavin a pace or two
behind; and then my legs shaped themselves into the half-remem-
bered complexities of the curtsey, but somehow I couldn't get low
enough.

'Sir – may I present Miss Christina Howard.'

He had actually paused, and my knees trembled, and I thought
I was going to crash over in front of him. Was I supposed to rise?
I didn't know. I stayed as I was. There was a moment of absolute
silence, and although I didn't dare lift my eyes, I could feel his
gaze fastened on me. But it wasn't me, it was the dress.

'How unusual . . .' My eyelids flicked up, and I met his look
fully. I could feel myself flush with something near anger, but this
was one place I could make no retort. Then, astonishingly, the
soft, plump finger was under my chin, tilting my face upwards,
almost causing me to lose that precarious balance. 'How charming
. . .' The words melted me; I could feel myself begin to smile with
gratitude. Did one smile at Royalty?

Margaret was saying something in a low tone close to his ear.
He was nodding. 'Ah, yes . . . our dear Bishop's daughter. So
tragic . . . he had done so much good for China.'

I knew my father had never met the Prince in his life, and the
Prince could not know that my father considered that the

Christians had done little, if any good, for China, in all the years
they had laboured there – and that thought pained him more than
any kind of death. But the words were well meant, and to console
me. All I could think of was that my knees wouldn't hold me in
that position much longer. Was I expected to reply?

Apparently not. The Prince and Margaret moved on, and then
Gavin's gaze was on me as I rose stiffly. I had the overwhelming
conviction that he knew what I had been thinking. In a flash I
was suddenly at one with my grandfather, knowing that I should
never have come, angry that this unknown man, however distinguished, should claim some knowledge of my father, should
presume to patronize me, even if he had only meant to be kind
to this oddly dressed female. The gratitude vanished. I was done
with curtseying and posturing; I wished I were back by the fire
at Cluain. And somehow Gavin understood all this.

The rest of the evening was a kind of torture. As I suspected,
I was taken in to dinner by that lone man, Major James McCulloch-Johnstone. He made conversation for the requisite amount
of time, all about things that I didn't know anything of – his
regiment, his family, which I had to assume was distinguished, his
guns. Did I ride? – did I collect anything special? – did I know
the Lovats? – had I heard that John Singer Sargent was to paint
Lady Campbell's portrait this coming winter? He was making an
effort, because for some reason the Prince had chosen to single me
out, to call me charming. I heard my tight little replies: remembering Angus Macdonald, I refused all the wines; I was angry
and lonely – so terribly lonely. Gavin was far away down the
table, and only now at Cluain would the lamps and candles begin
to be lighted. There was no waste at Cluain, and here the twisted
silver candelabra were placed every three feet along that enormous
table, and there was more food placed on the table, and toyed
with, than would have fed one of my father's mission houses for
a month. I decided then that I must be very like my grandfather;
I loved abundance, I loathed waste. The hungry energy of those
Macdonald ancestors scratching a living from their bare Western
Isle was eating at my bones and heart. I counted this moment,
this night of being complimented and flattered by a prince, as the
moment when I received my identity, I became a Scot, and a
Macdonald. A kind of fierce pride stiffened my backbone then,
and when McCulloch-Johnstone finally gave up on such unpro-
mising material, and my left-hand neighbour, an Englishman who
seemed to have a title but whose name I couldn't remember,
began to talk to me, I gave him little chance. I found myself

launched into a kind of mad diatribe on the barley crop, and
whisky, and even – how ill-bred he must have thought it – the
selling of whisky. I could see the raised eyebrows, the long face
grow longer.

'And tell me, Miss . . . er . . . Miss Howard, what did you do
with your time in China?'

'In China? – oh, one mostly watched people die. You know
– the usual thing – revolutions and beheadings, and people dropping in the streets of starvation. Yes, one sees a lot of people die in
China.'

He was unutterably shocked. I could see by his face that he
thought I was in this company by some terrible mistake. In another
minute I might begin to talk about votes for women. He turned
away hastily, and I sat in silence for the rest of the meal.

And he was right – it was a terrible mistake that I had come.
The interminable meal dragged on, course after course. The flame
of the candles swam before my eyes; down the table James
Ferguson nodded to me, his face flushed with wine and triumph.
Was this, perhaps, his supreme triumph? – had he ever known a
moment of victory in business that equalled this social exultation?
His daughter – clothed in silk and emeralds and her own beauty,
hostess at a table with the Prince of Wales at her side. From this
time on he could only wait for the coronet of a marchioness for
his daughter and the courtesy title of an earl for his grandson.
Was there anything else he wanted? – would he then be satisfied?
From him I looked down the length of the table to Gavin. He sat
quite still, talking to neither of the ladies beside him; his face wore
that look of weary detachment I had marked the first time I had
seen him. He was staring at his wife, and there was no triumph
in that gaze. I read a kind of stern sadness, controlled as if he
almost could not bear what he saw. But what did he see?

The dinner was over at last, and the ladies withdrew. If possible
this was even worse. Margaret led us upstairs; in passing, she
smiled at me. It was that same radiant smile she always had,
guileless as a child's. She seemed almost to be trying to say to me
that this was no different from any other visit I had made to
Ballochtorra, and that we would gossip about it later over the tea
cups. But now she had more demanding, difficult guests than me
to deal with, and I would understand. I did understand, but it
did not make it any easier for me to wait my turn at the pier glass,
to see once again the strangeness of the garments I wore. The
sheer size of the flounces and ruffles about me, the spilling over
of powdered bosoms above the tightly corseted waists, the dazzle

of diamonds and emeralds nearly as big as Margaret's, the glow of rubies even more precious, cloyed my senses. There was a heavy perfume on the air, the tangible scent of money and rank and privilege. It wasn't envy I felt, only a kind of disgust with myself for ever having felt pleased to be invited for this occasion. In the midst of it all I suddenly thought of Callum, and a kind of wholeness came back upon me. I loved, and I loved the right kind of man. I thought of how his lips would have curled in half-laughter at the sight of us all herding about. It made me want to laugh too. I almost did when I overheard, as I was surely meant to, the remark of one woman to another as we passed on our way back to the drawing-room to await the gentlemen. 'I did not know, did you, my dear Lady Amelia, that it was meant to be a costume ball. How novel! – very droll – a Chinese Scot.'

A few of the men joined us later, after the port had gone round. The new billiard room was waiting for the Prince, and in a smaller room adjoining, card tables had been set up. The Prince did not care to dance any longer, they said; no one was impolite enough to add that it was probably because he was too stout. But in the gallery above the main hall a discreet orchestra was playing, well screened by potted palms. I sat by myself in the drawing-room; none of the other ladies spoke to me and I suppose they thought it odd that I was there alone. I didn't care. I would just have to wait out the hours until it was permitted to leave. How did one leave when the guest of honour was staying in the house? What had the invitation cards said – 'Carriages at Three a.m.'? The Sunday Lad would have eaten his head off in the stable by then, and the Ross MacKinnons beginning to yawn over the food in the servants' hall. Since the servants were seated in accordance with the rank of the master, then the MacKinnons would be placed very low indeed. But they would claim, and rightly, that they were not servants at all.

Once James Ferguson strolled near my chair. 'Good evening, Miss Howard. I hope you are enjoying yourself.'

'Very much,' I lied. We both knew it was a lie. 'It's a very splendid company.'

He could not resist saying it. 'Aye, very splendid. My little girl has done very well.' Then, looking hard at me, at the Chinese gown, at the tartan sash and the two clan brooches, 'And when will Angus Macdonald be ready to sell Cluain, do you think?'

I lifted my head. 'My grandfather will never sell Cluain.'

'Well then, he will not live forever. I hear he has been poorly this past winter. It will be sold when he is gone.'

'Don't be too sure, Mr Ferguson.'

'So then, lass? You think you have it for yourself? Well, it's nothing for an inexperienced girl. Or a man who doesn't know what he's about. Well, you may give Angus Macdonald the message. James Ferguson will meet his price whenever he is ready.'

'Give the message yourself, Mr Ferguson.' I got to my feet, almost brushing him aside. 'I am no messenger boy!'

I went through the hall quickly. Neither Margaret nor Gavin was in sight. I thought I was at the point when I would damn etiquette, and ask for The Sunday Lad to be brought around; and then I thought again. My grandfather would expect me to bear through whatever the evening held; I would not let him down, nor would I admit my defeat before these people. I would not let the valley know that I had left before the proper time. Because the valley would know everything about this night.

I avoided the rooms where the people strolled, and the cards were played. No one danced; those who had been invited after dinner had arrived, and became part of the company. The large rooms seemed almost crowded. After that huge dinner, supper was already being set up. It was an animated gathering, but curiously joyless. To the people who watched from beyond the windows, it must be a strange sight. Where were the traditional Scottish dances, the men in their dress kilts and ruffled jabots, the women with the tartan sashes? – where was the piper? But perhaps His Royal Highness was tired of such ceremonial, and wanted only his cards, with high stakes. It was an English gathering, however many of the company bore lordly Scottish names.

I found the room I sought, the small one almost at the end of the passage that ran the length of the main building. I had thought I would find it empty, and it was. No one would miss me, and I would wait until the first carriage came to the door. And then go and get the monkey fur, and home to Cluain. Home.

'Are you tired of it all, too, Kirsty?'

I swung round. 'Gavin!' He was seated in a deep armchair, facing the long windows and the very last of the light that silhouetted the opposite heights of the glen. The moon was already there, waiting for the sky to darken.

'Shouldn't you be with your guests?'

'Shouldn't you be out enjoying yourself? No one can have failed to notice that the Prince thought you charming. Other women have made whole careers of less than that.'

'Gavin – don't laugh at me – not you!'

He got to his feet slowly. 'It's the last thing in the world I would

do – laugh at you. You're a proud and courageous woman, Kirsty.
If you wanted to, you could have charmed every man in the house,
and made all the jewels and finery look silly.'

'Oh! – the little country maid? I can't play that role, Gavin.
It doesn't suit me. It wouldn't suit my grandfather to have me
do it, either.'

'No – it wouldn't suit. So you wait it out, as I do. Well, it won't
be long.'

I was standing by one of the french windows that looked out
on to the principal terrace. This was the new part of the house,
and down below, nearer the river, the old tower stood, a kind of
stern reminder of what this place had first been built for. From
here, the music was faint, almost ghostly.

'Take the White. First move to you, Kirsty.'

I looked back at Gavin. Between the windows there was a
marble chess table, and he was now standing beside it. I took the
couple of paces to bring me opposite him, and looked down at
the table. I spent some minutes examining the set; I had seen a
similar one before – a Cantonese ball-mounted set, carved in
Indian ivory of exquisite quality and delicacy. Not really a set to
play with, but to look at. I held up one of the pieces against the
light from the window, marvelling at the intricacy of balls set
within balls – the eternal Chinese enigma.

'How beautiful,' I said. 'How really beautiful.'

'One of the few things I own at Ballochtorra. It belonged to
my father.' He prompted me again. 'Take the White Queen,
Kirsty.'

'How did you know I played?'

'William's sister? How could you not?'

I acknowledged the fact with a nod, replaced the piece I was
holding, and made my first move. His followed rapidly. My next
I made almost without thought. The rest was part of the pattern.
We followed it through, perhaps both of us knowing, and yet I
was unsure. Compelled, I made each move as before, Pawn,
Bishop, Knight. Gavin's moves now seemed like an oft-told tale.
We reached the point I knew we must reach.

'Check to the Queen, Kirsty.'

I looked at him. 'Did you play with him? – with William?'

'We played quite often.'

'This game? – these moves?'

'This game? – I don't remember this particular game. No – I
don't think we did, ever.'

'But you played this game now ...'

'Why not?'

'Because ...' Suddenly I shivered. William's presence was too tangible. I looked hard at Gavin, trying to reassure myself that this was a living, independent being, his own man, not an instrument of a dead man, not an old man like my grandfather, not a grieving sister, playing and replaying endlessly the last game.

'Kirsty ...'

'Yes?'

'Kirsty ... I'm going. This is a kind of farewell. I could hardly have gone to Cluain ...'

'You're going? – you mean to London? When the house is ready?'

'No, not to London. Never to London. I'm going, Kirsty.'

'Going where?'

'God knows. I'm leaving. That's what I mean. Leaving. I have to leave for my soul's sake – for what that's worth.'

'Gavin – what are you saying? *Exactly.*'

'Exactly? I'm saying that when this tiny farce is over, when His Royal Highness has set the accolade upon my wife's shoulders as the most beautiful woman, the best hostess – whatever the nonsense is, then I'm leaving. Leaving Ballochtorra, leaving everything. Leaving – God forgive me – leaving my son.'

'You *can't*!'

'I must. Even leaving a son is better than appearing a fool in his eyes. In a very little time Jamie will know that my father-in-law pays for everything here. In a little time more he will know what a pretence it is between his mother and father. I can't be here to witness it. I would rather be dead than see his knowing – the contempt – in his eyes.'

I knew. At once I knew. There was no need to ask. 'Where will you go? What will you do?'

'Who knows? Anywhere – it doesn't matter. What I do doesn't matter. I'll never find an organ to play, but there's always a ditch to dig – a boulder to move – somewhere in the world. Anywhere – away from here. Lost.'

'You can't be lost, Gavin. No ...'

'To them ... yes. Margaret will miss the convenience of me – for a while. I will never formally take my seat in the House of Lords, and so my father-in-law will lose something. But one day my son will. Perhaps by then he will understand. The only hope I have is that he will somehow understand why I had to go. But you see, *I* matter too, Kirsty. I can't live with myself as things are. Can I expect to live with my son?'

'Can you live without him?'

'I will have to try. Better that than be an object of scorn to him –'

'Other men don't mind. Other men marry for money, and make no bones of it. They exchange a title for money, and it seems to men like James Ferguson, and most others, that it's a fair exchange.' Why did I argue with him? I knew the truth.

'It was never that sort of exchange. It was a small enough rank, and there wasn't so much money then. We loved each other . . . I'm sure of that. And somehow we lost it. How did we lose it, Kirsty? How could I have let it happen?'

'Could you have helped it?'

'I could, if I'd known. Is one always too young to know these things at the right time? The first acceptance of help from James Ferguson was the beginning of losing what we had – and yet could I have expected a woman like Margaret to go on enjoying poverty? She was not made for it – I should have known that.'

'There'll be a scandal . . .'

'Of course there'll be a scandal . . . but it will only dawn on people gradually that I am not coming back from whatever part of the world they'll say I've gone to. By then Margaret will be firmly established as a London hostess. I won't even be missed.'

'You'll be missed.' I looked down at the board. 'You're being too extreme, Gavin. There isn't any need . . . you could stay on here alone, if that's what has to be.'

'On James Ferguson's money? No, there've been too many years of that. If I stay any longer I won't have the courage to go. I will never be happy away from this place, this strath. Every day I stay the resolution will grow weaker – I will find excuses to delay. Just as I'm delaying now. I tell myself it's for Margaret – just to see her through this. I say I'll have just one more summer of Jamie before they send him off to school and make a stranger of him. And the excuses will go on, and on . . .'

I fingered the elaborately carved figure of the White Queen. 'There's no way out of this check, Gavin. I have played the same game too often. William . . .'

'Yes, William . . . I don't forget William.'

I looked straight at him. It had grown much darker. There was no light now but the moon.

'Was William her lover, Gavin?'

The sudden clatter of the pieces falling to the parquet as his hand swept them off the board was my answer, the terrible,

deliberate crunching of the delicate ivory as they splintered under
his feet. It was one of the most awful things he could have done
– the destruction, in his despair, of something loved and prized,
a part of himself. His hand now partially covered his face, needing
to screen it.

'I don't know. That's the worst of it. *I don't know!* That's
what will kill me if I stay – never knowing. Or knowing too well.
Guessing. Which one? – this one, or another? When? How? Was
William one of them? *I don't know . . .*'

I turned away from him, sick. The taste of deceit was in my
mouth, and the terrible memory of the letters that had told too
little. William . . . what would he have done? He might have
loved, and not counted the cost, not reasoned the error. I suddenly understood much more because I loved Callum Sinclair.
Did I stay at Cluain for him – or for the sake of Cluain itself?
Had William deceived both my grandfather and himself that he
too stayed for the sake of Cluain? The words came back . . .
'there is an enchantress.' Had he been bewitched and enchanted,
as I was, sick with longing, lost to reason? Was there a kind of
madness here that both William and I had experienced in our
separate ways? Was that why his hand had touched me so
strongly, why his presence was all about me at every turn, so that
he even played over and over this wretched last game of chess?
It was almost as if he tried to speak to me. 'Not you, too, Little
Sister. Here is your check. There is no way out, unless it is to lose
. . . unless it is to damnation . . .' But William had never said
that. I was being too fanciful, letting myself be carried along on
the wave of Gavin's anguish for his own loss. Why should the
sense of damnation cross my spirit at this moment? There was
nothing wrong in my love for Callum . . . nothing wrong . . .
nothing wrong. And yet why did I feel this breath of ice, as if
William's cold hand was touching mine across the chessboard, not
a warning, but a terrible confirmation that I also must lose. *'Check
to the Queen, Kirsty.'*

It was not William's hand that touched me, but Gavin's.
'Listen . . . !'

And eerily, upon the stillness of that hour that had crept past
midnight, when the moon held its own, came the sound of the
pipes. It was below us, and farther over, at the old part of the
house. Both of us went to the window, again the crunching sound
of ivory under our feet, and Gavin flung open the long window.
The rush of chill air met us, and the sound of the pipes, stronger.

The moon cast unreality upon the scene; the whole deep glen

was in shadow and bold relief. The light blended the old and the new of the buildings into one. In that instant it was a fairy castle, frozen in time and pale golden light. All along that upper terrace, from all the french windows of the new wing, the guests came, the silks and the flash of jewels as brilliant as they had been by candlelight. They drifted, that splendid company, the Prince's figure conspicuous among them, to the balustrade.

It was a sight from the ages that met us. The platform of a tower of the old building was below us, and clearly in our view. The moon struck fire from the shining steel of the two crossed swords, laid at right angles on the ground; it caught the drone of the pipes, and the silver of the clan badges. The piper and the dancer both wore full dress – lace at the throat and sleeves, velvet jacket, jewelled dirk at the garter of the stocking. The kilt and the plaid each wore was different. Even from this distance, though, I knew at once the Sinclair tartan. But no matter what he had been wearing, I would never have mistaken the figure.

My lips formed his name soundlessly. 'Callum!'

It was performed with beautiful precision, the sword dance. The pipes skirled, and his slippered feet leapt between the blades; the kilt and the plaid flared about his body, the arms extended outward and bent at the elbows, and so clear was the moonlight that I could even see the grace of the upraised fingers. It was a heart-stopping sight, there upon that ancient battlemented tower, with no room for mistakes, and no forgiveness from his audience either, if one slippered foot should even brush one of the blades. The first murmurs among the watchers had died. Even on that gathering, to whom little was new, he was making his impact. And the word had spread quickly. From the back of the house, from the kitchen and stables, the sound of the pipes had drawn them, those who knew the dance, and those, like myself, who had never seen it before. For most of them, it must have been the first true satisfaction of the evening – an entertainment for a prince, but in the traditional manner, and executed with flawless precision and grace.

But this was not the Callum I knew, the man who would have scorned to dance for a prince. Who was this stranger in finery I would not have expected him ever to put on – the kind of dressed-up travesty of the old sensible Highland garb that now was romanticized beyond recognition? And had I ever thought to see him dance? Perhaps . . . perhaps at a wedding when the whisky had been passed around, and there were other feet to tap the rhythm with the piper, perhaps before the huge fire of an ancient hall like Cluain's. But here, like some hired entertainer, dressed in costume? The grace and skill I might have expected; his presence here, never.

'Is he drunk?' I whispered at last to Gavin. It was the only explanation.

'No – not drunk.'

'What then?'

'Mad.'

The word was said with conviction, and harsh bitterness. With its saying, the pipes died out on their wailing note, and the dance was done. There were shouts and whistles of appreciation from those who had drifted round from the back of the house; they had carefully separated themselves by a long space from the guests clustered around the Prince. A few urged Callum on to other things. I heard a polite handclapping among the privileged group. The Prince puffed on a half-smoked cigar, and he continued to stand, as if he also waited for more. Perhaps he had been entertained, after all. Certainly, the whole event had had the novelty of the unexpected, and the most supremely appropriate setting. But it should not have been Callum Sinclair there.

But Callum was finished. I was glad to see there was nothing of a bow to acknowledge the applause. I wished that I did not feel a shame for him – one should not feel shame for someone who was loved – but I did. One more thing to be endured on this interminable evening, the evening when I seemed to be losing everything, the night when I was learning the bitterness and price of becoming myself. With a kind of dreadful fascination, wondering how deep the hurt could go, I watched as Callum lightly vaulted the battlements of the tower, and leaped to the balustrade of the lower terrace. He must have leapt the slippery rocks of mountain streams much more dangerous, but that instant when his figure was outlined against the sky was dramatic and slightly theatrical. There were little gasps from the women. And then he was running lightly up the steps to the upper terrace, and heading directly for where the Prince stood. The run slowed to a walk. I couldn't believe it. Was Callum Sinclair, the proud, lonely man, who asked for no favours, going to bow before the Prince and be grateful for a word or two – something to boast of after? I didn't want to look. It was like the shattering of a dream. I stared out across the glen, unwilling to witness the falling of an idol.

But it was the shocked murmur that forced me to look again. The Prince had advanced slightly, graciously willing to accept the bow, perhaps to offer the hoped-for few words. But Callum had simply passed him by as if he did not exist. It was to Margaret, who had been standing by the Prince's side, that he went. The people about her drew back slightly, as if they couldn't believe the scene. She and Callum were isolated in the midst of that circle when he made his low bow to her. And then she, as if she had also entirely lost all sense, instead of gesturing towards the Prince, held out her hand to Callum. I had never thought to see him bow low to kiss a woman's hand, but he did it then, and it was for all the world to see.

Then he was walking quickly along the terrace, his back to the Prince; the same light run down the steps, the same effortless leap from the balustrade. The swords were gathered up quickly, and he and the piper vanished down through the trapdoor that gave access to the tower. They had gone, like two ghosts of the night, leaving behind consternation and scandal, and hurt in me such as I had thought I could never feel. Is there a precise moment when one remembers the wish to die? – the first time it comes? I knew it then. But death is not so easy. One has to live the next seconds, and the minutes and the days.

Perhaps it was worse for Gavin, beside me, but I doubted it. He had begun to live with it long ago.

'So she has Sinclair too. Are there none she will leave alone? – no one she will not claim for her own. Is she never satisfied? How many more? – *how many!*'

Then he took my hand and led me back to the darkened room where the ivory pieces were the final, devastating reminder of William. 'I'll help you get your wrap, and send for the MacKinnons. Don't wait for who should leave first. All the etiquette has been smashed. The evening is over.'

8

The late days of August and early September stayed warm, and the barley stood high and golden; then it began to be touched lightly with brown, and was dry when I put my fingers to the heavy sheaves. 'It is time to begin,' my grandfather said. So they were saying at each farm all over Speyside, and labour was needed everywhere. Everyone on Cluain worked, of course, and the call went out to other straths and as far as Inverness, and the itinerant workers came, bringing women and children with them – the children old and strong enough worked beside their parents, and the young ones tumbled barefooted among the stubble, following the line of workers who moved with sickles through the fields. It was hard work, that endless stooping under the sun, but most seemed to enjoy it – enjoy the warmth of the days, the company, the songs, enjoy the food sent out on the wagons to wherever the workers were in the fields at noon, and the communal eating in the barns where the barley would eventually be stored, and where the itinerants now slept. Mairi Sinclair's kitchen had never been so busy, and she had several extra women to help – my first and only offer of help was shrugged aside, and those days were strangely quiet and dull for me in the midst of all the activity. My grandfather did not come for his evening meal till the last of the workers had left the fields. I watched the Cluain workers on the road home and the itinerants gather in the barns – whisky had passed around in the last minutes in the fields, and tired women sang songs to sleeping infants as they carried them back. 'The whisky eases an aching back and gives a good night's rest,' Angus Macdonald said. 'Not too much, or they would not be at their work tomorrow, but enough to warm their hearts.' My grandfather made no economies in the food or the whisky. It was always Cluain's best.

It should have been a happy time for me, a time to perceive and enjoy, as these people did, the endless cycle of life in this strath, the celebration of another year's crop. But I felt myself dry and brittle as the stooks of barley standing in the suddenly arid-looking fields.

My unhappiness was Callum Sinclair, of course. I had not spoken with him since the night when he had taken Margaret Campbell's hand on the terrace of Ballochtorra, and the story had sped up and down the strath, and beyond, of that supreme act of folly, the insult to the Prince – and most talked of, Margaret Campbell's calm acceptance of both. They said afterwards that the Prince had not shown more than momentary surprise, had rather seemed more amused than insulted. But Margaret Campbell had dared much by not rebuffing that gesture from Callum, and it seemed that no one could talk of anything else.

I could not even come face to face with Callum, much less speak to him. He seemed to have no place in the work of gathering the harvest – the only man at Cluain so exempted, and since that was not remarked on, I thought it was probably part of his agreement with my grandfather. He showed no sign of repentance for his act, and would remain independent to the last. He would appear again at Cluain when the harvest was in, and the malting ready to begin, and not before. He rode back and forth on that road that passed through Cluain with no sign that anything had changed, or there was more reason than before to mark his passage – I saw him a number of times – him, the pony, the setter and sometimes Giorsal. I knew by now that there were many other ways to pass along the strath – the track by the river, paths that by-passed the house. But Callum Sinclair would have scorned to hide from anyone, to avoid the comments – if any dared to offer them to his face – and the looks, which could say even more. So he travelled the road as before, and I was more intensely aware of him than ever; I seemed to know his coming long before the familiar shapes appeared, and I was sick with hurt and envy as I watched him pass from sight. It would be Margaret Campbell who knew where he went, and when, and she seemed to care as little for the scandal of it as Callum did. But at least she did not ride that road, or if she did, I never saw her.

Giorsal I did see, though. In those too often wakeful nights that blended to the dawn, and I sat at one of the windows of the tower room watching for the first of the sun, hearing the first stirrings about Cluain as the cattle were brought to be milked, as the ranges were stoked in the kitchen in preparation for the day's cooking – several times I saw Giorsal. Callum was flying her before there was danger from any shooting parties on the moors; it could only have been Giorsal, the great dark lightning streak in the sky, that plummeting stoop to her prey. The strath was her territory; she roamed its sky, wheeled and circled and lazed upon its air currents. Her only enemy was the gun, and before there could be danger, she would disappear, off in the direction of Ben Cullen. My whole spirit called after her. Only once did my grandfather speak of what pre-empted everything else in my thoughts. It was two days after the party at Balloch-torra; I sat toying with the food on my plate and saying nothing.

'Well, then . . . can you not hold your head up? Will you let the world see the pining of a love-sick girl for a man that's worth nothing? He has shamed and disgraced himself and his mother, and that woman up there who flaunts – '

'Enough, Grandfather! I will thank you to say nothing more about Callum Sinclair. He has done what he has done – and that takes courage. A mad courage, if you like. He has told the world that he loves a woman. But he never said that he loved *me*! I told you that he would have none of me. What a fool I was to think he would look at me when there was Margaret Campbell.'

'Margaret Campbell is a married woman, and should have more decency and pride. Where does she stand now before the world — before her son? There is shame for them both, but more for her.'

'Oh, leave them be,' I cried at him. 'It is their own affair. Margaret Campbell has not ruined herself. But she has ruined Callum. She will go and leave him here, and then he will be wretched.'

'And will you be waiting when he comes down from his dream world? Will you look to take her leavings?'

'There will be no leavings. When Margaret Campbell goes Callum Sinclair will not be free of her. I think he will never be free again. He may go also, but not with her — because of her. He may never see her again, but he will not be free of her. His sort, once they have given themselves, can never be free. I think he will leave Cluain.'

'And as well if he did. If it were not for his mother I would —'

'I don't want to hear!' I said. I stabbed the food with my fork. 'I don't want to talk about Callum Sinclair. And my head is high — never higher. You will not see me weep. It is a worse kind of feeling than when William and my father died, but no one will see me weep. And I hope he *does* go. If I could, I would make it a little easier for myself. But if he stays, then I will have to bear that, too.'

'Have a care, Kirsty. Have a care. No point to ruin *your* life.' It was said quite gently, and he was indeed more gentle with me in those next days. I worked in the office, and no words passed between us that did not concern business matters. But even sitting there at the desk with my back to the window I knew the sound of Callum's pony, and I could never stop myself looking around. If my grandfather was not there I would rise and watch him out of sight, as I had always done. I did not weep, ever. There was nothing but a kind of aching silence in my heart. Those were the nights when I played chess with fierce concentration, striving to wipe out the memory of that scene on the terrace. And those were the nights that my grandfather at last began to go down before me. Game after game I won, and he began to struggle, to put out his best efforts. But the terrible hurt had to be assuaged somehow. I could not lose everything.

So it had been a relief when the time of the harvest came. I welcomed the distraction of it, the bustle of the carts leaving with the food. I did not often go into the fields among the workers — just enough so that my presence was seen and felt there, but never dallying in case I might overhear talk – talk about Callum and Margaret. I rode beside my grandfather, and his very appearance was enough to silence even the rowdiest of the children. I began to see him fully in those days as the man he appeared to be in the strath; he was just, not unfeeling, even generous when his help was needed. And yet the jokes fell silent on the lips as he passed, and the children gazed after him in shy awe. I often thought that the minister up in the kirk might have envied the respect that Angus Macdonald seemed able to command without words.

No one saw Gavin Campbell in those days. The Prince had left after the allotted four days, the servants departed from Balloch-torra, and a strange quiet descended on the castle. I heard from Morag that Gavin left Ballochtorra early with Jamie and a gillie, and spent each day on the moors shooting. Occasionally, from down at Cluain, we heard the sound of guns, but it was not always from Ballochtorra moors. There were other shooting parties in the district, working over rented moors. They would pass along the road, looking curiously at Cluain and the distillery, talking about it. For some reason I resented that. They were strangers to me, as the hired servants had been, when all the faces in the strath were growing familiar. I almost looked forward to the time of the snow, when they would be gone. But when they were gone, I thought, so would Margaret Campbell, and Jamie. Perhaps Callum would be gone, also. And Gavin would be gone, probably forever. It was a time of waiting, these last days of the summer. And I waited to see what my life would become when the summer was finally over.

2

There was something else astir in the strath, something that called my grandfather from the harvest fields, and brought Samuel Lachlan several times down from Inverness – hurried visits without the usual overnight stay. The little man looked grey and fretted, I thought, as I sat and ate a midday meal with him in the dining-room of Cluain, and lingered with him over his tea when my grandfather had to hurry back to the fields. Neither of them said anything before me of the reason for the unusual activity – the talk was of the harvest, the weather, an occasional uninterested reference to the shooting season, and Samuel Lachlan's persistent enquiries for details of the Prince's visit; to these I made guarded, agonized replies, and knew that my grandfather's attention was always on me at these moments. But whatever lay behind the visits, and the long sessions of talk in my grandfather's office, the telegrams sent back and forth to summon Samuel Lachlan once again, or announce his coming, I knew who had instigated them. It was James Ferguson.

That burly authoritative figure changed subtly in those days also. He stayed for only one night of the Prince's visit, perhaps not wishing to stress too much of his daughter's association with 'trade', and lower her standing. Besides that, he did not shoot, and was lost in that company which talked of little else. So he left Ballochtorra on the day after the party, and I wondered what he had made of the scene on the terrace. Margaret had been greatly daring – the risk of offence to the Prince had been great. But Edward did not leave, and the shooting party went on, and perhaps there was faint amusement at Margaret Campbell's strange, rustic lover. The story, embroidered, I was sure would go about the London drawing-rooms that winter, but as long as the Prince continued to grant his company, Margaret was safe. In those few hushed moments it must have seemed to James Ferguson that his daughter was about to throw away all that he had so carefully planned and paid for. Yet the Prince had chosen to smile instead of frown – he must have liked his hostess very much. So James Ferguson departed, perhaps not pleased, but at least reassured.

But he was back again a very few days after the Prince's party had left, and it was not for pleasure – and the reason somehow concerned my grandfather. Ferguson waited overnight at Ballochtorra until Samuel Lachlan could be summoned from Inverness, and the three spent the most of the next day closeted in my grandfather's office, though James Ferguson returned to Ballochtorra for his midday meal, and did not sit with us at table at Cluain. He returned for some hours more in the afternoon, and then a carriage from Ballochtorra came to take him to the station. The Sunday Lad was harnessed to take Samuel Lachlan to get the same train, but from the looks on the faces of the two men as James Ferguson departed Cluain, I did not think they would share the same compartment. And, of course, it was Samuel Lachlan's unshakable rule to travel second class.

And the next week James Ferguson was back again, and so was Samuel Lachlan, this time by appointment; the same sessions of talk took place in the office, the same arrangements over the meals. This time James Ferguson did not even stay overnight at Ballochtorra. He nodded to me absently, rather curtly, when I encountered him in the yard on that occasion, as if he had almost forgotten my identity. He wore then an air I had never expected to see on him – the bluff, expensive look of the successful man of business who now sets out to enjoy his success seemed diminished – though I noticed that when he realized that my eyes lingered on him for a time his rounded figure automatically straightened, and a smile flashed on as if he had touched a switch. He raised his hat elaborately to me as the Ballochtorra carriage drove off; I thought that he had not liked the fact that I had surprised his expression of abstraction.

Samuel Lachlan stayed that night at Cluain. After supper, which was late, since the harvest had now begun, and my grandfather had had to go to the fields after Ferguson had left, I waited for the old man to climb the stairs to his bed before I voiced my question. Angus Macdonald had played one weary, absent-minded game of chess with me, and I had won easily. I rose and took the board away without his saying so.

'Grandfather – is James Ferguson trying to buy Cluain? He said to me – '

He cut me short. 'James Ferguson will never buy Cluain. Now mind your own business, Kirsty.'

I was not offended. I took my time about lighting my own candle. 'He once gave me a message for you, and I said I would not deliver it. I gave him an answer – I said Cluain was not for sale.'

He gave me a long, concentrated look. 'You would be right in that. You had no business to say it, but, by God, Gurrl, you would be right.'

The weather held, the last of the barley was cut, and the stooks stood upright, drying in the fields. It would be a matter for the Cluain men to gather them into the barns when the seasonal workers had gone. The evening the last field was cut, a long table was set in the neatly swept yard of Cluain, and the food was brought from the kitchen – such mountains of it as I had never seen before – great sides of beef and pork and ham, turkey and goose, blackberry and apple tarts, cream and sugar, iced cake laced with brandy. That night every soul who had worked at Cluain during the harvest, and the children who had played around their feet, sat down to eat. And this night Angus Macdonald placed no limit on the whisky and beer.

'They will sleep it off,' he said. 'They will remember it, and next year those I ask will come again. The idlers I notice and mark, and those are never welcome again at Cluain.'

I wondered why he always cloaked his generosities with some other motive. I noticed that even that night he did not sit as a

familiar man with his men, nor beam with paternal pride on them.
No one would ever see his face, flushed and triumphant, as I had
seen James Ferguson's face on the night of the party at Ballochtorra. The next day, Angus Macdonald would look about his
world with a coldly sober eye, and have no indiscretions to regret.

Nor did Morag join the group. After she had helped with the
serving and clearing away, I found her standing a little behind
me, her face impassive, the glow of the lantern light and the bonfire in the yard burnishing her hair. She looked beautiful, and
rather stern.

'You don't join them, Morag?' The whisky had passed around
freely, and there was singing, and a piper, and some couples rose
to their feet, and went, a little wildly, through the sets of some
Highland dances.

'Not I, mistress. Young men make free when there's whisky
taken.'

'One day you'll have to choose your young man, Morag. You'll
not spend your life unwed – not you.'

'Aye, that is so. But he shall be *my* choice. The man I want.
None other.' Then she stepped nearer me in the half-darkness;
her voice was barely a whisper above the exultant cries of the
dancers. 'Do you wait for him still, mistress? Do not. He is not for
you and surely you must by now know it.'

I should have turned and left her, but I didn't. 'I don't wait
for anyone, Morag.'

'You do, mistress. You do. You still think that when she has gone
he will turn to you. It is useless. Have you looked on his face these
last weeks?'

'I have not.'

'Then if you had, you would know. He is a man gone mad. He
is lifted out of himself. He always has been different from every
other man, but now the difference is greater, and it comes out of
him like a light. He walks and he moves – but he sees and feels
nothing. Nothing but her . . . There was a poem your grandmother
read to me once. I did not understand it, and it made me frightened. Those last words, I cannot remember them clearly, but I was
a wee girl, and they frightened me. Something . . . Och, how did
it go? – I repeated them in bed that night, and they made me
shiver. Something . . . Do you know it, mistress? – "Circle him
thrice . . ." '

Yes, words to make one shiver.

'I know it.

'Weave a circle round him thrice,
And close your eyes with holy dread,
For he on honey-dew hath fed,
And drunk the milk of Paradise.'

'Ay, that's it. The milk of Paradise . . . exactly so. Once a man
has tasted that, it seems to me, he will drink no other. He rides
out to meet her. They come and go separately, but they meet. To
be sure, he must go without his drink these next few days – a
taste of the long thirst that is to come. She has gone with Sir
Gavin to a grand party given at Cawdor Castle – the Campbell
of Cawdor who is chief of his clan. She is not one to be missing
such a thing for some lover here in the strath – and no doubt His
Royal Highness will be among the company. Those kind, the
gentry, they merely smile at the little things they do among themselves to pass the time. The story of her lover here in the Highlands will not go against her when she is among the London
crowd – since he is so handsome, and well-spoken, and could pass,
the way they saw him that night, as a Scottish gentleman. He is
a distillery worker who flies a falcon – a sport for princes and
gentlemen. It will make an amusing tale, I've no doubt, this winter
in London. Very original, Lady Campbell will be thought. And
he – he will break his heart, and he will not look on another
woman. He will be waiting on her now – you see, he is not among
this company. He will spend his days upon the moors, flying his
hawk until she returns. And she will take her time. There is another
shooting party to go to, at some place beyond the Moray Firth.
Lady Campbell does not neglect such activities. Is she not bored
here? – and that is the only reason that Callum Sinclair is chosen
to ease her boredom. And he will be waiting, poor fool.'

I should not have listened, but I let the voice, quiet, calm, continue. 'They meet in the old bothy of his grandfather – Mairi
Sinclair's father. He has a part of it new-roofed, and the track to
it so wild and rough that none do ever go that way. It is the track
that goes up beyond his own cottage, away up there towards the
slopes of Ben Cullen, towards the top of the glen past the waterfall.'

'How do you know this?' I choked on the words, but I had to
say them. Everything else receded – the firelight, the pipes, the
songs, the cries of the dancers; I heard nothing but the voice near
my ear.

'I use my head and my eyes, mistress. I was born at Cluain. I
know this strath – its every stream and glen almost as well as Callum

Sinclair. *I* am no fool, mistress.'

I turned and looked at her. 'And you think I am!'

A weird little smile came to her lips. 'I would not see you commit folly.'

It was clear that Morag had found no one among the young men to linger late with over the whisky and beer that night, because she was up before the herdsman had gone to bring in the cows to milking the next morning. I saw her from where I sat by the tower window; she was wrapped against the chill of the early morning in a plaid, but I knew that quick, light, high-stepping walk, and the one glimpse of the red hair that the plaid revealed. I did not think about it very much – Morag was like Mairi Sinclair in her ways. They both did the work that was to hand, and no one would have dreamed of questioning their comings and goings. So I marked her crossing the yard, and thought no more of it; after that I did not even notice which way she went. My gaze was searching the valley for a sight of Giorsal; but it was overcast, and the clouds were low. In the mist that tumbled down from Ballochtorra there was the feeling of rain – a change in the weather. My grandfather would be in a great hurry today to get in the stooks of barley. Once more Cluain and Angus Macdonald had been lucky; the barley was cut and would soon be in the barns, and the itinerant workers would struggle off in twos and threes that morning, their wages in their pockets, and perhaps some Cluain whisky for those especially favoured. I thought, as I watched that mist blot out the mountains, that if the weather turned cooler now, the malting would begin, and Callum would return to the distillery. And then I cursed myself for the vain wish that lay behind the thought.

But the thought of Callum would not be wiped out – never had been in all the weeks of the summer when I had grown into the world of Cluain. Had it actually begun, I wondered, on that first evening, the first time I had seen him there beneath the beeches below Ballochtorra? No, people of intelligence did not fall in love with the image of a man merely glimpsed. But was love ever intelligent? – if I applied logic to my own madness, then all it was revealed as was just that – madness. But why had that moment of first sight remained so intensely with me – and now, when I thought of it, it could have been one of the times when he had ridden with Margaret Campbell, and had, that evening, watched her husband return home from a journey, and known that their freedom to meet must now be more restricted. I grew slightly sick at the thought. I heard again Morag's whispered words of the night before. 'They meet in the old bothy of his grandfather . . .' I did not believe it; they could not have established anything so permanent as a trysting place – nothing except the heather and the moors and deep rock shelters of the Ballochtorra crag. But as an animal will lick and probe its wound endlessly, feeling the hurt and yet not knowing how to stop, so did I. I had to know.

I lingered over the midday meal that day, drinking tea after my grandfather had gone back to the office. The itinerant workers had begun to shake off their night's revelry, and with a last hand-out of food from Cluain's kitchen, were starting back along the road to the bridge at Ballochtorra, and from there on to the next strath.

'The weather's turning against them, though,' Morag remarked as she stacked dishes on the sideboard. 'The next farmers may not be so fortunate as the Master.' I noticed that Neil Smith had let Big Billy and his flock out from the pen by the warehouses; the gander was thoroughly enjoying harassing the strangers that he had been kept away from for so long. 'Many were on their way very early, to try to get another day's work, at least.'

'You were abroad early also, Morag.'

She did not pause in her task of loading the tray – the tureen, the dishes, the knives and forks neatly and competently, without noise, as she did everything. 'A sick child one of the women had, mistress. And Mistress Sinclair bade me take the little one some extra medicine before the family left. They were to go early, and Mistress Sinclair left it ready for me last night . . . I often do these errands for her. For all her cleverness with the herbs, she is still stiff with strangers. Once she knows which mixture to make, she has little to say to those she treats.'

I nodded. It would be so. 'It seems odd,' I said, really for the sake of talk, 'to see so many on the road. The strath will be quiet now they're leaving.'

'Och,' Morag tossed her head lightly as she lifted the tray, 'there'll be enough coming and going for a while – as long as the shooting lasts. But when the snows come it is quiet enough. The gentry all run south then. Ballochtorra will be empty until the late spring. And Sir Gavin may come back alone, for Lady Campbell, they say, has made plans for the fashionable races – Ascot, is it? – and such things . . .' And with that she deftly balanced the tray on one hand, and pulled the door closed behind her, leaving me alone.

Leaving me to the disquiet of my thoughts, which could hardly now be borne. I took my plaid and went into the herb garden, and paced its walks – back and forth, back and forth. The tall thyme and the lavender nodded to me, but leaves were beginning to dry, and blow off the roses that climbed the wall. How quiet and deep the snow would lie on this garden. The white cat ran before me. Out here the cat seemed a kitten again; he scurried among the beds, and lay in wait to pounce on me, to grab with his paws for the swinging end of the plaid. I watched his pranks, and wondered how Mairi Sinclair could have used such an innocent creature to make him seem the instrument of the destruction of that silly white dress, the dress that seemed so far back in time now. What had she used? – the sharpened claws of a rabbit, or a bird? It might have deceived anyone who had not liked cats, had not known their ways. And there I paused. In my turns along the path I had seen that black figure seated in a chair by the kitchen range, Bible in hand, seemingly oblivious of my presence. It struck me that I had never seen her seated before; but she was human like us all, and must need rest. The harvest time had been gruelling for her, and she had tended more than one sick person among the workers. Morag sang by the scullery window as she washed the dishes. The cat made another playful dash for the plaid, and it occurred to me that no one could ever prove that it had been Mairi Sinclair who had wreaked her dislike of me upon that white dress. But Mairi Sinclair knew cats and their ways, and suddenly it seemed too clumsy an effort for her. So I looked from that still, black figure by the range, to the shining red hair of the singer by the scullery window. Morag did not like cats – so she said. But Morag said a great deal, and knew a great deal. She said she knew where Callum and Margaret met.

Suddenly I knew what I would do. I already wore my plaid, the new serge skirt sent from Morag's aunt, and the usual boots. I needed nothing else. I went out by the seldom-used door from the herb garden into the road, and then on to the stableyard. Both those watchers, the one by the kitchen range and the one by the scullery window must have heard the slam of the door. The song that had floated over the gentle rattle of the dishes stopped.

Ailis's big eyes greeted me as if she already had foreknowledge of our destination; if she had really known she would have thought me foolish. I slipped an ordinary saddle across her back, and hurried with the harness before John Farquharson could come to help me. If the track was as rough as Morag said, and there was the burn to cross near a waterfall, then I would need both feet in the stirrups.

Big Billy was quiet as I went by the warehouses. Perhaps he was worn out by the morning's exertions; perhaps he just knew that there was no longer any sport to be had from me.

3

It was as Morag had said. The track past Callum's cottage narrowed and went higher, skirting the edges of the burn, and weaving among boulders. The dry weather had dropped the level of the flow, but I could see how it would cascade when the floods of the spring thaws came, or a thunderstorm broke over the mountains. We went higher than I thought, and closer to Ben Cullen – the terrain grew rougher and tighter, the glen narrowed almost to a gorge. The water spilled green on mossy rocks. It would be a poor land up here when I did find the bothy, poor, starved land that the cousin that Mairi Sinclair's father had willed it to would never have bothered with. The waterfall, when I came to it, was a gentle trickle, but it foamed into a deep pool. Stunted trees tried to meet each other across the burn; I saw the dark leaves of holly and the more tender leaves of laurel. The snow would lie here in the winter, but they would have shelter from the biting winds. I saw the way across, the fording place just below the pool, and if Ailis had not been what she was, and the water so low, I would not have liked to take that path; below it again was a sheer rock fall, and more boulders. But I turned her, and she led me across, calmly, quietly, and, as if she knew the way, she found the track on the other side. In the dry weather the ground had hardened, but this way was not unused. We emerged from the gorge at last, and out on to more open land – that is, free of trees, windswept, wild, and choked with gorse. It rose above my head, and if it had not been for the faintly defined track, I would never have found the place.

It was a tiny Highland 'butt and a ben' – the traditional two-roomed cottage, rough stoned, and the stones mortared with mud. The searing winds and rains up here had long ago taken most of the whitewashed plaster, and the gorse grew almost to the door. It was no longer land even fit for sheep to graze. I thought of Mairi Sinclair, as I sat quietly on Ailis and looked at it; she had been born here, and been a girl here, had walked this hard track all her young life. I remembered Morag's story of how she had been beaten by her father until the life almost left her. I thought of the last terrible downhill climb, over the ford by that deep pool, bearing the burden of her unborn child. Having made this journey, I now began to understand many things about Mairi Sinclair, gazing about at the grim, barren land, just looking at the place where she had grown from child to young woman, where she had been formed to the hardness of the granite. Hard and passionate, holding forever to whatever belief, whatever love, whatever hate.

I saw all the rest of it too, in those few minutes. I slipped from Ailis's back, and led her to the second half of the ruined house – that with the gable and almost gone, and a quick roof of boughs and straw thrown over it to form a rough stable. It had been recently used – there were fresh droppings on the ground that the fastidious Callum would never allow to collect in depth, the fresh straw spread; there were two hitching rings fastened to the solid wall that would be the back of the fireplace in the other room; there was even a bag with feed in it. The space where the entry had been to this room from the other had been freshly blocked with stones, and plastered with mud. I left Ailis tied loosely there, and with a useless determination to see it all, I went to the door of the little house. That too, had been freshly mended, the rotten wood replaced, the lintel propped up, the catch was new, though there was no lock. Inside was emptiness – that is, if I could ever see emptiness in the place so imbued with the presence of those who had recently used it. The thatch was loose and rough enough, but sufficient to keep out the rain of the summer – and if it leaked in one place, they could move to another. The stone walls had been swept clean of dust and cobwebs, and newly whitewashed; the floor was the bare earth, but laid deep with clean straw. The old, tiny windows had been sealed so that no birds or rodents could enter and defile this place. I looked at it all with mute acceptance, wanting to close my eyes, and not being able to. I did not even have to touch the ash in the old fireplace. It was fresh and powdery, the smell of peat recently burned lay on everything. As if they were before my eyes I saw them there, Margaret and Callum, their hands upon each other, their white bodies on that clean straw. I saw the passion of Callum's face. *'For he on honey-dew hath fed, And drunk the milk of Paradise.'* The milk of Paradise. I turned and closed the door carefully behind me.

Afterwards I didn't remember how long I stood outside, registering the knowledge of what I had seen. There were no more dreams now, no more doubts. Whatever Margaret Campbell felt, I knew that for Callum to have gone this far, then he was gone very far indeed. The instinct I had had about him, that if I only waited he would be mine, had been totally wrong. Not for me would the earth floor be lovingly laid with a blanket of clean hay; not for me would the peat fire burn. I took it in in a dazed, superficial kind of way; I realized vaguely that with time the hurt would only be deeper. I stumbled towards the stable and with a kind of idiot's half-seeing gait. With a rough pull I jerked Ailis's head out of the feed bag, resenting her, somehow, for eating what I could not taste.

'Greedy beast! Isn't there enough at Cluain for you!'

She looked at me with indignant eyes, and the slowness of her walk seemed to mock my impatience. But her broad back received me as willingly as always, and soon I found my arm about her neck, and I leaned forward and lightly kissed her between the ears. 'No – I understand. There's not enough at Cluain for me, either.'

At an ordinary time I would have noticed it sooner. But we were down at the ford below the waterfall before I was fully aware of the tremble through all her limbs; the leisurely pace had become something more, a dragging, leaden pull – one leg deliberately placed after the other, and she seemed to wait upon each step, as if not trusting herself to make another. When we reached the ford she would not descend to the water-line; she tossed her head in a violent denial, almost the last energy she seemed to have left. Then I slipped down from her back, and stroked her head, wondering how I had not noticed before the sweat beginning to stand out darkly on her coat. 'Ailis? – what is it?' The usually knowing, intelligent eyes looked at me with dull incomprehension.

I led her with infinite care across the stones of the ford, my ankles and skirt deep in the water. She did not want to come. Something in that great spirit had become afraid, confused; the pool looked so deep, and below the ford the rocks of the gorge seemed more jagged.

But we were across, and the downward track faced us. I trembled almost as much as Ailis did, but with a nervous energy and desperation that were not in her. I dared not mount her again, nor force the pace. The way was so rough that if once she slipped, I doubted I would be able to raise her heavy little body. I took my plaid, folded it, and laid it along her back, the best kind of blanket I could devise.

I prayed on the way down that I would see smoke rising from Callum's chimney, hear Dougal barking in the yard. But the cottage was closed and silent as before, and beyond giving a couple of shouts as I drew near, I didn't waste any time there. Ailis followed me obediently; I had the feeling that if once we stopped she would lose the will to go on. Her eyes looked with a kind of dumb wonder when finally we reached the place where the track to Callum's cottage joined the road. She was not so far gone that she did not know this place, and the firm, level surface of the road that led back to Cluain. Momentarily she raised her head and looked at me. I encouraged her with a light whisper. 'Soon home, Ailis. Home!' But the even surface of the road made the trembling wobble of her tough little legs all the more painfully obvious.

Several people came to the doors of their cottages as I passed. There were offers of help, offers to shelter Ailis in their own lean-to stables. But I knew that above all she needed the reassurance of her own place, and I kept her going. It would be time to lay her down in straw when she reached the familiarity of Cluain. A woman sent one of her sons with me, to walk the rest of the way. He put his strong young shoulder against Ailis's, so that now she was supported on both sides. At last we were past the warehouses and into the stableyard. I had sent the lad on ahead to warn John Farquharson, and the loose box was open, and ready, spread with fresh straw. He rushed forward to take off the saddle and harness.

'Easy, lass – easy,' he murmured. And to me, 'What has happened, mistress?'

I shook my head. 'Just bed her down, please, John, and give her nothing. Not water – not anything, yet.'

And then I ran, using all the pent-up need of the slowness of the journey back. I burst in at the kitchen door, and Mairi Sinclair looked up from her task of setting the dishes for the supper she and Morag ate at the big scrubbed table.

'Mistress Sinclair, will you come at once . . . please! It's Ailis. There's something terribly wrong with her!'

The dark eyes met mine, lingering only a moment. There was a kind of wonderful assurance in her calm. She nodded. 'I will bring what may be needed.'

There had been neither foreknowledge or surprise in that gaze. It was the instinctive, experienced, unpanicked reaction of the healer to a cry for help. It was from Morag the exclamation came – not of questioning, but a little yelp of pain as she placed her hand carelessly against a hot pan on the range. But by then I was already on my way out, and Mairi Sinclair was reaching for the keys to the herb room, and flinging her plaid about her shoulders.

For the first time since I had come to Cluain we moved together, in common purpose.

We sat there by the loose box through the night, Mairi Sinclair and I. At first she squatted by the pony, feeling her, looking into her mouth, opening the eyelids that wanted to close; she put her

hand, and then her ear, to Ailis's heart. She stayed there for a
long time, saying nothing, just watching; she did not reach for
anything from the basket of medicaments she had brought from
the herb room. She raised her head only when the shadow of
Angus Macdonald fell across her.

'I don't know what it is, Master. Never have I seen anything
like it – such strange symptoms in an animal – one thing going
against the other. The heart is too fast, and yet she is sluggish. It
is beyond my knowledge to prescribe anything for her. I am
afraid of what I do not know. You must send for the veterinarian,
Master.'

'What – have you lost your courage, Mistress Sinclair? You've
saved animals that veterinarians have given up.'

She was stubborn. 'I give my medicines when I believe I know
what I am giving them for. When I am ignorant, I say so. And
I say I do not know what ails the animal. What I know is that
you set great store by this one.'

'My granddaughter sets great store by Ailis, Mistress Sinclair. I
trust your skills. We will wait until morning before we send for
the veterinarian. He will not come this evening, in any case, and
if he's been at the bottle, it were better he did not come at all.'

'You place a burden on me, Master.'

He looked down at her, hardness in his face. 'And when has
Cluain not placed its burden on you, mistress? This is nothing
new.'

And then he left us.

I remember Morag brought us things to eat in a basket, and
hot jugs of tea. My grandfather sent a flask of whisky, which Mairi
Sinclair refused, but I did not. We sat on stools and as it grew
dark a lantern was brought, and placed between us. On her last
visit that night, Morag brought Mairi Sinclair her Bible, and she
read it, the pages held low to the light. But I noticed, as time went
on, that she almost ceased to read; her lips moved soundlessly
over the words, reciting the endlessly familiar chapter and verse.
She needed no lamplight.

There was nothing to do for Ailis except to give her the knowledge
of our presence. There was little to see, except that from time to
time she still trembled, and her eyes were closed, and she sweated
under the blankets. Occasionally Mairi Sinclair would rise and
kneel beside her, bending low to listen to the heart beat, rolling
back the eyelids. Several times she returned to her stool and nodded
to me. 'She holds – she holds, yet.' And when I went to pat the
sweating, heavy little body, Ailis would faintly flicker an eyelid,

and once she struggled to rise. Instantly, Mairi Sinclair was there beside me, and together we forced the pony back. When she was quiet again, I went and paced the dark stableyard to exercise some warmth back into my cold and cramped limbs. But Mairi Sinclair seemed to need no such thing. Once more, at the coldest time of the night, I sipped a quarter cup of whisky, expecting to find the woman's eyes upon me disapprovingly, but there was no reaction. With her plaid about her she seemed the immemorial figure of the woman who watches by a bedside, waiting for the hours to decide on life or death. She must have sat in that fashion so many times in her life.

Once, across the glow of the lamp, I whispered to her. 'Did you sit this way with William?'

She shook her head. 'Your brother did not like me, mistress. It did not calm him to have me by his bed.' She said it as if she had known for most of her life that there were some who did not like her, for whom her presence did no good. There was a stoic acceptance of that, as of other things. 'It was Morag who sat with him, and fetched and carried. I thought it might help him a little to see a young face beside him. She was very attentive.'

We said no more. I sat hunched upon my stool, a plaid and a blanket about me. And before dawn I must have nodded in sleep. I woke with Mairi Sinclair's hand upon my shoulder, her face bent close to mine. I felt a sudden start of fear. 'Ailis . . . ?'

'It is past. She sleeps naturally. The heart beat is normal now. The sweat is over. Now I may go and prepare a little bran mash for her, and put a gentle sedative in it. She should rest easy through the day. And when that is done, I will send Morag to warm your bed, mistress. It is time you went to your own rest.'

So I stayed alone with Ailis, sitting in the straw beside her, in those last minutes while Mairi Sinclair went back to the kitchen and her tasks. The sky was lightening rapidly. I heard footsteps in the yard, and hastily brushed away the tears that had come as a relief in the privacy of those moments. Neil Smith's red, unshaven face looked down at me.

'The little lass is all right, then?' he said. 'You will have her for a long time yet, mistress. These wee ponies live to a terrible great age. Mistress Sinclair has made her right again.'

'Mistress Sinclair refused to dose her . . .'

'Then you may be sure that was precisely what she should have done. Mistress Sinclair has strange powers . . . if she will not dose, then it is best left alone. Good morning to you, mistress.'

I looked after his squat little figure, wondering why I should ever have disliked him. He and Big Billy were as much part of Cluain as its very walls. And his words came home: 'You will have her for a long time yet . . .' Through the open door of the loose box I watched the light grow steadily, outlining the far distant rim of the Cairngorms. The hurt of Callum came flooding back with the sweetness of the relief that Ailis would live. And Neil Smith thought I would be with Ailis at Cluain for a long time, the pain and pleasure of its life mixed as it had been this night.

My grandfather came from his room as I climbed to the tower stairs. I had never seen him in the long flannel nightshirt, and the plaid used as a robe about his shoulders. Perhaps he had spent his own vigil by his bedroom window, watching the light in the stableyard. Perhaps he saw the traces of tears yet on my face, and the relief and the weariness there.

'It is not the last long night you will spend sleepless at Cluain, Kirsty. You learn, Gurrl. You learn.'

3

I came down to eat the midday meal after my grandfather had left. My eyelids still drooped with half-finished sleep; I felt curiously numb. I wanted to drift on the tide of my fatigue and not to think. The thoughts, the remembrances would only bring the probe and the pain again. But before I sat down to eat, I visited Ailis in her box. She was standing, steadily enough, and looking slightly aggrieved; I guessed that Mairi Sinclair had kept her on tight rations that morning, and she was hungry. I didn't dare feed her; just stroked her nose, and fended off John Farquharson's questions about what might have brought on Ailis's attack. I remembered all through the night that Mairi Sinclair had asked nothing except if I knew had Ailis been feeding on any wayside herbage, and to that I could truthfully answer that she had not. I knew the more lengthy questioning would come, and with it I might have to say where I had been. So long as Ailis had recovered, I felt disinclined to tell anyone, not my grandfather or Mairi Sinclair, about the journey up to the ruined bothy above the waterfall.

I did not linger in the stable. I had woken to the sound of steadily beating rain, the straight rain that comes with no wind, and will not move on with the clouds. The stableyard was full of puddles; no one was to be seen out about the distillery. Big Billy kept his flock within their pen. I shook off the Inverness cape I had worn to the stable in the kitchen hall, and regretted the splashes it left on Mairi Sinclair's scrubbed flagstone floor. It was the kind of day that mud gathered on one from nowhere.

Morag served me hot soup, and a beef stew kept warm on the range. It was already growing late; the afternoon seemed dark after the golden days of the harvest. I began to sense what the winter would be like.

As if she knew my thoughts, Morag nodded towards the window and the steady downpour. 'Aye, mistress, I'm thinking we may have seen the end of the summer. It is well the barley is in the barns. The days will start to close in quickly now.' She took the empty soup bowl, and began to ladle out the stew. 'There's not many will be stirring on a day like this.'

As she set the plate before me I answered, just to show a kind of spirit I did not truly feel, 'Oh, not many, I agree.' I dug into the steaming meat. 'But everyone is not deterred. I saw Lady Campbell out on her mare – down by the river. Wet through, I'd say. So you see, Morag, perhaps she is less inclined to party-going than you think. She and Sir Gavin must have come directly back from the gathering at Cawdor.'

'Lady Campbell.' The lid of the stew dish clattered a little as she replaced it. 'Lady Campbell? – is that so, mistress? Well, she'll hardly have much company on a day like this. I'll leave the stew, shall I, mistress, if you should like some more? I've the vegetables to see to for supper . . .'

But when I carried the dishes through the kitchen into the scullery it was deserted. The carrots and cabbages were laid there ready for preparing. And Morag's plaid was gone from the line of hanging pegs in the kitchen passage.

Perhaps I dozed that afternoon by the fire. I remember I built it up, and took some needlework, which bored me, and settled before it. I wore my cashmere shawl and the red slippers. I would be waiting so when my grandfather came in.

It was odd that this once I should have missed his coming, when so many times I had seemed to know it before the figure on the pony even appeared along the road. But it was the thundering bang of the knocker at the front door which roused me. The piece of sewing had slipped from my lap. I did not wait for Morag or Mairi Sinclair to attend it.

Callum was still mounted on his pony. He was bareheaded, and rain streamed down his face, the bedraggled, mud-caked setter tried to find what shelter he could within the doorway, his tail hanging and a whimper in his throat. I let my eyes slowly travel upwards to Callum's face. I had never seen anything so awful – like stone set in a deathmask of suffering.

'The mare has broken a leg. She is up there screaming, and may drown. Have someone go up with a gun and put her at rest. John will know where it is – the place just below the waterfall on the way up to the old Sinclair croft. Up beyond my cottage. Tell them to shoot the mare, and leave her where she is. I will see to the rest.'

I could say nothing. One hand held the reins, and with his other arm he supported the sodden burden. The tweed cape I had seen her wear to protect her from the rain as she had splashed along by the river early that afternoon was wrapped about her, covering her head and face. The hand-made boots, fitted to the delicate ankles, hung limply from the familiar cinnamon-tan riding habit; the cream-coloured lace on her petticoat was mud splattered and soaked. I remember the horror of standing there, watching the rain stream off the heels of those boots, the unheeding rain.

'Margaret . . .'

'Dead. I'm taking her to Ballochtorra.'

He flicked the reins, and the pony moved off; the dog was close by, as always, but keeping far enough back to avoid the mud kicked up by the pony's hooves. The rain became an obliterating curtain. I seemed paralysed there in the doorway, with the rain dripping down on my head from the eaves. I opened my mouth. The sound that came was a weird low moan, much like the whimper in the throat of the dog.

9

The tales drifted to us in the next two days, while the rain hung on the strath, not the streaming, heavy rain of the day Margaret had died, but gentler, sometimes no more than a light sheet of mist. They were not spoken of within the household of Cluain – it was Mairi Sinclair's son the stories concerned, and even Morag knew enough to keep silent about that. It was a very silent household. My grandfather spoke less even than usual; our chess games were concentrated and swift, and ended soon, and I found myself going earlier to the tower room, where Morag had already completed her tasks, and made no excuse to linger. There were no songs rising from the scullery window. Even, for those days, the flow of those who came to seek Mairi Sinclair's aid ceased, as if no one could quite face her with this new, terrible thing which must be borne, but not spoken of. And yet, calmly, the night that Callum had brought Margaret's body to the door, Mairi Sinclair set out in that drenching rain to deliver the first child of a young distillery worker's wife. No one knew at the cottage what had happened, and the talk was normal, at least as normal as it ever was in the presence of Cluain's housekeeper, whom the whole strath held in some awe. But she was gentle, and soothing and efficient, bringing her own clean linens from Cluain, hanging a sheet soaked in a solution of carbolic at the doorway of the tiny room where the child was born. The grandmother complained that there was unnecessary washing of hands, and too much water to keep boiling. She was outraged that she was not allowed to handle the child or the mother without washing her hands and wrapping her person in linen which Mairi Sinclair supplied. When the young wife screamed in the pains of labour, Mairi Sinclair gave her a mild infusion of henbane, and the woman was lulled, though still awake.

It was about dawn, they said, and the child had been born and bathed, and slept peacefully, before Callum Sinclair came to the door of the cottage. He refused to come inside, and Mairi Sinclair stood in the road in the rain to speak briefly with him. When she came back inside, they said she seemed no different – but there never was any telling with Mairi Sinclair. She washed again, took more clean linen, and went to tend the mother. Then finally she gave the young woman a potion that would give her complete sleep, and rest her tired and wracked body; and very gently she moved the cradle where the eyes of the woman would fall on the baby when she woke. In the last moments before sleep, the moments of emotional weariness when the tension and pain are at last gone, the mother lifted her eyes once more to Mairi Sinclair. 'I shall call him Callum . . .'

'No, do not call him Callum. You would be better with any other name.' And she did not explain.

And in her usual fashion, before she left, she ordered the young father to see that the fire was kept up, but the window open, that his mother was not to smoke her pipe over the cradle of the baby, and everyone who touched the mother or the child must first wash their hands. She left a solution of carbolic.

He dared to grip her hand in thanks, and offer a black shawl which his wife had knitted as a gift against this time, knowing, as they all did, that Mairi Sinclair never accepted money. But she shook her head. 'Your mother will find it warming this winter.'

'Then let me walk with you back to Cluain.'

Mairi Sinclair had looked at him with eyes that he swore afterwards he could never forget. She lifted her face, and he saw an expression of pain that not even his wife's trials during the night had produced. 'Thank you, I will go alone. It grows light. And what harm can come to me in this strath – now?'

I heard this story, and others, from John and from Neil Smith, and the others who moved about Cluain – the outside people who perhaps were hoping in turn to have my version of what Mairi Sinclair herself said, or thought – as if anyone could ever know that. The stories drifted down first from the servants at Ballochtorra, and were added to by those who lived along the road to Callum's cottage.

First there had been the shock of Callum bringing Margaret back to Ballochtorra. He had taken her to the stableyard, because he had to have help in getting down from the pony. But they said that he would not then relinquish her body until he had finally laid it upon her own bed, and he himself had taken a towel and dried that cold, wet face, and tried to smooth the hair. Then he had gone downstairs, to wait on Gavin. What had been said between the two men when finally Gavin had been found, had visited Margaret's room, and come to the library where Callum waited, no one ever heard, even those who had listened too closely. The tone of the men's voices had never risen above a murmur – that, I thought, itself was a deadly thing. That conversation had been ended by the sudden scream of Jamie, who had discovered what had happened to his mother before Gavin had had time to tell him. That scream must have rung in Callum's ears as he left Ballochtorra, riding back past Cluain in the darkness, gathering a lad from the stable, and another from a cottage along the way. With them he had gone to the place below the waterfall where Margaret's mare lay. John Farquharson had hours ago put the mare down with one of my grandfather's guns. He was waiting for Callum at his cottage, and had joined the three on the uphill trek. They had taken a field gate, and dragged the mare's body, lashed to it, down that impossible track, and there, not too far from Callum's cottage, they had dug a pit. It was hard work, and the rain poured down; the hole had inches of water in the bottom. Callum went to the cottage and brought whisky for them, the young lads taking their share. But they said he himself did not drink. And when the hole was ready Callum dismissed them, saying he would do the rest himself. He had, he said, Gavin

Campbell's permission to bury the mare. They did not dispute him.

This I heard, and was told, but the rest was my own, and shared with no one but Mairi Sinclair.

She came to me as I lingered over my tea at the breakfast table the next morning. Morag had cleared away all the rest of the dishes, poked the fire and laid more peat on it against the dampness of the day, and had retired, unusually silent. I stayed on, wondering how I would fill the hours of this day, and hoping they would be easier than the sleepless hours of the night before. Would I ride to Ballochtorra and see Gavin? I shrank from it. Would I just ride, and hope to weary myself to the point of sleep? But Ailis was not yet well enough. I felt the dry prickle of my eyelids, and longed for them to close, but they would not. I thought of the one person who had locked in her herb room that which could give me sleep, and give me a little surcease from the pain and yet she was the one person I could not bring myself to ask it of.

But she came herself. She came quietly, and closed the door of the dining-room behind her. Then she moved close to the table, so that her voice was very low when she spoke. I knew where she had been the whole of the night before – Morag had spoken at supper of her having been called to the delivery. The only words I had had from Morag that morning was that the mother was well, and the child strong and healthy, and that Mistress Sinclair had returned just before breakfast and had gone immediately to her tasks at the range. Now I looked at this woman, and wondered if the gauntness of her features was in her part due to the many nights she must have spent so, without sleep, and returning at once to her usual tasks. The seamed and cracked hands all at once became a badge of honour.

'Mistress, may I speak with you?'

Involuntarily, I rose to my feet. The occasion seemed to demand it. 'What is it, Mistress Sinclair?'

'I spoke with my son this morning, very early. He left this with me.' She now lifted her hand and held out the leather pouch that I recognized as the one Callum used to carry the meat for Giorsal, ready against the time when the peregrine had failed to kill, and must be lured back to feed.

'Left it? He has gone? Where . . . ?'

'I did not ask. It is his own business. He will be back . . . naturally, he will come back.' There was no need for her to say anything else; it seemed inevitable that there must be an Enquiry.

She fumbled with the pouch nervously, and I knew how she must have hated having to come to speak to me this way. 'He asks of you, mistress . . .'

'Yes . . . ?' I knew I was too eager.

'He asks if you would have the goodness to go and feed the bird. He says the bird knows you, and will take food if you offer it. But you must be careful to wear the gauntlet – there is a second one for the right hand in the shed. And you must not take off the hood.'

She put the pouch upon the table. 'It should be fed every day until he returns. But you know this, too. There is no one else, I think, he could ask. No one knows the bird so well – now.' We both thought of Margaret then, and both recognized the thought. I nodded, and looked away from her, so that she was spared any gesture of thanks. All I heard was the door closing again softly behind her. And then I went and touched the pouch. How well, how cruelly well, Callum knew me, his servant in all but the way I wanted to be.

The second I opened the door to the hut where Giorsal sat on her long perch she bated off – flying up on the jesses, and screaming at me. I stood very still by the doorway until she calmed down and found her position back on the perch again. It seemed miraculous that she did; if she had not, and had hung upside down on the jesses, I would have had to have taken her in my own hands and lifted her back. When she had ceased screaming, I talked softly to her; she seemed almost to know my voice, though I could hardly believe that. What did I say? – I used her name a great deal, but I know I talked about Callum, about Callum and Margaret. I told her about the baby being born the night before, about Margaret being dead of a broken neck. Mostly I talked about what it is like to love when it is not returned. What does one say to a hawk? – I told her that loving like that was as if she herself could never fly again, as if her beautiful wing feathers, stretching and spreading in confidence, were suddenly damaged, and she would plunge to earth. After a while, the hooded head bobbed and nodded to the rhythm of my voice, and I stepped nearer her, and took up the long feather Callum used to stroke her with. I kept on talking as I stroked, and at last she stopped pacing the length of the perch, and stood still, soothed and slightly hypnotized.

Wearing Callum's gauntlet was like plunging myself into his being; but it was necessary. I took out pieces of the cut-up meat. At first Giorsal would not leave the perch, but pulled at the meat from her stand there; at last hunger and her sense of confidence overcame reluctance. She stepped on to the glove, and perched there, tearing away at the meat greedily, waiting impatiently until the next piece was offered between my gloved fingers. It was almost more than my strength to do this – to take the weight of the bird, and the fierce tugging as she tore at her food. The hardest time came when I had to offer her the breast of the grouse which was included in the bag – hawks, I remembered Callum saying, had to have some feathers in their diet for cleansing their stomachs. As often as I had watched Callum feed her a plump pigeon on days when it was too windy or wet to fly her, still I never expected to have to make the offering myself. Once through the glove I felt the fierce sharpness of her beak, and the terrible strength of her claws as she sought a tighter grip in order to tear at the bird. Hooded, she seemed frustrated in the business of preening and eating the bird, but I could not remove it because I would never have the skill to get it back on. Callum, as always, expected a great deal. Thankfully, at last she finished what was in the bag. When no more food was forthcoming, she reluctantly went back on the perch; I lowered my aching arm.

I was glad it still rained, and wondered, had it been fine, if Callum would have expected me to attach the jesses to my own fist and carry her to the block by the burn, so that she could bathe and dry off. He would expect anything, I thought – anything but that I lose his falcon. No, I could not risk the block at all, even if Giorsal did without her bathing until Callum returned. I did not know the Falconer's knots. She could be gone in one swift rise, and hooded, dash herself to death against a tree or a rock. No, he could not have meant that. She must stay safely in the hut, and I must go every day to feed her, and clean the tray under the perch. She must stay safely in her calm, dull darkness, and Callum would come back, because, even more than Margaret, who had been his passion and his madness, he loved this bird.

When it was all over and the door to the hut closed, I leaned against it and found myself trembling with fatigue and fear. But I had held Callum's falcon upon my hand. The smallest welling of improbable pleasure and hope rose in me.

2

It still rained the next day, and when Margaret Campbell was buried those who attended manoeuvred awkwardly with umbrellas, and the slope of the kirkyard was slippery with mud as we made our way from the kirk to the open grave. It was just across the

path from where Christina and William lay; it would be the next
in the row of shiny marble stones bearing the Campbell name.
During the service, at which Gavin had forbidden any music, and
for the time he stood by the open grave, almost no one dared to
look directly into his face. All the time, in the kirk and in the
graveyard, he held Jamie tightly by the hand, even at that grim
moment when he had to scatter the customary earth upon the
coffin. There were no flowers, except those that Jamie himself
carried, the September roses from the garden of Ballochtorra, all
of them golden, Margaret's colour. He simply laid them by the
side of the grave, ready to be put in place when the grave should
be filled. It was then, for the first time, that he turned his face
against his father's side, and wept. They hurried down the path
to the waiting carriage.

And all the time Gavin did not look right or left, did not seem
to see any of the hands of condolence outstretched to him. Neither
he nor Jamie wore the customary black, nor were there black
bands on hats or sleeves. He had refused to plume the horses of
the hearse in black. There were reports of a terrible explosive
scene between Gavin and James Ferguson at this lack of con-
formity to the ritual that death then demanded. Gavin had refused
to see those who came to call at Ballochtorra, and James Ferguson
had received them alone in the darkened drawing-room. The day
before Margaret was buried the talk was that Gavin had taken
Jamie riding all day on the moors, and so had been absent when
the carriage had arrived at Ballochtorra bearing the hereditary
chief of his clan, the Thane of Cawdor, who had come to offer
condolences. It seemed that even James Ferguson was not quite
unshaken by this meeting. The scandal of Gavin's odd behaviour
spread.

I watched those two, Gavin and Jamie, hurry down the path.
They went immediately into the carriage, and so had to wait for
the unhurrying James Ferguson to join them. It was he who
lingered for the handshakes, who replied to the formal phrases. He
seemed a curiously shrunken figure, the lines newly graven in the
red puffiness of his face. He appeared more nervous than sorrow-
ing, his tongue licking his lips. He tarried too long, and suddenly,
to everyone's shock, Gavin slammed the door of the carriage, and
ordered the coachman to start on. This left Ferguson to ride back
in the second carriage with his solicitor. It was known that Gavin
had issued no invitations to anyone to return to Ballochtorra with
them. But James Ferguson flung them about him like seed; anyone
of any consequence was welcome at Ballochtorra to eat and have

a dram. He could not stop being James Ferguson.

'Let us away then, Kirsty,' my grandfather murmured close to my ear. We tried to slip past the knot of people at the gate of the kirkyard, but James Ferguson had seen us.

'You'll come, Macdonald. You'll come to Ballochtorra.'

'Not this day, Mr Ferguson. My own hearth is close by. I have sent a message to the Master of Ballochtorra of my own and my granddaughter's sympathy. You have it also.'

Ferguson turned oddly pale. He came very close to us and his words were intended for my grandfather only, but I heard them.

'Telegraph for Lachlan to come. I will be at Cluain tomorrow morning.'

My grandfather frowned. 'This is a strange time for you to be discussing business matters. It should wait . . .'

Ferguson licked his lips again. 'The matter will not wait. It will not wait on anything now.'

We were silent all the way back to Cluain, the depression of the kirkyard settled on us like the misty rain; it was not a full year yet since my grandfather had stood there by William's open grave. I shook off my wet coat and hung it in the kitchen passage before I went to the tower room to change into my slippers. The fire was laid, but not lighted. I was tired and cold. I had been up very early to collect the leather pouch which Mairi Sinclair had left ready in the pantry. The walk to Callum's cottage to feed Giorsal had been hard going in the soft ground. But she had greeted me this time almost without fuss, reacting at once to my voice, eagerly looking for the meat, eating her fill from the piece held between my gloved fingers with greedy ferocity. I wondered how long she would bear with the silent boredom of the hut, how long she would listen to the cries of other birds about her before she began to scream for the freedom of her own flight, for the joy of her own kill, the function for which she had been created. I almost began to envy the simplicity of the instinct of creatures so sure of what they are intended to be. To have no doubts, no choices . . . But my father would have rejected such a doctrine, and have opted, always, for the freedom of the soul to bestow love, even to have it rejected, to suffer if one must. Anything, he would have said, than not to feel; and somehow he and Callum would have made strange agreement on this point. And, to grant her the last justice, so must Margaret Campbell.

My grandfather was waiting in the dining-room for the midday meal, still wearing his Sunday clothes. He looked fidgety, and turned to me with an air of relief when I entered. 'Well, then – have a dram. It will take the chill off.'

I accepted it; but the chill of death was something even whisky couldn't touch, the chill of the look on Gavin's face, the shiver that had wracked me at the sight of the golden roses lying in the mud and rain. The Inverness paper had arrived. My grandfather did not try to keep it from me. There was a picture of Margaret, blurred, though nothing could really blur those lines of beauty. *Baronet's wife killed in fall from horse. Daughter of James Ferguson* . . . The item was small, and brief and discreet, mentioning that Gavin was the heir to the Marquis of Rossmuir, telling again the story the paper had so recently used of the visit of the Prince of Wales. It said nothing of the scandal or surmise that was already raging in the whole district, and reaching the London papers. How she had died, and where, and who had brought her back to her husband was not mentioned.

'There will be a Fatal Accident Enquiry,' my grandfather said.

'Yes.' I did not want to talk about it, but he persisted.

'The post-mortem certificate was that she died of a broken neck from the fall. That much is simple. But I hear that the police have been making enquiries. It seems probable that they will want an Enquiry before a Sheriff . . . Callum Sinclair will have to appear.'

'Yes.' He spoke as if he had to be sure I was prepared. It would only become more ugly; they would make it more ugly. They would defile that mountain croft that Callum had kept so clean because he had loved Margaret – and they would defile it with words that must come from Callum's own lips.

10

The next day the clouds scudded past on the rising wind, and after the rain and the mist, I noticed, as I walked up to feed Giorsal, that some of the birches had turned golden, as their leaves shook dry of their moisture. An autumn look had come on the land. Sometimes the sun broke through, reaching to, and suddenly illuminating a deep fold in the mountains, outlining a ridge I had never noticed before. There seemed to be no more guns on the moors; the land was silent, save for the wind.

And when I came back to Cluain it was almost time for the

midday meal, and John was rubbing down The Sunday Lad after the trip to Ballinaclash to fetch Samuel Lachlan; the door of the room he always used at Cluain was open, and, as I passed on the way to the tower room, I saw Morag making up the bed. They anticipated a long session with James Ferguson. And it was a trap from Ballochtorra that I saw tucked away at the side of the stables, out of view of the road. James Ferguson was already with them, then, and did not want his presence advertised to those who might pass.

And the usual procedure of James Ferguson leaving while my grandfather and Samuel Lachlan ate together was upset. As I was getting ready to go down to the meal Morag appeared in the door-way, with that silent way she had of suddenly being where one did not expect her.

'Excuse me, mistress. The Master is taking his meal with Mr Lachlan and Mr Ferguson, and there is business they have to discuss. Mistress Sinclair has sent me to tell you that there is a tray ready for you in the parlour.'

'The parlour – but I could have eaten in the kitchen.'

I was following Morag down the stairs, and she turned swiftly and shot a look back at me that seemed almost to pity my sim-plicity. 'That would never do, mistress. Mistress Sinclair would never permit it – and the Master would not be pleased.' And so I was put back in my place, perhaps an unnecessarily exalted place in Morag's eyes, but nevertheless, my place. And there was the big silver tray laid on the long table in the drawing-room, immaculately set with a snowy linen cloth. I sat in one of the straight-backed Jacobean chairs, and ate mechanically, aware that the walk had made me hungry, but that food, since that moment when Callum had appeared at the door with Margaret's body cradled in his arms, had seemed to have no taste. This room had a window that looked up the road towards Ballochtorra. I thought about Gavin and Jamie, and I thought about James Ferguson's presence at Cluain's table at this time. Something was stirring, and I would only know the nature of it when my grand-father chose to tell me. But it came to me then that, with Margaret dead, Gavin would not leave the strath. I suddenly knew how it would be. He would take no more money from James Ferguson. If Margaret's dowry reverted all to her father, or was placed in trust for her son, I knew that it would matter nothing to Gavin. If he had to walk out of Ballochtorra, with Jamie, and toss the keys to James Ferguson, he would do it. I thought of that poor bit of farmland, still undrained, that he had dreamed of that day with me. This might be the way the tenth baronet of Balloch-torra, and heir to the Marquis of Rossmuir, would choose to live, eccentric, and out of his time, but his own man at last, and his son his own.

The meeting between the three men continued all afternoon. Twice I saw Morag cross the yard to the office with the loaded tea tray, but finally, as the hour for supper drew near, I heard the trap from Ballochtorra being made ready. My grandfather and Samuel Lachlan accompanied Ferguson to the trap; there was still some talk among them, but no handshakes. Ferguson gave an odd backward glance as the trap drove off, but the two men were already deep in talk again, and didn't even seem to mark his going. There was late sunlight for the few moments it took them to cross the yard to the house; my grandfather's mane of hair was silvered in it, and stood almost upright in the wind. I noticed then that little piles of leaves had collected in the corners of the usually immaculate yard.

Downstairs the two men gave me the sudden impression of old age at the end of a long day. They had almost finished their first whisky when I came in, and I thought that it had been mostly drunk in silence, as if each needed the respite. Samuel Lachlan's black clothes were greenish in the lengthening rays of sun that streamed in the windows; he got to his feet momentarily, and adjusted his glasses on his nose, which, I suppose, was the only sign of pleasure he ever permitted himself. But he said to me what I might have said of him, 'You look tired, Kirsty.'

My grandfather answered for me. 'Och, it's the harvest, and this damnable business at Ballochtorra. Well –' as if that disposed of the matter, 'the wind is drying. We need it after the rain.' To back up his statement the window rattled suddenly in a sharpening gust.

They took their second dram more slowly, but my grandfather did not have his usual place in the settle before the fire. It was very uncharacteristic of him, the way he paced between the window and the sideboard, his glass left there, sipping each time he came back to it. There was a kind of frenetic mood upon him that I had never witnessed before; something either troubling or exciting him. I wished it were not so; I wished, too, for a respite, a time of peace. There was yet much to come – so much more. All that the Inverness paper had hinted was yet to come.

Finally, it was Samuel Lachlan who spoke. 'Kirsty – there is something we have to say to you –'

He blinked through his spectacles. 'We agreed that she should know, Angus. We agreed.'

'Very well. But let us have our dram, at least, man. We've earned our spell away from it – '

'Christina must know.'

'A while yet, man – a while !'

Morag brought in the first serving dishes, and Samuel Lachlan hurried to take his place at the table. How he must look forward to Cluain's food after those meals sent round from the chophouse. But when the food was set before him, he seemed less interested. He ate slowly, and forgot to have gravy, forgot even the endless salt he craved. He was so slow, in fact, that Morag put her head inside the door several times to see if we were ready for the next course.

At last he spoke, and my grandfather seemed content to let him do so.

'Kirsty – Ferguson is going broke.'

'Going – ' Then the door opened, and Morag appeared once more. This time she removed the meat dishes, and I went to the sideboard and served the apple tart that Samuel Lachlan loved. Morag closed the door, and he poured the cream with absent-minded lavishness.

'Going broke,' he repeated.

I could hardly believe it; did people who had castles and yachts on the Clyde go broke? But James Ferguson was clever, a self-made man. He could surely never fall into some pit he had not seen before his feet.

'Why?'

'Stretched too thin. There must be two dozen distilleries that have extended him credit – for far too long. He has accepted orders from America, with some advance payment – orders for millions of gallons that he now can't fill. He has indulged in over-production of his own patent grain whisky, storing it up, extending, advertising, sending his salesmen all around the world. And now the malt that he needs for his blends – from the cheapest to the best – is locked up in warehouses all over the Highlands, and he hasn't the money to buy out the stuff, or pay the Excise on it. Even if the distillers would extend credit still further, there's still the Excise, and Her Majesty's Excise doesn't give credit – and the tax is the largest part of the bill.'

'But didn't he *know* this would happen?'

'He knew – and didn't pay much attention to it. There was a big loan being raised in the City – London. He won't admit so much, but the merchant bankers he was getting it from have done a more thorough investigation of the affairs of James Ferguson than he thought possible. The loan is now refused. He has creditors everywhere, and no cash. It will be, he now says, only a matter of days until the news of the refusal of the loan leaks out. He has been up and down the Highlands begging for more credit, begging for the distilleries to pay the Excise on what he takes from the warehouses, and once the whole picture is put together there will be a rush to sell by the shareholders. Once that starts, the share prices will drop to the bottom. If he ever has the chance of raising money by pledging his own shares, they themselves are about to be made almost worthless. *That* is why he will be broke.'

'And he owes Cluain?'

My grandfather broke in. '*No one* owes Cluain. Not after the first twenty years did anyone ever get a penny's worth of credit from Cluain. I am not in business to store unpaid-for whisky in my warehouses. The buyers come and they pay, literally, cash on the barrel. Even the great James Ferguson has had to pay. I store it for them, and they are free to take it after the legal minimum, and they pay the Excise.'

'Then he has whisky paid for and stored with you. Why doesn't he use it?'

'He has none. Not a gallon. His has all been taken. In this last year he has drawn out every barrel he owned. Telling me, always, that his business with England and America was so good he had to make up his blends as young as he could, to meet the demand. But I had a suspicion all along that he was drawing so quickly on his stock here because it might have been the only whisky he had already paid for. Why – I've even had trouble getting him to return the casks . . .'

'Then if he owes Cluain nothing, why does he keep coming? What has all the talk – '

Again Morag was back, removing the tart plates, placing the cheese, leaving the tray with tea. She was as quiet and deft as always, but I thought it odd that she came so often. Usually the task of clearing was done by myself. For some reason Samuel Lachlan liked to be waited on by me – perhaps he enjoyed the change after the years of boys rushing over with his tray from the chophouse. Lachlan waited quietly, took his Cheddar made in Mairi Sinclair's dairy, and piled the butter on her brownish golden biscuits. His poor false teeth worked hard at the task. He even sipped his tea a little without talking any more. I resigned myself to wait. His former impatience to tell me whatever was to be told had evaporated. There was enough to think about, besides savouring the relief that Cluain was not touched by James Ferguson's madness. I had not known until that moment how much store I had placed in the independence of Cluain, its self-sufficiency. There was danger there, of course – the kind of dangerous pride that my grandfather exhibited, his satisfaction at being able to snap his fingers at the world, and owe no man. But he had worked for it – oh, yes, he had worked for it. And now James Ferguson stood helpless in the ruins of his own monumental pride. As if Lachlan read my thoughts he spoke suddenly.

'Ah, well, that is often the way of it when a man gets in deeper than he knows.' At last he was finished with his cheese and his tea, and he stood and moved back to his place at the settle. At once my grandfather poured two more whiskies, and handed one to Lachlan. 'Yes,' Lachlan said, as if he had never stopped, 'if one will build castles and restore churches, and have a private railroad carriage, and a house in Belgrave Square, then there must be something very solid behind it. I have followed his career with interest –' He rubbed his thin nose. 'Yes, great interest. He was a wealthy enough man when his daughter married Campbell, but after that he would have had to be much more than merely wealthy to support the kind of things he did. But he had a name for making money, and he paid good dividends, and the shareholders came running. He built and he expanded. How much he speculated in other things one does not know. But I – well, I myself was never tempted to buy a single share of Ferguson's. No, not a single share.' He recited all this carefully, as if again retelling to himself, and perhaps for my benefit, a lesson long ago learned. Lavish spending disturbed him greatly. And yet I could not hear a note of satisfaction in his recital. He did not rejoice in the downfall of James Ferguson. Any edifice that crumbled was another attack on the sacred idea of capital.

He sipped his whisky quietly, waiting for Morag to be done with the last of the dishes, and when she was gone, finally, the crumbs swept from the table, the tray removed, he resumed.

'Yes, Kirsty, there has been much talk. Very much talk. And I have myself travelled too much for my age in these past weeks, in the matter of James Ferguson. I do not like too much to commit myself to paper in making enquiries. Discretion, and a quiet talk over a dram, with nothing recorded, is the better way. I have been back and forth between Cameron's and Macquarie's, and both distilleries are very inconveniently located. But both are solid – very solid. Solid men of business in each of them, and each held by the family. They keep their books and do their business at the distilleries, and there are no castles. They keep good horses, but there are no thoroughbreds in their stables. The young men of the families marry sensibly, and settle down in new houses near the distillery. Their wives keep good tables, but there is no waste. They fatten their own pigs, and silk dresses are for Sundays only. Yes, they are solid.'

I did not much like the sound of it. Where, in all the respectable mass, the great solidity, was there room for a falcon to spread her wings, to swoop, to soar, to stoop? Where would there have been a chance for a man like my grandfather to come from his poor Western Isle, and declare that on this piece of land he would make his kingdom? Was the day, then, of one's own private kingdom gone – was there no room, any more, to be free? No, I didn't like the sound of all these solid people.

'Then why does James Ferguson talk to you? He owes you no money. Why have you had to make these visits to Cameron's and Macquarie's on his behalf?'

'I did nothing on behalf of James Ferguson. I simply did not trust what the man was saying. He spoke for others, and he was in a state where he might have said anything – '

'But to what purpose?'

Now Samuel Lachlan gestured to my grandfather, as if deferring to him as Master of Cluain. 'He proposes, Kirsty, that Cameron, and Macquarie, and Cluain should join together to take on the business of Ferguson's. If the three distillers announced that they were joining up with Ferguson, Distillers, then the rest of the world need never know how much he was giving up in order to have us come in. Cameron and Macquarie are bigger than Cluain – ours would be a minority share, but a biggish share. And for Ferguson it would be a face-saving action. It would stop a run – at least this is what we think – by the shareholders. James Ferguson would have a seat on the board, for the time being, but with little or no voting rights, it would be nominal. We have his word, and would have it in a private letter from him before we moved further, that he would resign in about six months' time, giving ill-health and his daughter's death as reasons. Face-saving only. His name would still remain. But Ferguson's would belong to Cameron, Macquarie and Cluain.'

I gasped in utter disbelief. 'But Ferguson's is huge, isn't it? Would it . . . well, it would need a great deal of money to keep it going. Can Cluain . . . ?' I didn't dare ask the question of these two men.

Samuel Lachlan answered me. 'It would be close. Yes, there's no doubt it would be close. But we would be getting Ferguson's at a rock-bottom price. We would have a great organization for blending and distribution already made – yes, and the market lies that way, Kirsty, no matter how the malt men may despise the product. And as to Cluain's position in this . . . as I said it would be tight. But do not think Cluain has no resources. They have been carefully built up, husbanded. Like Cameron's and Macquarie's, all our goods are not in the shop window. Your grandfather . . . well, Angus?'

'No, not in the shop window, but in good, fine whisky. We have a certain production run each year, Kirsty. So many hundred thousand gallons. For the last ten or so years I have undersold the production run. I have my own warehouse – just casks marked with numbers and the workers do not know which distillery they have been sold to. In fact, they are Cluain's own unsold. The finest twelve-year-old malt, the first of it just ready, and each year more and more added, and maturing. And out of the operating profits I have set aside the Excise tax. That, and a little more besides, is Cluain's capital. And then there is Samuel. He will come in with more capital, if I wish to move forward with the matter. But not one of us – not Cameron's, Macquarie's – will move without the other two. And if we don't move, Ferguson sees no prospect of making an arrangement with others – and has not the time for it. He will simply go bankrupt – that is, he will go bankrupt publicly. The other way he has a chance simply to disappear, to fade out. In the end, as far as money is concerned, it is the same. He is broke.' My grandfather was not like Lachlan; he did not even try to keep the satisfaction out of his tone.

I pressed my hands together, and rocked forward, looking into the fire. 'And a few weeks ago, he was telling me that he would buy Cluain any time you wanted to sell. The Prince's visit – the cost of it! And all the time he was waiting on a loan simply to stay in business.'

'A kind of madness,' Lachlan said. 'It got to the point where he could not stop. James Ferguson has never been known to gamble at cards or horses, or anything else. But a gambler he is. He is so used to everything coming as he tosses the coin, that he is quite unable to stop it. He went on spending like a fool, when the coffers were empty. A dangerous man – dangerous to himself, and to everyone associated with him. He used shareholders' money for reasons other than business. If we do not proceed, he will be lucky if he is merely bankrupt. There could be a gaol sentence for misrepresentation.'

I suddenly looked up, looked at my grandfather. 'Then why –
why, in God's name, are you even prepared to associate with him?
Even if he is powerless, what is it you are looking for?'

'Looking for . . . ?'

I gestured to the room, the whole world of Cluain about me,
and my voice rose. 'Isn't this enough? What more could you
want?'

'Och, I was afraid you would not understand. I thought you
had more of a head for business than this. Understand me, Kirsty.
This is a chance to own Ferguson's. To be a world name in whisky.
To –'

'To be a fool!' I almost screamed the words at him. 'Wasn't this
what James Ferguson first dreamed? To be a world name in
whisky. Well, he's that, and it's lying in ruins about him. He is so
fevered he cannot even properly mourn the death of his only child.
Ferguson's is his child. That, and his pride, are more to him than
anything else. And you tell me – two old men . . .' It was cruel,
and I saw my grandfather's face flush with anger and affront,
'that this is what you are even tempted into. *Why?* You have a
whole world here. No one can touch Cluain. No one may lay a
finger upon it, except by your leave. You have a pile of gold stored
up there in those warehouses, and you are going to gamble it just
as James Ferguson would have done. You have been Master of
Cluain since the day you first won the deed to it from the Campbells. Are you now going to *give* Cluain to some little group that
goes under the name of *Ferguson?* You tell me there are young
men in the Cameron and Macquarie families. Do you think they
will let you have your own way completely? Will you be able to
run Ferguson's the way you've run Cluain? – everything exactly
as you want it? No compromise? No letting down of standards?
Your precious twelve-year-old will be thinned out to nothing to
help out the pile of rot-gut neutral spirits that James Ferguson
has run off. The name of Cluain will mean nothing. It will be
Ferguson's! Those young men – those solid young men – will be
here, looking over your stock, selecting what they want, three-
year-old, four-year-old. Breaking your heart. And because you will
be tied to them, hand and foot, you will not be able to stand out
against them. You will go with them, because you have to. And
why? Forget Ferguson – why do you hand over your heritage to
the Camerons and Macquaries? They will decide, whether you
like it or not, that Cluain can expand – can produce more whisky,
and still more. There will be more stills put in, and men to manage
them. And Cameron and Macquarie men at that. And what will

become of you . . . ? Where will the Master of Cluain be then?'

I thought he cringed a little, but his face was turned away from me. 'And what else is there to do? Where else am I to turn? If William had lived – but he didn't. There is only you . . . and you're a woman.' Now he looked back at me, and his tone was nearly one of pleading. 'It is mostly for your sake. You have said we are two old men, and that we are. What will you do when neither of us is here?'

'Are you saying Cluain will be mine? Are you saying that precisely?'

He paused. 'It is no easy thing for a woman – especially a young woman – to run a business. It is not a woman's world. But there is a prospect . . . Well, there is one of the young Cameron men yet unmarried. Personable, Samuel says. Intelligent. He has travelled, Kirsty . . .' His tone grew more eager. 'He has been in America, and places like Paris and Rome. He is very sharp in business, they say. He would make any young woman a fine husband. You could do much worse, Kirsty. And Cluain – '

'No!' My hands went to my mouth to try to keep down the words that came rushing. But I heard myself screaming, screaming as if I had been struck. 'No! You must be mad! The two of you – mad old men! Do you think I could marry because it would fit in nicely with the whole plan? Tell me! Tell me if that was part of all your visiting back and forth? Oh, God! – that is what happens to women in China! Do you think my father would have permitted such a thing – even thought of it?'

'It is not unknown,' my grandfather said curtly. 'Marriages are arranged on much worse terms than these.' He was stiff and embarrassed; the value of property was being questioned, and the value of Cluain being weighed against the capricious wishes of a young woman. I began to see what this madness was; if William had been here there would have been none of it. Two old men, I had said. It was true. They were two old men and between them they had only me with which to envisage the future – me, unmarried, without a child, without a son . . . 'Cluain is no mean dowry, Gurrl.'

'Dowry! Whoever asked for a dowry? And given on condition that I marry a good solid young man who has travelled, personable, was what you said, wasn't it? – and no doubt wearing a good suit.'

'There is something wrong with a good suit?' Samuel Lachlan chided me.

'No – nothing. But everything . . .' I closed my eyes and there was the vision of a man in a kilt growing frayed at the edge, and sheepskin dark with rain. 'No, nothing wrong with a good suit – but I cannot marry a good suit.'

'You're hasty, lass. You need time to think.'

'And is there time to think?' I flung back at him. 'You tell me it is a matter of days before Ferguson's position will be known to the shareholders. And in a matter of days I am expected to say I will marry someone I've never seen – who has never seen me? Grandfather, did you set me down in the balance sheet of Cluain? I wonder what price I was valued at? Was my stock high or low?'

'It was never a precise condition . . . just a suggestion. The young Cameron had heard of you – from others, it seems. Husbands like that are not picked up for the asking. You would show good sense to consider – '

'I'm showing the best sense I've ever done in my life. You remember your mother, Christina? Did *she* marry where she was bidden? Did she found a family, and carry on after her husband was dead? Did she begin a distillery out of nothing, and lose it for no fault of her own? Would you say she lacked the courage of a man – or three men? Did she breed you – from a husband of her own choosing? I tell you I will not be part of the balance sheet. If you make your arrangement with Cameron's and Macquarie's, then do it. But count me no part of it. If I have to leave Cluain tomorrow, then I'll leave. I will not be sold as part of the furnishings. On these terms, I do not want it. I can't lose what I never had. You can't take it away from me.'

'Truly spoken, mistress. Who would have supposed you had such fire in your guts?'

We all turned. As we had talked together the room had grown darker, and there was only the light from the peat logs to glow upon our faces. It had been sufficient; in these last minutes we had not really wanted to look at one another. But now we turned. Morag stood with a candle by the open door, and in silence she moved forward with her graceful gestures, and laid the candle down on the sideboard. Her cap was off. The red hair streamed in its wonderful abundance on her shoulders.

'How right you are, mistress, to know you cannot lose what was never yours.'

For a moment longer my grandfather was shocked into silence. Then his voice rose with a growl of fury. 'What do you think you're about, miss? What kind of business is this?'

'The business of Cluain, Master. The business of Callum Sinclair.'

'And how so his business? And what do you know of it?'

'How would I not know of it? Do you think I am blind and deaf? Have I carried trays to you these past weeks in the office, have I served you here all day with Mr James Ferguson, and not known what was discussed, what was going on? Because women wait on men, Master, it does not mean that they must be stupid. And I would have had to be deaf indeed not to have heard Mistress Kirsty's fine speech of what she would not do for you. Women continue to surprise you, do they not, Master?'

'Impertinence, miss! You get above yourself. Where is Mistress Sinclair? Does she not know how to keep order in her kitchen?'

'Mistress Sinclair has retired to her room, Master. She has had long nights recently, and has need of rest. But she does keep order in her kitchen. I have learned very much from Mistress Sinclair. At this moment I should be washing the dishes in the scullery. There are times, though, that the dishes must wait on other things, and Mistress Sinclair disobeyed. *She* does not own me, no more than you do.'

My grandfather took a deep breath, as if struggling for patience. It would not have surprised me to see him rise and give Morag a smart clip on the ear. For a second he glanced at me, and then back to Morag. Did he think that some spirit of perverse madness had suddenly possessed all the females of Cluain? What had happened to this well-ordered world? Samuel Lachlan was leaning forward in astonished wonder.

'You are bold, miss, and you try my temper. What *have* you come to say — what is all this business about women? And again, what business is it of yours what we discuss here, or in the office? What business?'

'If you had listened, Master, you would have heard my answer. It is the business of Cluain. And the business of Cluain is Callum Sinclair's business. Must I say more, Master? Will you put right what should have been right years ago, or will you have me force your conscience further? Will you open the book yourself, Master? I have waited for this time — for years I have waited. But there was always the grandson. And then he was dead, and there was this girl, your granddaughter. And there is also Callum Sinclair. Will you speak now, Master?'

In the candlelight my grandfather's face had turned a yellowish colour; it was not fury that he struggled to control now, but an emotion that threatened to make him incoherent. A garbled sound came from his throat. For an instant he clutched at his chest, as if in pain, and then his hand went back to grip the side of the settle. There was no question now that he might rise to strike Morag. I did not think he was capable of moving.

At last his words came, in a kind of gasp.

'Kirsty – Kirsty, fetch Mistress Sinclair!'

I ran. He seemed to be ill – and yet it was more than that. I had forgotten to bring a candle – the light from the open door reached only halfway up the curve of the staircase. From there I groped and fumbled; in the passage at the top the faint light from the sky helped me. I counted the doors to reach Mairi Sinclair's and I pounded loudly to waken her.

'Mistress Sinclair – will you come? My grandfather asks for you to come!'

But she had not been asleep. Almost immediately she flung open the door, and I had a glimpse of a bare, stark room, without comfort. There was a fireplace, but she did not permit herself a fire. A candle burned on a small table, and a single, straight-backed chair was before it. The familiar black book lay open. She wore the same long white nightgown and the plaid in which I had seen her on my first night at Cluain. Her black, silver-streaked hair was loosed, straight, and as shining as Morag's.

'The Master is ill?'

'I – no, I don't think he's ill. But he asks you to come – at once.'

Without a word she went to the table and picked up the candle. Shielding it against the draught of her movements, she lighted me down the stairs. Then she stood with her plaid tightly drawn across her in the door of the dining-room, unwilling to come farther.

'Come in, Mistress Sinclair. Sit down.' She moved farther into the room, but she ignored my grandfather's motion towards a chair.

'There is something wrong?'

He gestured helplessly. 'It concerns you.'

'It concerns Cluain, Master,' Morag interjected. 'And it concerns Callum Sinclair.' She stood exactly as she had been when I left, facing the two men with no sign of faltering in whatever she had come to do. I had never seen such beauty upon her – the apricot-stained skin, and the glowing eyes. In the deep quiet that attended her words she turned and went then to the table where the big Bible had its place. It had always seemed to me a part of the furnishings of the room, built like the walls themselves, immovable. But Morag lifted it, heavy even for her strong arms, and brought it to the exact centre of the dining table on my side, placing the brassbound edge precisely parallel to the line of the table.

Mairi Sinclair's face clenched in anger as she observed all this. She made an instinctive movement, which she checked, as if she too longed to strike Morag. 'How do you *dare*?' she demanded of the girl. 'No one touches that Book!'

'I dare because you do not dare, Mistress Sinclair. I would dare very much for the sake of Callum Sinclair.'

'And what have you to do with my son? What has *this* to do with him?'

'I make your son my business, mistress, because that is the way I would have it. I must do for him what you have so far failed to do. Have you not waited, also, mistress? Or have the years made you fearful? Have you stayed silent all this time only to find now that you have no tongue in your head? Have you believed that Cluain must come to him because it is his due – his right? Did you trust the final decency of this old man? – his honesty? Well, I have to tell you, mistress, that there is no honesty in him. He and Mr Lachlan between them are settling the future of Cluain, and your son's name is not even mentioned.'

Mairi Sinclair looked around all of us slowly. 'What the Master does is his own affair. It has nothing to do with my son.'

Morag threw back her head with a gesture that set the candle-flames flickering. 'Fool! You are a fool! *This* is the time. If you do not speak now it will be gone forever. *Demand!* It is his! – and they are giving it away! You have allowed yourself to be a servant all your life. But you cannot let that happen to your son, cannot let him be so cheated. How can you have that Heaven you pray for if you have done so ill by your own flesh? I tell you, if Callum Sinclair were not from home I would have him here this moment, and then see if any of you would dare to pass him by! Well, Master, will you speak? Will you open that Book and let all here read, or shall I tell them what I have seen written?'

'Bitch!' he said. 'Prying, deceitful little bitch! How have you read from that Book?'

'The keys, Master – the precious keys of Cluain. Always kept about your person, and yet trusted to Mistress Sinclair and then to myself because it never seemed to enter your head that I could be other than she. Do you not understand that what is locked must always arouse curiosity? While the Mistress was alive it was never locked. Often in this room, when I was a wee girl, I can remember her opening it. In her failing years she read from it often. I learned some of my letters from that Book. She was very patient with me. I can remember her pointing out where the names of your two grandchildren were recorded. I saw your daughter's name – the day she was born, the day she married, the day she died. All written there. I could barely understand all those names, but I learned to read them – William and Christina. And then the Mistress died, and the Book was locked. And never opened – never! You do not remember the times, Master, when you were ill, and you sent me to fetch a dram of whisky? And gave me the keys, to be returned to your bedside at once. Did you think I would not remember the brass key with the fancy end to it – I had thought it so beautiful when I was a wee girl, and the Mistress had shown me how cunningly it locked the big Book. Children do not forget secret things. I was fourteen years old when you first trusted me with the keys. No doubt you thought of me as just such another as Mairi Sinclair. But I am not. I saw the little brass key, and I opened the Book, and I looked at the back where the names are written. I held the knowledge to myself, and I waited. Shall I speak now, Master? Is there need to?'

'No!' Mairi Sinclair gestured violently towards my grandfather. 'What have you done? What wrong, foolish thing have you done! I said never – *never*!'

But he was shaking his head. 'It was done long ago. The night my wife died and I sat down to record her death, I knew that since I could no longer hurt her, there was something else to be recorded. What I hoped for then, I do not know. I could see the names of my two grandchildren there – but they were far away in China, unknown, perhaps never to be known.' Before he put his hand in his pocket to bring out the bunch of keys, I saw him again hold his chest. Then he extended the keys to me. There was infinite weariness in the gesture.

'Here, Kirsty. Open it and read for yourself. We need no more talk from this meddlesome piece here.'

'Angus . . .' Lachlan said.

'It is done, Samuel. What has been will never be undone. Kirsty will open it.'

I sat down where Morag had placed the Bible. The key was small but easily recognizable by its elaborate design. But the whole bunch was cumbersome, and I fumbled as I tried to insert the small key in the lock. As if she were performing any other service, Morag calmly lighted another candle, and brought it to the other side of the Bible. Then, with a turn, the locked clasp was free.

Morag could not restrain herself. She leaned across me. 'There at the end!' It was her hand that turned the printed pages until the plain ones were reached. 'You see, it goes far back in the family. It is the Macdonald family Bible, not the Campbells'.' Her finger traced eagerly the history of a family, written in many hands, over many generations. 'You see here, how it traces back to Ranald, younger son of John, First Lord of the Isles. The Mistress taught me it all – she was proud of it. How it goes, splitting and splitting, and it grows too wide and far-placed for any to keep account of it. So it becomes just the family – the Master's own family of Macdonald, on Inishfare, his own father, his brother – himself. When they were born, when they died. His daughter, born here at Cluain, and her death. Your brother's birth, in China, and your own, and then recorded last of all, long beyond its time, his own son, the date and birthplace ... Cluain.'

The last entry was in my grandfather's hand. *Callum Sinclair Macdonald.* And the date of birth given was nearly thirty years ago.

I took my hands slowly off the Book, and looked at my grandfather.

'It is true?'

He inclined his head. 'It is true.'

The sickness and the pain were almost beyond bearing. I clamped my lips together so that I would not cry out, but there was no controlling the cold trembling that took possession. I wanted to run from here, and yet my legs would not lift me from the chair. Where could I hide from the gaze of them all? I turned my head from side to side, shaking it like a bewildered animal. The truth of all that I had ever sensed between myself and Callum was now laid cruelly bare, the feeling of something forbidden and dark that had not, could not be, fully comprehended. A blood relationship so close, and yet when I had pulled him down against me in the heather, he had been the sum of all my desires. I had hunted and followed him through the strath all summer. He had tried to shake me away, and he had not succeeded. What perverse blackness had possessed me, like an evil, rank growth. Half-brother to my own mother, and yet I had looked for him as a lover, had schemed and planned for him as a husband. How twisted and perverted could natural desires grow? – and grow from innocence? I had told myself that I could outwit all other loves that possessed him, and I had endured even the knowledge of his love for Margaret. I had said I would be stronger than that knowledge, overlook it, forget it; I knew how to wait. Well, now I knew that the waiting was over – and still it went on. The hunger was there, and must be denied. It would be forever. I had lost, not only my hope of love, but the very right to feel it. It must not be offered; it could never be accepted.

Dumbly I read again those words. *Callum Sinclair Macdonald.* There was no wiping them out. Why was I even surprised to see them? The truth, revealed now, was startlingly plain. Why had I not seen it? I had been blinded because Callum so much resembled Mairi Sinclair. But were not the eyes, and the skin and the hair as much my grandfather's – and William's, and my own? When I had looked in the mirror, why had I only seen William's face, never Callum's? The blindness of love was infinite.

I found the strength to get to my feet. I could even face them all, and when I looked around I wondered why I should have been so concerned only for myself. Others felt, and they suffered. The impact of those words was visible about me; in those moments Samuel Lachlan had risen and had come to look for himself, because, in fact, no one had actually spoken that name. Now he shuffled back to the settle, and he showed his trembling, as much as I.

For me, then, Samuel spoke. 'Why did not you tell us, Angus? It would have made a difference.'

'Would have.' My grandfather looked about us all. 'Aye, it might have made a difference if it had been right at the start. But I was a coward then, and I let myself listen to Mairi Sinclair's words. She would have none of it. She would not have the scandal settle about my wife and daughter. I might never have known, even, that she was with child, if her father had not beaten her to the point where the whole strath knew of it, and knew why he had beaten her. She was bent on going away, but my wife insisted on taking in this young girl, and I had not the courage to say what was the truth. Mairi Sinclair threatened then that if I spoke to my wife she would go – she would be off to Glasgow, or some place else, and get work there, and no one would ever hear of her again. Thinking what wrong I had already done her, did I have the right to bring more hardship on her and the child? At least they would be safe and sheltered at Cluain. Then all I could hope for was that the child would be a girl. A girl would have been easier to provide for. But it was a son – my only son – and I could make no claim to him then. Cowardice denied me what I had most wanted in the world.'

For a moment he leaned back and closed his eyes, and there was remembrance of times long past, but always lived with. 'It happened because I stayed some nights up on the shielings in those years. I could afford less farm help then, and I used to take my turn up there to let one of the older ones come down to his family. Mairi Sinclair was there also. It is to my shame that I allowed myself to do what I did, but I feel no shame, and have never felt shame, in having loved her. It was the only time we

were together – that one summer. Since she has been in this house
she has lived alone. When my wife died, I asked her to marry me,
and thus her son could, by adoption, become my own. But she
would have none of it. Some rubbish about refusing to profit from
her sin. As if it could be counted profit . . . So many years had
passed. It would have been a marriage in name only, and she
refused the falsehood of it, and I had to respect that. And as for
sin . . . she was not guilty, that girl of long ago. Seventeen, she
was, and innocent. Intelligent and knowing, far beyond her schooling. Long black hair . . . She said I had no rights in her life, or
her son's. And I had not. The man who acts as I did, has no rights.
He can ask, but he cannot demand.'

Shakily, Samuel Lachlan motioned me with his glass. I went
and poured another whisky for him and didn't care, nor did anyone seem to notice, how much I spilled.

'But your *son*, Angus! A son for Cluain. I remember . . . I
remember the time your wife took Mairi Sinclair into Cluain and
I did not think it wise. But your wife was a very determined –
and a very soft – woman. I remember the child being born. If I
had known . . . It would have been better, Angus, if you had
spoken. *I* could have done something! *I* could have persuaded
Mairi Sinclair that she owed something to her son . . . This girl
here – ' His gesture towards Morag indicated distaste, but considerable respect. 'This girl here is right. I question her motives, but
she is right. There should be no settlement of Cluain's future
without telling Callum Sinclair this. He has rights . . . Perhaps no
rights in law, but in nature.'

'And nature has always been between us, Samuel. It was as if
Callum's knowledge of me as a coward and an adulterer was there
from the moment that his eyes were fully opened. He grew up in
this house, but he could have been as far from me as my grandchildren in China. Do not forget, Samuel, that when my wife died,
he was a grown lad already, and past my possessing. He would
take nothing from me. Not the smallest gift. Not the least help.
All he would take from me was knowledge, and he milked me of
that, whatever I had to give. He took it all, as he took knowledge
from everyone. He had all his mother's intelligence. He seemed
his mother's son entirely. Independent, proud, stubborn – no, obstinate. Many times I believed he hated me, and perhaps that is
the truth. But he never tried to hide it. There was no currying
favour with the Master of Cluain. I could have made life easier
for him as he grew up, but he did not choose the easy way. He
learned all I had to teach him – the farm, the distillery. He already

had his mother's way with animals and nature. And then there came the day he walked out of his strath and went to school in Edinburgh on money provided by his mother, and his own savings from wages. Neither he nor she would take a shilling beyond what they had earned – and doubly earned – in work for Cluain. Nor will he take it to this day. The privileges he seems to have are his by right and agreement. When I asked him to return to the distillery we both knew it must be on his terms. He takes no favours from me – expects none. Since he has rejected everything else I have offered, I have no reason to believe that if I told him the truth, offered him a share in Cluain, he would not throw it back in my face. You see, I know him – and I know myself. He would know that if I made such an offer it would not be because I loved him as a father should love a son, but because Cluain needed him. I have tried to love him – it is not in my heart. And once he knew, if there was revenge in his heart, he could have it simply by refusing Cluain. That would be the surest way . . .'

'And he would refuse it, Master. I know my son.'

Could we have forgotten Mairi Sinclair just because she had remained silent? She stood there, the dark eyes deepened in that half-light, tall and majestically straight, a compelling, handsome woman, and one did not wonder at the magnetic quality she would have possessed at seventeen, beautiful then, and with knowledge beyond her years, different from other girls as she was from other women now. I imagined her up on the shielings, staying apart from the others when the fires burned at night, and there was laughter among the young people, and banter she could not join. The last flush of the twilight on the mountain, and the Master of Cluain for her companion. Not the man we saw now, but a younger man by thirty years, still struggling to make Cluain what it was, still with dreams unrealized, still hungry with wants and hopes. And perhaps it had been the same way with the black-haired girl, the girl with gifts already apparent, and beauty, and the beginnings of wisdom in her face, the girl from a crofter's cottage, as fierce in her pride as in her poverty. Not a girl to flirt, beg, nor afterwards to tell, even though her life was almost beaten from her. Nor one to deny life to the child she carried. How could we have forgotten her, even for a few seconds?

'You should never have written that name, Master. If I had known it was written, the Book, even that sacred Book, would have been destroyed. Not even that – there are acids that would have burned the paper, leaving only a cipher for the prying eyes of scheming little girls – little girls who know only the face of what they see, not the heart of it. It should never have been written, Master.'

He sighed. 'I wrote it after my wife died, remember. Perhaps I wrote it in remorse, knowing that then the truth could not hurt her – but great-souled woman that she was, I think she could have borne the truth, and perhaps Callum would have been less perverse with her than me. Perhaps I had some notion of it as a last testament. If those unknown grandchildren could not be mine, then after my death, the truth would be clear. I looked at that name again – Callum's name – on the day that I made the entry of William's death. But Callum and I were so far apart that he seemed no more to me than that other grandchild, still in China. And then she came . . .'

'Master, remember that it would have been a useless cruelty to have told the Mistress. Remember that I swore to you the time when you forced from me the admission that it was your child I carried, that if you ever spoke to the Mistress, then I would be gone from Cluain that same day, and so would the child. Could you have two women of your acknowledged loving under the one roof? Could you have expected me to stay? In the beginning it was a penance every time I had to meet the Mistress's eyes, but I stayed because I wanted my child brought up here, not in some city tenement. What punishment I bore would have to be my own, not his. But he would not be your son. He was no one's son but mine.

'And yet, I have always thought that he knew. As he grew, the knowledge seemed to come to him, though it was never spoken by me. It is, as you say, Master, as if he were born knowing, and perversely used the knowledge to punish you – to withhold from you what we all knew you most wanted, your own son. If he never accepted any gift, it was because he could never bring himself to thank you for it. Callum could thank no one. It is a hard fault, Master, and one that I am cursed with. I can give no thanks, but neither can I accept thanks. I do what I can, what I see to be right, as the Lord gives me to see. When your grandson came – so easy he was, so charming, and you both going along together as if it were he, not Callum, who had been here all his life, I felt myself possessed of jealousy and greed. I wanted your thoughts only for Callum. I prayed very long over that, and I believed my soul was finally freed of it. Then your grandson died, and I felt as if a judgement had been made on both of us, to see your happiness so destroyed. But then this girl came to take his place, and I suffered my jealousy and greed once again. I fought it, and

prayed, and I began to see that my son was never to profit from
the wrong I had done. And I knew what wrong he was committing
with that woman, Margaret Campbell. It was wrong – compound-
ing wrong. It seemed to stem from me, as if I had given him the
seed of evil. For what fault I am not yet free of, I can only pray
for forgiveness.'

'And I say *damn* your prayers for forgiveness, Mairi Sinclair!'
Morag cried it with the fierceness of pent-up anger. 'You and this
old man here – so concerned with your souls and your consciences!
What of your son? Until you have told him, face to face, what his
position is in this household, you have no right, between you, to
be worrying about your salvation and your repentance. It has gone
beyond that. Now it is a matter for Callum. Will you take from
him his inheritance because your soul is troubled? And you,
Master, will you now weakly slide along into some plan for joining
with other distillers, and leave your own son out of it because long
ago you had not the courage to acknowledge him? Do you not
stand high enough in your own estimation to be able to afford
this gesture? Is the Master of Cluain so small a man that he
cannot make others accept his son? Think on it, Master, because
if you do not tell him, then most surely *I* will. And can any of you
deny now what you have seen written there?'

'But he *knows*!' I had found my tongue at last. 'He knows!
Even if he has not heard it in words from his mother or my grandfather, he most certainly knows.'

Morag turned on me. 'You are sure of that?'

'Certain. And by the certain, sure way that a woman knows.
I'll say it before all of you, because I am not – I cannot – be
ashamed of it. If I could have had him, Callum Sinclair would
have been my husband. *Yes* – I wanted him in that way. But he
would not give himself to me, and he went his own way, and he
followed another woman to the moment of her death. But even if
he had not loved Margaret Campbell, he would never have been
mine. I see it now – so clearly. But I could not before. He tried to
tell me – he *tried*. Even if there was nothing to prove whose son
he was, he sensed it, and he tried to stop me from loving him. As
if he could! I went on, and I kept my hope. Now I know what
held us apart, and there never was a hope at all.'

I did not care that they all knew now the way I had loved
Callum. Let them know the dangers they had run of a dark and
forbidden love growing up; let them know how close I had come
to the ultimate disaster. I remember how he had called back to
me that day on the mountain : *'Forget this day, Kirsty. Forget it!'*

His instinct had tried to save me; if he had known for certain he would have said it in words. But we were alike, Callum and I; we had both persisted in our loves against reason and against hope.

Now I went back deliberately and seated myself again in front of the Bible, reading once more the names – William's and my own, set down before Callum's, which should have preceded them. 'So there is something to be put right, Grandfather. I can see that so long as there was William, you still might have hoped for a legitimate heir for Cluain – but even so, justice would not have been done. I think you have made it too easy for yourself all these years since my grandmother died. When Callum was a child, his mother could speak for him, force conditions on you. But when Callum was grown, there was no excuse, before God, not to tell him the truth. He should have been given a share in Cluain – on whatever pretext you or he wanted to present to the world. Either that, or a chance of honestly refusing it. Of saying no to you! But you kept placing your hope in William, and pushing aside an old shame. How can either of you speak for Callum now? – most especially *now*, when my brother no longer gives you even the faintest reason to hold off. When William died, Grandfather, your last excuse died with him. There is more shame to you now that you talk of bringing in Cameron's and Macquarie's, and even of marrying me off to one of them – and your own son is left out.'

'He will refuse. He will take nothing from me.'

'Then let me hear it from Callum himself! Let us all hear it. Do we need Morag to do this task for us? I will tell him myself if you do not. I will tell him, and then I will leave Cluain. Because I *have* loved him. Do you understand love, Grandfather? I doubt that you do. This was a wrong love, a wrong and twisted thing. I could not stay here, and see him day after day, and have the knowledge of it fester in me. But before I go, I will tell him – I swear it! And I will not see Cluain parcelled off without his consent. If he wants to let it go, then let him say so. But in all that you are now deciding for Cluain, remember that the Camerons and the Macquaries will not stand still after your death. They will chip away at what Cluain is, at what you have built up. It is how these things always go, no matter what promises are made, what contracts are signed. You *must* know for the Camerons and the Macquaries you have one great counterweight. Dear God, in Callum Sinclair you have a *man*!'

Then I could stand it no longer. I put my face in my hands, and prayed that I would not weep here and now for all that I had lost, and for all that I was throwing after it. Callum would not be mine. I felt the awful bleakness of it. There was nothing left to love.

'Is there some whisky in this house? I have need of a dram or two. I have just come from Edinburgh . . . and from Ballochtorra.'

Callum's voice. My head flew up, and my spirits seemed to bound with pleasure; and then came the dull remembrance. He stood in the doorway of the kitchen passage, his body slumped against the frame, with the look of exhaustion upon him. He had never seemed more like his mother. His eyes seemed sunken with sleeplessness; I wondered if he had thought to take any food at all since Margaret had died; his face and lips were pinched and white. There was silence as he advanced into the room, and took, uninvited, a chair at the table. My own chair scraped back as I rushed to the decanter, to be there before Morag. But she already had her hand on it, and I banged it loudly against the glass as I pulled it from her.

'I will pour,' I said. I had had enough of Morag. She was right in her demand for justice for Callum, but she did it with no sense of disinterest. I wondered why I had never seen ambition before in those bright, knowing eyes, the ever-present willingness to help, the thirst for knowledge. For a young girl in this quiet, slow strath she knew so much, and she had kept her most important knowledge to herself until it could be made to serve herself. I wanted no more of her.

I poured a large glass of whisky, and spilled a little water into it. I placed it on the table before Callum. He took it slowly, and drank a little, and then set it down.

'You need some food,' I said. 'Morag will bring you something.'

'Morag will bring nothing. She will stay where she is. And I need no food.'

He took another drink. 'I wonder what Cluain is coming to? I have come in and stabled the pony, and no one has heard me. Not a dog barks. Big Billy's flock do not open their mouths. A man can be too well known to a household. You're all so full of your own concerns, you have ears for nothing. I've been standing there near half an hour. Not hiding – just standing there where any of you could have seen me if you cared to look. It made too interesting hearing to interrupt. It isn't often a man gets a chance to hear the truth about himself – good and bad. Mostly, it seemed to be bad.'

'If you'd had the decency to declare yourself . . .' my grandfather began.

Callum's weary gesture of dismissal silenced him. 'Do you want to talk *now* about decency, Mr Macdonald?' He looked around us all. 'Well, between you, you've left almost nothing unsaid. I've never heard such a lot of pious prattling in my life . . . no, I'm sorry.' He turned himself sideways and reached for my hand, pulling me down into the chair next to him. 'I'm sorry, Kirsty. That wasn't for you. I'm sorry about everything. For me, this summer has been the whole climax of my life – it has been . . . *everything*. For you, it has been hell. The kind of hell that I live in now. Yes, I did try to stop it, but how can you tell someone not to love? I didn't want you hurt, but I didn't understand how deep it went with you. Forgive me for not allowing you the feelings I had myself for Margaret. I did you an injustice. If I had guessed that it was more than a light fancy, I would have said more. I would have stopped it. Because I knew that I would leave Cluain when Margaret went, at the end of the summer. Oh –' he gestured with the glass. 'I knew I would not be with her. I wouldn't have followed her to London like a love-sick boy, though that's what I was. And I could not wait here to be a summer diversion for her again next year. I was not completely blind, even if I was in love. I did not blame her – she never fully knew what she was to me. But I knew I could not endure it here without her. I would go away, and in time you, Kirsty, would love someone else, and no damage would be done. But that was what I thought. If I had dreamed it could hurt you so, nothing would have stopped me speaking.'

'You knew then – about my grandfather?'

'My father.' We could have been speaking alone together in that room. Suddenly all the barriers were down. The first free and unconstrained speech we had ever had, and it took place before an audience. It didn't matter. All the pretence was gone, the striving. The love was still there. Like the name written in the Book, it could not be wiped out, even with the acid of my pain; but it had undergone a strange transmutation. I looked at Callum with other eyes, but not less loving eyes.

'My father. Yes, I knew – or guessed. Not that anything ever was said, and I didn't suspect that he could be capable of the kind of sentiment that would cause him to write my name where he did. Perhaps we had a chance, and lost it – long ago. But only between two people related as closely as we are could the kind of feelings we had exist. I could not have been so involved with someone not close to me. I would simply not have cared. It seems I can only love or hate. Most of the time I thought I hated him – overbearing, arrogant, too full of himself and Cluain. And then at times I knew great pity for him, growing old alone, sitting her at nights alone, going to his bed alone. If my mother thinks she has saved her soul by refusing to marry him, then she should look into her heart for a little Christian charity towards him. For all she says of praying, she has not forgiven him – or herself. She had her own revenge, my mother, and called it penance. All these years, however she tries to deny it, she must have believed Cluain would be for me. Who else was there? We quarrelled, the old man and I, and still he had to call me back. I was glad when William came. I was released. The old man had company, and hope. And I was free. I was no longer possessed by a future which might be dictated for me. I neither had to accept nor refuse Cluain. Then everything changed again when William died – and Margaret came to me. It all changed so suddenly that my head spun with trying to comprehend. I lived in a haze of joy so long as I had Margaret, and I was so blind to what you felt. I knew it was going to hurt like death when it came to an end. And like death it is. I'm sorry, Kirsty. I would never have let it be this way for you if I hadn't been so wrapped in my own joys and woes.'

The exhausted face looked at me with a kindliness I had never experienced before. Suddenly I put my hand on his, as it lay on the table, just gently put it on his, not gripping. It might have been William I touched.

'We will both survive,' I said. 'One does not die so easily. I will leave Cluain, and you will stay, because you must. But we will both survive.'

'I will not stay at Cluain,' he answered. 'Not for anything. Not for this old man, or anything he can give me. I gather there is some talk of a merger with Cameron's and Macquarie's – well, I will not stay for that either. There is nothing anyone can give me now. So it is you who must stay, Kirsty. You who will have to battle out Cluain's future. They will try to arrange a marriage. But take nothing you do not want yourself – accept no one and nothing in which there is not willingness and love. Once you have known love, you will either seek it again, or live without it. You will not take what pretends to be love – not for money, or convenience, nor for the sake of peace. You and I, Kirsty – we are not made for peace, it seems. It is not a family inheritance.'

Samuel Lachlan could contain himself no longer. His glasses came off, and his glass tipped wildly, so that the whisky spilled on his trousers.

'Do you mean, Sinclair – Callum – that you will not stay at Cluain? That you refuse, should Mr – your father – offer? That you would not stay and take over? – when the time comes, of course.'

Callum seemed not to hear him. He was looking at me very directly, a way he had not looked almost since the first time we had encountered each other, a look that searched my face, with tenderness, with compassion. Then I felt his hand, which had rested under mine, quietly, slowly, fold over, until it encompassed mine, held it, gathered it to him, for what comfort it would offer. 'I'm sorry, Kirsty,' he said again. 'I'm leaving you an uneasy future. Cluain is no gift, but a burden. I'm sorry.'

It was only then he looked beyond me to the two men. 'No – I am not staying. My years of service to Cluain are ended. We cannot unmake the past – my father and I. It is too late, for both of us. We cannot stop being what we are, and what we are will not live together. So go on and make what plans you must. I will not be part of them. I will be going as soon as you can find a man to replace me.'

'You are certain?' my grandfather said. He looked at Callum and his face twisted with bitterness. The pretence was gone from between them also. It must be almost impossible for Angus Mac-donald to comprehend that Callum could be willingly leaving behind a chance to be master of Cluain, even though, to this moment, he himself had not formally offered it. He looked very old, the lines of age unnaturally harsh. I thought that for thirty years he must have carried at the back of his mind the thought of Callum, perhaps unconsciously believing that if every other plan failed there was the ultimate heir to Cluain. And now thirty years were gone, and so was Callum. He was left with me.

'It turns to ashes,' he said. 'A man works all his life . . . for what? You and I, Samuel, what have we laboured for?'

The other man looked more bewildered than ever. All around him, the forces on which he had based his life, the sanctity of hard work, the sacredness of capital, of possessions, was being challenged. Before him were two young people, and in these last minutes he had heard each of us refuse what had taken Angus Macdonald and himself a lifetime to build. He shook his head, mute.

'Well then, Callum Sinclair, let us not detain you,' my grand-father said. 'I am still capable of a day's work in the distillery. We are about to begin malting, and I have a fair knowledge of how it's done. I have not yet lost my eyes and nose for good whisky. Let us not keep you a day longer than needs be. If Cluain does not satisfy you, then let us not hold you here against your will. Another man will be found. There are many who would be glad

to come to Cluain. Do not trouble yourself that we shall not continue to make good whisky without your help.' It was the final
dismissal.

Mairi Sinclair made only one sign of protest. Her hand went
out suddenly in a gesture, as if she would have kept Callum
seated there, as if she would have kept him forever. Then slowly
it fell again to her side. She also was losing Callum. For her also
the years at Cluain without him stretched ahead.

Almost at the same instant as her hand fell, the real protest
came from Morag. 'Callum – you are *mad*! You cannot do this
thing! You cannot throw away such a prize. Think of it! –
Cluain! Is it not everything a man could want? A fine house, a
fine farm – a famous distillery. Look at those two old men! – you
have only to nod your head, even now, and it is yours. Do not
believe what he says about going. He would have you – and
gladly. He is pushed – he *needs* you. Och, you have lost your
sense over this dead woman. In time – in a very little time, you
will find that she did not matter. Frivolous, light-minded creature
she was. You will wonder how you could ever have given time or
thought to her. She was not worth more than her looks.'

Callum turned slowly towards her. After her struggle with me
over the decanter, Morag had retreated to the kitchen-passage
door, almost beyond the candlelight, where Callum had stood, as
if she would remain unnoticed, and not be sent away.

'And what is it to you, Morag, how I choose to give my time,
where I choose to give my love? I gave both – gladly. Never mind
what Margaret was. She gave me back things no woman has ever
given me. Her death has not taken them away. They remain
forever.'

'Then you are doubly a fool! Your sense is in your loins, not
in your head. You ask what it is to me? My life – that is what it
is! Since you came back here, since I was fifteen, I have waited
for you, Callum Sinclair. I have waited, and learned to do and
be everything that a wife for a man like you should be. Do you
think there have not been others after me? – Yes, *see* me! If I
had had the clothes of Margaret Campbell, and the soft hands,
and rode a mare like hers, would you not have noticed me sooner?
My hands are rough, but my face is not, nor my body. There has
never been anyone else for me but you, Callum. I cannot *stand*
to see you throw away Cluain. I have counted on you – and it. It
was to be your future. And mine. Even Angus Macdonald must
see this. Together, you and I, Callum – we could make a whole
generation to succeed at Cluain. Children . . . sons. I could give

you *everything* – and Cluain what it most needs. No, you cannot throw it away. I will not let you! It is too much if what I have done is for nothing.'

'And what have you done, Morag?'

She was silent for a time. I stared at her, fascinated. She was like a creature suddenly broken from a shell; the red lips were full and passionate; there was now no winning smile, but the wilful stance of a woman in the full spate of her needs and desires, someone who sees the fruits of a long toil about to be snatched from her. She was so different from the faded, resigned old-age acceptance of Samuel Lachlan and my grandfather. There was no acceptance in Morag; she was fighting.

'What have I done?' she repeated, at last. 'I have loved you, Callum Sinclair. *That* is what I have done. I have loved you lawfully, keeping myself for you. It has not been like the love of that woman, Margaret Campbell, who sought to pass an idle summer and bewitched you out of your senses. She who lost a lover when Master William died, and looked about for the one to take his place. No, my love has not been like that, nor like the love of this girl here, who has loved where she should not have done – well, it is not her fault, but she is foolish, and was love-sick, and would not listen to me when I tried to tell her that you were not for her. I have loved you the way a woman should, ready to do anything for you, to be anything. And I have waited. So you see, you cannot leave Cluain. You can't leave me.'

Callum drank from his glass again. 'How old are you, Morag?'

She drew herself to her full height. 'Old enough. Nearly eighteen.'

He shook his head. 'It's a sad waste, Morag. You think I haven't seen you? I have. I have seen you about my mother's kitchen, and I have seen no woman, but a child with a scheming heart. There is no innocence in you, Morag. You talk of Margaret Campbell – but what did you know of her? It is the evil minds of those like you who make her seem sullied and corrupt. She was not that. She was never capable of a calculated gesture. She was simple – even guileless, no matter what the world says of her. She never stopped to consider that friendship with a man, laughter, enjoyment, could lead to love. And when love came, she took it gladly, whole-heartedly. You do not understand that kind of love. You never could. You don't know what love is, Morag. You have waited, and planned. Planned for what? – I don't know. So far as I'm concerned, it's all wasted. Turn your talents elsewhere. I will leave.'

'I have said, Callum Sinclair,' Angus Macdonald broke in, 'that we have no need of you here.' How cold and tired his voice had grown; I sensed the anger of his rejection taking hold.

'I will go,' Callum replied, 'as soon as I am permitted to go. There may be legal procedures which require me to stay some time yet.'

'An Enquiry?' My grandfather said it with contempt. 'And what will that be but a formality? Because the sheriff is a friend of the Campbells he will gloss it over. But of course you will have to describe what happened, since you were with her. However carefully you choose your words, the whole countryside will know what you were about. The relationship between you and Margaret Campbell was already a scandal. You could hardly claim you were in attendance on her as a groom.'

'I will never pretend I was anyone's groom! But there will be more than a police glossing over of her death. The reason for her death is quite clear. She broke her neck when the mare stumbled on the rocks below the waterfall, and pitched her down on her head. She did not live beyond that second. But there was more than that. It was not a normal fall the mare took. I was riding after Margaret and I saw it clearly. The mare did not slip – she staggered. And at a bad place. I had noticed there was something wrong and I called to Margaret to dismount. But she seldom paid heed to advice like that. She went ahead, crossing the ford, and it was there the mare's legs suddenly folded under her, and she and Margaret together fell down on the rocks below.'

'The mare was ill?' My grandfather leaned forward. 'It is not like Ballochtorra to send an unfit animal out from its stables.'

'The mare was well enough when she went out. I told you I have just come from Ballochtorra. I have spoken to Gavin Campbell, as I had to do before, to get his permission to act in the first place. Before the mare was buried, up there by my cottage, I removed her stomach. Then I took it to a pathologist in Edinburgh – a friend I made when I was at school. I did not tell him the full circumstances. He trusted that I would make the right use of the information he gave me. And the law will probably be about my neck for taking things into my own hands. But I wasn't absolutely certain. If I had been wrong, there would only have been more gossip and speculation, and Margaret's son would have suffered all the more – without need. If I had waited to call the constable from Grantown, and all the rest, the countryside would have been ringing with the news. And perhaps I had been wrong. I hoped I had been wrong. But I wasn't.'

'What did the man find, then?'

'Hemlock — more than a trace of digitalis — foxglove. Henbane — hyoscyamine. The mare had taken enough hemlock to have eventually killed her. She had eaten while we — while Margaret and I were in the cottage. That staggering walk was the beginning of the vertigo that comes from the drug — so the pathologist tells me.'

His voice had faltered as he recalled the details of the scene. He leaned back and sipped again from his whisky. 'There was a feed bag with oats there. I had made a rough little stable of the second half of the croft — just to shelter the animals from the weather, perhaps to shelter them from prying eyes if anyone came that way. But people never went up that track except on purpose — the gorse up there is above head high, and they would only come looking for a strayed sheep. I never saw any — so that is unlikely. But also I never left any feed there. Why should I? I did not want to advertise our presence — the use of the place more than I had to. But the feed bag was there that day, when I tied up the mare and my pony. Margaret had dismounted and gone into the cottage. I did not say anything to her about the feed bag. I thought it was some kind of cruel hint from someone who knew we met there, and who wanted to make an ugly joke. Nothing we did there was ugly — and I did not want to make it seem so to Margaret. But I can never forgive myself for not taking the feed bag beyond reach of the mare. There is no doubt she ate from it.'

'Och, what nonsense,' Morag cried. 'You are making a big and tragic event because your fancy woman has been killed, and you want to make someone else suffer for it. The countryside is filled with hemlock in the wild places. Where it is not cut it will sprout and grow wild and big. Every child knows that.'

Mairi Sinclair intervened. 'Hemlock is a rank, evil-smelling plant — repellent. Only hungry animals would graze on it. Horses from the Ballochtorra stable would never touch such a thing in its wild state. As to the henbane — I do not know. It was in the oats. It would have been a potent dose.'

'How do you know it was in the oats?'

'I know. I know the mare could never have grazed on enough of it to make such a concentration in the stomach to kill her. Mice may die of nibbling at hemlock — not horses. It was not a natural fall she had. Was she dead when John went to shoot her?'

Callum shook his head. 'She was not. But she was not screaming and struggling as an animal would do who is in great pain from a broken leg. The drugs would have been having their full effect by then. John told me she was lying very still, and she hardly opened her eyes when he came near her. I asked him to say nothing, and he agreed. *He* trusted me, too. I thought of the oats myself, and I went up at first light the next morning to bring the bag down. But it wasn't there. I have no proof that the mare got the hemlock from the oats – or the henbane, or digitalis, or belladonna. What I have to know – and I may never know – is who it was who knew that Margaret and I met there. If it was meant simply as a warning – the warning of some narrow-minded zealot that the wages of sin is death, then it succeeded. But it was meant for the mare – and now Margaret is dead! God, if only she had dismounted when I called to her! If she had never crossed the ford . . .' He wiped his hand across his forehead. 'The Enquiry may reveal nothing but these facts – and I cannot produce the bag of oats. But I will not leave the strath until I know every single person who knew that Margaret and I met there. I *will* know!'

'I knew,' I said. 'I knew – and I went there the day before Margaret died.'

Callum shook his head in disbelief. 'Kirsty! – *you* couldn't . . .'

'I did not. I told you I knew. I went there. Even with all I had seen, even after the night of the Prince's ball, I still did not quite believe. But when I saw the cottage – how could I not believe it then? The feed bag was there, and in the few minutes I stood at the door of the cottage Ailis got to it. She did not have time to take very much. She lived.'

'How did you know, Kirsty? – about the croft?'

'Morag.'

She did not flinch under all our eyes. She stood erect, blazing with anger and passion.

'Yes, I knew. And so did half the strath.'

'But you told *me* about it the night the harvest feast was spread, Morag. You told me where to go, and what to look for. And very early the next morning, just at first light, you left Cluain. I saw you. Later you told me you had gone with something Mistress Sinclair had given you for a sick child of one of the workers.'

Mairi Sinclair's words were sharp and dry. 'I did not send her.'

Morag's head went up farther. 'And so – what if she did not send me? What business was it of yours to enquire? I have no life of my own? Is Callum Sinclair the only one who may go to meet a lover if he chooses?'

Callum leaned both arms on the table, and put his chin in one hand, rubbing it wearily. He did not look at Morag any longer. 'And what is all this you have said about keeping yourself for me?'

He sighed, and I thought he would rather not have gone on. 'Morag – Morag, don't lie! There was or there was not a sick child? There was or there was not a lover to meet?'

When Morag made no attempt to answer, I spoke. 'She meant it for me. She dangled the knowledge of the croft before me that night like bait, and she went with the feed bag the next morning, knowing that I could not resist seeing the evidence for myself. To those like Morag, I must seem such a fool – but who in love is not foolish? I went, as she guessed I would. There was nothing so obvious as poison for *me* – but something to tempt Ailis. Who knew what could have happened? Everyone knows that Ailis will eat anything presented to her, for as long as it's there. She could have fallen anywhere along the track – most of the glen is narrow, and boulders most of the way – some of it dangerous to a rider like myself. A fall – perhaps a night in the open. Ailis too drugged to get back to Cluain. Perhaps dead. Perhaps myself hurt, and with luck, some rain. Who knows that I would not have followed on the way William went? It took three days and two nights to find him.'

'What has this to do with Margaret?' Callum demanded sharply. He forced himself upright in the chair.

'Yes . . . what?' I was asking it, of myself, remembering, trying to recall each moment of the day that Callum had hammered on the door, and Margaret's slackly hanging boots had dripped rain, almost on my face.

'I remember I got up very late that day – the day Margaret died. We had been up all night in the stable with Ailis – Mistress Sinclair and myself. And as I was getting dressed I saw Margaret riding along by the river. It was a surprise to see her – Morag had told me she and Gavin were at Cawdor, and were going on to some other place. It was such a terrible day – the rain pouring down. I guessed where she was going. And just to show Morag that I did not care as much as she supposed – what a stupid pretence that was – I told her I had seen Margaret out riding. Morag hurried with my meal, I remember, and talked about having vegetables to prepare. But when I went out into the scullery, she wasn't there.'

'What are you saying, Kirsty?' Callum said impatiently. 'Make yourself plain, for God's sake!'

'I'm *trying*!' I snapped back at him. I was weary of it all myself. 'I think it is coming plain.' I looked at Morag. 'It was meant for me, wasn't it, Morag – for Ailis? Margaret didn't matter, not that much. Callum could never have married her, and she would be gone soon. But I was here – and in your mind, I stood in the way of Callum having Cluain. Did you rush up the mountain that afternoon I told you I had seen Margaret out riding? – knowing as well as I did where she would be going on an afternoon like that? Did you go to get the feed bag before her mare or Callum's pony could get to it? You had not expected anyone there so soon – she was supposed to be away at Cawdor. And it was too late. Margaret and Callum were there before you, and Margaret's mare had eaten the oats. And Margaret fell with the mare.'

'You are *accusing* me? You have not the slightest proof!'

'No – I haven't. But are you as clever at getting the keys to Mistress Sinclair's herb room as you were in getting the key to the Bible? It would have had to be a strong, prepared dose of hemlock – the juice only, to mix with the oats. And a little digitalis, just to make sure? – a little henbane.'

'So it's hemlock from Mistress Sinclair's room now, is it? Then why should it not have been Mistress Sinclair who put the bag of oats there? Why should it be me? Did she not have reason to dislike Margaret Campbell, who had led her son into what she calls the paths of unrighteousness? Does she not have the skill to mix such a compound – and the keys to the herb room are hers, not mine.'

'It was a very unskilful mix, the pathologist said. Too strong to be normal – that is, if the mare had grazed on it,' Callum answered. 'Surely my mother knows better how to administer a poison if she is determined to do it. It does not fit.'

'Nothing fits,' Samuel Lachlan said. 'It is a tangle of supposition. And what, Kirsty, do you mean by Morag intending you to follow William?'

'It was thought, wasn't it, that William had a good chance to live when he was found and brought back after the shooting accident? He was young – strong. He had the best attention – and the will to live?'

My grandfather half rose from his seat. '*What* are you saying? My grandson had every care. Nothing was spared.'

'No – nothing. A surgeon from Inverness to remove the bullet, even a doctor from Edinburgh, a renowned nurse and herbalist to bring down the fever, to bring him back to health. But he died. I think . . . I think he died because Morag knew how to get the keys of the herb room. She had a little knowledge, picked up from Mistress Sinclair – enough to be dangerous. And William's name came before Callum's in the Bible – as mine does. No – I don't think it possible she could have planned the accident with the gun. It doesn't seem possible. But she knew her opportunity when it came.

Remember, Mairi Sinclair did not actually do much nursing of
William. She prepared the food, and gave the medicine the doctors
ordered, and her own remedies as well. But it was Morag who
fetched and carried to him, who sat up there with him in the tower
room. Mistress Sinclair herself told me that William did not like to
have her by him. I think Morag added enough to these brews and
medicines to turn the balance – a little of this, a little of that – to
confuse the doctors and Mistress Sinclair. All of it deadly if given
in too strong a dosage. Enough to defeat William's struggle for
life.'

A wild laugh broke from Morag. 'You are joking! You make
these mad accusations against me, but there is not the least proof.
Is all this come from the fact that one little pony was ill – and
recovered? – and Margaret Campbell's mare had eaten from a
poisonous plant? It is all fancy – all this about Ailis and Margaret
Campbell's mare. All about Master William's death. Your grief and
your thwarted love has sent your imagination reeling. I would have
a care if I were you. Accusations like these must have a proof, and
I will not sit still under them.'

'There is proof. The proof that Callum has brought, serious
enough for him to offer it at the inquest.'

'*That* is no proof against me! I have already said that it would
far more likely have been Mistress Sinclair who did that. That is
what most will say. As for your brother . . . Do you know more than
the doctors? Were you here when he died?'

'I only have what proof he sent me. I did not come to Cluain
uninvited just to have a roof over my head. Something unnatural
had happened to my brother. Something not explained. God knows,
it was slight enough, the proof he gave – but perhaps all that a man
who felt he was dying had strength to provide. Something that
would not be discovered and destroyed. It was sent to me in China.
It was that which brought me to Cluain.'

Now I had risked everything. The meaning of those words of
William's would never be plain. Had they been the last fevered
thought of Margaret, of her terrible, though strangely innocent
power to wreck and destroy? Or had they literally meant what
they had tried to say, and as strength had waned, been left unfinished? Who could ever know what had been in William's mind?
And I was challenging Morag with them.

'There *is* no proof – no proof!'

'It exists, Morag. It exists. But I had to come to Cluain to be
certain. I had to find out many things I could not have known.'

'None exists!' Her tone rose close to panic. 'I made sure. There was no writing – nothing.'

'You made sure, Morag? Why did you have to make sure of anything, if there was nothing to hide? It is there in writing – but something you couldn't read, and not in a letter, which you might have suspected and destroyed. The words are written in Mandarin characters on a scroll – a scroll with the drawing of a bird on a bare branch. You will remember that. You packed and sent that scroll to me in China. *You* brought me to Cluain.'

Now my grandfather got to his feet. He walked towards Morag with slow steps, the heaviness of his body menacing. But she did not shrink from him.

'*My* grandson. I entrusted him to you. Was there murder done so that you could secure Cluain for the man you wanted to marry?'

'Murder, is it?' Morag tossed her head. 'Better ask that of Mairi Sinclair! I don't know what proof your granddaughter imagines she has, but there is nothing to it, or why would she have waited this long time to bring it out? Oh, no, Master, I shall not be so easy. You may make your accusations until the breath has left your body, and I shall deny them. And I will point to Mairi Sinclair, who had equal, and more, chance than I to do any mischief that might have been done.'

The slight flaring of panic had left her; her confidence grew with her argument. 'After all, who am I? I merely do what I am told at Cluain. I carry out Mistress Sinclair's instructions. I don't care what is written or not written on a heathen scroll. There will be no proof that *I* have done wrong. All I have confessed to is opening the Bible and knowing what it contained. That – and the crime of loving Callum Sinclair.'

'You confessed before us all, that you made sure there was no proof of anything amiss before you packed William's belongings,' Callum said. 'There is more than fancy in what Kirsty is saying.'

Morag looked directly at me. 'Does that writing name my name? Does it?'

I could only shake my head. 'It names no name.'

'There! *Now* bring your proof. Shout it to the whole country. A fine business it will make. Will they dig up your grandson's body from the kirkyard, Master, to see if it contains poisons? How will you like that? Your name and the Campbell name – if Callum goes on with his nonsense – linked in the courts by a servant girl who is accused of causing two deaths. Or will it be Mairi Sinclair who is finally accused? – she who will then become known as your one-time lover? It will be a fine scandal to take into your declining years – and it will not change anything – not as you wish it changed. It will not bring your grandson back – '

Samuel Lachlan interrupted her, speaking directly to me. 'The nature of this proof you say you have, Kirsty? It is not definite? Has William made an accusation? – of some specific thing – named some specific person?'

'No. Morag is right. There is only a fragment . . . obviously written when he was in a high fever, to judge by the characters. There is no name – no crime that a court of law could fasten on to. That is why I have not spoken of it. I hoped to find out for myself – to be a little more sure. But in the cold light of day there is still so little. The pathologist's report that Callum brought back – but no bag of oats to go with it. There is William's scroll with his few words splashed on it. "*She has killed* . . ." is what he wrote, and even what he wrote is open to question. Even my father's translator was not quite sure . . .'

I stopped, because Samuel Lachlan was shaking his head. 'It will not do.' He rubbed his nose pensively. 'If ever there was enough evidence assembled to bring either of these women to trial – and I doubt that – you know what the verdict would be. *Not proven.* The Not Proven verdict is uniquely Scotland's law. The question would forever remain, no matter how sure *we* are that Mairi Sinclair could not have done such a thing. But there is also little proof that this girl here *did* do it. Unless you can find a witness who saw her on the way to, or at the cottage that day, you will achieve nothing. And then, what did she do, but cause harm to a horse? The matter of William is more delicate still. Two doctors attended him, and neither suspected foul play. Doctors are notoriously conservative in these matters. They do not like their judgements questioned. You would find it difficult to get an exhumation order on the strength of those few words William wrote. Were they dated? – were they signed?'

'No.'

He shook his head again. 'It will hardly stand up. I doubt that any of it would get past a Court of Enquiry. And do you want it to? Do you want it, Angus?'

'I want – ' Callum cut in. Samuel Lachlan silenced him with a lift of his hand.

'*You*, Angus. You have everything to consider before you make a move. The reputation of Mistress Sinclair. The good name of Cluain. The scandal that must attach to such a hearing, when a name like Lady Campbell's is involved. You would have every newspaper in England with its representative here. If once the accusation is made publicly – if even the present facts are brought out, you will never know a moment's peace again.'

'You are suggesting,' Callum said, 'that the whole thing be ignored? For the sake of hushing up a scandal!'

'Are you seeking vengeance, Callum – or justice?' Lachlan said. 'Consider your own mother, and her position in this. Justice is an abstract thing – but vengeance can become a monster that turns and consumes itself. The dead will not come back. The living will suffer, and, even so, the guilty may go unpunished. Think well about it. Perhaps it would be the better part of justice if your friend in Edinburgh were told that the mare had indeed grazed on poisonous herbage . . .'

'Then you mean me to stand up at an Enquiry and say that before my eyes the mare stumbled at the middle of the ford, and pitched them both down. *That* is what you want me to say? – and you call yourself a man of the law.'

'That much would be the truth. And it is because I am a man of the law that I count myself also a man of sense. It is revenge that is senseless, Callum. You have lost your . . .' He stumbled over the difficult words. '. . . the woman you love. Your natural instinct is to hit back. Think of those you will have to injure with that action – and this girl, *if* she is guilty, I think – yes, I think this girl would go free. Her kind do. She would make a most impressive witness in the hands of a good advocate. Juries are impressionable. Set her beside your mother – I beg your pardon, Mistress Sinclair, but this must be said. Your mother will be spoken of as the one-time lover of Angus Macdonald. Set this girl beside the story of your liaison with Lady Campbell. Beside those facts, this girl will appear as innocent as a babe. I know juries, Callum. They judge – but they do not always give justice.'

'I will face what I must,' Mairi Sinclair said. 'Do not consider me in this. "Blessed are they who hunger and thirst after justice, for they – " '

'It is the Bible that is abstract here, not justice,' Callum said to her. 'For God's sake – I *must* consider you, since you've never considered yourself.'

Morag stepped away from my grandfather, and paused in the doorway. She raised both her arms until her hands rested on the doorframe. Her confidence was supreme. 'Well, then, I will leave you to your considerations. And let us hope that you will hear the sense of what Mr Lachlan has said. For believe me, I will make it hard on all of you. I will be just as Mr Lachlan says I will be – I will be that and more. And you will all rue the day you raised a voice against me.' Then her contempt got the better of her control.

'You are fools – all of you! But you, Callum – you are the greatest fool of all. You did not see what was before your eyes. You would not stoop to pick up what was under your hand. There was Cluain, which you could have demanded as a right. And there was me, whom you could have had for the asking. And what did you choose? Your wilful, prideful ways. Cluain was thrown away because it would have meant a few years of putting up with that old man there. I was not good enough for you – you preferred that foolish woman who could give you nothing but her body. You did not see me beneath your feet, for gazing up at the sky. Like that hawk you fly. Well, your pride is like that bird's, and you look too high. But you will fall to the ground, as she must, some day. Och, you will fall. Believe me, you will fall.'

Then she lowered her arms, and very gently closed the door behind her.

When she was gone, Mairi Sinclair moved, almost mechanically, to build up the fire. In silence we all watched her poke the embers and lay on more peat and wood. Then she went to where the Bible still lay open; she closed it with great care, locked it, and then she took the bunch of keys to my grandfather.

'The keys, Master.'

It was as if she were indicating that the ritual of Cluain would continue, must continue. It was more enduring than the present storm. Then she went back to her place at the end of the table, and waited.

Callum turned and said quietly to me, 'Kirsty . . . Kirsty, you have come all the way from China for this . . . for *this*.'

I stretched out my hand to him and once again touched him. It was not the touch of desire, but of knowing, of loving and knowing the love returned. It was not now desire; I knew I had his trust.

'Yes, for this. And worth it – for *this*.'

How does one mark the end of one relationship, and enter another? With no further words, Callum and I did in those moments. They were the last moments of grace we had.

My grandfather went slowly back to his place on the settle. For long minutes he stared into the fire. 'That is your true opinion, Samuel – that we should leave things be. Not attempt to prosecute the girl . . .'

'It is.'

He sighed. 'William is gone. Better leave him in peace.' The sigh was like a faint echo of the wind outside, a gusting, moaning sound. 'Perhaps it might be the better thing to leave ourselves whatever peace we may yet be permitted. Perhaps better to forget it all. Forget Ferguson, forget Cameron's and Macquarie's. Perhaps Kirsty is right. Expansion is just to become another Ferguson. Perhaps peace is what we need. There are not so many years of Cluain left to me. We will try to hold on to our senses – and perhaps to gain our peace. Honour – honour I let slip from me many years ago. I could have had a son. I have no son . . .' His great eyebrows hooked together as he looked at Callum. 'That is so, is it not? I have no son?' It was the final question.

Callum got to his feet, and went to the decanter and poured for himself. He drank at one gulp. 'That is so, Mr Macdonald. You have no son. I will go, when I am permitted to. I must. I will live only so long as I can live freely – come freely, go freely. My falcon is mine only so long as she chooses to be. The day she chooses to go on the wind, to fly on, and never return, then she is mine no longer. We live together on those terms. *I* can live no other way. And when I fall, I will fall hard, as Morag said. I know it – I accept it. I can be no permanent part of Cluain. That burden must fall on Kirsty.'

He replaced his glass. 'And now, Mr Macdonald, I am going up to my cottage. I will wait to hear from you. It is *you* who must go to Gavin Campbell and give him your reasons for proceeding or not proceeding with this thing. I have told him what I know. And whatever you say, whatever your arguments, it must ultimately be he who decides in the matter. If he says I am to tell the whole story at the Enquiry, then I will. And all of us must bear the consequences. If you want to preserve this peace you suddenly crave, for once Cluain will have to make common cause with Ballochtorra. It rests with him – and with you. Good night, Mr Macdonald.'

When he reached the door he turned and looked at me. 'Good night, Kirsty. Good night!' The way he spoke, it might just as well have been goodbye.

He still hesitated in the doorway, as though there was something he had still to say. Then the door of the kitchen passage crashed open, and banged against the wall. The wind of it swept through the room, and sent the candle flickering wildly.

Neil Smith, red-faced and frantic, glared in upon us. 'Is it deaf you all are? Are you so gone in your drink you cannot hear or see? Get out of here and get the place roused. Can you not hear the screams of the horses? The stable's afire!'

I suppose we all cried or shouted something in that first second: I knew only my own word, 'Ailis . . . !'

2

We should have heard the horses – except that their screams seemed almost part of the wind, the howl of its gusts. The tumult of our hearts inside that room had been too great to allow other sounds, perhaps we had, as Neil Smith said, been too far gone – but not in drink. He had seen, he shouted back to us as we ran through the kitchen passage, the glow from the window of his cottage. And the high garden wall had kept the same sight from us.

'Never mind water – the horses first,' Callum shouted. He seemed to have taken charge; my grandfather was momentarily bewildered. 'And you, Kirsty, run up to Farquharson's cottage and rouse them out. Have them send the lads on to the other cottages. We need every man here.'

As he raced to help Neil Smith open up the doors of the loose boxes, I caught at his arm. He checked impatiently. 'Ailis first,' I said. 'Ailis.'

'Very well – Ailis!'

And then my grandfather came to life. He rushed to join the two men, and for a moment I stood and watched, wondering if it could be done. And what had I asked Callum? – his own pony was probably tethered in one of the empty stalls. But we were fortunate in Cluain's stables. Built of stone, like the distillery and warehouses, with slate roof, and all the loose boxes opening into the yard, instead of two rows of stalls into a central passage, as it would have been in a bigger stable. It was the hay that was the danger; the hay was alight in the lofts above, stray wisps were blowing in the wind, and pieces falling among the bedding straw of the fear-maddened horses. Most of the animals were untethered, but it needed skill to get them to back away out of the boxes when a rain of fired hay seemed to fall between them and the freedom of the yard. But one or two, those of uncertain temper, were tethered, and someone would have to go past those lunging heels and take the halter and turn and lead them out. In the last instant before I started running I saw Callum pull off his coat. Ailis, sensible creature that she was, was already free, and retreating into the kindly darkness beyond the roaring threat. Then I saw Callum plunge past the heels of the worst of the huge Clydesdales, the one called Trumpeter, and fling his coat over the crazed animal's eyes. The fight was on. I didn't look any more. A single blow from one of those enormously powerful legs, and Callum would not live.

I saw something else, though, as I ran. Morag stood alone in the middle of the stableyard, just where the tidal edge of the light from the blaze fell upon her. She stood quite still, calm in the midst of the clatter of the hooves of the freed horses and the calls of the men, wrapped in her plaid against the wind, watching as if it were some interesting spectacle, but none of her business. Perhaps it wasn't – now. She glanced at me as I ran past her, but she made no attempt to move, no attempt either to leave or to take some action to help. I knew it was useless to urge her.

Before I reached John Farquharson's cottage the door had opened, and he was out, still buttoning his trousers over his night-shirt. 'I've already sent the two lads up the road, mistress,' he called to me. 'I've told them that *everyone* is to come. We'll get the horses out all right, but the building will be hard to save. The pump is ready in the cooperage – but we'll have to get the line down to the river . . .' His words trailed off as he ran past me. From the doorway his wife called, 'I'm dressing, mistress. The lads will bring whatever women can leave their bairns. It must not touch the distillery, mistress.'

It was all of them, it was the whole world of Cluain, their jobs, their families, their loyalties. And as I turned to follow John back, I glanced upwards, and the first lights were beginning to come on at Ballochtorra. There would be more men on the way. As I came back within the shelter of the walls of the farthest warehouse I could already hear, distinguishable among all the clamour, Big Billy's honk of alarm and indignation; but he was well away from it, separated by the width of the road, and Neil Smith would never forget him and his flock. And there, in the darkness which was already beginning to be lightened by the glow of the fire, I felt a nudge on the shoulder, a muzzle rub along my cheek. 'Ailis . . . is this as close as you'll come? Well, stay then, good girl. And don't wander too far off.' I did not attempt to tether her to any of the posts or gates; she would feel more easy that way and I did not have to worry that she would stray far from Cluain. 'There'll be horses to look for all over the strath tomorrow . . .'

And there would be. I counted the open doors of the loose boxes, saw the horror of the inferno in the hay, above in the lofts and on the floor. There was a series of ominous explosive sounds, like the retorts of a gun, as individual slates cracked in the heat. But I could see no sign of a horse still left within those fiery shells. I thought they were all clear, and most of them had disappeared into the friendly darkness. Some would have jumped fences they had never thought to try before, some would stay by the roadside, a safe distance from the fire, some we would have to search the hills for, and some, too panic stricken, would injure themselves, and have to be put down. There, in the midst of the small crowd of men that had now reached the yard from the cottages, and the growing number of women joining them, I knew the first real moment of fear. There had not been time until now to take in the full implication of what yet could happen. And I cursed the wind that blew, and brought the heat of the flames to my face.

By the time the pump and hose line to the river was hooked up, the men had arrived from Ballochtorra. The stable hands, coachmen and gardeners went to work as if they knew what they were doing; the indoor servants were almost more hindrance than help, and I could hear my grandfather cursing one or two of them. It was a big, wheeled handpump, kept for such emergencies, and like everything else at Cluain, old, but in good repair. The river was in full spate after the rains, so we did not, after the pump was ready, lack water. What was needed was the pressure and the energy to raise it the height to the buildings themselves, high enough to wet down the roofs of the house and the distillery. I suddenly knew then the good reasoning behind the placing of the warehouses on the other side of the road. Distance now was everything. It worked for and against us. The distance to the river, which protected the house and distillery when the river was in flood, seemed now impossibly far to pump the water, the distance for the jet of water to reach the tower room of the house was too great. But distance from the other buildings protected the warehouses. All the men took turns at the pump, while the others rested; the hay in the loft of the stables was now consumed, but the timbers were on fire. One of the faces I saw rushing by me in the now smoky haze that overhung us, intent on making his way down to the river, was Gavin Campbell. He didn't see me, and I didn't try to detain him. I stood for a moment with Samuel Lachlan, who leaned, trembling, against the garden wall. I tried to comfort him; he just kept shaking his head. 'Such a loss! — such a loss! All the horses saved though . . . Sinclair had to fight with those two brutes . . . Angus is doing too much. He's too old . . . too old. *I'm* too old. There should be another pump . . . Angus should have had another pump.'

'There wouldn't be men to work it,' I said.

'Another pump,' he insisted. 'Oh, I'm too old.' And he was. His frail body still shook from the exertion of that first effort to open up the stables and free the horses, shook from excitement and fear. At last I managed to persuade him to give up his post at the garden wall, and come around into the road outside the house. There, incongruously, he was ensconced in a chair from the drawing-room. The small group of women who had come from the distillery cottages, and some of the young maids from Ballochtorra, come to watch the spectacle, had been organized by Mairi Sinclair, who was now wearing a black coat over her nightgown. Methodically, she was overseeing the removal of the most valuable pieces of the furniture from the ground floor of the house. It was no small task. The great hall table had to be left – it would have needed eight men to lift it. And so also the sideboard from the dining-room. I myself brought out the Bible, and set it down on a settle placed opposite Samuel Lachlan. 'Watch it now, Mr Lachlan – and should I go and start bringing the ledgers and files from the distillery office? – no, I can't. My grandfather has the keys.'

'The distillery! The distillery will not take fire – not the distillery!' He was imploring.

'A precaution, only . . .'

'A precaution, oh, yes.'

'Since you are here, Mr Lachlan,' Mairi Sinclair broke in, 'would it trouble you to place your eye on these things. That light-minded lot down from Ballochtorra might take a fancy to one or two.' She had loaded the settle with silver trays, and teapots and jugs and tongs. There, under the settle, were the fire-dogs with the Cawdor crest. My grandfather's chess set was laid beside them.

'Yes, mistress – yes,' Samuel Lachlan replied. I had never heard such meekness from him. The stable was smoking now, smoke that even the wind did not immediately clear; smoke full of menace, because no one could see the swift lick of flame that might still curve about a timber. While I stood there, and Samuel Lachlan huddled in his chair, a stream of water from the hose, meant to be directed towards the roof of the house, fell short of it, and reached over the garden wall, and on to me. I staggered for a moment; it did not touch the old man. Suddenly, now that the flames were gone, and the heat no longer there, I was drenched and cold. Then, leaving Samuel Lachlan, I walked around the corner of the garden wall. The smouldering building was hard to see – the wind drove the smoke into my eyes, and they watered. I shivered in my wet dress.

'They all were got out, Kirsty.' Callum's voice beside me. I looked up. 'Ailis was first. But I haven't seen her.'

'Ailis is all right. She is taking care of herself. She always does.'

One side of his face was horribly swollen; even though it was darkened by soot, I could see the distortion. And there was blood, already caked and dried, at the hairline above his left eye.

'You've been hurt!'

'No. I was slammed into a post getting one of the Clydesdales out. But no horse perished, Kirsty. That's what matters. Your grandfather will have to build new stables, but his heart will not be broken. If we stand by till the wind has dropped, and keep the pressure on the hose up, the distillery and the house are safe. We can just hope – or pray, as Mr Lachlan seems to be doing – that no spark takes hold on the distillery. Every piece of wood there is saturated by forty years of alcohol.'

'How did the fire begin?'

'Time enough to ask that when we know we have it beaten. Everything will wait on that.'

'Callum . . . ?'

He had already turned away from me, answering some call from the midst of the men. There was some trouble with the hose; my grandfather was ordering it to be extended, but to make the coupling the pressure would have to be reduced.

'Callum . . .' He was gone. His figure melted into the group about the hose. I didn't even know what I had meant to say to him. It was part of the chaos of that whole scene – I saw and knew only parts of it, fragments, my impressions scattered like the burning hay in the wind, like the distraught horses dispersed over the countryside. Then I pulled myself up. I was standing and staring, but doing nothing, less useful than Samuel Lachlan, who at least guarded part of Cluain's treasures. So then I went into the house and placed myself under Mairi Sinclair's direction. She nodded to me, as if she knew my helplessness. 'Go to your grandmother's room, and bring whatever you can that seems valuable – take one of the trays to carry on. I have cleared the silver from the pantry. If you see anyone upstairs in the house who is not the wife or child of one of the Cluain workers, order them out, or we shall have small items missing when we come to count.'

'It won't spread to the house,' I said, even as I went off to obey her. 'They just have to watch the stable now, and keep wetting it down.'

She answered me with my own word. 'Precautions . . .'

So I went to my grandmother's room, and began passing out to the waiting arms and aprons and trays of the Cluain women and children the precious things that Mairi Sinclair had stored away there, all the softening touches that the rest of the house lacked, the mirrors, the pictures, the little ornaments, the rolled-up rugs. These last were carried down between two of the strongest women who offered themselves. The little girls were given the ornaments

to carry, one at a time, carefully, down the stairs. I grew weary
of it, because, looking from the window, it all seemed unnecessary.
The fire was not out completely, but it was controlled and there
was nothing very combustible left to feed it. They would have to
keep watch on it all night, and when daylight came, to start cutting
away at the smoking timbers.

'Shall we start to take down the books, Mistress Kirsty?' one
of the women asked me. I looked at the two bookcases there,
crowded with volumes, and decided against it. There was a sudden
sound of china shattering on the staircase, and the instant, nervous
giggling. Well, it was inevitable that some things would be broken,
and everyone was not familiar with those strange stairs, curving,
and without a rail. It occurred to me then, when I thought about
the books, to go down and ask Mairi Sinclair if she had removed
her own herb and medicine books from the herb room. How one
missed Morag in all this; her quickness and intelligence would have
been worth the strength of six of these women.

I went and spoke to Mairi Sinclair about clearing the herb room.
She shook her head. 'Not unless it is necessary. After what has
been said tonight, do you think I want to unlock that door?'

'But your books – your own records! They are more valuable
than anything that's upstairs.'

'Perhaps it would have been better for us all if they had never
been. But go, mistress, and stay with Mr Lachlan. I will try to
bring a hot drink soon. He does not seem well. One of the women
will come with me to the kitchen and make tea to pass out. The
men need something now. I will tell the others to go – they are
getting careless. A vase has been broken, and the leg of a chair
damaged. The frame of a mirror chipped . . .' She grieved over a
mirror, she who never looked into one. I did as she said, and went
to stay with Samuel Lachlan. Before I went I brought from the
passage the Inverness cape for him. He accepted it about his
shoulders without comment. He sat, bemused, amidst the great
jumble of what had been taken from the house – china, chairs,
bedding, silver, like a strange old spider in the middle of a fantastic
web of collections. Who would have thought that the bare starkness
of Cluain had contained so many riches?

I stood with him for a while, talking about anything that came
to mind, but he hardly seemed to hear me. He was muttering under
his breath, his own litany of incantations about carelessness and
waste, of bad stewardship. 'But it's only the stables, Mr Lachlan,'
I said impatiently. 'We have been lucky it was no more.'

'Waste!' was the only reply I got. I went to the corner of the wall. Here the wind blew straight at me, and the smoke was carried with it. Ironically, now that the hay no longer blazed, it had been necessary to bring lanterns so that the men could see to move about. Clouds were scudding before the wind, blotting out the light that might have helped them, but too swiftly, I thought, to bring rain. Rain would have helped us, and yet made the operation more difficult. Down at the river they would be standing in mud. I wondered where Gavin Campbell was. I wondered if I should go and ask my grandfather about taking the books from the distillery office. I didn't know where he was – or Callum. I started for the thickest group of men standing before the ruin of the stable.

Halfway across the yard I heard Neil Smith's voice – his tone carrying all the agony of a man who sees his life's work betrayed before his eyes.

'God Almighty! – Look, Macdonald! – look! The back end of the warehouses!'

I was amongst those who crowded to the road to look along it, and there, in the warehouse farthest from the yard and the distillery, was the terrible glow. The iron bars across the high, small windows were outlined against it.

I was one of the ones near to Neil Smith as we gathered closer to the warehouses. The main doors were flung open wide – I think it was he and I together who rushed to free Big Billy and his flock from the pen close to those doors. In the first minutes the big gander went about biting every leg he found available, unwilling to believe that he and all his family were not the personal objectives of the holocaust.

It had become a holocaust. There is no way that water can fight spirits once they are alight. Useless to get up the extra length of hose, useless to urge the men at the river to pump. Water was only the means of diluting the stream of fire, perhaps spreading it farther. It already flowed, the deadly stream released by the explosion of casks soaked for long years in sherry and whisky; it ignited the columns and beams already impregnated by contact with the saturated casks. And all the doors – the doors big enough to allow for the passage of the distillery drays, had been opened right through to the end, where the fire had begun. With the wind blowing, it created a natural funnel for the flames, a lateral chimney by which fire fed on fire.

I witnessed the anguish of Neil Smith as he came out of his cottage, after the geese had been released. I remember the grip of his hand, biting into my arm, the old broken nails still having the power to hurt. 'God help me! I didn't think to take the warehouse keys with me when I went running to the house first. Someone has been in and taken them from the board. Look at the doors – standing wide open to the world! It's the end of me!' Then he looked up, realizing at last whose arm he clutched. 'It's the end of Cluain, lass!'

My grandfather directed the added lengths of hose to be run along the road at the side of the warehouses, and the water to be played upon the roof – but there was nothing he could do about what was happening inside. The small jet of water was futile against the force of energy set alight within. There was one great explosion in the end warehouse, and suddenly, through the ventilation holes at floor level, the stream of fire flowed. It followed the drainage channels, and finally reached the place where the burn flowed beside the buildings. It caught. The burn itself was afire, fed by the endless stream of alcohol from inside the warehouse. It was a sight I could not wholly believe in, even though I saw it myself. The burn ran with fire, and where it was channelled under the road, at the little bridge, there was a weird gap of blackness between the two fiercely burning streams. It ran on down to the river, finally to be diluted by that much greater torrent, to nothingness.

For a moment, close to my ear, I heard Callum's shout. The roar of the flames was already greater than anything the stable fire had produced. 'It's still in the end warehouse. The doors have to be shut. It's the only hope we have to save anything. If I can close the doors we have a chance to soak them with enough water to stop the spread to the rest. Go and tell your grandfather to bring the hoses up through the warehouses. I'll try to close the doors one by one.'

He was gone, escaping my clutching hands, escaping my cries. Neil Smith and I stood and watched as he ran through the open main door of the warehouses, the stacked casks high on each side making his figure ever smaller and smaller. Did we see it – did we actually see it – or was it fantasy? In that last second before he reached the end doors – those massive doors had to be swung and closed against the force of the heat and energy generated within that inferno, the draught that sucked the fire in upon itself and stoked it – did Neil Smith and I see that figure for a second? – that slender figure with fiery hair, the momentary dark figure silhouetted against the blaze, the figure of a young woman, who only began to run as the fire raced to engulf her? Was it she whom Callum also saw? What else could have made him rush within the raging territory of the last warehouse, beyond the door that might have meant safety? We never really knew – Neil Smith and I. What we thought we saw was Callum's running figure, and then the shape that might have been Morag, suddenly outlined, helplessly caught, the sleepwalker awakened too late from sleep. They did not meet, those two figures – I would swear to it. Before Callum reached the last doors, the end warehouse, feeding totally upon itself, erupted. The whole mass went in one explosion of blazing alcohol. An enormous fire ball shot up, devouring support columns, beams, and roof. The air all around was sucked towards the dreadful centre. Slates crashed in upon the burning casks, the ventilation holes choked, so that the liquid spilled back upon itself, finding other ways to run, into the forward warehouses. The door to the last warehouse was engulfed before Callum could reach it. And after that, there was no distinguishing one part from another. It raced like the wind, explosion upon explosion, the slates raining down on the men who stood dumbfounded in the road at the side of the building, helpless, speechless. All I could feel was the tightening grip of Neil Smith's fingers upon my arm. No smoke now, but fire consuming fire, raging, pouring, as fuel was added to unquenchable fuel.

'Callum . . . ?'

It seemed so few minutes before it was consumed. The whole stored wealth of Cluain disappeared before our eyes, and in the midst of it was the man who might have been its future wealth. We never even had a glimpse of Callum again.

My grandfather went on. I don't know from what source he gathered his strength, but he did. He saw forty years consumed in minutes, but he still had the energy to direct the men to bring the hose back to the distillery and wet it down. The distillery before the house. Then the house was again soaked, stone walls and roof, a fairly hurried operation because they had to return to the distillery, which was much more vulnerable. The sparks from the warehouse flew upwards, and I stood rooted, dreading to see the first glow from within the distillery. But with a fire so hot, there was very little left of the warehouses – it was quick, and powerful and sure. It flared and died almost as rapidly. And my grandfather continued to direct the whole operation to safeguard the distillery as though he were unmoved by the holocaust which consumed his life and his work, and by the cries of Neil Smith, who watched his neat cottage, attached to the warehouse, also disappear.

It wasn't until I told my grandfather – when the fire in the warehouse seemed to fold in upon itself, when the burn ceased to run with fire, that Callum had gone into the warehouse, and was dead, that he turned aside. Without an order to any other man to take over, he abruptly turned aside. He went back into the house, into the dining-room, Samuel Lachlan grabbing unavailingly at him. We stood there, still, unspeaking, and my grandfather kept his back turned to the windows, so that even the enormous, dying glow of the warehouses was just, for his eyes, a reflection on the walls.

We moved some chairs back in, Mairi Sinclair and I, and she poked some life into the peat turfs, and laid some fresh. I remember forcing my grandfather down into a chair, keeping his back carefully to the garden, so that he might not watch the glow that still lighted the sky. Gavin Campbell came; I don't think he said anything, just took my grandfather's hand for a moment. My grandfather didn't seem to notice his presence. I helped Mairi Sinclair bring bread and ham from the kitchen, and we served it on the thick kitchen crockery. She seemed now not to care for the good china stacked up outside in the road, or Cluain's silver. I also helped her carry out food for the men standing about in the stableyard, still pumping water on the distillery. There were plenty of women about in the kitchen would have done the task just as well, but it seemed right that if my grandfather was not there, I should appear.

Then I came back to the dining-room, and began to pour whisky into glasses that one of the women had brought in from the road. I passed it round, and to Neil Smith, who still stood in the doorway, halfway between our group and the men in the yard. He really belonged nowhere, and his world was just as much finished as ours.

'Grandfather,' I said, 'I have sent whisky with the food to the men. It grows cold, and they must still keep wetting down the distillery.'

He looked at me with dulled eyes. 'Aye – that's right. Don't spare it, Kirsty. I have a few casks in the cellar – Excise paid, mind you, Neil Smith.' He rose to his feet and went to pour more whisky from the decanter. 'No, let us not spare it this night. We might as well drink the best – here, Samuel, your glass.' The old man was rocking in his chair, sipping at the whisky, and keeping up a continual little moaning sound, that might be his substitute for weeping. 'And you, Campbell, you drink Cluain's whisky this night, and savour it. Because when these few casks are done, there will be no more for a long time. And tell Callum . . . Tell Callum Sinclair – My God! – Callum . . .'

Now he stopped. His back was towards us as he stood at the sideboard. The action was so slow that I actually saw the glass slipping in his hand, and his desperate fight to hold on to it, and himself. Then it fell to the ground and smashed. He held himself upright, hands pressed on the edge of the sideboard, for a few seconds longer, then that burly body crashed down, and one hand lay among the broken glass and the spilled liquid of his life.

II

Two days later Angus Macdonald was buried in the plot between his wife and his mother Christina. Next to Christina was William's grave, and beside that was the grave of Callum Sinclair.

Mairi Sinclair had protested. 'You cannot. It is not right, now.'

'If it is not right now, it shall never be. Is it not now time we all laid down our pride and our fears, and admitted to the truth? I intend Callum to lie beside William, and close to his father. And his headstone will be marked Callum Sinclair Macdonald – as my grandfather wrote it in the Bible. It is long ago time that all who care to know, should know. He is dead – shall we bury him in some corner of the kirkyard? He must lie with his family. Do you dare to say no?'

If she wept, I could not tell it. She was as silent and withdrawn as ever. How silent the whole house was. Samuel Lachlan sat in his chair by the fire; how frail he seemed after the bulk of my grandfather; how deep was the quiet without Morag's voice to break it. I made my journeys to feed Giorsal, and she was becoming tamer to my hand. I had John shoot me a rabbit or a pigeon for her each day. I stood in the shed with Giorsal, stroking her with the feather, as Callum had done, and it was there I did my weeping alone, where no one could see, or hear. Cluain in these days had need of a calm presence. I could no more afford to indulge grief than Mairi Sinclair.

Gavin sent the Ballochtorra landau for the journey to the kirk-yard; it had to be borrowed, since the Cluain trap had gone in the stable fire. But The Sunday Lad had been found, and it was he who was between the shafts, not one of Ballochtorra's horses. Gavin came with the carriage to Cluain to escort us to the kirk, and to take Samuel Lachlan. Again there was the confrontation between myself and Mairi Sinclair when I insisted that she break the habit of a lifetime, and ride beside me.

'We are burying your son, and my grandfather this day, Mistress Sinclair, in the same family grave – marking them with the same name. Will you have me pass you on the road as you walk to your son's funeral? A time of change has come at Cluain. It is as well to recognize it.'

'Yes, a time of change. It is as well to recognize it. I will be packing my things tomorrow, mistress. I would be grateful if you could keep my books for a little time until I have found a place to take them. Of my other belongings, there is little enough.'

'Your books will stay at Cluain forever – as you will, Mistress Sinclair. I think your grief has turned your senses.'

'I cannot stay where I am not wanted. *You* cannot want me here. I take no charity . . .'

'None is offered. Cluain has need of both of us, and well you know it. It is unthinkable that you should leave. I do not offer you charity – or ease. Cluain will use both of us hard. It will make its demands, as it always has done. You do not exist away from Cluain. As my grandfather could not – nor Callum. We have lost very much. Let us not lose more than we need.'

All she did was nod, and turn away. But when the Ballochtorra carriage arrived I found her waiting in the hall, wearing, as always, the plaid about her head. We did not speak all the way to the kirk-yard, nor back again, but she rode beside me.

Those two burials were hard. The anchor of Cluain was gone, and, almost, its hope. I wondered where I would turn now. With my hand on his arm, and more to support him than anything else, I felt Samuel Lachlan tremble. And then I looked across Callum's open grave at Gavin's face, and remembered that beyond the crowd that surrounded us now, just across the path, Margaret lay. The grass had not even started to sprout on that grave; and she lay so close to two men who had loved her. And Gavin's eyes met mine, then; we both seemed to know what the other thought, and the thought was the same.

Gavin escorted us back to Cluain, and Samuel Lachlan, as though he dreaded the thought of the empty, quiet house, asked him to come in.

'Angus was more than ten years younger than me,' Samuel Lachlan said. 'I had not thought to be the one left.'

And then he picked up the Inverness paper, which had arrived while we were gone. There was a picture of the remains of the warehouse at Cluain, and an article about the fire which I did not even want to read. But the main headline was reserved for something else. PANIC RUSH TO SELL SHARES. FERGUSON'S BANKRUPT?

He held it towards Gavin. 'What do you make of this?'

'What am I to make of it? I'm sorry for James Ferguson. I'm not sorry for myself and my son.'

'You mean you're *glad*?' Samuel was dumbfounded; how could anyone not mourn the fall of a capitalist's kingdom?

'I think it may be my son's salvation. Ferguson can make no claim on him now. There is nothing for Ferguson money to buy. And Ferguson does not understand any other relationship, so he will leave my son alone. Jamie will be what I am – that is, a poor man. I think he will be no worse for it.'

'But – Ballochtorra . . . ?'

'Ballochtorra cannot be run without money. The servants have had their notice – I gave them that the day my wife was buried, before I knew about Ferguson's difficulties. I suppose, if Ferguson goes into liquidation, the receiver might justly claim the contents of Ballochtorra – the horses and all the rest of it. But the title to the house and lands has to stay with me. If it's possible to find a buyer, I'll try to sell the house. The land, such as it is, must be kept for Jamie. There will be no gamekeepers, of course. But the grouse moors are there, and will stay, even though they might not provide a worthy day's shooting for a prince. They could be rented perhaps . . . We'll see.'

'And you?' Samuel was so shaken by the events of the last day that his reserve and probity seemed to have dropped from him. I had not thought him capable of asking such questions of someone who was almost a stranger to him.

Gavin took the tea I poured, and munched on the ham sandwich as if he suddenly found himself hungry. 'We'll do as I've always wanted to. There's a little money – I'll borrow the rest – and I'll drain the only piece of Ballochtorra land that's worth trying to do anything with. It could raise a crop or two – it *could* make pastures. We would not be hungry, Jamie and I. And the gatehouse will soon be empty.'

'The gatehouse!' Samuel Lachlan was thunderstruck. 'And you are the heir to the Marquis of Rossmuir!'

Gavin actually laughed. I heard the sound with pleasure; it broke the silence of mourning in this house, a sound that would help to bury the past.

'And the present Marquis of Rossmuir wishes he had some place as comfortable, no doubt. Though I can't speak for the old gentleman; I've never met him. But it will do very well for Jamie and me . . . until we can sell the house, or find a tenant. And then the money will build us a small house on the land I want to farm. I know the place where I want to build. It is out of sight of Ballochtorra – which is no great loss. Jamie will fish the river, and we will be able to keep a gun or two. I've always noticed that small houses are warmer than big ones. We will manage, Jamie and me. And he will not go to school in England. It is the one piece of news that has made him happy since his mother died. He will have a pony – not the thoroughbred he has now. A garron – one of the kind we breed around here. Far safer – far tougher. What he really longs for, of course, is that I should buy Ailis for him.'

'I will never sell Ailis.'

'You suppose I don't know that? But let him dream. In time he will love his own pony – and he will love it better for having to take care of it himself. So you see, Mr Lachlan, that Ferguson's going bankrupt is a bad blow for James Ferguson, but I cannot think it is wholly a disaster for his grandson.'

'But . . . he will be an *earl*!'

Again Gavin laughed. Why did the sound affect me so much? It was like the spring of hope, of new life. He saw no adversity before him, or Jamie. I sipped my tea and thought of his remark about small houses, and how he and Margaret had lost each other in the vastness of Ballochtorra.

'Yes, an earl. I must try to explain it to him soon. That poor old man can't live much longer. They say he is pitifully weak, and can hardly see or hear. So Jamie will be an earl. I think his grandfather has given him the impression that a coronet will appear like magic – a real coronet. But children forget easily. If he can fish his river, and ride his pony on his own moors, I think the coronet may not matter so much. I'm sorry his grandfather will think it is such a come-down for his only grandchild. But James Ferguson will never see it any other way. Without money and power, he is a ruined man in every respect. If I give my life to it, I will see that Jamie does not become that kind of man.'

Then he took his hat and went. I saw him motion to the coach-man to give up the reins, and he himself took them. The sullen look on the man's face indicated that he had had his notice along with the others, and thought also that Sir Gavin had indeed come down in the world, and had no business to appear so cheerful about it.

'I will send John tomorrow with the landau,' I called to him. 'He can walk The Sunday Lad back.'

'Use it as long as you like. Ferguson's can't begrudge you that little favour. I don't think the Receiver will be in by tomorrow.'

I went back to Samuel Lachlan at the fire, and suddenly the house was silent and empty again. I fought, in a moment's panic, against the depression that started to come over me, the loneliness, the sense that now the fight was just beginning. And I had need of Gavin's laugh, his cheer, the sense of courage he imparted. But I had to go back to the old man by the fire, and try to give to him what I had hardly begun to scrape together for myself.

'Extraordinary!' Samuel muttered. 'I do believe he means it!'

'Means what?'

'He really doesn't care about the money. Imagine having to do without Ferguson's money, and not caring!'

'It's possible some men are like that. Like Callum – who didn't want Cluain. *He* would have parted with what he loved rather than be a James Ferguson. It's possible, Mr Lachlan . . . it's possible.'

He shook his head. 'I don't understand it. Give me some whisky, Kirsty. The kirkyard was cold . . .'

And he warmed his bones before the fire, and on Cluain's whisky, remembering, perhaps, what my grandfather had said – that when those few casks were empty, there would be no more until Cluain's next distilling came of age. At that moment, I had no idea when that might be.

2

Even after they combed the wreckage of the warehouse there was nothing found that even suggested the body of Morag MacPherson. 'But I saw her!' Neil Smith kept saying. He repeated it again and again, to the Excise officers who came to investigate the fire, and to the police. 'I saw her there, right at the end, in the last warehouse where the fire started. And that was a laid fire – the doors opened all through like that. Deliberately set. Well, Mistress Howard here will tell you the same thing. She stood beside me – '

I had to tell them that I could not swear that we had seen Morag MacPherson in those seconds – something that appeared to be the figure of a woman outlined against the inferno behind her. The blaze had been so intense it had almost seemed to sear the eyes. Callum, I knew, had never reached her – if she had been there.

'If she had been there,' one exciseman said, 'we would have found the remains. No one could have escaped from where you thought you saw her. And if it is arson . . .'

'It *was* arson! Do I go leaving my warehouses open to who wishes to walk inside? Is it for this I have built my reputation in the service? I tell you that girl started the blaze in the stables as a distraction – and then she waited her chance to start the fire that really destroyed Cluain.' Neil Smith was indignant and shamed.

And afterwards, when he had walked off up the road to the cottage of one of the workers where he was temporarily lodged, the exciseman turned to me. 'Well, we all knew it was past time for Neil Smith to retire – but he *had* built a fine reputation in the service, and it being so quiet up here, and he never leaving the place – no family, no distractions, and never touched a dram in his life. But to go and leave the keys . . . no matter *what* was taking place outside the cottage. If the sky had been falling on him, he should have thought of his keys first. It will go badly with him, Miss Howard. He cannot expect to stay in the service now.'

'He will stay at Cluain, however,' I said. 'No one could imagine him leaving.'

'You will build again, then?' The man was looking at me with frank curiosity. 'You will go into production?'

'Why not?' I answered. 'There is a distillery, isn't there? The men haven't lost their skills overnight because of a fire! We will find warehousing.'

'It will have to be adequate, Miss Howard. Bonded is bonded. It must be secure, and with accommodation for Excise officers. It isn't like the old days, you know, when Mr Macdonald first set up. They say that in those days he had a fence and a shotgun. That sort of thing won't do now.'

'It will be done exactly as it should,' I retorted. 'Cluain has never been in trouble with the Excise, has it? It has never been short on quantities? Well – that is how it will go on.'

And the exciseman, staring at me, was wondering how it was to be done, just as I was. But he said no more about it. It was my business. No doubt the word would run through the whole Excise service that Angus Macdonald's granddaughter was just as tough and irascible as the old man, that he would not be dead while she lived. But I was not Angus Macdonald, and this was not the Cluain of forty years ago, a simpler, more trusting world, where things could begin small, and be permitted to grow. The distillery waited – but that was all. Its product had to be stored and guarded, it had to be serviced. There was so much, and it had to come from me.

But once I could bring myself to look beyond the fearful ruin of the warehouses, I was calmed. The world of Cluain was still here, damaged, but essentially the same. The sleek cattle grazed the river meadows, the barley was safely stored. This was no dubious heritage Angus Macdonald had left in my hands.

And as I went back to eat dinner with Samuel Lachlan after that interview with the exciseman and the police, I pondered the fate

of Morag. Had we really seen her, Neil Smith and I? Was it a
trick of the fire? – unnatural shadows thrown for a few seconds
only that had deceived us? No young body had been found crushed
and charred in the wreckage. It was not possible she had found
some other way out. There was no other way. I imagined her, as
calmly as she had stood in the stableyard watching the race to
bring the horses out, then going, in the midst of the incoherent
pattern of that first fire, into Neil Smith's cottage, taking the keys,
and making her way right back to the very end of the warehouses –
the place hardest to reach with the hose, the place where it would
least be noticed. And there setting the first small blaze, which she
knew would take hold. And then as calmly opening wide and
hooking back each set of doors as she returned through the building,
leaving the front door itself open to the wind. And then, with the
same unhurried calm, replacing the keys on Neil Smith's rack – for
that was where they had been when he had thought to look – just
before the fire took his cottage. He still held the keys to the
blackened, roofless ruin.

And where was Morag now? Had she just walked as far as
Grantown and taken the first train from there in the early morning?
– before news of the fire had come, before anyone thought to look
for a young girl? With a plaid half over her face, she would not
be in any way remarkable. I thought of her, and the future. She
would go, probably to Glasgow, and lose herself in its teeming
warrens until the search and enquiries about her would die away.
She could turn her hand to so many things, could Morag, and
her tongue and wit would not betray the background of Cluain.
But Morag did not care for crowded places. In time she would go
off – Canada or Australia. Clever as she was, and knowing her own
worth, she would not give herself to anyone who asked; when it
came to marriage, Morag would choose well. She was beautiful,
and young, and clever. And how her heart must have been filled
with rage and hate to do what she had done. It was formidable
to think of that lovely face, its skin flushing apricot in excitement
and passion, the shining red curls – and the kind of inner madness
of greed and cunning it had masked. She had dreamed of being
Mistress of Cluain, of having Callum. And yet, had I not dreamed
the same dream? How different were we? It was a sobering,
humbling thought.

I shivered in the September wind as I scurried across the yard
from the distillery office; light drops of rain blew into my face.
No, I did not think that Morag MacPherson had died in the fire.
Somewhere she went on, planning, under another name, a future

just as great as she had sought here at Cluain. And, being Morag, I thought it was very probable that she would find it.

3

I faced Samuel Lachlan with the facts as we sat before the fire that night.

'Mr Lachlan, I have told all the workers that they will stay on. I have told them that we might have to miss a season's production, and that they might have to turn their hands to anything that comes — building labourers, farm workers, anything that Cluain needs. But they need not leave their cottages, and their wages will be the same as if they worked in the distillery and the warehouses. I cannot let them go . . . they will be needed, more than needed, when we are back to full production.'

'And where will you get the money?'

'You will lend it to me, Mr Lachlan.'

'On what surety?'

'Cluain.'

'I charge a high interest rate. What would I do with Cluain if you fail?'

'If I fail you will own a fine farm – and distillery buildings. You will own the assets of Cluain.'

'The assets of Cluain would not pay me back what you need to start again. The insurance will cover what you will owe to the blenders whose whisky was stored in the warehouse, but Cluain's wealth rested in those barrels of unsold spirits which Angus Macdonald held for himself. Have you any idea how much money you are asking for?'

'No – I thought you would tell me.'

'You expect me to be broker and banker at the same time? You ask a lot, young woman.'

'Yes, I ask a lot. My grandfather asked a lot of you the day he walked into your office in Inverness and asked you to take his case for no payment, but the justice on which it rested. And then he borrowed from you to make his beginnings. Was he really asking for *less*, in those days, than I am asking for now?'

'But he was . . . well, he was Angus Macdonald.'

'And I am Angus Macdonald's granddaughter. You're going to say that a woman cannot run a distillery? Have any tried? Have any failed? Yes – I know, my great-grandmother failed, but she was on a poor little island out in the Hebrides. There was no Cluain for her.'

'If you were married . . .'

'If I were married I might be married to some fool who would spend your money foolishly. Men have failed also, Mr Lachlan. Ferguson's is now in the hands of the Receiver. A year ago, would you have said it could happen?'

'I told you I watched Ferguson closely. I heard the stories of him. And I never bought a penny share of his stock.'

'Would you buy *my* stock? Would you buy the stock and seed of Angus Macdonald? That is all I have to persuade you with. I am ignorant, yes – I'm too well aware of that. So have others been, and they have learned. Look at me, Mr Lachlan. Do you see any of Angus Macdonald in me? The men will stay with me, and I will learn – from you and from them. There are all those ledgers in my grandfather's office from which I will learn. I expect long days – and nights – of work. I welcome them. You will see no grand living here, Mr Lachlan. And no silk, even for Sundays. What do you say, Mr Lachlan?'

'It is a risk. A huge risk. And what is in it for me? I am old. I may be dead before you sell your first cask.'

'That too is a risk, Mr Lachlan. And what is in it for you? – am I presumptuous if I say that in it for you is the right to sit where you now sit, at Cluain's fireside – the right to guide Cluain, as you have done for forty years. You can always go back to your rooms in Inverness, Mr Lachlan – and I've no doubt I could go and find buyers. There would be buyers, I haven't any doubt, for a fine farm, and a distillery in good working order, with skilled distillery hands ready. Oh, I think there are plenty who would take it off my hands. Let us start with the Macquaries and the Camerons. *They* know the value of Cluain – even just as a name, a reputation. Yes, I think I could sell it all. And then you and I, Mr Lachlan, we both would have lost it. I would have some money in my pocket, instead of debts. And you would avoid a big risk. But what would we lose, both of us?'

'You will be cheated. Men will try to cheat you because you are a woman.'

'Let them try! They'll not do it a second time. Do you forget what I learned in China? There, I knew by exactly how much each was *allowed* to cheat. It is quite a skill, Mr Lachlan. Not learned in an accountant's office. And, yes, I will make mistakes with the farm – but I will listen to advice. Has no man ever left his crops too late? – or a storm come before they were ready? Well, these are the problems my grandfather fought, and I would want to try to fight. It would be easier if I did not. I would have money, and some comfort, and no doubt, in time, a husband who liked the bit of money I brought with me. And you would still have *your* money, safely invested wherever it is invested. Or we both can have Cluain. Which, Mr Lachlan – which?'

'You press me very hard, woman. Very hard.'

'I am Angus Macdonald's granddaughter, Mr Lachlan. Would you expect anything else?'

'Yes – you are Angus Macdonald's granddaughter. And that is where I will put my money.'

I went and got him a whisky. 'It is your own private reserve, now, Mr Lachlan. For as long as Cluain's whisky lasts, it is for you alone. For ourselves, for the first years, we will make do with an inferior product. You will live – you will live to drink these last casks, and by that time the first of Cluain's new distilling will be fit for drinking. You are like Ailis. You will live to be a terrible great age – at Cluain.'

'Ah –' He shrugged off the words. 'There will be little enough time for me to be at Cluain. Do you realize, Kirsty, how I will have to work to get this money to lend you? I must be back to Inverness tomorrow to draw up the papers. Everything must be in order. I will be back next week . . .'

And every week, I thought, so long as he lived. And he must be ever welcome at Cluain's fireside – however old, however irritable. Angus Macdonald's granddaughter must always make sure of that.

12

It was early the next morning when I rode up to Callum's cottage on Ailis. It was the first time she had been ridden since her illness; there was the bouncy freshness of a young pony in her step, but, as always, no trace of skittishness. It was a grey morning, chill, with a light wind. I held my plaid closely about me, glad to leave behind the yard of Cluain, where the smell of the charred timbers and the earth soaked with spirits still hung, despite the wind. Ailis did not hesitate as I turned her head up the track that led to Callum's cottage; if she thought at all of the fearful journey when she had last come down here, she did not show it. I carried a pigeon, shot by John that morning, in the pouch. Giorsal would not eat any but fresh-killed meat.

I checked Ailis before we crossed the burn to the cottage, looking at the scene, thinking that already, in the few days it had been untenanted, it seemed to wear an air of desolation. There were leaves gathering before the door of the cottage, and against the walls; in a few weeks weeds would grow there. If there were not regular fires kept up in the range, the damp would begin to creep in, and as the winter snows began to drift down from the heights, the field mice would find an entry, and settle, and the rooks nest in the chimney. I could not bear the thought of it falling into ruin – like that other cottage up there, where Mairi Sinclair had grown up. I wondered, sitting there on Ailis, if Neil Smith would come up here to live. He would no longer be with the Excise, but he would stay at Cluain, I knew. He could have Callum's pony for the trek up and down to Cluain – I was sure Mairi Sinclair would agree to that. I looked about me. It was so lonely here, in this little clearing by the burn, the silence so complete. I wondered if Neil Smith would mind the loneliness, he who had always lived so close to the centre of Cluain's life. Would he want to bring Big Billy and the flock with him? And where would we make a pool for them? – the burn was too swift and too narrow. And I realized as I sat there, looking at the place that had been Callum's own, and would be forever that way in my heart, that the practical, everyday problems of Cluain were already impinging. What I had promised Samuel Lachlan last night must be carried out. There could be no waste at Cluain. To think of it inhabited by any other than Callum was like pressing on a raw wound, but some arrangement must be made. I pictured it as I knew it – the books stacked haphazardly on the shelves, the untidy roll-top desk. I would ask Mairi Sinclair to come up here and select that which she did not wish to leave to another. For myself, I did not think I could ever enter that door again.

I put Ailis in the empty stable. Giorsal greeted me with a harsh cry, and ran up and down on the perch. She had ceased bating off at my arrival. It signalled food to her, and she welcomed me, welcomed, also, the release from the boredom of sitting on her perch. She was growing very restless. It was too many days since she had sat on her block, too many since she had bathed and preened herself. She danced up and down the perch in greedy anticipation. She spread her wings for me, as if to remind me that she had them, that flight was being denied her. I slipped on the gauntlet, and took the first piece of pigeon out of the bag. Without hesitation, she stepped on to my fist, and began to pull with a claw and beak at the piece of bird I held between my fingers. It was strange how quickly I had become used to handling the piece of pigeon, watching her pull a few feathers away, and then swallow the rest. It offended me now no more than seeing the uncooked meat in the pantry at

Cluain. This was Giorsal's natural food; with it, she stayed healthy.

But she would not finish the whole pigeon. I kept extending the pieces to her between my gloved fingers, but finally she moved back on to the perch, and took up again the restless pacing, up and down, up and down. Even when I stroked her with the feather she was not appeased. She looked towards me and uttered her strange cry.

'Come now, Giorsal. It is time.'

First of all I removed the hood; it would be easier here where she was on the perch, and I had both hands free for the task. I could not hope to match Callum's dexterity with his teeth and one hand. When the hood came off I left her alone for a few minutes, talking all the time to her though, while her eyes grew accustomed even to this amount of dim light after the long darkness. I sweated with nervousness as I released the jesses from the swivel, and twined them through my fingers, trying to remember how Callum had done it. She did not at once realize what had happened, and I had to entice her with a piece of fresh-cut carcass meat to move forward from the perch on to my fist. Then, as she pulled and tugged at the meat, I took by first steps backwards away from the perch. She stopped in surprise. I saw her wings begin to flex up, and wondered what I would do if she bated off my hand, and would not return, finally hanging head downwards, and swinging from the jesses. She would sense, of course, that I was frightened. A timid, uncertain handler was an invitation to trouble from a hawk. Desperately, I did not want to botch these next few minutes. If she did not completely trust me, if I had not learned enough from watching Callum's calm, sure handling of her, there would be trouble and danger for her before I got her into the open. If she spread her wings here and tried to escape me, she could damage their tips, and perhaps be hampered in flight. If the hood were back on her she would be calm, but with either course I would have difficulties.

I opened the door very slowly, so that she did not see too much of the sky at once. But the light streamed on her, the pupils of those big eyes contracted in response to it. Again she raised her wings, and I felt a powerful tug on my fist. But we were safely past the doorjamb, and in the open. Here her wings could stretch, and she might attempt a flight, but with no harm, except for the possibility of pulling me off balance.

But she was wonderfully quiet, just raising her head to the sky, seeing her world again, sensing it, smelling it. I swear that she took her time to look around the clearing, and up beyond it, where the folds of the mountains could be seen. She felt she would soon be among it all again, but she was in no hurry. In all my nervousness

I also paused; Callum had shown me one of the noblest sights seen by man, the flight of the falcon. And now I looked at that wonderful, proud head as it slowly turned, and I was grateful. No span of time, no dimming of memory, would ever take this from me.

The next was the hardest, and the most dangerous – dangerous for Giorsal. If I bungled it, she would be dead in a very short time, and she would be a trapped and maimed creature for whatever time she did live; she would die miserably, tangled in a tree or thicket.

So I took the piece of fresh grouse meat, shot illegally on Ballochtorra's moors that morning, the piece I had saved for this moment. I put it between the thumb and first finger of my left hand, where Giorsal sat; I twitched it a little, to make her notice it. Her eyes were full of her world, and her crop was full already, but the scent reached her, and she began to pull daintily at it, as if it were something to play with. While she was absorbed, I reached into the bag with my right hand, and groped about for the scissors. They were small, with blunted ends, but a sharp cutting edge, borrowed from Mairi Sinclair who used them for preparing dressings. I had explained what I needed them for, and she had shaken her head, even as she tried to sharpen them still more. 'I doubt they'll cut through. They are not meant for leather.'

'I will have to try. I don't know how to manage any other way.'

But they cut; Callum had kept the leather oiled and supple. First the bewits that held the bells – a little tinkling sound as the one attached to the left leg hit the ground. The second was difficult, because it was on the leg with which Giorsal was gripping the meat. But finally I had manœuvred the scissors between her leg and the leather, and cut through. The second bell hit the ground, and rolled among some stones. She ceased eating on hearing the noise. She stayed for a long minute, looking down and around her. Then she turned to the meat again. This time I went to the upraised leg first; if I could cut the jess off that without alarming her, the task was almost done. She stopped eating again, and looked around at me, cocking her head, and swivelling to try to understand this strange new thing that was happening. But I had reached in clean and near to the leg, and the whole jess fell away. The second one was simple. Giorsal was still holding up her leg, with claws extended, seeing its odd nakedness, without bell or jess, when I reached and cut near the second leg, the one with which she gripped my fist.

'Goodbye, Giorsal . . .' I lifted my arm with the motion I had seen Callum use when he cast her off. She lifted her wings, and momentarily hovered, the wings brushing my face, as if she did not quite know what to do with this freedom. Where were the long streamers which had been her shadow from her first year of life? – where was the sound of the bells? But finally the sense of joy gained in her, and she was up, rising quite slowly, trying her wings. She circled the clearing a few times, as though making up her mind in which direction she would fly first. There would be no need for her to hunt today. She would soar, and float and stoop, making mock passes at the birds of passage, pretending, playing. Then she would bathe, and preen, and dry. And tomorrow, when she felt hunger, she would kill, and she would be on her own, and free.

But in case she did not kill, I would come back for three days and leave fresh pigeons for her here in the clearing, on the block. She would not so soon forget where her shelter was, where she had returned each time from hunting with Callum. By then, she would either have adapted to the wild state, or she would have failed, and she would die. But better to die out here, in the country she loved, in her own element, than live her days, hooded, in a darkened shed, on a perch. No one but Callum could have cared for her properly; none would now try.

She rose a little higher above the trees of the clearing, above the high rocks behind it, as if to take her bearings, to remind herself of the lay of her territory. She hovered a little there, and all at once she came down. Just in time, as she came at me, I raised the gloved hand. There she clung, perhaps three seconds, perhaps five, wings still outstretched, her black eyes boring into mine. And then she was off, swift and high this time, higher and higher, up and off along the wind, tearing down the glen towards the crag of Balloch-torra, where she had been born.

I dropped my hand. She was gone – that most beautiful of birds in flight, that graceful, swooping creature, that shadow of death to the other birds of the strath – she was gone. But she had returned, once, for those magical seconds, to my hand, bestowing the gift of her freedom upon me. I knew then, fully, the joy Callum had had in her. I was truly melded with him, for just this one time.

This, rather than his burial, was our real parting. 'Goodbye.'

I picked up the cut jesses, the bewits, the little tinkling Indian bells. I couldn't make myself go into the cottage to leave them, so I put them in the pouch. They would go back to Cluain with me. They would join William's scroll in the leather trunk that had come from China – one which I would seldom open.

It was then his figure came from the shadow of the trees near the burn. He did not look at all like Callum, and yet an odd resemblance was there in his figure, his bearing. I had not seemed to notice before how tall he was. He wore the green Cawdor kilt and stockings, a hazy green tweed jacket that seemed to fade into his background. But there was the blond hair, streaked lighter in parts, from going without a hat, and the strangely brilliant blue eyes. No, Gavin did not look like Callum, except in the familiarity of the way he moved about this terrain, the long easy stride of the hill walker, the economy of movement, the quietness.

'She paid you the supreme compliment, didn't she, Kirsty? — Callum's peregrine — to come back to your hand.'

'I have been feeding her . . .'

'That is not everything. I held my breath when she came back. No jesses — no bells. A free creature.'

'She had to be free. There is no one else who could manage her. And it is right that she be free. Callum could never bear to be tied. I know I did what he wanted.'

'You did it magnificently.'

'I was frightened. I was afraid I would bungle it. If the jesses had stayed on, she would have tangled in some tree, and probably hung head down until she died. I could never have forgiven myself for that.'

'But you did it — and she is free.' He moved closer. I noticed now his pony tethered on the other side of the burn. 'I called at Cluain, and Mairi Sinclair told me you had come up here. It is unlike her to part with such information. She keeps such a close mouth, always.'

I drew off the glove, and I couldn't help the sigh that came. Was it fatigue after the strain of the effort, the fear? — was it the sadness in the knowledge that both Giorsal and Callum were finally gone?

'None of us is unchanged by these last days, Gavin. Perhaps she had kept a close mouth all these years because of Callum. Now everyone knows he was my grandfather's son. There is less reason for silence at Cluain now — and yet, how silent it is. How unnervingly silent! So quiet that I hear a kind of creaking inside of me. I wonder if it is fear, or loneliness — or what. There is so much to do. And so much I know I did not do in the past, so much I misjudged. Will I do it again?'

He put his hand on my shoulder. 'Hush, Kirsty, hush . . . Weep when you must, but do not weep for anything you have done.'

'I loved him — I loved Callum. And I should not have.'

'No love is ever wasted — or lost. *I* have to keep telling myself that too. *I* have to keep asking myself where I misjudged, where I failed her. But Callum loved you, Kirsty. As his falcon did — in the way that a creature, a near-wild creature, sometimes does. The falcon came back to your hand, Kirsty. Never forget it. It was as if Callum, in the only way he could, was back with you — for that instant. No one should forget such things. And no love should ever be forgotten, no matter what went wrong. It is precious – beyond price.'

His tone was soft as he went on. 'How does that falconer's rule go . . . something about an eagle for an emperor, a falcon for a queen – '

'A king,' I corrected him.

'A falcon for a queen, Kirsty. And a queen you are – this territory is yours, just as surely as it is the falcon's. There are those who in nature are noble – you, and the falcon. Not made for mean or small things. They only know great joys and loves – great griefs. When they fly, they fly high and sure and swift. When they fall, they don't stumble, they crash. If they should fall, it is the end – and they accept it. You and the falcon, Kirsty. I can never forget that sight . . .'

I brought Ailis from the stable, and Gavin and I started down the track. It was wild and lovely, as were the high moors and the deeply shadowed glens, and I would miss them. But the girl who had ridden Ailis through all the valley this summer was gone; she had vanished with the fire, and the flight of the falcon. What woman would come to take her place I was not quite sure; a woman of affairs, who would run Cluain as I had promised it would be run, a woman who must now grow larger in spirit, in heart, so that there was not only room for Callum, and William, and – yes, Angus Macdonald – but for the others who would come to join them.

I looked back at Gavin. 'Tell Jamie I have a gift for him.'

'What is it?'

'I am giving him Ailis.'

I was glad he made no protest. Instead he came forward and our two ponies stood side by side. 'Ailis will be the most precious thing Jamie will ever possess.' Then his hand sought mine – momentarily, a touch only. 'And me, Kirsty – will there ever be anything for me?'

I looked, not at Gavin, but upwards, my eyes reaching up, searching for Giorsal; but I got no sight of her. I turned and looked back. The clouds had lifted higher with the wind, and on the highest, farthest fold of the Cairngorms that I could see, what had fallen as rain in the glen the night before, up there lay in a glistening white band, the first snow of the coming winter.

'Who knows? Perhaps in time . . . in time . . .'

Epilogue

So it was that the lands of Cluain and Ballochtorra were joined again through Gavin and myself. That old man, dying so slowly in Edinburgh, finally lost his hold on life, and when King Edward VII was crowned, it was I, not Margaret, who had the right to be seated in Westminster Abbey and wear a marchioness's coronet. But Gavin and I were not there; Gavin had never formally taken his seat in the House of Lords, and we had no notion to spend the money for the extravagance of the robes, and the cost of the journey. Nervously, Samuel Lachlan suggested to Gavin that he might be permitted to pay, but we did not even consider it. There was endless building going on at Cluain, and the debt to repay. There seemed not even time for such a trip, even if we allowed Samuel Lachlan to pay. I think he was disappointed; he had looked forward to the gossip we would bring back. We celebrated Coronation Day with a picnic on the moors, in a place, not high and lonely, but easily accessible to the road. We went there by trap, because Samuel Lachlan could not walk far, and because I was expecting my first child. Only Jamie talked about his memories of the time when the Prince, who was now the King, had visited Ballochtorra.

But as the children came, Jamie still retained his special place with me – as much loved as they, perhaps even more. He was my link back, through Margaret, to William and to Callum. He had always been a child of grace, and he grew into a beautiful young man. We gave him the tower room at Cluain; I had moved from it into my grandmother's room after Angus Macdonald's death. I wanted no more of the sweeping view of the strath up to Ballochtorra, down to the river. I think Gavin himself was not unhappy that the other wing of Cluain cut off the sight of Ballochtorra. We both lived with our own ghosts, Gavin and I.

The buildings of Cluain continued, never stopping, never quite ready, it seemed, to take the new season's production of whisky. Two excisemen and their families came to take the place of Neil Smith, because we were growing so fast. With the loan only half paid off, Gavin and I contracted another one for a second distillery building, with four pot stills. This meant extra warehousing. 'Have a care, Kirsty. You will become like James Ferguson,' Samuel Lachlan said. But he advanced the money, and we continued to repay him, and to pay the interest. And he continued to come to

Cluain, more and more frequently, living on to a great age, as I had predicted. He lived to drink up his own special reserve casks of Cluain's whisky, and the new distilling was a very respectable age before he tasted it. He enjoyed it all, I thought, in his own odd way – the ceaseless activity, the difficulties, the small triumphs. He seemed to enjoy seeing Gavin and me together at Cluain. It was not as peaceful a place as it had been. Young children are noisy, and need room to play, and more servants. Samuel Lachlan didn't seem to mind. They played about him like puppies, and I never forgot the day, not long after I married, when he came to Cluain dressed in heathery tweed, because Jamie had teased him by saying that only rooks went on the moors in black suits. Samuel Lachlan never went far on the moors, not for very long, but he loved Jamie. And Jamie seemed to give back that love, unselfconsciously. Samuel Lachlan came into the golden age of his life, with Cluain, and love and companionship.

Mairi Sinclair remained at Cluain, but she mellowed only slightly with the years, always retaining that awesome dignity and her own austere habits, even as Cluain changed about her, becoming a hard-used, slightly untidy household of books and pictures, music and flowers. But as my children struggled to stand and take their first steps, I noticed it was her skirt they would reach for, her hand they would clutch, as readily as mine. They grew up respecting her, but without fear of her. In unguarded moments, when I saw her eyes upon each of them, it seemed to me that the anguished hunger of her expression was gone. I came to believe that she, too, lived those years with more happiness than she had ever known.

Jamie finally went to school, protestingly, in Edinburgh, and it was at Edinburgh University he got his degree in science. Samuel Lachlan wanted to pay for him to go to Cambridge, and Jamie had refused. 'Edinburgh's best,' he said, with youthful Chauvinism, 'and besides, Cambridge is too far from home.' He surprised everyone then, with his degree in his hand, by saying that he wanted to stay on at Cluain and work in the distillery. Samuel Lachlan was doubtful. 'It looks well to have an earl's name on the letterhead – but we already have a marquis! Can an earl *work* in the distillery?'

'I'm a chemist,' Jamie said, and he went to work. And the distillery workers never called him anything but Master Jamie. 'Whisky is becoming *the* world's drink, Mr Lachlan,' he had said, so earnestly, as if we were just discovering the brew. 'I want to be in whisky.' He worked his full hours in the distillery, and in his spare time he roamed the strath with the pony Samuel Lachlan had given him after Ailis had died, and he fished the river, and hunted the moors. He learned to play the organ from Gavin, competently enough, but without his father's distinction. Samuel Lachlan paid for the organ repairs, when they became necessary. Samuel used to go to listen to Jamie's organ lessons with Gavin, and then began to stay to hear Gavin play. It came late to him in life, that discovery of music.

And then Jamie was killed in the Somme offensive in 1916, and there was a grave in Flanders for him, and only a memorial tablet to mark his name in the kirk at Ballochtorra.

After Jamie's death Samuel Lachlan failed quickly. He loved my children, but he loved none as he had loved Jamie. 'I am too old,' he said, as he had said when my grandfather had died. 'I am too old still to be living, and Jamie was too young to die.' Watching the grieving of that old man was worse than Gavin's sadness. I urged him to give up the rooms he clung to in Inverness, his symbol of independence, and come to Cluain. He agreed, after argument, but he did not very long survive Jamie. It was strange to hear his will read, made out so carefully in his lawyer's language. Gavin and I had worked so hard to repay the debt, and the interest – but that was according to Samuel Lachlan's principles, and that was what I had promised. His will, the latest one made directly after Jamie was killed, left his entire estate to me. He was buried in the kirkyard of Ballochtorra, and another granite headstone rose there.

No one ever bought Ballochtorra, though the moors were rented each year for the shooting. Gavin made no attempt to keep it in repair. 'Shall I beggar my children to keep up a front that no one needs?' he answered Samuel Lachlan's criticisms of a building falling into ruin. 'It started as a small fortress-castle. The rest is James Ferguson's creation. Why should I try to preserve *that*?'

Gavin had had his own satisfaction in the reclamation of the river meadows beyond the bend of Ballochtorra – meadows where cattle as sleek as any Cluain had ever had now grazed.

So the terraced garden of Ballochtorra blurred over with weeds, and young saplings took hold. The putty in the windows dried out, and the panes fell and crashed; the roof began to let in the snow and rain. The ivy crept in. The rooks nested in all the crannies of its crenellated towers, their raucous cries a part of our lives. Almost every Sunday I walked with Gavin and our children through the kirkyard of Ballochtorra, and I saw the granite headstones, and every spring, when the snows thawed, I went to cut the long grass on those graves, and let the wild flowers reach to the light. And every spring I looked for falcons bringing food to an eyrie on the crag of Ballochtorra. I cherished the thought that Giorsal had found a mate, and had made her nest up there somewhere on the rock shelves near where she had been born; I made myself believe that her descendants came back there to mate and to nest. Sometimes I did see the high, hovering speck of a falcon. And I never forgot that overpowering moment of wonder when one of that kind, a peregrine named Giorsal, had clung, willingly, to my outstretched hand. Gavin was right; one does not forget.

And we did not beggar our children; we did not keep up a front. Perhaps we learned, at last, the true meaning of the Cawdor motto — *Be Mindful*.